James Terry White

The national cyclopaedia of American biography

James Terry White

The national cyclopaedia of American biography

ISBN/EAN: 9783742889560

Manufactured in Europe, USA, Canada, Australia, Japa

Cover: Foto ©Raphael Reischuk / pixelio.de

Manufactured and distributed by brebook publishing software
(www.brebook.com)

James Terry White

The national cyclopaedia of American biography

THE NATIONAL
CYCLOPÆDIA OF AMERICAN BIOGRAPHY

VOLUME VI.

THE NATIONAL
CYCLOPÆDIA OF AMERICAN
BIOGRAPHY

BEING THE

HISTORY OF THE UNITED STATES

AS ILLUSTRATED IN THE LIVES OF THE FOUNDERS, BUILDERS, AND DEFENDERS
OF THE REPUBLIC, AND OF THE MEN AND WOMEN WHO ARE
DOING THE WORK AND MOULDING THE
THOUGHT OF THE PRES-
ENT TIME

EDITED BY

DISTINGUISHED BIOGRAPHERS, SELECTED FROM EACH STATE
REVISED AND APPROVED BY THE MOST EMINENT HISTORIANS, SCHOLARS, AND
STATESMEN OF THE DAY

VOLUME VI.

NEW YORK
JAMES T. WHITE & COMPANY
1896

THE NATIONAL CYCLOPÆDIA OF AMERICAN BIOGRAPHY

PROMINENT CONTRIBUTORS AND REVISERS.

Abbott, Lyman, D. D., LL. D.,
Pastor of Plymouth Church, and Editor of "The Christian Union."

Adams, Charles Follen,
Author of "Dialect Ballads."

Adams, Charles Kendall, LL. D.,
President of Cornell University.

Alexander, Hon. E. P.,
Ex-General Southern Confederacy.

Alger, Rev. William Rounseville,
Author.

Andrews, Elisha B., D. D., LL. D.,
President of Brown University.

Avery, Col. Isaac W.,
Author "History of Georgia."

Ballantine, William G., D. D.,
President Oberlin College.

Baird, Henry Martyn,
University City of New York.

Bartlett, Samuel C., D. D., LL. D.,
President of Dartmouth College.

Battle, Hon. Kemp P.,
Late President of University of N. C.

Blake, Lillie Devereaux,
Author.

Bolton, Sarah Knowles,
Author.

Bowker, R. R.,
Writer and Economist.

Brainard, Ezra, LL. D.,
President of Middlebury College, Vt.

Brean, Hon. Joseph A.,
Supt. Public Instruction, Louisiana.

Brooks, Noah,
Journalist and Author.

Brown, John Henry,
Historical Writer.

Brown, Col. John Mason,
Author "History of Kentucky."

Burr, A. E.,
Editor "Hartford Times."

Burroughs, John,
Author.

Candler, W. A., D. D.,
President Emory College, Ga.

Capen, Elmer H., D. D.,
President Tufts College.

Carter, Franklin, Ph. D., LL. D.,
President Williams College.

Cattell, William C., D. D., LL. D.,
Ex-President Lafayette College.

Clapp, W. W.,
Formerly Editor "Boston Journal."

Clarke, Richard H., LL. D.,
President New York Catholic Protectory.

Coan, Titus Munson, M. D.,
Author.

Cooley, Hon. Thomas M., LL. D.,
President Interstate Commerce Commission.

Cravath, E. M., D. D.,
President Fisk University.

Crawford, Edward F.,
Staff "New York Tribune."

Curtis, George Ticknor, LL. D.,
Author and Jurist.

Deming, Clarence,
Author.

De Peyster, Gen. J. Watts,
Historian.

Dix, Morgan, D. D., LL. D.,
Rector Trinity Church.

Dreher, Julius D., Ph. D.,
President Roanoke College.

Donnelly, Hon. Ignatius,
Author.

Douglass, Hon. Frederick W.

Dudley, Richard M., D. D.,
President Georgetown College, Ky.

Dunlap, Joseph R.,
Editor "Chicago Times."

Durrett, Col. R. T.,
Historian of the West.

Dwight, Timothy, D. D., LL. D.,
President Yale University.

Eagle, James P.,
Governor of Arkansas.

Eggleston, George Cary,
Author and Editor.

Eliot, Charles W., LL. D.,
President Harvard University.

Fetterolf, A. H., LL. D., Ph. D.,
President Girard College.

Field, Henry Martyn, D. D.,
Editor "New York Evangelist."

Fisher, Prof. George P., D. D., LL. D.,
Professor of Divinity, Yale University.

Garrison, Wendell Phillips,
"Evening Post."

Gates, Merrill E., Ph. D., LL. D.,
President Amherst College.

Gilman, Daniel C., LL. D.,
President Johns Hopkins College.

Greeley, Gen. A. W.,
United States Signal Service and Explorer.

Hadley, Arthur T., M. A.,
Professor Yale University.

Hale, Edward Everett, S. T. D.,
Author.

Hamm, Mlle. Margherita A.,
Journalist.

Hammond, J. D., D. D.,
President Central College.

Harding, W. G.,
Of the "Philadelphia Inquirer."

Harper, W. R.,
President University of Chicago.

Harris, Joel Chandler (Uncle Remus),
Author.

Harris, Hon. William T.,
United States Commissioner of Education.

Hart, Samuel, D. D.,
Professor Trinity College.

Haskins, Charles H.,
Professor University of Wisconsin.

Higginson, Col. Thomas Wentworth,
Author.

Hurst, John F., D. D.,
Bishop of the M. E. Church.

Hutchins, Stilson,
Of the "Washington Post."

Hyde, William De Witt, D. D.,
President Bowdoin College.

Irons, John D., D. D.,
President Muskingum College.

Jackson, James McCauley,
Author and Editor.

Johnson, Oliver,
Author and Editor.

Johnson, R. Underwood,
Assistant Editor "Century."

Kell, Thomas,
President St. John College.

Kennan, George,
Russian Traveler.

Kimball, Richard B., LL. D.,
Author.

Kingsley, William L., LL. D.,
Editor "New Englander and Yale Review."

Kip, Rt. Rev. William Ingraham,
Bishop of California.

Kirkland, Major Joseph,
Literary Editor "Chicago Tribune."

Knox, Thomas W.,
Author and Traveler.

Lamb, Martha J.,
Editor "Magazine of American History."

Langford, Laura C. Holloway,
Editor and Historical Writer.

Le Conte, Joseph, LL. D.,
Professor in University of California.

Lindsley, J. Berrien, M. D.,
State Board of Health of Tennessee.

Lockwood, Mrs. Mary S.,
Historical Writer.

Lodge, Hon. Henry Cabot,
Author.

Longfellow, Rev. Samuel,
Author.

MacCracken, H. M., D. D., LL. D.,
Chancellor of University of the City of New York.

McClure, Col. Alexander K.,
Editor "Philadelphia Times."

McCray, D. O.,
Historical Writer.

McElroy, George B., D. D., Ph. D., F. S.,
President Adrian College.

McIlwaine, Richard, D. D.,
President Hampden-Sidney College.

McKnight, H. W., D. D.,
President Pennsylvania College.

Morse, John T., Jr.,
Author "Life of John Adams," etc.

Newton, Richard Heber, D. D.,
Clergyman and Author.

Nicholls, Miss B. B.,
Biographical and Historical Writer.

Northrup, Cyrus, LL. D.,
President University of Minnesota.

Olson, Julius E.,
Professor University of Wisconsin.

Packard, Alpheus S.,
Professor Brown University.

Page, Thomas Nelson,
Author.

Parton, James,
Author.

Patton, Francis L., D. D., LL. D.,
President Princeton College.

Peabody, Andrew P., D. D., LL. D.,
Harvard University.

Pepper, William, M. D., LL. D.,
Provost University of Pennsylvania.

Porter, Noah, D. D., LL. D.,
Ex-president of Yale University.

Potter, Eliphalet N., D. D., LL. D.,
President Hobart College.

Powderly, T. V.,
Master Workman, Knights of Labor.

Prime, Edward D. G., D. D.,
Editor "New York Observer."

Prince, L. Bradford,
Governor New Mexico.

Prowell, George R.,
Historical Writer.

Ryder, Rev. Charles J.,
Secretary of American Missionary Society.

Sanborn, Frank B.,
Author.

Schaff, Philip, D. D., LL. D.,
Author.

Sharpless, Isaac, Sc. D.,
President Haverford College.

Stott, W. T., D. D.,
President Franklin College.

Shearer, Rev. J. B., D. D.,
President Davidson College, N. C.

Small, Albion W., Ph. D.,
President Colby University.

Smith, Charles H. (Bill Arp),
Author.

Smith, George Williamson, D. D., LL. D.,
President Trinity College.

Smith, William W., LL. D.,
President Randolph-Macon College.

Snow, Louis Franklin,
Professor Brown University.

Stockton, Frank R.,
Author.

Sumner, William G.,
Professor Political Economy, Yale.

Super, Charles W., A. M., Ph. D.,
President Ohio University.

Swank, James W.,
Secretary American Iron and Steel Association.

Tanner, Edward A., D. D.,
President Illinois College.

Taylor, James M., D. D.,
President Vassar College.

Thurston, Robert H.,
Director Sibley College.

Thwing, Charles F., D. D.,
President Western Reserve University.

Tuttle, Herbert, LL. D.,
Professor Cornell University.

Tyler, Lyon G.,
President College of William and Mary.

Venable, W. H., LL. D.,
Author.

Walworth, Jeannette H.,
Author.

Warren, William F., S. T. D., LL. D.,
President Boston University.

Watterson, Henry,
Editor "Louisville Courier-Journal."

Webb, Gen. Alexander S., LL. D.,
President College of the City of New York.

Weidemeyer, John William,
Historical Writer.

Wheeler, David H., D. D.,
President Alleghany College.

Winchell, Alexander,
Late Professor University of Michigan.

Wise, John S.,
Ex-Congressman from Virginia.

Wright, Marcus J.,
Historian and Custodian of Confederate Records
in United States War Department.

TYLER, John, tenth president of the United States, was born at Greenway, Charles City co., Va., March 29, 1790. He was the second son of Judge John Tyler and Mary, his wife, only child of Robert Booth Armistead of York county, Va. In early boyhood he attended an "old-field school," and was graduated at William and Mary College in July, 1807. James Madison, the president of the college, and Judge Tyler had been college-mates of Thomas Jefferson, and the political principles of the rising statesman came naturally to favor "states-rights." At college he showed a strong interest in ancient history. He was also fond of poetry and music and was a skilful performer on the violin. In 1809, before attaining his majority, he was admitted to the bar. He was elected to the legislature and took his seat in that body in December, 1811. He was here a firm supporter of Madison's election; and the war with Great Britain, which soon followed, afforded him an opportunity to become conspicuous as a forcible and persuasive orator. The bank had always been unpopular in Virginia, but the Virginia senators at Washington ignored the instructions to the legislature and favored its re-charter in 1811. On Jan. 14, 1812, Tyler introduced resolutions in which the senators were taken to task, and the binding force of instructions was formally asserted. Tyler married, March 29, 1813, Letitia, daughter of Robert Christian, and a few weeks afterward was called into the field at the head of a company of militia, to take part in defence of Richmond, now threatened by the British. His military service lasted but a month. He was re-elected to the legislature annually until, in November, 1816, he was chosen to fill a vacancy in the house of representatives, caused by the death of John Clopton. As a member of the house, during the fourteenth and fifteenth congresses, he soon made himself conspicuous as a strict-constructionist. He voted against the bill introduced by Calhoun in favor of internal improvements on the ground of its unconstitutionality and its lack of a principal of uniform application among the states. He voted against the bill changing the *per diem* allowance of $6 a day to members of

congress for an annual salary of $1,500. He also opposed the passage of the national bankrupt law, and condemned the course of Gen. Jackson in Florida. He was a member of the committee for inquiring into the affairs of the national bank. In the next canvass he rested his election on his speech against the bank, which he distributed among his constituents; and was re-elected to congress without opposition. In the debates over the admission of Missouri, Tyler took the ground that slavery was an evil, but that congress had no constitutional power to permit slavery in the states and prohibit it in the territories, when, by the express language of the constitution, the territories had all the rights of the old states on their admission into the Union. He held with Jefferson and Madison, that as the Northern states had secured emancipation by the sale and diffusion of their slaves, it was unfair, under pretext of saving Missouri from its establishment, to darken the cloud over Virginia by confirming its existence there. The deepening of slavery in the old Southern states would make the laws concerning the slaves all the more rigorous, and abolition itself under such circumstances would still leave Virginia a negro-ridden community. On the other hand, no argument was more absurd than the objection that the increase of the "slave states" could possibly keep pace with the progress of the North, constantly accelerated by the heavy emigration from Europe. The adoption of a "compromise bill" admitting Missouri without restriction, but prohibiting slavery in all the territory north of the line 36° 30', seemed to Tyler a surrender of the whole question at issue; and against the opinion of Calhoun, of Clay, and nearly the whole Southern representation, Tyler voted in the negative. At this congress the attack was made for the first time upon the tariff, which had been passed in the interest of protecting Northern manufactures, and Tyler made the opening objections. Such power did the young orator exhibit in this speech that Judge Baldwin, then chairman of the committee on manufactures, went to his seat and prophesied on the strength of what he had heard, great political advancement in the future. In 1821 Tyler declined a re-election to congress on account of impaired health, and returned to private life. But in 1823 he was again elected to the house of delegates of Virginia. The next year he was nominated to fill the vacancy created in the U. S. senate by the death of John Taylor, but his friend, Littleton Tazewell, a much older man in politics, was elected. In the legislature in 1824, he opposed the attempt to remove William and Mary College to Richmond, and received his reward in being afterwards made successively rector and chancellor of the college, which prospered signally under his auspices.

In December, 1825, he was chosen by the legislature to the governorship of Virginia, and in the following year he was re-elected by a unanimous vote. Before the presidential election in 1824, William H. Crawford was the only candidate of the Republican party whose opinions were unequivocal against the American system of high tariffs, national bank, and internal improvements. He accordingly received the support of Jefferson and all the Virginia leaders, including John Tyler. When Crawford, by reason of a stroke of paralysis, was deemed out of the contest, Tyler and the rest of the strict-constructionists preferred John Quincy Adams to either Henry Clay or Andrew Jackson. When Adams came out in the same colors, the strict-constructionists, who had adhered to Crawford, remained neutral for a time, but were finally forced into co-operation with the followers of Andrew Jackson—the majority of whom were members of the old Federal party. Tyler went along with the rest of the Crawford men, but from the first his support of Jackson was coupled with the condition of Jackson's sustaining the Republican doctrines as maintained in Virginia. Parties now assumed new names. The friends of Adams and Clay took that of National Republicans, while the friends of Jackson and Crawford assumed that of Democrats. But each party claimed to be the true representative of the old Republican party of Jefferson. Firmly devoted to his principles, Tyler would not be a partisan. He never attached any importance to the widely prevalent story of a corrupt bargain between Adams and Clay. When the Clay and Adams men in the legislature momentarily united in 1827 with a majority of the Crawford men and elected Tyler senator over John Randolph, some zealous friends of Jackson attempted to show that there must have been some secret and reprehensible understanding between Tyler and Clay. He subsequently supported Jackson for president in the fall of 1828, as a choice of evils only. Tyler strongly condemned Jackson's policy in his first administration; still, in the presidential election of 1832, he supported him again as a less objectionable candidate than either Clay or Wirt. Tyler disapproved of nullification and condemned the course of South Carolina, as both "impolitic and unconstitutional." But he condemned the tariff measures of the administration for the same reasons, and for the additional one that they were the cause of the errors of South Carolina. Jackson's famous proclamation of Dec. 10, 1832, was denounced by him as "sweeping away all the barriers of the constitution," and as establishing in principle "a consolidated, military despotism." Under the influence of these feelings he undertook to play the part of mediator between Clay and Calhoun, and suggested to them the idea of the compromise tariff of 1833.

On the so-called "force bill," clothing the president with extraordinary powers for the purpose of enforcing the tariff, which had caused all the trouble, Tyler showed the courage of his convictions. The vote stood: yeas 32, nay one (John Tyler). The tendency of successive defections was to bring Tyler and his friends into closer and closer conditions with Clay and the National Republicans. Tyler opposed the removal of the deposits from the United States Bank. He voted in favor of Clay's proposition to censure the president, but his entire opposition was founded on a theory of states-rights, which was really repugnant in principle to all the views expressed by Clay and the National Republicans in 1828. In 1836 no common candidate could be agreed upon. The states-rights men nominated Hugh White of Tennessee for president, and John Tyler for vice-president. The National Republicans, wishing to gather votes from the other parties, nominated for president Gen. William Henry Harrison, who, as a soldier, was not identified with any political party. The Democratic friends of Jackson nominated Van Buren, who received many National Republican votes in the election. There was a great deal of bolting among the states. Massachusetts threw its votes for Webster for president, and South Carolina for Willie Mangum. Virginia, which voted for Van Buren, rejected his colleague, Richard Johnson, and cast its electoral vote for vice-president on William Smith of Alabama. White obtained the electoral votes of Tennessee and Georgia, twenty-six in all, but Tyler made a better showing; he carried, besides these two states, Maryland and North Carolina, making forty-seven in all. No one of the candidates for the vice-presidency having received a majority of the electoral college, the choice devolved on the Democratic senate, who chose R. M. Johnson. In the course of the year preceding the election, an incident occurred, which emphasized more than ever Tyler's hostility to the Jackson party. Benton had resolved to have "expunged" from the journal of the senate the resolution of censure passed by that body in 1834 upon Jackson, for removing the deposits from the United States Bank, and his friends in the general assembly of Virginia passed through that body a resolution instructing the Virginia senators to support Benton. This procedure placed both Tyler and his colleague in the senate in embarrassing positions; for both had been the champions in

favor of the right of instructions. Leigh, however, would not obey the resolutions of the legislature, and made his disobedience unpardonable in the eyes of the Virginia people by holding to his seat; Tyler, too, would not obey, but he reconciled the people to him by resigning, in 1836, the three unexpired years of his term. He maintained that an adhesion to the doctrine of instructions did not carry with it the obligation to violate the constitution. On the seventh anniversary of the Virginia Colonization Society, Tyler was chosen its president. While maintaining the sovereignty of the states over the subject of slavery, he had been ever foremost in all

heard, great political advancement in the future. In 1821 Tyler declined a re-election to congress on account of impaired health, and returned to private life. But in 1823 he was again elected to the house of delegates of Virginia. The next year he was nominated to fill the vacancy created in the U. S. senate by the death of John Taylor, but his friend, Littleton Tazewell, a much older man in politics, was elected. In the legislature in 1824, he opposed the attempt to remove William and Mary College to Richmond, and received his reward in being afterwards made successively rector and chancellor of the college, which prospered signally under his auspices. In December, 1825, he was chosen by the legislature to the governorship of Virginia, and in the following year he was re-elected by a unanimous vote. Before the presidential election in 1824, William H. Crawford was the only candidate of the Republican party whose opinions were unequivocal against the American system of high tariffs, national bank, and internal improvements. He accordingly received the support of Jefferson and all the Virginia leaders, including John Tyler. When Crawford, by reason of a stroke of paralysis, was deemed out of the contest, Tyler and the rest of the strict-constructionists preferred John Quincy Adams to either Henry Clay or Andrew Jackson. When Adams came out in the same colors, the strict-constructionists, who had adhered to Crawford, remained neutral for a time, but were finally forced into co-operation with the followers of Andrew Jackson—the majority of whom were members of the old Federal party. Tyler went along with the rest of the Crawford men, but from the first his support of Jackson was coupled with the condition of Jackson's sustaining the Republican doctrines as maintained in Virginia. Parties now assumed new names. The friends of Adams and Clay took that of National Republicans, while the friends of Jackson and Crawford assumed that of Democrats. But each party claimed to be the true representative of the old Republican party of Jefferson. Firmly devoted to his principles, Tyler would not be a partisan. He never attached any importance to the widely prevalent story of a corrupt bargain between Adams and Clay. When the Clay and Adams men in the legislature momentarily united in 1827 with a majority of the Crawford men and elected Tyler senator over John Randolph, some zealous friends of Jackson attempted to show that there must have been some secret and reprehensible understanding between Tyler and Clay. He subsequently supported Jackson for president in the fall of 1828, as a choice of evils only. Tyler strongly condemned Jackson's policy in his first administration; still, in the presidential election of 1832, he supported him again as a less objectionable candidate than either Clay or Wirt. Tyler disapproved of nullification and condemned the course of South Carolina, as both "impolitic and unconstitutional." But he condemned the tariff measures of the administration for the same reasons, and for the additional one that they were the cause of the errors of South Carolina. Jackson's famous proclamation of Dec. 10, 1832, was denounced by him as "sweeping away all the barriers of the constitution," and as establishing in principle "a consolidated, military despotism." Under the influence of these feelings he undertook to play the part of mediator between Clay and Calhoun, and suggested to them the idea of the compromise tariff of 1833.

On the so-called "force bill," clothing the president with extraordinary powers for the purpose of enforcing the tariff, which had caused all the trouble, Tyler showed the courage of his convictions. The vote stood: yeas 32, nay one (John Tyler). The tendency of successive defections was to bring Tyler and his friends into closer and closer conditions with Clay and the National Republicans. Tyler opposed the removal of the deposits from the United States Bank. He voted in favor of Clay's proposition to censure the president, but his entire opposition was founded on a theory of states-rights, which was really repugnant in principle to all the views expressed by Clay and the National Republicans in 1828. In 1836 no common candidate could be agreed upon. The states-rights men nominated Hugh White of Tennessee for president, and John Tyler for vice-president. The National Republicans, wishing to gather votes from the other parties, nominated for president Gen. William Henry Harrison, who, as a soldier, was not identified with any political party. The Democratic friends of Jackson nominated Van Buren, who received many National Republican votes in the election. There was a great deal of bolting among the states. Massachusetts threw its votes for Webster for president, and South Carolina for Willie Mangum. Virginia, which voted for Van Buren, rejected his colleague, Richard Johnson, and cast its electoral vote for vice-president on William Smith of Alabama. White obtained the electoral votes of Tennessee and Georgia, twenty-six in all, but Tyler made a better showing; he carried, besides these two states, Maryland and North Carolina, making forty-seven in all. No one of the candidates for the vice-presidency having received a majority of the electoral college, the choice devolved on the Democratic senate, who chose R. M. Johnson. In the course of the year preceding the election, an incident occurred, which emphasized more than ever Tyler's hostility to the Jackson party. Benton had resolved to have "expunged" from the journal of the senate the resolution of censure passed by that body in 1834 upon Jackson, for removing the deposits from the United States Bank, and his friends in the general assembly of Virginia passed through that body a resolution instructing the Virginia senators to support Benton. This procedure placed both Tyler and his colleague in the senate in embarrassing positions; for both had been the champions in

favor of the right of instructions. Leigh, however, would not obey the resolutions of the legislature, and made his disobedience unpardonable in the eyes of the Virginia people by holding to his seat; Tyler, too, would not obey, but he reconciled the people to him by resigning. In 1836, the three unexpired years of his term. He maintained that an adhesion to the doctrine of instructions did not carry with it the obligation to violate the constitution. On the seventh anniversary of the Virginia Colonization Society, Tyler was chosen its president. While maintaining the sovereignty of the states over the subject of slavery, he had been ever foremost in all projects to put a stop to the slave-trade and to ameliorate the condition of the slave. And, as early as 1832, he had, as chairman of the senate committee, proposed a code for the District of Columbia, one section of which prohibited the slave-trade in the District. In the spring elections of 1838, Tyler was again returned to the Virginia legislature. On the advice of Clay, the majority of the Whigs determined to go for William Rives in preference to Tyler. Naturally indignant at this treatment, the personal friends of Tyler would not yield, and no election ensued at this legislature on account of the deadlock which resulted. Before the Whig convention at Harrisburg the old issues of bank, tariff, and internal improvements were distinctly surrendered by Clay, Webster, Adams, and all the leaders of the old National Republican party. Clay especially had gone so far in conciliating Southern sentiment as to be considered the Southern candidate. The Northern representatives sought to defeat his election by again putting up Gen. Harrison, to whom the South could not well object, as he was a Southerner, but who was preferable to Clay in the eyes of the manufacturers, since, although approving the compromise tariff of 1833, he had not been the mover of it. They succeeded in defeating Clay, and Gen. Harrison became the candidate of the Whig party for the presidency. Tyler was the choice of everybody for the vice-presidency. Borne upon a great wave of popular excitement, "Tippecanoe and Tyler too" were carried to the White House. It is idle to suppose there were not causes for the great enthusiasm manifested, apart from the clap-trap of politics. There was not a department of the government which was not in confusion, not an office which was not the seat of peculation, and not a principle of the constitution which had not been scorned and insulted by the course of the men in authority, under Jackson and Van Buren. A deep-seated conviction of the necessity of reform prevailed, and this conviction swept the Democrats from power. The triumph of the Whigs was followed by startling results. A collision between their varying factions was unavoidable. Clay hurried the quarrel. Without waiting for Harrison's inauguration, he at once assumed the dictatorship of the Whig party and revived the old National Republican measures which in his letters and public speeches he had declared "obsolete." Matters had already come to a rupture between Clay and Harrison when the latter died one month after his inauguration. The presidency, thereupon, devolved upon the vice-president, whose views were even more fixed against the policy proposed than Harrison's. The national bank was announced by Clay as the great cardinal object of the new Whig administration. But neither in his inaugural address nor in his message calling the congress in extra-session on May 31, 1841, had Harrison indicated that the bank would be agreeable to him. Tyler privately submitted several financial projects to his cabinet, which, while they avoided recognizing the power of congress to create corporations in the states, really accomplished all that a national bank could have effected respecting the finances and business of the country. A measure similar in all respects to the plan which Harrison favored was finally adopted by the Whig cabinet and recommended to congress by Thomas Ewing, the secretary of the treasury. Clay forced a fight on the constitutional question by substituting a bill differing from the cabinet bill in allowing the bank to establish its branches at will in the states. Despite the opposition of the senators from Virginia and Massachusetts, the bill in this objectionable form passed both houses of congress. The president was not only by all his past life committed against the principle of Clay's bill, but he had, in an interview with Clay himself, at the beginning of the extra-session of congress assembled in obedience to a proclamation of the late president, clearly forewarned him of the folly of his course. He therefore vetoed the bill, but by withholding the veto until the ten days allowed by the constitution had nearly expired, he afforded another signal proof of his wish to harmonize with the Whigs. He could not yet fully believe that the Whigs would be so blind as to deliberately sacrifice the result of the recent election by a conflict with their own president. As Clay's objection was against requiring the assent of the states to the establishment of the bank, or its branches within them, the president thought that the Whigs might be satisfied with a proposition which by limiting the bank to dealings in exchanges would, under a recent decision of the supreme court of the United States, avert the necessity of obtaining the expressed consent of the states for branches. In accepting this distinction Tyler made no surrender of his consistency; for it was a distinction made by the law of nations, which was itself founded on the voluntary consent of states. But as the will of a free state or nation is not subject to a coercive code, Tyler made provision for the possible interdiction by a state of branches of the bank within it. He wrote a suitable reservation upon the margin of the paper that had been made the basis of the bill, which with this reservation was carried to the Whig caucus. Now the bill, as adopted by congress, did not contain the marginal words, and a second veto followed. Some of the Whigs seem really to have hoped that such a storm would be raised as would frighten the president into signing the bill, or resigning his office. Threats were fulminated against him on all sides; private letters warned him of plots to assassinate him, and Clay in the senate referred to his resignation in 1836, and asked why he should not follow that example now. The adjournment of congress

was fixed for Monday, Sept. 13, 1841. The second veto was sent to congress on Sept. 9th. On the 11th all the cabinet, save Webster, resigned. The members were fully aware that according to the president's view all vacancies happening during the session had to be filled and sanctioned by the senate during the session. Yet, if the five cabinet officers who resigned could have been satisfied by a delay of their resignation until Tuesday morning, of two days only, a larger opportunity would have been afforded Mr. Tyler of performing the work of making an almost entire cabinet, which, on the part of his predecessor, had required months to adjust. The president would make no bargain of any kind, but before sending in his veto message he had submitted it to his cabinet, and professed his willingness to incorporate in the paper a declaration against a second term which the Whig papers were continually charging as the object of his conduct. The cabinet members opposed his insertion of such a paragraph, and yet he encountered shortly the attacks of some of the very men who gave him the advice and who were foremost in ascribing to him the ambition of a re-election. Some of the leading Whig members of congress now issued addresses to the people, declar-

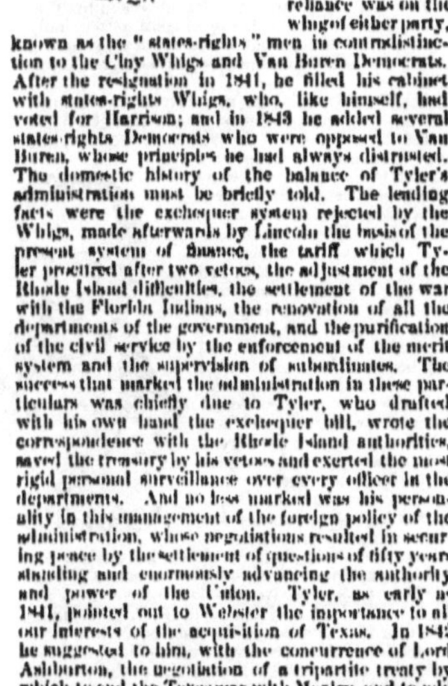

ing "all political connection between them and John Tyler at an end from that day." Daniel Webster, who warmly condemned the course of Clay, adhered to the president. During the next two years, while the Whigs controlled congress, Tyler received little support from that party, and the case was not changed much for the better when the Democrats, controlled by the Van Buren wing of the party, succeeded to the seats which the Whigs had vacated. Tyler's reliance was on the whig of either party, known as the "states-rights" men in contradistinction to the Clay Whigs and Van Buren Democrats. After the resignation in 1841, he filled his cabinet with states-rights Whigs, who, like himself, had voted for Harrison; and in 1843 he added several states-rights Democrats who were opposed to Van Buren, whose principles he had always distrusted. The domestic history of the balance of Tyler's administration must be briefly told. The leading facts were the exchequer system rejected by the Whigs, made afterwards by Lincoln the basis of the present system of finance, the tariff which Tyler procured after two vetoes, the adjustment of the Rhode Island difficulties, the settlement of the war with the Florida Indians, the renovation of all the departments of the government, and the purification of the civil service by the enforcement of the merit system and the supervision of subordinates. The success that marked the administration in these particulars was chiefly due to Tyler, who drafted with his own hand the exchequer bill, wrote the correspondence with the Rhode Island authorities, saved the treasury by his vetoes and exerted the most rigid personal surveillance over every officer in the departments. And no less marked was his personality in this management of the foreign policy of the administration, whose negotiations resulted in securing peace by the settlement of questions of fifty years standing and enormously advancing the authority and power of the Union. Tyler, as early as 1841, pointed out to Webster the importance to all our interests of the acquisition of Texas. In 1842 he suggested to him, with the concurrence of Lord Ashburton, the negotiation of a tripartite treaty by which to end the Texas war with Mexico, and to add California and the West to the Union in return for the concession to Great Britain of the line of the Columbia river, as her boundary on the northwest, and the release to Mexico of the spoliation claims. He sent Frémont on his exploring expeditions to the West, despite the protest of Col. Abert and the higher grade officers of the engineer corps, thus enabling that competent officer to make known the passes of the Rocky Mountains. To Tyler also belongs the credit of encouraging the missionary Whit-

man in his plan of transporting caravans of emigrants to the West to counteract the work of the Hudson Bay Fur Co. After Upshur's death in 1844, it was Tyler, and not Calhoun, that secured the mastery of the Texas question. Calhoun was in entire ignorance of the efforts of the president to get Texas until nominated secretary. Then he thought it was an "unpropitious time" to carry through so important a measure, and he declared that he had remonstrated with his friends against accepting office under Tyler. He suffered nearly three weeks to elapse before he reached Washington, after his nomination as secretary of state. And when the treaty of annexation by which the act was sought first to be accomplished was defeated in the senate, Calhoun advised Tyler to abandon the project. The final annexation of Texas was distinctly a crowning victory for President Tyler's policy. Tyler left the government on March 4, 1845, but before he departed he had the happiness to announce to congress the successful negotiation of the first treaty with China by Caleb Cushing. When his term expired, the condition of the government was the happiest possible. A balance was found in the treasury of $8,000,000; and but one defaulter, and he for the small sum of $15, had come to light during his four years of office. Tyler, during his administration, was a strong advocate of civil service reform, and the chief missions were for years filled with persons politically opposed to him. After leaving the White House, Tyler took up his residence on an estate three miles from Greenway, where his father had lived, in Charles City county, Va. To this estate he gave the name of "Sherwood Forest," and there he dwelt during the remainder of his life. He ceased to take an active part in politics, but even in his retirement he exerted a great influence upon public opinion in Virginia. He made a number of addresses, which rank high as literary productions. He had borne great and undeserved misrepresentation, which by his sensitive nature was keenly felt. He was, therefore, greatly gratified to find his popularity in Virginia and the South return in a few years. When Lincoln was elected, and South Carolina seceded, the Virginia people relied much upon his approved sagacity and elected him to the state convention in January, 1861. In order to preserve the Union, he suggested a peace conference of the states, which met at Washington in February. Of this distinguished body Tyler was the president, but his best efforts could not avert the impending clash. When war was certain, he voted in the state convention to repeal the ordinance of the convention of 1788, which expressly provided that the powers granted by the people of Virginia to the Federal government might be resumed "whensoever the same should be perverted to their injury or oppression." Tyler was a delegate to the provisional congress, and was member-elect of the Confederate house of representatives, but died before he could take his seat in the latter body, on Jan. 18, 1862.

TYLER, Julia Gardiner, wife of President Tyler, was born on Gardiner's Island, near East Hampton, N. Y., May 4, 1820. She was educated at the Chegary Institute, New York city, and after a short time spent in travel in Europe, she went to Washington with her grandfather, David Gardiner, in 1844. A few weeks after her arrival they accepted an invitation from President Tyler to attend a pleasure excursion down the river, which took place Feb. 28th, on the war steamer Princeton. The festivities on the occasion were sadly marred by the explosion of a gun on the vessel, causing serious loss of life. Among those killed was Miss Gardiner's father. His body was taken to the White House, and the young lady was thrown into the society of the president owing to the peculiar circumstances attending her father's death. President Tyler's first wife had died shortly after he entered the White House, and the president paid Miss Gardiner marked attention, which resulted in their marriage in New York city, June 26, 1844. For the succeeding eight months of President Tyler's term she presided over the White House with tact, grace, and dignity. After Mar. 4, 1845, Mrs. Tyler retired with her husband to the seclusion of their country place, "Sherwood Forest," on the banks of the James river, Va. She remained in Virginia until after the civil war, her husband having died in the second year of the strife, and then went to reside with her mother at Castleton Hill, Staten Island. After several years' residence there she removed to Richmond, Va., where she died, July 10, 1889.

LEGARÉ, Hugh Swinton, lawyer, attorney-general, and secretary of state, was born in Charleston, S. C., Jan. 2, 1797. His father was of French Huguenot stock. A physical infirmity that debarred him from all manly sports gave him a taste for books at an early age, and it is said the chief object of his ambition was to become an orator. He entered the College of South Carolina, Columbia, S. C., where he particularly distinguished himself in the study of the ancient classics. He was graduated in 1814, and then applied himself to the study of law, not neglecting to embellish his mind with the treasures of literature. After three years thus spent, he went to Europe, and when in Paris rendered himself familiar with the French language. Subsequently he went to Edinburgh, and for a considerable time devoted himself to mathematics, natural philosophy, and chemistry. In the spring of 1819 he commenced a traveling tour, spending about a year in visiting different parts of England, Scotland, Holland, Belgium, and France. Returning home in 1820, he engaged in cotton-raising on John's Island, at the same time commencing the practice of law in Charleston, besides giving some attention to politics. He represented Charleston in the legislature 1820-22 and 1824-30. He was then elected attorney-general of South Carolina, and during the nullification excitement ardently supported the union in public speeches. Amid the labors of his profession he continued to employ himself in writing, and together with Stephen Elliott published the "Southern Review," a quarterly magazine. He was the principal contributor until the death of Elliott, when he became sole editor. At the end of the eighth volume the magazine was suspended. At a later period he was also a most able contributor to the "New York Review," conducted for several years by Joseph G. Cogswell, LL.D., probably the most learned bibliographer in the country. Some of Legaré's legal arguments have been pronounced equal to the most profound juridical learning and acumen of the profession. In 1832, being appointed *chargé d'affaires* of the United States to Belgium, he took up his residence for about four years at Brussels, after which he made a tour to Northern Germany, being thus enabled to enlarge his knowledge of civil law and of the German language. On returning to his own country in the autumn of 1836, he intended, with these increased qualifications, to pursue his professional labors. His friends, however, antici-

pating his return, had elected him to congress as a Union Democrat, and he took his seat in the extra session of 1837 that was called to deliberate on the financial embarrassments of the country. He greatly increased his reputation in debates that followed, but his course in opposition to the sub-treasury project caused his defeat in the next election. He returned to his profession, in which he was very successful, receiving a most liberal patronage, not only in the great number of cases committed to his care, but in their magnitude. In the presidential canvass of 1840 he favored the election of Gen. Harrison. In September, 1841, he was appointed by President Tyler attorney-general of the United States, and, after the withdrawal of Daniel Webster, Legaré succeeded him as secretary of state, May 9, 1843. A few weeks later he went north with President Tyler and other high officers to attend the unveiling of the Bunker Hill monument in Boston. He was one of the most accomplished scholars of the South, and one of the few Americans of distinctly literary tastes and pursuits who have attained eminence in politics. Chief Justice Story said of him: "His argumentation was marked by the closest logic; at the same time he had a presence in speaking I have never seen excelled." His writings were collected and published with a memoir in 1846, in two octavo volumes, by his sister, Mary Swinton Legaré, who founded the Legaré College and School for the Higher Education of Women at West Point, Lee co., Ia. He died suddenly at Boston, June 20, 1843, being at that period only forty-six years of age, but possessed of a ripeness of intellect not usually attained before the age of threescore years.

FORWARD, Walter, secretary of the treasury, was born in Hartford county, Conn., Apr. 17, 1786. He had the advantage of an excellent education, and while still a young man, in 1803, removed to Pittsburg, where he settled, and for a time ably edited a Democratic newspaper, called the "The Tree of Liberty." Meanwhile he devoted himself to the study of law, and at the age of twenty was admitted to practice in Allegheny county courts. He was encouraged by ample success, and soon became well established in his profession. He continued actively in the practice of law until 1822, when he was elected a member of congress to fill a vacancy, and occupied the position for three years. Up to this time he was a Democrat, but in 1824, during the contest for the presidency between Jackson and John Quincy Adams, he worked for the latter, and was recognized as an active Whig. In 1837 he took an active part in a convention to revise the constitution of the state of Pennsylvania. In March, 1841, President Harrison made him first comptroller of the U. S. treasury, an office which he filled until appointed by Pres. Tyler to the post of secretary of the treasury. His report in 1842, relating to the tariff, was pronounced to be an able document. Sec. Forward continued in the cabinet until 1843, when he retired, and returned to his profession. In November, 1849, President Taylor appointed him *chargé d'affaires* at Copenhagen, Denmark. He remained there two years, when he resigned the position, in order to accept the office of president judge of Allegheny county district court, to which he had been promoted by popular election. He was considered by the oldest members of the local bar the ablest judge of his time in Western Pennsylvania. While attending to the duties of his office he was suddenly taken ill in Pittsburg, Pa., and died within forty-eight hours, on Nov. 24, 1852.

BIBB, George M., secretary of the treasury, was born in Virginia in 1772. He received his early education in the town schools, and was sent to Princeton College, where he was graduated at the age of twenty. He then studied law, and was admitted to practice at the bar. He shortly after removed to Kentucky, where he settled, and began his professional life. He entered into politics, and being recognized as a man of more than usual ability, rose rapidly to public preferment. He became a member of the legislature of the state, was afterward elected to the state senate, and was then made chief justice of the state, and twice re-appointed. In 1811 Bibb was elected a member of the U. S. senate, succeeding Henry Clay in that position, and he remained a member of that body during the twelfth and thirteenth congresses. In 1829 he entered the twenty-first congress, having been again chosen senator from Kentucky, and in the twenty-second congress served with Henry Clay as his colleague. He continued in the senate until 1835, when he was succeeded by John Jordan Crittenden. On June 15, 1844, President John Tyler appointed George Bibb secretary of the treasury, and he continued to fill that office until the beginning of the administration of James Knox Polk, when he was succeeded by Robert John Walker. On retiring from the treasury department Bibb continued to practice law at the capital, and for a time held a subordinate position in the office of attorney-general of the United States. During the latter part of his life he resided in Georgetown, D. C. George Bibb published, in 1808–11, "Reports of Cases at Common Law and in Chancery in the Kentucky Court of Appeals." He died in Georgetown, Apr. 14, 1859.

SPENCER, John Canfield, secretary of war and of the treasury, was born at Hudson, N. Y., Jan. 8, 1788, son of Judge Ambrose Spencer. He was graduated from Union College in 1806, was secretary to Gov. D. D. Tompkins in 1807–08, and in 1809 began legal practice at Canandaigua, N. Y., where he remained for thirty-six years, and was postmaster in 1814. He was made master in chancery in 1811, brigade judge-advocate in the army on the frontier in 1813, and in 1815 assistant attorney-general and district attorney. While in congress, as a Democrat, 1817–19, he wrote the report of the committee on the U. S. Bank, which was afterward used by President Jackson at a time (1833) when the opinions of its author on this subject had greatly changed. He was in the assembly 1819–20, speaker the latter year, state senator 1824–28, a supporter of DeWitt Clinton, and active with J. Duer and B. F. Butler, in the revision of the New York statutes. He was for a time connected with the anti-Masonic party, and was special attorney-general, under a law passed for the purpose, to prosecute the supposed abductors and murderers of William Morgan, but had a difficulty with E. T. Throop, then acting governor, and resigned in May, 1830. In 1832 he was sent to the legislature for another term. As secretary of state and superintendent of schools, 1839–40, he did much to advance public instruction. In October, 1841, he entered President Tyler's cabinet as secretary of war. Thurlow Weed, speaking of Spencer, says, "He entered the cabinet with the notion of being able to bridge over the breach between Tyler

and the Whigs of New York. In this he was perfectly sincere, though, with our knowledge of his political eccentricity of character, none of us doubted that from the moment he entered the cabinet he would zealously espouse and warmly defend Tyler's views and policy." The New York "Tribune," then just started, said of Spencer's appointment: "A matter of surprise to many, but we trust a subject of regret to none; New York should have some voice in the cabinet counsels, and no abler and worthier hand could be found than our present secretary of the state of New York. With a wide and well-estab-

lished fame as among the soundest and ablest American lawyers, he possesses a reputation for purity of purpose and dignity of aim rarely enjoyed." While holding this position a terrible affliction fell upon him; his son, a midshipman on the U. S. schoolship Somers, headed a mutiny, and was hanged at the yard-arm, Dec. 1, 1842. When the big gun burst on the Princeton in 1843, killing Secretaries Upshur and Gilmer and the father of President Tyler's future bride, two other persons and two seamen, the cabinet was reconstructed, Calhoun made secretary of state and Spencer secretary of the treasury. In a short time Spencer resigned, and his place was filled by Bibb of Kentucky. Spencer had been practically ignored and insulted for some time by Tyler. The New York "Evening Post" said that "the cause of the change was Spencer's declining to deposit $100,000 as secret service money with a confidential agent at New York to fit out a naval expedition against Mexico. As he could discover no act of congress directing such a disposition of public money, Mr. Spencer declined to give the order, or allow it to be given to his subordinates, and the next day he received a peremptory order to transfer the money. Seeing the game was up, Mr. Spencer coolly wrote a second refusal, and that day he sent in a written resignation, and remained in the department just twenty-four hours afterward, having in that short space squared all the ends of his concerns with it." The last day of the session Tyler withdrew the nomination of Reuben Walworth for the supreme bench and substituted John Canfield Spencer. Objection was made, and Walworth's name was reinstated, but the senate confirmed nobody. Thus practically closed the career of one of the most indefatigable men in the land; too industrious, almost, to feel domestic bereavement. Toward the close of January, 1844, Spencer's nomination for district judge over New York, Vermont, and Connecticut, to succeed Smith Thompson, was rejected by 26 nays to 21 ayes. Among those who voted against Spencer were Bayard, Benton, Berrian, Choate, Clayton, Crittenden, and Dayton. For him were Buchanan, Colquitt, King, McDuffie, Sevier, and Silas Wright. Spencer put many useful things into the laws of New York, and he served the state well, but he never was an attractive man, because his ambition was kiln-dried. Nathan Sargent says that Spencer was "a man of great abilities, industry, and endurance, curt manners and irascible temper, and before being tendered a position in Tyler's cabinet he had written an address upon Tyler's treachery to the Whig party more severe than anything that appeared from any other quarter, and fairly flayed the president, lashing him as with a whip of scorpions; yet, after this, Tyler could offer him, and he accept, the place of secretary of war; and second, that of secretary of the treasury. It is but just to say of him that he rendered the country important service in the treasury department, which he administered with ability, assiduity, integrity, and faithfulness seldom equaled since the days of Hamilton." In 1845 he removed to Albany. In 1849 he received the degree of LL. D. from Union, of which he had been a regent from 1840. He edited De Tocqueville's "Democracy in America," (2 vols., 1838), bore a prominent part in organizing the N. Y. Asylum for Idiots, and served as a member of state commissions. He died at Albany, May 18, 1855. A review of his legal and political career, by L. B. Proctor, appeared in 1880.

GILMER, Thos. Walker, secretary of the navy, and twenty-second governor of Virginia, was born in Virginia in 1802. He resigned the governorship, Feb. 18, 1844, to accept the portfolio of secretary of the navy in President Tyler's cabinet, and served but ten days, being killed by the explosion of a gun on the steamer Princeton, Feb. 28, 1844. (For a more complete biography, see Vol. V., p. 449.)

HENSHAW, David, merchant and secretary of the navy, was born at Leicester, Mass., Apr. 2, 1791. His ancestors were among the original proprietors of the town, his grandfather, Daniel Henshaw, emigrating there from Boston in 1748, while his father, David Henshaw, was a revolutionary patriot and for many years, during the prime of his life, was a highly respected magistrate. An early American ancestor was Joshua Henshaw, who lived in Dorchester in 1664; and his uncle, William Henshaw, was a soldier in the revolutionary war. David Henshaw, the subject of this sketch, spent his boyhood on his father's farm. He attended the free schools of his native town and afterward Leicester Academy. At the age of sixteen he became an apprentice to a drug house in Boston, and soon after he became of age he established himself in a store of his own, in connection with his brothers and David Rice, which was very successful, and continued in that business until 1829. He devoted all his leisure time to reading and study, and taking an interest in politics, he became noted as one of the best political writers of his time. His natural talents in connection with his mental culture, enabled him to hold a prominent and leading position in the Democratic party, not only in his own state, but in New England, and, indeed, in the Union. Besides his political essays, he contributed to the periodical and daily press. After retiring from business, in 1826 and 1830 Henshaw represented the district in both houses of the legislature of the commonwealth. In 1830 he was appointed collector in the custom house at Boston; in 1839 he was sent to the house of representatives from Boston, and served through one term. At the same time he interested himself in a number of railroad projects. Even before the charter was obtained, he expressed a willingness to invest his whole fortune in the Boston and Worcester Railroad. Through his agency in devising and pushing forward this road, as well as those between Boston and Providence and Boston

and Albany, the business of Boston has been placed ten years in advance of what it would otherwise have been. On July 24, 1843, he was appointed secretary of the navy by President Tyler, but he held the office only a few months, as the appointment was not confirmed by the senate, and he was succeeded by Thomas Walker Gilmer. He spent the last years of his life at his ancestral home in Leicester, and died there Nov. 11, 1852.

MASON, John Young, secretary of the navy, and attorney-general of the United States, was born in Greenville county, Va., Apr. 18, 1799. In his boyhood he studied in the common schools of his neighborhood, and was afterward sent to the University of North Carolina, where he was graduated in 1816. He fixed upon the profession of law as his future vocation, and went to Litchfield, Conn., where there was a law school of celebrity, and where he remained three years, when he was admitted to the bar. He settled in Southampton county, Va., and began practice, which soon became extensive and lucrative. He was elected to the Virginia assembly while still a young man, and continued to serve in that body for a number of terms. In 1829 he was a member of the state constitutional convention, and in 1831 was elected a member of the U. S. house of representatives, where he remained until 1837, when he was appointed judge of the U. S. district for Virginia. Tyler, on his accession to the presidency, Apr. 4, 1841, after the death of President Harrison, retained the cabinet which had been appointed by Harrison until 1843, when he made a reorganization, which included Thomas Walker Gilmer of Virginia for secretary of the navy. With the other new members, Gilmer was confirmed by the senate, Feb. 15, 1844, but thirteen days afterward, on Feb. 28th, by an explosion of a gun on board the steamship of war Princeton, on the Potomac river, he and the secretary of state, Judge Upshur, lost their lives. The position of secretary of the navy was filled by Com. Lewis Warrington until March 14, 1844, when John Young Mason received the appointment, and was at once confirmed by the senate. On the accession of James Knox Polk to the office of president, Mason was appointed by him on March 5th, and promptly confirmed by the senate, attorney-general of the United States. He continued to hold this position until Sept. 9, 1846, when he succeeded George Bancroft as secretary of the navy, the latter having been appointed minister to the court of St. James.

At the end of the Polk administration, Mason went to Richmond, Va., and settled there in the practice of law. In 1850 he was a member of the constitutional convention of the state of Virginia, and presided over the deliberations of that body. In 1853 Franklin Pierce became president, and he appointed Mason U. S. minister to France. He was reappointed by President Buchanan, and remained abroad during the rest of his life, dying in Paris, Oct. 3, 1859.

GRANGER, Francis, postmaster-general, was born in Suffield, Conn., Dec. 1, 1792. He was the son of Gideon Granger, postmaster-general under the administrations of Presidents Jefferson and Madison. He was sent to Yale College, where he was graduated in 1811. His father removed to New York state and settled at Canandaigua, where Francis was admitted to practice at the bar. He entered politics and was elected a member of the New York state legislature, where he served for a number of years. In 1836, when Harrison was first nominated for the presidency,

Francis Granger was on the same ticket with him as a candidate for vice-president. Harrison, however, received only seventy-two electoral votes and the ticket was defeated. In 1838 Granger went to congress. In 1841, when Harrison was elected president, Granger was appointed by him postmaster-general, entering upon his official duties on March 6th of that year. He retired from the position in September, 1841, when John Tyler assumed the presidency, and was offered a diplomatic post abroad, but declined it. He was again sent to congress and continued in that service until 1843, when he retired from public life. Granger had the honor of giving his name to a political party, called the "Silver-grays," so named from the beautiful silver-gray hair which crowned his head. Granger was a member of the peace convention of 1861. In 1817 he married Cornelia Van Rensselaer, who died in 1823, leaving two children. He died in Canandaigua, N. Y., Aug. 28, 1868.

WICKLIFFE, Charles A., postmaster-general, was born in Bardstown, Ky., June 8, 1788. He received his education in an excellent school in his native place, and, having graduated, went into an office to study law, and in 1809 was admitted to practice at the bar, and established himself at Bardstown, where he soon obtained a lucrative business. At the beginning of the war of 1812, Mr. Wickliffe entered the service of the United States, and during the battle of the Thames, which occurred Oct. 5, 1813, he acted as aide to Gen. Samuel Caldwell. This battle took place at the Moravian settlement on the Thames river, Ontario, Canada, between the American forces under Gen. William H. Harrison and the British army, with 2,000 Indian allies under the great chief, Tecumseh, the whole body being commanded by Gen. Proctor. Tecumseh was killed during the fight, as is believed, by Col. Richard M. Johnson, who decided the battle by a brilliant charge of cavalry. During this engagement the British lost heavily in killed and wounded, besides 600 prisoners captured, and a large quantity of cannon, stores, etc. Wickliffe distinguished himself during this battle, as Gen. Caldwell, who was his commander, was with his brigade in the thick of it. In 1814 Wickliffe was elected to the state legislature of Kentucky, and served until 1823, when he was sent to congress, where he remained during the next ten years. In 1834 he was again elected to the state legislature, and was made speaker. Two years later he became lieutenant governor, and in 1839 was for a time acting governor of Kentucky. When John Tyler succeeded Gen. Harrison as president of the United States, he appointed Wickliffe postmaster-general, his commission dating from Sept. 13, 1841, and he remained in this position until March, 1845, when President Polk sent him to Texas to make an investigation into the feeling there with regard to annexation. In 1861 Wickliffe was a member of the peace congress, and he took his seat in the house of representatives in the same year as a Union Whig. In 1864 he was a delegate to the Chicago National Democratic convention. Charles Wickliffe was an unpopular man among those who were not of his own standing in society, on account of his possessing a manner which was autocratic and disagreeable, and especially obnoxious to those socially beneath him. An idea of the estimation in which he was held by the lower classes may be obtained from the fact that they nicknamed him "The Duke." He died in 1869.

NELSON, John, attorney-general, was born in Fredericktown, Md., June 1, 1791. He was the son of Roger Nelson, who was a brigadier-general in the revolutionary army, and was left for dead on the field of Camden, but recovered and afterwards became a member of congress and district judge of Maryland. John Nelson was sent to William and Mary College, where he was graduated in 1811. He took up the study of law, and two years later was admitted to the bar and began practice. Very little is recorded of his after-life except that he was a Democrat in politics; was a member of congress two years, from 1821; was appointed U. S. minister to the court of Naples in 1831 by President Jackson, of whom he was an enthusiastic supporter; and attorney-general of the United States by President Tyler, Jan. 2, 1844, succeeding Hugh S. Legaré, who died in office; and retired with that administration, March 4, 1845. John Nelson died in Baltimore, Md., Jan. 28, 1860.

PORTER, James Madison, secretary of war, was born in Selma, Pa., Jan. 6, 1793. He was the son of Gen. Andrew Porter, who fought through the revolution, and was personally commended by Gen. Washington on the field for his conduct at the battle of Germantown. He was also a brother of David Rittenhouse Porter of Pennsylvania. Like the latter, he was educated for the bar. During the war of 1812 he served in the field, having volunteered as a private, although he was afterwards a commissioned officer. He settled in eastern Pennsylvania, where he opened an office, and obtained a very large practice, not only in that section, but in the surrounding counties, both in his native state and New Jersey. In 1838 he was a member of the Pennsylvania constitutional convention. In 1843 President Tyler sent his name to the senate for the office of secretary of war, but he was rejected. He was one of the founders of Lafayette College, Easton, Pa., and was for more than twenty-five years president of the board of trustees of that institution. He was a

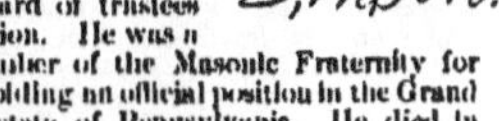

prominent member of the Masonic Fraternity for many years, holding an official position in the Grand Lodge of the state of Pennsylvania. He died in Easton, Pa., Nov. 11, 1862.

UPSHUR, Abel Parker, jurist, secretary of state and of the navy, was born in Northampton county, Va., June 17, 1790. He received a classical education at Nassau Hall, from which he was graduated in 1802, after which he went through a course of legal training in the office of William Wirt, LL.D., of Richmond. In 1810 he was admitted to practice at the bar, and practised in Richmond, Va., during the next fourteen years, when he removed to his estate in Northampton county, but did not relinquish business in the courts where he had been accustomed to practice. He became a candidate for the state legislature, and was elected to that office. In 1826 he received the appointment of judge in the general court of Virginia. In 1829 he was a member of the state constitutional convention that was called to revise the state constitution, and was again made judge of the general court, this time by election to that office, which he continued to hold, with credit to himself and with satisfaction to the public, until 1841. On Sept. 13, 1841, President John Tyler appointed Judge Upshur secretary of the navy, and he continued in charge of that department until June 24, 1843, when he was appointed secretary of state. He held the latter office until his sudden and tragic death, when he was succeeded by John C. Calhoun. Judge Upshur was a fine constitutional lawyer, a man of decided talents, and possessing more than ordinary mental powers, and an able writer on legal topics. He was a pro-slavery Democrat in politics. On Feb. 28, 1844, President Tyler, Secretary of State Upshur, and Secretary of the Navy Thomas W. Gilmer, with other officials, were on board the U. S. war steamer Princeton, in the Potomac river, when a large wrought-iron gun, with which experiments were being made, exploded, killing Judge Upshur, secretaries Gilmer, Maxey, and others. Judge Upshur was the author of a number of essays and speeches, which were published, and also of an important work entitled "Brief Inquiry into the True Nature and Character of our Federal Government; Review of Judge Joseph Story's Commentaries on the Constitution" (Petersburgh, Va., 1840). He died near Washington, D. C., Feb. 28, 1844.

HOUGHTON, George H., clergyman, was born at Deerfield, Mass., Feb. 1, 1820. After a school education he studied at the New York University, where he was graduated in 1842; he then pursued a theological course privately. He took orders in the autumn of 1845, acting as assistant to Dr. Muhlenberg for a time, and then began to officiate at a private house in New York for a small number of persons. In 1849 they were organized as the Church of the Transfiguration, and through the benevolence of one of the members of the parish, a building was erected for them on Twenty-ninth street near Fifth avenue, which was occupied on Sunday, March 10, 1850. It is one of the most picturesque structures in any city in the country. Until May, 1854, the entire pew rents of this church were used for reducing the debt incurred in purchasing the ground and building. The pews are rented, not sold, and there are 150 free seats, these latter being in the chapel part of the edifice. The congregation, which for some years struggled toward prominence, is now one of the largest and wealthiest in New York. Dr. Houghton held the position of instructor of Hebrew in the General Theological Seminary of the Protestant Episcopal church for twelve years. In 1859 he received the degree of D.D. from Columbia College. His publications have consisted of occasional sermons. His attainments in Hebrew are such that he has established a wide reputation as a teacher of that language. Dr. Houghton's church has become widely known as "the Little Church Around the Corner," through the fact of his having performed there the burial service over the remains of the eminent and admired George Holland, when the rite was refused him by another clergyman. The incident which brought this about was peculiar. Mr. Joseph Jefferson, renowned on account of his "Rip Van Winkle," went to this clergyman with the request that he would open his church for the burial of Jefferson's brother actor. To this the clergyman objected, on the ground that the latter was a professional player. He thought, however, that Mr. Jefferson could meet with more success at "the little church around the corner," and by that name Dr. Houghton's church has been generally known ever since. Dr. Hough-

ton's ministrations in his present parish work commenced with only six persons, and now he has reared a fine church and drawn about him a numerous and devoted congregation. This has been done by great labor; but also by the fascination of his personal character and the beauty of his Christian life. As a man he is everywhere cherished, as a citizen he is respected by all with whom he comes in contact, and as a pastor he is sincerely beloved by all his people. The Church of the Transfiguration was Dr. Houghton's first and has been his only charge, and with it has always been identified in the public mind; neither the doctor nor the "Little Church Around the Corner" seeming complete when considered apart the one from the other.

DRAKE, Alexander Wilson, engraver and art director, was born near Westfield, N. J., in 1843, son of Isaac and Charlotte Osborn Drake. In his boyhood he displayed a decided talent for art, and at an early age began the study of wood engraving in New York under John W. Orr, the leading wood engraver in America at that time. Afterward for several years he continued this study under William Howland. In the prosecution of his art he also studied drawing, first with August Will, and later in the evening classes at Cooper Union and the National Academy of Design, then the only two art schools of importance in New York. After a number of years spent in wood engraving, he took up drawing on wood for engravers. Later he taught drawing at Cooper Union, and devoted several years to the study of art from nature, in water colors, black and white, and oil. In 1865 Mr. Drake established himself in the business of wood engraving, doing work for publishers. In 1870 he was made art superintendent of "Scribner's Monthly," which in 1881 became known as the "Century Magazine," and with which Mr. Drake has since been continuously connected. The liberal policy of the publishers of this magazine made it possible for Mr. Drake to give full scope to his progressive ideas, and he introduced new methods and radical innovations that helped to revolutionize the art of wood engraving, and the success of his efforts is illustrated in the high standard which the art has reached in the "Century Magazine" and "St. Nicholas." Mr. Drake also deserves great credit for his encouragement of pen drawing and illustration in general. He has been identified with many of the important art movements in this country for the past twenty-five years. He was one of the organizers of the great Bartholdi Loan Exhibition, held for the purpose of raising funds to build the pedestal for the Statue of Liberty. He was also on the committee of the Washington Centennial Loan Exhibition, and one of the art committee for the erection of the Washington Memorial Arch. Mr. Drake has contributed several short

stories to the "Century Magazine," which show him to be a writer of charming fancy and originality. Several of his poems have also appeared in different periodicals. He is an untiring collector, and has a most remarkable collection of old masters, old hammered brass and copper, and curious old rings. He was one of the founders of the Grolier and Aldine Clubs; and is a member of the Century Association, the Players' Club, the Architectural League and Municipal Art League of New York, and the Cosmos Club of Washington, D. C.

CHASE, William Thomas, clergyman, was born in Hallowell, Me., July 11, 1839, third child of William and Mary (Roberts) Chase. He comes of old English stock, one of his ancestors, a son of Sir Richard Chase, of Chesham, Eng., having been among the first settlers of Hampton, N. H., in 1640. The great-grandson of this early settler, a Harvard graduate, and the only other clergyman of the line, was a Congregational minister in Kittery, Me. While he was still in his boyhood, his father, who was a farmer, was killed by an accident, and this sudden bereavement gave his mother a nervous shock from which she never fully recovered. Thrown thus early on his own resources, his way through school and college was attended with many sacrifices and privations. With a manly spirit he took the chief burden of the education of a sister, as well as his own, teaching school in winter, and working on a farm in summer. In this way he succeeded in getting through his preparatory studies, and entered Waterville College, in 1860, at the age of twenty-one. The war breaking out soon after, he entered the army as chaplain of a colored regiment, and was stationed at Port Hudson, La., both before and after its surrender. While there, he prevailed on Gen. Andrews, commanding the post, to permit the building of schools for the colored troops, and devoted himself to teaching them. After a year's service in the army he returned to college, and was graduated in July, 1865. A year was now spent in teaching, and then he entered Newton Theological Institution, graduating in 1869. His first pastorate was in Dover, N. H., from 1869–74. In 1874 he was called to an important church in Lewiston, Me., and in 1879 to a large and influential church in Cambridge, Mass. In 1884 he was induced to settle in Minneapolis, Minn. While there, he received from the Chicago University, in 1894, the title of D.D. After five years in the West he returned to New England, occupying the pulpit of the famous Ruggles Street Church in Boston for two and one half years, when he was called, in 1891, to the Fifth Baptist Church of Philadelphia. Dr. Chase has brought incessant energy and devotion to his work. His pastorates have laid upon him exceptionally heavy burdens. At Lewiston he inspired the church to lift a debt of $33,000, which was crushing it. At Cambridge the church was burned, and a splendid building was erected in its place. At Minneapolis a still more magnificent structure was erected. Amid all these labors, the spiritual part of his work has never been neglected, and his ministry has been characterized by constant additions. Dr. Chase has sustained important relations with the great missionary activities of his denomination. He has served as a member of the executive committee and board of managers of the American Baptist Missionary Union, as a member of the board of managers of the American Baptist Publication Society, trustee of the Newton Theological Institution, and president of the Baptist Education Society of Maine. He has been called repeatedly to deliver sermons and addresses before the national conventions of the denomination with which he is connected.

ABBOTT, David, pioneer, was born at Brookfield, Mass., Dec. 5, 1765, was educated at Yale College, and practiced law in Rome, N. Y., until 1788, when he removed to Ohio. He was the sheriff of Trumbull county when it included the entire Western Reserve, and a member of the convention which formed the constitution of the state in 1802. Subsequently he was repeatedly a member of the legislature, and, in 1812, one of the presidential electors for Ohio. In 1808 he became the first landowner in what is now Erie county. He was a man of eccentric habits, and had no difficulty in adapting himself to the primitive conditions of a newly-settled country. He had an Indian's love of the forest, and delighted in nothing so much as in prolonged fishing excursions upon Lake Erie, during which he several times traversed the entire distance from Fort Niagara to Detroit in an open boat. On one occasion, in a frail skiff, with but a single companion, he was caught in a furious storm, driven a hundred miles diagonally across the lake, and thrown, half drowned, upon the Canada shore. The boat had been kept afloat only by the constant bailing of his companion, but once on land, they were in a scarcely better condition, being in a wide forest remote from any human habitation. By dint of persevering effort, the boat was at last repaired with twigs and the inner bark of trees, and again launched upon the lake; and, finally, at the end of more than a month, during which they subsisted solely upon fish and wild berries, the voyagers reached their homes; Abbott to find that his funeral sermon had been preached, and that his wife had gone into mourning. Subsequently he did his fishing nearer shore, and died comfortably in his bed in the year 1822.

BATTERSON, James Goodwin, insurance president, was born in Bloomfield, Conn., Feb. 23, 1823. He was given an academical education, and was prepared for, but did not enter, college. The business of the father, who was a dealer in building stone, naturally interested the son; and wisely improving his opportunities, he gained an intimate knowledge of the geological formations of different rocks, as well as their adaptability for special uses, which knowledge contributed in no small degree to his subsequent success in life. He first went into the printing and publishing house of Mack, Andrus & Co., Ithaca, N. Y.; then returned to his home in Litchfield, and commenced the study of law in the office of Judge Seymour, but in 1845 he opened in business as an importer and dealer in granite and marble, transferring his headquarters to Hartford, where he has since resided. From a comparatively small beginning, his business has increased until now it is one of the largest in the United States. He owns and operates extensive granite quarries at Westerly, R. I., and Concord, N. H. He erected the magnificent capitol at Hartford, the Connecticut Mutual Life Insurance Co.'s building at Hartford, the Mutual Life and Equitable Life Insurance Co.'s buildings at New York, the W. K. Vanderbilt residence at Newport, R. I., and the Library of Congress at Washington, D. C. Mr. Batterson was the

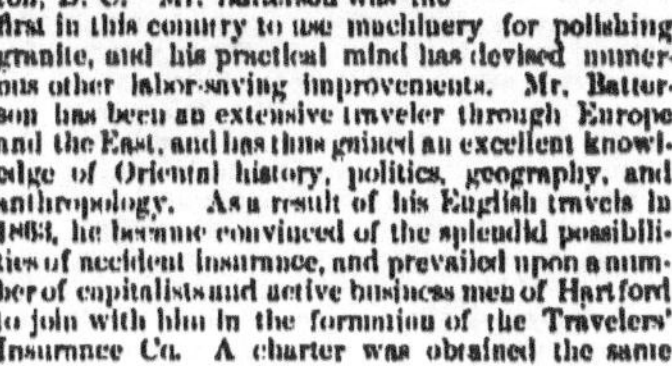

first in this country to use machinery for polishing granite, and his practical mind has devised numerous other labor-saving improvements. Mr. Batterson has been an extensive traveler through Europe and the East, and has thus gained an excellent knowledge of Oriental history, politics, geography, and anthropology. As a result of his English travels in 1863, he became convinced of the splendid possibilities of accident insurance, and prevailed upon a number of capitalists and active business men of Hartford to join with him in the formation of the Travelers' Insurance Co. A charter was obtained the same year for insuring against accidents in traveling, and $250,000 was secured as capital. The next year the charter was amended to allow the company to insure against accidents of all kinds. The sudden growth and prosperity of the new business brought forth a swarm of rival companies. In the winter of 1864 over a dozen accident insurance companies were organized in the western states, and early in 1865 some twenty-five accident companies applied for charters, and soon the railroad companies began to start accident organizations of their own. In 1866 a new corporation was formed, known as the Railway Passengers' Assurance Co., composed of representatives of all the leading accident companies, to consolidate the railway-ticket business under one management, which, however, a few years later was incorporated in the ticket department of the Travelers' Insurance Co. The success of the latter was largely the result of incessant labors and the severest economy from the time of its start in an up-stairs room, furnished solely with an old table, a pine desk, and a few chairs. A few years after the company was started, when its accident field seemed likely to be more than filled, Mr. Batterson added a regular life department, the success of which has been equally pronounced. Mr. Batterson has been the moving and controlling force in the management of the Travelers' Insurance Co. since its inception in 1863. Both Yale and Williams Colleges have conferred upon Mr. Batterson the degree of M.A. The first was given at the suggestion of his intimate friend, Dr. Bushnell, in view of the exceptional service he rendered in promoting and upbuilding the educational interests of Hartford. Besides the presidency of the Travelers' Insurance Co., Mr. Batterson is president of the New England Granite Works, senior member of the firm of Batterson, See & Eisele, granite dealers of New York, and is officially connected with numerous other corporations. He is a formidable debater, a capable actuary, and a thorough student of economics. His judgment in art is good, as is evidenced by his fine collection of pictures, which cover a remarkable range of schools and subjects. Mr. Batterson married Eunice Elizabeth, daughter of Jonathan Goodwin, Esq., of Hartford. His son, James G. Batterson, Jr., is vice-president of the New England Granite Works, and his daughter, Mary Elizabeth, is the wife of Charles Cofling Beach, M. D.

ANDREWS, Sherlock James, jurist, was born at Wallingford, Conn., Nov. 17, 1801. He was graduated at Union College in 1821, after which he continued his studies at Yale, and acted as assistant to Prof. Silliman in his lectures. He was admitted to the bar, and removed to Ohio in 1825, where he soon took high rank in his profession. He had few equals in his power over a jury, whom he seemed to sway at will, by his wit, eloquence, and eccentricity. It is related that he was once employed by a clergyman to bring against a parishioner a suit for slander. The opposing lawyer, who was an avowed atheist, had stated to the jury that the suit was an attempt to levy blackmail; that all clergymen were mercenary, and there was nothing in religion but money. As he rose to reply, Mr. Andrews drew his watch from his pocket, and holding it out to the jury, said: "The gentleman asserts that there is nothing in religion but money; in other words, that this watch never had a maker, and this beautiful world, and the glorious heavens over our heads came into being without a Creator; that all this magnificent frame of earth and sky is the result of chance and accident. If that be so, has he no fear that chance may some day catch hold of him, and whirl him into some region where all is everlasting chance and chaos?" He said no more, made not the remotest allusion to the case of his client, but without leaving their seats the jury rendered a verdict for the clergyman, with handsome damages. In 1840 Mr. Andrews was elected to congress, and in 1848 was appointed a judge of the superior court of Ohio, and was a member of the constitutional conventions of 1848 and 1873. He subsequently declined a nomination for the governorship of the state. He died Feb. 11, 1880.

BOYD, Isaac Snedecor, manufacturer, was born in Lauderdale county, Miss., Feb. 22, 1843. His parents removed three years afterward to Sumter county, Ala. His great-grandparents, John and Jane Boyd, came to America in 1769 from county Down, Ireland, on the same vessel with one Tygert family, and settled in South Carolina. His grandparents, Nathan Boyd and Elizabeth Tygert, were infants on the vessel, only six months old, and were married Jan. 20, 1792. Their children were one daughter and nine sons, nearly all becoming Methodist preachers. One of these, Rev. L. M. Boyd, the father of Isaac, went from Newberry district, S. C., to Green county, Ala., when quite young, and in 1837 married Sarah Emily Snedecor, a descendant of an old and aristocratic family of Kentucky. She was of superior culture and Christian endowments, and gave to her son the qualities that overcame adverse circumstances. He early displayed a love of truth and integrity. At his first school he bore the reputation of being the most truthful boy of 100 pupils. At eleven years of age he joined the Methodist church, and from that time lived a consistent Christian life, holding responsible positions in the church, and becoming secretary of the Church Conference and recording steward of the First Methodist Episcopal Church South in Atlanta, Ga., the leading Methodist church, South. He had an academic education, but before completing it he, from a sense of duty, enlisted in the fall of 1862 as a private in the 36th Alabama regiment of infantry, C. S. A. At the great battle of Chickamauga's famous "River of Death,"

he fell in the front badly wounded, and will carry to his grave the leaden memento of that bloody struggle. Owing to this wound he was assigned to post duty until the surrender. The war left him with deficient education and without means. For a few months he assisted his old preceptor in teaching. Late in 1865 he began farming and did this three years, after which, on account of the unsettled condition of labor, he went into the fire and life insurance business, at which he was eminently successful from the start. In 1869 he removed to Georgia, and though young and a stranger, won the confidence of the best people of the state. In 1871 he located in Atlanta, where he built up an extended and lucrative life and fire insurance business. In 1884 he retired from insurance, and began the successful manufacture of furniture. His partner was Thomas N. Baxter, but the firm was soon incorporated as the Boyd & Baxter Factory, of which he was the president, and whose success was very great. The factory was thoroughly equipped and beautifully located in a grove of oaks, and the business extended throughout the South. They were the largest and leading furniture manufacturers of the southern states. He married, November, 1871, Mrs. Mary Lucy Holliday, daughter of John Ray of Newnan, Ga., who died in November, 1891. In the fall of 1893 he married Nannie Seawell of Nashville, Tenn., a lady of brilliant artistic and literary accomplishments. In the fall of 1892 the Boyd & Baxter Furniture

Factory was leased to capitalists, who organized it into the National Furniture Factory. Mr. Boyd has taken rank among the best citizens of the progressive city with which he has become identified, his business and personal excellencies having made him a leader, while his sagacity and worth are universally recognized.

COOKE, Josiah Parsons, chemist, was born at Boston, Mass., Oct. 12, 1827, a lineal descendant of Maj. Aaron Cooke, who emigrated to America from England in 1630, and was one of the earlier settlers of Dorchester, afterwards Northampton, Mass. His father was a lawyer, and one of the oldest members of the Suffolk (Mass.) bar. He was prepared for college at the Boston Latin School, and entered Harvard in 1844, from which he was graduated in 1848. He went abroad for one year, and in 1849 returned to the university to accept the position of tutor of mathematics. He was subsequently appointed instructor in chemistry, and after filling this position one year, succeeded to the Erving professorship of chemistry and mineralogy. The course of chemistry under his direction has developed from a meagre beginning until the opportunities offered for study and research are nowhere excelled. He did not originally have any systematic scientific training, but acquired his love of chemistry from lectures given by the elder Silliman at the Lowell Institute. He began his first lectures at Cambridge, with the apparatus he had collected in a small laboratory in his father's house while a lad. He took the initial step in introducing laboratory instruction in the undergraduate course of an American college, and has been successful in his undertaking to render the inductive methods of experimental science a legitimate means of liberal culture in the preparatory schools as well as the college. He has published, in connection with his teaching, "Chemical Problems and Reactions, to accompany Stöckhardt's Elements of Chemistry," "Elements of Chemical Physics," and "Principles of Chemical Philosophy," and to him more than to any other chemist, may be accorded the credit of having made chemistry an exact and disciplinary study in American colleges. He has delivered a number of popular lectures in different cities, Lowell, Worcester, Brooklyn, Baltimore, and Washington, besides five courses at the Lowell Institute, Boston. His course of lectures given before the Brooklyn Institute, were afterward published under the title of "Religion and Chemistry; or, Proofs of God's Plan in the Atmosphere and its Elements." He aimed to demonstrate in these discourses that the argument for design is not invalidated by the theories of evolution. In 1872 he delivered an entertaining and valuable course of lectures on the "New Chemistry," which was subsequently published in the International Scientific Series, and was translated into most of the European languages. His discourse on "Scientific Culture," delivered at Harvard University, printed in the "Popular Science Monthly," and afterwards republished in London, was one of the most able contributions to the literature of scientific education that have recently appeared. He has written a number of minor papers, which are valuable contributions to the bibliography of science. As director of the Harvard Chemical Laboratory he published a number of contributions to chemical science. His many mineral analyses, with description of new species, have appeared in the "Proceedings of the American Academy of Sciences and

Arts," and the "American Journal of Science," with both of which he was editorially connected. In 1882 he was awarded the degree of LL.D. from the University of Cambridge, England, and in 1889 from Harvard. He was elected foreign honorary member of the Chemical Society of London, and a member of many learned societies in America and Europe. His scientific publications include: "Chemical Problems and Reactions," "Elements of Chemical Physics," "First Principles of Chemical Philosophy," "The New Chemistry," and "Fundamental Principles of Chemistry." His literary contributions comprise: "Religion and Chemistry," "Scientific Culture, and Other Essays," and "The Credentials of Science the Warrant of Faith." His life was wholly absorbed in his studies, and was little given to social intercourse. His work created a profound impression throughout the world, and gave him a high place among the world's thinkers. He died in Cambridge, Mass., Sept. 3, 1894.

WINSTON, Joseph, soldier, was born in Louisa county, Va., June 17, 1746. He was descended from a family originally of English blood, the earliest American member of which was one of five brothers who emigrated about the middle of the 17th century from Winston Hall in Yorkshire, and settled in Hanover county, Va. He received a fair education, and at the age of seventeen joined a company of rangers under Capt. Phelps which, on Sept. 30, 1763, was drawn into an ambuscade by the Indians and defeated by them. Young Winston's horse was killed under him, he himself was twice wounded, and left in an almost helpless condition. He managed to conceal himself, however, until the Indians were gone, when a comrade came to his aid and carried him on his back for three days until they at last reached a friendly frontier cabin. He recovered from his wound in time, but the ball never being extracted, it occasionally caused him pain. He was an early and devoted friend to the cause of independence and, in 1755, took part in Braddock's defeat. In 1769, failing to obtain a grant of 10,000 acres south of the Guyandotte river, he emigrated to North Carolina and settled in what is now Forsythe county. He was a member of the Hillsboro' Convention which met Aug. 21, 1775, and all hopes of reconciliation with the royal government being now ended, he erected a provisional form of government for the state. In 1776 he was created ranger of Surrey county and major of militia and served in Rutherford's expedition against the Cherokees. The following year he was a member of the House of Commons from Surrey, and assisted in making a treaty with the Cherokees at Long Island which, although made without taking any oath, has never yet been violated. In 1780 he served with Col. Davidson in pursuit of Bryan's forces and was with Cleveland in his movements against the loyalists on New River. He commanded a portion of the right wing in the fierce and bloody battle of King's Mountain on Oct. 8th, when the Americans succeeded in driving the British from their lofty position. Over 200 of the British were killed and 890 were captured, while but 88 of the Americans were killed and wounded. The legislature of the state voted Joseph Winston an elegant sword for his distinguished services on that day. In February, 1781, he led a party against a band of Tories and defeated them; he then took part in the battle of Guilford Court House, the effects of which were almost a victory for the Americans. In 1793-95 and again in 1803-07 he was a member of congress. The county seat of Forsythe county, N. C., was named after him. He was a man of stately form, old school manners, and commanding presence. He died within the lofty mountains of Stokes and Surrey, in the neighborhood of Germantown, N. C., Apr. 21, 1815, leaving many worthy descendants.

BENHAM, Robert T., revolutionary soldier, was born in Virginia about 1745. He probably entered the Continental army at the beginning of the war, but the first authentic record of him dates from about July, 1779, when he held the rank of captain, and was in command of a company at Fort Pitt, now Pittsburg. The fort being short of provisions, he was at that time dispatched, with Maj. Rodgers and seventy men, in a couple of keel boats, down the Ohio and Mississippi to New Orleans, for clothing and military supplies for the garrison. About the middle of October the laden boats arrived, on their return trip, at the sand-bar which is formed by the waters of the Little Miami, and stretches entirely across the Ohio to the Kentucky shore, about five miles above Cincinnati. Both rivers were on a freshet, and the Little Miami was pouring into the Ohio with great velocity. As Maj. Rodgers approached along the Kentucky bank, he perceived a number of canoes, filled with savages, driven out of the mouth of the Little Miami by the rapid current directly towards the southern extremity of the sand-bar, on which several Indians were already collected. Evidently they were a hunting or war party of Ohio red-skins, about to go upon a raid into Kentucky. His own boats were hidden by the undergrowth that grew along the banks of the river, and, deeming himself unobserved, he landed sixty-five of his men, with the intention of surrounding the united Indians when they should have come together upon the sand-bar. This he proceeded to do, but, before he reached the spot, he was suddenly encircled by a force of savages of more than treble his own numbers, who poured upon him a close rifle fire, and then, throwing away their guns, rushed upon them with their tomahawks. His men were panic-stricken, and scattered in all directions, leaving their commander and about forty of their comrades dead upon the ground, or badly wounded, and soon to be dispatched by the savages. The remainder of the force broke through the Indian lines, and fled into the forest, encumbered there by a dense undergrowth, which, in the approaching darkness, would afford them protection. But the Indians were in close pursuit, firing as they followed. Among the fugitives was Capt. Benham, who, however, had not gone far before an Indian ball passed through his hips, shattering the bones, and bringing him to the ground. Fortunately a large tree, recently blown down, lay near by, and dragging himself with difficulty in among its top branches, he soon saw the Indians pass him unobserved, in their eager pursuit of his comrades. By midnight all was quiet, but on the following morning the savages returned from their fruitless pursuit, to strip the dead and rifle the one boat they had captured—the other having put out from shore, and escaped down the river. Left thus alone, and unable to move, Benham was in danger of famishing; but he made no sound, for he knew well that if discovered he would be instantly dispatched—it being the Indian custom to slaughter all prisoners who would encumber a march. He had staunched his flowing wound as well as he could, by binding about his hips pieces of his underclothing, and now he lay in the fallen tree-top till the evening of the second day, looking forward to death as a thing inevitable. But just at dark, happening to glance up at the sky, he observed a raccoon coming down a neighboring tree, and reaching quickly for his rifle, he fired, and brought the creature to the ground, where he hoped it would lie until the following day, when he might manage to crawl to the spot, build a fire, and, on its flesh, put off for a little time his expected death from starvation. Scarcely had the report of his rifle

died away, when he heard a human cry, coming, as he thought, from a distance of not more than a hundred and fifty yards. He silently reloaded his rifle, to sell his life as dearly as possible, and while doing so, heard the cry again, this time nearer than before. Still he made no reply, but softly drawing back the hammer of his gun, peered intently through the branches that concealed him, for a first shot at his adversary. Then, still nearer, came a third halloo, followed by the words, " Whoever you are—for God's sake, answer me!" It was the voice of one of his own men, named John Watson, who, in his flight, had received a shot through both his arms, completely disabling them. It was a joyful meeting to the captain, for it put him suddenly in possession of a sturdy pair of feet. One man was the complement of the other: Benham was all arms, Watson all legs; and each had a brain of his own, which was especially fortunate, seeing that abundant mental resources would be required to extricate them from the untraveled wilderness where they were, alone, surrounded by hostile savages, and more than a hundred miles from any friendly human being. But the situation of the two was not now altogether desperate. They were no longer in danger of immediate starvation, for Benham could kill the game, while Watson could, with his feet propel it from where it fell, to a fire that Benham had built of twigs, gathered in the same manner. Thus they lived for several weeks, till Benham's wound was sufficiently healed to permit him to hobble short distances on crutches. Then by easy stages they journeyed about five miles to the mouth of Licking river. There they built a hut on the present site of Newport, and waited, in the hope of being rescued by some friendly boat passing down the Ohio. But they waited long, for few at that period were venturing into the "dark and bloody ground of Kentucky." November came with heavy rains and furious storms, and at length with chilling sleet and drifting snows, the foretellings of the terrible winter of 1780—the coldest ever known on this continent—but the sound of no friendly oar broke the stillness of the river solitudes. At last, when the 27th of that month had arrived, and the two men had been six long weeks in the forest wilderness, a boat hove in sight coming down the river. Instantly Benham hoisted his hat upon a pole, and shouted with all the strength of his lungs to attract the attention of the voyagers. Soon he perceived that his signals were seen, for every oar was manned, and the boat propelled with all speed—to the opposite side of the river. It was a common stratagem of the Indians to exhibit false signals of distress, and thus decoy unsuspecting boats to their destruction. The river  was wide, and at the distance the crew could not distinguish Benham and Watson from Indians, so they stretched to their oars, and rowed rapidly down the river. As the two deserted men saw the boat receding from them, their hopes gave way to despair, for the place where they were was much frequented by Indians, and should they escape discovery, they could not, in their open hut, survive the rigor of the coming winter. But as Benham continued to wave his hat and shout after the receding voyagers, the crew brought their canoe to shore, took Benham and Watson on board, and paddled them down to the boat, where their story was believed, and they were given every possible attention. In due time they arrived at the Falls of the Ohio (now Louisville), where Benham remained until fully recovered of his wound, when he made his way back to Pittsburg. He subsequently served throughout the Indian war—was with the expeditions of Harmar and Wilkinson, and shared in the defeat of St. Clair in Wabash county, and the victory of Wayne at Fallen Timbers. The war over, he settled in Campbell county, Ky., where in 1794, he was one of the first judges of the county court, but he soon removed to Warren county, Ohio, where he lived, greatly respected, "in a double cabin, about a mile below Lebanon, on what is now known as the Flarney farm," and there he died, a few years prior to the last war with Great Britain.

COXE, Tench, political economist and father of the American cotton industry, was born in Philadelphia, Pa., May 22, 1755. He came of a distinguished family, his mother being a daughter of Tench Francis. After receiving an academic education, he began the study of law, but his father determined to make him a merchant, and in a short time he was put in the counting-house of Coxe & Furman. In 1776 he was made a member of that firm. During the early part of the revolution he took sides with the royalists, and when Howe evacuated Philadelphia he was arrested, and released on parole. Subsequently he became a Whig, served in the Annapolis convention in 1786, and in 1788 was a member of the Continental congress. He joined the Federalist party on its formation, and from 1789 until 1792 served as assistant secretary of the treasury. In 1792 he was made commissioner of the revenue, but was removed by Adams, whereupon he joined the Republican party. During the presidential canvass of 1800 he published the letter which Adams had written him in reference to Pinckney, and for this he was denounced as a renegade and traitor by the Federalist leaders and press. From 1803 until 1812, by appointment of Jefferson, he served as purveyor of public supplies. It is not, however, his political services that gave Tench Coxe the greatest claim to remembrance. He has frequently, and with justice, been called the father of the American cotton industry. He first essayed, in 1789, to transport an Arkwright machine from England to the United States, and for many years, with voice and pen, constantly urged the planters of the South to undertake the culture of cotton. He was a prolific writer, and his writings cover a wide and varied field; but he was at his best in dealing with statistical and economic subjects. His best known works are: "An Inquiry into the Principles for a Commercial System for the United States" (1787); "Examination of Lord Sheffield's Observations on the Commerce of the United Provinces" (1792); and "View of the United States" (1787–94). His papers, dealing with the workings of the treasury department, will be found in the "American State Papers." He died in Philadelphia, Pa., July 17, 1824.

DUVALL, Alvin, jurist, was born in Scott county, near Georgetown, Ky., March 20, 1813, the son of John Alvin Duvall, a native of Maryland, an officer in the war of 1812, and a member of the Kentucky legislature of 1827. He gave his son Alvin the best education that the schools of the times and the state afforded. He was graduated with distinction from Georgetown College in 1838, and subsequently studied law under Gov. James F. Robinson at Georgetown, completing his legal course at Transylvania University, near Lexington, in March, 1840. In 1850 he was elected a member of the legislature, and two years later appointed circuit judge, to fill an unexpired term of a deceased judge of the district. At the expiration of his term in 1854, he was elected judge of the court of appeals, holding this office until 1864, when he was again a candidate for the office. By order of Gen. Burbridge, who was then military governor of the state, his name was stricken from the poll-books three days prior to the election, and by the same order Judge Duvall was arrested and imprisoned, along with other prominent men in the state, on the ground that he was a sympathizer with the Confederate cause. In order to avert this unjust decree, Judge Duvall went to Canada, where he remained two months, subsequently returning to Georgetown, where he resumed his law practice. In 1866 he was appointed reporter of the court of appeals, and published two reports of that court, the first and second, which the bar of this state, as well as other states, have highly commended for their accurate, concise, and comprehensive digest of opinions delivered. When the Democratic party was reorganized, after the close of the civil war, he was appointed clerk of the court of appeals. Judge Duvall had one of the largest law practices in the state of Kentucky. He was a hard student, a man of high scholarship, with a well-poised mind, ever ready with his legal knowledge, and was regarded as one of the ablest jurists in Kentucky. His legal opinions were widely quoted, and the soundness and equity of his decisions were never questioned. Judge Duvall was married in 1843 to Mrs. Virginia Holtzclaw, of Scott county, Ky., who, with eight children, survives him. He died at Frankfort, Ky., Nov. 17, 1891.

CHURCH, Frederick Edwin, artist, was born in Hartford, Conn., May 4, 1826. Early in life his talent for art was prominent, and after some preliminary studies in that direction, he placed himself under the tutelage of Thomas Cole, R.A., to whom may be directly traced the primal success of the art of landscape painting in this country, and resided with him in the Catskills. While his society and instruction furthered the artistic development of Church, the latter showed from the first a marked individuality of style. He soon became well known as a landscape painter, and critics awarded him praise for accuracy of drawing and great mechanical dexterity, and a vivid appreciation of nature. He spent a short time in Switzerland, and in 1853 visited South America, to study the picturesque aspects of that remarkable country. His "View of Niagara Falls," now in the Corcoran Art Gallery, Washington, D. C., is recognized as the first satisfactory production by art of this wonderful phase of nature; it won a prize at the French Exhibition, 1867. He conceived an original idea of painting icebergs, and went in a small boat to study this architecture of the sea; the result of which was his marvelously true work, "The Icebergs," owned by Sir Edward Watkins, M.P., London. He has traveled extensively in this country and abroad, studying nature, and giving to the world numerous productions of a high character, the fruit of his skilful and ready brush. He

is a student and reader of a thoughtful turn of mind, and a ready and pleasing conversationalist. He spent three years in the selection of his picturesque estate on the Hudson, and finally succeeded in satisfying his artistic eye. The magnificent chateau which adorns the romantic environment of Hudson, Columbia co., is one of the most elegant of the many handsome residences that add so much glory to the Rhine of America. He was his own architect, and is constantly adding new beauties and improvements to his already complete establishment, where his friends find cordial welcome and generous hospitality.

BASS, Edward, first Protestant Episcopal bishop of Massachusetts, and seventh in succession in the American episcopate, was born in Dorchester, Mass., Nov. 23, 1726. He was given a liberal primary education, entered Harvard, and was graduated in the class of 1744. He engaged in teaching immediately after his graduation, and was licensed to preach in Congregational churches. In 1852 he applied for orders in the Protestant Episcopal church, and was ordained both as deacon and priest by Bishop Sherlock in London, whence he had journeyed for the purpose. Upon his return, in May, 1752, he was installed rector of St. Paul's Church, Newburyport, Mass., which place he made his home during his life. Upon the colonies withdrawing their allegiance from Great Britain, Mr. Bass yielded to the popular sentiment in favor of independence, and omitted the prayers as set down in the prayer-book for the royal family, and, in consequence, lost the annual stipend contributed to the clergy by the Society for Propagating the Gospel in Foreign Parts. He, however, continued the services of the church until the war was over, and then applied for arrearages of stipend, but the society refused. This action led him to publish his defense in a pamphlet which was issued in London in 1786. The University of Pennsylvania conferred on him the degree of S.T.D. in 1789. In 1796 a convention of clerical and lay delegates from the newly organized Protestant Episcopal Church in Massachusetts, unanimously elected Mr. Bass to become bishop of the diocese. He was consecrated in Philadelphia by Bishop White, assisted by Bishops Provoost and Claggett, May 7, 1797, and his jurisdiction extended over the churches in Rhode Island and New Hampshire, he continuing, in addition to his duties as bishop, to exercise his care as priest of his parish at Newburyport, where he died Sept. 10, 1803.

PARKER, Samuel, second Protestant Episcopal bishop of Massachusetts, and tenth in succession in the American episcopate, was born in Portsmouth,

N. H., Aug. 17, 1744, son of William Parker, an eminent lawyer and jurist. The son was prepared for college in his native city, and entered at Harvard. He was graduated in the class of 1764. He then prepared for orders in the Protestant Episcopal church, teaching in the meantime. In October, 1773, he was offered the position of assistant rector of Trinity Church, Boston. In order to accept the offer, he was obliged to go to England to be ordained, and on Feb. 25, 1774, was made deacon, and three days later was ordained priest, both ceremonies being performed by Dr. Terrick, lord bishop of London. Upon his return to America, in November, 1774, he assumed his duties. When the revolution took place in 1776, he was the only Episcopal clergyman to remain at his post, and side with his countrymen, and in 1779 he was made rector of the parish. At the close of the war he sought to revive and give aid to the scattered Episcopal churches of the diocese, which had been deserted by their rec-

tors, and did much to encourage them, through his office as agent for the Society for the Propagation of the Gospel. In 1803 the general convention unanimously elected him to succeed Bishop Bass in the episcopate of Massachusetts, and he was consecrated at Trinity Church, New York city, Sept. 14, 1804, by Bishop White, assisted by Bishops Claggett, Jarvis, and Moore. On returning to Boston, he was prostrated by an attack of the gout, from which he never recovered, and which affliction rendered it impossible for him to perform one single episcopal act. In 1789 the University of Pennsylvania conferred upon him the degree of D.D. Bishop Parker died Dec. 6, 1804.

EASTBURN, Manton, third Protestant Episcopal bishop of Massachusetts, was born in Leeds, England, Feb. 9, 1801. His parents removed to the United States when he was a child. His brother was James Wallis E., who wrote the hymn, "O, Holy, Holy, Holy, Lord." In his youth Manton Eastburn was of a religious turn of mind, and had a decided taste for theological discussions. In 1817 he was graduated at Columbia College, and entered the General Protestant Episcopal Theological Seminary in New York. He was ordained in 1822, and officiated as assistant minister in Christ Church for several years thereafter. In 1827 he became rector of the church of Ascension, and on Dec. 29, 1842, was

made assistant bishop of the diocese of Massachusetts. Upon the death of Bishop Griswold of the Eastern Diocese, he became bishop of Massachusetts. He took large interest in missionary work, and upon his death bequeathed his property to the domestic missions in Massachusetts, and to the endowment of a Protestant Episcopal Theological School at Cambridge, and to the American Bible Society. Among his publications were, "Four Lectures on Hebrew, Latin, and English Poetry," delivered before the New York Athenæum (1825); and a portion of a volume of "Essays and Dissertations on Biblical Literature" (1829); also "Lectures on the Epistles to the Philippians" (1833). He delivered the oration at the centennial anniversary of Columbia College in 1837. He edited Thornton's "Family Prayer" (1830). He died in Boston, Mass., Sept. 11, 1872.

PADDOCK, Benjamin Henry, fourth Protestant Episcopal bishop of Massachusetts, was born at Norwich, Conn., Feb. 29, 1828, son of Seth B. Paddock, for twenty-three years rector of Christ Church, Norwich. He entered Trinity College, Hartford, where he was graduated with highest honors in the class of 1848. After his graduation he taught for one year in the Episcopal Academy, Cheshire, Conn., and subsequently entered the New York General Theological Seminary, and was graduated in 1852. He was, upon graduation, ordained a deacon by Bishop Brownell, of Connecticut, and immediately afterward returned to New York city, to serve as assistant minister in the Church of the Epiphany, in charge of the Rev. Dr. Locke Jones. He was, on Sept. 27, 1853, ordained a priest at Norwich, Conn., by Bishop Williams. He then accepted the rectorship of St. Luke's Church, Portland, Me., now the cathedral church of Bishop Neeley. After remaining there three months, he resigned his pastorate on account of ill health. In 1853 he accepted a call to Trinity Church, Norwich, Conn., a church founded years previously by his illustrious father. He remained with this charge for seven years, and in 1860 assumed the rectorship of Christ Church, Detroit,

Mich. At a special meeting of the house of bishops in 1868, he was elected missionary bishop of Oregon, but declined the appointment. In 1869 he was called to Grace Church, Brooklyn, N. Y., and remained in charge of this parish until 1873, when he was elected bishop of Massachusetts by the convention which met in Boston that year to name a successor to Bishop Manton Eastburn. His chief competitors were Dr. Henry C. Potter (afterward elected bishop of New York), Dr. James De Koven of Wisconsin, and Dr. George Leeds of Baltimore. After several ballots he was elected, and the election would have been made unanimous but for one dissenting voice. His name was, in 1891, brought into prominence by his refusing to open the pulpits of his diocese to the Anglican monk, Father Ignatius. He was the author of numerous magazine articles, sermons, canonical digests, etc., and was a learned scholar, and one of the most brilliant speakers in the Protestant Episcopal church. Bishop Paddock died in Boston, Mass., March 9, 1891.

BROOKS, Phillips, fifth Protestant Episcopal bishop of Massachusetts. (See Vol. II., p. 304.)

LAWRENCE, William, sixth Protestant Episcopal bishop of Massachusetts, was born in Boston, Mass., May 30, 1850. His father was Amos A. Lawrence, one of the founders of the city of Lawrence, Kan., which was named for him. His grandfathers were Amos Lawrence (q. v.) and William Appleton. After completing a preparatory course in the Boston schools, he entered Harvard, where he was graduated in 1871, when he studied at Andover for a year, and afterward for a year in the Philadelphia Divinity School. He was graduated at the Episcopal Theological School in Cambridge in 1875, and after spending a short time in Lawrence, Mass., became assistant to Dr. Packard at Grace Church, in that place, where he was ordained by Bishop Paddock, June 11, 1876. After Dr. Packard's death, that same year, he was elected rector, and continued in the rectorship until 1884, when he resigned, to accept the chair of homiletics at the Episcopal Theological School, at Cambridge, and on the death of Dean Gray, in 1890, Prof. Lawrence was elected to succeed him. His pastoral work was remarkably successful. He built up the parish, and impressed all whom he met as a man of rare executive ability, combined with eloquence and greatness as a preacher. He was also preacher at Harvard University (from 1888 to 1891). He received the degree of S.T.D. from Hobart College in 1890, and that of D.D. from Harvard in 1893. He was elected bishop of Massachusetts to succeed Bishop Phillips Brooks, on May 4, 1893, and was consecrated in Trinity Church, Boston, Oct. 5, 1894. Bishop

Lawrence is the author of a life of his father, Amos A. Lawrence, who was one of the benefactors of the theological school. This institution was founded in 1867 by B. T. Burr, for the education of young men for the Episcopal ministry. It aims at a high standard of scholarship.

WAGNER, William, philanthropist, was born in Philadelphia, Pa., Jan. 15, 1796, son of John Wagner, a cloth merchant and importer, distinguished as a man of great energy and probity, and who lived to an advanced age. His grandfather, Rev. M. Tobias Wagner, came to Pennsylvania from Würtemberg in 1742, and located at Reading as a Lutheran missionary. He was a great-grandson of Tobias Wagner, chancellor of the University of Tübingen, 1662. The boy evinced a great love of nature, and early commenced his study of science by making collections of curious natural specimens, which formed the nucleus of his afterward valuable collection deposited in the museum of the Wagner Free Institute of Science. His school training was acquired at the famous Academy of Dr. Abercrombie, where he was graduated with honor in 1808. He desired at this time to take up the study of medicine and surgery under the celebrated Dr. Physick, but his father advised him to a mercantile training, and he found employment in the counting-room of his brother-in-law, Mr. Shipley. Soon after, however, being offered a position in the office of Stephen Girard, he accepted the fortunate opportunity of so desirable a position. Mr. Girard took a marked interest in the lad, and rapidly promoted him, entrusting him with responsibilities belonging to a man of mature years. During the term of his clerkship he maintained his studies in French, Latin, and mathematics. In 1818, when twenty-two years old, he was sent as assistant supercargo on a trading voyage of two years' duration. This experience was full of adventure and incident. At the various ports at which they called, he made extensive collections of minerals, shells, plants, and organic remains that afterward found places in the museum. After leaving Mr. Girard, he engaged in coal mining in Schuylkill county and various other business ventures. In 1840 he retired from commercial pursuits. He was married on March 9, 1841, to Louisa Binney, and they went abroad soon after.

They traveled for two years, during which time he added largely to his collections. Upon his return he began the arrangement and classification of his specimens, and upon the completion of this work, in 1847, he began his course of scientific lectures to such listeners as would gather at his beautiful rural home. The number so increased that the accommodations in the house, shaded piazzas, and extensive lawn of his home were illy fitted for his ardent listeners, and in 1852 he secured a hall, and this in 1855 had evolved into the Wagner Free Institute of Science, with an able corps of well-known lecturers as assistants. On May 6, 1865, an edifice was dedicated, and Mr. Wagner, under charter authority granted by the commonwealth of Pennsylvania, transferred the building, its collections, cabinets, apparatus, and library to trustees, on condition that the property shall forever be used for instruction in natural science. Other valuable property was afterward conveyed to the corporation, and still further provisions made in the last will and testament of the founder. The total amount so contributed has been estimated at not less than half-a-million of dollars, while no money value can be placed on the vast collections preserved in the museum. Prof. Wagner continued to act as president of the institute until his death, which occurred Jan. 17, 1885.

CHOATE, Rufus, lawyer, was born in Essex, Mass., Oct. 1, 1799. John Choate, who became a citizen of Massachusetts in 1667, was his earliest ancestor in the United States. His grandfather, John Choate, was a member of the Massachusetts Legislature from 1741 to 1761, and for the five years following was a member of the council. Choate's father, David, was a man of pronounced character and intellect, and, although not a professional lawyer, he is said to have conducted a suit against himself,

making a sound and eloquent argument, and won the case. His wife was Miriam Foster, by whom he had several children. The son, Rufus, was always precocious. He could repeat large portions of the "Pilgrim's Progress" before he was six years old; was perfectly at home in the village library, and read the Bible with avidity. He was graduated first in his class from Dartmouth College in 1819. His inclination to study law was kindled by the great speech of Daniel Webster in the Dartmouth College case (1818), and he entered the Cambridge (Mass.) Law School in 1821, having spent one year as tutor at his alma mater. Thence he went to Washington, D. C., and pursued his studies in the office of William Wirt, then attorney-general of the United States. Studying after that at Ipswich and Salem, Mass., he was admitted to the bar in 1823, and practiced at Danvers, Mass., for five years. In 1825 Mr. Choate married Helen Olcott, of Hanover, N. H. He removed to Salem in 1828, and was elected to congress in 1830, where he at once distinguished himself by a speech on the tariff. He was re-elected in 1832, but when the winter session of 1834 was finished, he resigned, and settled in law practice at Boston, Mass. In 1850 he went to Europe, traveling throughout England, Belgium, France, and Germany. He was the acknowledged leader of the Massachusetts bar, and was regarded by the younger members of the profession with a love equal to their reverence. His legal career will be noted further on; his political history may be despatched in a few words. He was elected to the U. S. senate by the Massachusetts legislature to fill the unexpired term of Daniel Webster in 1841. In that body he spoke upon the Oregon boundary, the tariff, the U. S. Bank Bill, and the Smithsonian Institution, and vehemently opposed the annexation of Texas to the United States. He advocated the nomination of Daniel Webster for the United States presidency as a candidate of the Whig party, in 1852, and was an influential member of the convention for revising the Massachusetts state constitution in 1853. He acted with the Democratic party in the support of James Buchanan for the presidency in 1856. In 1859 his health failed, and he sailed from Boston for Europe, but died *en route*. During all his active life Mr. Choate was enthusiastically addicted to the cultivation of literary pursuits, and if he had not been eminent as a lawyer, would doubtless have left some permanent impressions upon American literature. His works (orations and speeches) were edited, with a copious memoir, by S. G. Brown, in 1862: (Boston, 2 vols.). The reputation of a mere lawyer, however great, is proverbially evanescent, but any careful study of the record of Mr. Choate makes it apparent that no mere advocate has ever arisen in the United States who has been his superior. That he possessed genius in the best sense of that often misunderstood term is

unquestionable, as it is that this was habitually manifest in the exercise of his profession. It will be conceded beyond this, by any one qualified to give judgment, that he was profound in the knowledge of the law, that he was both an acute and a comprehensive reasoner, and that his practical sagacity in the conduct of a case was not to be excelled. Nor do those judges go too far who have ranked him as the superior in natural powers, and the equal in effectiveness, as a pleading lawyer, of Lord Erskine, of England. He was a man of striking personal appearance—in his youth the very ideal of manly beauty; in his adult age, even down to the end of his days, his was a figure and face which fastened the attention of all in whose company he was cast. As an effective orator he has had few American equals; his power over juries was literally immense, and he often used it, not merely to please, persuade, astonish, and convince them, but, if need were, to overcome them. Traditional illustrations of his success are numerous, and of the most fascinating interest. In personal bearing and intercourse, however, he was urbanity itself. Wit he had in abundance, and employed it to good purpose. His logic, once his premises were granted, was inexorable, and his rhetoric, in his best efforts, fairly flaming. So continuous, so almost uninterrupted, were his legal victories, so manifold his resources, extending even to the strength of expression he could throw into his face, that imputations on his intellectual conscientiousness were not at all uncommon. "Why," said an old farmer, listening to an argument of Mr. Choate directed against his own interests, "why, that fellow can *cant* his countenance so as to draw the tears out of your eyes." But few lawyers, in truth, have ever had a higher ideal than his of what is due, in the nature of the case, to men whose cause they undertake, or permitted that ideal to dominate them more exclusively. While he is to be remembered as one of the most eloquent forensic advocates of any age or country, he is also to be regarded as a man of unsullied honesty of heart and purpose. Consult "Recollections of Eminent Men," by E. P. Whipple (Boston, 1886). Mr. Choate died in Halifax, N. S., July 13, 1859.

CORAM, Thomas, philanthropist, was born at Lynn Regis, Dorsetshire, Eng., in 1668. Nothing is known of his boyhood and youth, save that he was a shipwright in Taunton, Mass., in 1694, and owned a considerable tract of land. In 1708 the first record of his benevolent instinct is recorded, in that he gave to the Taunton authorities fifty-nine acres of land as the site for a church or school-house. In the deed of gift he is described as "of Boston in New England, sometimes residing in Taunton, in the county of Bristol, shipwright."  He also gave a library to Taunton. The Book of Common Prayer used in the church of that town was presented to him by Mr. Speaker Onslow, which fact points to his having enlisted the sympathy of others in his good works. He also appears as the master of a ship, as it is recorded that he was shipwrecked, plundered, and maltreated by wreckers at Cuxhaven, while a passenger on the Sea Flower. The affidavit accompanying the record describes him as "of London, mariner and shipwright." At this time he was engaged in the supply of stores to the navy. Soon after, he retired from a seafaring life, and devoted himself and his accumulations entirely to charitable objects. His experience in, and knowledge of, America gave him a special interest in the plantations, and he was a promoter of English colonization, notably in Georgia. He made a friend of Lord Walpole of Walterton (an uncle of Horace Walpole), who testified warmly to his honesty, disinterestedness, and knowledge of the subject of charity. That his logic was plain sense, his eloquence the natural language of the heart, is the estimate made of him by Dr. Brocklesby. After seventeen years of exertion, he succeeded in obtaining a royal charter for the establishment of the Foundling Hospital in London, of which Handel was one of the noblest benefactors. Capt. Coram expended his fortune in benevolent enterprises, and in his old age was dependent on the charity of friends. He greatly promoted American commerce by securing an act of parliament granting a bounty on naval stores of colonial production. His scheme for the education of Indian girls was interrupted by his death, which occurred March 29, 1751.

HAMER, Thomas Lyon, congressman and soldier, was born in Pennsylvania in 1800, the son of a poor farmer. He passed his boyhood days on the borders of Lake Champlain, where he witnessed the naval fight between McDonough and Capt. Downie. When seventeen years old he removed to Ohio, where he taught school, and at the same time studied law. He was admitted to the bar in 1821, and commenced the practice of his profession at Georgetown, in that state. He was elected a member of the state legislature, and served on important committees, being returned for several consecutive years, and serving as speaker of the house for one session. In 1832 he was elected to represent his congressional district at Washington, as an independent Democrat, his opponent in the canvass being Owen T. Fishback, the Whig nominee; Thomas Morris, the regular Democratic candidate (afterward U. S. senator); and William Russell, the present member, who had represented the district from 1827 to 1833, but who, on this occasion, was supported only by a few anti-Masons. His unsurpassed eloquence, effectively used on the stump, won his election, and as a member of the twenty-third congress, he appointed Ulysses S. Grant a cadet to the West Point Military Academy. He was re-elected to the twenty-fourth and twenty-fifth congresses, and on the outbreak of the war with Mexico, he enlisted as a private, and was elected major of the 1st Ohio Volunteers; but, on landing at Vera Cruz, presented to the commanding officer his commission, signed by President Polk, as brigadier-general, dated July 1, 1846, the day after he enlisted. He at once assumed his rank, and served in every engagement, up to and including the battle of Monterey, commanding his division after Gen. William Butler had been wounded. He died at Monterey, Dec. 3, 1846, and in recognition of his gallant services, congress presented a sword to his nearest male relative. His remains were conveyed to his home at Georgetown, O., and buried in the village cemetery.

JUNEAU, Laurent Solomon, the founder of the city of Milwaukee, was born near Montreal, Can., Aug. 9, 1793. His parents were French. He dropped Laurent from his name in early life, and was always known in Wisconsin as Solomon. He was introduced to the locality by Jacques Vieau, agent of the Northwest Co., who made his winter home at Milwaukee in 1795. He had married Vieau's daughter, Josette, and took up the land now occupied by the city of Milwaukee, Sept. 14, 1818, and succeeded to his father-in-law's trade. While Juneau is regarded by all local historians as the real founder of the town, he was not in reality the first settler, having been preceded by many other French traders, and conspicuously by Jean Baptiste Mirandeau, a college-bred French creole blacksmith and trader, of whom it was said: "He came to make Milwaukee his home and conducted all his affairs accordingly. He never sold whisky to the Indians, as was the custom of most Indian traders. He brought his wife, library, idols, and household gods with him to found a home in the wilderness, not knowing whether he would ever have a civilized neighbor or not." The Indians ceded to him a large tract of land before they transferred it by treaty to the Federal government, but Mirandeau's death left matters in an unsettled condition, and Juneau seems to have profited by that event, to get possession of the Mirandeau tract originally staked off by the Indians. While the historians have been disputing about awarding the honor of the first settlement of Milwaukee to various persons, her citizens have recognized the founder of the city to be Solomon Juneau, who made the first survey of the village, built the first bridge, was the first postmaster, the first president of the village, the first mayor, and donated the ground for the first public square, on which the present costly court house stands. There is a township called Juneau and a county named after him; there is a Juneau Park overlooking Lake

Michigan, on which the Juneau Monument now stands; a Juneau Democratic Club; and one of the principal residence thoroughfares in the city is known as Juneau Avenue. Juneau was the agent of the American Fur Co. of which John Jacob Astor of New York was the head and from which he laid the foundation of the largest fortune that has ever been accumulated by legitimate business in this country. At that time Wisconsin was an unexplored wilderness inhabited by savage tribes of Indians, traders and missionaries, and was known on the maps as a part of the Northwest Territory, ceded by the state of Virginia to the Federal government. There was no civil government and no one to govern. Bishop Berkeley might have had Solomon Juneau and his class in mind when he wrote the famous line:

"Westward the course of Empire takes its way,"

for Juneau was the first to rear the banner of civilization on the west shore of Lake Michigan and lay the foundations, broad and deep, for a splendid empire, whose watchword is liberty, religion, and law. His predecessors had been simply Indian traders, with no intention of making a home. "At that time," said orator Holton at the unveiling of the Juneau Monument, "he was a man of great personal beauty. He was six feet in height; his curly hair was black as the raven's wing; his eye dark, large, benign, and beautiful; his form, broad, manly, and symmetrical; his presence by nature majestic and commanding; his voice clear, strong, and trumpet-toned. He was an accomplished singer." Shakespeare's description may be aptly applied to him;

> " A combination and a form, indeed,
> Where every god did seem to set his seal,
> To give the world assurance of a man."

Juneau was married to Josette Vieau, when she was fifteen years old; she bore him fifteen children. Her mother was a pure-blood Meuomluee squaw. This child of the forest is described as a remarkable woman, with great influence over the different tribes with which Juneau did business. He lost possession of his property and died in poverty and debt at the age of sixty-four, while attending an Indian payment at Shawano in the northern part of the state, and his remains were cared for and buried by the Indians, always his firm friends. He was a devoted Catholic. Two wealthy and liberal merchants of Milwaukee, Charles T. Bradley and W. H. Metcalf, in 1887 caused his remains to be removed to Milwaukee and erected a fine bronze statue in the public park that bears his name, overlooking the most charming bay on Lake Michigan, and presented it to the city, to stand as a testimonial forever, to perpetuate the virtues, honesty, and public enterprise of Solomon Juneau. The date of his death was Nov. 14, 1856.

RUSSELL, Addison Peale, editor, state officer, and author, was born in Wilmington, Clinton co., O., Sept. 6, 1826. The son of a manufacturing merchant, he was brought up to hard work, and his early education was limited to the common schooling of his native village. At the age of about sixteen he was indentured to a printer in the office of the "Gazette" at Zanesville, O. In 1845 he became editor and publisher of the "News," a Whig paper issued from Hillsborough, O. Two years later he removed to Lebanon, O., where he was connected with the "Western Star." These associations with the political press led to his being selected to serve at the clerk's desk in the senate of Ohio, in the year 1850. Returning to Wilmington, he bought a half interest in the "Clinton Republican," and, in 1855, while editing that paper, was elected by the Republicans of Clinton to represent them in the state legislature. He served as representative for two years. In 1857 he was elected secretary of state by the Republicans; and was re-elected in 1859. The statutes of Ohio at that time required a financial agent for the state, to reside in the city of New York. To this important position Mr. Russell was appointed in 1862 by Gov. Tod, and re-appointed by Gov. Brough in 1864, and again by Gov. Cox in 1866. At the close of this useful and highly responsible career of official life, in 1868, he retired from public affairs, leaving an unspotted record. Drawn by strong natural tastes toward literary pursuits, Mr. Russell was, from boyhood, a reader and writer.

The first-fruits of his inclination to productive letters was a small anonymous volume by D. Appleton & Co., New York, entitled "Half Tints: Table d'Hôte and Drawing-room." Since its appearance in 1867, the author has been engrossed in study and literary labor in quiet retirement at his old home in Wilmington. In the year 1875 his unique and admirable "Library Notes" made its appearance from the press of Hurd & Houghton, New York. This gained a wide reputation, and was so much in demand that a second edition, revised and enlarged, was brought out in Boston in 1879. The author's third book—a model of its class—was published in 1881 by Robert Clarke & Co., Cincinnati, and is entitled "Thomas Corwin: A Sketch." The fourth work came out in 1884, published by Houghton, Mifflin & Co.—a companion volume to "Library Notes"—bearing the modest title "Characteristics." Next appeared, in 1887, the charming anonymous volume of essays, very happily named "A Club of One." This wise and witty little volume, the product of Mr. Russell's fertile heart and brain, is read and appreciated by men and women of culture on both sides of the Atlantic. The same may be said of his next work, "In a Club Corner," published in 1890, by Houghton, Mifflin & Co. Mr. Russell's last work (1895), brought out by the same publishers, is entitled "Sub Cœlum: A Sky-built Human World." While it is a fanciful description of a highly improved condition of human society, it is really a strong protest against the apparently growing materialistic and socialistic tendencies of the day. It is truly an original work, and many readers and some critics have pronounced it the author's masterpiece.

McLELLAN, Isaac, poet, was born at Portland, Me., May 21, 1806. When he was only six years old his parents removed to Boston, and in 1819 he and Nathaniel P. Willis were sent together to Phillips' Academy, Andover, Mass., to prepare for college, Willis subsequently going to Yale College, while McLellan went up to Bowdoin College. Here he found himself in the next class to Nathaniel Hawthorne and Henry Wadsworth Longfellow, with the latter of whom he struck up a friendship that endured until Longfellow's death in 1882. He was graduated in 1826, and returned to Boston, where he took up the practice of the law for a number of years, during which time he renewed his ties with Willis, who was then editing the "Monthly Magazine," and contributed many poems and prose articles to his friend's periodical. He became associate-

editor of the "Daily Patriot," which was afterwards merged into the "Daily Advertiser," and a little later commenced the publication of a monthly magazine that was finally consolidated with the "Weekly Pearl." He was also a constant contributor to the "New England Magazine" and the "Knickerbocker." McLellan was a passionate lover of field sports and his leisure time was employed in wild-fowl shooting along the New England coast, and it was not long before his zeal for all kinds of out-door recreation stirred his muse to the outpouring of poems on sporting subjects, many of which attained wide popularity through their vigor and inspiring sentiment, and brought their author the sobriquet of the "poet-sportsman." In his writings he testifies that neither of his renowned classmates, Longfellow, Hawthorne, and Willis, had any taste for rod or gun, though they loved to roam along stream and through forest. Sargent Smith Prentiss, however, who was another former schoolfellow, shared his tastes, and the two would often ramble together through the woods on a Saturday afternoon in pursuit of game. In 1838 Mr. McLellan went on a sporting tour in Europe, and for two years fished and shot in nearly every country on that continent. On his return he abandoned the practice of the law as well as his editorial labors, and retired to the country, where he could give himself up unrestrainedly to his passion for sport. The shooting resorts most frequented by him were Plymouth, Cohasset, and Daniel Webster's rural retreat, Marshfield, Mass., where through the great statesman's generosity, he was able to spend two seasons as an occupant of one of the farm houses on the estate. In 1851, resolving to continue his literary pursuits once more, he took up his residence in New York city, where he became acquainted with many kindred spirits who used to congregate at the offices of the "Spirit of the Times." For years he made expeditions during the season along the coasts of Virginia and North Carolina for the purpose of wild-fowl shooting, and in later days went gunning along the Shinnecock and Great South Bay, L. I., finally settling near the latter resort at Greenpoint in 1870. Although on the verge of fourscore and ten years of age, Mr. McLellan is still to be found in the field as well as at the desk, his love of the sportsman's life being unquenchable, and as a poet of rod and gun has practically no rival to-day. Besides numerous contributions to sporting journals, he is the author of various works in book form: "The Fall of the Indian" (Boston, 1830); "The Year" (1832); "Journal of a Residence in Scotland," from the MSS. of H. B. McLellan (1834); "Mount Auburn" (1843), and "Poems of the Rod and Gun" (New York, 1886).

WORTHEN, Amos Henry, geologist, was born at Bradford, Orange co., Vt., Oct. 13, 1813, the son of Thomas Worthen and Susannah Adams. His mother was a descendent of Henry Adams, the founder of the Adams family in Massachusetts, who settled at Mt. Wollaston (now Quincy), Mass. President John Adams, one of his descendents, erected a plain granite monument to his memory, with the following inscription: "In memory of Henry Adams, who took his flight from the dragon persecution in Devonshire, England, and alighted with eight sons near Mt. Wollaston. One of the sons returned to England after taking time to explore the country. Four removed to Medford and the neighboring towns; two to Chelmsford. One only remained, Joseph, who lies here at his right hand, who was an original proprietor in the township of Brainton Incorporated in the year 1639." Thomas Worthen was a farmer and brought up his

large family upon his farm, giving them the best educational advantages the common schools of the state afforded. Young Worthen was graduated from the academy at Bradford village, and before he had attained his majority was married, on Jan. 14, 1834, to Sarah Kimball of Warren, N. H. He soon afterward emigrated to Kentucky and joined his brother Enoch, who was living at Cynthiana. He subsequently taught school at Camminsville, O., and in 1836 removed to Warsaw, Ill., where he afterwards resided. He first engaged in business there as forwarding and commission merchant, and later in the dry-goods business. He could hardly have selected a better situation to pursue his predilections for scientific studies than Warsaw, or one more calculated to sustain the enthusiasm of a naturalist. The geode formations in this locality present some of the finest specimens of Keokuk limestone, and tons of them, principally collected by Prof. Worthen, have been shipped abroad for various cabinets. In 1842 he removed to Boston on account of business depression, which was caused by the Mormon agitation. He took with him a fine collection of geodes, which were then rare in collections. Instead of selling them he exchanged them for a cabinet of sea shells,

which he took with him when he returned to Warsaw in 1844. The science of geology was then in its infancy, and when Prof. Worthen began his investigations, the facilities for study were few, especially in the West. He pursued his studies while engaged in business, and by comparing his specimens with various fossils, became an expert palæontologist. He had, meanwhile, through correspondence and exchanges, made the acquaintance of a number of scientific men, and in 1851 was elected a member of the American Association for the Advancement of Science. At its fifth annual meeting, which was held at Cincinnati, O., in February, 1851, the Illinois legislature passed a law authorizing a geological survey of the state and appropriating $3,000,000 a year for the purpose, which sum was, in 1858, increased to $5,000,000. Prof. Worthen was appointed assistant to Prof. Norwood, the noted scientist, who was made geologist of this state. In 1855 he became assistant to Prof. Hall, who was geologist of the surveying in Iowa, and did valuable service both actively and by the loan of his fine collection of carboniferous crinoids. On March 22, 1858, Prof. Worthen was appointed state geologist by Gov. William H. Bissell of Illinois. The work, which had languished under Prof. Norwood's management, assumed a new impetus when Prof. Worthen took charge of affairs. He at once began active labors in the field and was assisted in the prosecution of his investigations by his large collection of geological specimens, of which he had a finer assortment than any scientist of the period. He continued at the head of the survey until 1877, when it was abolished. It is said of Prof. Worthen that, like Gen. Grant, he never withheld the word of praise and credit from his assistants and co-laborers. He associated with himself an able corps of assistants in every department, and had as his co-laborers, J. D. Whitney in mineralogy, Leo Lesquereux in coal measures and coal plants, and such men as Newberry, Ulrich and others in the various departments of palæontology. Prof. Worthen's most important discoveries were among the lower carboniferous, and in this connection he made some remarkable palæontological discoveries of fish remains and terrestrial flora. When the geological survey of Illinois was abolished in 1877, Prof. Worthen was appointed curator of the State Historical Society and Museums of Natural History, which office he retained up to the time of his death. In a record of his work given in the "Geological Survey of Illinois" (1890), the writer says of him: "He was a brother indeed to the great naturalist he so much admired and loved, Prof. Agassiz. He had the same intense love of natural science as that great teacher. Like him, he could not exist without collecting a museum. He had the same remarkable powers of instant observation. Like him, he gathered and brought home from the formations to which he devoted his life-work, a collection of fossil remains of greater variety than has ever before or since been brought together by one individual. He had the same disinterestedness, the same consecration to science, the same readiness to oblige even the humblest and most modest, the same superiority to self-interest, the same sincerity and absence of all pretension, and the same enthusiasm in all that was noble. As with Agassiz, so with Worthen, never was a life more richly filled with study, work, and thought. Like Agassiz, Worthen had no time to make money." His bibliography numbers a great many scientific papers that embrace a wide range of subjects. On Jan. 16, 1863, Prof. Worthen was elected a member of the American Philosophical Society of Philadelphia; on Apr. 17, 1872, was made a member of the National Academy of Science; and on Oct. 15, 1871, was appointed correspondent of the Imperial Royal Geological State Institute of Vienna. He was also connected as a member and correspondent with various literary and scientific bodies. He died at Warsaw, Ill., May 6, 1888.

BATTLE, Burrill Bunn, jurist, was born in Hinds county, Miss., July 24, 1838, the second child of Joseph and Nancy (Stricklin) Battle. His father, Joseph J. Battle, was born in Wake county, N. C., where he resided until manhood, and his grandfather, Burrill Battle, was a lineal descendant of Elisha Battle, a founder of the Battle family in America, who in 1743 removed into Edgecombe county, N. C., from Virginia. The mother of Burrill Bunn Battle, also a native of North Carolina, was a daughter of Bolin Stricklin, a planter. The son emigrated with his parents to Lafayette county, Ark., in 1844. Here he attended the common schools of the neighborhood until 1852, when he entered Arkansas College, Fayetteville, where he was graduated in 1856. He entered the law department of the Cumberland University at Lebanon, Tenn., in 1857,

graduating in 1858. In the same year he was licensed to practice law by the judges of the supreme court of Tennessee, and in the fall of 1859 by Len B. Green, judge of the sixth judicial circuit of Arkansas. He at once began the practice of his profession at Lewisville, the county seat of Lafayette county, where he remained until the outbreak of the civil war. In 1861 he enlisted in the artillery service of the Confederate states, in a battery which for two years formed a part of the division commanded by Gen. Frank Cheatham, and afterward for the remainder of the war in a battery attached to the division commanded by Gen. Patrick Cleburne. He remained a private during the entire war, and never lost a day from his gun on the field of battle, except in the engagement in front of Nashville, which occurred while he was on detached service. He participated in the battles of Shiloh, Perryville, Murfreesboro', Chickamauga, Missionary Ridge, and with the one exception mentioned all the other battles fought by the Army of the Tennessee, until Gen. Hood was removed from its command. At the close of the war he returned to his home at Lewisville, Ark., where he continued to practice law until 1869, when he removed to Washington, Hempstead co., in the same state. In 1871 he was elected a Democratic representative in the general assembly of the state. On Nov. 29, 1871, Mr. Battle was married to Mrs. Josephine Witherspoon, daughter of John S. Cannon, a prominent citizen of southwest Arkansas. In 1879 Mr. Battle settled in Little Rock, the state capital, where he engaged in the practice of his profession continuously until 1885, when he was elected to fill a vacancy upon the supreme bench of the state, occasioned by the death of Associate Justice John R. Eakin. In 1890 Mr. Battle was re-elected to the same position for the full term of eight years, by the largest vote cast for any candidate in that election. His standing as a lawyer, and character as a man, were such that he not only received the unanimous nomination of the Democratic party, to which he always adhered, but the endorsement of the "Agricultural Wheel," an organization of farmers then figuring extensively in state politics, a compliment which was accorded to but one other Democratic candidate. In September, 1894, he was re-elected without opposition associate justice of the supreme court of Arkansas for another term of eight years. Giving careful and close attention to the study of law; always cautious in forming and giving opinions; and with a well-balanced and discerning mind, stored with general knowledge, Judge Battle was peculiarly adapted to the honorable position to which he was called. He is a member of the Missionary Baptist Church.

ATWATER, Amzi, pioneer, was born at New Haven, Conn., May 23, 1776. His parents were in narrow circumstances, and he was employed at farm labor, with little opportunity for study, till he was eighteen years of age. Then he visited an uncle in Westfield, Mass., who taught mathematics to a class of young men, and of him he learned the art of surveying. At the age of nineteen he set out on foot and alone for the then wilderness of western New York, and there fell in with the party who were going out, under Moses Cleaveland, to survey the Western Reserve. He joined them, taking charge of the cattle and pack-horses, and conducting the animals all the way by land to Cleveland, O. He then acted as lineman and assistant surveyor in laying out the Western Reserve, and during the following two years ran the township lines for the Holland Land Company in western New York. In 1800, he settled permanently at Mantua, O., and on the organization of Portage county, in 1808, was elected one of the county judges. About thirty days before his death he wrote to a friend: "I have run *the line of life* through some of the swamps of adversity, and over many of the plains of prosperity. My provisions hold out well, and perhaps I have enough to carry me through to the end of my line, which I have good reason to believe will soon be completed." He died June 22, 1851.

SMITH, Samuel A., manufacturer, was born at Sidney Plains, Chenango co., N. Y., Aug. 21, 1852. His father, William A. Smith, M.D., was born at Guilford, Chenango co., N. Y., in 1830. He was a graduate of Geneva College; enlisted at the opening of the civil war, and served until its close. He had charge of the last prisoners held by the Union army. Samuel passed his early boyhood at Norwich, N. Y., but upon his father's return from the war went to Newark, Essex co., N. J., to reside. He attended the public schools of that city for a term, and completed his education at the Grace Church School, after which he engaged in business in New York city. In 1877 his father was elected county clerk, and he took a clerkship in the office, remaining there during his father's term, being retained by his father's successor, under whom

he was appointed deputy county clerk, a position he held until elected to the county clerkship by a large majority in 1887. The term expired Nov. 15, 1892, and he declined a renomination to the county clerkship, as well as one for member of congress, and settled down to business pursuits. He has been a prominent figure in club and social circles; from a business standpoint he has proved an able and efficient official.

DURAND, Marie, soprano-singer, was born in Charleston, S. C., about 1846. She studied music in New York city, and made her earliest appearance at Chicago, Ill., in Mozart's "Don Giovanni." Later she entered on musical studies at home and in Europe, and sang in the opera-houses of Brussels and St. Petersburg. Returning to the United States, Miss Durand sang in New Orleans and several other places. She afterward went to Europe, sang at Italian theatres, and for a season was engaged at St. Petersburg. In 1884 she was with the Italian Opera company in London, and later re-engaged at St. Petersburg. Since then she seems to have retired from the stage. Her success at home was not remarkable.

RICHARDSON, Henry Hobson, architect, was born at Priestley's Point, St. James's Parish, La., Sept. 29, 1838. His father was an American planter, whose earlier ancestors were Scotchmen. His mother was Catherine Caroline Priestley, a granddaughter of Rev. Dr. Joseph Priestley, of England. He was intended for the army, but his father's death necessitated a change in his plans. Mr. Richardson was graduated from Harvard College, Mass., in 1859. Ten years later he was graduated from the Ecole des Beaux Arts, at Paris, France, having been obliged to practice his profession to some extent during the intervening period, on account of the loss of his property during the civil war. He was then associated in his profession with Charles D. Gambrill

—the firm name being Gambrill & Richardson. Mr. Richardson's early works gave but faint promise of the genius he afterward exhibited. Some of these were the depôt of the Boston and Albany Railroad at Springfield, Mass., and the Agawam Bank building, and the Church of the Unity in the same city. In general, the buildings of this earlier period were experimental, but he soon developed the architectural style which was so peculiarly his own. His later more important and well-known works included nearly every kind of building, all of them creditable to his education and discipline. No single feature of his later work surpassed the noble beauty of the tower of the Brattle Square Church. From year to year he developed greater facility in adaptation and in expression, and an increasing refinement appeared with a gain in dignity and strength. This is shown in the whole series of buildings from the time Trinity was begun until his death. His dwelling-houses and railroad stations form the only exception to the general development of Mr. Richardson's art. The senate chamber, the room for the court of appeals, and the western staircase of the New York state capitol at Albany; Sever Hall and Austin Hall, at Cambridge, Mass.; the county buildings, at Pittsburg, Pa.; the Chamber of Commerce building, at Cincinnati, O.; large warehouses, at Chicago, Ill.; private dwellings, at Washington, D. C.; the Oakes Ames Memorial Hall, and other buildings at North Easton, Mass.; Craig Memorial Library, at Quincy, Mass., and other village library buildings throughout New England, illustrate the growth and vigor of his genius. The crowning work of his professional career, however, was Trinity Protestant Episcopal Church, at Boston, Mass., wrought out in the last years of his life, while he suffered from an incurable disease. This noble building announced not only to the American public, but to the world, a new departure in ecclesiastical architecture, which will doubtless command more, rather than less, admiration from its beholders as time goes on. A suggestion from the tower of Salamanca was developed into greater size and dignity, with a freshness and originality which was peculiarly his own. A short time before his death he was elected an honorary and corresponding member of the Royal Institute

of British Architects, in which reference was made to the exceptional constructive skill shown in the stable erection of so large a central tower as Trinity. As he read the letter he exclaimed, "If only they could see Pittsburg!" He did not live to see this completed, but the designs alone were worthy in themselves of all the satisfaction and pride he took in them. His delight was in the Romanesque architecture of southern France. His strong feeling for harmony is characteristic in the Harvard Law School, which is one of the most beautiful structures. On removing from New York, Mr. Richardson established his house and workroom in Brookline, building additions from time to time as his work increased, and employed a large number of students, with whom he was always on the most sympathetic terms. It was Mr. Richardson's habit, when once the general design and purpose and spirit of the composition had been made clear, to leave to each draughtsman the working out of his particular share of the plans; but he kept all the work in view, going from man to man, encouraging by suggestion and comparison. Enthusiastic himself, he imparted his enthusiasm to his workers, so that they would work all night to complete plans within the time limit of competition. The following anecdote illustrates his unostentatious kindliness: He traveled in Europe one summer with Phillips Brooks, who greatly admired a piece of statuary he saw in Italy, but its price made Mr. Brooks reluctant to purchase it. Mr. Richardson urged him to obtain it, and determining to do so, he revisited the studio, only to find that an American had purchased it the day before. His disappointment was great, but he made up his mind to forget it. Upon Mr. Brooks's return, he found the wished-for statue in his

library, presented by his friend, Mr. Richardson. During the last ten years of his life he endured great physical suffering, which did not, however, seem to impair at the very last the vigor and growth of his powers. But brief and incomplete as his life must seem, he had lived and worked long enough to leave to his profession, at a time when it was needed, a standard of excellence in endeavor and achievement, an inspiration to whatever is best in his art, than which no worthier monument could be found. He died at his work at Brookline, Mass., Apr. 28, 1886.

VASSAR, Thomas Edwin, clergyman, was born at Poughkeepsie, N. Y., Dec. 8, 1834, son of William and Mary (Hageman) Vassar. After completing his theological studies under Rev. Rufus Babcock, and others, he was ordained to the Baptist ministry, at Poughkeepsie, Jan. 28, 1857. His first settlement was with the church at Amenia, in his native county, where he remained eight years. While pastor there the civil war broke out, and he was elected chaplain of the 150th New York Volunteers, a Dutchess county regiment. He was with the regiment one year, and participated in several battles, including the battle of Gettysburg. At the close of the war he was called to the First Baptist Church, of Lynn, Mass., where he remained eight years. His later pastorates were with the Flemington, N. J. Church, the South Church, of Newark, N. J., and the First Church, Kansas City, Mo., where he now ministers to a large and growing congregation. He has done considerable work in the way of lecturing; has served on many educational and missionary boards of his denomination, and has written a good deal for publication. His biography of his uncle, John Ellison Vassar, has had a very wide circulation in Great Britain, as well as in this country, and one or two of his later volumes have been well received. Madison (N. Y.) University (now Colgate) conferred on him the degree of D.D. in 1882.

LEA, Isaac, naturalist, was born at Wilmington, Del., March 4, 1792, of Quaker parentage. At fifteen years of age he went into business with his brother in Philadelphia. Out of business hours he made frequent excursions into the surrounding country, for the purpose of collecting specimens in mineralogy, a study in which at that time he took a deep interest. In 1815 he was elected a member of the Philadelphia Academy of Natural Sciences; before which he read his first scientific paper, three years later, describing the minerals in the neighborhood of Philadelphia. In 1821 he became a partner in the publishing house of his father-in-law, Matthew Carey, a relation in which he continued uninterruptedly for thirty years. He contributed frequently to the early numbers of the "American Journal of Science," and in 1828 published in the "American Quarterly Review" a noteworthy article on the Northwest Passage. He took the ground that the passage could only be effected by sailing from West to East, a prophecy which, as is well known, was justified by the event. In the meantime, he had taken up the study of Unio, a genus which was afterward to become his specialty, and in 1827 had contributed to the "Journal of the American Philosophical Society" a paper describing six new specimens. In 1832 he went to Europe, where he became acquainted with the eminent scientists of his time, acquiring thereby valuable additions to his knowledge and his collections. He named, classified, and amplified the collection of Unionidæ at the British Museum, London and assisted in doing the same at the Jardin des Plantes, Paris. In 1852 he revisited Europe, rendering as well as receiving favors from scientific men and institutions; in particular, arranging for Bowin and Petit the Unionidæ in their collections. After his return to this country he devoted himself exclusively to scientific pursuits until his death. A friend of Dr. Lea's thus describes his methods of work: "Dr. Lea habitually, during a period of nearly half a century, spent many hours of the night in his studies and his writings, seldom relinquishing them before midnight. These night studies were continued with little intermission until he was nearly eighty years old, and they were gradually and finally abandoned only in compliance with the warnings of his medical adviser. . . . . During the last few years of Dr. Lea's life, after he relinquished much of the active work in his mineral cabinet, his time was usually spent in his library, in the happy enjoyment of life, surrounded by his books referring to his favorite studies: mineralogy, geology, and conchology. He enjoyed especially the company of his scientific friends, and his interest in discussing scientific subjects was maintained until his final illness." His greatest contributions to science were made in the department of conchology, by the classification and description of the Unionidæ; his collected papers upon this single genus amounting to thirteen quarto volumes. At the same time he was a thorough student of mineralogy and geology, being first to discover fossil footprints in the new red sandstone formation, and the first American to engage in microscopic mineralogy. He devoted much time to the microscopic examination of crystals, and was an expert judge of the value of precious stones, of which he possessed a large collection. Besides being a member of thirty or more learned societies in this country and Europe, he was president of the Philadelphia Academy of Science from 1853 to 1858, and of the American Association for the Advancement of Science in 1860. His collections were bequeathed to the National Museum at Washington, and the results of most of his researches have been published. The degree of LL.D. was conferred upon him by Harvard in 1852. His death occurred at Philadelphia, Pa., Dec. 8, 1886, in his ninety-fourth year.

HARKNESS, Albert, educator, was born Oct. 6, 1822, in Mendon, Mass., now the town of Blackstone. In his boyhood, while living on the farm, he attended the district school for ten or twelve weeks in the year. In 1836 he attended the Uxbridge High School for a single term, and in 1837 the Worcester Academy. In 1838, after a year's study at home, mostly without a teacher, he entered Brown University, where he at once attained high rank in his class. He was graduated as valedictorian in 1842. He then engaged in the work of private instruction, but at the opening of the Providence High School in 1843 he became one of its teachers. He was senior master from September, 1846, until August, 1853, when he went to Europe for study and travel. After a year's study at Bonn and Berlin, he received the degree of Ph.D. at Bonn, being the first American to receive the degree of that university. The subject of his thesis was: "*Comparantur Studia Graeca et Latina quae in Nova Anglia cum eis quae in Borussia sunt.*" He then spent one semester at the University of Goettingen. During the summer of 1855 he traveled in Germany, France, Switzerland, Italy, Greece, and England. On his way to Greece he received notice of his election to the Greek chair in Brown University, and he began his work in the following September. Twice since that time (in 1870, and in 1883) he has had leave of absence for a year to visit Europe. He has lectured before the Franklin Lyceum, before audiences at the college, before the Historical Society, the Rhode Island Institute of Instruction, the American Institute of Instruction, the American Philological Association, and elsewhere. He was president of the Franklin Lyceum in 1849; of the Rhode Island Alpha Chapter of the Phi Beta Kappa from 1871–73. He was one of the founders of the Philological Association, one of its first vice-presidents in 1869, and president in 1875. He is a member of the Archaeological Institute of America, and in 1881 was a member of the first committee appointed to consider the expediency of establishing an American School of Classical Studies at Athens. This school

began in 1882. Prof. Harkness was elected director of the school in 1884. In his visits to Europe he made a careful study of educational questions. At the German gymnasia and universities, and at the English universities he enjoyed peculiar privileges of inspecting academic work. He began his career as an author in 1851 with the publication of the "First Latin Book." His later works are the "Second Latin Book," the "First Greek Book and Greek Reader," the "Latin Grammar," two "Latin Readers," an "Introductory Latin Book," "Practical Introduction to Latin Composition," "Elements of Latin Grammar," editions of "Cæsar's Gallic War," of "Cicero's Select Orations," and of "Sallust's Catiline," a "Preparatory Course in Latin Prose Authors," a "Latin Course for the First Year," and an "Easy Method for Beginners in Latin." The publication of this series marked an era in classical education in America. The merits of his works have been recognized by the highest educational authorities in Europe. Prof. Harkness is also the author of scientific papers embodying some of the original results of his philological investigations, which were published in the "Transactions of the American Philological Association," and have been noticed with great respect by American and European philologists. The degree of LL. D. was conferred upon Prof. Harkness by Brown University in 1869. In his ecclesiastical relations he is a Baptist, and a member and deacon in the First Baptist Church of Providence. He married on May 28, 1849, Maria Aldrich Smith. They have two children, Clara Frances, wife of Prof. Poland (B. U., 1868) of Brown University, and Albert Granger Harkness (B. U., 1879) formerly professor in Madison, now in Brown University.

TEALL, William W., lawyer and financier, was born at Manlius, N. Y., Apr. 23, 1818. He was educated at Cazenovia Seminary, Hamilton Academy in Madison county, Bartlett's High School at Utica, Union College, and the Law School of Yale University, completing his legal studies in the office of Noxon & Leavenworth, well-known lawyers of the state. He was admitted to the bar in 1839, and opened an office in Syracuse, soon gained a lucrative practice, and in 1842 was admitted to practice as attorney, proctor, and solicitor in the U. S. court of the northern district of New York, and in the same year became surveyor of the Saratoga Mutual Fire Insurance Co. In 1842 he was appointed by Gov. Bouck agent of the Indians on Onondaga reservation, and

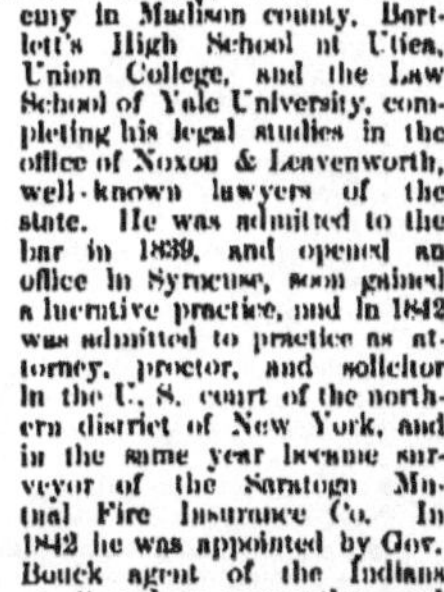

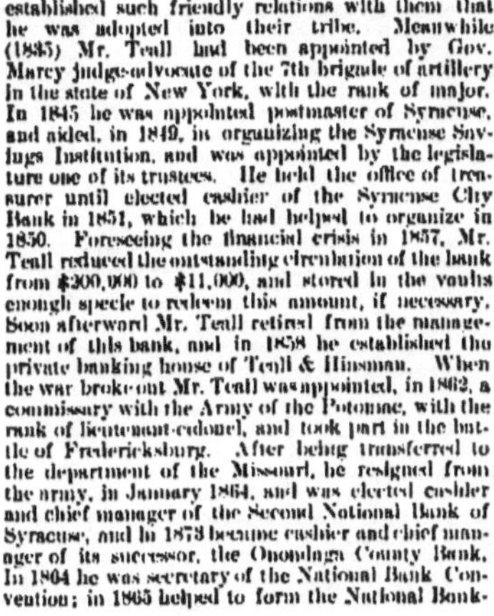

established such friendly relations with them that he was adopted into their tribe. Meanwhile (1835) Mr. Teall had been appointed by Gov. Marcy judge-advocate of the 7th brigade of artillery in the state of New York, with the rank of major. In 1845 he was appointed postmaster of Syracuse, and aided, in 1849, in organizing the Syracuse Savings Institution, and was appointed by the legislature one of its trustees. He held the office of treasurer until elected cashier of the Syracuse City Bank in 1851, which he had helped to organize in 1850. Foreseeing the financial crisis in 1857, Mr. Teall reduced the outstanding circulation of the bank from $300,000 to $11,000, and stored in the vaults enough specie to redeem this amount, if necessary. Soon afterward Mr. Teall retired from the management of this bank, and in 1858 he established the private banking house of Teall & Hinsman. When the war broke out Mr. Teall was appointed, in 1862, a commissary with the Army of the Potomac, with the rank of lieutenant-colonel, and took part in the battle of Fredericksburg. After being transferred to the department of the Missouri, he resigned from the army, in January 1864, and was elected cashier and chief manager of the Second National Bank of Syracuse, and in 1873 became cashier and chief manager of its successor, the Onondaga County Bank. In 1864 he was secretary of the National Bank Convention; in 1865 helped to form the National Bank-

ers' Express Co., and was one of its directors; in 1866 aided in organizing the United States Accident Insurance Co., of Syracuse, and in that same year became the largest stockholder in the Empire Windmill Manufacturing Co. In 1869 he was secretary of the second National Bank Convention, and prepared and published the proceedings of that body. In 1870 he became a director of the Lake Ontario National Bank at Oswego; in 1871, secretary of the Abel Loom Co.; in 1873, a trustee of the Citizens' Savings Bank of Syracuse, which he had aided in founding; and also cashier of the Onondaga County Bank. In 1879 he established the Onondaga County Real Estate Agency, and managed it in connection with his own business, until July, 1883, when he became trustee, secretary, and treasurer of the Sanderson Brothers' Steel Co., which is largely owned by English capitalists. Mr. Teall is a member of St. Paul's Episcopal Church, and is active in carrying on local charities. He is an earnest supporter of the Democratic party. He was married on May 14, 1850, to Sarah Montgomery Sumner, a great-granddaughter of Joseph Montgomery, a member of the continental congress for two years. Of six children, five are living, of whom Oliver Sumner Teall, who was born in 1852, and was educated chiefly at Yale College and the Albany Law School, is prominently identified with the political and social life of New York city.

DUSTIN, Hannah, patriot, was born in 1659, and married Thomas Dustin of Haverhill in 1677. The Indians, who lived at the head of the Merrimac river, attacked the settlement on March 15, 1697, when Mrs. Dustin, ill in bed, bade her husband take the children and escape to a place of safety. Mrs. Dustin was dragged from her bed, and with her nurse and baby, only one week old, obliged to go with the Indians on a weary march of several days, into the wilderness. After they had gone a few miles, as the child was troublesome, an Indian dashed its brains out against a tree. Until then Mrs. Dustin had wept and lamented her fate, but instantly she dried her tears and resolved to be avenged and to escape. They halted at last on an island in the Merrimac river, about six miles above the present site of Concord, N. H. The captives were kept in a wigwam with a dozen Indian men and women, with whom they found an English boy named Samuel Leonardson, who had been captured the year before. On the 30th of the month Mrs. Dustin instructed the boy to ask his master where to strike "to kill quickly," and she listened eagerly to the minute directions the Indian gave, not only for killing, but for scalping in a scientific manner. That night, when the Indians were sleeping soundly, she seized a tomahawk and killed nine of them, each at a single blow, the boy slaying the chief in the same way. She struck one squaw who fled badly wounded, and one boy she purposely spared. On viewing her work, she thought her friends would disbelieve her story of slaughter, and she thereupon took the scalps of her enemies. Then with her nurse and the English boy, she got into a bark canoe and floated down to the falls, where they followed the river through the woods and, after incredible hardships and suffering, she reached her family and friends at Haverhill. The general court of Massachusetts, after examining her story, and finding it true, took her scalps as trophies of her courage and presented her and her boy companion with £50 each. Col. Nicholson, then governor of Maryland, also gave her a suitable present. In 1874, the commonwealths of New Hampshire and Massachusetts caused a granite monument to be erected, on the tablets of which they inscribed the names of Hannah Dustin, Samuel Leonardson, and Mary Neff, the nurse.

CLEMENS, Samuel Langhorn, author (familiarly known under his pen-name "Mark Twain"), was born in Florida, Monroe co., Mo., Nov. 30, 1835. His father, soon after his birth, removed to Hannibal in the same state, where, until he was twelve years of age, he attended the village schools. The death of his father, a man of strong character and fine intellect, left the mother and children without means, as he had lost all by endorsing for friends. The young Samuel, in order to contribute to the support of the family, entered the office of the Hannibal "Courier" as an apprentice. Here he remained for nearly three years, during a portion of  the time assisting in editing the "Courier." At the conclusion of his apprenticeship he visited the East, and worked at his trade successively in New York, Philadelphia, Cincinnati, and St. Louis. In 1857 Mr. Clemens returned to Hannibal, and carried out his long cherished ambition to become a steamboat pilot. In course of time he received his pilot's license, and worked in that capacity until 1861. This period of his life is graphically described in "Old Times on the Mississippi." At the outbreak of the war of the rebellion he served for a few weeks in the Confederate army, and then went with his brother to Nevada, of which territory the elder Clemens had been appointed secretary. He acted for a short time as his brother's private secretary, and then engaged in silver mining, but without success. In 1862 he became city editor of the Virginia City "Enterprise," to which journal he contributed a number of articles, signing himself "Mark Twain." This *nom de plume* was taken from the speech of the leadsmen on the Mississippi river in making soundings. Mr. Clemens remained with the "Enterprise" for two years, during a portion of the time reporting the legislative proceedings from Carson, and then removed to San Francisco, where he became a reporter for the "Morning Call." In 1865 he engaged in mining in Calaveras county, but soon returned to San Francisco, and renewed his connection with the "Call." In 1866 he visited the Hawaiian Islands, and wrote for the Sacramento "Union" a series of brilliant letters, several of which were afterward incorporated in "Roughing It." Upon his return to the United States he lectured with success in California and Nevada, and then appeared upon the lecture platform in the eastern states, also attracting attention by the publication of a humorous volume entitled, "The Jumping Frog and Other Sketches." In 1867 he joined a pleasure party which had chartered the Quaker City, and visited France, Italy, and Palestine. Upon his return to the United States he published, under the title of "The Innocents Abroad," a humorous account of the trip, which, sold by subscription, proved instantly successful, and gave its author an international reputation. In 1870 Mr. Clemens married Miss Langdon, a wealthy lady of Elmira, N. Y., whose brother, Gen. Charles J. Langdon, had been one of his companions during the trip of the Quaker City. Following his marriage, Mr. Clemens became editor and part proprietor of the Buffalo, N. Y., "Express." He soon, however, retired from journalism, and removed to Hartford, Conn., where he has since resided. Since 1872 he has given his time to literary work, appearing occasionally on the lecture platform, and making frequent and extended sojourns in Europe. A complete list of his books includes, besides those already named, "Roughing It" (1872); "The Gilded Age," written in conjunction with Charles D. Warner (1874); "Sketches, Old and New" (1875); "Adventures of Tom Sawyer," dealing with his boyhood experiences in Missouri (1876); "Punch, Brothers, Punch" (1878); "A Tramp Abroad" (1880); "The Stolen White Elephant" (1882); "The Prince and the Pauper" (1882); "Old Times on the Mississippi" (1883); "Adventures of Huckleberry Finn" (1885); "A Yankee at the Court of King Arthur" (1889); "The American Claimant" (1891); "Tom Sawyer Abroad" (1894); and Pudd'nhead Wilson (1895). He has now (1895) in preparation a volume of European sketches, also a novel entitled, "Personal Recollections of Joan of Arc." "The Gilded Age," "The Prince and the Pauper," "Pudd'nhead Wilson," and the "Yankee at Arthur's Court" have been dramatized, and have met with remarkable success upon the stage. All of his books, with a single exception, have been published by subscription, and of them nearly 1,000,000 copies have been sold. Most of them have been translated into German, French, Italian, Norwegian, Danish, and other tongues. As many copies of his books have been sold in Great Britain as in America. Mr. Clemens has also attracted attention as an inventor, and for some years more than 100,000 of his scrap-books have been sold annually. In 1884 he founded in New York city the publishing house of C. L. Webster & Co., which has published the "Memoirs" of Gen. U. S. Grant, and many other notable works. Mr. Clemens long since took rank as the foremost humorist of his time. His humor is unctuous and natural. He is a shrewd and kindly student of human nature, and his style is strong and terse. He is a man of marked personality and rare conversational powers. In manner he is generous, kindly, and democratic.

NYE, Edgar Wilson, humorist, was born at Shirley, near Moosehead Lake, Me., Aug. 25, 1850. Of his ancestry he himself says: "The Nyes are proverbially reticent about their genealogy. Some of them claim to be of French extraction, and I have a cousin who says that he is a descendant of Marshal Ney, that being the spelling of the family name in an early day. I had some curiosity a few years ago, and tried to learn all I could of this matter. I traced our people back to the European police courts and even beyond that, discovering at last, in France, our  Coat of Arms, but I lost it from the line where it was airing last summer." When he was little over two years old, his parents removed to St. Croix county in Northern Wisconsin, where the boy received a thorough academical education, after completing which he studied law, and was admitted to the bar in 1876. Chance, however, threw in his way a position as reporter on an evening paper in Laramie city, Wyoming Ter. This he held for a year, and then practised law for some time, being a justice of the peace for a period of six years. Some amusing stories are in circulation in connection with his judicial labors at Laramie, which partake somewhat of the delightful airiness of fairy tales and doubtless owe their origin largely to Mr. Nye's reputation for humorous originality in action as well as in fancy. He also held other offices, among them that of postmaster of Laramie, his resignation of which, addressed to President Arthur, escaped from official hands at Washington, and finding its way into print, was copied, as he himself declares, "from

Japan to South Africa and from Beersheba to a given point." He was never enamored of the law, however, and in course of time drifted back into journalism, and as a special writer for current humorous literature, became especially successful. Combining good business methods with a degree of diligence and pleasure in his work which soon put him beyond the usual trials and griefs of struggling writers, albeit there was a time when his remuneration was but $1 a column. Still, he tells us, "The columns were short and the type large, and he was glad to get the dollar." He used the pseudonym of "Bill Nye" in his writings, and it was not long before the name was known throughout the length and breadth of the land. In association with James Whitcomb Riley, the "Hoosier poet," he began in 1885 to give readings from his works, and this somewhat novel partnership was highly successful. He has since continued to lecture and travel extensively throughout Canada and the United States, visiting Europe betweentimes, in the meanwhile publishing several volumes of collected sketches, one in collaboration with Mr. Riley. Much of his work has been printed in the newspapers belonging to the American Press Association with mutual profit to author and publishers. His publications in book form are: "Bill Nye and the Boomerang" (Chicago, 1881); "The Forty Liars" (1883); "Baled Hay" (1884); "Bill Nye's Blossom Rock" (1885); "Thinks and Remarks by Bill Nye" (1886); "Fun, Wit, and Poetry" in conjunction with Riley, (1891); "Bill Nye's History of the United States" (1894); "Bill Nye's History of England" (1895). In 1891 he produced "The Cadi," a comedy which met with moderate success, and in 1895, in collaboration with Paul M. Potter, "The Stag Party." Mr. Nye married on March 7, 1877, Miss Clara Frances Smith, by whom he has two sons and two daughters.

SHILLABER, Benjamin Penhallow, pen-name "Mrs. Partington," humorist, was born July 12, 1814, in Portsmouth, N. H. He received his education in the public schools of his native town, and left when fifteen years of age to enter a printing office. After serving for two years he went to Boston where he followed his trade in newspaper offices, until he went on a voyage to British Guiana. A year's experience sent him back to newspaper work, and in 1840 he became connected with the Boston "Post," where he continued for ten years. In 1847 he began writing his "Sayings of Mrs. Partington," achieving unusual success from the very first. He then accepted an editorial position on the

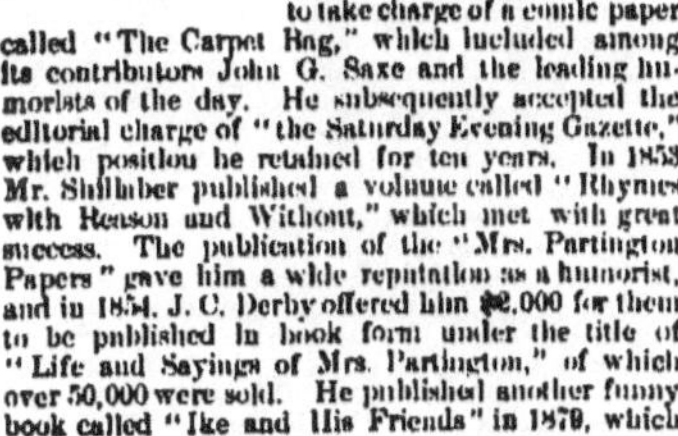

"Post," but resigned it in 1851 to take charge of a comic paper called "The Carpet Bag," which included among its contributors John G. Saxe and the leading humorists of the day. He subsequently accepted the editorial charge of "the Saturday Evening Gazette," which position he retained for ten years. In 1853 Mr. Shillaber published a volume called "Rhymes with Reason and Without," which met with great success. The publication of the "Mrs. Partington Papers" gave him a wide reputation as a humorist, and in 1854, J. C. Derby offered him $2,000 for them to be published in book form under the title of "Life and Sayings of Mrs. Partington," of which over 50,000 were sold. He published another funny book called "Ike and His Friends" in 1879, which

was followed by the Ike Partington series. In 1882 he published "Wide Swath," a collection of verses including "Lines in Pleasant Places." In addition to these he has published "Knitting Work," "Partingtonian Patch Work" "Cruises with Captain Bob," and "Double Runner Club." During the intervals between the books he contributed sketches and essays to the various periodicals, which have uniformly had a large success. His wife, Mrs. Lydia Shillaber, published a cook-book which had a wide circulation. Mr. Shillaber suffered severely from gout in his late years, from which he died, March 25, 1890, at Chelsea, Mass.

LOCKE, David Ross, humorist, was born in Vestal, Broome co., N. Y., Sept. 20, 1833. He received a common-school education, learned the trade of printer in the office of the Cortland "Democrat," and while still a young man obtained employment as local reporter and journeyman printer upon various journals in western cities until 1852, when he was successively editor and publisher of the Plymouth "Advertiser," Mansfield "Herald," Bucyrus "Journal," and Findlay "Jeffersonian," all of the state of Ohio. It was

in the "Jeffersonian" that he began the "Nasby Letters" in 1860, which were continued until the close of the war. They were letters purporting to be written by Petroleum Vesuvius Nasby, who desired to be postmaster. With quaint satire, reckless in style but remorseless in logic, he laughed to scorn the pretensions and fallacies of slavery and its political sympathizers. They at once engaged public attention, and soon brought the writer a national reputation. President Lincoln is reported to have said, that next to a dispatch announcing a Federal victory, he read a Nasby letter with the most pleasure. Chief-Justice Chase said that the Nasby letters formed the fourth force in the reduction of the rebellion. After many adventures in the journalistic field Mr. Locke took editorial charge of the Toledo "Blade," and obtained a proprietary interest in the paper, which he retained until his death. He was a striking exception among literary men in that he combined great business capacity with literary talent and vivid imagination. In 1873 he became a member of the firm of Bates & Locke, newspaper advertising agents, in New York city. While on a European tour in 1881 he met his old friend, James Redpath, who interested him in Irish politics, a subject on which Mr. Locke delivered several lectures. He opened the columns of the "Blade," also, to the advocacy of the Irish cause. Mr. Locke has been thoroughly successful as an editor, author, lecturer, and man of business. He published "Nasby" (1865), "Swingin' Round the Cirkle" (1866), while "Echoes from Kentucky" and others of his letters have since appeared. He removed to New York in 1871, and became managing editor of the "Evening Mail," while still retaining his connection with the "Blade," but after several years in New York he returned to Toledo. He also published: "The Naval History of America's Life Study," "The Struggles of P. V. Nasby," "The Morals of Abou Ben Adhem," "A Paper City," and "Hannah Jane." He died at Toledo, O., Feb. 15, 1888.

HALPIN, Charles G., humorous writer, was born near Oldcastle, County Meath, Ireland, Nov. 20, 1829. His father, an Episcopal clergyman of extraordinary ability, was editor of the Dublin "Evening Mail," and a peculiar aptitude for literature ran in the family. Charles, who was a favorite of the father, early gave promise of unusual abilities, and entered Trinity College, Dublin, at as early an age as the rules of the college permitted, and was graduated with distinction in 1846. He began the study of medicine, but soon abandoned it for the more congenial vocation of journalism. He contributed to the press in Ireland and England, until feeling that his powers were cramped, he emigrated to the United States in 1849. He established himself in Boston, where he was joined by his young wife, whom he had left to follow as soon as he had secured a position. His first work was on the Boston "Post," but he shortly became leading editor of the "Carpet-Bag," a humorous journal, which was being conducted by Benjamin Shillaber ("Mrs. Partington") and Dr. Shepley. After its failure in 1852 he removed to New York, where he became associated with Henry Raymond upon the "Times," after being engaged a few months upon the "Herald." But he shortly secured an interest with John Clancy in the New York "Leader," to which he devoted his best efforts. His political articles and humorous sketches were so well appreciated that the circulation of the paper increased enormously, and it became a political power. He had remarkable power for fictitious invention, and under a wager produced a long account of the resuscitation of Hicks, the pirate, executed on Bedloe's Island, which created great excitement. His pen was versatile and prolific, turning out articles of every description, which he adapted to the needs of the various journals of the day. To the "Tribune," which printed his first article, he contributed poetry, including the famous lyric:

> "Tear down the flaunting lie!
> Half-mast the starry flag!"

which has long been falsely attributed to Horace Greeley. When the civil war broke out he renounced the liberal income he was receiving, and enlisted as lieutenant in the 69th regiment under Col. Corcoran, and so rapidly mastered the details that he was promoted to be adjutant-general on the staff of Gen. Hunter, with whom he served during the greater part of the war. Maj. Halpin prepared the first order for the enrollment of a negro regiment, which brought upon him also the ban of outlawry by the Confederates, which directed the immediate execution of both general and adjutant should they be captured. When Maj.-Gen. Halleck became commander-in-chief Maj. Halpin was transferred to his staff, and, in addition to preparing all the official correspondence, he contributed much by his pen to moulding the public mind to military necessities. Under the pen-name of "Miles O'Reilly," in the assumed character of private in the 47th New York, he wrote a number of amusing articles which were an immense success, and did great good to the service. His poem, "Sambo's Right to be Kilt," was as astonishing as its arguments were unanswerable, and regiments of blacks became not only possible, but a necessity. His eminent services were recognized by both the commanding officers, and his promotion was urged. It was delayed by official jealousy, but, finally, upon his resignation he was brevetted brigadier-general. Few sons of the soil could have sacrificed more for the Federal cause

than Halpin, and he deserved all the rights of one "born free." Upon his return to New York he served upon the staff of Gen. Dix, where he attracted the attention of the Citizens' Association by his articles exposing the corruption of the city government, and as soon as he was released from the army he was offered the conduct of "The Citizen," the organ of the reform movement then inaugurated. He accepted the position, and shortly purchased the entire paper, which he conducted until his death. His irrepressible activity enabled him to find time to contribute articles to other papers, and to engage in hunting down corruption in the political arena, even though it led him to battle against an organization which had formerly been his home. His first victory was his election to the registership by a coalition of Republicans and Democrats, and this was followed by other triumphs. Col. Halpin in all his writings worked for a purpose. He made no pretense to finish and adornment of style, and rarely read his productions except to correct proof. His love songs are exquisite works of art, which are only excelled by his poems in memory of those who fell in the war for the Union. His works include: "Life and Adventures, Songs, Services, and Speeches of Private Miles O'Reilly, 47th Regiment, New York Volunteers;" "Baked Meats of the Funeral: a Collection of Essays, Poems, Speeches, and Banquets by Private Miles O'Reilly." He is the author of "Lyrics by the Letter H," R. B. Roosevelt collected "The Poetical Works of Charles G. Halpin" after his death. His unremitting literary labors made him subject to insomnia, for which he took opiates. By an unfortunate mistake of the druggist, he took an overdose of chloroform when attacked by a severe pain in the head, from which he died Aug. 3, 1868.

LANDON, Melville D. (Eli Perkins), author and lecturer, was born in Eaton, N. Y., Sept. 7, 1839, son of John Landon, and grandson of Rufus Landon, a revolutionary soldier from Litchfield county, Conn. He was educated at the district school and neighboring academy, where he was prepared for admission to the sophomore class at Madison University. He passed two years at the university, pursuing the class course, when he was admitted to Union College, and was graduated with the class of 1861, receiving the degree of A. M. in 1863. He at once obtained a position in the treasury department by appointment from Secretary Chase, and this brought him to Washington, D. C., at the outbreak of the civil war. Mr. Landon helped Gen. Cassius Marcellus Clay to organize the "Clay Battalion," and he served in its ranks. This was before the arrival of any of the northern regiments sent to the defence of the national capital. He afterwards resigned from the treasury department to accept a position on the staff of Gen. A. L. Chittain, commanding the post of Memphis, Tenn. He resigned from the army in 1864, to engage in cotton-planting in Arkansas and Louisiana, where the next year he had under cultivation 1,700 acres of cotton. In 1867 he went abroad, making the tour of Europe, traversing Russia, and sailing down the Volga to Kazan. While in Russia, his old commander of the "Clay Battalion," then U. S. minister to St. Petersburg, made him secretary of legation. In 1870, upon his return to America, he published a history of the Franco-Prussian war, and followed it with numerous humorous writings for the public press under the pen name of "Eli Perkins." He was a regular contributor to the "Commercial Advertiser" during 1872, and his humorous contributions to that paper gave "Eli Perkins" a world-wide reputation. He has published, "Saratoga in 1891," "Wit, Humor and Pathos," "Wit and Humor of the Age," "Kings of Platform and Pulpit," "Thirty Years of Wit and Humor," "Fun and Fact," and "China and Japan." Mr. Landon is president of the New York News Association, but he occupies much of his time as a public lecturer, and is known by his humorous contributions to nearly every prominent lyceum course in the United States.

BAILEY, James Montgomery, editor and humorist, was born at Albany, N. Y., Sept. 25, 1841, the son of a humble carpenter. He received a common school education, and then learned his father's trade. His natural abilities were more than sufficient offset to further education that was denied him. His father died when he was three years old and the mother subsequently married Daniel Smith of Rome, N. Y., where James passed his boyhood. Removing to Danbury, Conn., in 1860, he was employed at his trade for two years, and in 1862 enlisted in the 17th Connecticut volunteers, serving until the end of the civil war. He was captured at Gettysburg, and for a short time was prisoner of war at Belle Isle. Before he entered the service of his country he had been an occasional contributor to newspapers, and while in the service he wrote many letters that were widely read because of their striking originality and quaint humor.

After being mustered out of the service in 1865, he returned to Danbury and purchased the "Times," and in 1870 consolidated it with the "Jeffersonian," which he acquired that year, and changed the name to the "Danbury News." His exquisitely humorous treatment of every-day affairs was an innovation in newspaper circles, and gave him the name of the "Danbury News Man," under which title his witticisms were quoted in almost every newspaper in the country, and even across the water. He was original, and was successful in opening up an entirely new vein of humor, which gave his paper, the "Danbury News," a national reputation, and created a circulation of over 40,000 copies weekly, which is probably the highest ever reached by a village newspaper. His sketches were afterward published in book form, and attained a remarkable popularity. It is pertinent to remark that Bailey was the originator of many subjects for the humorist that have now become threadbare and worn by incessant use. One day he hailed a passing peddler with the query, "Have you got charcoal in your wagon?" "Yes sir," said the expectant driver. "That's right," said Bailey. "Always tell the truth and people will respect you." That joke has been written up as original by almost every humorist of later years. His first book entitled "Life in Danbury," was published in Boston in 1873, which was followed soon by "Mr. Phillipp's Goneness," "They All Do It," "England from a Back Window," and "The Danbury Boom." In 1873 he published a novel volume entitled "The Danbury News Man's Almanac," which was as suc-

cessful as his volumes of sketches, and gave him high rank as a humorous author. In 1874 he visited Europe for his health, and upon his return entered the lecture field, where he was in great demand. The "Danbury News Man" was as wise as he was droll and his writings show that he had a very thorough knowledge of human nature. The "Danbury News" continued under his management as editor and proprietor, until his death, which occurred March 4, 1894.

BURBANK, Alfred Post, elocutionist, was born in Chicago, Ill., July 10, 1846. He was educated at the University of Chicago, and when only seventeen years old enlisted in the Federal army, and served in Tennessee. For many years he was principal of the old Dearborn and the Douglas public schools in Chicago, but subsequently became a professional reader, and appeared with great success in all parts of the United States and London. For a time he went on the stage, creating the part of the Claimant in "Mark Twain's" dramatic sketch of that name. He afterward played the part of Dick Fennel in Pinero's "Sweet Lavender" in New York city and throughout the country. He dramatized Dickens's "Tale of Two Cities," and made extracts from it upon the platform with great effect. He made three tours in partnership with "Bill Nye," the humorist, but was compelled to abandon travel, owing to increasing ill health. He was a member of the Delta Kappa Epsilon Society and of the Lotos Club, to which organization he had belonged for many years, and was one of its best entertainers. He died in New York city, June 23, 1894.

SHAW, Henry Wheeler, pen-name "Josh Billings," humorist, was born Apr. 21, 1818, in Lanesborough, Mass. His father, Henry Shaw, was an influential and well-to-do man who was a member of the Massachusetts legislature for twenty-five years, and was also a member of congress at the time of the birth of his son. He gave careful attention to the early training of Henry, who at fourteen was prepared for college and entered Hamilton College in 1832. He only remained one year, when he became restless under the restraints of conventionalism, and declining the position of private secretary to John Quincy Adams, he abandoned college life and fled to the edge of civilization. He started for Mexico and engaged in the various occupations of steering steamboats, keeping a country store, teaching school, acting as auctioneer, and at one time driv-

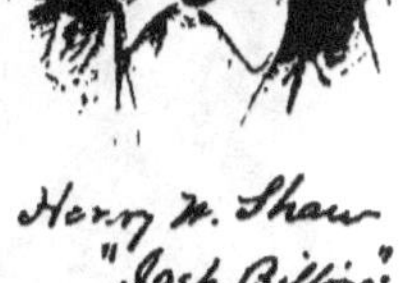

ing cattle. But he became weary of this irregular life, and returned to Poughkeepsie in 1858, when he became an auctioneer. His scholarly temperament however, soon led him to literature, and he accepted an editorial position upon a local paper and wrote humorous articles under the name of "Josh Billings." His humor did not receive the recognition he desired. As he expressed it, "I didn't strike it and I concluded I was boring with a pretty poor gimlet," and he abandoned the work for awhile, but returned to it the next year, when he adopted a phonetic style of spelling, "slewed round the spelling," as he expressed it, which more resembled his style of pronunciation. Under new spelling he sent a previously published article, "An Essa on the Muel," to a New York paper. It had instant success, and was copied far and wide. His first book was published in 1866 under the title, "Sayings of Josh Billings," which was followed by "Josh Billings on Ice," both of which had an enormous sale. But his greatest success was a travesty on the "Farmers' Almanac," published by the Thomas family. This he published in 1870 under the title of "Josh Billings' Farmers' Allminox," and it had a circulation of 90,000 the first year, 117,000 the second, and 100,000 the third year. From that time until his death his career was one of continued financial success. For a long time he wrote for the "New York Weekly" at a salary of $4,000 a year, and he contributed numerous articles to the "Century" under the pen-name of "Uncle Esek." His humor was dry and homely, but it had a practical philosophy which appealed to the average mind. In 1863 he began to lecture and delivered about eighty lectures a year, for which he received frequently $150 each. They were a series of pithy sayings strung together without much connection, but being full of odd wisdom with a practical moral, and delivered in an awkward manner peculiarly his own, which made their humor irresistible, he became at once a favorite from one end of the country to the other. In addition to those mentioned he published "Every Boddy's Friend" in 1876, "Josh Billings' Complete Works" in 1876, "Josh Billings' Trump Karals," in 1877, and "Josh Billings' Spice Box" in 1881. He wore ill-fitting clothes, and had a melancholy look which gave him a peculiar appearance, but possessed a geniality which won for him a host of warm admirers. His health gradually gave way and he removed to California, where he died suddenly at Monterey, Oct. 14, 1885.

GRISWOLD, Alphonso Miner, journalist and humorist, was born in Oneida county, N. Y., in 1836, of New England ancestry. He attended the academy in his native town and was graduated at Hamilton College. In 1858 he became a reporter on the "Buffalo Republic and Times," edited by Henry W. Faxon, and soon was advanced to editorial writer, in which position he developed marked talent as a humorous writer, under the nom-de-plume of the "Fat Contributor." In 1859 he became editorial writer on the Detroit "Advertiser." Later he was made editor of the Cleveland "Democrat;" associate-editor of the "Cleveland Plain-Dealer," succeeding Artemus Ward; and in 1863 city editor of the Cincinnati "Times." His health and eyesight becoming impaired, he temporarily retired from editorial work, and became the manager of Lawrence Barrett, then a young and struggling actor. On March, 15, 1865, in Cincinnati, he made his first appearance as a humorous lecturer, and was so warmly received that he continued on the lecture platform for eighteen years, appearing during that period in all parts of the United States and Canada. In 1872 he

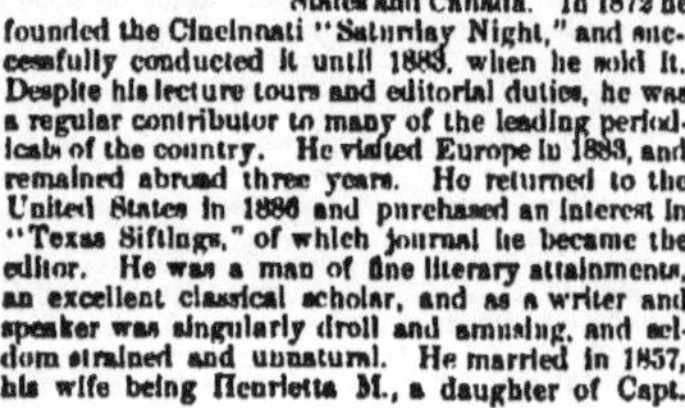

founded the Cincinnati "Saturday Night," and successfully conducted it until 1883, when he sold it. Despite his lecture tours and editorial duties, he was a regular contributor to many of the leading periodicals of the country. He visited Europe in 1883, and remained abroad three years. He returned to the United States in 1886 and purchased an interest in "Texas Siftings," of which journal he became the editor. He was a man of fine literary attainments, an excellent classical scholar, and as a writer and speaker was singularly droll and amusing, and seldom strained and unnatural. He married in 1857, his wife being Henrietta M., a daughter of Capt.

A. J. Benson of Boston. He resumed his lecturing tours soon after his return from Europe. He died suddenly of apoplexy on March 14, 1891, at Sheboygan Falls, Wis., where he had lectured on the previous evening.

COZZENS, Frederick Swartwout, humorist, was born March 5, 1818, in New York city. His father was a prosperous merchant, who gave his son every advantage. The son early developed a taste for literature, but his father wished him to lead a mercantile life, and trained him to business. He began with his father in the grocery and wine business when he was twenty-one, and developed it into one of the leading houses in the wine business. He became interested in native wine-making, and made connections with Western grape-growers, and was instrumental in introducing the Longworth wines from Ohio. His taste for literature led him to devote his leisure to writing, which he followed as a pastime. In 1847 he contributed a number of humorous sketches and poems to "Yankee Doodle," and afterward wrote a series of articles for the "Knickerbocker Magazine," which he collected and published in 1853 under the title of "Prismatics," using the pen-name of "Richard Haywarde," which

was the name of one of his ancestors. Subsequently he contributed to the "Knickerbocker Magazine" the "Sparrowgrass Papers," which were a series of very funny sketches, describing the adventures of a city man unused to country life, who had purchased a rural home. This was afterward published in book form (1856), and had an enormous circulation, and gave Mr. Cozzens a wide reputation as one of the first humorists of the country. He published in 1858 "Acadia; a Sojourn among the Blue-Noses," and the same year contributed to the New York "Ledger" "The True History of New Plymouth." He conducted, in connection with his business, a trade-paper called the "Wine-Press," for which he wrote a pleasant miscellany of choice essays and sketches in the line of practical æsthetics, in addition to much information on wine-making and his hobby, the native culture of the grape. Mr. Cozzens continued to edit this periodical for seven years, until the breaking out of the civil war, when it was abandoned. In 1867 he made a collection of the sprightly essays from its pages, which he published in book form under the title "Sayings of Dr. Bushwhacker and Other Learned Men." The next year he wrote a "Memorial of Fitz Greene Halleck," which was read before the New York Historical Society, and afterward printed by them. He resided in Yonkers at the time the "Sparrowgrass Papers" were written, and it was there that most of its scenes were laid, but after a failure in business he removed to Rahway, N. J. In addition to what is mentioned, he published a "Memorial of Col. Peter A. Porter." He was on a visit to Brooklyn when he was stricken down suddenly, and died Dec. 23, 1869.

NEAL, Joseph Clay, humorist, was born Feb. 3, 1807 in Greenland, N. H. His father, a retired clergyman, who had been principal of a school in Philadelphia, died when his son was two years old. Joseph was early attached to editorial life, and contributed articles to various periodicals until 1831, when he became editor of the "Pennsylvanian." The labor proved too severe for his delicate constitution, and he was forced, in 1844, to relinquish his post and go abroad. Upon his return he established "Neal's Saturday Gazette" which achieved great success, and which he continued to edit until his death. In 1846 he married Alice Bradley, who was a woman of fine literary taste and culture, and greatly assisted him in his work. Mr. Neal's humor lays in the delineation of small spendthrifts, pretenders to fashion, bores, and the frayed-out gentleman; a

quaint vein of speculation ran through his human dialogues, which gave them great popularity. There were several series of these sketches contributed to the papers which Mr. Neal edited, and also to the "Democratic Review." They were first published under the title of "City Worthies," but were afterwards collected into several volumes under the name of "Charcoal Sketches or Scenes in a Metropolis," and republished in London under the auspices of Charles Dickens, to whose earliest writings they compared favorably. A collection of these "Charcoal Sketches" appear in the middle of a volume of "Pickwick Papers" edited by Charles Dickens, introduced by the editor as from a "Nameless Person," but without giving credit to Mr. Neal. They were followed by "Peter Ploddy and Other Oddities." Mr. Neal died in Philadelphia, July 18, 1847.

WHITCHER, Frances Miriam, humorist, was born Nov. 1, 1811, in Whitestown, N. Y. Her father, Lewis Berry, was a farmer, who, though in straitened circumstances, gave personal attention to the education of his children. Frances was very precocious and could repeat long pieces of poetry before she was three years old, and had even learned the alphabet. She had from birth a keen sense of the ridiculous, and as a child was the terror of the neighbors on account of the charcoal sketches and doggerel in which she caricatured them. When four years old she was sent to the village school, where she developed her remarkable cleverness in original illustration. Her slate was covered with caricatures of the peculiar features about her, which she seemed unable to keep from drawing. Her copy book followed no set copy, but was filled with little poems interspersed with verse of her own, and the margins were adorned with heads and various devices. In drawing she never had a master, and received only a few hints from a relative. Itinerant professors of drawing who passed through the village were incapable of improving such an endowment as hers. From her earliest childhood she made rhymes, one of which, a parody on "My Mother," was particularly humorous. She first became a contributor to "Neal's Saturday Gazette" in 1846, when she concealed her identity. Its editor, Joseph C. Neal, the well-known author of "Charcoal Sketches," was struck with the originality of her work, and began a correspondence with his unknown contributor, soon discovering that she was so sensitively modest and unaware of her remarkable talent as a humorist that she was ready to abandon writing. Mr. Neal encouraged her despondent genius, and induced her to continue in her work. When her best known effort, "Widow Bedott's Table Talk," first appeared in Neal's paper the authorship was attributed to Mr. Neal himself, no one being able to believe that sketches so full of humor, and so remarkable for minute observation of human nature, were the work of an unpracticed pen. To "Godey's Lady's Book" she contributed "Aunt Maguire" and "Letters from Timberville," besides writing many articles for other periodicals of the day. In 1847 she became the wife of Rev. Benjamin Whitcher, an Episcopal clergyman, the incumbent of a church at Elmira, N. Y., whither she removed the following spring. It was while she presided over the parsonage at Elmira that she achieved her greatest fame as a humorous writer, but in the midst of her popularity she drew upon herself the ill-will of many of her husband's parishioners, who fancied they were the originals of her sketches, and the ill feeling became so marked and general as to necessitate a removal to another parish. Mrs. Whitcher returned to her native town in the fall of 1850, and continued her literary work, but her health declined shortly afterwards, and after a year and a half of severe suffering, she died Jan. 4, 1852. She left uncompleted a novel entitled "Mary Elmer," which was begun while at Elmira. After her death her writings were collected into book form. "The Widow Bedott Papers," with an introduction by Alice Neal, the wife of her first publisher, appeared in 1855, and "Widow Spriggins, Mary Elmer, and other Sketches" appeared in 1867.

LEWIS, Charles Bertrand, journalist and humorist, was born at Liverpool, O., Feb. 18, 1842. His father, George C. Lewis, a contractor and builder, was a man of considerable education. After attending the common schools of his native town, Charles went to the Agricultural College of Lansing, Mich., after which he learned the trade of printer in the office of a weekly newspaper in that city. He worked for some years as a compositor, and then accepted the editorship of a paper at Jonesboro', Tenn. While on his way to his new home, he took passage at Cincinnati on an Ohio river steamboat, the boiler of which exploded, and he was severely injured. He lay in a hospital at Cincinnati for many weeks, and then concluded to return to Lansing, where he became foreman of the "Jacksonian." One day, in the absence of the editor, he wrote and published a humorous article, entitled "How It Feels to be Blown Up." The article was widely copied, and attracted the attention of the editor of the Detroit "Free Press," who, in 1869, offered Lewis the position of legislative reporter on that journal. When the legislature adjourned he went to Detroit, and his quaint and humorous descriptions of local events were soon quoted everywhere, and gave the "Free Press" a more than national reputation, while he, under the odd nom-de-plume of "M. Quad," became one of the best-known humorists of his time. His connection with the "Free Press" continued for twenty-two years, and during the greater part of that time he held a proprietary interest in the paper. Among his notable contributions to the "Free Press" were the series of sketches entitled "His Honor and Bijah," another dealing with the mirthful doings of the "Lime-Kiln Club," and still another detailing the joys and sorrows of "Mr. and Mrs. Bowser." He also wrote many thousands of descriptive and character sketches, full of sentiment and pathos.

Upon May 1, 1891, he became a member of the editorial staff of the New York "World," at a salary of $10,000 a year. He is a prodigious worker, and a writer of wide scope and fertile imagination, which explains his enduring popularity. He has traveled widely and written much upon scenes and incidents dealing with the war of the rebellion. A play of his, entitled "Yakie," was produced in 1884.

WILDER, Marshall Pinckney, humorist, was born in Geneva, N. Y., Sept. 19, 1859, son of Louis de V. Wilder M.D. He attended school in Hartford, Conn., and Rochester, N. Y., and early gave evidence of that brilliancy of mind and decision of character which have enabled him to overcome grave handicaps and encompass an enviable success. It is related that while a school boy, at Rochester, he, resenting the officiousness of a certain policeman in interfering with ball playing in the public park, with true American independence, carried the matter to the mayor, and by dint of persuasive eloquence, secured written permission for himself and friends to enjoy unmolested the national game. Upon the completion of his education he came to New York, and was for a while employed with Bradstreet's Commercial Agency. He mastered stenography with the intention of making it a profession, but subsequently altered his plans, although finding it now a most useful accomplishment, enabling him, as he expresses it, "to catch ideas on the wing." Being naturally of a most sociable nature, he was in great demand at evening parties and entertainments, and soon discovered a remarkable ability to render recitations, especially those of a humorous nature. His popularity increased to such an extent that he determined to adopt this line as a profession, charging in the beginning 50 cents for an evening's entertainment and later $5. To-day he commands his own prices and is universally in requisition. As a humorist he is inimitable; his impersonations indicating a dramatic insight of the first quality and being rendered the more forcible by a mobility of feature which permits of expressing every grade and degree of feeling. His amiability of character and the refinement of his entertainments have endeared him to every audience; and, despite the smallness of his stature, he is a very great man indeed. Mr. Wilder has traveled extensively, met many people of distinction, and been everywhere welcomed with the utmost courtesy. The Prince of Wales received him with great consideration and favorably commented on his talent. Among his many distinguished friends he counts Pres. Cleveland, Ex-Pres. Harrison, Wm. E. Gladstone, and Chauncey M. Depew. The late George W. Childs said truly, "No young man is more popular;" and Mr. Spurgeon could not forbear the tribute, "He makes men better with his humor." It is related that, presenting a letter of introduction from the late Henry Ward Beecher to Pres. Cleveland, Mr. Wilder was honored by an immediate audience, although many distinguished guests were waiting their turn. His success is the just fruit of his own industry and perseverance. He made a lifelong friend of Mr. Beecher, but had been previously refused admittance at his door on six occasions, when he sought an opportunity to give an entertainment in Plymouth Church. But he was not discouraged, and Mr. Beecher recognized his worth. He has written one book, "The People I've Smiled With," which is a witty and highly readable account of interviews with the many worthies he has met in the course of his career, showing talent as a writer quite commensurate with his histrionic ability.

SWEET, Alexander Edwin, humorist, was born in St. John, New Brunswick, Canada, March 28, 1841, son of James R. Sweet, who was a merchant of that city. In 1849 the family removed to Texas, settling in San Antonio, where the son acquired his primary education. In 1858 he was sent to College Hill Collegiate Institute, Poughkeepsie, N. Y. After a year and a half he went to Germany to complete his studies at the Polytechnic School, Carlsruhe, Baden. He was married to a lady of that city, and returned to Texas in 1862, where he joined the Confederate army, serving principally on the Rio Grande and in the Indian Territory. After the war he studied law, and practiced his profession in Texas for several years with very limited success, and then drifted into journalism; first on the San Antonio "Herald," afterward as local editor of the San Antonio "Express," and finally as associate-editor of the Galveston "News," after having been its San Antonio correspondent for several years. An alliterative managing editor on the "News" gave Mr. Sweet's San Antonio letter the heading of "San Antonio Siftings." The items were widely copied, and when Mr. Sweet started a paper of his own in Austin, Tex., in 1881, it was given the name of "Texas Siftings," of which much-quoted humorous journal he has been the editor continuously from its first issue. Besides furnishing all the editorial matter in "Texas Siftings," Mr. Sweet contributes regularly to several syndicates. In 1888 "Texas Siftings" was removed from Texas to New York. Among the better known productions of Mr. Sweet's pen are the "Bill Snort Letters," which have been widely copied. These political satires have created a popular belief in the real existence of Col. Snort, and it was a frequent incident in the experience of Pres. Cleveland in his travels to be annoyed by people who insisted that Col. Snort was with the party. Mr. Sweet is a very rapid and copious writer. He claims to turn out more copy than any other contemporaneous humorous writer, save possibly Lewis (M. Quad) of the Detroit "Free Press."

RILEY, James Whitcomb, the "Hoosier Poet," was born in Greenfield, Ind., in 1853. He left school early, having acquired a taste for a roaming life from accompanying his father, who was a lawyer, in his circuits from court to court. His father wished to make him a lawyer, but the wandering life seemed to call him, and he adopted the profession of a strolling sign-painter. He even at times pretended to be blind to secure sympathy and trade, being led about from place to place by a little boy. So cleverly did he carry out this rôle, running his hand over the surface of the board as if taking the measurements, and then falling to work, that wondering crowds gathered to see the "blind sign-painter." He "fell in" on one of these tramps with a "patent medicine man," with whom he joined for-

tunes; his share of the business being to collect and amuse the crowd by funny songs to a banjo accompaniment, while his partner sold his nostrums to the people. In this way he acquired the language and dialect of the "Hoosiers," which he has used so effectively in his verse. James began early to rhyme, his first effusion being a four-line valentine with comic illustrations, when barely as high as the table upon which he wrote it. He next became a member of a troupe of barn-storming Thespians, and turned his talent to improvising songs and adapting plays. He had remarkable imitative powers, and a poem, "Leonainie," in imitation of Poe, deceived even the foremost literary critics. He had announced, on its publication, that it was a poem found on the fly-leaf of a book of Edgar Poe's, and discovered by a relative who had migrated to Indiana many years before. This subterfuge was the means of securing him a position on a newspaper in Indianapolis, in which his first dialect poems appeared. His popularity was immediate, and his fame spread far and wide. His collected poems have passed through many editions. They are entitled: "The Old Swimmin' Hole, and 'Leven More Poems," by Benj. F. Johnson, of

Bonne (1885); "The Boss Girl, and Other Sketches" (1886); "Character Sketches and Poems" (1887); "Afterwhiles" (1888); "Pipes o' Pan at Zekesbury" (1889); "Green Fields and Running Brooks," and "Rhymes of Childhood" (1893). Mr. Riley has written in prose as well as verse, and some very charming sketches have come from his pen, but it is as a poet he is best known and loved. He is the poet of human nature, which he depicts in a quaint and simple way that reaches the heart. Some of his happiest efforts are his poems of childhood, which breathe his love of children in every line. There are few children who are not familiar with the story of "Little Orphant Annie," with its ghost suggesting refrain, "An' the gobble-uns 'll git you, ef you don't watch out," and it has an appeal to children of a larger as well as those of a smaller growth. Mr. Riley's muse has touched with an indescribable pathos and tenderness, the most commonplace events and experiences of life, and his poems will live as long as hearts are responsive to nature, and the ideals of love and home. Mr. Riley is still unmarried (1895).

JOHNSON, Samuel William, chemist, was born in Kingsboro', Fulton co., N. Y., July 3, 1830. He is a descendant of Robert Johnson, one of the founders of the town of New Haven. He received his early education in the common schools and Lowville Academy, when he entered the scientific school of Yale College in 1850, where, for eighteen months, he studied agricultural chemistry under Profs. Norton and B. Silliman, Jr. His home was upon a large, well-managed farm, giving him the advantage of a wide range of practical agricultural knowledge. During the winter of 1851–52 he was instructor in the natural sciences in the New York State Normal School at Albany, and after spending the following winters in work in the laboratory at New Haven, he gave two years to study at Leipsic and Munich, under Erdmann, Von Robell, Liebig, and Pettenkofer. From Germany he went to England, studying under Frankland during the summer of 1855. He was appointed chief assistant in chemistry in the Yale Scientific School in September, 1855, and professor of analytical chemistry in 1856, succeeding Prof. John A. Porter in the chair of agricultural chemistry in 1857. He became professor of theoretical and agricultural chemistry in 1875, which chair he has since held. Prof. Johnson was a member of the state board of agriculture of Connecticut when first established in 1866, and after two years of service was appointed chemist to the board. He began as early as 1873 to agitate the establishment of a state agricultural experiment station, which was organized by act of the legislature, passed in 1877, Prof. Johnson being appointed director. Though confined for many years to two small rooms, and the works of references and applia．．s being mostly loaned from Yale College and the professor's private laboratory and library. Its work has been of incalculable benefit to the farmers, as the reports of the institution show. The single thought that animates these reports is to deal with those particular features of agriculture of most immediate interest to farmers. One of the predominant crops of the state being grass, the things most needed for profitable returns are economical and efficient fertilizers. These are, therefore, most largely presented. A brief summary of two or three of these reports will serve to illustrate their nature.

The report of 1886 directs attention to the importance of the relations of the mechanical constitution of soils to the growth of plants. While still a student, Prof. Johnson began writing for the agricultural papers. One of the earliest of his publications was an address before the State Agricultural Society of Connecticut in 1856 on "Fraud in Chemical Fertilizers," which brought about the adoption of measures to protect buyers against imposition through adulterated fertilizers. Among the best known of Prof. Johnson's writings on the special subjects of

Sheffield Scientific School.

his studies are: "How Crops Grow" (1868); "How Crops Feed" (1870), and "Peat and its Uses as Fertilizer and Fuel" (1866). The former book found great favor in America and Europe, having been republished in England under the joint editorship of Profs. Church and Dyer, of the Royal Agricultural College at Cirencester, and translated into German, under the direction of Prof. Liebig. Versions have also been made in Italian, Swedish, Russian, and Japanese. "How Plants Feed" deals exclusively with the subject of vegetable nutrition. These books are commended to students of agriculture, whether on the farm or in the school. Prof. Johnson has also edited Fresenius's "Quantitative Analysis" (1864), and his "Qualitative Analysis" (1869). Prof. Johnson stands deservedly high as an authority on the application of chemistry to agriculture. He is a member of the National Academy of Sciences, and of the American Academy of Arts and Sciences. The "American Agriculturist" names Prof. Johnson as one of the trio, Gossman, and the late Dr. Cook of New Jersey being the other two, "who have done so much for agricultural science and experimentation." Prof. Johnson is a devoted student of science, and is eminently practical in the direction and purpose of his work. He is pleasant and modest in his manners, has a wide knowledge of human nature, and "a practical conception of what farmers want of agricultural experiment stations." As a writer, his style is clear and concise, but most delightfully smooth and finished.

CLIFTON, Josephine, actress, was born in New York city in 1813. She received a patient and careful training for the stage, and made her début as a professional actress as Imogene in "Bertram" at the Bowery Theatre, Sept. 21, 1831. Her great beauty and abundant talent, combined with the advantages she had received, won her instant success. During the following season she was leading lady at the Chestnut Street and Walnut Street theatres in Philadelphia. She appeared in the most important cities of the country, and in 1834 visited England making her début as Belvidera at Drury Lane, London, on Oct. 4th. She was the first actress of American birth to visit England as a star, but her reception was a very cordial one. Returning to the United States, she resumed her tours as a star. In 1837 N. P. Willis wrote for her the tragedy "Bianca Visconti," first produced at the Park Theatre, New York. During her earlier years Charlotte Cushman was her only serious rival in such rôles as Bianca, Belvidera, Mrs. Haller, and Jane Shore; but as she advanced in life she grew obese and lymphatic, and was finally compelled to retire from the stage. In July, 1846, she became the wife of Robert Place, the manager of a New Orleans Theatre. She died suddenly in New Orleans, La., Nov. 23, 1847.

DAW, George Weidman, lawyer, was born in Cohoes, Albany co., N. Y., May 24, 1855. His father was Peter Ferris Daw, a lawyer of some prominence in the place. His paternal ancestors were descended

from a French family of the Huguenot stock, who, in the latter part of the seventeenth century, emigrated from the city of Rochelle in France, in company with many others of the same religious sympathies and views, and found refuge from persecution near the city of New York, at a place named by them and ever since known as New Rochelle. Mr. Daw's uncle, Harry Daw, was one of the earliest and most prominent citizens of Buffalo. Mr. Daw, through his grandmother, Esther Denison (born 1776), is a descendant of Capt. Geo. Denison, a noted officer in the Indian wars of Connecticut, whose wife was Ann Borsdaile, an English lady of rank, and whose father, William Denison, came to America in 1631, and settled in Roxbury, Mass. After the death of his first wife, Capt. George Denison returned to England, served under Cromwell in the army of the parliament, was wounded at Naseby, and nursed at the home of John Borsdaile by his daughter, Ann, whom he subsequently married, and returned to Roxbury, Mass., finally settling at Stonington, Conn. He died and was buried at Hartford, Conn., in 1694, leaving behind him the reputation of a splendid Indian fighter and a man of great force of character. He was described as the Miles Standish of his settlement, but was a far better soldier than his prototype. As leader of the volunteer forces he visited vengeance on the Indians and broke their power for ever. Mr. Daw attended the public school in Cohoes until the age of fifteen, when he went to the public school in Albany to fit himself for college, and was graduated at the Albany High School, but his father's sudden death upset his plans. In 1877 he went to Troy and studied law in the offices of Messrs. Smith, Furman & Cowen, and was admitted to the bar in 1880. After two years a partnership was entered into with Eugene L. Pelter, which continued until 1890, since which time he has practiced alone. Mr. Daw has occupied many important local positions, among them that of attorney for the excise board of Troy, 1883–86. He was one of the organizers, and is now (1895), a director of the Peoples' Bank of Lansingburgh, besides being a director of the R. T. French Co. of Rochester, N. Y. He takes an active interest in politics, having been secretary of the Rensselaer county Republican committee from 1880–84, and acting chairman during the Blaine campaign of 1884. He was one of the organizers of the Rensselaer Union Club, now known as the Troy Republican Club; is a member of the Troy Club; a vestryman of Trinity Church; was the originator, and is now a director of the Riverside Club of Lansingburgh; a director in the Beacon Electric Light Co. of Lansingburgh, and a director in several other local organizations. He was married May 10, 1882, to his cousin, E. Eugenia, only daughter of Daniel Weidman of Albany. Two daughters are the issue of the marriage.

LEMEN, Lewis Erastus, physician, was born in St. Clair county, Ill., Apr. 1, 1849, son of Silvester Lemen, a farmer, and leader in the Baptist church. His grandfather, Rev. James Lemen, was the first white child born in Illinois, one of the founders of Shurtleff College, the founder of the Bethel Baptist Church in St. Clair county, Ill. Five of his brothers were Baptist preachers of the heroic type, and their father fought as a patriot in the revolutionary war and performed other services of importance to the government, relative to the early settlement of the western territory. Young Lemen attended the district schools of his native county, working on his father's farm when not in school until his sixteenth year, when he entered Shurtleff College, and after a three years' course he entered the St. Louis Medical College, and was graduated in 1871 an M.D. Upon graduation he was appointed assistant physician of the St. Louis City Hospital, and after one year of practical training he began to practice medicine in St. Louis. Owing to failing health, he was obliged to remove West in 1874, and located in Georgetown, Col., and in the spring of 1883 he located in Denver. In 1883 he was made surgeon for the Omaha and Grant Smelting and Refining Co., and of the Globe Smelting and Refining Co. upon its organization in 1887; and for a number of years surgeon of the Union Pacific Railroad, and of the Denver City Cable Railway Co. since 1885. He is consulting surgeon of the U. P. D. and G. Railroad. He is president of the staff and surgeon to the St. Joseph's Hospital, consulting surgeon to St. Luke's Hospital, and president of the staff of surgeons of the Cottage Home. Dr. Lemen lectured for two years in the medical department of the University of Denver. For one year he held a chair in the Gross Medical College, and for the past three years he has occupied the chair as professor of clinical surgery in the University of Colorado. Dr. Lemen is a member of the American Medical Association, Colorado State Medical Association, Denver and Arapahoe County Medical Association, American Academy of Railway Surgeons, and the American Association of Railway Surgeons. He has served as president of the Denver Medical Association, was appointed health commissioner of Denver in 1893, and in 1880 was appointed commissioner of the Colorado State Insane Asylum, and is president of the board of commissioners. In 1887 the honorary degree of A.M. was conferred on him by Shurtleff College. He is a prominent member of the Masonic Fraternity, having taken the thirty-second degree. He is a Knight-Templar and a Shriner. Dr. Lemen was married May 5, 1875, to Lizzie, daughter of Henry T. Mudd, St. Louis, Mo. She died in 1876. On Apr. 13, 1882, he was married to Elsie, daughter of Wm. H. James of Leadville, Col.

MAXIM, Hiram Stevens, inventor, was born in Sangerville, Me., Feb. 5, 1840, son of Isaac Weston and Harriet Boston (Stevens) Maxim. The family originally lived in the county of Kent, England, and were French Huguenots, who found in England a refuge from religious persecution. They came to the English colonies in America about 1650 and settled in Plymouth county, Mass. The men were soldiers with Wolfe and Montgomery at Quebec, and when the colonists declared their independence, they espoused the cause, resigned their commissions under the British flag in the colonial militia, and fought in the revolutionary war against the king. About 1785 two brothers, sons of Nathan Maxim, left Wareham, Mass., and taking with them apple tree sprouts, settled in Maine on the banks of the Kennebec, at Wayne, Kennebec county, planted the apple sprouts and built for themselves log cabins. Later they built frame houses, making the brick for the chimneys on the spot. When established at Wayne they sent for their father; and one of the brothers, having married Eliza Ryder of Martha's Vineyard, Mass., became the father of Isaac Weston Maxim, who was born in 1814, and upon his marriage migrated still farther to the east and settled in the woods in the town of Sangerville. Here they endured many hardships which the son, as a boy and a youth, shared with his parents. They were entirely dependent on their own exertions for everything, and with no money were forced to make from raw material, all the necessities of life. The mother was an expert spinner, weaver, dyer, and seamstress, and the father a trapper, tanner, miller, blacksmith, carpenter, mason, and farmer. Amid such surroundings and with continual daily object lessons of industry, thrift, courage, and determination, the boy early displayed remarkable aptitude with his only working tool, the universal Yankee jackknife, and the product of his skill in mechanical objects excited the wonder and interest of the locality. His parents did not encourage the latent genius, and bound him an apprentice to coach-building. Filial duty kept him at the uncongenial occupation for four years, but upon his release he forsook it and found employment in a machine shop at Fitchburg, Mass. Soon mastering the alphabet of mechanical engineering he took up the study of mechanical drawing, and from the Fitchburg shop he went to Boston as the foreman of a philosophical instrument manufactory, and thence to New York where he gained experience in iron-working and ship-building at the Novelty Iron Works Ship-Building Company. His inventions up to this period embraced various improvements in steam engines and the Maxim Automatic Gas Machines, which came into universal use. In 1877 he turned his attention to electricity. In 1878 he produced an incandescent lamp which would burn 1,000 hours. He was the first to design a process for flashing electric carbons and the first to "standardize" carbons for electric lighting. In 1880 he visited Europe and exhibited at the Paris Exposition of 1881, his self-regulating current machine, receiving the decoration of Chevalier de la Légion d'Honneur. In 1883 he returned to London as the European representative of the United States Electric Light Company. An incident of his boyhood in which the recoil of a rifle attracted his attention to an apparent loss of power, led him in 1881–82,

to utilize the force of the recoil to good account in a gun which loads itself automatically, and fires at the rate of 770 shots per minute by the power of the previously wasted force. The Maxim-Nordenfelt Gun Company, with a capital of $9,000,000 is represented in Europe by Mr. Maxim. In 1883 he patented his electric training gear for large guns, which is used in all parts of the world. In 1889 he began to turn his attention to flying-machine construction, and in it made remarkable headway. This, however, was not suffered to interfere with his greater interests in the Maxim gun, which he has successfully introduced to the various ruling governments of the world, and by most of which it was at once adopted. His residence at Baldwyn's Park, Dartford Heath, near Bexley, England, is a picturesque estate of 500 acres. Here he has his laboratory and library, and on this estate he made his later experiments (1894) with his flying machine, which he announces as a certain solution of aerial navigation, even if his own present machines actually fail; and the great works at Erith, Kent, even apart from his aerial problems, are among the sights of Europe and bear impressive testimony to the genius and will-power of a tireless inventor. At the International Patent Office of Europe he has taken out over 100 different patents relating to petroleum and other motors and smokeless gun powders. He took up his residence in England to avoid what he claimed to be unfair treatment accorded him and his inventions by the government of the United States. Mr. Maxim was married in 1880 to Sarah, daughter of Charles Haynes, of Boston, Mass.

ALGER, William Rounseville, author and clergyman, born at Freetown, Mass., Dec. 30, 1822. Thrown at an early age upon his own resources, he obtained work in the cotton mills at Hooksett, N. H. His desire for knowledge was such that he devoted the greater part of his leisure time to study. Fastening pages of his grammar on a post in the mill, he committed them to memory as he tended his machines, and in odd moments of rest, which the care of the machinery frequently permitted, he worked out problems in arithmetic and algebra, with a bit of chalk on a strip of wood, or read a page in some history or romance. At the end of five years, having fitted himself, and saved sufficient money to pay his tuition, he entered the academy at Pembroke, N. H., where he remained one year. He then went to the academy at Lebanon, and from there, after a half year's instruction, to the Harvard Divinity School, where he was graduated in 1847. On Sept. 8, 1847, he was ordained over the Mount Pleasant Congregational Society in Roxbury, and in 1852 Harvard University conferred on him the honorary degree of A.M.

In 1855 he resigned the pastorship of the Roxbury church to accept a call from the Bullfinch Street Society of Boston, over which he was installed on the first Sunday in January of that year. In 1857 he accepted an invitation to deliver the Fourth of July oration before the city authorities of Boston, and improved the occasion—although pro-slavery feeling was then at its height—by an uncompromising protest against the slave power in the South, and its upholders at the North. The board of aldermen refused to pass the customary vote of thanks, but seven years later, in 1864, the vote was passed. In 1868 he was chosen chaplain of the Massachusetts house of representatives. In the autumn of 1868 the members of his church, and others of the liberal faith, organized a society for the holding of free services in the Boston Music Hall, and there he preached every Sunday to audiences of from 2,000 to 3,000 persons. In 1871 he sailed for Europe, to enjoy a short season of rest and recreation, but while in Paris his health broke, in consequence of overwork, and for months his recovery was doubtful. A year of entire rest, however, with the best of care, made him stronger than before, and in May, 1872, he resumed his preaching in the Music Hall, continuing it until September, 1873, when he resigned. In December, 1874, he accepted a call from the Church of the Messiah, in New York, and continued there until 1878. He has since held pastorates in Chicago, Ill., and Portland, Me., and is now (1890) residing in Boston, Mass. He has written numerous books of exceptional interest and value, the best known of which are perhaps his "Critical History of the Doctrine of a Future Life," and his "Poetry of the Orient;" and he has also been a frequent contributor to the leading American magazines. He is a writer of rare insight, and remarkable power and originality.

FOWLER, George W., printer, was born in Westfield, Mass., Oct. 15, 1844, of an honored ancestry. After receiving a thorough education in the public schools of his native town, he learned the printer's trade in the composing rooms of the Westfield "News-Letter." During the civil war he was in the employ of the Springfield "Republican." In 1864 he removed to Hartford, Conn., and spent eight years in the employ of the Hartford "Times." In 1873 he organized the printing firm of Smith, Fowler & Miller, which in 1881 was incorporated as the Fowler & Miller Co., and from that time he was its president and controlling spirit. Possessed of rare executive ability and sound business judgment, he has made his company one of the leading printing establishments of the city and state, and many of the city and state documents are entrusted to them. He is chairman of the state commission, appointed by the governor for the care of the East Hartford bridge over the Connecticut river. For eight years he was a leading member of the board of aldermen of the city, and has been at the head of the board of selectmen for twelve years, resigning in May, 1894, to accept the position of town collector, and in June assumed the duties of city collector. Mr. Fowler has taken an active interest in the welfare of the community, and in appreciation of that fact, has for several years received the nominations of both parties. He is a prominent society man, and very popular among the members of the leading fraternal orders. He married M. Louise, daughter of Judge William P. Rowles, of Tennessee.

MAURY, Matthew Fontaine, hydrographer and meteorologist, was born in Spottsylvania county, Va., Jan. 14, 1806. At an early age he removed to Tennessee with his parents, and was placed at the Harpeth Academy, then under the charge of Rev. James H. Otey, who afterwards became bishop of Tennessee. When nineteen he entered the U. S. navy as a midshipman, making his first voyage in the frigate Brandywine, to France, with Gen. Lafayette. He accompanied the vessel to the Pacific, where he was transferred to the Vincennes, in which vessel he completed the circumnavigation of the globe. He again sailed as passed-lieutenant to the Pacific in the sloop-of-war Falmouth, when he was transferred as lieutenant to the Potomac. While at sea he devoted his leisure to mathematics, in which he found he was not proficient enough for the requirements of his profession, and to extend his knowledge of modern languages at the same time, he used Spanish text-books. In pursuing his studies he was greatly inconvenienced by the number of different volumes employed, and with a view to saving others a like difficulty, he prepared, amid the annoyances and interruptions of a life at sea, a work on navigation. "Maury's Navigation" was commenced in the steerage of the Vincennes, and completed in the Potomac, and published in 1885, when it met with universal acceptance, and was adopted as a text-book in the navy. During this interval of active service he married Ann Herndon, a sister of Lieut. Herndon, of the U. S. navy, who rendered such conspicuous service upon the sinking of the Central America, which he commanded. In this same year he was appointed astronomer to the South Sea Exploring Expedition, but, upon the withdrawal of Com. Jones, he declined the appointment. In 1839, while on his way from Tennessee, to join a surveying vessel in New York harbor, the stage-coach was overturned and his leg was broken, which resulted in permanent lameness, and disabled him for active service. During his long period of imprisonment from his disabled leg, he amused himself writing a series of articles on the abuses in the navy, which were published in the "Southern Messenger" under the title of "Scraps from the Lucky Bag, by Harry Bluff." His forceful style produced an immediate impression, and resulted in great reforms, and ultimately in the establishment of the Naval Academy. His advocacy of the establishment of a navy-yard at Memphis, Tenn., resulted in an act of congress to build it. He made the first observations on the flow of the Mississippi river, and proposed a system of observations which would give every day, by telegraph, the state of the river and its tributaries to captains of steamers on the river. He made studies in regard to the enlargement of the Illinois and Michigan canals, by which war vessels might pass from the gulf to the great lakes, for which he received the thanks of the Illinois legislature. He was the first to suggest what is known as the warehouse system. His thirteen years' service at sea gave him an opportunity for extended meteorological and hydrographical study, and soon after his retirement from the exploring expedition, he was appointed chief of the Hydrographical Bureau at Washington, and upon its union with the National Observatory in 1844, he became superintendent of the combined institutions. To him is due many of the present methods employed in the weather bureau. He devoted much study to the ocean currents, and collected from the log-books of the ships of war data upon which he determined the direction of winds and currents of the ocean, which he published in 1844 in a paper read before the National Institute, which was afterwards printed under the title of "A Scheme for Rebuilding Southern Commerce." Recognizing the need of systematizing the observations and records which were taken differently by the various nations, Lieut. Maury proposed a maritime congress, which, at the earnest advocacy of the United States, was held at Brussels in 1853, at which was recommended a uniform style of abstract log, to be kept by all vessels, in whatever service. At the close of the congress the merchants of New York presented him with $5,000, and a service of plate. The result of his studies upon the winds and currents, was his "Physical Geography of the Sea," which was of the utmost value to the maritime world, and was immediately translated into nearly every language, making its author at once famous throughout Europe. Humboldt declared that Lieut. Maury had founded a new science, and the governments of almost every nation in Europe conferred upon him orders of knighthood, and other insignia of honor. He was made a member of the Academies of Sciences of Paris, Berlin, Brussels, St. Petersburg, and Mexico. Lieut. Maury described with great carefulness the course of the gulf stream, showing the best course to be followed in crossing the Atlantic. He also instituted deep-sea sounding, and discovered the great plateau under the Atlantic. He

first suggested to Cyrus W. Field the feasibility of telegraphic communication between Europe and this country by means of a cable laid on the bed of the ocean, and indicated the route upon which it was finally laid. His services to the scientific knowledge of the country have hardly been surpassed. In 1855 he was given the rank of commander, which position he held at the outbreak of the civil war in 1861. He resigned, to follow his native state, Virginia, out of the Union, at the same time refusing generous offers, made by both the Grand Duke Constantine of Russia, and his Imperial Highness Prince Napoleon, on condition of his settling in their respective countries. In 1862 he established a naval submarine battery service at Richmond, but before much progress had been made, he was sent to England, after having attained the rank of captain in the Confederate service, and continued his studies, making a number of important discoveries, among them several improvements in the application of magneto-electricity to torpedoes. He was also appointed one of the navy agents for the Confederate states, and while in Europe, fitted out several armed cruisers. At the close of the war he went to Mexico, where the Emperor Maxmillian, a former friend of his, appointed him to a place in his cabinet. He also served for a time as commissioner of emigration, declining all other honors offered him, owing to a distrust of the stability of the French government there. This distrust finally became so great that he returned to England, where he was joined by his family from Virginia. While in Europe the University of Cambridge conferred upon him the degree of LL.D., and he was invited by Napoleon III. to accept the superintendency of the Imperial observatory at Paris. In 1868 he was offered the professorship of physics in the Military Institute at Lexington, Va., which he accepted. He returned to this country, and performed the duties of his professorship until his death, at the same time conducting a physical survey of Virginia, which was published in Richmond in 1868, under the title of "The Physical Survey of Virginia." The results of this survey established through routes by rail, and a great

free water-line, uniting the East and West. It also established a system of observations and reports of crops, which greatly promoted foreign commerce. With William M. Fountain he prepared and published "The Resources of West Virginia." In 1871 he accepted the presidency of the University of Alabama, but on account of ill health, returned to his professorship at Lexington. Besides the works mentioned, he has published a series of text-books on astronomy and political and physical geography, prepared during his English exile. But the work which has made Maury famous is his official work as head of the hydrographical board at Washington, which resulted in the Maury "Wind and Current Charts," and two large volumes of "Sailing Directions." These works, owing to their clear indications of the best ocean routes, shortened voyages to such an extent as to save several million dollars annually to the commerce of the world. The amount of labor they involved may be judged from the fact that 1,159,353 separate observations on the force and direction of the wind, and over 100,000 observations on the height of the barometer at sea, were necessary for the wind chart alone. He also published "Letters on the Amazon and the Atlantic Slopes of South America," "Relations Between Magnetism and the Circulation of the Atmosphere," "Laws for Steamers Crossing the Atlantic." Com. Maury is also the author of several addresses delivered in various parts of the country, among which may be mentioned those before the Geological and Mineralogical Society of Fredericksburg. In 1836, and Southern Scientific Convention at Memphis, on the Pacific Railway. He died in Lexington, Va., Feb. 1, 1873.

BOTTY, Henry C., jurist, was born in New York city, Dec. 27, 1854, of Dutch parentage. He received his early education in the public schools, and subsequently in the Christian Brother's School of De La Salle Institute, New York, where he was graduated in the class of 1869. At the age of fifteen he entered upon the study of law in the law office of Ex-senator Lewis S. Goebel, a practitioner of good repute and prominence in the city, and continued his clerkship with him for several years. In the year 1873 he was admitted to Columbia College Law School, in order to perfect his studies in the law, and was graduated with honors in the year 1875, he being then a little over twenty years of age and one of the youngest graduates of a class of several hundred students. In January, 1876, shortly after attaining his majority, he was duly admitted to the practice of law by the New York supreme court, and subsequently in the U. S. courts. He has been actively engaged in the general practice of the law in all its branches in his native city ever since his admission to the bar, and by diligent attention to his business and devotion to his clients' interests, he has won the con-

fidence and esteem of all who came into contact with him, so that he now enjoys a large and lucrative practice. He is prominently identified with a number of benevolent, social, and other organizations in New York. Being a firm believer in the principles of the Republican party, he became identified with it as soon as he attained his majority, and has been ever since a strong and consistent Republican, having rendered valuable services to his party. In recognition of his sterling Republicanism and his ability as a lawyer, he was twice nominated for the office of civil justice in the years 1881 and 1887, and was strongly supported for the office by Democrats and Republicans alike but was defeated. In 1892 he was nominated for county clerk of New York city. The entire ticket, however, although headed by Benjamin Harrison for president, was defeated by an overwhelming Democratic majority. On July 16, 1895, Chief-Justice Simon W. Ehrlich of the city court of New York died, and on July 30, 1895, Gov. Morton filled the vacancy by appointing Mr. Botty to the bench. The appointment was well merited, and will add dignity and ability to the bench. The term of office of the appointee will expire Jan. 1, 1896.

ZOLLARS, Thomas Jefferson, was born in New Hagerstown, O., July 7, 1839, son of Daniel Zollars, a farmer, real-estate operator, and capitalist.

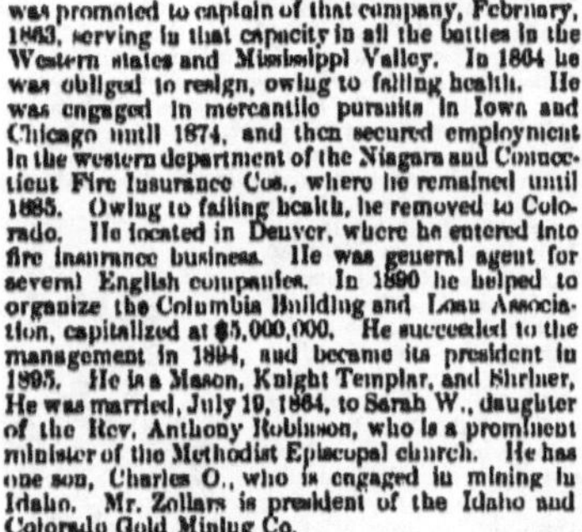

Mr. Zollars's maternal grandfather, Frederick Druckmiller, was in the war of 1812, and his great-grandfather, Jacob Zollars, fought in the revolutionary war. After a preparatory course in the public schools of his native town, he entered the Wesleyan University at Mt. Pleasant, Ia. When Abraham Lincoln issued his call for volunteers, he enlisted in company F, 1st Iowa Infantry, and served until that regiment was discharged in August, 1861. He participated in the battle of Wilson Creek, Mo., in which Gen. Nathaniel P. Lyons was killed. He helped to organize company F, 4th Iowa cavalry in November, 1861, and was made first lieutenant, and was promoted to captain of that company, February, 1863, serving in that capacity in all the battles in the Western states and Mississippi Valley. In 1864 he was obliged to resign, owing to failing health. He was engaged in mercantile pursuits in Iowa and Chicago until 1874, and then secured employment in the western department of the Niagara and Connecticut Fire Insurance Cos., where he remained until 1885. Owing to failing health, he removed to Colorado. He located in Denver, where he entered into fire insurance business. He was general agent for several English companies. In 1890 he helped to organize the Columbia Building and Loan Association, capitalized at $5,000,000. He succeeded to the management in 1894, and became its president in 1895. He is a Mason, Knight Templar, and Shriner. He was married, July 19, 1864, to Sarah W., daughter of the Rev. Anthony Robinson, who is a prominent minister of the Methodist Episcopal church. He has one son, Charles O., who is engaged in mining in Idaho. Mr. Zollars is president of the Idaho and Colorado Gold Mining Co.

GRANT, Mrs. Anne, author (commonly styled "of Laggan," to distinguish her from Mrs. Grant of Carran), was born at Glasgow, Scotland, Feb. 21, 1755. Her father, Duncan MacVicar, was an officer in a highland regiment; her mother a descendant of the ancient family of Stewart, in Argyleshire. In the year 1758 mother and daughter sailed for the United States, and settled at Claverack, N. Y., where the husband was stationed with a party of highlanders. Here Anne was taught to read by her mother, and learned to speak Dutch. In 1760 MacVicar conducted a company of soldiers from Claverack to Oswego, and his wife and child went with the party. In her "Memoirs of an American Lady," Mrs. Grant declared: "I am convinced that I thought more in that fight, that is, acquired more ideas and took more lasting impressions, than ever I did in the same space of time in my life." In her sixth year Anne was familiar with the Old Testament, and also read with eagerness and pleasure Milton's "Paradise Lost." In the summer of 1762 her talents attracted the attention of Madam Schuyler, wife of Gen. Philip Schuyler, of Albany, N. Y., with whom she resided for several years. A few years after the conquest of Canada her father resigned his position in the British army, and settled in Vermont, receiving a grant of land from the English government, to which he made large additions by purchase. Because of ill health and mental depression, he decided to return to his native Scotland in 1768, and Anne left America with the family, never to see it again. When the war of the American revolution began, her father's property in Vermont was confiscated by the Colonial authorities, and reduced pecuniary circumstances, made him chiefly dependent upon his limited pay as barrack-master at Fort Augustus, to which position he had been appointed in 1773. In 1779 his daughter was married to Rev. James Grant of Laggan, in Inverness-shire, Scotland. By the greatest application the young wife forthwith acquired a sufficient knowledge of the Gaelic language to converse freely with the people in their own tongue. Here, in the simple life of a secluded highland parish she passed many years, and became the mother of twelve children. Her husband died in 1801, leaving his widow and considerable debts behind. Mrs. Grant was now urged to collect and print the poems which she had previously written, and 3,000 subscribers for the book were obtained in advance of its publication under the patronage of the celebrated Duchess of Gordon. The volume was entitled "The Highlander and other Poems," and its profits enabled the authoress to discharge those debts which had hung so heavily over her. She now abandoned the small farm at Laggan, and removed to the neighborhood of Stirling. Here, besides pursuing her literary labors, she received many young ladies into her family. One of her pupils was the mother of the Duke of Argyll, and another the late Mrs. Cruger

of New York city. In 1806 Mrs. Grant's second book was published by the Longmans of London, entitled "Letters from the Mountains." They had been written to her correspondents from the manse at Laggan during a long series of years, and had such vivid descriptions of highland scenery, character, and legends, that they proved exceedingly popular, and rapidly passed through several editions. Through the exertions of Miss Lowell of Boston Mass., and a few other ladies, moreover, an American edition of the book was published in that city, and the sum of £300 remitted to Mrs. Grant as the proceeds. Mrs. Grant's best known work was doubtless the "Memoirs of an American Lady" (Madam Margarita Schuyler), already referred to. This was not begun until the year 1807, but was printed by the Longmans in 1808. Besides her youthful recollections of Mrs. Schuyler, it contains the most vivid descriptions of the simple manners of the descendants of the Dutch settlers in the province of New Amsterdam and New York, sketches of the history of New York, and anecdotes of the Indians. Her pronounced toryism makes the book at this time all the more piquant. "What the loss of the Huguenots," she remarks, "was to commerce and manufactures in France, that of the loyalists was to the religion, literature, and amenity of America." The second and third editions appeared in London in 1809 and 1817, and it was reprinted the same year in Boston, and in New York city. Editions were also printed in New York in 1836 and 1846, and at Albany, N. Y., in 1876. This charming picture of Colonial life greatly delighted Sir Walter Scott and Robert Southey, the former saying that the description of the breaking up of the ice in the upper Hudson river was "quite Homeric." "Exceedingly instructive concerning the manners and customs which prevailed in New York colony at the close of the eighteenth century," was the comment upon the volume by William H. Seward. In 1810 Mrs. Grant removed to Edinburgh, and her residence there was frequented by Lord Jeffrey, Sir Walter Scott, Henry Mackenzie, and other men of that order. Her "Essays on the Superstitions of the Highlanders" was issued in 1810. Such was her knowledge of the Gaelic people, language, and literature, that the earlier volumes of the Waverley Novels were frequently attributed to her pen. She published "Eighteen Hundred and Thirteen," a metrical work, in 1814; and "Popular Models and Impressive Warnings for the Sons and Daughters of Industry," her last production, in 1814. She lived twenty-three years after its issue. In 1824 she received the gold medal of the Highland Society for one of her Gaelic translations. In 1820 an untoward fall produced permanent lameness, and in 1828 she received from the British government a pension of £100, in consideration of her literary talents. Her letters, with a memoir by her son, appeared in London, England, in 1844, 1845, and 1853. The edition of the "Memoirs of an American Lady," printed by J. Munsell (Albany, N. Y., in 1876), was edited by James Grant Wilson, her godson, and has a memoir of Mrs. Grant from his pen. She died in Edinburgh, Nov. 7, 1888, and was buried under the shadows of the "castle in that city." Near her grave is that of Thomas De Quincey.

WALLACE, William Harvey Lamb, soldier, was born in Urbana, O., July 8, 1821. When a lad of eleven years he removed with his father to Illinois, and there attended school until he had acquired a fair general education. He then devoted himself to the study of law, and was admitted to practice in 1846. The call for volunteers for the Mexican war was being made that year, and the young lawyer abandoned his prospects for winning distinction at the bar, and volunteered as a private in the 1st Illinois regiment. He won promotion to adjutant during the war, and participated in the battle of Buena Vista, and several minor engagements of the campaign. Upon the return of peace he took up the practice of law, and was in 1853 elected district attorney. His career as a lawyer was again disturbed in 1861 by the outbreak of the civil war, and he at once volunteered his services to the government as colonel of the 11th Illinois regiment of volunteers. He was engaged in the battles of Fort Henry and Fort Donaldson. At Fort Donaldson he commanded a brigade of McClernard's division, made up of the 17th, 45th, 48th, and 49th Illinois, and McAllister's battery, and at noon of Feb. 13, 1862, led the assault on the middle redoubt of the Confederate works, but after reaching within forty rods of the battery, and for an hour maintaining the stand, was obliged to fall back. On the 15th he again led his brigade, augmented by the 11th and 20th Illinois, and resisted the desperate charge of the Confederates in their last effort to escape from the fort by breaking the Federal lines. Wallace held in check the enemy until reinforced by Gen. Lew. Wallace, and subsequently by Gen. Grant, who directed the final movements, resulting in the capture of Fort Donaldson Feb. 16, 1862. For this battle he was made a brigadier-general of volunteers. He next was on the field of Shiloh in command of Gen. C. F. Smith's division, and for six hours met the assault of Gens. Polk and Hardie, and his division was the last to leave the field. Gen. Wallace in this defence was mortally wounded, and died at Savannah, Tenn., Apr. 10, 1862.

HILL, Nathaniel Peter, senator, was born in Orange county, N. Y., Feb. 18, 1832. He is descended from an old English family which became a large landholder in the north of  Ireland about 1573, from lands granted on account of the active part taken by Sir Moses and Peter Hill, under the Earl of Essex, in suppressing O'Neill's rebellion. His great-grandfather, Nathaniel Hill, came to this country in 1730 and went to the Scotch-Irish settlement west of the Hudson, in what is now the town of Crawford, Orange co., N. Y., where he became a large landed proprietor. His grandfather, Capt. Peter Hill, was an officer in the revolutionary army, and made a brave defense of Fort Montgomery at the time it was captured by the British. His father, Nathaniel P. Hill, was a member of the New York legislature in 1816, 1819, 1820, and 1825; was sheriff 1820, 1822; judge of the court of common pleas, 1823, 1825; was presidential elector in 1836, and voted for Martin Van Buren. The distinction of peacemaker which had been given to his father, Capt. Peter Hill, belonged to a still greater extent to him. The son entered Brown University in 1852, was graduated in 1856, and remained there afterwards as instructor and professor of chemistry, in all, eleven years. He went to Colorado on a professional visit in 1864, and becoming interested in the great problem of extracting the gold and silver from the refractory ores of that state, soon after resigned his professorship in Brown University, and made his permanent home in Colorado in 1867. As manager of the Boston and Colorado Smelting Co., he was the first to successfully treat the ores of Colorado, and stands alone in the work he did in the early days to put mining and smelting in that state on a sound basis. He was elected U. S. senator in January, 1879, and served for the full term of six years. His known probity of character and sound judgment had often suggested him to his neighbors for various offices, and his election as senator came without a struggle, and was an unsought honor. His career in the senate was remarkable for his constant effort in the interests of the common people. No question ever came up in the senate during his term in which the interests of the capitalists or great monopolies of the country were arrayed against the interests of the masses of the people, that Senator Hill was not found working with untiring zeal for the latter. In fact, his warfare upon the powerful monopolies of the country probably prevented his succeeding himself as senator. Throughout his term he was an ardent advocate of silver coinage, and spoke and wrote extensively on the subject. He was essentially the originator of the best plan for a government telegraph which has yet been devised, and his speeches on that subject displayed the most thorough research. At the close of his senatorial term he assumed the active management of several large enterprises, all of which have been remarkably successful. He has since held but one public office, as one of the three members of the International Monetary Commission, to which he was nominated by Pres. Harrison and confirmed by the senate.

GODFREY, Benjamin, founder of Monticello Seminary, was born at Chatham, Mass., Dec. 4, 1794. He came of an old New England family. At the early age of nine years he ran away from home and went to sea, his first voyage being to Ireland, where he spent nine years. The war of 1812 brought him home, and he spent part of the time during that conflict in the U. S. naval service. After returning from Ireland he lived for a time with his uncle, Benjamin Godfrey, with whom he studied and obtained a fair education, including a knowledge of navigation. He subsequently became master of a merchantman, and made voyages to Italy, Spain, the West Indies, and other countries. On his last voyage he was shipwrecked near Brasos, Santiago, and lost nearly all his fortune. In 1824 he engaged in the mercantile business at Matamoras, Mex. He accumulated a handsome fortune, and was transferring the silver, some $200,000, across the country on the backs of mules, when he was robbed of the whole of it by guerillas. Undeterred by this great misfortune he again started in business, this time in New Orleans, where he was again successful and remained there until 1832, when he came North, settling in Albion, Ill., where he engaged in business with W. S. Gilman. It was in the warehouse of Godfrey & Gilman that E. P. Lovejoy lost his life while defending his property against a pro-slavery mob (see vol. II. 328). In 1833 Mr. Godfrey united with the Albion Presbyterian Church, of which he subsequently became an elder. Later he transferred his connection to the Monticello Church. Extensive travel and observation had revealed to him the power of female influence over society, and to use his own words, "being desirous to act the part of a faithful steward of what God had placed in my possession, I resolved to devote so much of it as would erect a building, to be devoted to the moral, intellectual, and domestic improvement of females." This was the germ of Monticello Seminary. Upon the original building, erected four miles north of Albion, he expended $53,000. After it became a chartered institution he acted as one of its trustees until its death. The institution opened its doors for the reception of pupils on Apr. 11, 1838, and from that time has been a phenomenal success. Its original building was destroyed by fire some five years ago, and replaced by one costing $250,000, and unsurpassed in architectural beauty, modern improvements, and appointments, and complete equipment by any educational institution in the country. Capt. Godfrey led an active business life and engaged in vast enterprises, including the building of the Albion and Springfield Railroad. In this enterprise he lost heavily, but notwithstanding this misfortune and his large benefactions, he died a wealthy man. Capt. Godfrey was twice married; first to Harriet Cooper, of Baltimore, Md., Nov. 27, 1817, by whom he had twelve children. He was married again Aug. 15, 1839, to R. E. Petit, of Hempstead, Long Island, by whom he had three children. Capt. Godfrey died at his suburban residence in Godfrey, Ill., Aug 13, 1862. His widow survived him some twenty years, when the homestead descended to the children of his youngest son, Benjamin Godfrey Jr., also deceased.

BALDWIN, Theron, missionary and first principal of Monticello Seminary, was born at Goshen, Litchfield co., Conn., July 21, 1801, son of Elisha and Clarissa (Judd) Baldwin, and a descendant of Nathaniel Baldwin, one of the first settlers of Milford, Conn. He was graduated at Yale College in 1827, having taken rank among the foremost scholars of his class, and then entered the theological school. He was soon led to select Canada as a place for future missionary work, but meanwhile, and largely owing to his influence, an association had been formed by the students with the intention of selecting one of the new states in the Mississippi Valley and uniting their labors in founding churches, schools, and other institutions of learning, especially a college. Mr. Baldwin's adhesion to the enterprise was considered indispensable, and, finally consenting, he and his life-long friend, Julian Sturtevant, were ordained to the ministry in 1829, and under the auspices of the American Home Missionary Society proceeded to Illinois in advance of the rest of "the Illinois Band," as the association of young students came to be called. His first year was spent in preaching, including tours on horseback over the prairies, among the scattered settlements, and as secretary to the Illinois State Sunday-school Union. In 1831 he went East to solicit funds for Illinois College, opened at Jacksonville in 1830, and in June of that same year was married to Caroline Wilder of Burlington, Vt. Mr. Baldwin had made a thorough study of systems of education, and when Capt. Benjamin Godfrey was proposing to found Monticello Seminary, he made it a condition that Mr.

Baldwin should become its first principal. Another trip to the East was then undertaken, the leading seminaries for young ladies in New England and New York state were visited and their methods of government and courses of study examined, teachers of rare force of character and accomplishment were engaged, and when Monticello opened, it had more of the essentials of a college than any other institution for women, west of the Alleghanies, having been organized and equipped in accordance with Mr. Baldwin's belief that women should have the same educational advantages as men. His work in connection with the seminary was supplemented by that of his wife, to whose efforts in raising money for her tuition, many a young girl was indebted. Previous to the year 1843, some half dozen collegiate institutions had been founded in the states of Ohio, Indiana, Illinois, and Wisconsin, by Presbyterians and Congregationalists, and it was felt that these could be best fostered and aided by a single organization. In 1843 such an agency was formed under the name of the Society for the Promotion of Collegiate and Theological Education at the West. Some years later it passed into the control of the Congregational denomination, and is now known as the College and Education Society. Mr. Baldwin was chosen its first secretary, and removed to New York to spend the rest of his life in labor with voice and pen, in urging the necessity of planting a Christian college of high grade in every new state. He foresaw the future greatness of California, and prophesied its connection with the East by means of a railway, when few even among the wise could be found who believed that the Pacific coast would ever be so thickly settled as to need colleges. His yearly reports and the addresses delivered by eminent educators and clergymen at the annual meetings of the society constitute a most valuable contribution to the history of higher education. He received the degree of D.D. from Marietta College. His death occurred Apr. 10, 1870, at Orange, N. J.

Theron Baldwin

FOBES, Philena, educator, was born in Onandaga county, N. Y., Sept. 10, 1811, daughter of Philander Fobes, a native of Bridgewater, Mass. His earliest ancestors in this country were John Fobes and John Washburn —on his mother's side. They came from England in 1632 and '35, and were among the original settlers and proprietors of Bridgewater. Her mother, Nancy Warner, of Cummington, Mass., was of Puritan descent. Miss Fobes received her education mostly in Albany, and at Courtland Seminary, New York, where she was graduated. She taught for three years in the Seward Seminary, Rochester, N. Y. In 1837 Miss Fobes went to Monticello to take charge of a department, and she aided in the arrangement of the curriculum of that seminary, which opened in April, 1838, one of the pioneer institutions of learning in the West. Dr. Baldwin continued principal of this seminary until 1843, but his necessary absence much of the time, left Miss Fobes its active head and inspiration. In 1843 she was chosen principal, holding the office until 1866, making twenty-seven years of life-work at Monticello, with the exception of the year 1854, which she spent abroad, returning with a store of reminiscences which have been helpful in her work. After resigning her charge at Monticello in 1865 and leaving in 1866, Miss Fobes spent some years in Rochester, N. Y., and New Haven, Conn. In 1886 she took up a permanent residence in Philadelphia, where she maintains a lively interest in the benevolent and educational movements of the day. In a large measure due to her influence and exertions, Monticello Seminary stands pioneer in the West: in the erection of buildings adapted and equipped for educational work; in adopting and requiring a course of study with examinations for admission, and diplomas for graduation; and in providing independent instructors for each department. Her aim was to base her instructions upon the great principles of religion, that the education furnished should be substantial, practical, and develop both the physical, intellectual, and moral powers, and prepare its subject for the sober realities and duties of actual life.

Philena Fobes

HASKELL, Harriet Newell, third principal of Monticello Seminary, was born at Waldboro', Lincoln co., Me., Jan. 14, 1835, of English and Scotch-Irish antecedents, her maternal grandfather having been one of the first settlers of her native town, receiving deed of lands from Gen. Henry Knox. In 1848 she entered the Castleton Classical Seminary at Castleton, Vt., taking there a diploma for full classical course which would give entrance to the junior class at Vermont University had women been admitted; from there, in 1851, she went to Mount Holyoke Seminary, where she was graduated in 1855. She at once began her career as an educator, as principal of high schools in Maine and Boston. In 1862 she was called by unanimous vote of board of trustees of Castleton Seminary in Vermont, to become principal; heretofore in this old school, founded in 1766, only men had been principals. Miss Haskell's versatility and energy received recognition in the responsibility of the position. She resigned in 1867 to assume the same position in Monticello Seminary at Godfrey, Ill. Miss Haskell raised the institution to the highest standard, and on Nov. 4, 1889, saw it burned to the ground in one hour's time. Here her native courage and energy were put to the severest test. She was the only woman on the board of trustees, and while the other members seemed overwhelmed by the calamity and despaired of raising funds necessary for the rebuilding of the institution, she at once thought out plans for the erection of a temporary structure, and raised a large amount of the money necessary to build it, herself donating the sum of $1,000, though she was personally a heavy loser by the fire. She

Harriet N. Haskell

then called the board together, and seeing what she had accomplished, they gave her the heartiest approbation, and in the course of eight weeks the work had been so vigorously pushed, that the scattered pupils were called together, their work resumed, and the senior class, was graduated in June at the usual time, the corner stone of the permanent structure being laid on commencement day. Had it not been for Miss Haskell's persistent energy and success, it is probable that the usefulness of Monticello would have been indefinitely if not permanently suspended. The present school building is one of the most beautiful in the United States, and the chapel, donated by William Henry Reid of Chicago, in memory of his wife, Eleanor Irwin Reid, is considered a model of architectural beauty. It may be well seen through the work that she has accomplished, that Miss Haskell is a leader. As an educator, she has few equals. As a woman, she has a happy combination of strength of character, gentleness and kindness of heart, and as a Christian, her life is an example. Through these united qualifications, she has attained the highest success.

JOHNSON, Charles P., lawyer, was born in Lebanon, St. Clair co., Ill., Jan. 18, 1836. His ancestors, from Virginia and Pennsylvania, were among the pioneers of the western territory. His education

was obtained chiefly at the common schools, though prior to his settling in St. Louis he was for one year a student at McKendree College. The best part of his education, however, was procured at "the case," as he not only thoroughly learned the printer's trade, but also published, in his eighteenth year, a weekly paper at the town of Sparta, Ill. In 1855 he established himself in St. Louis, and commenced the study of law, and was admitted to the bar in 1857. In 1859 he was elected to the office of city attorney, his term expiring in 1860. On the outbreak of the civil war he enlisted under the first call for troops, and served as lieutenant for three months in the 3d Missouri regiment. During this time he was actively engaged in raising the 8th Missouri regiment, which he tendered to Mr. Lincoln in person. He was also the bearer of dispatches from Gen. Lyon to Pres. Lincoln. The officers of the 8th Missouri elected him to the majorship of the regiment, but he declined, because of delicate health and his lack of military knowledge. In 1862, although declining the nomination for congress, he accepted the candidacy to the legislature. There he was assigned to what at that time was the most important position in the body, the chairmanship of the committee on empancipation, his zeal, energy, and powers as a debater, soon giving him the leadership of the house. In 1865 he was again elected to the legislature, but in the fall of 1866 he accepted the appointment of circuit attorney for the city and county of St. Louis, which position he filled for six years. During this time he laid the foundation for his subsequent brilliant career at the bar. In the selection of the joint Democratic and liberal Republican ticket of 1872, he was presented as a candidate for lieutenant-governor. He was elected, and during the time he served, became noted for his marked ability as a parliamentarian and presiding officer. A few years later Gov. Johnson's interest was aroused in opposition to the evils of public gambling in St. Louis, which had become a ruling element in the politics of that city. For this purpose he again became a member of the legislature in 1881, and the consequences of his work in that body are matters of history. Throughout his entire public career, Gov. Johnson showed himself to be a man of broad and liberal views, possessing in addition the power to embody in legislative enactment what is necessary for a practical accomplishment of desired ends. He was a zealous supporter of every measure or movement looking to the development and advancement of his city and state. From the expiration of his last term in the legislature, Gov. Johnson has declined all nominations for public office which were tendered him, returned to the practice of law, giving his entire attention to that profession, and devoting himself almost exclusively to criminal law. His reputation as an advocate and orator extended throughout the entire West. In 1892 he was tendered and accepted the professorship of criminal law in the law department of the Washington University of St. Louis.

MARKLE, John, coal operator, was born at Hazleton, Pa., Dec. 15, 1858, and is the son of the late George B. Markle, whose biography will be found elsewhere in this work, and who was pre-eminent in the development of the coal industry in the anthracite region. Our subject attended private and public schools in his native city, until his twelfth year, when he entered the Alexander Military Institute at White Plains, N. Y., where he remained three years. The following two years he attended Landerbach's Academy in Philadelphia, and afterwards entered Lafayette College in the class of '80. He was graduated in the mining-engineering course, after which he was appointed general superintendent of his father's firm, in the region of Jeddo. In time succeeding his father, who was compelled to retire on account of ill health. During the entire period of his management of the affairs of the firm, of which he is now a partner, he has shown talent and executive ability of a high order and is the daring projector of the Jeddo tunnel, one of the most important improvements so far introduced into the coal industry in the anthracite regions. This tunnel is being made at vast expense, and when completed will be the most important advance in the matter of mining that has marked the decade of late rapid improvements, and will open several coal fields, heretofore practically shut out from development. Mr. Markle is president and chief engineer of the company.

CONNELL, William Lawrence, business man, was born in Minooka, near Scranton, Pa., Oct. 14, 1862, son of James Connell. He was educated in the public schools of Scranton, and by private instruction. In 1881 he entered the furniture business of Hill, Keiser & Co., at Scranton, and in 1886, with B. A. Hill, purchased the interests of the firm which was afterward continued under the name of Hill & Connell, and became one of the leading furniture houses of the state. Mr. Connell is a director of the Scranton Axle Works, and treasurer and manager of the business of the Enterprise Coal Co. He has served two terms as member of the common council of Scranton, one term as chairman of the same, and was elected mayor of Scranton in 1893.

Mr. Connell is a gentleman of rare personal gifts, embodying a remarkably fine and commanding presence, with mental qualities of a high order. In his official career he is stern and unrelenting to incorrigibles, merciful to the unfortunate, disposed to deal leniently with first offenders, and has made an unsurpassed chief magistrate. Favoring all public improvements calculated to secure the advancement of the municipality and welfare of its inhabitants, he exercises proper economy and watchful care over expenditures to prevent waste.

ANDERSON, Richard Clough, soldier and pioneer, was born in Hanover county, Va., Jan 12, 1750. Entering the Continental army as a captain, he served with great gallantry throughout the revolutionary war, specially distinguishing himself at Brandywine, Germantown, and Trenton; in this last battle crossing the Delaware in advance of the main body of the army, and driving the enemy before him. Retiring at the close of the war with the rank of lieutenant-colonel, he removed to the wilderness of Kentucky, near Louisville, and became one of the most active and influential of those heroic men who wrested that state from the savages. He was a member of the important convention of 1788, and in 1793 was chosen a presidential elector. In 1797 he built a two-masted vessel, and shipped from Louisville the first cargo of produce that ever went from Kentucky direct to Europe. About 1785 he married Elizabeth Clark, a sister of Gen. George Rogers Clark, and by her became the father of Richard Clough Anderson and Robert Anderson. He died near Louisville, Ky., Oct. 16, 1826. His biography has been written by E. L. Anderson (New York, 1879).

ADAMS, John B., clergyman, was born in Plainfield, Conn., in 1802, and was graduated at Yale in 1821. He was engaged continuously in pastoral and missionary labor until June, 1861, when he was appointed chaplain of the 5th Maine volunteers. He was present at nearly all the battles of the army of the Potomac, from the first Bull Run to the close of the civil war, and his services were such as to receive public commendation from his general officers and the governor of Maine. He died of disease contracted in the discharge of his army duties, Apr. 26, 1866.

HARTRANFT, Chester David, clergyman and educator, was born in Frederick township, Montgomery co., Pa., Oct. 15, 1839. His father was the proprietor of extensive flour mills in Philadelphia. His ancestors on both sides came to this

country from Germany about 1734, under the stress of religious persecution, those on the father's side being Schwenckfelders, from Silesia; those on the mother's being Lutherans, from the Palatinate. The son removed with his parents from Frederick to Philadelphia in 1846, so that the foundations of his education were laid in the city schools. In 1856 he was graduated from the Philadelphia High School, a semi-collegiate institution, conferring a baccalaureate degree. He then studied for one year at the Hill School in Pottstown, Pa. During this period he was an omnivorous reader, especially in the field of English literature; an earnest student in all prescribed topics; and a frequent speaker, and even lecturer, before students' clubs; a leader in athletic sports; and ardently interested in the political discussions of the time. His success in mathematics led to his nomination for a vacancy at West Point; but his age was at that time below the standard. From 1857 to 1861 he was in the regular course at the University of Pennsylvania, where he was graduated with honors. Throughout the first years of his college study Dr. Hartranft had the career of a lawyer in view; later this gave place to a determination to specialize as a teacher of history. Though always religiously inclined, he did not avow his Christian faith until his third year at the university, when he joined the Second Dutch Reformed

Church in Philadelphia. The outbreak of the civil war led to the formation of a military company in the university, of which he was chosen captain. Later, he held the same rank in the 18th regiment of the Pennsylvania militia, raised in Philadelphia. Had not unforeseen hindrances intervened after the battle of Gettysburg, he would have served either as colonel of a then newly organized regiment of infantry, or as major of artillery. From the university he went to the theological seminary of the Dutch Reformed church at New Brunswick, N. J., where he was graduated in 1864, his first pastorate being over the Dutch Reformed Church of South Bushwick, N. Y., now a part of Brooklyn, where he remained two years. In 1866 he was called to the Second Dutch Reformed Church in New Brunswick, N. J., and there labored for twelve years. During these pastorates he displayed his versatility and capacity for work, not only in the usual lines of preaching and general pastoral care, but in an enterprising, and at that time novel, organization of the Sunday-school for systematic study and teaching, and of the whole church for a variety of philanthropic and evangelistic objects. In New Brunswick, also, he found opportunity for the special exercises of his unusual musical gifts and attainments, which had been recognized in 1861 by an honorary degree of Mus. D. from Rutgers College. He formed and trained a chorus choir of fifty voices, and a chorus of children. He was for ten years the conductor of an oratorio society, giving many of the best choral works. His own specialties as a performer included the violin and the organ, as well as the voice. He was at the head of a large plan for a musical conservatory, which was in successful operation for three years, until given up in the business depression of 1873. In this enterprise the late Dr. Leopold Damrosch, and the organist, Samuel P. Warren, were actively interested. In February, 1879, Dr. Hartranft became Waldo professor of ecclesiastical history in the Hartford Theological Seminary (then called the Theological Institute of Connecticut). This chair gave him the opportunity to utilize the remarkable accumulation of historical and technical theological knowledge with which his mind was already stored. It also gave impetus to the prosecution of further study in all branches of sacred learning. His treatment of theological encyclopædia and of biblical theology as parts of a seminary course was more extensive than had before been attempted in America. Indeed, their development in Hartford was the signal for their recognition in many other seminaries. The special interest of Dr. Hartranft in the expansion of the scope of theological education was first expressed publicly in an address delivered in 1879 at New York, entitled, "Aims of a Theological Seminary." In the reorganization of the course of study at Hartford, from 1885 onward, he took a leading part. In 1888 the office of president was revived, and he was elected to it. His inaugural address, entitled, "Some Thoughts on the Scope of Theology and Theological Education," was delivered on May 10th of that year. This became a kind of basis for the new pedagogic system of the institution, which was at the time somewhat novel in America, and which still maintains its uniqueness in several particulars. From this point onward the influence of Dr. Hartranft's masterly mind is to be traced in every part of the institution's life. To him is specially due the formation and arrangement of the extensive library which, in 1894, was established in the fine building erected for it through the liberality of the late Newton Case. This collection numbered at that time nearly 60,000 volumes, being the second in size in the state. Dr. Hartranft had also been the originator of a choral society in Hartford in 1882, which still flourishes. In 1889 he secured the opening of the seminary to women on the same terms as to men. From the same year he was also particularly interested in the university extension movement in Hartford, which proceeded partly under the auspices of the seminary and partly outside. At the same time, also, he was active in the formation of a learned society called the National Academy of Theology, in which theological professors of all denominations united. In 1892, in consequence of the fuller subdivision of topics in the seminary faculty, Dr. Hartranft was transferred to a new professorship—that of biblical theology, retaining his place as president. Dr. Hartranft has published comparatively little. In 1887 he edited the Anti-Donatist writings of St. Augustine, and in 1890 the ecclesiastical history of Sozomen, for the American series of the Post-Nicene fathers. Since 1884 he has been at work, under the patronage of the Schwenckfelders, on an exhaustive publication of all the accessible information and documents concerning their founder, Caspar Schwenckfelder von Ossig, one of the great actors in the German reformation. In pursuance of this object Dr. Hartranft had made several visits to Europe, one of which covered more than a year, and has already accumulated an enormous mass of literary material, most of it entirely unedited and unknown, and some of it having very important bearing on the religious history of the early sixteenth century. None of this material has as yet (1894) been published. The most salient of Dr. Hartranft's characteristics is his remarkable breadth of culture. There is hardly a branch of learning, be it linguistic, physical, historical, æsthetic, or philosophical, in which he has not made independent and useful researches. His powers of mental acquisition are phenomenal, coupled with fine capacities of analysis, systematization, and original re-arrangement. These qualities, combined with conspicuous energy of body, mind, and spirit, an unfailing enthusiasm and strong personal magnetism, have given Dr. Hartranft unusual success as a teacher. As a public speaker, he is distinguished by great impressiveness of manner, copiousness of expression, and power to appeal to and sway the wills of his auditors. Williams College, at its centennial, conferred upon him the honorary degree of S.T.D. Dr. Hartranft was married on June 20, 1861, to Anne Frances, daughter of the Rev. J. F. Berg, D.D. Of their five children, but one son, Frederick Berg Hartranft, survives.

HOOK, Frances, soldier. She received a superior education, and was an accomplished young woman. When her brother joined the 65th Home Guards of Illinois, she enlisted also, under the name of Frank Miller. At the end of the three months' service she was mustered out with the remainder of her regiment, her sex not having been discovered. She then enlisted in the 90th Illinois, and was subsequently wounded in a battle near Chattanooga, and when trying to escape, was again wounded in the leg, and taken prisoner. The Confederates, on discovering her sex, treated her respectfully, and while in prison at Atlanta she received a letter from Jefferson Davis, offering her commission as lieutenant in the Confederate army. As soon as she was released she joined the 2d East Tennessee cavalry, and fought gallantly with them near Murfresboro', and with them waded the Stone river into the place on the Sunday when the Federal troops were repulsed. During this battle she was severely wounded in the shoulder, and her sex being reported to Gen. Rosecrans, he ordered her dismissal from the service. She had performed valuable duty as scout to the army of the Cumberland, and her intrepid bravery, and her entreaties to remain, so touched Gen. Rosecrans, that he personally arranged for her return to her parents. Notwithstanding her dismissal, she afterward joined the 8th Michigan at Bowling Green, and remained connected with this regiment. She was a true patriot and gallant soldier.

PEAVEY, Frank Hutchison, capitalist, was born in Eastport, Me., Jan. 18, 1850; son of Albert D. Peavey, who was a vessel owner, and in partnership with Geo. Peavey, his father, one of the most extensive dealers in pine lands and saw mills in eastern Maine. At the age of fifteen Frank went to Chicago to seek his fortune, and was employed as messenger boy, and later as book-keeper in the Northwestern National Bank of that city, where he remained two years. In 1867 he accepted a position in a general store in Sioux City, Ia., the largest on the Missouri river at that time, in which city he remained for eighteen years. His career as a grain merchant began in 1875, under the firm name of F. H. Peavey & Co., starting in business with one elevator. He now (1895) owns and controls over 400 country elevators, scattered from Chicago to the Pacific coast; and his firm owns and controls the largest number of terminal elevators of any concern in the country. The capacity of the Peavey elevators is 16,500,000 bushels, which is the largest elevator capacity controlled by any one man in the world. In addition to the elevator capacity that he owns and

controls, he is also the largest stockholder and president of the Globe Elevator Co. of Duluth, Minn., which has 5,000,000 bushels capacity. The success of his grain and elevator business is due to wise and careful management, strict avoidance of speculation, and the application of solid business principles. In nine years it had become so extensive that more central headquarters were demanded, and in the fall of 1884 he removed to Minneapolis, and has since that time made his residence in that city. He is a director in the Northwestern National Bank of Minneapolis. He was one of the organizers of the Security National Bank of Sioux City, and up to the time of his removal from the city was its president. In 1872 Mr. Peavey was married to Mary, daughter of George G. Wright of Des Moines, Ia. They have three children: two daughters and one son.

BROWN, John, senator, was born in Staunton, Va., Sept. 12, 1757. He belonged to a noted family, his father, of the same name, being for forty years a prominent Presbyterian minister of Virginia; his brother James, jurist, was U. S. senator from Louisiana, and minister to France; and another brother Samuel was a distinguished physician of Kentucky, whose son, Benjamin Gratz Brown, became governor of Missouri. During the retreat of the American army through New Jersey, Princeton College, where John was a student, was closed. John immediately joined the retreating forces, crossed the Delaware, and served under Washington and Lafayette until the close of the war. He then completed his education at Washington College, Lexington, Va.; afterwards studied law, while supporting himself as a teacher, and was admitted to the bar in 1782. Removing to Frankfort, Ky., in 1783, he secured a large legal business, and attained great popularity as a prominent actor in the most critical period of the commonwealth's existence. He was a member of the convention of 1786; addressed the people on the subject of the Mississippi in 1787; was the same year elected to the state legislature of Virginia; was a member of the Continental congress in 1787–88; and served in the Federal congress from March 4, 1789, until Nov. 5, 1792. He was one of the last survivors of the old congress, and the first U. S. senator from the Mississippi valley, serving from Nov. 5, 1792, until March 3, 1805, presiding *pro tempore* in 1803. He was active in the Indian affairs of the western frontier, and did much to promote the admission of Kentucky into the Union, and to secure for the West the navigation of the Mississippi river. With the majority of his state he opposed the ratification of the Federal constitution, and was a warm supporter of President Jefferson's policy. He died in Frankfort, Aug. 29, 1837.

MERRILL, George Robert, clergyman, was born in Newburyport, Mass., Dec. 26, 1845. His parents were working people in modest circumstances, of Norman-French ancestry, who came to New England in the Puritan emigration. He was fitted for college in the Brown High School of his native city; was graduated at Amherst College in 1865, having met his college expenses by teaching at East Corinth and Blue Hill in Maine, Beemerville, N. J., and the Amherst public schools. Never having had any other purpose than to enter the ministry, he began theological studies at the seminary in Bangor, Me. Early in 1866 he accepted an appointment as missionary of the American Missionary Association, and was located at Hampton,

Va. In July of that year an unexpected train of providential circumstances brought him to Henrietta, a suburb of Rochester, N. Y., and the care of the Congregational Church in that place was joined with attendance upon the lectures at Rochester Theological Seminary. He was ordained at Henrietta, Jan. 2, 1867, the sermon being by an honored instructor, Prof. W. S. Tyler, of Amherst College. From 1870–73 he was stated supply of the Presbyterian Church at Medina, N. Y.; from 1873–76, pastor of Plymouth Church, Adrian, Mich., and engaged with Rev. J. G. Fraser, D. D., in the publication of "The Fellowship," a religious paper for Ohio and Michigan. From 1876–79 he was pastor of the Second Church, Biddeford, Me., and engaged in preparation of Sunday-school lessons for the "Union Bible Teacher," then published by Hoyt, Fogg & Donham of Portland. From 1879–80 he was pastor of the First Church, Painesville, O., from which place he removed to the pastorate of the First Congregational Church in Minneapolis, Minn., Dec. 1, 1886. He was married May 1, 1867, to Eunice Thurston Plumer, of Newburyport, Mass., who died Nov. 29, 1883; and on May 10, 1885, to Mary Morse House, of Painesville, O. He received the degree of M.A. in course from Amherst College, and the honorary degree of D.D. from Ripon College in 1893. He has published occasional sermons and is an infrequent contributor to the papers of his denomination.

HOWELL, John Adams, naval officer and torpedo inventor, was born in New York, March 16, 1840. He was appointed a midshipman in September, 1854, and was graduated at the U. S. Naval Academy, in 1858. He was commissioned as lieutenant in April, 1861, and during the civil war served with the North Atlantic and West Gulf squadrons. As executive officer of the steamsloop Ossipee, he took part in the battle of Mobile Bay, on Aug. 5, 1864, and received honorable mention in the official dispatches. He was promoted to be lieutenant-commander in

March, 1865, commander in March, 1872, and in March, 1884, was advanced to the rank of captain. In 1877 he was a member of the naval advisory board. In 1872 he began work upon a submarine torpedo, which he finally perfected in 1891, and which is believed by naval experts to be the best now in use. The Howell torpedo is shaped like a spindle, the central portion being cylindrical, and the shell is constructed entirely of brass or bronze. It is propelled by a fly-wheel of steel, weighing 130 pounds, which also steers the shell in the horizontal plan. The fly-wheel is geared to two shafts, one on each side of the torpedo, which carry the propellers, and when set in motion it will continue to rotate for several hours. The propellers, by revolving in opposite directions, prevent the torpedo from rolling. The submersion is controlled by a horizontal rudder, operated automatically. The discharging gear for sending the torpedo from the ship towards the enemy consists of a frame extending from the ship's side, under which the torpedo is hung. The torpedo when detached from the frame does not drop vertically into the water, but is swung outward in the arc of a circle. This gives it an impulse without changing the angle of its longitudinal axis with the surface of the water. The explosive charge, which is of gun-cotton, is placed in the forward end of the torpedo, and is fired by a detonating cap placed under a percussion firing-pin. The outer end of the firing-pin is provided with fan-shaped, corrugated beams which receive the impact blow and are so shaped and arranged as to prevent glancing or sliding along on the object struck. The force of the blow shears off the soft metal-pin and thus permits the firing-pin to be drawn down on the detonator by the spring. The Howell torpedo has several times been severely tested by naval boards and always with success. Large numbers of the torpedoes have been ordered by the U. S. government, and it has recently been adopted by several foreign governments.

WOODRUFF, Wilford, fourth president of the Mormon church, was born in Avon, Conn., March 1st, 1807. He received his early education by attending at the academy at Farmington. He was quite young when he was led to join the Mormon church, and was ordained to the priesthood when twenty-six years old. He followed the fortunes of the church in its successive removals from New York state westwards. He was ordained one of the twelve apostles Apr. 29, 1839, at Far West, Mo., and was known in the order as "The Banner of the Gospel" on account of his eloquence as a preacher and successful work as an evangelist. He was sent on missions to all points in the United States, and to the English-speaking people of Europe. He traveled upwards

of 150,000 miles on these evangelical tours. When President John Taylor died in 1887 Woodruff succeeded him as President of the Church of Jesus Christ of Latter Day Saints, he having been previously the president of the twelve apostles. He served as a member of the lower house of the legislature of Utah of 1867, and as a member of the upper house continuously from 1868 to 1876. In 1843, when the Mormons were located at Nauvoo, Ill., they published the "Times and Seasons" and Woodruff was a member of the editorial staff. In 1843, while in Liverpool, England, he edited the "Millenial Star." He was a polygamist at the time when there was no law against it in the United States, but as a law-abiding citizen relinquished its practice when it became unlawful according to civil authority.

NICHOLS, James, underwriter, is a native of Fairfield county, Conn., where he was born Dec. 25, 1830. He passed his boyhood and youth in Newtown, in that county, where his education was obtained. He was educated for the legal profession, and was admitted to the bar at Danbury in 1854,

and a few months later removed to Hartford, where he was appointed assistant clerk of the superior court for Hartford county. He retained this position a little over two years, and then returned to the practice of his profession in the same city, a portion of the time alone, and afterward in partnership with Julius L. Strong, a member of congress. In 1860 he was elected judge of probate for the district of Hartford, and performed the duties of that office for three years with ability and good judgment, and to the entire satisfaction of the community. Again resuming practice in 1863, he continued his profession until 1867, when fire insurance having greater attractions for him than the law, and a field being opened that would give scope to the exercise of his ability in that line, he became the adjuster and special agent of the Merchants' Fire Insurance Co., of Hartford. Here his business traits and abilities were soon appreciated, and he became secretary and a director of the company. This company, the stock of which was valued at $250 per share (two and a half times its face value), was overwhelmed in the great fire in Chicago in 1871, and ceased doing business. The National Fire Insurance Co. (which had been incorporated in 1869) was organized soon after, principally by the stockholders of the Merchants', and Mark Howard, president, and Judge Nichols, secretary of the Merchants', were respectively chosen president and secretary of the National. Judge Nichols continued as secretary until the death of Mr. Howard in 1887, when he was elected president. Under the able management of Presidents Howard and Nichols the company has made extraordinary advances, paid steady and satisfactory dividends, built up large assets and an ample surplus, and has the reputation of being one of the best managed companies in the country. The greater growth has been accomplished under the management of President Nichols, and to his efforts and those of his able coworkers are due these most gratifying results. Judge Nichols has from time to time held many positions of trust in the community in which he lives, and is a director and vice-president of the Charter Oak National Bank, a director in the Phœnix Mutual Life Insurance Co., and trustee of the Society for Savings.

HARE, George Emlen, professor and theologian, was born in Philadelphia, Pa., Sept. 4, 1808, a nephew of Robert Hare, the celebrated scientist. He was graduated from Union College, Schenectady, N. Y., 1826. He studied theology and was ordained a deacon of the Protestant Episcopal Church by Bishop White, Dec. 20, 1829, and before receiving his orders as priest in 1830, he was chosen rector of St. John's Church, Carlisle, Pa. Trinity Church, Princeton, N. J., elected him their rector in 1834, and St. Matthew's Church, Philadelphia, Pa., in 1845. While rector of St. Matthew's, he also under-

took the instruction of the diocesan training-school, and as that institution rapidly developed into the present Divinity School of the Protestant Episcopal Church in Philadelphia, he was in 1852 appointed professor there, first in Biblical learning, afterward in New Testament literature, which position he still (1894) holds. He was a member of the Old Testament company of the American committee on Bible revision, and published "Christ to Return" (Philadelphia, in 1840). He received the degree of S.T.D. from Columbia College in 1848, and that of LL.D. from the University of Pennsylvania in 1873. He is the father of Bishop William Hobart Hare. (See Vol. III., p. 408.)

CORBIN, Margaret, patriot, was born about 1750. When Fort Washington was attacked at the battle of Monmouth, her husband, who belonged to the artillery, was killed while serving his gun. Seeing him fall, she at once took his place, and performed his duty. Congress took notice of her heroic conduct, and in July, 1779, passed the following resolution: "*Resolved,* that Margaret Corbin, wounded and disabled at the battle of Fort Washington, while she heroically filled the post of her husband, who was killed by her side serving a piece of artillery, do receive during her natural life, or continuance of said disability, one-half the monthly pay drawn by a soldier in the service of these states;" and the next year, on learning of the total loss of her arm, the board of war recommended "that she now receive, out of public stores, one compleat suit of cloaths, or value thereof in money."

TAYLOR, George Herbert, lawyer and author, was born in Berkshire, Vt., May 10, 1858, son of John Taylor, a Yorkshire Englishman, and Sarah Dowler, a Scotchwoman. His father, with many others of his countrymen, came to America in 1840 to better his condition, and settled on a farm, at that time but a Vermont wilderness. For eighteen years he laid sturdy blows to the stalwart forest trees, so that when in 1858 he died, more than seventy acres had been cleared and made ready for the plow. In a little log school-house, surrounded by towering maples, for three months each year, until he was twelve years of age, the son received such instruction as the teachers of that day and locality were competent to give. Then for six years he labored on the farm; his only books his Bible and the "Seven Wonders of the World;" his only tutor Nature itself. At eighteen, alone and without assistance, he set out to get an education, and for eight months attended the academy at Richford, Vt. In the summer following, during vacation, he found employment as freight brakeman on the Central Vermont Railway. In this situation he was injured, so that he has carried a crippled and partially useless right arm ever since. This accident placed him

$600 in debt, and able to do only the lightest kind of work. The railroad then gave him clerical employment for twelve years. He had to give up all hope of a college education, but developed a taste for history and biography, and was fond of writing newspaper sketches. For ten years he was the local correspondent of various newspapers published in the state. In rummaging through an old attic one day he found a copy of "Blackstone," which he read and re-read many times before he had thought of taking up the law as a profession. His first story was published in 1884, "How She Hated Him." About this time he removed to the West, and took up the study of the law as a profession, and was admitted to the bar in 1886 in the city of Minneapolis, Minn., where he has been a successful practitioner in all the courts of the state. His writing has been done almost entirely between the hours of eight o'clock P. M. and midnight. There have been published of his writings the following: "Fifteen Years a Mystery" (1885); "John Ottenberg's Mistake" (1885); "My Revenge" (1887); "Erastus Corning, a Story for Boys" (1880); "An Agreement and What Came of It" (1892); "William Livingston, or the-Man-with-the-White-Face" (1893); besides numerous sketches about fishing and hunting. Those attracting most attention were: "A Day in the Adirondacks" (1885); "Trout-Fishing in Wisconsin" (1885); "Hunting the Ruffled Grouse in Wisconsin" (1885); "A Bear Hunt in Vermont" (1887); and "Hunting in Minnesota" (1889). He was married in 1876 to the daughter of Daniel Tilden, of West Lebanon, N. H.

CROES, John James Robertson, civil engineer, was born in Richmond, Va., Nov 25, 1834. His father, Rev. Robert B. Croes, was the youngest son of Bishop John Croes of New Jersey. His mother's father, James Robertson, a native of Scotland, was a banker in Philadelphia and for several years a member of the Pennsylvania legislature. Mr. Croes began his professional life in 1856 in the service of the New Jersey Railroad and Transportation Co.; was engaged on the construction of the Brooklyn water works, 1857–60, and the Croton water works extensions, 1860–63; was principal assistant engineer of the Washington aqueduct, 1863–65; and from 1865–70 was in charge of construction of storage reservoirs in the Croton water-shed. From 1872 to 1878 he was in charge of the topographical surveys and the development of the street and sewer systems of the 23rd and 24th wards of New York city, comprising the territory north of the Harlem river. Between 1878 and 1895 he had an extensive expert practice in design and construction and consultations on works of water supply, water power, sewerage, and irrigation in all parts of the United States. He was one of the board of experts selected by the New York aqueduct commissioners in 1888 to report on the plans for the great Croton dam, and in 1895 was appointed one of the commissioners of the state of New York for the acquisition of the Palisades of the Hudson river by the United States. He has been a large contributor to the civil engineering journals and to the publications of professional societies and to "Johnson's Universal Cyclopedia." Among his published reports, those on the water supply of Newark, N. J., 1879, of Syracuse, N. Y., 1889, and on the prevention of floods at Johnstown, Pa., 1891, have been extensively circulated and highly commended for their thorough treatment of the subjects discussed. He is a member of the American Society of Civil Engineers, of which he was for ten years the treasurer and then vice-president, the American and the New England Water Works Associations, the Institution of Civil Engineers and the Imperial Institute of England, and the Union League Club and Century Association of New York city. Since 1890 he has also given a great deal of attention to the question of rapid transit in cities and been engineer to several commissions for laying out rapid transit roads. The suburban rapid transit road in the northeastern part of New York city was built after his plans and under his supervision. This was the first of such roads which was located chiefly on its own purchased right of way and so constructed as to admit of running heavy trains at high speed.

BURNZ, Eliza Boardman, educator, was born at Rayne, Eng., Oct. 31, 1823, removing with her parents to America in 1837. At fifteen years of age she taught her first school in Salem, Mass., two years after the Choctaw Indians had taken their departure for the Indian territory. For many years she taught in various parts of Tennessee, Mississippi, and Alabama, and afterward in the public schools of Cincinnati. In 1846 her attention was first called to the system of shorthand as invented by Isaac Pitman of England. She at once recognized the possibilities of such a method, and sought to have it introduced in all institutions of learning, not only for its own merits but as an aid in mastering the language. At the close of the civil war she went to Nashville, and engaged in teaching the newly freed colored people to read by means of books printed with a phonetic alphabet. She came to New York city in 1860, where she again devoted herself to teaching phonography and to the preparation of a more satisfactory text-book of the art. For three years she conducted classes at the Mercantile Library, and from 1872 to 1889 instructed the free evening classes at Cooper Union which were established solely at her instigation. At that time, 1872, there were not half-a-dozen women in New York engaged in the stenographic profession. Her success as a teacher and publisher of shorthand works was continuous, and she also sought to reform orthography by the same means. When the international congress of spelling reform met in Philadelphia, in 1876, Mrs. Burnz had already published a phonetic alphabet which contained no new letters, but which had added characters composed of marked letters and diagraphs sufficient to have a regular representative for each sound of the language. This alphabet and the print are known as the Anglo-American. She also adopted the partially amended spelling recommended by the English and American philological associations and has printed thousands of tracts presenting reasons for a simplification of orthography. Mrs. Burnz was the organizer of the "Leag for Short Spelling," which has its headquarters at 24 Clinton Place, New York, and she is now its secretary. In the summer of 1891 she devised a plan for pronouncing print, which should not deviate from the common spelling, and the "Step by Step Primer" was begun. The book was published in September, 1892. The following is a specimen of Burnz's Pronouncing Print:

Of do done was
says eye one bird
eat high know use

Mrs. Burnz is the only woman author of a special method of shorthand with text-book. She has held the office of librarian of the New York State Stenographers' Association. She has been twice married, is the mother of four children, and the grandmother of eight.

BROOKS, James, statesman and journalist, was born in Portland, Me., Nov. 10, 1810, son of Capt. James and Elizabeth (Folsom) Brooks. His father, English by birth but American in his sympathies, commanded the brig Yankee, a privateer, which was lost with all on board during the war of 1812. His mother's ancestors, the Folsoms, were among the earliest families in New England, having settled in the Massachusetts Bay Colony in 1633. At the death of his father, his mother, a woman of energy and character, but with no means of support save the pension allowed to her by the U. S. government, was left with three children dependent upon her. James was sent to the public schools, but at the age of eleven was "bound" until he should attain his majority, after the custom of the day, to a storekeeper at Lewiston, Me. His employer recognized his worth, and released him from his obligations. Entering Waterville College, now Colby University, and, supporting himself by teaching school, he was duly graduated at the head of his class in 1831. After passing a rigid examination he was appointed teacher in a Latin school at Portland, and at the same period he commenced the study of law in the office of the celebrated John Neal, and began to write anonymous letters to the Portland "Advertiser." Though admitted to practice at the bar of Maine, an offer of $500 a year from the latter journal determined his life's career. He soon became noted as a political writer and

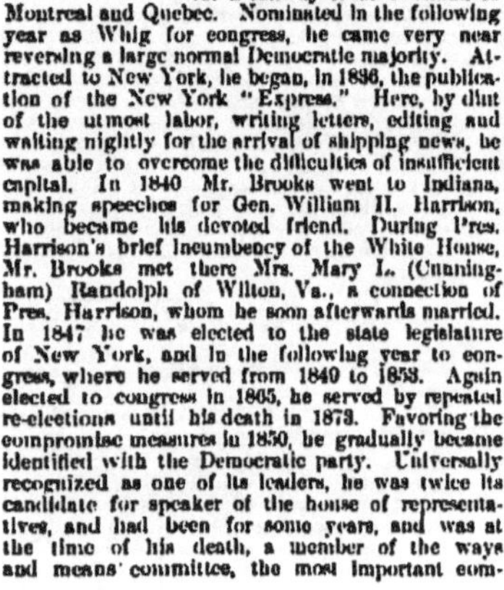

speaker, and when but twenty-one years of age was elected to the legislature. He went to Washington the next year, and made the initial effort in Washington correspondence in his series of spirited letters which were extensively copied in this country and Europe. His correspondence was a revelation in journalism. He traveled in the South and in Europe, mainly on foot, as correspondent for his newspaper. An evidence of his broadness of mind, even at that age, is shown by the fact that in 1835, when again elected to the Maine legislature, he introduced the first proposition for a railway from Portland to Montreal and Quebec. Nominated in the following year as Whig for congress, he came very near reversing a large normal Democratic majority. Attracted to New York, he began, in 1836, the publication of the New York "Express." Here, by dint of the utmost labor, writing letters, editing and waiting nightly for the arrival of shipping news, he was able to overcome the difficulties of insufficient capital. In 1840 Mr. Brooks went to Indiana, making speeches for Gen. William H. Harrison, who became his devoted friend. During Pres. Harrison's brief incumbency of the White House, Mr. Brooks met there Mrs. Mary L. (Cunningham) Randolph of Wilton, Va., a connection of Pres. Harrison, whom he soon afterwards married. In 1847 he was elected to the state legislature of New York, and in the following year to congress, where he served from 1849 to 1853. Again elected to congress in 1865, he served by repeated re-elections until his death in 1873. Favoring the compromise measures in 1850, he gradually became identified with the Democratic party. Universally recognized as one of its leaders, he was twice its candidate for speaker of the house of representatives, and had been for some years, and was at the time of his death, a member of the ways and means' committee, the most important committee of the house. In 1867 he was a member of the New York state constitutional convention, and at various periods had been sent as delegate to political national conventions. In 1869 he was appointed by Pres. Johnson government director of the Union Pacific Railroad. In 1872 Mr. Brooks was unjustly accused, along with Oakes Ames, James G. Blaine, James A. Garfield, and other congressmen, of complicity in the "Credit Mobilier" scandal. For political reasons it was necessary to involve some prominent Democrat, and he was chosen as the scapegoat, and along with Ames, a Republican, censured by the forty-second congress. This injustice aggravated a chronic trouble with which he was suffering, and resulted in his death the following spring, thus preventing the reversal of the censure in his case. As an instance of the regard he commanded from his constituents, he was returned to the forty-third congress by the largest majority ever polled, up to that time, for any congressman in New York city. His death, however, occurred before the opening of the session. Mr. Brooks was the author of "A Seven Months' Run Up and Down and Around the World" (New York, 1872), a compilation of his letters contributed to the "Express" during his last trip abroad. During his career he enjoyed the friendship of Webster, Clay, and the leading men of both political parties, and was well informed upon all questions affecting the history of his country. He was well-read and spoke four languages; his mental powers were wonderfully trained, his will inflexible, and his perseverance equal to any difficulty; he had remarkable ability to grasp situations and state them clearly. After his death a prominent authority has said: "Mr. Brooks was an able writer. For perspicuous narrative, terse comment, apt reflection, ready information, courteous tone and dignified manner, he was as remarkable as for unflagging labor, untiring enterprise, an intuitional knowledge of the salient points of affairs. He attained success as an editor, an author and a politician, and could have attained greatness in any one of the three professions to which he might have chosen to devote the whole, not a part, of his very clever, thoroughly trained powers. Personally he was most popular—because a considerate, pure and worthy gentleman—one whose fine social qualities and whose amiability in all the relations of life had won for him the regard and esteem of all who had the honor of his acquaintance." He died at his residence, in Washington, on Apr. 30, 1873.

BROOKS, Erastus, statesman and journalist, was born in Portland, Me., Jan. 31, 1815. He was the younger brother of James Brooks, whom he resembled in pertinacious industry, indomitable courage, and successful struggle with adversity. He began his active career at the age of eight years, working in a Boston grocery store for his board and clothes. In the meanwhile he obtained the rudiments of an education in an evening school, and was later apprenticed to the compositor's trade. He expended his savings in perfecting his education, and while yet very young entered Brown University, where he took a partial course, paying all his expenses by working at the case. On the completion of his studies he founded a paper, called the "Yankee," at Wiscasset, Me., but soon after removed to Haverhill, Mass., where he first taught school for a while, the poet, Whittier, sitting in judgment on his work, as one of the school-board of the town, and later became editor and proprietor of the Haverhill "Gazette." In 1835 he began in Washington, D. C. his sixteen years' career as correspondent, contributing news of the capital to the New York "Express" and other papers. In 1840 he joined with his brother in the editorial management of the "Express," subsequently assuming the entire control. During the epidemic of cholera in New York, when all who could left the city, he edited the "Express" almost single-handed; was one of the first to use the telegraph in newspaper reports, availing himself of the offer of Ezra Cornell to use the new telegraph line between New York and Albany, and receiving and publishing news from the legislature before Mr. Bennett's pony express had reached the city. He was one of the founders, and for many years chairman, of the executive committee of the associated press. In 1843 he made the tour of Europe on foot, from Queenstown to Moscow, contributing letters to the "Express," which, like his Washington correspondence, attracted wide attention.   On his return voyage the vessel was wrecked off Sandy Hook, he being one of the few passengers to escape the catastrophe. As editor of of the "Express" he took an active part in the agitation against the exemption from taxation of Catholic church property, on the ground that, being held in the name of the bishops, it should properly be included under the laws governing personal holdings in realty, and was drawn into a vigorous debate with Archbishop Hughes.   As an outcome, he was elected to the state senate on the "American ticket," assisting in the further discussion of the question in the legislature. A full account of this discussion was published in book form, under the title, "Controversy on Church Property." In 1856 he was nominated for governor by the same party, and although leading his ticket several thousand votes in many counties, was defeated by John A. King.   Mr. Brooks was subsequently a member of the national Democratic conventions which nominated Fillmore, Bell, and Seymour; a member of the New York state constitutional convention of 1866–67, serving as chairman of its committee on charities; also a member of the constitutional commission of 1872–73. As member of the assembly for Richmond county in 1878, '79, '81, '82, and '83; Mr. Brooks was easily leader of his party in that body. He was continuously a member of the committee on ways and means, being its chairman in 1882; and was also on the committees on cities and rules. A political syndicate, composed of John Kelly, Augustus Schell, and others, purchased the stock of the "Express" in 1877, and thereafter, except for his legislative duties, Mr. Brooks led what he expressed as a "busy idle life," finding sufficient employment for his active powers in furthering schemes of charity and public weal. He was for many years a member of the state board of health.   He was a trustee of the New York Institution for the Instruction of the Deaf and Dumb, and of the Nursery and Child's Hospital, several times visiting the legislature in their behalf. In the National Charities' Association, and in all movement instituted for the benefit of the Indians, he was an active agent.   So great was his interest in the Indian cause that he rose from his sick-bed to attend the Indian conference at Lake Mohonk, thereby contracting pneumonia, from which he died.   He was an old-time friend of Ezra Cornell, and for many years a trustee of Cornell University. He gave to this institution the benefit of his varied experience and fine executive ability. After his death the trustees erected a tablet to his memory in the university chapel, with the inscription: "The Honorable Erastus Brooks, LL.D., 1815–1886. One of the first elected trustees of Cornell University. Though closely occupied with many important public trusts, and with absorbing duties as editor of a leading metropolitan journal, and though residing at a greater distance from the university than any other member of its governing board, he never, during the twenty years he was connected with it, was absent from one of its meetings.   In grateful memory of his devotion to the university—and of his wisdom in its councils—his fellow-trustees erected this tablet."   Throughout his varied experiences, and the cares and responsibilities of his public and official career, Mr. Brooks remained the same humble Christian, polished gentleman, and helpful friend and adviser to the least of his associates. Thoroughly acquainted with the principles of parliamentary bodies and the public issues of his day, he was a ready debater and a trenchant speaker, yet withal, of calm temper and excellent judgment.   It is suggestive and interesting, that the two brothers, James and Erastus Brooks, should have been, both of them at various times, in the legislative halls with which their careers were almost identified, the candidates of their party for presiding officer, and that they should have been, after reaching the maturity of their powers, in almost every session on the most important committee—that of the ways and means—of these legislative bodies.   Both were members of the two state conventions for the revision of the state constitution which were held during their lifetime. Both were noted for the force and purity of their style, whether in speech or in written language.   Mr. Brooks married Margaret Dawes, daughter of Judge Cranch, chief justice in the District of Columbia, and left surviving him three children, one son and two daughters. He died, universally regretted, at Richmond, S. I., on Nov. 25, 1886.

BROOKS, James Wilton, lawyer and author, was born in New York, Apr. 19, 1854, son of James and Mary Louisa Brooks. His early education was obtained at private schools, at home and abroad, and he then entered Yale College, where he was graduated in the class of 1875. He studied law at the Columbia Law School, and was admitted to the bar in 1881. He met with success in his practice at the start, and attained a just popularity, professionally and socially. In 1882–83 he was elected to the state legislature, sitting, though from another part of the state, as one of the youngest members of the house, in the same session with his distinguished uncle, Erastus Brooks. Mr. Brooks subsequently resumed the practice of his profession, also becoming interested in several business and publishing enterprises.   He has written considerably for the public press, and his contributions are ever well received. In 1890 the degree of LL.D., was conferred upon him by St. John's College, Annapolis, Md., the New York "Sun" remarking at the time, "Few scholars have ever achieved the enviable learned distinction of the doctorate at his years." 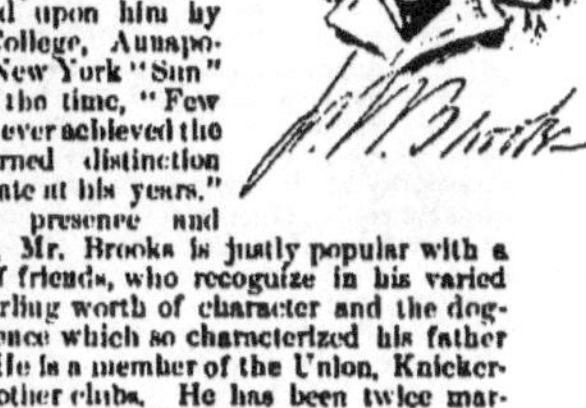
Of pleasing presence and wide culture, Mr. Brooks is justly popular with a large circle of friends, who recognize in his varied career the sterling worth of character and the dogged perseverance which so characterized his father and uncle. He is a member of the Union, Knickerbocker, and other clubs. He has been twice married, his first wife dying in 1888. He was married in 1893 to Florence, daughter of the late Henry James Miller, for many years president of the Cincinnati Gas and Coke Co.

ALEXANDER, Robert Carter, lawyer and journalist, was born at West Charlton, Saratoga co., N. Y., July 7, 1857. His father, Alexander F. Alexander, and his mother, Margaret (Bunyan) Alexander, both belonged to a Scotch community, which settled western Saratoga county in the closing decade of the last century. The son's early education was obtained in the district school, and he was prepared for college at the Charlton Academy and the

Union Classical Institute in Schenectady. He was graduated at Union College in 1880, at the head of his class, taking also the graduating prizes for oratory and for essay writing. While in college he had been an editor of the college paper, and had long cherished the ambition to follow the journalistic profession. Circumstances, however, were not favorable to his embarking at once in that profession, and he chose the law. He was graduated from the Albany Law School in 1881, with the degree of LL.B., and in May of that year was admitted to the bar. He continued the study,

R. C. Alexander.

and began the practice of his profession in the office of ex-Gov. Lucius Robinson in Elmira, N. Y., until 1884, when he removed to New York city, and entered upon the active practice of the law, making a specialty of real estate, surrogate's practice, and the law of corporations. Among the most important of the enterprises which he organized and shaped, was the Adirondack League Club, probably now the largest and wealthiest sporting club in the country, owning some 120,-000 acres of forest land in the western Adirondacks. He has been a trustee and officer of the club ever since its organization. In 1897 he became the counsel of the late Col. Elliott F. Shepard, and in the following year conducted, in Col. Shepard's behalf, the negotiations by which the latter became the owner of the "Mail and Express," a paper which the brilliancy of James and Erastus Brooks, and the genius of Cyrus W. Field, had made the leading paper of New York. Mr. Alexander became actively associated with Col. Shepard in the new enterprise, and was made secretary and treasurer of the "Mail and Express" corporation, as well as its legal counsel. The old inclination toward a newspaper career, indulged in a desultory way ever since Mr. Alexander left college, now had fuller scope. He familiarized himself with every department of the paper, and from the first, did more or less work on the editorial page. Upon the death of Col. Shepard, in 1893, the management of the paper practically devolved upon Mr. Alexander, and he found it necessary to give nearly his entire time and attention to its literary and financial interests. In February, 1895, he became editor-in-chief of the paper, still retaining, however, his connection with the business department as treasurer of the corporation. Mr. Alexander wields a powerful and facile pen, and has already, by his brilliant work, taken a prominent place among the older men in his profession. Since his accession to the editorial chair of the "Mail and Express," the paper has been strengthened and brightened until it is recognized as one of the most influential Republican organs in the country. Mr. Alexander is also a graceful and eloquent speaker, and his voice is frequently heard on the political platform, and at public dinners. In 1890, at the age of thirty-two, he was elected a life trustee of Union College, in recognition of his constant interest in, and services in behalf of, his alma mater. In 1888

he organized the graduates of New York city and vicinity into the Union College Alumni Association of New York. While practically withdrawn from the active practice of the law, Mr. Alexander maintains intimate relations with the members of that profession, being a life member and an officer of the State Bar Association, and a member of the City Bar Association, and a number of clubs, and other social organizations, and is a director in several business corporations. He has several times been urged to accept various political offices, but has preferred to hold aloof from politics, except from the standpoint of the editorial sanctum. Mr. Alexander possesses, to an unusual degree, the rare quality of making and holding friends, and to this quality, added to his ability, and his modest, unpretentiousness of character, must be ascribed the honors to which he has attained at so early an age. Mr. Alexander married, in 1884, Annie Clare of Schenectady, N. Y.

MORGAN, Abner, revolutionary soldier, was born at Brimfield, Mass., Jan. 9, 1746. He was graduated at Harvard College in 1778, and began the practice of law in Hampshire and Hampden counties, but on the Lexington alarm—being at that time a member of the general court, or legislature of Massachusetts—he enlisted, and was elected major of the first regiment of Continental troops raised by Massachusetts for the war of the revolution, Col. Porter in command. The regiment was mustered in at Watertown, and joined Gen. Arnold at Albany, marched to Quebec, and participated in the storming of that city, under Gen. Montgomery; was in the retreat. At Crown Point, July 8, 1776, he drew up an address of officers taking farewell of Gen. Sullivan on his withdrawing from the army of Canada; was commissioned brigade major Aug. 29, 1778; was commissioned justice of the peace by Gen. Hancock, 1781; assessor of U. S. direct taxes, 1798; selectman of Brimfield twenty-two years, and member of the state legislature eighteen years; practiced at the bar of Springfield and Worcester for fifty-four years. He died at Lima, N. Y., Nov. 7, 1817.

THOMPSON, John Reuben, poet and journalist, was born at Richmond, Va., Oct. 23, 1823. His education began at home, and was continued in a school at East Haven, Conn., where he was sent to prepare for college. He entered the University of Virginia at the age of eighteen, and was graduated with high honors in 1845; but continued the study of law there, under the direction of Joseph A. Seddon, an eminent lawyer of Richmond, receiving the degree of LL.B. the following year. He practiced in Richmond two years, and, although equipped with every material for success, did not find his work congenial, and gave it up to follow the bent of his genius—literature. Accordingly, in 1847 he accepted the editorship of the "Southern Literary Messenger," a monthly magazine, established in 1835, whose

long and brilliant career has had no parallel in the South, and which was then unsurpassed in literary merit throughout the entire country. Poe had been its conductor years before, and had made it a vehicle for many of his extraordinary productions. Mr. Thompson brought a great deal of zeal and energy into the editorial chair, and its high character was fully maintained during the twelve years of his management. Much encouragement was offered to

Southern writers, and among its contributors were Paul H. Hayne, Henry Timrod, Philip P. Cooke, and John E. Cooke; and o. the North, Donald Grant Mitchel (Ike Marvel), whose "Reveries of a Bachelor" and "Dream Life" first appeared there in 1849–50. In connection with his professional pursuits, he frequently delivered poems and lectures at college commencements, before lyceums, and on other occasions. Among his poems thus read first in public, are: "Patriotism" (1856), "Virginia" (1856), "The Greek Slave," delivered at the unveiling of the Washington statue in Richmond (1858), and "Poesy" (1859). In 1854 he went to Paris to live, where, on account of his attachment to the diplomatic family of Minister Mason, he had special opportunities for forming the acquaintance and friendship of men of culture. During this absence he contributed articles on his European observations to the "Messenger," which were afterward put in book form and printed; but the whole edition was lost by fire in the publishing house of Daly & Jackson, one copy only being saved. Mr. Thompson remained in charge of the "Messenger" until 1859, when, on account of delicate health, he went to Augusta, Ga., to assume the editorship of the "Southern Field and Fireside." Later he was connected with the Richmond "Record," a new weekly journal. In 1863 he went to London, in poor health, but the voyage benefited him, and he was engaged to write for the London "Index," and contributed also to "Blackwood's Magazine." Soon after the war he returned, still in poor health, and making New York his home, became literary editor of the "Post" until his death. He was a diligent and careful worker, and an accomplished and graceful writer, of both prose and verse. His fugitive pieces were never collected, but they are very popular in the South, especially in Virginia, his native state. While in New York he grew more and more feeble, and in the winter of 1872 went to Colorado, in a vain effort to benefit his health. Returning to New York the following spring, he died there, Apr. 30, 1873.

BECKWITH, John Watrous, second Protestant Episcopal bishop of Georgia and eighty-sixth in succession in the American Episcopate, was born in Raleigh, N. C., Feb. 9, 1831. He was graduated from Trinity College, Hartford, Conn., in 1852, was ordained deacon, May 24, 1854, and priest in May, 1855. He was rector of churches in Wadesboro', N. C., and in Anne Arundel county, Md. In 1861 he removed to Mississippi, and in that same year became rector of Trinity Church, Demopolis, Ala. For a time he served as chaplain in the Confederate army, and by his eloquence obtained great influence over the soldiers. In 1865 he became rector of Trinity Church, New Orleans. In 1867 he received the degree of S. T. D. from Trinity College, and in that year was elected bishop of Georgia. He was consecrated in St. John's Church, Savannah, Apr. 2, 1868. He was one of the most eminent men the Protestant Episcopal church in the South has produced, and used his exceptional talents and executive ability with marked success in building up the parishes impoverished, or wholly destroyed, by the ravages of war. The churches in his diocese multiplied under his administration, and their benevolent work broadened considerably. Bishop Beckwith was noted for his genial and courtly manners, but particularly for his oratorical gifts. In his later

years he spent his summers at Riverdale, on the Hudson, and took especial interest in a home for orphans, founded and endowed by the Appleton family of New York. He published some addresses and sermons. He died in Atlanta, Ga., Nov. 23, 1890.

WORCESTER, Joseph Emerson, lexicographer, was born in Bedford, N. H., Aug. 24, 1784. His father, Jesse Worcester, was a highly cultivated man and an author, but had retired to a small farm. The son's early life was spent on this farm, but he was a thoughtful youth, and early displayed a strong love of knowledge and a quiet determination, which were the predominant traits of his character. He gained possession of a grammar, which he mastered by himself, and embraced every opportunity for gaining knowledge that came within his reach, but his environment was discouraging, and his difficulties would have overcome a less indomitable spirit. He spent his nights in study, and when he became twenty-one years old, he resolved to obtain a liberal education, and after incredible difficulties, entered Yale College in 1809. His unremitting study enabled him to graduate in two years, when he be-

gan teaching school in Salem, Mass. All the time not absolutely needed in the school, he devoted to study and literary work, which was first confined to the department of geography. During the next year he engaged upon a "Geographical Dictionary, or Universal Gazette," which was published in Andover in 1817, and a new edition, greatly enlarged, in 1823. This was followed by "A Gazetteer of the United States." He then removed to Cambridge, Mass., where he resided during the remainder of his life. In 1819 he published "Elements of Geography, Ancient and Modern," which was very favorably received, and passed through many editions. He then published "Sketches of the Earth and its Inhabitants," and in 1820 issued a new edition of the history, with an historical atlas, which was used very extensively as a school text-book. In 1825 he contributed to the American Academy a paper on "Longevity, and Expectation of Life in the United States." His first publication on lexicography was an edition of Johnson's Dictionary with Walker's Pronouncing Dictionary combined, which appeared in 1828, and the following year he was induced to prepare an abridgement of Webster's large Dictionary. He was strongly disinclined to undertake this task, as he was preparing a work of his own, but he reluctantly yielded to the persuasions of the publisher, though it was a regret ever after. In 1830 he produced his own work, a comprehensive "Pronouncing and Explanatory Dictionary," which had such a copious vocabulary and other substantial merits that it had an immediate and overwhelming success. The next year Dr. Worcester went abroad, visiting the literary centres of Europe, where he remained seven months, collecting books on philology and lexicography, and obtaining the rest which his arduous labors had made imperative. Upon his return he assumed the editorship of the "American Almanac," which he continued for eleven years. During all these years he had been engaged upon a "Universal and Critical Dictionary," which he finished in 1846. It was almost immediately printed in London, where it was claimed to be compiled from the materials of Noah Webster. This literary fraud Dr. Worcester was compelled to refute in a pamphlet issued in 1858. In 1847 an enlarged edition was published, which was still further improved in 1849 and 1855. The continued and laborious work of so many years began to tell upon his eyesight, and in 1847 it gave way, and for two years Dr. Worcester was forced to suspend his work. This was a sore trial to a man of his energy and mental activity, but he bore the affliction with remarkable patience. A cataract formed in each eye, and, though three operations were performed upon the right and two upon the left, only one upon the latter eye was successful. He only partially regained his sight, but in this disabled condition he resumed his labors. The most elaborate and important of Dr. Worcester's literary labors, one to which all his previous works were preparatory and introductory, was the "Dictionary of the English Language," which was issued in 1860. In the explanation of technical terms the author was aided by many able experts, and it presented the ripe results of years of conscientious research, shaped by unerring judgment and good taste. It was the first dictionary that employed illustrations. It was received with great favor, which more than met the author's expectations, and called forth unmeasured approval from the most learned men in literature and philology at home and abroad. Dr. Ezra Abbott says of him, "There is no lexicographer whose judgment deserves higher consideration." He simply endeavored to preserve the language as it was, and not to improve it, and as the Webster dictionary has gradually abandoned the original plan, there is little essential difference between them at the present time. Dr. Worcester was a member of the Massachusetts Historical Society, the American Academy, and the American Oriental Society, and honorary corresponding member of the Royal Geographical Society of London. He received the degree of LL. D. from both Brown University in 1847, and Dartmouth College in 1856. In 1841 Dr. Worcester married Amy Elizabeth, daughter of the Rev. J. McKean, D.D., of Boylston, professor of rhetoric and oratory in Harvard University, but had no children. He died in Cambridge, Oct. 27, 1865.

LENNOX, Charlotte Ramsay, author, was born in New York city in 1720, daughter of Col. Ramsay, lieutenant-governor of the colony. Her primary education was acquired in the best schools of the city of her birth, as her father's position gave to the child unusual advantages. When she was fifteen years old, her mother being dead, she was sent to England to complete her education. The relation to whose care she was consigned never informed her that her father died during her voyage. Left thus without a protector, Lady Rockingham took her up, receiving her into her household; but an obscure love affair ended the friendship, and the Duchess of Newcastle became her patroness. She first appeared before the public as an actress, and Walpole spoke of her acting as "deplorable." She married an employee of William Strahan, the well-known London printer, who introduced Mrs. Lennox to Samuel Johnson. He, with his companions of the Ivy Lane Club, commemorated, in the spring of 1751, at Devil's Tavern, by Temple Bar, the birth of her first novel, "Life of Harriot Stuart," printed by Strahan. Mr. and Mrs. Lennox and a female acquaintance met with the club, and it is said that Johnson "encircled her brow" with a crown of laurel, specially prepared by himself, and the company did not break up until St. Dunstan's clock was nearing eight. In 1747 Paterson had published a thin volume of her poems, dedicated to "the Lady Isabella Finch," her maiden effort. Then, following her "Life of Harriot Stuart" came "The Female Quixote" and "Shakespeare Illustrated;" then a translation of Sully's "Memoirs." Johnson was her lifelong friend. He wrote the dedications to two of her works: "The Female Quixote" and "Shakespeare Illustrated;" quoted her in his dictionary, and drew up a tale of 1775, the "Proposal," for a complete edition of her works, and reviewed her writings repeatedly. Richardson, Goldsmith, and Fielding were equally her literary sponsors. It may be said that she was not equally popular with her own sex, who, while they admired her works, disliked her. Her husband died shortly after she had published her first novel, and thereafter she had only her literary gifts to give her a livelihood. Her works not already mentioned include: "Henrietta," "Euphemia," and "Sophia," novels; and "The Sisters," and "Old City Manners," comedies. A portrait by Reynolds, engraved by Bartolozzi, appeared in Harding's "Shakespeare." Mrs. Lennox was supported in her declining years partly by the literary fund and partly by the Right Hon. George Rose, who, after her death, on Jan. 4, 1804, in Dean's Yard, Westminster, paid the expenses of her burial.

SMITH, Samuel Francis, clergyman and author, was born in Boston, Oct. 21, 1808. His father and grandfather were both Bostonians, while the grave-stone of his great-grandmother, Ann McMillan, is still visible in Copps Hill burying-ground. He studied at the Boston Latin School, and was graduated at Harvard College with the famous class of 1829, numbering among its members Oliver Wendell Holmes, Prof. Pierce, and James Freeman Clarke. He immediately entered An-

dover Theological Seminary, graduating in 1832, and in this year wrote the hymns most widely known, "My Country, 'tis of Thee" and "The Morning Light is Breaking," besides many others. After one year spent in editorial labors in Boston, he was ordained pastor of the First Baptist Church in Waterville, Me., Feb. 12, 1834, at the same time becoming professor of modern languages in Waterville College, now Colby University. He held this double office eight years, then removed to Newton Centre, Mass., in January, 1842, where he has since resided. At this date he became editor of the "Christian Review," a quarterly publication, which he managed from 1842 to 1848, being at the same time pastor of the First Baptist Church in Newton, an office which he filled until his resignation on June 30, 1854. For the next fifteen years he was editorial secretary of the American Baptist Missionary Union, at the same time preaching regularly on the Sabbath, chiefly for feeble churches. In 1875 he visited Europe, spending one year in travel, extending his visits, in 1880, to India and the Burmese empire. On these tours he visited many missionary stations of the various Christian denominations, not only in France, Spain, Italy, Austria, Turkey, Greece, Sweden, and Denmark, but also in Burmah, India, and Ceylon. He has since been engaged chiefly in literary labors. Among his publications are a "History of Newton" (950 pp., 8vo.); "Missionary Sketches," "Rambles in Mission Fields," "Life of Rev. Joseph Grafton," and three collections of hymnology, original and translated: "Rock of Ages" (1860, new ed., 1877); "Lyric Gems" (the latter a publisher's title, Boston, 1843); and "The Psalmist," a Baptist hymn-book (1843). Besides these, he has edited many works for the press, and written innumerable articles and poems for reviews, magazines, and newspapers. While still pursuing his collegiate and theological education, he translated from the German "Conversations-Lexicon," fully enough matter for an entire volume of the "Cyclopædia Americana." His poems have never been printed in a separate volume, but are very numerous. His hymns number more than 100, largely occasional, and are found in the psalmody of all the Christian denominations. His love for acquisition of foreign languages, and his facility in that line of attainment, has extended over many years, so that he has read books in fifteen different tongues. His national hymn, "America," written in 1832, has found its way wherever an American heart beats, or the English language is spoken, and has probably proved useful in stirring the patriotic spirit of the American people. It is as popular after sixty-two years of its existence as it was when it was first sung in Park Street Church in Boston. Many thousands of the late Dr. Holmes's admirers will remember the lines in his famous "Reunion Poem," "The Boys":

> "And there's a nice youngster of excellent pith;
> Fate tried to conceal him by naming him Smith!
> But he shouted a song for the brave and the free—
> Just read on his medal, 'My Country, of Thee!'"

Dr. Smith married, Sept. 16, 1834, Mary White Smith, of Haverhill, Mass., granddaughter of Rev. Hezekiah Smith, D.D., who was a chaplain in the revolutionary war for six years, and an intimate friend of Washington. He died at his home, Nov. 16, 1895.

RAVENSCROFT, John Stark, first Protestant Episcopal bishop of North Carolina, was born in Prince George county, Va., in 1772. He was the only child of Dr. John Ravenscroft, a gentleman of fortune, who had been educated for the medical profession. Two months after his birth his parents removed to Great Britain and settled in the south of Scotland. His father died in the latter part of 1780. His mother availed herself of the excellent opportunity which Scotland afforded, of giving her son a thorough classical education, and after finishing his course in a grammar school he was placed in a seminary of a high grade in the north of England. Soon after entering on his seventeenth year, his friends deemed it advisable for him to return to Virginia for the purpose of securing the remains of his father's property. This he did, and having a desire to study law, he entered William and Mary College with this object, and also to acquire a more perfect acquaintance with the sciences. It does not appear, however, that he ever procured a license to practice his profession. He married and settled in Lunenburg county, Va., where, although he sustained an honorable reputation among his fellowmen, so great was his neglect of the outward forms of religion, that, according to his own statement, from the year 1792 to 1810, he was not present at a place of public worship more than six or seven times; but a short time subsequent to the latter period, his attention was diverted to the duties of a religious life. He first connected himself with the Methodists; but, after having had his mind directed to the Christian ministry in 1815, he became a member of the Protestant Episcopal church. In 1817 he was admitted to holy orders by Bishop Moore of Virginia; became the minister of St. James' Church,

Mecklenburg county, in that state, and resided there, zealously and usefully occupied in the labors of his profession, until the year 1823, when he was elected bishop of North Carolina. He was consecrated, Apr. 22, 1823, and promptly entered upon the highly important functions of his new office, which he performed with his characteristic energy, until his constitution and strength completely failed him. In person Bishop Ravenscroft was large and commanding, with a countenance somewhat austere in its general aspect, but susceptible of the most benevolent expression. His manner corresponded with his personal appearance, especially when exercising his ministerial functions; being remarkably dignified, and so solemn and impressive, as to inspire all present with reverence. Two volumes of his sermons were published after his death. He died, March 5, 1830.

IVES, Levi Silliman, second Protestant Episcopal bishop of North Carolina, 1831–53. (See Vol. V., p. 409.)

ATKINSON, Thomas, third Protestant Episcopal bishop of North Carolina and fifty-eighth in succession in the American Episcopate, was born at Mansfield, Va., Aug. 6, 1807, the sixth child of Thomas and Mary (Tobb) Atkinson, and great-grandson of a clergyman of the Church of England. He entered Yale College, but was expelled for refusing to disclose the names of some fellow students who were concerned in a carousal in which he, however, had taken no part. He then entered the junior class at Hampden, Sidney, in 1825, and was graduated at the age of nineteen. He studied law and was admitted to the bar in 1828, but after practising successfully for several years, decided to enter the church, and on Nov. 18, 1836, was ordained deacon

in Norfolk, Va., by Bishop Meade. He became assistant at Christ Church in that city, and in 1837 was consecrated priest, after which he officiated as rector of St. Paul's, Norfolk, and at St. Paul's, Lynchburg. In 1838 he was called to St. Peter's Church, Baltimore, and was so acceptable to the churchmen of that city that Grace Church was built for him and he became its rector in 1852. In 1850 a controversy arose in Maryland over the right of the bishop to administer the holy communion at his visitation, one party claiming that a rector could not rightfully vacate the trust of such administration at such a time. Dr. Atkinson took a leading part in the debates in the diocesan convention and moved resolutions sustaining the bishop, which were adopted by an overwhelming majority. On May 26, 1853, he was elected bishop of North Carolina, and was consecrated in St. John's Chapel, New York city, on Oct. 17th. The work to be done in his diocese required talents of no common kind, for the church in North Carolina had been divided by the teachings of Bishop Ives, and these talents were displayed by Bishop Atkinson who, by his wise administration, brought order out of confusion. With Bishop Lay he attended the General Convention of the Episcopal church in 1865, and by his calm but forcible utterances did much to hasten the reunion of the northern and southern dioceses. Bishop Atkinson resided in Raleigh for a time after his consecration and then removed to Wilmington. In 1873 Dr. Theodore Benedict Lyman became his assistant. Bishop Atkinson received the degree of D.D. from Trinity College in 1846, and that of LL.D. from the University of

North Carolina in 1862, and from the University of Cambridge, England, in 1867. He was a man of great dignity, but was so affable that the most humble could approach him freely; self-reliant, but cautious; intensely intellectual, but free from intellectual narrowness. The diocese prospered greatly under him. He was married in 1828 to Josepha, daughter of John and Jane Wilder of Petersburg, Va., by whom he had three children. He died at Wilmington, Jan. 4, 1881, and was buried under the altar of St. James' Church, of which he was at one time rector. A commemorative sermon was preached before the diocesan convention in 1881, by Bishop Lay of Easton, and was published in pamphlet form.

LYMAN, Theodore Benedict, fourth Protestant Episcopal bishop of North Carolina and 103d in succession of the American Episcopate, was born at Brighton, Mass., Nov. 27, 1815. He was graduated from Hamilton College in 1837 and entered the General Theological Seminary, New York city,

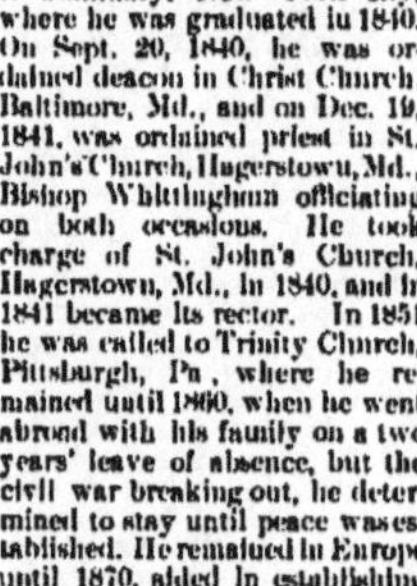

where he was graduated in 1840. On Sept. 20, 1840, he was ordained deacon in Christ Church, Baltimore, Md., and on Dec. 19, 1841, was ordained priest in St. John's Church, Hagerstown, Md., Bishop Whittingham officiating on both occasions. He took charge of St. John's Church, Hagerstown, Md., in 1840, and in 1841 became its rector. In 1851 he was called to Trinity Church, Pittsburgh, Pa., where he remained until 1860, when he went abroad with his family on a two years' leave of absence, but the civil war breaking out, he determined to stay until peace was established. He remained in Europe until 1870, aided in establishing

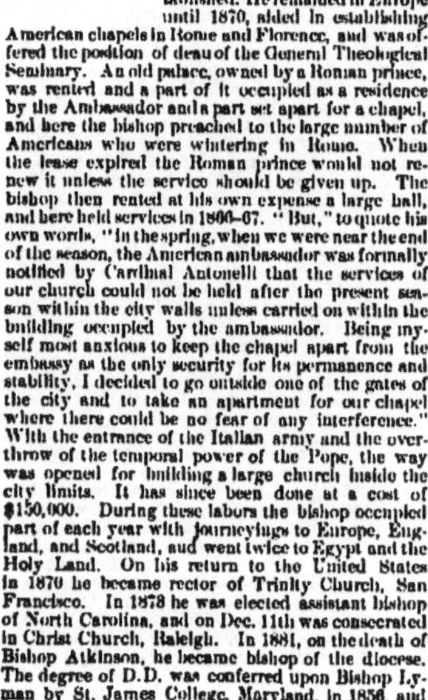

American chapels in Rome and Florence, and was offered the position of dean of the General Theological Seminary. An old palace, owned by a Roman prince, was rented and a part of it occupied as a residence by the Ambassador and a part set apart for a chapel, and here the bishop preached to the large number of Americans who were wintering in Rome. When the lease expired the Roman prince would not renew it unless the service should be given up. The bishop then rented at his own expense a large hall, and here held services in 1866–67. "But," to quote his own words, "in the spring, when we were near the end of the season, the American ambassador was formally notified by Cardinal Antonelli that the services of our church could not be held after the present season within the city walls unless carried on within the building occupied by the ambassador. Being myself most anxious to keep the chapel apart from the embassy as the only security for its permanence and stability, I decided to go outside one of the gates of the city and to take an apartment for our chapel where there could be no fear of any interference." With the entrance of the Italian army and the overthrow of the temporal power of the Pope, the way was opened for building a large church inside the city limits. It has since been done at a cost of $150,000. During these labors the bishop occupied part of each year with journeyings to Europe, England, and Scotland, and went twice to Egypt and the Holy Land. On his return to the United States in 1870 he became rector of Trinity Church, San Francisco. In 1873 he was elected assistant bishop of North Carolina, and on Dec. 11th was consecrated in Christ Church, Raleigh. In 1881, on the death of Bishop Atkinson, he became bishop of the diocese. The degree of D.D. was conferred upon Bishop Lyman by St. James College, Maryland, in 1856, and

in 1886 he was given charge of the American Episcopal churches in Europe. He was twice married. His first wife was Miss Anna Albert of Baltimore; his second wife Miss Robertson of Charleston. He died of apoplexy, at Raleigh, N. C., Dec. 13, 1893.

CHESHIRE, Joseph Blount, clergyman, was born in Edenton, N. C., Dec. 29, 1814. On his mother's side he is descended from a family which has been prominently connected with the Protestant Episcopal church in North Carolina ever since the organization of the first parish vestry in 1701. He was educated at the Edenton Academy, one of the two incorporated institutions of learning of ante-revolutionary foundation in North Carolina. In his sixteenth year the death of his father so reduced the means of the family, that he was taken from school and placed in a store as clerk. While employed in this capacity his contributions to the Edenton paper attracted such favorable attention that it was thought best to give him an opportunity of further education. He was therefore sent to the Episcopal School in Raleigh, then under the head mastership of that eminent scholar and educator, Joseph G. Cogswell. After pursuing his studies here for a year or two, he studied law with the late Thomas Devereux, reporter to the supreme court of North Carolina, and was admitted to the bar in 1837. He practiced on the Edenton circuit for a year or two, but just as success began to crown his efforts, he found himself drawn to the ministry, and abandoned the law. He studied under the personal direction of Bishop Ives, and was ordained deacon in 1840, and priest in 1841. After acting as missionary in Halifax and Bertie counties for a year or two, he settled down to the care of Trinity Church, Scotland Neck, and Calvary Church, Tarboro', in 1841 and 1842. In 1869 he resigned the former, but still ministers in the latter whenever his strength will permit, having ceased to be the active rector in 1889. He received the degree of D.D. in 1861. He has always held a high place in the esteem of the people of the diocese and of the state. For many years he represented his diocese in the general conventions, and he has exhibited one of the longest, most faithful, and successful pastorates in the history of any religious denomination in the state.

CHASE, Pliny Earle, astronomer, was born at Worcester, Mass., Aug. 18, 1820, the eldest child of Anthony and Lydia Earle Chase, both of Massachusetts. His first American ancestor was Aquilla Chase, who came from England. After studying in the public schools of Worcester, and at the Friends' School, Providence, R. I., the son entered Harvard, and was graduated with high rank in 1839. He taught school, both in Leicester and Worcester, and afterward in Philadelphia, where he also engaged in mercantile pursuits. In 1871 Mr. Chase was appointed professor of natural science in Haverford College, near Philadelphia, and in 1875 was transferred to the chair of philosophy and logic. Upon the organization of Bryn-Mawr College, he was appointed lecturer on psychology and logic there. He received the degree of M.A. from Harvard in 1844, and the degree of LL.D. was conferred upon him by Haverford College. Much of his time was devoted to study and scientific research. The Magellanic medal of the American Philosophical Society was awarded to him in 1864 for his paper on the "Numerical Relations of Gravity and Magnetism." He was a member of the above society for twenty-five years, during a part of which time he acted as vice-president and secretary. He contributed 130 papers to the proceedings, which indicate a wide range in philology, meteorology, physics, and mental philosophy. He published in 1844 "The

Elements of Arithmetic," Parts I. and II., which was followed in 1848 by "The Common School Arithmetic," and in 1884, "Elements of Meteorology for Schools and Households." For many years a manager of the Franklin Institute, in Philadelphia, he contributed to the "Journal," also to "Silliman's American Journal of Arts and Sciences," the "London, Dublin, and Edinburgh Philosophical Magazine," and the "Comptes Rendus," of Paris. In 1874 he was elected a fellow of the American Association for the Advancement of Science. In 1844 he married Elizabeth Brown Oliver, of Lynn, Mass., a niece of Goold Brown, the grammarian, and had six children. He died in Haverford, Pa., Dec. 17, 1886.

SMITH, John Lawrence, scientist and physician, was born near Charleston, S. C., Dec. 16, 1818, the son of Benjamin Smith who emigrated from Virginia to South Carolina. He received a classical education at Charleston College, which was supplemented by a thorough course at the University of Virginia. Here he devoted himself particularly to higher branches of physics and mathematics—chemistry he followed as a pastime. When he had completed his collegiate course, he selected civil engineering as a profession and studied its various branches for two years, and also embraced in his category mining engineering and geology. He was employed  as assistant engineer on a railroad projected between Charleston and Cincinnati. This profession not proving congenial to his tastes, he began the study of medicine at the Medical College in the city of Charleston which, at that period, had a most able faculty. He then went abroad and for three years pursued his medical course, but science was always nearest his heart. He studied physiology under Flourens and Longet; chemistry under Orfila, Dumas, and Liebig; physics under Pouillet, Desprez, and Brequer; and mineralogy and geology under Eli de Beaumont and Dufrenoy. In 1844 he returned to America, having thus early in his career earned a reputation for original scientific researches, principally in connection with fatty bodies. His paper, "Spirmaceti" (1842), at once stamped him as an experimental inquirer. Upon his return to Charleston he at once began the practice of medicine and gave a course of lectures in that city on "Toxicology." But the state of South Carolina now commanded his services as assayer of the bullion that was introduced into commerce from the gold fields of Georgia and North and South Carolina. He also gave a great deal of his attention at this period to agricultural chemistry. Pleasing in this study were the unrivaled marls upon which the city of Charleston now stands, the great agricultural worth of which immense beds of fertilizers he was among the first to discover. He also discovered phosphate lime in these marls, and did not neglect his researches in geology and mineralogy. He made valuable and complete investigations into the meteorological conditions and character of soil affecting the growth of cotton. This report was of such importance that at the request of the Sultan of Turkey he was appointed by President Buchanan to teach the Turkish agriculturists the proper method for the successful management of the cotton crop in Asia Minor. He found the arrangements not to his liking when he reached Turkey, and was on the point of returning home when the Turkish government offered him

the independent and lucrative position of mining engineer. For four years he filled this place so satisfactorily to the government that when he left he was honored with the decorations of the empire and was the recipient of munificent presents. His labors were of permanent advantage, and Turkey continues to receive large revenues from the results of his discoveries. The papers published, relative to these discoveries, at once gave him a foremost rank in the scientific world. His discoveries on emery in Asia Minor led to its discovery in America, and have been of great practical value. His paper, "Thermal Waters of Asia Minor," is interesting and important to science. In 1851 he invented the inverted microscope. Upon his return from Europe he was at once elected to the chair of chemistry at the University of Virginia. While there, in company with his assistant, Prof. George J. Brush, he accomplished a much needed work, the revision of the "Chemistry of American Minerals." In 1854 he was married to Sarah Julia Gutherie of Louisville, Ky., daughter of James Gutherie, secretary of the treasury, and from this date adopted that city as his home. He was soon after appointed to the chair of chemistry in the medical department of the University of Louisville, which he occupied until 1866. After resigning this office he took a position as scientific manager of Louisville Gas Works, of which he was afterwards president. He had a laboratory for the manufacture of chemical re-agents and rare pharmaceutical preparations. In this laboratory he was assisted by Dr. Edward R. Squibb. He led a life of comparative leisure in Louisville, devoting his time mainly to scientific researches; being particularly interested in the study of meteorites. His collection was inferior to none in this country and is now in the possession of Harvard University. John P. Morton & Co. of Louisville, published an interesting and valuable work from his pen, "Scientific Researches of Prof. Smith." He made many valuable contributions to scientific literature, his published papers numbering 150; the more important were collected by himself and published under the name of "Mineralogy and Chemistry." The National Academy of Sciences presents every two years the Lawrence Smith medal, valued at $200, to any person making satisfactory and original investigations. Hubert A. Newton was the first to receive this medal, Apr. 18, 1888. Dr. Smith was a prominent member of the Baptist Church of Louisville, which is indebted to him and his wife for many munificent donations. In 1867 he was appointed commissioner to the Paris Exposition, and made an able report on the "Progress and Condition of Several Departments of Industrial Chemistry." He was also appointed commissioner to Vienna in 1873, where he discharged his duties with ability, and as usual returned to his own country covered with honors. He was a man noted for his important original researches, and received the highest honors at home and abroad that science can confer. In his elegant residence at Louisville he had his private laboratory, and up to the time of his death, devoted several hours each day to experiments and research. His remains rest in Cave Hill cemetery, near those of James F. Gutherie, under a unique monument designed by his wife, upon which are recorded some of his numerous honors. Unfortunately he left no heirs. He died at Louisville, Ky., Oct. 12, 1883.

SILLIMAN, Benjamin Douglas, the Nestor of the New York bar, was born at Newport, R. I., Sept. 14, 1805, member of a family that has been prominent in Connecticut for nearly two centuries. His great-grandfather, Ebenezer Silliman, was for twenty-eight years a member of the upper house of the colonial legislature, and was judge of the superior court of the colony for twenty-three successive years. His grandfather, Gen. Gold Selleck Silliman, an able and prominent lawyer, and a man of great influence, was attorney of the crown in Fairfield county, who heartily espoused the patriot cause and served throughout the war, taking an efficient part in the battles of Long Island, Harlem, White Plains, Danbury, and elsewhere. Three days after the battle of Long Island, in which as colonel he commanded a regiment, he was promoted by Gen. Washington to the command of a brigade of five regiments. Gen. Silliman had command of the defences of the Connecticut coast adjoining New York, and by his energy incurred the active resentment of the enemy, who succeeded in capturing him in his house at night and keeping him a prisoner on parole for a year. The father of Benjamin Douglas, who was named after Gen. Silliman, was, like his father and grandfather, a graduate of Yale, and after practicing law with great success at Newport, R. I., removed to New York to engage in business, and (about 1823) settled in Brooklyn, where for some years he was postmaster. The mother of Benjamin Douglas Silliman was a daughter of the Rev. David Ely, D.D., of Huntington, Conn., who was a trustee of Yale College for twenty-one years. Benjamin Douglas Silliman naturally received an academic training, and entered Yale College, where so many of the family on both sides of the house had been graduated, and in which his uncle, Benjamin Silliman, was professor of chemistry and natural history. Among his classmates (in the class of 1824) was Rev. Richard Falley Cleveland, father of President Cleveland. On leaving college Mr. Silliman studied law in New York in the office of Chancellor Kent and his son, William Kent, and was admitted to the bar at the May term of the supreme court in 1829. He immediately opened an office in New York, and with the exception of a visit to Europe in 1848, has steadily practised his profession in that city and in Brooklyn, his place of residence; his practice embracing cases in the state and federal courts, the supreme court of the United States, common law, in equity and admiralty, his clientage including many large and important corporations. The principles on which his professional life is based are well summed up in a paragraph in an address delivered before the graduating class of Columbia Law School in 1867, in which he said: "No man can consistently, with personal honor or professional reputation, misstate a fact or a principle to the court or jury. The man who would cheat a court or a jury would cheat anybody else. Measured by the lowest standard, that of expediency, no lawyer can afford to act meanly or speak untruly." Mr. Silliman was in early life a Whig. In 1838 he was elected to the legislature, and while a member of that body introduced and procured the passage of the bill incorporating Greenwood Cemetery. In 1839 he was sent as a representative of the congressional district, comprising Kings, Richmond and Rockland counties, to the national convention which nominated Gen. Harrison for the presidency. In 1843 he was nominated for congress by the Whigs, and although he led the whole ticket at the polls, was defeated. In 1853 he was nominated for the state senate by the same party, but declined the nomination. He had previously represented Kings county in the state legislature. When the Republican party was formed, Mr. Silliman became connected with it, and on the organization of the Eastern District of New York, was appointed by President Lincoln to the office of U. S. district attorney for that district. In 1872 he was appointed by the governor and senate a member of the commission for revising the state constitution, and took a prominent part in the deliberations, being chairman of one committee and a member of others. In 1873 Mr.

Silliman was nominated by the Republican party as their candidate for the office of attorney-general of the state, and received a flattering support at the polls, although the Republican ticket failed of election. Mr. Silliman has been largely identified with the social, political, and benevolent institutions of his time, and his circle of friends has included the most eminent men in every profession. He was for more than twenty years the president of the Brooklyn Club, was president of the Yale Alumni Association of Long Island, is a trustee of Greenwood Cemetery, a director of the Long Island Historical Society, was president of the New England Society of Brooklyn from its organization until 1886 (when he declined a re-election), for nearly twenty years was one of the managers of the House of Refuge for juvenile delinquents in New York, was a vice-president and one of the founders of the Bar Association of New York City, and a director in other benevolent and literary institutions. He received the degree of LL. D. from Columbia College in 1873 and from Yale College in 1874.

BIDDLE, James, commodore, was born in Philadelphia, Feb. 18, 1783. He was the son of Charles Biddle, of Philadelphia. After obtaining a preparatory education, he passed through the course of study at the University of Pennsylvania. Here he is said to have made great progress in his studies, and especially to have acquired a taste for literature, which remained with him, and was fostered during his whole life. On leaving the university, young Biddle and his brother Edward obtained midshipmen's warrants, and were attached to the frigate President, which was at that time fitting out at New York, and which sailed for the West Indies in September, 1800. This voyage was fatal to young Edward Biddle, who died at sea of a fever, after a short illness. On the return of the ship to the United States, the trouble with France being over, and the navy being reduced to a small peace footing, James Biddle was fortunate enough to be retained as a midshipman. Early in 1802 he sailed on board the frigate Constellation, Capt. Murray, for the Mediterranean, with a squadron engaged in the protection of American vessels against Tripolitan cruisers. The Constellation returned home in the spring of 1803, and Biddle was transferred to the frigate Philadelphia, Capt. Bainbridge, which sailed for the Mediterranean in July of that year. Here she met with an unfortunate disaster which ended her career; on Oct. 31, 1803, off the coast of Tripoli she struck upon a rock not laid down on any charts extant, and unknown to any American vessels which had previously frequented that coast; every effort to float her being ineffectual, the colors of the Philadelphia were hauled down, and the first lieutenant, accompanied by midshipman Biddle, was dispatched to inform the enemy's gunboat of their surrender. The officers and crew were carried in shore, and consigned to prison. After being detained for about nineteen months, peace with Tripoli was signed, and in September, 1805, Capt. Bainbridge and Biddle, who had not separated after the loss of the frigate, returned together to Philadelphia. Biddle was now promoted to a lieutenancy, and, after remaining home for a few weeks, was ordered to the command of a gunboat, on board of which he cruised for privateers on the southern coast; he also assisted in making a survey of the harbor of Beaufort, S. C. In 1807, being on furlough, he was allowed to make a voyage to China, as first officer of a merchant ship. On his return he was detailed to the Delaware flotilla, employed in enforcing the embargo. In 1809 he was second lieutenant of the President, Capt. Bainbridge, and the following year took charge of the Syren, sloop-of-war; later he joined the Constitution, Capt. Hull, and after that was on the President again for a time. In the winter of 1811 Lieut. Biddle was bearer of dispatches from the U. S. government to the American minister to France, and remained in Paris

nearly four months. Soon after his return war broke out between the United States and Great Britain, and, after some delay, he was appointed first lieutenant of the sloop-of-war Wasp. This vessel, on Oct. 18, 1812, captured the British sloop-of-war Frolic, which was taken charge of by Lieut. Biddle, but both vessels were afterward captured by a British seventy-four. Lieut. Biddle was taken, with the other officers and men of the Wasp, to Bermuda, where they were detained for a short time, and then released. On returning to the United States, Biddle was promoted to the rank of master-commandant and put in command of the Hornet. In January, 1815, the Hornet sailed for Tristan d'Acunha, and on the voyage attacked and captured the British brig Penguin, armed with sixteen 32-pound carronades, two long 12's, a 12-pound carronade on her topgallant forecastle and swivels. She had 132 men. The Penguin was completely riddled with shot, and her masts so crippled as to be incapable of repair or strengthening, and she was accordingly scuttled. In this action Biddle was severely wounded. Sailing for the Cape of Good Hope, the Hornet encountered a British line-of-battle ship, and was chased, being obliged to throw over shot and heavy spars, and cut away the sheet anchor and cable to lighten the ship. Finally they were obliged to throw over all their guns but one long gun, nearly all the shot and spare spars, while running at their best speed under fire all the time. The Hornet eventually succeeded in getting away, and sailed for San Salvador to refit, where Commandant Biddle heard that peace had been concluded. During his absence, he was promoted to the rank of post-captain, and on his arrival home a public dinner was given to him by the citizens of New York, and a service of plate by those of Philadelphia. Capt. Biddle continued on active duty after the close of the war; in 1817 he was sent by the government on the Ontario, sloop-of-war, to the Columbia river to take possession of Oregon territory. In 1822 he commanded the Macedonian on the West India station. From 1826-32 Com. Biddle was cruising either on the South American station or in the Mediterranean. From 1838-42 he was in charge of the naval asylum near Philadelphia. He negotiated the first treaty between the United States and China, in 1845, being at the time flag-officer of the East India squa-

dron. During the Mexican war he commanded on the Pacific coast. Com. Biddle died in Philadelphia, Oct. 1, 1848.

ALLEN, David Oliver, missionary, was born at Barre, Mass., Jan. 6, 1800. He received his education at Amherst College, from which he was graduated in 1823, and after teaching a short term at Lawrence Academy he entered Andover Theological Seminary, but left in 1827, to go as a missionary to India. He established schools in the province of Bombay, and superintended a translation of the Scriptures into the Mahratta language. After twenty-five years of zealous service his health broke down, and he returned to this country in 1853. He subsequently wrote a valuable history of India. He died in Lowell, Mass., July 17, 1863.

DORR, Julia Caroline Ripley, poet, was born in Charleston, S. C., Feb. 13, 1825, daughter of William Young and Zulma de Lacy Thomas Ripley. Her mother was the daughter of French refugees, who fled from San Domingo during the insurrection of the slaves near the close of the eighteenth century. She died when her daughter was an infant. The father was a prosperous merchant of Charleston, S. C., a native of Vermont, to which state he returned with his daughter in 1830, and engaged in developing the Rutland marble quarries, giving his daughter every advantage that a refined home and surroundings of culture and refinement afforded. Her poetic instinct manifested itself when she was a mere child, but she never saw her poems in print until she became a grown woman. In 1847 she was married to Seneca M. Dorr, a native of New York, and a man of wide culture and literary tastes. Mr. Dorr sent one of her poems to the "Union Magazine" without her knowledge, and it was accepted and published much to her surprise. In 1848 she won a $100-prize, offered by "Sartain's Magazine," for a short story entitled "Isabel Leslie," her first published prose tale. In 1857 Mr. and Mrs. Dorr took up their residence in Rutland, Vt., and from that time her pen was constantly busy. "Farmingdale," published under the *nom de plume* of "Caroline Thomas;" "Lanmere;" "Sibyl Huntington;" "Poems;" "Expiation;" "Friar Anselmo, and other Poems;" "The Legend of the Baboushka;" "Daybreak, an Easter Poem;" "Bermuda, an Idyl of the Summer Islands;" "Afternoon Songs;" and "Letters to Alice," and "Letters to Philip," followed each other at intervals between 1854 and 1885. Her latest book is a so-called "complete edition" of her poems, published by Chas. Scribner's Sons (1892). Her husband died in 1884, and the next year she became the leader of a band of women who founded the Rutland Free

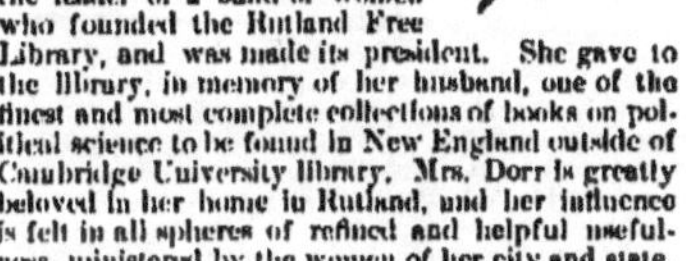

Library, and was made its president. She gave to the library, in memory of her husband, one of the finest and most complete collections of books on political science to be found in New England outside of Cambridge University library. Mrs. Dorr is greatly beloved in her home in Rutland, and her influence is felt in all spheres of refined and helpful usefulness, ministered by the women of her city and state.

AIKEN, John, was born in Vermont in 1797. He was an influential citizen of Massachusetts, a member of the governor's council from 1844 to 1851, a trustee of the Andover Theological Seminary, and for fifteen years one of the board of commissioners for foreign missions. He died Feb. 11, 1867.

EGGLESTON, Edward, clergyman and author, was born at Vevay, Ind., Dec. 10, 1837. His father, a Virginian, was a lawyer of prominence and scholarly tastes, who died when Edward, the eldest of four children, was nine years old. His mother was descended from an old Kentucky family that gave prominent ministers to the Baptist church. Edward inherited a delicate constitution, and suffered much during his early years. Until he was ten years of age he had the reputation of being a dull boy, but he really had, in all, not more than two years of schooling, and gained his education mainly from reading. When he was seventeen years of age he attended Amelia Academy in Virginia, but his education was chiefly obtained at home, where he acquired a knowledge of several languages, and an intimate acquaintance with the best French and English literature. At school he was recognized as captain by all his schoolmates, and his word was law, although physically the inferior of most of the boys, but he asked no odds of any one, and took his knocks manfully. His companions looked up to him, recognizing his superior knowledge and ability, and admired him on account of his being perfectly just, and absolutely without fear or favor. In the vain hope of finding some occupation suitable to his health, his childhood was passed in a continual change from school to farm, from farm to store, and back again to school. He became a member of the Methodist church when eleven years old, and perhaps the strict austerity and pietism which he practiced helped to undermine his health. In 1856, when for the twentieth time his life was despaired of, he went to Minnesota, dividing his time between farming, surveying, and photography. Upon his return, when but nineteen years of age, he entered the Methodist ministry, beginning as a circuit-rider over a four weeks' circuit, with his usual persistency. Six months of this work forced him to seek health again in Minnesota, where he held pastorates at St. Paul, Stillwater, Wynona, and St. Peter's. While pastor of a church at St. Peter's he married a lady to whose wisdom and excellence he attributed much of his later usefulness. At the age of twenty-four he was pastor of the most prominent church of his denomination in the state of Minnesota. His health, however, repeatedly broke down, and he was forced three times to give up his preaching and follow secular pursuits, to support his family, until he reluctantly abandoned the ministry. He early evinced a taste for literature, and in 1866 removed to Evanston, Ill., where he became associate editor of the "Little Corporal," of Chicago, to which he had already contributed a series of "Round Table Stories." A few months later he became editor-in-chief of the "National Sunday-School Teacher," of that city. The paper was then in its infancy, but under his able management its circulation increased from 5,000 to 35,000. During this time he was a favorite speaker at Sunday-school conventions, and gained a wide reputation as a successful manager of Sunday-school Institutes, for which he wrote several practical works, notably "The Sunday-school Manual," and "Sunday-school Conventions and Institutes." At this period he wrote many stories for children, which were published in the magazines and reprinted in book form in 1870, under the title of "The Book of Queer Stories." For several years, under the name of "Pen-holder," he was the regular western correspondent of the New York "Independent," and in May, 1870, he was called to New York, to assume the literary editorship of the "Independent," and at the close of the year, upon the retirement of Theodore Tilton, was made superintending editor. In July following he resigned, to take editorial charge of "Hearth and Home," and through his able management, and introduction of popular stories, this periodical has attained its present wide-spread popularity. His "Hoosier Schoolmaster" was the first of the stories that brought the paper prominently into notice. This has been translated into French and Danish, and sells as readily at the present time as it did twenty years ago. It had a circulation of over 20,000 the first year of its publication. "Huldah the Help," which appeared in the second number of "Scribner's Magazine," was his first story for grown people. In 1872, Mr. Eggleston resigned his editorship, and, removing to Brooklyn, devoted himself solely to literary labor. He accepted a pastorate over the "Church of Christian Endeavor," an independent organization, which effected much good among the masses. He retained this position until 1879, when he was forced to resign from failing health, and return to literature. He retired to Lake George, where he built a beautiful house called "Owl's Nest," where he has written most of his books. His works comprise, in addition to those already mentioned, "The End of the World," "The Mystery of Metropolisville," "The Circuit-Rider," "Christ in Literature," "Christ in Art," "Roxy," "The Graysons," and a "History of the United States." With his daughter, Mrs. Lillie Seelye, he published "Famous American Indians," in five volumes. The "Nation" says: "Mr. Eggleston's stories have held, from the beginning, a great popularity with a large circle of readers, and it has been in many ways well deserved."

ABBEY, Edwin Austin, artist, was born in Philadelphia, Pa., in 1852. He was educated at the Pennsylvania Academy. He showed an early aptitude for drawing, and by the time he was twenty years old had become so skilful a draughtsman that he was taken into the employ of the publishing firm of Harper & Bros., New York city, as an illustrator of Harper's Weekly." Soon after he was transferred to "Harper's Magazine," to which he continues a frequent contributor. He has attracted considerable attention as a water-colorist by such pictures as "The Widower" (1883), and "Reading the Bible" (1884); but he is best known as an illustrator in black and white. English life in the eighteenth century furnishes him with his favorite themes, and to the end of interpreting them vividly and truly in all their details, he has made his home in England since 1883. His illustrations of Herrick's poems, and of Goldsmith's comedy, "She Stoops to Conquer," are particularly fine. Apropos of the latter, Henry James

writes: "Mr. Abbey has evidently the tenderest affection for just the old house and the old things, the old faces and voices, the whole irrevocable human scene, which the genial hand of Goldsmith has passed over to him, and there is no inquiry about them that he is not in a position to answer. He is intimate with the buttons of coats and the buckles of shoes; he knows not only exactly what his people wore, but exactly how they wore it, and how they felt when they had it on. . . . . , His drawing is the drawing of direct, immediate, solicitous study of the particular case, without tricks or affectations or any sort of cheap subterfuge, and nothing can exceed the charm of its delicacy, accuracy, and elegance, its variety and freedom, and clear, frank solution of difficulties." Mr. Abbey's greatest fame, however, is as an illustrator of Shakespeare, in which capacity he has produced for "Harper's Magazine" pen-and-ink drawings which are absolutely inimitable. Mr. Abbey has been elected to membership in the New York Water-Color Society, and the London Institute of Water-Colors.

SCOLLARD, Clinton, poet and educator, was born at Clinton, Oneida co., N. Y., Sept. 18, 1860. His father and grandfather were both natives of New York; the former has been a practising physician for over forty years. Young Scollard, after completing his preparation for college, entered Hamilton, from which he was graduated in 1881 with the degree of A.B., and A.M. in 1884. In the latter year he went to Cambridge, Mass., to continue his literary studies, and subsequently made four trips to Europe, extending his travels to Egypt, Greece, and the Holy Land. Mr. Scollard passed the autumn of 1887 at Cambridge, Eng., attending lectures at the University. He was professor of rhetoric and elocution in Hamilton College, 1891-93, and was appointed to the chair of English literature in 1893. He has published six volumes of poems, namely: "Pictures in Song," "With Reed and Lyre," "Old and New World Lyrics," "Giovio and Guilia," "Songs of Sunrise Lands," and "The Hills of Song;" also two volumes of travel sketches in prose, viz., "Under Summer Skies," and "On Sunny Shores."

HAWKS, Cicero Stephen, first Protestant Episcopal bishop of Missouri, and forty-fourth in succession from Bishop Seabury, was born in New-Berne, N. C. May 26, 1812. He was graduated from the University of North Carolina in 1830, and began the study of law, which was soon abandoned for that of divinity. He was ordained deacon Dec. 8, 1834, and priest July 24, 1836, by Bishop B. T. Onderdonk, and became rector of Trinity Church, Saugerties, N. Y. In 1837 he was rector of Trinity Church, Buffalo, N. Y., and in 1843 rector of Christ Church, St. Louis, Mo., and held this position until Feb. 1, 1854. In 1844 he was elected bishop, and was consecrated Oct. 20, 1844. The churches in the diocese were in debt, and the distances to be traveled were very great, and later, the growth of the diocese was checked by the civil war; these, and other obstacles, requiring incessant mental and physical toil on the part of Bishop Hawks. During the cholera epidemic of 1849 he was conspicuous in caring for the afflicted, and his services were recognized by the gifts of a purse from Christ Church and a residence from the citizens of St. Louis. He published "Friday Christian; or, the First Born of Pitcairn Island," and wrote for various periodicals. He died in St. Louis, April 19, 1868.

ROBERTSON, Charles Franklin, second Protestant Episcopal bishop of Missouri, was born in New York city, March 2, 1835. A short interval of attempt at commercial life closed with definite inclinations toward the ministry, and after a course at Yale, he completed his preparation for clerical duty in 1859, at the General Theological Seminary of the Episcopal Church. He was ordained deacon in the Church of the Transfiguration by Bishop Potter in 1862. A six years' pastorate followed at St. Mark's Church, Malone, N. Y. After the removal of a few days to a parish in Batavia, he learned of his election as second bishop of Missouri by the diocesan convention. He was consecrated in Grace Church, New York city, Oct. 25, 1868. Feelings yet embittered by the war, and a section disorganized by its ravages, were the conditions awaiting Dr. Robertson's influence. At this time there were only twenty clergymen in the diocese, and but five parishes in St. Louis. He was then thirty-three years old, and possessed youth, fine health, and energetic zeal. Individual in his methods, the emerging of the diocese out of poverty and debt into vigorous growth is as much due to his executive ability as to the prosperous development of the state. The number of clergymen pertaining to the diocese increased to sixty-two, and nine additional parishes were founded before his death. He received the degree of S.T.D. from Columbia College in 1868; its equivalent, that of D.D., from the University of the South, in 1883; and LL.D. the same year from the University of Missouri. Research in points of doubt among American records often filled his leisure hours, and he stood among the first members of the Missouri Historical Society through his cultivation and efficiency. His active interests extended beyond those of clerical labor; to the welfare of Missouri and the cause of temperance he gave his earnest and practical thought. Bishop Robertson published a number of historical papers. He died in St. Louis, May 1, 1886.

TUTTLE, Daniel Sylvester, third Protestant Episcopal bishop of the diocese of Missouri, and eighty-fourth in succession in the American Episcopate, was born at Windham, Greene co., N. Y., Jan. 26, 1837. He was the son of Daniel Bliss Tuttle, born in 1797, whose father, Charles, came from Wallingford, Conn. His mother's maiden name was Abigail Clark Stimson. The rector of the Episcopal Church at Wallingford encouraged him in his studies, helped him prepare to enter Delaware Academy, at Delphi, and influenced him in the choice of a profession. In 1853 he entered Columbia College, and in 1857 was graduated; entered the General Theological Seminary, and, while pursuing his studies, was private tutor in the family of Bishop Horatio Potter. In June, 1862, Mr. Tuttle was ordained deacon, and from 1863 to 1867 labored at Morris, Otsego co., N. Y., first as assistant, and then as rector, being ordained priest in 1863. In 1866, although not yet thirty years old, he was elected missionary bishop of Montana, with jurisdiction in Montana and Idaho. He was consecrated in Trinity Chapel, New York, May 1, 1867, and in two months' time was in Utah, where but three communicants of the Episcopal church were to be found. Bishop Tuttle soon gathered into the schools he established in Utah, numbers of children of Mormon parents, and prosecuting his work in Idaho and Montana, spent a year at Virginia City and another at Helena, where he commended himself to the miners by his strength and fearlessness. In 1868 he declined an election to the diocese of Missouri, believing that he was needed more on the frontier. In September, 1869, he made his home in Salt Lake City, and initiated a quiet warfare against Mormon influences. In 1880 Montana was set off as a separate diocese, at his suggestion, and he remained bishop of Utah, with jurisdiction over Idaho. In 1884, rather than miss his appointments in the mining camps of Idaho, he declined the honor of representing Columbia College at the tercentenary of the University of Edinburgh. On the death of Bishop Robertson, of Missouri, Bishop Tuttle was elected his successor, and since 1887 has lived in St. Louis. His degree of D.D. was conferred by Columbia College in 1866.

FENNELL, James, tragedian, was born in London, Dec. 11, 1766, and made his début as an actor in Edinburgh in 1787. Soon after he was seen as Othello at the Convent Garden Theatre, London. He was a vigorous and versatile actor, and soon won an eminent position in his profession. He came to the United States in 1797, making his American début in Annapolis, Md., and for a time disputed with Cooper the supremacy in tragic rôles on this side of the sea. Wine and women in the end wrought his ruin. He retired from the stage in 1814, and died an imbecile in Philadelphia in June, 1816. An "Apology" for his life, a curious book, was published some time before his death.

AUGUSTUS, John, philanthropist, was born in Boston, Mass., about 1785. He was a shoemaker in moderate circumstances, but devoted a large part of his time and means to reclaiming and befriending the criminal and outcast classes. It was his custom to visit the Boston police-courts every morning, and to become bail for those charged with petty crimes whom he thought capable of reformation; and such was his judgment of character that he was very seldom mistaken. This he did for many years, and the amount of good he accomplished is beyond computation. He was accustomed to say that "the blessing of the friendless is the only coin that is current in the better country." He died in Boston, penniless, but greatly respected and beloved, June 21, 1859.

COUDERT, Frederic René, lawyer, was born in the city of New York in 1832, the son of Charles Coudert, who was born in Bordeaux, France, 1795, and after an adventurous career in the service of the Bonapartes, escaped to America in 1824, where he settled for the remainder of his life. He was an officer in the Guard of Honor attached to the old Imperial Guard of Napoleon I., was wounded in the famous three days' battle at Leipsic, participated in the battles of Montereau and Montmirial, and served actively in the desperate engagements fought prior to the entry of the allies into Paris. After the Restoration, through the influence of La Fayette, he became involved in a conspiracy to place the Duke of Reichstadt, Napoleon II., on the throne of France. The conspiracy failed, he was tried, and condemned to be shot, but through some informality in the trial the execution was postponed, and after many months spent in prison, he escaped to England. Two years afterward he returned to France in disguise, which was discovered, but through the assistance of influential friends he escaped to the United States. He was awarded two decorations for his devotion to the cause of the Bonapartes; one being the Legion of Honor, and the other a medal presented by the Second Empire for services rendered to the First. This was the medal which Napoleon I., when dying at St. Helena, desired to have presented to the companions of his glory, and which, in accordance with his wishes, was awarded by Louis Napoleon to every surviving officer and soldier of the First Empire. Louis and Joseph Bonaparte were entertained at his house during their visit to America. Frederic René Coudert received his early education at his father's school in New York city, and at the age of fourteen entered Columbia College, graduating with the highest honors in the class of 1850, his ad-

dress on that occasion attracting marked attention from the press. At the age of twenty-one (1853) he was admitted to the New York bar, having in the meantime busied himself with newspaper work, teaching, and translations. His brothers, Louis and Charles Coudert, Jr., soon joined him in the practice of law, and together they formed the firm of Coudert Brothers, which is one of the oldest and largest law firms in New York, and already by 1891 numbered as its clients several of the governments of Europe. Of late years there have been but few cases involving nice questions of law in which the advice of Mr. Coudert has not been sought. His success as a jury lawyer has been pronounced; he has the happy faculty of quickly recovering himself in a trial if the facts seem to change or the evidence go against him, and he at once leads the jury to believe that that particular adverse evidence was exactly what he had contemplated as a possibility. As a mark of his fairness, courtesy, and popularity, he was selected by his fellow-members of the bar to be their spokesman in opposition to the civil code, which was so persistently urged upon the legislature. He was also selected to write the memorial of Charles O'Conor, and again honored by being elected president of the Bar Association of New York city, and represented the Chamber of Commerce at the International Congress at Antwerp for the framing of international rules of general average. As a speaker he commands the closest attention of his professional brethren; his style is clear, and his ready wit enlivens the most tedious subjects, so that he has become famous as an orator. As he has also the power of appealing to the judgment and convincing the intellect, he is in great demand as a speaker, and it would be impossible to give a complete list of his orations and after-dinner speeches. One of the most notable was his address at the Centennial celebration at Columbia College, 1887. He lectures at times for charitable purposes, and has treated as his platform subjects: "Edmund Burke," "Lying as a Fine Art," "Manners and Morals," "The Church and the Bar," "Young Men in Politics," "The Protection of Foreign Trade-Marks," etc., etc. Among his notable public addresses are those on the arrival of Bartholdi's statue of Liberty and the inauguration of the statues of La Fayette and Bolivar. He has written largely for the leading periodicals upon subjects outside of his profession. He has taken an active part in the political work of the Democratic party, and during the Tilden and Hayes campaign, his services were in constant requisition. After the election he was appointed by the Democratic committee to go to New Orleans, La., and assist in securing a fair count of the vote in that state. He was a strong political supporter of Samuel Tilden, and in 1879 an ardent supporter of Gov. Robinson. During that campaign he made an eloquent speech in favor of "Democratic Union," and was the only speaker who claimed the rapt attention of the noisy crowd. He supported Mayor Grace in both his campaigns, and took a prominent part in the election of Mr. Cleveland in 1884; was president of the Lawyers' Campaign Club, and made many speeches in favor of the candidate. He has himself positively refused political preferment, and has several times declined nominations which signified election to the bench of the supreme court, and in 1888 refused an appointment to the bench of the court of appeals. Aside from this, he has held many positions of trust and honor. In 1877 he was appointed delegate to represent the interests of American commerce at the International Congress on the Law of Nations, held at Antwerp. In 1882 he attended another session of that congress held in Liverpool, and recently represented the United States as one of its counsel before the international tribunal appointed to determine the Behring Sea controversy. For ten years he was president of the French Benevolent Society; was the first president of the United States Catholic Historical Society, and held the office several terms; was president of the Young Men's Democratic Club of New York city; and for many years president of the Columbia College Alumni Association; for three years he was government director of the Union Pacific Railroad; for several years vice-president and president of the Manhattan Club; for a number of years trustee of Seton Hall College, New Jersey; trustee of Columbia and Barnard Colleges; member of the visiting committee of Harvard College; and director in numerous social and charitable organizations. He was awarded the degree of LL.D. from Seton Hall College in 1880, from Fordham College in 1884, and the degree of J.U.D. from Columbia College in 1887, having been chosen by his alma mater to deliver the oration at the celebration of the one hundredth anniversary of the establishment. From the French government he received the cross of the Legion of Honor, and likewise received similar honors from the governments of Italy and Bolivia. He is a man who has avoided rather than sought public functions, but has been sought in spite of himself. Of courteous, kindly manners and heart, his life has ever been a benefit to those with whom he was connected.

DUFF, Mary Ann Dyke, actress, was born in London, Eng., in 1794. When scarcely fifteen years old she was known far and wide as one of the most beautiful girls of the neighborhood. Owing to the poverty of her parents, she adopted the stage as a profession, and she and her two sisters became dancers

at the Dublin Theatre, where their grace and beauty attracted immediate attention. Whenever the Dyke sisters appeared, the theatre would be thronged. At a charitable performance given at Kilkenny in 1809, the poet, Tom Moore, was presented to Mary Dyke, and he immediately fell passionately in love with her. It is said that she was his first sweetheart, and a number of his lyrics and songs refer to this beautiful Mary. After a while he poured forth his great love for her, but she did not reciprocate his affection, and rejected him. It was this that led Moore to pen his celebrated love-song, beginning:

"Mary, I believed thee true,
And I was blessed in thus believing."

He afterwards transferred his affections to Mary's sister, Elizabeth, whom he wedded, and it was then revealed that Mary's rejection of him was due to her love for one John R. Duff, an actor of the Dublin Theatre, whom she shortly afterwards married. They immediately sailed for America, and on Dec. 31, 1810, she made her first appearance in Boston, at what was then the Federal Street Theatre, in the rôle of Juliet to her husband's Romeo. She did not create a very marked impression as an actress, but her marvelous beauty became the talk of the town. Not being satisfied to be accepted merely as a beauty, she studied and worked hard to gain applause for her art, until her shortcomings were overcome. She next appeared as Lady Anne to the "Richard III." of the renowned George Frederick Cooke, and her success was more marked. It was not, however, until February, 1818, that she really stamped herself as a great actress. At that time she appeared again as Juliet, and was at once pronounced an actress of the first magnitude. She played much in Philadelphia, Boston, and New York, scoring the most brilliant and lasting triumphs. In the latter part of 1828 she returned to London, and acted with Macready at Drury Lane Theatre; but the next year she again came to America. In 1831 Mr. Duff died, leaving his wife with ten children, almost penniless. These were hard times for her, but she continued on the stage until 1836, when she married John G. Sevin (or Seaver), and two years later renounced her profession and went to New Orleans to live. Finding herself unhappily married, she passed her days in deepest retirement. Suddenly, in 1854, she disappeared from New Orleans with her husband and children, and nothing was ever heard of her again during her life. She spent the remainder of her days at the home of her youngest daughter in New York city, a sad, subdued, and broken-spirited old lady. It was not until twenty years after that the world learned the secret of her later life and death, and then it was discovered that the greatest actress of her day was buried with her daughter in an unknown grave in Greenwood cemetery, beneath a small white marble stone bearing the simple inscription:

Mother
and
Grandmother.

By Junius Brutus Booth, Mrs. Duff was called "the greatest actress in the world." John Gilbert said: "Without exception, she was the most exquisite tragic actress he ever saw. Her beauty was worshiped. She swayed audiences as never did woman before. Her tenderness touched hearts, her grace enthralled them, and her career was as brilliant as her life was stainless. She died in New York, Sept. 5, 1857.

DUTTON, Edward P., publisher, was born at Keene, N. H., Jan. 4, 1831. He removed with his parents to Boston in 1833, was educated in the public schools of that city, and, after some four years at the Latin school, entered his father's store to learn the routine of jobbing dry goods. His health soon broke down, and he was directed to seek restoration in Southern Italy. He went in a sailing-vessel to Genoa, and after a sojourn of six months, returned home by the way of Switzerland and France completely cured. On his return in the fall of 1852 he engaged in the publishing and selling of books under the firm name of Ide & Dutton, Boston, Mass. In the spring of 1858 Mr. Dutton bought out the interest of Mr. Ide, and continued the business as E. P. Dutton & Co. In 1864 he bought out the stock and good-will of the retail business of the publishing house of Ticknor & Fields, historically known as the Old Corner Book-store, and admitted as a partner Charles A. Clapp, at the time in the employ of that firm. About 1866 they bought the business of the General Protestant Episcopal Sunday-School Union and Church Book Society of New York city, and made this business a branch of the Boston house. In 1869 they sold out the Boston store, and removed to New York city, taking up with their other business the New York business of J. R. Osgood & Co., Boston. They were located at 713 Broadway from

1869–82, when they removed to Twenty-third street with the current of trade, Mr. Dutton and Charles A. Clapp being the partners of the firm. They made a specialty of theological and children's books, and the publications connected with the Protestant Episcopal church. All the works of Phillips Brooks and Henry Codman Potter have the imprint of the house, as have those of many of the other eminent Episcopal divines, published during the last forty years. They became the American agents for the color work done by Ernest Nister in Nuremberg, Germany, and the illustrated books which bear the imprint of E. P. Dutton & Co. are examples of the artistic excellence of that work. Mr. Dutton was married in 1856 to a daughter of Jacob Sleeper of Boston, Mass.

CARTWRIGHT, Peter, clergyman, was born in Amherst county, Va., Sept. 1, 1785, of very poor parents. His father served as a patriot soldier in the war of the American revolution. Shortly after the colonies gained their independence, the family removed to Kentucky. The wilderness through which they passed was filled with hostile Indians, and there were 200 families banded together, with a hundred young men, well armed, as a guard upon their journey. Their first place of abode was Lancaster, Lincoln co. His mother being a member of the Methodist Episcopal church, sought and obtained acquaintance there with two travelling Methodist ministers. In 1793 the family removed again, this time to Logan county in the southern part of the state. The father, though not a religious man, was not opposed to religion, and permitted Methodist preachers to use his cabin for holding services. The mother connected herself with a Methodist church some miles distant from their home, in a region known as Rogue's Harbor. Refugees from almost all parts of the Union were gathered here, who had fled from the scenes of their law-breaking to escape merited punishment. Murderers, horse-thieves, highway robbers, and counterfeiters abounded; indeed, formed the majority of the inhabitants. There was no newspaper printed south of the Green river, no mill short of forty miles, no school worth the name. Sunday was set apart for hunting, fishing, horse-racing, card-playing, and dancing. In all these young Cartwright indulged to his heart's content, unrestrained by his father, but to the grief and against the remonstrances of his mother. A race-horse and a pack of cards, given him by his father, nearly formed his ruin. He was sent at one time to school, but his education was limited. When he was sixteen years old he began to reflect on the life he was leading, and by the prayers and agency of his mother, his reflections were continued and deepened. On a given day in the horse-lot, in great agony of mind, and trying to pray, he imagined that he heard a voice from heaven saying, "Peter, look above!" Shortly after (1801) at the Lane Bridge camp-meeting, among weeping multitudes, an impression was made upon his mind as though a voice said: "Thy sins are all forgiven thee," and he was thence onward at peace with God. Some time before this he had returned the race-horse to his father, and brought his cards to his mother to be burned. Straightway he joined the Methodist church, and began to speak and exhort in local meetings. His autobiography records the fact that from the year 1801 extensive religious movements prevailed through almost all inhabited parts of the western country, for some years, and in them the Methodist camp-meeting system had its origin. Cartwright soon came to be known in these meetings as the "Kentucky Boy." His only theological training appears to have been derived from the diligent study of the Bible and habitual prayer, along with the experience derived from his continuous labor in religious gatherings. In May, 1802, he received a certificate from the preacher-in-charge that he was permitted to exercise his gifts as an exhorter in the Methodist Episcopal church, "so long as his practice is agreeable to the Gospel." The family removed again, in 1802, to Lewiston county, Ky. When he applied to the presiding elder for letters of recommendation to the local Methodist Episcopal church in the latter region, he found that the paper which he had received authorized him to travel through all the region to which he was going to hold meetings and organize classes, in a word, to form a new Methodist circuit, and upon his doings he was to report at the Fourth Quarterly Meeting of the Red River circuit. This was done in the fall of 1803, the new sphere of influence being named Livingston circuit. In October of that year he threw himself fully

into the ranks of circuit preachers, the discipline of the church, at that time, allowing a single man $80 per annum, "and in nine cases out of ten he could not get half that amount." At the conference in October, 1804, he was sent as the junior preacher to the Salt River and Shelbyville circuits. In 1805–06 he was on the Scioto (Ohio) circuit, state and district. At the conference in 1806 he was ordained a deacon by Bishop Asbury, and Oct. 4, 1808, was made an elder by Bishop McKendree. On Aug. 18, 1808, he married Frances Gaines, upon her nineteenth birthday. Circuit-riding and preaching at stated quarterly and camp-meetings in Kentucky and Tennessee now filled his life. He was made presiding elder in the fall of 1812 by Bishop Asbury at the Tennessee conference. In the fall of 1813 he was elected delegate to the second general conference of the church in America, to be held at Baltimore, Md., in 1816, and from that time he was always present at the quadrennial gatherings of the denomination in the United States, with one exception, when he was absent solely because of affliction in his family. In fifty consecutive years he failed in attendance only at a single annual conference, and then for a kindred reason. His occupancy of the presiding eldership in his church covered more than fifty years, and during that period the Methodist Episcopal church in the country rose in numbers from 72,784 to 1,756,000 members. Determining to remove from Kentucky in 1823, he set out to explore the state of Illinois for a home, and on Nov. 15, 1824, reached Pleasant Plains in that state with his family. This was ever afterward his place of residence. His reasons for the removal were characteristic, and were characteristically expressed: "First, I would get rid of the evil of slavery. Second, I could raise my children where work was not thought a degradation. Third, I believed I could better my temporal circumstances, and procure lands for my children as they grew up. Fourth, I could carry the Gospel to destitute souls." He had been transferred to the Illinois conference, and appointed to travel the Sangamon (Ill.) circuit. He had charge of other circuits in the state for the remainder of his life. During his residence in Illinois he was twice chosen a representative to the state legislature. In the Illinois conference of 1832 he was placed on the superannuated list for a year, but finding at the expiration of a few hours that there was no one to take the presiding eldership of a new district, at his own suggestion the vote by which he was put upon the superannuated list was reconsidered, and despite his years of toil and the infirmities incident to his exposures, he was given the new appointment, and discharged its arduous duties most successfully. In the General Conference of 1844 at New York city, he resisted to the utmost of his ability the division of the denomination into the Methodist Church North and the Methodist Church South, and he also struggled hard against those tendencies in the church by which the merely itinerant character of its clergy was largely laid aside for the more stable and fixed tenure of local pastorates. He was known, moreover, for many years as an inflexible opponent of slavery, and a champion of the cause of African colonization from the United States. By common consent, Peter Cartwright is recognized as a notable type of the pioneer or backwoods preacher of the Christian communion to which he belonged. Beyond that, his work for the extension of that denomination was far-reaching, and his influence in its councils was not small. His personal traits were of the most positive nature. Physically, mentally, and morally he was a man in the best sense of the word. Few books of a similar genius are of more significance and value than his "Autobiography" (New York, 1856). Rev. Dr. Abel Stevens's writings upon Methodism may also be consulted concerning him, and "The Backwoods Preacher" (London, 1869). His death took place at Pleasant Plains, Ill., Sept. 25, 1872.

AUSTIN, Jane Goodwin, author, was born in Worcester, Mass., Feb. 25, 1831. Two years later her widowed mother removed to Boston, where the

subject of this sketch was educated in private schools. Her father, Isaac Goodwin, Esq., was not only a lawyer and author of legal manuals, but also a well-known antiquarian, and an authority upon Pilgrim history. Her mother was a highly educated woman, well known in later life as a song maker. Both parents were born and bred in Plymouth as all their progenitors had been, and in emigrating from the old colony they carried their family records and traditions with them, not forgetting the romantic story of Dr. Francis Le Baron, the "Nameless Nobleman," from whom both Mr. and Mrs. Goodwin were descended. These stories and associations naturally seized upon the mind of a rather precocious child, and as soon as Jane could wield a pen, she began to write stories of the Pilgrims and of the Le Barons for her own amusement. As the years went on, many of these and other stories were published under various *nom de plume*, and a literary career seemed already opening before the young girl, when at the age of seventeen she was married to Loring Henry Austin of Boston, himself a descendant of a well-known family of patriots in the revolutionary war. It was not for some thirteen years after her marriage that Mrs. Austin resumed her pen, but it was then with energy and success. For many years she was a contributor to leading magazines of the country, and her work is to be found scattered through the volumes of the "Atlantic," "Harper's Monthly," "Putnam's Magazine," "Emerson's Magazine," the "Galaxy,"—that brilliant but ephemeral constellation—and other periodicals of less permanent fame. Her last volume, called "David Alden's Daughter and Other Stories," is a collection from these sources, and others may yet be compiled. It was in the "Galaxy" that "Cipher," Mrs. Austin's first work appeared and met with much approval. It was soon followed by "The Shadow of Moloch Mountain," and then came "Dora Darling" and

"Outpost," stories of the civil war, and "Moonfolk," a book for children. After this, as has been the case with many authors, the early methods seemed inadequate; there was a period of inaction and of study, and as its result we have "Nantucket Scraps," an exhaustive account of that unique little island; "Mrs. Beauchamp Brown" in the No Name Series, and "The Desmond Hundred" in the Round Robin Series. Finally, as the result of the author's full maturity of power, came the "Pilgrim Books," which have made the name of Jane G. Austin so widely known. The proper sequence of these volumes is, "Standish of Standish," "Betty Alden," "A Nameless Nobleman," and "David Alden's Daughter and Other Stories." Mrs. Austin began work in 1893 upon a book to be called "Next Door to Betty," which, in period of historical sequence, was to follow "Betty Alden," and deal largely with Capt. Benjamin Church and the Indian wars, but death came to her before she had finished the work. Mrs. Austin spent her summers mostly at Plymouth, dividing her time between the graves of her ancestors on Burying Hill, and the homes of her surviving kindred in the town. In winter she lived in Boston, to which city she was strongly attached. She was a good deal in society, especially in the literary circle, and enjoyed receiving her friends in her own home. Occasionally she was persuaded to read a paper to some society or to join in an "Authors' Reading," a form of amusement very fashionable at the "Hub." Her mornings, however, were devoted to work or to the study of Pilgrim history and the rare volumes of genealogies and family history, of which she had an unusually fine collection. Mrs. Austin died in Roxbury, Mass., March 30, 1894.

DELAFIELD, Richard, banker and merchant, was born at New Brighton, S. I., Sept. 6, 1853, the son of Rufus King Delafield. His mother was Eliza, daughter of the late William Baml. Rufus was a prominent merchant of New York, and was the brother of Gen. Richard Delafield and of Dr. Edward Delafield. The family of Delafield or Dela-Feld, is one of the most ancient in France, antedating the year 1000. The Counts de la Feld, in Alsace, long resided at the castle that bears their name, situated in a pass of the Vosges mountains. Hubertus de la Feld was the first of his name who emigrated to England, coming over with the Conqueror. The Delafields of America are descended from John Delafield, who came from England during the last century, and settled in New York. He married a daughter of Gen. Joseph Hallet of Hallett's Cove (now Astoria). John Delafield was the father of a numerous family, of whom seven sons and three daughters grew up. Three of the sons, Joseph, Henry, and Edward, died within three days of each other, each being over eighty years of age, and were all buried at the same time, Feb. 16, 1875, in Greenwood Cemetery, Brooklyn. Richard Delafield (great-grandson of John Delafield) was educated at the Anthon Grammar School, New York. In 1873 he entered a New York mercantile house as clerk, eventually became manager, and in 1880 commenced business in the California trade. A man of high social and business standing, he has been for many years recognized as one of the leading and most prosperous merchants of New York, and has been connected with many of the leading commercial, social, and other institutions of the city. He is senior partner and capitalist of his firm in New York, St. Louis, and San Francisco, is a director of the National Park Bank of New York and ex-president of the New York Mercantile Exchange. He is prominently identified with the Episcopal church, and is a vestryman of Trinity Church Corporation. He is well known in musical circles, and was president of the Staten Island Philharmonic Society and secretary of the New York Symphony Society. He is a member of the Society of the Sons of the Revolution, of the Merchants', Union League, Tuxedo, and New York Athletic Clubs, and of several social organizations. He was a member of the Committee of One Hundred at the New York Columbian Quadro-Centennial Celebration, as appointed by the mayor of New York city. He has been for many years identified with, and taken an active part in, benevolent and charitable institutions, being president of the Sea-Side Home of Long Island, and also a member of the committee of Varick Street Hospital. He is also president of the Commission of the World's Columbian Exposition of the State of New York for the first Judicial District.

FITCH, John, inventor, was born in East (now South) Windsor, Conn., Jan. 21, 1743. His father was a hard-working farmer, and until his tenth year the boy only went to a village school, where he learned to read and write; and from that time forward he was kept hard at farm work, although he was so small and weak that it was said he could only thrash out two bushels of wheat a day. His love of knowledge is said to have been remarkable. He especially devoted himself to arithmetic and geography, and before he was seventeen years old studied surveying, and with so much success that he was able to earn enough to buy a few books, which he read assiduously. When he was seventeen he left home to seek his fortune. At first he tried the sea, but he found it a hard service, and bound himself apprentice to a clockmaker. He was unfortunate in the conditions which surrounded his early life, as his father is said to have been very parsimonious, while the clockmaker was still meaner and almost starved him, at the same time denying him every opportunity to learn his trade. At the age of twenty-one he left this service, and started as a clock-cleaner and brass-smith. He was so industrious that, despite the fact of his having no capital, in two years he had saved £50. But before he was twenty-five years of age he made the mistake of his life in marrying a woman who was much older than himself, who proved to be bad-tempered, and made his existence miserable. Fitch is described as being one of the mildest, kindest, and most patient of men, and he put up with the unhappiness brought upon him by his wife's behavior for a long time, but eventually he abandoned his home, leaving his wife and infant son, and becoming a wanderer. He offered himself as a farm-laborer, but, on account of his weak frame and apparently poor constitution, met with no success, and the same was the case when he tried to enlist as a soldier. He managed to earn a precarious livelihood by roving about the country cleaning clocks from house to house. At length he reached Trenton, N. J., where he lived for a while on the most frugal fare by making brass buttons. During the revolution he worked at repairing muskets, and for a while served in the field. He joined the New Jersey troops, and was with Washington during the severe season at Valley Forge. Near the end of the war he set out for the West, having the intention of becoming a surveyor. He was captured by the Indians, after having made extensive surveys in Kentucky. By this time he had gathered together some property, the most of which he had with him on his expedition, and when his party was attacked by the Indians two of his companions were killed, nine were taken prisoners, and all his goods were destroyed. Fitch was fortunate enough to escape with his life, and, after severe trials, to be set free, and in 1785 he was living in Bucks county, Pa. Up to this time he had never seen nor heard of a steam engine, and it is stated of him that his first idea with regard to the application of steam to locomotion was obtained by seeing a neighbor drive rapidly past him in a chaise drawn by a powerful horse. The notion of propulsion by the power of steam flashed upon his mind, and he began to work at the idea, coming to the conclusion that the force could be better applied to a vessel than to a carriage. He now began to study books, and to consult men who were well-informed with regard to machinery; and in the same year completed his first model of a steamboat, and invited a number of distinguished personages to come to the shores of the Schuylkill, and see it tried. His first model had wheels at the sides; but later in July, 1786, he produced a boat with a steam-engine of three-inch cylinder, with paddles. The boat moved very slowly; the engine being much too small for the hull, and a clumsy and incomplete machine, made by common blacksmiths. He did, however, succeed in demonstrating the possibility of a boat moving upon the water by a steam-engine. From this time he persevered himself, while making every effort with the Continental congress and the Pennsylvania legislature to obtain financial aid to assist him, and losing no opportunity of recommending his views to the scientific and public men of his day. He met, however, with the usual ill success of inventors, obtaining no money, and gaining the reputation of being insane. At length he devoted himself to the engraving of a map of the Northwestern territory, and printed off impressions of this on a cider-press. By this means he succeeded in getting together nearly $1,000, and formed a company. He also obtained from the states of New York, Delaware, Pennsylvania, and Virginia the right to use their waters for fourteen years for the purpose of navigation by means of steam. Fitch's second boat made its trial trip on the Delaware, at Philadelphia, Aug.

27, 1787, and during the next two years he improved greatly on the invention. In 1790 he ran a boat between Philadelphia and Burlington with the speed of eight miles an hour. But in the meantime his resources were exhausted, and as there was no money forthcoming his stockholders became discouraged, and he was obliged to abandon his project. In 1793 he went to France, intending to build a steamboat there, but it being the period of the revolution, the time was unpropitious, and he was obliged to abandon the idea. It is stated that he left his plans and specifications with the American consul at L'Orient while he visited London, and that during his absence his drawings and papers were loaned by the consul to Robert Fulton, who was at that time in Paris, and who had them in his possession for some months; the inference being that, as has been not infrequently the case, Fulton obtained his reputation as being practically the inventor of steamboat navigation from the ideas which he obtained after the inspection of Fitch's drawings and specifications. In 1794 Fitch was obliged to work his passage home to America as a common sailor. Two years later, however, with the indomitable perseverance which had characterized him up to that time, he succeeded in constructing another steamboat from a ship's yawl, and this, which was worked by a screw propeller, was tried on the Collect Pond, in New York city— the present site of the Tombs prison. In 1798 Fitch made a three-foot model of a steamboat, which he tried upon a small stream in Bardstown, Ky. Here he for a while owned some land, but, probably on account of not having been able to pay the taxes, it was occupied by others; and here he gave up his struggle. Some time before this he had prophetically said: "You and I will not live to see the day, but the time will come when the steamboat will be preferred to all other kinds of conveyance; when steamboats will ascend the western rivers from New Orleans to Wheeling; when steamboats will cross the ocean. Johnnie Fitch will be forgotten, but other men will carry out his ideas, and grow rich and great upon them." In 1817 the question of the invention of the steamboat being raised before a committee of the New York legislature, the original patents, drafts, specifications, and models by Fitch and Robert Fulton were exhibited; and the report was finally made by the committee that "the steamboats built by Livingston and Fulton were, in substance, the invention patented to John Fitch, in 1791, and Fitch, during the term of his patent, had the exclusive right to use the same in the United States." But Fitch had been dead twenty years, and it is not recorded that his heirs ever gained any advantage on his invention. Some time during the summer of 1798 he committed suicide. He had been sick for a few days, and his physician had ordered opium pills, of which he was to take one each day. Instead of doing this, he took twelve at once. He died in a tavern, without a relative or friend near him, and was buried in Bardstown, where no stone marks his resting-place.

ALLEN, John, pioneer, was born in Rockbridge county, Va., Dec. 30th, 1772. When he was eight years of age his father removed to Kentucky, and his youth was spent among perilous scenes of Indian warfare which inured him to danger, and developed in him every manly quality. In 1791 he began the study of the law, and, being admitted to the bar in 1795, settled at Shelbyville, and soon took high rank in his profession. In 1812 he raised a regiment of riflemen and joined Gen. Harrison on the Canada frontier. He was engaged in the battle of Brownstown, Jan. 18, 1813, and commanded the left wing of the American army at the disastrous battle of the River Raisin, where he was killed while bravely rallying his troops, Jan. 22, 1814. Kentucky named a county in his memory.

ADAMS, John Frederick, clergyman, was born at Stratham, N. H., May 23, 1790. He was licensed to preach in 1812, and joined the New England Methodist conference. He was assigned to duty in the thinly-settled districts of Maine, where he soon distinguished himself for zeal and a rude eloquence that was very effective. His appointments were sometimes fifty miles apart, and to keep them he often rode through rain and snow, all day without food, and all night with no other bed than the back of his horse. He was a power for good, and his well-known zeal and ability gave him a wide influence in his denomination. He believed in the abolition of slavery, and had the courage of his convictions. He died, greatly esteemed, in Greenland, N. H., June 11, 1881.

PARTRIDGE, William Ordway, sculptor, was born in Paris, France, Apr. 11, 1861, son of George S. Partridge, an American who was temporarily a resident of Paris, and prominent in the American colony during the existence of the second empire. He was a connoisseur and amateur of ability. His mother is of the old Boston families of Caillu and Derby. The childhood days of the son were spent principally in France and Germany. He began to draw at a very tender age, and his art-passion for form developed early. At the age of seven he was brought to America and attended successively the Cheshire Military Academy and the Adelphi Academy in Brooklyn. At the age of fifteen he carved from a piece of soft limestone an ideal head of a woman. He entered Columbia College, where he remained one year, having in the meantime developed a talent for reading in public. His studies at the college, public readings to help in his support, and the hours devoted to art, proved too great a task and his health deserted him. In the fall of 1882 he was sent abroad to recuperate. In Naples he took up modeling in a shop where copies of famous statues were supplied. In Florence he studied under Galli. He returned to America in 1885, where he found himself thrown upon his own resources. He did not yet feel competent as a sculptor to venture his work on the market, so he accepted a position at Wallack's Theatre, New York, and filled his part very acceptably. His Steerforth in "David Copperfield" was notable. After the play he spent his time in modelling in clay. For his mother he produced a successful study of the head of a wrinkled old woman. He gave up the stage and aided financially by his guardian, Dr. A. W. Catlin, he devoted himself to sculpture. About this time he made the acquaintance and gained the friendship of Thomas

Davidson, the writer and lecturer on art and philosophy. For a time they lived together, teacher and scholar, devoting much time to the study of Greek art. He now began to sell small pieces of work, increasing his income by public readings, being especially successful before Boston audiences, where his interpretations of Keats and Shelley interested such critics as Phillips Brooks, W. J. Rolfe, Henry Clapp, and others. In 1887 Mr. Partridge married Mrs. Augusta Merriam of Milton, Mass., and went abroad, where, while at Rome, he worked in the studio of Pio Welonski. In 1879 he obtained from the city of Chicago, after competition, the commission for a statue of Shakespeare for Lincoln Park, which was an artistic success. In 1880 the Hamilton Club of Brooklyn gave him an order for a statue of Alexander Hamilton. The two statues were wrought in Paris. Of his Hamilton, a critic said: "Mr. Partridge's Hamilton does not come from Athens, it comes from Poughkeepsie. . . . He is actually delivering a speech, and has just said something." Mr. Partridge made a bust of Dr. Edward Everett Hale that has been widely admired. A bust of his wife has also attracted attention; as has a Madonna exhibited in the Paris Salon of 1892, and which was finally purchased in Chicago. Of this work a critic said: "It expresses the beauty of past conceptions wedded to the larger view of woman which prevails among the best minds of to-day." In 1894 Mr. Partridge received an order from the Union League Club of Brooklyn for an heroic equestrian statue of Gen. Grant, the model of which has been described as "simply a citizen doing his ghastly duty without flinching." He has also executed an ideal head of Christ which found a home in Chicago. Mr. Partridge is the author of three books on art, namely: "Art for America," "The Technique of Sculpture," and "The Song Life of a Sculptor." He is also professor of fine arts in the Columbian University at Washington. Mr. Partridge had, in 1893–94, three studios in France: two in Paris, and one at Anvers which was formerly the workshop of Daubigny, the eminent French painter. He closed his studios in France and returned permanently to America on the completion of his Shakespeare and Hamilton; and in his studio at Milton, Mass., is working upon his equestrian statue of Gen. Grant.

MARSHALL, Humphrey, soldier, was born in Frankfort, Ky., Jan. 13, 1812, son of John Jay Humphrey (1785–1846), an eminent lawyer and jurist. His grandfather was Humphrey Marshall, the statesman (1756–1841). He was appointed a cadet to the U. S. Military Academy at West Point in 1829, and was graduated in the class of 1832. He served as lieutenant of the mounted rangers in the Black Hawk expedition, and then resigned from the army to study law. Upon being admitted to the bar, he practiced in Frankfort, and afterward at Louisville. He joined the state militia, was made captain in 1836, major in 1838, and lieutenant-colonel in 1841. He raised a company of volunteers in 1836 to take part in the defence of the Texas frontier against the Indians. He disbanded his forces before reaching the scene of the trouble, upon hearing of the victory of Gen. Houston at San Jacinto, and returned home. At the outbreak of the war with Mexico, Col. Marshall, commanding the 1st Kentucky volunteer cavalry, embarked on June 9, 1846, for the seat of war, and under Gen. Taylor won distinction at the battle of Buena Vista, where he led the cavalry charge. He afterward retired to his farm in Henry county, Ky., after declining several important nominations, both state and national. He was elected a representative to the thirty-first congress in 1849, and re-elected to the thirty-second congress. President Fillmore nominated him, in 1852, as commissioner to China, which post was immediately raised to a first-class mission, and he was promptly confirmed by the senate. Upon his return, in 1854, he was elected on the American ticket to represent his district in the thirty-fourth congress, and returned to the thirty-fifth, serving on the committee on military affairs. He was member of the National American Council in New York city in 1856, where he succeeded in striking from the rules of the society the pledge to secrecy. In the presidential campaign of 1860 he canvassed his state for John C. Breckinridge, and upon the secession of the Southern states raised a large number of volunteers for the Confederate army, accepting from that government a commission as brigadier-general. He was made commander of the army of eastern Kentucky, with instructions to operate in the mountain passes on the Virginia border. He met the Federal army under Gen. Garfield at Middle Creek, Floyd county, Jan. 10, 1862, and after a desperate battle of nine hours, was forced to retire. In May, 1862, he defeated the Federal forces under Gen. Cox at Princeton, Va., and opened to the Confederate service the Lynchburg and Knoxville railroad, for which he received the thanks of Gen. Lee. He soon after resigned from the army, and opened a law office in Richmond, Va. He was elected to the Confederate congress, serving on the military committee. After the war he was one of the first of the Confederatists to apply for a removal of disabilities by congress, and, returning to Louisville, Ky., he acquired a large law practice. He died March 28, 1872.

GRIDLEY, Jeremiah, attorney-general of Massachusetts, was born in Boston, Mass., March 10, 1702. He went to Harvard College, where he was graduated in 1725. Having settled in Boston, he taught in a grammer school there for some years. In the meantime he studied theology and occasionally occupied a pulpit. Afterwards he studied law and was admitted to the bar, and soon became eminent as a lawyer. He was a member of the general court from Brookline and opposed the measures of the British ministry. However, this did not interfere with his standing, and he was appointed attorney-general for the province of Massachusetts Bay. In this capacity, in 1761, he defended the "writs of assistance," for which the custom house officers had applied to the superior court, and which authorized them to enter houses under suspicion of obtaining smuggled goods, at their own discretion. Gridley had for an antagonist in this case the celebrated patriot, James Otis. Besides holding his legal position, Gridley was colonel of militia, grand master of the Freemasons of the colony and president of the Marine Society. As early as 1731 Mr. Gridley was editor of the "Weekly Rehearsal," a newspaper published in Boston for one year. He is said to have possessed an extensive acquaintance with classic literature, and a strong mind and quick intelligence; while his thorough acquaintance with canon and civil law placed him at the head of his profession. He died in Brookline, Mass., Sep. 10, 1767.

GRIDLEY, Richard, brother of Jeremiah, was born in Boston, Mass., Jan. 8, 1711, and was a soldier of repute, having a particular reputation as an artillery officer. During the siege of Louisburg, in 1745, he served as an engineer; and in 1755, at the beginning of the French and Indian war, was chief engineer and colonel of infantry in the British army. He was in the expedition against Crown Point, and the fortifications of Lake George were constructed under his direction. After having served under General Amherst, 1758, he was present with Wolfe on the Plains of Abraham at the capture of Quebec. At the end of the war, the British government gave him the Magdalen Islands as a reward for his services, with half pay for his life. In 1775 Col. Gridley joined the patriots, and received the appointment of chief engineer and commander of artillery of the colonial army at Cambridge. It is said of him that he planned the works of Bunker Hill on the night before the battle of June 17, 1775, and that he fought during the entire engagement under heavy fire and was severely wounded. In the following September congress made him a major-general, and he had command of the Continental artillery until November of that year. He died in Stoughton, Mass., June 20, 1796.

EVANS, Oliver, inventor, was born at Newport, Del., in 1755. He was a descendant of Evan Evans, D. D., the first Episcopal minister of Philadelphia, who died in 1728. His parents were in humble circumstances. He was in his youth apprenticed to a wheelwright and soon exhibited great mechanical talent and a strong desire to acquire knowledge. His attention was at an early period drawn to the possible application of steam to useful purposes. At an early age he designed a non-condensing engine, in which the power was derived from the tension of high pressure steam, and proposed its application to the propulsion of carriages. About the year 1780 Evans joined his brothers, who were millers by occupation, and employed his inventive genius in improving the mill machinery. His inventions included the "elevator," the "conveyor," the "hopper-box," the "drill," and the "descender," and so successful was he that over twenty pounds of flour were saved to every barrel, thus reducing the cost of attendance one half. In 1786 he applied for a patent for the application of the steam engine to driving mills, but was refused it. In 1800 he commenced the construction of a steam-carriage to be driven by a non-condensing engine, but changed his plans and adapted it to driving mills. When but twenty-four years old he invented a machine for making the wire teeth used in cotton and woolen cards, turning them out at the rate of 3,000 per minute. A little later he invented a card-setting machine. He continued to improve his engine, of which he had sent plans and specifications to England in 1794, thereby enabling Vivian and Trevithick, through whose hands they passed, to claim credit for the invention, and in 1804 employed one of them in the transportation of a large, flat-bottom boat in Philadelphia, and named the old machine "Oruktor-Amphibolis." This was used as a dredging machine; it weighed about 40,000 pounds, and was propelled very slowly from the works to the Schuylkill river. The engine was then applied to the paddle-wheel at the stern, and drove the craft down the river as far as the Delaware. This is believed to have been the first instance in America of the application of steam power to the propelling of land carriages. He was desirous of building a railroad between Philadelphia and New York, but was prevented by the lack of money. He wrote "The Young Steam Engineer's Guide," and "The Young Millwright's Guide," a work which remained standard many years after his death. Evans has sometimes been called the Watt of America, and while he never succeeded in accomplishing in America as great a success as had rewarded Watt in Great Britain, he was undoubtedly one of the most ingenious mechanics that America ever produced. He died in New York, April 15, 1819.

HILYARD, George Dilwyn, builder. was born in New York city, Feb. 8, 1830. His father was John Hilyard of Burlington county, N. J.; his mother Ann Whitson, whose mother was Hannah Smith, of Smithtown, L. I. John Woolman, the journalist, was an uncle of Mr. Hilyard's grandmother, and his ancestors have since been members of the Society of Friends and were among the early settlers of southern New Jersey. His father and grandfather were prominent builders. His great-uncle, Eber Hilyard, built Fort William on Governor's Island, New York harbor.

Being left an orphan early in life, he was educated at the Friends' Institute, Westtown, Pa., and grew up in that strict orthodox faith. He was apprenticed to his uncles, James and Joseph Hilyard, where he learned all the branches of the trade, including masonry. After completing his apprenticeship he remained in his uncle's employ as superintendent. In 1856 he started in business for himself and by his industry and strict economy accumulated a fair competence. He made no effort to compete with other contractors in the construction of public buildings, knowing that politics, for which he had no taste, entered largely into the arrangements. During his long business career he has constructed some of the best and most substantial buildings in the city, all of which would bear the most rigid scrutiny. Through his efforts many thousand dollars have been annually added to the wealth of the city. Under the auspices of the Society of Friends he erected the building for the colored mission at 135 West Thirtieth street, and the 21st ward mission at 305 East Forty-first street. He was made trustee and treasurer of the latter and has filled the position with honor and fidelity. While leading a quiet, unobtrusive life he has maintained the principles inculcated by those of his faith and has enjoyed the confidence and respect of the business community. For many years he has been a worthy member of the Society of Mechanics and Tradesmen, and has largely promoted the interests of that organization. On Oct. 14, 1868, he married Elizabeth Wills, who died April 13, 1879, leaving two children. On Jan. 4, 1883, he married Anna Wills, by whom he has one son.

PRESCOTT, William Hickling, historian, was born at Salem, Mass., May 4, 1796. He was the grandson of William Prescott, the distinguished soldier of the revolution to whose memory a statue was erected on Bunker Hill. His father was a lawyer of means and culture, and gave careful attention to his son's education. Upon the removal of the family to Boston in 1808, he was placed under the tuition of Dr. Gardiner, a pupil of Dr. Parr. In his school-days he had a passion for mimic warfare and for the narration of original stories, which might be indicative of his historical bias. He had a healthy aversion to persistent work, though he made good use of his permission to read at the Boston Atheneum, an exceptional advantage, at a time when the best books were not easily accessible. In 1811 he entered Harvard College with a fairly thorough mental equipment, but almost at the outset of his career, met with an accident which affected his whole subsequent course of life. A hard piece of bread, thrown at random in the Commons Hall, struck his left eye with such force as to fell him to the floor, and immediately destroyed the sight of the eye. He resumed his college work with success in classics and literature, though he abandoned mathematics, in which he could not obtain even average proficiency. After graduating honorably in 1814, he entered his father's office as student of law, but in January the injured eye showed dangerous symptoms, and it was determined that he should pass the winter at St. Michael's, and in the spring seek medical advice in Europe. During his visit to the Azores, which was constantly broken by confinement in a darkened room, he began the mental discipline which enabled him to compose and retain in memory large passages for subsequent dictation; and apart from his gain in culture, his journey to England, France, and Italy during the following year was scarcely beneficial. The injured eye was found to be hopelessly paralyzed, and the sight of the other depended upon the maintenance of his general health. His further study of law seemed out of the question, and upon his return to Boston he remained at home, listening to a great deal of reading. On May 4, 1820, he married Susan Amory, and resolved to devote his life to literature. He had not hitherto displayed any remarkable aptitude, but having once determined his future occupation, he set himself strenuously to the task of self-preparation. With almost amusing thoroughness he commenced the study of "Murray's Grammar," the prefatory matter of "Blair's Rhetoric," and "Johnson's Dictionary," reading at the same time, for purpose of style, a series of standard English writers. A review of Byron's "Letters on Pope," in 1821, constitutes his first contribution to the "North American Review," to which he continued for many years to send the results of his slighter researches. He next turned to French literature, mitigating its irksomeness by incursions into the early English drama and ballad literature. Of the quality and direction of this thought he has left indications in his papers on "Essay Writing," and "French and English Tragedy." In pursuance of his method of successive studies, he began in 1823 the study of Italian literature, passing over German as demanding more labor than he could afford, and so strongly did he feel the fascination of the language that for some time he thought of selecting it as the chief sphere of his work. In the following year, however, he made his first acquaintance with the literature of Spain, under the influence of his friend and biographer, Ticknor, who was then lecturing upon it, and while its attractiveness proved greater than he had anticipated, the comparative novelty as a field of research served as an additional stimulus. In the meantime his aims had gradually been concentrating. History had always been a favorite study with him, and Mably's "Observations sur l'Histoire" appears to have had considerable influence in determining him in the choice of some special period for historic research. The selection was not made, however, without prolonged hesitation. The project of a history of Italian literature held a prominent place in his thought, and found some tentative expression in his article on "Italian Narrative Poetry," published in 1824, and in the reply to Da Ponte's criticism; but he had also in contemplation a history of the revolution which converted republican Rome into a monarchy, a series of biographical and critical sketches of eminent men, and a Spanish history from the invasion of the Arabs to the consolidation of the monarchy under Charles V. It was not until 1826 that he recorded in his private memorandum, begun in 1820, his decision "to embrace the gift of the the Spanish subject." It was a bold choice, for he not only had an absolute dislike of investigation of latent and barren antiquities, but his eyesight was fast failing, which, by others than Milton, has been deemed indispensable to an historian. He could only use the eye which remained to him for brief and intermittent periods, and as traveling aggravated his affliction, he could not expect to make personal research amongst unpublished records. He was, however, in possession of ample means and admirable friends to amply supply necessary materials, and began without hesitancy the grand work of "The History of the Reign of Ferdinand and Isabella." Mr. English, one of his secretaries, has furnished a picture of him at this period, seated in his study lined on two sides with books and darkened by green screens and curtains of blue muslin, which required readjustment with almost every passing cloud. In a letter to the Rev. George E. Ellis, he describes the difficulties under which he worked. "I obtained the services of a reader who knew no language but his own. I taught him to pronounce the Castilian in a manner suited, I suspect, much more to my ear than to that of a Spaniard, and we began our wearisome journey through Mariana's noble history. I cannot even now call to mind, without a smile, the tedious hours in which, seated under some old trees at my country residence, we pursued our slow and melancholy way over pages which afforded no glimmering light to him, and from which the light came dimly struggling to me through a half intelligible vocabulary. Though in this way I could examine various authorities, it was not easy to arrange in my mind the results of my reading, drawn from different and often contradictory accounts. To do this I dictated copious notes as I went along, and when I had read enough for a chapter (from thirty to forty and sometimes fifty pages) I had a mass of memoranda in my own language which would easily bring before me at one view the fruit of my researches. These notes were carefully read to me, and while my recent studies were fresh in my recollection, I ran over the whole of my intended chapter in my mind. This process I repeated at least half a dozen times, so that when I finally put my pen to paper it ran off pretty glibly, for it was an effort of memory rather than of composition. Writing presented to me a difficulty even greater than reading. Thierry, the famous blind historian of the Norman conquest, advised me to cultivate dictation; but I have

usually preferred a substitute that I found in a writing-case made for the blind, which I procured in London forty years ago. It is a simple apparatus, often described by me for the benefit of persons whose sight is imperfect. It consists of a frame of the size of a sheet of paper, traversed by brass wires as many as lines are wanted on the page, and with a sheet of carbonized paper, such as is used in getting duplicates, pasted on the reverse side. With an ivory or agate stylus the writer traces his characters between the wires on the carbonated sheet making indelible marks which he cannot see on the white page below. This treadmill operation has its defects; and I have repeatedly supposed I had completed a good page and was proceeding in all the glory of composition to go ahead, when I found I had forgotten to insert my sheet of writing paper below, that my labor had all been thrown away, and that the leaf looked as black as myself. Notwithstanding these and other whimsical distresses of the kind, I have found my writing-case my best friend in my lonely hours, and with it have written nearly all that I have sent into the world the last forty years."

The rate of progress in preparation was therefore necessarily slow. He still continued his yearly experimental contribution to the "North American Review," elaborating them with a view as much to ultimate historical proficiency as to immediate literary effect. The essays on "Scottish Song," "Novel Writing," "Molière," and Irving's "Granada" belong to this preparatory period. The death of his daughter in 1828 led him aside to the study of Christian evidences, with the result that he convinced himself of the fundamental truth of Christianity, though he did not accept all the tenets of orthodoxy. On Oct. 6, 1829, he began the actual work of composition, which was continued until June 25, 1836. During this period he interrupted his work to write the essays on "Asylums for the Blind," "Poetry and Romance of the Italians," and "English Literature of the 19th Century." Another year, during which time his essay on "Cervantes" appeared, was spent in the final revision for the press, in which labor he was assisted by Gardiner, the son of his old schoolmaster, who criticised the style, and Folsom, who verified the facts. Upon its publication in Boston its success was immediate and marked. It was speedily republished in England, where its success was equally great. From the position of an obscure reviewer, Prescott found himself elevated to the first rank of contemporary historians. Daniel Webster spoke of him as a comet which had suddenly blazed out upon the world in full splendor, and American, British, and Continental reviews were no less laudatory. Its reception determined the nature of his future work. Hitherto he had inclined to the history of literature rather than to polity and action, on the ground that it was more in consonance with his previous studies and more suitable for his special powers. A close examination of his work in the department of literary criticism does not bear out this estimate of his own genius, and the popular voice in approving his narrative faculty, gave the required impetus in the right direction. After coquetting awhile with the project of a life of Molière he decided to follow in the track of his first work with a "History of the Conquest of Mexico." Washington Irving, who had already made preparation to occupy the same field, generously withdrew in his favor, and in May, 1839, Prescott began reading upon the subject, and completed the work in 1843. During these five years he reviewed Lockhart's "Life of Scott," "Kenyon's Poems," "Chateaubriand," "Bancroft's United States," Marlotti's "Italy," and Madame Calderon's "Life in Mexico." He also made an abridgment of "Ferdinand and Isabella" in anticipation of its threatened abridgment by another hand. In 1843 his "Conquest of Mexico" was published with a success proportionate to the wide reputation won by his previous work. The whole edition was sold in four months, the London and Paris edition having a similar reception. The careful methods of work which he had adopted from the outset had borne admirable fruit. While the study of authorities had been no less thorough, his style had become more free and less self-conscious, and the epic qualities of the theme were such as to call forth in the highest degree his picturesque narration. It was only a step to the "Conquest of Peru," and scarcely three months elapsed before he began to break ground on the latter subject, though actual composition was not commenced until the autumn of 1844. While the work was in progress and before the close of the year, his father died, a heavy blow to him, inasmuch as the elder and younger members of the family had continued to share the same home upon almost patriarchal terms, and the breach was therefore in an association extending over 48 years. In 1848 he was elected as corresponding member of the French Institute in place of the Spanish historian, Navarette, and also to the Royal Society of Berlin. The next winter he arranged his articles and reviews for publication, and issued them almost contemporaneously in London and New York. After minor interruptions—his removal from Bedford street to Beacon street, visits to friends, and a renewed failure of sight — he completed the "Conquest of Peru," in November, 1846, and it was issued in the following March. His misgivings as to its reception were at once set at rest, and it was speedily translated into French, Spanish, German, and Dutch, in addition to the English issue, in New York, London, and Paris. He was now over fifty, and his sight showed serious symptoms of enfeeblement. Although it had been of very intermittent service to him, it had by his careful regimen so far improved that he could read with some regularity, during the writing of the "Conquest of Mexico," though in a less degree during the years devoted to the "Conquest of Peru." Now, however, the use of his remaining eye had been reduced to an hour a day, and he was forced to conclude that future plans must be formed upon the expectation of blindness. He had for many years been collecting material for a history of Philip II., but he hesitated for some time to attempt a work of such magnitude, occupying himself meanwhile with a memoir of John Pickering for the Massachusetts Historical Society, and the revision of Ticknor's "History of Spanish Literature." But in March, 1848, he set himself with characteristic courage to the accomplishment of the larger project, though with the intention of writing memoirs rather than a history, as admitting of less elaborate research. He was fortunate in obtaining the aid of Don Pascual de Gayangos, then professor of Arabic literature in Madrid, who enabled him to obtain material not only from the public archives of Spain, but from the muniment rooms of the great Spanish families. With the extended range of information thus given to him, he began his history in 1849, but finding himself still unsettled in his work, he decided in the spring of the following year to carry out his long projected visit to England. His reception was of the most cordial and gratifying kind, and, returning reinvigorated for his work, he dismissed his idea of memoirs in favor of the more elaborate form, and in November, 1855, issued the first two volumes of his uncompleted "History of Philip II." Its success eclipsed that of any of his former works, and his fame was greatly increased and extended. This was his last great undertaking, but as the light of new sources of information made Robertson's "Charles V" inadequate to take its place as a link in the series, he republished it in an extended and improved form in 1856. A slight attack of apoplexy on Feb. 4, 1858, foretold the end, though he persevered with the preparation of the third volume of "Philip II," for the press. He never entirely recovered from this attack, and in January, 1859, as he stepped into an adjoining room, he was seized with another stroke, and expired at two o'clock on the same day. In personal character Prescott possessed many admirable and amiable qualities. As an historian, he stands in the direct line of descent from Robertson, whose influence is clearly discernible, both in his style and method. His power lies in the clear grasp of fact in selection and synthesis, and in the vivid narration of incident. For critical analysis he had small liking and faculty; his critical insight is limited in range, and he confines himself to the concrete elements of history. Few historians have had in a higher degree that artistic feeling in the broad arrangement of materials which insures interest. The romance of history has seldom had an abler exponent. Humboldt said of "Ferdinand and Isabella," that it was an enduring history and could never be surpassed. The portion of history selected by Prescott had not been covered by previous writers, and had only been touched upon by Italian writers, and not until the treasures concealed in the tragic Annals of Llorente and the political disquisitions of Mariana, Sempere, and Capmany were unlocked, could any faithful narrative of this particular era be given to the world. Prescott had unusual facilities for research in the many and rare works purchased in Spain by his friend George Ticknor in connection with his own work in Spanish literature. He also collected an enormous number of unpublished documents through the agency of A. H. Everett, Arthur Middleton, and Obadiah Rich. Prescott spent his fortune liberally in the collection of every scrap which could let light in upon his subject, and gained access to secret depositories, which never before had been opened to the eye of the exploring historian. Prosper Merimée says of Prescott: "Of a just and upright spirit, he had a horror of parade. He never allowed himself to be drawn away by it, and often condemned himself to long investigation to refute even the most audacious assertions. His criticism, full at once of good sense and acuteness, was never deceived in the choice of documents, and his discernment was as remarkable as his good faith. If he may be reproached with often hesitating, even after a long investigation, to pronounce a definite judgment, we must at least acknowledge that he omitted nothing to prepare the way for it, and that the author, perhaps too timid to decide always, leaves his reader sufficiently instructed to need no other guide." Prof. C. C. Felton wrote: "It is a saying that the style is the man; and of no great author in the literature of the world is that saying more true than of him whose loss we mourn. For in the transparent simplicity and undimmed beauty and candor of his style were read the endearing qualities of his soul, so that his personal friends are found wherever literature is found, and love of him is co-extensive with the world of letters, not limited to those who speak the Anglo-Saxon mother language, to the literature of which he has contributed such splendid works, but co-extensive with the civilized language of the human race."

SCOTT, Irving Murray, shipbuilder and iron-master, was born near Hebron Mills, Baltimore co., Md., Dec. 25, 1837. His father, who was a farmer and a prominent member of the Society of Friends, was a man of fine mind and strong character, and the son inherited many of his sterling qualities. His boyhood was passed on his father's farm, and at an early age he evinced marked mechanical ability. He was educated in the public schools, and afterwards at Milton Academy, under John Emerson Lamb, where he studied for three years. Upon leaving school his father offered to defray the expense of his preparation for one of the learned professions, but he preferred to enter the field of mechanics and was accordingly apprenticed to the machinist trade in Baltimore, learning the iron and woodworking trade under Obed Hussey, inventor of the reaping machine, and studying marine engineering with the firm of Murray & Hazelhurst. After the completion of his service he worked for some time in Baltimore, being mainly employed in supervising the construction of steam engines, and giving his leisure hours to study. Three nights a week he spent at the Mechanics' Institute, where he took a course in mechanical drawing, the fourth in the study of German and the fifth at lectures. In 1860 Mr. Scott was engaged as draughtsman by the Union Iron Works of San Francisco. In his new field of labor his advance was rapid and after becoming, in 1861, the chief draughtsman, he rose, in 1863, to be superintendent and then general manager of the works, which position he still retains (1895). In 1865 he became a member of the firm of Booth & Co. When he first became associated with the Union Iron Works only twenty-two men were employed; now they furnish employment to 1,400 men and represent an invested capital of $2,000,000. They were for many years chiefly engaged in the construction of mining machinery, and in this department of mechanics long held the first place on the Pacific coast. In 1880 Mr. Scott went on a trip around the world with James Fair, and while in Europe made a close and exhaustive study of the industries and industrial establishments of the several countries which he visited, giving special attention to the shipbuilding plants of France and England. Upon his return home the Union Iron Works were enlarged and greatly improved. They now cover twenty-five acres on the water front of San Francisco and are the most complete of their class in the United States. The firm was made into a corporation in 1882, and in 1884, at the instance of Mr. Scott, it engaged in shipbuilding. Since that time the company has built for the U. S. government

the San Francisco and the Charleston, unarmored cruisers of 3,750 and 4,130 tons burden respectively, and the Monterey, a powerful coast defence vessel. It has built the Oregon, of 10,200 tons, and a line-of-battle ship of the first class. The company has also built many vessels for private persons. Mr. Scott, besides devoting his ability and energy to building up the Union Works to their present proportions, has engaged successfully in mining and banking, and is a trustee or director in many institutions. To him was largely due the development of the Clipper Gap Iron Co., probably the richest in California. As president of the Art Association and of the Mechanics' Institute; regent of the University of California; trustee of the Leland Stanford, Jr. University, and of the Free Library, his influence has made itself felt. He was one of three appointed to receive the Japanese embassy in 1879 and was appointed to extend the welcome of the citizens of San Francisco to Gen. Grant on his world-embracing tour. In April, 1891, he was made president of the California commission to the World's Fair. He is a liberal patron of art, and for some years has been president of the San Francisco Art Association, as well as of the Washington Irving Literary Society, the Addisonian Literary Society, and the Howard Street Literary Society, and was chosen in 1880 to be president of the Authors' Carnival. He is a wide and constant reader and an acute and original thinker, and his contributions to the magazines and reviews upon labor and other industrial problems have at different times attracted much attention. In politics he is a Republican, having been a member of the Young Men's Republican Club from 1865 to 1872, and is one of the leaders of his party in California. Since 1890 he has strenuously advocated the erection on the Pacific coast of a government plant for the construction of heavy ordnance and the adoption of a more complete and effective system of harbor defence. In 1892 he paid a second visit to Europe to supplement his knowledge of shipbuilding and the construction of marine machinery. Mr. Scott was married in 1863 to Laura, daughter of John R. Horde, of Covington, Ky., and is the father of two children. He is a fluent writer and an eloquent speaker, his address before the Mechanics' Institute in 1869 receiving the personal congratulations of William Seward. He also delivered the orations at the unveiling of the statues to Francis Scott Key and Starr King, erected in Golden Gate Park. He was made a member of the states prison board by Gov. Stoneman, while Gov. Perkins appointed him on his staff with the rank of civil engineer. He is a member of the Pacific Union and Burlingame Clubs, and of the Lawyers' Club of New York.

PATTISON, Granville Sharp, anatomist, was born near Glasgow, Scotland, in 1791. He was educated in that city, and at the age of seventeen began the study of medicine. Four years later he accepted the position of assistant to Allan Burns, the founder of surgical anatomy in Great Britain, and henceforth devoted himself to the study and teaching of anatomy, and it is probable that no anatomical teacher of his time attained a higher reputation. His forte as a teacher lay in his knowledge of visceral and surgical anatomy, and in applying this knowledge to the diagnosis and treatment of diseases and accidents and operations. His earnest manner and clear demonstrations made him very popular in the lecture-room. He possessed a singularly attractive eloquence that left a lasting impression upon his auditors. Early in his professional career he edited Allan Burns's "Surgical Anatomy of the Head and Neck," and performed several important surgical operations, tying, it is said, upon one occasion, the omohyoid muscle instead of the common carotid artery. He had little taste, however, for surgery, and abandoned it entirely in his latter years. His first lectures on anatomy were delivered at the Andersonian Institute, Glasgow, and in 1818 he went to Philadelphia, and being disappointed in obtaining the chair of anatomy, which had been promised to him by the University of Pennsylvania, he was tendered and accepted the chair of anatomy in the University of Maryland, which, through his brilliant teaching, soon reached a high degree of prosperity. In 1828, upon the organization of Loudon University, he was called to the chair of anatomy there. This position he soon resigned, on account of a misunderstanding with the demonstrator of anatomy. He subsequently returned to Philadelphia, and accepted the professorship of anatomy in Jefferson Medical College, which position he held from 1831 to 1840; when he went to New York city, to assist in founding the medical department of the University of the City of New York, a project into which he entered with all the energy and enthusiasm of his nature. He continued his connection with this university until his death. He was actively interested in the establishment of the Grand Opera House, New York city; was fond of music, hunting, and fishing, and, but for his naturally indolent nature and love of ease, would, no doubt, have attained a pre-eminent reputation as an anatomist. He was a frequent contributor to the "American Medical Recorder;" published a translation of J. W. Masse's "Anatomical Atlas," edited Jean Cruveilhier's "Anatomy of the Human Body," and published several pamphlets on personal subjects. He died in New York city, Nov. 12, 1851.

GRAY, George, senator, was born at New Castle, Del., May 4, 1840. He was graduated from Princeton College with the class of 1859, and later  spent a year at the Harvard Law School. From 1869 to 1879 he practiced law in Delaware, becoming during that period one of the leaders of the bar of the state. A close student of public affairs, he early became active in politics. He was attorney-general of Delaware from 1879 to 1885, and as a delegate from Delaware took a prominent part in the Democratic national conventions of 1876, 1880, and 1884. When Mr. Bayard became secretary of state, Mr. Gray was chosen his successor in the U. S. senate and at once took his seat in that body. In 1887 he was re-elected senator for the full term of six years. After the death of Morrison Waite, the appointment of Mr. Gray as chief-justice of the supreme court was strongly urged upon the president; but his claims were rejected on account of his age, an older man being thought more desirable for the place. During his period of service in the senate, where he has served upon many important committees, he has gained a reputation as a careful and painstaking worker, and has come to be regarded as one of the foremost orators of that body. His delivery is fluent and his manner easy and graceful. In the session of 1890-91 he led the Democratic opposition to the Federal elections bill, and his speech upon that measure, which occupied several days in its delivery, was regarded as a masterly effort. Mr. Gray is above six feet in height, besides being a strikingly handsome man. He was married many years ago to the daughter of Dr. Charles Black, of New Castle, Del., a beautiful and accomplished woman. They have a family of five children, three sons and two daughters.

THOMSON, Samuel, physician, was born at Alstead, N. H., Feb. 9, 1769. He received what little education he had at home, but early in life removed to Boston, where he began the practice of medicine. He was the originator of what is called the Thomsonian system of medicine, which consisted in the use of herbs. He agreed with the hydropaths and homœopaths in asserting the great curative forces in nature — the most important principle in medicine established during the century; and was largely instrumental in forcing the regular school to diminish the quantity of drugs administered, and otherwise to modify its practice for the better. His opposition to the reckless and frightful use of mercury, and the indiscriminate bloodletting then in vogue, entitles him to grateful memory. He was  also the originator of the steam bath. He was outrageously persecuted; at one time he was arrested on the charge of murder, the result of alleged malpractice from the use of his simple herbs. He was imprisoned in Newburyport for months, though he was acquitted finally. This incident illustrates the bigotry of the time. He is the author of "Materia Medica and Family Physician," "New Guide to Health and Family Physician." He died in Boston in 1843.

BADGER, Joseph, missionary, was born at Wilbraham, Mass., Feb. 28, 1757. His early education was obtained at home from his parents. At the age of eighteen he joined the revolutionary army, and remained in the service until the end of 1778, when he was honorably discharged. Being paid in the depreciated continental currency, he had scarcely money enough on leaving the service to buy himself an ordinary coat; but, poor as he was, he resolved to acquire an education, and, at the age of twenty-two, entered the family of Rev. M. Day, father of President Day of Yale, and began studying the elements of spelling, reading, writing, and arithmetic. By the hard labor of his hands he managed to pay his way through college, and in 1785 was graduated from Yale. He then studied for the ministry, and, having been ordained in 1787, he was, in 1800, sent by the Connecticut Missionary Society to the wilds of Ohio. There, for more than thirty years, his labors were severe and his hardships many. He traveled on foot or horseback through regions where there were neither roads nor bridges, and sometimes no settlements for a whole day's journey. At one time, as he was journeying at night and alone through a dense forest, and, in the midst of a heavy rain, he was met by a bear, whose flashing eye and ominous growl told him what he had to encounter. Letting his horse loose, he climbed a tree, and there, beyond reach of Bruin, he slept soundly until morning. During the war of 1812 he was appointed brigade chaplain in the U. S. army, and his knowledge of the country rendered his services of great value to Gen. Harrison, whose friendship he retained until his death. At the close of the war he resumed his missionary work. In 1826, owing to his extreme poverty, the government granted him a pension of $90 a year, but he continued his missionary work until his infirmities would allow him to labor no longer. Then, in 1835, he went to live with a daughter in Perrysburg, O., and there died May 5, 1846.

AUSTIN, Stephen F., Texas patriot, was born in Wythe county, Virginia, Nov. 8, 1793, the son of Moses Austin, an enterprising pioneer from Connecticut. Stephen was liberally educated in Connecticut and at Transylvania University, Lexington, Ky., and was taken to Missouri by his father in 1799. He served in the territorial legislature of Missouri when very young. His father had been granted permission by the Mexican government to plant a colony of 300 families in Texas, and on his death in 1821, the son resolved to carry out his plans

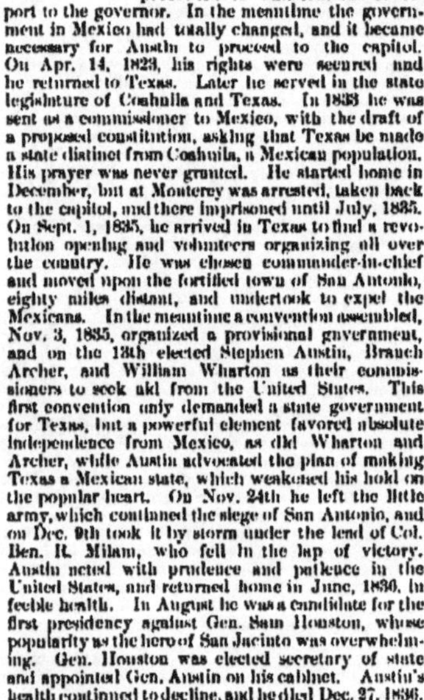

if he were so allowed. He went to San Antonio, Tex., in August, 1821, and was duly recognized as his father's successor, and granted permission to select a district for colonization. He chose the country between the La Vaca and the San Jacinto, ten leagues from the reserved coast, and hastened to the United States to secure immigrants. On Jan. 1, 1822, he arrived on the Brazos with a few settlers, others coming by water. In March he proceeded to San Antonio to report to the governor. In the meantime the government in Mexico had totally changed, and it became necessary for Austin to proceed to the capitol. On Apr. 14, 1823, his rights were secured and he returned to Texas. Later he served in the state legislature of Coahuila and Texas. In 1833 he was sent as a commissioner to Mexico, with the draft of a proposed constitution, asking that Texas be made a state distinct from Coahuila, a Mexican population. His prayer was never granted. He started home in December, but at Monterey was arrested, taken back to the capitol, and there imprisoned until July, 1835. On Sept. 1, 1835, he arrived in Texas to find a revolution opening and volunteers organizing all over the country. He was chosen commander-in-chief and moved upon the fortified town of San Antonio, eighty miles distant, and undertook to expel the Mexicans. In the meantime a convention assembled, Nov. 3, 1835, organized a provisional government, and on the 13th elected Stephen Austin, Branch Archer, and William Wharton as their commissioners to seek aid from the United States. This first convention only demanded a state government for Texas, but a powerful element favored absolute independence from Mexico, as did Wharton and Archer, while Austin advocated the plan of making Texas a Mexican state, which weakened his hold on the popular heart. On Nov. 24th he left the little army, which continued the siege of San Antonio, and on Dec. 9th took it by storm under the lead of Col. Ben. R. Milam, who fell in the lap of victory. Austin acted with prudence and patience in the United States, and returned home in June, 1836. In feeble health. In August he was a candidate for the first presidency against Gen. Sam Houston, whose popularity as the hero of San Jacinto was overwhelming. Gen. Houston was elected secretary of state and appointed Gen. Austin on his cabinet. Austin's health continued to decline, and he died Dec. 27, 1836.

ALEXANDER, James Waddel, clergyman, was born in Louisa county, Va., March 13, 1804.

He was the eldest son of Archibald Alexander, and, on his mother's side, a grandson of James Waddel, the "blind preacher," made famous by William Wirt. He was graduated from Princeton College in 1820, and appointed tutor in that institution in 1824. He resigned that post the next year, and settled as pastor of a church in Charlotte county, Va. Here he remained two years, and in 1828 accepted a call to the First Presbyterian Church, Trenton, N. J. In 1832 he resigned this charge, and became the editor of the "Presbyterian," and in 1833 was called to the professorship of rhetoric and belles lettres at Princeton College. Here he remained until 1844, when he was chosen pastor of the Duane Street Presbyterian Church, New York. In 1849 he was appointed professor of ecclesiastical history and church government in Princeton Theological Seminary, where he remained until 1851, when he returned to his former parish in New York city. He wrote upwards of thirty volumes for the American Sunday-School Union, and also a biography of his father, Dr. Archibald Alexander. He died at the Virginia Springs, July 31, 1859.

FANNIN, James W., soldier, was born in Georgia about 1800. He was educated at West Point, and in 1834, with money partly furnished by his friends, he emigrated to Texas, and became a slave-holder and planter. When a conflict with Mexico became imminent, he raised a company and hastened to the West, where at the battle of Conception he won the title of "the hero of Conception." At the subsequent reorganization of the army, the executive council at San Felipe selected Fannin as one of the recruiting officers, virtually setting aside Gen. Houston as commander-in-chief, which act but reflected the general demoralization of the state at that time. Gov. Smith, who had been deposed by the council, refused to surrender his office, which was likewise claimed by Lieut.-Gov. Robinson. The contradictory orders issued by the two, greatly confused the army, Gen. Houston recognizing the authority of Smith, and Fannin that of Robinson,

while the council itself was also divided. From whatever cause, it is evident that Fannin committed various blunders, which eventually cost him his life, and the lives of his faithful companions. In January, 1836, he set out to reinforce Dr. James Grant, who was in command of an unauthorized expedition to Matamoras. Upon learning at Refugio of the destruction of Grant's party, Fannin retreated to Goliad, where he erected a line of defence. Subsequently he marched toward Victoria, and on March 19th was attacked, and was forced to surrender, on the banks of the Coleta river. The terms of the surrender were, however, most honorable, and it was solely through the treachery of Santa Anna, the Mexican general, that the Texans, after giving up their arms, were, one and all, put to death. Fannin was a man of strong domestic affections, a brave patriot, and one that must always hold an important place in the history of his adopted state. The Texans honorably avenged the massacre of Fannin and his men in the decisive battle of San Jacinto, where the battle-cry was: "Remember the Alamo! Remember the Goliad!"

AVERY, Waitstill, revolutionary patriot, was born at Groton, Conn., May 3, 1745. After being graduated from Princeton in 1770, he removed to Mecklenburg county, N. C., was admitted to the bar, and took an active part in the political agitation that followed the battle of the Alamance. In 1775 he was a member of the celebrated Mecklenburg Convention, which was the first public body to announce a desire for independence from Great Britain. In 1776 he was elected to the state legislature, and in 1777 appointed attorney-general of the state. In the following year he was given command of a regiment of state troops, and served with credit in that capacity until the close of the revolutionary war. He died May 8, 1821.

MURDOCH, James, E., actor, was born in Philadelphia in 1812, and made his first appearance on the stage at the Walnut Street Theatre in that city as Frederick in "Lover's Vows," on Oct. 13, 1829. A year later he was seen at the Chestnut Street Theatre as Young Norval, and his subsequent

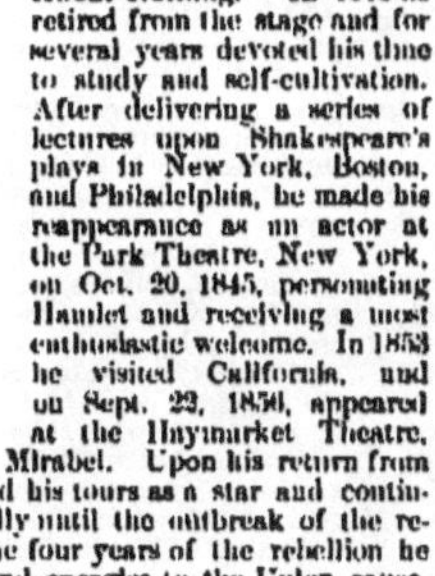

advancement was constant and unimpeded. He made his first appearance in New York at the Park Theatre in 1838 as Benedick in "Much Ado About Nothing." In 1842 he retired from the stage and for several years devoted his time to study and self-cultivation. After delivering a series of lectures upon Shakespeare's plays in New York, Boston, and Philadelphia, he made his reappearance as an actor at the Park Theatre, New York, on Oct. 20, 1845, personating Hamlet and receiving a most enthusiastic welcome. In 1853 he visited California, and on Sept. 22, 1856, appeared at the Haymarket Theatre, London, as Young Mirabel. Upon his return from England he resumed his tours as a star and continued them successfully until the outbreak of the rebellion. During the four years of the rebellion he devoted his time and energies to the Union cause, nursing the sick and wounded on the field and giving entertainments in aid of the sanitary commission. He reappeared on the stage in Cincinnati in October, 1865, but his final retirement soon followed. His more recent appearances before the public have been as a lecturer. At his best he was one of the most finished and scholarly actors of his time, his versatility making him almost as effective in tragedy as in comedy. His Mercutio, Benedick, and Claude Melnotte have never been equaled on the American stage. He is now a resident of Cincinnati.

FENTON, William Matthew, lawyer, was born at Norwich, Chenango co., N. Y., Dec. 19, 1808; his father, Joseph S. Fenton, being a prominent banker of that place, an elder in the Presbyterian church, and one of the first citizens in wealth and social position. The eldest of nine children, Mr. Fenton early showed remarkable aptitude for study, and at fourteen entered Hamilton College, from which he was graduated in 1827 at the head of his class. He then entered his father's bank, but his health becoming impaired by close confinement,

he undertook a sea voyage, shipping from Charleston, S. C., as a common sailor. Four years later he was mate of a merchantman, and declined the captaincy of a similar craft. In April, 1836, he married Adelaide Birdsall, daughter of Judge Birdsall, of Norwich, and in July of the same year removed to Michigan, residing for two years at Pontiac, and afterwards in Genesee county, where he purchased the site of the village of Fenton. In 1839 he undertook the study of law, and in 1841 was admitted to the bar with Andrew Parsons, afterwards governor. Entering politics as a Democrat, he was soon recognized as a leader. In 1844 he was defeated for the legislature, but at the next election was returned to the state senate. From 1848 to 1852 inclusive, he served as lieutenant-governor with Govs. Ransom and Barry, and was twice nominated for circuit judge. In 1850 he removed to the city of Flint, his home until his death, and in 1852 was made register of the land office at that place by President Pierce, holding the position until the removal of the office to Saginaw. In 1856 he traveled in Europe, and in 1858 was elected mayor of Flint. On the outbreak of the war he telegraphed to the governor of the state $5,000 for the equipment of troops, and early in 1861 was appointed a member of the state military board. He was shortly after made major of the 7th Michigan infantry, which, in the main he recruited, and which, in little more than thirty days, reached South Carolina during the capture of Port Royal. On Apr. 16, 1862, at Wilmington Island, Ga., on landing from the steamer Honduras during a reconnaissance, he was engaged in a successful and spirited encounter with the 13th Georgia; and on June 16th led a brigade in the assault on Secessionville, James Island, S. C. In March, 1863, he tendered his resignation on account of failing health, resuming the practice of the law, in which he ranked high. In 1864 he was Democratic candidate for governor, in opposition to Gov. Crapo. A successful business man, he was founder and president of the Citizens' National Bank of Flint, and built the handsome business block in the city which bears his name. He died May 12, 1871, in consequence of injuries received as chief of the fire department.

GROIN, William M., U. S. senator, was born in Tennessee in 1805, the son of a Methodist preacher. He was educated at Transylvania University, in Kentucky, and for several years practiced medicine in Tennessee and in Mississippi. About 1833 he was appointed marshal of Mississippi, and relinquished the practice of his profession. In 1841 he was elected to congress. In 1847 he was appointed to superintend the erection of the custom house at New Orleans, La. His love for political life led him to California, where he took a leading part in the affairs of the Pacific coast. It has been asserted that his record shows that even then he was imbued with disunion sentiments. Certainly, in October, 1861, U. S. Gen. Sumner, who had been called eastward from San Francisco, sailed with his staff and with Senator Groin to Panama, and before reaching that port, on learning that some of his officers had been approached, arrested Groin and Calhoun Benham, who forthwith retired to their rooms and threw overboard a quantity of maps and papers, a fact unknown for half an hour afterward. Sumner took both as prisoners with him to New York, where they had a brief residence in Fort Lafayette, and were then taken to Washington, but were discharged. Groin, however, at once disappeared from the political history of California, spent some time in Mississippi, and then went to France to labor for the southern Confederacy. The latter part of his life was spent in California in retirement, but he died in New York in the fall of 1885, and was buried in San Francisco.

BOKER, George Henry, author and diplomat, was born Oct. 6, 1823, in Philadelphia, Pa. His father was a wealthy banker, who gave his son every educational advantage. Henry early displayed a fondness for literature, and after his graduation from Princeton, in 1842, having studied law for a few months, astonished his friends by choosing literature as his profession. In 1847 he made an extended tour in Europe, when he devoted himself to preparation for his chosen work. His first production, "The Lesson of Life and other Poems," appeared immediately after his return. The next year he published "Calaynos," a tragedy, the interest in which turned upon the hostile feeling between the Spanish and Moorish races. This was his first tragedy, and it

was received with great favor, and was acted the following April with success at Sadler's Wells Theatre, London. Mr. Boker's second tragedy, "Anne Boleyn," appeared shortly afterwards, and was also produced upon the stage. It was followed by "The Betrothal," "Leonore de Guzman," "The Widow's Marriage," and a comedy, "All the World a Mask," all of which have been produced with success. In the difficult line of dramatic composition Mr. Boker has achieved a large success, both at home and abroad. His "Francesca da Rimini" is a famous example of his work, which was made more famous by its superb representation in the hands of Lawrence Barrett. Its popularity for thirty years after its composition is a proof of its merit. In 1856 he collected his writings into two volumes of "Plays and Poems," which contained, besides those already mentioned, "The Iron Carver," "The Podesta's Daughter," "The Song of the Earth," "A Ballad of Sir John Franklin." As a lyric writer and a writer of sonnets, his abilities are of a high order. There is nothing sensational about his writings; they are models of good taste, which he adhered to at the risk of his popularity. He was intensely devoted to the union cause, and wrote numerous songs and lyrics during the civil war, which were collected into a volume in 1864, under the title "Poems of the War." Among the most notable of these were "On Board the Cumberland," "Battle of Lookout Mountain," "The Black Regiment," and "The Soldier's Dirge," for Gen. Kearney. In 1869 appeared "Königsmark; the Legend of the Hounds and other Poems," which included "Our Heroic Themes," a poem read in 1865 before the Phi Beta Kappa Society of Harvard. Later he published "Street Lyrics," and "The Book of the Dead," in 1882. In 1871 he was appointed U. S. minister to Turkey, where he was made an honorary member of the Greek Syllagos, a literary society which bestows its distinctions only on foreigners of high reputation in literature. In 1875 he was sent to the more important post of minister to Russia. He met with such favor that it is reported that Gortschakoff said to his successor: "I cannot say I am glad to see you. In fact, I am not sure that I see you at all for the tears that are in my eyes on account of the departure of our Boker." Mr. Boker presents something unique in his wonderful versatility. While he was a man of wealth, he was an author, a poet, a society man, a patriot, a politician, and a mechanic. So skilful was he in the use of tools, that he could have gone into a machine shop and earned his living. George Parsons Lathrop says of him: "He takes place with Motley on our roll of well-known authors, and it is even more remarkable that he should have cultivated poetry in Philadelphia, where the conditions were unfavorable, than that Motley should have taken up history in Boston, where the conditions were wholly propitious." Besides his poetical works, Mr. Boker wrote vigorous and eloquent prose, chiefly in the form of patriotic appeals, which were embodied in the "Reports of the Union League Club," of which he was the secretary from its first establishment until he was made its president. He was identified with the politics of his state, and took an active part in support of Republican measures and candidates. Mr. Boker's dramatic compositions avoid the stilted periods of the classic drama, but have the action befitting the stage and the finish requisite for the drawing-room, while his blank verse is smooth and his dialogue spirited. His latest work was a volume of sonnets, which appeared in 1882. The "Nation" says of him: "For a long time his position has been settled and secure." He died in Philadelphia, Jan. 2, 1890.

WYETH, Nathaniel Jarvis, pioneer explorer, was born in Cambridge, Mass., Jan. 29, 1802, son of Jacob Wyeth, a graduate from Harvard in the class of 1792. The son was given a classical education, intending to enter Harvard. He decided, however, to engage in business enterprises. In 1824 he married Elizabeth Jarvis Stone. In 1826 he entered the employment of Frederick Tudor, who was the pioneer storer of ice for shipment to tropical countries, and by his energy and inventive genius practically revolutionized this industry. In 1831, his attention having been attracted to the great Northwest, he retired from the ice business, and organized an expedition to march over the continent to establish a colony in Oregon. Though but twenty-nine years of age, he was foresighted enough to see the value of acquiring a territory so vast and important; and that thus to acquire it, it was necessary to colonize it with Americans. The question of ownership of this territory was then in dispute. The interests and influence of the Hudson Bay Co. were predominant. On Dec. 19, 1831, he wrote to Edward Everett, then secretary of state, expressing the hope that congress would "aid good men to form a settlement in that region, and assume the government of the colony." On March 11, 1832, he left Boston with a company of twenty-one men, fully armed and equipped, by way of Baltimore, Pittsburg, Cincinnati, St. Louis, and Independence, Mo., and reached Oregon, Oct. 29, 1832. Of the entire company only eight reached the Columbia. The casualties were from disease brought on by starvation, exposure, accidents, and attacks by Indians, but the chief loss was from desertion. The active part taken by the survivors in the bloody fight of Pierre's Hole with the Blackfeet is described in Washington Irving's "Bonneville." Of these eight, one died shortly after reaching Oregon, and the other seven asked to be released from their five-years' contract of colonization. Entirely alone he spent the time to Feb. 8, 1833, acquainting himself with the topography and resources of the country. He then recrossed the continent with two half-breed Indians as guides and servants, reaching Fort Leavenworth, Kansas, Sept. 27, 1833, and by March 8th he was in Boston preparing for a second expedition. On Nov. 20th he chartered a ship, and had her loaded for the Columbia trade. On May 5, 1834, he left Liberty, Mo., with sixty men; from Feb. 14th to Aug. 6th he built Fort Hall on Lewis river (now state of Idaho), and on Sept. 23d located his colony near the present site of Portland, Ore. He also built Fort William on the Columbia, and established a settlement on Wappatoo Island. About this time he was prostrated by an illness, which threatened to terminate his career. His men became discouraged and demoralized in the absence of their leader, upon whom their hopes rested. The Indians took advantage of the demoralization, and the Hudson Bay Co., seeing in Wyeth's persistent energy and pluck a formidable competitor for the trade and possession of this country, were silent abettors of the persecution and ultimate destruction of this expedition. Gov. Polly, of this company, writes in 1838, "We have compelled the American adventurers to withdraw from the contest." Of Nathaniel Wyeth, Washington Irving wrote: "He had once more reared the American flag in the lost domains of Astoria, and had he been enabled to maintain the footing he had so gallantly effected, he might have regained for his country the opulent trade of the Columbia, of which our statesmen have negligently suffered us to be dispossessed." Nathaniel Wyeth lived to see Oregon a territory of the United States, and although he died before it was admitted as a state in 1859, his last years must have been happier in the knowledge that he had done much to make the occupation of this territory possible to his fellow-countrymen. Dr. Marcus Whitman led his great caravan of about 200 wagons and 800 souls by way of Fort Hull, the route four times traveled over by Wyeth between 1832–36, and there he established a trading-post; and it was not until 1846 that Frémont occupied Oregon by way of this same route. He died Aug. 31, 1856.

WYETH, Louis Weiss, jurist, was born in Harrisburg, Pa., June 20, 1812, son of John and Louisa (Weiss) Wyeth, natives respectively of Massachusetts and Pennsylvania. His paternal grandfather, Ebenezer Wyeth, was a farmer and soldier in Capt. Samuel Thatcher's company, Col. Gardner's regiment, which took part in the fight of Concord, Apr. 19, 1775. Louis Weiss was educated at Harrisburg; began the study of law at eighteen, and three years thereafter was admitted to the bar at Carlisle, Pa. In 1833 he located at Harrisburg, and removed to Guntersville, Ala., Apr. 29, 1836. Here he continued the practice of his profession, and became one of the most successful attorneys in this part of the country. In 1837 he was appointed county judge by the governor, and was afterward elected by the legislature for a term of six years. He held the office, however, only about six months, when he resigned, and resumed his practice. In 1874 he was elected judge of the fifth judicial circuit, and was re-elected until he declined to serve. Later he was urged to accept a judgeship of the supreme court of Alabama, but declined. He was married Apr. 9, 1880, to Euphemia, daughter of John Allan, a Presbyterian minister, who came from England, settled in Georgia, and finally at Huntsville, Ala. Three children survive: Mary, wife of Hugh Carlisle; Louisa Weiss,

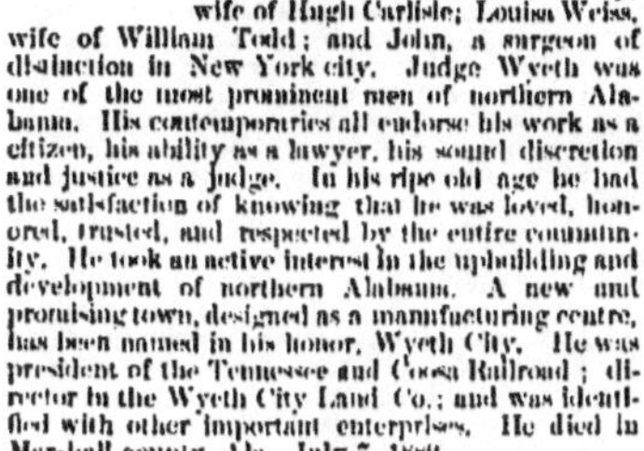

wife of William Todd; and John, a surgeon of distinction in New York city. Judge Wyeth was one of the most prominent men of northern Alabama. His contemporaries all endorse his work as a citizen, his ability as a lawyer, his sound discretion and justice as a judge. In his ripe old age he had the satisfaction of knowing that he was loved, honored, trusted, and respected by the entire community. He took an active interest in the upbuilding and development of northern Alabama. A new and promising town, designed as a manufacturing centre, has been named in his honor, Wyeth City. He was president of the Tennessee and Coosa Railroad; director in the Wyeth City Land Co.; and was identified with other important enterprises. He died in Marshall county, Ala., July 7, 1889.

WYETH, John Allan, surgeon, was born in Marshall county, Ala., May 26, 1845, son of Louis Wyeth, lawyer and judge of one of the judicial districts of Alabama, who died in 1889, at the age of seventy-seven. The grandfather of Louis Wyeth was Ebenezer Wyeth, a farmer and private in Capt. Samuel Thatcher's company of Massachusett's militia, which attacked the British, and drove them into Boston on the retreat from Lexington on Apr. 19, 1775. Thatcher's company was in the regiment of Col. Gardner, who was killed at Bunker Hill. In this company of eighty men, of whom a list is given in Paige's "History of Cambridge," "In commemoration of their patriotism in marching to the alarm on Apr. 19, 1775," there were five Wyeths. The founder of this family in America was Nicholas Wyeth (or Wythe, as the name sometimes appeared in the middle of the seventeenth century), who settled and became proprietor of lands in what is now Cambridge, Mass., in 1645. His mother was Euphemia Allan, daughter of John Allan, a Presbyterian clergyman who settled in Tennessee, having emigrated from England. He afterward removed to Huntsville, Ala. The son was educated

in the common school at Guntersville, Ala., and was one year at the Military Academy at Lagrange, Ala. He served as a private soldier in the Confederate army, took part in sixteen engagements, was confined as a prisoner of war at Camp Morton, Ind., and published an article on the treatment of prisoners at this prison in the "Century Magazine," April, 1890. He commenced the study of medicine in 1867, was graduated at the University of Louisville in 1869, took the degree of *ad eundem* at Bellevue Medical College, 1873; was appointed assistant demonstrator of anatomy in this college, 1873, and prosector to the chair of anatomy, 1874; published an article on "Dextral Preference in Man" (1875); was awarded the Alumni Association prize in 1876, for "the best essay on any subject connected with surgery or surgical pathology," his subject being "Amputations at the Ankle Joint;" won the first prize of the American Medical Association in 1876 for an essay on "The Surgical Anatomy and Surgery of the Common, External, and Internal Carotid Arteries;" and gained the second prize of the same association in 1878 for an essay on the "Surgical Anatomy and Surgery of the Innominate and Subclavian Arteries." He was appointed surgeon to Mount Sinai Hospital, 1880, founded the New York Polyclinic, a school of clinical medicine and surgery for practitioners, in 1882; became professor of surgery in that institution, and in 1893, president of the faculty. He is author of "A Text Book on Surgery" (1888); "Bloodless Amputation at the Hip Joint" (1890); "Osteo-Plastic Operation for Correction of Deformities of the Nose and Palate" (1892), an historical sketch entitled "The Struggle for Oregon" in "Harper's Magazine" (1892), and a considerable number of contributions to various scientific periodicals. He was twice president of the New York Pathological Society, and in 1893 first vice-president of the American Medical Association. In 1886 he was married to Florence Nightingale Sims, daughter of the eminent surgeon, James Marion Sims.

BLODGETT, Henry Williams, jurist, was born at Amherst, Mass., July 21, 1821, son of Israel and Avis Blodgett. His first American ancestor settled in Cambridge in 1635. With his parents he removed from Massachusetts to Illinois in 1850, and settled on a farm about thirty miles west of Chicago. Here he worked upon the farm, and was carefully instructed in the rudiments of an English education by his mother, there being at that time no schools accessible. When seventeen years old, he went back to his native state to complete his educational course, and attended for one year at the Amherst Academy, devoting himself principally to the study of surveying and civil engineering. Upon his return to Illinois he taught school and worked as a land surveyor, alternating with work on the farm. In the fall of 1842 he began the study of law in Chicago, and was admitted to the bar in January, 1845. In February he located in Waukegan, Ill., and there began the practice of his profession. In April, 1850, he was married to Alathea, daughter of Amos Crocker, of Hamilton, N. Y. He was elected a representative to the Illinois legislature in November, 1852, and served for two terms in the house. In 1858 he was elected a state senator, and served for four years. To him is due the legislation in Illinois giving married women entire control of their separate estates. He was made attorney for the Chicago and Northwestern Railway Co. in June, 1853, and served in that capacity until December, 1860. He was the originator of the Chicago and Milwaukee Railroad Co., and served as its attorney, director, and president. He was at one time local solicitor for the Michigan Southern, the Fort Wayne, and Rock Island Railroad Cos., and at the same time general solicitor of the Northwestern Railroad Co. He resigned his several railroad positions in 1869 to serve as U. S. district judge for the norther district of Illinois, to which position he had been appointed by President Grant, taking the bench in January, 1870. He remained in this position until December, 1892, when he resigned, to accept an appointment by President Harrison as one of the counsel of the United States in the Behring Sea arbitration, which was to meet in Paris, Feb. 23, 1893. He attended the session of the tribunal of arbitration, and at its close returned to the United States and retired to private life at his old home in Waukegan, Ill.

AUDUBON, John James, naturalist, was born near New Orleans, La., May 4, 1780. His father was a French admiral, who about the middle of the eighteenth century emigrated to Louisiana, bought a plantation, married a lady of Spanish descent, and reared a family. While a little boy, John James showed a remarkable interest in the birds that flew about his father's estate, and made a collection of living birds. His first attempts to draw and paint were inspired by his wish to keep in memory the beautiful plumage of some of his birds that died. In this art he was encouraged by his parents from the time he could talk, and he displayed so much talent that, at the age of fourteen, after his mother's death in a negro insurrection in San Domingo, his father took him to Paris, and placed him in the studio of the famous painter, David. This great artist's forte lay in painting battle pieces, but young Audubon paid no attention to such studies, persisting in devoting himself almost exclusively to painting birds. At the age of seventeen he returned to Louisiana, when his father, who had originally intended him for the navy, recognized the talents and tastes of the youth, and made him a present of a farm at Mill Grove, in Pennsylvania, on the banks of the Schuylkill. Here he fell in love with a Miss Lucy Bakewell, the daughter of an Englishman who owned property adjoining his own. Upon the advice of Mr. Bakewell, who thought him not practical enough, Audubon removed to New York and engaged with a business house, but he soon demonstrated his unfitness for commercial

pursuits, and returned. He formed a partnership with Ferdinand Rosier in 1808, and sold his farm, buying a stock of goods with the proceeds, married Miss Bakewell, and started for Louisville, Ky. The trip to Louisville, made on a flat boat, was their wedding journey. But Audubon could not be confined to the routine of business, and abandoned it to his partner, spending his time roaming the woods, collecting birds and making drawings of them. Here he met Alexander Wilson, the great ornithologist, who was soliciting subscriptions for his work on American birds, and who was greatly astonished when shown drawings superior to his own and of birds he had never seen. Although Wilson, in his description of this visit, spoke disparagingly of Audubon, and exhibits a spirit of jealousy towards his rival, whom he had met so unexpectedly, he did without doubt receive great assistance from Audubon's wider knowledge of the country. The partnership business naturally did not succeed, and was dissolved in 1812, when Audubon finally settled in the village of Henderson, on the banks of the Ohio river. From here, for fifteen years, the "American woodman," as he liked to be called, made excursions into the forests, and from the Great Lakes to the extremest point of Florida, from the Alleghanies to far beyond the Mississippi, he hunted birds, seeking new varieties and copying them in the size of life, measuring every part with the utmost nicety of mathematics. "It was no desire of glory," he said himself, "which led me into this exile. I wished only to enjoy nature." He made another unsuccessful business venture with his brother-in-law in New Orleans, and was afterwards in dire straits, being obliged to give drawing lessons and make money on portraits. It is said that his wife encouraged and assisted Audubon, while all other friends considered him mad to give himself up so entirely to such unprofitable work, and she even became a governess in New Orleans in order to obtain money with which

to educate her children. Finally she established a school at Bayou Sara for the purpose of assisting her husband and lightening his expenses, thus enabling him to carry out his plans. Upon the death of his father he fell heir to an estate in France and about $17,000 in money, but the trustee who had charge of the estate failed, and not one penny ever came into his hands. On one occasion Audubon paid a visit to some relatives in Philadelphia, carrying with him 200 of his designs. Being obliged to leave Philadelphia for some weeks, on his return, to his horror and despair, he discovered that they had been totally destroyed by mice. He was obliged to start once more into the forest to renew these examples, and it took him three years to repair the damage. During his stay in Philadelphia, in 1824, Audubon made the acquaintance of Prince Canino, the son of Prince Lucien Bonaparte, who strongly urged the naturalist to publish his designs. Audubon was impressed with the idea and finally determined to do so, proposing to issue several volumes of engravings, colored and in life size, with other volumes of printed description, the price of the work being fixed at $1,000. He issued his prospectus in 1827 in England, for his "Birds of America," which was to be published in numbers, each containing five plates; the whole work to consist of four folio volumes. At the time the prospectus was issued he had not enough money to pay for even the first number, but through the influence of Sir Thomas Lawrence, the painter, he was enabled to sell some pictures, which provided for the engraver's first bill. He was obliged to be his own publisher, besides personally soliciting subscriptions from the public, but his enthusiasm was positively infectious and won for him strong friends and supporters. In 1828 he went to France, where he spent two months canvassing, and the next year returned to America for the same pur-

pose. His wife was devoted to him through all these trials, and frequently traveled with him, assisting in getting subscriptions. He was received in Europe with great distinction, and obtained in all nearly 170 subscribers, of whom, however, he lost nearly one-half, owing to the financial disaster of 1837. He made many friends among the eminent men abroad, including Herschel, Sir Walter Scott, and "Christopher North," in England, and Cuvier, Humboldt, and St. Hilaire, in France. In 1830 the first volume of his work appeared in London, consisting of 100 colored plates. The volume excited enthusiasm wherever it was exhibited, and the King of France and the King of England both wrote their names at the head of the list of subscribers. The principal learned societies of London and Paris added Audubon to the number of their members, and the great naturalists, Cuvier, Humboldt, Wilson, and others, were warm in the expressions of their praise. During the publication of his work, Audubon made several trips across the Atlantic, collecting material through the States, and, in particular, being enabled to study the birds on the coast of Florida, in a vessel provided for him by the Government of the United States. The work, when completed, consisted of four large folio volumes of colored engravings and five of letter-press, and was finished in 1839. In 1840 he left England for the last time, and bought a beautiful residence on the Hudson, near the city, which he named Minnie's Land, in honor of his wife, and which afterwards became "Audubon Park." During the next four years he was engaged at his home in preparing for the press an edition of his great work on smaller paper, in seven volumes, which he completed in 1844. At about this time Audubon exhibited in New York a wonderful collection of his original drawings, containing several thousand examples, all of which he had studied in their native homes, all drawn of the size of life by his own hand, and all represented with their natural foliage and accessories around them. In 1846 Audubon issued the first volume of his work on the "Quadrupeds of America," much of the material for which he gathered in the woods, accompanied by his two sons, Victor and John, who with the Rev. John Bachman, of Charleston, S. C., completed the work. When Audubon died, his name passed into history as the "great 'American woodsman,' the unequaled painter, and gifted historian of nature." His wife lived until 1874, and wrote the biography of her husband, which was published in New York in 1868.

Audubon was buried in Trinity Church cemetery, near his home. A movement to erect a monument to the great naturalist, at the present writing (1895), promises to meet with success. Audubon is described as having been tall and remarkably well formed, and, at the age of sixty-five years, his natural vigor appeared to be in no degree abated. His forehead was high, his nose long and aquiline, his chin prominent, and his mouth characterized by energy and determination; his eyes were dark gray, set deeply in his head and as restless as the glance of an eagle. His manners were extremely gentle and his conversation full of point and spirit. Besides his eminent talent as an artist, Audubon was a vigorous and picturesque writer. Some passages of his, descriptive of the habits of birds, are among the finest pieces of writing of that character ever produced in America, and have been made familiar to the public through the medium of reading-books. Audubon was whole-souled in his generosity. He freely parted with choice specimens after he had described them. To this trait the National Museum at Washington owes its possession of the "Audubon types," which were presented by the naturalist to his friend, Spencer F. Baird, who transferred them to their present place of deposit, when he became head of the Smithsonian Institution. At the time of his death Audubon was a fellow of the Linnæan and Zoölogical Societies of London, of the Natural History Society of Paris, of the Wernerian Society of Edinburgh, of the Lyceum of Natural History of New York, and an honorary member of the Society of Natural History of Manchester, and many other scientific bodies. Audubon's great work on birds is confessedly the most important and the finest in execution of any publication of that character ever issued. Copies of it sell at auction at from $1,000 to $1,500, according to condition. His death occurred at his home on the Hudson, Jan. 27, 1851.

DAVEISS, Joseph Hamilton, lawyer (widely known as Joe Daveiss), was born in Bedford county, Va., March 4, 1774, of Irish and Scotch ancestors. He was the son of Joseph and Jean Daveiss, both of Virginia, and at the age of five his parents removed to Kentucky, then an almost unbroken wilderness, and settled in what was then Lincoln county, near the present town of Danville. Owing to the lack of educational facilities he was taught by his mother, but at the age of eleven or twelve years he was sent to a grammar school, remaining there three years. He excelled in mathematics and the classics, and always stood at the head of his class. He had an unusual talent for declamation and public speaking. He was recalled on the death of a brother and sister, and returned home to assist his father on the farm. He was not fond of agricultural pursuits, and was in the habit of shirking his duties to continue his education by reading. At the age of eighteen young Daveiss volunteered in the Indian campaign under Maj. Adair. His term of service expired in six months, and concluding to study the law, he entered the office of George Nicholas. He was a most laborious and indefatigable student. In connection with his legal studies he read history and miscellaneous literature, so that when he was admitted to the bar in 1795 his mind was richly stored with various and profound knowledge. He commenced the practice of his profession at Danville and soon commanded a splendid business in all the courts in which he practiced. Soon after removing to Frankfort a few years later, he was appointed U. S. attorney for the state of Kentucky. In the year 1802 he went to Washington to argue an important suit, being the first Western lawyer who ever appeared in the supreme court of the United States, and there his speech excited the greatest admiration of the bench and bar and placed him at once in the foremost rank of the profession. During this trip he visited the principal cities of the North and East and made the acquaintance of the most distinguished men of America. In 1803 he was married to Anne Marshall, a sister of the chief-justice of the United States. In 1808 Daveiss appeared in open court before Judge Inness and moved for process to compel Aaron Burr to attend and answer a charge of high misdemeanor in organizing from within the jurisdiction of the United States a military expedition against Mexico, a friendly power. This motion was grounded upon the oath of the attorney, setting forth with great accuracy the preparations then being made by Burr, and imputing to him designs, which subsequently proved to have been well understood by him. After considering the application for two days, the court overruled the motion, but Burr appeared in court the next day and requested the motion be granted, and asked for an immediate investigation. Daveiss's witnesses could not be produced and the prosecution was ultimately abandoned. In 1801 he removed to Lexington, where he continued in the practice of his profession until his untimely death. In the fall of 1811 Daveiss joined Gen. Harrison's army in the campaign against the Indians and received the command of major. He took prominent part in the battle of Tippecanoe, in which he was shot while leading a cavalry charge against the savages, dying a few hours afterwards, Nov. 7, 1811. Daveiss county, Ky., was named in his honor, the spelling being afterwards changed to Daviess.

BLODGETT, Delos Abiel, capitalist, son of Abiel and Susan Richmond Blodgett, was born in Otsego county, N. Y., March 3, 1825, of New England ancestry. When he was four years of age the family removed from Otsego to Erie county, where they settled on a farm. From then until he was twenty years of age he resided with his parents, assisted in the farm work, and attended the district and select schools. At the age of twenty he left home, and as a raftsman and boatman worked his way down the Alleghany, Ohio, and Mississippi rivers and finally landed in New Orleans; his health failed him and he decided to return North, going to McHenry county, Ill., to which point his parents had in the mean time removed. In the fall of 1848 he started for western Michigan then just coming into notice as an important lumbering state; he landed in Muskegon and found employment in the lumber woods in that vicinity. Two years later he entered into the logging and lumber business on his own account, and from that time his career has formed a large part of the history of the development of western Michigan. He has been continually and extensively engaged in lumbering as well as farming, banking, and real estate. He still has large holdings of timber lands in Michigan, Washington, Oregon, and most of the Gulf states, and is largely interested in real estate in Grand Rapids and Chicago. Mr. Blodgett has never been a candidate for any public office nor a member of any secret society. Politically he is a staunch Republican, and his counsel, his labors, and his cash have always been freely given in behalf of his party. He was a delegate in 1880 to the National Republican Convention held at Chicago, and again in 1892 a delegate at large to the National Republican Convention held at Minneapolis, Minn. In matters of religion he is an Agnostic, believing in "one world at a time." On Sept. 9, 1859, Mr. Blodgett was united in marriage to Jennie Wood, of Woodstock, Ill., who died in October, 1890, leaving a son, John Blodgett, and a daughter, Mrs. Edward Lowe, both of Grand Rapids. On June 3, 1893, Mr. Blodgett married Daisy, daughter of the author, Prof. William Henry Peck, of Atlanta, Ga. Though far from robust in physique or health he has been an indefatigable worker, a man of great activity and surprising energy. To his industry as well as his business integrity and great courage, is his marked business success due; a success that has left no rancor in the minds of his employees or competitors, because it has never been at the expense of any one else and has never changed his manners or his kindliness toward others. His large business interests have never closed his ears or his hands to the needs of his fellowmen. A worthy cause, no matter in what department of charitable, religious, social, educational, or political work, is sure of his prompt and generous assistance. He is a close observer, a student, appreciating the progress of humanity.

WARD, James Edward, ship owner, founder of the Ward line of steamships, was born in the city of New York, Feb. 25, 1836. His father was James Otis Ward, of New York (where he established one of the first sailing vessel lines), formerly of Roxbury, Mass., the family having a lineage there dating as far back as 1643. At an early age he began an active business career, and was the foremost representative of American shipping interests engaged in foreign trade. Mr. Ward commenced business under the firm name of James E. Ward & Co. in the year 1856, establishing the well-known Ward line of sailing packets for Havana. The firm has been in successful existence since that time. In the year 1875 he had in the freighting business of the world, afloat under the American flag, some forty sail, principally in the trade to the West Indies, and notably the Havana line. In 1866 he commenced the first regular steam communication between New York and Havana with the steamship Cuba. The steamship Liberty followed some time after, and in 1875 various freight steamships were under charter in the Cuban trade under the Ward flag. In the year 1877, when steam had made great inroads in the general carrying trade, he became convinced that the day of wooden sailing-vessels in the trade of the West Indies was near its end. With his far-seeing business penetration he contracted with the great American shipbuilder, John Roach, for the construction of two iron steamships for the Havana line, and proceeded to sell the fleet of sail. This new departure resulted in the dispatch of the first-class iron steamships Saratoga and Niagara, of 2,300 tons each, fitted for passengers and for the handling of cargo in all respects in advance of anything then afloat under the American flag. The Saratoga was shortly sold to the Russian government for a naval cruiser, in which service she has since continued an object lesson of the value of the merchant marine as a naval reserve. The second Saratoga was immediately commenced, and launched in the latter part of 1878, a model of beauty, of some 2,500 tons, surpassing her predecessors in power, speed, and passenger accommodations. In 1879 the steamship Santiago was built, a new departure for the accommodation of trade and travel to the south side of Cuba. In 1880 the famous steamship Newport, of 2,800 tons, was built, with speed and elegance of fittings surpassing all in advance of her building. She completed the Havana fleet. Mr. Ward had thus given the island of Cuba for the entire north and south coasts, in both accommodations and tonnage, a high-water mark, up to which her trade must yet grow. The results met his expectations. The line prospered, its full capacity occupied through the increase of the island's commerce with this country. In 1883 the Cienfuegos was built for the south route, and thus the Ward fleet continued to increase, until to day ten first-class iron and steel steamships, of some 80,000 tons, regularly steam between New York and points in the island of Cuba, Mexico, and Nassau, the product of an enterprising spirit, begun in 1856 with a monthly sailing of small vessels from 200 to 400 tons each. Mr. Ward was always a strong advocate of the American flag over American-built ships, taking a most active and patriotic interest in any effort to promote the extension of the American merchant marine in the foreign trade. He was an active promoter and supporter of the American Shipping and Industrial League, which did so much to arouse the country and congress to action in its fiftieth session for the revival of its marine supremacy on the ocean, which he had seen wrested from the nation's grasp in the span of his business life by the English and other great maritime powers of the world. He was married to Harriet Augusta Morrell, Oct. 1, 1857. He died at his country seat, Great Neck, L. I., July 24, 1894. One daughter survived him, Florence, wife of Alphonse Alker, of New York.

LOOMIS, John Mason, merchant, was born at Windsor, Conn., Jan. 5, 1825, son of Col. James Loomis, a farmer, merchant, and miller. He was colonel of the 1st regiment of Connecticut state militia, and a great admirer of John Mason, a famous New England soldier, in admiration of whose powers he named his son. He is the descendant of an old English family, of which the pioneer in America was Joseph Loomis of Braintree, England, who came to this country on the ship Susan and Ellen, reaching Boston July 17, 1638. The records at Windsor show that he bought a piece of land at the confluence of the Farmington and Connecticut rivers, in what is now Hartford county, Feb. 24, 1640, and this estate is still in possession of

the family. His mother, Abigal Sherwood (Chaffe) Loomis, was a native of Greenfield Hill, Conn., a descendant of a family noted for its high social standing and the large number of successful practitioners it furnished to the medical profession. The son received his early education in the common schools and academies of Connecticut, and he afterwards had some practical business training in his father's store. He came of fighting stock, however, and at the age of eighteen became captain of a company of militia. Before this time he had been appointed a midshipman in the navy. Becoming tired of waiting to be detailed for service, he shipped in the China tea trade and served in the various grades of a sailor. In 1846 he went to Chicago, and

thence to Milwaukee, where he found employment as a clerk and bookkeeper in a lumber yard. His first year's salary was $62. In 1848, at the suggestion of his employers, he bought their stock, giving his note for the purchase. He prospered from the start, and with the exception of his army service during the civil war, has been in the lumber trade ever since. In 1849 he married Mary, daughter of Milo Hunt, of Chenango county, N. Y. In 1852 Mr. Loomis transferred his business to Chicago. At the outbreak of the civil war, in 1861, his business was as extensive and profitable as the trade of any lumber firm in the Northwest. When the war broke out Gov. Yates appointed him to the command of the 26th Illinois Infantry, as colonel. At the close of its three years' service the regiment re-enlisted for the war, and on accepting the service Gov. Yates said: "When I selected Col. Loomis as commanding officer of this regiment it was not because he raised it. I selected him for his ability to command, for his military talent, and for his devotion to his country; and I have not mistaken the man. He has been equal to the emergency. The names of New Madrid, of Island No. 10, of Iuka, Corinth, Farmington, Vicksburg, Jackson, Tunnel Hill, and Chattanooga, are inscribed on your battle-worn flags." While in the field Col. Loomis was in command of the brigade to which his regiment was attached, and he was known as a fighting colonel, rigid in discipline, honored and loved as a father, and trusted as a leader. There was no march too long, no fatigue too great, no effort too supreme for the 26th Illinois infantry so long as Col. Loomis was at its head. On leaving the army, in 1864, Col. Loomis found his business affairs gone entirely into other hands, and he was utterly without money. Grave as was the situation, Col. Loomis was undaunted, and soon began in the lumber business anew as a commission merchant. His efforts soon secured a good patronage, and two or three years of close economy gave him capital enough to begin the purchase of pine lands in Michigan. He organized the Père Marquette Lumber Co., and has since directed its management; and through this and other lumber interests he has accumulated a large fortune: much is invested in real estate and in the business districts and finer residence quarters of Chicago. After the fire of 1871, Col. Loomis was a member of the board of direction of the Chicago Relief and Aid Society. He served the society as auditor in 1873, and was a member of the auditing committee from 1874 to 1881, and has given freely of his time and means in behalf of this great charity. He became an active member of the Citizens' Association of Chicago soon after its organization in 1874. He is a member of the committee on military affairs, and served as its chairman from 1879 to 1883. During Col. Loomis's administration not less than $50,000 was raised by popular subscription under his direction, and applied to the purchase of arms, clothing, and equipments for the national guard. In connection with other members of the Loomis family he, in 1878, incorporated the Loomis Institute of Windsor, Conn., for the free education of all persons between the ages of twelve and twenty years who can read and write, and who understand the elements of arithmetic, grammar, and geography; giving preference to those belonging to the Loomis family by name or consanguinity. Under the provision of an act of the Connecticut legislature, the Loomis family is accumulating a fund for the endowment of the Institute which will eventually amount to from $1,500,000 to $2,000,000. In addition to the monetary gifts and bequests made by will and the investment of large funds in good paying real estate for the benefit of the institute, the five members of the family who are parties to the compact have devised the old homestead at Windsor for a building site. The trustees are authorized to select fifty acres of this estate for institute ground, and provision is made for its permanent maintenance. This land, which is known as "the Island," is not only of large money value but possesses great historical attraction, especially to the Loomis family, in whose possession it has been for seven generations. Col. Loomis, by reason of his army experience, takes a deep interest in the veteran soldiers' organization, and is active in their support. He was one of the charter members of the Loyal Legion, and in 1884 succeeded Gen. Sheridan as commander of the Illinois commandery. He is a member of the George H. Thomas Post, G. A. R., and holds the honorary position of colonel for life of the military association of the survivors of the 26th Illinois Infantry veteran volunteers. Col. Loomis is a member of Grace Episcopal Church. He is a member of the Chicago, Calumet, Union, Washington Park, Tolleston, and other clubs. In politics he is a Republican, and is active in the selection of good men for office, and the securing of good government. His home in Chicago is one of the finest residences in that city of palatial homes, and is a model of good taste and domestic comfort.

HOWE, Robert, soldier, was born in Brunswick county, N. C., in 1732. His ancestry was English, and he received but little early education. He married when very young, and apparently married well, as he was able to visit England, where he lived for two years, visiting among his relatives and connections. In 1766 he returned to America and entered the British service, being commissioned by Gov. Tryon captain of Fort Johnson in North Carolina. In 1772 he was a member of the colonial assembly, and in 1774 a delegate to the congress which was held at New Berne, where he so conducted himself as to bring himself in conflict with the colonial government. In 1775 Howe was appointed colonel of the 1st North Carolina regiment and was proclaimed by the governor of the colony as a traitor. In December of the same year he was ordered to Virginia, where he aided the patriots of that colony in driving Lord Dunmore from the country. He was now promoted to brigadier-general, and joined Gen. Henry Lee in his expedition to the South, being received with public honors as he passed through North Carolina. So bitter was the feeling of the Tories against him that Sir Henry Clinton sent Lord Cornwallis with a large detachment of troops to ravage his plantation in Brunswick county. During the defense of Charleston, Gen. Howe commanded the North Carolina contingent, and later he was commander-in-chief of the southern department. In 1777 he received his commission as major-general, and in the following year commanded an expedition against Florida, which was unsuccessful. He attempted to defend Savannah in 1778, but having a very small force, was surprised in the night by Lieut.-Col. Campbell and forced to evacuate the place. For this act he was severely criticised, but on being summoned before a court-martial he was honorably acquitted. Among the animadversions on his conduct, however, that of Gen. Christopher Gadsden, of Charleston, most irritated him, and he at once challenged its author. They fought at Cannonsburg, Aug. 13, 1778, when Howe shot Gadsden in the ear and the latter fired in the air. The result of the duel was a reconciliation. Maj. André wrote a humorous account of the duel in eighteen stanzas, to the tune of "Yankee Doodle." He was now removed from the South and sent to the northern department, and in 1779 he co-operated with Gen. Wayne in his attack upon Stony Point on the Hudson. Thereafter he was on duty in the vicinity of West Point and

the Hudson Highlands until near the close of the war. On two occasions Gen. Howe was specially appointed by Washington to discharge the important duty of quelling a mutiny—first in the New Jersey line and then in that of Pennsylvania, and he always had the unbounded confidence of the commander-in-chief. In May, 1775, congress appointed him to treat with the western Indians. On his return from the accomplishment of this duty, he was not only received with public honors in North Carolina, but was elected to the legislature of that state. Unfortunately, however, he was attacked with fever, and died before taking his seat, on Nov. 12, 1785.

O'BRIEN, Fitz-James, author, was born in Limerick, Ireland, about the year 1828. His father was a barrister in comfortable circumstances, and his mother a lady of remarkable beauty and culture. He received his education at the University of Dublin, but was not trained for any particular profession. He very early displayed a taste for literature, and while at college wrote two poems, entitled "Loch Ine," and "Irish Castles," which appeared anonymously in the "Ballads of Ireland," in 1850. On leaving college he went to London, where, in the course of about two years he dissipated his inheritance, which is stated to have been about £8,000. In 1852 he considered it advisable to seek his fortune in the New World, and bringing letters to several prominent literary men, 

was enabled to make an auspicious entrance into society and literature, and it was not long before his brilliant abilities were recognized and he became a general favorite. His first literary work was for the "Lantern," published by John Brougham. T. B. Aldrich says he first met O'Brien trimming the wick of the "Lantern," which went out shortly afterward. He contributed in a desultory way to the "Home Journal," "Evening Post," "New York Times," and the "American Whig Review." His associations circled around Willis and Morris, while he led the life of a literary soldier of fortune, with expensive tastes and habits of extravagance which made Grub Street a hard road to travel. His most important literary association was when he became a regular contributor to "Harper's Magazine," in 1853. His first article was entitled "The Two Skulls," a philosophical and scientific production, which was followed by sixty-six other articles in prose and verse. He was a prolific writer for "Harper's Weekly," and contributed to the "Saturday Press" dramatic sketches which were incisive and informing. He possessed a showy dramatic sense acquired in his London days. To "Putnam's Magazine" he was a contributor from its inception, several of his best efforts appearing in the magazine. He was a diligent writer for "Vanity Fair," to which he contributed that grisly fancy "The Wharf Rat," and the "Song of The Locomotive." Two of his most remarkable productions were "The Diamond Lens" and "The Wondersmith," which appeared in the "Atlantic Monthly." They electrified the literary world and set up a model of excellence which gave a marked improvement to periodical literature. All this time he was writing for the stage, of which he was passionately fond. He was intimate with James Wallack and wrote for him bright and spirited plays, some of which, notably "A Gentleman from Ireland," still holds the boards. At the instance of Jefferson he adapted "The Tycoon," for Laura Keene. At one time he traveled with the Matilda Heron Co. as literary assistant, visiting Boston and other cities. When the war broke out he joined the 7th regiment and became captain, but he was disappointed in not being called into active service, and upon the return of the regiment he left it to recruit a volunteer regiment called the McClellan Rifles. He was subsequently appointed to the staff of Gen. Frederick Lander, and went to the front in Virginia, where he distinguished himself by his energy and bravery. In a skirmish with Col. Ashley's cavalry he was severely wounded, and died on the night of April, 1862, at Cumberland, Va. His body was brought home and buried with impressive honors in Greenwood. His intimate friend, William Winter, made a collection of his poems and sketches to which he added the personal recollections of the author's old associates. This was published in Boston in 1881. O'Brien had great personal magnetism; his literary genius was extraordinary, and his intellectual activity incredible. His poem "A Fallen Star," was written between midnight and morning at one sitting. "The Sewing Bird," was written in two days during one of his fits of depression, but when he received the $100 for which he sold it, he was as merry as a lark. In addition to those mentioned, his best poems are "The Zouaves" and "The Lost Steamship."

ADAMS, Jonathan, civil engineer, was born in Taunton, Mass., July 8, 1798. At an early age he began the business of engineering, his first employment being upon the Chesapeake and Ohio canal, a work which had been recommended by Washington ; but on the introduction of railways he devoted himself to that branch of his profession. Many of the important lines in New York and New England were constructed under his supervision, and for fifty years he ranked as one of the most skilful railroad engineers in this country. He died, Sept. 6, 1873.

GREENLEAF, Franklin Lewis, manufacturer, was born in Boston, Mass., Oct. 7, 1847, son of Gardner Greenleaf. He was educated at the Boston Latin School and at Chauncy Hall. In 1865 he went to Colorado, where he engaged in general merchandising, and also became interested in mining. After remaining in Colorado, for three years, he removed to Minneapolis, Minn., where he engaged in the wholesale and retail boot and shoe business for seven years. In 1875 he commenced the manufacture of flour, forming the firm of H. F. Brown & Co., and purchased the Dakota mill ; in 1878 he formed the firm of Hinkle, Greenleaf & Co., and operated the Humboldt and Florence mills. These mills had a capacity of 2,200 barrels of flour per day. In 1890 he withdrew from the firm, and continued to operate the Florence mill, under the name of the Florence Mill Co. In the same year he formed the partnership firm

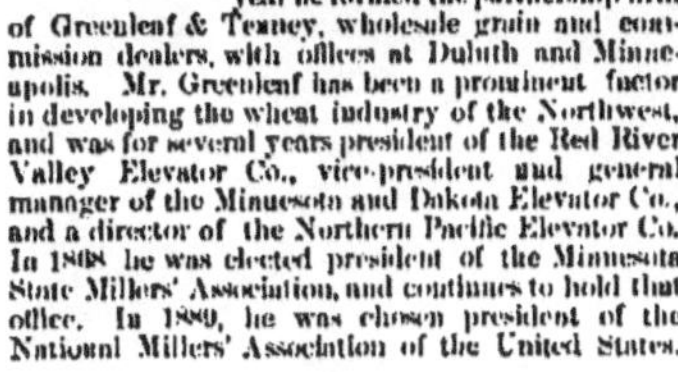

of Greenleaf & Tenney, wholesale grain and commission dealers, with offices at Duluth and Minneapolis. Mr. Greenleaf has been a prominent factor in developing the wheat industry of the Northwest, and was for several years president of the Red River Valley Elevator Co., vice-president and general manager of the Minnesota and Dakota Elevator Co., and a director of the Northern Pacific Elevator Co. In 1888 he was elected president of the Minnesota State Millers' Association, and continues to hold that office. In 1889, he was chosen president of the National Millers' Association of the United States.

In 1891, he was elected president of the National Transportation Association, and from 1865 to 1889 was vice-president of the Minneapolis chamber of commerce, and was elected as its president in 1889, 1890, and 1891, consecutively. In 1888 he served as alderman in the city council.

VANDERBURGH, Charles Edwin, jurist, was born in Saratoga county, N. Y., Dec. 2, 1829. His father was a farmer, and the son attended the district school during the winter months and worked on the farm in the summer until fifteen years old, when he prepared for college at Courtland Academy, Homer, N. Y. He was admitted to the sophomore class of Yale College in 1849, and was graduated with the class of 1852. He then became principal of the Academy at Oxford, N. Y., and in connection with the management of the school, took up the study of law. He was admitted to the bar in 1855, and the next year removed to Minneapolis, Minn., formed a partnership with

F. R. E. Cornell, which became one of the leading law firms of the new state. In 1859 Mr. Vanderburgh was elected judge of the fourth judicial district, which position he held for over twenty-two years. His thorough legal training, habits of close investigation, and discrimination, in the application of legal principles, led him to sound conclusions, and his decisions were seldom reversed. He ranks very high as an equity judge. In 1881, the death of Judge Cornell created a vacancy on the bench of the supreme court of Minnesota, and Judge Vanderburgh was elected to fill it. He served two terms, twelve years in all, retiring from the bench Jan. 1, 1894. He was twice married. His first wife was Julia Mygatt, of Oxford, N. Y., to whom he was married in September, 1857. She died in 1863, leaving two children, William Henry and Julia Vanderburgh. In 1873, Judge Vanderburgh was married to Anna, daughter of John Culbert, of Fulton county, N. Y. In political faith he is a republican, but in no sense a partisan. He was brought into national prominence in 1860 by reason of his decision in the case of the slave woman Eliza Winston, owned by Col. Christmas of Mississippi brought to Minneapolis by her master on a visit, and there by a writ of Habeas Corpus brought before Judge Vanderburgh, who declared "that slavery was a local institution, and that a slave brought into a free state by its owner became free." He therefore advised the woman that she was free to choose whether to remain with her former owner or to leave him. She chose the latter. A body of abolitionists active in the matter thereupon took her in charge, and in spite of protests and considerable force enabled her to escape to Canada. The Judge has for many years been a prominent member and officer of the Presbyterian church and active in philanthropic and evangelical work.

BADGER, Milton, clergyman, was born at Coventry, Conn., May 6, 1800. He was graduated at Yale in 1823, and, after studying theology at Andover, Mass., entered the Congregational ministry in 1828. For the next seven years he officiated as pastor of a church at Andover, and in 1835 was appointed one of the secretaries of the American Home Missionary Society. He held this office for nearly thirty-five years—most of the time being the senior secretary—and did not resign until forced to relinquish work by old age and many infirmities. He died March 1, 1873.

James Monroe

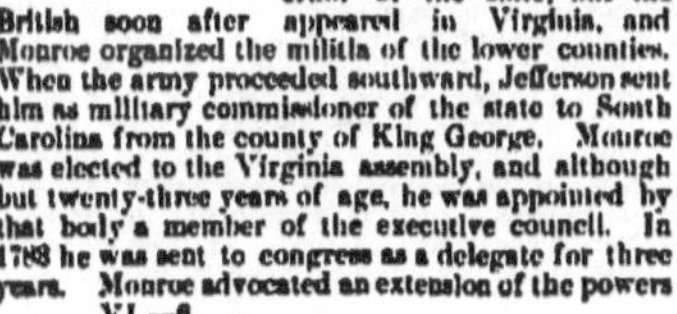

MONROE, James, fifth president of the United States, was born in West Walden county, Va., Apr. 28, 1758. He was descended from English ancestry, the first of the name having been an officer in the army of Charles I., who emigrated with other cavaliers to Virginia in 1657. The future president was educated at William and Mary College. He left in 1776 to enter the army. He was soon commissioned lieutenant, and was active in the campaigns on the Hudson river. He was engaged in the affair at Trenton, N. J., where with a small detachment he captured one of the British batteries. He was wounded on the shoulder in this action, and for his gallant conduct was promoted to a captaincy. In 1777 Monroe was appointed aide-de-camp to Lord Stirling, with the rank of major. During that and the following year he fought at Brandywine, Germantown and Monmouth, but by having accepted a staff position he forfeited his rank as a commissioned officer in the regular army. Returning to Virginia, he began the study of law under the supervision of Thomas Jefferson, at that time governor of the state, but the British soon after appeared in Virginia, and Monroe organized the militia of the lower counties. When the army proceeded southward, Jefferson sent him as military commissioner of the state to South Carolina from the county of King George. Monroe was elected to the Virginia assembly, and although but twenty-three years of age, he was appointed by that body a member of the executive council. In 1783 he was sent to congress as a delegate for three years. Monroe advocated an extension of the powers of congress, and in 1785 moved to invest that body with authority to regulate trade between the states. It was this resolution, which was referred to a committee, and on which a favorable report was made, that led to the convention at Annapolis and the subsequent adoption of the Federal constitution. Monroe was appointed a member of the commission to decide upon the boundary between Massachusetts and New York. He also exerted himself in devising a system for the settlement of the public lands. In 1785 Monroe married a daughter of Lawrence Kortright, of New York, a lady who was justly celebrated for her beauty and accomplishments. Three years later Monroe was re-elected to the general assembly, and in 1788 was chosen a delegate to the Virginia convention to decide upon the adoption of the Federal constitution. He was apprehensive that the instrument, as submitted, conferred too much power upon the general government, and was one of the minority in that state, but this course of action was warmly approved by the great mass of the people of Virginia, and in 1790 Monroe was chosen from that state as senator. In the senate he at once became a prominent representative of the anti-federal party, with which he acted until the expiration of his term. In May, 1794, Monroe was appointed minister plenipotentiary to France, and was received in France with respect, and even enthusiasm, but his marked sympathy with the French republic was displeasing to the administration. John Jay had been sent to negotiate a treaty with England, and the course pursued by Monroe was considered injudicious, as tending to throw serious obstacles in the way of the proposed negotiations. On the conclusion of the treaty Monroe's alleged failure was presented in its true character to the French government, and in August, 1796, he was recalled under an informal censure. Soon after his return to America, Mr. Monroe published a review of the conduct of the executive in the foreign affairs of the United States, which served to widen the breach between himself and the administration. He

VI.—6

remained on good terms with Washington and Jay, however. From 1799 to 1802 Monroe was governor of Virginia, and at the close of his term was appointed envoy extraordinary to the French government to negotiate, in conjunction with the resident minister, Mr. Livingston, for the purchase of Louisiana. The result was that within a fortnight after his arrival in Paris the entire territory of Orleans and district of Louisiana was secured for $15,000,000, an acquisition of territory whose worth was almost inestimable. In the same year Monroe was commissioned minister plenipotentiary to England, but was soon sent to Madrid as minister extraordinary and plenipotentiary to adjust the controversy between the United States and Spain in relation to the boundaries of the new purchase of Louisiana. In this he failed, and in 1806 he was recalled to England, where a treaty was concluded for the protection of neutral rights, but which was deemed ambiguous in relation to certain important points and which omitted any provision against the impressment of seamen, and in consequence of these faults the president sent it back for revisal, pending which Monroe returned to America. In 1810 Monroe was appointed to the general assembly of Virginia, and in 1811 was again governor of the commonwealth, but in the same year assumed the position of secretary of state, to which he was appointed by President Madison. After the capture

of Washington, in 1814, Monroe was appointed to the war department, which he took without relinquishing his former post. He improved the condition of the army greatly by his judicious administration and even pledged his private means to sustain the public credit, which was completely prostrated. It was this latter act which enabled the city of New Orleans to successfully oppose the attack of the enemy. Monroe continued to serve as secretary of state to the end of Madison's administration in 1817, when he succeeded to the presidency as a candidate of the party then generally known as democratic-republicans, by an electoral vote of 183 out of 217. During a tour which Monroe made through the Middle and Eastern states for the inspection of arsenals, naval depots, fortifications and garrisons, he found that the party spirit which had been lately so rampant, was greatly allayed. He was careful, however, in making appointments to the offices within his gift, to select none but his most devoted adherents. John Quincy Adams was recalled from the Court of St. James to become his secretary of state. The other members of his cabinet were William H. Crawford, of Georgia, secretary of the treasury; John C. Calhoun, of South Carolina, secretary of war ; Benjamin W. Crowninshield of Massachusetts, secretary of the navy, and William Wirt, of Virginia, attorney-general. In the meantime the influence of the revolution had affected other nations. The Spanish colonies in

South America threw off their allegiance to the mother-country and declared themselves independent. Under pretext of having commissions from these new republics, adventurers seized Amelia Island, off the harbor of St. Augustine. A similar haunt for buccaneers—for these worthies had soon begun to smuggle merchandise and slaves into the United States—had existed for some time at Galveston, Tex. Both of these establishments were now broken up by order of the United States government. The condition of the South American republics excited great sympathy in the minds of the people. Some advocated giving them aid, while others were anxious that congress should at least acknowledge their independence. Cruisers bearing the flags of these republics were fitted out in some of the ports of the United States to prey on Spanish commerce. In regard to the Florida trouble, it was somewhat serious. It originated in the conflict between the South American republics and their mother-country, and in the fact that privateers bearing the flags of these republics were fitted out in some of the southern ports of the United States to prey upon Spanish commerce. All of this led to a lingering war, and the Georgia settlements were pillaged by bands of Seminoles, refugee Creeks, and others, and, finally, a boat ascending the Appalachicola was attacked, and more than fifty persons, men, women, and children were massacred. This brought orders from Washington to Gen. Jackson to invade the Indian territory, which he did with small ceremony, hanging some of the hostile chiefs whom he captured, and seizing the only Spanish fort in the disturbed part of Florida, on the ground that its officers were aiding the Indians in their hostility to the United States. He also captured Pensacola. These arbitrary proceedings were brought to the consideration of the government at Washington by the Spanish minister, with the result that Florida was ceded to the United States for the consideration that the United States assumed a debt of about $5,000,000, which American citizens had claims against the Spanish government. In March, 1822, new interest was awakened in behalf of the South American republics. Great efforts had been made by Henry Clay during their struggle to induce congress to acknowledge their independence, but it was then thought premature. Now the bill was passed. The next year the president declared in his message to congress that " As a principle, the American continents by the free and independent position which they have assumed and maintained are henceforth not to be considered as subjects for future colonization by any European power." This has since been known as the " Monroe doctrine," though its authorship, it would seem, belonged rather to Monroe's secretary of state, John Quincy Adams. The last year of Monroe's administration was signalized by the visit of the venerable Marquis de Lafayette to the United States as the invited guest of the nation. On Mar. 4, 1825, Monroe retired from office and returned to his residence at Oak Hill in Virginia. He was chosen a justice of the peace and as such sat in the county court. In 1829 he became a member of the Virginia convention to revise the old constitution, and was chosen to preside over the deliberations of that body but he was compelled by ill health to resign his post in the convention and to return to Oak Hill. In addition to his bodily infirmities, Monroe suffered under the misfortune of pecuniary embarrassment, and although he had received $350,000 for his public services, yet in his old age he was harassed by debt. Monroe's wife died in 1830 and in the summer of that year he removed his residence to that of his son-in-law, Samuel L. Gouverneur, in the city of New York, where he died. In 1858 his remains were removed with great pomp to Richmond, Va., and reinterred on July 5th, in the Hollywood cemetery. It is justly said of Monroe that he held the reins of government at an important period and administered it with prudence, discretion and a single eye to the general welfare. He went further than any of his predecessors in developing the resources of the country. He encouraged the army, increased the navy, augmented the national defences, protected commerce and infused vigor and efficiency into every department of the public service. His honesty, good faith and simplicity were generally acknowledged and disarmed the political rancor of his strongest opponents. In person, Monroe was tall and well-formed, with a light complexion and blue eyes and the expression of his countenance was an accurate index of his simplicity, benevolence and integrity. He died in New York city July 4, 1831.

MONROE, Elizabeth (Kortright), wife of President James Monroe, was born in New York city in 1768, the daughter of Captain Lawrence Kortright, of the British army, who remained in New York after the peace of 1783. Elizabeth was educated in her native city, and is supposed to have married Mr. Monroe in 1789, and settled in Philadelphia after their marriage. In 1794 she went with her husband to France, where he occupied the post of U. S. minister, and during her residence there Mrs. Monroe visited the wife of the Marquis de Lafayette, who was confined in the prison of La Force, hourly expecting to be executed, and finally effected her release. Mrs. Monroe returned to America with her husband, and subsequently accompanied him abroad a second time, when he went to France as minister to London and to Spain. On their return to America they resided in Virginia, and subsequently in Washington, where as the wife of the secretary of state, and, later, of the president, Mrs. Monroe was as prominent in society as her delicate health would permit. She is said to have been an elegant and accomplished woman, possessing "a charming mind and dignity of manners which peculiarly fit her for her elevated station." Mrs. Monroe died at Oak Hill, Va., her husband's residence, in 1830.

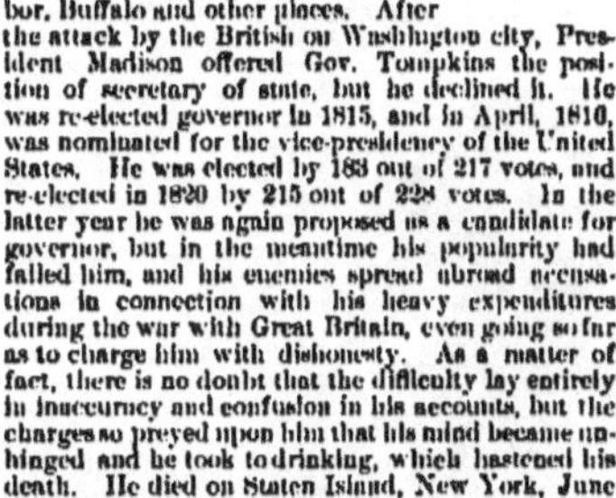

TOMPKINS, Daniel D., vice-president of the United States, and governor of New York (1807–16), was born in Westchester county, N. Y., June 21, 1774. He was the son of the revolutionary patriot, Jonathan G. Tompkins, who died in May, 1833, aged eighty-six, at Fox Meadows, or Scarsdale, on the river Bronx, in Westchester county, N. Y., the family homestead. Young Daniel went to Columbia College, where he was graduated in 1795, studied law and settled in New York city as a lawyer. During the party struggles of 1799–1801, Mr. Tompkins was a conspicuous republican and became a leader of the party in New York state. He was elected to the constitutional convention of 1801, was a member of the assembly, and in 1804 was elected a member of congress, but resigned, having been appointed a justice of the supreme court of his state. On June 9, 1807, Mr. Tompkins resigned this position also, having been nominated a candidate for governor by the democratic wing of his party. He was elected, and re-elected in 1809 and 1811. In 1812, the abolition of the United States Bank being about to cause the establishment of the Bank of North America in New York, a financial policy which he believed to be corrupt, Gov. Tompkins made use of the extreme powers of his office, and which no other governor ever used except himself, before or since. Acting within his constitutional rights, he prorogued the legislature of the state. The effect, however, was only temporary, and when the legislature met again the obnoxious bill was passed. During the war of 1812 Gov. Tompkins became very popular on account of the activity of his patriotism and the importance of his services. He succeeded in organizing the militia, while he sustained the United States government credit with his own personal funds at a time when New York banks refused to lend money on United States treasury notes without his endorsement. Indeed, he used his large means in advancing money in all directions to enable the prosecution of the war. It was he who sustained the Military Academy at West Point, paid for recruiting in Connecticut, and sustained the workmen who were manufacturing arms at Springfield, Mass.

He succeeded in equipping 40,000 militia, and sent them to the defense of Plattsburgh, Sackett's Harbor, Buffalo and other places. After the attack by the British on Washington city, President Madison offered Gov. Tompkins the position of secretary of state, but he declined it. He was re-elected governor in 1815, and in April, 1816, was nominated for the vice-presidency of the United States. He was elected by 183 out of 217 votes, and re-elected in 1820 by 215 out of 228 votes. In the latter year he was again proposed as a candidate for governor, but in the meantime his popularity had failed him, and his enemies spread abroad accusations in connection with his heavy expenditures during the war with Great Britain, even going so far as to charge him with dishonesty. As a matter of fact, there is no doubt that the difficulty lay entirely in inaccuracy and confusion in his accounts, but the charges so preyed upon him that his mind became unhinged and he took to drinking, which hastened his death. He died on Staten Island, New York, June 11, 1835.

CALHOUN, John Caldwell, secretary of war (1817–25), vice president (1825–31), and secretary of state (1843–45), was born in Abbeville District, S. C., March 18, 1782, a descendant of a race of Calvinists. His grandfather, James Calhoun, emigrated from Donegal, Ireland, to Pennsylvania in 1733, bringing his family with him. He afterward removed to Virginia, settling on the Kanawha, and in 1756 settled in South Carolina, establishing the "Calhoun Settlement." His son, Patrick, married Martha Caldwell, daughter of an Irish Presbyterian emigrant, and they became the parents of John C. Calhoun. John's father died while he was a child, and the boy spent his youth on his mother's farm, receiving but little schooling until he was placed under the care of his brother-in-law, Rev. Dr. Waddell, a Presbyterian clergyman, who prepared him for college. He entered Yale college in 1802, graduating at the age of twenty-two with honors and the approval of President Dwight, who prophesied that he would attain great eminence. He subsequently devoted three years to the study of law, studying in South Carolina and in Litchfield, Conn., graduating from the latter place, and was admitted to the bar in South Carolina in 1807. He engaged in the practice of law at Abbeville, but soon relinquished his profession to devote himself to politics. He was elected to the state legislature, served two terms, and in 1811 was elected to congress, taking his seat at a time when war with Great Britain was imminent. He was placed on the committee of foreign affairs, wrote the report that was presented to the house, urged a declaration of war, and upheld the American cause with great enthusiasm. Randolph opposed the report and the war. But Calhoun would not compromise; in his first speech he said, "The law of self-preservation is never safe, except under the shield of honor." In the same year he married his cousin Floride, whose comfortable fortune enabled him to pursue the career upon which he had entered, with the assurance of a competence, whatever misfortunes might befall him. After the war, in 1815, the country was confronted with various important questions, which gave Calhoun an opportunity to develop his original views. He urged the bank bill, organized the tariff of 1816, so favorable to his native state, urged a system of roads and canals, though he afterward modified his views on these questions, declaring that remedies that were proper and suitable for a certain state of things were not advisable for another. In 1817 President Monroe appointed him secretary of war, in which office he displayed great energy and ability, and won an undisputed fame. He straightened out the confused affairs of the department, reduced the expenditure of the army without sacrificing its efficiency or comfort, drew up a bill for organizing the department, and established a system that is still in force to a large extent. In 1824 Mr. Calhoun was elected vice-president of the United States by a large majority, and this period of his life may be said to be the beginning of his career as a constitutional statesman. In 1837 he said, "The station, from its leisure, gave me a good opportunity to study the genius of the prominent measure of the day, called then the American system, by which I profited." He referred to Mr. Clay's system, the bank, the protective tariff, the internal improvement system and general welfare rule, all flourishing at that time. In 1828 Jackson was elected president, and Calhoun was re-elected vice-president. In the early part of his career Mr. Calhoun advocated broad and patriotic views, but in after years he became a leader of distinctly southern interests, though it is probable that he thought they involved the benefit of the whole country. He sided with South Carolina against the protective system, and his "Exposition," with amendments, was adopted by the legislature of that state. He hoped that President Jackson would veto the tariff bill, but as he did not do so, Calhoun removed to South Carolina in 1829, and had passed in the legislature the famous resolution "that any state in the Union might annul an act of the Federal government." Virginia, Georgia, and Alabama gave in their adhesion, and the dissolution of the Union seemed imminent. Mr. Calhoun delivered an address on the relations of the states to the general government, in 1831, drew up a report for the legislature in the same year, an address to the people of the state at the close of that session, a letter to Gov. Hamilton on state interposition, in 1832, and an address to the people of the United States by the convention of South Carolina in 1832, in all of which he maintained the doctrine of state interposition, or "nullification." Mr. Calhoun's relations with the president became strained, he lost much of his popularity, and in 1831 resigned the vice-presidency, but was soon afterward elected to the senate. He stood alone as the champion of his state, defending its ordinance of nulli-

fication, both political parties and the administration being opposed to him. But Calhoun had the courage of his convictions, and was indifferent to personal consequences. In November, 1832, the president issued his proclamation, which was followed by the "force bill," and in the following February Calhoun made a powerful speech against it, followed by a reply from Daniel Webster, who dwelt with considerable length upon certain resolutions proposed by Mr. Calhoun. The latter brought forward his resolutions, and made a speech of great power and brilliancy, to which, however, Mr. Webster did not reply. The issue was on the first resolution: "That the people of the several states comprising these United States are united as parties to a constitutional compact, to which the people of each state acceded, as a separate and sovereign community, each binding itself by its own particular ratification; and that the union, of which the said compact is the bond, is a union between the states ratifying the same." Many of the democrats and whigs held that the constitution was a compact, but denied the right of nullification by a state, and many denied the right of secession. There were some who believed in the right of secession, but not of nullification. It was claimed for the doctrine of nullification that it was a remedy within the Union, reserved to the state—a remedy for evils—to declare void an unconstitutional law, and to save the Union, not dissolve it. During the last term of President Jackson Mr. Calhoun acted with the whig party on the bank and tariff questions. He claimed to lend the "state-rights" men, who acted from principle, and who were not governed by party motives nor ambition. He called an extra session of congress in 1837, in connection with the financial panic of that year, advocated a total separation of the government from the banks, and was favorable to the constitutional treasury plan. In 1838 Mr. Calhoun made his famous speech on slavery. He regarded slavery as a natural relation, and the abolition movement caused him great anxiety. If it proved successful he believed that the fate of the southern people "would be worse than that of the Aborigines," and that the fruitful fields of the South would be reduced to their primeval condition. "To destroy the existing relations," he said, "would be to destroy the prosperity of the Southern states, and to place the two races in a state of conflict, which must end in the expulsion or extirpation of one or the other." He looked upon social and political equality as the necessary consequence of emancipation, but believed that such equality must forever be impossible between the races. In 1841 Mr. Calhoun was a leader of the democratic party, and discussed the tariff question in a series of brilliant speeches, taking the ground that a tariff for revenue only was constitutional and proper. On Aug. 5, 1842, the closing words of his speech on this subject were: "The great popular party is already rallied almost en masse around the banner which is leading the party to its final triumph. The few that still lag will soon be rallied under its ample folds. On that banner is inscribed: Free trade; low duties; no debt; separation from banks; economy; retrenchment, and strict adherence to the constitution. Victory in such a cause will be great and glorious; and long will it perpetuate the liberty and prosperity of the country." In 1843 Mr. Calhoun was appointed secretary of state, and during his term of office established the rights of the United States to Oregon and Washington territories, which resulted in the treaty of 1846. He prophetically spoke of the future triumphs of steam and electricity, in a speech delivered in that year in connection with the Oregon affair, and said: "Providence has given us an inheritance stretching across the entire continent from ocean to ocean . . . . our great mission as a people is to occupy this vast domain; to replenish it with an intelligent, virtuous, and industrious population, to convert the forests into cultivated fields; to drain the swamps and morasses, and cover them with rich harvests; to build up cities, towns, and villages in every direction, and to unite the whole by the most rapid intercourse between all the parts. . . . Secure peace, and time, under the guidance of a sagacious and cautious policy, 'a wise and masterly inactivity,' will speedily accomplish the whole. . . . War can make us great; but let it never be forgotten that peace only can make us both great and free." On retiring from the state department, Mr. Calhoun was elected to the senate, and did all he could to prevent the war with Mexico. During the progress of the war the Wilmot proviso was proposed by the anti-slavery party, which declared that slavery should never be allowed in any Mexican territory acquired by treaty. This caused great agitation throughout the country, and on Feb. 19, 1847, Calhoun expressed his views in the following resolutions: " That the territories of the United States belong to the several states composing the Union, and are held by them as their joint and common property; that congress, as the joint agent and representative of the states of the Union, has no right to make any law or do any act whatever, that shall directly, or by its effects, make any discrimination between the states of this Union, by which any of them shall be deprived of its full and equal right in any territory of the United States, acquired or to be acquired." The question was not settled until 1850, when the compromise measures were passed, and Mr. Calhoun's last speech was on this subject on March 4, 1850, the speech being read for him. Henry Clay said of Mr. Calhoun: " He possessed an elevated genius of the highest order." Daniel Webster said: " He was a man of undoubted genius and of commanding talent. All the country and all the world admit that. . . . He had the basis, the indispensable basis of all high character, and that was unspotted integrity, unimpeached honor and character. If he had aspirations, they were high and honorable and noble. . . . I do not believe he had a selfish motive or selfish feeling." Edward Everett said: " Calhoun, Clay, Webster! I name them in alphabetical order. What other precedence can be assigned them ?" In private life Mr. Calhoun's character was above reproach. He was a devoted husband and father, a sincere friend, a good neighbor and citizen. His manners were simple, his morals rigid, his habits temperate, his nature genial, his conversation brilliant. As a statesman he has left a reputation for purity and greatness. He published " A Disquisition on Government," and " A Discourse on the Constitution and Government of the United States." Mr. Calhoun's residence at Fort Hill was the abode of hospitality and elegance. Mr. Calhoun died in Washington, D. C., March 31, 1850.

SOUTHARD, Samuel Lewis, secretary of the navy and governor of New Jersey (1832–33), was born at Baskinridge, N. J., June 9, 1787. His father removed from Long Island, where the family had resided, and settled in New Jersey, where he devoted himself to farming. He was justice of the peace, member of the state assembly and member of congress. When about twelve years of age young Samuel began his education at a classical academy in his native village, and became interested in the profession of teaching, to which for some years he devoted himself. In September, 1802, he entered the junior class at Princeton, and was graduated with honors two years later. Soon after leaving college he taught for a time in Morris county, and then obtained a tutorship in the family of Col. John Taliaferro, a member of congress from Virginia, at his plantation in King George's county, near Fredericksburg. Here he remained for five years, instructing the children of Col. Taliaferro and his relatives. He also began the study of law, and in 1809 was admitted to practice. By his pupils in Virginia he was held in the highest esteem and affection, and as they grew to manhood they never failed to regard him highly for his talents and his kindly manners. While in Virginia Mr. Southard made the acquaintance of Monroe, Jefferson and Madison. He married Rebecca Harrow, a ward of his patron. In 1811 Mr. Southard settled in Flemington, Hunterdon Co., N. J., and, devoting himself to the practice of law, soon acquired a good business, besides being appointed prosecuting attorney of the county. In 1814 Mr. Southard was elected a member of the assembly of the state, and immediately after, one of the justices of the supreme court. He sat on the bench for five years, being, at the same time, the reporter of the decisions of the court. In 1820 he was a presidential elector, and in the same year was elected one of the senators from the state of New Jersey, in which body he took his seat Feb. 16, 1821. It has been claimed that Mr. Southard was the actual originator of the Missouri compromise resolutions, which were presented by Henry Clay. In 1823 Mr. Southard was appointed secretary of the navy, in which position he remained until March 3, 1829; during some of that period being both secretary of the

treasury and secretary of war, besides fulfilling the duties of his own office. During the period of the election of James Monroe to the presidency, in 1816, and that of the election of Jackson, in 1828, the party conditions assumed quite a new shape. The old federalists became disorganized and ceased to act as a party, and in 1824 the old party organizations were practically powerless, while the new ones had not become sufficiently well-formed to be influential. It happened, therefore, that both Jackson and Adams were voted for by democrats and federalists. After the inauguration of Mr. Adams considerable hostility toward him was shown in congress and throughout the country. Mr. Southard was one of his supporters, and New Jersey gave Mr. Adams a decided majority. Jackson, however, was elected, and was the first chief magistrate after Washington who was really elected by the people. In 1829 Mr. Southard was put forward as a candidate for senator of New Jersey, but failed of election. He was soon after, however, chosen attorney-general of the state, and settled in Trenton. In the meantime, in 1822, he had been chosen one of the trustees of Princeton College, and in 1832 received the degree of LL.D. from the University of Pennsylvania. In the latter year he was elected governor of the state of New Jersey; but in 1833, having been elected U. S. senator, he assumed that office, which he held until 1842, when he resigned, being president of the senate in 1841. Mr. Southard was both scholarly and eloquent. In 1827 he delivered the anniversary address before the Columbian Institute at Washington ; and in 1830 discharged the same function before the Newark Mechanics' Association. He was also selected to deliver a discourse on the professional character and virtues of William Wirt. While in the senate he took an active part in its proceedings, and spoke frequently. While personally admired within his party, he possessed no talents as a party leader, having no skill in organization or administration. In 1838 Mr. Southard was appointed president of the Morris Canal and Banking Co., and from that time had his residence in Jersey City. He died at the house of his wife's brother, in Fredericksburg, June 26, 1842.

WIRT, William, attorney-general, was born at Bladensburg, Prince George's Co., Md., Nov. 8, 1772. His father, a Swiss, died while he was an infant, and his mother, a German, when he was not 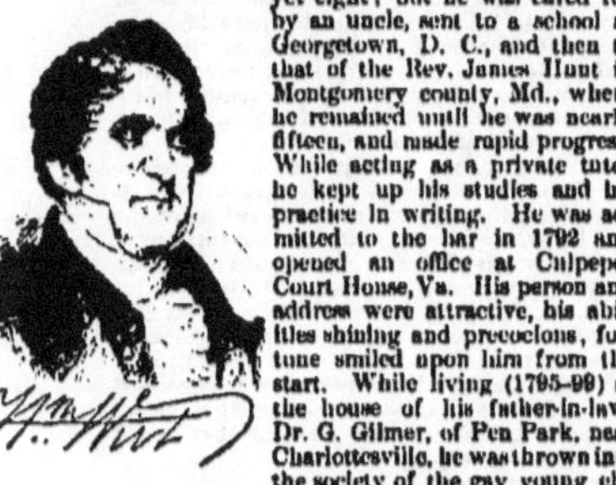 yet eight; but he was cared for by an uncle, sent to a school at Georgetown, D. C., and then to that of the Rev. James Hunt in Montgomery county, Md., where he remained until he was nearly fifteen, and made rapid progress. While acting as a private tutor he kept up his studies and his practice in writing. He was admitted to the bar in 1792 and opened an office at Culpeper Court House, Va. His person and address were attractive, his abilities shining and precocious, fortune smiled upon him from the start. While living (1795–99) at the house of his father-in-law, Dr. G. Gilmer, of Pen Park, near Charlottesville, he was thrown into the society of the gay young element of the state, and being of a naturally vivacious disposition and an agreeable personality, he was gladly welcomed, and easily held his own in the dissipations of the time. This course gave him a reputation as a *bon vivant* among his professional brethren, who failed to see in their gay companion anything which suggested an ambitious lawyer. Before it was too late Wirt saw the error of his course, and breaking away from the temptations to which he had been exposed, settled down to a sober life and a course of reading which in great measure supplied the deficiencies of his early education which, especially in law, was exceedingly meagre for one who had to meet such opponents as Thomas Jefferson and James Monroe. On his wife's death in 1799 he went to Richmond, where he met the great men of the state, was presently made clerk of the house of delegates, and in 1802 chancellor of the eastern district, an office which he held but six months. In this year he married again. In 1803 his "Letters of a British Spy" appeared in the Richmond "Argus" and as a volume, added greatly to his reputation; the tenth edition (1832) had a sketch of the author by P. H. Cruse. After two years and a half at Norfolk he returned to Richmond in 1806. In 1807, by President Jefferson's appointment, he was a counsel in the trial of Aaron Burr; one of his speeches, which lasted four hours, was vastly admired and was among the finest efforts of his life. This speech greatly extended his fame, and is perhaps the one which has made him best known to succeeding generations, as its florid periods and its occasional pathos made it a prime favorite for academic declamation, and although it may be said to be worn to shreds by the constant repetition, it yet has the power to charm even a critical reader. His essays, collected as "The Rainbow," were first printed in 1804 in the Richmond "Enquirer," as was, two years later, "The Old Bachelor," gathered in two volumes (1812). To the latter several writers of less fame contributed; J. P. Kennedy called it Wirt's best book, but other critics were not of that opinion. His "Life of Patrick Henry" (1817) was widely circulated rather than highly esteemed; it had all the gorgeousness of his earlier oratory. His only experience as a legislator was in 1808. In 1816 he was appointed by President Madison U. S. district attorney for Virginia, and in 1817 by President Monroe U. S. attorney-general. This post he held with great repute until 1829, residing at Washington. Judge Story ranked him "among the ablest and most eloquent of the bar of the supreme court." He took part in many leading cases, among them that of Dartmouth College, 1819; in this he was not at his best, and the honors went to Webster who won the case. His most noted extralegal addresses were that of Oct. 19, 1826, on the deaths of Jefferson and Adams, and one at Rutgers College in 1830, which was reproduced in England, Germany and France. In 1829 he removed to Baltimore. In 1881 appeared his letters and those of J. Q. Adams on the anti-Masonic movement; the next year he was the candidate of that party for the presidency and received a popular vote of 33,108, and the electoral vote of Vermont only. Harvard gave him the degree of LL.D. in 1824. He was president of the Maryland Bible Society and a devout and consistent Presbyterian. See his Life by J. P. Kennedy, 2 vols., 1849. Extracts from his speeches and sketches (e. g. "The Blind Preacher") were long and widely diffused through the medium of Readers and Speakers, and his name still lingers among those which occupy the borderland between greatness and passing popularity. His second wife, Elizabeth Washington Wirt, born at Richmond, Va., Jan. 30, 1785, was a daughter of Col. Robert Gamble. She put forth in 1829 "Flora's Dictionary," a quarto remarkable in its day, combining botany with an epistolary guide and a dictionary of quotations. Mr. Wirt died at Washington Feb. 18, 1834.

THOMPSON, Smith, secretary of the navy and associate justice of the U. S. supreme court, was born in Stanford, Dutchess Co., N. Y., Jan. 17, 1768. He received a liberal education, and was sent to Princeton, where he was graduated in 1788, studied law with Chancellor Kent in Poughkeepsie, and as was usual at that time continued his education by teaching. In 1792 he was admitted to the bar, and for a while practiced in Troy. Afterward he returned to Poughkeepsie, and in 1800 was elected a member of the state legislature. The following year he was one of the delegates to the constitutional convention of the state of New York. In the same year he was offered the position of district attorney, but declined. In 1802 he was made associate justice of the  state supreme court, a position which he continued to hold until 1814. In the meantime he could have had the mayoralty of the city of New York, where he resided at the time, but this he rejected. In 1814 he was made chief justice of the supreme court of New York, and continued to hold that office until 1818, when President Monroe appointed him secretary of the navy, and he assumed the position Nov. 9th of that year, succeeding Benjamin W. Crowninshield, of Massachusetts, who had held over. Mr. Thompson resigned in September, 1823, having been appointed a justice of the United States supreme court, to succeed Judge Brockholst Livingston, and he continued to hold this high office until his death. Judge Thompson was a man of great learning, both legal and general, and his private life was pure and exemplary. At the time of his death he was the oldest vice-president of the American Bible Society. He received the degree of LL.D. from Yale and Princeton in 1824, and from Harvard in 1835. He died in Poughkeepsie, N. Y., Dec. 18, 1843.

ENGELMANN, George, botanist, was born at Frankfort-on-the-Main, Feb 2, 1809. He was descended from a long line of clergymen, who for several generations filled pastorates at Bacharach, on the Rhine. His uncle, Frederick Theodore, was an early American viticulturist and one of the pioneer Germans of Illinois. He pursued the ordinary course of gymnasial instruction at Frankfort, and in these schools first acquired his taste for scientific knowledge. In 1827 he entered Heidelberg University, and in 1828 transferred himself to the University of Berlin. After studying here two years he removed to Würzburg, from which university he received the degree of M.D. in 1831. His graduation thesis was entitled, "De Antholysi Prodromus," a morphological dissertation on the study of monstrosities, illustrated by himself. It was a valuable contribution to teratology, and holds an important place in the literature of morphology. The original MS. of this thesis is preserved in the library of the herbarian of Harvard University. A portion of the year 1832 he passed in Paris, where he met Louis Agassiz. Here he pursued the studies of medicine and science, and during the latter part of the year started for America, being strongly influenced in taking this step by the hope of finding new flora for

the pursuit of his botanical studies. He traveled through various parts of the country on horseback, and finally, after several years spent in roaming, in 1835 settled in St. Louis, Mo., then a small frontier town. Here he engaged in the practice of medicine, in which he was eminently successful, and soon became one of the leading physicians of that rapidly-growing city. His botanical researches were continued and pursued as a recreation. He made a number of collections, which with his own scientific descriptions he sent to the European museums, and added from these collections to his own herbarium. In 1837 he made a botanical excursion to Arkansas, the outcome of which was his first botanical work, "A Monograph of North American Cuscutaceæ," which was first published in 1842, in the "American Journal of Science," and immediately placed him on a prominent footing in the scientific world. In 1849 he published his "Plantæ Fendlerianæ." His work upon the cactus family was considered most important, as well as particular and difficult. He established for the first time, the arrangements of the plants upon floral and carpological characters; the same may be said of his untiring study of North American vines, of which he characterized a dozen species, now of vast importance to grape growers both in America and in Europe. His study of the cactus family became so celebrated, that most of the specimens brought in by the government surveys were sent to him to be classified; and it must be acknowledged that all that is principally known of the American species and forms of Vitis is due to his investigations. He made several long journeys to the Rocky Mountains, and the Appalachian Mountains in Tennessee; to New Mexico, Colorado, and North Carolina; and also to the Pacific coast in search of more unexplored floral fields. Dr. Engelmann's meteorological observations were another important feature of his scientific work. His last publication was a digest of the thermometrical part of these observations, given before the St. Louis Academy of Science.

He was first president of that body, and subsequently served several terms in this capacity. He visited Europe several times with his family. He was a public-spirited citizen of St. Louis, interested in all that concerned the welfare of the city. He was an able, voluminous, and ready writer upon general scientific and botanical subjects, and a recognized authority in all the apartments of his favorite science. His valuable botanic collection, which contains the original specimens from which many of our western plants have been described and named, was donated to Shaw's Botanical Garden, St. Louis, Mo. This gift induced the founding of the Shaw School of Botany as a department of Washington University, St. Louis, where an Engelmann professorship of botany has been established. He was a member of numerous scientific societies at home and abroad; and one of the original members of the National Academy of Science. Dr. Engelmann died at St. Louis, Mo., Feb. 4, 1884.

ISAACS, Myer S., lawyer, was born in the city of New York in 1841. He is the eldest son of Rev. S. M. Isaacs, and received from his parents an exceptional home-training. He attended Forrest's Collegiate School, and in 1856 matriculated at the New York University, where he was awarded all prizes of freshman and sophomore years, and was graduated valedictorian in 1859. In 1862 he was graduated from the New York University Law School, and was admitted to the bar the day he became twenty-one years old. He adopted as his particular department of practice real estate law, wills, and trusts, and his firm of M. S. & I. S. Isaacs has won a place among the leaders in that branch. Mr. Isaacs was for three years vice-president of the Real Estate Exchange, and of the Republican Club, and is one of the executive committee of the University Alumni Association. While warmly interested in politics, he has held public office only once, when, in 1880, he was appointed by Gov. Cornell, judge of the marine court of the city of New York. In 1881 Judge Isaacs was elected to the central committee of the Alliance Israélite Universelle. In 1865 he became one of the founders of the Hebrew Free School Association, of which he was president from 1881–92. In 1873 he took the initiative in organizing the United Hebrew Charities. He also took a leading part in organizing a hospital for chronic sufferers, subsequently crystallized in the Montefiore Home; in the foundation of the Hebrew Technical Institute (the outcome of the United Hebrew Charities, Orphan Asylum, and Hebrew Free School Association), and of the Purim Association, of which he was the first president. He called the meeting of December, 1881, to consider the condition of the emigrants fleeing from Russia, and was one of the committee of the aid society which founded and assisted colonies in Kansas, Dakota, and New Jersey, and he was chairman of the committee in charge of the Crémieux Memorial of 1880, and took part in the obsequies of Lasker, and in the Montefiore memorial service. He is president of the Baron Hirsch fund, a contribution of $2,400,000 for the exiled Russian and Roumanian Hebrews who settle in the United States. He was one of the founders and is vice-president of the Educational Alliance, which erected a public building on the plan of the Cooper Union, designed for the elevation of the population in the seventh and tenth wards of the city of New York. He has for several years lectured before the classes of the law school of the New York University on the "Examination of Titles to Real Estate," and kindred subjects, and received from that college the degrees of A.M. and LL.M. Judge Isaacs has published the following pamphlets: "The Persecution of the Jews in Roumania" (1875); "The Jewish Question in Russia" (1882); and American Israelites" (1886).

LEE, Charles Arnold, journalist, was born at Pawtucket, R. I., Dec. 14, 1845, son of Nehemiah W. Lee. On his father's side he is descended from Richard Lee of England, who settled in the southerly part of Rehoboth, Mass., some time between the years 1690 and 1700. The descendants of this Richard Lee settled in Cumberland (once a part of "Rehoboth North Purchase," in the colony of Massachusetts). His mother was the youngest daughter of Arnold and Nancy Thayer Taft of East Douglas, Mass., representing in her ancestry the well-known Taft family, the earliest settlers of Mendon, Mass., and the Thayers of Uxbridge. Graduating at the Lonsdale High School in 1863, he entered the "Gazette and Chronicle" office, of which he became part proprietor in 1875. Since 1878 he has been editor of the paper, and since 1883 its sole proprietor. He founded the Rhode Island Press Association in 1879, and has since been its secretary and treasurer; was president of the Suburban Press Association of New England, 1885–88, and of the National Editorial Association in 1889. In 1890 and 1891 he was elected to the Rhode Island general assembly. He is a Republican, a Universalist, and, since 1877, a representative to the supreme lodge, Knights of Pythias. He enjoys a high reputation as a writer, speaker, and presiding officer, and is said to have a larger personal acquaintance with newspaper men than any other provincial editor.

GRIFFING, Josephine Sophie White, philanthropist, was born in December, 1816, at Hebron, Conn. She was descended, on her father's side, from Peregrine White, who was the first child born of Pilgrim parents in New England, and on her mother's, she was the lineal descendant of Peter Waldo, the founder of the sect called the Waldenses. Soon after her marriage, in 1838, she moved to Ohio, where she made her house a refuge for fugitive slaves. In 1849 she began speaking in public at the anti-slavery conventions which for years were interrupted by all sorts of riotous proceedings. She possessed great ability and persuasiveness as a public speaker, and did much to enlighten and change public sentiment. Her history is not only interwoven with that of abolition but with that of woman suffrage; and later she became an active member of the Woman's Loyal League and its outgrowth, the Sanitary Commission. In connection with the last she lectured through the West, and organized societies for the relief of the soldiers and freedmen. While engaged in this work her mind was roused to the condition of the thousands of slaves who, in 1863, were pouring into Washington, and to the need of an organized system of protection, help, and education. She went to Washington and submitted her plans for their relief and employment to Pres. Lincoln and Sec. Stanton, who approved them and gave her their assistance. Through her efforts, in December, 1863, a bill for a bureau of emancipation was presented to the house of representatives, but it was not passed until March, 1865. While this was pending, by her energetic solicitations for money and supplies and the use of her own property, she greatly relieved the suffering of thousands hidden away in alleys and stables, attics and cellars, many of them old and infirm and unable to work. She opened at once industrial schools for the women, who were clothed with the garments when finished, and three ration houses where 1,000 could be fed daily. She caused old barracks to be made into comfortable shelter for them and distributed army blankets and wool, given her by the personal order of Sec. Stanton. Large supplies of food and clothing she also obtained from the northern aid societies. The bill having been passed, and the freedmen's bureau established, her plans were adopted, and the freedmen and women sent, at government expense, to homes at the North, and employment offices opened in New York city and Providence, R. I. Private generosity assisted in this work, and congress appropriated $106,000 for the purchase of supplies of which more than half were distributed by Mrs. Griffing at her own house. In about two years she personally arranged and superintended the departure of over 7,000 freedmen and women from Washington. It would be impossible to state the whole number she assisted, but at one time there were in Washington 30,000 of these homeless people. To Horace Greeley, who alone of the prominent men of the day refused her recognition and encouragement, she gave a summary of her work as follows: "A freedmen's bureau; sanitary commission; church sewing societies; orphan asylums; old people's home; hospital and almshouse for the sick and blind; minister-at-large to visit the sick, console the dying and bury the dead." She was president of the Universal Franchise Association, and secretary of the National Woman Suffrage Association. After the bureau was abolished she continued to work for the freedmen, at request of such men as Sumner, Stanton, Wade, Wilson and others, and only relinquished it when failing strength compelled her. She died in Washington, Feb. 18, 1872. Of her Mr. Garrison said that she belonged to the honorable women "whose self-abnegation and self-sacrifice in the cause of suffering humanity having been absolute, and who have nobly vindicated every claim made by their sex to full equality with men in all that serves to dignify human nature."

THOMPSON, George Kramer, architect, was born at Dubuque, Ia., Oct. 15, 1859, son of John H. and Sophia B. Thompson of West Virginia. They went, in the early fifties, to Dubuque, Ia., where his father established commercial interests, and became a prominent citizen of the West. The son, George K., showed in early boyhood decided inclination to mechanical pursuits, and after completing a common-school education in his native city, attended Shattuck Military Academy, and later Franklin and Marshall College. In 1879 he entered the office of Frederick C. Withers, architect, New York city, and in 1882 accepted an engagement as assistant in the office of Kimball & Wisedell, of the same city. In the autumn of 1883 he opened an

office on his own account in New York, and during the interval, until he formed a partnership with Francis H. Kimball in 1892, he had a large and varied practice, designing many works of importance in various parts of the country. The competition for, and the final execution of, the Manhattan Life Insurance building, in connection with his distinguished associate, Mr. Kimball, has been the most important of his career up to the present time (1895), and has also been crowned with so much success that the result has secured for him an enviable position in his profession.

CHAPIN, Edwin Hubbell, clergyman, was born in Washington county, N. Y., Dec. 29, 1814. While he was a boy his parents removed to Burlington, Vt., where he attended school, studying law later in Troy, N. Y. From Troy he went to Utica, and as by this time his mind was tending in the direction of a ministerial career, and as he had already become interested in the Universalist belief, he accepted a position as editor of a periodical publication established in the interests of the Universalists. He devoted his spare time to the study of theology and ecclesiastical history, and in 1837 was ordained as a Universalist clergyman. He accepted the offer of a church at Richmond, Va., where he remained for three years. He was then called to Charlestown, Mass., where he remained during the next six years. In 1847 he united with Hosea Ballou in charge of a Universalist church in Boston, but the following year accepted a call to the Fourth Universalist Church of New York city, with which he was destined to pass the remainder of his life. The church at that time was in the neighborhood of the City Hall and was not proving particularly attractive, but soon after the advent of Mr. Chapin it began to fill up until it became necessary to find other and larger quarters. It was obvious, as the new

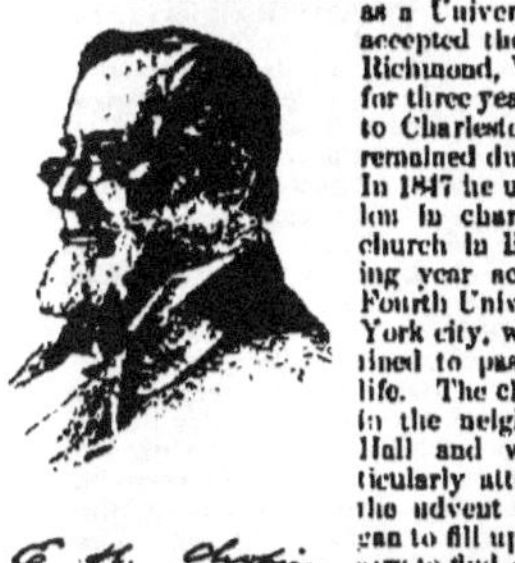

pastor became known, that a power for good had entered the religious service of the metropolis. The building known as the Dusseldorf Gallery, on Broadway near Bleecker street, was secured, and here Mr. Chapin preached to large audiences with remarkable effect. As an orator he had distinguishing qualities unlike those of any other preacher, and indeed of any other public speaker. The rapid flow of his eloquence, the brilliancy and originality of his illustrative metaphor, and the fine effect of his vocal and elocutionary powers made him altogether a most effective and interesting public orator, while the matter of his sermons evidenced intellectual study and culture. After a number of years spent in his Broadway church, which was crowded at every service, another removal to a still larger building became necessary, and in 1866 the congregation removed to the Church of the Divine Paternity, at Forty-fifth street and Fifth avenue, where Dr. Chapin continued to preach until his death. In the meantime, he had come to be recognized as a citizen who was an essential factor in all public undertakings of a benevolent, patriotic, or religious character. His versatility enabled him to speak well on any subject which he undertook. In such speaking he was both persuasive and encouraging, and became exceedingly popular. He was a member of many important societies and public organizations, a trustee of Bellevue Medical College and Hospital, and for a long time editor of the "Christian Leader." He published a number of works, including the following: "Hours of Communion" (New York, 1844); "Discourses on the Lord's Prayer" (1850); "Characters in the Gospels" (1852); "Moral Aspects of City Life" (1853); "Discourses on the Beatitudes" (1853); "True Manliness" (New York, 1854); "Duties of Young Men" (1855); "The Crown of Thorns—A Token for the Suffering" (1860); "Living Words" (Boston, 1861); and "The Gathering," which was the memorial of a meeting of the Chapin family (Springfield, Mass., 1862). During his latter years his health was feeble. He failed slowly, and died in New York city, Dec 27, 1880. A most beautiful charity, the Chapin Home for Aged and Indigent Men and Women, reared in his memory, became a monument to the esteem and honor in which he was held.

ELDREDGE, Barnabas, manufacturer, was born at Munson, Geauga co., O., June 19, 1843, son of Franklin and Eliza (Vandyke) Eldredge. The first American representatives of the family were Edward, Zenas, and Asael Eldredge, who, in their youth, emigrated from Wales to Cape Cod, Mass. Edward, born Sept. 9, 1737, subsequently removed to Sharon, N. Y., where he died March 28, 1821, and where the family was prominent for several generations. His wife, Adna Hammond, of Dartmouth, Mass., was born May 25, 1735, died Dec. 25, 1825, and was one of the same family as Jabez Hammond, author of the "Political History of New York." Of their nine children, Barnabas Eldredge, who was born Sept. 29, 1768, and died Sept. 5, 1843, was a member of the New York state assembly in 1821, and was married to Theodosia, daughter of Josiah Wadsworth, of Poughkeepsie, N. Y. Their son, Franklin Eldredge, born Dec. 17, 1801, was married Nov. 26, 1822, to Eliza Vandyke (born Oct. 3, 1802, at Middleburgh, N. Y., died at Munson, O., Aug. 1, 1879), a descendant of Hendrick Vandyke, who, emigrating from Holland to New York in 1636, was a distinguished character among the early Knickerbocker colonists. After his marriage, Franklin Eldredge removed from Sharon to a farm on the Western Reserve of Ohio. Here the son was reared, receiving his early education in the country schools, and working on the farm until 1861, when he went to Cleveland, to pursue an advanced course of study. Leaving the Cleveland High School shortly before graduation, he became connected with the shipyards of Stephens & Presley, pursuing at the same time a course of study in a commercial college, from which he was subsequently graduated. Shortly afterward he engaged in the hardware business in Cleveland, as a member of the firm of Van Tassel & Eldredge, where his attention was first attracted to the sewing-machine trade. In 1866 he entered into a partnership with his brother, who already carried on an extensive sale of sewing machines in Detroit, Mich., and in 1869 he abandoned the hardware business in Cleveland, and moved to Detroit, to become an active partner in the conduct and management of the sewing-machine business. Their trade here extended over a large territory, and they had remarkable success in establishing the Domestic sewing machine, then being introduced in the market. Remaining in Detroit until 1874, Mr. Eldredge then went to Chicago as the general manager of the Domestic Co., having under his control all the territory lying between the western line of Ohio and the Rocky mountains and all the southern states.

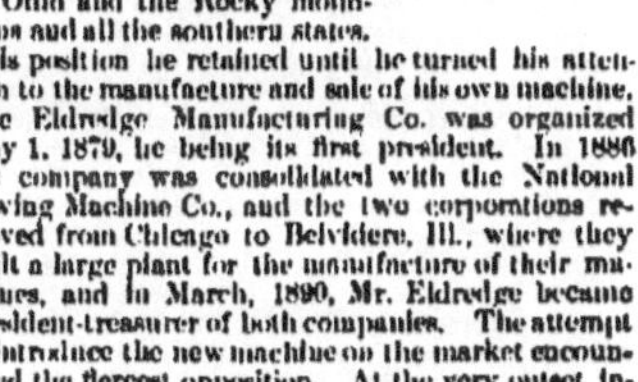

This position he retained until he turned his attention to the manufacture and sale of his own machine. The Eldredge Manufacturing Co. was organized May 1, 1879, he being its first president. In 1886 the company was consolidated with the National Sewing Machine Co., and the two corporations removed from Chicago to Belvidere, Ill., where they built a large plant for the manufacture of their machines, and in March, 1890, Mr. Eldredge became president-treasurer of both companies. The attempt to introduce the new machine on the market encountered the fiercest opposition. At the very outset infringement suits were brought whenever a pretext could be obtained for doing so, and the defense of these involved great expense, and led to serious business embarrassment. The persistence, and courage of Mr. Eldredge at length overcame all obstacles, however, and he was free to give his entire attention to the development of the industry. From a small beginning in 1879, the business in 1894 had grown to a magnitude in which from 500 to 600 men were employed in turning out annually from 60,000 to 80,000 sewing machines, the product of which amounted to nearly $1,500,000. The goods were sold throughout the entire world, the plant ranking as the largest sewing-machine factory in the West. In 1865 Mr. Eldredge was married to Marie Presley, daughter of the junior member of the firm by which he had been first employed.

ANDROS, Sir Edmund, colonial governor of New England, was born on the Island of Guernsey, Dec. 6, 1637. He was brought up as a page in the English royal family, served during its exile in the army of Prince Henry of Nassau, and was attached to the household of the Princess Palatine, grandmother of George I. After the restoration he gained some distinction in the war against the Dutch, and in 1672, having meanwhile married an heiress, was made major of a regiment of dragoons. This was the highest promotion he had reached before he came to New York, as the Duke of York's lieutenant in 1674, except that the proprietors of Carolina had comprehended him in their scheme by making him a land-grave with an endowment of four baronies of 12,000 acres of land each, with four castles in Spain. Andros took possession of New York when it finally fell into the hands of the English after its short reoccupation by the Dutch. He began his administration by laying claim to a part of the territory of Connecticut, on behalf of the Duke of York, but it was not allowed. In the King Philip's war he was charged by the New England colonists with indifference to their danger, and it was even alleged that he allowed the Indians to obtain their ammunition from Albany, but in August, 1676, he sent a force to Kemaquis (in the present state of Maine), to build and occupy a fort, and the officer in command entered into communication with the neighboring Indians and procured the release of fifteen English captives. In 1680 he was found laying claim for his master, the Duke of York, to Fisher's Island, off New London Harbor, which claim was also resisted by the Connecticut authorities. In January, 1681, Andros went back to England, and was succeeded by Thomas Dongan, in August, 1683. But Andros returned to America, landing at Boston on Dec. 20, 1686, and bearing with him a royal commission for the government of all New England. He was now "governor-in-chief," to put in practice, as opportunity should serve, the theory of rules by which King James II. of England became owner of all the land in New England, and might if it pleased him, oust all the holders from property which their families had acquired at great cost and hardship, and had peaceably possessed for nearly sixty years. Andros had gotten the honor of knighthood in England, and had risen to the command of a regiment in the royal army. He forthwith demanded the surrender of the Rhode Island charter, which had been given him. He also instituted at Boston the worship of the Church of England, frightening the sexton of the "Old South Meeting House" into opening the doors and ringing the bell, so that Episcopal worship was afterwards held there on Sundays and other holidays of the church, at hours when the building was not occupied by the regular congregation. It was moreover charged against him that he or his officials corrupted juries: taxes were arbitrarily imposed upon the people, and the demand was made upon the landholders that they take out new patents for the ownership of their lands. Quit rents were insisted on for the conformation of land titles. Portions of the common lands of towns were also enclosed, and given to friends of the governor. Andros browbeat his council. He also exercised the same despotic government in the district of Maine, which was included in his commission as in that of Massachusetts. The New Hampshire colony and that of Rhode Island submitted with little or no resistance. He next assumed the government of Connecticut, and the story of the non-surrender of her charter, and of its being hidden in the Charter-Oak at Hartford, which was long current, is now regarded as apocryphal by the best historians. This assumption consolidated New England under one despotism. The governor resumed his attacks on ancient laws and vested rights in Massachusetts, and when he returned to Boston speedily entered upon the business of vacating the prior land bills. Writs of intrusion were served on some of the most considerable of those persons who did not come forward to buy new land patents. The governor built a fort on Fort Hill, commanding the harbor, and felt that the great features of his administration were satisfactorily settled. It was at this time (June, 1688), that he received from James II. another commission, which made him governor of all the English possessions on the mainland of America, except Pennsylvania, Delaware, Maryland, and Niagara, and extended the territory and dominion of New England southward to latitude 14°, this taking in New York and the Jerseys. The governor at once went south to take possession. Meanwhile the Rev. Increase Mather, minister of the Second Church at Boston, and president of Harvard College, having gotten away from America in disguise, was in England presenting colonial complaints against Andros to the King, and had been well received by James, who was then courting Dissenters, although no decided measures of relief were promised him. Meanwhile Gov. Andros led an abortive military expedition into Maine, 1688, to chastise recalcitrant Indians, and by its ill-success increased his unpopularity. When the news of the Prince of Orange's arrival in England to overthrow King James reached Boston (April, 1689), Andros saw such threatening signs in the local political atmosphere that he at once withdrew within the walls of Fort Hill. And well he might, for the colonists were now in earnest. On Apr. 18th, the townspeople assembled, deposed him from his governorship, and imprisoned him with fifty of his followers. On June 27th, Andros with several others was impeached before a colonial counsel by the newly formed house of deputies, and was denied admission to bail. In November following, the new ministry in England sent an order to Boston for the forwarding of Andros to Great Britain. There the colonists made their charges against him, but he was not tried, the American agents singularly enough declining to sign the statement of grievances which was prepared for them by their legal counsel. Andros and his fellow culprits were therefore set free. In 1692 he was again in America, this time as royal governor of Virginia, where for six years he had a remarkably prosperous administration, encouraging manufactures and cotton culture, and with others laying the foundation of William and Mary College, which, next to Harvard University, is the oldest seat of learning in the United States. Commissary James Blair (1656–1743), its first president and the highest ecclesiastical officer in Virginia, became involved in controversy with Andros, whom he called an enemy to religion, the church and the college. Charges were preferred against him, and he was finally removed, but was made governor of the island of Guernsey in 1704. This position he occupied for two years, and then took up his residence in London, England, where he died, Feb. 24, 1714.

KIEFT, Wilhelm, third governor of New Netherlands (New York), was born in Holland about the year 1600. Not much information can be gotten of his early life. He landed on Manhattan Island, March 28, 1638, with his commission from the Dutch West India Co., as successor of Wouter Van Twiller, to find that rumors to his disadvantage had preceded him. It was said that he had failed in mercantile business in Holland, and that according to Dutch custom, his portrait had been affixed to the gallows, in consequence. That, in Dutch estimation, was a lasting disgrace. After that, it was alleged, he had been sent by his government as minister to Turkey, and entrusted with money to free some Christian captives, but the captives were not liberated nor the money returned. He siezed the reins of authority, however, in his new position, with the air of a master, using the liberty given him by his commission to fix the number of his council in the choice of one man, alone, for its membership, the favored individual being Dr. Johannes La Montaigne, a learned and highly bred Huguenot. But Kieft gave to La Montaigne only one vote at the council board, reserving two votes for himself. The governor, however, graciously declared himself willing to admit to the council chambers, an invited guest when special cases should be tried in which either he himself or La Montaigne was supposed to be interested, but it was to be judged a high cause to appeal from the council to any other tribunal. When Kieft wrote his first letter to Holland, he gave to the West India Co. a formal and dolorous account of the condition in which he found the colony, saying: "The fort is open at every side except the stone point; the guns are dismounted; the houses and public building are all out of repair; the magazine for merchandise has disappeared; every vessel in the harbor is falling to pieces; only one wind-mill is in operation; the farms of the company are without tenants and thrown into commons; the cattle are all sold or on the plantation of Van Twiller." Abuses existed in every department of the public service. Law seemed fast becoming obsolete. The new governor's measures of reform were begun by the issued proclamations written in a plain hand, and pasted on posts, trees, barns and fences. No guns or powder were to be sold to the Indians upon pain of death. Illegal traffic in furs was forbidden. Retailing liquors was limited to "moderate quantities." Hours were fixed for laborers to stop work; sailors were ordered not to leave their ships after nightfall. All the vices were forbidden. No one was to leave the island without a passport. The weekly meeting of the council was fixed for Thursday. No attestations or other public writings should be valid before a New Netherland court, unless they had been written by the colonial secretary, Van Tienhoven, whose salary had been fixed at $250 per annum. The governor vehemently espoused the cause of Dominie Bogardus, pastor of the Dutch Church, who had been complained of, for irregularities, to the classis of Amsterdam in Holland. He instituted the custom of ringing the church bell nightly at nine of the clock, to announce the hour for retiring; also every morning and evening, to call persons to and from labor, and on Thursdays to summon prisoners to court. In some respects he brought order out of chaos. He selected Pearl street, then a mere road on the bank of the river, for the best class of dwellings on account of its fine river prospect. Kieft also encouraged gardening after the most approved European standard, besides stocking the farms with fine cattle. Peter Minet, the first Dutch governor, having led out to America a company of Swedes, settled in the Delaware Bay country, and claimed ownership of all territory on the west of the Delaware river from Cape Henlopen to the Trenton Falls, and as far inland as they might wish. Kieft wrote to him a letter of remonstrance, and then notified the Dutch West India Co. of these proceedings; but the company had not the means of resisting this aggression, and his representations brought about no prevention of the Swedish movement. The governor next proceeded (1638–39) to purchase from neighboring Indian chiefs nearly all the territory now comprising the county of Queens on Long Island. Shortly after, he acquired a large tract of land in Westchester, including the present town of Yonkers. Portions of these lands were also deeded away to enterprising settlers, and by reason of a liberal system then adopted by the Dutch West India Co., rapid impulse was given to the settlement of the province. But the state of morals in New Amsterdam (New York) was by no means healthy. Prosecutions and punishments for dishonesty and public executions for murder were not infrequent. Kieft was on the alert, but from his irritable nature commanded no respect and had to enforce obedience. He proceeded to levy a tribute of maize, furs, or "sewan" upon the Indians. If they refused to pay it, he threatened to compel them to do so. At this time the Dutch had a small fort at the mouth of the Connecticut river, and in it a small garrison, but it gave no protection against the encroachments of the Connecticut colonists upon the domain in that region which was claimed by the New Netherlanders, and Kieft's efforts to prevent the settlement of that part of the country and of the eastern portion of Long Island by the "Yankees" were vain. Hearing rumors that the Indians intended to attack New Amsterdam, with whose inhabitants they had up to this time been on good terms, the governor made himself the aggressor, and forthwith blunderingly attacked the Raritan tribe and slew some of their number, sowing the seed of a long and bloody war. Meanwhile, the West India Co. in Holland agreed upon the continuance of a liberal policy toward new settlers, the fruit of which was the charter of Freedoms and Exemptions (1640), operating decidedly for the benefit of the inhabitants, and Kieft constantly issued new municipal regulations of which there was great need. The tapping of beer during divine service and after one o'clock at night was forbidden. Measures were taken to prevent the deterioration of the currency. Two annual agricultural farms were fixed on, one of cattle and one of hogs. The first liquor ever made in this country was in 1640 produced from a private still erected by the governor on Staten Island, and he secured for Cornelis Melyer permission from De Vries, patroon of Staten Island, to erect a small redoubt upon the eastern headland, where a flag was raised whenever a vessel appeared in the bay, this being the first instance of a marine telegraph in New York harbor. In June, 1641, his inconsiderate treatment of the Raritan Indians fruited in their attack on De Vries' unprotected plantations on Staten Island. The governor forthwith fell to stirring up the Hudson river Indians by exterminating the others. An Indian murdered a Dutchman on Manhattan Island by way of revenge for the previous murder of his uncle; and while the governor would at once have proceeded to declare war for this fresh attack, he was persuaded to submit the case to a meeting of patroons, masters, and heads of families, which he summoned to meet him at the fort. This was the pioneer of popular meetings on Manhattan Island. His inclination to do this is attributed by the historian to the fact that he was told by friends that he was accused of exciting these hostilities in order that he might make wrong reckonings with the West India Co. Twelve men were selected at this meeting to co-operate with the governor and council. They soon demanded reforms in his administration. Kieft made a show of acceding to their wishes, but fulfilled no promise of reform, and at once issued a proclamation that he should call no more meetings, and forbade any one else to call them. Then he sought to execute his purpose of chastening the Indians who had sheltered the murderer of Manhattan Island, but this military expedition against them was not especially successful. It was about this time (April, 1642) that in view of rumors of intended attack upon all New England settlements by the Indians, that the town of Greenwich in Connecticut, deemed it best to swear allegiance to the New Netherland government, and gain its protection, whatever that might be worth. Greenwich inhabitants were accordingly invested by Kieft with all the rights of patroons. Further complications arising out of New England aggressions upon the New Netherlanders' lands ensued, but the questions at issue were left unsettled, although they were the subject of complaint from the States General of Holland to the government of England. The outcome of ecclesiastical dissensions in New England was now the settling, under Kieft's jurisdiction, of Newtown, L. I., by some of the best of its subsequent population, who left the New England towns of Lynn and Ipswich (in Massachusetts) for the milder rule of the Dutchman. Kieft now erected at the West India Co's. expense, the first tavern in New Amsterdam. This was followed by the erection of a new stone church, seventy-two feet long, fifty feet wide, and sixteen feet high, at $1,000 for the job, within the walls of the fort—on its front a marble slab, with the inscription: "Anno Domini, 1642, William Kieft, Directeur General. Heeft de gemeente desen tempel doer bouwen." In 1787, when the fort was demolished to make room for the government house, this slab was found buried in the earth, was removed to the belfry of the old Dutch Church on Garden street, and remained there until the burning of the church in 1835, when it totally disappeared. An official interpreter between the Dutch and the English colonists who had settled among them, was now appointed at an annual salary of 250 guilders. Indian troubles multiplied, and in the winter of 1643 (Feb. 26th) came the disgraceful and impolitic massacre of the savages at Hoboken, opposite New Amsterdam, by Kieft's express order, which was afterward most signally avenged. The bloody strife was carried into Long Island and the governor was justly held responsible for the slaughter and destruction that succeeded. The New Amsterdam inhabitants were so maddened that they talked of deposing him and sending him in chains to Holland. But a quasi truce between his opponents and himself followed, in consequence of his concessions. It was only for a time. Quarrels broke out afresh, and by 1645 it was found by the directors of the West India Co. that, since

the year 1526, their North American province, instead of proving to them a source of revenue, had actually cost them over 550,000 guilders, above returns. This determined Kieft's recall, and after disgraceful contentions with his best friends, if indeed he had friends in New Amsterdam, including fierce dissension with Dominie Bogardus, pastor of the church, the headstrong governor sailed for Holland, Aug. 16, 1647, bearing with him more than $100,000 which he had gathered together during his term of office; Peter Stuyvesant, his successor as governor, having reached New Amsterdam on the previous 11th of May. With him went Dominie Bogardus and certain of the colonists, against whom proceedings had been initiated by Kieft and Stuyvesant as well. The vessel, the Princess, was lost in a storm on the rocky coast of Wales, England, and only about twenty persons escaped death, Kieft and his treasure sinking beneath the waves, together with the clergyman and eighty-one other souls.

DRAKE, Elias Franklin, capitalist, was born at Urbana, O., Dec. 21, 1813, son of Henry and Hannah Spining Drake. His grandfather, Ithamar Drake, removed from Pennsylvania to Ohio about the close of the eighteenth century, and with his wife and four children settled in Warren county, where he engaged in farming. His father, Henry Drake, was a physician, but died soon after beginning his practice, leaving a widow and four children, of whom Elias Franklin was the second. The widow took up her residence on the farm of Mathias Spining, her father, and being a woman of strong character bravely undertook the education of her children. The son Elias when but seven years old began his life-work, laboring on the farm in summer and attending school in winter. He also found occupation for some months in a printing office at Lebanon, but the confinement impairing his health, he returned to the farm. In 1828 he became a clerk in a general store in Lebanon, where he remained three years and occupied every moment of his spare time in reading and study. In 1832 he formed a partnership with three other young men and conducted a general store, but soon found the business would not support so many partners, and Mr. Drake withdrew. He then took a clerkship and continued to reside in Lebanon until he had attained his majority in 1834. He then went to Columbus as chief clerk of the state treasurer. He was sent officially by Gov. Lucas to Washington on state business and had an interview with President Jackson. This was in 1836, and he returned in time to cast his first presidential vote for William Henry Harrison. While in the treasury department Mr. Drake began the study of law under the preceptorship of Noah Swayne. He was admitted to the bar at Delaware, O., in 1837. The same year he became cashier of the Bank of Xenia,

and filled the position for eleven years. During this time he was one of the most influential citizens, being a member of the town council, colonel and aide-de-camp in the militia, captain of the fire company, chief officer of two turnpike roads, trustee of the Presbyterian church, president of the Dayton and Xenia Railroad, and of the Dayton and Western Railroad, and largely interested in the construction of the Little Miami, Columbus, and Xenia Railroad. He was president of the county agricultural society and member of the Whig central committee. He organized the home league for the protection of American industry, which was pledged not to buy any goods other than of American manufacture, and for three terms served his district in the state legislature, and was for one term speaker of the house. In 1841 Mr. Drake was married to Frances Mary, daughter of Maj. James Galloway, of Xenia. She died in 1844, leaving one child, Sallie Frances, who became the wife of Charles Rogers. In 1848 he accepted the presidency of the Columbus Insurance Co. In 1856 he married Caroline Matilda, daughter of Alexander McClurg, of Pittsburg, Pa. She died Jan. 25, 1895, leaving several children. Soon after his second marriage he became interested with Andrew DeGraff in railroad building, and was connected with the leading railroad enterprises of that period in Ohio. In 1860 he transferred his field of operation to St. Paul, Minn., and constructed the first ten miles of railroad built in the state. In 1864 he removed his family to St. Paul. He built the St. Paul and Sioux City Railroad and the Sioux City and St. Paul Railroad and their tributaries, and was for more than sixteen years president of the companies, which were the only railroads in Minnesota that withstood the panic of 1871. In 1880 he retired from railroad management and devoted himself to the care of his rapidly accumulating properties in the West. In 1882, with his family, he made the tour of Europe. He served for many years as director of the Merchants' National Bank, the St. Paul Trust Co., the St. Paul Fire and Marine Insurance Co., and other financial institutions. He was from its organization a member of the chamber of commerce, and served for a term as president of the Minnesota Historical Society. He was a member of the Republican national conventions that nominated Mr. Lincoln at Baltimore in 1864, and Mr. Garfield at Chicago in 1880. At the latter convention he introduced the resolution that broke the unit rule and secured the nomination of Garfield. In 1878 he was elected to the state senate of Minnesota and during the session was instrumental in securing to the state 500,000 acres of land under a half-forgotten law of congress, the act of Sep. 4, 1841, which granted to certain states public lands for internal improvements. Mr. Drake went to California in November, 1891, with the hope that a change of climate would arrest failing health. His hopes were not fulfilled, and he died at San Diego, Feb. 14, 1892.

BLEWETT, Benjamin T., educator, was born in Warren county, Ky., Sept. 17, 1820. His early life was spent alternately on a farm and at school until his thirteenth year, after which he taught the younger members of his family during the winter months, going to school during spring and summer. When eighteen years of age he was admitted to the school of Josiah Pillsbury, and prepared for college. He became a Baptist two years after, and having decided to preach, determined to have a good collegiate education. He entered Georgetown College, August, 1841, as a freshman. Not having sufficient means to carry him through college, he went to the academy connected with the college as principal at a salary of $350 a year; he kept it for two years, then again attended college, graduating in 1848. In 1848 he married. In January, 1853, he resigned the position he had held in the academy, and after his graduation removed to Russellville and took charge of Bethel High School. Here he found scope for his almost miraculous energy. He was given the management of the enterprise. The school-house was not completed, and the control of it was put into his hands. After a year of incessant toil the building was finished, furnished, and formally dedicated to learning and religion, Jan. 3, 1854. At first came discouragements and disappointments, but the high school prospered. Mr. Blewett now decided to supply the felt want of a Baptist college in southern Kentucky, and, with the consent of the trustees, obtained a new charter, and the Bethel High School was transformed into Bethel College; Mr. Blewett, as principal of the high school, becoming president of the latter. This college continued prosperous until the war, when it closed temporarily. After this President Blewett resigned in 1861, seeking another field of labor. Upon leaving Russellville he took charge of Braken Academy, Augusta, Ky., spending ten years, and successfully conducting a first-class school. In 1870 he assumed charge of a young ladies' academy in St. Louis, Mo. This school, built up under the auspices of the Baptists, had become embarrassed with debt. President Blewett bought it, and at sixty-nine years of age, is now (1895) conducting a seminary for young ladies. His two sons are principals of public schools in St. Louis, each having thirty teachers and 1,200 pupils. His two daughters are associated with him in the St. Louis Seminary. The Baptists of southern Kentucky may well feel indebted to Mr. Blewett for their noble college. The greater part of his prime was devoted to its up-building; his extraordinary energy and vigorous mental powers were brought in play, his perseverance was untiring, and his small fortune also was devoted to the institution, and his name deserves honoring by those enjoying the fruit of his labors.

BRENNAN, Thomas, lumberman, was born in Burnchurch, Kilkenny, Ireland, November, 1838. As a lad he lived in the same parish with John Ireland, afterward archbishop of the Roman Catholic see of St. Paul, with whom a warm acquaintance and friendship was ever maintained. Young Brennan came to America when a mere lad and settled in Wisconsin, where he lived upon a farm until he was nineteen years old, when he left the farm and became roadmaster on the St. Paul and Duluth Railroad. He drove the first spike on the Northern Pacific Railroad at Northern Pacific Junction. Later he became superintendent of the Duluth road, but resigned the position in order to accept the superintendency of the Manitoba Railroad. In 1881 he gave up railroading

to engage in the lumber business, and so successful was this venture that he came to be known as one of the largest operators in the Northwest, in which he acquired a large fortune. He was ever a devoted son of the Roman Catholic church, and identified with every movement made by the bishop and archbishop which called for his operation. His sympathies were easily aroused and always found practical expression in good deeds, performed in so delicate a way as to leave his beneficiaries doubtful as to the source of the benefaction. He was a member of the Society of St. Vincent de Paul Orphan Asylum, president of the Irish-American Club, a member of the Celtic American Club, and of the Contractors' and Builders' Association. Mr. Brennan was married in 1867 to Mary Agnes Kelly of Dodge county, Wis. Overwork and climatic influences finally undermined his health and he sought restoration in the milder climate of Arkansas. He visited the Hot Springs and while there died, March 1, 1889.

QUINCY, Edmund, author and reformer, was born in Boston, Mass., Feb. 1, 1808. He was the second son of Josiah Quincy, president of Harvard. The atmosphere of literature and culture in his home early gave him a taste for literature, which he indulged even before he entered college. He was noted for the sprightliness of his compositions during his course at Harvard, from which he was graduated in 1827. He was associated with William Lloyd Garrison and Mrs. Maria Weston Chapman in the conduct of the "Non-Resistant," a paper which, while not the official organ of the Abolitionists, represented the peaceful methods to which they had pledged themselves. Mr. Quincy was the chief editor, and furnished most of the original articles, Mr. Garrison confining himself to the "selections," and the general oversight. The paper lived only two years, but its significance for the philosophic historian is, that it is indicative of the millennial character of the reformatory ferment that pervaded the period. He was one of the most active members in the Non-Resistant Convention in 1840, at which the Abolitionists adopted this principle. Mr. Quincy wrote an admirable biography of his father, and in 1850 published a novel, entitled, "Wensley," which Whittier pronounced the best book of the kind since Hawthorne's "Blithedale Romance." He was one of the ablest and most effective contributors to the anti-slavery press, to which he devoted his best powers. He died in Dedham, Mass., May 17, 1877.

SHEPARD, Edward Morse, was born in New York city, July 23, 1850. His father, Lorenzo B. Shepard, died in New York city in 1856, after a distinguished, though brief, career as a lawyer and politician. Three years after his father's death Mr. Shepard removed to Brooklyn, N. Y. He obtained his education in the public schools, studied one year at Oberlin College in Ohio, and in 1869 was graduated from the Free College of the city of New York. He studied law in the office of Man & Parsons, and three years after his admission to the bar established an office of his own. In 1876 he entered into partnership with Albert Stickney, the firm name being Stickney & Shepard. In 1890 he formed a partnership with John E. Parsons under the name of Parsons, Shepard & Ogden. Mr. Shepard took an active part in the organization of the Young Men's Democratic Club of Brooklyn, serving during the years 1883, '84, and '85 as its president and for two earlier years as chairman of the executive committee. He was counsel in 1887 in investigating official abuses in Brooklyn. He was appointed civil service commissioner by Mayor Low, and originated the civil service code which has since been pronounced the most practical and effective of any yet adopted in America. For two years under Mayor Chapin he was chairman of the civil service commissioners of Brooklyn. In 1884 and 1885 he was forest commissioner of New York state and prepared the plan of the forest preserve of New York. He has made frequent addresses and written magazine articles and monographs on historical, economic, and literary subjects, and in 1888 published in the "American Statesman" series "The Life of Martin Van Buren." The organizations of which he is a member are the Cobden Club of England, the Manhattan, University, Reform, and Church clubs of New York, and the Hamilton, Brooklyn, and Riding and Driving clubs of Brooklyn. He is a member of Holy Trinity Episcopal Church, trustee of the Packer Institute, and regent of the Long Island College Hospital. In the early part of 1892 Mr. Shepard was at the official head of the Democratic uprising in Kings county to prevent the nomination of David B. Hill and to secure the nomination of Mr. Cleveland for the presidency. In the fall of 1893, by articles in periodicals and by public speeches and also by effective political organization he led a revolt of about one-third part of the Democratic party in Kings county against party abuses in local affairs, the result of the movement being the overwhelming defeat of the old organization of his party. In November, 1893, the governor of New York placed in the hands of Mr. Shepard and Gen. Tracy, lately the secretary of the navy, the prosecution of the extraordinary election frauds at Gravesend. The general direction of these prosecutions was in Mr. Shepard's hands. They resulted before the end of March, 1894, in the imprisonment at Sing Sing of John Y. McKane, a famous political boss, and the imprisonment in the Penitentiary of twenty other offenders; the complete destruction of the political power of McKane and his following; and later a complete security against a repetition of the abuses by the legislative incorporation of Gravesend into the city of Brooklyn.

ADAMS, Ezra Eastman, clergyman and author, was born at Concord, N. H., Aug. 20, 1813. He was graduated at Dartmouth College in 1836, and passed the succeeding thirteen years in Europe, mostly in France, where he was seamen's chaplain at Havre. Returning to this country, he was made pastor of a church at Nashua, N. H., until 1860, when he removed to Philadelphia, and founded the Broad Street Church. In 1867 he was made professor of theology in Lincoln University, Pa., and in 1870 became editorially connected with the "Presbyterian," published at Philadelphia, both of which positions he held until his death. He was the author of several poems of merit, and contributed freely to the "Presbyterian." He died at Oxford, Pa., Nov. 3, 1871.

DAVIES, Charles William, steel and copper plate engraver and stationer, was born at Whitesboro', N. Y., June 21, 1854, only son of David and Sarah (Jones) Davies, both members of the Congregational church. His father was a carpenter and builder, who came to this country from Wales in 1828 at the age of six years, and settled in central New York state. Charles completed a course in the public schools and entered as a student into the Whitesboro' Seminary. Here he continued to take elective studies until he was twenty years of age. Upon leaving school he went to Utica, N. Y., and served as an apprentice in a jewelry store. He felt a natural inclination toward engraving, and after working under one of the engravers of that city long enough to acquire a thorough knowledge of the art, he formed a partnership with his employer, which continued for two years. He then went to Syracuse, N. Y., and started in business for himself. But no sooner had he gained a foothold than he was burned out, thus being reduced to a state of most embarrassing poverty; yet, possessed of unflinching courage, he faced the world determined not to surrender. At this time he was drawn toward the West and set out for Minneapolis. He stopped at Grand Rapids, where he worked a while at his trade, and finally reaching his destination, without friends, standing, or resources, in a new city. He was determined to succeed, and began business in his own name. With a capital of 50 cents he converted a store box into a table, and with a few tools and plenty of pluck he began business as the pioneer engraver of Minneapolis, November, 1881. Under his tireless and persistent care his business has grown until its patrons are not only of his own city but throughout the entire Northwest. He was married in 1885 to Clara Getz of Delaware, O., a woman reared in a Methodist home and of strong Christian character. Their home, always open to their friends, is filled with books, music, and rare works of art. They have two children, Marion and Clifford.

HART, Joel, T., sculptor, was born in Clark county, Ky., in 1810. Not having facilities for a school education, he obtained what learning he could from books at home. He was apprenticed to a mason until 1830, when he removed to Lexington, Ky., where he worked in a marble yard. At this time he met with S. V. Clevenger, also a stone-cutter, with whom he worked for a number of years. He was inspired by Clevenger to model busts in clay, and soon developed unusual talent. He studied anatomy at the old medical college in Lexington, for the sake of exactness in his art. His first effort of note in his new profession was a bust of Cassius M. Clay, a young man of his own age. The Ladies' Clay Association of Richmond commissioned him to execute a statue of Henry Clay, upon which he worked three years. He went to Florence, Italy, in the fall of 1894 to transfer his work to marble, and the statue now stands in Richmond, Va. The city of New Orleans ordered a colossal bronze statue of Clay. Thirty years of his life were spent in Florence, during which time he made many busts of note. Of his ideal pieces the most appreciated are, "Angelina," "Il Penseroso," and the "Triumph of Chastity," which is considered his masterpiece. He died in Florence, Italy, March 1, 1877.

HIGBY, William Riley, banker, was born in Bridgeport, Conn., Aug. 6, 1825, son of Hervey and Charlotte (Baldwin) Higby, and grandson of Maj. Samuel Higby. His father was a leading citizen of Bridgeport, and held many positions of honor and trust. His maternal ancestry were Huguenots, who fled to this country about the time of the massacre of St. Bartholomew. William was educated in the private schools at Bridgeport and New Haven, and began business life as teller and bookkeeper in the Connecticut Bank in 1844. After seven years' service in this position he engaged in the manufacturing business, which was destroyed by fire a few months later. In 1851 he assisted in the organization of the Pequonnock Bank and was its first cashier. He officiated in this position until 1869, when he resigned to engage in fire insurance, associating with him two years later T. B. De Forest. Mr. Higby has held many positions of responsibility and trust in town and city affairs. He was city treasurer 1853–57, for eleven years was treasurer of the town, and twelve years a member of the board of fire commissioners. For nearly twenty years he has been a director, and is now vice-president, of the Connecticut National Bank, and for over thirty years has been a trustee of the Bridgeport Savings Bank, and is a director and president of the Bridgeport Gas Light Co., succeeding his father who was an efficient officer of these institutions. Mr. Higby has been director, secretary, and treasurer of the Mountain Grove Cemetery Association since 1861. He became a master Mason in 1852, and was the first Templar in Hamilton Commandery in 1855. He received in 1855 the several grades of the A. A. S. R., including the 33d°, and in 1878 was received into the Royal Order of Scotland. Mr. Higby has occupied all the principal positions in all the bodies of the A. A. S. R. at Bridgeport, and since 1868 has been grand treasurer of the Connecticut grand commandery. He is one of the two active members of the state of Connecticut in the supreme council of the A. A. S. R. for the northern jurisdiction of the United States. He has always manifested a deep interest in Masonic matters, and is one of the few 33d Masons in the state. An eminent writer says of Mr. Higby, "Among the prominent features of his character are fidelity to principles and causes which he may espouse, without regard to popular clamor on the one hand or popular favor on the other." He married in 1846 Mary, daughter of Lyman Johnson, and they have two daughters.

REID, James, president of the College of Montana, was born in Dundas county, Ontario, Canada, of Scotch-Irish ancestry. He worked upon his father's farm, attended the neighboring public schools, where he also taught, and eventually entered Toronto and McGill (Montreal) Universities. He was graduated from the latter in 1881, receiving his diploma from the Presbyterian College during the same year. He next studied at Union Theological Seminary, New York city, and at the theological schools of Edinburgh. Upon his return to America, he was for a time engaged in connection with the First Presbyterian Church, Bay City, Mich. Mr. Reid spent 1889–90 in post-graduate work at Union Theological Seminary, going from there to the pastorate of the Presbyterian Church at Deer Lodge, Mont.; also the seat of the College of Montana. In 1890 he was appointed president of the college, in which capacity he did much to forward that institution's best interests. President Reid is well known throughout the state as an educator, lecturer, and preacher. He was the first president of the Montana state council of education; was president of the State Teachers' Association in 1894; and a member of the state board of education.

ROWAN, John, jurist and statesman, was born in Pennsylvania in 1773. His father, William Rowan, at the close of the revolutionary war, went to Kentucky and settled in Louisville, at that time a mere village. The next spring they removed further West, settling on Green river. At the age of seventeen he entered the classical school at Bardstown. Upon leaving school he went to Lexington and commenced the study of law, and in 1795 was admitted to the bar. He soon attained a high rank in his profession, and Kentucky even at that date contained many men of talent, learning, and eloquence—yet he was considered one of the foremost. He was a member of the convention that formed the present constitution of Kentucky in 1799. He was made secretary of state in 1804, and two years later was elected to congress. He was appointed judge of the court of appeals in 1819, and while on the bench delivered a learned and forcible opinion on the power of congress to charter a bank of the United States. He resigned his seat in 1821; in 1824 he was elected to the U. S. senate, in which he served six years. The last public office Mr. Rowan filled was that of commissioner to adjust the claims of United States citizens against Mexico, under the convention of Washington of April, 1839. Upon the organization of the Kentucky Historical Society in 1838, he was elected president, and held that office until his death, which occurred in Louisville, Ky., July 18, 1843. Rowan county, Ky., was named in his honor.

PHIPS, Sir William, colonial governor of Massachusetts, was born at Woolwich, Me., a small settlement near the mouth of the river Kennebec, Feb. 2, 1651. He was one of twenty-six children of James Phips, gunsmith, who had emigrated from Bristol, England, at an early period in the history of the colonies. While he was very young he was a shepherd boy; at eighteen he bound himself to a ship-carpenter and remained with him four years. In 1673 he removed to Boston, and for a year worked at his trade, learning meanwhile to read and write. Here he also married about this time Mrs. Hull, widow of a Boston merchant, and by the connection thus formed laid the foundation of future prosperity. He then engaged in ship-building and in trading by sea, but his ventures were not successful, nor was it until 1684–87 that he got his start in life by recovering sunken treasures from the sea near Port de la Plata in the Bahama islands, to the amount of £300,000, under the patronage of the English Duke of Albemarle, his own share being some £1,600. King James II. was advised to seize the whole cargo, instead of taking the tenth which by law belonged to him, but he refused to do so, and instead promised to Phips the royal countenance and favor. This

promise was fulfilled in part, in the conference upon Phips of knighthood, and a request that he remain in England, with a further engagement that he should have honorable employment in the public service. The latter proposal Phips declined and was forthwith appointed sheriff of New England by his royal master. But he found when he reached Boston, Mass., that his patent as sheriff would not put him in possession of the office, Sir Edmund Andros being the colonial governor, and after a timebe returned to England, where he received from James II., then in exile, an offer of the government of New England, which offer he was shrewd enough to refuse. Returning to Boston in 1689, he offered his services to Gov. Bradstreet for the Indian war then raging on the frontiers. About this time (March, 1690) he became a member of the North Church in Boston, of which the Rev. Cotton Mather was minister, in whom he found a steadfast friend; and this year in the service of the colony he headed successful expeditions against Port Royal in Acadia, whence French privateers had fitted out to prey upon Massachusetts commerce. The place surrendered to Phips at his first summons. Previous to sailing he was, for the first time, made a freeman. In the more ambitious scheme of the capture of Canada by the Massachusetts colonists (also in 1690) Phips commanded the naval force of thirty-two vessels carrying 2,000 men, for operations against Quebec on the river St. Lawrence. But his vessels met with a most mortifying repulse at Quebec, and from that and other causes the expedition ended in failure, at a cost to the colony of Massachusetts of £50,000. Disheartened by this result, Phips was yet ready to proceed to London on colonial matters, ostensibly to secure aid for another movement against Canada, but really (as has been claimed) to solicit the restoration of the colonial charter, which had been taken away by the British authorities in 1684. The issue of this visit, and of the exertions which he made in company with Increase Mather, then agent

of the colony of Massachusetts in England, was the assurance of a new charter for the colony, and the appointment of Sir William Phips as governor, his connections also making him captain-general of the colonies of Connecticut and Rhode Island. He reached Boston with this instrument May 14, 1694, Mather returning with him. He at once, without authority, instituted a special commission of oyer and terminer for the trial of alleged witches, of whom, following the manifestations at Salem, there were then in jail and awaiting trial nearly 100, and it was by that court that the execution of the twenty Salem witches, so called, was ordered. In August of the same year, the governor sailed with 450 men for Pemaquid river, in the present state of Maine, where a stockade fort had previously been erected by Gov. Andros. This had been destroyed by the Indians in 1689, and as the French and Indians were at this time troublesome, Phips rebuilt the fort, this time substantially. This proceeding, however, brought him into collision with his own colonists, and his reputation not only as a military man but as a civil administrator began to decline, largely because of personal peculiarities of temper. Quarrels ensued, and in a street encounter with the captain of the frigate which had brought them to Boston from England, the governor knocked down his antagonist and beat him with his cane, after which he put him into jail, and then sent him to the secretary of state in London. His appointment as captain-general of Connecticut and Rhode Island also brought perplexity to him; he had a serious altercation with Brenton, the royal collector of customs in Boston, and offered him personal violence, and was speedily involved moreover in bitter controversy with Gov. Fletcher of New York about the surrender of a fugitive from Fletcher's jurisdiction, whom Phips would not give up to him upon demand. Upon representations from individuals in the colony, the governor soon found himself summoned to England by the English privy council, that he might clear himself of the accusations brought against him by his opponents. He sailed for London, in obedience to this order, Nov. 19, 1694, after an administration of but two years and a half. He appears to have succeeded in defending himself satisfactorily, and received assurances of his restoration to the governorship, but was suddenly taken ill; and on Feb. 18, 1695, he died of malignant fever.

HORNBLOWER, Josiah, engineer, was born in Staffordshire, England, Feb. 23, 1729. Having a taste for mathematics and mechanics, his early studies were in these directions, and his elder brother being an eminent engineer, he adopted that profession, and with him went to Cornwall in 1745, where he aided him in setting up steam pumping engines for the mines. Through this and other experience he became accomplished in mining and machinery, and having emigrated to the United States in 1753 he built, near Belleville, N. J., the first steam-engine ever constructed in this country, and which was used in connection with the copper mines near that town. Of these mines he was manager for five years, during that time being also commissioned as captain and employed in the defense of New Jersey against the inroads of the French and Indians during the war of 1755. During the revolutionary war he was a member of the lower house of the New Jersey legislature, of which he was speaker in 1780. The British made a futile attempt to kidnap him, and in 1781 he was elected to the upper branch of that body, of which he continued a member until 1784, when he was elected a member of the Continental congress. During the latter part of his life he was judge of the Essex court of common pleas. He died in Newark, N. J., Jan. 21, 1809.

MITCHELL, Donald Grant, author, was born at Norwich, Conn., Apr. 12, 1822. He was the grandson of the distinguished jurist, Stephen Mix Mitchell, through whose efforts Connecticut was able to establish her claim to the tract of land known as the Western Reserve. His father was the pastor of the Second Congregational Church in Norwich. Donald was prepared for college at the boarding-school at Ellington, Conn., by Dr. John Hall, said to be the original of some of the traits portrayed in the hero of Mitchell's only novel, "Dr. Johns." From this school he entered Yale College, where he was graduated in 1841, when, his health being somewhat impaired, he spent the next three years upon his maternal grandfather's farm in Salem, Conn., where he probably received his impressions of country life, which he has so beautifully portrayed later in his books. He became much interested in agriculture, and wrote a number of letters to the "Albany Cultivator," and took the prize given by the New York Agricultural Society for a plan of farm buildings. In 1844 he went to Europe, spending one-half the winter on the island of Jersey and in the following spring rambling over England on foot, visiting every county and contributing letters to various journals. After spending a year and a half on the continent, he returned, and began the study of law in New York. With the materials gathered during his continental trip he published "Fresh Gleanings; or, a New Sheaf from the Old Fields of Continental Europe, by Ike Marvel," which was a delightful volume of leisurely observation of the Old World. Mr. Mitchell's health not being able to bear the confinement of a law office, he again visited Europe in 1848, traveling through England and Switzerland, and was in Paris during the revolution of that year, the experiences of which he recorded in "The Battle Summer," published the next year. Upon his return to New York he began the publication of "The Lorgnette," a weekly periodical in the size and style of "Salmagundi," which was afterward issued in book form. This was issued under the *nom de plume* of "John Timon." Although it attracted much attention from its brilliancy and style, the author's *incognito* was preserved for nearly a year. At this time Mr. Mitchell brought out his more popular work, "Reveries of a Bachelor," a delightful contemplation of life from the slippered ease of the chimney-corner. The basis of this work was originally a contribution to the "Southern Literary Messenger," under the title "A Bachelor's Reverie." This was followed in 1851 by "Dream Life," written in the same vein of hazy reminiscence in which every one finds the story of his own life. Some one has said that these compositions are to American literature what a wood fire is on a dreary day. They are all warmth and cheer and light. They somewhat resemble Irving's "Sketch Book" in their tender sentiment, and in the elegance and delicacy of their diction, which has placed them among the classics of American literature. In 1850 he married Mary, a daughter of Wm. B. Pringle, of Charleston, S. C., and great-granddaughter of Rebecca Motte. In 1854 Mr. Mitchell was appointed U. S. consul to Venice, where he began collecting material for a history of the Venetian Republic. This was never written, but the material appears in his later writings, and in "Titian and his Times,"

VI.—7

delivered as a lecture before the Yale Art School, of which Mr. Mitchell has been a trustee since its establishment, and was later included in his volume of miscellaneous writings, entitled "Bound Together." He returned in 1855, and bought a farm in the neighborhood of New Haven, Conn., which he named Edgewood, and which has subsequently become well known to the public through his books on rural life. In them he conveys much practical information, together with a delightful æsthetic flavor of sentiment and literary refinement. These are "My Farm of Edgewood," "Wet Days at Edgewood," "Rural Studies, with Hints for Country Places." These works were preceded by "Fudge Doings," which appeared originally in the "Knickerbocker Magazine." He has been an occasional contributor to "Harper's Magazine" and the "Atlantic Monthly," besides writing for other periodicals and delivering lectures and addresses on subjects connected with literature and agriculture. In 1868 he edited the "Atlantic Almanac," and the next year became the editor of the "Hearth and Home." He was appointed one of the judges of Industrial Art at the Centennial Exposition of 1876, and was also appointed U. S. commissioner to the Paris Exposition of 1878, in which year Yale conferred upon him the degree of LL.D. In addition to the books mentioned, Mr. Mitchell published: "Seven Stories with Basement and Attic" (1864); "About Old Story-Tellers" (1869); and "Pictures of Edgewood" (1877); also a series of literary papers delivered before various educational institutions, and published under the general title of "English Lands, Letters, and Kings," *i.e.:* "From Celt to Tudor" (1889); "From Elizabeth to Anne" (1890); "Queen Anne and the Georges" (1895). Many of his books concealed the name of their author under the name "Ike Marvel."

WRIGHT, Carroll Davidson, statistician, was born in Dunbarton, N. H., July 25, 1840, the son of Rev. Nathan Reed Wright. He was educated in the public schools of Vermont and New Hampshire, and the high school at Reading, Mass. In 1860 he entered upon the study of law. In 1862 he enlisted as a private in the 14th regiment New Hampshire volunteers, and became colonel of this regiment in December, 1864. His principal service was as acting assistant adjutant-general of a brigade in Gen. Sheridan's Shenandoah Valley campaign. He left the army in March, 1865, and was admitted to the New Hampshire bar in October of that year, but, on account of ill health, did not begin practice until August, 1867, and then at Boston, being, in the autumn of 1867, admitted to the Massachusetts and U. S. courts. He served in the Massachusetts state senate during the years 1872–73, and in the latter year secured the passage of a bill to provide the establishment of trains for workingmen on suburban roads. He was chief of the Massachusetts Bureau

of the Statistics of Labor from 1873 to 1888, and in 1880 was appointed supervisor for the U. S. census for Massachusetts, and also special agent of that census on the factory system. In 1885 he was commissioned by the governor of Massachusetts to investigate the public records of towns, parishes, counties, and courts. In January, 1885, he was appointed commissioner of labor by the president, which office had been created in June, 1884. Col. Wright was a Republican presidential elector in 1876.

In 1875, and again in 1885, he had charge of the decennial census of Massachusetts. During the year 1879 he was lecturer on the ethical phases of the labor question at the Lowell Institute in Boston, and in 1881 university lecturer on the factory system at Harvard University. He has been university lecturer at Johns Hopkins, the University of Michigan, and the Northwestern University in Illinois. He is a member of various scientific societies at home and abroad. He was given the degree of A. M. by Tuft's College in 1883, and in 1894 the degree of LL. D. was conferred upon him by Wesleyan University. Among the books which he has published are the following: " Annual Reports of the Massachusetts Bureau of the Statistics of Labor" (1873-88); "Census of Massachusetts" (1875); "Statistics of Boston" (1883); "Factory System of the United States" (1883); "Census of Massachusetts" (1885); "Reports of the U. S. Commissioner of Labor" (1886-94); and numerous pamphlets. By special act of congress he was in October, 1893, placed in charge of the eleventh census, in addition to his duties as commissioner of labor. In August, 1894, under the provision of law, he served as chairman of the U. S. strike commission to investigate the Chicago difficulties occurring in that year.

WOODBURN, Benjamin Franklin, clergyman, was born in Crescent Township, Allegany co., Pa., March 23, 1832, son of William Woodburn (born 1777, died 1859), who was a farmer and during his lifetime held various offices of trust in his community. His paternal grandfather emigrated from the north of Ireland during the revolutionary war and served two years in the army. He settled in Cumberland county, Pa., near Carlisle, but removed to the banks of the Ohio river in 1794. A block house was then located on the opposite bank to protect the settlers from the incursions of the Indians. His mother's maiden name was Veazy; her ancestors came from Baltimore, Md. The son acquired a good common school education, supplemented by a course at a commercial college. At the age of 18 years he became clerk on a steamer on the Arkansas river, and was employed on boats plying the Ohio, Mississippi, Cumberland, and other rivers for eight years, as clerk and captain. In 1854 he was married to Margaret Shouse of Shousetown, Pa. In 1859 he determined to fit himself for the ministry and entered the sophomore class of Jefferson College, and was graduated with the first honors of his class in 1862. He was graduated in 1865 from the Western Theological Seminary, Allegheny City, and was ordained as pastor of the Mt. Pleasant, Pa., Baptist Church the same year. In March, 1870, he became pastor of the

Sandusky Street Baptist Church, Allegheny City, Pa. He celebrated his twenty-fifth anniversary in 1895. Dr. Woodburn identified himself with the interests of the community in establishing the Allegheny General Hospital; he has been president of the institution since its opening in 1884. He is a member of the board of controllers of public schools, has served on the high school committee, and is chairman of the committee that manages the Citizens' and Public School Library. In 1881 the University of Lewisburg conferred upon him the degree of D. D.

ROBERTSON, Robert Henderson, architect, was born in Philadelphia, Apr. 29, 1849. His father, Archibald Robertson, although born in the United States, was the son of Scotch parents, his mother, Elizabeth Henderson, being a native of Scotland. The son's early life was spent in Philadelphia, where his father was engaged in mercantile enterprises. On reaching the age of eighteen, he entered the class of 1869 at Rutgers College at New Brunswick, N. J., and after graduation he entered the office of Henry Sims, a well-known architect of Philadelphia. Upon the death of Mr. Sims, Mr. Robertson removed with his family to New York, where he entered the office of Edward T. Potter, and later that of George B. Post. At this time, when there were no architectural schools in America, Mr. Robertson was most fortunate in being able to pursue his studies under the direction of such men. They were of the first rank, and of wide experience. Here was laid the foundation for Mr. Robertson's subsequent success. After several years of office work under such supervisors, he went into active practice, in which he continued alone until 1875. In that year he entered into a partnership with William A. Potter, who had a short time before been appointed by President Grant supervising architect of the U. S. government at Washington, and with whom he remained associated until 1880. Both during this partnership and since, Mr. Robertson has acquired a wide experience in his profession, not only in designing but also in the practical details of building. His career has been at once busy and prosperous, his practice being confined to no especial class of buildings. He stands among the first practitioners of his art in

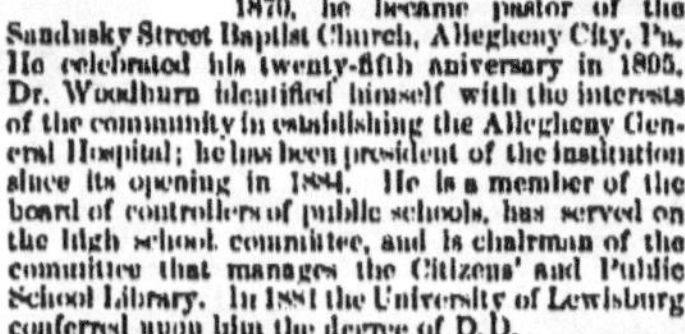

America, and his reputation is based not only on his thorough mastery of the practical phases of architecture, but also on his artistic gifts. In appearance he is tall, well built, and with a well-developed physique, having given no small attention to athletics, and being a most enthusiastic hunter and fisherman. He is a fine musician, being a highly prized member of the Mendelssohn Glee Club, of which he has for many years been the president. Mr. Robertson was married early in life to Charlotte, eldest daughter of Dr. Thomas M. Markoe, a distinguished physician of New York. They have one child, Thomas Markoe Robertson.

DRAPER, William Franklin, manufacturer, was born at Lowell, Mass., Apr. 9, 1842, eldest son of George and Hannah Thwing Draper. George Draper was a manufacturer of cotton machinery, a man remarkable for strength of character, energy, and intellect, and left a record of usefulness excelled by few of his contemporaries. His grandfather, Maj. Abijah Draper, of Dedham, fought in the revolutionary war. The son received an education intended to fit him for Harvard University. His school life was interspersed with periods of labor in machine shops and cotton-mills, the last three years before the outbreak of the civil war being entirely given to studying the manufacture and operation of cotton machinery. On Aug. 9, 1861, young Draper enlisted in a local company that his father was instrumental in raising, and the youthful volunteer was chosen second lieutenant of Company B., of the 25th Massachusetts regiment. His war experience extended over nearly four years' campaigning. He became signal officer on the staff of Gen. Burnside, and in this position he went through the battles of Roanoke Island, Newbern, and Fort Macon, when he was promoted first lieutenant and returned to his regiment. In August, 1862, he was commissioned captain in the 36th Massachusetts, and joined his regiment just after the battle of South Mountain,

Md. With them he went through the rest of the Antietam campaign, and the battle of Fredericksburg, and was then with the 9th corps sent to Newport News. After this several months were spent pursuing Morgan's cavalry and sundry guerillas in Kentucky. In June, 1863, he joined Grant's army at Vicksburg, taking part in the capture, and subsequently in the march to Jackson and the fighting in that locality. His regiment was reduced from fighting and sickness from 650 in June, to 198 in September. During this campaign he was appointed major of the regiment. In August, 1863, he returned to Kentucky and marched through Cumberland Gap into East Tennessee. While staying there through the winter, the siege of Knoxville took place, and the battles of Blue Springs, Campbell's Station, and Strawberry Plains were fought, Maj. Draper commanding the regiment after Oct. 10th, in the place of Col. Goodall, who was wounded. In the spring of 1864 his corps was removed to Annapolis and partially recruited, and then joined the army of the Potomac. In the battle of the Wilderness, on May 6th, he was shot through the body while leading his regiment in the capture of a rifle pit. After having been left

on the field as hopelessly wounded, and subsequently captured by and recaptured from the enemy, he was saved and sent to the hospital in Washington. He was commissioned lieutenant-colonel from this date, but his regiment was too small from loss in the severe fighting to muster a full colonel. After partially recovering from the wound he joined his regiment during the siege of Petersburg, and took command of a brigade at the Weldon Railroad engagement. A month later, at Poplar Grove Church and Pegram Farm, his division was severely engaged and cut off from the rest. His regiment was the only one of the brigade that came out as an organization; and they brought back the colors of several others. He was again wounded in the shoulder by a nearly spent ball. On Oct. 12, 1864, his service expired and he accepted a discharge. He was brevetted colonel and brigadier-general for "gallant service during the war." Gen. Draper then accepted employment from the firm of E. D. & G. Draper, manufacturers of cotton machinery. In April, 1868, Mr. E. D. Draper retiring, his interest was bought by Gen. Draper, who became a partner with his father under the firm name of George Draper & Son. Continuing in successful manufacturing, Gen. Draper grew in business reputation, and since his father's death, in 1887, has been the head of the firm of George Draper & Sons, widely known as the leading introducers of improvements in cotton machinery in this country. Besides this position he has been directly connected with many other large manufacturing concerns, and is now president or director in various corporations, covering the manufacture of machinery, cotton cloth, shoes, electrical goods, etc., and railroads, gas and water companies, and insurance. Gen. Draper has also shown marked legal ability, which has helped his firm through numerous patent suits, as well as strong inventive talent, having personally patented more than fifty inventions. Mechanically he is known as the first expert in this country on splicing machinery, and has written standard articles on this and other mechanical subjects. Gen. Draper served on Gov. Long's staff during the three years the latter held office. He was a delegate to the convention nominating Pres. Hayes, and was afterwards an elector-at-large, voting for Pres. Harrison. He was chairman of the committee on resolutions at the Republican state convention, in 1887. In 1888 Gen. Draper was a candidate for the Republican nomination for governor, being strongly backed by the soldier vote. He was defeated in the nomination by Gov. Ames, after an interesting preliminary struggle. In economic circles he is known as a student and thinker. The protective tariff has been his especial field of research, and he has personally investigated at great length economic conditions both in Europe and this country. His pamphlet and magazine articles on the tariff have been widely read and discussed. He has twice been president of the Home Market Club, founded by his father, which is the strongest and most influential protective organization in New England, and second nationally only to the American Protective Tariff League. He is also a member and officer of the Arkwright Club, which represents the great cotton manufacturing industry. He is a member of the Loyal Legion and Grand Army, is a Knight Templar, member of the Sons of the Revolution, the Society of Colonial Wars, the Union and Algonquin Clubs of Boston; the Metropolitan and Army and Navy clubs of Washington, the Hope Club of Providence, and many others. Gen. Draper was nominated by acclamation for representative in the fifty-third congress from the eleventh Massachusetts district, and was elected by over 2,500 plurality. He was a member of the foreign affairs and patent committee of the house, and took a prominent part in debate. At the present writing (1894) he has been unanimously renominated, with a probability of re-election by double his former plurality.

GILLIS, James Henry Lawrence, commodore U. S. navy, was born near Ridgeway, Pa., May 14, 1831, of Scotch ancestry, his father being an officer in the war of 1812, and afterward one of the pioneer settlers of the western section of the state. He entered the U. S. navy in 1848, cruised in the West Indies and on the coast of Africa, and was graduated from the U. S. Naval Academy in 1854, previous to which he spent five years in active service. In 1859, while a lieutenant on board of the U. S. steamer Supply, at Montevideo, he saved the lives of three men, whose vessel, the Argentine schooner Filomena, had been wrecked in a pampero. "These wretched beings," writes an eye-witness, " were clinging to the masts of their submerged vessel, and on them was fastened the gaze of the thousands who lined the shores. The storm was still raging, and none dared to attempt a rescue until Lieut. Gillis appeared on the scene, when, calling for volunteers among the American seamen, he was soon in charge of a boat manned by ten of these brave fellows, and after three hours of almost superhuman exertions, succeeded in rescuing his despairing fellow-beings

from their awful position. For this act of heroism he was publicly crowned with laurels and received the thanks of the government of the country, and thirty years after, the officers of the Argentine navy presented him with a handsome medal of steel and gold mounted in diamonds, commemorative of this exploit. He participated in the first naval encounter of the civil war between the U. S. frigate St. Lawrence and the Confederate privateer Petrel, and continued in active service until the taking of Mobile, when his vessel, the monitor Milwaukee, was one of the twenty-two blown up by the torpedoes in Mobile bay. After this he volunteered for and was given command of a naval battery on shore, and assisted at the taking of Spanish Fort. He was afterwards promoted for gallantry by act of congress, and received the special commendation of the secretary of the navy. It is a remarkable fact that during the whole of the war he lost neither a man nor an officer. This led to a belief among the sailors that he bore a charmed life, and that he insured the safety of all who sailed with him. This belief was confirmed by his extraordinary experience while in command of the U. S. steamer Wateree. This vessel alone of all those in the harbor of Arica escaped total destruction by the tidal wave which accompanied the earthquake of 1868. The receding waters left the Wateree safely lodged between the hillocks half a mile inland, uninjured, and none on board any the worse for the involuntary cruise. For his services to those rendered destitute by the catastrophe, he afterwards received the thanks of the English government. In 1881, while in command of the U. S. steamer Lackawana, he successfully arbitrated and concluded a treaty of peace between the rival kings of Samoa: Malietoa and Tamasese. In 1888 he was appointed acting rear-admiral, and placed in command of the South Atlantic station. In 1892 he was ordered as member of the lighthouse board, on which duty he remained until his retirement, May 14, 1893, he having reached the limit of age on the active list.

RICE, Frank Sumner, lawyer and author, was born at Elmira, N. Y., Feb. 3, 1850, oldest son of Remick Chauncy Rice, a direct descendant of the English Puritan, Edmund Rice, who removed from Berkhampstead, England, and settled at Sudbury, Mass., in 1639. The name is well and favorably known throughout New England from the earliest colonial times in connection with many offices of trust and emolument. Mr. Rice was educated at Lafayette College (class of 1870), studied law, and was admitted to the bar at Saratoga Springs in 1877. He married in 1880 Mary, daughter of Rev. Augustus W. Cowles, who for thirty-six years was president of Elmira College. In 1886 he removed to Colorado and became prominently identified with several mining corporations of great importance. He is president of the Gold Bug Consolidated Mining and Milling Co., vice president of the Monte Christo Co., and treasurer of the New Castle Coal and Coke Co. These enterprises are capitalized at $2,350,000 and have greatly stimulated the mineral development of the state. Mr. Rice has won a distinguished position in the legal literature of the country by the publication of the "Annotated Code of Civil Procedure," a work adjusted to the code practice of the western states; and by a recent and more ambitious undertaking in three volumes entitled "Civil and Criminal Evidence." The last is regarded as a classic on the subject.

RAMBAUT, Mary L. Bonney, educator and reformer, was born in Hamilton, N. Y., June 8, 1816, daughter of Benjamin and Lucinda Wilder Bonney. Her father was in the war of 1812, and later a colonel of the 163th regiment of the New York State Militia. Her parents were greatly esteemed for intelligence, integrity, and piety. Their deep interest in the extension of Christian education was a strong influence in moulding the character of their children. Her grandparents, Benjamin Bonney and Abel Wilder, both of Chesterfield, Mass., were in the revolutionary war (1775), the former serving as a member of the legislative assembly at Boston, and the latter as a soldier of the army, standing by the side of Gen. Warren when he fell at the battle of Bunker Hill. The daughter was educated in the public schools of the town and for years in the ladies' department of Hamilton Academy, a school of high rank in the state. Later she entered the Troy Female Seminary, conducted by Emma Willard, from which she was graduated in 1834. She soon commenced her life-work and taught in Jersey City, in New York city, in De Ruyter, N. Y., and in the Troy Female Seminary. In 1842 she went to South Carolina and taught successfully six years at Beaufort and Roberville. In 1850 she planned the establishment of a ladies' seminary in Philadelphia, and invited her friend, Harriette Dillaye, also a graduate and teacher of the Troy Female Seminary, to join her in the enterprise. In September of that year they opened the Chestnut Street Female Seminary, Miss Mary Bonney and Miss Harriette Dillaye, principals. They conducted this school a third of a century, during which time it became one of the leading schools of the state. In 1879 Miss Bonney became thoroughly aroused by the injustice of the policy of our government toward the Indians. She presented the subject to her friend, Mrs. A. S. Quinton, and they entered into a covenant by which Miss Bonney was to furnish the means, and Mrs. Quinton to find the workers and organize a campaign in their behalf. They succeeded in arousing the churches and the press of the land to a sense of the injustice of the government in their treatment of their wards that resulted in the formation of the Woman's National Indian Association, which so influenced legislation as to lead to the new and improved policy of the government as expressed in the "Dawes' Indian Severalty Bill," which opened to the Indians citizenship and all its attendant blessings. Up to 1894 the association had planted directly or indirectly thirty-five missions in the wild destitute tribes; had built homes by loan funds for sixty-eight Indians; given libraries to schools and individuals; given professional education to bright Indians; and done a great amount of other work, chronicled and unchronicled, in their behalf. Miss Bonney was the largest financial contributor during the first four years; became its first president, and was ever a liberal patron of its growing work. In 1883 Miss Bonney and Miss Dillaye, in connection with two of their teachers as associate principals, transferred the Chestnut Street Seminary to Ogontz, near Philadelphia, the elegant country seat owned and formerly occupied by the celebrated financier, Jay Cooke, under the name of Ogontz School for Young Ladies. In 1888 Miss Bonney, having taught fifty years, and served thirty-eight years as senior principal of the Chestnut Street and Ogontz School, resigned her position and retired. The same year, when in London as a delegate to the World's Missionary Convention, she was united in marriage with Dr. Thomas Rambaut, a friend of many years, a delegate to the same convention, and a well-known educator, pastor, and preacher. Since his death in 1890, Mrs. Bonney Rambaut has resided at her brother's home in Hamilton, N. Y., a university town. Of her educational work it has been said that "to an unusual degree she taught her pupils how to think. With clear perceptions, logical processes and conclusions that could be firmly held and vigorously pushed, she not only impressed her own strong nature on her pupils, but equipped them with her methods, to go out into the world as independent thinkers and actors."

CARLETON, Frank Henry, lawyer, was born at Newport, N. H., Oct. 8, 1849, son of Henry G. Carleton, senior editor of the "New Hampshire Argus and Spectator," which position with his associate, Matthew Harvey, he held for forty years. The son was graduated at Kimball Union Academy, at Meriden, N. H., in 1868, and at Dartmouth College in 1872. In 1870 he was principal of an academy in Mississippi. After graduating from college he became one of the editorial staff of the "Manchester (N. H.) Daily Union." In 1873 he became city editor of the "St. Paul (Minn.) Press," and was for some years Minnesota correspondent of the "Chicago Inter-Ocean" and New York "Times." In 1875 he read law in the office of Gov. Cushman Davis at St. Paul, and shortly after became clerk of the municipal court at St. Paul. In 1880 he became secretary to Gov. John Pillsbury and rendered efficient service in connection with the settlement of the repudiated Minnesota railroad bonds. In 1883 he became a member of the law firm of Cross, Hicks & Carleton at Minneapolis, Minn., which partnership relations have only been interrupted by the election of Judge Henry Hicks to the bench, the firm now being Cross, Carleton & Cross. From 1883 to 1887 he was assistant city attorney of Minneapolis. During this time he had the personal management of the very many hotly-contested prosecutions instituted under the patrol limit charter and ordinances. The patrol limit principle was an entirely new method of dealing with the saloon question and had its origin in a recommendation of Mayor George Pillsbury that liquor saloons be permitted only in the "down town" parts of the city where there was a continuous police patrol, and that they be entirely excluded from the residence portions of the city. This new principle was bitterly contested by the liquor interests and many politicians, and every inch of ground in its favor was gained only at the end of legal prosecutions. The principle was a new and astonishing one to the lawyers, and for years Mr. Carleton was confronted in a series of litigations by many of the ablest lawyers, until the principle has become a permanent one in Minneapolis and has been extensively copied in other cities as a practical solution of many of the evils of the saloon question. Mr. Carleton has a large and varied practice before the courts of the state and the U. S. courts, and is a hard worker. He is a great reader in topics outside of his profession and is an occasional lecturer and contributor to periodicals. He is one of the five directors of the Minnesota Home Missionary Society. He was married March 24, 1883, to Ellen, daughter of Judge Edwin Jones of Minneapolis, and has four sons.

HORRY, Peter, brigadier-general in the war of the revolution, is supposed to have been born in South Carolina. Nothing is known of his early life or of his military history. He was a brigadier-general, serving under Gen. Francis Marion, and in combination with Rev. Mason Weems, wrote in 1824 a "Life of Marion," of which a number of editions were published. Gen. Horry, who supplied the facts for this volume, afterwards complained of the sensational treatment which they received at the hands of Weems, and disclaimed all responsibility for the authorship of the book. A manuscript autobiography of the life of Gen. Horry was in existence in 1844, and was referred to by William Gilmore Simms in his "Life of Marion." A good many extraordinary stories regarding Horry appear in the latter work. According to these, Horry seems to have been descended from Huguenot stock. There were two brothers of the names Hugh and Peter. The former was Marion's favorite, although he had the highest esteem for Peter Horry. The latter was very ambitious and, although no rider, was desirous of commanding cavalry, rather than infantry. A good many amusing anecdotes are told of him. One was in connection with the fact that he had an impediment in his speech, which prevented him from ordering his men to fire on an important occasion. At another time, he was riding through a swamp and got caught in an overhanging tree, while his horse slipped from under him, and it was with great difficulty that he could be saved, as he was unable to swim. The most of Horry's fighting, as indeed was the case with that of Marion, appears to have been skirmishing and generally guerilla warfare. In this he was courageous and competent.

MANLEY, Joseph Homan, lawyer, was born in Bangor, Me., Oct. 13, 1842, where his parents were temporarily residing. They returned to Augusta soon after this date, where he was brought up and where his ancestors for six generations had resided. At the age of eleven he was sent to the "Little Blue School" for boys, at Farmington, Me., remaining there four years. Ill-health interrupted his plan of a collegiate education, but when nineteen he began the study of law in Boston, and in 1863 was graduated from the Albany Law School with the degree of LL.B. The same year he returned to Augusta and became the law partner of H. W. True. In 1865 he was admitted to practice in the U. S. and circuit courts, and was appointed commissioner of the U. S. district court of Maine. During this and the following year he was in the Augusta city council acting as president of that body in 1866. From 1869 to 1876 he was in government employ as agent of the Internal Revenue Department and spent the three following years in Washington as agent of the Pennsylvania Railroad in its relations with the treasury department.

In the spring of 1878 he purchased a half interest in the "Maine Farmer," and acted as general editor of that paper until his appointment by President Garfield in 1881 as postmaster of Augusta. This position he held under two administrations, resigning in 1892 to take, at Mr. Harrison's request, a position on the Republican national executive committee, of which he is now (1894) chairman. Mr. Manley was delegate to the Republican national conventions of 1880, '88, and '92, and has served as chairman of the state committee for eleven years. He is a trustee of the Augusta Savings Bank, a director of the First National Bank, and the Edwards Manufacturing Co., is treasurer of the Augusta Water Co., and the Electric Light and Power Co., and is thoroughly identified with the social and commercial life of the city. Mr. Manley married Susan, daughter of ex-Gov. Cony, in 1866, and has four children.

STOBAEUS, John Baptist, manufacturer and inventor, was born at Melliurichstadt, Bavaria, Germany, July 12, 1844, the son of Christopher Stobaeus, who was born at Schwabach, Bavaria, June 20, 1800, and emigrated to the United States in 1852. He settled in New York city and engaged in business as a pharmacist. He died Aug. 22, 1878, and was buried in Evergreen cemetery, near Newark, N. J. The son was educated in the public schools and high school of New York, and in 1859, under the direction of Dr. Baumgarten and Dr. Drechsler, he entered the McDowell Medical College, St. Louis, Mo. He remained

there until the beginning of the civil war in 1861, which broke up the college, and all the students enlisted on one side or the other, the larger part joining the Southern army. Young Stobaeus enthusiastically espoused the Union cause, and although but seventeen years of age, enlisted at the first call for three months' volunteers in the 5th Missouri regiment (U. S. reserve corps). He at once took part under Gens. Wool and Lyon in the struggle which retained the state of Missouri in the Union. His active service began with the battle at Camp Jackson, in which the Confederates under Gen. Price were routed, and he also fought in the battles of Booneville, Lexington, and Berlin, being wounded at the latter. He was afterwards detailed to act as hospital steward on the steamer White Cloud, which patrolled the Missouri river, and was honorably discharged at the expiration of his term of service. He remained on hospital duty for some time afterward, and although anxious to re-enlist for three years, was refused on account of being under age. In January, 1862, he returned to New York, and assisted his father in the drug business. The following year he engaged with Charles Cooper & Co., of New York, manufacturers and dealers in chemicals, and in 1864 they erected a small factory in Hoboken, N. J., of which he was given the superintendence. His medical education and pharmaceutical experience proved of great advantage to him in the business which was destined to be his life-work, and at this time he supplemented it by taking the chemical course at Cooper Institute, New York, where he was graduated. In 1867 he became superintendent of the business of his firm at Newark, N. J., and the following year began the erection of the present extensive works. In 1870 he was admitted to an interest in the firm, and took up his residence in Newark, where he has since lived. In 1889 Mr. Cooper retired, and since that time the business has been conducted by Jacob Kleinhaus and Mr. Stobaeus, the original firm name being still retained. The manufacturing department remains under the direct superintendence of Mr. Stobaeus, and the works rank among the largest in this country, covering four city blocks, and giving employment to about 125 men. They manufacture a general line of chemicals, their specialties being anhydrous ammonia for manufacturing artificial ice, ethers, wood alcohol, gun cotton, nitrate of silver, photographic chemicals, retiuing of photographers' waste, sulphuric and other acids, and liquified carbonic acid gas. The latter was first commercially made here by Mr. Stobaeus, and introduced in connection with

compressors and apparatus invented and patented by him, for use in drawing different beverages and in the art of brewing, which it has almost revolutionized. The firm also owns the only original copies of the Thorwaldsen bas-reliefs which were obtained at great expense from the Thorwaldsen Museum at Copenhagen. From these, photographic copies of great merit are taken and sold throughout this country and Europe. They also control the celebrated Columbia chemical fire engine, patented by Dr. Henry P. Weidig, chemist of the company, which is charged with water, liquified carbonic acid gas, and anhydrous ammonia, which chemicals form carbonate of ammonia, the best extinguisher of fire and perfectly harmless in its action even to the most delicate fabrics. Mr. Stobaeus takes an active interest in public affairs, and acts with the Republican party. He was for several years vice-president of the Newark board of trade, and in 1894 became a member of the board of health of the city. He was married June 18, 1872, to Jenny Seibold, of New York city, who died Apr. 27, 1873. Mr. Stobaeus was again married in the Evangelist Protestant Church, Apr. 2, 1883, to Lucy, daughter of Charles Schmetz, a manufacturing jeweler of Newark, N. J., by whom he has had five children, Frank, William, John Baptist, Jr., Gertrude and Johanna.

STODDART, James Henry, actor, was born at Barnsley, Yorkshire, Eng., on Oct. 13, 1827, the second of five brothers. His father, of the same name, was an actor of ability and note, and was long the leading man of the stock company playing at the Theatre Royal in Glasgow. When a mere lad the son began his career as an actor in boys' parts under the tutelage of his father. His début as an adult was made when he was eighteen years of age, and for eight years thereafter he was a member of a traveling company playing in the provincial cities of England and Scotland, with growing reputation as a conscious, capable, descriptive actor. His merit was such that Copeland, the manager of the leading Liverpool theatre, trusted him to play first old man in the support of the visiting stars. Mr. Stoddart came to America in 1853, on the advice of Morehouse, an American, and for four years played character parts in the famous company of the elder Wallack in New York city. In 1856 he became a member of Laura Keene's Company, playing at the Olympic Theatre, and three years later joined the company of Dion Boucicault at the Winter Garden Theatre. He returned to the Olympic Theatre in 1861, and remained there until 1867, when he joined Lester Wallack's Company, and continued

a member of it until 1874. Following this, he traveled as a star with success for two seasons, and then joined the Union Square Company, and remained with it until its disbandment, when he joined the Madison Square Company, and has ever since (1895) remained under the management of Mr. A. M. Palmer. During a long and arduous professional career, Mr. Stoddart has created many parts. His failures have been few, and his successes many. His Moneypenny in the "Long Strike," Seth Preen in the "Lights o' London," and his Curate in "Saints and Sinners," are recalled by old theatre-goers with especial pleasure and delight. As an actor he is always tender, impressive, and delicate, and finished in his art. It is said of him, "His appreciation of marked individuality is clear and unerring and his ability to realize it is only bounded by the limitation of the stage itself. To realize divergent individualities commands every force the actor possesses. Out of this severe test Mr. Stoddard has won for himself the position of an artist who has never done himself discredit or his other self on the stage injustice, who in a long life of labor can say that he has always done his best, and that that best was always good." He was married many years ago to Miss Conover, formerly a member of Wallack's Company, and has long made his home on a farm owned by him at Rahway, N. J.

DURYEA, Harmanus B., assemblyman, was born at Newtown, Queens co., N. Y., July 12, 1815. The Duryea family in this country sprang from a Huguenot whose name was Joost Durie, who emigrated from Mannheim, in the Rhine Palatinate, in 1675, accompanied by his mother and wife, and settled on Long Island. The family resided at first at what is now New Utrecht, but afterwards in Bushwick and in Brooklyn. Jacob, the second son of Joost, was the first to sign his name Durye. He died in 1758. His son, Joost, in 1709, was a farmer and lived at Jamaica. His brother, Abraham, was a New York merchant, and was active throughout the Revolution. He wrote his name Duryee. Later it was changed to Duryea. The oldest son of Joost, John Duryea, was a flour merchant in New York in the latter part of the last century. He was twice married, his second wife being the daughter of Cornelius Rapelyea ; the second son of John was Cornelius Rapelyea Duryea, who was the father of the subject of this sketch. Harmanus Duryea received a common school education, and in 1825 the family removed to New York city and afterwards to Brooklyn. Harmanus began to study law in the office of Thomas W. Clerke, afterwards a judge of the supreme court of the state. He was admitted to the bar in 1836, and went into partnership with Judge Greenwood and began to practise. In 1842 he was appointed supreme court commissioner for Queens county, and soon after corporation counsel for the city of Brooklyn. In June, 1847, Mr. Duryea was elected district-attorney for Queens county, and re-elected for the following two terms. In 1857 he was elected member of the assembly for Kings county, and in the following year was re-elected, being at that time the only Republican member of the assembly south of Albany. For many years Mr. Duryea was a member of the Brooklyn board of education. In 1831 he was elected a member of the Hamilton Literary Association and was its president for a number of terms. Mr. Duryea's military associations began in 1836, when he became connected with the militia of Kings county, and served as lieutenant, captain, colonel, brigadier-general, and finally major-general of the second division of the national guard of the state of New York. He held this position for many years, resigning it in 1869, when he was the senior major-general of the state. It was through Gen. Duryea's influence that many improved regulations were enacted, and through all his military life he was actively engaged in the improvement of the state soldiery. He served on state boards for the revision of laws and regulations and was for three terms president of the State Military Association. At the outbreak of the civil war in 1861, Brooklyn at once organized the 13th, 14th, and 28th regiments, the 14th volunteering for the war, in which connection Gen. Duryea's talents for organization and his long military service rendered him invaluable.

RYAN, Patrick John, R.C. archbishop of Philadelphia, was born at Cloneyharp, county Tipperary, Ireland, Feb. 20, 1831, son of Jeremiah Ryan. His early education was received at the Christian Brothers' School at Thurles. Having at an early age evinced a strong predilection for the priesthood, he was, at his father's death, entrusted to the care of a kind friend at Dublin, where he commenced his classical studies at the school of Mr. Naughton, of Richmond street, in the parish of Rathmines. Here he showed especial talent for declamation, and in 1844 was selected by a deputation of his fellow-students to deliver an address before the patriot O'Connell, then imprisoned in Richmond Bridewell. Resolving to devote himself to a missionary calling in the United States, Patrick John Ryan entered Carlow College as an affiliated subject of the Most Reverend Peter Richard Kenrick, then presiding over the diocese of St. Louis. His marked proficiency as "first premium man," strict observance of college discipline, and earnest piety soon earned for the young student the successive minor orders, and afterward the higher grade of sub-deaconship. During this time he contributed many articles to the Irish periodicals and newspapers, although the authorship was known but to a few of his intimate friends. For a year or more after his arrival at St. Louis the young deacon directed the study of aspirants to the ministry. He also preached regularly, though not yet a priest, being under age, in the pulpit of the cathedral at St. Louis. In 1853 he was ordained priest. He was afterward rector of the cathedral, and was subsequently appointed pastor of St. John the Evangelist's Church, and in due course of time became vicar-general of the diocese. While in his ministerial capacity he for twenty years allowed few Sundays or chief festivals to pass by without preaching his anticipated sermon. During the civil war he looked after both the bodily and spiritual comfort of the many prisoners in the city of St. Louis. In 1868 Father Ryan accompanied the archbishop of St. Louis to Rome, stopping for a short time in Dublin, where the former preached three sermons. After reaching Rome, where they had audience with Pope Pius IX., Father Ryan preached the English lenten sermons in a church upon the Piazza del Popolo, and also gave two celebrated panegyrics upon St. Patrick

and St. Agnes. On Apr. 14, 1872, Father Ryan was consecrated coadjutor bishop of St. Louis, with the right of succession, his title being Bishop of Tricomia, *in partibus infidelium*. In 1883 he was one of the U. S. prelates commissioned to represent the interests of religion in Rome, where his sermons again attracted large and appreciative audiences, made up of all denominations. On Jan. 11, 1884, he was promoted to be titular archbishop of Salamis, and became archbishop of Philadelphia in the same year, after he preached the dedication sermon in Rome on the occasion of laying the foundation stone of St. Patrick's Church. Father Ryan's success as a pulpit orator was largely due to his well-modulated voice, powers of emphasis, and graceful action, which are more than equaled, however, by his sound good sense and impassioned eloquence. It is difficult to determine whether his dogmatic or moral sermons were more admirable. He was also a zealous and indefatigable worker in the affairs of the parish. His most memorable discourses include one upon the consecration of the Most Reverend Stephen Vincent Ryan as bishop of Buffalo, one shortly after the great fire at Chicago, one at Chicago in memory of Bishop Foley, and one at the dedication of St. Patrick's Cathedral in New York city. Upon two occasions he delivered the annual inaugural address at the State University of Missouri, and to the great admiration of all his hearers, many of whom were non-Catholics, he twice lectured at their invitation before the assembled senators and representatives of the Missouri legislature. He lectured, with gratifying success, in all the principal cities in the United States, many of his discourses afterwards appearing in pamphlet form. The most notable of these was a remarkable treatise on "Modern Skepticism." Several of Archbishop Ryan's lectures and addresses will soon be published by a New York house.

FISHBACK, William Meade, governor of Arkansas, was born at Jeffersonton, Culpepper co., Va., Nov. 5, 1831, third child and second son of Frederick and Sophie (Yates) Fishback. His paternal grandfather, Martin Fishback, a revolutionary soldier, was descended from Frederick Fishback, a planter, who settling in Maryland at an early date, owned the land upon which Frederickstown afterward stood, his wife's father, named Hager, owning the site of Hagerstown. His maternal grandfather was Col. William Yates of Petersburgh, Va., whose wife (born Stith) was directly descended from the author of Stith's "History of Virginia," one of the earliest settlers of that colony and a contemporary of Capt. John Smith. Our subject received his early education at the schools of his native village and vicinity, subsequently entering the University of Virginia. After his graduation in 1855, he studied law in the office of Luther Spellman of Richmond, and was admitted to the bar in 1858. His first venture in law practice was in 1858, while on an extended visit to Illinois. Here he became acquainted with Abraham Lincoln, who, attracted to the young man, entrusted to him some important legal business. In 1858 Mr. Fishback took up a permanent residence at Fort Smith, Ark., where he engaged in the practice of his profession. Meanwhile Lincoln, with offers of other business, urged him to return to Illinois, which, however, he did not do, preferring the Arkansas climate. In 1861 he was elected delegate to the state convention which passed the ordinance of secession. Although so pronounced a Union man that the secession press of Arkansas denounced him as an abolitionist, he was opposed to the policy of coercion, thinking that it would provoke civil war. Upon Pres. Lincoln's call for troops to coerce South Carolina, Mr. Fishback, by advice of his constituents, voted for secession in the hope that when the North saw the withdrawal of all the Southern states, it might be forced into accepting the Crittenden compromise. All efforts at compromise failing, however, when the war broke out he went North, and during the occupation of Little Rock by the Federal troops in 1863, he established a newspaper there called the "Unconditional Union." While editing the paper, he, as commander, was raising the 4th Arkansas cavalry for the Federal service. When about 900 men had enlisted, he was elected to the U. S. senate by the Union legislature, and thus was never mustered into service. Under the proclamation of Pres. Lincoln the reorganization of the state had been at length accomplished, Mr. Fishback having such influence with the convention in charge that he was called upon to write the greater part of the constitution of 1864, sometimes called the "Fishback Constitution." He was advised that if the word "white" as a pre-requisite to voting was not stricken out, the state would not be received into the Union, and he would not get the seat in the senate to

which it was known he would be elected. Believing, however, that it would not be safe to confer the suffrage upon such a large mass of ignorance, he refused to strike it out. His was the first case from the South of an effort to restore representation in congress. Pres. Lincoln's cabinet recognized the senators, but other leaders of the party in power, headed by Sumner and Wade, took the ground that as the state had run down like a watch, and could only be wound up by some extraneous power, that power was congress, and that no Southern states should be wound up unless with negro suffrage. He was therefore not seated. In 1865 he was appointed treasury agent for Arkansas, a position which he refused to accept until told that by so doing he could save the people many millions of money. His conduct of that office added largely to his popularity. In 1874 he was elected to the constitutional convention which framed the present constitution, and in 1877, 1879, and 1885 served in the legislature. He is the author of what is known as the "Fishback Amendment" to the constitution of Arkansas, by which the legislature is forbidden ever to pay certain fraudulent state bonds issued during reconstruction. During the summer of 1892, contrary to the policy of his opponents, he made no canvass for the nomination for governor. His cause was taken up by the people, however, and he received 540 votes out of 628 in the nominating convention, while his plurality at the polls was larger than that received by any other governor since reconstruction times. Immediately after election he accepted the urgent invitation of the national Democratic committee, and coming North, made a number of speeches in New York and Indiana, which met with gratifying success. His administration was marked by continued prosperity. It was at the instigation of Gov. Fishback that the governors of the Southern states met in convention at Richmond, Va., in April, 1893, one of the most important and distinguished assemblies ever held in America, and of which he was made president. In 1857 he was married to Adelaide, daughter of Joseph Miller, a prominent merchant of Fort Smith, Ark., who was robbed and murdered on board a Mississippi river steamboat in 1850. Five children were born to them, three sons and two daughters. Mrs. Fishback died at Fort Smith, Dec. 6, 1881. As a lawyer Gov. Fishback ranks with the best, while as a debater and public speaker he has few equals. No man is better known throughout his state; his history being part of its history.

LITTIG, John M., banker, was born in Baltimore, Md., July 4, 1843. His early education was in the public schools, and afterward in the Baltimore City College, whence he was graduated in 1860. Mr. Littig devoted a few months to teaching, and then secured a position in the Chesapeake Bank of Baltimore. He began his banker's life as a "runner," but his genius for banking business caused him to be rapidly advanced to the position of discount clerk; then book-keeper, then teller. He was soon after elected cashier of the Chesapeake Bank, where he remained until 1879, when the bank ceased its existence, after paying its depositors and stockholders in full. In December, 1879, he was elected cashier of the Marine Bank of Baltimore, which in 1880 was converted into the National Marine of Baltimore. Mr. Littig is a director in the Metropolitan Savings Bank of Baltimore, member of the finance committee, and president of the North Norfolk Land Co. of Norfolk, Va. Mr. Littig has been twice married: first to Sallie Edmondson Sterett, by whom he has two children, Louisa Gettings Littig and Sallie Sterett Littig. His second wife was Mary Clare Ross, who has borne him also two children, Clara Littig and Charles Ross Littig.

GUNNING, Josiah Henry, clergyman, was born at Oak Hill, near Shepton Mallet, Somersetshire, England, March 1, 1840. His father, John Brewer Gunning, was of a family quite eminent in English history, and came to America about 1843, accompanied by his wife, son, and two daughters. The son was sent to the public school in New York city, and subsequently upon the removal of the family to St. Catherine's, Ont., entered the academy there. In 1850 the family having returned to New York, he attended Fergusonville Academy, Delaware county, N. Y., where he was prepared for college. In 1858 he entered as a student of medicine, attending lectures in the medical department of the University of the City of New York, and was graduated an M.D. March 4, 1861. On the breaking-out of the civil war he applied for examination for the medical department of the U. S. navy, and was commissioned assistant surgeon Apr. 1, 1862, and after a brief service on the U. S. receiving ship North Carolina, was detached and ordered as medical officer to the U. S. S. Tahoma. He served on this vessel all through the war under Captains J. C. Howell, Alexander Semmes, and David Harmony. During the scourge of yellow fever which swept through the fleet at Key West, Fla., 1862–63, he succeeded in confining its ravages and finally stamping it out of the ship altogether. The fleet surgeon, Dr. G. R. B. Horner, complimented him personally for this service. While under the command of Capt. Semmes, he was several times in close quarters with the enemy while on boat expeditions up the bay and in the rivers around Tampa, and also at Cedar Keys, Fla. In each of these he was deliberate and cool, never losing control of himself or of his work. In 1864 he was married to Josephine, only daughter of Capt. Anthony Holmes, U. S. navy. In 1866, having spent a year at the Naval Hospital in Brooklyn, N. Y., he resigned from the service and commenced private practice. In 1867 he was appointed lecturer on medicine in the medical department of the University of the City of New York, resigning in 1869 to accept a position in the service of the Department of Charities and Corrections of New York city as physician to the out-door poor. In 1869 his wife died and he entered Union Theological Seminary with a view to entering the ministry. In 1871 he was ordained by a council called by the First Baptist Church of Middletown, N. Y., and served them as their pastor for three years. On his settlement with this church he was married to Tillie Jacacks, a graduate of the Normal College of New York and a teacher in the public schools. In 1874 he accepted a call to the pastorate of the First Baptist Church of Morristown, N. J. After three years of service there, he accepted a call to the First Baptist Church in Titusville, Pa., which he resigned after two years' service and returned to New York city. In 1880 he accepted a call to the First Baptist Church of Nyack, on the Hudson, where he rebuilt the church edifice, drawing the plans and superintending the work, and greatly strengthening the congregation in numbers and financial resources. In 1883, his wife having died, he accepted a call to the Harvard St. Baptist Church of Boston, Mass., in which pastorate he was eminently successful, adding large numbers to the membership. He added a dispensary to the church with a full corps of attendant physicians, established a reading-room for young men and women, and inaugurated a series of class instruction in Biblical and scientific studies. He was prominent in the establishment of the Medical Dispensary of the " North End," accepting the position of manager and superintendent for several years. For over five years he acted as president of the College of Physicians and Surgeons of Boston, and president also of the faculty. Before going to Boston he invented and patented an ingenious instrument known as the Pulsating Pen, for which he received the bronze medal of the American Institute Fair for superiority over other writing devices. In 1891 he accepted the pastorate of the Bedford Avenue Baptist Church of Brooklyn, N. Y., succeeding Rev. Hiram Hutchings, made pastor *emeritus*. His early love for the practice of medicine had, however, by no means deserted him, and on March 1, 1894, he opened an office for the practice of his profession in order that he might relieve his financially straightened people of paying him a salary, and continued to supply the church on Sundays, also attending the week-day prayer meetings. Dr. Gunning was acting president of the Rockland County Historical Society, and the first health officer of the village of Nyack, when it became a corporation. He is a member of Kings County Medical Society, a member of the Grand Army of the Republic, having served as chaplain of the Department of New York, and a Knight of Pythias, having served on the staff of Gen. James Caurnhan, the commander-in-chief, as chaplain of the military rank.

NEWHOUSE, Finley De Ville, missionary, was born in Rochester, Fulton co., Ind., July 27, 1857. His ancestors on both sides were of purely English stock. His father, Rev. John Newhouse, is a minister of the Methodist Episcopal church in the N. W. Indiana Conference, of which he has been a member nearly half a century. The son was educated in De Pauw University, Greencastle, Ind., and was graduated in 1880, taking honors in history. During his college course he achieved unusual success as an orator, as well as a student of the Greek language and literature, to which he gave special attention, reading much more than the regular course required. Receiving the degree of B.A. at graduation, he was given the degree of M.A. in 1883, and of D.D. in 1892. Soon after his graduation Dr. Newhouse was sent by William Taylor to the American College at Concepcion, Chili, S. A., where he filled the Greek chair. In addition to his college duties he did considerable preaching, both in English and Spanish, and while yet in Chili was admitted as a minister to the N. W. Indiana Conference of the Methodist Episcopal church. His health became seriously impaired, and in the fall of 
1884 he returned to the United States, and was almost immediately appointed pastor of the Methodist Episcopal Church in Williamsport, Ind. Here he was united in marriage to Ida Kate Fox. The following fall, at the request of the missionary secretaries of his church, he consented to a transfer to British India, and was made pastor of a large English church in Allahabad, capital of the N. W. provinces. The health of Mrs. Newhouse becoming feeble, they again returned to the United States in 1889, and Mr. Newhouse was stationed at the Fifth Avenue Methodist Episcopal Church in Goshen,

Ind. Still in search of health, they went in 1890 to Huron, S. D., where he was pastor of the First Methodist Episcopal Church for three years. During this pastorate a heavy church debt was lifted, a valuable parsonage property was acquired, and 357 were added to the church membership. In the fall of 1893 Dr. Newhouse received a call from the Franklin Avenue Methodist Episcopal Church, Minneapolis, which he accepted. He is the author of a college romance entitled, "The Three C's," and has published a book of lectures under the title, "Why I am a Protestant." He has also written much for his church papers, and several articles from his pen have been published in the magazines of the country.

OLNEY, Charles Fayette, educator, was born in Hartford, Conn., Aug. 27, 1831; son of Jesse and Elizabeth (Barnes) Olney. His father was a celebrated geographer, author, educator, and lecturer. (See Index). His mother was descended from an unbroken line of Puritan ancestors. His paternal grandfather, Jeremiah, and grand-uncle, Stephen, who led the advance column at Yorktown, were revolutionary officers, while another grand-uncle, Capt. Joseph Olney, was a distinguished commander in the naval service. The father of these patriots, Thomas Olney, was the first American ancestor, and emigrated from Hartfordshire, England, in 1633, settled on a grant of land comprising forty acres in Salem, Mass., and was elected one of the leading officers of the colony. Becoming converted to the peculiar views of Roger Williams, he soon gave up all his Salem privileges, traversed the wilderness with

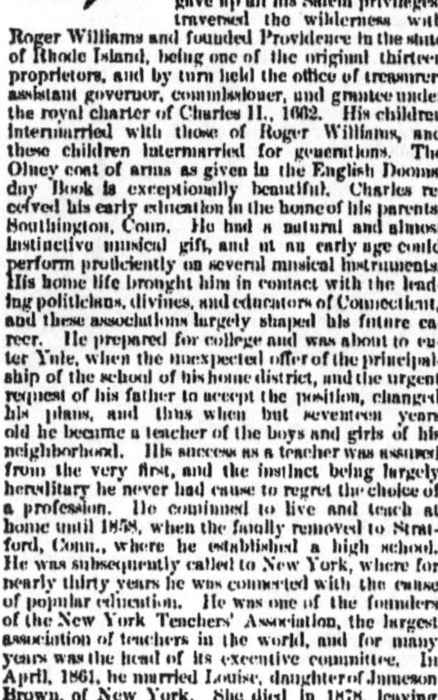

Roger Williams and founded Providence in the state of Rhode Island, being one of the original thirteen proprietors, and by turn held the office of treasurer, assistant governor, commissioner, and grantee under the royal charter of Charles II., 1662. His children intermarried with those of Roger Williams, and these children intermarried for generations. The Olney coat of arms as given in the English Doomsday Book is exceptionally beautiful. Charles received his early education in the home of his parents, Southington, Conn. He had a natural and almost instinctive musical gift, and at an early age could perform proficiently on several musical instruments. His home life brought him in contact with the leading politicians, divines, and educators of Connecticut, and these associations largely shaped his future career. He prepared for college and was about to enter Yale, when the unexpected offer of the principalship of the school of his home district, and the urgent request of his father to accept the position, changed his plans, and thus when but seventeen years old he became a teacher of the boys and girls of his neighborhood. His success as a teacher was assured from the very first, and the instinct being largely hereditary he never had cause to regret the choice of a profession. He continued to live and teach at home until 1858, when the family removed to Stratford, Conn., where he established a high school. He was subsequently called to New York, where for nearly thirty years he was connected with the cause of popular education. He was one of the founders of the New York Teachers' Association, the largest association of teachers in the world, and for many years was the head of its executive committee. In April, 1861, he married Louise, daughter of Jameson Brown, of New York. She died in 1878, leaving

him childless. From this time he took refuge in collecting works of art, antiquity, and curiosity, and being fond of travel, thousands of interesting and beautiful objects were brought from far and near, forming one of the most notable art collections in America, unique in its kind. In 1887 he married Mrs. Abbie Bradley Lamson, of Cleveland, O., a friend of his boyhood, and then took up his residence in that city, where he has added to their beautiful home an elegant Grecian art temple, dedicated in December, 1893, as the Olney Art Gallery. He is a member of the National Geographical Society, the Sons of the American Revolution, and the Cleveland Chamber of Commerce; he is president of the Cleveland Vocal Society, of the Cleveland Sociological Council, of the Society for the Promotion of the Atmospheric Purity of Cleveland, of the Pilgrim Institute, of the Sacred Music Society of the Pilgrim Church, and of the Cleveland Brush and Palette Club. He is also a trustee of the Cleveland School of Art, and of the City Missionary Society, and vice-president of the Cleveland Art Association.

CLARK, Addison, president of the Add Ran Christian University, Thorp Spring, Texas, was born in Titus county, Tex., Dec. 11, 1842, son of J. A. Clark, who came to the state in 1839. Hattie De Spain, whom he married, came from Alabama about the same time. The ancestral lines trace back to the Scotch Dissenters and French Protestants. The son was a student from early childhood. The schools of the country were few, and not of the best, but this lack was made up at home. Both parents were liberally educated, so with music, choice books, and pictures of the mother's painting, the boy passed beyond the primary grade, and became a companion for his parents. He had few boy companions. When he left home for school he took his place at once with young men. Much of his time between the age of twelve to eighteen was spent either with private teachers or in schools that promised collegiate instruction. The thorough, competent teacher, whether in a cabin or under the shade of a tree, was to him a college. The civil war interrupted his studies. He entered the Confederate army among the first, and took his place among men, and soon became a commander of men. At the close of the war he was fortunate in securing a competent instructor in Elder Charles Carlton, a graduate of Bethany College, Virginia,

and a teacher of many years' experience, with whom he remained as student and teacher two years. He had chosen teaching and preaching as a life-work. His degree of LL.D. was conferred without his seeking it. In 1873 he and his brother, Randolph Clark, founded an institution of learning at the little village of Thorp Spring, in Hood county, Tex., and christened it Add-Ran College, the term "Add-Ran" being a compound of the war names of the two brothers. He, being the elder brother, was made president, and resolved to make the institution a college in more than name only, and it is due to his wonderful executive ability, his capacity to work in every department, a will to meet all obstacles, a constitution to endure all things, and, above all, a faith that will not allow failure, that this college has become the Christian university of Texas. The institution continued under the brothers' management until 1889, when they turned it over to the Church of the Disciples, and a board of trustees was elected, who re-chartered it, under the name of Add-

Ran Christian University. This institution has done much for the cause of higher education in Texas, and her graduates are filling positions of honor and trust all over the state. It has ever been her policy to secure the most thorough and competent teachers available in the several departments. Ex-Senator J. J. Jarvis is president of the board of trustees, and he is one of the best financiers in the state. Under his wise management, the institution has been placed upon a firm financial basis. The president, with a faculty devoted to the work, is gaining a reputation as among the most faithful educators in the Southwest. In the session of 1892–93 there were 445 matriculates. A post-graduate department has been added, which is under the supervision of Chancellor James Lowber, and graduates of institutions in different parts of the United States and Canada, and even in England, are matriculating in this department. The university grants no honorary degrees whatever. The Bible is made a text-book in this institution. The university is located at the village of Thorp Spring, a pleasant health resort, three miles from Granbury, the county seat of Hood county. The university building is a substantial stone structure, and can well accommodate 600 students. The authorities of the institution believe in the co-education of the sexes, and have provided a commodious building, called "The Girls' Home," where the young ladies attending the university are properly cared for by an experienced matron. The boys are also well provided for, and Thorp Spring may be strictly called a university town.

LOWBER, James William, educator, chancellor of Add-Ran Christian University, was born in Nelson county, Ky., 1847. His early years were spent on a farm, but from boyhood he was ambitious of intellectual and moral improvement. In addition to the ordinary books of the country school, others on art, science, philosophy, and religion were sought after, and their contents devoured with avidity; so that, notwithstanding his inheritance of poverty, his large, active brain, sustained by an excellent physical constitution, enabled him to overcome every obstacle to his ambition, and placed him in circumstances to enter systematically on a course of education. Much of the expense at college had to be met by manual labor, but none the less his progress was rapid, so that, when only in the junior class, he was selected by the president of the college to teach a class in Greek, the Greek professor having recommended him as the most thorough student in that language in the university. Indeed, he has made it a point to excel in every department of study he takes up. For months before his graduation he stood at the front in every study. In linguistic acquirements he has made much progress, having studied some seventeen different languages. Five universities have conferred certificates of graduation, and he has been honored with the degrees of A.B., A.M., Sc.D., Ph.D., and LL.D.; no one of which was honorary, but all the result of strict examinations. After completing his college studies, he spent twelve years in the class-room as teacher; while devoting himself mainly to the ministry he has had several calls to the presidency of colleges, and is frequently called on to deliver the annual address at institutions of learning. Dr. Lowber is also an ardent temperance advocate, and interested in the temperance movements of the day, and his addresses have been highly complimented. His reputation is

such that he has been invited from England to enter the lecture field, and devote his time to the cause of temperance in that country. He was one of the first in America to advocate the science of Christian sociology, and started a few years ago a social reform movement, which has attracted a good deal of attention. "The Struggles and Triumphs of Truth," "The Devil in Modern Society," and "The Who and the What of the Disciples of Christ" are works from the pen of Dr. Lowber that have had wide circulation. His contributions to the religious and scientific journals are always of a high order of excellence, and greatly valued. His most recent work is entitled "Culture," which is designed to show the relations of all departments of learning to the principles of the Christian religion. It is a book of 544 pages, and it is seldom that so extensive a field of investigation is covered in as brief a space. The versatility of the author is most apparent. He has laid under contribution the works of the masters of science, philosophy, religion, literature, and art, ancient and modern, to set forth in contrast the transcendent claims of Jesus of Nazareth as the model and teacher *par excellence* for the regeneration and elevation of human society in all its departments. This book will doubtless be extensively circulated. In 1892 he was elected chancellor of the Add-Ran Christian University. In 1882 he was married to Maggie De Baun of Kentucky, who has been a great support to him in all his literary, social, and religious work.

FIELD, Marshall, merchant and financier, was born in Conway, Mass., Aug. 1835. He is of Puritan descent, his earliest American ancestors having settled in New England about 1650. But the name Richard de Field is mentioned in Normandy, France, which was settled by the Normans in 912, hence, the name is of Norman extraction, as it does

not occur in the early records of the ancient Britons or the Saxons. (See work entitled "Norman People," published in London, 1874.) His father was a farmer, and he received the thorough industrial training of a New England country boy, and with it a common school and academic education. Having manifested a preference for commercial pursuits, at the age of seventeen he went to Pittsfield, in his native state, as a clerk in one of the dry-goods establishments of that city. In this capacity he mastered the details of trade, and in 1856, soon after attaining his majority, removed to Chicago. Entering the employ of Cooley, Wadsworth & Co., one of the pioneer mercantile houses of the young western city, he displayed a genius for business, and rendered such valuable service to his employers, that in 1860, he was admitted to a partnership in the firm which became known as Cooley, Farwell & Co., and later as Farwell, Field & Co. This partnership being subsequently dissolved, the firm of Field, Palmer & Leiter was formed in 1865. Two years later Mr. Palmer retired, and the business, which had by this time assumed vast proportions, was conducted until 1881 under the firm name of Field, Leiter & Co. At that date Mr. Field purchased Mr. Leiter's interest, and has since continued the business as Marshall Field & Co. Prior to the Chicago fire in 1871, the sales of the great establishment of which Mr. Field was the head, amounted to $12,000,000 a year. Since that time the sales have steadily increased until they reach (1895) the enormous aggregate of $35,000,000 a year. The Chicago fire destroyed for

Mr. Field and his associates property valued at $3,500,000, their business at that time being all carried on in a single large building; this building has been replaced by a larger one, which has since been exclusively devoted to the retail trade. The wholesale business of the firm is now carried on in a massive granite edifice, covering an entire block, and one of the most notable buildings of its kind in the world. Besides the two mammoth establishments in Chicago, Mr. Field has branch houses in England, France, and Germany. His investments outside of real estate, railways, stocks, and bonds, are large, in addition to his mercantile interests. While he has avoided anything that might appear ostentatious, he has been liberal in the bestowal of charities, exercising always a careful discretion in selecting the objects of his beneficence. One of his most considerable donations has been the gift of a tract of land, valued at $200,000, to the University of Chicago, and he assists in practically all the commendable movements of a public character inaugurated in the city, requiring expenditures of money. After the World's Columbian Exposition was closed, the people of Chicago began a movement for the permanent preservation of many of the exhibits in a suitable building. This was made possible by Mr. Field's gift of $1,000,000, conditional on the raising of $500,000 by others. This was done, and on June 2, 1894, the Field Columbian Museum was formally opened, with becoming ceremonies, which were simple in accordance with Mr. Field's manner of evincing himself more by actual deeds than by imposing display. This museum will ever remain an enduring monument of his generous endowment, as its contents embrace the elements of ethnological science as well as natural history.

LODGE, James Llewellyn, clergyman, was born in Montgomery county, Md., June 12, 1840, son of Llewellyn and Martha Lodge. He was educated chiefly at Columbian College, Washington, D. C., and was licensed to preach by the Rockville (Md.) Baptist Church in the fall of 1859. In October, 1864, he was ordained. His first pastorate was at Sater's, Baltimore co., Md. He was next called to an important pastorate in Pittsburgh, Pa., and from Pittsburgh, he went to Shelbyville, Ky., and from there to Modest Town, Va. In all these fields he labored with success, especially in Modest Town, where his great success attracted the favorable attention of his brethren throughout the state. In November, 1874, he became pastor of Summit Avenue Baptist Church of Jersey city, N. J. Here he stayed five years. His work here won for him great distinction in the North. While he was pastor the church was greatly increased in numbers and a large debt was paid off. From Jersey

City he went to Newark, where he stayed but a few months, being compelled in 1880 by ill health to leave the North and seek recovery in Maryland. In 1882, having somewhat recovered, he accepted a charge in Washington, D. C., where he labored for three years, when in 1885 his health failed utterly and he retired to his country seat in Montgomery co., Md. He continued to supply local churches and did a large amount of itinerant missionary work. Dr. Lodge has contributed extensively for the leading journals of the Baptist denomination, for reviews, and on literary topics for the secular press, and is known all over the United States as a writer of great

force, clearness, and polish. He is particularly distinguished for his pulpit eloquence, which is of a high order, logical, philosophic, and yet aflame with enthusiasm. Wake Forest College, North Carolina, conferred upon him in 1878 the degree of D. D. In 1864 he was married to Alice Virginia Warfield. They have had eight children. The eldest son, Dr. Lee Davis Lodge, is a graduate of, and professor in, the Columbian University, Washington, D. C.

SMART, James Henry, president of Purdue University, Lafayette, Ind., was born at Center Harbor, N. H., June 30, 1841, son of William Hutchings Smart (physician) and Nancy Farrington Smart. He received most of his early education at the Concord High School and by the instruction of private tutors, and was given the honorary degree of A. M. by Dartmouth in 1870 and the degree of LL. D. by Indiana University in 1883. From 1859 to 1863

he taught in the New Hampshire schools; from 1863 to 1865 he was principal of the intermediate schools at Toledo, O., and from 1865 to 1875 was superintendent of the city schools at Fort Wayne, Ind. He was superintendent of public instruction in the state of Indiana for six years, and in 1883 became president of Purdue University. He has also served as trustee of Indiana University and of the State Normal School, and for twenty-seven years was a member of the Indiana state board of education. In 1872 he was appointed as assistant commissioner for Indiana to the Vienna Exposition; in 1870 was one of the U. S. commissioners to the Paris Exposition; in 1881 was president of the National Teachers' Association, and in 1890 of the American Association of Agricultural Colleges and Experiment Stations; while in 1891 he was appointed U. S. representative commissioner to the International Agricultural Congress at the Hague. President Smart has published "An Ideal School System for a State," "The Institute Systems of the United States," "Commentary on the School Laws of Indiana," "The Schools of Indiana," twelve sets of school reports for the state of Indiana; and many other papers. He was married July 21, 1870, to Mary Swan, of Albany, N. Y.

SMITH, Samuel G., clergyman, was born in Birmingham, England, March 7, 1852, son of the Rev. Wm. Smith, a prominent minister in the Methodist church, removed to America in 1858 and settled in Iowa. The son was graduated from Cornell College, Iowa, in the classical course in 1872, and subsequently received the degree of Ph. D. from Syracuse University, on examination in 1882. He entered the Upper Iowa Conference in the fall of 1872. Soon after he was elected principal of Albion Seminary. After three years he resigned to enter the pastorate. His charges have been: Osage, Ia., for two years; Decorah, two years. In 1879 he removed to St. Paul to become pastor of the First Methodist Church. In 1882 he was appointed presiding elder of the St. Paul district. In 1883 he was elected a delegate to the general conference. Failing health compelled him to retire from the St. Paul district in the fall of 1884, and he spent most of the following year in Europe. In 1885 he was re-appointed to First Church, St. Paul, by unanimous request of that church. On Jan. 1, 1885, he resigned that pulpit and withdrew from the M. E. Church at the request of friends in St. Paul, and became pastor of the Peoples' Church of St. Paul, hold-

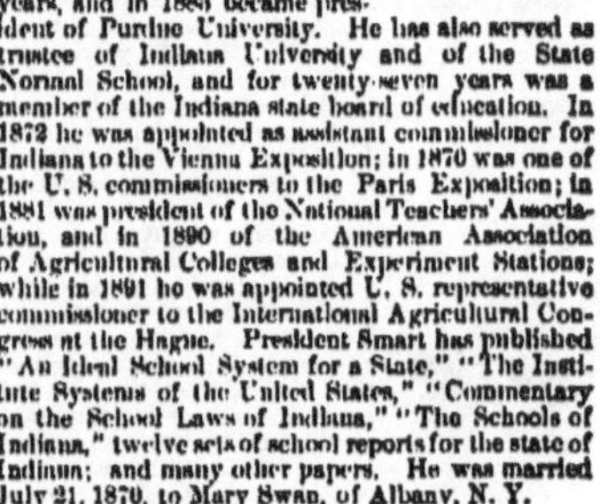

ing services in the Opera House until a large and most complete edifice was erected. Dr. Smith has been closely identified with the social and political life of Minnesota for fifteen years. He has served for three years on the school board, resigning on account of the pressure of other duties. For the past six years he has been a member of the state board of corrections and charities, having been appointed by three successive governers. During the past three years he has been lecturer on sociology in the University of Minnesota. He has also for many years lectured at Chautauqua assemblies and on other lyceum platforms. During several tours in Europe he has studied the life and art of the leading nations, including a tour devoted to penal and charitable institutions, in which he visited sixty of the leading prisons and asylums by appointment of Gov. Nelson as official visitor from Minnesota. He is a man of genial disposition, sympathetic heart, and practical turn of mind. His theology is one which can be applied to the problems of every-day life. As a preacher he has but few equals, having the advantage of a thorough education coupled with unusual natural ability. He is exhaustless in his pulpit resources. His church, which is among the largest in America, is always a centre of educational influence, Christian culture, and spiritual power.

WALKER, William Henry, banker, was born at Utica, N. Y., Aug. 20, 1826, son of Stephen Walker, a master mechanic and builder. The father removed to Buffalo when the son was a mere lad, and there he and a brother entered into business as architects and builders, many of the fine residences and business houses in the city being erected by the firm. The son was educated in the private schools of Buffalo and at the Buffalo Academy. His first business education was acquired as a clerk in the store of Orrin P. Ramsdell, a dealer in boots and shoes. After several years' clerkship he was admitted as partner, and the business of Orrin P. Ramsdell & Co. was soon thereafter entirely wholesale. In 1876 the firm was dissolved, and Mr. Walker established himself in the same line, and soon took position as one of the largest dealers in western New York. His cousin, Edward C. Walker, William A. Joyce, and Stephen Walker, are now (1894) partners in the firm of Wm. H. Walker & Co., which occupies one of the finest fire-proof buildings in Buffalo. In 1884 Mr. Walker was elected president of the Merchants' Bank of Buffalo, and under his management the bank has paid regular dividends on its capital of $300,000, and earned besides, a surplus of over $200,000. Mr. Walker is vice-president of the Buffalo General Hospital, trustee of the real estate of the Y. M. C. A., trustee of Hobart College, Geneva, N. Y., trustee of the Crocker Fertilizer and Chemical Co., and holds various other positions of honor and responsibility. In 1892 he was nominated as a presidential elector for New York on the Republican ticket, and received the second largest vote given to any elector on the ticket.

EDWARDS, George Clark, manufacturer, was born at Watertown, Conn., June 29, 1846. He was a descendant of John Edwards, a prominent member of the liberal party, who left England about the year 1600 and settled at Chestnut Hill, near Bridgeport, Conn., and was a descendant of Roderick the Great of Wales. After a thorough education in the public schools and at Watertown Academy, he entered the drug and chemical business at Waterbury, Conn., at the age of eighteen, and in January, 1871, engaged in the same business on his own account in Philadelphia. In 1874, on account of impaired health, he was obliged to relinquish business, and most of the time during the next two years was spent in travel. He returned to Waterbury, and in 1876 began the manufacture of wood alcohol. This business had been originally started at Black Rock, Conn., and abandoned as impracticable. After a careful study of the original process, Mr. Edwards, bringing to his aid his knowledge of chemistry, immediately put into execution plans for its manufacture on a large scale, though against the advice of many learned men who frankly told him that he was wasting his time and money in the venture. For that purpose the Burcey Chemical Co. was formed and began business at Waterbury, which was soon after removed to Binghamton, N. Y., where better facilities were offered. Special apparatus was brought from France to carry out the work, and the business was a success from the start.

In the carbonizing of wood what had been previously thrown away as useless was made a useful and valuable adjunct in the manufactures and arts. Mr. Edwards, the pioneer in this line of manufacture, was manager, secretary, and treasurer of the company, which became one of the large industries of the country. In 1880 Mr. Edwards accepted the position of secretary and treasurer of the Holmes & Griggs Mfg. Co., manufacturers of brass and German silver, at New York. Being of a progressive disposition, Mr. Edwards searched for auxiliaries for the business, and assisted by Col. C. E. L. Holmes, his brother-in-law, the president of the former company, he purchased a controlling interest in the Rogers & Brittin Silver Co., of Bridgeport, Conn., and the name was changed to the Holmes & Edwards Silver Co., who acted as consumers of metals manufactured by the former company. Soon afterwards Col. Holmes died, and Mr. Edwards, seeing a brilliant future in the manufacture of silver-plated flat wares, sold out his interests and resigned his position in the Holmes & Griggs Mfg. Co., and removing with his family to Bridgeport, gave his whole attention to, and assumed personal charge of, the business of the Holmes & Edwards Silver Co., and became its president, treasurer, and controlling spirit. Under his management the business had a steady growth which necessitated frequent additions to its facilities until it ranked as the largest of its kind in the United States, if not in the world. This company is the sole manufacturer of the sterling silver inlaid spoons and forks that have attained such a wide celebrity and have taken the highest awards at all the exhibitions. The government report of the World's Columbian Exposition says: "The Holmes & Edwards Silver Co. are entitled from a practical standpoint to the credit of having made the most marked progress in the development of the art of increasing the durability of silver-plated spoons and forks that has been made since the first introduction of silver-plated ware." In 1887 he organized the Bridgeport Chain Co., for the manufacture of the "Triumph" weldless wire chain. He is also incorporator of the Miller Wire Spring Co., and is president and treasurer of both these corporations. In 1893 he exhibited at the University College of Liverpool the machine for making the weldless chain and it so attracted the leading manufacturers of England that a company known as the Weldless Chain Co. was organized, and purchased the foreign patents to manufacture the chain. Mr. Edwards is a director of the City National Bank, trustee of the Bridgeport Savings Bank and a director in the Y. M. C. A. He never held public office, but has always been active in promoting the public welfare as a private citizen. He married in 1872 Ardelia daughter of Israel Holmes (q. v.), who was founder of the brass and German-silver manufacture in this country.

WOODS, William Stone, banker and financier, was born in Columbia, Mo., Nov. 1, 1840, of Kentucky ancestry, his father having removed to Missouri during the early history of that state. When the boy

was five years old his father died leaving a wife and five children with almost no means of support. Without other education than that which the district school afforded, William was at once compelled to go to work, and for several years he toiled at farm and other manual labor, his earnings going to the support of the family. As he grew older he alternately taught and attended school, until 1861. Through his own efforts he paid the expense of a good education and was graduated from the Missouri State University. His first ambition was to be a physician, and in March, 1864, he was graduated as a doctor of medicine from Jefferson Medical College, Philadelphia. After a few years' successful practice, however, he gave up the profession for an active business life, for which he was especially fitted by nature. In 1868 he engaged in the wholesale grocery trade with towns west of Omaha, pending the construction of the Union Pacific Railroad. This was a successful venture, and enabled him to make his first venture in banking, which was destined to be his principal occupation in life. In 1869 he started a bank in Rocheport, in his native county, with $7,000 capital. This he conducted successfully as cashier until 1881, building up the capital by reinvestment of profits to $50,000. He then removed to Kansas city, Mo., and among other things organized the firm of Grimes, Woods, LaForce & Co., wholesale dry-goods dealers. He also bought an interest in the Kansas City Savings Association, and became its president and manager. In 1892 he merged this institution into the bank of commerce with a capital of $200,000, and as the president managed the affairs successfully until 1887, when he reorganized it as the National Bank of Commerce with a capital of $2,000,000, becoming its president likewise, which position he has continued to hold. A conservative banker, with no liking for speculation, and deeply interested in his occupation, Dr. Woods has now bravely and worthily won a high reputation in Kansas City. He has educated to the banking business a large number of young men, relatives and nephews, who are now occupied in the West in institutions of this class, in most of which Dr. Woods is interested. His keen perception of opportunities for favorable investment has led him to take an interest in many other enterprises beside that of banking. At one time he invested largely in cattle and was joint owner of large ranches in South Dakota, and during the early years of Kansas City, long before the "boom," he invested largely in real estate, being to-day the owner of much valuable business property, which is covered with buildings and rented to good advantage. With others, in 1890, he organized the Kansas City, Pittsburgh, and Gulf Railway Co., of which he was made vice-president. Dr. Woods has been wonderfully successful in all his operations. He is a man of very decided character, and is noted for his keen foresight as well as his liberality to the needy, which latter quality was splendidly shown in his donation, in 1890, of $50,000 to the Orphans' School at Fulton, Mo. In 1886, Dr. Woods was married to Binn, daughter of E. W. McBride, of Paris, Mo., a successful business man, judge, farmer, and trader in central Missouri. One daughter has been born to them.

CORBETT, Henry Winslow, senator and capitalist, was born in Westborough, Mass., Feb. 18, 1827, the youngest son of Elijah and Melinda (Forbush) Corbett. His father was a pioneer manufacturer of edged tools and a man of skill and inventive genius. His first American ancestor came to New England early in the seventeenth century. In England the family trace their genealogy to Roger Corbett, a military chieftain who won honor and distinction under William I. in the conquest of the country. His early boyhood was spent in Washington county, N. Y., where he attended the district school. He was then admitted a pupil in Cambridge Academy, where he pursued the regular academic course and was graduated. He then took position as a clerk in Salem, the county seat. In 1844 he removed to New York city, where he engaged in the dry-goods business. After the discovery of gold in California, he was entrusted with a stock of goods which he shipped around the Horn to Portland, Ore., conditioned on his following the cargo and remaining in Oregon three years to effect their sale and the establishment of a business on the coast, he then to return and divide the profits. He left New York, Jan. 20, 1851, by way of Panama, and reached Portland, Ore., March 5th. Within fourteen months Mr. Corbett had disposed of his entire stock and returned to New York with $20,000 net profits for division. The next year he returned to Portland to make that city his home. He became interested in the establishment of various transportation lines in Oregon and California, and was an earnest advocate of the project to build the Northern Pacific Railroad. He helped to organize and was an early president of the Portland board of trade, and was prominently connected with the board of immigration. He helped to found the Children's Home and the Boys' and Girls' Aid Society, and has been the most earnest advocate of a place for the disposition of first offenders to the care of a society rather than in the associa-

tion of hardened criminals in state prisons and jails. He took an active part in the organization of the Republican and Union parties in the state, was a delegate from Oregon to the Chicago convention of 1860 which nominated Lincoln for president. Not being able to reach Chicago in time, Horace Greeley represented him by proxy. In 1866 he was elected to the U. S. senate for the term commencing in 1867, and served throughout the term, having a place on the committee on commerce, Indian affairs, and District of Columbia. He was an earnest advocate of specie payment and funding the national debt. His first business, established in Portland in 1851, has since been continued and developed into the largest hardware business in the city, and is conducted under the firm name of Corbett, Failing & Co. Mr.

Corbett is the owner of some of the first business blocks in the city, and his business principle has been to keep his capital in active business for the benefit not only of himself but of the community at large. His rule as to charity has been inflexible, and one-tenth of each year's earnings have been devoted to meeting the charitable demands of the next. He was the first merchant in Portland to close the doors of his store on Sunday, and while it was a startling innovation in those pioneer days it was at no less of custom. Mr. Corbett was married in February, 1853, to Caroline Jagger of Albany, N. Y. Their son, Henry Corbett, after graduation, took a place in his father's bank as clerk, won his way to the place of cashier, and gave promise of being an able successor, but died in 1895, at the age of thirty-eight, leaving three sons. In 1867, just prior to taking his seat in the senate, Mr. Corbett married for his second wife Emma Ruggles, of Worcester, Mass., who soon acquired a prominent position in Washington society.

FEININGER, Charles William Frederick, composer, was born at Durlach, Germany, July 31, 1844. He was brought to the United States by his parents when in his ninth year, and emigrated to South Carolina. Later, he was sent to Leipzig Conservatory, Germany, to complete his musical education. On his return home, during the civil war, he served a short time in the Federal army, and after the conclusion of peace, taught music and conducted orchestral performances. In 1874 Mr. Feininger went to Brazil, and spent several years visiting other portions of South America. He has written symphonies and overtures for orchestra, an operetta, choruses, and songs. Some of his orchestral compositions have been performed in Germany.

WINSTON, George Tayloe, president of the University of North Carolina, was born at Windsor, Bertie co., N. C., Oct. 12, 1852, the son of Patrick H. Winston, a leading lawyer and planter, and Martha Elizabeth Byrd Winston, of Scotch-Irish ancestry, and a relative of Col. William Byrd, governor of Virginia, and the author of the "Westover Manuscripts." The Winstons came originally from England and settled in Virginia, but subsequently emigrated to many other states. Accounts of the family are given in all the lives of Patrick Henry, the great Virginia orator, whose mother was a Winston. The subject of this sketch entered the University of North Carolina in 1866, being the youngest student in the college. In 1868 the university closed, and young Winston receiving an appointment as midshipman in the U. S. navy from President Andrew Jackson, entered the Naval Academy at Annapolis in 1869. He resigned his commission in 1870; being at the time the first scholar in his class, and in 1871 entered Cornell University at Ithaca, N. Y., where he was graduated in 1874 with much honor, having previously received the highest prize for Latin scholarship. After his graduation he was appointed instructor in mathematics. On the reorganization of the University of North Carolina in 1875, Mr. Winston was elected assistant professor of literature, taking charge of the departments of Latin and German. At the end of a year he was promoted to a full professorship. In 1884 he spent some time in Europe in the study of Roman customs and antiquities, and in 1885 he became professor of Latin, that department in the university having been enlarged.

The scholarship of Prof. Winston has been noted by all the institutions of North Carolina. Davidson College conferred upon him the degree of A.M.; Trinity College that of Ll. D., and the teachers of the state have twice elected him president of their assembly. In 1891 he was unanimously elected president of the University of North Carolina. Under his presidency the attendance steadily increased from 198 in 1891 to 380 in 1894.

NETTLETON, Alured Bayard, soldier and journalist, was born at Berlin, Delaware co., O., Nov. 14, 1838, son of Hiram Nettleton, an intelligent farmer. He was descended from John Nettleton, who emigrated from Kenilworth, England, in 1662, and who was one of the founders of the plantation or settlement of Killingworth, Middlesex co., Conn., in 1663. On the side of his mother, Lavina Janes (or Jaynes), the direct line included Lieut. Elijah Janes, who served in the revolutionary army from 1777 to 1782, having enlisted at the age of seventeen, and was severely wounded in one of the engagements which preceded the surrender of Burgoyne. Prior to his fifteenth year young Nettleton, during the usual intervals of regular work on the farm, attended the neighboring district and select

schools. At sixteen, after a course of training in a business academy, he entered upon some years of commercial experience as clerk and book-keeper for a leading lumber manufacturing firm in Michigan. During this period, as opportunity offered, he prosecuted his studies privately. In 1859 he entered the class of 1863 in Oberlin College. There he remained partly supporting himself by teaching winters, until his junior year, when in April, 1861, at the first outbreak of the war of the rebellion, he enlisted in the Federal army with a number of fellow-students. The first quota of troops from Ohio being already full, the acceptance of his company was deferred, but in July following he again enlisted, this time as a private in the 2d Ohio cavalry. Chosen first lieutenant by his company he went to the field in the autumn of 1861, and served at the front from that time until June 15, 1865, following the surrender of the Confederate armies. With his regiment he served in fourteen states and one territory, campaigning from the Indian territory to the Virginia coast. He shared in seventy-two battles and minor engagements, including Grant's campaign of the Wilderness, the siege of Richmond, and Sheridan's battles of the Shenandoah, having four horses shot in action. He was successively promoted in the field to the rank of captain, major, lieutenant-colonel, and colonel of his regiment, and for gallant service rendered in Sheridan's Shenandoah campaign in 1864, he was at the age of twenty-five brevetted brigadier-general by the president. He served successively under Schofield, Burnside, Sheridan, Meade, and Grant, and in the cavalry division of Major-Gen. Custer. From the last-named officer he received especial commendation for courage and efficiency. Upon leaving the army Gen. Nettleton studied law and then entered upon the work of journalism, to which he subsequently devoted many years of his life. He was first editor and part owner of the "Daily Register" of Sandusky, O.; was at one time managing editor of the "Philadelphia Inquirer;" and later was several years editor and proprietor of the "Daily Tribune" of Minneapolis, established by him. He received successively the degrees of A.B. and A.M. from Oberlin College, of which he was for twenty years a trustee. From 1870 to 1875, as a co-adjutor of Jay Cooke, he was prominently identified with the projection and construction of the Northern Pacific Railroad, and from 1875 to 1880 was interested in mining and manufacturing. In 1880 he became a citizen of Minnesota, from which state in 1890 he was appointed by Pres. Harrison, assistant secretary of the treasury. Upon the death of Secretary Windom in 1891, Gen. Nettleton became acting secretary of the treasury, in which capacity he served for a considerable period. He was appointed by the president in 1890 a member of the board of management of the government department of the World's Columbian Exposition of 1893. Always an ardent Republican, he in 1868 was a delegate to the national Republican convention which placed Gen. Grant in nomination for the first time. Since his residence in Minnesota he has been active in placing on the statute books of that state a body of laws for restricting and suppressing the liquor traffic, which are not anywhere excelled for efficiency. Gen. Nettleton was married on Jan. 8, 1863, to Melissa, daughter of Emeline (Harris) and Dr. Laman Tenney, the latter formerly of Vermont. He is a member of the Congregational church.

ALTMAN, Henry, merchant, was born in Rochester, N. Y., Aug. 12, 1854, son of Jacob Altman, a successful business man. In his early childhood he removed with his parents to Buffalo, N. Y., where his elementary education was obtained in the public schools. He prepared for college at the Buffalo Academy, from which he was graduated in the summer of 1869. In the following autumn he entered Cornell University at Ithaca, N. Y., then just established. While there he held prominent positions in his class and in various societies. He was a member of the "Alpha Delta Phi" fraternity, one of the organizers of the Cornell navy, and bought the first shell purchased for a Cornell crew. He was graduated from the university in 1873, taking the degree of bachelor of science. His class was the second graduated after a four years' course. Mr. Altman has always taken an active interest in the affairs of the university since his graduation and was president of the Alumni Association one term and vice president two terms. He has presided over the class of '73 at all its reunions, and has attended 23 commencements of his alma mater. As a member of the "Alpha Delta Phi" fraternity he presided over the first convention held with the chapter at Cornell. After leaving college Mr. Altman entered business in Buffalo and early won success. As one of her most public-spirited citizens he is given prominence in citizens' movements and in commercial and social enterprises. The revision of the charter of the city of Buffalo in 1890 led to the creation of a

board of school examiners in connection with the department of education, which proved a long step in taking the schools out of politics and making them more efficient. Mr. Altman was the only Republican selected by Mayor Bishop, Democrat, as a member of this board, and for several years he gave a great deal of his time to the interests of the schools of Buffalo. Mr. Altman has taken a lead in all movements of a public character in Buffalo. He is a member of the Buffalo Republican League and has served as its president. He was influential in the organization of the University Club of Buffalo, is a trustee of the Buffalo Library Association, a noble of the Mystic Shrine, a 32° Mason, and a member of the Buffalo, the Saturn, and the Falconwood Clubs, and of various societies. On July 4, 1888, while in London, Mr. Altman was married to Mrs. Sadie Rayner, of Baltimore, Md.

PENDLETON, George, business man, was born in Camden, Me., Feb. 22, 1800, the youngest son of John Pendleton, a captain in the war of 1812, and a descendant of Maj. Brian Pendleton, who came with his family to Watertown, Mass., in 1632 from the town of Pendleton, England. When twelve years of age he was a gunner's boy to his father, who, in command of the land forces, stationed cannon upon the top of Camden mountain to repel the British fleet as they entered the Penobscot river. He received a common-school education, and taught school for some time. When a young man, he was secretary to Com. Warrington, upon the frigate Constellation, and while in this service he took part in the reception to Gen. Lafayette, upon his visit to

this country in 1825. While his father was still living, he purchased the prospective interests of his brothers and sisters in his father's property, and engaged in general mercantile, milling, and other business. In the financial reverses that followed the panic of 1837, he made a settlement with his creditors, upon the basis of fifty cents on the dollar, but when, afterward, he had retrieved his fortune, he voluntarily settled in full all of these canceled obligations. In 1849 he was placed by President Fillmore in charge of the custom house at San Francisco. At the close of Fillmore's administration, he purchased a country home in the village of Gorham, Me., being attracted by its educational advantages for his family of eight children. He was a strong advocate of temperance. In politics he was a Whig, joining the Republican party at the beginning of its history. He was pronounced in his views against slavery, and long before the proposition was suggested by Lincoln, he publicly favored the solution of the slave question by the purchase of all slaves by the government. As a delegate to the Harrisburg convention, at the nomination of Gen. Harrison, he proposed a resolution, that the term of the president be extended to a period of six years, and that he be ineligible to re-election. The resolution was defeated, but, from that time, the proposition has continued to gain in favor. He was a man of conspicuous integrity of character, of broad views, with cultivated and cordial manners. In 1831 he married Susan Johnson of Canterbury, Conn., a descendant of the early Johnson family of Massachusetts, and on her maternal side, of the historic Huntington family of Connecticut. Mr. Pendleton died in Detroit, Mich., Aug. 27, 1875.

COLLINS, Lewis, jurist, was born in Fayette county, Ky., Dec. 25, 1797, son of Richard Collins, a soldier in the revolutionary war. At an early age he was apprenticed to the printing trade, and in 1820 became proprietor and editor of the Maysville "Eagle." This he conducted in conjunction with the book business, with much tact, ability, and energy for twenty-seven years. From 1851–54 he was first presiding judge of the Mason county court. On Apr. 1, 1823, he was married to Mary, daughter of Maj. Valentine Peers, an officer of the Virginia army. He died in Lexington, Ky., Jan. 29, 1870.

STEPHENS, Lon V., financier, was born in Boonville, Mo., Dec. 21, 1858, son of Joseph Lafayette and Martha (Gibson) Stephens. His father was a lawyer with a large practice, a capitalist, a banker, and a man of affairs, prominent in church, civic, and state activities. The son studied first in the public schools of Boonville, and then for three years at the Cooper Institute, three years at the Kemper family school of the same town, and for one year at Washington and Lee University, Virginia. From the latter he was graduated as a lawyer. While yet a boy, young Stephens had learned the printer's trade. In later life he entered upon editorial life in the conduct of the Boonville "Advertiser." He was thus well grounded in a practical newspaper education. Nervous, quick, and of unusual pertinacity, he applied himself to the pursuit of numerous avocations; found time to receive instructions as a banker in the Boonville Bank, presided over by his father, took a course in telegraphy and became an expert operator, and was eventually given charge of the Western Union Telegraph Co.'s main office in Boonville. Thus he became a student, a printer, an editor, a bank assistant, and a telegraph operator, and, after his law course, a lawyer. As a student he was always ahead of boys of the same age, especially in mathematics. In 1878 he made his first European tour; visited all the capitals and made quite a stay in Paris, studying the features of that year's exposition. Returning to Boonville he became bookkeeper of the Central National Bank, which position he filled for two years, when he was made assistant cashier and director. He remained in Boonville until 1897, having taken charge of the bank, became owner and editor of the Boonville "Advertiser," an interested holder of railroad properties, and a steward in the M. E. Church, South. In that year the Fifth National Bank of St. Louis failed. Thousands of depositors were panic-stricken by the announcement. For a time it seemed as if everything was lost. The government had taken possession of the bank, and little information could be had as to the extent of the losses to depositors. There was a demand for a man of the best financial ability to take charge of the affairs of the defunct enterprise, and the appointment to the receivership by the U. S. comptroller of the currency was watched with painful interest by those involved. Mr. Stephens's name had been suggested by the leading bankers and financiers of Missouri as that of a fit and competent man. His appointment followed soon afterward, and he promptly qualified for his duties. As soon as he assumed the management of affairs he began to show his remarkable training and ability. He so performed his duties that he succeeded in obtaining for the depositors every dollar that was due them, and in this point made the best record in the history of the treasury department. When, therefore, a year later the treasurer of the state defaulted, and a man of recognized ability, honesty, and financial acumen was required to fill the position declared vacant by the governor, Lon V. Stephens was instantly appointed, and from every side resounded praise for Gov. Francis's selection. Mr. Stephens's administration of the affairs of the treasury of the state was, as every one predicted, brilliant, and it was not a surprise when he was nominated by his party three years later, for that office, nor wondered at when the official account of the state election revealed the fact that he had received the greatest number of votes that up to that time had been cast for any man in the state of Missouri. For some time Mr. Stephens was an aide-de-camp on the staff of Gov. John Marmaduke, and was paymaster-general on the staff of Gov. D. R. Francis. He has taken an active interest in every public enterprise in Boonville and central Missouri. Charities and public welfare find in him a liberal contributor. He donated a large sum at one time to establish "Stephens' Scientific Hall," in connection with the Central College of Fayette, Mo. Mr. Stephens is a Mason in high standing and a Knight Templar. In politics he is a Democrat, and one of his speeches, entitled, "Why I am a Democrat," made during a political canvass, was extensively copied by the press of the country. Altogether Mr. Stephens is a fine type of the American citizen, representing the nation in what might be called its inter development. He was married in October, 1880, to Margaret, daughter of J. M. Nelson, one of the wealthiest citizens of central Missouri, and a sister of T. C. Nelson, president of the St. Louis National Bank. She is widely known for her beauty and accomplishments.

McMURRAY, Patrick Early, manufacturer, was born in county Leitram, Ireland, March 4, 1841, son of a farmer. His mother, Margaret Early, was a direct descendant on the maternal side of Brefy O'Rourke, one of the early kings of Connaught. The son came to the United States in 1857 and located in New Haven, Conn., where he learned the trade of carriage-making. At the outbreak of the civil war he enlisted in the 9th Connecticut regiment, serving for three years, when he was honorably mustered out of the service at Hartford, Conn. He resumed his business as carriage-maker, and in 1867 emigrated to California, remaining on the Pacific coast for seven years. He then removed to Jacksonville, Fla., where with his brother, John McMurray, he established the business of manufacturing wagons and carriages, under the firm name of McMurray & Co. It took the lead of the whole South in the business, and outranks every establishment of the kind south of Atlanta, Ga. In 1877 McMurray was elected city marshall of Jacksonville. From 1880 to 1882 he served as alderman. In 1888 he was elected state senator for two years. While in the state legislature he secured the passage of a mechanics' lien law, and the charter which enabled the city of Jacksonville to extend its corporate limits. During the yellow fever epidemic of 1888 in Jacksonville, he remained in the stricken city, and served as one of the members of the sanitary and auxiliary association, in whose charge the affairs of the city were placed during the prevalence of the epidemic. His active and beneficent labors at the time greatly endeared him

to the people of Jacksonville. He was appointed postmaster in 1889 by Pres. Harrison, and so conducted the affairs of the office as to secure the approbation of the entire community, and differences in political faith were forgotten in the business-like manner in which the mail service was administered under his direction. The terrible conflagration of 1891 destroyed the post-office building, yet Postmaster McMurray had the mails of the next day privately assorted and delivered, to the astonishment and admiration of the citizens, not yet recovered from the panic into which the great fire had thrown them.

He is a member of the Jacksonville board of trade, of the O. M. Mitchell Post, G. A. R., of the Benevolent Protective Order of Elks, and of the Catholic church. His business occupies an entire city block on which is erected a fine brick factory and salesrooms. He was married in November, 1875, to Kate Scanlan, a native of Branford, Conn.

KROEGER, Ernest Richard, was born in St. Louis, Mo., Aug. 10, 1862. His father, one of the most eminent literary men in the West, superintended his early musical education, after which he had as instructors several celebrated musicians, notably W. Goldner of Paris in composition, and Charles Kunkel in pianoforte playing. Up to his twenty-third

year Mr. Kroeger was employed in mercantile business, but in the meantime he prosecuted his musical studies with great energy and enthusiasm, finally entering upon a musical career on Nov. 1, 1885. As a pianist he has been heard frequently in concerts, and in conjunction with Mr. Charles Kunkel has made a great specialty of duo playing upon two pianofortes. He was for eight years organist of Trinity Episcopal Church, and has been for the same length of time organist of the Church of the Messiah (Unitarian), both of St. Louis. In the latter church Mr. Kroeger has conducted a fine chorus choir for five years, which has rendered works by such composers as Beethoven, Bach, Handel, Mendelssohn, Mozart, Gounod, Spohr, Dvorak, Haydn, Schubert, Weber, and others. As a conductor, in addition to the chorus above mentioned, he has had charge of the musical features of the McCullough Club, has been director of the "Amphion" Male chorus, and is at the present time leading the Morning Choral Club, composed of fifty ladies. But it is as a composer that Mr. Kroeger has achieved his greatest reputation. His works, published and unpublished, are in nearly all branches of music. They include many pianoforte pieces, songs, church music, and other smaller compositions. In larger fields, Mr. Kroeger has written a great deal of chamber music, notably his "Quintet for Pianoforte and Strings," given with great success at the Music Teachers' National Association at Detroit in 1890, also a "Symphony for Orchestra," "Four Symphonic Overtures," and a "Pianoforte Concerto." One eminent musical critic says: "His work is based upon the modern romantic style, such as Raff, Scharwenka, and Moszkowski have been developing. The compositions by Mr. Kroeger prove him to be a thorough artist, that his knowledge of counterpoint is profound, and that he does not need to wander about for the effects he wishes to produce. His compositions are full of sparkling originality and are artistically developed. Mr. Kroeger, in his many beautiful works, shows that he is able to use the modern school and even some of the Wagnerian effects without forgetting that a composer's individuality must be kept uppermost in all his writings. He is an American writer who not only possesses contrapuntal skill, but a decided gift for melody." He has been twice elected on the committee of Examiners of American Compositions in the Music Teachers' National Association, and his reputation as a composer, performer, and teacher is continually growing.

BREWSTER, Lyman Dennison, jurist, was born in Salisbury, Conn., July 31, 1832, the son of Daniel Brewster, and his ancestry is easily traced to its first representative, who landed from the Mayflower at Plymouth Rock in 1620. His early education was in the common schools, and he was prepared for college at the Williams' Academy at Stockbridge. He was graduated from Yale College in 1855, and in 1857 visited England and the continent of Europe, and returning the following year, began the study of law with Roger Averill, of Danbury, Conn. He was admitted to the bar on June 21, 1858, and practised his profession from 1859 to 1879, being in partnership with Mr. Averill, his old preceptor. He was judge of probate in 1858, judge of court of common pleas from 1870 to 1874, member of the state legislature in 1870, 1878, and 1879, and a prominent member of the state senate in 1880 and 1881, being chairman of the judiciary committee. In 1878 he was appointed by Gov. Hubbard a member of the committee to simplify legal procedure in the state. He is a member of the American Bar Association, and in the spring of 1893 was appointed one of the commissioners on uniform state laws. He has been counsel in many important cases, among others the Tilden will contest, as counsel for the heirs. He was married Jan. 1, 1868, to Sarah Amelia, daughter of Gen. W. Ives, of Danbury, Conn., in which city he still (1894) continues the practice of his profession. He has been chairman of the supply committee of the Danbury Public Library since its organization in 1870.

BENTON, Herbert E., lawyer and politician, was born in the town of Morris, Conn., July 31, 1849. His American lineage dates back to early colonial times, his ancestors having participated in both colonial and revolutionary wars. He obtained an ordinary school education and then entered Gen. Russell's Military School at New Haven, where he prepared for college. Entering the class of 1872 in Yale, he was graduated from the law school of that university in 1875. It was during his college course that, as one of the editors of the "Yale Courant," he

began the career in journalism in which he afterward achieved marked success. His first practical newspaper experience was as an assistant editor of the "New Haven Daily Press," of which Prof. Cyrus Northrop was at the time proprietor and editor-in-chief. Leaving the "Press" in 1875 he became night editor of the "New Haven Daily Palladium," in which capacity he served until his appointment as editor-in-chief of that paper in 1880. He was conspicuous in journalism for the immense amount of work that he performed with apparent ease, and for his great foresight and judgment in affairs. As a vigorous political writer he never became offensively or unfairly partisan. A serious affection of the eyes compelled him to abandon the editorial chair in 1885, and he accepted an appointment to the clerkship of the court of common pleas for New Haven county, in which position he remained until January, 1893, when he resigned and devoted himself to the practice of law, which profession he is still following. Mr. Benton began his political career early in life. Like most other young men fresh from college, he was inflated with a desire to reform parties and existing affairs, and therefore went on the stump in 1872 for Horace Greeley. It was his only heresy as a Republican, however, and he declares himself thankful that the attack occurred at an early age. He has since been an uncompromising advocate of the principles of the Republican party. From 1880 to 1892 he was continuously a member of the New Haven city government, serving two years as councilman, four years as alderman, and six years as police commissioner. He was the nominee of the Republican party for state representative in 1887, and in 1888 was tendered the nomination as state senator. He attested his personal popularity by running far ahead of his ticket, although failing of an election. He was especially active in the presidential campaign of 1888, and had at his command any office in the gift of the victorious party, but declined federal appointment. He was elected chairman of the Republican state central committee in 1890, and re-elected to the same position in 1892 and 1894. For two terms Mr. Benton has served as president of the Republican League of New Haven, one of the leading political organizations of Connecticut.

ANDERSON, Richard Clough, statesman, was born in Louisville, Ky., Aug. 4, 1788. His father, of the same name, was a gallant soldier and pioneer, while his mother was Elizabeth Clark Anderson, the sister of Gen. George Rogers Clark, the Northwestern explorer. Young Anderson received his early education in the frontier schools, and was then sent to William and Mary College, Va., where he was graduated in 1804. He afterward studied law in the office of Judge Tucker, and on being admitted to the bar began practice in Louisville. He soon stood in the front rank of his profession as an able advocate and counsellor. His natural tastes and the suggestions of his friends took him into the field of politics. He was elected a member of the Kentucky legislature, in which body he continued to hold a seat for a number of years. In 1817, he was elected to a seat in the Federal congress, where he continued four years. At this time exciting debates were taking place on the important question of the admission of Missouri as a state, and in these Mr. Anderson took a prominent part. In 1822, he declined a re-election, but accepted his return to the legislature of his own state. He was chosen speaker of the assembly, but in 1823 resigned on being appointed by President Monroe the first U. S. minister to the new republic of Colombia, South America. During his residence at Bogota, he gained a high reputation among the citizens, and in 1824 was able to negotiate an important treaty. The following year, having lost his wife by death, he visited Kentucky for a time to arrange for the education of his children; but returned to his post in the autumn of the same year and remained there until the spring of 1826. President Adams then appointed him a member of the diplomatic congress, held at Panama, to consider the welfare of the South American republics. On his way to fulfil this duty, Mr. Anderson was taken ill at the village of Tubaco, where he died on Jan. 24, 1826. He was succeeded in his office as minister to Colombia by Gen. William Henry Harrison, afterwards the ninth president of the United States.

CHAFFEE, James Franklin, Methodist Episcopal clergyman, was born in Middlebury, Wyoming co., N. Y., Nov. 5, 1827. His parents, Chaffees on both sides, belonged to New England stock, having been among the colonists emigrating from old England prior to 1650. When our subject was seventeen years old, the family removed to Illinois, so that the whole period of his minority was passed on the frontiers of civilization, where he built up a hardy frame upon a constitution inherited from temperate and laborious ancestors. His educational opportunities were such only as the common schools afforded, supplemented by hard study and a wide range of reading. He was received into the ministry of the Methodist Episcopal church in 1848. For the next nine years he shared the life of the itinerant ministry. His first charge was to the Carthage circuit, which included the city of Nauvoo. Successive appointments were at Oquawka, Monmouth, and Knoxville, Lewiston and Jefferson streets, Chicago. During the first years of his ministry he married Calista Hopkins, who has endured with him the toils and responsibilities, and shared with him the felicities of a Methodist preacher's itinerant life. He took up his residence in what is now the city of Minneapolis in the fall of 1857, and was stationed at St. Anthony. Here he conducted for eight weeks without ministerial help, a series of meetings which yielded 100 accessions to the church. In the spring of 1859 Mr. Chaffee was appointed to the Jackson Street Church, St. Paul, but returned to Minneapolis in the fall of 1860 to the then only Methodist church in the city. At the outbreak of the civil war he was appointed chaplain of the 5th regiment of Minnesota Infantry. Severe sickness compelled him to resign his post from before Corinth, after a service of only six weeks. In the fall of 1862 he was appointed presiding elder of the Minneapolis district, which then included the whole northwestern frontier of the state. For two years he traveled throughout this extensive field, strengthening the feeble churches and gathering others, upon the annual salary of $550. Two years later the Minneapolis and St. Paul districts were consolidated, and Elder Chaffee was made presiding elder of the new district, continuing for three years. Elder Chaffee was appointed to the pastorate of the Centenary Church, Minneapolis, in 1867, continuing its pastor for three years. In 1870 he was appointed to the Minneapolis city mission, and devoted himself to the organizing of the Seventh Street Methodist Episcopal Church, procuring the building of a convenient church edifice, which afterwards became the Thirteenth Avenue Methodist Episcopal Church. For the next few years Elder Chaffee filled a pastorate at Duluth, another at Faribault,

another at St. Paul, and was presiding elder of the Winona district. In 1879 he was appointed, by special request, to the pastorate of the Hennepin Avenue Methodist Episcopal Church, and continued in it for three years. During the next four years he was presiding elder of the Minneapolis district. Among the churches he helped to organize were the Twenty-fourth Street Methodist Episcopal Church, Simpson Church, Bloomington Avenue, Forest Heights, Western Avenue, Taylor Street, and Lake Street Methodist Episcopal Churches. Since 1887 Dr. Chaffee has been presiding elder of the Winona district until one year ago, when he was appointed to the Minneapolis district to commence his third term. In 1867, 1879, 1880, and 1891, he was elected delegate to the general conference and each time as leader of the delegation. The general conference of 1892 elected him a member of the general missionary committee, the term of which will not expire until the meeting of the general conference in 1896. His most important general service has been in connection with the educational work of the church. At the conference held at Mankato in 1871 he was elected agent of Hamlin University. For the last five years Dr. Chaffee has been president of its board of trustees. He assisted in the organization of Asbury Hospital, which, largely through the liberality of Mrs Sarah Knight, the daughter of his old friend, T. A. Harrison, has been equipped and opened as a public hospital, under the management of the Methodist churches. Dr. Chaffee is president and financial agent of the institution. He has been a prolific writer. Besides conducting the editorial work of the "Methodist Herald" for several years, he has been a frequent contributor to the local and periodical press. Not alone does the discussion of theological and church subjects engage his pen, but speculative and scientific ones as well. Especially is he strong in meeting the cavilers at religion on scientific grounds. In theology he is liberal within the limits permitted to a loyal believer in the doctrines of his church. Of a family of nine children born to Dr. and Mrs. Chaffee, but two survive. Their daughter, Carrie, is the wife of H. M. Farnham, Esq., and his son, Hugh, is connected with the Security Bank. While the Methodist church has claimed and received the chief labor of Dr. Chaffee's long and active career, he has been an active participator in all the stirring events which have given to Minneapolis during his residence in it a marvelous growth and expansion, especially in those of education, morals, and charity. An effective and persuasive preacher of righteousness, he has been a loyal, enthusiastic, and helpful citizen.

MACDONALD, John Louis, lawyer and congressman, was born in Glasgow, Scotland, Feb. 22, 1838, son of John and Margery McKinley Macdonald. His father was a prominent physician, in comfortable circumstances, and emigrated to Nova Scotia when the son was quite young, and in 1847 they removed to Pittsburg, Pa., where he obtained an academic education. In the spring of 1855 the family removed to St. Paul, Minn., locating, in the fall of that year, in Belle Plaine, Scott co. Here he studied law, and in the spring of 1859 was admitted to the bar. At the first state election, after his admission, he was elected judge of the probate court of Scott county, and held that office for two years. He then held successively the offices of county superintendent of schools and prosecuting attorney of the county. In 1860–61 he edited the "Belle Plaine Enquirer," and in the fall of 1861 removed to Shakopee, where he established the "Shakopee Argus," and edited it until 1862. During the civil war he was commissioned to enlist and muster in volunteers for the Federal army. In 1869–70 Mr. Macdonald was a member of the house of representatives of Minnesota, and from 1871 to 1876 he was a member of the state senate. In both branches he served on judiciary and other important committees. He introduced and secured the passage of the constitutional amendment which requires that any law amending or affecting the provision that the railroads of the state shall pay a percentage upon their gross earnings in lieu of taxation, shall be referred to the people and adopted by a majority of their votes before taking effect, thereby introducing the principle of the "referendum" in the making of state laws. In 1872 he was the candidate of the Democratic party for the office of attorney-general of the state, but was defeated with his party ticket. In 1875 he was elected mayor of Shakopee. In 1876 he was elected judge of the eighth judicial district for a term of seven years, and in 1883 he was re-elected without opposition, and served until 1886, when he resigned to return to the practice of law. He was in the same year elected a representative in the fiftieth congress from the third district of Minnesota, notwithstanding the district had been previously Republican by 3,000 majority. He served on the committee on public lands, merchant marine, and fisheries. His speeches on the tariff question, land grants, and forfeitures were fearless and to the point. Mr. Macdonald was a friend of the old soldiers, and in congress was active in securing just pension bills. He was renominated by his party in 1888, but failing of election, at the expiration of his term he removed to St. Paul, where he has since been engaged in the practice of his profession. Mr. Macdonald, being an ardent advocate of the free coinage of silver, joined the Peoples' party in 1892. He was married June 22, 1861, to Mary, daughter of P. Hennessy, of Belle Plaine.

BIGELOW, Horace Ransom, lawyer, was born in Watervliet, N. Y., March 13, 1820, son of Erastus and Statira Ransom Bigelow. His grandfather, Otis Bigelow, was a revolutionary soldier and patriot of the Connecticut branch of the family. Erastus Bigelow removed, with his family, about 1822 to Troy, N. Y., and shortly afterwards to Oneida county. Our subject attended school at Saugerfield and Utica. His father being a farmer of limited means, he worked upon the farm and taught school during the winter season. He then studied law in Utica with Charles A. Mann and John H. Edmonds. On being admitted to the bar, he formed a partnership with Edward S. Brayton, which lasted until 1853, when he removed to the West. He was for a time clerk of the recorder's

court, and also of the supreme court held in Utica. In company with Judge Flandrau, he removed to St. Paul, Minn., in 1858, where they opened a law office as Bigelow & Flandrau. Mr. Bigelow taught in the Jackson school for a time, but finally gained a practice that proved profitable. In 1860 he entered into partnership with John B. Brisbin as Brisbin & Bigelow, afterwards with Greenleaf Clark, as Bigelow & Clark. In 1870 the firm became Bigelow, Flandrau & Clark; then Bigelow, Flandrau & Squires. In 1886 Mr. Bigelow retired from the firm and devoted his time to his growing private business. He was attorney for the first division of the St. Paul and Pacific Railway Co., and its successor, the St. Paul, Minneapolis and Manitoba, until absorbed by the Great Northern Railway Co. He was likewise attorney for the Chicago, Milwaukee, and St. Paul Railway Co. until he withdrew from practice. He was for a number of years president of the Ramsey County Bar Association. He was one of the commissioners in the construction of the county court house of St. Paul; and was for many years a director of the First National Bank. Mr. Bigelow was married in June, 1862, to Cornelia Sherrill of New Hartford, Oneida co. He died at his home in St. Paul, Nov. 14, 1894.

KNOX, Henry Martyn, banker, was born in Knoxboro', Oneida co., N. Y., July 10, 1830, son of John and Sarah (Curtis) Knox. His father was a prominent citizen, having been a bank president, college trustee, and merchant. His first American ancestor came from Strabane, County Tyrone, Ireland, of Scottish lineage. The son was educated at the public school and the academy of his native village, and was there prepared for college, entering Hamilton College in 1847 and graduating with his class in 1851. He was a classmate of Charles Dudley Warner of Hartford, and Penoyer Sherman of Chicago, and among his college contemporaries were Dr. Thomas Hastings, of New York; Elliot Anthony, of

Chicago; Breese Stevens, of Madison; and Rev. Dr. Wilbur Paddock, of Philadelphia. His three brothers were prominent public men, William being a noted Presbyterian divine, John Jay, U. S. comptroller of currency, and Charles, president of the German Theological School, Newark, N. J. (See Index.) Upon leaving college he took the position of teller in his father's bank at Vernon, N. Y., and served there for two years. In 1853 he removed to New York city and became a clerk in the Merchants' Bank, Wall street. In 1856 he resigned and removed to St. Paul, Minn., and with his brother, John Jay Knox (see vol. III., 15) established a private banking business there. The business was discontinued just after the breaking out of the civil war, 1861, and he was appointed by the government national bank examiner for Minnesota and northern Wisconsin. He was afterwards chosen cashier of the First National Bank of St. Paul, where he remained until 1876, when he resigned and made the tour of Europe. In 1878 Mr. Knox was appointed by Gov. Pillsbury the first public examiner for the state of Minnesota, under a law creating the office. He was re-appointed by Govs. Pillsbury, Hubbard, and McGill, serving in all ten years. To the duties of this office were added that of superintendent of banks, both of which positions, with their novel, complex, and difficult requirements, Mr. Knox acceptably filled. In 1888 he resigned to accept the position of vice-president of the Security Bank of Minnesota, in Minneapolis, one of the largest financial institutions of the Northwest, which position he now (1895) occupies. Mr. Knox has always been a consistent Republican in national politics, and an active promoter of educational and religious institutions. He was one of the founders and active promoters of the public library and of the Young Men's Christian Association of St. Paul, and for many years was a trustee of Macalester College. He is a ruling elder of the House of Hope Presbyterian Church of St. Paul, having been chosen in 1857, and is the oldest in term of service of its board of elders. He was a delegate to the first Pan-Presbyterian council held in Edinburgh, Scotland, 1877. At that time he visited Paris, Munich, and Copenhagen in the interests of the U. S. treasury department. He also attended the third Presbyterian council held in Belfast, Ireland, in 1884. He was a member of the joint committee of co-operation between the Northern and Southern Presbyterian churches raised by the general assemblies of the two bodies, and meeting in Baltimore and Atlanta in 1888-89. He was also a member of the general assembly's committee on its relations with the theological seminaries, meeting in 1893-94, at Saratoga, Chicago, Pittsburg and Cincinnati, and was a supporter of the minority report. Mr. Knox was married in 1857 to Charlotte, daughter of Rev. Dr. Samuel W. Cozzens of Milton, Mass. Two of their children survive, a daughter and a son. The son, Henry Cozzens Knox, is cashier of the Paterson National Bank, Paterson, N. J.

WEEKS, Thomas Edwin, dental surgeon, was born at Massillon, O., May 5, 1853. He received his early education in the public and high schools of Mansfield, O. In 1873 he commenced the study of dentistry in the office of Dr. W. F. Semple in Mt. Vernon, O., where he remained for three years, then removing to Council Bluffs. In June, 1880, he again removed to Minneapolis, Minn. In 1881 he became a member of the firm of Bowman, Weeks & Jenison. Dr. Weeks retired from this firm in 1891 and opened an independent office. He was a charter member of the Minneapolis Dental Society and of the Minnesota Dental Association, to which he has been a frequent contributor of valuable papers and clinics. Dr. Weeks has been elected to honorary membership in various dental societies outside of the city and state. He has always been in sympathy with all movements tending to elevate dentistry, and has given them a liberal share of time and energy. He was appointed demonstrator of operative dentistry in the dental department of Minnesota College Hospital, in the first year of its establishment, and held the position for two years. In 1885 he was appointed lecturer on practical dentistry. In 1886 the Minnesota Hospital College conferred on him the honorary degree of Doctor of Dental Surgery and appointed him to fill the chair of operative dentistry. This position he retained till the college surrendered its charter, becoming a department of the University of Minnesota, when he was reappointed by the board of regents. In 1892 dental anatomy and operative technics were added to this chair. Dr. Weeks has contributed frequently to the programmes of dental societies and is the author of the first text-book of dental technics ever published: "Weeks' Manual of Operative Technics." He is much interested in dental education, was instrumental in organizing the National School of Dental Technics, and is at present vice-president of that body, also chairman of its board of control. He is also one of the associate editors of the "Dental Review."

McKINLEY, William, clergyman, was born in Glasgow, Scotland, March 24, 1834, son of George and Margaret McDonald McKinley. His paternal grandfather, John McKinley, lived in the north of Ireland, but moved to Scotland during the political troubles of 1798. His maternal grandfather, Angus McDonald, was a Scotch Highlander and British soldier in the wars of the French revolution. In 1841 young McKinley emigrated with his parents to the United States, settling in Baltimore county, Md., and in 1849 he accompanied an uncle to Illinois, where he spent the next six years in teaching and attending school and in private studies. He was chiefly educated at private schools in Maryland, and at Rock River Seminary, Mount Morris, Ill., supplemented with a brief period at Beloit College, Wisconsin; left the latter institution on account of ill health, and in 1855 came to Minnesota. He was licensed to preach in the same year, and in 1856 was admitted on trial in the Minnesota annual conference of the Methodist Episcopal church; received into full membership in 1858, and ordained elder in 1859. During the last named year he was married to Amy Sumner, who died in 1871. He was again married in 1876 to Alice Hayward. Mr. McKinley served successively as pastor

in the following charges: Northfield, Minn.; Trempealeau, Wis.; Hokah, Minn., one year each; Taylor's Falls, four years. He was for one year chaplain in the army. Other pastorates held by him were at First Church, Minneapolis, two years; First Church, Winona, three terms, nine years; Jackson Street, St. Paul, three years; First Church, Duluth, two years; Knoxville, Tenn., one year; Church of Christian Endeavor, Brooklyn, N. Y., one year; Red Wing, three years; Hamline and St. Paul, five years. He was presiding elder of Winona district, two years, and of St. Paul district three years, which office he now holds. He was elected delegate to the general conference of the Methodist Episcopal church in 1876, 1880, and 1892. The degree of D.D. was conferred on him by Hamline University in 1884.

EUSTIS, William Henry, mayor of Minneapolis, was born at Oxbow, Jefferson co., N. Y., July 17, 1845, son of Tobias Eustis, wheelwright. He was educated at the district schools of Hammond, N. Y., and at Wesleyan University. He was graduated at Columbia Law School in the year 1874, and began the practice of law with Judge Putnam at Saratoga Springs in 1875. In the year 1881 he removed to Minneapolis, Minn., where he soon identified himself with the interests of that growing city, and in November, 1890, was elected to the mayoralty, where his faithful and efficient service has given satisfaction to all parties. Mr. Eustis is unmarried. He is a member of the Methodist Episcopal church.

PROTHEROE, Daniel, musical conductor and composer, was born at Ystradgynlais, Swansea Valley, South Wales, Nov. 24, 1866. He received a general education at the Swansea Normal College, and his musical education under the direction of that famous instructor and composer, Dr. Joseph Parry. Early in life Mr. Protheroe showed a wonderful aptitude for music, winning prizes in local Eisteddfodau when but five years of age. From the national Eisteddfod of 1880–81 he carried away the laurels as a contralto singer, receiving golden encomiums from the critics, who predicted for him a brilliant future. When but eighteen years of age he was chosen to lead the Ystradgynlais Choral Society, and with that organization succeeded in vanquishing at the Llandeilo Eisteddfod some of the ablest conductors of the land. The result of the contest gave him a national reputation in Wales. In 1886 he came to America and settled at Scranton, Pa., where shortly

after his arrival he was appointed conductor of the Scranton Cymmrodorion, and under his management the society so greatly improved and advanced, that in 1887 a choir embracing Scranton's best musical talent was formed to compete at the Pittsburg Eisteddfod, where they were awarded the prize for the second competitive chorus, and the following year took the first prize of $1,000 at the Wilkes Barre Eisteddfod, at which Carl Zerrahn and his colleagues pronounced the choir the finest of its kind in the United States. The choir has since then given concerts in connection with the famous Gilmore and Cappa bands. The high excellence attained by this organization is mainly due to the ability of its brilliant young leader. At present Mr. Protheroe devotes his time entirely to teaching as an occupation congenial to his taste and for which he is exceptionally well qualified. His instruction is principally confined to the piano, voice culture, harmony, and composition. He is musical director of the Elm Park Methodist Episcopal Church and Holy Rosary Church choirs; is an associate of the Society of Science, Letters, and Art; received a senior honors certificate from Trinity College, London, Eng., and the degree of Mus. Bac. from the University of Trinity College, Toronto, Canada. He has been successful in winning altogether about 100 Eisteddfod prizes. Among his popular compositions may be mentioned the cantata, "The Lord is my Shepherd," for solo and chorus; "Mass in F," for solo and chorus; "The Crusader," "Thermopylae," "The Dew Drop;" Glees entitled, "The Rivulet," "Myfanwy," "Evening Song," etc., and the songs: "The Sweet-Voiced Bell," "Ave Maria," "The Hero," "Doubting," etc.; also a number of piano compositions. Prof. Protheroe married on Apr. 26, 1892, Hannah Harris, of Scranton.

CLARK, Enoch W., banker, was born in East Hampton. Mass., Nov. 16, 1802, a descendant of Capt. William Clark, who came from England in 1630, and removed to the town of East Hampton in 1639. At the age of sixteen our subject removed to Philadelphia, and entered the office of S. & M. Allen, one of the leading financial houses, with main offices in Philadelphia and New York, and branches in Charleston, Louisville, Albany, and other cities. When he arrived at his majority, in 1823, Mr. Clark, through the influence of Solomon Allen, head of the firm, became a partner in a branch house which he established in Providence, R. I. He there met with marked success in the banking business, but after several years he left the Allens, and went into other business, in which he was unfortunate. In 1833 he removed to Boston, and resumed the banking business in connection with the Allens. The parent house failed in 1836, and he returned to Philadelphia in January, 1837, and entered into partnership with his brother-in-law, Edward Dodge, the firm name being E. W. Clark & Co. The financial results were reasonably large, but during seven years Mr. Clark's share amounted to enough only to pay the debts incurred in Boston. Mr. Clark visited St. Louis in 1843 and 1844, and in the latter year established, with his Philadelphia partners and his brothers, J. W. Clark and L. C. Clark, then in business together in Boston, the house of E. W. Clark & Bros. in that city. From there he went to New Orleans, and with the same parties and George W. Farnum, of Philadelphia, established the house of E. W. Clark, Bros. & Farnum. In 1847 the different houses united in forming the house of E. W. Clark, Dodge & Co., in New York, so that from the above dates until his death in 1856, his houses occupied the most important business centres, and their transactions were on a very large scale. In the years intervening between 1844 and his death in 1856 Mr. Clark amassed a considerable fortune. Jay Cooke became a partner in the house about 1844, after being for some time a clerk, and Mr. Clark's son Edward was admitted in 1849, and Clarence in 1854. Mr. Clark withdrew from the really active management of the house about 1850. He died in August, 1856, after suffering for a year from a painful disease, having its origin in nicotine poisoning.

CLARK, Edward W., banker, was born in Providence, R. I., Jan. 28, 1828, the oldest son of Enoch and Sarah (Dodge) Clark, and came with his parents to Philadelphia in January, 1837. He received his education principally at the Central High School of Philadelphia, and entered the banking house as office boy in 1844. In 1849 he became a member of the firm, which at that time included Jay Cooke. The firm was dissolved on Dec. 31, 1857, but it was immediately reorganized, Jan. 1, 1858, under the same name, with the following partners: Edward W. Clark, Clarence H. Clark, F. S. Kimball, and

H. H. Wainwright. Mr. Clark was elected president of the Lehigh Coal and Navigation Co. late in the year 1867, an action which exhibited the thorough confidence of the directors in his financial ability. He retained his interest in the banking house until 1877, when he was made a receiver of the Lehigh and Wilkes-Barre Coal Co. The responsibilities of that position, added to those of the presidency of the Lehigh Coal and Navigation Co., compelled his withdrawal from the firm. Having succeeded in winding up the receivership in the latter part of 1881, and contemplating an early resignation from official connection with the Lehigh Coal and Navigation Co., Mr. Clark re-entered the firm of E. W. Clark & Co. on Jan. 1, 1882. C. H. Clark and F. S. Kimball retiring, the house was reorganized at that time, still under the old name, by which it had been honorably known for nearly half a century, with the following partners: Edward W. Clark, Sabin W. Colton, Jr., Edward W. Clark, Jr., J. Milton Colton, Edward E. Denniston, and H. M. Sill. Clarence H. Clark, Jr., became a partner on Jan. 1, 1884. Mr. Clark has been in the banking business since 1844, excepting the five years from 1877 to 1882, and most of that time as senior and head of the firm of E. W. Clark & Co. He has been a director of the Fidelity Insurance, Trust, and Safe Deposit Co. since its organization, and of the First National Bank for many years, also of many railroad, coal, and other companies. The firm had large dealings in government securities during the period of the civil war. In these securities the firm did more than any other house in Philadelphia, excepting Jay Cooke & Co., and materially helped to maintain the Federal credit during the critical war times. Mr. Clark was politically an advanced and early Republican in principle, even before the party was formed; a staunch supporter of the Union cause, and a constant adherent of the party during the later periods of its history. He takes a warm interest in public affairs, and is always ready to aid all measures for improvement, whether moral, municipal, or political, but seldom appears conspicuously in such movements, preferring to do his share in the work quietly and unobtrusively. Mr. Clark was married July 19, 1855, to Mary Sill, of an old Philadelphia family. They have six children, of whom three sons are associated in business with their father.

WHITFORD, William Clarke, president of Milton College, Milton, Wis., was born in the town of Edmeston, Otsego co., N. Y., May 5, 1828, son of Capt. Samuel and Sophia Clarke Whitford, both of whose English ancestors were among the first settlers of Rhode Island. His early life was passed on a farm in Plainfield, in the same county, where he attended a neighboring district school, working on the farm during the summer. At thirteen he developed an extraordinary fondness for reading, and at sixteen began a three years' course of instruction at Brookfield Academy in an adjoining town. He next entered De Ruyter Institute, Madison county, N. Y., where he prepared for admission to Union College, Schenectady, N. Y., from which institution he was graduated in 1853. Meanwhile, in order to obtain means by which to finish his education, he taught one term in Milton Academy, Wisconsin, and two years in Union Academy, Shiloh, N. J. He was also occupied for one summer in preparing for publication an elaborate map of several towns in Madison county, N. Y. Upon the completion of his college course, he entered Union Theological Seminary, New York city, graduating in 1856. In April, 1856, he was ordained to the ministry of the Seventh-day Baptist Church, at New Market, N. J., and at once accepted a pastorate at Milton, Wis. Here he remained for three years, in which time the membership of the church was more than doubled. In 1858, during the last year of his pastorate, he accepted the principalship of the academy of that place. Under Mr. Whitford's administration, the attendance of this institution, already large, was materially increased, and mainly due to his efforts. During the civil war 312 of its young men joined the Union army. In 1869 the academy, through the exertions of Mr. Whitford, was incorporated by the state as a college, he being elected president of its board of trustees and of its faculty. The latter position he has held (1895) for over thirty-six years, during which time many of the institution's graduates have become prominent in public affairs; additional buildings were provided; old debts wiped out, and a comfortable endowment secured. Mr. Whitford also served several times as a visitor, appointed by the state, at the State University and the state normal schools. For nine years he was a member of the board of regents of the latter schools; for one year president of the State Teachers' Association of Wisconsin; for four years the chief editor of the "Wisconsin Journal of Education;" and during thirty years has delivered many addresses on educational subjects in the state and elsewhere in the East and the West. In 1868 he was elected a member of the lower house of the state legislature, serving as chairman of its committee on education. He has also often been sent as a delegate to conventions of the Republican party of the state. In 1877, he was chosen state superintendent of public instruction, and two years later was re-elected, holding the office four years in all. He labored to improve the condition of the country schools; to establish them in the newer portions of the state; to introduce a full graded system; to make more efficient the supervision of all public schools in the state; and to provide for such schools better accommodation as to warmth, light, seats, and ventilation. Many of his suggestions with respect to these points

were subsequently adopted also in other states of the Union, and by the U. S. commission of education. Mr. Whitford has held influential positions in the denomination to which he belongs. He was twice elected president of its general conference, and once chairman of its northwestern association; delegate of this body to other religious organizations; inaugurated its scheme in 1872 for raising a large memorial fund to aid its institutions of learning, and served as its agent four years in raising this fund. He has been corresponding secretary of its education society; for several years was a member of its committee to furnish a denominational exhibit at the World's Fair, and its representative at the parliament of religions held at Chicago in 1893. He was also editor of its "Quarterly," a magazine; and has been for six years corresponding editor of the "Sabbath Recorder," its principal paper, having in charge the departments of history and biography. His sermons delivered among this people at their prominent meetings would form a good sized volume. A work on the "Bibliography of Wisconsin Authors" gives a list of thirty-seven of his works that have been published, being, in the main, books, pamphlets, and long articles appearing in periodicals. Among these are his reports as state superintendent of public instruction: "History of School Supervision in Wisconsin;" "Historical Sketch of Education in Wisconsin for the Centennial Exposition at Philadelphia in 1876;" "Co-education of the Sexes in Our Schools;" "Education of Work;" "Text-book Legislation in the Different States;" "Grading System for the Country Schools of Wisconsin;" "Plans and Specifications for School-Houses;" "The Principles of Church Discipline;" "History of the Seventh-day Baptist Institutions of Learning in America;" "Christ the Student's Model;" "History of Milton College;" "Lessons from a Four Months' Trip in Europe;" "Christianity in the Higher Schools," Mr. Whitford not only received his first degree from Union College, but also his second degree, M. A. He received the degree of D.D., from Blackburn University, Illinois. Dr. Whitford has been twice married; first to Elmina Coon of Lincklaen, N. Y., a graduate of De Ruyter Institute, whose death occurred within six months after marriage; second, to Ruth Hemphill of Alfred, N. Y., a graduate of Alfred University, who taught for many years in conjunction with her husband. One surviving child, Milton Clark Whitford, was the fruit of the last marriage. Mr. Whitford has made repeated visits to the Southwest of our country and in Mexico, and has in preparation a work descriptive of the leading features, the historical events, and the inhabitants of these regions. In 1891 he made an extensive tour of Europe, visiting nearly all the countries in it, studying its people and their customs, and examining its many places of historical interest.

GRUBE, Bernhard Adam, Moravian missionary, was born in Germany in 1715. He was educated at Jena, where he fell under the influence of the Unitas Fratrum, and came to America in 1746. He labored long among the Indians and translated into the Delaware tongue a "Harmony of the Gospels," 1767, and a collection of hymns. He died at Bethlehem, Pa., March 20, 1808.

PRIEST, Henry Samuel, jurist, was born in Ralls county, Mo., Feb. 7, 1853. His father intended him for the church, but his own tastes led him to the bar. After a course of general study in the country schools and at Westminster College, Mo., he entered upon the study of the law. He was admitted to practice at Hannibal, Mo., in November, 1873. He opened an office at Moberly in the same state and began the practice of his profession, in which he was from the beginning rewarded with marked success. In 1880 he became the assistant attorney of the Missouri Pacific Railroad Co., which position he left to become general-attorney of the Wabash Railroad Co. in 1883. In 1890 he was appointed general-attorney of the Missouri Pacific Co. Although throughout a large portion of his professional career he gave especial attention to railroad litigation, he never relinquished general practice. He was appointed to the position of U. S. district judge for

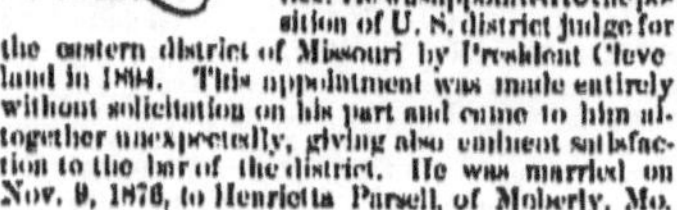

the eastern district of Missouri by President Cleveland in 1894. This appointment was made entirely without solicitation on his part and came to him altogether unexpectedly, giving also eminent satisfaction to the bar of the district. He was married on Nov. 9, 1876, to Henrietta Pursell, of Moberly, Mo.

HAYES, Warren Howard, architect, was born at Prattsburgh, Steuben co., N. Y., Aug. 22, 1847. On his father's side he is of New England stock, being descended from George Hayes, of Windsor, Conn., who emigrated from Scotland to Derbyshire, Eng., and thence to Windsor, Conn., in 1680, where descendants of the family still live. Many honored names represent the family in professional and official life, Pres. Rutherford Hayes being among the number. Upon his mother's side, Mr. Hayes' progenitors are the Robsons and Straughans, of Northumberland county, Eng., who emigrated to Geneva, Ontario co., N. Y., early in the nineteenth century. The boyhood of Mr. Hayes was spent on the farm of his father, George Goundry Hayes, who was at that time one of the most successful agriculturists in that section, owning and tilling large farms in Yates, Steuben, and Ontario counties. The son's studies were begun at the age of five in the "district school," and continued for seven years. This was supplemented at the select school in Italy, N. Y., at Watkins' Academy, and at Genessee Wesleyan Seminary at Lima, N. Y. In 1868 Mr. Hayes entered the sophomore class of Cornell University, and was graduated in 1871, having successfully taken the courses in architecture and civil engineering, including the natural sciences and modern languages. He also, during his college course, took two President White first prizes for proficiency in mechanics and physics. The succeeding

ten years were given to the successful practice of his chosen profession, architecture, at Elmira, N. Y., where, in May, 1881, he was united in marriage to Miss M. F. Beardsley. In September, 1881, he opened an office in Minneapolis, Minn., where from that time to the present (1894), he has maintained a widely extended and successful practice. Many of the finer business and public buildings in Minneapolis and St. Paul have been erected by him, as well as notable structures in other cities. Mr. Hayes shows especial originality in ecclesiastical architecture. Among the churches which he has designed are the First Congregational Church at Rockland, Plymouth co., Mass.; Union Congregational Church at Rockville, Conn.; First Baptist Church at Portland, Ore., and Wesley Methodist Episcopal Church, Minneapolis, Minn. At the present time Mr. Hayes has in process of erection the Fowler Methodist Episcopal Church, illustrated on a previous page herein, a most complete and finely equipped edifice, and named for Bishop C. H. Fowler. All the above buildings, and many similar ones, notably the Central Presbyterian Church of St. Paul, Minn., and First Presbyterian of Galesburgh, Ill., are planned on Mr. Hayes' original "diagonal plan" of auditorium, developed by him in the winter of 1882, and first used in several leading churches in Minneapolis. Its beauty and success were popular from the first. It has become widely known and used, until now it may justly be said to be the most practical and successful form of church auditorium known in modern architecture. It insures superior qualities with respect to acoustics, facilities for sight, ventilation, light, access, and ease of combination with the chapel, bringing all within sight of, and within short distance from, the speaker. The diagonal auditorium is the result of much study on the part of the originator, to whom it has brought great credit and enduring fame. On Oct. 26, 1886, Mr. Hayes was married to Mrs. Lillie Cook Van Norman, of Hamilton, Ont., his first wife and daughter having died four years previous. From this second marriage three children were born to them: Edith, George Edson, and Helen, who, with Mary Van Norman, the step-daughter, form the present family.

EATON, Theophilus, first governor of New Haven colony, was born at Stony Stratford, Buckinghamshire, England, about 1591. His father was a clergyman and it had been the hope of Eaton's friends to see him in the ministry, but he was permitted to follow his own preferences, and became a merchant in London. Here he rose to opulence and attracted the notice of his government, by which he was sent in a diplomatic capacity to Denmark. He remained there for several years. Returning to England, he settled again in London, and was a parishioner of the Rev. John Davenport, rector of St. Stephen's Church in Colman street in that city. These two men, it is said, lived in uninterrupted intimacy; they were rarely separated from each other; their history runs in one channel; their names are inseparably associated. Eaton sailed for America with Davenport and a number of friends in "two ships," and reached Boston, Mass., June 26, 1637, in the height of the troubles of the Antinomian controversy and the Pequot war. The stay of the party at Boston was but brief, for they preferred to found a new colony rather than to settle in one whose beginnings were already made, for good and sufficient reasons; although efforts of the Massachusetts settlers to retain them were repeated and earnest. But having taken some months for inquiry and deliberation, Eaton having gone to Quinnipiac (the present New Haven, Conn.), in the fall of 1637 and left a few men there to prepare for the advent of the rest of the party, these people, headed by Eaton and Davenport, sailed from Boston for that place, March 30, 1638, and reached it on Apr. 15th. Prior to this, (November, 1637) Eaton had contracted with the Indians for land, out of which since that time seven townships have been made, the price paid being thirteen English coats. As one historian says, "with a wiser judgment of the safe way of proceeding in such affairs than Gorges exercised when he planned a government beforehand for his province, or Locke when he made a constitution for those who might people South Carolina, the settlers at Quinnipiac gave themselves a year to learn from experience the arrangements suitable to their social organization," and then elected twelve men of their number, of whom Eaton was one, "to begin the church." These twelve selected from their own number "seven pillars," of whom Eaton was also one, to perfect the business, and then having organized their associates in the church, nine in number, as freemen acting as a court, Eaton was made a "magistrate" for one year, and four other persons chosen with him to be "deputies." This office he held by successive re-election, its title becoming that of governor, until Oct. 27, 1643, when he was chosen to that office over the new community formed by the union of several other settlements with that at New Haven for purposes of civil government. Prior to this, however, Eaton and the New Haven settlers had "intended to employ themselves in the commercial industries to which they had been used, having chosen their site at New Haven with reference to its convenience for this purpose. With the same view they also purchased lands and established a plantation on Delaware Bay, near to a fort which had been erected by some Swedes. But their commercial undertakings did not prosper; and as one after another of the agricultural communities grew up and passed them, their employments came to assimilate themselves to those of the rest of the country." Under the auspices of the New Haven government, moreover, Southold on Long Island was established; Stamford, in Connecticut, was founded; and an attempt was made at Greenwich, Conn., still nearer the New Netherland border, although this frontier town was for some time in revolt. In 1646 Gov. Eaton proposed to Kieft, Dutch governor of the New Netherlands, to settle all differences with him by arbitration, but Kieft was soon afterwards displaced by Peter Stuyvesant, and nothing came of Eaton's suggestion. Theophilus Eaton has been spoken of as a man "handsome and commanding in figure, strict and severe in religious matters, but affable and courteous." At his death, when money was worth three times as much as in our day, his wearing apparel was inventoried at £50 sterling and his plate at £150. His "Turkey carpet," "tapestry coverings," and "cushions of Turkey work" were among the articles of show which helped him to maintain "a part in some measure answerable to his place." He died in New Haven, June 7, 1658.

FICKLING, Francis William, lawyer, was born on Hilton Head Island, Beaufort co., S. C., Jan. 20, 1811. He was graduated at Brown University, studied law, and practiced in his native region, where he took very high rank in his profession. As an equity lawyer he had few equals; his opinions were practically decisions. Gifted, eloquent, and perspicuous, he was considered one of the chief ornaments of the South Carolina bar. He died at Columbia, S. C., Feb. 17, 1887.

ROBINSON, Sumers Corson, manufacturer, was born at West Creek, Cumberland co., N. J., March 21, 1831, son of Morris and Mary Robinson. His father was a farmer, in straitened circumstances, and was unable to give to the son any educational advantages save six winters' schooling at the district school. His summers and mornings and evenings were devoted to hard work on the farm. When fifteen years of age he left the farm, and was apprenticed to the village carpenter, with whom he served three years. In the meantime, much against the will of his employer, he joined the Methodist church. This caused him severe persecution from his employer, and to avoid it he ran away and went to sea. While absent, his father repented of his harshness, and asked him 
to return. This led to reconciliation: the lad came back and completed his term of apprenticeship; and at the age of twenty-one he received his first wages as a carpenter. The next year he married Maria, daughter of Levi Dare, a prominent citizen of Cumberland county. He continued his occupation of carpenter until he was twenty-six years old, when he took up the business of contractor and builder. In 1857 he went to Leavenworth, Kan., where he found profitable employment at his trade for nine months. Upon his return to New Jersey for his family, the opposition offered by his wife's father to her settling in so wild a place as Kansas then was, determined him to locate in some other section of the West, and in 1858 he took his family to Minnesota and located at St. Anthony. After eight years of success as a contractor and builder in St. Anthony, he removed to the new and growing city of Minneapolis, where he continued to thrive. Here he formed a partnership, and entered into the manufacture of building material on a large scale. The business resulted in the Bardwell, Robinson Co., the largest manufacturers of building supplies in the state. His son, Charles N. Robinson, became a member of the concern in 1884. Mr. Robinson is an ardent Republican in politics, and a prominent Methodist in religion. His charities to churches and schools are large, but unostentatious,

and his advice is specially valued in all the societies and organizations devoted to building up the interests and purposes of his accepted denomination. His hospitality is unbounded, and at his elegant home in Minneapolis he is the centre of a large circle of devoted friends. He has one daughter, Mary Robinson, wife of William Wolford.

JOY, Charles Frederick, lawyer and congressman, was born in Morgan county, Ill., Dec. 11, 1849, of New England parentage. His father, Charles Joy, soon after his marriage journeyed from New Hampshire to Illinois, using as the principal means of conveyance a four-wheeled covered vehicle, not unlike those used for carryalls in country villages in the West, or prairie schooners on the western plains.

After reaching Morgan county, Ill., he with two of his brothers purchased a large tract of land and commenced life. The son spent the years of his minority on the growing farm, being educated in the household and at the country schools which the section afforded. The father was an unswerving Union man, and the first farmer in his country to raise a flag in the political campaign which resulted in the election of Abraham Lincoln to the presidency. He died in 1864. After the death of his father the son formed the determination to obtain a college education, and to this end prepared for admission to college, under the direction of Rev. E. B. Tuthill, the Congregational clergyman of Joy Prairie Church; was admitted to Yale College in 1870; and in June, 1874, was graduated with honor. He studied law and was admitted to the bar in St. Louis in 1876. On Sept. 10, 1879, he married in Salem, Conn., Arabel, the eldest daughter of Rev. Jairus Ordway, the Congregational clergyman of that place, and took her to his adopted home, St. Louis. She lived but a few months, however. Mr. Joy has always been a Republican, and at each election has taken an active part in the campaign, contributing of his means and with his voice toward the success of the political tenets in which he believes. He frequently refused office, preferring to devote himself entirely to his professional duties. In 1892, however, in a strongly Democratic district, after a short campaign of more than usual activity, he was elected over his Democratic opponent to congress, where he took his seat on March 4, 1893.

STEERS, Henry, shipbuilder, was born in New York, Sept. 14, 1832. He passed his examination for admission to the Free Academy, now the College of the City of New York, but having decided to begin at the foundation in training for the profession of his father and grandfather, he did not enter on the advanced studies of that institution, and at the age of sixteen became an apprentice of his uncle, George Steers, then general manager for William H. Brown, at that time engaged in the building of the Atlantic and the Arctic for the Collins line of mail steamers between New York and Liverpool. He continued his apprenticeship with his father and uncle when they became partners in 1850. He rapidly acquired skill in the use of tools and the practical handicraft of the trade, also studying draughting and modeling, so that before he attained his majority he had become a master-workman, and was frequently put in charge of gangs of workmen, most of whom were older than himself, his services being also frequently hired by other firms, in the supervision of labor by contract. He joined his father and uncle on the yacht America at the Isle of Wight, and was on the yacht in her celebrated race. On attaining his majority he continued in the employ of G. & J. R. Steers until the final closing of the business of that firm early in 1857. Owing to the financial crisis, which paralyzed the shipbuilding interests, he did not deem it prudent to undertake business on his own account, and for about two years devoted himself to draughting and modeling for different shipbuilders. Early in 1859 he hired a part of the shipyard of William H. Brown on the East river, between Eleventh and Twelfth streets, and began in a small way at first his career as a master-shipbuilder. During the first year Mr. Steers built a small steamer, the Seth Grosvenor, for the American Colonization Society, to be used in the colony of Liberia, Africa, and a pilot-boat, the Charles H. Marshall, which gained a high reputation for speed and sea-going qualities. In 1860 he removed his shipyard to Greenpoint, L. I. At this time a company, formed by Marshall O. Roberts, of New York, and other gentlemen, was organized for the transmission of the U. S. mail, and for passenger and freight business from New York along the Atlantic coast, across the peninsula of Florida, and by the Gulf of Mexico and the Mississippi river to New Orleans. This company contracted with Mr. Steers for the building of a steamer of 1,000 tons, to run between Cedar Keys and the west coast of Florida. Before she was finished the indication of a disturbance in the relations of the Southern with the Northern states became so alarming that the company decided to suspend their operations, and entered into negotiations with Paul Forbes of the great American house of Russell & Co., at Canton, China, for the sale of the steamer as she was on the stocks. Mr. Steers had introduced certain new ideas, both in the lines of the vessel and her frame, the latter of which, designed to increase its strength, were novel in shipbuilding, though not novel as mechanical devices, having been used in the trestle work of modern bridge building. These innovations by so young a man, whose ability had only been displayed in the construction of a pilot-boat and a steamer of about 100 tons burden, evoked criticisms of a decidedly unfavorable character from master-shipbuilders of long experience, and from mechanical engineers who claimed to be experts. These criticisms led to some hesitancy on the part of Mr. Forbes to close the contract. He was, however, so impressed by the confidence expressed by Mr. Steers, and the reasons given for it by him, that he made the purchase, and waited for the completion of the vessel. When she was launched it was found that the calculations of Mr. Steers for her draught without her machinery were not at fault by a single inch. The steamboat, when completed, was a decided success, and made a remarkably quick voyage to China, and became at once distinguished as the fastest vessel in China. He afterward built for the same firm another steamer which made the quickest time to China ever recorded, and a number of steamers for the China coast and river trade. He also built the yachts Henrietta, for James Gordon Bennett, and Hope, for Ives of Providence, which achieved a national reputation, and the steamers Massachusetts and Rhode Island; he also built and reconstructed the yachts Idler, Palmer, Magic, Dreadnaught, and many others. During the civil war he built the steam frigate Idaho, which was acknowledged by naval officers to have been the best

vessel of her class ever built for the government outside of their yards. From 1866–75 he was building principally for the Pacific Mail Steamship Co. the steamers China, Arizona, America, Great Republic, Alaska, Japan, Golden Rule, and several others; these vessels were the largest wooden steamers ever built in this country. During 1878 and up to 1875 he was associated with John Roach in the shipyard at Chester, Pa. Mr. Steers retired from active work as a shipbuilder in 1878. In 1880 he was chosen president of the Eleventh Ward Bank, which was organized from the banking department of the New York Dry Dock Co., of which his grandfather, Henry Steers, Sr., the builder, was the first superintendent. He is also president of the Williamsburg Gas Co., and of one of the city street railroads. In 1882 Mr. Steers was appointed a member of the U. S. Naval Advisory Board, a body constituted under an act of congress, requiring that two of the members should be from civil life. The appointment of Mr. Steers was an honorable and deserved tribute to his ability as a practical shipbuilder. While a member of this board he designed the U. S. steamer Dolphin, and notwithstanding the efforts of the enemies of John Roach, her builder, to condemn her on her several trials, she proved to be one of the most useful and efficient vessels in the navy, making a trip around the world, and returning to the United States with hull and machinery in perfect condition. The U. S. steamers Chicago, Atlanta, and Boston were also designed by the board of which he was a member, and the success of these vessels is chiefly due to Mr. Steers's suggestions.

DEERING, John William, merchant, was born in Saco, Me., Aug. 7, 1833, the eldest son of James Madison Deering, a leading merchant and the second mayor of that city, a descendant of one of the first settlers of Maine, who emigrated from England with Tucker and Cleeves to Pine Point, Scarboro', in 1680. Mr. Deering was educated in the public schools and at Thornton Academy in his native city. At the age of sixteen he went to sea before the mast, and owing to special fitness, ability, and executive force, became master of a first-class ship in the European trade at the age of twenty-three years. He continued in the China and European freighting business until he came to Portland in 1867. Since then he has been engaged in the southern pine lumber business and in building vessels. Mr. Deering was elected mayor of Portland in 1883 and and again in 1885 by the Democrats; and in both of these terms of office the affairs of the city were so excellently administered as to draw forth hearty commendations from men of all parties. In 1894 Mr. Deering was the Democratic candidate for representative in congress in opposition to Thomas B. Reed, receiving the nomination by acclamation in an unusually large convention of delegates. He was appointed collector of customs for the port of Portland and Falmouth by Pres. Cleveland, Feb. 9, 1895. He is president of the Portland Marine Society, and a member of the Athletic and Bramhall social clubs. His religious faith is Unitarian. He was married in October, 1863, to Mary, daughter of Samuel and Elizabeth Small of Portland, and granddaughter of Elder Rand, one of the most noted divines in the Free Baptist church in Maine. They have three children, a son and two daughters. Mr.

Deering's success in life may be attributed to more than ordinary native ability and executive powers, supplemented by strict honesty in both business and political relations. He is a man of broad ideas, well posted on the leading questions of the day, exceptionally well informed on all matters pertaining to the shipping interests of the country, and a strong and convincing public speaker.

BAIRD, Matthew, locomotive-builder, was born near Londonderry, Ireland, in 1817, of Scotch-Irish parentage, his parents emigrating to Philadelphia when he was but four years of age. His father, a copper-smith by trade, gave him an education in the common schools of the city. Soon after leaving school the son was appointed assistant to one of the professors of chemistry in the University of Pennsylvania. In 1834 he went to New Castle, Del., into the copper and sheet-iron works of the New Castle Manufacturing Co., from which position he became superintendent of the railroad shops at that place. In June, 1838, he became foreman of the sheet-iron and boiler department of the Baldwin Locomotive Works at Philadelphia, in which position he remained until 1850. Subsequently he engaged for a couple of years in the marble business with his brother John,

returning in 1854 to the Baldwin Works as partner of Matthias Baldwin, and upon the death of the latter, in 1866, he became the sole proprietor of the establishment. He at once reorganized the institution, joining with himself as partners Messrs. George Burnham and Charles Parry, under the title of M. Baird and Co. This business relation was maintained until his withdrawal from active business in 1878. Mr. Baird designed many improvements in mechanical appliances and especially in locomotive machinery. In 1854, when bituminous and anthracite coal came into general use as fuel for locomotives, he invented various devices for consuming the smoke and securing the most beneficial results from it, his inventions being adopted on all roads where bituminous coal was used for generating steam. Mr. Baird was eminently a public-spirited man. He was one of the incorporators and directors of the American Steamship Co., a large investor in the Pennsylvania Railroad Co., a director of the Texas and Pacific Railroad Co., and of the Philadelphia and West Chester Railroad Co. He was also a director in the Pennsylvania Steel Co., and the Andover Iron Co. For many years he was one of the directors of the Central National Bank, a manager of the Northern Home for Friendless Children, and to calls for charitable and benevolent purposes he always responded with an unstinted hand. He was a firm supporter of the Union during the civil war, and the immense capacity of the Baldwin Locomotive Works was tasked to the utmost in turning out locomotives for the use of the government in the transportation of armies, supplies, and munitions of war. He was also much interested in religious and educational matters in Philadelphia. He died, after a useful and busy life, May 19, 1877, leaving a large estate.

HALEY, Thomas Preston, clergyman, was born in Lafayette county, near the city of Lexington, Mo., Apr. 19, 1832. His fraternal ancestors were from the north of Ireland,—his mother's family were English, Carver by name, and came over on the May Flower. The son removed with his parents to Missouri when quite young, settling on a farm in Randolph county, in the central part of the state. He worked on the farm in the summer, attending country schools throughout part of the winter. Of religious parentage, his thoughts naturally inclined to religion, and at the age of fourteen he became a member of the Christain church. Before he was seventeen years of age he was a country school teacher. After teaching two terms he entered the academy at Huntsville, the county seat, where, under Rev. Bartlett Anderson and Prof. Asa Grant, he completed the course and was prepared to enter the Missouri University. After a brief interval of teaching he entered this institution, under the presidency of James Shannon. His college studies were completed in 1853. In November of

the same year he was ordained to the ministry of the church in which he grew up. During the years of 1854-55 he was a "missionary pastor" in the district embracing the whole of northeast Missouri. In this work he was remarkably successful, gathering together and organizing many of the now prominent churches in that part of the state. In the spring of 1855, May 1, he was united in marriage with Mary McGarvey, a beautiful and accomplished woman of Fayette, Mo., the sister of the Rev. Prof. McGarvey, of Kentucky University. In the year 1858 Mr. Haley became pastor of the church of Lexington, Mo., where he continued until August, 1864, when he was called to the pastorate of the Second Church in Louisville, Ky. Here he maintained a most successful pastorate until the fall of 1869, when on account of a protracted throat trouble he resigned and returned to Missouri. During the time of his retirement from active pastoral work Mr. Haley secured the money to purchase and partly endow the "Missouri Female Orphanage School of the Christian Church," at first established at Camden Points but later removed to Fulton, Mo. With returning health Mr. Haley spent five years as pastor of the First Christian Church, at St. Louis, Mo. He has now, however (1894), been the pastor of the First Church of Kansas City, Mo., for thirteen years. Though three-score years of age, he is in the meridian of his strength, and conducts the labors of a large pastorate. In the year 1887 his wife died, and in the spring and summer of 1888 he made an extensive tour of Western Europe, visiting the great capital cities of the old world. During his sojourn in England he preached several times in London, Southampton, Chester, and Southport. In July, 1892, Mr. Haley was married to Mrs. Mary Campbell of Kirksville, Mo. By his first marriage three sons and two daughters were born to him. His sons are intelligent and successful in their respective professions, and his daughters are both happily married to active business men. Mr. Haley is the author of several small volumes, chief of which is "The Dawn of the Reformation," a collection of historical and biographical sketches of the ministers and churches of his denomination.

JAYNE, Trafford Newton, lawyer, was born near St. Charles, Minn., Nov. 3, 1868, son of Havens Brewster Jayne, his grandfather being Joseph Brewster Jayne. He is a lineal descendant, through his grandfather on the maternal side, of William Brewster, of the Mayflower. On the Jayne side, William Jayne came from England in an early day, and settled on Long Island. His father died when the son was four years old, and the mother had a hard struggle to support herself and two children. Young Jayne was chiefly educated in the country schools, living on a farm for five years after his father's death. He next attended the High School in Winona, Minn.; at twelve years of age was a freshman in the High School proper; and at the end of that year left school, and learned telegraphy. He soon entered into work, taking first a night office, but by promotion was at the age of fourteen years made cashier of the C. M. and St. Paul Railroad at Winona, Minn., at a good salary. At sixteen he was cashier of the C. and N. W. Railroad at Mankato, Minn., with salary increased. Here he began to appreciate his lack of education, and in July of his eighteenth year commenced preparation for the University of Michigan. He resigned his position as cashier on July 19, 1886, and studied from that time until the following September, when he entered college at Ann Arbor, Mich. He took three years of the course in the regular literary department and one in the law department, accomplishing the four years' course in three years. He was also fairly prominent in athletics during his college course, being on the university base-ball team, and in 1889 beating the champions of both Michigan and Ohio at tennis. He held several college honors, and at the age of twenty was president of the University Republican Club, numbering 600 members. In 1889 he left college, having expended all his funds, and returned to Minnesota. His college expenses had been met in a large degree with his own earnings. In addition to other college work, he had learned stenography and typewriting, which, after his departure from college, at once secured him a position in St. Paul as chief clerk and stenographer in a law office there. In January, 1890, he was admitted to the bar, being just past his twenty-first year. He practised alone in St. Paul until November, 1890, when C. B. Palmer, one of St. Paul's oldest attorneys, took him into partnership, and he was thus able to get much practice in court from the start. In December, 1891,

Mr. Palmer decided to go to New York, and as Mr. Jayne was offered the attorneyship of the Wilber Mercantile Agency in Minneapolis, he removed to that city on Jan. 1, 1892. The work proving too much for one man, he formed a partnership with Robert Morrison, under the firm name of Jayne & Morrison. Since that time the business has increased greatly. They have had charge of several large matters running up to hundreds of thousands. Their cases number already over 700, although their partnership has existed but three years. Their business is equaled by but few firms in the city, their court work being especially large, and but few cases placed in their hands have been lost. Among their clients are some of the largest wholesale dealers in the city. At the age of twenty-three, Mr. Jayne was elected president of the Minnesota Union of Christian Endeavor Societies, the association at that time numbering 30,000 young people. As an active member of the Methodist Episcopal church, he has charge of a mission in the city, and endeavors to make his religion a business, and to make his business religious.

BAILEY, Ezra Brewster, financier, was born at Franklin, Conn., March 20, 1841, son of Aaron and Eliza (Brewster) Bailey, and ninth in direct descent, on the maternal side, from Elder William Brewster, of the Mayflower, through his eldest son,

Jonathan Brewster, who joined the Connecticut colonists, and settled in early life at Norwich, in that state. His ancestors, on his father's side, are of an old English family, and among the first settlers of America. Mr. Bailey's early life was spent on the ancestral farm, of which he became the proprietor, and he obtained his education in the district schools of Franklin and the High School at Norwich. He early acquired habits of industry and economy, which have been the keystone of his successful business career. While still in his minority, his patriotism led him to enlist in company B, 20th Connecticut regiment, in September, 1862. While in camp, however, he was stricken with typhoid fever, and obliged to remain at home, and was unable thereafter during the war to carry out his desires on account of ill health. In 1867 he removed to Windsor Locks, and devoted one year to farming and tobacco raising. In 1868 he was made assistant-postmaster in the same town, at the same time having charge of a large store. He afterwards made an engagement with a large publishing firm in Springfield, Mass., as supervisor of agencies. His duties took him all over the northern states and Canada, and he built up a large and profitable business in the four years he was connected with the firm. In 1873 he became secretary and treasurer of the E. Horton & Son Co., manufacturers of the celebrated "Horton Lathe Chuck," of Windsor Locks, organized that year. In 1875 he severed his connection with that company, and removed with his family to Franklin, and for four years devoted all his time to agricultural pursuits and the raising of Jersey stock. In 1880 he resumed control of the E. Horton & Son Co., and since that time has been its general manager, and is now president and treasurer. He is also officially connected with many other financial, industrial, and commercial enterprises of Windsor Locks and Hartford. He is the president of the Windsor Locks Electric Lighting Co., in the establishment of which he was intimately concerned; a director of the Connecticut River Co., who own the Enfield and Windsor Locks water-power; a director of the Windsor Locks Savings Bank, and of the Dwight Slate Machine Co., of Hartford. He was an incorporator of the Windsor Locks Water Co., and is a director of the J. R. Montgomery Co. He served in the state legislature in 1880-83-87, the latter year in the senate, where he was chairman of important committees. Mr. Bailey is an ardent Republican, and has held many positions of trust in the town and state. In 1890 he was appointed to his present position, that of U. S. collector of customs to the port of Hartford. Mr. Bailey is a member of the American Society of Mechanical Engineers, and of the Connecticut Society of the Sons of the American Revolution, and stands high in Masonic circles. He married, in 1871, Katie, daughter of Eli Horton, the inventor of the celebrated Horton lathe chuck, and by her has a son and a daughter. Mrs. Bailey is eighth in descent from John and Priscilla Alden, prominent characters in early Puritan history.

DUNN, James H., surgeon, was born at Fort Wayne, Ind., May 20, 1853. His parents, natives of Dublin, Ireland, came to the United States in 1846, locating finally in Winona county, Minn., in 1855. Dr. Dunn received his education in the common and high schools of Winona, entered the First State Normal School in 1869, and was graduated in 1871. He then engaged in teaching, and was instructor in the Minnesota State Teachers' Institute until 1874, when he began the study of medicine, and was graduated from the medical department of the University of the City of New York in 1878. He was then instructor in the natural sciences in the Second State Normal School for two years, after which he entered upon a large country practice in Scott and adjoining counties. In 1884 he went to Europe to pursue post-graduate studies, spending two years at Heidelberg, Vienna, and Paris. On his return he located in Minneapolis, where he secured a large practice, chiefly as a surgeon and consultant. He is a member of the Minnesota Academy of Medicine, the State Medical Association, and several other local and national medical and scientific societies, and was president of the State Medical Association in 1888.

He has been an enthusiastic medical teacher for the past ten years; was city physician and surgeon in charge of City Hospital in 1886 and 1887; and is now professor of genito-urinary diseases, and adjunct professor of clinical surgery in the medical department of the University of Minnesota; and attending surgeon to St. Mary's, Asbury, and the City Hospitals. His practice is chiefly surgery and genito-urinary diseases, in which departments he has had large experience and success. He is a contributor to several medical journals. He was married in 1885 to Agnes, daughter of J. L. Macdonald, of St. Paul, and has one son, James L. Dunn, born in Minneapolis, Aug. 29, 1887.

BACON, Frederick Hampden, lawyer, was born at Niles, Mich., May 5, 1849, son of Nathaniel Bacon, a circuit and afterwards supreme-court judge of Michigan. His paternal great-grandfather was a lieutenant in the revolutionary war. On his mother's side he is descended from the Lord family, of whom John Lord, the historian, and his uncle, Nathan Lord, president of Dartmouth College (1793-1870), were her near relations. Of this same family, several members served in the American navy in the war of 1812. The son was educated in the public schools of Niles, and at the University of Michigan, which institute he left during his junior year. He then studied law, and was admitted to the bar of Berrian county, Mich., in 1871, and practiced there until 1874, when he removed to St. Louis, Mo., where he continued the practice of his profession, and gained a high position at the bar of that state. While in Michigan he was circuit court commissioner. Mr. Bacon was married in 1882 to Clara Cleland, of Niles, Mich., of English ancestry. He is a member of the Presbyterian church, and has been for fifteen years a deacon in the First Presbyterian

Church at St. Louis. As a Mason he stands high in the order, and is a member of several other fraternal societies. In 1888 Mr. Bacon prepared and published a law treatise, "Benefit Societies and Life Insurance," which became the standard work on the subject. He published a new and enlarged

edition in two volumes in 1894. Besides this work, Mr. Bacon in his early life was a successful editor of several local newspapers.

KINCAID, William, Joseph, manufacturer, was born on a farm in Burke county, N. C., Jan. 3, 1841, of Scotch-Irish descent, his first American ancestor having emigrated from the North of Ireland about 1750 and settled in Tryon, now Lincoln county, N. C., but his great-grandfather, John Kincaid, and

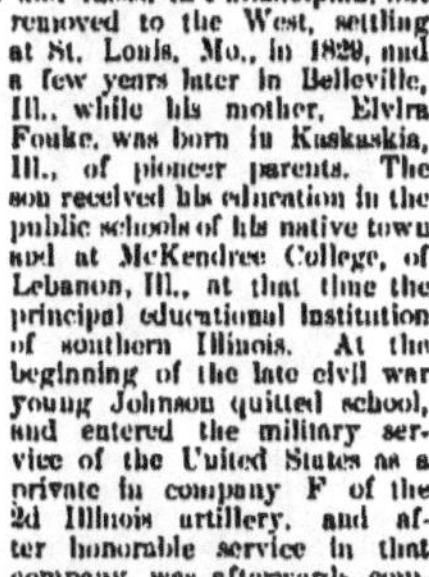

grandfather, James Kincaid, were soldiers in the American revolution. Young Kincaid commenced to earn his own living at the age of thirteen; since then he has needed the financial assistance of no one. Upon the outbreak of the civil war in 1761, he volunteered as a member of Company G, 1st North Carolina regiment, which was subsequently known as the 11th Bethel regiment. In 1862 he was appointed first lieutenant of his company, and after the battle of Gettysburg, where he was severely wounded, was promoted to a captaincy, having served during the entire war. At the close of the war Capt. Kincaid, bankrupt in both money and health, commenced life afresh as a salesman in a jobbing dry-goods house in Baltimore. At the end of the first year, however, in 1866, he opened a small general store at Wilson, N. C., which he conducted with profit until 1871, when he removed to Georgia, and established himself at Griffin. Here he continued the mercantile business with increased prosperity until 1883. He then organized the Griffin Manufacturing Co., for the manufacture of cotton goods, and five years later the Kincaid Manufacturing Co., for the same purpose. He is president of both companies, which have been successful under his management.

JOHNSON, John Davis, lawyer, was born at Belleville, Ill., Apr. 19, 1844. His father, Henry Johnson, was born and raised in Philadelphia, but removed to the West, settling at St. Louis, Mo., in 1829, and a few years later in Belleville, Ill., while his mother, Elvira Fouke, was born in Kaskaskia, Ill., of pioneer parents. The son received his education in the public schools of his native town and at McKendree College, of Lebanon, Ill., at that time the principal educational institution of southern Illinois. At the beginning of the late civil war young Johnson quitted school, and entered the military service of the United States as a private in company F of the 2d Illinois artillery, and after honorable service in that company, was afterwards commissioned as a first lieutenant in the 38th Missouri infantry. At the close of the war he received an honorable discharge from the military service of the Union, and applied himself to the study of the law. In 1870 he was admitted to the bar, and began the practice of his profession at St. Louis, Mo. At a later date he formed a law partnership with his elder brother, Chas. P. Johnson, one of the leading criminal advocates in the West. Under the name of Chas. P. & Jno. D. Johnson the firm existed for

many years. John D. Johnson devoted his energies exclusively to the civil practice, earning for himself the reputation of being one of the best practitioners in the state of Missouri. Of commanding presence, genial manners, never-failing courtesy, a hard student, thoroughly versed in all branches of the law, an easy, graceful, and convincing speaker, and a tireless worker, no man, in the profession or out of it, has commanded greater respect. He was frequently tendered judicial positions, but as often declined them, preferring the practice of his profession to the exacting labors of the bench. His successful career enabled him to accumulate a comfortable competence before arriving at middle age. Mr. Johnson's favorite sports were hunting and angling, in which he was as successful as in professional pursuits.

GWYNN, Joseph Kean, state commissioner, was born at Spring Station, near Midway, Woodford co., Ky., Jan. 19, 1854. He is a son of William Gwynn, who was a native of Woodford county, and by occupation a farmer and breeder of fine sheep and cattle, and was an elder in the old-school Presbyterian church. His mother was Angelina Kean, born in Mississippi, and married to William Gwynn at Midway in 1851. When the son was six years old his parents located near Elizabethtown, Hardin co., Ky., where he was educated principally in the common schools, but completed at Lynnland Institute, a college of some reputation in Kentucky, and situated near Glendale. At the age of sixteen he had the misfortune to lose both parents, which event left him the eldest son of a family of eight children, the support and education of which he and an elder sister assumed. He remained on the farm, keeping the family together for two years, at the conclusion of which the elder sister having married, he engaged in mercantile life for a short period in Louisville, but realizing that his earnings from this source would be insufficient to complete his own education, and to procure that of his brothers

and sisters, he retired from mercantile life, and himself engaged in teaching, keeping always two or more of his brothers and sisters with him while so doing. He established a high-school at Louisville, and conducted both the school and a newspaper successfully until 1880. In the latter part of that year his newspaper establishment was destroyed by fire, and he purchased the "Versailles Gazette," his only competitor in the town, but that too was destroyed by fire within six months. In the early part of 1887, a well defined and vigorous emigration movement was set on foot in Missouri, and he was made the secretary of the Southwest Missouri Immigration Society, with headquarters at Clinton. In this capacity he became widely acquainted with the representative men of the state, and made a conspicuous success of the enterprise. After prosecuting this work for two years, he went to the Panhandle of Texas, and engaged in development work there. He organized the counties of Floyd and Motley, and established the county seats of Floydada and Matador respectively, continuing in this work until 1890, when he was chosen the executive commissioner of the World's Fair board for the state of Missouri. While at the World's Fair he was made secretary of the national organization of World's Fair state executive officers, in which capacity he was brought in close contact with the executive commissioners of all the states in the union, and also with most of those from foreign countries. At the close of the Fair, in 1893, Mr. Gwynn was made secretary and general manager of the St. Louis Fair Association. Mr. Gwynn was married at Versailles, Mo., on Aug. 31, 1885, to Lou, daughter of Shores Hunter, of Morgan county, the family being of English extraction.

DAGGETT, Aaron S., soldier, was born at Greene Corner, Me., June 14, 1839. He is descended from an ancient and honorable paternal ancestry, having an established record as far back as A. D. 1100. His mother was Dorcas, daughter of Simon Dearborn, a lineal descendant of Gen. Henry Dearborn. His more immediate ancestors came from Old 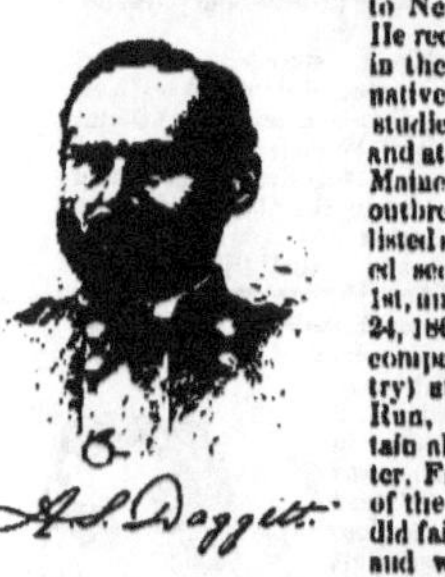 to New England about 1630. He received his early education in the common schools of his native town, continuing his studies at Monmouth Academy and at the Maine Wesleyan and Maine State Seminaries. At the outbreak of the civil war he enlisted as a private, was appointed second lieutenant on May 1st, and first lieutenant on May 24, 1861. He commanded his company (E. 5th Maine infantry) at the first battle of Bull Run, and was promoted captain about three weeks thereafter. From this first engagement of the regiment Capt. Daggett did faithful and gallant service, and was promoted major on Apr. 14, 1863. On Jan. 18, 1865, he was commissioned lieutenant-colonel of the 5th regiment, U. S. veteran volunteers, Hancock corps. He was brevetted colonel and brigadier-general of volunteers, March 13, 1867, for "gallant and meritorious services during the war," and received the brevets of major U. S. army for "gallant and meritorious services at the battle of Rappahannock Station, Va.," Nov. 7, 1863, and lieutenant-colonel for "gallant and meritorious services in the battle of the Wilderness, Va." Immediately after the battle of Rappahannock Station, the captured trophies, flags, cannons, etc., were escorted by those who had been most conspicuous in the action to Gen. Meade's headquarters, Col. Daggett being in command of the battalion of his brigade, having been chosen by Gen. Upton, who wrote of him as follows: "In the assault at Rappahannock Station, Col. Daggett's regiment captured over 500 prisoners. In the assault at Spottsylvania Court House, May 10th, his regiment lost six out of seven captains, the seventh being killed on May 12th, at the 'angle,' or the point where the tree was shot down by musketry, on which ground the regiment fought from 9:30 A. M. until 5:30 P. M., when it was relieved. On all these occasions Col. Daggett was under my immediate command, and fought with distinguished bravery." Gen. Upton also wrote to the governor of Maine as follows: "Maj. Daggett served his full term in this brigade with honor both to himself and state, and won the reputation of being a brave, reliable, and efficient officer. His promotion to a colonelcy would be a great benefit to the service, while the honor of his state could scarcely be entrusted to safer hands." Col. Daggett was subsequently recommended for promotion by Gens. Meade, Hancock, Wright, and D. A. Russell. He was in every battle and campaign in which the 6th corps, army of the Potomac, was engaged, from the first Bull Run to Petersburg, and was twice slightly wounded. On July 28, 1866, without his knowledge or solicitation, he was appointed a captain in the regular army, on recommendation of Gen. Grant; has since been promoted major, and lieutenant-colonel. In the regular service he has won the reputation of being a fine tactician, and of being well versed in military law. Not only as a soldier, but in many other ways has Gen. Daggett distinguished himself. As a public speaker, the following was said of him by the Rev. S. S. Cummings, of Boston: "It was my privilege and pleasure to listen to an address delivered by Gen. A. S. Daggett on Memorial Day of 1891. I had anticipated something able and instructive, but it far exceeded my fondest expectations." Gen. Daggett is noted for his courteous and genial manner, and his sterling integrity of character. He is a member of the Presbyterian church.

FREY, Henry B., lumberman, was born in Crawford county, Pa., Oct. 5, 1845. His paternal ancestors in America were Pennsylvania Dutch, while his mother's family are of New England Puritan stock. Both parents were born in Crawford county, and farmers. The son was brought up on the farm, and inured to hard work, interrupted by attendance at the district school in winter. When the boy was thirteen years old the father died, leaving his mother and two younger children, with a farm greatly burdened with debt. The farm was sold, and the family broken up, the son going to a farm about twenty miles from his old home, where he lived and labored until 1862, when the farmer enlisted in the army, and the boy, then seventeen years old, was left in charge of the farm, which he conducted for two years. In March, 1864, he enlisted as a soldier in the 2d Pennsylvania cavalry, and served until the close of the war. On returning to Pennsylvania he determined to go West, and located in Saginaw, Mich., where he found employment at lumbering for one year. He then removed to St. Anthony Falls, Minn., where he worked in the saw-

mills and the lumber district up the river. He went into the lumbering business on his own account in 1870, the business being known as Patten & Frey, Minneapolis. In October, 1882, he purchased his partner's interest, and combined it with the firm of Nelson, Tenney & Co., uniting manufacturing with the lumbering business. In 1893 their mills cut over 100,000,000 feet of lumber. In 1894 the business was further consolidated, and is known as the Minnesota Logging Co., which corporation controls one-half of the timber in Northern Minnesota, and owns the Brainerd and Northern Minnesota Railroad, which is being pushed into the woods as the timber is cut, and transferred over its route to the Mississippi river, and to market. Mr. Frey is recognized as one of the sterling business men of Minneapolis, and besides attending to his large private interests, gives much time and aid to the furtherance of all movements calculated to benefit the city and body politic.

RUCKER, Howard Lewis, educator, was born on a farm near Jacksonville, Morgan co., Ill., Jan. 12, 1852, son of Harris Ahmed and Sarah Fletcher Rucker. His paternal grandfather, Ahmed Rucker, lived in Kentucky, and was a Methodist minister in Virginia and Kentucky. Earlier ancestors came from Lorraine, France, and were among the early settlers in Virginia. His maternal grandfather, John Rucker, was a Methodist clergyman in Amherst county, Va. His maternal grandmother, Betsy Burton, was born in Orange county, Va. Her mother came from Wales. In 1856 young Rucker removed with his parents to Clinton, De Witt co., Ill., where he spent the next six years in school. During the succeeding nine years Mr. Rucker's time was employed in farm work, a part of each year being devoted to schooling under the best teachers he could find. In 1872 he took a position in a district school, though his slight frame and youthful appearance made the trustees doubtful as to the applicant filling the position, the boys having proved too unruly for his predecessor, but young Rucker proved perfectly satisfactory. He spent two years in teaching, then entered a drug store, and at the end of six months his employer supplied the capital and established him in business at Kenney, Ill., giving him unlimited time in which to repay the funds advanced. At the expiration of two years he repaid the loan and sold out the drug business. In 1876 he married Alice Trowbridge, of Kenney, and removed to Ashland, Cass co., Ill. He spent some months in the commission business, and a term as teacher. With O. W. Clark he established a business college at Mattoon, Ill. In 1880. From that time Prof. Rucker devoted himself to this work, and has organized the following business schools: Mendota, Ill., 1883; Marshalltown, Ia., 1884; Grand Island, Neb. 1885; Minneapolis, Minn., 1886; Aberdeen, S. D., 1888; Grand Forks, N. D., and Brainerd, Minn., 1889; Menominee, Mich., Marinette, and West Superior, Wis., 1890; Stillwater, Minn., Mankato and Austin, Minn., 1891; Fargo, N. D., Merrill and Portage, Wis., 1892; Menomonie, Neenah, and Kenosha, Wis., and Boone, Ia., 1893; and Galena, Ill., 1894. All except two of the above were in successful operation in 1895. He resides in Minneapolis, and is president of the University of Commerce and Finance there. In the various schools established by Pres. Rucker, more than 10,000 pupils have been under instruction. This work has been accomplished without a dollar of endowment. To these thousands of young people the educational work has proved an inestimable boon. Mr. Rucker has made large donations in the form of scholarships to pastors and religious societies, to be given out at their discretion, and he has extended his work into fields hitherto unoccupied.

GREENWOOD, John, jurist, was born in Providence, R. I., Nov. 6, 1798. At the age of ten years he removed with his father to New York state and commenced preparation for college. He acquired a good knowledge of Latin, Greek, French, and English literature, and attended chemical and philosophical lectures, but, instead of entering college, accepted an invitation to study law in the office of Aaron Burr. In three years he made such rapid progress as to be given the preparation of the cases in Burr's immense chancery practice. He had the opportunity of meeting such men as Chancellor Kent, Chief-Justice Spencer, such lawyers as Josiah Ogden Hoffman and Thomas Addis Emmit and other notables. Completing his legal studies in the office of Eli King of New York city, he was admitted to the bar in October, 1819, and at once opened an office in Nassau street, near Maiden Lane. He entered upon a good practice, which continued to increase, and formed a partnership with a Mr. Everson. In 1823 he removed to Brooklyn, though his business continued principally to lie in New York city until 1837, when his Brooklyn practice had so increased that he gave up his New York office and formed a partnership with Gen. H. B. Duryea. He was a warm advocate of the interests of Brooklyn, and rendered invaluable service in obtaining a city charter against strong opposition in New York city, and on the formation of the government he was selected as city judge. He was corporation counsel in 1842, but in the following year was appointed first judge of the Kings county court, having previously served several years as supreme-court commissioner and master in chancery. His manner as a judge was exceptionally able, and his charges to juries never failed to convey the respect, if not always the assent, of both litigants. His great forte was ability to present a subject to the jury in such form that it could be easily understood. He was not only a good lawyer and judge and fine political speaker, but an admirable orator. His experience of men was wide and his recollections given in conversation were choice bits of narrative and illustrated with a grace and charm which made him a most agreeable companion. He was twice married; first, in 1822, to Catharine Dobblu of New York, who died twelve years after, leaving him two sons, and one daughter; and in 1836 to Miss Lammer, of German extraction, who died in 1881, leaving three daughters and two sons. Judge Greenwood died Dec. 11, 1887, in the ninetieth year of his age.

GREEN, William Henry, clergyman, a distinguished Hebrew scholar, was born at Groveville, near Bordentown, N. J., Jan. 27, 1825. He was graduated at Lafayette College, Easton, Pa., in 1840, was tutor there for two years, 1840–42, and instructor in mathematics for one, 1843–1844; but studied theology in Princeton Theological Seminary, and immediately after his graduation in 1846 was appointed instructor in Hebrew. He was pastor of the Central Presbyterian Church, Philadelphia, 1849–51, and then became professor of Oriental and Old  Testament literature in Princeton Seminary, which position he still holds, having declined the presidency of the university in 1868. He published "A Grammar of the Hebrew Language" (New York, 1861), enlarged edition (1889); "Elementary Hebrew Grammar" (1866), new edition (1871); "The Pentateuch Vindicated from the Aspersions of Bishop Colenso" (1863); "The Argument of the Book of Job Unfolded" (1874); "Moses and the Prophets" (1883); "The Hebrew Feasts in their Relation to Recent Critical Hypotheses Concerning the Pentateuch." He was chairman of the American Old-Testament Co., of the Anglo-American committee on the revision of the authorized translation of the Bible, and received the degree of D.D. from the College of New Jersey in 1857, and that of LL.D., from Rutgers College, New Brunswick, N. J., in 1873.

SHELBY, Joseph, soldier, was born at Lexington, Ky., in 1831. He was educated in the schools of his native place, and when nineteen years old emigrated to Lafayette county, Ind., where he became the owner of a rope factory. He was rapidly growing rich in this business when the outbreak of the Kansas border troubles induced him to side actively with the pro-slavery party. He had hardly resumed his work when the civil war commenced in earnest and he relinquished everything to organize a company of cavalry, which at once marched to Independence, Mo., and soon afterward joined Gen. Sterling Price's forces in the western part of that state. The subsequent history of Gen. Shelby's military career is the history of the entire war west of the Mississippi river. He was an active participant in every hard-fought battle, and was conspicuous as a raider, many of the most important and terrific raids of Gen. Price's army being under his command. In 1862 he became colonel of cavalry, in January, 1863, colonel in command of a brigade, and in May, 1864, a brigadier-general. At the battle of Pea Ridge, March 4, 1864, Gen. Shelby particularly distinguished himself, as he did also at Cone Hill, Westport, and at Newtonia, Ark., where the last battle of the war west of the Mississippi was fought. At the close of the war, when Kirby Smith, in command of the department, was anxious to surrender, Gen. Shelby was a zealous advocate of further resistance. His protest was unavailing, however, and the surrender was made at Shreveport, La., and the army disbanded. Gen. Shelby then gathered about him 600 men, for the most part Missourians, devoted to their leader, and determined to go into Mexico and take part in the contest then raging between Maximilian and Juarez. They made a journey across Texas that was memorable for the entire absence of depredations or other warlike accompaniments. Once in Mexico they allied themselves with the imperialists, although Gen. Shelby was later invited to the command of the states of Nueva Leon and Coahuila. Had this latter offer been accepted, thousands of Confederates would in all probability have joined him, and with such a force he might have been able to save Maximilian or to have become a power in Mexico's affairs. As it was, his services were refused by Maximilian, and giving up all idea of further military life, his men entered heartily into the colonization schemes. Gen. Shelby, with headquarters at Cordova, became a large freight contractor. Among those in the colony with him were Gen. Sterling Price, Gen. Stephens of Lee's staff, Gov. Reynolds, Gov. Allen of Louisiana, Gen. Lyons of Kentucky, and Gen. McCausland of Virginia. Freighting soon proved unprofitable, however, and Gen. Shelby went to Vera Cruz, where a vessel was fitted out for him, and he was instructed to sail for Havana in furtherance of the colonization plan. He loaded his ship with agricultural implements exported from America and returned to Mexico. Meanwhile Maximilian, whose forces were meeting with defeat on every side, sent for Shelby and asked him how many American soldiers he could now summon to his assistance. "Not a corporal's guard," replied the general, "you are too late." In 1867, Gen. Shelby returned to the United States and to his home in Lafayette county, Mo. Later he removed to Bates county, where he now resides. In March, 1894, Gen. Shelby was appointed by Pres. Cleveland U. S. marshal for the western district of Missouri, at Kansas City. During the great railroad strike of 1894, when asked by Gov. Stone what right he had to appoint U. S. deputy marshals to protect railroad property, he made this patriotic and characteristic reply: "I am acting under the instructions of the attorney-general of the United States; ask him." His reputation for courage and efficiency has lost nothing by his return to allegiance to, and his acceptance of office under, the U. S. government. Gen. Shelby is a thorough Southerner, both in sentiment and appearance. Although he has been in comparative retirement since the war, he has kept in touch with the political issues of the day, and is known throughout his state as an ardent Democrat. In 1858 he married Miss Betty Shelby. Of his eight living children, his oldest son, Orville, resides in Oklahoma, and the second, Joseph, is a resident of Kansas City, holding a position in the grain-inspecting office.

WILLIAMS, James Baker, manufacturer, was born in Lebanon, Conn., Feb. 2, 1818, in the house which has been the home of his ancestors for nearly two centuries, and is still standing. This house was, during his ministry of fifty-four years, the home of Rev. Solomon Williams, D. D., (first cousin of Jonathan Edwards the elder), who was the theological perceptor of the first Gov. Jonathan Trumbull. During the revolution a regiment of French cavalry was quartered upon the premises. It was also the birthplace of Rev. Eliphalet Williams, of East Hartford, Ezekiel Williams of Wethersfield, and of William Williams. Our subject was the son of Solomon and Martha (Baker) Williams, the former being for many years a manufacturer of gunpowder. His father was a student of Yale with the Rev. Dr. Porter of Farmington, Conn., (father of the late Pres. Porter), and Gov. Joseph Trumbull, but on account of illness did not complete his course. His paternal ancestor, Robert Williams, came from Yarmouth or Norwich, England, and settled in Roxbury, Mass., now a part of Boston, about the year 1634. Dr. Joseph Baker, his maternal grandfather, was a surgeon of the Connecticut troops in the revolutionary war under Gen. Putnam. His ancestry were connected, both directly and collaterally, with some of the most distinguished revolutionary and colonial characters, among others Gov. Welles of Connecticut and Col. Ephraim Williams, the founder of Williams College, Rev. Elisha Williams, third president of Yale College, and his brother, Rev. Solomon Williams, from whom he is in direct line of descent, as was his father's uncle, William Williams, one of the signers of the Declaration of Independence, and his father's cousin, Thos. S. Williams, late chief justice of Connecticut. The educational opportunities of the subject of this notice were necessarily limited, and the greater part of his education was obtained by close study at home after the day's work was over, continued during many years. At the age of sixteen he became clerk in a country store at Manchester; at the age of twenty engaged on his own account in the drug business; and two years later added the manufacture of shaving soap. In order to obtain better business facilities, he removed in 1847 to Glastonbury, where soon afterwards his brother William became associated with him under the firm name of J. B. Williams & Co. From a small beginning this enterprise soon obtained rank as the leader in its line. In 1885 the business became a joint stock family corporation with Mr. Williams as its president. Mr Williams is still active in the counsel and management of the great industry established by him over half a century ago, and takes pardonable pride in the immense proportions the business has attained. While he has had no taste for public life, he has several times represented his town in the state legislature. He is president of the Williams Brothers' Manufacturing Co., manufacturers of silver and nickel ware; is officially connected with the Vermont Farm Machine Co., of Bellows Falls, Vt., and was president of the latter corporation for a number of years. Mr. Williams has been deeply interested in religious work for more than half a century, is an active member of the First Congregational Church, and since 1859 has been one of its deacons. In 1846 Mr. Williams was married to Jerusha, daughter of David Hubbard, who died in 1860. In 1869 he married Julia, sister of his first wife. Two of his sons, David, who has represented his town in the state legislature, and Samuel, are officially connected with the J. B. Williams' Co., and another, James, is superintendent of the Williams Bros.' Manufacturing Co.

WELBY, Amelia B. Coppuck, poet, was born in St. Michael's, Md., Feb. 3, 1819. While she was an infant she was taken to Baltimore by her father, who was a journeyman mechanic, and remained there until 1834, when the family removed to Louisville, Ky. Here she was surrounded by a great deal that was grand and beautiful in nature, and developed her poetical talent. In 1837, under the name of "Amelia," she began to contribute her poems to the Louisville "Journal." They attracted much attention for their sweetness and melody, and she published her first volume, entitled "Poems by Amelia," before she was eighteen years of age. Her education was not thorough, her mind was not disciplined by study, nor was her reading extensive; yet, in spite of all these disadvantages, her poetry is perfect in rhythm and harmony. In 1838 she married George B. Welby, a prominent merchant of Louisville. A slight imperfection in her upper lip, which gave a peculiar piquancy to her expression, greatly added to her personal charms. E. A. Poe says; "None equal her in the riches and positive merits of rhythmical variety, conception, and invention." George D. Prentice and R. W. Griswold were unmeasured in the praise of her work. A second edition of her works appeared in 1846 since when numerous editions have appeared. She died in Louisville, May 3, 1852.

ALLEN, Elizabeth Akers, author, was born in Strong, Me., Oct. 9, 1832. Her ancestors were of the pioneer settlers of New England. Thomas Mayhew, the first governor of Martha's Vineyard, being a direct ancestor of her paternal great-grandfather, Thomas Chase, who was himself one of Paul Jones' men. He shipped on board one of the first privateers fitted out in Massachusetts in 1775, and was one of the 400 Americans captured on the high seas and imprisoned at Plymouth, England. In the "Old Mill prison" for two years, and exchanged through the efforts of Benjamin Franklin, the minister to the French court. They went to L'Orient, France, and a crew, among whom was Mr. Chase, was selected from them by John Paul Jones, and shipped on the Bon Homme Richard. He made with Jones six

or seven cruises. Elizabeth Chase began to write at a very early age, her first attempts being kept secret from her friends. When her work was discovered and published without her knowledge she was a mere child. When fifteen years old, she began to offer articles to the press, under a feigned name. These were collected in a book, under the title of "Forest Buds," by "Florence Percy," a name which she has ever since tried to shake off. She afterwards wrote for the "Atlantic Monthly," beginning when that magazine was under the editorial charge of James Russell Lowell. In 1860 she married Paul Akers, the sculptor. He died the next year, and left her penniless, homeless, and broken in health and spirit. The war was in progress, and her friends, mostly resident on the Southern side, could not be reached. The few marbles left by her husband could not, in those exigent times, be sold. She labored on, however, and in 1866 Ticknor & Fields, of Boston, published her second volume of poems. She included in this volume her "Rock me to Sleep, Mother," which has been many times set to music, and become very popular. It was first published in the Philadelphia "Saturday Evening Post," the manuscript having being sent by her to that paper in 1860, when she was in Rome. Its popularity brought out several claimants of authorship, and the matter became a subject of much controversy. The facts, however, never admitted of much doubt. In 1865 she married E. M. Allen, a merchant of New York city, but retained "Elizabeth Akers" as a pen-name. In 1874 she entered, as literary editor, the office of the "Daily Advertiser," Portland, Me., an evening paper, owned and edited by H. W. Richardson. Here she worked nearly seven years, supplying at times all the departments of office work, from that of editor-in-chief to that of proof-reader. In 1885, she sent out a volume of domestic prose sketches, a volume of verses, "The Silver Bridge," and later, another volume of verses, entitled "The High-Top Sweeting." A small collection of her verses was published in Dublin. Mrs. Allen has made three visits to Europe, in the last two visiting out-of-the-way places, and studying the everyday life, manners, and labors of the people. In speaking of her life and its work, she says: "I believe in labor as a saving grace, in equal rights and equal morals for men and women, in the right of women to decline marriage without being killed or ridiculed for it, in the abolition of wife-beating, drunkenness, political corruption, gambling, and custom-houses, and in the prevention of cruelty to all creatures, dumb and otherwise."

AKERS, Benjamin Paul, sculptor, was born in Saccarappa, Me., July 10, 1825. His father was a wood-turner of limited means. The son was nicknamed St. Paul for his serious cast of mind, and adopted the name Paul by which he is known to the art world. After attending the local public schools he worked for his father six years, and first developed his artistic ability in original designs for ornamental woodwork. He at this time exhibited a talent for portraiture, cutting out of a bit of marble with a carpenter's chisel the features of a neighbor before ever having seen a bust or a bas-relief. It was not until he was nineteen that he had access to a library of books, and he eagerly availed himself of the opportunity. To Hyperion he gives the credit of first arousing his enthusiasm for art. After reading Plato, Aristotle, and Dante, he devoted himself to German and French literature, and after some crude attempts with both brush and pen, he went to Portland and entered the composing-room of the "Transcript." Notwithstanding his love for literature he felt that this was not his vocation, and accidentally seeing a marble bust by

Brackett exhibited in a shop window determined that sculpture was the path of his genius. In 1849 he went to Boston, where he received lessons in plaster-casting from Carew. Returing home to Salem Falls he spent the winter upon a bust of the village doctor, producing a marvelous likeness, and later a head of Christ, which was of remarkable impressiveness. This was subsequently ordered in marble by the U. S. minister to the Hague. The following spring he opened a studio in Portland in connection with Tilton, the landscape artist, where he devoted himself to executing portrait busts.

Among the busts which aided his reputation are Longfellow, Samuel Appleton, Prof. Cleveland, and Prof. Sheppard of Boston, John Neal, Rev. Dr. Nichols of Portland, and Gov. Gilman of New Hampshire. He also produced some ideal heads, notably "Charlotte Corday." In 1852 Akers went to Florence, Italy, where he executed two bas-reliefs, "Night" and "Morning," for Samuel Appleton, and several portrait busts. He also wrote critical essays on art and contemporary artists, which revealed such knowledge of the principles and requirements of art that they attracted marked attention. In 1858 he returned to Portland, where he modeled his first statue, "Benjamin in Egypt," which was exhibited at the Crystal Palace in New York, and unfortunately destroyed when that building was burned. During the winter of 1854 he lived in Washington, D. C., where he executed busts of Pres. Pierce, Judge McLean, Edward Everett, Gerrit Smith, and a medallion head of Sam Houston, which particularly attracted attention and praise. He also modeled an ideal head, "The Drowned Girl," which was a work of exquisite delicacy, designed to be one of a series to illustrate Hord's "Bridge of Sighs." He felt that he belonged in Rome, and in 1855, taking with him a number of busts to be cut in marble, he embarked for Italy and took a studio in the Via del Crecle, which became immortalized through Hawthorne's "Marble Fawn," Kenyon's studio being none other than Paul Akers's. In it also are described his "Milton," and the "Dead Pearl Diver," now owned by the city of Portland. His growing reputation necessitated larger quarters, and he took rooms once occupied by the famous Canova. While in those rooms he conceived and executed his finest works, among which are "Peace," "Una and the Lion," "Girl Pressing Grapes," "Isaiah," "Diana and Endymion," and "St. Elizabeth of Hungary." During this time he obtained permission from the authorities to make a cast of the mutilated bust of Cicero. He restored the eyebrow and ears and modeled a neck and bust. In 1856 he traveled in Switzerland, Germany, and France, and spent four months in Great Britain, where he made studies for his colossal head of Milton, which when completed was pronounced "a poet's ideal of a poet." Browning said of it, "It is Milton the man-angel." He devoted much time to the study of painting, architecture, and geometry, even formulating an elementary work with diagrams in color. He realized that science is a requisite of art, appreciated that mysterious something, in what is called consummate art, which still eludes the touch of science and, child-like, plays with powers which terrify the intellectual world. A certain broad humanity and catholicism characterized him, and took form in an endeavor to establish in New York a free gallery to contain copies in marble of the chief works of ancient art. But in the midst of his plans, his health, which had always been delicate, began to fall, and being obliged to suspend work he returned in 1858 for a year's visit to his home and went back to his work with health partially restored, but with a courage surpassing his strength, and completed a statue of Commodore Perry for Mr. Belmont, which was placed in Central Park. In 1860 he was again forced to recruit his failing health, and returned to Portland, where he married Elizabeth Chace, who under the pen-name of "Florence Percy," was gaining reputation as a poet and author, and has since attained wkle fame as Elizabeth Akers Allen (q. v.) Too feeble for work, his final effort, a bust of the Rev. John Frothingham, was finished with the aid of his brother Charles. Paul Akers's career was remarkable in that he awakened to a consciousness of his powers amid surroundings in great contrast with his nature, and achieved eminence through the strength of the innate force within him. He died with his mind filled with conceptions of new and greater works, and as he expressed it, "just begun." Under his supervision a large number of copies in marble of the famous works of the Vatican and the Capitol were made for Edward H. King of Newport, Conn., who afterwards presented the collection to the Redwood Library of that place. A visit to Philadelphia upon the advice of his physician did not benefit him, and he died there, May 21, 1861.

HORTON, Albert, Howell, jurist, was born near Brookfield, N. Y., March 12, 1837, youngest son of Dr. Harvey A., and Mary (Bennett) Horton. The ancestor of the American branch of the Horton family was Barnabas, born in Mously, Leicestershire, England, July 16, 1600, who came to Hampton, Mass., between 1633 and 1638, removed to New Haven, Conn., in 1640, and later to Southold, L. I. After a preparatory course in the public school, and in the academy at Goshen, N. Y., he entered the University of Michigan at Ann Arbor in 1856, but was compelled to leave in his second year by reason of an affection of his eyes. He studied law and was admitted to practice in 1860 in Brooklyn, N. Y. The same year he removed from Goshen, N. Y., to Atchison, Kans. In April, 1861, he was elected city attorney of Atchison upon the Republican ticket, and in the following September was appointed district judge of the second judicial district of the state by Gov. Charles Robinson, a position to which he was twice elected without opposition, and which he resigned to resume the practice of his profession. From 1861 to 1864 he was one of the editors of the "Weekly Champion," a newspaper published at Atchison.

In 1868 he was a Republican presidential elector, his services being rewarded in May of the following year by his appointment by Pres. Grant to be U. S. attorney for Kansas. In November, 1872, he was elected a member of the house of representatives of Kansas from Atchison, and in November, 1876, state senator from Atchison county, which position he resigned Jan. 1, 1877, to accept an appointment by Gov. Osborn to the position of chief justice to the supreme court of Kansas. The same year he was elected chief justice to serve an unexpired term; in 1878 he was re-elected for the full term of six years; and was re-nominated and re-elected in 1884 and 1890. He was long president of the Alumni Association of Michigan University for the Southwest. In June, 1889, the university conferred upon him the honorary degree of LL. D. On Apr. 30, 1895, he resigned his position of chief justice to resume the practice of his profession at Topeka, Kans., as a member of the law firm of Waggener, Horton & Orr. He was married on May 28, 1864, to Anna Amelia Robertson of Middletown, N. Y., by whom he had four children. His wife dying in 1883, he was married a second time, Nov. 18, 1887, to Mary A., widow of Addison Prescott, one of the pioneer bankers of Topeka.

SLAVENS, Luther Clay, lawyer, was born in Putnam county, Ind., Aug. 13, 1836, son of Hiram and Sarah (Holland) Slavens. His parents were
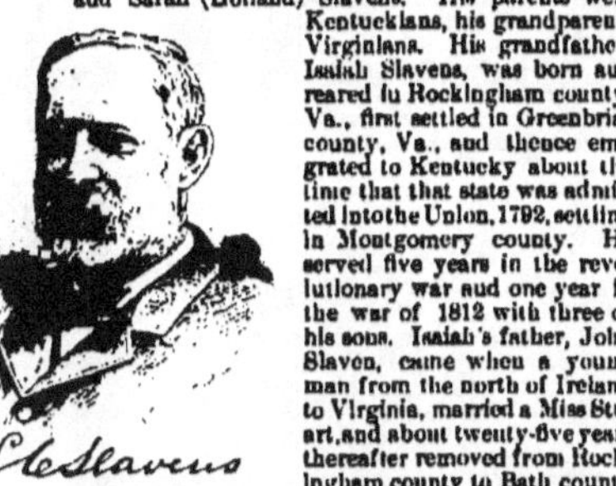
Kentuckians, his grandparents Virginians. His grandfather, Isaiah Slavens, was born and reared in Rockingham county, Va., first settled in Greenbriar county, Va., and thence emigrated to Kentucky about the time that that state was admitted into the Union, 1792, settling in Montgomery county. He served five years in the revolutionary war and one year in the war of 1812 with three of his sons. Isaiah's father, John Slaven, came when a young man from the north of Ireland to Virginia, married a Miss Stuart, and about twenty-five years thereafter removed from Rockingham county to Bath county near the headwaters of Jackson river. Luther Clay Slavens passed his early life upon a farm. He was educated at Depauw University, Greencastle, Ind., graduating in the classical department in 1858, and in the law department in 1860. On Jan. 8, 1861, he was married to Sallie Boggs, daughter of Isaac Shelby of Tippecanoe county, Ind. Her grandfather, David Shelby, was also raised in Rockingham county, Va. He was one of the first settlers of Pickaway county, O., represented that county in the Ohio legislature over twenty years, and was a first cousin of Gen. Isaac Shelby of revolutionary fame, the first governor of Kentucky. Soon after his marriage to Miss Shelby, Mr. Slavens removed to Covington, Ind., where he practised his profession until the close of the civil war, when he removed to Kansas City, Mo. Here he has steadily continued the practice of the law, and justly ranks among the leading lawyers. He has never sought nor held political office. He was once appointed city counsellor of Kansas City, and served for one year. He was a member of the national Republican convention at Chicago, in 1880, and was one of the "306" who from the first ballot to the last steadily voted for the nomination of Gen. Grant. He has for several years been a member of the board of trustees of the Syracuse University of Syracuse, N. Y., having supervision of its legal business respecting investments in the West. Both he and his wife, as were their parents before them, are members of the Methodist Episcopal church.

HOWARD, James Leland, manufacturer and merchant, was born in Windsor, Vt., Jan. 10, 1818, son of Leland Howard, a prominent Baptist clergyman of rare abilities. His paternal ancestors came to this country from Swansea, England, and were among the original property holders of the town of Milford and Mendon, Mass. Benjamin Howard, his great-grandfather, was born in Mendon, Aug. 23, 1713, but in the latter part of his life removed to Jamaica, Vt., where he died Oct. 29, 1783. Calvin Howard, son of Benjamin, and father of Leland, was

born in Mendon in 1762, and removed, with his father to Jamaica, where he lived a farmer. Leland was born at Jamaica, October, 1798. He married Lucy, daughter of Capt. Isaiah Mason, of Ira, Vt., and James Leland Howard was the eldest of their eight children. He received a common school and academic education, and in 1833 entered upon a mercantile life in the city of New York. Five years later he removed to Hartford, Conn., where in 1841 he formed a partnership with Edmund Hurlburt, for the manufacture and sale of carriage and saddlery hardware. Mr. Howard eventually bought his partner's interest, and after conducting the business for a short time alone, he took his brothers into partnership with him under the firm name of James L. Howard & Co. This firm was one of the first in the United States to engage in the manufacture of railway car trimmings, and to this business the firm devoted its entire energies and resources with marked success. In 1846 the firm built an extensive block and factory on Asylum street, where the business of railway supplies is still carried on. In 1876, the state having granted a special charter, the partnership was changed into a corporation retaining the old name of James L. Howard & Co., and Mr. Howard became and still remains its president. Mr. Howard is eminently a man of affairs, and the financial and business interests of Hartford have always engaged his earnest attention. He has been a director of the Phœnix Bank since 1854; was one of the incorporators and has been a director of the Travelers' Insurance Co. from the date of its organization in 1864; is vice-president of the Hartford County Fire Insurance Co.; and since 1880 has been president of the Hartford City Gas Light Co. He is also a director in several manufacturing companies. In February, 1846, Mr. Howard was appointed agent of the Mutual Benefit Life Insurance Co. at Hartford, and in his counting-room were held some of the first conferences which resulted in the organization of the Connecticut Mutual Life Insurance Co. Always interested in political affairs, though never seeking office, he was elected to many official positions, acting

successively as councilman, alderman, police commissioner, park commissioner, and for many years as member of the high school committee; and also as member of the building committee, and treasurer of the moneys appropriated for the erection of the present Hartford High School building. Originally a Whig, he became a Republican when the party was organized in 1856, and has always remained an earnest and steadfast supporter of its principles. In 1876 he was chosen to the office of lieutenant-governor of Connecticut. With that courtesy and fairness for which he is everywhere respected, he presided over the deliberations of the senate with dignity, and retired from office holding the esteem of his associates regardless of party lines. In early life he became a member of the First Baptist Church of Hartford, but his religious activities have extended beyond the limits of his own church to numerous organizations of the Baptist denomination. He was the first president of the Connecticut Baptist Social Union, and held that office by successive re-elections for several years; is president of the board of trustees of the Connecticut Literary Institute at Suffield, Ct., was president of the Connecticut Baptist Convention from 1871 to 1876; of the American Baptist Publication Society from 1873 to 1877; of the American Baptist

Home Mission Society from 1881 to 1884; of the American Baptist Historical Society from 1890 to 1893; is president of the Connecticut Baptist Education Society, and a member of the Board of Managers of the American Baptist Missionary Union. He is a trustee of Brown University, Providence, R. I.; of Shaw University, Raleigh, N. C.; of Spelman Seminary, Atlanta, Ga.; of the Newton Theological Seminary, Newton, Mass., and of the American Baptist Education Society. In 1894 Brown University conferred on him the honorary degree of A. M. In June, 1842, Mr. Howard was married to Anna, daughter of Joseph Gilbert, some time treasurer of the state of Connecticut. They had five children, three of whom are now living. Amid all his many cares of business, he has always retained a strong love for his family and its home life, in which he has found the source of his greatest happiness.

WILKINS, Beriah, financier, congressman, and editor of the "Washington Post," was born in Union county, O., July 10, 1846, of English and Scotch ancestry. His grandfather, Beriah P. Wilkins, a native of Saratoga county, N. Y., was one of the pioneer settlers in Ohio and became prominent in the public affairs of the state during the early part of the present century. His father, Alfred F. Wilkins, was an active and influential man, and filled various positions of trust and responsibility. As a civil engineer he assisted in laying out the national road, one of the great public highways in the internal improvements of the country before the time of railroads, and which extended from Washington city to the borders of Indiana. He had also much to do in central Ohio, with surveying the allotment of land in that region, made by the general government to the state of Virginia. He was married in 1848, to Harriet Stuart, a descendant of the Scotch Covenanters. The son obtained his education in the public schools of Union county, and was graduated from the High School at Maryville, O. He then engaged in mercantile pursuits, and during the civil war, although a minor, served a term of enlistment in the army. Very early in his career he developed a marked interest in financial matters, and in 1869, organized at Uhrichsville, O., the Farmers' and Merchants' Bank, of which he was cashier and general manager the succeeding twelve years. In the meantime he took a large interest in politics, made a diligent study of current questions of public interest, served as a member of the Democratic state central committee, and in 1879 was elected to the Ohio state senate. In 1882 he was chosen to represent the sixteenth Ohio district in the forty-eighth congress, and was re-elected to the forty-ninth and fiftieth congresses. His knowledge of monetary matters and his successful experience as a banker eminently fitted him for the responsible position of chairman of the committee on banking and currency, which he filled with recognized ability. In January, 1889, before the expiration of his third term in congress, Mr. Wilkins, in connection with Frank Hatton, purchased the "Washington Post," the leading morning newspaper at the national capital, established in 1877 as a Democratic journal. Under the new ownership it became independent in politics and entered upon a broader and more successful career than it had ever before experienced. It at once attracted attention on account of the judicious management, the force and originality of its editorials, and its comprehensive news service. It grew rapidly in circulation, influence, and popularity, and soon took rank with the leading newspapers in this country. It has the service of the New York Associated Press and the United Press Association, thanks to which, together with its special service, its news facilities are unsurpassed. Probably no newspaper in this country is more influential in moulding public opinion on current questions of general interest than the "Post." The prosperity of this journal is largely due to the executive and administrative ability of Mr. Wilkins.

BERWALD, William Henry, was born at Schwerin-Mecklenburg, North Germany, Dec. 26, 1864. He was graduated from the public schools of his native town at eighteen years of age, and studied music at Munich and Stuttgart under Prof. Joseph Rheinburg, the well-known German composer and teacher. He then entered the Conservatory of Music at Stuttgart. He was conductor of orchestra and chorus for two years in Russia, after which, in September, 1892, he came to America and entered the Syracuse University 

as instructor upon the piano and professor in the history and theory of music. In June, 1893, he was made full professor.

BURRITT, Elihu, reformer, was born at New Britain, Conn., Dec. 8, 1810, being the youngest son in a family of ten children equally divided between the two sexes. The first traceable American ancestor was William Burritt, a native of Glamorganshire, Wales, who settled in Stratford, Conn., and died there in 1651. His descendants at the time of the war of the revolution took opposite sides, one branch going to Canada with other loyalists. Both the grandfather and father of the subject of this sketch, each bearing the same Christian name, took part in the struggle. The father, like most of the early settlers in New England, plied his trade, that of a shoemaker, in winter and handled the plow and sickle in summer. Young Elihu left the common school at the time of his father's death in 1825, and was some time after apprenticed to a blacksmith. From an early age he displayed an extraordinary capacity for mathematics. He received strong encouragement from one of his brothers, Elijah Burritt, who was himself a fine mathematician and an astronomer of much eminence, and under the impetus of his cordial interest Elihu, at the age of twenty-one, began his first systematic course of self-instruction. He acquired a strong liking for languages, and studied with such intense zeal after the close of his apprenticeship that at the end of a year his health gave way, forcing him to abandon the calling of a teacher which he had begun under his brother, who kept a small boarding school. He mastered Homer's "Iliad" with the aid solely of a Greek lexicon with Latin definitions, and devoted the winter of 1832 to the study of various other tongues. Then for a short time he became a commercial traveler with the idea of benefiting his health, and subsequently established himself in the grocery trade, but this venture was broken up by the commercial crash of 1837. After walking to Boston with the idea of taking ship to England and using his earnings to buy Oriental works there, he went to Worcester, Mass., and returned to the anvil and to his studies, which he prosecuted with increased energy with the help of books from the valuable library of the Antiquarian Society of that town, and in the course of a year or two had acquainted himself not only with most of the languages of Europe, but with many of the Oriental tongues, including Hebrew, Chaldaic, Syriac, and Ethiopic. These varied acquirements, so astonishing in a man of his youth and humble station, soon procured him the familiar appellation of the "Learned Blacksmith," and led to his being requested to deliver a lecture in the winter of 1841. This he did, taking for his subject "Application and Genius," and contending that genius, so far from being inborn, does not really exist, and that all attainments are nothing more than the result of persistent will and application, thus giving utterance to what is at least a great half-truth. The anti-slavery movement was then beginning to gather strength, and Elihu Burritt at once became a warm advocate of its doctrines; and so, his thoughts coming to be drawn into the field of active philanthropy, his studies in languages were after awhile perforce discontinued. Starting to write a description of the analogy which he perceived between the configuration and functions of the earth and those of the human frame, the conviction grew upon him that differences in the climate and natural resources of countries lying in the same parallel were preordained, through the necessity of an interchange of each country's productions, to form a

natural bond of union between them. This was the awakening in Burritt's mind of an idea which was thenceforth to shape the actions of his whole life—that of universal brotherhood. He thereupon prepared a radical "Peace Lecture" out of the subject, and delivered it before a Baptist society in the Tremont Theatre at Boston. He then started a weekly paper at Worcester, calling it the "Christian Citizen," advocating anti-slavery, peace, temperance, and self-culture. In 1846, in consequence of the part which he played in the settlement, through correspondence between the com-

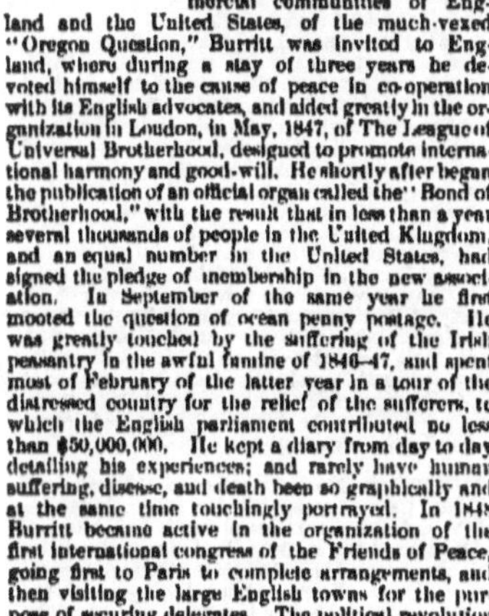

mercial communities of England and the United States, of the much-vexed "Oregon Question," Burritt was invited to England, where during a stay of three years he devoted himself to the cause of peace in co-operation with its English advocates, and aided greatly in the organization in London, in May, 1847, of The League of Universal Brotherhood, designed to promote international harmony and good-will. He shortly after began the publication of an official organ called the "Bond of Brotherhood," with the result that in less than a year several thousands of people in the United Kingdom, and an equal number in the United States, had signed the pledge of membership in the new association. In September of the same year he first mooted the question of ocean penny postage. He was greatly touched by the suffering of the Irish peasantry in the awful famine of 1846–47, and spent most of February of the latter year in a tour of the distressed country for the relief of the sufferers, to which the English parliament contributed no less than $50,000,000. He kept a diary from day to day detailing his experiences; and rarely have human suffering, disease, and death been so graphically and at the same time touchingly portrayed. In 1848 Burritt became active in the organization of the first international congress of the Friends of Peace, going first to Paris to complete arrangements, and then visiting the large English towns for the purpose of securing delegates. The political revolution in the French capital, however, caused a postponement and change of locale, and the conference eventually was held at Brussels in September, the Belgian government giving official recognition to it, while both English and Continental journals hailed it as a "Peace Congress." After its close the League of Universal Brotherhood united with the London Peace Society to petition the English parliament through Richard Cobden in favor of international arbitration. When Cobden's motion was finally put in the house of commons, over seventy members voted in its favor, a remarkable tribute to the intrinsic worth of a doctrine then so subversive of all generally received ideas on the subject of war and international rivalry. The second congress was held in Paris in 1849, with Victor Hugo presiding. The great French poet on this occasion made a speech which has since been widely read and quoted, on account of its inspired spirit of prophecy. "A day will come," he declared in tones of earnest conviction, "when those two immense groups, the United States of America and the United States of Europe, will be seen placed in the presence of each other, extending the hand of fellowship across the ocean—exchanging their produce, their commerce, their industries, their arts, their genius—clearing the earth, peopling the desert, improving creation under the eye of the Creator, and uniting for the good of all, these two irresistible and infinite powers—the fraternity of men and the power of God." Shortly afterwards the American reformer returned home and was received with enthusiastic demonstrations of respect and delight. He proceeded on a lecturing tour through most of the states of the Union, returned to Europe, attended the peace congresses at Frankfort-on-the-Main in 1850, London, 1851, Manchester, 1852, and Edinburgh, 1853, meeting everywhere with signs of the increased hold which the doctrines of universal brotherhood and international arbitration had acquired over the minds of all classes. Immediately after the Edinburgh congress he returned to America and devoted himself to agitating ocean penny postage, addressing public meetings in different states, seeking to enlist members of congress in Washington in favor of reform, and then touring the Southern and Western sections of the country on its behalf. Then passing through Canada he obtained petitions to the British parliament in many of the principal cities, and in August, 1854, once more found himself in England. His efforts to arouse public opinion met with such success that the English government made material reductions in the postal charges to Australia, India, Canada, and other colonies, as well as to France. The Crimean war put an end to the movement for universal peace, and Burritt turned his attention to the slavery question in his native land, and while yet in London assumed the editorship of a paper published in Philadelphia, the "Citizen of the World," through the columns of which he advocated compensated emancipation. Recrossing the Atlantic he spent several winters in traveling through the United States, addressing meetings from Maine to Iowa, and called a convention in August, 1856, at Cleveland, O., to which came delegates from various parts of the country, including a few even from the South. A resolution was passed favoring the organization of The National Compensated Emancipation Co. All such schemes were, however, nipped in the bud by John Brown's raid on Harper's Ferry. Burritt's contention was that the extinction of the evil of slavery by compensation "would have recognized the moral complicity of the whole nation in planting and perpetuating it on this continent. It would have been an act of repentance, and the meetest work for repentance the nation could perform. But it was too late. It was too heavy and red to go out in tears. Too late! It had to go out in blood, and the whole nation opened the million sluices of its best life to deepen and widen the costly flood. If, before these sluice-gates were opened to these red streams, so hot with passion, one *bona fide* offer had been made by the North to share with the South the task, cost, and duty of lifting slavery from the bosom of the nation, perhaps thousands who gave up their first-born and youngest-born to death might have looked into that river of blood with more ease and comfort at their hearts. Although the earth has drunk that red river out of human sight, it still runs fresh and full, without the waste of a drop, before the eyes of God; and the patriot, as well as the Christian, might well wish that he could recognize in the stream the shadow of an honest effort on the part of the North to lift the great sin and curse without waiting for such a deluge to sweep them away." Full of grief at the failure of his plans, he then returned to his farm at New Britain. In 1868 he once more crossed to Great Britain, and made long tours on foot through England and Scotland, with the purpose of acquainting himself with the agricultural pursuits and problems of the kingdom, and so enlarging his own and his countrymen's knowledge. He wrote two volumes descriptive of these walks, which were published in London. In 1865, without his solicitation, he was appointed U. S. consular agent at Birmingham, was superseded under Grant's administration, and after a brief visit to Oxford, where he formed the acquaintance of Max Müller, returned to his New England home in 1870, and there spent the declining years of his active and laborious life. Elihu Burritt's character was just such a one as furnishes the best possible kind of model for youth to study and endeavor to emulate. His character was above reproach, his aims of the purest and highest, his will-power indomitable, his appetite for work insatiable. We cannot do better in this connection than quote his own words: "All that I have accomplished, or expect or hope to accomplish, has been, and will be by that plodding, patient, persevering process of accretion which builds the ant-heap, particle by particle, thought by thought, fact by fact. If I was ever actuated by ambition, its highest and warmest aspiration reached no further than the hope to set before the young men of any country an example in employing those invaluable fragments of time called 'odd moments.'" The poet Longfellow has borne his tribute of praise likewise: "I always had a great admiration for the sweetness and simplicity of Mr. Burritt's character, and was in perfect sympathy with him in his work. . . . . Nothing ever came from his pen that was not wholesome and good." Of his unfailing efforts in the cause of peace, to which he devoted the best energies of his life, it is sufficient to say that, if not so successful as he would have wished, they have yet led to very important results, both during and since his life-time. One has only to call to mind the Geneva tribunal, which settled the Alabama difficulties; the Washington treaty, which disposed of a vexed question between England and the United States; the Paris Behring Sea tribunal, which prevented a possible rupture between the same countries over the seal fisheries question; and the still more recent representations of the Powers and the United States to Turkey in favor of an arbitration committee to regulate the Armenian troubles; to perceive how powerful and good has been the life-work of this single-minded and zealous reformer. It remains to be recorded of Elihu Burritt that, unlike most reformers, he was never a bigot; but, broad-minded and charitable, he could respect the opinions of others even when they were diametrically opposed to his own convictions. He had the faculty of mak-

ing friends among all classes, and was in his own person a true apostle of his great creed of the brotherhood of man. His published works are "Sparks from the Anvil" (London, 1845); "Miscellaneous Writings" (1850); "Olive Leaves" (1853); "Thoughts of Things at Home and Abroad" (Boston, 1854); "Handbook of the Nations" (New York, 1856); "A Walk from John O'Groats to Land's End" (London, 1864); "A Walk from London to Land's End and Back" (1864); "The Mission of Great Sufferings" (1867); "Walks in the Black Country" (1868); "Lectures and Speeches" (1869); "Ten Minute Talks" (1873); and "Chips from Many Blocks" (1878). His life has been written by Charles Northend (New York, 1879). He died at his home at New Britain, Conn., March 9, 1879.

KINNEY, Thomas Tallmadge, journalist, was born at Newark, N. J., Aug. 13, 1821, the only son of William Burnet Kinney, who was U. S. minister to the court of Sardinia during the administration of President Taylor. He was graduated at Princeton College in 1841, having developed a strong inclination for natural science during the course, which attracted the attention of Prof. Joseph Henry, whose assistant he became in his senior year, their intimacy subsequently ripening into a life-long friendship. After graduation Mr. Kinney immediately entered the office of J. P. Bradley, afterward associate justice of the U. S. supreme court, and was his first law student. Soon after his admission to the bar Mr. Kinney relinquished the practice of his profession, and entered the field of journalism, reporting the proceedings of the legislature, and the political conventions of the period, for his father's paper, the Newark "Daily Advertiser." He introduced many improvements in the machinery and processes of news-gathering which were novel at the time, and some of which subsequently culminated in the organization of the Associated Press. He afterward became a partner and finally sole proprietor of the "Daily Advertiser." In 1860 he was a dele-

gate to the Republican convention in Chicago, and labored earnestly for the first nomination of President Lincoln, after which he invariably declined political office, including the offer of a foreign mission from President Arthur, afterward repeated by President Harrison. Mr. Kinney was one of the original incorporators, and for many years the president of the New Jersey Society for the Prevention of Cruelty to Animals; a member of the geological board of the state; president of the board of agriculture from 1878-82; trustee of the State Institution for the Deaf and Dumb; a member of the board of proprietors of East Jersey; and a hereditary member of the Society of the Cincinnati, organized by the officers of the revolution. He is also actively identified with many local institutions, being president of the Fidelity Title and Deposit Co., of which he was one of the founders, director in the National State Bank, the City Ice Co., the Electrical Light and Power Co., and other organizations.

CUMMINS, Maria Susanna, author, was born at Salem, Mass., Apr. 9, 1827. Her father, Judge David Cummins, took personal interest in her education, and supervised her studies. Her intimate association with him during her earlier years did much towards determining the direction of her literary work, and his encouragement helped to develop her aspirations.

She attended Mrs. Charles Sedgwick's school at Lenox to finish her education, after which she began to contribute short stories to the "Atlantic" and other magazines. When she was twenty-seven she published "The Lamp Lighter," which was instantly popular, over 40,000 copies being sold within two months. It was republished in England, where it was received with even greater approbation, and the sale reached upward of 120,000 copies. The work is one of the noted successes in American fiction, being exceeded only by novels like "Ben Hur" and "Uncle Tom's Cabin." Had Miss Cummins written nothing else, she had earned her title to fame; but she followed this with "Mabel Vaughan," in 1857, which is by many critics considered even superior to her first book. She followed this with "El Fureidis," a story of Palestine and Syria, in 1860, and "Haunted Hearts," in 1864. Miss Cummins's work had behind it the motive of a strong moral conviction. Her characters were true to life, and by their thoroughly humane quality appealed to the hearts of her readers. She died at Dorchester, Oct. 1, 1866.

HOWARD, Benjamin Chew, congressman, third son of Col. John Howard, was born at Belvedere, Baltimore Co., Md., Nov. 5, 1791. He was for eight years a member of congress and for nearly twenty years the reporter of the supreme court of the United States. In 1861, he was the Democratic candidate for governor of his state, but withdrew his name at the very last moment to prevent a disturbance. The degree of LL.D., was conferred upon him in 1869, by Princeton College, of which he was a graduate. He died on his ancestral estate, Belvedere, March 6, 1872.

BREWSTER, Simon L., banker, son of Elisha Belcher and Eunice (Hull) Brewster, and a descendant of Elder William Brewster, who came over with the Pilgrim Fathers in the Mayflower in 1620, was born in Griswold, Conn., July 27, 1811, and received his education in the common schools. At the age of twenty-one he engaged in manufacturing in Jewett City, Conn., where he continued for about ten years, when he removed to Rochester, N. Y., engaging in merchandizing until 1859, when he retired from business. He had for many years been connected with the Traders' National Bank as one of its directors and as vice-president. In 1863 he was elected president and took charge of the bank. Under his administration the business of the bank grew from a discount line of less than $300,000 to over $3,000,-000; the surplus fund from a few thousand dollars to over $700,-000. During the past twenty-five years, his son, Henry C. Brewster, has been associated with him in the management of the bank, as its cashier. In 1844 he was married to Editha Colvin. In addition to the son above referred to, he has one

daughter who is unmarried. Mr. Brewster has never held any public office, except one term as a member of the board of supervisors of Monroe county. He is at present a director in the Flower City Hotel Co., and a trustee of the First Unitarian Church. The bank of which he is president was first organized as the Eagle Bank of Rochester, and incorporated March 27, 1852. On July 23, 1856, the Manufacturers' Bank of Rochester was organized, and about Apr. 25, 1859, the two banks were consolidated, as the Traders' Bank of Rochester, with a paid-in capital of $250,000. The Traders' Bank was re-organized under the national banking law, and commenced business as a national bank, March 22, 1865, and the charter was extended for twenty years, March 22, 1885. The officers have remained unchanged since 1868 except that on Jan. 21, 1886, Charles H. Palmer was elected assistant cashier.

HALEY, Elijah, clergyman, was born near Oxford, England, Apr. 7, 1836. He was educated in the national school under the care of the established church. When fourteen years old he was by chance brought under the influence of primitive Methodist preaching and the religious experience thus gained changed his plans of life. He felt that his vocation was to preach the gospel as he now understood it, and at the age of nineteen he was licensed as a primitive Methodist local preacher. He served in this capacity until 1871, when he was called to the regular ministry in Barnsley circuit, Yorkshire. He served on the itinerancy for four years and was then by reason of his age refused admission into the conference, the rule limiting the age of candidates to twenty-five years and under. This resulted in his determination to accept the pressing invitation of a friend, and find for his family a new home in America.

In 1876 he located in Illinois, where he joined the state conference then presided over by Bishop Wiley. He was stationed at Dawson, 1876–77; Chesterfield, 1878; and Raymond, 1879–81, when he was transferred to the Minnesota conference and assigned to High Forest, remaining three years, 1882–85; served at Kasson two years, 1886–87; and at Eyota, 1888–89. He was in 1890 transferred to the Bloomington Avenue Church, Minneapolis, where he has carried on a very successful work, paying off a large debt and restoring peace and prosperity to a weak and divided congregation.

VANDERBILT, John, state senator, was born in Flatbush, L. I., in 1819, son of John and Sarah Lott Vanderbilt. After receiving a good school education he studied law, was admitted to the bar and became one of the firm of Lott, Murphy & Vanderbilt, of which Henry C. Murphy, one of the leading men of Brooklyn, was senior member. On May 1, 1844, Gov. William Bouck appointed Mr. Vanderbilt first judge of the court of common pleas of Kings county, as the successor of Judge Greenwood, resigned. Two years later this court was abolished under the constitution of 1846, and Judge Vanderbilt retired from the bench. In 1852 he was nominated on the Democratic ticket for the state senate and being elected, filled his term to the satisfaction of his constituents. While senator, he was appointed on important commissions, one to investigate the harbor encroachments of New York, and another on the affairs of Union College in relation to Pres. Nott. In 1858 he received the Democratic nomination for lieutenant-governor, but was defeated with his party. He married Gertrude Phœbe, daughter of John Lefferts of Flatbush, who survived him and gained much credit for her literary talent and patient spirit of research as shown in her "Social History of Flatbush," published in 1882. He was always exceedingly popular throughout the section and was commonly called "Kings county's Favorite Son." For several years before his death Judge Vanderbilt was retired from active service, owing to the effects of a stroke of paralysis, and died at his home in Flatbush, May 16, 1877.

ABBOTT, Jacob, author and educator, was born in Hallowell, Me., Nov. 14, 1803. He was one of three brothers, and the father of four sons, who, as educators and authors, have had a deep and wide influence upon the American mind. Having been prepared for college at the Hallowell Academy he was graduated from Bowdoin in 1820, and studied theology at Andover from 1821 to 1824. He began teaching in Portland Academy, and soon afterwards was appointed tutor in Amherst College, in which position he continued until 1825, when he was made professor of mathematics and natural philosophy in that institution. On May 8, 1826, he was licensed to preach by the Hampshire Association. Three years subsequently, on May 18, 1829, he married Harriet Vaughan, of Hallowell, Me., and directly afterwards removed to Boston, where, on June 1st of that year, he opened the Mount Vernon School—one of the first institutions in the country to give to young women an education equal in excellence to that given to young men. At this school Mr. Abbott put into practice the principles—very radical at that time —which always characterized his teaching. He made the school self-governing. He enforced but one rule, and that rule was adopted by the scholars themselves. At the side of his desk was a metallic plate upon which in gilded letters were the words: "Study Hour." The plate was movable, and when in an upright position it was the signal for silence and study; when it was inclined halfway down, any scholar might leave her seat or whisper, but she could do nothing to disturb the others; when the plate was altogether down, all restraint was suspended, and the pupils were left entirely to their liberty. All serious cases of wrong-doing were managed by Mr. Abbott, by appealing, directly and openly, to the conscience of the offender. Minor transgressions were tried, half in jest and half in earnest, by a jury of the young ladies themselves, who were pretty sure to inflict some slight, but effective punishment. By such novel methods Mr. Abbott secured for his school a discipline better, perhaps, than that of any other in the country. He continued as principle of this school until 1834, when he entered upon the broader fields of preaching and authorship. On Sept. 16, 1834, he took pastoral charge of the Eliot Congregational Church at Roxbury, Mass., and the same year produced the first of the three remarkable books entitled, "The Young Christian Series." These books grew out of his experience in conveying religious truth to his pupils, and they are models of the graphic description and simplicity of statement that are best adapted to young readers. They achieved at once a remarkable popularity and determined Mr. Abbott's vocation as an author. Henceforth, though he was for a time associated with his brothers in the conduct of the Abbott Institute in New York, authorship was his principal pursuit, he producing during the remainder of his life, more than 200 volumes, very many of which were republished in England, Scotland, Ireland, Germany, Holland, France, and India. It is probably no exageration to say that his books have had many millions of readers, and that thousands of the leading men of this country have received their first impulse to a high moral character, and a manly and useful life from some one of his volumes. Speaking of the "Young Christian" he once said, "I made the book fit the human nature around me, and consequently it fitted human nature elsewhere." And this remark applies to all his works. He was constantly studying life, especially human life, and these studies he transferred to his books, until his very fictions became facts—fact in its broad sense of truth to nature. It is this trait, together with his own childlike humility, truthfulness, playfulness, genuineness, and intuitive discernment which he infused into his books, that has given them their exceptional popularity. The profoundest truths he makes clear to the simplest intellect by speaking, after the manner of the Great Master in parables. The latter part of his life he passed at Farmington, Me., in a quiet, rural retreat, to which he gave the name of "Two-acres;" and it is hard to find a more beautiful picture than that which one of his sons has drawn of these closing years—the good man at rest, the work of his life done, his pen laid aside except to write letters to his children and grandchildren or an occasional article for some public journal; but still giving gratuitous instruction to the children of his poor neighbors, and lessons in French to the young ladies of the village. "When his hand wearied of his pen," says the account, "he would lay it down, even upon an unfinished page, and go out to the path he was making, or the shrubbery he was trimming, or to the shop where he would have a collection of rustic canes or pretty paper-knives in process of manufacture. When he wanted rest of a different character, he would seek it on the sofa, over the newspapers, or some entertaining novel or other new volume." Thus his life passed peacefully away until Oct. 31, 1879, when he died, beloved and honored by all who knew him, and by millions who did not know him except through the books he had written.

PILLSBURY, Fred Carleton, mill owner, was born at Concord, N. H., Aug. 27, 1852. He was educated at the high school of his native city, and in 1870 removed to Minneapolis, where he engaged as clerk for his uncle, John S. Pillsbury, in the hardware business. On Oct. 19, 1876, he married Alice, daughter of D. M. Goodwin, a prominent physician of Minneapolis, and about the same time was admitted a partner in the milling firm of Chas. A. Pillsbury & Co. An experience of fourteen years as an active manager of the largest milling business in the world gave him a mastery of the business, so upon the sale of that great property  he joined with other gentlemen of the city in organizing the Northwestern Consolidated Milling Co., of which he became a director and one of the managing committee Next to the Pillsbury-Washburn syndicate, this is the largest milling business in the country. It owns and operates the Crown Roller, Pettit, Northwestern, Columbia, and Galaxy mills, with a daily capacity of about 10,500 barrels of flour, and a daily consumption of wheat of over 50,000 bushels. Mr. Pillsbury was a director in the First National Bank, the oldest and largest bank in the city, also in the Swedish-American Bank, one of the latest. He was president of the Minneapolis, Lyndale, and Minnetonka Railway, a suburban steam line, until that company was absorbed in the present electric system of rapid transit. He was for two years president of the State Agricultural Society, during which time he gave the management his personal attention, and subjected it to the strictest business methods, so that the society was placed on a firm financial basis, its annual exhibitions being the best in the country. He had a decided taste for rural life, delighted in fine horses, and surrounded himself with blooded cattle. His summer home on the shores of Lake Minnetonka, and his farm, well stocked with choicest cattle, sheep, and blooded horses, were his special delight. He possessed a fine artistic faculty, and had embellished his home with rare examples of the sculptor's and painter's art. He was the first to introduce art into Minneapolis on a large scale. Mr. Pillsbury was a very active member of the Minneapolis Club. His charities were very liberal but unostentatious. He died from malignant diphtheria, May 13, 1892.

CONVERSE, Dexter Edgar, manufacturer, was born in Swanton, Vt., Apr. 21, 1828, son of Orlin and Lonisa Couverse of New Hampshire, and both of English descent. His grandfather, Paine Converse was descended from Edward Converse, who came to America with Gov. Winthrop in 1630. The family history traces the name Converse, originally De Cougiers, back to French or Flemish origin, its entrance into England dating from the Norman Conquest. The American descendants are settled throughout New England, and are largely identified with all lines of commercial and manufacturing enterprises. The father of our subject died when the boy was three years old, and his mother having married again, he was reared by his uncle, Albert G. Brown, of Canada, being engaged with him in the manufacture of woolen goods, until he reached his majority, and received his education at the common schools. At twenty-one he secured a position in a cotton mill at Cohoes, N. Y., where he remained five years. In 1854 he went to Lincolnton, N. C., where he was superintendent of a cotton mill for a few months. In February, 1855, he settled at Bivingsville (now Glendale), S. C., where he lived until 1891, when he removed to Spartanburg. While at Bivingsville, he purchased an interest in the cotton mill there, and soon became its manager. The mill then contained only 1,300 spindles and twenty-six looms, which formed the nucleus, however, of his present extensive works and the beginning of his successful career as a cotton manufacturer. The Bivingsville soon became the Glendale mills, and in 1886 was incorporated as the D. E. Converse Co. The mill now has 17,-000 spindles, 510 looms, and in

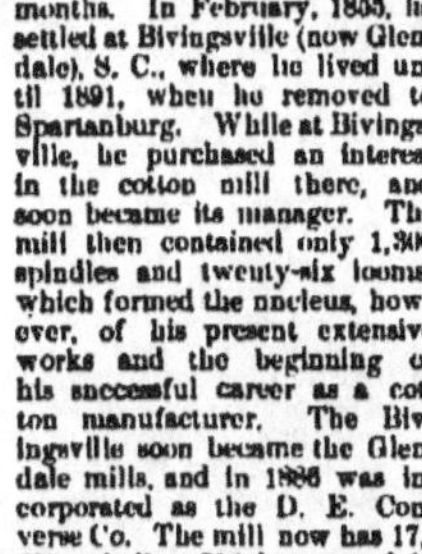

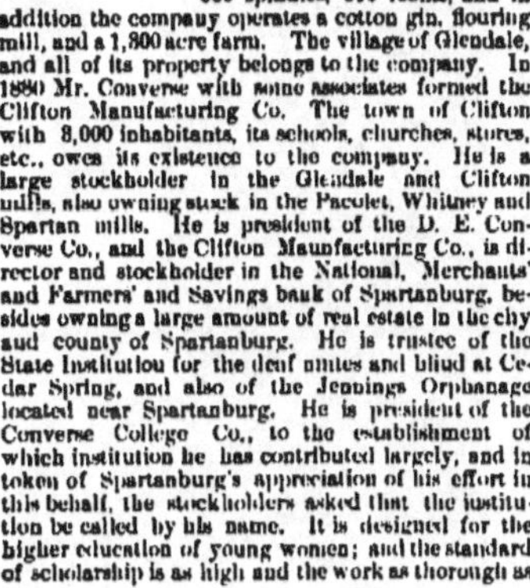

addition the company operates a cotton gin, flouring mill, and a 1,800 acre farm. The village of Glendale, and all of its property belongs to the company. In 1880 Mr. Converse with some associates formed the Clifton Manufacturing Co. The town of Clifton with 8,000 inhabitants, its schools, churches, stores, etc., owes its existence to the company. He is a large stockholder in the Gleudale and Clifton mills, also owning stock in the Pacolet, Whitney and Spartan mills. He is president of the D. E. Converse Co., and the Clifton Maunfacturing Co., is director and stockholder in the National, Merchants' and Farmers' and Savings bank of Spartanburg, besides owning a large amount of real estate in the city and county of Spartanburg. He is trustee of the State Institution for the deaf mutes and blind at Cedar Spring, and also of the Jennings Orphanage located near Spartanburg. He is president of the Converse College Co., to the establishment of which institution he has contributed largely, and in token of Spartanburg's appreciation of his effort in this behalf, the stockholders asked that the institution be called by his name. It is designed for the higher education of young women; and the standard of scholarship is as high and the work as thorough as

that required in colleges for men. Mr. Converse is a Republican with regard to national issues, although a Democrat in state and local politics. He is one of the most prominent business men in South Carolina, is largely identified with the business interests and enterprises of Spartanburg, and is the chief promoter of cotton manufacturing in the South. During the civil war he was enrolled in the confederate ranks but was detailed to attend to his factory for the product of which the country had need. Mr. Converse married Helen A. Twichell of Cohoes, N. Y.

WILSON, Benjamin Frank, first president of Converse College, was born near Mayesville, Sumter co. S. C., March 12, 1862, of Scotch-Irish descent. His ancestors, who fled from Scotland to avoid the religious persecution incident to signing the "League and Covenant," first emigrating to the north of Ireland and from there to the Black river settlement in Williamsburg county, S. C., in the sixteenth century. Mr. Wilson's parents were Benjamin F. Wilson, born June 21, 1830, and Rebecca Wilson, born in Marion county, S. C., in 1830, and a daughter of William Thomas Wilson. His paternal grandfather, James Harvey Wilson, was one of the first settlers of Sumter county. Until seventeen years of age the son lived upon his father's cotton plantation. He received his early education at the country schools, and in 1880 entered Davidson College, North Carolina, from which he was graduated in 1884, having completed five years' course in four. During his college career he was the recipient of many honors, receiving medals both in his junior and senior years, and being elected valedictorian of his class. In the fall of 1884 he entered the theological seminary of the Presbyterian Church at Columbia, S. C., and the next year he entered the theological seminary at Princeton, N. J., from which he was graduated in 1887. During his course there he took postgraduate work in psychology and historic theology under Drs. Patton, McCosh, and Hodge, respectively. He also took the second Greek prize during his first year, and in his second year he won the first scholarship prize in Hebrew. In the summer of 1887 he was invited to churches in Spartanburg, S. C., and in Birmingham, Ala. He accepted the call to the First Presbyterian Church of Spartanburg, and continued with great success as its pastor until 1890. The summer of 1888 he spent in the University of Berlin, Germany, pursuing philosophical and philological studies. In 1889 Mr. Wilson was elected alumnus orator by his alma mater. In the spring of 1889, he was elected pastor of the First Presbyterian Church of Richmond, Ky., and at the same time to the chair of Christian apologetics of the Central University of Richmond, Ky., both of which invitations he declined. In the winter of 1889 he was elected president of Converse College, and organized a well-appointed institution of learning, for the higher education of women, which in its standard of scholarship has maintained the highest record of any college for women in the Southern states, and has in its third year enrolled 300 students from 16 states and Canada. The college now has twenty-five officers and teachers selected from some of our best colleges and universities. July 30, 1890, Pres. Wilson was married to Mrs. Sallie Foster, daughter of J. C. Farrar, formerly a prominent merchant of Charleston, and the widow of the late J. A. Foster of Spartanburg. Pres. Wilson is a member of the Sigma Alpha Epsilon Fraternity. He is a contributor to the "Quarterly Review," and other periodicals, is a talented educator, preacher, writer, and a strong executive officer.

ARCHER, Henry Hayes, street railway manager, was born at Rokeby, Chester co., Pa., July 1, 1800, of English descent. He attended the common schools until fourteen years of age, and then began his career as a laborer with pick and shovel for the Pennsylvania Railroad Co. Later he learned telegraphy, and in 1876 was operator for the same company, and in 1877–78–79 was employed on a construction train for maintenance of way in the track department, and in 1880–81 was employed as brakeman. In the winter of 1881–82 he entered the employ of the Wilmington and Northern Railroad of Delaware, and successively held the positions of passenger brakeman, conductor, and train dispatcher, until 1885, when he entered the service of the Baltimore and Ohio Railroad as yardmaster, continuing

in that position until 1888. He was then engaged by the Wilmington City Railway Co. as assistant superintendent, eighteen months later was made superintendent, and three years after was appointed general manager and treasurer, continuing until November, 1892, when he removed to Scranton to accept the position of general manager of the Scranton Traction Co., the revenues of which have increased over twenty-five per cent. under his efficient management. Mr. Archer is president of the Valley Railway Co. of Scranton, and vice-president of the People's Railway Co. of Scranton, and the system of which he is manager comprises thirty-eight miles of road, owned by seven distinct companies, though operated by the Scranton Traction Co. Mr. Archer is a member of the Methodist Episcopal church, is a prominent Knight-Templar and Elk, and in politics a Republican.

LIVERMORE, George, author, was born in Cambridge, Mass., July 10, 1809. He was a descendant of John Livermore, who emigrated from Ipswich, England, in 1634, and settled in Watertown, Mass. The boy attended the public and private schools at Cambridgeport until he had reached the age of fourteen years, at the same time preparing for college. At one private school he had Oliver Wendell Holmes as a fellow-pupil. Young Livermore did not go to college, however, but at the age of fourteen, entered a store at Cambridgeport kept by two of his elder brothers. But in 1827–28, he passed through two terms at the Deerfield Academy. While still a mere boy he showed remarkable precocity, and was a voluminous reader, always employing his savings and spare time in purchasing and reading books. In 1829 he went to Waltham, where he acted as a salesman in a dry-goods store for a year, and from that time for some years he moved about from one place to another taking whatever service offered, but in all that time he devoted his leisure to reading and studying. In 1838 he formed a partnership with an older brother in business as wool merchants, which resulted successfully. On Oct. 1, 1839, Mr. Livermore married Elizabeth Cunningham Odiorne, of Cambridgeport. Meanwhile he was accumulating a library which grew to possess considerable importance and value. In 1842 he received a copy of Eliot's "Indian Bible," as a gift from his brother, who purchased it for $25. Copies of this book have since been sold for more that $1,000. Gradually Mr. Livermore began to be recognized as an antiquarian and man of letters, and also as a writer for the newspapers and reviews of bibliographical and historical topics, his articles being very gladly accepted by publishers. Eventually, he gathered one of the finest collections of Bibles in the country. In 1843 he assisted in the editorship of Grahame's "History of the United States," and the same year he visited Europe, where he made the acquaintance of Samuel Rogers, Wordsworth, and many other distinguished authors. In 1846 and thereafter, Mr. Livermore was a frequent contributor to the "Cambridge Chronicle," a weekly newspaper published in Cambridgeport. There he published his article on the "New England Primer." Later on he appeared in the "North American Review," in a series of papers on "Public Libraries." He was made a trustee of the State Library of Massachusetts, in 1849. In 1850 he received from Harvard College the honorary degree of M.A. Mr. Livermore was always deeply interested in political affairs of his state and of the nation, but he never took office. In 1855 he was elected a member of the American Academy of Arts and Sciences. Mr. Livermore lost nearly all his property in 1857, but the outbreak of the civil war brought about such a demand for goods which were manufactured by his firm that he soon realized a large fortune, of which he gave freely to the cause of the Union. During the latter part of the war, Mr. Livermore's health broke down and he died in Cambridge, Mass., Aug. 30, 1865.

McILWRATH, William, merchant, was born at Belfast, Ireland, June 10, 1834. He was second youngest of a family of eight children born to Samuel and Annie Gray McIlwrath. His boyhood life was one of labor. He learnt first the trade of linen weaver, and afterwards that of baker and confectioner. In 1856 he came to America and first settled at Fulton, Calloway co., Mo. At the breaking out of the civil war of 1861 he was in a border state where feeling ran highest and divisions of families and communities were widest. In 1862 he enrolled in the 9th cavalry regiment, M. S. M. From Aug. 22d of that year until Dec. 4th he was in command of his company operating with the Federal forces under Gen. Pleasanton in driving the Confederate Gen. Price out of the state in what was known as the "Price Raid." He was soon promoted to first lieutenant, and was detailed for duty at Paris, Mo., as provost-marshal. He filled this important position from December, 1862, to August, 1863; and then was sent to Chillicothe, Mo., in the same line of duty. This position he held until Au-

gust, 1864. He was mustered out of the service in April, 1865, and returned to Chillicothe and engaged in the grocery business. A year or so later he was appointed postmaster of Chillicothe, and during his three years' of service gave up business and devoted his whole time to official duties. In 1869, upon retiring from official life, he established himself in a general book and stationery store, and when the legislature of the state of Missouri, by special act of March, 1887, established the State Industrial Home for Girls, the governor named Mr. McIlwrath as one of the board of control for the long term of six years, and at the first meeting of the board he was elected president, and held the position until the end of his term. In all that pertained to the successful and practical establishment and the subsequent working of the home, in supervising the plans and construction, and in making its success large and creditable, Mr. McIlwrath has been the central figure. In local educational matters he has also been a progressive factor. In 1886 he was made a member of Chillicothe's Board of Education, and afterward its president. Since the inauguration of the new board the wards of the city, four in number, have been supplied with proper buildings through the efforts of Mr. McIlwrath and his co-workers.

KELLEY, William Darrah, congressman, was born in Philadelphia, Pa., Apr. 12, 1814. He was a descendant of John Kelley, a major in the war of the revolution. The death of his father, in his childhood, left the family in such straitened circumstances that he was obliged to leave school at eleven years of age, and go to work, first as an errand-boy, and afterward as copy-holder to a printer. At thirteen he was apprenticed to a jeweler, with whom he remained seven years. Having thus become master of his trade, he practised it in Boston for five years, during which he made a number of public speeches as a free-trader and Democrat. In 1840 he returned to Philadelphia to study law in the office of Col. James Page, who had been attracted to him by his speeches. In five years he rose to be deputy prosecuting attorney for the state, and in 1846 he became judge of the court of common pleas by appointment, and in 1851 (under a new law), by election. In this position he rendered a number of important decisions. In 1854 his anti-slavery sympathies, coupled with a change in his views respecting free-trade, carried him into the Republican party, and two years later he was nominated for congress on that ticket, but was defeated. He was a delegate to the convention which nominated Lincoln for the presidency in 1860, and was the same year elected representative to congress from the fourth congressional district, which he represented from that time on, without interruption, until his death. As a congressman, he was an ardent advocate of arming the slaves, a member of the committee of ways and means for twenty years, and so thoroughly identified with the protective tariff, particularly in its relations to the industries of his own state, that he became known as " Pig Iron Kelley " all over the country; frequently, it is said, receiving letters addressed to " Hon. P. I. Kelley." Besides a number of books and pamphlets on political subjects, he published " Letters from Europe " (1880), in which is embodied the results of investigations made by him during a number of trips abroad. He died at Washington, D. C., Jan. 9, 1890.

O'NEIL, John, manufacturer, was born in Boston, Mass., Jan. 20, 1849, son of Morgan O'Neil, a native of county Cork, Ireland, and so prominently identified with the struggle for independence in 1848 that he was compelled to flee to the United States to escape the consequences of his patriotism. He had inherited his love of country from his father, who was engaged in the uprising of 1798 and only escaped transportation through the eloquent pleadings of a nobleman before the castle authorities. When Morgan O'Neil emigrated to the United States he brought with him as his wife Catherine Harde, a native of the same county, and together they landed in Boston in 1848. He began his new life as a manufacturer of men's clothing and met with unusual success. His son was educated in the Boston public schools, graduating from the grammar school when sixteen years of age. He at once apprenticed to the trade of wood-turning and thoroughly learned his craft and became a master workman. He removed to Jacksonville, Fla., in November, 1870, where he found employment at his trade and was soon a partner in the business. He was afterwards joined the establishment of Penniman & Co. as partner, and his experience, judgment, and skill soon made the firm one of the most prominent in the state. On the death of Mr. Penniman he bought the interest and became the sole owner. His saw-mills, planing-mills, and wood-turning factories consume millions of feet of lumber, and find ready markets in all directions from Jacksonville extending into other states. Mr. O'Neil was married on July 5, 1885, to Minnie, daughter of Samuel Owens of South Carolina, and they have three children. He is the owner of large tracts of land in and around Jacksonville, besides extensive timber lands throughout the state, and is largely interested in the material welfare of his adopted city.

FESS, Simeon Davidson, educator, was born near Lima, O., Dec. 11, 1861, son of Henry Fess, a farmer. When but four years of age his father died, leaving the family almost destitute, they barely escaping dependence upon public charity.  The boy obtained a meagre elementary education at a country school, and at the age of eighteen he entered a select school at West Newton, and continued for one year. He then became a student in the Ohio Normal University where he was graduated A.B. in 1889, bearing first honor in his class. While pursuing his studies here he taught several terms of school in the country, and during the last two years of his under-graduate work, he served as tutor in the university, and on graduation was appointed to the chair of history and science. In 1893 he received the degree of LL.B., and has since had charge of the law department in the university. Prof. Fess has published " A Compendium of U. S. History " (1891); and " Outlines of Physiology and Hygiene" (1893). The former of these has now (1895) passed its second edition, and the latter bids fair to be widely used in schools. He is favorably known throughout Ohio and adjoining states as an instructor at teachers' institutes, and as a popular lecturer. He has been prominent in the work of the Y. M. C. A., being a member of the Ohio state executive committee of that organization, and having been a delegate to the International convention held at Philadelphia in 1888. He superintends the Methodist Episcopal Sabbath-school of Ada, and teaches a class numbering about 800. In 1890 he was married to Eva Caudas, daughter of Capt. B. A. Thomas, of Rushville, O.

THOMPSON, John, banker, was born in Berkshire county, Mass., in 1800, the son of a well-to-do farmer, who instilled into his mind the maxim, " hard work and plenty of it." He worked on the farm until his nineteenth year, attending school during the winter season. He completed his education at Hadley Academy, then a famous institution, and at twenty engaged in teaching in Hampshire county, and later took charge of a school in Albany, N. Y. He was for three years agent of the Yates & McIntosh lottery, a venture authorized by the state legislature for the benefit of Union College. His net earnings in the employ of this firm aggregated something over $1,000, and with this insignificant capital he made his start in Wall street. In a few years he had accumulated $10,000, when realizing the need of a journal giving reliable information on the currency of the country, which at that time consisted of state bank issues, he established " Thompson's Bank Note Reporter," the pioneer journal of its kind. In time its circulation exceeded 125,000 copies per week. His bold denunciation of bad banking and fraudulent issues of currency notes involved him in several lawsuits, the most prominent of which was in 1838 with Moses Y. Beach, owner of the "Sun," whom he sued for blackmail, the jury awarding him the full amount of damages, $10,000, without leaving their seats. In 1882 he opened a small office on Wall street, and took the initiative in the establishment of the national banking system, whose adoption by the government was greatly due to his influence and advocacy. Foreseeing the perils that must inevitably follow the lack of a staple and solid currency, he forwarded communications upon the subject to Pres. Lincoln and Sec. Chase. His suggestions were favorably considered and formed the groundwork for the national bank system as put before congress in 1863. In the latter part of this year he established the First National Bank of New York city, the first in the country, with but two stockholders, members of his own family. For a time it was debarred from the privileges of the clearing house, through the opposition of the other banks, which, however, were soon glad to award them. In 1878 he severed his connection with this bank and set about organizing The Chase National Bank, of which he was subsequently vice-president. He was a member of the Stock Exchange, but seldom went on the floor. His death occurred Apr. 20, 1891, in New York city.

THOMPSON, Frederick F., banker, was born in New York city, 1836, the son of John Thompson, a banker of that city. After a thorough preparation for college, in 1852 he entered Williams', and subsequently founded there the Lambda chapter of the Delta Psi fraternity. In 1854 he left college to go abroad on an important business mission for his father, but afterward returned to college, was restored to his class, and received his degree, his name appearing on the list as a regular graduate of the class of 1856. In 1857 he was married to the daughter of M. H. Clarke, governor of the state of New York, and subsequently established the banking-house of Thompson Brothers, and the same year succeeded to his father's business. At the outbreak of the civil war he secretly organized and drilled large bodies of colored troops, and afterward entered the service himself as captain of the 37th New York artillery. As a business man he has been eminently successful, and founded the National Currency Bank of New York city, which institution was afterward profitably closed, and also with others established the First National of Detroit and the Columbia Bank at Chatham, N. Y. He is also connected with other financial corporations, and is interested in the construction of the Nicaragua canal, and many manufacturing enterprises. He has been prominently connected with educational and benevolent work, was one of the chief movers in building the Ontario Orphan Asylum, and the buildings of Williams College, Vassar, and Teachers' Colleges, and others. He is trustee of Williams and Vassar Colleges, the Ontario Orphan Asylum, New York Dispensary, and numbers of libraries and associations. To the students of Vassar College he is known as "Uncle Fred." He supports a free course of amusement lectures in Williamstown, and is a generous beneficiary, in an unostentatious way, to numerous educational institutions. He has never enter-

tained any aspirations for political life, but is a member of several clubs and scientific societies, among them the American Institute, Historical, Geographical, Photographic, Microscopical, and Archæological.

BROWN, John, clergyman, was born in New York city, May 19, 1791. He received his early education in his native city, entered Columbia College, and was graduated, Aug. 7, 1811, as the valedictorian of his class. He selected the ministry as his profession, and studied theology under the Rt. Rev. John H. Hobart, the assistant bishop of the Protestant Episcopal diocese of New York. He was licensed as a lay reader to Fishkill, Oct. 12, 1812, and continued as such in the old parish of Trinity Church until Apr. 18, 1814, when he returned to New York city, and was ordained to the diaconate in St. Mark's Church in the Bowery. On Sept. 18th, of the same year he accepted a call to Trinity Church, Fishkill. On Nov. 15, 1815, he was ordained to the priesthood by Bishop Hobart, in Trinity Church, New York city. During the summer of 1815, after officiating twice on Sunday in his own parish at Fishkill, he established a third service in Newburgh. He found but two communicants in the village. A room was obtained in the Bath Hotel, in South Water street, where the services of the young minister were favorably received. In 1815 he received

a call to the rectorship of St. George's Church, Newburgh, which he accepted. Dr. Brown also organized St. Thomas's Church, New Windsor; was chosen its rector, devoting one-fourth of his time to the New Windsor parish—until 1847. He organized St. John's Church at Monticello; Grace Church at Middletown; and the churches at Cornwall and Marlborough. He revived the church at Goshen; also St. Andrew's at Walden; St. Peter's at Peekskill; and St. Philip's at Garrisons; holding services at intervals at these places until the churches were strong enough to support rectors. He attended to the work of his parish without assistance until Feb. 1, 1859, when an assistant minister was appointed. On Feb. 6, 1878, he resigned the rectorship, and was made rector emeritus. Dr. Brown received the degree of M.A. from Columbia College in 1815, and the degree of D.D. from Hobart College in 1841. He was elected a trustee of the General Theological Seminary in 1832, and continued a member of the board until his death. During his ministry he preached special sermons on the occasion of the death of ten presidents of the United States. Jan. 14, 1856, he presided at the obsequies of Uzal Knapp, the last of the life guards of Washington. Aside from his distinguished services to the church, Dr. Brown exhibited a devotion and zeal in other matters second only to his fidelity and love for his priestly calling. He served as one of the trustees of the academy, and was president of the board from 1832 until the property was transferred to the school trustees of the village. He was a member of the first board of trustees of the common schools, the president of the first horticultural society of Newburgh, and was chaplain of the 19th regiment there. He became a member of the Masonic fraternity in 1817, in Hiram lodge, and from 1879 until his death, he was chaplain of Hudson river lodge. Dr. Brown's life was a singularly eventful one—full of sacrifice and zeal in the work of the Master. His influence was ever exerted in the encouragement and support of various benevolent, educational and ennobling movements of the day. People of all sects and denominations recognized the perfectness, the beauty, the worth of such a life as his. Dr. Brown married, Nov. 15, 1819, Frances Elizabeth, daughter of Robert Ludlow, of Newburgh, and had ten children. His wife died, Apr. 19, 1871. He died at his home in Newburgh, N. Y., Aug. 15, 1884.

LENAGHAN, John Francis, merchant, was born in county Armagh, Ireland, Aug. 31, 1854. His father, Thomas Lenaghan, was a prominent farmer, and a direct descendant of the O'Neills, the chiefs of Ulster. His mother, whose maiden name was Alice McCoy, was the daughter of a well-to-do farmer of Armagh. The son came to the United States in 1867, and entered Rockhill College, Ellicott City, Md. He remained there until 1871, when he became a clerk in a grocery house in Washington, D. C. Having mastered its details in three years, he went to Ireland, and after spending some time with his family, set out on an extensive tour of Europe. He returned to the United States in 1875, and began business in Washington, D. C., as a wholesale dealer in butter and cheese. In 1880 he added the wholesale wine and liquor business to his trade, and was accumulating wealth rapidly when, in 1883, a destructive fire swept his house out of existence, and almost ruined him. He resumed business at the earliest opportunity, and continued until 1885, when he removed to Orlando, Fla., then one of the most promising towns in the state, and engaged in the wholesale grocery trade. His business increased so rapidly that he was compelled to remove to Sanford in 1890, to secure better shipping facilities, and be in communication with the large areas in south Florida over which his business extended. He now (1898) occupies an immense brick warehouse, filled with goods received direct from the manufacturers. In July, 1892, he formed a partnership with Dr. C. C. Haskell, the former treasurer of the Southern Florida Railroad, for handling butter and cheese at wholesale, and this he has added to his grocery business, now the largest in south Florida. Mr. Lenaghan was married July 8, 1890, to Dora G., daughter of Dr. James N. Butt of Orlando, Fla. She is a native of Elizabeth City, N. C., her family having been settlers of that place for several generations.

QUINCY, Josiah (1st), was born at Braintree, Mass., in 1709, younger son of the third Edmund Quincy. He was graduated at Harvard in 1728, entered into trade, and was much abroad until his fortieth year. In 1755 he and T. Pownall were Massachusetts commissioners to treat with New York as to military defenses against the French, who were then building Fort Ticonderoga, and threatening that region. He was a warm patriot, and was much shocked when his son undertook the defense of the "criminals charged with the murder of their fellow-citizens," i. e., Capt. Preston and the soldiers, who had fired on the crowd at the Boston massacre. He built the house, still in possession of his posterity, at Quincy (then Braintree), and died there in 1784.

KETCHAM, Isaac A., inventor, was born in Huntington, L. I., in 1827, the only son of John Ketcham. He received a good education, and, while still a young man, showed a capacity for invention, and the application of new devices in machinery, which made him generally known among those interested in mechanics. He had the honor of plan-ning the first iron-clad torpedo boat, which was built by the U. S. government in 1864. The new vessel, called The New Era, was very formidable, although she did not carry a gun, and was used on the James river, and in other places, for the purpose of clearing the harbor of obstructions. He next invented a device by which an endless cable could be used in adjusting torpedoes or batteries across channel-ways for harbor protection. Mr. Ketcham's inventions were brought before the U. S. navy department by Pres. Lincoln's special request, but the department, which was at that time under the supervision of Gideon Wells, secretary of the navy, paid little attention to his devices, and reported against them. Mr. Ketcham married a daughter of Thomas S. Robbins of Huntington, L. I., and had two sons, the elder, George F. Ketcham, a physician, the younger an artist.

GLOVER, Charles Carroll, banker, Washington, D. C., was born in Macon county, N. C., Nov. 24, 1846. He had the advantage of good parentage, his grandfather, after whom he is named, having been one of the foremost citizens of Washington in the early years of this century. His father was following the profession of a surveyor in North Carolina when he met and married Caroline Percy. The lad returned to Washington in July, 1855, received an education at a private school, and in 1862 entered Franck Taylor's book store as clerk. Three years later he entered the banking house of Riggs & Co., where he acted as receiving and paying teller for a number of years, when, about 1873, he was taken into partnership. Since he has been a member of the firm he has seen the deposit account of the institution increase from $700,000 to between $4,000,000 and $5,000,000, while his own fame as a financier has grown in the same proportion. The splendid development of the Washington and Georgetown Railroad Co. was due to his judgment and foresight. At a time when the interests of the company were being jeopardized by stockholders who, living out of the city, were gradually making a very valuable franchise worthless, Mr. Glover stepped into the breach. Although he owned but thirty shares he finally secured, by every honest effort, from adroit argument to earnest plea, all the proxies he could find. He interested Mr. George Riggs in the stock and with the latter's co-operation obtained control, defeated the old board of directors, and infused new blood into the corporation. From that time the popularity, carrying capacity, and earning power of the road increased, until to-day it stands one of the richest corporations in the United States, operating three lines of cable system, equipped with the most complete and powerful motive plant, and owning large blocks of real estate, worth hundreds

of thousands of dollars. Mr. Glover has also found opportunity to work with unflagging energy for public interests. The acquisition of the national park of 1,500 acres within the district limits is due in part to his unselfish labors. The bill to be introduced in congress was framed by James Johnston and Calderon Carlisle, and discussed at Mr. Glover's residence, where a few days later the project was heartily endorsed. The first steps toward the accomplishment of the reclamation of the flats and the extension of the water supply were also inaugurated by Mr. Glover. He secured and donated to the district two acres of valuable land on Fort Reno for the site of a reservoir. He was also instrumental in the presentation to the district of the land necessary for the construction of Arkansas and Arizona avenues, in the western portion of the county. The fact that Mr. Glover has for twenty years been an intimate personal friend of many of the leading legislators of the land has enabled him to exercise a vast amount of influence for the good of the city. He has enjoyed the confidence of every president since Grant occupied the White House, and has suggested to those high in authority the best means for the advancement of the nation's capital. Formerly the treasurer of the Washington Gas Light Co., and a director of the National Union Fire Insurance Co., Mr. Glover resigned these positions because of the multiplicity of his duties, and has also recently retired, for the same reason, from the vice-presidency and directorship of the Washington and Georgetown Railroad Co. He did not leave the latter corporation, however, until the vast system of improvements had been successfully inaugurated. Even now, besides his large interests in Riggs & Co.'s Bank, he is vice-president and director of the National Safe Deposit Co., a trustee of the Corcoran Gallery of Art, a director in the Columbia Fire Insurance Co., a trustee of the Children's Hospital, the executor of George Bancroft's estate, a vestryman of Epiphany Church, and the president of the Washington Stock Exchange. A firm believer in the great future of Washington, Mr. Glover is the owner of large tracts of suburban property, some of which, purchased years ago, are now immensely valuable. His handsome country home is situated near the site of the proposed National University, while his city residence, on Lafayette square, is a model of taste and refinement. He was married on Jan. 10, 1878, to Anna, daughter of the late Rear-Admiral Poor, U. S. N., and of the three children born to this marriage two survive—Elizabeth Lindsay and Charles Carroll, Jr. Still in the prime of life, vigorous and active, Mr. Glover can look foward to many years of usefulness in a community whose interests he has done so much to forward.

HEALD, Edward Payson, educator, was born in Lovell, Oxford co. Me., Feb. 5, 1843, and comes of American lineage extending in an unbroken line for 260 years. His ancestors, both on the father's and mother's side, came from England with Gov. Winthrop and were among the first of the Puritans to land at Massachusetts Bay. The Healds settled near Boston in 1630, and have resided in New England ever since. After acquiring a thorough English and classical education, our subject commenced his career as a teacher at the Portland (Mo.) Business College and applied himself so diligently to his chosen profession that he soon became known beyond his state. In 1868 he went to California, and, though only in his twentieth year, opened a business college in San Francisco, the first of the kind on the Pacific coast. This pioneer experiment has continued to prosper, and now ranks as one of the leading schools of its class in the United States. Mr. Heald has repeatedly visited every large city in Europe and America for the purpose of familiarizing himself with the best methods of business education. The moral and educational power exerted by a few commercial schools in our large centres has been chiefly instru-

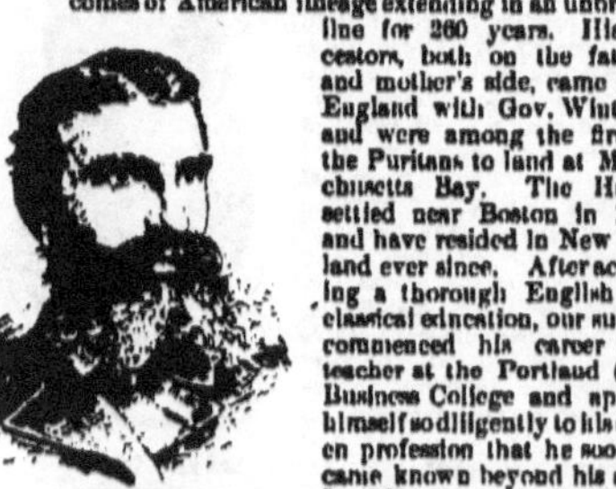

mental in opening the world of business to women, and Heald's Business College has been foremost in this work. The college employs a large faculty, and the attendance frequently runs up to 500 students, many of whom come to it from South America, the Hawaiian Islands and distant parts of the Pacific. The name of Mr. Heald has been often mentioned for political honors, which, however, he has invariably declined.

HENDERSON, Peter, horticulturist, was born in Pathhead, Scotland, June 9, 1822, the youngest of the three children of James and Agnes Gilchrist Henderson. His father was a land steward and horticulturist, highly respected in the community in which he lived for his industry and integrity. From him Peter inherited many of the strong traits of his character, and his vigorous constitution; to his mother he owed his intellectual endowments. His maternal grandfather, Peter Gilchrist, after whom he was named, was a shepherd, and subsequently a florist and nurseryman. He was an unusually well educated man for one of his station in life, and was much given to reading and study. Peter was educated at the parish

schools, and there first gave evidence of the wonderful industry that characterized his after life. At the age of sixteen he was apprenticed in the gardens of Melville Castle, located near Dalkeith. These gardens were under the direction of George Stirling, and were considered the best training school in Scotland. In 1840 he competed for and won the medal given by the Royal Botanical Society of Edinburgh for the best herbarium of native and exotic plants, a competition open to the whole of Great Britain. In the spring of 1843 he sailed for America, and after meeting with some discouragement, first obtained employment in the nurseries of George Thorburn, of Astoria, L. I. After remaining there one year, he took a position with Robert Buist, Sr., of Philadelphia, then the leading florist in the United States. In 1847, having accumulated a capital of $500, he formed a partnership with his brother, James, who had about the same amount, and together they started the market-garden business in Jersey City, renting about ten acres of land, upon which were three small green-houses. They subsequently dissolved partnership, and Peter, finding his taste for fancy gardening increasing, began to turn his attention more particularly in that direction. In 1864 he removed his business to South Bergen, and there erected what was then considered the model range of green-houses, which were an example for the florists of the United States for many years. These buildings were torn down and reconstructed in 1880, as time had shown that they could be improved. At the time of Mr. Henderson's death his establishment covered five acres in solid glass. In 1862 he opened a seed store on Nassau street, New York city, and in 1871 established the seed business known throughout the world under the name of Peter Henderson & Co. He had as much skill in the management of this business as he had shown in the culture of flowers, was constantly introducing new varieties, and his talent for advertising was remarkable. He was the first to introduce the plan of sending his surplus plants to auction, and subsequently established the system of growing plants for auction only, which has since become a legitimate part of the business of horticulture in New

York. For a number of years he personally prepared and superintended all the matter for his plant catalogues, and after the establishment of the seed department wrote the important parts of that catalogue. He also did much towards the development of beauty and variety of color in the common flowers by cultivation and careful selection. Peter Henderson may fitly be called the "father of horticulture and ornamental gardening" in the United States, for he certainly occupied a unique position in the history of this industry. His biographer has said of him: "In horticulture, either here or abroad, he has no prototype. The annals of the profession may be searched in vain to find where any one man attained the same degree of eminence which Peter Henderson secured at one and the same time in three distinct divisions of horticulture. To have been either the leading florist, great seed merchant, or the versatile horticultural writer, would have been fame enough for most men. So when it is considered that he held almost the highest rank in all three departments, we begin to understand how wonderful his genius and his industry must have been." He wrote for a number of horticultural journals, and in 1869 declined the flattering offer of $6,000 per annum to become editor of "Tilton's Journal of Horticulture." His "Gardening for Profit," published in New York (1866), was the first book ever written exclusively on market-gardening in the United States, and his later works are the standard American authorities on the subjects of which they treat. Mr. Henderson's works have reached an enormous circulation, his "Gardening for Profit" having attained a sale of over 100,000 copies. One of his chief characteristics was the remarkable kindness and consideration he showed to young men seeking his assistance. He was popular and widely known both in America and Europe. At his death his family received nearly 8,000 letters of sympathy and condolence from all parts of the world. Mr. Henderson was twice married; his first wife was Emily Gibbons, of Bath, England, who died, leaving him three children. He afterwards married Jean, the daughter of an old friend of his named Andrew Read. He died at Jersey City, N. J., Jan. 17, 1890.

KENNA, Edward Dudley, lawyer, was born at Jacksonville, Ill., Nov. 17, 1861. His father, Michael Edward Kenna, whose parents came from near Nenagh, county Tipperary, Ireland, was born in Kingston, N. Y. His mother's maiden name was Ellen Pilcher, born in Morgan county, Ill., whither her parents had removed from Kentucky. Her paternal grandfather was with the Tennessee Rifles at the battle of New Orleans and participated in the battles of Lundy's Lane and Chippewa Falls; and her great-grandfather was a lieutenant in the Continental army with Gen. Anthony Wayne at the taking of Stony Point, N. Y. The Pilchers appear to have come originally from Wales. Our subject was educated in the common schools of Springfield, Mo., studied law, and was admitted to the bar May, 1880; removed to St. Louis in 1881, and since November, 1889, has been general attorney of the St. Louis and San Francisco Railway Co. On Sept. 15, 1895, he was appointed general solicitor of the Atchison, Topeka and Santa Fe Railroad system, succeeding Mr. G. R. Peck. He was married June 2, 1894, to Madeline, daughter of Richard C. Kerens of St. Louis, Mo., and is the father of one child. Mr. Kenna ranks as one of the ablest corporation lawyers of the Southwest. His rise in his profession has been almost phenomenal, he being the youngest general solicitor of any railway in the country.

KENLY, John Reese, soldier, was born in Baltimore, Md., in 1822. He attended private schools in that city, studied law, and was admitted to the bar in 1845. At the outbreak of the war with Mexico he raised a company of volunteers and became their captain. He took part in the battle of Monterey, and when Col. William H. Watson fell, during that engagement, he quickly rallied and re-formed the battalion. On the expiration of his term of enlistment, he returned to Baltimore, where he was tendered the commission of major. He immediately resumed active service until the close of the war, and then received the thanks of the state for gallantry in the field. Afterward he continued his law practice until the outbreak of the civil war, when he was appointed to the colonelcy of the

1st Maryland regiment, June 11, 1861. He was at Port Royal in May, 1862, and aided in saving the force under Gen. Banks from capture. Col. Kenly was severely wounded at the time, and taken prisoner, but was exchanged on Aug. 15th, and a week later became brigadier-general, with the command of all the Baltimore troops outside the forts. After the battle of Antietam he joined McClellan, and was present at Hagerstown and Harper's Ferry. He participated in the recapture of Maryland Heights in 1863, and thereafter, until peace was declared, he commanded various brigades in the 1st and 8th army corps. He was brevetted major-general of volunteers March 13, 1865, and after being mustered out of service, again received the thanks of his native state, and was honored with the presentation of a sword from the corporation of Baltimore. Since then he has practiced his profession with success, and has written "Memoirs of a Maryland Volunteer in the Mexican War," (Philadelphia, 1878).

KEENAN, Henry Francis, author, was born at Rochester, N. Y., May 4, 1849. He received a high school education and during the war of the rebellion served as a private soldier in the Federal army. At the battle of Drury's Bluff, Va., he was severely wounded. In 1868 he became a reporter on the Rochester, (N. Y.) "Chronicle," and by brilliant work won rapid promotion. Subsequently he found employment on the Chicago "Times," the Philadelphia "Times" and "Press," and the New York "Star." He also acted at different times as the Washington and Paris correspondent of various journals. In 1883 he left journalism and for some years gave his time to more pretentious work. He was then editor of the New York "Graphic," where he did all the literary work of the paper, editorial and comic. He has published several novels: "The Money Makers, a Social Parable" (1885); "Trajan" (1885); "The Aliens" (1886); and "One of a Thousand" (1887); all of which possess merit and were well received. In 1888 he purchased a farm near Mamaroneck, N. Y. He is now (1891) a member of the staff of Scranton, (Pa.) "Daily Truth." The "Nation" said of him: "he can construct a plot, conceive rather brilliant and original characters. . . he commands a wealth of picturesque and poetical expression." He made his first reputation by a fictitious account of a balloon voyage.

ABBOTT, John Stephens Cabot, author and clergyman, was born at Brunswick, Me., Sept. 18, 1805. After being graduated at Bowdoin College and Andover Theological Seminary, he was ordained to the Congregational ministry in 1830, and took charge of the church at Worcester, Mass. He continued to preach until shortly before his death, holding successively pastorates at Roxbury and Nantucket, Mass., and Fair Haven, Conn. His first essay at authorship was the "Mother at Home," a series of lectures which grew out of the "familiar talks" he was accustomed to address to a "Maternal Association" in his church at Worcester.

The "talks" excited so much interest in the small society of ladies he addressed, that he decided to write them out and submit them to a larger audience. The publishers to whom the MS. was presented were about to bring out a much more elaborate work on the same subject from a celebrated doctor of divinity, and they questioned the success of so unpretentious a book by an unknown author. But the title was good, and their printers were standing nearly idle, so they concluded to risk a small edition. The elaborate work died almost as soon as it was born, while the little book bounded at once into a large circulation, was republished in England, and translated into nearly every Continental language, and even into the dialects of India and Africa. This remarkable success decided Mr. Abbott to adopt the career of authorship. After writing a small book on "Practical Christianity," he entered the field of history, and produced in rapid succession several works, which, whatever may be thought of their value as historical studies—have demonstrated that fact may be made as interesting as fiction. His "Life of Napoleon Bonaparte," probably attracted more readers to the magazine in which it appeared as a serial than any merely fictitious narrative has ever done. After the publication of this work he produced others of a similar character, which had a like popularity, and he continued the active use of his pen to the very last—writing, while lying in his bed, a few days before his death, a leading article for the "Christian Union." Mr. Abbott's great success as preacher and author, was due to his habit of systematic work and unintermitting industry. He was an indefatigable worker. He would preach twice on a Sunday, lecture at least once during the week, and furnish to the press not less than two volumes a year, besides frequent contributions to the periodicals. He generally rose early, and often had accomplished two hours of solid work before the major part of the world knew that the sun had risen. After breakfast he once more entered his study and he did not again emerge from it until dinner time. His afternoons he devoted to visiting his parishioners—finding in this both rest and recreation—and his evenings he gave to the enjoyment of his family. It was his rule not to work after supper, but this rule—like those of a Greek grammar—had as many exceptions as examples. He was an assiduous student, but like his brother Jacob, consulted nature quite as much as he did his library. He read a book as a bee sips a flower—extracting its sweets and then tossing it aside. In writing history he was accustomed to read up his subject until it was thoroughly familiar, then closing his eyes, he would transport himself into the scene he was about to describe, and paint with his pen what he had seen in mental vision. He had a rare power of abstraction,

VI.—10

and the ability to come out of the past and return to it almost instantly. He would leave the death-bed of De Soto, or a battle-field of Napoleon, to answer a question about his household, or receive a chance visitor, and then return to his unfinished picture without displacing a figure or altering a color. But, as has been true of very many literary workers, much of his success was due to the efficient aid of his wife. She was his amanuensis, looked up his authorities, conducted his correspondence, corrected his proofs, and relieved him of the greater part of the drudgery incident to a literary career. She was in truth a "help-meet" for him. Next to his wife, the most potent helper Mr. Abbott had in his work was an equal temper. He was never discomposed, never in a hurry. However hard pressed he might be by publisher or printer, he always wrote with a quiet mind. His books, while not such as are accounted great, have had a great influence. But his personal influence was greater than that of his books, for he was a good man. In his last illness he looked forward to the close of his life with all the impatience of a school-boy awaiting his vacation. To a nephew he said, a few hours before his death, "You cannot conceive how inexpressibly happy I am to know that before to-morrow's sunrise the angels will take me to my long home." He died at Fair Haven, Conn., June 17, 1877.

BERRY, A. Moore, lawyer, was born at Greenville, S. C., Dec. 5, 1849, son of Rev. Larkin M. and Martha Bishop Berry. He received an academic education at Lincolnton, N. C., and at the age of twenty years removed to Missouri, where he secured the position of deputy clerk and recorder of deeds of Livingston county. During the period of this official employment, by diligence and determined application, he qualified himself for admission to the bar. He removed to St. Louis in 1872, and acquired a law practice. In 1874 he married Ella, daughter of William M. Leftwich, D.D. In 1877 his legal and literary attainments secured his appointment as law reporter of the court of appeals, which position he filled for twelve years, with such distinguished ability as greatly enhanced his reputation with the bench and bar throughout the state and elsewhere. He resigned this position in order to have it filled by a friend, a distinguished jurist, who, because of defective hearing, had been obliged to resign his position on the bench. During his incumbency of that office he prepared and published twenty-eight volumes of "Missouri Appeal Reports." Early in his career as a lawyer, an eminent judge of national reputation said of Mr. Berry,

"Few men have succeeded so well in establishing a high official reputation, while gaining numerous personal friendships, founded not less upon his rare social gifts than upon the substantial evidences of sterling character and unusual ability. As a lawyer, he is a devotee, as well as a successful expounder of principles, rather than an undiscriminating searcher after precedents. Of a nature at once genial and determined, quick of perception, and prompt in action, his methods form the surest basis of successful advocacy. His analytical habits of thought, cultivated by the necessities of his public and professional duties, render him a safe counsellor and a formidable opponent." Mr. Berry is the president of the Southern Saving-Fund and Loan Co., and the general counsel of banks and business corporations of great magnitude. As a successful lawyer and business man he occupies an enviable position, won by acts worthy of emulation; while his literary knowledge and his wonderful command of language, coupled with his social gifts, make him one of the most charming and most sought-for after-dinner speakers of his city.

DISSTON, Henry, manufacturer, was born at Tewkesbury, England, May 24, 1819, son of Thomas Disston, of Tewkesbury and Derby, at which latter place he was engaged in the manufacture of lace machines, and where the son early acquired a thorough knowledge of mechanics. In 1833 the family emigrated to America, and three days after landing in Philadelphia, the father died from a sudden stroke of apoplexy, leaving the fourteen-year-old boy penniless, and with a younger sister dependent upon him for support. He at once apprenticed himself to a saw-making firm, and within a few years' time had mastered all the details of that manufacture. When he was eighteen years of age the firm failed, and being unable to obtain in cash some of the wages due him, he took in payment a small stock of unfinished bricklayers' trowels. These he finished up and sold, thus realizing his first capital, about $350, with which he at once embarked in business on his own account. The Disston Keystone Saw Works were then started in 1840, in a room and basement on Broad street, Philadelphia. He built his own furnace, wheeled the first barrow of coal from the wharf at Willow street, made his own tools, and, in fact, ran the entire business without help. Having made his first lot of saws, he himself put them on sale, but it was a long time before he could make people believe that an American saw was anything but a poor imitation of the English article. He was discouraged many times, but never lost heart. He often sold a saw at a profit of but one per cent. Upon taking a room in a factory at Front and Maiden streets, his effects were levied upon for the rent of the building, for, although he himself owed nothing, he was merely a sub-tenant. Money was advanced by an old friend, who appeared at this opportune moment, and a new landlord taking the building, operations were resumed. He borrowed $200, which, while enabling him to branch out a little, made him the more determined to succeed. Soon afterwards the boiler in the building exploded, the structure was destroyed by fire, and young Disston was severely injured. Within ten days, however, he removed into a new building adjoining the old shop. The tariff of 1861 gave his saws their first great start. During the next year he decided to no longer import English steel, and to this end he utilized the scraps of his own establishment. Hitherto all waste material had been shipped to England for that purpose. Rolling-mills directly adjoining the works on Laurel street were therefore established, together with a melting department, and in the new adjunct was produced all the iron and steel used in the several factories. During the civil war he engaged extensively in the manufacture of military accoutrements, receiving large orders for this class of goods. His devotion to the government was testified in various ways. He sent twenty-five men, fully equipped, to the army, paying their wages during their military service as though they were still working for him, and reserving their positions until their return. By 1864 his business had grown to $35,000 a month, when fire again destroyed everything. Within fifteen days after the disaster, however, saws were being manufactured on the old site under a roof of canvas. Substantial buildings were quickly erected, and soon the establishment at Front and Laurel streets covered eight acres. The complete area covered by the works is twenty-four acres, some sixteen of which are at Tacony, on the Delaware river. Besides creating a new industry, Mr. Disston founded an industrial university, where a dozen useful trades are taught. In later years his sons became active factors in the firm's success. Hamilton, the elder, served seven years before he was taken into the counting-room, while Albert now deceased, Horace, William, and Jacob, the other partners, each also served his time before admission to the firm. In 1847 a file factory was started at Tacony in order to supply the saw-works with files. Like the saws, these tools soon won their way into public favor, large quantities of them being produced annually. At Tacony, too, were manufactured the brass and wood-work used for the numerous tools turned out by the city establishment, while another most important branch of the business is sheet-steel, of which as much as 100 tons have been produced in a single week. The Disston saws are now regularly exported to Great Britain and her colonies, and, indeed, to every part of the globe. A man of profoundly religious temperament, Mr. Disston was a life-long member of the Presbyterian church, the Oxford Presbyterian Church being founded largely, if not wholly, through his generous gifts. He was a member of St. George's Society, Masonic, and a trustee of the Presbyterian Hospital. During the presidential campaign of 1876, he was one of the electors from Pennsylvania. Mr. Disston's great success in business was due to integrity of purpose, native ability as a mechanic, and indomitable perseverance. Mr. Disston died at his home in Philadelphia, March 10, 1878. Since his death the enterprise inaugurated by him has been ably maintained by his sons.

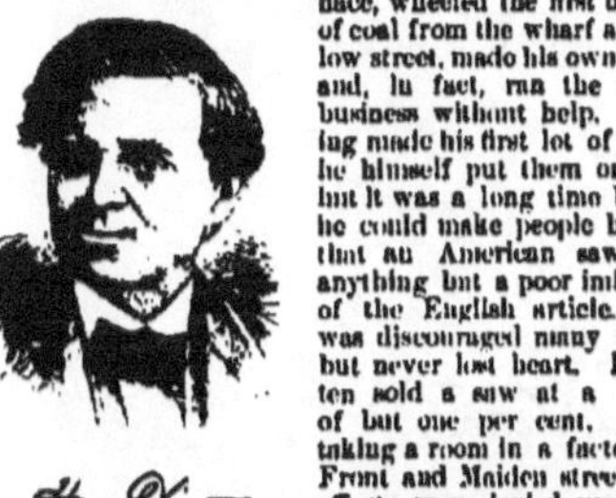

HORN, Charles Edward, composer, was born in the parish of St. Martin's-in-the-Fields, London, June 21, 1786. He was taught the elements of music by his father, a German musician. In 1809 Horn made an unsuccessful attempt as a barytone singer at the English Opera House in London. Thereafter he studied solfeggio, and five years later again sang in Storace's opera "The Siege of Belgrade" and similar musical pieces; this was followed by his appearing as a vocalist and conductor at sundry minor theatres in Great Britain and Ireland. On the production of a mutilated representation of Weber's opera "Der Freischutz," at Drury Lane, Horn undertook the part of Caspar, which he sang and acted "after a fashion." In 1831–32 he directed the music at the London Olympic Theatre. In 1827 Horn came to the United States, sang at concerts and oratorios and brought out a number of so-called English operas in New York, Philadelphia, and other cities. These were compounds audaciously made up from various composers, and interspersed with some of his own or Braham's songs. These operas were advertised as "The Barber of Seville," "Cinderella," "The White Lady," "Guy Mannering," "The Magic Flute," "Don Giovanni." In this edition of "The Magic Flute" the Queen of the Night had no place, Sarastro sang a melody from "La Bayadère," and all Mozart's concerted music was omitted. Later Horn brought forward an oratorio entitled "The Remission of Sin," which was revamped in London under the name of "Satan," where it was hissed and whistled off the stage. In 1840 he ventured to produce in New York city an opera, "Ahmed al Kamel," that outlined two representations. Horn went to London in 1831, and directed the music at at one of the minor playhouses; in the following

year he returned to the United States. He then taught music in New York city, and for about a year was connected with a music business, under the firm name of Davis & Horn. In 1845 he recrossed the ocean, and for a season played the violin in the orchestra of the Princess' Theatre, London. He returned to America in 1845, settled in Boston, Mass., and for the season of 1847–48 was conductor of the Handel and Hayden Society. Horn wrote some vocal music that became popular, and is not without merit. His best composition is a duet, "I know a Bank whereon the Wild Thyme Blows," that is occasionally sung during the performance of Shakespeare's "Midsummer Night's Dream." "Cherry Ripe," "Through the Wood," "Even as the Sun," and "I've been Roaming," had considerable popularity. Horn's abilities as a musician and singer were of little account; he was besides a bad actor. He always prided himself on being "a true-born Briton," and had nothing in common with the countrymen of his father. He died in Boston, Mass., Oct. 21, 1849.

WALL, Joseph B., lawyer, was born in Hernando county, Fla., Jan. 23, 1847, the eldest son, by a second marriage, of Judge Wall, who was for many years probate judge of the county, and among its first settlers in 1846. The son was educated at the public schools until his eighteenth year, when, feeling that he could render good service to his native state, he threw down his books, entered the Confederate army as a private in the 2d Florida reserves, and served until the close of the war in April, 1865. He then studied law in the University of Virginia, and after graduation in 1869, returned to Brooksville, Fla., for the practice of his profession. Mr. Wall removed to Tampa, Fla., in 1873, and formed a partnership with H. L. Mitchell, who was subsequently elected to the state supreme bench, and afterwards became governor of Florida. Wall was appointed state attorney for the sixth judicial district in 1874 for four years, being the first Democrat appointed to office by Gov. Hart, who was an ardent Republican. On the expiration of his state attorneyship in 1878 he devoted himself to his private practice, to improving the city, and managing his landed interests. He was made a brigadier-general in the national guard of the state in 1880 by Gov. Bloxham, elected to the state senate from Hillsborough county in 1886, and became president of the senate in 1889, after the adoption of the new constitution, which abolished the position of lieutenant-governor. His management of the business of the senate made him popular throughout the state, and won him many encomiums. He was elected first president of the Florida State Bar Association in 1887 and vice-president of the Florida Field Sports Association in 1889, and was

one of the fifteen Democratic senators who left their seats in the senate and retreated to Thomasville, Ga., in 1891, in order to prevent the election of Wilkinson Call to the U. S. senate. This famous retreat became historical, and those taking part in it were humorously designated as the "Babes in the Wood." As chairman of the Tampa board of public works he has done a great deal for the city, the handsome city hall having been erected during his term, the streets paved, and many other improvements made. He was urged to accept the position of circuit judge, but felt compelled to decline the honor on account of his private practice and landed interests. Gen. Wall's knowledge of the law is broad and thorough.

He uses law and logic in his cases instead of pyrotechnic displays, is an able speaker, a close, clear reasoner, and an incisive analyzer of evidence. Genial and unpretentious in manner, a warm friend and a magnanimous foe, he stands in the front rank of his profession in the state. He has been twice married: first, in the autumn of 1869, to Miss Ederington, of South Carolina; and in 1875 to Miss F. Lykes, of South Carolina, who now reigns in his home.

CORT, Thomas, manufacturer, was born in Spratton, Northants, England, 1854, son of Thomas Cort, a shoe manufacturer. The son was self-taught, and when but nine years old commenced to learn the trade of shoemaker with his father. In 1869 father and son came to America, settling in Newark, N. J., where they commenced the manufacture of shoes. The son went to Philadelphia in 1872, where he followed up his trade, and where in 1874 he was married to Kate Keller Grubb, a native of that city. In 1874 he settled in Newark and began business for himself in the manufacture of high-grade walking and lawn-tennis shoes, being among the first engaged in this specialty in America. The business grew rapidly, and by making the very best work and putting in the market none but superior shoes, he has made for himself a wide reputation and large sales. Mr. Cort is a member of the Order of Elks, a Mason, and belongs to several social and political clubs in Newark. He was elected alderman of the city for his ward in 1893, and has made a reputation as a careful and conscientious legislator.

MITCHELL, Lucy Myers Wright, archæologist, was born in Orcomiah, Persia, March 20, 1845, daughter of Rev. Austin H. Wright, an American missionary to the Nestorians, who lived with that people for twenty years. In 1859 the daughter was sent to America to be educated, and attended Mount Holyoke Seminary. In 1864 her father was on a visit to America, having brought his son, John Henry Wright, to be educated, and the daughter urgently requested to be allowed to return with him to Persia, where she remained until the sudden death of her father, in 1865, when she returned to America. In 1867 she was married to Samuel S. Mitchell, of Morristown, N. J., afterward an artist of considerable repute. Her life after her marriage was spent largely in Syria, Germany, Italy, and England. She had acquired a vernacular knowledge of Syriac, Arabic, French, German, and Italian languages, and was largely interested in philological researches. While a resident of Tübingen she prepared a dictionary of the modern Syriac language, which, however, was not published, the manuscript being now the property of the University of Cambridge, Eng. She followed with deep interest the philological studies of her brother, Prof. John Henry Wright, of Harvard. In 1873 she took up with great enthusiasm the study of classical archæology, which she pursued in Rome, Florence, Munich, Berlin, and London. While residing in Rome (1876–78) she gave popular lectures to ladies on Greek and Roman sculpture, accompanied by visits to the Roman collections. In 1883 she published "History of Ancient Sculpture," and its companion volume of plates, "Selections from Ancient Sculpture," in New York and London, which were received with great favor by students and friends of art, and the press of Berlin, London, and New York were equally liberal in their praises of its worth. In 1884 she was elected an active member of the Imperial Archæological Institute of Germany, only one other woman enjoying the distinction with her. In 1884–86 Mrs. Mitchell resided at Berlin, and there made a special study and collection of material for a work on Greek vases and vase-paintings. She studied the ancient Greek language, that she might have its aid in the literature relating to her subjects. She at the same time studied modern Greek, and gained a practical knowledge of photography in anticipation of faithful research and study when the next season she should visit Greece. During the winter of 1886–87 her husband took her to the shores of Lake Geneva for rest, with the hope of checking the inroads of disease. She did not, however, gain any permanent help, and died March 10, 1888, at Lausanne, Switzerland.

PRIESTLEY, Joseph, scientist, was born in Fieldhead, near Leeds, Eng., March 24, 1733. His father, Jonas Priestley, was a woolen cloth-dresser in very moderate circumstances. His paternal grandfather was a clergyman, whose high, moral character became a sacred tradition in the family. His parents were non-conformists, and he was brought up with quiet strictness. His mother died when he was a child, and he was reared and educated by his aunt, Mrs. Keighley. With a view of impressing him with a clear idea of the distinction of property, she made him return a pin which he had picked up at a relative's. At the age of twelve he was sent to a neighboring endowed school, where he made rapid progress in classics, while on holidays by way of variation he studied Hebrew with a dissenting minister, who afterward took the entirecharge of his tuition. As his health was not good, it was thought that commercial life would be better for him, and, with this in view, he learned French, Italian, and German without assistance; but his aunt had set her heart on making a minister of him, and the mercantile situation at Lisbon was declined. Priestley in his twentieth year, from 1752–55, studied at the dissenting academy in Daventry, with the intention of becoming a clergyman, but at the end of that time was refused entrance into the ministry because of his liberal views. Though brought up in the principles of Calvinism, he could not realize the experience he supposed to be necessary to conversion. He could not repent of Adam's transgression, a difficulty which he never surmounted, and his candid mind began to doubt whether he was so much entangled in Adam's fall as he had been taught; accordingly he was refused admission to the Independent church, where his aunt attended. At Daventry he remained three years, taking a prominent part in the free discussions that formed the chief part of the exercises, and he soon came to embrace what is called the heterodox side of almost every question. His intellectual preparation is noteworthy. Besides being a fair classic scholar, he had learned Chaldee and Syriac and begun to read Arabic. He had also mastered "Elements of Natural Philosophy," and various text-books in logic and mathematics. His speculations at this time were philosophical rather than scientific. Under the influence of Hartley's "Observations on Man," and Collins's "Philosophical Enquiry," he exchanged his Calvinism for a system of "necessarianism," which realized the inviolable connection between cause and effect in the moral world as well as the physical. During

these early years he began his enormous industry as a writer, and in particular laid down the lines of his "Institutes of Natural and Revealed Religion." In 1755 he preached at Needham Market in Suffolk, with slight success, but in 1758 he obtained a more congenial congregation at Nantwick, where he established a school. It is noteworthy that he varied his elementary lessons with experiments in natural philosophy, and he is probably one of the very first teachers to appreciate the importance of physical science in early culture. From 1761–67 he taught the languages and *belles-lettres* in a dissenting academy at Warrington, where he spent six of his happiest years, pursuing his scientific studies, enjoying congenial intercourse with various Manchester men, whose sons helped to form the "Manchester school." In addition to his school work, he preached regularly during this period, and was finally ordained as a minister, and married the daughter of Isaac Wilkinson, an iron-master at Wrexham. His attainments as a scholar now began to be recognized, and in 1766 the University of Edinburgh gave him the degree of LL.D., and he was also chosen a member of the Royal Society. In 1767 Dr. Priestley was installed over a church at Leeds, and in the same year, at the instance of Franklin, whose acquaintance he had previously made during a visit to London, he published his "History and Present State of Electricity, with Original Experiments." While a minister at Leeds he was constantly engaged in literary, theological, and scientific investigations, all of which bore important fruit. Now he changed his Arianism for definite Socinian views. In addition to his preaching and teaching he carried on his chemical researches with results which at the time were considered startling. Chemistry, as the term is now understood, was then unborn. Living next door to a brewery, he experimented with the "fixed air" (carbonic acid), and succeeded in forcing it into water. Thus began the researches which gave impetus to experiment and controversy throughout the country. At this time he wrote various political papers, always in favor of popular rights, and in favor of the American colonies. In 1769 he engaged in a controversy with Sir William Blackstone, which caused the latter to make many important changes in his recently published "Commentaries," and in 1772 he published the "History and Present State of Discoveries Relating to Vision, Light, and Colors." From 1772–80 he acted as literary companion to the Earl of Shelburne, a position which gave him abundant leisure for study and scientific experiments. He traveled extensively on the continent, and resided for a considerable period in Paris, but upon the completion of his "Disquisitions on Matter and Spirit" the connection was dissolved as his patron feared to share the unpopularity of his views. It was during these years that he made his greatest discoveries in chemistry. In 1772 he discovered nitric oxide; in 1774, oxygen, hydrochloric acid, and ammonia; in 1775, sulphur dioxide, silicon, tetrafluoride, and carburetted hydrogen gas; in 1776, nitrous oxide; and in 1779, carbon monoxide. He also demonstrated that the prolonged passage of electric sparks through a given bulk of air forms an acid, and this later led to the discovery of nitric acid by Cavendish. He was compelled to construct his own apparatus, but he did his work so well that many of his devices are in use at the present time. The results of his researches he elaborately and accurately described in "Experiments and Observations Relating to Natural Philosophy," published between 1779 and 1786. He was also at this time a constant and voluminous writer upon theological subjects, and engaged in frequent controversies, in nearly all of which he was successful. In 1780 Dr. Priestley became pastor of an independent church in Birmingham, and in 1790 aroused bitter hostility by his bold defense of the French revolution and of individual liberty. Indeed, so intense became the feeling against him that on July 14, 1791, a mob attacked and burned his church and house in Birmingham, destroying his library, apparatus, and manuscripts. The venerable scholar made his escape to London, and after a long and costly litigation succeeded in securing partial compensation for his great loss. On Apr. 7, 1794, he sailed for the United States. On his arrival in New York he was invited to deliver a course of lectures on experimental philosophy, but this invitation he declined, as he also did a subsequent offer of the professorship of chemistry in the University of Pennsylvania. His sons were already settled at Northumberland, Pa., and there they built for their father a home and laboratory, where he actively continued his work as an author and scientist until his death. He delivered series of lectures in Philadelphia in 1796 and 1797; gave valuable aid to Thomas Jefferson in founding the University of Virginia, and a few years before his death was tendered the presidency of the University of North Carolina. Dr. Priestley's writings, besides those already named, include: "Rudiments of English Grammar" (1761); "Course of Lectures on the Theory of Language" (1762); "Familiar Letters to the Inhabitants of Birmingham" (1790); "Letters to Rt. Hon. E. Burke, Occasioned by His Reflections on the Revolution in France" (1791); "Discourses Relating to the Evidences of Revealed Religion" (1796); "General History of the Christian Church to the Fall of the Western Empire" (1802-3); "Answer to Mr. Paine's 'Age of Reason'" (1795); "Comparison of the Institutions of Moses with those of the Hindoos and Other Nations" (1799); "Notes on all the Books of Scripture" (1803); and "The Doctrines of Heathen Philosophy Compared with Those of Revelation" (1804). His "Theological and Miscellaneous Works" were published in twenty-six volumes, between 1817 and 1832. In 1860 a marble statue in his honor was placed in the museum at Oxford, and in 1874 another statue was unveiled in Birmingham. See also "Memoirs of Dr. Joseph Priestley to the Year 1795, Written by Himself; With a Continuation to the Time of His Decease by His Son, Joseph Priestley" (1806-7); and also, "Life of J. Priestley," by John Corry (1805). The interest in Dr. Priestley's life lies in the fact that his career affords a typical illustration of mutual relation and interaction of some great factors of human progress at a critical time. As a non-conformist minister, born into a Calvinistic circle, educated in an independent academy, developing into a Socinian divine, yet maintaining always the most friendly relations with clergymen, priests, and orthodox ministers, he gives us an insight into the condition of English religion before they had hardened into their modern form. As a pioneer in the investigation of gases, and the discoverer of oxygen, he helped to erect chemistry into a science. As a professed materialist, whose doctrines seem to merge matter into force, he prepared the way for the modern agnostic, who declines to look behind phenomena. As a politician, he anticipated nineteenth century radicalism. He died Feb. 6, 1804, in Northumberland, Pa.

MILLS, Henry Edmund, lawyer, was born in Montrose, Susquehanna co., Pa., June 24, 1850, son of Bartlet Himes Mills, a prominent temperance editor, and organizer and lecturer in the order of Good Templars. His first American ancestor was Samuel Mills, born 1622, a freeholder of Dedham precinct, now Needham, Mass. In 1645 Samuel had a son, Benjamin; Benjamin had a son, Benjamin, Jr.; Benjamin, Jr., had a son, Nehemiah; Nehemiah had a son, Nehemiah 2d, who had several children, among them Josiah, born Oct. 7, 1763, at Roxbury, Mass.

Josiah, who was the father of Bartlet Himes, was in the revolutionary war, first as drummer, afterward as a soldier in a Massachusetts regiment, was in the principal battles of Valley Forge and Yorktown, and was a pensioner. His mother was a Halsey, tracing back directly to Thomas Halsey, who came from Hertfordshire, Eng., to Lynn, Mass., afterward settling in Southampton, L. I., where are now found numerous Halseys. His maternal grandmother was Cordelia Sayre, whose ancestor, Thomas Sayre, came from Bedfordshire, Eng., to Lynn, Mass., in 1638, and afterward, in 1640, was one of the original settlers of Southampton, L. I. Mr. Mills was educated at Shurtleff College, Upper Alton, and was graduated in 1869. He taught a country school for one year, when he took up the study of law at the St. Louis Law School, where he was graduated in June, 1872. He was admitted to the bar in 1871, one year before his graduation. He was married Aug. 30, 1877, at St. Louis, Mo., to Emma Brown Sprague, whose parents were among the earliest settlers of the Muskingum valley, emigrating thither from New England, where they served in the revolutionary war. Mr. Mills has served as alderman of his city, but has avoided all political offices, giving his whole time to his profession. He is the author of "Law of

Eminent Domain," published in 1878, which called for a second revised edition. This work has received favorable comment from law periodicals and the courts, and is a standard reference-book on the subject.

PHILLIPS, Adelaide, actress and prima donna, was born at Stratford-on-Avon, England, Oct. 26, 1833. When she was about seven years old, her father left England for Canada, and soon afterwards removed to Boston, Mass., which became their home from that time. Adelaide began her artistic career when only seven years old, in the Tremont Theatre in Boston, where she was required to sing and dance, and represent five characters. A few months later she was engaged at the Boston Museum, belonging to the company of which the famous Warren was a member. She remained there for some years, a favorite with everyone for her pleasant manners and good nature, a child of the stage, whom all united in protecting from harm and evil. Her voice, which had received careful cultivation, was a good contralto, and her teachers were convinced that a great future lay before her in Italian opera. When Jenny

Lind was in Boston in 1851, her attention was called to Miss Phillips. She heard her sing, and at once advised her to study under her own famous teacher, Garcia. Her advice was accompanied by a check for $1,000, which enabled Miss Phillips to go to London in 1852, and to put herself under Emanuel Garcia's instruction for two years. In order that she might master the Italian language, and obtain the necessary dramatic training, she went to Italy. In a few months an engagement was concluded for her at Brescia in Lombardy, where she made her début as Arsace in "Semiramide." Her appearance was most successful, and procured her engagements for a time, but was followed by a season of great disappointment. A favorite with the Italians, she was yet unable to procure engagements, and she decided to return to the United States. She did so in 1855, and made her operatic début in Philadelphia again as Azucena. At once she became a most popular artist, and for years in this country and abroad had a very successful career. She maintained her family from her early years, and made for them a charming home at Marshfield, Mass., where she permitted herself, at rare intervals, the rest she so much needed. Her goodness and her generosity were the delight and help of her family and many pensioners; while her unselfishness and hard work brought to a premature grave, a life which was most valuable to the world and her friends. Her ill health was due in great measure to her impulsive nursing of a chorus girl, ill of yellow fever. She herself took the fever, and never regained her vigor. Even when her health began to fail seriously, she kept on with her arduous work, and when, in 1882, she went abroad, hoping that rest and change would restore her to strength, it was too late, and she died at Carlsbad, Germany, Oct. 3, 1882.

JUNGMANN, John George, Moravian missionary, was born at Flochenheim, Germany, Apr. 19, 1720. The family came to America in 1732, and took a farm in Berks county, Pa.; here he was attracted by the Moravians and joined them. After long and faithful labors in his own province he went to Ohio as assistant to David Zeisberger, and with him was arrested by the British and taken to Detroit in 1781. The massacre at Gnadenhutten ruined what was left of this mission, but he remained in the West until 1785, chiefly in what is now Michigan. His later years were spent at Bethlehem, where he died, July 17, 1808.

McDONALD, Edward Francis, congressman, was born in Ireland, Sept. 21, 1844. He came to America with his parents in 1850, and was educated in the public schools of Newark, N. J., where his parents had made their home. When the civil war broke out in 1861, he was a lad of seventeen years, and left his bench in a machine shop, where he had been learning the trade, to enlist in the service of his adopted country. He joined the 7th New Jersey volunteers. During his first months in the army he was stricken with typhoid fever, and was honorably discharged Dec. 30, 1862. Upon his recovery he re-enlisted, and served under McClellan and Hooker in the peninsular campaign and through the seven days' fight before Richmond, as sergeant of his company. Returning home at the close of the war, he took up the business of machinist and toolworker, which occupation he followed for twelve years. In 1874 he was elected to represent Hudson county, N. J., in the state legislature. He was afterward made director-at-large of the freeholders of his county, and was twice re-elected. He also served a term as town treasurer. In November, 1880, he was elected state senator, and in 1890 was elected to represent the seventh congressional district of New Jersey in the fifty-second congress, and served throughout the first session up to the time of his death. He was a useful member of the committee on military affairs in the house, and was a candidate for re-election to the fifty-fifth congress on the eve of his sudden death. Representative McDonald was married, and had six children. In religion he was a devout Roman Catholic, and in politics a Democrat. Mr. McDonald in his brief life demonstrated what could be accomplished by one of even the most humble origin. As a legislator he was incorruptible, while in the very midst of political corruption. His learning was self-acquired, during a hard struggle for daily bread, and was wide in range; his nature was singularly sympathetic, and his manner magnetic. As an orator, his services were in constant demand during political campaigns, while his ability as a political leader was acknowledged, even by his opponents. He died at his home in Harrison, N. J., Nov. 5, 1892.

HARRIS, Samuel Arthur, banker, was born at Goshen, Elkhart co., Ind., Oct. 25, 1847. His father, Thomas G. Harris, was one of the best known lawyers of the state, and president of the Salem Bank at Goshen. The son received his education in the public schools of his native place, and afterward spent two years in the East and in Europe. In 1868 he located in Minneapolis, where he secured employment as clerk in a hardware store, and afterward with lumber dealers. For a few months he was clerk in the State National Bank, and when the Hennepin County Savings Bank was organized in 1870 he became a stockholder and trustee, and was appointed assistant cashier. In this position he remained for nine years, and then resigned to take a similar position with the Northwestern National Bank, where in the spring of 1880 he was advanced to the position of cashier, and seven years later became president. Under his administration the institution prospered exceedingly, enlarged its capital to $1,000,000, and changed a large part of its real estate security to cash, that made its assets more available in an emergency. In 1890 he resigned the presidency of the bank, and spent some months with his family in travel. In 1891 he became treasurer of the Globe Elevator Co., one of the largest corporations of its kind in the country, having his office in Minneapolis; and in December of the same year was elected president of the National Bank of Commerce. He found this bank also encumbered with real estate and other dead assets, and his first work was to turn them into available shape. This was accomplished in six months, and the bank, with a cash capital of $1,000,000, is one of the four large banks of Minneapolis. He has been president of the Clearing House Association, and also of the Dual City Bankers' Club; he was for some years a member of the executive council of the American Bankers' Association, a director of the Minnesota Loan and Trust Co. from the time of its organization, and has been for a long time treasurer of the Globe Gaslight Co. On Sept. 18, 1872, Mr. Harris was married to Anna, daughter of the Rev. Daniel Stewart, of Minneapolis. They have two sons and one daughter. He is an elder in the Westminster Presbyterian Church, and has given considerable time and attention to evangelistic and mission work. He was for many years treasurer of the Presbyterian Alliance. In every public enterprise, looking to the advancement of the material interests of Minneapolis, he is among the foremost and most liberal supporters.

DREW, Francis A., merchant, was born at Lismore, county Waterford, Ireland, June 7, 1848, the third son of William Henry and Catherine Mary Drew. He was educated by private tutors until the age of fifteen, when he was sent to the college of the Trappist monks at Mount Melleray, where he studied for two years. He was then sent to the Catholic University of Ireland, in Dublin, where he entered to study medicine; attended lectures at the University School of Medicine, and for hospital practice at the Mater Misereordis and St. Vincent's Hospitals. During the Fenian excitement of 1867 and 1868 he, with other students, was suspected of being in sympathy with the movement, and not wishing to incur the displeasure of the authorities, determined to leave the country. Being informed that the position of house-surgeon in a hospital of Lima, Peru, was at the disposal of the famous Dr. Stapleton of Dublin, he made application for it, but on account of his youth was rejected. He then left for New York, and in a short time finally removed to St. Louis, where, after experiencing all the disappointments that new arrivals generally encounter, he secured employment as book-keeper. Having learned by hard work enough of the paint, oil, and glass business to warrant him in starting independently for himself, he obtained the agency for one of the largest and oldest plate and window glass importing houses in New

York, and also of a foreign encaustic tile house, laying the foundation of his present business. At the end of the first year his business having outgrown its limits, he opened a large store, where he remained for four years, then, removing to one still larger, he remained for twelve years, when, to meet the requirements of his business, he was again compelled to obtain more extensive quarters. Mr. Drew is a member of the University, Marquette, and Mercantile Clubs, a director of the Merchants' National Bank, and treasurer of the Catholic Orphans' Board. He has also been a director of the Mercantile Library Association, and has traveled extensively in Europe. Though his father was a Protestant up to the time of his marriage, and never completely severed his connection with that faith, he allowed his wife, a Catholic, to bring up all the children in her faith; Mr. Drew has always adhered to the Catholic church. His political views are Republican, though in no sense extreme. He was married on Sept. 2, 1872, to Emma, second daughter of George Barnett by his first wife, who was a daughter of Edwin Lewis, surgeon in the royal navy of Great Britain and Ireland, and who was at the time of his marriage in active service on board her majesty's ship Emulous.

MARTIN, William, clergyman, was born in Mecklenburg county, N. C., March 9, 1807, of Scotch-Irish Presbyterian parentage. His paternal grandfather came to America from Scotland, and took part in the campaign of Braddock against the Indians in 1775, and later engaged in the revolutionary war, and commanded a company of troopers under Col. Campbell in the battle of King's Mountain, N. C., Oct. 7, 1780. His father died during William's infancy, and he was educated by his mother, a woman of superior ability. At the age of sixteen he became connected with the Methodist church, and in 1828 was admitted on trial as a traveling preacher in the South Carolina conference, and was for sixty years thereafter identified with the progress of Methodism in the Carolinas, Georgia, and Alabama. He manfully overcame the impediments of his early education and improved his opportunities so well that in a short time he was appointed to preach in the large cities of Georgia and South Carolina. He had previously been serving as a missionary to the Indians and the negro slaves; and preached among the remote scattered settlements on the borders of civilization; his only method of traveling being on horseback, by which means he traversed thousands of miles. Mr. Martin was instrumental in the establishment of the Wayside Hospital at Columbia, S. C., at the commencement of the civil war, which proved a great boon to the Confederate soldiers wounded during the war. He was appointed superintendent of the central bureau for the relief of the Confederate army, by which the comfort of the soldiers on the field and the prisoners of war was greatly promoted. Mr. Orr appointed Mr. Martin to take charge of the donations of food and clothing that were contributed from all quarters to Columbia when that city was devasted by Gen. Sherman during the civil war. He organized a system of distribution which he personally superintended and succeeded in greatly alleviating the sufferings of the people. He next devoted his attention to restoring the waste and ruin war had brought to the churches, and through his untiring efforts as agent and pastor, in the course of a few years a handsome building was erected on the site of the burned Washington Street Church, the chapel was rebuilt, and a mission church erected in another section of the city. Mr. Martin has held the highest official position of trust and responsibility in the Methodist church and its institutions of learning. He was agent of the American Bible Society, financial agent of the Columbia Female College, president of the Columbia Bible Society, etc. He also contributed to the various church papers, was editor of the "Temperance Advocate," and author of a book entitled, "Incidents in the Life of a Pastor." He died at Columbia, S. C., Jan. 10, 1889.

JOY, Edmund L., lawyer and business man, was born in Albany, N. Y., Oct. 1, 1835, son of Charles and Harriet (Shaw) Joy, grandson of Nathaniel Joy, a soldier in the war of the American revolution, and great-grandson of Nathaniel Joy, who was killed in the French and Indian war. His first American ancestor, Thomas Joy, came from Yarmouth, England, in 1630, with a colony of 900 persons, including John Winthrop, governor of Massachusetts Bay, and settled in the vicinity of Plymouth. Edmund was educated at Anthony's Classical Institute and the Albany Academy, where he was prepared for college. After graduation from the University of Rochester, he studied law and was admitted to the bar of New York in 1857. His father removed from Albany in 1857 and settled in Newark, N. J., where he conducted an extensive business as a packer and smoker of provisions. The son, in 1857, removed to Ottumwa, Ia., where he established himself in the practice of his profession. He was appointed city attorney in 1860.

At the outbreak of the civil war he took an active interest in raising and equipping troops and securing volunteers, and in 1862 went to the front as a captain in the 36th Iowa infantry, and served in the South-west, notably throughout the Vicksburg campaign. In 1864 he was appointed major and judge advocate, U. S. volunteers, by Pres. Lincoln, and assigned to the 7th army corps, which was commanded by Maj.-Gen. Steele. He was subsequently made judge advocate of the department of the Arkansas, with headquarters at Little Rock. He had much to do in this capacity with the organization of a judicial system for Arkansas and the Indian Territory, and aided in the organization of a state government under a new constitution for the state of Arkansas. At the close of the war, broken in health, he returned to the home of his father at Newark, N. J., and became interested with him in business, which, upon the death of his father in 1878, he continued on his own account during the remainder of his life. In 1871 he was elected to represent his district in the legislature of New Jersey, and re-elected the following year, was made chairman of the judiciary committee. In 1877 he became a member of the board of education of the city of Newark, continuing in that position, for eleven years, being president of the board during the years 1885, 1886, and 1887. He was a member of the Newark board of trade, its president in 1875 and 1876, and its treasurer from 1879 to the time of his death. He was a delegate to the national Republican convention of 1880, and in 1884 and 1885 served as a government director of the Union Pacific Railroad Co., by appointment of Pres. Arthur. He was one of the founders of the Manufacturers' National Bank of Newark, and was identified with other financial institutions of that city as well as of New York. He was a remarkably able speaker and a man of deep religious convictions, great energy, and intellectual capacity, excellent judgment, and keen wit. In 1862 he married Theresa R., daughter of Homer L. Thrall of Columbus, O., a well-known physician, professor in Starling Medical College, and for many years previously in Kenyon College. They had two sons, Edmund Steele and Homer Thrall, and two daughters, Helen Adele and Harriet Shaw, wife of Robert D. Martin of Chicago. Col. Joy died at his home in Newark, N. J., Feb. 14, 1892.

KELLEY, Benjamin Franklin, soldier, was born at New Hampton, N. H., Apr. 10, 1807. At the age of nineteen he settled in Wheeling, W. Va., where he was engaged in mercantile pursuits until 1851, when he was appointed freight agent of the Baltimore and Ohio Railroad. He became prominent in the affairs of his adopted state, and was active in saving West Virginia to the union. Having had some experience as a commanding officer in connection with a local military organization, when the call for volunteers was made, he at once raised the 1st Virginia regiment of volunteers, of which he was commissioned colonel May 25, 1861. This was the first regiment of loyal troops raised south of Mason and Dixon's line. Two days after he received his commission he left Wheeling with his regiment for Grafton, which was at that time in possession of the Confederates under Gen. Porterfield, who retreated to Phillips at the approach of the Federal troops. Col. Kelley attacked him a few days later, and after a short engagement, won one of the first battles of the civil war. He was severely wounded in the breast during the battle, but, at the expiration of sixty days, was able to resume his command, having meanwhile been brevetted brigadier-general. On Oct. 23d he captured Romney, and for gallant conduct was complimented by Pres. Lincoln and Gen. Scott. He was appointed to the command of the department of Harper's Ferry and Cumberland, but on account of his wounds, was relieved at his own request. He served with distinction throughout the entire war, and from the beginning to the end was successful in all the battles in which he was engaged, and in recognition of meritorious and gallant services at Cumberland and New Creek, was brevetted major general of volunteers March 13, 1865. At the cessation of hostilities he served for a term as internal revenue collector of West Virginia, and was subsequently appointed by Pres. Hayes superintendent of the Hot Springs in Arkansas, and in 1883 was appointed examiner of pensions. He died at Oakland, Md., July, 1891.

OLDS, Edson B., statesman, was born in Burlington, Vt., in 1819, son of Gamaliel Smith Olds, clergyman and educator (1777-1848). With his parents he removed to the state of Georgia where his father was for several years professor of mathematics and natural philosophy in the University of Georgia, at Athens. Here he had the advantages of a thorough course at this celebrated school where he was duly graduated. He adopted the profession of medicine and in 1841 removed with his parents to Cincinnati, O., where he commenced practice as a physician and surgeon. He became popular, and soon gained a large acquaintance and influence. He was elected as a Democrat to represent his district in the thirty-first U. S. congress and was re-elected to the thirty-second and thirty-third

congresses, where he served on important committees and was a prominent and pronounced defender of the institution of slavery as it then existed in the southern states, and in favor of an equal chance for its introduction in the new territories. The anti-slavery sentiment became so strong that he was not returned to the thirty-fourth congress. However, his local reputation as an able legislator secured for him a place in the Ohio state legislature, where he served for six years in either house, and was for one session president of he state senate. In 1862 he was accused, by the general government, of disloyalty, and arrested and imprisoned in Fort Lafayette, New York harbor. While so imprisoned his constituents renominated him for the Ohio legislature and he was elected. The charge of treason not being sustained, he was released and took his seat in the state legislature. After the close of the war Dr. Olds built a church and made the one condition in its management "that it should be free from the heresy of regarding slavery and rebellion as sins." He died at Lancaster, O., Jan. 24, 1869.

SARGENT, Winthrop, territorial governor of Ohio, was born at Gloucester, Mass., May 1, 1753, grandson of Judge Epes Sargent, and cousin of L. M. Sargent. He was graduated at Harvard in 1771, and in 1775 left the command of one of his father's ships to enter the army, and served as captain of artillery under Gen. Knox from March, 1776, taking part in many of the battles, and rising to be a major. After the war he was concerned in the Ohio company, and was made surveyor-general of the northwest territory in 1786, and secretary the next year. He was adjutant-general of the army in the expeditions of Gens. St. Clair and Wayne, 1791 and 1794, and was wounded in the former. During the years preceding the admission of Ohio as a state, 1798-1801, he was its governor. He was a member of the Cincinnati, of the Philosophical Society, and of the Academy of Arts and Sciences. He wrote "Boston," a poem, 1803, and part of Dr. B. S. Smith's "Papers Relative to Certain American Antiquities," 1796. He died while travelling on the lower Mississippi, June 3, 1820.

FLOWER, George, pioneer, was born in Hertfordshire, Eng., about 1780, and became a prosperous farmer. Fired with the reports of the magnificent prairies of America, he sold his property, and, early in 1816, came to this country in quest of them. Unless he had been well off, he never would have found the land of his dreams, for it was nearly two years before his eyes rested on it. Almost two months were taken up by the ocean trip, and the fourth month of his absence from home had begun before he started on his horseback ride of 1,500 miles to the far West. Of the difficulties and hardships of this journey it is impossible, in this age of easy travel, to form any adequate idea. It was mostly through an unsettled country, and he had to carry with him a sufficient quantity of clothing and food to supply his needs. The passage of the numerous swift rivers was so perilous and terrifying that the memory of his narrow escapes haunted him in dreams to the end of his life. Added to the hardships of his ride, he had to endure great discouragement as to the realization of his hopes, for even at Cincinnati, then regarded as very far west, not a person had ever heard of the prairies. At last the brother of Gov. Shelby, of Kentucky, assured him of their existence, for he had just crossed the splendid prairies of Illinois. As it was then November, and too late to continue his hazardous journey, Flower turned back 1,000 miles to Virginia, and presenting his letter of introduction from Lafayette to Thomas Jefferson, spent most of the winter at the latter's hospitable home. On his way thither he had, at a horse-race in Nashville, a very characteristic view of the unique Andrew Jackson, whom he describes as outdoing all competition by his "violent gesticulations and imprecations." In the spring Flower was joined by Morris Birkbeck, a friend and farmer, from England, who brought with him his nine children and Miss Andrews, a friend of his daughters. The journey, as far as Pittsburg, was accomplished in the stage-coach, and the rest pleasantly on horseback. A little romance enlivened their progress, for Mr. Birkbeck having offered himself in marriage to Miss Andrews, and been refused, the embarrassing situation was relieved by her marrying the other pioneer, George Flower, the rejected suitor giving away the bride, when the party continued the trip in great content. At the end of the summer their efforts were rewarded by the sight of a splendid prairie, dotted here and there with oaks. "The whole," as Flower describes it, "presenting a magnificence of park scenery complete from the hand of nature," and fully equalling their hopes. They selected for their home a spot in Edwards county, Ill., and formed what is termed in the annals of the Chicago Historical Society, the "English Settlement," which received the name of Albion. George Flower left an interesting account of the growth of this frontier town: the first building, of the log-cabin order, being a tavern and blacksmith-shop combined, in order to keep man and beast in working order. He lived to see Albion become a prosperous and beautiful town. He died at Grayville, Ill., Jan. 15, 1862.

EATON, Charles H., tragedian, was born in Boston, June 10, 1813. He studied for the stage, and made his début as a professional actor as the Stranger at the Warren Street Theatre in Boston, October, 1833. He was most cordially received, and when the Kembles soon after visited Boston he was invited to play with them. He appeared as Master Walter to Fanny Kemble's Julia, and fairly divided honors with that experienced and accomplished actress. He first appeared in New York in July, 1833, and in Philadelphia in November of the same year. His New York début was made as Richard, and he was greeted with crowded houses for several weeks. He at once became a popular and profitable star, and during the next ten years played in all parts of the United States. In 1842 he commenced an engagement in Pittsburgh. On the second night he played William Tell to a crowded house. Returning to his hotel after the performance, he was seized with vertigo while ascending the stairs to his apartments, and fell to the floor below, sustaining injuries from which he died a few days later. Death thus cut short the career of one who promised to be the greatest actor of his time. He was a handsome man, of classical features, and impressive presence. During his career he played a long and varied list of parts, among them Shylock, Damon, Sir Edward Mortimer, Sir Giles Overreach, Othello, Macbeth, and Hamlet. He did nothing badly, and in many rôles he was superb. His acting, always virile and effective, showed the impress of a strong and original intellect, and as a reader of Shakespeare he was surpassed by no other player of that period.

DUNN, Elias Bound, meteorologist, was born in Brooklyn, N. Y., March 23, 1855. He is a descendant of an old New York family of merchants, whose founder was one Arthur Dunn, born in New York in 1640. He received his education in the public schools of Brooklyn. Upon his leaving school, he was for some years in the printing business. When eighteen years old he adopted the study of weather forecasting, in which science he has earned a world-wide reputation. He entered the U. S. army in 1873, and was assigned to the signal-service weather bureau, being first stationed in New York city. Upon the establishing of a weather bureau station at Denver, Colo., he was transferred to that station, and later, to the station at Toledo, O. Afterwards he was for two years signal officer at New Orleans, where he made a special study of floods. From New Orleans he went to Cincinnati, O., as chief weather observer, and there he predicted the freshets in the Ohio valley in 1883. For this rare service he received from Gen. Hazen, the chief of the bureau, from the Cincinnati Chamber of Commerce, and from the board of trade of that city, special commendatory letters and resolutions of thanks. He also predicted the great overflows of the Mississippi in 1889 and 1893. From Cincinnati he was transferred to the main office of the bureau in Washington, D. C. In 1884 he was made chief of the weather bureau under the U. S. Department of Agriculture in New York city. At this station Signal Officer Dunn has been remarkably successful in forecasting the weather, notwithstanding the fact that the location lies between two great storm tracks, having telegraphic communications only on one side. He thus has to depend on incoming vessels for definite information from the sea, and this is almost always too late for the work of forecasting. Generally, however, his prophecies are strictly accurate, and in the forecasts for successive days he is remarkably accurate. Gaining knowledge from experience, he has made prognostications for twenty-four, forty-eight, fifty-two, and even sixty-four hours, especially as affecting the locality of Long Island, the Hudson river valley, Connecticut and northern New Jersey—so reliable that his reports are valued by the farmers in arranging for planting and gathering their crops. Mr. Dunn has prepared numerous books and pamphlets upon weather and climatic influences, which are of great value. The state educational department secured his services in preparing weather maps, which are issued twice a day, for use in the public schools. These maps give the pupils such a thorough knowledge of the topography of the atmosphere that they can predict the probabilities of the weather from the well-established rules laid down by the weather bureau, with some idea of what the climatic conditions may be over the whole country. Since the adoption of the map in the schools of this country, the same studies have been introduced into the schools of England. At the request of the authorities, he also prepared a chart showing the relations between the death rate and the weather conditions, which was of great service in showing the means of ameliorating the epidemic of the "grip" in the city of New York. Mr. Dunn was married at New Orleans, La., on June 17, 1878, to Ida, daughter of John and Sarah Perkins.

COMBE, George, phrenologist and moral philosopher, was born near Edinburgh, Scotland, Oct. 21, 1788. He was the son of a brewer, who gave his son all possible educational advantages. After passing through the high school, he entered the university, from which he was graduated when sixteen years of age, and began to study law. He became a writer to the signet in 1812, and shortly after became a notary public. His career as a lawyer was eminently successful, his conscientiousness and shrewdness gaining him a large and lucrative practice. He continued to practise until 1837, when he resolved to devote himself to popularizing his views on education and phrenology. As early as 1816 he had made the acquaintance of Spurzheim, and had become a convert to his system of phrenology. The result of this determination was his "Essays on Phrenology," published in 1819, and his "Elements of Phrenology," in 1824, which reached a ninth edition in 1862. But his most important production is "The Constitution of Man," published in 1828, in which he endeavored to demonstrate the essential harmony of the nature of man with the surrounding world, and the necessity of studying the laws of nature. Combe's doctrines were violently opposed, being considered by many inimical to revealed religion. He numbered among his supporters Cobden, Robert Chambers, and George Eliot, who assisted him to establish the "Edinburgh Phrenological Journal." With his brother Andrew, he conducted this journal for nearly twenty-three years, and contributed a large number of its important articles. In 1833 he married Cecilia Siddons, a daughter of the celebrated actress. They went to Germany on a lecturing tour in 1837, and the next year came to the United States, where for nearly two years he lectured, visiting all the great cities of the Union, and delivering 158 lectures. He said, that of all nations whose heads he had examined, the Americans had the organ of veneration the least developed. When Father Miller was under examination, being *incognito*, Combe said, "Father Miller could not easily make a convert of this man to his hare-brained theory; he has too much good sense." His writings roused popular interest in the science of healthy living, and left their impress on New England life and education. He returned to England in 1840, and published his "Moral Philosophy," and in 1841 his "Notes on the United States." Besides these works, he wrote "Principles of Criminal Legislation" (1854); "Phrenology Applied to Painting and Sculpture" (1855); "The Currency Question" (1855); "The Relation

Between Science and Religion." Combe's ideas on popular education were put into experimental shape in a secular school which he founded in 1848, where the sciences were taught, including physiology and phrenology; but it was too much in advance of the time, and, after a few years, had to be abandoned; but all his subjects, except phrenology, are now taught in the board schools of the United Kingdom and in the common schools of the United States. After his death, which occurred in Moor Park, Surrey, Eng., Aug. 14, 1858, the trustees of his estate, and of that of his brother Andrew, founded a physiological lectureship in the city of Edinburgh.

STEARNS, John Newton, temperance reformer, was born in New Ipswich, N. H., May 24, 1829. He was given a good English education, and had been prepared at the village academy for entrance at college, when ill health prevented further confined study, and he worked on the farm of his father, studying and teaching until he reached his majority, when he removed to New York city, and engaged in literary pursuits. He purchased a popular juvenile publication, "Merry's Museum," and was for fifteen years its editor and proprietor. He was known to its readers as "Robert Merry," and had a large following among the little folk, to whom he imparted much valuable information, and especially taught lessons in temperance. He had signed the total abstinence pledge when a mere lad, and was a member of the Coldwater Army and of the Cadets of Temperance long before he came to New York. On coming of age, he entered the ranks of the Sons of Temperance, which organization was then in its infancy. Being a zealous and untiring worker, he gained rapid promotion in the order, and reached the highest place of usefulness and honor within its gift. He traveled thousands of miles at his own expense, and spoke in nearly every town in the state of New York. In 1865, at the National Temperance Convention, held at Saratoga, he proposed and planned, and the convention organized, the National Temperance Society and Publication House, which went into operation in 1866, and Mr. Stearns was elected corresponding secretary and publishing agent. He also, in 1865, became editor of the "National Temperance Advocate," and of the "Youths' Temperance Banner." He has, in thirty years (1895) of official management of the publishing house, and in the editing of its temperance literature and large-circulating periodicals, shown himself to be a man of determination, method, and unflinching courage. Mr. Stearns has been president of the New York State Temperance Society, Grand Worthy Templar of the Grand Temple of Honor of the state, Most Worthy Templar of the Supreme Council of the Templars of Honor and Temperance of North America, and Most Worthy Patriarch of the National Division Sons of Temperance of North America; and, as a member of the order of Good Templars, has attended the Right Worthy Grand Lodge for many years. He is the only man in America who is a delegate or representative in the highest bodies of the three great national organizations of Good Templars, Sons of Temperance, and Templars of Honor. Among his most popular works are: "The Temperance Chimes" (1867); "The Temperance Speaker" (1869); "The Centennial Temperance Volume" (1876); "The Prohibition Songster" (1885); "One Hundred Years of Temperance" (1885); "Temperance in All Nations"

(1893). In 1893 he brought about the holding of the World's Temperance Congress in Chicago. He died on Apr. 21, 1895, at his home in Greenpoint, Brooklyn, N. Y.

PIERPONT, John, clergyman, was born in Litchfield, Conn., Apr. 6, 1785. He was the great-grandson of James Pierpont, one of the founders of Yale College. After completing his early education at home he entered Yale College, from which he was graduated in 1804, when he taught school in the academy at Bethlehem, Conn., after which he became tutor in the family of Col. William Allston of South Carolina. He returned in 1809 and studied law in Litchfield, where he was admitted to the bar in 1812. He devoted most of his time to law in Newburyport, Mass. The sedentary life undermined his health and he relinquished the profession for mercantile life, which he pursued in Boston and afterward in Baltimore. This not proving congenial or successful, he gave up business in 1816 and studied theology first at Baltimore and then at the Cambridge Divinity School. Upon his graduation

in 1819 he was ordained pastor of the Hollis Street Church in Boston, where he ministered until 1845. He was an abolitionist and an ardent advocate of prohibition legislation and reform in legislation on imprisonment for debt. His unyielding fidelity to his convictions caused dissensions in his parish, which brought about his arraignment before an ecclesiastical council in July, 1838. The controversy continued for seven years, when after sustaining his position and exonerating himself, he requested his dismissal. He was afterward called to the Unitarian Church at Troy, N. Y., where he remained four years, when he accepted a call to the Congregational Church in Medford, Mass. This pastorate he held until 1856. He was a candidate of the Abolition party for governor, and was nominated for congress in 1850, by the Free Soil party. At the beginning of the civil war he became chaplain of a Massachusetts regiment, although seventy-six years of age, but was compelled to resign on account of his feebleness. He was then given a clerkship in the treasury department at Washington, which position he held until his death. In 1816 he published his "Airs From Palestine," which was reissued with other poems in 1840. "Warren's Address at the Battle of Bunker Hill," is known by every schoolboy. He also published a number of sermons and addresses. Mr. Pierpont was a graceful poet and a rare scholar. He died at Medford, Mass., Aug. 26, 1866.

BROMFIELD, John, merchant, was born at Newburyport, Mass., Apr. 11, 1779. His father, John Bromfield, was a direct descendant of Edward Bromfield, the first of this family to settle in America in 1675. He settled at Boston, Mass., and his mansion-house, surrounded by spacious grounds, was situated on the street that now bears his name. The family of Bromfields was distinguished in the annals of English history, and William Bromfield, one of the ancestors, was appointed lieutenant of ordnance in the Tower by Queen Elizabeth, and owned large estates in the vicinity of London. The subject of this sketch received his primary education from his brother, and in 1792 entered Dumener Academy in Byfield. At the age of fourteen he obtained employment in the counting-house of Larkin &

Hurd, of Charlestown. In 1809 Mr. Bromfield went to China as agent for Theodore Lyman, Sr. He was joint supercargo of the Atahualpa with William Sturgis, and remained in China as Mr. Lyman's agent after the departure of the ship. He acquired quite a fortune during his residence abroad, which was augmented, as he said, "beyond his hopes or desires." Unlike the majority who accumulate wealth, he felt disposed to devote the greater portion of his fortune to philanthropic works. He cared little for wealth or display, and desired that his gifts should be bestowed without the author being known. He left $10,000 to the city of his birth for planting and preserving trees in the streets, and keeping the sidewalks in order, gave $25,000 to the Boston Athenæum, and at his death willed over $100,000 to various charitable institutions. Mr. Bromfield never married, as he lived much within himself, and found his chief companionship among his books. He was a profound thinker, an able financier, and a prudent business man. He systematically avoided society, lived with economy, and gave liberally of his income to his relations. His charitable contributions were incessant, and always given in secret. The practical kindliness of his nature is well shown in the following story of one of his generous deeds. On one of his winter passages to Europe he found the sailors suffering extremely from handling frozen ropes with their naked hands. Having been brought up to do things as well as read about them, he took one of his thick overcoats, and made with his own hands a pair of mittens for every sailor. He died at Boston, Mass., Dec. 8, 1849.

HORSFORD, Eben Norton, chemist, was born in Moscow, Livingston co., N. Y., July 27, 1818. He studied at the Rennselaer Polytechnic Institute, and was graduated in 1838 from that institution as civil engineer. During the next year he was employed in the geological survey of the state of New York; and in 1840 received the appointment of professor of mathematics in the Albany Female Academy. Here he continued during the next four years, at the same time holding an appointment to deliver an annual course of lectures at Newark College, Delaware. In 1844 Prof. Horsford went to Germany, where he remained during the next two years, engrossed in the study of analytical chemistry, and having the good fortune of being able to carry on experiments in the laboratory at Giessen conducted by Prof. Liebig. He returned to the United States in 1847, and was elected to the Rumford professorship of science applied to the arts, at Harvard. It was his influence which caused the foundation by Abbott Lawrence of the Lawrence Scientific School in Cambridge, devoted principally to the departments of analytical and applied chemistry. For sixteen years Prof. Horsford devoted himself to the application of analytical chemistry in this institution, and then resigned to become president of the Rumford Chemical Works in Providence, R. I. Prof. Horsford, during his skilled experience as a chemist, made a number of useful discoveries; one of the most important of which had reference to the preservation of the phosphates in connection with the preparation of white bread, and also in the production of the "acid phosphate," now sold by every druggist. It is important, in regard to the career of Prof. Horsford, to record his connection with Wellesley College, inasmuch as he provided for it an endowment for its library, and for continuous supplies of apparatus for the departments of physics, chemistry, botany, and biology, and also established a system of pensions for the president and heads of departments, with the condition that the beneficiaries must be women. By this liberal endowment, the officers to whom it applies are given one year in seven for travel or sojourn in Europe, and after twenty-one years of service receive a progressive increase of salary; and after twenty-six years of service a pension of $500 a year for life. Prof. Horsford's literary work in the interest of science has included a large number of contributions to scientific periodicals, and to the journals and proceedings of scientific societies. He was one of the first to announce to the world, as long ago as 1860, the successful results of the application of oil to rough seas. He also became generally known as a chemical expert, and his services were frequently in demand in courts of law; this being particularly the case during the important and protracted vulcanized rubber litigation. At the Vienna International Exposition of 1873, Prof. Horsford was one of the U. S. government commissioners. He was also one of the jurors in the Centennial Exhibition at Philadelphia in 1876. Prof. Horsford's father, Jerediah Horsford, was a missionary among the Seneca Indians; and in his childhood Eben Horsford, who was with his father, learned much about the Indian language. He published not only a work on the "Indian Names of Boston," but also a printed reproduction in English, German, Iroquois, and Algonquin, of the manuscript Indian dictionary of David Zeisberger — a work of great importance in its elucidation of Indian philology.

GOTTSCHALK, Louis Moreau, musician, was born in New Orleans, La., May 8, 1829. He was of German-Jewish lineage. At the age of twelve his parents sent him to Paris, where he received instruction on the pianoforte and in harmony from several noted musicians. In 1845, on the conclusion of his studies, he appeared in Paris at several concerts, and three years later toured as a virtuoso through France, Switzerland, Italy and Spain. In Paris he published a number of pianoforte compositions that displayed considerable novelty and were well received. In 1853 Gottschalk returned to his native land, giving concerts in Boston, New York, and Philadelphia. Later he made prolonged tours through the length and breadth of the Union and published salon-pieces that found ready sale. Among them were "Le Bamboula," "La Savane," "La Danse des Ombres," and "The Cradle Song." After visiting Mexico, the West Indies, Buenos Ayres, Montevideo, etc., he went to Brazil and made his abode in Rio de Janeiro. It was there, during one of his public performances, that he was suddenly attacked by mortal illness. In 1881 appeared in the Boston "Atlantic Monthly" his "Notes of a Pianist." Gottschalk played with neatness, expression, and singular charm of manner. His arrangements were sufficiently scientific to compel the regard of musicians. Most of his performances were confined to his own compositions; their melodies were novel, treated with more or less originality and considerable effect, founded on Creole songs, South-American airs, and Louisiana plantation ditties. Of the old masters he interpreted next to nothing, and carefully

shunned playing the pieces of living composers. He left unfinished several operas and symphonies, and published a number of songs. Gottschalk died at Tijuca, near Rio de Janeiro, Dec. 18, 1869.

RUNKLE, John Daniel, mathematician, was born at Root, Montgomery co., N. Y., Oct. 11, 1822. He became an eager student and early formed the purpose of acquiring a college education. His first practical training was in the rudiments of knowledge as taught at the time in the district school and the practical kindergarten of his father's farm where, out of school, he mastered its rugged tasks. When sixteen years old he first took up the higher branches of mathematics, no teacher being available before that time in the remote country place. Three months at a private school taught by a senior student from Union College, first fanned into flame the latent spark of his genius. He never despaired of gaining a college education, and in mathematics had, self-taught, gone over and mastered the whole ground covered in a college course. In 1847 the opening of the Lawrence Scientific School made a way for him to carry out a plan which his age had deterred him from adopting at any other college. He entered in 1848, and found himself far advanced in the work of the school. In astronomy he worked and studied under Dr. Bard in the Cambridge Observatory. Through Prof. Pierce he, in 1849, received a position upon the American Ephemeris and Nautical Almanac, a department just established by the U. S. government. This position he held until 1884. He completed his scientific course in 1851, receiving, besides his degree of B.Sc., that of A.M. In 1855 Mr. Runkle published in the "Smithsonian Contributions to Knowledge," a set of astronomical tables. In 1858 he established the "Mathematical Monthly," discontinued in 1861. When the Massachusetts Institute of Technology was started in 1865, he was made professor of mathematics and has since continued to hold the position. In 1868, on account of the illness of President Rogers, Prof. Runkle was made acting president of the corporation, and in 1870 president of the institute. During his administration he added each year some new feature or study to the curriculum of the school, calculated to lead to an increase of interest in the institution and add to its prosperity. He first introduced physical laboratory work and conceived and established the mining laboratory and by his trip to Colorado and Utah in 1871, with a party of students, organized the first Summer School of Mines. In 1872 he established the Lowell School of Practical Design and in the next two years the mineralogical laboratory and the gymnasium and drill room. In 1876 he added a woman's chemical laboratory and the same year an organic laboratory. After visiting the Centennial Exposition at Philadelphia in 1876, and viewing the models and plans of the Imperial Technical School at Moscow, he founded the department of Mechanic Arts—to which the czar of Russia presented a complete set of patterns. In 1878 he resigned the presidency and made a two years' trip abroad as relief from official work. He visited many of the Continental scientific schools, looking for suggestions and new methods. Upon his return he gave the results of his research in a lengthy paper read before the Society of Arts. He also resumed his old position as professor of mathematics, Prof. Rogers having in the meantime been re-elected president. He received the degree of A. M. from Harvard in 1851, Ph. D. from Hamilton in 1869 and LL. D. from Wesleyan in 1871.

WARING, George E., Jr., sanitary engineer, was born in the town of Poundridge, Westchester co., N. Y., July 4, 1833, son of George E. Waring. His boyhood was passed in Stamford, Conn., where his father was a manufacturer of stoves, agricultural implements, etc. He was educated in the public and private schools of Stamford, and subsequently attended Bartlett's School (College Hill), Poughkeepsie, N. Y., from 1847 to 1849. He spent about a year (1850–51) in the hardware business, in New York, then returned to Stamford and managed a country grist-mill until the spring of 1853, when he became a pupil of Prof. Mapes in scientific agriculture. During the winters of 1853, '54 and '55 he lectured before farmers' clubs, etc., on improved methods of farming. In the spring of 1855 he undertook the management (on shares) of Horace Greeley's famous farm at Chappaqua, N. Y. Early in 1857 he hired Fred. Law Olmstead's farm on Staten Island. In August of the same year he was appointed drainage engineer of Central Park, and gave up his farm at the end of the season. He employed the first laborer, and, after the adoption of the Olmstead and Vaux plan, broke the first ground for the improvement of the park. He had charge of most of the agricultural work of the park until May, 1861, when he was commissioned major of the 39th New York volunteers (Garibaldi Guard), and went with them to Virginia. He served with his regiment in Miles's brigade (reserve), near the first battle of Bull Run. Early in August he was transferred to Gen. Frémont's department as major of cavalry. In St. Louis he raised a battalion of cavalry, called the Frémont Hussars, which was (Jan. 9, 1862) consolidated with other troops, forming the 4th Missouri cavalry, of which he was commissioned colonel. In March, 1865, he was mustered out of the service. From May, 1862, until the end of his service, he commanded brigade, part, or division—usually on outpost service. In 1862 he commanded a cavalry brigade under Davidson, in South Missouri and northern Arkansas. At Union City, Tenn., 1863, he had a command numbering 6,500 men of all arms, mainly cavalry. In 1864 he commanded the 1st brigade of the cavalry division of the 16th corps, and went with his command on the Sooy Smith, Grierson, and Sturgis expeditions against Forrest in Mississippi. Immediately after the war he engaged in oil and coal enterprises, which were unsuccessful. In the spring of 1867 he removed to Newport, R. I., and took a fresh start in life as a market gardener and florist, and later, as a farmer. He had control of "Ogden Farm," belonging to George F. Tyler, for ten years, and during this time wrote the "Ogden Farm Papers" for the "American Agriculturist." In 1868 he originated the American Jersey Cattle Club, and edited the "Herd Book." This work he continued until 1882. He gave up his gardening operations in 1872, and farming in 1877, in order to devote his whole time to engineering work—largely what is called "sanitary engineering." His most important works in this connection have been the sewerage of Ogdensburg, 1871; the main sewer of Saratoga Springs, 1874; the sewerage of Memphis, 1880; the Buffalo trunk sewer, 1882–86; and the sewerage of San Diego (Cuba), 1887. He has made plans and executed work for the sewerage of many other towns, and the system of sewerage first introduced in Memphis has been very largely used in all parts of the country. He is the author of the following books: "Elements of Agriculture" (1854); "Draining for Profit and Draining for Health" (1868); the "Handy Book of Husbandry" [now called the "Book of the Farm"] (1869); "The Sanitary Draining of Houses and Farms" (1874); "The Sanitary Condition of City and Country Dwelling-Houses" (1877); "A Farmer's Vacation; Travels in Holland, Normandy, Brittany, and the Channel Islands" (1875); "The Bride of the Rhine," "Two Hundred Miles in a Moselle Row-Boat" (1876); "Whip and Spur" (1875); "Village Improvements and Farm Villages" (1877); "Tyrol and the Skirt of the Alps" (1870); "Sewerage and Land Drainage" (1889); "Modern Methods of Sewage Disposal" (1894). In 1895 Wm. L. Strong, the Reform mayor of New York city, appointed him commissioner of street cleaning, and his vast experience and entire independence of the demands of party, enabled him to re-organize the department, and demonstrate the wisdom of applying business methods to the work in hand. Col. Waring is an honorary member of the Royal Institute of Engineers (Holland); member of the Institution of Civil Engineers (England); fellow of the Sanitary Institute of Great Britain, and corresponding member of the American Institute of Architects.

SEELYE, Julius Hawley, fifth president of Amherst College (1877–90), was born in Bethel, Conn., Sept. 14, 1824. He entered Amherst College, from which he was graduated with high honors in the class of 1849. The next three years he spent at the seminary in Auburn, N. Y., in the study of theology. In 1852 he went to Germany, where he continued his theological course for one year at Halle. He was ordained by the classes of Schenectady, N. Y., in 1853, as pastor of the First Dutch Reformed Church in Schenectady, and continued in charge of that church until 1858, when he was elected professor of mental and moral philosophy at Amherst. In 1872 he made a voyage around the world in company with Dr. Edward Hitchcock and Abijah Fitch, of Auburn, N. Y., during which time he visited India, by invitation, for the purpose of delivering a series of lectures defending Christianity, which were largely attended by native educated Hindoos, and afterwards published in their language, as well as in German and Japanese. In 1874 Gov. Washburn appointed him one of a commission to revise the laws of the state of Massachusetts on taxation. The same year he was chosen to represent his district in the Forty-fourth congress, being elected over the nominees of both the great parties by independent votes of Republicans and Democrats alike, and at an expense to him of only one postage stamp. He served through the first session with distinguished success for a representative of the people, and yet bound to no party, and was especially useful as a member of the committee on Indian affairs, and was already considered as sure to be his own successor, when the death of President Stearns made him the natural successor to the presidency of Amherst, and, although he was bitterly opposed by half the faculty; firstly, on personal grounds, mainly on account of his autocratic and overbearing manner, as manifested as a member of the faculty; and secondly, on political grounds, in that, as a Republican, he had opposed the Electoral Commission and the subsequent declaration of the election of Rutherford B. Hayes as president; he was unanimously selected by the trustees of the college, and duly installed in 1877. His well equipped mind and vigorous personality soon won the affection of the students, and commanded the respect of the faculty, even though many disagreed with his policy at times. His aim as an educator was toward character-building, and thus educating and training the whole man, and much to the surprise of his early opponents, he soon demonstrated his sympathy with the students. He early established a system of self-government through a "College Senate," by which the students from the four classes had a large share in maintaining discipline, and which became known as the Amherst system. This system has been productive of good results, and numerous colleges which first looked upon the experiment with distrust, have since adopted it. President Seelye introduced other radical changes, and the faculty soon after committed to him almost absolutely the immediate government of the college. He made the personal acquaintance of every student, and in most cases could address each by his Chris-

tian name. He gave the greater part of his time to studying the student, even at the expense of that spent in the class-rooms, and was looked upon by the students as the very ideal of a large, strong, healthy man, physically, intellectually and morally. He was a member of one of the Greek letter fraternities, and a firm advocate of the secret society system. In addition to his work as a teacher, President Seelye did much to increase the material prosperity of Amherst, aggregating $825,000, and to erecting new buildings for college purposes. He attracted large gifts of money, securing an endowment for the presidency from Chester W. Chapin; for the professorship of history and political economy from Henry Winkley; and for a professorship of biology from Mrs. V. G. Stone. He was a trustee of the Clarke Institute for Deaf Mutes, and of Smith College for Women, of which latter institution his brother, Laurens Clark Seelye, is president, and was one of the board of visitors dealing with the question of the Andover theology, his stand being non-partisan and conservative. Union College gave him the degree of D. D. in 1862, and Columbia that of LL. D. in 1876. He published a translation of Dr. Albert Schwegler's "History of Philosophy" (1856), and his own "Lectures to Educated Hindus" (1873), "Christian Missions" (1875). He revised and edited Hitchcock's "Mental Science," "Moral Science," and "Empirical Psychology," and, during his presidency, re-wrote "Moral Science." His last book was "Cit-

izenship" (1894). Among his noteworthy contributions to the reviews were: "The Electoral Commission," "Counting the Electoral Votes," "The Moral Character in Politics," "The Need of a Better Political Education," "The Currency Question," "Should the State Teach Religion?" "Prohibitory Laws and Personal Liberty," and "The Recognition of God in Our Constitution." After the death of his wife, in 1881, President Seelye did not, apparently, recover from the shock. He suffered from erysipelas and nervous prostration, the result of overwork, care, and responsibility. He went abroad twice for rest and medical advice, and in 1890 tendered to the trustees of Amherst his resignation, which was reluctantly accepted, and he was succeeded by Merrill Edmund Gates, who had been president of Rutgers College. He continued to reside in Amherst, and to serve the college as lecturer on the History of Philosophy. It was one of his greatest pleasures to have Amherst alumni call on him, and even in his declining days he seldom made a mistake in recognizing them, and in calling them by name. President Seelye died May 12, 1895.

MOTT, James, philanthropist, was born in North Hempstead, L. I., June 20, 1788. He was a Quaker by ancestry and training. Having received a good education, while still a young man he received an appointment as teacher in a boarding-school in Dutchess county, N. Y., which was kept by members of the Society of Friends. He remained there, however, only for a short time, when he removed to New York city; and, having married, he settled in Philadelphia in 1810, where he became a partner in business with his father-in-law. In this he remained during the next forty years, at the end of which time he had acquired a competency and retired from business. He became prominent in the early days of anti-slavery as an associate of William Lloyd Garrison, Wendell Phillips, and other prominent anti-slavery agitators. He organized, with others, the National Anti-Slavery Society in Philadelphia in 1833. In 1840 he was a delegate from the Pennsylvania Society to attend the World's Anti-Slavery Convention in London. He presided over the first Woman's Rights National Convention, which was held at Seneca Falls, N. Y., in 1848. He had much to do with the organization of the Friends' College at Swarthmore, near Philadelphia. He died in Brooklyn, N. Y., Jan 26, 1868.

VARNUM, James Mitchell, lawyer and soldier, was born at Dracut, Middlesex co., Mass., Dec. 17, 1749. He was descended from George Varnum, who settled near Ipswich, Mass., before 1635; and his father, Samuel Varnum, held large estates on the Merrimac river. He studied for a short time at Harvard and was graduated in 1769 at Rhode Island College (now Brown University), taking the negative side in a debate at commencement, "Whether British America can afford to become an independent state?" He studied law under Oliver Arnold, attorney-general of Rhode Island, was admitted to the bar in 1771, and commenced practising at East Greenwich, R. I., where he had one of the finest houses in the colony, and entertained Washington, Lafayette, Greene, Sullivan, and other leaders. Mr. Varnum had also a great taste for military life and was made colonel of the Kentish Guards in 1774, and of the 1st Rhode Island infantry in May, 1775. He served at the siege of Boston and about New York, and on the reorganization of the army in October, 1776, was recommended by Washington for retention. He was made brigadier-general of state troops Dec. 12, 1776, and of the Continental army Feb. 21, 1777. At his suggestion slaves were enlisted and emancipated, the Rhode Island legislature making some compensation to their owners. Gen. Varnum rendered good service on the Hudson and in New Jersey, was engaged at Red Bank and Monmouth, described the sufferings of the army at Valley Forge in letters quoted by Sparks, and in July, 1778, was ordered to Rhode Island, where his brigade bore the chief part in the fight with Sir R. Pigot. He had a remarkably active though brief military career. In March, 1779, there being too many general officers, he resigned his commission in the army, and resumed his practice. The legislature of his own state, however, forthwith appointed him major-general of Rhode Island militia. He was active and eloquent as a Federalist in the Continental congress, 1780–82 and 1786–87. At home he opposed the craze for paper money, was instrumental in having some of the acts for its issue declared unconstitutional, and defended the judges who were impeached for this cause. In August, 1787, he became a director of the Ohio Company of Associates, and in October was appointed a supreme court judge of the Northwest territory. Reaching Marietta, O., in June, 1788, he delivered on July 4th an oration which was published by the company, and helped in framing a code of laws for the territory. Elkanah Watson called him "one of the most eminent lawyers and distinguished orators in the colonies." He was one of the first members of the Society of the Cincinnati. (See an article by A. B. Gardiner in the "Magazine of American History" for September, 1887.) He died at Marietta, O., Jan. 10, 1789.

ALLEN, Ebenezer, revolutionary soldier, was born in Northampton, Mass., Oct. 17, 1743. At the age of twenty-four he removed to Poultney, Vt., and in company with a brother-in-law, began the first settlement of that town. In 1775 he went to Tinmouth to live, and was sent to the conventions in the New Hampshire grants in 1776, and to those that formed the state constitution the following year. He was appointed captain of a company of minute-men, and served in Col. Herrick's regiment of rangers during the revolutionary war. He distinguished himself for gallantry at the battle of Bennington, Aug. 16, 1777, in the month following led the attack against the British post on Mount Defiance, and subsequently captured fifty of Burgoyne's rear-guard on their retreat from Ticonderoga. He was commissioned a major for his gallantry, and his after-exploits won for him a high reputation as a partisan leader. In 1788 he removed to South Hero, Vt., and resided there until 1800, when he went to Burlington, where he died, March 26, 1806.

BOWEN, John Eliot, author, was born June 8, 1858, in Brooklyn, N. Y., and was the fifth of the seven sons of Henry C. Bowen and Lucy M. (Tappan) Bowen. He was graduated from Yale College in 1881, and then spent two years in travel and study in Europe and the East, where he made himself acquainted with events connected with the occupation of the English in Egypt, which afterward proved of immense value to him. On his return to America he took a position in the editorial department of "The Independent," and so great was his devotion to his studies that, amidst the pressure of his office duties he found time to pursue a post-graduate course of study at Columbia College in history and political economy, and was presented with the degree of Ph.D. in 1886. "The Conflict Between the East and West in Egypt" formed the subject of his doctor's thesis, which was published in "The Political Science Quarterly," and afterwards in book form. During his connection with "The Independent" he proved himself of incalculable service to the paper, being fertile in plan and suggestion, and the special merit of its literary features may be largely credited to his unwearying activity. His bright fancy, clothed in a clear, strong style, found expression in many excellent stories and poems which were published in the magazines. His poeti

cal translations of Carmen Sylva's "Songs of Toil," published with an introductory sketch of the royal authoress (New York, 1877), were well received by the public. "John Bowen was more afraid to do wrong than many a man is of death," was said of him by one of his intimate associates. This statement strikes the key-note of his character, which was affectionate, simple, warm-hearted; and at the same time judicial fairness was the crown of his gentle spirit. He was grandly independent on the side of right, always asking, "How does that accord with the law of God and the law of righteousness?" He died on the day that had been set for his marriage in the summer of 1890.

HUNNEWELL, James Frothingham, merchant and antiquary, was born in Charlestown, Mass., July 3, 1832, son of James and Susan Hunnewell. The homestead, which he still occupies (1895), is a large house with picturesque rooms and contents, and a garden with old trees which retains some of the little remaining original surface of the Bunker Hill battle ground, the left of the British attack having reached it. The Hunnewell family have lived in Charlestown since 1698, and the Frothinghams have been there since about 1630. The boy's early education was chiefly in private schools, trouble with his eyesight preventing a college course. In 1849 he began business life with his father, a merchant of long standing and high credit, who, in 1826, established a mercantile house in Honolulu, still flourishing. The business was with distant foreign ports, especially with the Hawaiian islands, and with the west coast of America. About 1866, when American foreign commerce had seriously declined, both father and son retired from active business. In 1869 the father died; the son has constantly been engaged in business enterprises and the care of property, realizing that fully as much care is needed to keep it in order as to acquire it. Meanwhile he has been much interested in antiquarian and historical subjects and has devoted a great deal of time and

labor to them, but without pecuniary return. His travels at home and abroad have been extensive, and these and his tastes have led him to make notes about the condition of a great number of places and objects important in art or history, among them fully 400 cathedrals, abbeys, and churches of special note. Since boyhood he has been a collector of books, and he has an unusual library representing art, antiquities, and history, including what are called historic bindings. In his native town he was three times elected a trustee of the public schools, and eight terms trustee of the public library. For about forty years he has been an officer of the First Parish, and much of the time chairman of its standing committee. He has been president of the Gas and Electric Co. since 1887, and a vice-president of the Winchester Home (a charity maintained by union of denominations), a trustee of the Five-Cent Savings Bank, and director of the Bunker Hill Monument Association. In connection with Hawaii, he was many years president of the Hawaiian Club, and is treasurer of the American Endowment of Oahu College and a corresponding member of the Hawaiian Historical Society. For many years he was a director of the New England Historic-Genealogical Society and since 1867 a member of the American Antiquarian

Society. He is an officer in the ancient Society for Propagating the Gospel, a life member of the Archæological Institute of America, an original member and a director of the Bostonian Society, an honorary member of the Boston Marine Society, a member of the Prince Society and of the Boston Memorial Society. He is also a vice-president of the New England Mortgage Security Co. Besides clubs resigned, he is now a member of the Union, St. Botolph, Athletic, Odd Volumes, Massachusetts Reform, and Exchange. Results of his work, travels, and book-collecting appear in his published and privately printed volumes. Of the former are: "The Lands of Scott," "The Historical Monuments of France," "The Imperial Island, as "England's Chronicle in Stone" (John Murray, London); "Bibliography of Charlestown and Bunker Hill" (1880), and "A Century of Town Life, Charlestown, 1775–1887" (Boston, 1888). Privately printed by him are: "Civilization of the Hawaiian Islands, with a Bibliography;" Memorials of His Father, of His Mother, and of the First Church, and "Records of the First Church, 1632–1789," "A Relation of Virginia, 1609, by Henry Spelman," "A Journal of the Schr. Missionary Packet, Boston to Honolulu, 1826," by his father—a very remarkable voyage. Besides these are "Illustrated Americana," reprinted from the proceedings of the American Antiquarian Society, and several other papers read to clubs and societies, or for other purposes. On Apr. 8, 1872, he married Sarah Melville, daughter of Ezra Farnsworth, of Boston. They have one child, James Melville Hunnewell.

CARTER, William Thornton, financier, was born at Breage, England, Aug. 23, 1831. His parents were William and Mary Thomas Carter, and his ancestry on the paternal side traces back to the royal blood of England. He came to America in 1850, and joined his uncles, John and Richard Carter, pioneer anthracite coal miners at Tamaqua, Pa. He soon became interested in that business, and in 1861 purchased the Coleraine Collieries near Beaver Meadow, which he greatly enlarged and developed, and for thirty years was recognized as one of the largest and most successful individual coal operators in the country. In 1867 he purchased a large tract of land on the Lehigh Valley Railroad below Bethlehem, and founded the town of Redington, where he erected two large blast furnaces, machine and car shops which, in spite of depression in trade and suspension of business in mining and manufacturing, have been kept in continuous operation for over twenty-five years. Mr. Carter, in later years, became largely interested in developing and operating street railroads, especially the Ridge Avenue system of Philadelphia, which road was the first to adopt a uniform five cent fare, due largely to his influence. He was a director and one of the original subscribers to the United Gas Improvement Co., and owned the controlling interest in the First National Bank of Tamaqua, where he also controlled extensive machine shops. He was one of the projectors and financial supporters of the construction of the Poughkeepsie Bridge over the Hudson river, and its connecting railroads, and closely associated with many financial institutions in his own city. Throughout his entire business career he was governed by the strictest integrity and persistency of purpose, a man of remarkable foresight and keen judgment. In politics he was an ardent Republican, an extreme protectionist, and an earnest supporter of Blaine. He was a trustee of the Second Presbyterian Church, and associated with many church organizations and charities, a member of historical and genealogical societies, the Franklin Institute, the Union League, Art, and Rittenhouse Clubs of Philadelphia. In 1854 Mr. Carter was married to Miss Jewell of England, who died in 1864, leaving two children, Mrs. T. Chester Walbridge of Germantown, and Mr. Charles John Jewell Carter of Redington. In 1868 Mr. Carter was married to Miss Redington, a descendant of the pioneer Puritan settlers of New England, and a granddaughter of a revolutionary soldier. By this second marriage he has three children, Mrs. Joseph Leidy, William E., and Alice Carter. Since 1855 Mr. Carter had lived in Philadelphia, enjoying a quiet home life. He was a man of large culture, possessed a charming personality and was an unusually interesting conversationalist. He died at his home, Feb. 9, 1893.

TUDOR, Frederic, merchant, was born in Boston, Sept. 4, 1783, a son of Col. William Tudor. He entered early into business, and at the age of twenty-two was the owner of a vessel trading with the West Indies. In 1805 he originated the ice trade, beginning with a shipment to Mauritius, in which he risked his entire capital. The experiment succeeded, and he was encouraged to follow up his single cargo with many others larger and more profitable. During the war of 1812 the business was somewhat interrupted by the English cruisers, which were ever on the alert for prizes in the West Indian waters, but after peace was declared trade increased rapidly, and was extended to India in 1835. By him and his associates, notably the late Nathaniel J. Wyeth, were developed the marvelous processes of harvesting, handling, and storing ice, which are still in use wherever natural ice is obtained on a large scale. Mr. Tudor was also a successful horticulturist, and did much to beautify and attract attention to the peninsula of Nahant, now the leading attraction of the Massachusetts coast. He died at Boston, Feb. 6, 1864.

ALLEN, William Francis, educator, was born at Northborough, Mass., Sept. 5, 1830. His father was Joseph Allen, a minister of the old church of that town. He was graduated at Harvard in 1851, and spent the next three years as a private tutor in New York city. He then passed two years in Europe, studying history and antiquities, chiefly in Germany and Italy. On his return, in 1856, he taught for seven years in a private school in West Newton, Mass.; then was for two years in the South, in the employ of the Freedmen's and Sanitary commissions. While there he gathered materials for a collection of negro songs, published in 1867, under the title of "Slave Songs." After the close of the war he was one year at Antioch College, Yellow Springs, O., and one year at Eagleswood Military Academy, Perth Amboy, N. J. In 1867 he was appointed professor of ancient languages, and afterward of the Latin language and history in the University of Wisconsin, Madison, Wis.,—at various times since then the title of the chair has been altered —and later was professor of history. He wrote a number of books of standard merit, among them an edition of the "Annals of Tacitus," and a "Short History of the Roman People." He died suddenly on Dec. 9, 1889, greatly beloved by all who knew him.

ALLYN, John, clergyman, was born at Barnstable, Mass., March 21, 1767. He was graduated from Harvard in 1785, and, having studied theology, was ordained pastor of the Congregational church at Duxbury, Mass., in 1788. He preached there without an assistant for forty years, and with a colleague for an additional seven years, thus completing a ministry of nearly half a century. He died July 19, 1833.

SPEER, Emory, jurist, was born at Culloden, Ga., Sept. 3, 1848. His father is Dr. Eustace Speer, an eloquent divine, for many years a professor in the University of Georgia, and his grandfather was Alexander Speer, one of the foremost men in the Union party of South Carolina in nullification days. At sixteen Emory Speer entered the Confederate army. For his services in rescuing his state from negro domination, he was made solicitor-general by the first post-bellum Democratic governor. He was elected to the forty-sixth congress as an independent Democrat, but was soon ruled out of the party for his patriotic resistance to the then Democratic policy of loading appropriation bills with political legislation. He was returned to the forty-seventh congress, and immediately appointed a protectionist member of the ways-and-means committee, and was one of the conference committee between the house and the senate, whose report became the tariff bill of 1883. He was appointed U. S. attorney at Atlanta by Pres. Arthur, and won great professional distinction by convicting a band of Kuklux for beating negro voters after election, thus affording the supreme court (Ex parte Yarborough 110 U. S.) the opportunity of establishing the power of the national government to protect the voter at all times. While yet one of the youngest of the federal judges, Judge Speer won much national renown, especially in three cases in which he presided. One of them was the United States vs. Lancaster Hall and others, whom a number of conspirators of large influence were convicted for the murder of the agent of certain New York capitalists, to prevent them from protecting their rights in the U. S. courts. Judge Speer's rulings in Clarke vs. Central Railroad, involving $50,000,000, gave a tremendous blow to railroad financial wreckers, and his opinion in the case of the Brotherhood of Locomotive Engineers vs. the Central Railroad afforded labor organizations a position in the courts of such favor as they had never before enjoyed. This opinion was printed by the U. S. senate as a public document for the information of the people. Judge Speer is the author of a valuable legal work, "Removal of Causes," and he is regarded by the people of Georgia as one of their most eloquent and persuasive orators. He is president of the law department of Mercer University, one of the largest Baptist colleges in the South. He is himself a Methodist.

TREE, Lambert, diplomat, was born in Washington, D. C., Nov. 29, 1832, son of Lambert Tree, a government official in Washington. His grandfather, John Tree, was a soldier in the war of 1812. His paternal great-grandfather, Capt. Lambert Tree, was a soldier in the revolutionary war, captain of an artillery company, and was killed at the battle of Trenton by a Hessian bullet. His maternal grandfather, Joseph Burrows, a soldier in the war of 1812; and his maternal great-grandfather, Gen. Burrows, was also a functionary of the government, and removed with it from Philadelphia to Washington, serving in the patriot army throughout the revolutionary war. His first American ancestors on both sides came from England, their emigration to this country dating back to 1635. His mother was a reigning belle in Washington. He was educated in the best private schools of the national capital, entered the University of Virginia, and was graduated with honors in the class of 1853. He adopted the

VI.—11

law as his profession, studied in the office of James Mandeville Carlisle, and was admitted to practice in 1855. In February, 1856, he located in Chicago, and in six months became the junior in the law firm of Clarkson & Tree. In 1864 he served a term as president of the Chicago Law Institute, in which he had always taken an active interest. In 1870 he was elected to succeed Judge McAllister of the circuit court, who was promoted to the supreme bench. In 1878 he was re-elected for the full term without opposition. He resigned in 1875 on account of ill health, being ordered by his physician to Europe, where he remained several years. During his term upon the circuit bench many important cases were disposed of, notably the aldermanic bribery cases, which resulted in the imprisonment of a number of aldermen of the city, convicted of bribery, which conviction broke up a dangerous and corrupt ring. On his return from Europe he devoted his time entirely to his own private affairs. In 1864 he made the hopeless political race for state senator, as Democratic candidate, facing a Republican majority of nearly 20,000. In 1878, and again in 1882, with no chance for victory, he stood as the Democratic nominee for representative in congress from his district, and in each election succeeded in materially reducing the Republican majorities. He was a delegate at large for Illinois to the national Democratic convention of 1884, and came within one vote of defeating Gov. John Logan in the U. S. senatorial contest in the legislature of Illinois in 1885. In July, 1885, he was appointed by Pres. Cleveland U. S. minister to Belgium, and represented his country at the court of Brussels for three years, when he was transferred by the president to St. Petersburg, one of the four great foreign posts in the diplomatic service, soon afterwards represented by U. S. ambassadors. In 1889, just before the close of Pres. Cleveland's first administration, Minister Tree requested a recall, and returned home shortly after the advent of the administration of Pres. Harrison. During his entire residence in Brussels the most cordial relations existed between King Leopold and the U. S. minister, who with his accomplished wife, was in high favor at the Belgian court. In January, 1891, Pres. Harrison appointed Judge Tree one of the American members of the international monetary conference, which sat at Washington in the winter and spring of 1891-2. The propositions finally adopted were formulated by Judge Tree, who advocated them before the congress. While abroad as U. S. minister he represented his government as a member of several momentous international conferences, and was intrusted in negotiating a number of important treaties. His name

was one of those for which ballots were cast for the nomination for the vice-presidency in the national Democratic convention of 1892. He has been conspicuous in the interest he has manifested in the material advancement of Chicago, and is a large owner of realty in the business centre of the city which he has improved, and greatly increased in value. He originated the annual reward of medals to firemen and police conspicuous for acts of bravery, and the Lambert Tree medal was an example followed by other benefactors. He caused to be erected in Lincoln Park, a statue of Robert Cavalier de la Salle, the intrepid explorer; also, a magnificent statue in heroic size of an Indian warrior on horseback, both of which he presented to the park commissioners.

He is a trustee of the Mercantile Loan and Trust Co., a director of the Edison Electric Co., and interested in several private enterprises. He was one of the founders of the Chicago Club, a member of the Iroquois and Union clubs in Chicago; of the Union Club, New York city; the Metropole Club, Washington; and the Century Club, London. He is president of the Illinois state historical library board, and trustee for life of the Newberry Library of Chicago. Judge Tree was married in 1859, to the only daughter of H. H. Magie, one of Chicago's pioneers, who settled there in 1832. Their only child, a son, married the daughter of Marshall Field, of Chicago.

BLISS, Cornelius Newton, merchant, was born in Fall River, Mass., Jan. 26, 1833, of English ancestry, who first settled in this country about 1635. His father was from Rehoboth, Mass., and died while Cornelius was an infant. His mother remarried later Edward S. Keep of Fall River, and removed to New Orleans in 1840, leaving the boy behind in Fall River, where he remained until he was thirteen years of age, attending school. He then rejoined his mother in New Orleans, completing his education at the High School in that city, entered his step-father's counting-house, and continued there for about a year, after which he went to Boston, and about 1849 entered the service of James M. Beebe & Co., then the largest importing dry-goods and jobbing house in the United States. Here his industry and energy caused his continued advance until he became a partner in the house. The firm dissolved in 1866, and Mr. Bliss entered the commission house of John S. and Eben Wright & Co. of Boston, selling agents for some of the largest New England manufacturers, but soon after visited New York to establish a branch of the Boston house. Upon the death of the senior Wright the style became Wright, Bliss & Fabyan, of Boston, New York, and Philadelphia. The firm merged into Bliss, Fabyan & Co. in 1881, and became one of the most thoroughly accredited and established houses in the United States. They represent the Pepperell Manufacturing Co., the Otis Co., the Androscoggin Co., the Bates Mill American Printing Co., and many others. He is vice-president of the Fourth National Bank, director of the Central Trust Co. and the Equitable Life Assurance Co., vice-president of the Union League Club, and a governor and treasurer of the Society of the New York Hospital. While never actually in public life, Mr. Bliss has served as a delegate to city, county, and state conventions, and in 1884 was chairman of a committee appointed to attend the Republican national convention in Chicago, for the purpose of urging the nomination of President Arthur. In 1885 he declined to have his name

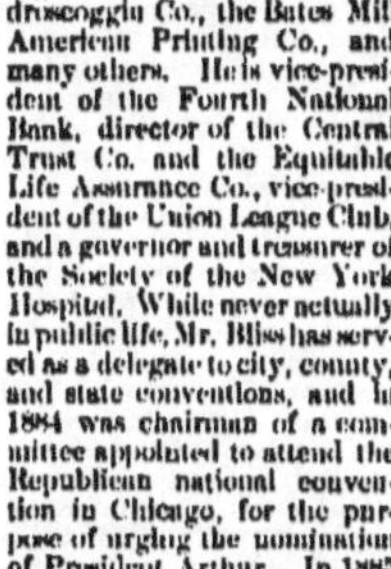

mentioned in the New York state convention at Saratoga as a candidate for the governorship, but he nevertheless received a large complimentary vote on that occasion. In 1891 he also declined to be a candidate before the convention. He was chairman of the New York state Republican committee in 1887, and again in 1888. In the presidential campaign of 1888 his great executive ability was displayed in the canvass which resulted in carrying the state for Harrison and Morton. In 1892 he was a member of the Republican national committee and member of its executive committee. Mr. Bliss is president of the American Protective Tariff League for the dissemination of protection doctrines to combat the influence exerted by the Cobden Club, and the American Tariff Reform Club in this country. He has also on several occasions been spoken of as a candidate for the mayoralty of New York city, but always declined to be a candidate. Mr. Bliss married, in 1859, Elizabeth, daughter of Avery Plumer of Boston, by whom he has two children living. He is considered an authority on general business principles, and on the political and economic questions of the day his advice and judgment are sought by men who have in their charge the shaping of public affairs. He is well known for his large and judicious charities.

ASHMUN, George, lawyer, was born in Blandford, Mass., Dec. 25, 1804. He was graduated at Yale in 1823, and began the practice of the law in Springfield, Mass., in 1828. He rose rapidly in his profession, and being elected to the legislature in 1833, served four terms in the state house of representatives, and two in the state senate between that date and 1841. In 1845 he was chosen to represent his district in congress, and by successive elections, held his seat until 1851, serving as a member of the committee on the judiciary, Indian affairs, and rules. In 1860 he was chairman of the convention which nominated Mr. Lincoln for the presidency and it is said that it was through his influence that Stephen A. Douglas was led to give a hearty support to the

Lincoln administration. He defended Webster's course, although did not approve the abandonment of the "Wilmot Proviso," and his speeches in reply to the attacks of C. J. Ingersoll and Charles Allen are masterpieces of eloquence, and gave him great eminence in the country. After Mr. Ashmun's retirement from congress, he withdrew largely from political life, but during the civil war he exerted all his influence in support of the Union. He was appointed a director of the Union Pacific Railroad, and in 1866 was chosen a delegate to the Philadelphia National Union Convention, but did not take part in its proceedings. He was much admired as a profound lawyer, a well-read scholar, and a polished gentleman. He died July 17, 1870.

GILMAN, Arthur, educator, was born at Alton, Ill., June 22, 1837, son of Winthrop Sargent Gilman, the family before the reformation lived in Norfolk county, England, the first American ancestor landing at Boston in 1638, but afterward making his home at Exeter, N. H., where the family became numerous. After the revolution Arthur Gilman's great-grandfather, Joseph Gilman, joined the company of patriots who purchased the Ohio region of the government, and settled at Marietta where he held various offices of importance. Washington appointed him judge of the Northwestern territory and his son, Benjamin Ives Gilman, became a member of the convention that framed the constitution of Ohio. The business of Benjamin Ives Gilman being ruined by Jefferson's embargo, he subsequently removed to the East, living first at Philadelphia, and afterward at New York, where his son, Winthrop Sargent Gilman, received his business education, and who in turn, went West and for some years engaged in business at Alton, Ill., and at St. Louis, Mo. At Alton his son, Arthur Gilman was born, but leaving the West in 1846, he was chiefly educated in New York, which became the family home. At the age of twenty young Gilman began business as a banker, and for a time received deposits and granted accounts, being the agent of Eastern capitalists and Western bankers. In this occupation he was most successful, but his health giving way he retired in 1862 to the Berkshire Hills, Mass., near Lenox, where he bought an estate and busied himself for a few years in agriculture and in performing the duties of visitor to the public schools. He also began to write for publication, and prepared the "Genealogy of the Family of Gilman in England and America," which was printed in 1869 by Joel Munsell of Albany, and which, as reviewed by Mr.

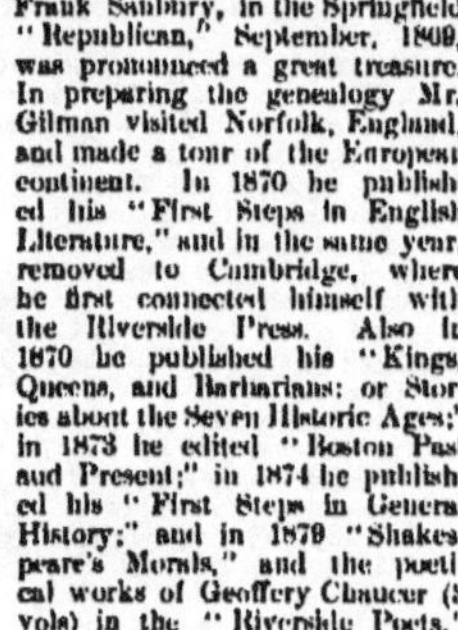

Frank Sanbury, in the Springfield "Republican," September, 1869, was pronounced a great treasure. In preparing the genealogy Mr. Gilman visited Norfolk, England, and made a tour of the European continent. In 1870 he published his "First Steps in English Literature," and in the same year, removed to Cambridge, where he first connected himself with the Riverside Press. Also in 1870 he published his "Kings, Queens, and Barbarians: or Stories about the Seven Historic Ages;" in 1873 he edited "Boston Past and Present;" in 1874 he published his "First Steps in General History;" and in 1879 "Shakespeare's Morals," and the poetical works of Geoffery Chaucer (3 vols) in the "Riverside Poets."

In consequence of family needs, Mr. and Mrs. Gilman, in 1877, made a plan for the systematic instruction of women by the professors of Harvard College, a society being formed to carry out the scheme. From its inception Mr. Gilman was the executive officer of this corporation, which legally entitled the Society for the Collegiate Instruction of Women, was familiarly known as the Harvard Annex. Its success, though not unexpected, was both immediate and great. No instructors were employed save those of Harvard College, the curriculum being identical with that of the college. In 1895 more than eighty Harvard professors were thus engaged, while the students, many of whom were doing very advanced work, numbered about 300. After the death of Longfellow, Mr. Gilman proposed through a Boston paper that a memorial should be built to the poet's memory on a lot opposite his historic home, and to carry out this idea a society was formed in which Mr. Gilman has been the only secretary. The immediate object of The Longfellow Memorial Association was the collection of $50,000 of which a large portion was soon received and a garden laid out between the Longfellow home and the river Charles, thus preserving the view so loved by the poet. Mr. Gilman's subsequent writings were all in the line of civil history. From 1880 to 1885 he edited Lathrop's "Library of Entertaining History," comprising India, Egypt, Switzerland, China, Spain, and the "History of the American People," the latter by himself, being in its way a popular classic. In 1887 he bought out with Dr. Schaff, the "Library of Religious Poetry," and edited "The Kingdom of Home," a large quarto volume of selected poems published by Lathrop. In 1882 he bought out the "Magna Charta Stories," in part written by himself, and in 1884, published the "Tales of the Pathfinders." In 1896 he completed the "Story of Rome," published by G. P. Putnam's Sons in their "Story of the Nation" series, Mr. Gilman helping also on Baring Gould's volume on Germany, Prof. Church's on Carthage, Stanley Lane Poole's on the Moors in Spain and on the Turks, and Prof. Mahaffy's on the Empire of

Alexander, and Rawlinson's "Egypt," all in the same series. In addition, Mr. Gilman wrote the "Story of the Saracens," "Short Stories from a Dictionary," "The Discovery and Exploration of America," "The Colonization of America," "The Making of the American Nation," and "The Story of Boston." Mr. Gilman's public labors were all connected with some branch of education, and he occasionally lectured before schools upon his chosen topic. In 1886 he purchased an estate adjoining the home of the Harvard Annex, and established an English classical school for girls known as the Cambridge School, and intended to carry out the most modern and most practical methods in preparing girls for college and in giving them a literary education. A unique feature of this deservedly popular institution is found in Margaret Winthrop Hall, and Howells House, two residences in which pupils from a distance receive every advantage of home life. In 1870 Mr. Gilman received the honorary degree of A. M. from Williams College. When the society for the Collegiate Instruction of Women was by special act of the legislature of Massachusetts made Radcliffe College Mr. Gilman was appointed regent of the new college.

BIDDLE, Nicholas, financier, was born in Philadelphia, Jan. 8, 1786. He was descended from ancestors who came from England with William Penn, and who took a distinguished part in the colonial struggles. His father, Charles Biddle, was a prominent actor in the revolutionary war, and his uncle was one of the early naval heroes. Another uncle served in the old French war, and was a member of the congress of 1744. He received his early education at an academy in Philadelphia where he advanced so rapidly that he was able to enter the class of 1799 in the University of Pennsylvania, and would have graduated at the age of thirteen but that it was not deemed advisable to allow his mind to be so rapidly pushed. Accordingly he was sent to Princeton where he entered the sophomore class, and was graduated as valedictorian in 1801. He entered upon the study of the law, but before finishing there he accepted the position of secretary of John Armstrong, minister to France, and accompanied him to Paris, where he was at the time of the coronation of Napoleon. His first experience in financial affairs was gained from having to audit and pay certain claims against the United States from the purchase money paid for Louisiana, when his youth and ability caused remark by the members of the French official bureau. Upon the completion of this duty he traveled extensively in Europe and returned to London, where he became secretary to Mr. Monroe the U. S. minister to England. Upon a visit to Cambridge he met a company of classical scholars and university professors, and in a discourse upon the modern Greek dialect, as compared with that of Homer, he astounded his listeners with his familiarity with the language and the exactness of his information. In 1807 he returned to Philadelphia and commenced the practice of law, devoting, however, much attention to literature, and contributing papers, chiefly upon the fine arts, to various publications. In association with Joseph Dennie in 1806, he undertook the editorship of a high-class magazine called the "Portfolio," which he continued alone upon the death of his associate, at the same time engaging in other literary work. He compiled a commercial digest and prepared for press the "Narrative of Lewis' and Clark's Expedition to the Pacific Ocean," for which he induced Mr. Jefferson to write the introductory memoir of Capt. Lewis. Being elected to the state legislature in 1810, he was compelled to turn the work over to Paul Allen who superintended the work, and other names were allowed to appear as the editors. He took a leading part in legislative affairs, especially in the effort to establish a system of common schools. In 1814 he was elected to the state senate when he gave ardent support to all measures for carrying on the war

with Great Britain. His first speech was made in favor of the United States Bank which attracted wide attention and was commended by Chief-Justice Marshall. This was his first step in his financial career. Among the able state papers from his pen was the report of the committee of the senate respecting the proposition of the Hartford convention. In 1817 he was the Democratic candidate for congress, but was defeated by the Federalists. When the United States Bank was rechartered in 1819, Mr. Biddle was appointed, by Pres. Monroe, a government director, and when Mr. Cheves resigned in 1823, he was appointed president, which position he held until the expiration of the charter. It is not denied that his administration of its affairs evinced the highest ability. The withdrawal of the government deposits by order of Pres. Jackson in 1833 precipitated a "bank war" which spread financial disaster throughout the country. Mr. Biddle resigned the presidency in 1839. In 1841 the bank suspended specie payments. In the discussion which followed Mr. Biddle asserted that the cause of the insolvency did not originate in the time of his presidency. In spite of this unfortunate conclusion of his financial career, he retained the admiration and confidence of the community. During the suspension of payment of interest on the state debt he published suggestions for its liquidation which were afterwards accepted. He was president of the Agricultural and Horticultural societies and of the board of trustees of the University of Pennsylvania and Girard College. To his taste Philadelphia owes two of its finest specimens of architecture, Girard College and the Bank of the United States. As a writer and orator he was a model of vigor and terseness. He was a highly accomplished scholar both in classical literature and in modern languages. C. J. Ingersoll says that he "was as iron-nerved a man as his great antagonist, Andrew Jackson, loved his country not less and money as little." He died Feb. 27, 1844.

BACKUS, Henry Clinton, lawyer, was born at Utica, N. Y., May 31, 1848. The old Puritan stock, to which the country is mainly indebted for its greatness, counted the Backus family among its members, the earliest representative of the name in this country being William, who, about 1637, settled in Saybrook, Conn., and afterward, in 1659, was, with his son Stephen, among the founders of Norwich, Conn., who received letters patent for the same. By consent of his fellow-planters he gave to this latter settlement its name. In 1700 his grandson, Stephen Backus the younger, an ancestor of Henry Clinton Backus, founded the town of Canterbury, Conn. Elisha the great-grandfather of Henry Clinton Backus took part in the battle of Bunker Hill, held the rank of major in the Revolutionary army and, in time of peace, emulated his forefathers by founding another town, that of Manlius, in Onondaga county, N. Y. His son Elisha was a colonel in the American forces during the war of 1812. Charles C. Backus, a son of the later Elisha Backus, became a member of the publishing house of Bennett, Backus & Hawley, at Utica, N. Y., and there issued also the "Baptist Register," afterward altered to the "Examiner and Christian Inquirer" of New York. He removed with his family to New York city about 1850 and became one of the originators of the American Express Co. Here Henry Clinton Backus was reared and received his education at one of the public schools. He studied for a while under private tutors and at Phillips Academy, at Exeter, N. H., where he prepared for Harvard. He entered that university in 1867, and was graduated four years later with the degree of A.B. Returning to New York, he took his degree of LL.B. at Columbia College Law School in 1873, and was admitted to the bar. He acquired experience in legal procedure and method with Sanford, Robinson & Woodruff and, after a year with this firm, entered the office of Beebe, Wilcox & Hobbs, then widely known for its immense admiralty practice. His taste and inclination leaned toward the civil rather than the criminal branches of the law. Hence Mr. Backus's reputation rests on his skill in probate and admiralty business, his grasp of legal lore and subtleties in connection with corporation and realty adjudication and his familiarity with constitutional and international law. He has become known for his powers of keen analysis and logical presentation of facts; and also for the unvarying courtesy with which he meets opposing counsel. This spirit of fairness has indeed won him the esteem of both bench and bar; while he has secured the confidence of clients by the strictly honorable observance of all the obligations of a lawyer toward those who seek his advice and assistance. In politics Mr. Backus is a Republican. He has frequently been solicited to accept nomination for public office but has steadily declined except when in 1893 he consented to stand for the New York Constitutional Convention.

For ten years he was a member of the New York Republican County Committee, during five of which he served on its committee on resolutions. While a member he introduced and effected an amendment to the New York County Republican Constitution whereby it was decreed that twenty-five voters in any assembly district might compel the polls at any primary election in that district to be open twelve hours instead of six. In 1891 he was chairman of the delegation of the thirteenth assembly district to the Republican County Committee of New York city and county and held the leadership of the district for a twelvemonth, declining, however, re-election the following year. Mr. Backus was a member of the original committee on the erection of the magnificent monument to Gen. Grant on Riverside drive in New York city. He is an active and popular member of the Chelsea Republican Club, of the New York City Bar Association, and of the New York State Bar Association; he was for some time a member of the New York Harvard Club, and he is a fellow of the American Geographical Society. As evidencing Mr. Backus's contempt for prejudice and narrow-mindedness, a striking proof of his moral courage is worthy of being recorded. Toward the close of the war, when the proscription of the negro, even in the North, still debarred him from equal enjoyment with other citizens of the United States of freemen's rights and privileges, Mr. Backus organized and taught a class of colored children in the Sunday-school of one of the large and fashionable churches in New York city. Few incidents in his career afford him more gratification. In 1890 he married Harriet Ivins Davis of New York, who is now a member of the board of managers of the New York Colored Orphan Asylum, in the work of which she has her husband's warmest sympathy.

KERN, Charles, county treasurer, was born in the Bavarian Palatinate in 1831. He inherited those traits by which his countrymen are known the world over, a straightforward character and a genial disposition, coupled with an indomitable energy. After going through the public schools of his town, he came to America, making his first home in Cincinnati. A few years later he removed to Terre Haute, Ind., where he engaged in the restaurant business. He was successful in this, and made so many friends, that in 1862 he was nominated for sheriff on the Democratic ticket, and was triumphantly elected, although Vigo county had up to that time been a Republican stronghold. His administration of the office was highly commended. Feeling, however, that the field for his energy was but a limited one, he removed to Chicago in 1865, where he again went into the restaurant business, and was burned out in the great fire of 1871. He immediately re-opened business, and met with splendid success. In 1868, only three years after he settled in Chicago, and again in 1870 and 1872, he was the nominee of the Democratic party for sheriff of Cook county, but was defeated each time with his party, although running ahead of his ticket. Nominated again in 1876 for the same office, he was elected, the only Democrat elected on the ticket. At the end of his term of office, for the administration of which he again received warm praises, he retired from office, to devote himself to his ever-growing commercial interests. In 1890 he was prevailed upon by his fellow Democrats to accept the nomination for county treasurer. He made a splendid race, and was elected for a term of four years, running again ahead of his ticket by 5,000 votes. In this capacity he made again a most enviable record for efficiency and economy. Mr. Kern has filled many honorary positions in the Democratic party, including president of the County Democracy, and vice-president of the Iroquois Club. He is one of the acknowledged leaders of the party. Mr. Kern is well known in society circles. He is a member of Ashlar lodge, Knights Templars, of the Washington Park Club, Germania Club, and a number of other societies of a social character. Mr. Kern is a sportsman of skill and prominence. He has been president of the State Sportsmen's Association, and has for many years held

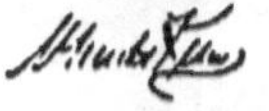

the position of president of the Audubon Club, earning considerable credit by introducing and aiding in the passage of laws for the protection of game, through the state legislature. Mr. Kern was married, July, 1852, to Mary Anne, daughter of Henry Richard Whitman, and they have two children, a daughter, Josephine, wife of James M. Dodge, and a son, Harry W.

HAMLIN, Teunis Slingerland, clergyman, was born at Glenville, Schenectady county, N. Y., May 31, 1847, son of Solomon Curtis Hamlin, a farmer, born in the same place, and whose father, Caleb Jewett Hamlin, came thither from his native place, Sharon, Conn. This Connecticut family of Hamlins were related to the Maine family. The Hamlins are of Huguenot blood, and their ancestors came into England from France with William the Conqueror in 1066. His mother was Christiana Slingerland, youngest child of Teunis Slingerland, a prominent business man of Albany, N. Y., of Dutch descent, and for many years identified with the First Reformed (Dutch) Church of Albany. Teunis, who was the only child, entered the district school one month before his fourth birthday. He

was prepared for college at the Academy in Charlton, Saratoga co.; entered Union College at Schenectady in 1864, and was graduated, with honors, in 1867. He was principal of the High School at Ypsilanti, Mich., one year, and in 1868 became principal of the Houghton public school in Detroit, but resigned after four months to prosecute theological studies. Mr. Hamlin was brought up in the Reformed (Dutch) Church of Glenville, of which his uncle, Rev. Elbert Slingerland, had been the pastor. During his junior year in college he united with the First Reformed (Dutch) Church of Schenectady, and in 1869 entered the theological seminary of that denomination at New Brunswick, N. J. The next year he went to Union Seminary, New York city, where he was graduated in 1871, and was licensed to preach by the Congregational Association of New York and Brooklyn. Mr. Hamlin was called to the pastorate of Woodside Presbyterian Church, Troy, N. Y., and was ordained and installed by the presbytery of Troy on Sept. 28, 1871. He remained in this pastorate thirteen years. In 1884 he accepted a call to the Mount Auburn Presbyterian Church, Cincinnati, O. Deep religious interest soon manifested itself, and the church grew rapidly in all directions, especially in the formation of a very vigorous Young People's Christian Union. In March, 1886, a unanimous call was extended to Mr. Hamlin by the Church of the Covenant in Washington, D. C., and he was installed on the 9th of the following November. This was a new Presbyterian church, organized only the October previous, and embracing a number of the most eminent men at the capital. The congregation was at this time worshiping in the chapel, but steps were at once taken to build the contemplated church edifice. Work was pushed rapidly, and notwithstanding the delay occasioned by the collapse of the magnificent tower, it was occupied for worship Feb. 24, 1890. It was immediately filled by a congregation embracing many distinguished families. In this pastorate Dr. Hamlin has been very successful, the membership of the church having increased more than seven-fold within nine years, and its influence being very widely felt. In 1886 Union College conferred upon Mr. Hamlin the degree of D.D. Two years later he delivered the baccalaureate at his alma mater. He has been one of the university preachers at Yale, Cornell, Princeton and at Vassar. On Nov. 11, 1890, he delivered an eulogium upon the late Dr. Ransome Bethune Welch before the faculty and students of the Auburn (N. Y.) Theological Seminary; and in June, 1895, an address on "Union College in the Ministry," at the centennial of that institution. He has written for many newspapers, magazines and reviews; his sermons have been numerously published, including a small volume entitled "Denominationalism *versus* Christian Union" (1892). He has always been active in ecclesiastical matters, and was chairman of the committee of his presbytery on the revision of the "Confession of Faith." He is one of the trustees of the United Society of Christian Endeavor. He is vice-president and president of the Open Air Workers' Association of America, chairman of the board of directors of the Memorial Association of the District of Columbia, and a trustee of Howard University at Washington. Dr. Hamlin was married, Feb. 4, 1873, to Frances E. Bacon of Ypsilanti, Mich. They have two sons, Elbert and Francis.

KARNES, Henry W., soldier, went to Texas from Tennessee in 1831, won distinction in the storming of San Antonio, Dec. 5th to 9th, 1835. He commanded the scouts on the retreat of Gen. Houston, fighting the Mexican advance on the Navidad, was captain of cavalry at San Jacinto, commanded in several Indian battles, 1836 to 1840, was a prisoner in Matamoros in 1836, also among the Comanches in 1837 or 1838. Karnes county, Tex., was named in his honor. He died in San Antonio, December, 1840.

PALMER, Thomas, lawyer, was born in Washington county, Ga., in 1859, the son of David Palmer, a wealthy planter of English and Irish extraction, and Margaret Collins. His father died before Thomas was born, and the widow removed to Madison county, Fla., when her son was an infant, and remained there until he reached man's estate. Mr. Palmer began studying law in 1883, and in six months was admitted to the bar. This was an unusual honor, and was so deemed by his fellow-citizens, for he was elected mayor of Brooksville, Hernando co., soon after, and became the law partner of Gen. J. B. Wall, one of the most eminent practitioners in the state. This partnership lasted two years, and was dissolved in order that Mr. Palmer might continue his law studies at the University of Virginia. After spending some time at the University, he returned to Brooksville, resumed practice for two years, when he again returned to the University of Virginia, and was graduated there in 1888. He married Ruby Brook, of Pleasant Hill, Ala., in April, 1889, and in September of the same year was

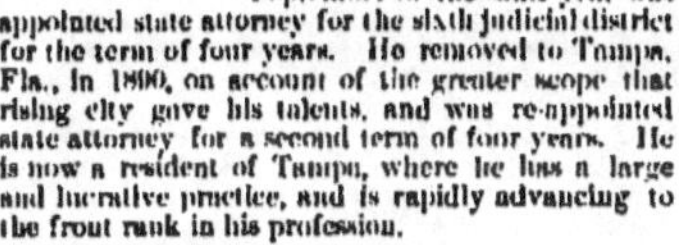

appointed state attorney for the sixth judicial district for the term of four years. He removed to Tampa, Fla., in 1890, on account of the greater scope that rising city gave his talents, and was re-appointed state attorney for a second term of four years. He is now a resident of Tampa, where he has a large and lucrative practice, and is rapidly advancing to the front rank in his profession.

DOREMUS, Sarah Platt, philanthropist, was born in New York city, Aug. 3, 1802. Her father, Elias Haines, and her mother, Mary Ogden, as also her grandparents, Robert Ogden and Sarah Platt,

devoted their lives and wealth to benevolence, so that consecration to Christian work was an inheritance. On Sept. 11, 1821, she married Thomas C. Doremus, a merchant of wealth and standing, and became the mother of nine children, Dr. R. Ogden Doremus, the celebrated professor in chemistry and toxicology, being her only son. In 1828 she began her first organized benevolent work, in labors for Greek women, then so oppressed by the Turks. With eight friends, she gathered large supplies, entrusting them to Dr. Jonas King as their representative, who became a devoted missionary in Greece. He was wont to call this band of ladies "The Nine Muses." In 1835 she took a vital interest in the Grande Ligne mission of Canada, so ably conducted by Mme. Henrietta Feller, of Geneva, Switzerland, and subsequently became the president of a society to promote the cause. Although Mme. Feller and her associates were Baptists, the broad, catholic spirit of Mrs. Doremus, brought up in the Presbyterian church, knew no sect in the pursuance of her benevolent work. In 1840 she commenced services in the women's ward of the New York city prison, called the "Tombs," nothing of the kind having before been attempted for the reclaiming of prisoners.

This work led to the formation of a society for discharged prisoners, called the Women's Prison Association, in which Catherine Sedgwick, the authoress, was a moving spirit. In this association she labored for thirty-seven years, a portion of the time as president, following many outcasts, individually, in the most successful yet self-denying methods. In 1841 she became a manager of the New York City and Tract Mission, a society having for its object the evangelization of the poor, to whose necessities she personally ministered. In 1849 she added to these labors by her connection with the City Bible Society, whose aim was to supply the destitute poor with the word of God, and through Bible readers to ameliorate their condition. In 1850, with many friends, she founded the House and School of Industry, an institution having a two-fold object: first, to give work to poor women, which was sold to them at a nominal price; second, to support a school, where children too poorly clad to attend public schools could receive instruction. In 1867 she was made the president, and was actively engaged in its interests until her death. In 1854 the claims of the poor pressed upon her in another direction, resulting, in connection with Mrs. Cornelius Du Bois, in the formation of the Nursery and Child's Hospital. This was the first organization of its kind where women who earned their daily bread could place their infants under watchful care during their enforced absence, or could seek the comforts of the hospital during the perils of maternity. In 1855 Dr. J. Marion Sims placed before her his plans for the establishment of a hospital to treat diseases peculiar to women. She readily responded to this call, and by repeated visits to the state legislature at Albany, secured the charter and appropriation for the institution known as the Woman's Hospital, the first ever founded in the world with this object in view. Religious services were established there, and sustained entirely through her direct instrumentality, prominent clergymen of the city rendering freely their ministrations. Filling at first the office of treasurer, which often obliged her to secure the needful income of the hospital, she became in 1864 the president, retaining the position at the time of her death. In 1860 she was mainly instrumental in founding the Woman's Union Missionary Society, the first organization of women in America to Christianize and elevate heathen women. For fifteen years her home was the headquarters of this society, demanding a consecration and service which cannot be estimated. In 1866 she aided in organizing the Presbyterian Home for Aged Women, and in 1876 became one of the committee to form the Gould Memorial in the interests of the Italo-American schools. Her labors in 1869 for the famine sufferers in Ireland, and her efforts for sick and wounded soldiers during the civil war were unequaled. Her private benefactions were countless, her home being a Bethel for returning or outgoing missionaries to foreign lands, to the sick and afflicted of every degree, and especially to the young, whose lives she filled with sunshine. All her labors for suffering humanity were so unostentatiously performed that much was not known until after her death. No outside duty was undertaken until the claims of her household were minutely discharged. From her youth she was a notable housewife, and her delicacies for the sick were among the crowning achievements of her education. She was skilled in all the accomplishments of the day, and her paintings and embroideries are preserved as evidences of her versatile talents. To the last day of her life she was to be seen making dainty fabrics with the dexterity and rapidity of the young. Her beauty was retained to old age, and her clear, cameo-cut features, her delicate complexion, with its soft color, and deep blue eyes, gave her a passport to all hearts. Her power to organize undertakings, broad and far-reaching, was only equaled by her execution of the minutest details. The motto of her paternal family: "With Sails and Oars," was strikingly exemplified in the skill with which obstacles were overcome, especially with a delicacy of health which might have precluded all active service. The secret of her success in every department of work was her entire consecration to the Lord's service. Mrs. Doremus died at her home in New York city, Jan. 29, 1877.

HANDY, James A., Methodist Episcopal bishop, was born in Maryland, Dec. 22, 1826. His mother died during his childhood, leaving him to the care of an uncle. His education was limited to four months in a night school. When he was eighteen, he joined the Moral Improvement Society, which gave him access to a small library. In 1853 he became a member of the African Methodist Episcopal Church, Baltimore, Md., and three years later became a trustee. He was licensed to preach in 1860, and filled pastorates in Maryland, Virginia, North Carolina, Louisiana, and the District of Columbia. In 1868 he was elected recording secretary of the missionary society of his church, a position he held four years. He was a presiding elder thirteen years, and in 1892 was ordained a bishop, his district comprising the churches of his denomination in Missouri, Kansas, Nebraska, Colorado, Wyoming, Montana, Utah, and New Mexico.

EVANS, Dudley, second vice-president and manager, Wells, Fargo & Co., was born near Morgantown, Monongalia co., Va., now West Virginia, Jan. 27, 1838, the son of Rawley Evans, whose ancestors were of Welsh origin, and came to this country in early colonial days. His great-great-grandfather was one of three brothers, who emigrated from Wales, and landed in Philadelphia about the year 1720, but subsequently removed to Virginia, was married near Mount Vernon, Fairfax co., and resided in Loudon county, where a son, John, was born. Col. John Evan's son, Dudley Evans, was colonel, under Gen. Harrison, in the war of 1812, and commanded a regiment of Virginia militia, stationed at Fort Meigs. Margaret, the only daughter, was married to Capt. John Dent, also an officer in the revolutionary war. Col. Dudley Evans, the subject of this sketch, is a great-grandson of John Evans, and is also a grandson, on his mother's side, of Moses Cox, who served as an officer in the war of 1812, stationed at Norfolk, Va. He was brought up on a farm about as most boys in those days were, alternating between school and play and work. When about fifteen he began attending the Monongalia Academy, where he was prepared for college, and entered the junior class at Washington College, Pa., now Washington and Jefferson, graduating in 1859. He subsequently removed to Louisiana, and was there when the war broke out. Having an inclination for more stirring scenes, he left for Virginia, and on his return homeward, he fell in with the Confederate troops then in camp near Beverly, Va., and remained there until the battle of Rich Mountain. He subsequently joined the army at Manassas, under the command of Beauregard and Johnston. After the battle of Seven Pines he was commissioned a captain in the Virginia state forces, which were afterwards turned over to the Confederate army. In the fall of 1862 he was taken prisoner, and among the force who captured him was one of his classmates, George B. Caldwell, then acting as adjutant in a Federal regiment. For a time he was confined in Camp Chase, O., then sent to Vicksburg, and there exchanged. In the spring of 1863 he was elected lieutenant-colonel of the Confederate cavalry, and took part in all the battles in the valley of Virginia in 1863-64. During the war, he was elected a member of the Virginia legislature by the soldier vote, and spent the winters of 1863-64 and 1864-65 in Richmond, and was there at the time of the evacuation. After the war closed, seeing no immediate prospect of bettering his condition, he left the scenes of distress and desolation, and started for California, with the intention of taking up the law as a profession, but on account of his political antecedents, was debarred by statutory enactment. He sought and obtained a situation in the organization of Wells, Fargo & Co., and was ordered to Victoria, B. C., where that company had an express and banking office. In 1871 he was appointed agent at Portland, Ore., and took charge of the business there, as well as acting as supervising agent for Oregon and Washington territory. He was afterwards made superintendent of the Northwestern division. In the beginning of the year 1888 he was transferred to Omaha, Neb., and placed in charge of the Northeastern division. Shortly afterwards he was made general superintendent of the central department. On Dec. 1, 1891, he was transferred to New York, in charge of the Atlantic department, where he has since continued as manager. On Aug. 11, 1892, he was elected one of the board of directors, and made second vice-president of the company, which position he still continues to hold.

HOGG, William James, manufacturer, was born in Philadelphia, Pa., July 5, 1851, the eldest son of William and Catherine (Horner) Hogg. His first American ancestor, William Hogg, a wealthy linen manufacturer of Scotland, came to Pennsylvania early in the nineteenth century, and settled in Northumberland county. His son, William Hogg, 2d, a staunch Scotch Presbyterian, removed to Philadelphia when a young man, and engaged in the manufacture of shawls and other woolen fabrics, and in 1832 began the manufacture of carpets, an industry then in its infancy, and in Hogg's establishment most of the successful carpet manufacturers of later days learned the business. In 1846, having amassed a competence, he was succeeded in the business by his son, William Hogg, 3d, who continued the business in connection with his younger brother, James, until 1850, when William continued the business alone within six months of his death, June 8, 1883. His son, William James, representing the fourth generation in America, and the third of the name who were notable as manufacturers of carpets in the United States, was educated at Dr. Faires's school in Philadelphia, and Lafayette College, Easton, Pa. He began his business life with his father, in 1868, and acquired an interest in the business in 1871. In July, 1879, he removed to Worcester, Mass., and in company with his father, bought the plant and business of the Crompton Carpet Co., changing the name to the Worcester Carpet Co., conducted by William James Hogg & Co. He retained his interest in the Philadelphia house until 1882, when he sold out, and bought his father's interest in the Worcester company, becoming its sole proprietor. In 1883 he built a new mill, enlarging the capacity of his plant one-third, and in 1884 purchased the Pakachoag Worsted Mills, adding to his business the business of spinning his own worsted yarns. Mr. Hogg produces the best grades of Wilton and Brussels carpets, and also rugs of the finest American make. He, in connection with Herbert L. Stockwell, purchased in 1887 the Stoneville Worsted Mills, at Auburn, Mass., for the additional supply of worsted yarns. Mr. Hogg was married in 1871 to Frances, daughter of George F. Happoldt, of Philadelphia, and his eldest son, William F., after finishing his education, was admitted to the business, making the fourth generation of carpet manufacturers in America, all inheriting the Christian name of William, as well as the business. Mr. Hogg is largely interested in real estate in Philadelphia and Worcester, on which he builds modern houses, opens streets, and improves generally. He is a director of the Quinsigamond Bank, and of the Worcester board of trade. He is a trustee of the Worcester Five-Cent Savings Bank, and is a stockholder in numerous banks and corporations. He is a member of the Congregational church, is a Mason, and a member of four social clubs. In 1891, Mr. Hogg, who always had a passionate fondness for horses and cattle, to further indulge his taste, purchased as a summer home "Hillside Farm," the former home of John B. Gough, the temperance lecturer, and on it he breeds fine horses and Jersey cattle. As a stock-raiser he promises a success as great as he has made as a manufacturer.

GUERNSEY, Lucy Ellen, author, was born at Pittsford, Monroe co., N. Y., Aug. 12, 1826. Her father was of New England stock, an early settler of Ontario county. She was carefully educated and when at school was fond of story writing. She began to write in 1852, and has been a prolific writer of children's story books, having furnished many of the juvenile tales published by the Sunday-school Union, which have proved exceedingly popular. "Irish Amy" being, perhaps, the best known. Besides her juveniles, she has published a series of books illustrating English history: "Lady Betty's Governess," "Winifred," etc.,

and a volume of Lenten meditations called "A Soul in Earnest." Her sister, Clara Guernsey, born at Pittsford, Oct. 1, 1836, has also written many books for the young and contributed to various periodicals. Her first story appeared in "Gleason's Pictorial" when she was fourteen. Of late years she has written and spoken in behalf of the Indian Six Nations of N. Y. The sisters have long lived together in Rochester.

OSGOOD, Howard, professor and Hebrew scholar, was born on Magnolia plantation in the parish of Plaquemine, La., Jan. 4, 1831, and educated in Harvard College, Cambridge, Mass. Though he grew up in the Protestant Episcopal church he afterwards joined the Baptist church and was pastor at Flushing, N. Y., 1856-58, and in New York city, 1860-65. After visiting Europe he was in 1868 appointed professor of Hebrew in Crozer Theological Seminary, Chester, Pa., and in 1875 in Rochester Theological Seminary, N. Y. He was a member of the Old Testament Co. of the American committee on Bible revision, and prepared "Leviticus" and "Numbers" for the "Schaff-Lange Commentary," 1876, besides a number of articles in "The Baptist Review."

WHITEHEAD, John, jurist, was born in Jersey, Licking co., O., September, 1819. Deprived by death of a father's care, his early years were passed in the home of his uncle, Asa Whitehead, a prominent lawyer of Newark, N. J. After receiving a thorough academic education, he became a student-at-law in his uncle's office. He was admitted to the bar in September, 1840, and began at once the practice of law, remaining with his uncle until 1843, when he opened an office for himself in Newark, where he followed his profession for more than twenty-five years. He has so thoroughly mastered the details and principles of his profession, that for years the younger members of the bar have consulted him in intricate cases, relying implicitly upon his application of the law to the case in hand, and, however busy he might be, the knowledge from his storehouse always seemed to be dispensed with pleasure. Mr. Whitehead has few equals as a historian and litterateur, and had he consulted his taste, the pursuit of literature might have over-shadowed his profession. He was an earnest advocate of the cause of education. As early as 1845 he was one of the members of the school committee, and when the Board of Education was formed, in 1851, he became its secretary and treasurer until 1855. He was then elected school superintendent, which position he filled for four years. He

was for a long time secretary of the State Society of Teachers and Friends of Education, and was also a

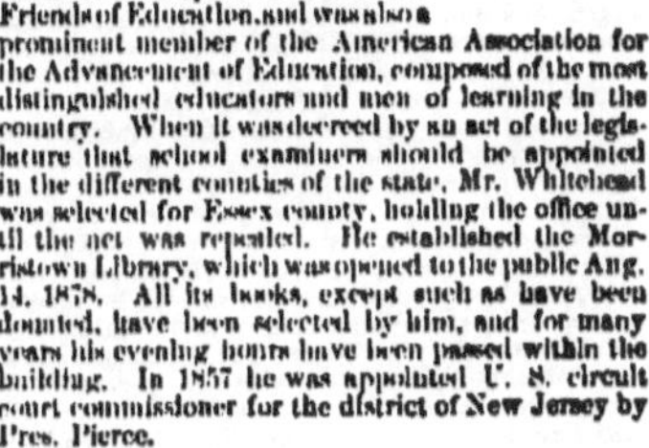

prominent member of the American Association for the Advancement of Education, composed of the most distinguished educators and men of learning in the country. When it was decreed by an act of the legislature that school examiners should be appointed in the different counties of the state, Mr. Whitehead was selected for Essex county, holding the office until the act was repealed. He established the Morristown Library, which was opened to the public Aug. 14, 1878. All its books, except such as have been donated, have been selected by him, and for many years his evening hours have been passed within the building. In 1857 he was appointed U. S. circuit court commissioner for the district of New Jersey by Pres. Pierce.

SANGSTER, Margaret Elizabeth (Munson), author, editor, and poet, was born in New Rochelle, N. Y., Feb. 22, 1838. She received her early education chiefly at Vienna, and in early childhood was precocious and gave evidence of literary talents. In 1858 she married George Sangster. She became a regular contributor to the leading periodicals of the day. Mrs. Sangster has been one of the popular American poets ever since the civil war. Twenty years ago her "Elizabeth, Aged Nine" and "Are the Children at Home?" were household words. They were published in the newspapers, the school readers and formed part of the repertoire of every elocutionist, "Our Own," which first appeared anonymously in "Harper's Bazar," has found a place in the poet's corner of papers throughout America, Australia, and England. Mrs. Sangster has been associate-editor of the New York "Hearth and Home," "Christian at Work," and "Christian Intelligencer." In 1882 she became editor of "Harper's Young People," and in 1889 succeeded Mary L. Booth as editor of "Harper's Bazar." She has also written some half dozen popular books for children. Mrs. Sangster remains at her New York office during

business hours and devotes the remainder of her time to her domestic and church duties. She is a prominent member of the Dutch Reformed church. Mrs. Sangster is a member of but one women's club, the Meridian. It has only thirty members, and no public meetings. She is particularly devoted to children, and all of her books except her bound volume of poems have been written for them. Her first was "Little Jamie," written when she was but seventeen years old. One of her later works, "Hours with Girls," was republished in England, and brought her an offer from an English publisher. Mrs. Sangster assisted Mrs. Terhune in conducting the women's council at Bay View, Mich. Mrs. Sangster is a woman of charming personality and of distinguished presence. The kindliness of her heart beams in her face and wins her a ready welcome in any company she favors with her society. In addition to her stories, she has published, "Manual of Missions of the Reformed Church in America;" "Poems for the Household;" "Home Fairies and Heart Flowers: Twenty Studies of Children's Heads with Floral Embellishments," accompanied with poems.

MAEDER, Frederick George, actor and playwright, was born in New York city, Sept. 11, 1840, the son of James Gaspard and Clara Fisher Maeder. He received his education in Trinity School, under the Rev. Dr. Morris. After leaving school, he engaged for a time in mercantile pursuits, but shortly after turned his attention to the stage, and made his first appearance as an actor in Portland, Me., Nov. 8, 1858, as Bernardo in "Hamlet," under the management of George Pauncefort. Two years later he was a member of John E. Owens's company in New Orleans. In 1861 he dramatized Dickens's "Great Expectations," which was first produced with great success in Montreal, Can. Soon after he adapted Miss Braddon's novel, "Nobody's Daughter," which also proved very successful, and in 1861 he became a member of the Wallack-Davenport combination. In the following year he assumed the management of a Washington theatre, where he produced his own adaptation of "Les Miserables." In 1863 he visited Europe, and traveled through England, Ireland, and Scotland, fulfilling a six weeks' engagement at the Prince of Wales Theatre in Liverpool. Returning to the United States, he produced the "Ticket-of-Leave Man" in Boston, and in 1864 he took part in "Solon Shingle" at the Broadway Theatre in New York. The late Lawrence Barrett was seen at one time in a dramatization of the poem of "Enoch Arden," made by Mr. Maeder; and the play of "Help," written for Joseph Murphy, gave that actor his first distinctive success. Mr. Maeder also dramatized "Shamus O'Brien," and wrote an Irish play entitled "Naun Cree." His last play was the "Cannuck," which, with the "Runaway Wife," he produced for McKee Rankin. He was a man of talent and culture, and an intelligent and earnest actor. He died in New York city, after a long illness, Apr. 8, 1891.

NORRIS, John, one of the founders of Andover Theological Seminary, was born in Salem, Mass., June 10, 1748. For many years he was a prominent merchant in Salem, and was also several times elected a member of the Massachusetts state senate. On March 21, 1808, he gave towards establishing the Andover Seminary the sum of $10,000, two merchants of Newburyport also giving towards the same object, $30,000. John Norris' widow, Mary Norris, who died in Salem in 1811, bequeathed $30,000 to the same institution, and the same sum to trustees for the benefit of foreign missions. Mr. Norris died in Salem, Mass., Dec. 22, 1808.

McALLISTER, Ward, lawyer, was born in Savannah, Ga., Dec. 28, 1827. His ancestors on the maternal side are of French descent, who came from Rochelle in a large ship chartered for the Carolinas by several Huguenot families of high rank and wealth. His grandfather, Matthew McAllister, was appointed, by Pres. Washington, U. S. district attorney for the state of Georgia, and he was also judge of the superior court of that state. His maternal grandmother was Sarah Charlotte Cutler, niece of Gen. Francis Marion, the "Swamp Fox" of the revolution, and wife of Benjamin Clarke Cutler, high sheriff of the county of Norfolk, Mass. The family tree on this side dates back over 200 years. His grandfather, Matthew McAllister, married Hannah Gibbons, sister of the millionaire Thomas Gibbons; their only son was Matthew Hall McAllister, the father of Ward, who also held the office of U. S. district-attorney for Georgia; was repeatedly elected mayor of the city of Savannah; and was the first U. S. circuit judge appointed for California. After receiving a thorough education, Ward McAllister was admitted to the bar of Georgia in 1850, but always showed more inclination toward the fine arts and society than to the practice of law. He and his father, however, joined his brother Hall in San Francisco where he had preceded them, and was winning both fame and fortune. The three

formed a partnership, and in a few years he had accumulated a sufficient fortune to retire from business with his father, leaving his brother Hall to continue the affairs of the firm alone. In 1853 he married Miss Gibbons, daughter of William Gibbons of Savannah, Ga., and soon after removed to New York city. He immediately became a prominent figure in the fashionable world, and being a man of the highest social culture and refinement, thereafter continued to be the acknowledged leader of New York society. His hobby was getting up and managing balls and dinners. Even as early as the time of his visit to California, as he tells in his book, "Society As I Have Found It," he gave a dinner in which he took great pride. He organized the series of dances known as "The Patriarchs," in 1872. The summers he spent at Newport, and was active in the same line that characterized his life in this city. He introduced what were known as "Dutch treats," otherwise called subscription picnics. Occasionally ho would visit the Bahamas in the winter, and then his energies continued in the line of getting up dinners and balls. He also traveled extensively abroad and was the author of one book, "Society as I have Found It," which attracted considerable attention at the time of its publication. Mr. McAllister was one of the oldest members of the Union League Club. He died in New York, after a brief illness, Jan. 31, 1895.

ROLLER, William Wallace, soldier, was born in Gowanda, Erie co., N. Y., Nov. 1, 1841, of German ancestry. His grandfather was an officer under Napoleon Bonaparte, taking part in the Russian campaign. He was educated in the public and private schools in the vicinity of his native town, and at the outbreak of the civil war enlisted as a private, Sept. 7, 1861, in Company A, 64th regiment, New York volunteers. His promotion was as follows: second sergeant, Nov. 15, 1861; first sergeant, March 1, 1862; sergeant-major, July 1, 1863; second lieutenant, Jan. 1, 1863; first lieutenant, March 31, 1862; and captain, Jan. 19, 1864. With his regiment Capt. Roller took part in the peninsular campaign, participating in the siege of Yorktown and the battle of Fair Oaks, where he was wounded while charging the enemy's line. He again joined his regiment at Harrison's Landing and was engaged in the second Bull Run, South Mountain, Antietam. Fredericksburg and Chancellorsville, where he was in command of Company D, and where he was again wounded. The 64th regiment distinguished itself at Chancellorsville, where, in company with four other regiments, it held an advanced line successfully against the persistent attack of a large force of the enemy, the brilliancy of the affair becoming a matter of history. Capt. Roller rejoined his regiment before his wound had thoroughly healed, and was made quartermaster for a time, after which, being promoted to a captaincy, he was placed in command of Company D, again participating in the battles of Auburn, Bristoe Station, Mine Run, the Wilderness, Morton's Ford, Po River, Spottsylvania Court House (where his brigade formed the front line), North Anna, Tolopotomy, Cold Harbor, the assault and siege of Petersburg, Jerusalem Road, Strawberry Plains, Deep Bottom, Reams's Station, Weldon Railroad, and

Hatcher's Run. He was placed in command of Fort Rice by general orders on Oct. 27, 1864. Capt. Roller was honorably mustered out, at his own request, Oct. 30, 1864, near Petersburg, Va., after which he entered Dartmouth College and took a partial course, subsequently going West and engaging in the furniture business at Ottawa, Kan. In June, 1874, he removed to Colorado Springs, Col., where he continued the same business. In 1880 he established himself in the real estate and loan business in Salida, Col. He was married on Feb. 27, 1871, to Claramond M. Hayes, who died, leaving one child, and on Sept. 24, 1884, he was again married to Nellie H. Arnold, and two sons and one daughter were born to them. An active and influential man in the community in which he lives, Capt. Roller is always foremost in every enterprise of a public nature, and is always on the side of right and morality. He is a member of the Loyal Legion, Colorado Commandery, and is a prominent Mason.

O'NEALL, John Belton, jurist, was born near Bobo's Mills, Newberry district, S. C., Apr. 10, 1793, son of Hugh O'Neall and Ann Kelly. His ancestors, both paternal and maternal, were of ancient Irish families. His grandparents were Quakers, settling in South Carolina early in life. The young man had unusual facilities for acquiring an education, and was graduated at South Carolina College in 1812 with the second honor of that institution; studied law, and was admitted to the bar in 1814. Becoming active in political affairs, he was elected to the South Carolina legislature as a member of the lower house, in 1816, when only twenty-three years old. He was returned to the legislature at three successive elections, and during the last two terms he was speaker of the house. In December, 1828, he was made associate justice of the court of appeals of the state, and elevated to a full judgeship in 1830. He remained on that bench when the change was made in the judicial system of the state and the court known as Court of Law. In 1850 he became president of the court of law appeals and of the court of errors. Upon the reorganization of a separate court of appeals, he was unanimously appointed chief justice of the state. His judicial duties claimed a large portion of his time, but Judge O'Neall was devoted to the science of agriculture, and gave much attention to its development and promotion, especially in his own district of Newberry, which owes much of its reputation for thorough cultivation of the soil to his continuous efforts. He was largely instrumental in the completion of the Greenville and Columbia Railroad. He was a prominent member of the Baptist denomination, and the best known and most highly honored layman of that denomination in the South. He was also known as the apostle of temperance in South Carolina, and was during his life a consistent advocate of total abstinence, instilling its lessons from the bench, in the church, and at the hustings. His advocacy of teetotalism was so earnest and unceasing, that he was credited with having done more voluntary labor for the cause than any other disciple of his times. He found time to perform the militia duty called for by his state, and rose to the rank of major-general. He wrote for the press on agriculture, temperance, religion, and education, and delivered lectures before conventions, public meetings, and at state and county agricultural fairs, many of which were published. He was author of "Digest of the Negro Law" (1848); "Annals of Newberry" (1858); "Bench and Bar of South Carolina" (2 vols., 1859). Judge O'Neall died at his home near Newberry, S. C., Sept. 27, 1863.

SHUEY, William John, publisher, was born in Miamisburg, Montgomery co., O., Feb. 9, 1827, the only son of Adam Shuey who was a pioneer of the Miami Valley, and a descendant of Daniel Shuey, who emigrated from the Palatinate and landed in Philadelphia in 1732. He was educated in the common schools and at an academy in Springfield, O., and for a time taught school near that city. In 1848 he received license to preach from the Miami annual conference of the church of the United Brethren in Christ, and was ordained in 1851 by Bishop Erb. He was pastor at Lewisburg, O., from 1849 to 1851; at Cincinnati, O., from 1851 to 1859; and at Dayton, O., from 1860 to 1862. From 1862 to 1864 he was the presiding elder of his conference. Having been an earnest advocate of an African mission, in 1854 he was appointed the first missionary of the United Brethren church to Africa, and in 1855, in company with Rev. Dr. D. K. Flickinger and Dr. D. C. Kumler, he made a voyage to the west coast of Africa for the purpose of selecting a site for a mission. This mission, situated near Freetown, Sierra Leone, now numbers nearly 6,000 members. In 1864 Mr. Shuey

was appointed assistant publishing agent of the United Brethren publishing house, located at Dayton, O. In 1865 he was elected senior agent, and in 1866 became sole agent, which position he has since occupied. Mr. Shuey has also been connected with all the important general interests of the United Brethren church, having been a delegate to eight general conferences, a member of the board of missions, a director of the Church-Erection Society, superintendent and treasurer of the general Sunday-School board, a member of the board of education, a trustee of Otterbein University, a member of the executive committee of Union Biblical Seminary, a member of the church commission for the revision of the confession of faith and amendment of the constitution, and a member of the general board of church trustees. He has also occupied other positions of honor and trust, both in the church and in the city in which he lives. In 1859 he became joint author with Rev. D. K. Flickinger of a volume entitled "Discourses on Doctrinal and Practical Subjects;" and has issued a number of pamphlets, besides writing constantly for the "Religious Telescope." In 1880 the title of D.D. was conferred upon him by Hartsville University, but was declined. His influence upon the denomination with which he is connected has been very marked, but has extended far beyond these limits. While devoted especially to the work of his church, he is a man of broad mind and liberal spirit, and belongs as well to the church universal. In 1848 Mr. Shuey married Sarah Berger, of Springfield, O., and has two children living.

QUACKENBOS, John Duncan, was born in New York city, Apr. 22, 1848. His great-grandfather, John Quackenbos, was a contractor to supply the Continental army with materials; his grandfather was Dr. George Clinton Quackenbos, a noted physician, and at one time health officer. His father was George Payn Quackenbos, author of Quackenbos' school books. He was graduated at Columbia College with first honors, June, 1868; received the degree of M.D. from the College of Physicians and Surgeons, New York, in March, 1871; the degree of A.M. from Columbia College, June, 1871; was appointed tutor in rhetoric and history, Columbia College in 1870; adjunct professor of the English language and literature in 1884; professor in University Faculty of Philosophy, and secretary of the faculty in 1890. He was elected member of the Geographical Society in 1883; member of the New York Historical Society in 1883; fellow of the New York Academy of Medicine in 1884; and member of the New York Academy of Sciences in 1890. His publications are: "Appleton's School History of World" (1876);

"History of Ancient Literature" (1878); was associate author of "Appletons' Elementary and Higher Geographies" (1880–81); "A History of the English Language," (1884); "Appletons' Physical Geography" (1889); "Appletons' Geography for Little Learners" (1889); "Appletons' School Physics" (1891); also author of various articles on natural hybridism among American and foreign salmonidæ, and on the salvelinus aureolus alpinus or so-called American salbling. He was also the first private importer of the Loch Leven trout (salmo levenensis) in 1887, of which 30,000 were planted in the waters of Sunapee Lake, N. H. He is also known in connection with efforts to promote fish culture in New Hampshire, and especially the development of Sunapee Lake, and the town of New London, N. H., as a summer resort.

DRAPER, John Christopher, physician, was born in Mecklenburg county, Va., March 31, 1835. He was the eldest son of the famous Dr. John W. Draper, the celebrated scientist (see Vol. III., 406). His mother was a daughter of Dr. Gardner, the attending physician of the emperor of Brazil, Dom Pedro I., and a descendant on her mother's side of a noted Portuguese family, De Piva Pereiras. He received his early education under the eye of his father, and entered the University of New York in 1852, but he left the classical department for the medical school, from which he was graduated in 1857. He served a year as house physician and surgeon at Bellevue Hospital, during which time he published two valuable papers on, "The Production of Urea," and "Experiments in Respiration." The following year he went to Europe, where he spent a year in travel and study, and upon his return in 1858 was elected to the chair of analytical chemistry in his alma mater, which he held until 1871. He was chosen professor of chemistry in Cooper Union in 1860, which he held for ten years, excepting three months during the civil war, when he was made surgeon to the 12th regiment, and accompanied them to the front. He was elected professor of natural sciences in the College of the City of New York in 1863, and three years later became professor of chemistry in the medical department of the University of New York, and held both chairs until his death. Dr. Draper brought from abroad an unusual equipment of the latest methods of study, and secured unusual facilities for the students. His success as an instructor has been very great, and the high order

of the college course is due to his earnest work. He was a member of the New York Academy of Medicine, and was a contributor to medical and scientific periodicals. Trinity College conferred upon him the degree of LL.D. in 1873. He edited the "Year-Book of Nature and Science" in 1872–73, and the department of natural science in "Scribner's" for three years. He also published, "Text-Book on Anatomy, Physiology, and Hygiene" (1866); "A Practical Laboratory Course in Medical Chemistry" (1882); and a "Text-Book of Medical Physics" (1885). He died in New York, Dec. 20, 1885, leaving a widow but no children.

DRAPER, Henry, scientist, was born at Hampden-Sidney, Prince Edward co., Va., March 7, 1837, the second son of Dr. John William Draper. Two years after the birth of Henry his father removed to this city to take the chair of chemistry in the New York University. He at first went through the primary school connected with the university, from which he passed into the preparatory school. At the age of fifteen he entered the collegiate department as an undergraduate, where he was distinguished for excellent scholarship. By the advice of his father, at the end of his sophomore year, he entered the medical department of the university, which his father had been prominent in establishing, and passed all his examinations satisfactorily, but not being of the age necessary for graduation his diploma was withheld, and with his brother he studied and recreated in Europe for one year, and upon his return took his medical degree in 1858. While in Europe he received an appointment upon the medical staff of Bellevue Hospital, which he held for sixteen months, but he then decided to abandon practice, and give himself to teaching. He was elected professor of natural science in the undergraduate department of the New York University in 1860, and in 1866 became professor of physiology in the medical department, and at the same time dean of the faculty. He resigned this post in 1873, and afterward taught advanced analytical chemistry in the academical department of the institution. Upon the death of his father in January, 1882, he was appointed to succeed him as professor of chemistry, but previous to the opening of the last fall term of 1882 he severed entirely his connection with the institution. But Henry Draper's

fame will not rest upon his professional labors, and we seek the key to his successful career in that education of his early life, which he did not get from the schools. He had, in his illustrious father, a companion, friend, and teacher from childhood, one of the most thoroughly cultivated and original scientific men of the day, who attended carefully to his instruction, and impressed upon him deeply the bent of his own mind in the direction of science. The boy was, in fact, immersed in science from his youngest years, and not merely crammed with its results, but saturated with its true spirit at his most impressionable period. He was taught to love science for the interest of its inquiries, and was early put upon the line of original investigation in which he acquired his celebrity. He inherited not only his father's genius, but his spirit and problems of research. Dr. John W. Draper was an experimental investigator of such fertility of resources and such consummate skill that the European savants always deplored his proclivity to literary labors as a great loss to the scientific world. Henry Draper inherited from his father in an eminent degree the aptitude for delicate experimenting, and a fine capacity for manipulatory tact. The elder Draper was one of the founders of the recent science of photo-chemistry. He worked early and brilliantly in the new and fascinating field of the chemistry of light, and more than forty years ago, by his extensive contributions to this subject, he prepared the way for those who entered to reap the fruits of his labors in the splendid field of spectrum analysis. Henry pursued the same line of research, and by his extension of it will have a permanent place among the discoverers of the period. His first important scientific investigation was made at the age of twenty, and was embodied in his graduating thesis at the medical college. It was on the functions of the spleen, which was illustrated by microscopic photography—an art then in its infancy. Soon after

receiving his degree he we went to Europe, and while there visited the widely known observatory of Lord Rosse, and studied the construction and working of his celebrated colossal reflecting telescope. This led him to consider the problem of using reflecting telescopes for the purpose of photographing celestial objects. On his return home he constructed a telescope of this kind of fifteen and a half inches aperture, and with it took a photograph of the moon fifty inches in diameter—the largest ever made. His success spurred him on to further improvements, so that he became an adept in grinding, polishing and testing reflecting mirrors. An equatorial telescope was afterward constructed by him, with an aperture of twenty-eight inches, for his observatory at Hastings-on-the-Hudson. The instrument was wholly the work of his own hands, and was designed mainly to photograph the spectra of the stars. After a long series of experiments, it was finished in 1872, and was pronounced by Pres. Barnard as "probably the most difficult and costly experiment in celestial chemistry ever made." He was the first to obtain a photograph of the fixed lines in the spectra of stars, and he continued the work until he had obtained impressions of the spectra of more than 100 stars. In 1874 he was appointed superintendent of the photographic department of the commission created by congress, for the purpose of observing the transit of Venus, and received from congress, in recognition of his services, a gold medal bearing the inscription, "He adds lustre to ancestral glory," which was the first time that the American government had made any such recognition of a scientific discoverer. In 1876 he made a negative of the solar spectrum, and in the following year announced, "the discovery of oxygen in the sun by photography, and a new theory of the solar spectrum." This was the most brilliant scientific discovery ever made by an American. He was a member of the principal scientific societies in America and Europe, and in 1882 was awarded the degree of LL.D. by both the University of New York and of Wisconsin. He died suddenly in the prime of a vigorous manhood. He had accomplished much, but with his ripened experience, his enthusiasm, his genius for investigation, and his large command of the facilities for research, still more was expected from him. As the names of the Herschels, father and son, will ever be connected in the history of modern astronomy, so also will the names of the Drapers, father and son, be jointly eminent in the advance of that more recent astronomy that has opened new and wonderful fields of study which even the Herschels hardly dreamed. Henry Draper died in New York city, Nov. 20, 1882, leaving no children. A biographical memoir was read before the Natural Academy of Sciences, Apr. 18, 1888, by Prof. George F. Barker, and afterward published in an octavo of sixty pages, with portrait, for private distribution.

DRAPER, Daniel, meteorologist, was born in New York city, Apr. 2, 1841, son of the eminent scientist and author, John William Draper; he is the only surviving member of this branch of the Draper family. On the maternal side, he is related to the celebrated De Piva Pereira family of Portugal; his maternal grandfather, Dr. Gardner, who was the attending physician to Dom Pedro I., emperor of Brazil, having married into the family. Mr. Draper received his early education at the primary department of the New York University, but left school to become his father's amanuensis, and under the latter's instruction he acquired that knowledge which has since made him famous, especially as a meteorologist. In the designing and construction of the observatory at Hastings-on-the-Hudson, he was associated with his brother Henry. Having a natural taste for mechanics, he served a five-years' apprenticeship in the Novelty Iron Works, New York, where he was employed during the building of the Roanoke and other ironclads for the U. S. government during the early part of the civil war. Through the recommendation and under the direction of Andrew H. Green, comptroller of New York city, he established in 1869 the meteorological observatory in Central Park, and was appointed its director. Through his efforts this has become one of the most important as well as one of the best equipped observatories in the world. For the work under his control he designed and patented a number of self-recording instruments, including the self-recording mercurial barometer, pencil thermometers (dry and wet), the sun thermometer, direction of wind, velocity of wind, force of wind, rain and snow gauges, etc. These have all proved of great advantage in ascertaining the various atmospheric changes, and have been adopted by many of the leading observatories in this country and in Europe. To supply the demand, Mr. Draper organized the Draper Manufacturing Co., of which he is president. In 1871 he began a series of meteorological investigations in connection with the observatory. Of these his considerations of the question, "Does the clearing of land increase or diminish the fall of rain?" showed that the prevalent impression of its diminishing was not founded on fact. Besides several researches concerning the variations in temperature, he took up the question, "Do American storms cross the Atlantic?" It was found that from 1869–75 eighty-six out of eighty-nine disturbances were felt on the European coast, and this led to the telegraphic announcement of storms from the United States to Great Britain. More recent investigation has shown the increased prevalence of pneumonia at times when the atmosphere is richest in ozone. His researches have earned for him the degree of Ph. D. from the University of New York, and they have been fully described in scientific journals in the United States and in Europe. He has published annual reports of his observations, which have proved valuable contributions to the scientific world. Mr. Draper is a fellow of the American Association for the Advancement of Science, a member of the Philosophical Society of Philadelphia, and other organizations. He married on Apr. 28, 1887, Ann Ludlow, of St. Louis, a descendant of the Huguenot families of Maury and La Fontaine, the latter of whom carried the manufacture of broad-cloth from France into England during the time of the persecution. Two daughters and a son resulted from this union.

KEELY, John Worrall, inventor, was born in Philadelphia, Pa., Sept. 3, 1837. He received but a scanty education, and learned the carpenter's trade at an early age, working at it in his native city until 1872. In that year he announced that he had discovered a new force by which motive power would be revolutionized. Acting upon this alleged discovery, he constructed what has since become known as the Keely motor, and on Nov. 10, 1874, first placed it upon exhibition before the public. A large number of capitalists and scientists witnessed its workings, and impressed by what they saw, advanced $100,000 to enable the inventor to perfect his discovery and apply the principle. Since then $400,000 more have been expended in experiments, but without practical or tangible results. Three years were spent in the construction of the first machine built, and when completed it was found to be worthless. Between 1874 and 1891 the inventor constructed and discarded 129 different models. Water was employed as a generator in the first models, but that has been discarded. His more recent experiments have been made with what he designates as a "liberator"—a machine equipped with a large number of tuning-forks, which he claims to disintegrate the air and release a powerful etheric force. In 1888 he was for a time confined in jail for contempt of court in refusing to disclose the secret by which he produced many remarkable effects in the presence of experts, but until the present time (1895) it is known only to Keely himself.

BRADFORD, James Henry, clergyman, was born at Grafton, Vt., Aug. 24, 1830, son of a Congregational minister, who held a charge for twenty-seven years. He is directly descended from the Rev. John Bradford, one time chaplain to the Queen of England, and prebendary of St. Paul's, London, who with others was burned at the stake at Smithfield, in 1558. Another ancestor is Gov. William Bradford of Plymouth colony, while his maternal grandfather, Thomas Dickman, was well known in Springfield, Mass., as a printer, postmaster, and the founder of a newspaper. Young Bradford was reared upon a farm, and received his early education at the district schools. At fifteen years of age he removed to Charleston, S. C., where he entered the drygoods house of W. G. Bancroft & Co. Returning to New England at the end of three years, he prepared for college at Williston Seminary, subsequently entering Yale Theological Seminary, but left to join the army as chaplain of the twelfth regiment of Connecticut volunteers. During this time Mr. Bradford participated in the two years' campaign in Louisiana, was with Sheridan for nearly one year in the Shenandoah Valley, and was present at the conflicts of Winchester, Fisher's Hill, and Cedar Creek. Throughout his entire army service he was never ill a day, wounded, nor captured. The war over, he assumed the duties of pastor and home missionary at Hudson, Wis., remaining there for two years. He was later chaplain and assistant superintendent of the Massachusetts Reform School for the same length of time, and for four years was superintendant and chaplain 

of the Connecticut Industrial School for Girls at Middletown, the latter being in those days the best school of its kind in America. Chaplain Bradford was vice-president of Gen Russell's C. C. Institute New Haven, and principal of the Student's Home Military School, Middletown, for one year each; superintendent and chaplain of the Massachusetts State Primary School, at Monson for three years; and, for a brief period, in Howard Mission, New York city. In 1881 he removed to Washington, D. C., where he engaged in labor in the educational and religious divisions of the census, and later in the pension and Indian bureaus. He has been chaplain of Garfield Post, G. A. R., from its inception; has served in the same capacity for one year in the department of the Potomac; for several years in the M. O. Loyal Legion; and has held almost weekly services in churches in and around Washington. Actively interested in the charities of the district, he has been a member of the board of associated charities from its organization, is a visitor and officer of one of its subdivisions; director and treasurer for the Temporary Home for Soldiers and Sailors; secretary of the Boys' and Girl's Home and Employment Association, and of the Manassas School for Colored Youth. Chaplain Bradford is especially interested in the conversion of children, his views upon the subject being given to the world from time to time through the medium of the religious press. In 1865 he married Ellen J. Knight. They have four children, two boys and two girls. Mrs. Bradford has established a wide reputation as the originator and manager of the Ben-Hur tableaux. In her voluminous correspondence in this connection, she is ably assisted by her husband.

HALE, Irving, soldier and electrician, was born in North Bloomfield, N. Y., Aug., 28, 1861, the son of Horace M., and Eliza Huntington Hale. In 1865 the family removed to Colorado, crossing the plains in the historic "prairie schooner," and making their home in Central City, where they lived until 1873, when they removed to Denver. Irvings's early schooling was received in his father's school at Central City. In 1877 he was graduated at the Denver High School, standing at the head of the first graduating class of that institution. Obtaining the appointment to the U. S. Military Academy by competitive examination, he entered West Point in 1880 and was graduated in 1884, first in his class, and with the highest record ever made at the academy to the present date (1895). He was assigned to the engineer corps as second lieutenant, and was stationed at Willet's

Point, L. I., until 1888, being promoted to first lieutenant in 1886, and appointed quartermaster and commissary of the battalion of engineers in 1887. In the same year he married Mary Virginia, daughter of Lieut.-Col. William R. King, of the corps of engineers, commandant of Willet's Point, and granddaughter of Col. and Brevet Brig.-Gen. I. C. Woodruff of the same corps. He represented the battalion of engineers in the division of the Atlantic rifle competition at Fort Niagara in 1888, and won the first division gold medal for the best total obtained in four days' known-distance and skirmish firing, as well as the first medal for the best two days' skirmishing. In September of that year he was detailed at the U. S. Military Academy as instructor in civil and military engineering. Not feeling satisfied with the prospects offered by the army, and desiring to make a specialty of electricity, he obtained in September, 1889, a six months' leave of absence, returned to Colorado to investigate the field for electrical engineering, and superintended the installation of the first successful electric road in Denver, which was started Christmas Day of that year. At the end of his leave of absence, in the spring of 1890, he resigned his commission in the army and entered the service of the Edison General Electric Co. After the consolidation of the Edison and Thomson-Houston Cos., forming the General Electric Co., he was appointed manager of that company for the district comprising Colorado, Wyoming, Utah, and New Mexico, with headquarters at Denver, which position he now holds. While most of his experience has been of a practical and commercial nature, he has carefully studied the theoretical side of electrical engineering, has contributed several valuable papers to scientific and engineering journals, and to the proceedings of the Colorado Scientific Society, of which he is an active member, and has received the honorary degree of Electrical Engineer from the Colorado State School of Mines.

PATCHIN, Jared, jurist, was born in Benton, Yates co., N. Y., Apr. 18, 1828. Three years after his birth his parents removed to Michigan, and settled in the vicinity of Detroit, in the Naukin schools of which city he received his first education, afterwards entering the University of Michigan at Ann Arbor, where he was graduated in 1852, was admitted to the bar in 1854. A year later he accepted the position of deputy county clerk under Judge Hawley, and held the office for several years, gradually attracting the notice of his superiors by his marked abilities and his grasp of legal technicalities. He eventually rose to be county prosecuting attorney, and his success in this position led to his speedy promotion to a circuit judgeship in 1868. After eight years' service on the bench he resigned on account of his health, to benefit which he made a sojourn in Florida, and became a member of its state legislature, serving with distinction until 1878. The desire to return to his old home grew too strong for him, and he returned to Detroit, where he had spent so many active years, and with renewed health took up his practice once more. While in the court room on Jan. 19, 1892, ex-Judge Patchin was stricken with paralysis, and expired at his home, Jan. 23, 1892. A meeting of the bar was called, and resolutions adopted. Judge C. I. Walker, Judge C. J. Riley, B. Prentiss, A. J. Chapin, and Judge H. N. Brevoot as committee. Courts adjourned, and the judges and members of the bar attended the funeral in a body.

BACON, John Watson, civil engineer, was born in Hartford, Conn., June 9, 1827, son of Leverett and Sarah (Watson) Bacon. His early education was obtained in the public schools, and in a private academy where he was fitted for college. He was graduated at Trinity College in 1846, being first in his class. Soon after he became principal of an academy at Essex, Conn., but soon resigned to begin the study of law with Isaac Toucey, of Hartford, where he remained until 1848, when he decided to adopt the profession of civil engineering. In this capacity he was employed on the first surveys of what is now the New York and New England Railroad, between Hartford and Willimantic, having charge, among other important work, of the construction of the Connecticut river bridge and the Union depot at Hartford. He spent two years on the surveys

and construction of the Danbury and Norwalk Railroad, and then assumed the position of superintendent of that part of the New York and New England Railroad between Providence, R. I., and Waterbury, Conn., for five years. He then went to West Virginia to take charge of the operation and development of extensive coal mines and salt works at West Columbia on the Ohio river. After remaining there two years he removed to Danbury, Conn., in 1859, where he made his permanent home. In July, 1859, he became superintendent and chief engineer of the Danbury and Norwalk Railroad, which position he held until January, 1877, when he was appointed by Gov. Hubbard railroad commissioner, to which position he was reappointed until 1887. He has taken an active interest in town and county affairs, originating and engineering the present waterworks of Danbury, while the organization of the Danbury Agricultural Society was due to his efforts, and he has been connected with it in an official capacity up to the present time. He has been director of the Savings Bank of Danbury for over thirty years, and upon the death of the late F. S. Wildman, its first president, he was elected to fill the vacancy. For several years he has been state commissioner of the official topographical survey of Connecticut, and has been a member of the American

Society of Civil Engineers since 1877. On Dec. 20, 1852, he married Caroline, daughter of Dr. Russell B. Botsford, for many years the leading physician of Danbury. The result of the marriage was three children: Sarah, Eliza (Mrs. G. Mortimer Rundle), and John Russell Bacon.

OSGOOD, Jason C., inventor, was born in Nassau, Rensselaer co., N. Y., Nov. 16, 1804. While he was still a boy his father removed to Madison county, where he purchased a mill. Young Osgood from his earliest years displayed a great taste for mechanics and remarkable ingenuity, and in connection with his father's business he was able to develop these traits. He made many little improvements in the machinery of the mill and soon showed that his ambition was to be a mechanic and an inventor. In 1833 he obtained his first patent for a horse-hair picking and curling machine and this invention created quite a revolution in that branch of industry. At about the same time he moved to Virginia, being employed on certain work by contract in connection with public improvements. In 1838 he took out a patent for a dumping and tilting wagon, the invention being afterwards applied to freight cars. Mr. Osgood removed to Troy in 1846 and continued to reside there until his death. In the meantime with Daniel Carmichael, of Brooklyn, he took the contract for deepening some of the state canals, and it was in connection with this work that he invented the celebrated Osgood dredging machine, which made his name known the world over. In 1855 he constructed the double dredger, which had a well hole for depositing its excavations. Mr. Osgood's "rock breaker" was invented by him in 1851, while he was engaged in dredging the Mississippi river at Des Moines rapids. It is stated that one of these machines moved 10,000 yards of rock on that river and became almost as famous in connection with his name as the dredger. In 1862 Mr. Osgood invented a canal dredger with an endless chain, which regulated the depth of dredging. His last important invention was the "ditcher," which was perfected in 1870 and so constructed that it could be run either by horse or steam power. Throughout his life he was engaged in public works and improvements and many of his novel ideas were perfected in connection with these labors. Among his important works were: deepening the canals of the state of New York; dredging Chesapeake Bay and Charleston harbor, S. C.; digging the canal through the dismal swamp; dredging the Mississippi, Missouri and San Juan rivers; and improving the Hudson river. In his leisure time Mr. Osgood interested himself in politics, so far as it was necessary to forward his views of the best interests of the city of Troy, where he lived. He was elected a member of the state assembly in 1852, and again in 1857 and in 1871. From 1861 to 1868 he served as a member of the board of fire commissioners of Troy. Many other public honors were tendered him, but he refused them all. He was exceptional among inventors from the fact that he was a shrewd, careful, and successful business manager.

REEVE, Tapping, educator and jurist, was born at Brook Haven, Suffolk co., L. I., in October, 1744. He was graduated at Princeton in 1763, and was a tutor there from 1767–70. He established himself at Litchfield, Conn., as a lawyer in 1772. Aaron Burr, whose sister he had married, lived with him until the war began, and was probably his first student. In 1776 he acted as a recruiting officer. In 1784 he opened his famous law school at Litchfield, which was long without a rival in America, and attracted pupils from every part of the country, among them many who became leaders. This he conducted alone until 1798, and then, until 1820, with the held of James Gould, who succeeded him. He was a judge of the Connecticut superior court from 1798 to 1814, and then, for a few months, chief justice. After a single term in the legislature, and one in the council, he declined further service of this kind. He was a Federalist, and the initiator of the movement to secure to married women, by legislation, the disposal of their own property. His "Law of Baron and Femme, of Parent and Child, of Guardian and Ward, of Master and Servant," etc. (1816), has been edited by different persons in 1846, 1857, and 1862. His "Treatise on the Law of Descent" appeared in 1825. His degree of LL.D. was conferred by Middlebury College in 1808, and by Princeton in 1818. His legal attainments were of a high order, and as a man he possessed the respect and esteem of the community. He died at Litchfield, Conn., Dec. 13, 1823.

COLT, Samuel, inventor, was born at Hartford, Conn., July 19, 1814, the third son of Christopher Colt, a wealthy manufacturer, and on the maternal side, the grandson of Maj. John Caldwell, president of the Hartford Bank from 1792 to 1819, president for twenty years of the first insurance company in that city, a member of the state legislature for twenty sessions, and a leading merchant of the Connecticut valley through nearly two generations. Heavy losses during and after the war of 1812 swept away the fortunes of the family, and at the age of ten Samuel entered his father's factory at Ware, Mass., whence he soon passed on to a school at Amherst, and on reaching his thirteenth year he shipped before the mast for Calcutta, making on the voyage a rough model of the revolving pistol that bears his name. At the close of the voyage, with cravings for adventure satisfied for the moment, he returned to the mill where he studied chemistry in connection with the processes of the business. When eighteen years old he ventured forth as a lecturer on nitrous oxide gas, and was then known as "Dr. Colt." His tours, which were extensive and contin-

ued for nearly three years, provided the means for further work on the revolving pistol. In the years 1835–36 respectively, he obtained patents in Great Britain and the United States for a rotating cylinder containing several chambers to be discharged through a single barrel. A company was formed to make the new weapon at Paterson, N. J. Two army boards reported against it. The inventor passed the winter of 1837–38 in the swamps of Florida, where he saw the value of the revolver tested in the war with the Seminoles. It had already become established in the affection of Texan rangers who had used it with great effect in winning Texan independence. In 1840 an army board reported unanimously in favor of the invention, but the demand was slow, and in 1842 the Paterson company was forced to the wall. In 1847, at the instance of Gen. Taylor, 1,000 of the pistols were ordered for use in the Mexican war. From new and improved models Col. Colt filled the contract by extemporizing a shop at Whitneyville, Conn. In 1848 he transferred his plant to Hartford, where to meet demands that poured in from all quarters of the globe, he completed, on land defended against spring freshets by a massive dyke, one and three-fourth miles long, the largest private armory then in existence. Machinery for the work was invented and made on the premises. His constant aim was to reach the most perfect attainable results by the most efficient means. He called around him a body of able assistants, who caught his spirit and became enthusiastic co-workers with him. Graduates from the armory, inspired by his love of mechanical excellence, have built for themselves highly successful establishments. These men, some of whom became famous industrial chiefs, have won wealth and distinction by adhering closely to the methods of their early teacher. In boyhood Col. Colt began to experiment with submarine explosives and foresaw the future use of the torpedo for harbor defense. Later he blew up ships in motion by electric batteries controlled from long distances. He urged upon the government the adoption of his system, but was too far ahead of the age to win official acceptance of his views. He was also the first to devise and lay a submarine electric cable, having thus, in 1843, connected New York city with stations on Fire and Coney Islands. With great resources at command he contemplated an addition to the armory of a plant for the manufacture of cannon on a large scale. But having accomplished much and with still more colossal schemes in mind, he was cut off suddenly in the meridian of his powers. Col. Colt married, June 5, 1856, Elizabeth H., eldest daughter of Rev. William Jarvis, of Middletown, Conn. Of their four children, two daughters and a son passed away in infancy, while the fourth, Caldwell Hart Colt, died in Florida, Jan. 21, 1894. Mrs. Colt for many years after her husband's death, managed with signal ability the affairs of his great estate, and added to the rare examples of successful business management conducted by women an illustrious record of achievement, and what is more, has at the same time attached to herself a wide circle of friends by her social graces, benevolence and sympathy. Col. Colt died at his home at Hartford, Jan. 10, 1862.

SLOAT, John Drake, naval officer, was born in New York city in 1780. He entered the united naval service as midshipman in 1800, but was mustered out

the following year upon the passage of the peace establishment act. He again entered the navy as sailing master in 1812, and served three years on the frigate United States. For his gallant services in the capture of the British frigate Macedonian he received a vote of thanks and a silver medal, and was promoted to a lieutenancy, but he was subsequently blockaded in the Thames river, Connecticut, and was obliged to remain inactive until the end of the war. After a long leave of absence he served on the schooner Grampus, suppressing piracy in the West Indian waters, during the years 1823–25, succeeding to the chief command in 1824. He captured the pirate Palmyra, and was active in the destruction of Foxhardo, the chief stronghold of the pirates in Porto Rico. Among his other notable captives was the pirate chief Colfrecinos, who was afterward executed by the Spanish authorities. His promotions followed rapidly. He was made master-commandant in 1826, and captain in 1837, and became commandant of the Portsmouth navy yard in 1840–44, when he was given command of the Pacific squadron. In anticipation of the occupancy of Monterey by the British admiral at the beginning of the troubles with Mexico, he took possession of that place, and when the war began, with wise foresight, occupied San Francisco and other important points, until relieved by Com. Stockton. In 1847–51 he was given command of the Norfolk navy yard, when he was placed in charge of the construction of the Stevens battery. In December, 1861, he was placed on the retired list, but was promoted to commodore in 1862, and to rear-admiral in 1866. He died in New Brighton, N. Y., Nov. 28, 1867.

RUSSELL, William Clark, author, was born in New York city, Feb. 24, 1844, his father being Henry Russell, well known as the author of the songs "Cheer, Boys, Cheer," "There's a Good Time Coming, Boys," "Life on the Ocean Wave," etc.; he finally retired from the concert-room and settled in England. His mother was a relative of the poet Wordsworth. Clark received his schooling in England and France. At thirteen years of age he went to sea, gaining during the seven or eight years he continued a sailor a fund of maritime knowledge which especially fitted him for the work he latter engaged in, that of writing nautical novels. "John Holdsworth, Chief Mate," his first serious effort in that direction, appeared in 1874, and was soon followed by the "Wreck of the Grosvenor," his most popular book. He has since written some twenty-five novels, besides several volumes of short stories. He has been at various times editorially connected with the Newcastle "Daily Chronicle," and the London "Daily Telegraph," but gave up all newspaper work in 1887, owing to ill health. He has probably done more than any contemporary English author to restore the prestige of the nautical novel. Besides his nautical stories, he published in 1871 "Book of Authors: a Collection of Criticisms," "Representative Actors," "A Book of Table Talk, of Poets, Philosophers, Statesmen, etc.," and "Life of Nelson" which made for him quite a reputation.

SABIN, Joseph, bibliographer, was born at Braunston, Northamptonshire, England, Dec. 9, 1821. He was of humble origin, and had little early education, but was apprenticed to a bookseller at Oxford, where he soon opened a shop of his own, and published in 1844 "The XXXIX. Articles, with Scriptural Proofs and References." He came to America in 1848, and for a time sold books in Philadelphia, Pa., but from 1861 was in New York, where he became well known to all lovers of the antique and curious in literature. He drew up the sale catalogues of a number of the most noted private libraries in the country, as those of Dr. S. F. Jarvis, 1851; E. B. Corwin and G. H. Hagerwell, 1856; W. E. Buxton, 1861; E. Forrest, 1863; J. Allen, 1864; T. W. Field, 1875, and W. Menzies, 1877. Bookhunting was his pleasure as well as his business, and few surpassed him in knowledge of his wide field. In person, or by proxy, he attended every important sale in America or England, making many ocean voyages in pursuit of rarities. With his sons, he reprinted several of the scarcer works bearing on the history of the New World; founded in January, 1869, the "American Bibliopolist," and conducted it for some years, and published thirteen parts, beginning in 1867, of a "Dictionary of Books relating to America." He died in Brooklyn, June 5, 1881.

SABIN, Elijah Robinson, pioneer preacher, was born at Tolland, Conn., Sept. 10, 1776. His father was mortally wounded at the battle of Trenton. His ancestor, William Sabin (or Sabine) emigrated in 1645, and settled at Rehoboth, Bristol co., Mass. Taken to Vermont in 1784, and brought up to the rough labors of the frontier, he became a Methodist minister in 1799, presiding elder of Vermont and most of New Hampshire in 1805, and later of a district which included the southern half of New England. He did much to introduce Methodism into the land of the Puritans, and was the first of that faith to be chaplain of the Massachusetts legislature. During the war of 1812 he was stationed at Hampden, Me.; when the town was taken by the British he was imprisoned on a vessel, whence his wife procured his release. He wrote "The Road to Happiness," and one or two other books, and died at Augusta, Ga., May 4, 1818, while seeking health by means of travel in a warmer climate.

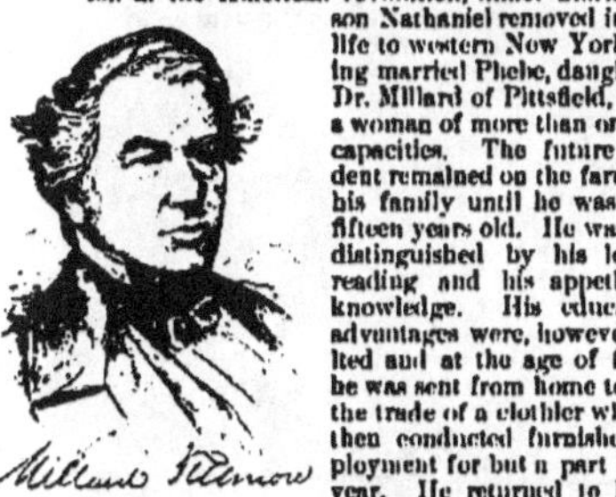

FILLMORE, Millard, thirteenth president of the United States, was born in Locke (now Summer Hill), N. Y., Jan. 7, 1800. For four generations his ancestors had been ploneers. John Fillmore, mariner, married Abigail Tilton at Ipswich, Mass., in 1701. John Fillmore, his son (the father having died at sea), was made administrator of his parents' small estate in 1723. After perilous adventures of his own, he settled at Franklin, Conn., then part of the town of Norwich. His son Nathaniel, the president's grandfather, located at Bennington, Vt., and fought as a lieutenant in the battle of Bennington in the American revolution, under Stark. His son Nathaniel removed in early life to western New York, having married Phebe, daughter of Dr. Millard of Pittsfield, Mass., a woman of more than ordinary capacities. The future president remained on the farm with his family until he was about fifteen years old. He was early distinguished by his love of reading and his appetite for knowledge. His educational advantages were, however, limited and at the age of fifteen, he was sent from home to learn the trade of a clothier which as then conducted furnished employment for but a part of the year. He returned to his father's home for the winter, but asked not to go again to his employer's because that employer had kept him for much of the time at other work than that which belonged to him. This resulted in his being placed elsewhere; but while he fitted himself to be a carder of wool and a dresser of cloth he attracted the attention and made the acquaintance of Walter Wood, a Cayuga county lawyer, and was enabled by his assistance to buy his time and devote himself to study. With Mr. Wood he read law and general literature and at the same time surveyed land for his patron. In 1821 he removed to Erie county, N. Y., and in 1822 read law in a Buffalo (N. Y.) law office, maintaining himself by teaching school. In the spring of 1823 he was admitted to the bar at Buffalo. He at once removed to Aurora, N. Y., where his father resided, and began the practice of his profession, winning his first case and a fee of four dollars. Here he remained until the spring of 1830, and for this period the cases in which he was employed were so well managed that his reputation steadily rose and he was led back to Buffalo at its close, where in a short time he formed a partnership with N. K. Hall, to which S. G. Haven was soon admitted. The firm of Fillmore, Hall & Haven became the leading law firm in western New York, appearing ordinarily in every case of magnitude in that portion of the state. In 1826 Mr. Fillmore married Abigail, daughter of Rev. Samuel Powers. In the fall of 1828 he had also been elected to the general assembly of the state from Erie county, going to the legislature as the successful candidate of the anti-Masonic party. He served in the legislature three successive terms, and during these years he, with others, secured the passage of the bill abolishing imprisonment for debt, which was drafted by him in connection with John C. Spencer. In 1832 he was chosen to the U. S. house of representatives from his congressional district. Serving one term he resumed his professional labor in Buffalo but in 1836 was re-elected and served continuously in the twenty-fifth, twenty-sixth and twenty-seventh congresses. He then declined further re-election although honored in the call of those which were given him by the largest majority ever gained in his district. In the twenty-seventh congress (1841–42) his party (whig) having come into power at the preceding presidential election Mr. Fillmore was appointed chairman of the committee of ways and means. The leading politicians of his state made an earnest endeavor to secure his nomination for the vice-presidency of the United States at the convention of their party in May, 1844, but unsuccessfully. Following this there was a general desire among the whigs of New York that he be nominated for governor of the state, to which he very reluctantly consented, and in September of that year he was by acclamation made the party's standard-bearer in the contest for that high office. He was disastrously defeated in the canvass by Silas Wright, the nominee of the democrats. On the 11th of November, writing to his illustrious contemporary, Henry

VI.—12

Clay, who was defeated in his presidential canvass at the same time, Mr. Fillmore said: "For myself I have no regrets. I was nominated much against my will, and although not insensible to the pride of success, yet feel a kind of relief at being defeated. But not so for you and the nation. Every consideration of justice, every feeling of gratitude conspired in the minds of honest men to insure your election, and although always doubtful of my own success, I could never doubt yours until the painful conviction was forced upon me." In the fall of 1847 he was elected comptroller of the state of New York, and entered upon the duties of the office Jan. 1, 1848. But soon after the transmission of his first annual report to the state legislature, Jan. 1, 1849, he resigned his position to enter upon his duties as vice-president of the United States, to which post he had been chosen in the November preceding (1848) with Gen. Zachary Taylor as the successful whig candidate for the presidency. The president dying in office (July 9, 1850) Mr. Fillmore at once assumed his constitutional duties as president, and faithfully discharged them until the end of his term, March 4, 1853. It is said that in his cabinet, made of Edward Everett of Massachusetts, secretary of state; Thomas Corwin of Ohio, secretary of the treasury; Alexander W. H. Stuart of Virginia, secretary of the interior; John P. Kennedy of Maryland, secretary of the navy; C. M. Conrad of Louisiana, secretary of war; P. S. Hubbard of Connecticut, postmaster-general, and John J. Crittenden of Kentucky, attorney-general, there was never a dissenting vote in regard to any important measure of his administration, and all of them united in a cordial testimony to him, when by the closing of his term their official relationships were severed. In the whig nominating convention for the presidency Mr. Fillmore's name was presented as a candidate but could not command twenty votes from the free states, a fact doubtless due to the official signature he had given as president to the fugitive slave bill of 1854 so called. In 1856 he accepted the nomination of the American party for the same office but only gained the electoral vote of the state of Maryland. Mr. Fillmore's active participation in public life closed with this candidacy and he retired to private life. His wife had died in 1853, shortly after the termination of his presidential career and in 1854 a daughter grown to womanhood was also removed from him by death. In May, 1855, he visited Europe, and while in England was the recipient of marked attention from eminent people. He however declined the degree of D.C.L. from the University of Oxford. In 1866 he made another visit abroad with his second wife, Miss C. C. McIntosh. The public and political action by which Mr. Fillmore's place is determined may be succinctly stated. With entire honesty of purpose, and sufficient independence and courage to take ground against his party if he conceived it to be right to do so, one notes this divergence in the early part of his congressional career, from the whig (Henry Clay) policy in favor of a United States Bank, and rejoices to find him a supporter of justice in advocating the receipt by congress of anti-slavery petitions. His labor in determining the legislation of the twenty-seventh congress, by which the tariff of 1842 was enacted, were exacting, arduous and most highly creditable. This may well be said, when it is recalled that John Quincy Adams rated that congress as the ablest he had ever known. In the report before alluded to, made Jan. 1, 1849, which he presented as comptroller of the state of New York, may be found the suggestion of a system of banking with the stocks of the United States as a basis for the issue of currency which was substantially carried out in the national banking system that came into existence in the early portion of the

civil war and continues to this day. When he became vice-president (1849) he found, as presiding officer of the U. S. senate, that John C. Calhoun of South Carolina had announced to that body in 1826 his opinion that the vice-president had no authority to call senators to order and that this was settled usage. Mr. Fillmore in a carefully considered speech declared that he regarded it as his duty to preserve decorum, and that he should, if occasion made it necessary, reverse the action of his predecessors. His position commanded the warm approval of the senate, and his speech upon the subject was ordered to be entered at length upon the senate journal. His presidential administration was not to be commended without qualification, if judgment be given by ancient political and party standards; but on the crucial question of slavery, especially in connection with the "fugitive slave law" heretofore referred to, his course cannot be approved by men whose conscience is sufficiently sensitive and enlightened to make them feel that a compact to do evil does not become a valid obligation, even if it be incorporated in a national constitution. The judgment of his countrymen upon this point was sufficiently decisive. Cheap postage was secured during his administration, and Japan was opened first to the United States and then to the world by the Perry expedition of 1853–54. He checked filibustering and in connection with the visit of Kossuth to the United States made himself known as a firm adherent of the "Monroe doctrine" of non-intervention by the United States with the affairs of foreign nations. As a citizen he was a model, taking the deepest interest in the civil, religious and intellectual development of the community which was his home. The biography of Millard Fillmore was published at Buffalo, N. Y., in 1856. He died in Buffalo, N. Y., March 7, 1874.

FILLMORE, Abigail Powers, wife of President Fillmore, was born at Stillwater, Saratoga Co., N. Y., in March, 1798, the youngest child of Lemuel Powers, a Baptist clergyman. Her father dying while she was an infant, her mother removed to Cayuga county, where Abigail was brought up in strict economy. She was studious and ambitious, progressed rapidly in her studies, and at an early age became a teacher. On Feb. 5, 1826, she was married to Mr. Fillmore, and removed with him to Erie county. Mrs. Fillmore continued to teach after her marriage, faithfully attended to her household duties, and aided her husband in his struggle to make a position for himself. In the spring of 1830 they removed to Buffalo, where she thoroughly enjoyed society and city life, being naturally sociable. When Mr. Fillmore became president her delicate health and her mourning for her sister prevented her from entering into the social gayeties of Washington, and the duties of hostess devolved upon her daughter. Mrs. Fillmore was fond of reading, and there being no books in the White House, President Fillmore asked an appropriation of congress, and appointed a room in the second story to be set aside as a library. Proud of her husband's success, Mrs. Fillmore made an effort to appear at the public dinners and receptions when her health would permit. She was intellectual, warm-hearted, and of a cheerful disposition. After her death her husband said: "For twenty-seven years, my entire married life, I was always greeted with a happy smile." Mrs. Fillmore at the expiration of her husband's term of office, was removed to Willard's Hotel, Washington, D. C., where she died March 30, 1853.

CLAYTON, John Middleton, secretary of state and senator, was born at Dagsborough, Del., July 24, 1796. He was the eldest son of James, descendant of Joshua Clayton, who came to Pennsylvania with William Penn in October, 1682. The father married Sarah Middleton of Virginian ancestry, and John M. was their second child. Receiving

some preparatory instruction at schools near his home, he entered Yale College on the day he was fifteen years old, and was graduated in the class of 1815, with the highest honors. Such was his love of books that during his four years' college course he took no vacations, but spent them all in study. Entering the office of his cousin, Thomas Clayton, in his native state, he began the study of law and afterward pursued it at the law school at Litchfield, Conn., studying, he said, fifteen hours per day for twenty months. He was admitted to the bar in Delaware, and in 1819 fixed his residence at Dover, the state capital.

From the first he took high position, although he came into competition with strong men. His power with juries was such that his political opponent and rival, James A. Bayard, said he had no superior in the country as a jury lawyer. His legal career lasted for ten years. In 1824 he entered the state legislature, and was subsequently secretary of state in Delaware, and state auditor. In 1828, in the fierce contest for the presidency of the United States between John Quincy Adams and Andrew Jackson, he threw himself warmly into the fight for the re-election of Mr. Adams, and the electoral vote of Delaware being so decided, the legislature chosen was also in accord with the friends of Clayton. He was therefore chosen senator, and entered the senate at the special session in March, 1829, contemporaneously with the opening of Jackson's eventful administration. His ability was quickly felt in that body. During the regular session of congress beginning in December, 1829, he took part in one of the most famous debates ever had in the senate—that upon "Foote's Resolution," which gave occasion for the great encounter between Daniel Webster and Mr. Hayne, of South Carolina. John Quincy Adams wrote in his diary of Mr. Clayton's speech, that "it was one of the most powerful and eloquent orations ever delivered in either of the halls of congress." He continued to be one of the most effective of the senators who antagonized the several radical measures of Gen. Jackson's two presidential terms. He made an energetic inquiry into irregularities in the U. S. post-office department and ultimately secured important reforms in it. He was conspicuous in promoting the prompt passage of the compromise tariff in 1833, by which John C. Calhoun and the South Carolina nullification party were afforded a door for retreat from their threatened rebellion. He effectually advocated the land act of 1833, and strongly supported the U. S. Bank in its application for recharter and in its resistance to the removal of the public deposits and of the pension fund. He voted for Henry Clay's resolutions condemning the removal of the deposits from the U. S. Bank, and was one of the U. S. senators named by President Jackson in his famous "Protest." In 1831 he was in the convention which revised the constitution of Delaware. In 1835 he was

re-elected to the U. S. senate, but in the fall of 1836 resigned and was made chief justice of Delaware. From 1833 to the date of his resignation, he had served in the U. S. senate as chairman of the standing committee on the judiciary. He resigned his judicial office in 1839, and entered the canvass of the whig speakers, who advocated the election of Gen. W. H. Harrison to the presidency. In 1845 he was again chosen to the U. S. senate from his state. He took a prominent part in urging the payment of the French spoliation claims and in the adjustment of the Oregon boundary question, supported the war with Mexico, after that had been entered upon, and pressed the nomination of Gen. Zachary Taylor for U. S. president in 1848. In March, 1849, he entered President Taylor's cabinet as secretary of state, but resigned in July, 1850, after the death of the president. During his service in the state department he negotiated, with Sir Henry Lytton Bulwer, the Clayton-Bulwer treaty between Great Britain and the United States, relating to the proposed construction of a ship canal in Central America to connect the Atlantic and Pacific oceans, and through an agent sent to Hungary, he expressed the sympathy of the people of the United States for Hungarian efforts after self-rule. Mr. Clayton was again elected to the U. S. senate in 1852, spoke on the 19th of March, 1853, in explanation of this treaty above referred to, which had been attacked by Senator Cass of Michigan, and on the 14th replied to speeches of the same character by senators Mann of Virginia and Douglas of Illinois. Senator Clayton married a daughter of Dr. James Fisher, of Camden, Del., in 1822. She died three years later and he never remarried. He died at Dover, Del., Nov. 9, 1856.

WEBSTER, Daniel, secretary of state. (See Vol. III., p. 36.)

EVERETT, Edward, secretary of state, senator, and thirteenth governor of Massachusetts, was born in Dorchester, Mass., Apr. 11, 1794. He was the son of Rev. Oliver Everett, from 1782 until 1709 pastor of the New South church in Boston, and brother of Alexander H. Everett, an eminent writer and diplomatist. Edward received his early education in the public schools of Boston, and entered Harvard, from which he was graduated in 1811. While in college he displayed his natural literary talent by editing the college publication known as the "Harvard Lyceum." After graduation he was for a while tutor in the college, pursuing at the same time studies in divinity. In 1812 he delivered the Phi Beta Kappa poem at Harvard, his subject being

"American Poets." This poem, written at eighteen, gave great promise that Everett's name might stand high on the list of American poets, but this promise was never fulfilled. He wrote but little poetry afterward, though one poem, "Alaric, the Visigoth," sustains his claim to rank among the poets in the English tongue. In 1813 he was made pastor of the Brattle street (Unitarian) church in Boston, where he speedily attained a high reputation for eloquence and spirit in his discourses. He also preached in Cambridge, and gained a wide reputation, young as he was, of being one of the most eloquent, and especially one of the most pathetic preachers in the United States. In 1814, having been chosen Eliot professor of Greek in Harvard, he went to Europe to fit himself for the duties of his position, remaining abroad during the next four years. He pursued a wide course of study, and formed a distinguished circle of acquaintances, including such eminent people as Scott, Byron, Jeffrey, Sir Humphrey Davy, and Romilly. M. Cousin, the French philosopher and translator of Plato, pronounced him "one of the best Grecians I ever knew." In 1819 Mr. Everett returned, and entered upon his duties at Harvard. From 1820 he edited the "North American Review," to which he contributed largely at that time, and also subsequently, when the editorship passed into the hands of his brother, Alexander H. Everett. In 1822 Edward Everett married the daughter of Peter C. Brooks, one of the wealthiest men of Boston, and two years later began his political career as a member of congress from the district of Boston. He sat in the house for ten successive years, but declined re-election in 1834. While in congress he voted on the whig side. In 1835 he was elected governor of Massachusetts, which office he held by successive re-election for four years. He missed further re-election in 1839 by only one vote out of over one hundred thousand. In 1840 he went to Europe, and while there was appointed minister plenipotentiary to the court of St. James, being further honored by receiving from Oxford University the degree of D.C.L., and from Dublin and Cambridge Universities that of LL.D. In 1845, owing to a change of administration, he was recalled from London, and during the next four years he was president of Harvard. In 1852 occurred the death of Daniel Webster, who was secretary of state, and Mr. Everett was appointed by Mr. Fillmore to fill out the few months remaining of the latter's term in that office. In 1853 Mr. Everett was elected U. S. senator, but he only held the seat one year, being obliged to resign on account of impaired health. In 1853, when the plan to purchase Mount Vernon by private subscription was organized, Mr. Everett was invited to deliver an oration on Washington in behalf of the undertaking. His accomplishment of this task was one of the most memorable events in the history of literature and forensic eloquence in the United States. The oration he delivered on that occasion has been pronounced one of the most powerful, comprehensive, and elegant ever written in any language, comparing favorably with those of Cicero, Demosthenes, and Edmund Burke. During the spring of 1856 and the summer of 1857, Mr. Everett delivered this oration in the principal cities and towns of the country more than one hundred times, with the result of turning into the treasury of the Mount Vernon Association nearly $60,000. In addition to this, during 1858 and 1859, he contributed to the "New York Ledger," owned and published by Robert Bonner, a weekly article for which the latter paid in advance $10,000 to the ladies of the Mount Vernon Association. The receipts for other addresses and lectures delivered for charitable purposes were nearly $100,000. He took an active part in the discussion of the political questions of his time, but he was more noted as an orator on literary and other public occasions. Collections of his speeches and addresses have been made at several periods. One of these, made in 1850, in two volumes, contained more than eighty addresses; a third volume appeared in 1858, and a fourth in 1869. One of the best of these is the Phi Beta Kappa oration, which was delivered at Harvard, July 4, 1826, on the fiftieth anniversary of the declaration of independence, and a day on which, within a few hours of each other, Thomas Jefferson and John Quincy Adams both passed away, even as their names lingered on the eloquent tongue of the great orator. In 1860, when the civil war was threatening, and the condition of politics had broken the people into half a dozen parties, Mr. Everett was candidate for vice-president, with John Bell, of Tennessee, for president, on what was known as the Bell-Everett or Union ticket. The election gave them the electoral votes of Virginia, Kentucky, and Tennessee—39 in all; the ticket received 590,631 votes out of a total 4,662,170. Throughout the war Mr. Everett was a consistent Union man, always retaining, however, a considerate feeling for the Southern people, whom he regarded as misguided and misled. His oration at the dedication of the National Cemetery, at Gettysburg, Pa., Nov. 15, 1863, was a magnificent production, in full accord with the gravity of the occasion, and couched in eminently fitting language. This address is worthy of being ranked among the greatest intellectual triumphs of its author. Edward Everett's last appearance was at a meeting held in Faneuil Hall, Boston, Jan. 9, 1865, for the purpose of assisting the people of Savannah, Ga. He was taken seriously ill after this fatiguing day, and never recovered, dying in less than a week thereafter. Perhaps the best summing up of Mr. Everett's intellectual gifts is to be found in an article by Geo. S. Hilliard, which was published in the "North American Review," in 1847, for even at that time Mr. Everett had reached a high eminence in the regard of his fellow-citizens. "The great charm in Mr. Everett's orations," says Mr. Hilliard, "consists not so much in any single and strongly developed trait, as in that symmetry and finish which on every page gives token of the richly endowed and thorough scholar. The natural movements of his mind are full of grace, and the most indifferent sentence which falls from his pen has that simple elegance which is as difficult to define as it is easy to perceive. His level passages are never tame, and his fine ones are never superfine. His style, with matchless flexibility, rises and falls with his subjects, and is alternately easy, vivid, elevated, ornamented, or picturesque, adapting itself to the dominant mood of the mind, as an instrument responds to the touch of a master's hand. His knowledge is so extensive, and the field of his allusions so wide, that the most familiar views, in passing through his hands, gather such a halo of luminous illustrations that their likeness seems transformed, and we entertain doubts of their identity." Mr. Everett died in Boston Jan. 15, 1865.

MEREDITH, W. M., secretary of the treasury. (See Vol. IV., p. 370.)

CORWIN, Thomas, secretary of the treasury and governor of Ohio (1840–42), was born in Bourbon county, Ky., July 29, 1794, the son of Mathias Corwin, who had removed from Morris county, N. J. His mother was a native of Long Island, and the daughter of a sea-captain. It was a common thing for eastern emigrants, who first settled in Kentucky, to remove over the river to Ohio, feeling that a slave state was no place to raise children. So it was with Mathias Corwin, who, four years after the birth of Thomas, settled in Warren county, on Turtle creek. Here he purchased a farm, and was so highly respected that for many years he represented his district in the state legislature. Thomas was ambitious, and desirous of obtaining an education, but his appeals to his father for opportunity to study were met by the statement that his services on the farm could not be spared. But shortly after, an accident, which laid the lad by with a broken leg, gave him leisure, which he improved by mastering the contents of a Latin grammar, the property of an elder brother, who was a clerk of court, and a man of considerable education. This renewed the boy's desire for an education, and being again refused any time to devote to study, he deliberately broke his leg again, that he might secure the leisure he wanted. Upon this his father withdrew his opposition, and the boy pursued his studies under his brother, who was his only teacher. He gained a thorough knowledge of the law, being quick to acquire and tenacious in retaining the information given in the text-books, and in 1818 was admitted to the bar. In 1822 he was elected to the state legislature, where he served seven years, distinguishing himself at the first session by a speech in opposition to the introduction of the whipping-post. In 1830 he was elected a representative in congress, where he soon became a whig leader. He remained in the house until 1840, when he was nominated by the whigs as a candidate for governor of Ohio. The campaign that followed was a remarkable personal contest. Corwin spoke two or three hours a day for over 100 consecutive days, with so much wit and eloquence that he carried the state on election day by a large majority. In 1845 he was chosen U. S. senator, and was exceptionally bitter and brilliant in invective against the supporters of the Mexican war. He was secretary of the treasury during the administration of President Fillmore, a representative in congress for two terms (1858–61), and U. S. minister to Mexico under President Lincoln from 1861 to 1864. In Mr. Corwin the social instinct was pre-eminent. It is said of him that so keen and brilliant was his wit that no one ever tired of his talk, and he often kept a party in constant laughter for hours at a time. He attributed whatever of talent he possessed to his Hungarian descent, of which he was extremely proud. The pronounced stand taken by him against the Mexican war hindered his political advancement, and he never had the faculty of saving money, so that in spite of his opportunities he died a comparatively poor man. He lived a busy life, was a faithful public officer, and was greatly loved in his adopted state. He died in Washington, D. C., Dec. 18, 1865.

CRAWFORD, G. W., secretary of war. (See Vol. IV., p. 371.)

CONRAD, Charles M., secretary of war, was born in Winchester, Va., in 1804. While he was a child his parents removed to Louisiana, and the boy was educated in New Orleans and afterward studied law, being admitted to the bar when he was twenty-four years old. He entered into political life, was elected to the state legislature through several terms, and in 1842 went to Washington as a member of the U. S. senate from Louisiana to fill the vacancy caused by the resignation of Alexander Mouton, who had been elected in 1837. Mr. Conrad remained in the senate until 1843, from which time until 1848 he continued to practice law in New Orleans. In the latter year he was elected a member of congress, and continued in the house of representatives until July 15, 1850, when he entered the cabinet of President Fillmore as secretary of war, and held that office until March 7, 1853, when he was succeeded by Jefferson Davis of Mississippi. Mr. Conrad returned to Louisiana and was practicing law at the time of the outbreak of the secession movement in 1860, when he began to exhibit a deep interest in the scheme of the southern Confederacy. In 1861 he attended the congress at Montgomery, Ala., as a member from Louisiana, and was also a member of the two Confederate congresses which existed during the war. In the course of this time, also, Conrad entered the Confederate army and rose to be brigadier-general. He died in New Orleans Feb. 11, 1878.

PRESTON, W. B., secretary of the navy. (See Vol. IV., p. 371.)

GRAHAM, William Alexander, secretary of the navy and governor of North Carolina (1845–49), was born in Lincoln county, N. C., Sept. 5, 1804, son of Gen. Joseph Graham. He was graduated from the University of North Carolina in 1824, became a lawyer, settled at Hillsborough, Orange Co., N. C., was much in the legislature from 1833, and several times speaker. In 1840 he was sent to the senate as a whig to complete an unexpired term and remained there until March, 1843. He filled the governor's chair 1845–49, and in the latter year declined a re-election and the mission to Spain. His services to the party were thought to be eminent, and Mr. Fillmore, on succeeding Gen. Taylor as president in June, 1850, called him into the cabinet to hold the portfolio of the navy. During his two years' tenure of this position he initiated Com. Perry's expedition to Japan. In 1852 he was the whig candidate for vice-president. After twelve years of retirement he entered the Confederate senate in 1864. In his last months of life he was a commissioner to adjust the northern boundary of Virginia. He died while on a visit to Saratoga, N. Y., Aug. 11, 1875.

KENNEDY, John Pendleton, secretary of the navy and author, was born in Baltimore, Md., Oct. 25, 1795. He came of prominent and wealthy ancestors, his mother, whose maiden name was Pendleton, being related to Judge Pendleton of Virginia and a descendant of Edmund Pendleton, who was a prominent member of the first Continental congress. From his youth up, young Kennedy had the advantages derived from the possession of wealth. He received a liberal education, graduating from the University of Maryland, at that time the Baltimore College. In 1812 he was in the United States service during the latter part of the war of 1812 with England, and studied law and was admitted to practice. From 1820 to 1823, he was a member of the house of delegates of Maryland. He was always a writer and during the early part of his life devoted his pen to the service of his political friends. He was a strong protectionist and wrote freely upon that subject. In 1838 he was elected a member of congress and again in 1841 and 1842. In 1846 he became again a member of the Maryland house of delegates and was elected speaker. On July 22, 1852, President Fillmore appointed Mr. Kennedy secretary of the navy, and he continued to occupy that position during the administration. The country was fortunate in having in this position, just at that time, a man of Mr. Kennedy's fine intelligence, education and broad grasp of affairs, as it was mainly through his efforts that Commodore Perry's expedition to Japan and the second Arctic Expedition of Dr. E. K. Kane were made

feasible. After his retirement from active politics, Mr. Kennedy continued to show an interest in the political discussions of the day by occasional contributions to the Washington "National Intelligencer," among which, a number of years before the outbreak of the civil war were articles from his pen, uttering a warning note on the possibilities of the existing political irritation between the North and the South, eventually resulting either in a dissolution of the Union or a sanguinary struggle between the two sections. When the southern states seceded Mr. Kennedy issued an appeal to the citizens of Maryland, showing how little that state had to gain by uniting its destinies with the South and how much by remaining steadfast to the Union. This appeal was described by Baron Gerolt, at that time minister from Prussia to the United States, as "one of the most statesmanlike and patriotic expositions of the subject he had seen." After the war Mr. Kennedy crossed the ocean and spent some time in England and on the continent, making three trips to Europe, altogether, before he died. He made the acquaintance of most of the literary men of the period and was especially intimate with Thackeray, being said to have written the fourth chapter in the fourth volume of "The Virginians" at the request of its great author, on account of his familiarity with the scenery of the part of Virginia described in it. Mr. Kennedy made his home in Baltimore when not in Washington or abroad and his residence there was a literary centre. He was a member of an organization styled the "Monday Club," which met every Monday at the house of some one of its members for social enjoyment and literary recreation. This club was peculiar in being composed of four doctors of law, four doctors of divinity, four doctors of medicine and four gentlemen of superior literary attainments and reputation. At the meetings of this club, Mr. Kennedy was said to be specially notable for the brilliancy of his conversational abilities. One of his earliest literary adventures, published in 1818, was the "Baltimore Red Book," a periodical publication, something after the style of Paulding and Irving's "Salmagundi." In this work Kennedy was associated with Peter Hoffman Cruse, who died of cholera in Baltimore in 1832. Kennedy at one time occupied as his town house the former residence of William Wirt; a curious coincidence, owing to the fact that he published his "Memoirs of the Life of William Wirt" prior to this period and that his occupying that particular house was purely accidental. Literature was more a pastime with Mr. Kennedy than a pursuit, and he never looked upon it as a source of pecuniary emolument. His first novel was "Swallow Barn," which was published in Philadelphia in 1832 and whose object was to give a description of the manners and customs prevalent in the "Old Dominion" during the last century. He was so careless, however, with regard to the success or reputation of his literary adventures, that when the first edition of his "Swallow Barn" was exhausted, he paid no attention to its republication, and it was not until some ten years later that a new edition of it appeared. His next novel was "Horse-Shoe Robinson, a Tale of the Tory Ascendency" (1835). These two books were written in his office in the city of Baltimore. In 1833 Kennedy was one of the umpires to decide as to the best tale contributed in answer to an offer of a prize on the part of a literary paper published in Baltimore, called "The Visitor." The prize was awarded to Edgar Allan Poe for his story, "A Manuscript Found in a Bottle." The prize was one hundred dollars and was the first success with which the gifted author of "The Raven" had been favored. He also gained at the same contest a prize of fifty dollars, offered for the best poem and which was won by his "Coliseum," but he was barred out on account of being the author of the successful tale. This incident brought Mr. Kennedy into an acquaintance with Poe, whom he recommended for an editorial position on the "Southern Literary Messenger," in which publication appeared some of his best stories. In 1838 Kennedy wrote and published his "Rob of the Bowl: A Legend of St. Inigoes." He also wrote

"At Home and Abroad, a series of Essays, with a Journal in Europe in 1867–68" (1872), and published a large number of discourses, orations and newspaper contributions. The uniform edition of all of Mr. Kennedy's works was published in New York in 1870, in ten volumes. Of Mr. Kennedy's ability, so able a critic as Alexander Everett said "His talent in this respect is probably not inferior to that of Irving. Some of his smaller compositions, in which our author depends merely on his own resources, exhibit a point and vigor of thought, and a felicity and freshness of style that place them on a level with the best passages of the "Sketch Book." During the latter part of his life, Mr. Kennedy occupied a residence on the banks of the Patapsco a few miles from Baltimore and in the immediate vicinity of a large number of cotton manufactories, in one of which he was largely interested. Mr. Kennedy was a member and constant friend of the Maryland Historical Society and also a trustee of the Peabody Institute, founded in Baltimore by Mr. George Peabody of London. On Sept. 8, 1870, a fine tribute to his memory was delivered by Robert C. Winthrop, which was afterward published. In 1871 appeared in New York his Life, written by Henry T. Tuckerman. Mr. Kennedy died in Newport, R. I., Aug. 18, 1870.

EWING, Thomas, secretary of the interior. (See Vol. III., p. 39.)

STUART, Alexander Hugh Holmes, secretary of the interior, was born in Staunton, Va., Apr. 2, 1807. He was the son of a revolutionary soldier, Archibald Stuart, who is said to have studied law in the same office with Thomas Jefferson, and afterward rose to high positions in the councils of the state. Alexander Stuart, after having been prepared for a university course, went to William and Mary College for a year, and then attended the University of Virginia, where he took the law course, graduating at the age of twenty-one, and being admitted to practice at the bar in the same year. The young man took great interest in politics, being a strong adherent of Henry Clay. He was in successful practice in Staunton when, in 1836, he was elected a member of the lower house of the Virginia state legislature, and was continuously re-elected until 1839, when he declined to serve. In 1841 Mr. Stuart was elected a member of congress, and in 1844 was a presidential elector on the whig ticket, and filled the same position on the Taylor ticket in 1848. On July 22, 1850, he as-

sumed the office of secretary of the interior, to which he had been appointed by President Fillmore, and in which he continued until the conclusion of that administration. Mr. Stuart was a member of the convention of 1850 which nominated Millard Fillmore for the presidency, and from 1857 to 1861 was in the Virginia state senate. He was a strong Union man in sentiment at the outbreak of the civil war and earnestly resisted the secession of his state, while he was one of the first of the southern leaders to promote reconciliation and political agreement after the war. But although elected a member of congress in 1865, he was unable to take his seat on account of the "iron-clad" oath. In 1868 Mr. Stuart was very active in his opposition and resistance to the objectionable features of the reconstruction acts. In 1876 he was elected rector of the University of Virginia, and, excepting a period of two years—between 1882 and 1884—he continued to fill that position until 1886, when he resigned. Mr. Stuart was a member of the board of trustees of the Southern Educational Fund founded by George Peabody. He was also for many years president of the Virginia Historical Society.

COLLAMER, Jacob, secretary of the Interior. (See Vol. IV., p. 371.)

HALL, Nathan Kelsey, postmaster-general, was born in Marcellus, Onondaga Co., N. Y., March 10, 1810. His ancestors were English, and his father removed from New England to New York shortly before the birth of the subject of this sketch. When the boy was eight years old the family settled in Erie county, and young Hall worked at the trade of a shoemaker, which was his father's, and part of the time on a farm, picking up his schooling in winter at the district schools of the neighborhood. In 1828 he went to Aurora, and into the office of Millard Fillmore to study law. He was admitted, in 1832, to practice at the bar, and Mr. Fillmore having removed to Buffalo, Mr. Hall settled there also and went into partnership with him, Solomon G. Hayden being afterward admitted to the firm, which became Fillmore, Hall & Hayden, and the most prominent law office in western New York, existing until 1847. In 1831 and until 1837 Mr. Hall held various local county and town offices in Erie county, including deputy clerk of the county, clerk of the board of supervisors, and city attorney and alderman of Buffalo. In 1839 Gov. Seward appointed him master in chancery, and in 1841 judge of the court of common pleas. He was elected a member of the state assembly in 1845, and in 1847 became a member of congress. On July 20, 1850, Mr. Hall became postmaster-general in the cabinet of Mr. Fillmore, and continued to hold that office until 1852, when he was appointed U. S. judge for the northern district of New York, a position which he held until his death. Judge Hall was a man of much more than ordinary ability, an able and upright judge, and thoroughly capable and qualified for administrative office. He died at Buffalo, N. Y., March 2, 1874.

HUBBARD, Samuel Dickinson, postmaster-general, was born in Middletown, Conn., Aug. 10, 1799. After preparing for college he was sent to Yale, where he was graduated at the age of twenty, and after leaving college entered a law office with the intention of devoting himself to that profession. He became suddenly wealthy, however, by inheritance, and giving up the law invested his capital, or a portion of it, in manufacturing. He became prominent in his neighborhood, interested himself in politics as a whig, and was sent to congress from his district in 1845, serving in the house of representatives four years. He was appointed postmaster-general by President Fillmore, and assumed the office Feb. 15, 1852, continuing in the cabinet until the close of that administration. Returning to Connecticut he devoted himself to educational and charitable objects, being president of the Middletown Bible Society until his death, which occurred at Middletown Oct. 8, 1855.

JOHNSON, Reverdy, attorney-general. (See Vol. IV., p. 371.)

CRITTENDEN, J. J., attorney-general. (See Index.)

BUTLER, William Orlando, soldier and candidate for vice-president (1848), was born in Jessamine county, Ky., in 1791, of a family memorable for military renown. His grandfather, a native of Ireland, emigrated to America about the middle of the last century and settled in Pennsylvania. He had five sons, who all entered the American army on the outbreak of the revolutionary war, and the patriotism and bravery of the whole family became so celebrated that Gen. Washington is said to have once given as a toast, "The Butlers and their five sons," while Gen. Lafayette said of them, "When I want a thing well done I order a Butler to do it." William O. was the son of Percival Butler, the fourth of these five brothers. He went to Transylvania University, where he was graduated in 1812, and was studying law in the office of Robert Wickliffe when the war with England broke out. Young Butler enlisted as a private, but was elected corporal before the army marched, and was soon made ensign. His regiment, under command of Gen. Winchester, advanced against the enemy near Frenchtown on the river Raisin, and fought two battles, one on Jan. 18, 1813, in which the Americans were victorious, and another four days later, when they were defeated and young Butler received a dangerous wound, being one of the few, however, who escaped the massacre by which the British Col. Proctor disgraced himself in violation of his word of honor. He was captured and carried through Canada to Fort Niagara, where he remained until 1814, when he was exchanged, and returning home was ordered South with the rank of captain to join Gen. Jackson. He was present at the attack on Pensacola and in the fighting before New Orleans on Dec. 23d. He also fought in the celebrated battle of Jan. 8th, and was brevetted major for his conduct on this occasion, while Gen. Jackson appointed him a member of his staff. In 1817 he returned to the study of the law, and was admitted to practice. He married and settled on his patrimonial estate at the union of the Ohio and Kentucky rivers, where he continued to reside for twenty-five years. He served in the legislature and also from 1839 to 1843 as a member of congress. He ran for governor for the state of Kentucky in 1844, but was defeated. He succeeded, however, in largely diminishing the usual majority of the whig party. On the outbreak of the war with Mexico, Col. Butler was created a major-general and marched with the Kentucky and other volunteers to the aid of Gen. Taylor. In the siege of Monterey, Butler was second in command, and while bravely leading his men during the street fighting, was wounded and carried from the field. After he had recovered he joined Gen. Scott and was present at the capture of the city of Mexico. Congress presented him with a sword of honor for his bravery at Monterey, and the state of Kentucky gave him another. Gen. Butler was in command at the battle of Saltillo and was commander-in-chief of the army, succeeding Gen. Scott, at the time of the declaration of peace, May 29, 1848. The national democratic convention the same year nominated Gen. Cass and William O. Butler for president and vice-president, but they were defeated by Van Buren and Adams. In 1855 he was offered the appointment of governor of Nebraska, but declined it. In 1861 he went to Washington as a member of the "Peace Congress." He published a collection of poems, called "The Boatman's Horn, and Other Poems." A life of him by Francis P. Blair, Jr., was published in 1848. He died in Carrollton, Ky., Aug. 6, 1880.

PARKER, George Washington, railroad president, was born in Springfield, Ill., Aug. 12, 1836, son of Leonard Buford Parker, born in Washington county, Pa., in 1786, a soldier in the war of 1812 under Gen. Jackson, and a member of his staff at the battle of New Orleans, a soldier in the Black Hawk war, and sheriff of Hardin county, Ky., whose father, Abraham Parker, born in Chester county, Pa., in 1758, was a revolutionary patriot. His mother, Elizabeth Fairleigh, was the daughter of Andrew and Letticia (Swan) Fairleigh, of Elizabethtown, Ky. In 1829 his parents removed to Paris, Ill., and were among the first settlers of that place. From there they went to Springfield in 1835, and in a few years to Fort Madison, Ia., where

his father died March 10, 1841. The mother, with her two sons, Andrew and George, then removed to Elizabethtown, Ky., and in 1844 she was married to Miles H. Thomas, a thrifty farmer of that place. The son, George, acquired his rudimentary education at the country schools in Hardin county, doing farm work during the summers, and at the Elizabethtown Academy, where he learned the trade of printer, serving in the office of the "Elizabethtown Register" four years. His first journalistic venture was the establishing of the "Elizabethtown Intelligencer," which he conducted successfully for two years, and then sold it to good advantage. He afterwards established the "Free Press" at Glasgow, Ky., and after one year sold it out, and with the proceeds pursued his legal studies, first with his cousin, Col. Thomas B. Fairleigh, at Brandenburg, Ky., for two years, and then at the law department of the University of Louisville, where he was graduated in 1861 with high honors. He began practice at Charleston, Ill., meeting with unusual success. In 1863 he was employed as local counsel for the St. Louis, Alton and Terre Haute Railroad; in 1865 was made general counsel, and two years later was elected its vice-president. In 1870 he removed with his family to St. Louis, and took charge of the road as vice-president and general manager, and in 1887 he was made president, and still holds the position. He was married, in October, 1863, to Aronella, only daughter of Dr. Aaron Ferguson, of Charleston, Ill. While a resident of Charleston, he was for a time president of the Second National Bank, and also mayor of the city. Mr. Parker was a member of the Illinois state legislature in 1869-70. After his removal to St. Louis he was made president of the Union Trust Co. of that city at the time of its inauguration. In 1891 his health failed, and he was forced to resign the presidency of the Trust Co., and seek rest and recuperation in the health resort at Carlsbad, Bohemia, at the same time making the tour of Europe. He is now vice-president of the Continental National Bank of St. Louis, with which he has been identified for many years.

MORGAN, Miles, soldier, was born in Bristol, England, in 1616. He was descended through a long line of Ivors, Llewellyns, and Morgans, from Cadivorfawr, a chieftain in Dyfed or Pembrokeshire, who died in 1080. His great-grandfather, Sir John Morgan, had a son, William, who is recorded as "apprenticed to a saddler" in Bristol, in 1559. That the descendant of a line of landed gentlemen should have been sent out as an apprentice is rather startling. Still there may have been loss of fortune to account for it; an explanation not at all improbable when we find this William's grandson (afterwards Capt. Miles Morgan) emigrating to the wilderness of America. He sailed from Bristol in one of the ships that carried emigrants to America, and arrived at Boston in April, 1636. He joined the expedition into the wilderness, led by Col. Pynchon, and settled at what is now Springfield, Mass. Here he built a fortified block-house on the Connecticut river, and soon after married Prudence Gilbert, who, in company with her parents, was a fellow-voyager on the same ship with him. Capt. Morgan fought in "King Philip's War," particularly at the sack of Springfield. His block-house was the refuge of the survivors, after the burning of the settlement, until dispatches could be sent to Hadley, and the standing army of the colony of Massachusetts Bay could be sent to their rescue. In 1879 the citizens of Springfield erected a bronze statue of him in the public square, to commemorate his services. Of his six sons, the second, Jonathan, was the father of Deacon David Morgan, who, with others, settled the town of Brimfield, Mass., in 1686. J. Pierpont Morgan, of New York city, who is at present (1895) senior partner of the London house of J. S. Morgan & Co., and Drexel, Morgan & Co. of New York city, is one of his descendants. He died at Springfield, Mass., in 1656.

LEWIS, Charles Henry, jurist, was born in Erie county, N. Y., Oct. 17, 1839, son of Orin and Betsy Lewis. In the summer of 1840 the family removed to the then new land of southern Wisconsin. The father erected a mill at Lewisburg, later Chemung. After two years the family removed to Boone county, Ill. In 1851 they went to Independence, Ia., where the father conducted a farm and a furniture store. Later, the father removed to Quasqueton, Ia., where he died. The son attended the district schools, and in 1859 began a course of study at Cornell College, Ia. In 1862 he enlisted as a private in Company H, 27th Iowa infantry. After one year's service he was made sergeant-major of the regiment, and in March, 1864, was promoted to adjutant of the regiment. The regiment was mustered out at Clinton, Ia., Aug. 5, 1865. At the close of the war he returned to Quasqueton, and for three years engaged in the mercantile and milling business. He then entered the law department of the State University at Iowa City, and was graduated with the class of 1869. He was married, March 31, 1869, to Emma E. Kellogg. In the spring of 1869 he located at Cherokee, Ia., and began there the practice of law. He served as county superintendent of schools, and as county recorder. In 1870 he was elected district attorney of the fourth judicial district of Iowa, and filled the position for four years. In 1874 he was elected presiding judge of the fourth judicial district of Iowa, then comprising twenty counties. In 1878 he was re-elected by an increased majority. In 1882 he was again re-elected by a still greater majority, and again in 1886, and continued to serve until January, 1891. In Judge Lewis's long career upon the bench, he won the favor, admiration, and respect of all. Judge Lewis is a strict temperance man, and was thorough in the enforcement of all laws. He, upon retiring from the bench, again took up the practice of law in Sioux City, and is in a fair way of building up a fortune, which his long service on the bench deprived him from accumulating.

SMITH, Eugene Allen, geologist, was born in Washington, Autauga co., Ala., Oct. 27, 1841. His father, Samuel P. Smith, M.D., was born in Jones county, Ga., of parents who came from North Carolina. His mother (née Adelaide J. Allen), was born in Windsor, Conn.; on her mother's side being a descendant of the Phelps and Loomis families of that place. Eugene A. Smith attended school in Prattville until 1855, when he went to Philadelphia, and soon after entered the public high school on Broad street. In 1859 he returned to Alabama, and became a student in the junior class of the University of Alabama in 1860. This college adopted the military system of government at this time, and young Smith was a member of the first corps of cadets. In the spring of 1862, he was detailed along with other cadets, to drill recruits at a camp of instruction in Greenville, Ala., and did not return to the university to graduate, although the degree of A. B. was conferred upon the members of this class. He was with one of the companies which he had been drilling, as first lieutenant, during the campaign through Tennessee and Kentucky, taking part in the capture of Munfordville, and the battle of Perryville. When the company went into winter quarters at Knoxville, he was detailed to the University of Alabama, as instructor in tactics, where he remained until the end of the war. In the autumn of 1865 he went to Europe, and remained three years in Berlin, Goettingen, and Heidelberg, attending lectures in chemistry, physics, botany, mineralogy, and geology. In the spring of 1868 he passed with the highest grade, *summa cum laude*, an examination for the degree of Ph.D. in Heidelberg, having for his main subject mineralogy and geology, and for minor subjects, chemistry and botany, and he remained another semester at Heidelberg in attendance on lectures. During the three years of his stay in Europe, he spent all his vacations and holidays in traveling, and visited Russia, Poland, Holland, and the Netherlands, most of the German states, Switzerland, the Tyrol, Austria, France, and Italy, and on his way back to America went to England and Scotland. He returned to America in the winter of 1868, and went immediately to the University of Mississippi, serving as assistant on the geological survey. Here he spent the next three years chiefly in making chemical analyses of soils for the survey, but he also made several excursions into the cretaceous and tertiary formations of the state, and in 1871 published his first paper, "On the Geology of the Mississippi Bottom." In the summer of 1871 he was elected to the professorship of geology and mineralogy at the University of Alabama. He married, in 1872, Jennie, a daughter of Landon C. Garland, chancellor of Vanderbilt University. In 1873 he was appointed state geologist of Alabama, and for ten years his work on the survey was done gratuitously. In 1880 he did some work for the tenth census, and furnished reports upon Alabama and Florida for the cotton culture volumes of that census. While visiting Florida on account of this work, he made the discovery that the greater part of the peninsula of Florida was underlaid by a substratum of the Vicksburg or Eocene limestone, which comes to the surface at intervals down the peninsula, through the overlying Miocene and later formations. The results of this trip were published in the "American Journal of Science" for April, 1881. He also wrote for the fourth report of the U. S. Entomological Commission, a general description of the climate, geological and agricultural features of the cotton-producing states. For many years Dr. Smith also had charge of the instruction in chemistry at the university. In 1888 a new chemical laboratory was erected, and under his direction fitted up with everything needful to make it one of the best equipped and most convenient laboratories in the South. Dr. Smith was appointed honorary commissioner from Alabama to the Paris Exposition of 1878. He is a member of the American Association for the Advancement of Science, served as secretary of the Geological section, and as a member of the committees appointed by that body on the International Geological Congress, and upon the Geological Congress Auxiliary of the Columbian Exposition. He has also served on the council of the American Geological Society, of which he is one of the original members. He prepared for the International Geological congress the report of the American sub-committee on the Marine Cenozoic.

READ, John, colonist, was born in Dublin, Ireland, in 1688. He came of a notable and wealthy family, but the death of his fiancée drove him, about 1725, to America, where he acquired large estates in the northern part of Maryland and Delaware. In 1742 he founded Charlestown, Cecil co., Md., as a rival to Baltimore, but it did not fulfil his expectations. He was a military officer of the colony, but spent the latter part of his life mostly on his estate in New Castle county, Del., where he died June 17, 1756, leaving three sons, who attained distinction respectively in civil pursuits, in the navy, and in the army.

SHERWOOD, Adiel, clergyman, was born at Fort Edward, N. Y., Oct. 3, 1791. His great-grandfather, Dr. Thomas Sherwood, emigrated from England to New York in 1683. He was graduated at Union College, Schenectady, N. Y., in 1817, and entered Andover Theological Seminary. He preached in Savannah, Ga., in 1818, and taught school two years at Waynesboro', Ga. He was ordained at Bethesda, Greene co. At the Sarepta Association, Ruckersville, Elbert co., Ga., he offered the resolution to form a state Baptist convention, which resulted in the Georgia state Baptist convention. In 1823, in the triennial convention at Washington city, he presented the resolution that started the organization of state conventions. He was pastor of churches at Penfield, Milledgeville, Macon, Greensboro', Griffin, Monticello, and Greenville, Ga. He was a great educator, teaching school and establishing a manual labor school in Eaton; offered the resolution that resulted in establishing Mercer University, and was in 1838 its professor of sacred

literature three years; professor in Columbian College, Washington D. C., in 1837; president Shurtleff College, Alton, Ill., in 1841; president Masonic College, Lexington, Mo., 1848-49; and president Marshall College, Griffin, Ga., in 1857. He received the degree of LL.D. from Union College. Dr. Sherwood was of most commanding person and had the largest intellectuality, and moral elevation. His spirit was Christian to the core, vital with a lovable sentiment, and full of sweet humility. Simple, modest, and learned, he was one of the early giants of his church. He had a creative mind and true business ability. He knew every president from Washington to Grant, and twenty of the governors of Georgia from Mitchell to Jenkins, was the personal friend of nineteen U. S. senators, and aided in educating thirty young Baptist ministers. He married, in 1821, Mrs. Early, widow of Gov. Early, and in 1824 Miss Heriot of South Carolina. Mr. Sherwood died in St. Louis, Mo., Aug. 18, 1879.

HALL, Charles Cuthbert, clergyman, was born in New York city, Sept. 3, 1852, son of William C. Hall, the head of a prosperous firm of importing druggists. The son was educated at his

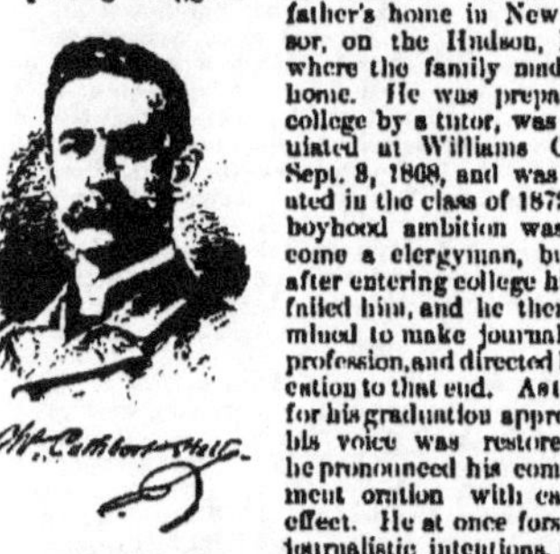

father's home in New Windsor, on the Hudson, N. Y., where the family made their home. He was prepared for college by a tutor, was matriculated at Williams College, Sept. 8, 1868, and was graduated in the class of 1872. His boyhood ambition was to become a clergyman, but soon after entering college his voice failed him, and he then determined to make journalism his profession, and directed his education to that end. As the time for his graduation approached, his voice was restored, and he pronounced his commencement oration with ease and effect. He at once forsook his journalistic intentions, and returned to his earlier plans of preparing for the ministry. He entered the Union Theological Seminary, in New York, in October, 1872, and was licensed to preach in 1874. He then devoted one year to study at the Presbyterian College at London, England, and at the Free Church College, Edinburgh, Scotland. On his return to America he was ordained to the ministry in December, 1875, and installed pastor of the Union Presbyterian Church, Newburgh, N. Y., where he succeeded Wendell Prime. Early in 1877 he accepted a call from the First Presbyterian Church, Brooklyn, N. Y., and was installed pastor May 10, 1877, as a successor to Daniel L. Carroll. He received the degree of D.D. from the University of the City of New York in 1889. Dr. Hall is a polished pulpit orator, is fond of music, and well versed in hymnology. He was a collaborator with Prof. S. Lasar in the compilation of the "Evangelical Hymnal," and is the author of two volumes of sermons entitled, "Into His Marvelous Light" and "Does God Send Trouble?" besides numerous sermons and addresses in pamphlet form. Dr. Hall was appointed Carew lecturer at the Hartford Theological Seminary for 1894, and has published his lectures in a volume entitled "Qualifications for Ministerial Power." He is a director of Union Theological Seminary, New York, a trustee of the Atlanta University, Georgia, and Williams College. In 1894 he received an urgent call to the chair of sacred rhetoric and pastoral theology at Andover Theological Seminary, Massachusetts, but it was declined, at the earnest solicitation of the First Presbyterian Church, to which Dr. Hall had so long ministered. After the call had been declined, the church signified its approval of their pastor's action by voluntarily raising the sum of $50,000 for the extension of the parish work. Dr. Hall married, in 1877, Miss Boyd, of New Windsor, N. Y., and has two daughters and a son.

RAWLE, Francis, colonial author, was born in England about 1660. He and his father, who was of the same name, were Quakers, and emigrated in 1686, to escape persecution in England, acquiring a tract of 2,500 acres near Philadelphia, where he founded the settlement known as "The Plymouth Friends." He held several offices, beginning, in 1688, with those of justice of the peace and of common pleas. Later he was a member of the council, of the assembly, and chairman of its committee, which in 1722 drew up the bill for the emission of paper money. He wrote "Remedies for the Restoring the Sunk Credit of the Province" (1721); "Ways and Means for the Inhabitants of Delaware to Become Rich" (1725), which is said to be the first book printed by Franklin, and in 1726 a "Just Rebuke to a Dialogue of James Logan," who had attacked his second pamphlet. These are supposed to be the earliest American works on political economy. Rawle died at Philadelphia, March 5, 1727.

BLANCHARD, Thomas, inventor, was born at Sutton, Mass., June 24, 1788. His original American ancestor was one of a body of thirty Huguenot families who, about 1710, fled to Massachusetts, and was granted by Gov. Joseph Dudley a tract of land in what is now the towns of Oxford and Sutton, in Worcester county. After about twenty years the settlement was broken up by the Indians, but subsequently the settlers returned. The father of Thomas Blanchard was a respectable farmer, who never gave any indications of mechanical genius, and the son seemed to be altogether misplaced, for he had no taste for farming, and there was nothing in the entire district to call out his inventive faculties. He received the ordinary common-school instruction, but he was accounted a dull boy, an impression no doubt largely due to an impediment in his speech, and to the fact that all his faculties seemed concentrated upon mechanical construction. He was noted as a boy for his efficiency in the New England accomplishment of whittling, making wonderful wind-mills and water-wheels with his knife. When thirteen years old he made an apple-paring machine with which, at the "paring-bees" held in the neighborhood, he could accomplish more than a dozen girls. When he was about eighteen years old, an elder brother started in a neighboring district a factory to make tacks by horse-power, and he employed the youth to head the tacks, which had to be done one by one by means of a vise. The boy was no sooner among the machinery than his dormant genius was aroused, and before many months he had constructed a machine by which he turned out 200 tacks in a minute, and more perfect in form than those made by hand. This machine he afterwards modified, so that it made 500 tacks in a minute, and experts assert that it is not capable of any further improvement. He worked at tack-making for some years, then sold his patent for $5,000, and turned his attention to the improvement of gun-barrels. On the Blackstone river, not far from his brother's factory, was an extensive armory, engaged in supplying guns to the government. The proprietor had introduced improvements by which with a simple lathe he could turn the barrel round, and of a uniform thickness, but to turn the irregular form of the butt baffled all his efforts, and those of every gun-maker in the country. The butt had to be reduced by hand-filing, and that cost $1 per gun. After a year of experimenting, the proprietor of the works heard of the rustic genius who had invented the tack machine, and sending for him, he told him what was wanted. Thomas looked at the machine, and began a low, monotonous whistle—a habit of his when in a deep study—and after a little time, suggested a simple, but altogether original, cam-movement. This being applied, removed the difficulty instantly, and turning to the young man, the delighted proprietor said: "Well, Thomas, I don't know what you won't do next! I would not be surprised if you turned a gun-stock." He had mentioned a thing that was neither round nor straight in any part of it, and to turn which was deemed impossible by mechanics. Thomas uttered another of his peculiar whistles, and stammered, "W-e-e will t-r-r-try that." He was two years in "t-r-trying" it, but by that time he had produced a machine which revolutionized the business of gun-making. The news traveled over the country, being received at first with incredulity, then with amazement, and orders began to pour in for the machine, and the young man's reputation and fortune were made. For eight or ten of these machines ordered by the British government he received $40,000. He was soon requested by the U. S. government to take charge of the stocking of guns at the Springfield armory, and at once proceeded to invent a machine for mortising into the stock every part of the gun—a thing deemed impossible by mechanics. The difficult part was the cutter. He invented an instrument that would cut on a straight line, bore a round hole, and cut down and round in any direction, so that when the mortise was completed the lock fitted closely to the stock. All his experiments were failures until he observed the cut of the borer-worm in an oak log. Splitting open the log, he studied the creature's operations with a microscope, and thus got his design—nature's own mechanical contrivance. Space will not allow even an enumeration of Mr. Blanchard's many inventions. His patents alone number twenty-five, and many of his contrivances were not patented. Before locomotives were thought of, he invented a steam-wagon; he also constructed a machine for bending large timber; an improved steamboat for ascending rapids; a machine for simultaneously cutting and folding envelopes; and various improvements in railroad machinery; in short, he was a mechanical prodigy. In his early years all his powers seemed to be centered in that of construction, but as he grew older his other faculties were developed, and his speech-impediment was conquered, so that he came to be recognized as a man of more than ordinary intelligence and culture. He died in Boston, Mass., Apr. 16, 1864.

CHAPPELL, Absalom H., author, was born in Hancock county, Ga., in 1801. He was educated at Mt. Zion, under Dr. Beman, and upon graduating went to New York, where he studied law, but returned and finished his studies under Judge Clayton, and was graduated at the law department of the University of Georgia. After practicing in Sandersville, Forsyth, and Macon, he settled in Columbus, where he married Loretta Lamar, the sister of the poet, Mirabeau Lamar. He took an active interest in politics, and was elected twice to the legislature, and once to the twenty-third congress, where he showed an extraordinary interest in the development of his native state, and rendered services which can hardly be estimated. He greatly assisted to develop the railroad interests of the state through a series of articles on the "Representative Business Men of the Day." When Prof. Morse was before congress endeavoring to get support for his telegraph scheme, it was Col. Chappell to whom the committee on ways and means referred the question, and it was he alone who prepared the report, which showed conclusively the wonderful advantages and possibilities of the telegraph system, and it might be said that it was almost entirely owing to his wisdom and foresight that the matter was brought to a successful issue. While occupied with the duties and responsibility of his profession, he found time to devote to literature, and published three books, which had a wide circulation, and gave him great reputation. These books contained "The O'Conor War," "Middle Georgia and the

Negro," "Gen. James Jackson," and "Gen. Anthony Wayne." During the war he took service in the ranks of his native state, and rose to the rank of colonel. He was remarkable for the perfect purity and simplicity of his character. He died in Columbus, Ga., in 1878.

MAC GAHAN, Janarius Aloysius, journalist, was born near New Lexington, O., June 12, 1844. His father died when he was a child, and his youth was spent on his mother's farm. He received his education in the common schools, and later attended a business college. From 1860 to 1868 he was a bookkeeper in Huntingdon, Ind., and St. Louis, Mo., at the same time corresponding for newspapers and commencing the study of law. In 1869 he visited England, traveled on the continent, and then resumed his law studies in Belgium. In 1870 he became correspondent for the New York "Herald," and was the only representative of a foreign journal in Paris during the reign of the commune, which he described in graphic letters that attracted wide attention. In 1871 he visited southern Russia, and then became the St. Petersburg correspondent of the "Herald." In 1872 he traveled with Gen. W. T. Sherman through the Caucasus, and later reported the proceedings of the Geneva conference. In January, 1873, having been refused permission to accompany the Russian expedition against Khiva, he made the journey across the Central Asian desert alone, reached Khiva in safety, and witnessed the fall of the city. While in Khiva he made the acquaintance of the younger Skabeleff, then a colonel, who remained his warm friend until death. He returned to Europe early in 1874, and published a book embodying his experiences and entitled "Campaigning on the Oxus," which is a brilliant and authoritative description of Central Asia. In July, 1874, he visited Spain, and until April, 1875, followed the operations of the Carlist insurrectionists. On one occasion, while wearing a Carlist uniform, he was captured by the Imperial authorities and sentenced to be shot, but was saved by the timely intervention of the

American consul-general. He left Spain for Cuba, where he reported the Virginius complications. In June, 1875, he sailed with Sir Allan Young, on the Pandora, for the Arctic seas in search of the lost crew of Sir John Franklin, the last expedition of its kind undertaken. His experiences during this journey are given in "Under the Northern Lights." In June, 1876, he visited Bulgaria as the correspondent of the "London News," and wrote a series of letters describing the Turkish massacres in that country, that aroused the indignation of the world, and led, in the end, to the declaration of war by Russia against Turkey. During the winter of 1876-77 he was in St. Petersburg, watching the preparations for war. Though severely injured by a fall from a horse, he was with the first Russian army corps that crossed the Pruth, and he followed the progress of the war from Plevna to San Stefano. His letters, permanently preserved in book form, give the most vivid and faithful account of the Russo-Turkish war extant. While the treaty of San Stefano was being negotiated, he fell ill of typhus fever, contracted from a friend whom he had nursed back to health, and died on June 9, 1878. He was buried at Scutari, on the Asian bank of the Bosphorus, but subsequently the legislature of Ohio made an appropriation for the transfer of his remains and their reinterment in his native place. He left a wife, a Russian lady to whom he was married in 1874, and one son, both now (1891) residents of New York city. To Mac Gahan belongs the chief credit for putting a new face on the Eastern question, and changing the map of the Balkan peninsula. He has been truly regarded as the liberator of Bulgaria, and on each recurring anniversary of his death, masses for the repose of his soul are said in every Bulgarian church. To extraordinary talent he added acute perception, intense activity, and entire fearlessness in the face of danger. He has been truly described by one who knew him well, as the "greatest and noblest of the knights-errant of the press."

SALTUS, Francis Saltus, poet, was born in New York, June 12, 1850. His father was a man in prosperous circumstances, who spared no expense in his son's education. His mother was a superb and enthusiastic musician, and his paternal grand-mother a woman of rare poetic talent and accomplishment.

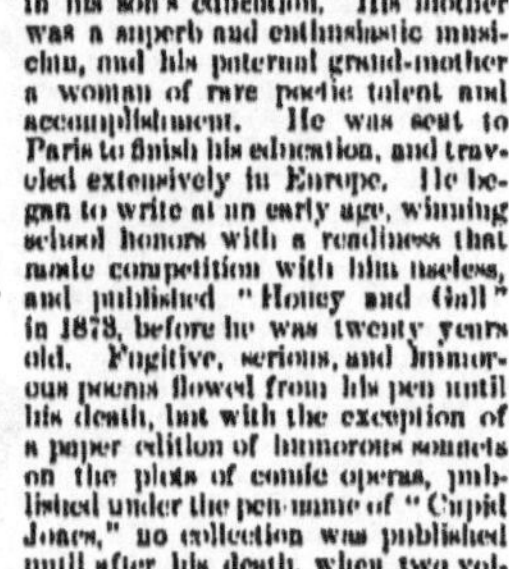

He was sent to Paris to finish his education, and traveled extensively in Europe. He began to write at an early age, winning school honors with a readiness that made competition with him useless, and published "Honey and Gall" in 1873, before he was twenty years old. Fugitive, serious, and humorous poems flowed from his pen until his death, but with the exception of a paper edition of humorous sonnets on the plots of comic operas, published under the pen-name of "Cupid Jones," no collection was published until after his death, when two volumes, "Shadows and Ideals" and "The Witch of Endor, and Other Poems," appeared. There still remain two volumes of miscellaneous poetry, one volume of sonnets, two volumes of French poems, one volume of poems in other foreign languages, one volume of children's poetry, and two volumes of comic verse. Besides these there was destroyed by a fire in a New York warehouse where his manuscripts were stored, a poem entitled "Nijni Novgorod," which would have made a large volume. He was a linguist of rare excellence, and the ease with which he mastered foreign languages, and the patois of out-of-the-way regions, was marvelous. The rapidity with which he worked, and his varied linguistic attainments can best be appreciated from his "Life of Donizetti." This is the most complete musical biography extant, and a work of such magnitude that it ordinarily would be the work of one man's lifetime. The manuscript is sufficient to make 700 printed pages, and involved much travel, a large expenditure of money, and a correspondence that became gigantic in its proportions. He gave much time to musical biography, writing monographs on Rossini, Bellini, and the "kings" of song. He was a contributor to numberless European papers, and his letters are widely quoted. He was prolific in those witty and humorous dialogues which enliven the daily press, often writing from fifty to 100 in a day. More than 10,000 of these were published, and a large number still remain in manuscript. Besides these he wrote crazy histories of the United States, France, Rome, England, and Germany, and a comic Robinson Crusoe, a comic cook-book and a comic Bible. He was also a writer of short stories in the vein of Theophile Gautier and Poe, but differing from them in thought and power. His originality and imagination, with his intimate acquaintance with French literature, have made these stories models of concise romance. There is enough material in his literary remains to fill at least fifty volumes. Moreover, he was a musical composer of great force and beauty, and was almost as prolific in this branch of art. He composed two operas, "Marie Stuart" and "Joan of Arc," besides several short comic operas. He composed some 2,000 fugitive pieces, all of which have merit, and some are veritable gems of melody. In improvisation Saltus was unrivaled. He could compose melodies with strange and beautiful harmony, without previous thought or study. His brilliant soul succumbed to a brief illness, and he died June 25, 1889. The work of Francis Saltus, in its prodigious amount, in its variety, in the originality of its thought, and the curious and vivid imagination displayed, gives evidence that our literature has produced a phenomenon.

THOMPSON, Zadoc, naturalist and historian of Vermont, was born at Bridgewater, Windsor co., Vt., May 23, 1796. His family were in straitened financial circumstances, and he was not able to avail himself of the educational facilities of the public schools, but he studied diligently in his spare moments, and having a natural aptitude for learning, with the assistance of Rev. Walter Chapin, he was able to prepare himself for college. To obtain the necessary means he did literary work, his first publication being an almanac for 1819. This enabled him to begin his course at the State University, at which he was graduated in 1823, having acquired a reputation for solid attainments in science. For many years he made astronomical calculations for the "Vermont Register," and afterwards, until his death, for "Walton's Register." In 1824 he published a "Gazetteer of Vermont," and the following year became tutor in the university, publishing an arithmetic during his spare moments. At one time he taught in the Burlington Academy, and later kept a private school for young ladies. He edited the "Iris" (1828), and the "Green Mountain Repository" (1832), and wrote a "History of Vermont" (1833). In 1833-37 he was at Hatley and Sherbrooke, Canada, where he prepared a "Geography of Canada." He received deacon's orders in the Protestant Episcopal church in 1836, but found his health too precarious to justify him in taking charge of a parish. In 1837 he became a teacher in the Vermont Episcopal Institute at Burlington, and in 1845 state geologist: this position he held for three years, collecting over 3,000 specimens, and putting forth in 1848 "Geography and Geology of Vermont." His most important work, "Natural, Civil, and Statistical History of Vermont," appeared by instalments in 1841-42-43, and with an appendix in 1853. This work was highly estimated at home and abroad, and permanently connected his name with the literature of his state. In 1845-47 he was made assistant geologist under Prof. Charles B. Adams. In 1850 he read a paper at Boston on the geology of his state, which was received with great commendation. In 1851 he was state commissioner to the London Exposition, and upon his return gave a very interesting account to the press under the title of "Journal of a Trip." In the same year he was appointed professor of chemistry and natural history in the University of Vermont, and two years later was commissioned state geologist and naturalist to take up the work so unwisely interrupted in 1847. Prof. Thompson entered upon this work with great earnestness, and suspended his labors in the university in order to make more rapid progress in it. For more than two years it absorbed all his time and labor, when he was attacked with an affection of the heart, which terminated his life, Nov. 19, 1860, at Burlington, Vt. Prof. Thompson was indefatigable in his scientific pursuits, heartily esteemed by every one who knew him. He was a man without an enemy, whose memory was a benediction. Besides the works above mentioned, he published a "Guide to Lake George, Lake Champlain, Montreal and Quebec" in 1845.

YOUNG, Charles Augustus, astronomer, was born at Hanover, N. H., Dec. 15, 1834. His father, Ira Young, held the chair of natural philosophy and astronomy in Dartmouth College, and his mother's father, Ebenezer Adams, had occupied the same po-

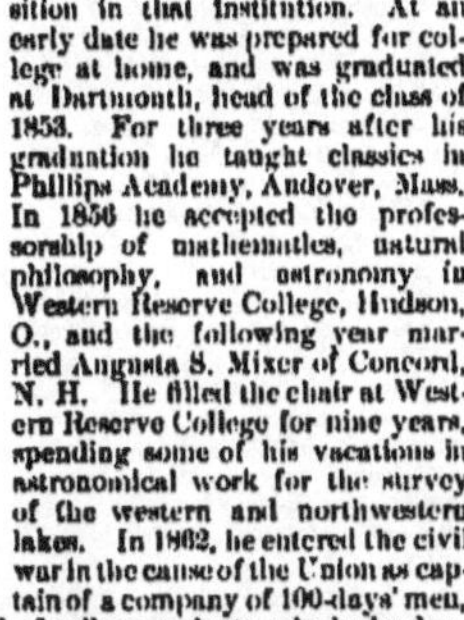

sition in that institution. At an early date he was prepared for college at home, and was graduated at Dartmouth, head of the class of 1853. For three years after his graduation he taught classics in Phillips Academy, Andover, Mass. In 1856 he accepted the professorship of mathematics, natural philosophy, and astronomy in Western Reserve College, Hudson, O., and the following year married Augusta S. Mixer of Concord, N. H. He filled the chair at Western Reserve College for nine years, spending some of his vacations in astronomical work for the survey of the western and northwestern lakes. In 1862, he entered the civil war in the cause of the Union as captain of a company of 100-days' men, chiefly composed of college students, who had volunteered at the call of the governor of Ohio. In 1865 he assumed the professorship of astronomy and natural philosophy in Dartmouth. He continued this connection until 1877, when he accepted the professorship of astronomy in the College of New Jersey at Princeton, where he still continues. He devised a form of automatic spectroscope which has been very generally adopted, and has made a great many new observations on the solar spectrum and prominences, and has also verified experimentally what is recognized as Doppler's principal as applied to light, demonstrating that the lines of the spectrum are slightly shifted to one direction or the other according as the source of light is moving toward the earth or away from it, by which method he has been able to calculate the velocity of the sun rotation. He has been engaged in several astronomical expeditions. In August, 1869, he had charge of the spectroscopic observations of the party which observed the solar eclipse at Burlington, Ia., and it was on this occasion that he discovered the bright "1474 line" which characterizes the spectrum of the corona. In December, 1870, he was a member of the coast survey party under the charge of Prof. Whitlock which observed the eclipse of the sun at Jerez, in Spain, and then for the first time observed the reversal of the lines of the solar spectrum; an observation, for which later, in 1891, he received the Janssen medal of the French Academie des Sciences. In 1872 he made solar spectroscopic observations at Sherman, Wy., in connection with a coast survey party, and prepared extensive catalogues of the lines reversed in the spectrum of the chromosphere, and of those modified in the spectra of sun-spots. In 1874 he was assistant astronomer in the party which observed the transit of Venus at Pekin, China. In 1878 he headed a party from Princeton which observed the solar eclipse at Denver, Col.; and again in 1887 took a party to Russia to observe the solar eclipse of that year in the neighborhood of Moscow, but was baffled by stormy

weather. He also made extensive observations of the transit of Venus in 1882 at Princeton. He gave elaborate instructions in his classes, delivered courses of popular lectures at the Peabody Institute of Baltimore and the Lowell Institute of Boston, and also delivered numerous scientific lectures in various cities, and regular educational courses at Mount Holyoke College, Williams College, St. Paul's School, and other places, besides contributing liberally to astronomical bibliography as a writer for scientific periodicals. He has also written an excellent popular treatise on the sun in the "International Scientific Series," and several text-books on astronomy for use in schools and colleges. He received from Hamilton College and from the University of Pennsylvania the degree of Ph. D., and that of LL. D. from Wesleyan and Columbia. He has been highly honored in his department of science both at home and abroad. He is a foreign associate of the Royal Astronomical Society of Great Britain, a member of the National Academy of Science, a fellow and ex-president of the American Association for the Advancement of Science, an associate fellow of the American Academy of Arts and Sciences, Boston, Mass., and an honorary member of the New York Academy of Sciences, and of the Philosophical Society, Philadelphia. He holds a distinguished place in the ranks of American astronomers.

CHICKERING, Jonas, pianoforte manufacturer, was born in New Ipswich, N. H., Apr. 5, 1797. His father was Abner Chickering, a blacksmith, and who had also a small farm. He was in humble circumstances, and at the age of seventeen his son, Jonas, went from home, and became an apprentice to a cabinet maker, with whom he served three years. His advantages of education had been few, but at an early age he displayed a talent for music, and when quite a boy became a proficient performer on the fife. From this instrument he went to the clarionet, which he also learned and in the last year of his aprenticeship he had an opportunity, for the first time, of seeing a pianoforte, there being but one instrument of the kind in New Ipswich. It fell to young Chickering to make some repairs on this instrument, and he made a thorough study of its structure. In 1818 Mr. Chickering went to Boston, where he obtained employment with a cabinet-maker, but a year later he began work with a pianoforte-maker. At this time the instrument, especially in America, was in its infancy. There were but few in the country, and most of these were of foreign construction. Although the demand for pianofortes was very slight, Mr. Chickering determined to embark in the business of manufacturing them, his great object being to make an instrument which

should remain in tune and fit for use without regard to atmospheric influence, conditions quite foreign to the instruments at the time in use. After working about three years as a journeyman, Mr. Chickering began business on his own account, at first with a partner, and then alone, until, in 1830, he associated with him Capt. John Mackay, a retired ship-master, who attended to the finances and business details, while Mr. Chickering had the entire direction of the mechanical part of the establishment. Soon the Chickering instruments began to attain a celebrity quite in excess of the hopes of their manufacturer. Business flowed in, and it became difficult to fill the orders received. In fact, their trade became so extended that in 1841 Capt. Mackay sailed from Boston to

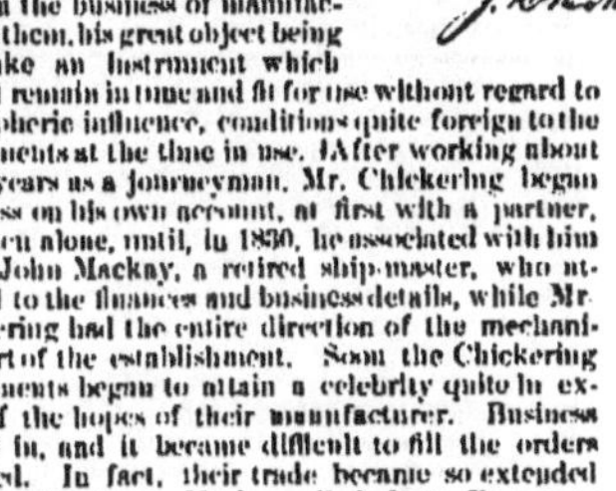

South America, with the design of obtaining an assorted cargo of the beautiful and costly woods to be found in that country; unfortunately, no tidings of him were ever afterwards received, and it was presumed that the vessel on which he sailed foundered at sea. By this time, Mr. Chickering had a large building, capable of containing 100 hands, with commodious and attractive store-rooms, where his instruments were exhibited. This building was destroyed by fire on Dec. 1, 1852, when Mr. Chickering bravely proceeded to the erection of a new edifice, which, at the time of its completion, was said to be the largest building in the United States, except the capitol at Washington, but Mr. Chickering died before the building was completed. It is estimated that before his death he had manufactured 14,000 instruments, and the number made per annum at his works at that time was about 2,000 pianos. Mr. Chickering invented and applied several important improvements on the instrument then in use, one of these being the casting of a complete frame for a grand piano at one time. After his death the manufacture of the Chickering piano was continued by his three sons, who were all brought up in the manufactory. His death was occasioned by the rupture of a blood-vessel while at the house of a friend on a mission of charity, and took place on Dec. 8, 1853.

SEWALL, Samuel E., chief justice of Massachusetts, was born in Boston, Dec. 11, 1757. He was the grandson of Joseph Sewall, "the good," minister of the Old South Church, and great-grandson of Samuel Sewall the chief justice of Massachusetts, who figured prominently at the time of the Salem witchcraft trials, and who publicly confessed his error. Samuel was graduated at Harvard in 1776, when he settled in Marblehead and devoted himself to the study of law, and soon became eminent in his profession, particularly as a commercial lawyer, for which he had fitted himself by unusual attention to the study of the law of nations. In 1797 and subsequently he was elected to congress where he was distinguished for his knowledge of commercial law. In 1800 he was elected to the bench of the superior judicial court, and held that position until 1813, when he was appointed chief justice. He was however, stricken down after occupying the position for only one year, and died at Wiscasset, June 8, 1814, when the bar erected a monument over his remains. Judge Sewall was high-minded, and correct in his principles, and as a judge was characterized by integrity and firmness, and was highly popular both with the bar and the people.

DURFEE, Zoheth Shearman, steel manufacturer, was born in Fall River, Mass., Apr. 22, 1831. He received an academic education and later learned the blacksmith's trade, which he followed for several years. In 1858 he was employed to study and make a report upon a new process of manufacturing steel direct from pig-iron, which had been invented by Joseph Dixon. While thus engaged he became interested in the Bessemer process, and made an exhaustive study of the whole subject of steel manufacture. In the course of his investigations he became convinced that Bessemer had been anticipated in his discoveries by William Kelly, an American, to whom patents had been granted by the U. S. government some years before. Mr. Durfee secured control of these patents and then visited England where he endeavored unsuccessfully to obtain the Bessemer patents for the United States. The added

knowledge of steel-making which he gained while in England led him to believe that an invention made by Robert Mushet was essential to both the Kelly patents, and during a second visit to England in 1863, he secured the Mushet patents for the United States. In the meantime he had organized a company for the introduction of the Kelly process in America, and in 1865 produced, at Wyandotte, Mich., the first steel rails made in the United States. In 1866 he replaced the cupola with the reverberatory furnace in melting the charge, and this change has since been generally adopted. In the same year the Pneumatic Steel Association was formed, and purchased the patents of rival steel inventors. Of this association Mr. Durfee was elected secretary and treasurer, and he remained its active manager until 1879. He made numerous improvements in machinery for the manufacture of steel and iron, and did more to advance the steel industry than any other American of his generation. The last years of his life were spent in New York city. He died at Providence, R. I., June 8, 1880.

NEALE, James Brown, lawyer, was born in Pittsburgh, Pa., Feb. 27, 1837, son of Dr. Samuel S. Neale, who was born in Burlington, N. J., January, 1792, and studied medicine with the celebrated Dr. Benjamin Rush of Philadelphia. He removed to Kittanning, Pa., about 1817, and was married, July 4, 1826, to Margaret, eldest daughter of Robert Brown, whose father, James Brown, Sr., served in the American army throughout the revolutionary war. James B. Neale was educated at the public schools of his native city and at Elder Ridge Academy. He early entered business as a clerk, then studied law, and was admitted to the bar in 1862. He commenced the practice of law in Kittanning, as a partner with his preceptor, E. S. Golden. He spent the year 1871 at the University of Leipzig, Germany,

and on his return to America resumed the practice of his profession, making his home at Kittanning, Pa. From 1876 until 1881 he was editor of the "Union Free Press," the Republican organ of Armstrong county. Gov. Hoyt appointed him president judge of the thirty-third judicial district of Pennsylvania in 1879, and the same year he was elected to the office at the fall election, as the candidate of the Republican party. He held the office for the full term of ten years, until January, 1890. On retiring from judicial office he resumed the practice of the law. Judge Neale was married, July 28, 1885, to Anna, daughter of Simon Truby, Jr., of Kittanning, Pa.

PYRLAUS, John Christopher, Moravian missionary, was born at Pausa, Saxony, in 1718. He spent five years, 1733–38, at the University of Leipsic, and developed a taste for linguistic studies. These he pursued while in America, from 1740–51, in connection with his ministerial labors. He became an authority on some of the Indian tongues, taught them to other missionaries as part of their preparation for their work among the aborigines, translated a number of hymns into the Mohican dialect, and prepared several vocabularies, etc., in German and Iroquois. The latter part of his life was spent in Germany, and he died at Herrnhut, May 28, 1770.

MEAD, Morris William, electrician, was born in Underhill, Vt., Oct. 28, 1854, son of Daniel Clark and Naomi E. (Terrell) Mead, whose ancestors for three generations had been residents of the same region of the state, and were farmers. His father studied law with Benjamin F. Butler, in Lowell, Mass., and was a political speaker of considerable local renown. He removed with his family to Pittsburgh, Pa., in 1861, and engaged in business. The son was educated in the public schools of that city, and the academy at Underhill, Vt., earning his own livelihood meanwhile, and was graduated at the Central High School, Pittsburgh, in 1873. After graduation, he read law for two years in the office of J. H. Baldwin. His father's death at the end of that time compelled him to seek remunerative employment, and he engaged in the oil business in Venango county for a time, and then with a florist and nurseryman establishment for two years, in Pittsburgh. In 1879 he was appointed operator in the fire-alarm telegraph office of that city, and within one year he was made assistant superintendent. Two years after he was promoted to the position of superintendent, acting at the same time as secretary to the board of fire commissioners, the only man who ever filled the double office. Upon the formation of the bureau of electricity in 1887, under the new city charter, Mr. Mead was made its superintendent, controlling as he does the fire alarm, police telegraph and telephone systems, as well as the enforcement of all laws and rules pertaining to the inspection of all electric wires in public and private buildings. Mr. Mead was president of the Pittsburgh Electrical Club for two years, a member of the New York Electrical Club, and director of the Young Men's Republican Tariff Club, the Americus Club, and the Pittsburgh Press Club. He is a 32d degree Mason, and a member of the Mystic Shrine, I. O. O. F., and other secret societies. He is a member of the National Electric Light Association, and honorary member of the International Fire Chief's Association, and a member of its electrical committee, which includes also the city electricians of Chicago and Boston. He was honorary assistant in the department of electricity of the World's Columbian Exposition in 1893. Mr. Mead was married, Nov. 11, 1886, to Ella, daughter of Joseph Norris, of Pittsburgh. He is a member of the Bellefield Presbyterian Church.

ADAMS, Charles Baker, educator, was born at Dorchester, Mass., Jan. 11, 1814. He prepared for college at Phillips Academy, Andover, entered Yale in 1830, and coming to Amherst during the second year of his course, was graduated there with the highest honors in 1834. From 1834 to 1836 he was a student at the Theological Seminary at Andover. During the latter year he accompanied Prof. Hitchcock on a geological survey of the state of New York, after which, until 1837, he was a tutor in Amherst College. In 1838 he was made professor of chemistry and natural history in Middlebury College, a position that he filled for nine years, during which time he also made a geological survey of Vermont. In 1847 he became professor of astronomy and geology at Amherst College. In the interests both of his health and his profession, he traveled in Central America and the West Indies between 1844 and 1851. In December, 1852, he visited St. Thomas, where he succumbed to the yellow fever, and died Jan. 19, 1853. He published eleven numbers of "Contributions to Conchology," monographs of "Stoastoma," and "Vitrinella," "Catalogue of Shells Collected in Panama," and, in conjunction with Alonzo Gray, "Elements of Geology." The zoölogical cabinet at Amherst, which, in some respects, is not equaled by any other scientific collection in the world, was solely the work of Prof. Adams, and stands as his sufficient monument.

GREATOREX, Henry Wellington, organist, was born at Burton-on-Trent, England, in 1811. His father was a noted musician, from whom the son received early instruction. Greatorex came to the United States in 1839 and settled in New York city as vocalist, organist, and teacher of singing and the piano-forte. For years he served as conductor of music, at Calvary Church, and at intervals sang at public concerts and in oratorios. For a brief time he lived in Hartford, Conn., and eventually went to Charleston, S. C. He published a collection of "Psalm and Hymn Tunes" (Boston 1851), that became popularly known as "The Greatorex Collection," and was noted for the merit of its music. To this collection Greatorex contributed some of the best melodies that are sung in our churches. Eliza Greatorex, his wife, is a noted painter. He died at Charleston, S. C., Sep. 10, 1858.

SEWARD, William Henry, banker, was born in Auburn, N. Y., June 18, 1839. He is the son of the eminent statesman of the same name. He was carefully educated at home, and entered business in a banking institution at Auburn in 1861, but shortly afterward enlisted in the volunteer service as lieutenant-colonel of the 138th New York infantry. He was an energetic officer, and was shortly promoted to the coloneley of the 9th New York heavy artillery. He was sent on an important mission to Louisiana in 1863. Col. Seward's regiment saw considerable service in the battle of the Wilderness, and took part in the battle of Cold Harbor. He was given command of Fort Foote, Md., and was engaged in the battle of Monocacy, where he received a slight wound, but not sufficiently serious to prevent his retaining his command. In 1864 he was commissioned brigadier-general, and was for

a season in command at Martinsburg, Va., but June 1, 1865, resigned his commission and returned to Auburn, where he resumed his banking business. He has held various positions of honor and trust in his native city.

SILVER, Thomas, engineer and inventor, was born in Cumberland county, N. J., June 17, 1813, of Quaker parentage. From his earliest boyhood he developed mechanical ingenuity, and it is said of him that at the age of nine years he constructed a boat, introducing devices which astonished scientific men. The ordinary education which he received seemed to lead in his case to no result except invention, and he made models of a great many devices, which, although afterwards placed in the patent office at Washington, and in the Kensington Museum in London, brought him no emolument. It is stated that the fact of the loss of the steamer San Francisco, in 1854, bound to California with troops, and which was caused by the engines becoming disabled in a severe storm, led to the invention of "Silver's marine governor," which was afterwards introduced not only into the U. S. navy and merchant marine, but also was adopted by Great Britain and France. This device was also employed on stationary engines, and especially in the cases of the New York "Herald" and "Tribune," and of the "Public Ledger," in Philadelphia. Mr. Silver was complimented very highly for this invention by the Royal Institute of London, and it is stated that Prince Albert, who was president of the Royal Institute, and greatly interested in that institution, and also in matters which came before it for consideration, said of Mr. Silver's invention : " It is so common-sense a thing that engineers must use it." Mr. Silver married a daughter of the late James M. Bird of Philadelphia, who survived him, and he also left a daughter, the wife of Thomas Chalmers, of New York. Mr. Silver died in New York, Apr. 12, 1889.

MORGAN, Lewis Henry, anthropologist, was born at Aurora, Cayuga county, New York, Nov. 21, 1818. His father, Jedediah Morgan, descended from James Morgan, who settled near Boston in 1646, and his mother was a descendant from John Steele, who resided near Cambridge, Mass., in 1641. Lewis Henry Morgan received an excellent preliminary education at Aurora, and entered Union College, at which he was graduated in 1840. He studied law, and was admitted to the bar in Rochester, N. Y., where he continued to make his home, and where he soon obtained a large and lucrative practice in company with his classmate, Judge George F. Danforth, with whom he was professionally associated. In 1855 Mr. Morgan became interested in a railroad which was projected to extend from Marquette, Mich., to the iron region on the southern shore of Lake Superior, and which was designed to aid in the development of its iron mines. The property became developed into one of great value, and he was induced to withdraw from his law practice and to make practical explorations in northern Michigan, at that time a wilderness. Here, curiously enough, he became interested in the habits and labors of the beaver and for several years, whenever he found the opportunity he followed that study, with the result of the publication, in 1868, of " The American Beaver and His Works," a book which has been described as coming nearer to perfection than any other work of its kind. Another interesting feature of Mr. Morgan's early life was the fact of his being a member of a secret society known as the Gordian Knot, which was the cause of his valuable investigations into the ethnology of the six nations. This secret society located upon the very ground of the ancient confederacy of the five nations, and had the notion of holding its council fires at night on the ancient lands of the Mohawks, Oneidas, Onondagas, Cayugas, and the Senecas. Gradually its members began to study the fragments of the history of the institutions and government of the Indians. But more than any of the others, Mr. Morgan became interested in the subject to that degree that it became at last a serious and devoted study which he continued to prosecute from the time of his arrival in Rochester. He wrote a number of papers which were read before the New York Historical Society and other institutions, some of which were published in book form in 1851, under the title of the " League of the Iroquois," in which the social organization and government of that confederacy were thoroughly explained. This was the first scientific account of an Indian tribe ever published, and won for Mr. Morgan the title of the father of American anthropology. He attended many councils of the Indians, and was regularly adopted into the tribe of the Senecas. Mr. Morgan also contributed to the " North American Review " between 1869 and 1876, important and valuable papers, under the titles of " The Seven Cities of Cibola," " Indian Migrations," " Montezuma's Dinner," and the ' Houses of the Mound-Builders." In 1878 Mr. Morgan made an excursion to the ancient and modern pueblos of Colorado and New Mexico, which was followed by the publication of a volume on " Communal Living Among the Village Indians." Mr. Morgan led a singularly varied life. His home in Rochester contained a fine library and collection of works on American ethnology, and was frequented by some of the leading scholars of his time. He was one of the founders of the literary clubs of his period and locality. In 1861 he was a member of the state assembly, and in 1867 a state senator. In public life he was the uncompromising foe of all vicious measures, while his own character was stainless. His investigations of the history of the Indian tribes and of their civilization deeply interested him in the unfortunate condition of existing Indians, and the unnatural methods pursued by an ignorant and faithless government in its relations with them, and he did everything in his power to improve their condition. From the vast amount of data regarding the kinship of the different tribes, which he collected during his travels and by correspondence, he compiled a work called " System of Consanguinity and Affinity of the Human Family," which was published by the Smithsonian Institute in 1869. Mr. Morgan was a member of the National Academy of Science and other social and scientific societies, both here and abroad, and in 1879 was elected president of the American Association for the Advancement of Science, and presided over its meetings in Boston the following year. In 1851 he was married to Mary A., daughter of the late Lemuel Steele of Albany, N. Y. He received the degree of LL.D. from Union College in 1873. Mr. Morgan died at his home in Rochester, N. Y., Dec. 17, 1881, and left his entire and considerable property in trust to the University of Rochester for the final establishment of a college for women.

ALLEN, William Howard, naval officer, was born in Hudson, N. Y., July 8, 1790. He was educated at the Hudson Academy and Doylestown College, Pennsylvania, and was appointed midshipman in the U. S. navy in 1801; and on July 24, 1811, was promoted to be lieutenant. He was second lieutenant of the Argus, and in an engagement with the Pelican, in 1813, Com. Allen being killed, Lieut. Allen assumed command. The Argus was captured, and Allen was taken prisoner to England, and detained there until too late for further service during the war. After serving on various ships, he was, in August, 1822, given command of the schooner Alligator, and dispatched on a cruise against the pirates who then infested the West India Islands. He was successful in the expedition, but was wounded in the breast on attempting to board a pirate vessel, and he died in the arms of victory, Nov. 9, 1822. It is stated that the news of his sudden death so prostrated his mother that she died from the shock a few days later. His remains were first buried at Matanzas, and afterwards removed to Hudson, his native city, by the U. S. government, and a monument was erected to his honor in 1883. One of Fitz-Greene Halleck's finest poems is a tribute to his memory, ending:

> " Pride of his country's banded chivalry,
> His fame their hope, his name their battle-cry,
> He lived as mothers wished their sons to live,
> He died as fathers wished their sons to die."

PINKERTON, Alfred S., lawyer, was born at Lancaster, Penn., March 19, 1856, son of William C. and Maria Fiske Pinkerton. At an early age the death of his father compelled him to rely on his own resources. His mother desiring to return to her native state, he accompanied her to Worcester, Mass. His nights and spare moments were devoted to books, and after an employment of several years in a large manufacturing establishment, and while also engaged in mercantile pursuits, he began a systematic study of the law, and was admitted to the bar in 1881. He immediately entered into practice in Worcester, and soon attained a recognized position in his profession. His practice has so far been largely in the civil courts in connection with equity and corporation business. In 1886 he was elected a member of the Massachusetts house of representatives, and served on a number of important committees. In 1890 he was elected to the state senate, representing the fourth Worcester district, and served with distinction on the committees of judiciary, probate, and insolvency, and constitutional amendments, of which latter committee he was chairman. He was re-elected in 1891, and was made chairman of the judiciary committee, and was also continued as a member of the committee on probate and insolvency. In 1892 he was unanimously elected president of the senate, and was re-elected to the same position in 1893 by the unanimous voice of Republicans and Democrats alike. Mr. Pinkerton has been a constant supporter of clean politics, an advocate of biennial elections, and in favor of sound business methods in state administration and in the management of corporations, deriving their privileges from the state. He is a polished, eloquent speaker, a keen, close, reasoning debater, and has ever commanded the attention of assembly or jury, while his services on the political and social platforms are in constant demand. He is a member of the Masonic fraternity, and of the order of Odd Fellows, being grand master of the grand lodge in 1888–89, the youngest man ever elected to that position in Massachusetts. Since 1890 he has represented the state in the sovereign lodge. He is a member of political and social clubs, but more devoted to books and law than to social gatherings. He is a director of several insurance and business corporations, and has law offices in both Boston and Worcester.

MATHER, Samuel, clergyman, was born in Boston, Mass., Oct. 30, 1706, the son of Cotton Mather. Samuel was graduated at Harvard College in 1723, and in 1732 was ordained colleague-pastor over the same church where his father and grandfather, Increase, had been pastors. In 1742 there was a difference of opinion among his parishioners concerning revivals, which was the cause of the establishment of another church in North Bennett street, of which Mr. Mather became the pastor. In 1773, Harvard conferred upon him the degree of D.D. Mr. Mather published "Life of Cotton Mather," "America Known to the Ancients," and "The Sacred Minister," a poem in blank verse, besides several sermons and essays. He died in Boston, June 27, 1785, and was buried with his father and grandfather, in Copp's Hill cemetery, that city.

KING, Horatio Collins, soldier, author, and editor, was born in Portland, Me., Dec. 22, 1837, son of Horatio King, postmaster-general under Pres. Buchanan. He is descended from Philip King who came from England and settled at Braintree, Mass., in 1680. His great-grandfather, George Klug, was clerk and sergeant of the Raynham Co., in the war of the revolution, and a man of great personal courage. Horatio C. King was graduated at Dickinson College, Carlisle, Pa., in 1858; studied law with E. M. Stanton, afterwards secretary of war, and was admitted to practice in New York city in May, 1861. Soon after the breaking-out of the war he entered the army as captain and participated with the army of the Potomac and the army of the Shenandoah for three years. He served on the staffs of Gens. Casey, Heintzelman, Augur, Wesley Merritt, and Thomas C. Devin, and received special mention for conspicuous gallantry at the battle of Five Forks. He was promoted to the rank of major, and was brevetted lieutenant-colonel and colonel for faithful and meritorious service. At the close of the war he resumed the practice of law, continuing until 1870, when he accepted the position of associate-editor of the New York "Star," of which Joseph Howard, Jr., was then the proprietor. Two years after he became associated with Rev. Henry Ward Beecher as business manager of the "Christian Union." He was for two years also publisher of the "Christian at Work," under the editorship of Rev. T. DeWitt Talmage. At the solicitation of Mr. Beecher he returned to the "Christian Union," remaining until 1878, when he resigned and resumed the practice of law. In 1883 he was appointed judge-advocate-general on the staff of Grover Cleveland, continuing until the close of his term of office. In 1895 he was the New York Democratic nominee for secretary of state. He has been conspicuous in the Grand Army of the Republic, in the Society of the Army of the Potomac, the Military Order of the Loyal Legion, the Masons, Elks, and other military and civic organizations.

CRAIG, James McIntosh, insurance actuary, was born in Philadelphia, Pa., Apr. 5, 1848. His father died when he was a mere child, and his mother with three children, had a desperate struggle for existence. She, however, maintained them, and gave to the son a good public-school education. When he was twelve years old, he had passed through a succession of accidents, each of which nearly cost him his life and out of which came to the boy a powerful impression of some over-ruling purpose to be wrought out in life by him. In 1860 he went to work for a manufacturer of gold and silver thimbles, and continued at that work for five years. He then spent a short time each as a jeweler, boat builder, woodcarver, and finally returned to his trade as a thimble maker. His ambition however, directed him away from the manufacturing business, and he, in 1866, entered the office of the National Life Insurance Co. of New York as office boy. As such he began the study of the principles and mathematical problems incident to life insurance, and also attended evening

high school and evening classes in mathematics in Cooper Institute. The studies of the evenings, supplemented by practical application of the principles there learned in his office work during the day, gave him an unusual insight into the business, and before he had left the position of office boy, he was in reality an insurance expert. His industry and application met with favor from the officers of the company, and he was promoted step by step for the six years he served the National company until he was qualified to do all the actuarial work of the company,

On June 1, 1872, he entered the employ of the Metropolitan Life Insurance Co., then in its youthful vigor. The spirit of the methods and plans of the new company, united his well-founded judgment of the proper methods of conducting life insurance, and he entered upon his new field with a willing heart. His work as actuary rapidly grew to immense proportions until he was the custodian of over three and a half million policies. He introduced a system that soon ran like clockwork, and the details of the office became a marvel of actuarial skill, which called forth the special commendation of the insurance department of the state. Mr. Craig was married Nov. 28, 1872, to Elizabeth H., daughter of William and Emily N. Morris of Jamaica, W. I., and they have five children and a pleasant home at Brooklyn, N. Y.

TILGHMAN, William, jurist, was born at Fausley, Talbot co., Md., Aug. 12, 1756, son of James Tilghman. The family removed about 1760 to Philadelphia, where he was educated, and read law under B. Chew; but his first ten years' practice was in Maryland, where he sat in the legislature 1788-91, in the senate 1791-93, and was an elector in 1789. He returned to Philadelphia in 1793, and from March, 1801, was chief judge of the U. S. circuit court until the post was abolished in the following year. In 1805 he became president of the court of common pleas, and in 1806, on the recommendation of his cousin, Edward Tilghman, was made chief justice of the Pennsylvania supreme court. In this office he won much honor, and was called by Horace Binney "a character as admirable as ever adorned the bench." In 1809 the legislature directed him to report on the English statutes in force within the state. He published two addresses, was made president of the Philosophical Society in 1824, and died at Philadelphia, Apr. 30, 1827. (See his life, by I. Golder, 1829.)

STONE, Ormond, astronomer and educator, was born at Pekin, Ill., Jan. 11, 1847. His father was a Methodist minister, and the son was educated in the public schools of the various towns in which he preached, until in 1859 he removed to Chicago, where Ormond entered the public schools, graduating from the high school in 1867. He had shown a fondness for mathematics from early childhood. When the Dearborn Observatory was erected with its great eighteen-inch refractor, then the largest in the world, young Stone sought out the director, Prof. Safford, and commenced with him in 1865 a course of instruction in mathematics and astronomy. With the exception of a year spent in teaching in Racine College, Wis., and a short period spent at the Northwestern Female College at Evanston, Ill., he continued his astronomical and mathematical studies until invited, in 1870, to become an assistant in the Naval Observatory at Washington. In 1875 the Cincinnati Observatory having been removed to a more eligible site, and an arrangement having been made by which the city agreed to maintain it in connection with the new university founded by Mr. McMicken, he was invited to become its director. He remained there until 1882, when he became professor of astronomy in the University of Virginia, and director of the Leander McCormick Observatory. He has made various contributions to astronomical and mathematical journals. He has edited the "Annals of Mathematics," from its beginning. While connected with the Cincinnati Observatory, Prof. Stone and his assistants observed nearly all the double stars between the equator and 30° south declination. Since 1890 he has been engaged in a study of the nebulæ including the determination of their positions, especial attention having been given to the great nebula in Orion. Quite a number of the younger American astronomers have been trained by Prof. Stone. He is a member of various scientific bodies. Prof. Stone married in 1871 Miss Catharine Flagler, of Washington, D. C.

KIRK, Edward Norris, clergyman, was born in New York city, Aug. 14, 1802, of Scotch-Presbyterian ancestry. He received his early education in the public and private schools of his native city, being graduated at Princeton College in 1820. He began the study of law, and continued it for eighteen months, but subsequently relinquished it for the ministry. To this end, he entered Princeton Theological Seminary, taking the four years' course, upon the completion of which he was appointed agent of the board of foreign missions, and traveled through the South in its behalf. He subsequently held pastorates at the Second Presbyterian Church in Albany, and at the Fourth Presbyterian Church. The organization of the latter was largely due to the revival labors

of Mr. Kirk in 1828. In this connection, also, was established a school of theology. Mr. Kirk resigned his pastorate in 1837, that he might seek rest and recreation in foreign travel, in which pursuit he preached both in London and Paris, establishing in the latter city the first American Protestant religious service. From 1842 to 1871 he had charge of the Mount Vernon Congregational Church, Boston, of which he was one of the organizers. He revisited France in 1856, and succeeded in erecting an American Protestant chapel. The year previous the degree of D.D. had been conferred upon him by Amherst College. For a number of years Dr. Kirk was president of the American Missionary Association, and secretary of the Evangelical conference. He was conspicuous as an author, his "Lectures on Revivals" (edited by the Rev. Daniel O. Mears) appearing in 1874, while among earlier publications were: "Memorial of the Rev. John Chester, D.D.," "Lectures on Christ's Parables," "Sermons," "Canon of the Holy Scriptures," translations of Gaussen's "Inspiration of the Scriptures," and Jean Frédéric Astie's "Lectures on Louis XIV., and the Writers of His Age."

SANDERSON, John, author, was born near Carlisle, Pa., in 1783. He first studied the classics with a clergyman, travelling some seven miles a day to receive his instruction. He studied law in Philadelphia in 1806, but finding the need for immediate support, became a teacher for some years at Clermont Seminary, afterwards marrying the daughter of the principal, and becoming a partner in the school. He contributed to the "Portfolio," and wrote occasionally for Duane's "Aurora." Aided by his brother, he wrote two volumes of the "Biography of the Signers of the Declaration of Independence," to which five volumes more were added by R. Wain and others, finishing the work in 1827; it was reprinted in 1865. His pamphlet, "Defense of Classical Literature as a Branch of Study in Girard College" (1826), had its effect on the managers of that institution, and prevented the exclusion of the classics therefrom. A visit to Europe in 1835–6, on account of ill health, gave rise to "Sketches of Paris, in Familiar Letters to His Friends" (1888), which was reprinted in London the same year as "The American in Paris," and translated into French by Jules Janin in 1843. The peculiar merit of his "Sketches" consists in their light tones of enjoyment. He caught the spirit of the place, and transfused it into the style of his letters, mingled with quotations from Ovid and Horace. To the "Knickerbocker Magazine" he contributed some papers entitled "The American in London." Returning to the United States, he held the chair of Latin and Greek in the Philadelphia High School from 1836 until his death in that city, Apr. 5, 1844. Though broken in health, he maintained a habit of cheerfulness, exercising his talent in humor and sarcasm. R. W. Griswold said of him in "Prose Writers of America" (1846): "He was not less brilliant in his conversation than in his writings, but he never summoned a shadow to any face, nor permitted a weight to lie on any heart."

ASHMUN, Jehudi, missionary, was born in Champlain, N. Y., on the western shore of the lake of that name, in April, 1794. He studied at Burlington College, or, as it was afterwards called, the University of Vermont, where he was graduated in 1816. For a short time thereafter he taught in a charity school, and then studied for the ministry, and after having finished his preparation for that office, was elected a professor in the Bangor Theological Seminary. He remained there, however, but for a short time, and removing to the District of Columbia, became a member of the Protestant Episcopal church, and editor of the "Theological Repertory," which was a magazine published in the interest of church matters. At this time, also, he became greatly interested in the matter of colonization, and published one number of a monthly journal, which was in advocacy of that plan. The work, however, was unsuccessful on account of want of patronage. Being appointed agent of the American Colonization Society, he was placed in charge of an expedition designed to reinforce the colony at Liberia, and embarked for Africa, June 19, 1822, arriving at Cape Montserado Aug. 8th of the same year. Having authority, in the event of finding no agent there, to assume that office, both in behalf of the society and for the navy department, he found that this was precisely the situation, and accordingly took the position of agent. He found the colony terribly disorganized and demoralized, mainly because of raids on the part of the savages. It became necessary, therefore, for him to act not only in the positions of legislator and administrator, but also as a soldier and engineer, to lay out fortifications and superintend their construction, meanwhile animating the emigrants to the highest determination for self-defense. This, too, while he was himself suffering under the fever of the country, at the same time being afflicted on account of the death of his wife. In November, his force only comprising thirty-five men and boys, the colony was attacked by 800 armed savages. Through the energy and desperate valor and skill of the agent, the assailants were repulsed, and a few days later, when they returned with their numbers still larger, they were utterly defeated. Meanwhile, the loss of the colony amounted to only four killed and four wounded. It is said that Mr. Ashmun displayed during these contests remarkable personal valor, besides a degree of generalship quite unexampled in a civilian and a minister of the Gospel. He remained in the colony for six years, but in 1828 his health had become so affected that he was obliged to return home. On March 20th of that year he embarked, being accompanied to the port by a large body of men, women, and children of Monrovia, who parted with him in tears. He left at this time in the colony a very different condition of things from what he had found six years before. There were now 1,200 freemen, forming a promising and comparatively prosperous colony. Mr. Ashmun arrived at New Haven, Aug. 10th, completely broken down by disease. He wrote the "Memoirs of Samuel Bacon," and made many contributions to the "African Repository." He died in Boston, Mass., Aug. 25, 1828. His life was written by R. R. Gurley (New York, 1839).

STUHR, William Sebastian, lawyer, was born in Brooklyn, N. Y., Oct. 1, 1859, the second son of William Stuhr, who was for many years a member of the board of freeholders of Hudson county, N. J. His parents removing to Hoboken, N. J., the following year, he received his early education at the Hoboken Academy, and subsequently studied four years in Europe. On his return, he entered the University of New York, and was graduated there LL.B. in 1879. He was admitted to the bar of New Jersey as attorney Nov. 7, 1880, and as counsellor three years later. Mr. Stuhr was elected corporation counsel of the city of Hoboken in 1883, and re-elected the following year. In May, 1888, he was elected assistant counsel to the board of freeholders of Hudson county, and on completing the work in hand, re-

signed Sept. 1st, believing the further continuance of the office unnecessary, and a useless expense to the county, and devoted himself to his law practice. His genial disposition, together with his ability and success, made him hosts of friends, and he was not permitted to live long in retirement. In June, 1889, he was elected chairman of the Jeffersonian Democracy of Hudson county, and in the fall of that year was nominated by them for state senator of the county; his nomination was also endorsed by the Republican party. After a bitter contest, the regular Democratic candidate, Edward F. McDonald, was declared elected, and took his seat at the organization of the senate of New Jersey, in January, 1890. Mr. Stuhr contested the seat, and being successful, was awarded his seat by vote of the senate, and he held it during the remainder of the session. Mr. Stuhr was married, Feb. 18, 1886, to Marietta, daughter of Thomas Miller, president of the New York Cement Co., who resides at Flushing, L. I. His wife was also a near relative of Gen. Pettigrew, who was at one time governor of South Carolina.

KING, Samuel G., mayor of Philadelphia, was born in that city, May 2, 1816, son of George M. King, a coppersmith, and Mary Gougler King. Mr. King's education was acquired in the schools and academies of his native city, and was completed at the Friends' School. By birth and education he was a Lutheran, but the influence exerted upon his youthful mind by the teachings of that Quaker school still clings to him. In religion he is broad and liberal, seeing good in all forms, freely allowing to others that which he claims for himself. After leaving school he entered upon a business career, from which he retired at the age of thirty-five with a high reputation for business integrity. In politics Mr King began at the bottom of the ladder, first as election inspector, ward committeeman, delegate to conventions, customs inspector, select councilman, and finally mayor of Philadelphia. In October, 1861, he was elected a member of the select council in which body he served for more than twenty consecutive years, having been re-elected seven times to that important office. His clear judgment, integrity, and spirit of progress gave him a commanding influence which was ever used for the public good. During his twenty years' service as a municipal legislator his name was prominently identified, either as the originator, intrepid leader, or able advocate of all the reform measures which have added to the fame of the city, its peace, progress, and prosperity. To him was largely due the fact that the Centennial Exhibition of 1876 was held in Philadelphia. Mr. King was inaugurated mayor of Philadelphia Apr. 4, 1881, having received a majority of 5,787 over William S. Stokley, who had been three times previously elected mayor. In his inaugural address he took a firm stand in favor of a non-partisan police force. The most radical act of Mayor King was the appointment of colored men as members of the police force; as previous to his term no colored man had ever worn the uniform of a policeman in Philadelphia, and his appointment of a number of them raised a storm of indignation such as no previous mayor ever encountered; but, conscious of the justness of his act, he went on in the even tenor of his way, resting his vindication to time and public opinion. During his term he earnestly recommended the establishment of a mounted police force for suburban districts, and since then put into operation a police patrol system, and the illumination of the streets by electricity, both established since he officially advised it. He also urged the building of more school-houses, a better water supply, a system for the reduction of the city debt, economy in public expenditures, improved street pavements, the improvement of the navigation of the Delaware and Schuylkill rivers, and other measures in the forward march of public progress. Mayor King was nominated for a second term, but was unable to overcome the normal majority of 20,000 cast against his party, although he cut it down to a very few thousands, about one-fourth the majority usually cast against Democratic candidates. At the expiration of his term he retired, with clean hands and a character unstained by the touch of corruption. Since his retirement from the mayoralty, Mr. King has been tendered the presidency of several trust companies and banking institutions, but declined them all, preferring the peaceful walks of a retired life. For years he has cultivated a taste for poetry, and his many productions in verse are full of delightfully expressed sentiments. His "Faith, Hope, and Charity," "Birds and Flowers," "To Fortune," "Green Leaves under the Snow," "The Old Oak," "Cricket on the Hearth" are compositions glowing with the inspirations of the true poet. His declining years are bright with the sunshine of a well-spent life. He can be pointed to as a shining example of a model public official, enjoying retirement at an age ripe with the fruits of honor, integrity, and industry. His patriotism is undoubted, his integrity unquestioned, his public services untarnished by stain, and he walks the streets of his native city, one of its most useful, honored, and respected citizens.

CLARK, Thomas, soldier and author, was born in Lancaster, Pa., Sept. 28, 1787. He was educated for the Roman Catholic priesthood at St. Mary's Seminary in Baltimore, but declining to take orders, he entered the army in 1812 as a lieutenant of artillery. He was subsequently promoted to captain of engineers, and during the latter part of the war was engaged in constructing the defenses of the Delaware river. On leaving the army, at the close of the war, he devoted himself to literature and mathematics. He wrote a history of the navy of the United States, which was highly commended by Jefferson and John Adams, and of which two editions were published. He became editor for an association of Philadelphia booksellers for the publication of Greek and Latin classics. His interlinear translations of Homer, Xenophon, Cæsar, Horace, etc., have gone through more than sixty editions in this country, besides having been extensively published abroad. In 1859 he published a "Practical and Progressive Latin Grammar." He also edited an edition of "Boyer's French Grammar," and a series of mathematical works. He died in Philadelphia, Apr. 28, 1860.

LAUGHLIN, John, lawyer, was born in Newstead, Erie co., N. Y., March 14, 1856, son of Bartholomew and Ellen O'Hara Laughlin, who emigrated from Ireland. The boy was brought up on a farm and attended the district school until nine years of age, when his parents removed to Wilson, Niagara co. In 1874 young Laughlin entered the Lockport Union School where he studied four years. He had by this time determined to study for the legal profession, and entered the office of Richard Crowley, U. S. district attorney for the northern district of New York. In December, 1880, he went to Washington, and took a position in the census bureau, but in the spring following went to Buffalo, where Mr. Crowley had just opened an office. He was admitted to the bar in October of that year, and subsequently entered into partnership with Mr. Crowley, the firm becoming Crowley & Laughlin. His first conspicuous appearance in court was in connection with the case of the government against the defaulting president of the First National Bank of Buffalo, Reuben Porter Lee. Soon after this he formed a partnership with Joseph E. Ewell and Daniel McIntosh, under the firm name of Laughlin, Ewell & McIntosh.

Mr. Laughlin's taste for public speaking naturally led him to participation in politics. He became a warm friend of James D. Warren, for years a Republican leader in Erie county and in western New York. In the presidential campaign of 1884 Mr. Warren was chairman of the Republican state committee, and upon his invitation, Mr. Laughlin accompanied the late James G. Blaine on his tour through the state. In the fall of 1887 he was nominated for senator in the Erie senatorial district, and was elected by a large majority, his opponent being Spencer Clinton, a lawyer of eminence. In the organization of the senate, Mr. Laughlin was made chairman of the important committee on canals, and was also a member of the judiciary committee. He was the youngest of his party colleagues in this body. In 1888 he was a delegate to the Republican national convention at Chicago, and supported the candidacy of Chauncey M. Depew, but on the latter's withdrawal voted for Mr. Harrison. Mr. Laughlin has always felt a deep interest in the subject of Irish home rule, and in 1886, was a delegate to the national land-league convention held at Chicago. Mr. Laughlin was re-elected to the state senate in 1889, and during his second term was connected with many important measures. He prepared and effected the passage of the school examiners's act, the police excise act, the free school book act, and he also drew up and introduced in the legislature amendments to the constitution, so arranging the terms of public officers as to separate local or municipal elections from state and national elections. This idea was subsequently taken up and extensively discussed with the result, that it was adopted by the constitutional convention of 1894, and is now a part of the constitution of the state of New York. Senator Laughlin retired from the senate at the end of his second term, and devoted himself to his extensive legal practice. He has not since held public office, but takes an active interest in politics, and is in demand as a speaker in every important campaign. He is an orator of much power, and is impressive in his delivery and finished in his style. He is equally effective on a platform or before a jury. The firm of which he is the head is now known as Laughlin, Ewell & Houpt. It has a large practice in the state and federal courts.

THACHER, Peter, clergyman, was born at Salem, Mass., July 18, 1651, son of Thomas Thacher. He was graduated at Harvard in 1671; taught there for a time, having Cotton Mather as a pupil; was in London in 1707, and resisted all temptations to conform to the Church of England; was ordained first minister of Milton, Mass., in June, 1681, and remained there until his death. He was prominent as a preacher and published sundry sermons and theological treatises between 1708 and 1728. His son, of the same name (1688–1744) was graduated at Harvard in 1706, married a sister of Thomas Prince, and was pastor at Middleborough, Mass., 1709–44. He died Dec. 17, 1727.

QUAYLE, William Alfred, president of Baker University, was born at Parkville, Mo., June 25, 1860. His early life was passed in Kansas, then in

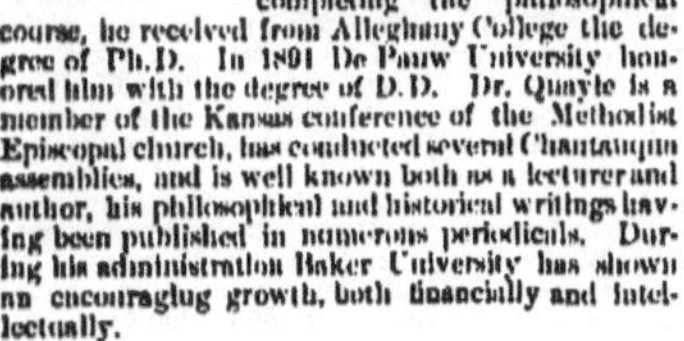

its pioneer stage. In 1880, he entered Baker University, and was graduated in 1885, serving as tutor for two years prior to his graduation, and in 1886, as adjunct professor of ancient languages. He was pastor of the Methodist Episcopal Church at Osage City in 1887, and in the following year returned to Baker University as professor of Greek, which office he held for three years, acting as vice-president during part of the last year. In 1890, he was elected to the presidency of the institution. The degrees of A.B. and A.M. were conferred upon Pres. Quayle by his alma mater, and on completing the philosophical course, he received from Alleghany College the degree of Ph.D. In 1891 De Pauw University honored him with the degree of D.D. Dr. Quayle is a member of the Kansas conference of the Methodist Episcopal church, has conducted several Chautauqua assemblies, and is well known both as a lecturer and author, his philosophical and historical writings having been published in numerous periodicals. During his administration Baker University has shown an encouraging growth, both financially and intellectually.

GIST, Mordecai, soldier, was born in Baltimore, Md., in 1743. He was a descendant of an illustrious family, whose name occurs frequently in the annals of the French and Indian war. His cousin, Nathaniel Gist, a man of great energy of mind and body, was a colonel in the war of the revolution, and it is related that a member of this family, Richard, saved the life of Washington, while *en route* to Fort Du Quesne, by rescuing him from the waters of the Monongahela river. He was educated at the private seminary of an Episcopal clergyman, who was stationed in the parish where the Gist family resided. In early life he was a merchant in Baltimore, where he became a leader among the young men of the city. On the breaking out of the revolution he put himself at the head of a company, the first recruited in Maryland, and led them forth to the defense of the rights of the colonies. In 1776 he was made major of a Maryland battalion, and participated in the battle of Long Island. After seeing considerable service in the North, he was appointed brigadier-general, with the command of the second brigade of the Maryland line, Jan. 9, 1779, and transferred to the South at the battle of Camden, S. C., where DeKalb lost his life, 1780. He was conspicuous alike for

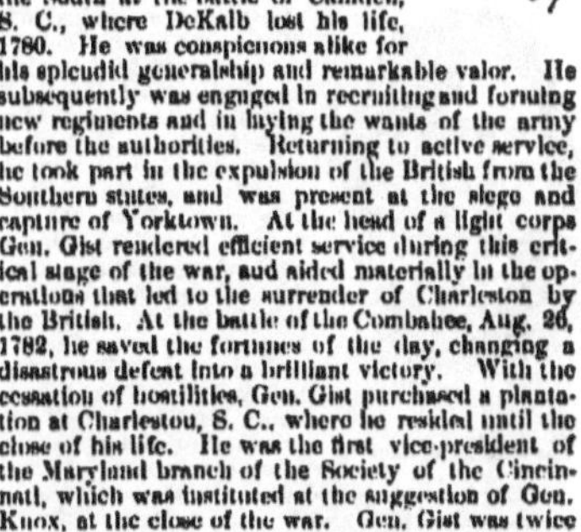

his splendid generalship and remarkable valor. He subsequently was engaged in recruiting and forming new regiments and in laying the wants of the army before the authorities. Returning to active service, he took part in the expulsion of the British from the Southern states, and was present at the siege and capture of Yorktown. At the head of a light corps Gen. Gist rendered efficient service during this critical stage of the war, and aided materially in the operations that led to the surrender of Charleston by the British. At the battle of the Combahee, Aug. 26, 1782, he saved the fortunes of the day, changing a disastrous defeat into a brilliant victory. With the cessation of hostilities, Gen. Gist purchased a plantation at Charleston, S. C., where he resided until the close of his life. He was the first vice-president of the Maryland branch of the Society of the Cincinnati, which was instituted at the suggestion of Gen. Knox, at the close of the war. Gen. Gist was twice married and had two sons, named Independent and States. He died in Charleston, S. C., Aug. 2, 1792.

COFFIN, Robert Barry, author, was born July 21, 1826, in Hudson, N. Y. He was descended from Tristram Coffin, and was great-grandson of Alexander Coffin, who was one of the original founders of Hudson. His father was a scholarly man who gave personal attention to his son's education, and encouraged him to read. This became so great a passion that the son spent all his savings in books, and before he was ten years old had collected quite a library. He attended the Collegiate Institute at Poughkeepsie, N. Y., for several years, where he began to indulge his taste for literary composition, contributing anonymously to various periodicals. To increase his income he became bookkeeper in a mercantile house in New York city, where he remained for four years, when failing health obliged him to go to the country. In 1852 with his brother he opened a book-store in Elmira, but this was also too confining for his delicate health. In 1854 he became a divinity student in preparation for entering the Episcopal ministry, and at the same time contributed to the "Churchman." He returned to New York in 1857, and the following year succeeded T. B. Aldrich as assistant editor of the "Home Journal," of which he had been a correspondent since 1849, and at the same time assuming the position of art critic of the "Evening Post." In 1863 he received the appointment of auditor's clerk in the New York custom house, which position he retained until 1869. He returned to the position in 1875 and retained it until the winter before his death. During this time he had opportunity to devote himself to his literary work, and produced humorous sketches over the signature of Barry Gray, which have been published in the periodicals. He published "My Married Life, or Hillside" and "Matrimonial Infelicities," in 1865; "Out of Town, a Rural Episode," in 1866; "Cakes and Ale at Woodside," in 1868; "Castles in the Air," in 1871; and "The Home of Cooper," in 1872. He was a regular contributor to "The Table," a monthly periodical devoted to gastronomy, and also to the "Caterer," a similar periodical published in Philadelphia. His humor was gentle and refined, and was greatly admired by a large class of readers. His health was precarious towards the end of his life, and he was a great sufferer. He died in Fordham, N. Y., June 10, 1886.

SMITH, Asenath Maria, philanthropist, was born in Montreal, Canada, Sept. 20, 1833, the daughter of Joseph and Fanny Holbrook. Her father was a prominent merchant. The daughter's education was principally acquired in public schools and Malone Academy. She was married to Pascal Smith,

Dec. 31, 1850, and at the age of eighteen she united with the Methodist Episcopal church. In the spring of 1853 her husband removed to Red Wing, Minn., where she at once identified herself with the Methodist Episcopal church and participated actively in religious and charitable work. From the time of her arrival at Red Wing to the close of the war she was president of the Women's Soldiers' Relief Society, and rendered beneficent services to the sick and wounded. In 1859 her husband removed to St. Paul, and Mrs. Smith identified herself with the principal missionary and charitable organizations of that city. She has been president of the Home for the Friendless since 1875, and is vice-president of the Foreign Missionary Society. She is a prominent leader of society and celebrated for her hospitable entertainment of a large circle of friends. Her husband died Nov. 27, 1880.

ALDEN, William Livington, diplomat and journalist, was born in Williamstown, Mass., Oct. 9, 1837. He is a son of the late Rev. Dr. Joseph Alden, formerly a professor at Williams College and at Lafayette College, Pennsylvania; afterwards president of Jefferson College, Pennsylvania, and still later president of the State Normal College at Albany. The young man was educated at Lafayette College, and studied law in the office of William M. Evarts after his graduation. At the expiration of four years' practice, he abandoned the domain of law, and adopted the vocation of journalism, for which he seemed to have a natural taste. Charles G. Halpine, of the New York "Citizen," made him one of his editorial assistants. Mr. Alden at once attracted attention in the field of metropolitan journalism by his humorous writings. He next became connected with the "World," and the "Graphic," and in 1865 joined the editorial staff of the New York "Times." Two collections of Mr. Alden's articles were published in book form, and he is the author of five volumes published by Harper & Brothers.

These are: "The Moral Pirates," "The Cruise of the Ghost," "The Cruise of the Canoe Club," "The Canoe and the Flying Proa," and "The Adventures of Jimmy Brown." A novel, entitled "A Lost Soul," a collection of short stories, entitled "Told by the Colonel," and a boy's book, entitled "Trying to Find Europe," have since been published by Mr. Alden in London. Mr. Alden is an enthusiastic canoeist. He was one of the founders of the New York Canoe Club, and the first commodore of the American Canoe Association. He made five visits to Italy, and resided there for some years. He learned to speak Italian fluently, and in 1885 Pres. Cleveland appointed him consul-genera' to Rome, an office which he filled during the latter's administration. On the expiration of his term, he was made chevalier of the order of the crown of Italy by King Humbert. Having been offered a position on the editorial staff of the Paris edition of the New York "Herald," Mr. Alden removed to Paris, where he resided for three years. He then became a resident of London, where he is at present employed in literary work. Mr. Alden is an active member of the New York Canoe Club, and is a canoe owner himself. He was one of the four who took the cruise recorded in "Canoeing in Kanukia." He introduced the nautilus canoe into the United States, getting drawings from Mr. Baden-Powell, and afterwards designed the well-known shadow canoe. He did much to popularize the sport at an early date, as far back as 1871, by writing many charming articles on canoeing for the "Times." An article on the modern canoe from his pen was published in "Scribner's Monthly" for August, 1872. Mr. Alden's bubbling good humor and quaint fun made him a very popular member at the early meets held at Lake George by the Canoe Association.

WOOD, Walter Abbott, inventor, was born in Mason, N. H., Oct. 23, 1815, son of Aaron Wood, a wagon-maker, who removed from New Hampshire to New York state, where he engaged in the manufacture of wagons and cast-iron plows, at that time newly invented by Jethro Wood, a relative. Young Walter worked in his father's shop until 1835, when he obtained a position in the machine shops of Parsons & Wikler, at Hoosic Falls, N. Y. He saved his money, and gathered together sufficient capital to start in business, in a small way, on his own account. He devoted himself particularly to the study of the mechanism of farming implements, especially the Manny reaper, then in use, and to which he added a number of improvements, and made a harvesting machine, known as Manny's reaper with Wood's improvements, of which in 1852 he made and sold nearly 200 machines. Stimulated by this success, Mr. Wood now devoted himself to inventions in the same line, and in particular to the manufacture of mowers, reapers, and self-binders; and so rapidly did the popularity of his inventions increase that in 1853 he sold as many as 500 of his machines. This seemed to be and was, at that time, an enormous sale, as the construction of agricultural implements, made on mechanical principles, with automatic attachments, was then in its infancy. No one could imagine the difference that a few years would make in all the processes of agriculture, through the ingenuity of inventors, who applied their abilities to the construction of machinery, which, with or without the aid of steam, should in its application to the various processes of agricultural industry completely revolutionize this vast business. Thus, mowers and reapers, steam plows, harvesters and horse rakes, made possible such great farming enterprises as were conducted on the Dalrymple and other farms in the West covering tens of thousands of acres. To this progress few have given such an impetus as Mr. Wood. As soon as he found that his implements were meeting with a large demand, he constructed enormous works, and began to manufacture on the largest possible scale. Between 1858 and 1869 his sales multiplied twelve times; that is to say, the 500 machines which he sold in the former year had become 6,000 in the latter. In the next sixteen years the latter number had been multiplied by eight, as in 1884 he sold more than 48,000 of his implements. It is stated that since he began business, Mr. Wood has taken out thirty patents, and manufactured and sold nearly three-quarters of a million machines. In 1866 he formed a stock company out of his business, calling it the Walter A. Wood Mowing and Reaping Machine Co., of which he became the president. This company, with its manufacturing establishment, is located at Hoosick Falls, N. Y. His machines received recognition at fairs and public exhibitions everywhere. Beginning at county and state fairs, they grew to achieve prominence, first, at the London World's Fair, 1862; then at the Paris Exposition of 1867; at Vienna in 1873; at the Centennial, in Philadelphia, in 1876; in Paris in 1878; and at Chicago in 1893. The reports which were made upon these exhibitions in foreign countries drew attention to his inventions, and his exportation business grew rapidly until it was estimated that ninety per cent. of all the agricultural implements sent abroad were made by his concern. He received a medal from Queen Victoria; the decoration of the Legion of Honor of France, from Emperor Napoleon III.; and the order of Francis Joseph from Austria. He was elected a representative in the forty-sixth congress in 1878, and was re-elected and served in the forty-seventh congress, his second term expiring March 4, 1883. Mr. Wood died, Jan. 15, 1892.

WALLACE, Horace Binney, author, was born in Philadelphia, Pa., Feb. 26, 1817, son of John Bradford Wallace, lawyer. Dividing his college course between the University of Pennsylvania and Princeton, he was graduated at the latter in 1835, and then studied in succession medicine, chemistry, and law. His short life was given to literary work and philosophic research. A novel, "Stanley," appeared without his name in 1838. With J. I. C. Hare, he edited six volumes of "Leading Cases" (1847–52). His part in this work, according to Horace Binney, displayed the "fruits of as accomplished a legal mind as any man in any country at his early age has shown," and Daniel Webster doubted "whether history displays, at thirty years, a loftier nature, or one more usefully or profoundly cultivated." To these eulogies must be added that of Comte, who pronounced him the "equal of the greatest American statesmen," and thought "he would have aided powerfully in advancing the difficult transition through which the nineteenth century has to pass." Beyond contributions to periodicals, and some collaboration with R. W. Griswold, Wallace published nothing more; but after his death, appeared "Art, Scenery, and Philosophy in Europe" (1855), and "Literary Criticisms, and Other Papers" (1856). He was abroad in 1849–50. In November, 1852, his eyes and brain being affected, he sailed for Liverpool; his disease grew worse, and he died by his own hand in Paris, Dec. 16, 1852.

GREEN, Seth, pisciculturist, was born in Rochester, N. Y. March 19, 1817. He obtained his early instruction in the common schools of that city. Being enthusiastically fond of hunting and fishing, and continuing to be addicted to these pursuits as he grew up, he became very expert as an angler and in the science of woodcraft. Mr. Green's success in following fishing and hunting as sports finally suggested to him the idea of making of them a life pursuit, and he established a large fishery on Lake Ontario at the same time opening a fish and game market near his home, of which he remained proprietor for several years. Gradually this novel business extended and he was obliged to appoint agents whom he had in scores scattered along the lakes and watercourses of that part of the state. Meanwhile, his natural powers of observation developed by the peculiarities of his life, and experience brought to his knowledge much in his particular line of natural history which had hitherto been unknown and which eventually brought about his important services to science. He first began his observations on fish spawning in Canada, in 1838, when careful observation led him to believe that artificial hatching in vast numbers could be accomplished by means of a comparatively simple mechanism. He accordingly fitted up a hatchery for experiments and devoted himself to the study of the process. Next experiments were tried previous to 1867 in the Connecticut river, with the result that twenty-five per cent. was the largest product of salmon or trout to be obtained artificially by the methods thus far employed. But, continuing his experiments, he gradually improved upon this, and in 1867 the fish commissioners of four of the Southern states arranged for a public trial, which took place at Holyoke, Mass., on the Connecticut river. In these trials he succeeded in hatching 15,000,000 eggs in a fortnight and in the next year he hatched 40,000,000. Since then he has been equally successful in stocking the waters of the Hudson, Susquehannah, Potomac and other large rivers in which he has been able to propagate fifteen of the more common species of fish and also to largely increase the product. Mr. Green's hatching box has been the prototype of every invention or application made since for the purpose of hatching fish spawn. One result of his activity and success in this vocation was to promote the study and practice of pisciculture in a number of different states, which appointed commissions and established hatcheries. In the New York state fish hatchery, of which Mr. Green was appointed superintendent,

the total number of shad hatched from 1870 to 1880 was 58,609,800. At the same time there were distributed 9,555,020 salmon trout. White fish and brook trout were also experimented with. As to the originality of Mr. Green's work it may be stated that, while fish eggs had been impregnated and hatched artificially before he commenced his operations, there was no record of any being hatched and raised to maturity by hand until it was done at his works at Caledonia, N. Y. He is the author of "Trout Culture," "Fish Hatching and Fish Catching," "Home Fishing and Home Waters, a Practical Treatise on Fish Catching." Mr. Green has been decorated with two gold medals and one silver medal by the Société d'Acclimatation of Paris, and a gold medal by the Internationale Fischerei Austellung of Berlin, and has received a bronze medal from the United States Centennial Commission. Besides these distinguished honors, he has received several diplomas from European societies. Mr. Green married, Feb. 14, 1848, Helen M. Cook, and has four children living, namely, Helen L., Alice G., Chester K., and William C. Green. He died in Rochester, N. Y., Aug. 20, 1888.

CHAFFEE, Jerome Bunty, U. S. senator, was born in Niagara county, N. Y., Apr. 17, 1825. At the age of twenty-two he had saved money enough from his wages as clerk in a country store to set up in business for himself, and he opened a dry-goods store at Adrian, Mich. During his stay there he took an active part in politics, and became an intimate friend of Zachariah Chandler, another drygoods merchant, doing business in Detroit. From Michigan he went first to St. Joseph, Mo., where he was engaged in banking; then to Elmwood, Kan., where he speculated in real estate; and finally to Denver, Col., of which place he was one of the founders. He succeeded in a variety of business enterprises, and became a leader in political affairs. He helped to organize the territory of Colorado, and was chosen speaker of its first legislature, and territorial delegate to congress. In 1876 he was elected one of Colorado's first senators, and in 1884 was chairman of the Republican National Committee. He died at Salem Centre, Westchester co., N. Y., March 9, 1886.

SHOCK, William Henry, naval officer, was born in Baltimore, Md., June 15, 1821. He received an academic education, and in January, 1845, was appointed third assistant engineer in the navy. He saw much active service during the Mexican war, and participated in the capture of Tampico under Com. Connor, and in the capture of Vera Cruz, under Com. Perry. In July, 1847, he was promoted second assistant engineer, and ordered to the steamer Engineer, home squadron. He was advanced to the rank of first assistant engineer in October, 1848, and in 1849 served as senior engineer of the coast survey steamer Legarce. In 1850-51 he was stationed at Philadelphia, where he had charge of the construction of the machinery of the steam-frigate Susquehanna. He was made chief engineer in March, 1851; directed the construction of the machinery of the Princeton in 1852, and in 1853 served as engineer inspector of the U. S. mail steamers, and also as chief engineer of steamer Princeton. In 1854-55 he was stationed at West Point, N. Y., engaged in the construction of marine engines, and the next year became chief engineer of the frigate Merrimac, and later of the Powhatan as fleet engineer of the East India squadron; from 1860-62 he was president of the examining board of engineers, but soon was assigned to special duty, superintending the constructing of river monitors at St. Louis. During the operations against Mobile he acted as fleet engineer to Adm. Farragut, and later was attached in the same capacity to the staff of Adm. Thatcher. During the service, besides performing services of the highest value, he designed and constructed an instrument for the destruction of submerged torpedo electric wires and also floating torpedoes, both of which proved very successful. In 1867-68 he became chief engineer at the Washington navy yard, and the following year was fleet engineer of the European squadron. In 1870 he was appointed inspector of machinery afloat, and was made a member of the board of visitors to the Annapolis Naval Academy. In 1870-71 he was acting chief of the bureau of steam engineering, receiving the formal thanks of the secretary of the navy for the manner in which he discharged the duties of the position. In 1873 he visited Europe, where he carefully inspected the various government dock-yards, and represented the U. S. bureau of steam engineering at the Vienna exhibition, where he was also appointed by the president one of the American judges of merit. On March 3, 1877, he was made engineer-in-chief of the U. S. navy, and filled that position until June 15, 1883, when he was placed on the retired list, and made Washington, D. C., his home. Chief-Engineer Shock has attained high rank as an inventor. In 1868 he invented a rotary projectile for smooth bore guns; in 1869 a relieving cushion for wire rigging for ships; in 1870 a projectile for small arms; and in 1874 steam radiators and attachments for heating purposes. He is the author of "Steam Boilers: Their Design, Construction, and Management" (New York, 1881), which is a standard work upon the subject, and he has long been a frequent contributor to scientific journals.

DUPUY, Eliza Ann, author, was born in Petersburgh, Va., in 1815, the daughter of a merchant and shipowner of that city, and a descendant of Col. Dupuy, who led a band of Huguenot exiles to a tract of land upon the James river, that had been granted them by James II. of England. Before she reached womanhood, her father, on account of pecuniary reverses, emigrated to Kentucky, and to help retrieve his fallen fortunes her first work, "Merton, a Tale of the Revolution," was written. After the death of her father, she commenced a strict course of study, and adopted the profession of a teacher. In her twenty-second year she completed "The Conspirators," an historical novel in which Aaron Burr is the principal character. Her other works are: "Celeste, or the Pirate's Daughter," "The Separation," "Florence, or the Fatal Vow," "The Concealed Treasure;" "Ashleigh, a Tale of the Revolution," and "The Huguenot Exiles." She also contributed a number of short stories to the "New York Ledger," under the name of "Annie Young." The latter part of her life was spent in Louisiana and Mississippi, and she died in New Orleans, Jan. 15, 1881.

TORREY, Charles Turner, reformer, was born at Scituate, Mass., in 1813, where his ancestor, James Totten, had settled after emigrating from Somersetshire in 1632. He was prepared for college at Phillips Exeter Academy, under the superintendence of Benj. Abbott, LL.D., and was graduated at Yale in 1833. He studied for the Congregational ministry, was pastor at Princeton and Salem, Mass., and published a "Memoir of W. R. Saxton" (1838). Later he went to Maryland in the service of the "underground railroad," which naturally brought him into collision with the local laws. He was arrested in 1843 for reporting a meeting of slaveholders, and the next year for trying to help slaves escape. Sentenced to a long term, he wrote "Home, or the Pilgrim's Faith Reviewed" (1846) during his confinement, and died of consumption in the state prison at Baltimore, May 9, 1846. His remains were taken to Boston, and interred in Mount Auburn, thousands attending the ceremony. His fate excited great sympathy in the North and England, and inspired the abolitionists with renewed zeal. His memoir, by J. C. Lovejoy, appeared 1847.

READ, George Campbell, admiral, was born in Ireland about 1788. He was brought to America when a child, entered the navy as a midshipman in 1804, and became a lieutenant in 1810. He acted with much gallantry in the fight between the Constitution and the Guerrière, Aug. 19, 1812, and received the sword of the vanquished Capt. Dacres. Two months later he took part in the duel of the United States with the Macedonian, and later in the war had command of the Chippewa. He was promoted to commander in April, 1816, and to captain in March, 1825. In later years he was in command of squadrons in the East Indies, on the African coast, and in the Mediterranean. One of his voyages was described by a subordinate in "Around the World" (2 vols., 1840). He was on the reserve list from September, 1855, was a governor at the Naval Asylum at Philadelphia, 1861-2, and was retired with the rank of rear-admiral, July 31, 1862. He died in Philadelphia, Aug. 22, 1862.

FRENEAU, Philip, poet, was born in New York city Jan. 2, 1752. His ancestors emigrated from France on the revocation of the edict of Nantes, and settled in Connecticut. He studied at Princeton, where he was graduated in 1771, in the same class with Pres. Madison, with whom he kept up a life-long friendship, and even before he left college had begun to write poetry. In 1776 he went to sea and visited the Danish West Indies, and two years later, Bermuda. During this time he wrote some of his longest poems. On his return he wrote for the "United States Magazine." In 1780 he visited the West Indies again, and was captured by an English cruiser, and consigned to the prison ship Scorpion an incident which he turned to account in his poem, "The British Prison Ship." He obtained his freedom in 1781 and returned home, and wrote prose and verse for the local papers. After peace had been declared he was for some time an editor, and again master of a vessel sailing to the West Indies and to Southern cities. In 1790 he was made editor of the New York "Daily Advertiser." Having attracted the attention of Jefferson, he received the appointment of translator of the state department, at the same time becoming editor of the "National Gazette." He was a caustic writer, and succeeded in arousing the animosity of Alexander Hamilton by charging that he used the patronage of his office to support the editor of his paper. For a short time Freneau published, at his home in Mount Pleasant, N. J., the "Jersey Chronicle." In 1797 he published in New York the "Timepiece and Literary Companion," which was issued in eight small quarto pages of the precise size of seven inches by eight. Freneau had a genius for newspapers, and for a long time it was sustained by his wonderful tact in administering to the tastes of the public. His prose essays are elegant papers, at once simple and elegant in style, independent in thought, playful, and humorous. They were for the most part written over the signature of Robert Slender, whom the author took the liberty of burying that he might publish his manuscripts. Freneau republished his series of "Tomo Checki, the Creek Indian in Philadelphia." This appears to have closed his literary life, although he lived thirty-five years longer. He lost his life in attempting to cross a meadow in the evening when he got lost and became mired in a bog and was found lifeless the following morning. Among his works are: "A Poem on the Rising Glory of America" (Philadelphia, 1771); "Voyage to Boston" (New York, 1774); "John Gage's Confession" (New York, 1775); "The British Prison Ship" (1781); "The Poems of Philip Freneau, Written Chiefly During the Late War" (1786); "A Journey from Philadelphia to New York by Robert Slender, Stocking Weaver" (1787); "The Miscellaneous Works of Mr. Philip Freneau" (1788); "The Village Merchant" (1794); "Poems Written between the Years 1768 and 1794" (1795); "Letters on Various Interesting and Important Subjects, by Robert Slender" (1799); "Poems Written and Published During the American Revolutionary War" (1800); "A Collection of Poems on American Affairs" (1815). Captain Freneau was a staunch Whig in the time of the revolution, a good soldier, and a warm patriot. The productions of his pen animated his countrymen in the darkest days of '76 and his humorous effusions cheered the desponding soldier as he fought the battle of freedom. The poems of Philip Freneau represent his times in the war of wit and words no less than of sword and stratagem of the revolution; and he superadds to this material a humorous, homely simplicity, peculiarly his own, in which he displays the local manners and rough ways of the times. He surprises one by his neatness of execution and skill in versification while his appreciation of nature is sympathetic and tender; but most worthy of notice is his originality, which marked out for itself new paths, and dealing with facts and realities, his compositions have a greater interest, than the vague expressions of many authors. Sir Walter Scott knew the verses on the "Battle of Eutaw" by heart, and remarked to Mr. Brevoort that the poem was as fine a thing as there is of the kind in the language and he also praised Freneau's Indian poems. Dr. John W. Francis says, that he was widely known and esteemed, and could talk intelligently upon the special and favorite topics of the leading men of his time as though he gave all his life to the study of the subject. He died near Freehold, N. J., Dec. 18, 1832.

WINTHROP, John, governor of Massachusetts, was born in Edwardston, England, Jan. 22, 1587. His grandfather, Adam Winthrop, was a wealthy clothier of Suffolk, who also had a city house in London, and who was at one time master of the famous cloth-workers' guild of London. He was a man of culture, energy, and great strength of character, which traits descended to his children. His daughters married men of eminence, and many of their children have become distinguished. His third son, Adam, who was a lawyer, was a graduate of Magdalen College, and for many years auditor of Trinity and St. John's Colleges. He married, for his first wife, a sister of the Bishop of Bath and Wells, who died, shortly after their marriage, without children. For his second wife he married Anne Browne, of Edwardston, whose only son, John, is the subject of this sketch. John's parents lived until within a few years of his coming to New England, the mother dying only a year before his embarkation. He was admitted to Cambridge in 1602, where he remained for two years, but his college career was brought to an abrupt termination by his early marriage to Mary, daughter of John Forth, of Great Stonebridge. She was the heiress of a wealthy family, which had a long pedigree of distinction and renown, and brought her husband "a large portion of outward estate." The records show that he was a magistrate at the age of eighteen, and that "he was exemplary for his grave and Christian deportment." Within eleven years after his marriage his wife died, leaving six children. His second wife

was a daughter of William Clopton, but she died a year and a day after marriage. He was always of a pious turn of mind, and these bereavements led him to contemplate becoming a clergyman, but he relinquished the idea, and gave himself up to the practice of the law and his duties as a magistrate. In 1618 he married Margaret, daughter of Sir John Tyndal, knight of Great Maplested, Essex. His profession was largely in the court of Wards and Liveries, which had jurisdiction over wards, widows, and lunatics, and he had several titled clients. In 1629 he lost his office, probably through his sympathy for those suffering under the unjust proscriptions of the crown, and having felt that evil times were upon the country, he began to consider the establishment of a "plantation" in New England. Winthrop saw that civil and religious persecution was assuming an intensity which could not fail to arouse the nation, and he was not of the material which could remain inactive. After great deliberation and consulting, he entered upon the undertaking with zeal, and secured a charter from the crown and completed the necessary arrangements with the "Massachusetts Company" for the transportation of his colony to New England. A plantation had already been established at Salem by the Massachusetts Company, and was under the leadership of John Endicott, who was directly responsible to the authorities of the home company in London. But it was now resolved to transfer the whole government to American soil, and the authority was vested in Winthrop, who was entrusted with the task of the transfer and establishment of the new government, "the Company having received," as the record says, "extraordinary great commendation of his integrity and sufficiency." He was elected governor by the company before leaving London, and embarked on Apr. 1, 1630, with about 700 persons, in a fleet of eleven ships, arriving in Salem June 22, when, after a few days' stay, he went to the settlement of Shawmut, which was afterward called Boston. His life and fortunes henceforth were linked with the colonization and civilization of the New World, upon which he exercised a greater influence than any other one man. He held the office of governor for twelve years, and administered the affairs with unusual wisdom and foresight. He became deputy-governor when Sir Harry Vane was appointed governor, and opposed him in the Anne Hutchinson controversy, upon which issue he was elected governor in 1637. The earnestness of his zeal for the welfare of the community made him hostile of the teachings of Anne Hutchinson and her followers, and he was active in their banishment. In 1644 he was impeached, but he triumphed, and his definition of liberty in the speech upon his acquittal has become celebrated. About 100 new arrivals were admitted to the company, but excessive privation drove about 100 back to England, while over 200 died before the following December. Winthrop wrote: "I do not repent my coming. I would not have altered my course though I had foreseen all these afflictions." In 1643 the colonies of Massachusetts, Plymouth, Connecticut and New Haven were united into a confederation under the name of The United Colonies of New England. He lived to see the city which he founded the capital of a confederation of which he was the first president, and "he closed his eyes upon a scene of rare prosperity, which he, laboring with many other good and able men, had been the chief instrument in creating." He was elected governor twelve times, and that he was not chosen continuously was due to his strong insistence upon the principle that true liberty requires wise and secure authority. He foresaw the folly and weakness of a loose democracy. He also perceived the error of "electing to office men who had

no learning nor judgment, though holy and religious," and allowing "some one or other of their ministers" to hold responsible places in the managing of state business. More than any Puritan founder, Winthrop embodied the broad forethought of combined liberty and law in both state and church, and the appellation of the "father of Massachusetts" is aptly applied. Winthrop began a journal a week after sailing from Southampton, a portion of which was published in Hartford in 1790. Subsequently a continuation was discovered in the tower of the old South Church, Boston, in 1816, and the whole was eventually published as "The History of New England from 1630 to 1649," in 1853. He is also the author of an essay entitled, "Arbitrary Government Described, and the Government of Massachusetts Vindicated from that Aspersion." A portrait of him, ascribed to Vandyke, is in the senate chamber of Massachusetts, from which the accompanying portrait is copied. He rendered the colonies the most efficient services by his judicious administration of its affairs, as well as by his good example in social life. When he first came to America his wealth was great, and he used it freely for the benefit of the public. It is said that he denied himself many of the luxuries of life, that he might set an example of frugality and temperance. Bancroft says: "It was principally the calm decision of Winthrop which sustained the courage of his companions." And Palfrey writes: "Among the millions of living men, descended from men whom he ruled, there is not . . . one who does not owe much of what is best in him to the benevolent and courageous wisdom of John Winthrop." He died in Boston, March 26, 1649.

EADES, Harvey L., leader of the Shaker Society in Kentucky, was born in Logan county, Ky., in 1806. His history is closely interwoven with that of the Shaker village in his native county. In the early part of the nineteenth century his parents, together with some other wealthy and prominent citizens of one of the highest agricultural districts in the state, became converts to the Shaker doctrine. They gave up their land, comprising thousands of acres, and put all their personal property into a common fund, and upon this land, which was now the common property of all who espoused their faith, they built a village, which has since been known as Shakertown. In this village they all lived. The husbands and wives were always affectionate and on good terms, but the men and women lived apart. The children were brought up as a common charge, and every fatherless and motherless child that could be found was taken in and given a moral and mental training. When they became of age, these children, if they so desired were allowed to leave the village, and become members of such churches as best suited them. Young Eades passed his childhood amid these surroundings, and after receiving his rudimentary education, was sent to Ohio for a more advanced course of study. Before returning to Shakertown he preached for a number of years throughout the East and West, about 1856 resuming his residence with the community. In 1872, when Jefferson Shannon, whose father had also been one of the founders of Shakertown, left the community, Elder Eades was placed at the head of both the financial and spiritual affairs. The community did not prosper under his administration as it had done under Shannon's management. Mr. Eades being a man of benevolent disposition and kindly heart, was frequently imposed on, and in this way large sums of money were lost. Shannon returned to the community, but never again assumed the management of affairs, Elder Eades continuing at the head until his death. He was a man of superior education and strong mental characteristics. He was at one time engaged in a debate with the Rev. J. R. Curd, a leading Cumberland Presbyterian minister of Warren county. The discussions were held in the church at Shakertown, and attracted thousands of people from the surrounding country, and considerable attention elsewhere. Elder Eades was a forcible, logical speaker, and presented his peculiar doctrines in a way that seemed unanswerable, in the numerous debates he held with ministers of other churches, and was always able to sustain his side of the argument. He was also the author of a number of religious and metaphysical books and pamphlets.

McREYNOLDS, Andrew Thomas, soldier, was born at Dungannon, Tyrone co., Ireland, Dec. 25, 1806. He emigrated to Pittsburgh, Pa., in August, 1830, where he became one of the original members and first ensign of the Duquesne Grays, which, organized in 1831, was the first independent volunteer company formed west of the Alleghanies. In 1833 he removed to Detroit, Mich., and in 1834 was appointed major on the staff of Maj.-Gen. Williams, then in command of all the militia in the territory. During the winter of 1834–35 Maj. McReynolds was one of four that organized the Brady Guards of Detroit, the first independent military organization west of Lake Erie subsequent to the war of 1812.

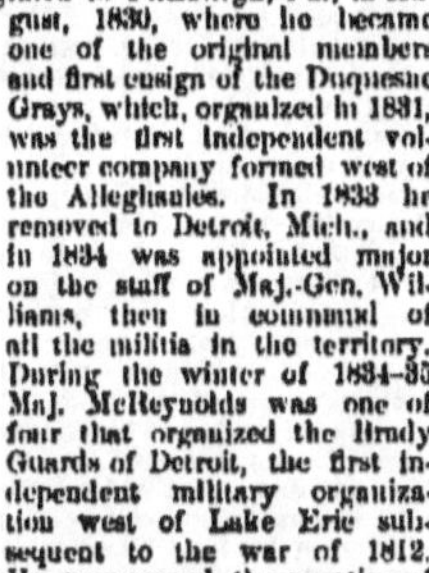

He commenced the practice of law in 1840, and soon rose to prominence in the profession. He organized the Montgomery Guards of Detroit, and was their first captain while in command of the regiment, also serving eleven years as lieutenant-colonel and colonel of the first regiment of Michigan militia. Having in March, 1847, received a captain's commission in the dragoon service of the U. S. army, he resigned the seat he was then occupying in the Michigan state senate, and served under Gen. Scott during the war with Mexico, and in 1832 volunteered under Gen. Scott to put down nullification in South Carolina. He was attached to the headquarters, his troops, 3d U. S. dragoons, in conjunction with those under Gen. Philip Kearney, as captain 1st U. S. dragoons, acting in squadron as bodyguard of the commanding general during the campaign that terminated in planting the American banner in triumph on the halls of the Montezumas. At the close of the Mexican war he returned to Detroit and resumed the practice of his profession until the outbreak of the civil war, when he tendered his services to Pres. Lincoln, was appointed colonel by him, and organized and brought into the field the "Lincoln cavalry," the first regiment of cavalry organized for the Federal army. He was mustered into the service for three years as colonel, June 14, 1861, in the city of Washington. Gen. McReynolds commanded his regiment during the first year of the war. Subsequently, was in command of a brigade for nearly two years, and of a division for six months, when his term of service having expired he, on Aug. 22, 1864, received an honorable discharge. He returned to his home in Grand Rapids, and again resumed the practice of his profession. Prominent in all the affairs of his state, he held many important civil positions. From 1834 to 1838 inclusive he was connected with the Bank of Michigan of the city of Detroit; in 1838–39 was an alderman of Detroit; during 1839–40 he represented Detroit in the state legislature; and in December, 1839, was a delegate from Michigan to the Harrisburg convention that nominated William Henry Harrison for the presidency, and is the only survivor of that memorable body, the first that the Whig party ever appointed to nominate a president of the United States. Under Pres. Tyler, Gen. McReynolds was Indian agent for three years; was state senator from Detroit in 1846 and 1847, and resigned to join his regiment in New Orleans, en route for Mexico. He was prosecuting attorney for Wayne county in 1851–52; was a candidate for circuit judge and associate justice supreme court on the Democratic ticket while a citizen of Detroit, but defeated at the polls; was a member and the first president of Detroit board of education, and was U. S. district attorney for the western district of Michigan, and while a resident of Grand Rapids was a candidate for congress in 1872, in the Greeley campaign, on the Democratic ticket, that resulted so fatally to the Democracy. He was afterward nominated for attorney-general of the state, but declined to accept; he has also been twice elected commander of his post—Custer Post, No. 5, G.A.R. of the city of Grand Rapids; and also department commander, department of Michigan G.A.R., as well as president of the Mexican Veteran Association of the state of Michigan, which position he has held for fourteen consecutive years; and vice-president of the National Association of Mexican Veterans.

JONES, Augustine, educator, was born Oct. 16, 1835, at South China, Me., son of Richard M. Jones, who died in 1842, leaving his only boy without money, but in care of an uncle. The son was, however, assisted in his education by the generosity of David Dudley of Presque Isle, Me. He was fitted for college at Yarmouth Academy, Me., and entered Bowdoin College in 1856, Thomas B. Reed being one of his classmates. Upon the graduation of young Jones in 1860, he became principal of Oak Grove Seminary, Vassalboro', Me. While still teaching he began the study of law and in 1863, entered Harvard Law School, and was graduated there in 1867, and in 1866 entered the law office of Gov. John A. Andrew, of Boston, Mass. He subsequently succeeded to the practice of Gov. Andrew, and in 1868 was administrator of the latter's estate. Mr. Jones practiced law in that office for twelve years, being associated for the latter part of that time with John F. Andrew, the son of the governor. In 1874, Mr. Jones was selected by the poet Whittier to represent the Society of Friends in a series of discourses on the Universal church, arranged by the Rev. James Freeman Clark, to be delivered at his church in Boston. Mr. Jones's discourse was published, and as it confined itself to the literature of the denomination produced quite an effect among the Friends by calling attention to their departure from the teachings of their early writers and fathers. He subsequently delivered before the Historic Genealogic Society of Boston an historical paper on Nicholas Upsal, which in 1874 was pub-

lished and appeared in the register of the society. In 1878 he was a member of the house of representatives of Massachusetts, where he served upon important committees. He entered upon his present position as principal of the Friends' School at Providence, R. I., in 1879, giving up a fine law practice to do so. Here his fifteen years' administration has brought some remarkable changes. The institution's endowments, through his personal efforts, have been considerably enlarged; music and art have become more prominent, and the standard of scholarship in all departments extended. In 1888 Mr. Jones published a pamphlet on "Peace and Arbitration," which ran through three editions and was distributed to the extent of 107,000 copies, in America and England. He was a delegate from the Peace Society of Boston, and from the Friends of New England,

to the Universal Peace congress held in London in 1890. He has taken an active interest in the improvement of the city of Providence. He is president of the Advance Club, which is devoted to public improvement, president of the Public Parks Association of Providence, and of the East Side Improvement Society for local improvements in the city. He read an address in 1891 before the Advance Club, on Parks and Tree-lined Avenues, which was published and widely circulated, one upon Robert Burns before the same Society in 1892, and another in the same year before the Rhode Island Historical Society on Moses Brown, one of the founders of Brown University, which was published by authority of the society.

SIMMS, William Gilmore, author, was born in Charleston, S. C., Apr. 17, 1806. He was of Scotch-Irish descent. His father, who had the same name, was a merchant of Charleston who, having failed in business, removed to Tennessee, where he held a commission under Jackson in the war against the Seminoles. His wife, Harriett A. A. Singleton, was of a Virginia family which came early to the state, and in revolutionary times espoused the Whig side. She died when her second son, William, was in his infancy and the boy was left, in the absence of his father, to the care of his grandmother. When his father went West he wished to take his son, which was resisted, and a lawsuit brought which resulted in the boy remaining in Charleston as he wished. On account of the straitened circumstances of the family, he did not have many early educational advantages, his entire course being confined to the public schools of his native town. He early developed his passion for literary composition, writing verses when only seven years old, and publishing a book, "Monody on Gen. Pinckney," when only nineteen. He worked as a clerk in a drug and chemical house for some time, and at one time intended to study medicine, but he relinquished this in favor of the study of the law and was admitted to the bar; but before he was twenty-one he realized that his taste led him in the direction of literary work, and he turned his thoughts in that direction. His first active engagement was as editor of the Charleston city "Gazette," in which he also held a proprietor's interest. He took strong sides against the prevailing doctrine of nullification, and although he displayed great spirit and industry, the enterprise proved a failure and he lost what little money he had invested in it. In 1827 he published a volume entitled,

"Lyrical and Other Poems," which was followed the same year by "Early Lays." The next year he issued another volume, "The Vision of Cortes, Cain, and Other Poems," and in 1830 "The Tricolor, or Three Days of Blood," a volume of verse in celebration of the French revolution. Upon the failure of his paper, Mr. Simms visited New York, and was introduced to the literary world of the metropolis, where he was warmly received. While in New York he published, through the Harper's, "Atalantis, a Story of the Sea," which was an imaginative poem written in easy, eloquent verse, interspersed with frequent lyrics. This was the best and longest of his poetical works, and achieved an unusual success. He now devoted himself to fiction, in which line he is best known, and the next year the Harpers issued his first tale, "Martin Faber, the Story of a Criminal," which was written in an intense passionate style, which commanded public attention at once. This was followed by a long series of stories, which appeared without interruption until a few years before his death. After the death of his first wife, which occurred shortly after their union, and before his visit to New York, he married the daughter of Mr. Roach, a wealthy planter of the Bauewell district in South Carolina, which placed him in affluence. He turned his attention to politics, and was for many years a member of the legislature, and in 1846 came within one vote of being elected lieutenant-governor of the state. The degree of LL.D. was conferred upon him by the University of Alabama. During the civil war he espoused the Southern side, and he suffered great loss of property when the Federal troops took possession of Charleston. He spent his time between his summer residence in Charleston and his plantation, Woodlands, at Midway, where he had a beautiful home amid the long-leaved pines peculiar to that region, and where he dispensed a wide hospitality. He was very helpful to young writers, which made him greatly beloved by the craft. The numerous writings of Mr. Simms are characterized by earnestness, sincerity, and thoroughness. He is vigorous in delineation, dramatic in action, poetic in his description of scenery, a master of plot, and skilled in the arts of the practiced story writer. His own taste led him to poetry and imaginative literature, which he freely introduced into his prose. Edgar A. Poe pronounced his novels the best produced in America since Cooper. In poetry Mr. Simms produced "Donna Florida," a metrical tale in the Don Juan style, but with nothing vicious in it; "Grouped Thoughts," "Lays of the Palmetto," "The Cassique of Accabee." In fiction his work might be divided as follows: revolutionary romances, the principal of which are the trilogy begun by "The Partisan," "Eutaw," "Guy Rivers," the first of a series of border tales, and "Beauchampe," covering the whole period of active warfare in South Carolina, and the careers  of the principal characters engaged; historical romances, among them "The Yemassee," which is considered his best story; "Pelayo," "Count Julien," "The Damsel of Darien," and "Vasconcelos," preserving the early history and local traditions of the South; moral and imaginative romances which include "Martin Faber," "Castle Dismal," and many others. In history Mr. Simms has produced a "History of South Carolina," "Civil Warfare of the South," and several biographies of eminent men which are handled *con amore*. In criticism Mr. Simms's pen has covered a wide field. He edited "Seven Dramas Ascribed to Shakespeare" with notes and preliminary essays. In periodical literature he has always been a liberal contributor, and himself founded and conducted several reviews and magazines, among which may be mentioned the "Southern Literary Gazette," and the "Southern Quarterly Review." In addition to these literary productions, Mr. Simms is the author of several orations upon public occasions. In 1859, and again in 1805, were published uniform editions of his revolutionary and border romances in seventeen volumes, to which were added two volumes of poetry. His last works were "The Ghost of My Husband" and "War Poetry of the South." He was forced by ill health to relinquish his pen, and succumbed to disease, June 11, 1870.

MOEN, Philip Louis, manufacturer, was born in Wilna, Jefferson co., N. Y., Nov. 18, 1824, the son of Augustus Réné and Sophie A. Moen. The

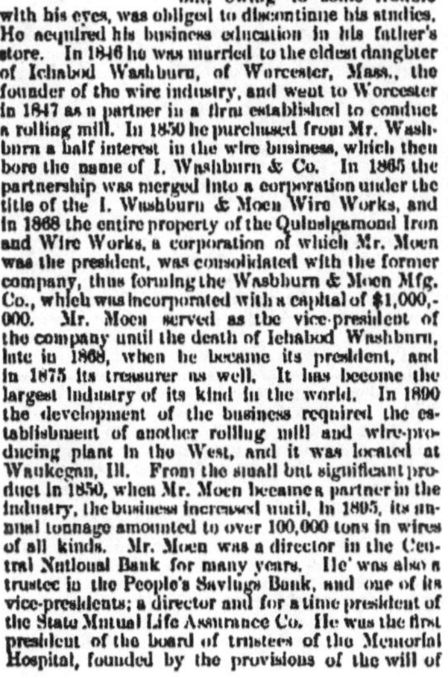

father of Augustus Réné Moen, emigrated from France to Northern New York, where his son, Augustus, grew up. After his marriage, Augustus Réné Moen removed to the Township of Carthage, where his first son, Philip, was born. After leaving Wilna, and with a brief sojourn at Houseville, N. Y., they removed to Collinsville, Conn., in 1830. In 1836 they made their home in Brooklyn, N. Y., and Mr. Moen established himself in the hardware business in New York, acting as the representative of English houses. The son was fitted for Columbia College under Dr. Charles Anthon, but, owing to some trouble with his eyes, was obliged to discontinue his studies. He acquired his business education in his father's store. In 1846 he was married to the eldest daughter of Ichabod Washburn, of Worcester, Mass., the founder of the wire industry, and went to Worcester in 1847 as a partner in a firm established to conduct a rolling mill. In 1850 he purchased from Mr. Washburn a half interest in the wire business, which then bore the name of I. Washburn & Co. In 1865 the partnership was merged into a corporation under the title of the I. Washburn & Moen Wire Works, and in 1868 the entire property of the Quinsigamond Iron and Wire Works, a corporation of which Mr. Moen was the president, was consolidated with the former company, thus forming the Washburn & Moen Mfg. Co., which was incorporated with a capital of $1,000,000. Mr. Moen served as the vice-president of the company until the death of Ichabod Washburn, late in 1868, when he became its president, and in 1875 its treasurer as well. It has become the largest industry of its kind in the world. In 1890 the development of the business required the establishment of another rolling mill and wire-producing plant in the West, and it was located at Waukegan, Ill. From the small but significant product in 1850, when Mr. Moen became a partner in the industry, the business increased until, in 1895, its annual tonnage amounted to over 100,000 tons in wires of all kinds. Mr. Moen was a director in the Central National Bank for many years. He was also a trustee in the People's Savings Bank, and one of its vice-presidents; a director and for a time president of the State Mutual Life Assurance Co. He was the first president of the board of trustees of the Memorial Hospital, founded by the provisions of the will of his father-in-law, Mr. Washburn, in memory of his daughters. This office he retained until his death. He was a trustee, and for several years the treasurer, of the Worcester Polytechnic Institute, to whose endowment he had been a generous contributor. In 1866 and 1867 he was president of the Worcester County Mechanic's Association. He was a trustee at the time of his death of the Free Public Library, of the Y. M. C. A., and of the Home for Aged Women. Mr. Moen was married, in 1856, to Maria S. Grant, his first wife having died in 1854. Mr. Moen died in Worcester, Apr. 23, 1890. A widow, one son, and two daughters survive him.

ESPY, James Pollard, meteorologist, was born in Westmoreland county, Pa., May 9, 1785, of Huguenot descent, the name having been originally spelled "Espie." His uncle, Col. Espy, was an officer in the revolution, a deputy to the provincial conference held at Philadelphia in June, 1775, a member of the council of safety in 1776, afterward prothonotary and one of the justices of the county, a member of the general assembly of the state, and one of the original trustees of Dickinson College. When quite young, James Pollard Espy removed with his parents to Kentucky, and subsequently to Ohio. Upon his graduation at Transylvania University, Lexington, Ky., in 1808, he began to, teach school in Xenia, O., also pursuing the study of law. He was admitted to the bar, and enjoyed four years' successful practice, but relinquished it to become principal of the classical school in Cumberland, Ind. In 1817 he assumed charge of the classical department of Franklin Institute, Philadelphia, and in 1836, during a visit to Columbus, O., he delivered a lecture upon the "Philosophy of Storms," which, as the result of his earliest researches into meteorology, excited much interest, and earned for him the name of the "Storm King." The lecture, greatly amplified, appeared in book form in 1841. The theory

was substantially as follows: "That every great atmospheric disturbance begins with the uprising of air which has been rarefied by heat. With the dilation of the rising mass, and its consequent fall in temperature, vapor is precipitated in the form of clouds. Because of the liberation of the latent heat the dilation continues until the moisture of the air forming the upward current is practically exhausted. The heavier air flowing in beneath finds a diminished pressure above it, and rushes upward with constantly increasing violence. This, by reason of the great quantity of aqueous vapor precipitated during this atmospheric disturbance gives rise to heavy rains." These views, which were undoubtedly correct so far as physical principles were concerned, were supported by observation, and found many adherents, both at home and abroad. In 1840 Mr. Espy, by invitation, visited England, for the purpose of explaining the theory before the British Association of Science. He was most cordially received, and subsequently went to Paris, where a committee, presided over by the illustrious Arago, had been appointed to welcome him, and where the "storm theory" aroused unbounded enthusiasm. "England had its Newton, France its Cuvier, and America its Espy," remarked Arago, in course of the debates. Upon Mr. Espy's return to America he was employed by the war department at Washington to prosecute his investigations in atmospheric currents and disturbances, the results of which were published in many volumes. He was at the same time connected with the Smithsonian Institute as corresponding member. During this period he established a service of daily bulletins in conjunction with the newspapers and the telegraph companies on the conditions of the weather in different localities, being the germ of the weather bureau, which afterward developed into an important branch of the war department. Mr. Espy believed that rains could be produced artificially by means of fires sustained long enough to bring about a powerful upward current, which would thus initiate the process promulgated by his "storm theory." Appropriations from congress and the Pennsylvania legislature having been granted him, he was at one time enabled to experiment in this direction, but was unsuccessful. Subsequent researches also led to significant modifications in his entire theory of atmospheric changes. Mr. Espy, as a member of the American Philosophical Society, received its Magellanic gold medal in 1836. During his residence at Cumberland, Ind., he was married to Margaret Pollard, of that place. He died at Cincinnati, O., Jan. 24, 1860.

BRADBURY, Albert Williams, lawyer, was born at Calais, Me., in 1840, son of Bion and Alice Williams Bradbury, a lineal descendant of Thomas

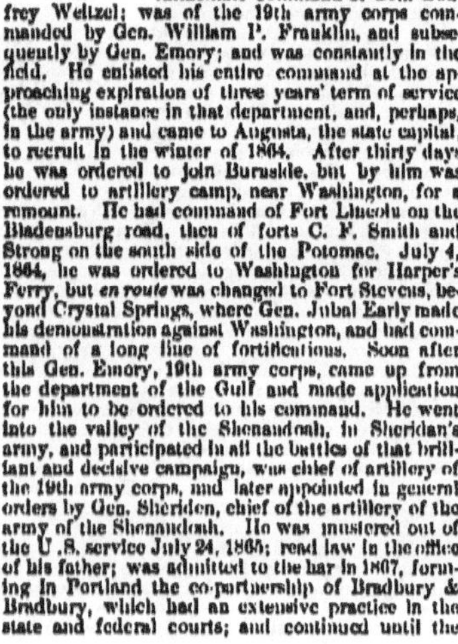

Bradbury, who came from Essex, England, in the early part of the seventeenth century, and great-grandson of Joseph Bradbury, an officer in the revolutionary army. He was educated at the public schools and academy of his native town, and was graduated at Bowdoin College in 1860. In August, 1861, he helped to recruit the 1st Maine battery, mounted artillery; was mustered in as second lieutenant in December; passed through the successive steps of first lieutenant, captain, major of 1st Maine mounted artillery, and brevet lieutenant-colonel of volunteers. He first served in Gen. Butler's department of the Gulf, under the immediate command of Gen. Godfrey Weitzel; was of the 19th army corps commanded by Gen. William P. Franklin, and subsequently by Gen. Emory; and was constantly in the field. He enlisted his entire command at the approaching expiration of three years' term of service (the only instance in that department, and, perhaps, in the army) and came to Augusta, the state capital, to recruit in the winter of 1864. After thirty days he was ordered to join Burnside, but by him was ordered to artillery camp, near Washington, for a remount. He had command of Fort Lincoln on the Bladensburg road, then of forts C. F. Smith and Strong on the south side of the Potomac. July 4, 1864, he was ordered to Washington for Harper's Ferry, but *en route* was changed to Fort Stevens, beyond Crystal Springs, where Gen. Jubal Early made his demonstration against Washington, and had command of a long line of fortifications. Soon after this Gen. Emory, 19th army corps, came up from the department of the Gulf and made application for him to be ordered to his command. He went into the valley of the Shenandoah, in Sheridan's army, and participated in all the battles of that brilliant and decisive campaign, was chief of artillery of the 19th army corps, and later appointed in general orders by Gen. Sheridon, chief of the artillery of the army of the Shenandoah. He was mustered out of the U. S. service July 24, 1865; read law in the office of his father; was admitted to the bar in 1867, forming in Portland the co-partnership of Bradbury & Bradbury, which had an extensive practice in the state and federal courts; and continued until the

death of the senior partner in 1887. Col. Bradbury has been city solicitor of Portland, and is senior member of the firm of Bradbury & M'Quillan. In May, 1894, he was appointed U. S. district attorney for Maine by Pres. Cleveland. Col. Bradbury has always taken an active interest in political affairs, and has been a prominent public speaker on the Democratic side in Maine and other states, besides delivering addresses upon many important occasions in various parts of the country.

WIGGIN, Kate Douglas, author, was born in Philadelphia, Pa., Sept. 28, 1857, the daughter of Robert Noah Smith, a lawyer, and Helen E. Dyer. Her ancestors were people of prominence in the church, in politics, and at the bar in New England. Her father's father was Noah Smith of Maine, who won considerable distinction as a statesman while serving for several terms as a member of the Maine legislature, and as clerk of the house of representatives in Washington. On her mother's side she is descended from Capt. Jonathan Knight, who fought in the first naval battle of the revolution, called the "Lexington of the Seas," and which resulted in the capture of the Margaretta from the British. Another of her ancestors was Mary Dyer, the Quakeress, who was hanged for continuing to preach her doctrines after the authorities had commanded her to stop; and still another, the famous Hannah Dustan. Soon after her birth the parents of Mrs. Wiggin removed to Hollis, Maine, and there, under their careful superintendence, her education was begun. Later, she attended Abbott Academy, Andover, Mass. In 1876 she went to California, and commenced the study of kindergarten methods in Los Angeles, under Emma Marwedel, who had gone there from Washington. After teaching for a year in the Santa Barbara College, she was then called upon to organize the Silver Street Kindergarten in San Francisco, the first free kindergarten west of the Rocky mountains. A society had been formed there by Felix Adler, who was then visiting California, but little was known of the practical methods of such work. Mrs. Sarah B. Cooper soon became interested in the movement begun by Mrs. Wiggin, and the two worked together for several years. Nora Archibald Smith, Mrs. Wiggin's sister, joined them, and in 1880, with her assistance, the California Kindergarten Training School was organized. The plan from the first proved a great success, and from the opening in Silver street, have resulted over sixty other like schools on the Pacific coast. In 1880 she married Samuel Bradley Wiggin, a lawyer of San Francisco, who died in 1889, shortly after their removal to the East. She then gave up teaching, but continued giving weekly talks to the training class, and visited all the kindergartens regularly, playing with the children, singing to them, and telling stories, while unconsciously gathering the rich material which she was afterward to weave into stories of greater influence for a wider public. Her first literary production was a short serial story, called "Half a Dozen Housekeepers," which appeared in the November and December "St. Nicholas" of 1878, but at that time there was no thought of relinquishing her kindergarten work for a literary career, and it was not until several years later that "The Story of Patsy" and "The Birds' Christmas Carol," written to raise money for her school, made their appearance. Their success was instantaneous and widespread. In 1888 Mr. and Mrs. Wiggin removed to New York, where her stories were republished, and met with immediate and extraordinary popularity. They were followed by "A Summer in a Cañon," "Timothy's Quest," and "A Cathedral Courtship." They were subsequently brought out in England, and have been translated in a number of foreign languages, and "Patsy" and "The Birds' Christmas Carol" have been put into raised type for the blind. Besides her literary ability in both prose and verse, she is an accomplished musician, and has composed a number of charming melodies for her favorite poems. Oliver Ditson & Co. published a book of her children's songs and games, called "Kindergarten Chimes," and in 1895 produced several songs. In the same year she was married to George Christopher Riggs. She has a summer home in Hollis, Me., but her winters are spent in New York, where she has been variously called the prima donna of literature, an irresistible wit, and the most accomplished woman engaged in philanthropic work in America.

CLARK, George, land proprietor, born at Hyde Hall, Otsego co., N. Y., in June, 1822, and educated at Flushing, N. Y. At one time he was the owner of more than 60,000 acres in central New York. He was the fourth of his name to possess the magnificent property granted to Lieut.-Gov. Clark of the province of New York by Queen Anne in 1740, and he would have been a very wealthy man but for his mania for buying and holding land. What with paying interest on mortgages and contending with his creditors in every court, Mr. Clark's affairs became hopelessly involved, and in 1887 he was forced to make an assignment. It was said to be the largest assignment of general property ever made in the state. He was a man of fine intellect, commanding physique, and a charming conversationalist, but he had a hobby of wearing the dingiest outer garments that he could procure. He wore for two years, it is said, a suit made of an old shawl belonging to his wife, and clung to the same high white hat for nearly six years. He was, however, particular about his linen, which was of the finest quality made. He spent much of his time at the Astor House in New York, where his long linen duster was a familiar sight. He allowed the fine old manor house, Hyde Hall, to go to partial decay, and at one time stored grain and housed cattle there, but his son, George Hyde Clark, lately renovated one wing of the hall, and now lives there. He died July 8, 1889, and was buried in the cemetery of Christ Church, Cooperstown, near the grave of James Fenimore Cooper, who was connected with him by marriage.

DANA, Edward Salisbury, mineralogist, was born at New Haven, Conn., Nov. 16, 1849, eldest son of James Dwight Dana and Henrietta Silliman (daughter of Prof. Benjamin Silliman). He was educated at New Haven, being graduated at Yale College in 1870; and spent the two following years in postgraduate study. In 1872 he crossed over to Europe, and pursued his studies for another two years at the universities of Heidelberg and Vienna. In 1874 he commenced the work of instruction as tutor of mathematics in Yale College; and it was not long before he was made assistant-professor, and finally professor of physics. At present (1895) he also holds the position of curator of the mineral cabinet, as well as that of trustee of the Peabody Museum. Since 1875 he has been an editor of the "American Journal of Science," issued at New Haven. He was elected a member of the National Academy of Sciences in 1884. He is author of the "Text-Book of Mineralogy" (1877); of the second and third appendixes to the fifth edition of the "System of Mineralogy" (1875 to 1882); of the "Text-Book of Mechanics" (1881); of the sixth edition of "Dana's System of Mineralogy" (1892),

and of an elementary work entitled "Minerals, and How to Study Them" (1895). He is also the author of numerous papers on mineralogy and crystallography, published for the most part in the "American Journal of Science."

BOYER, Henry Kline, legislator, was born at Evansburg, Montgomery co., Pa., Feb. 19, 1850, son of Ephraim Dull Boyer, a blacksmith by trade, and Rebecca (Kline) Boyer. Both parents came of old German families who resided in Montgomery and Berks counties for over a century and a half, though the Boyers were of French Huguenot origin, becoming Germanized through their settling in the Palatinate after the revocation of the edict of Nantes. Mr. Boyer obtained a rudimentary education in the public schools of his native place, and subsequently took a course at Freeland Seminary, now Ursinus College, Montgomery county, of which institution he is now one of the board of directors. At the age of sixteen he began teaching, and at eighteen became principal of the Kaighn's Point Grammar School, Camden, N. J., where he remained until 1871, when he was registered as a student-at-law in the office of the late Ex-Atty.-Gen. B. H. Brewster. He was admitted to practice at the Philadelphia bar in 1873, and practiced with success in the civil courts. In 1882 he was elected as a Republican to the state legislature, securing a re-election in 1884, and again in 1886, and was chosen speaker in the session of 1887. After having been re-elected again in 1888, he became the choice of Republicans and Democrats alike for the speakership in the session of 1889, the first time in the history of the state that such a compliment had been paid. Thus before he had reached the age of forty he had been chosen to preside over the house of representatives for two successive sessions. His labors met with approval on all sides. In the formation of standing committees and the assignment of members to service on them, he exhibited great knowledge of human nature and accuracy of judgment, so much as to be credited with having

never made a mistake in selecting a member for the position which he was best qualified to fill. His rulings in the chair were markedly impartial and fair, and were rarely questioned. At the state convention of 1889 he was unanimously nominated for the office of state treasurer, and was elected by a majority of close upon 61,000. In 1892 he was again sent to the legislature, and in the following session was chairman of the committee on ways and means. Among the measures which Mr. Boyer was largely instrumental in passing were the Bullit bill for the better government of Philadelphia; the board of health bill; the medical examiners' bill, and the bill regulating fraternal societies. In 1885 he assisted in framing the general revenue act, and also offered a successful amendment, regulating the taxation of corporation bonds. This section of the bill was afterwards pronounced unconstitutional by Judge Simonton of the Dauphin county court, but his decision was reversed by the state supreme court, in which course the latter was upheld by the U. S. supreme court. Mr. Boyer was the framer, in 1891, of a general revenue bill, which was passed without the aid of a conference committee, and is generally known as the "Boyer bill." Mr. Boyer has devoted much time to the study of history and literature, and in 1887 delivered the annual address before the literary societies of Ursinus College, which conferred upon him the honorary degree of A.M.

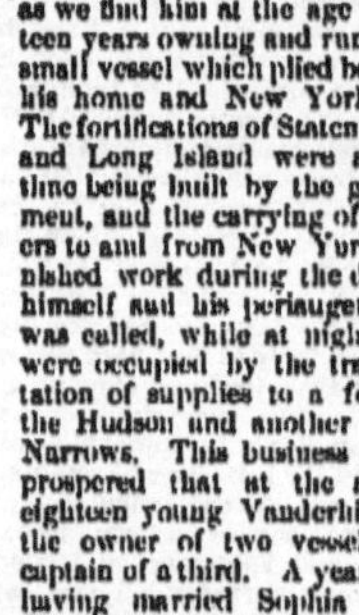

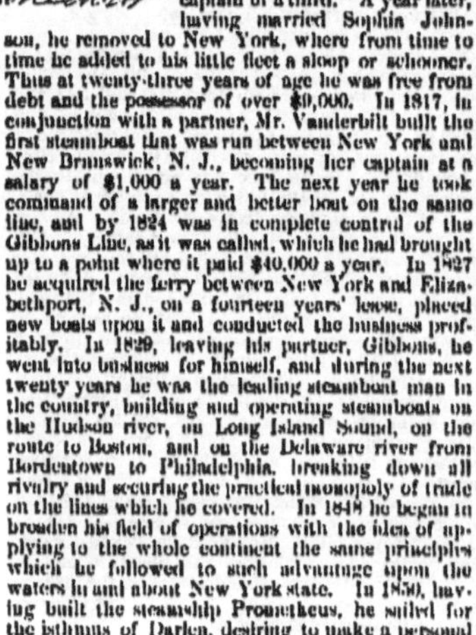

VANDERBILT, Cornelius, financier, was born at Port Richmond, Staten Island, Richmond co., N. Y., May 27, 1794. He was of Dutch ancestry, the first known representative of the family being Jan Aertsen Van der Bylt. The name Cornelius originated in that of the second wife of Jan Van der Bylt, Dierber Cornelius. The family name Van der Bilt or Bylt means simply "of the hill," Jan Vanderbilt signifying thus "John of the hill." Cornelius was certainly influenced by his surroundings, as we find him at the age of sixteen years owning and running a small vessel which plied between his home and New York city. The fortifications of Staten Island and Long Island were at that time being built by the government, and the carrying of laborers to and from New York furnished work during the day for himself and his periauger, as it was called, while at night they were occupied by the transportation of supplies to a fort up the Hudson and another at the Narrows. This business so far prospered that at the age of eighteen young Vanderbilt was the owner of two vessels and captain of a third. A year later, having married Sophia Johnson, he removed to New York, where from time to time he added to his little fleet a sloop or schooner. Thus at twenty-three years of age he was free from debt and the possessor of over $9,000. In 1817, in conjunction with a partner, Mr. Vanderbilt built the first steamboat that was run between New York and New Brunswick, N. J., becoming her captain at a salary of $1,000 a year. The next year he took command of a larger and better boat on the same line, and by 1824 was in complete control of the Gibbons Line, as it was called, which he had brought up to a point where it paid $40,000 a year. In 1827 he acquired the ferry between New York and Elizabethport, N. J., on a fourteen years' lease, placed new boats upon it and conducted the business profitably. In 1829, leaving his partner, Gibbons, he went into business for himself, and during the next twenty years he was the leading steamboat man in the country, building and operating steamboats on the Hudson river, on Long Island Sound, on the route to Boston, and on the Delaware river from Bordentown to Philadelphia, breaking down all rivalry and securing the practical monopoly of trade on the lines which he covered. In 1848 he began to broaden his field of operations with the idea of applying to the whole continent the same principles which he followed to such advantage upon the waters in and about New York state. In 1850, having built the steamship Prometheus, he sailed for the isthmus of Darien, desiring to make a personal investigation of the prospects of the American Atlantic and Pacific Ship Canal Co., in which he had purchased a controlling interest. This company projected a canal across the isthmus. Commodore Vanderbilt, as he had by this time come to be called, planned, as a result of this visit, a transit route from Greytown on the Atlantic coast to San Juan del Sud on the Pacific, which had the advantage over the old transit from Chagres to Panama, of saving 700 miles between New York city and San Francisco. In 1851 he placed three steamers on the Atlantic side and four on the Pacific side, to accommodate the enormous traffic which the discovery of gold in California had occasioned. The following year three more vessels were added to his fleet and a branch line established from New Orleans to Greytown. In this undertaking an attempt was made to send a side-wheel steamboat, called the Director, over the rapids in the San Juan river to Lake Nicaragua; by tremendous exertions the steamer was finally brought to the lake and the through line established. An enormous rush of passenger traffic followed, and the means of transportation were increased. Two steamers, the Clayton and Bulwer, were placed on the river, and a large one, the Central America, on the lake. On the Atlantic side were put the Prometheus, the Webster, the Star of the West, and the Northern Light, and on the Pacific side three others, a boat being started from New York every fortnight. In 1853 Commodore Vanderbilt sold out his Nicaragua route and the transit line, from which he had by this time netted over $1,000,000. Building the renowned steam yacht, the North Star, of 2,000 tons, he made a trip to Europe with his entire family: Phoebe Jane, wife of James M. Cross; Ethelinda, wife of D. B. Allen; William H. Vanderbilt; Emily, wife of W. K. Thorn; Eliza, wife of Geo. A. Osgood; Sophia, wife of Daniel Torrance; Maria, wife of Horace F. Clark; Frances, who died unmarried at the age of forty; Maria Alecia, wife of N. La Bau; Catharine, wife of Smith Barker, Jr.; and George Washington Vanderbilt. The Nicaragua Transit Co. to which the Commodore had sold a controlling interest in his shore route, grew rich and refused to fulfill their contract. He could have prosecuted them, but as such a prosecution would have been an international affair, involving much time and expense, he announced to them that he would not take legal measures against them, but would ruin them. He kept his word. He put on another fleet of steamers, and in two years the opposition line was bankrupt. He continued in the shipping business nine years longer, at the end of which the fortune he had accumulated thereby amounted to not less than $10,000,000. In 1856 he received a large subsidy for withdrawing his California line, but he kept up some time longer a trans-oceanic line from New York to Havre, which he had established when British ships were withdrawn during the Crimean war. In 1861 he presented the magnificent steamer Vanderbilt, which had cost

him $800,000, to the U. S. government to be used in the defence of the Union, for which patriotic generosity the thanks of congress were accorded him in joint resolution passed Jan. 28, 1864. For twenty years before this time Commodore Vanderbilt had been more or less interested in railroad matters, and it was the better promise of these enterprises which finally induced him to withdraw his capital and management from steamship navigation. In 1844 he had become interested in the New York and New Haven Railroad, the stock of which he continued to purchase heavily thereafter. These purchases having enlightened him as to the prospect of the railroad business in the vicinity of New York, he acquired stock in the Harlem Road, of which he became president in 1857. About this time the Hudson River Railroad, which had never paid a dividend, was quoted at thirty-three. In 1864 Vanderbilt secured control of that also, and working it in connection with the Harlem, brought it to a position where it paid an enormous profit. The same year he became a shareholder in the New York Central by investing therein $500,000, and after an inspection of the road, devoted all his resources to the purchase of Central stock until he, with other capitalists whom he had interested in the scheme, controlled the road. This was the beginning of the now celebrated Vanderbilt system, the almost immediate result being a combination including the three roads mentioned. Mr. Vanderbilt next turned his attention to the Lake Shore and Michigan Southern Railroad, of which he eventually became controller and chief owner, thus securing a direct connection between New York and Chicago and an entrance to the teeming trade of the great West. From this time he gave his personal

attention to his railroad properties, which in their consolidation had become the most magnificent system in the world, and in combination with the government of the city of New York, which paid half of the cost, he built what was known as the Fourth Avenue Improvement, a system of viaduct and tunneled approaches to the Grand Central Depot in Forty-second street. The completion of the life work of Commodore Vanderbilt may be said to have been the re-organization and consolidation of his railroad interests between New York and Chicago in his seventy-fourth year. His first wife, Phoebe Hand, dying in 1868, he married in the fall of 1869, Frances Crawford, a Mobile belle, who, during the remainder of his life, was a companion, adviser, and friend as well as a dearly loved wife. It was mainly through her influence that the principal benefaction of his life was accomplished, the founding of the Vanderbilt University at Nashville, Tenn., although he had previously given $50,000 to the Rev. Charles F. Deems of New York, to purchase the Church of the

VI.—14

Strangers in that city. The Vanderbilt University cost him $1,000,000, its construction being mainly directed by Bishop McTyeire, who was the religious adviser of Frances Vanderbilt, and who became its first president. On May 10, 1876, Commodore Vanderbilt was taken seriously ill. He rallied from the first attack, but there was a relapse in August, and throughout the year his condition was watched with the closest solicitude, the best obtainable medical skill being devoted to the effort of restoring him to health. He continued to fail, however, through the fall and winter. On the afternoon of Jan. 3, 1877, he was so visibly sinking that his children, relatives, and friends were called about his bedside, and the following morning he died. By his will his whole fortune, which was estimated at $100,000,000, was given to his eldest son, William Henry, with the exception of a bequest of $11,000,000 to the latter's four sons, and $4,000,000 to his own daughters. He died Jan. 4, 1877.

VANDERBILT, William Henry, financier, was born at New Brunswick, N. J., May 8, 1821, the first son of Commodore Vanderbilt, who was at that time engaged in steamboat operations in the waters of New York and vicinity. William was given, in addition to a common school education, such advantages as were then offered by the old Columbia College Grammar School, and at the age of eighteen years began to take care of himself by becoming a clerk in the house of Drew, Robinson & Co., Wall Street bankers. Speedily mastering the details of the business in which he was employed, he was soon recognized by his employers as a young man of more than ordinary promise, and was rapidly promoted. He supported himself on his salary, and

married, at the end of two years of office labor, Louise, daughter of Rev. Samuel Kissam, pastor of a Dutch Reformed church in the environs of the city of Albany. His employers contemplated taking him into partnership, but close confinement so far broke his health that it became necessary for him to give up in-door work. As the son had a natural taste for farming, his father purchased for him a small farm at New Dorp, S. I., where in 1842 he began the cultivation of seventy acres of unimproved land. In a very short time his farm was returning him a good income. He needed capital, however, and, curiously enough, on application to his father, who was already a millionaire, for a loan of $5,000, he was refused. The request was even made by a friend, as he was afraid to apply himself. It seems that up to this time the Commodore had not gained sufficient confidence in his son to trust him where business was concerned. William obtained elsewhere a loan of $6,000 by mortgaging his farm, and on being called to account for this action by the Commodore, told the simple truth, declaring at the same time that he was in a position to meet his engagement with his creditor. The result was that the Commodore sent him a check for $6,000 with orders to pay off the mortgage; and from this time on the former showed a different valuation of his son's character and abilities. The Staten Island Railroad having been nearly wrecked by bad management, it was found necessary to place it in the hands of a receiver, a position to which William H. Vanderbilt was appointed, thus beginning his career as a railroad manager. His success with this first enterprise was unqualified; in two years he paid off all the claims against the company, connected the road with New York by an independent line of ferry boats, and placed it upon a secure and permanent financial basis. The stockholders made him president and he continued to manage the affairs of the road with success for some time. He became the mainstay of his father in the latter's old age; was elected vice-president of the New York and Harlem Railroad Company in 1864, and the following year vice-president of the Hudson River Railroad Company, thus becoming the executive officer and confidant of the Commodore, whose comprehensive and far-reaching plans he carried out with entire success. William H. Vanderbilt was past forty years old before his father began to comprehend that in him he had not only one fully competent to carry out his own schemes, but one who in succeeding him would be certain to add honor to his name and fame. Immediately after the death of Commodore Vanderbilt, William Henry was elected president of the New York Central and Hudson River Railroad Company, with the minutest workings of which he was so thoroughly familiar that he assumed its control understandingly. By 1881 the business of the road had so increased that it required 15,000 men, 23,000 freight cars, 600 passenger cars, and 638 engines, while at some points as many as sixty trains passed each other daily. The management of the New York Central was combined in the hands of Mr. Vanderbilt with that of the Lake Shore and Michigan Southern and the Michigan Central, of both of which he was the president. He was also at one time in control of the Western Union Telegraph Company. To the judicious management of the vast interests in his charge, Mr. Vanderbilt applied the same watchful attention and economy with which he had successfully carried on his farm and brought out of insolvency the little Staten Island Railroad. By conciliation and compromise he averted the disastrous consequences which usually succeed a protracted war of rates, while at the same time averting a threatened strike of the laborers on his roads. Among his special achievements in extending the operations and the value of the Vanderbilt system were the acquisition of the Canada Southern and Michigan Central; the securing control of the Chicago and Northwestern, comprising with its

tributaries 4,000 miles of tracks; and the making connection with St. Louis by means of the Cleveland, Columbus, Cincinnati, and Indianapolis Railroad. In 1879, with the design of interesting other capitalists in the New York Central, and for the purpose of putting his own property into a shape in which it could be more readily handled. Mr. Vanderbilt sold 250,000 shares of Central stock to an English and American syndicate for $30,000,000, which he invested in U. S. government bonds, of which a year later he held $53,000,000. In 1880 he also sold out his interest in the Western Union Telegraph Co.,

resigned the office of president of the different roads in the Vanderbilt system, May 4, 1883, and sailed for Europe. About this time the "Nickel Plate" road was added to the Lake Shore system, while the West Shore was forced into bankruptcy and afterward acquired by the New York Central. Mr. Vanderbilt built on Fifth avenue a fine mansion for himself and four beautiful structures for his daughters. He inherited a great love of horses from his father and was at one time the owner of Maud S., the celebrated trotter. He added $200,000 to the endowment of Vanderbilt University, besides giving $100,000 to its theological school and $10,000 to its library. In 1884 he gave $500,000 for land and for the erection of new buildings for the College of Physicians and Surgeons in New York city. The train men and laborers of the New York Central Railroad kept out of the great railroad strike of 1877, and at its close Mr. Vanderbilt distributed $100,000 among them for their fidelity to their duty. He gave $50,000 to the Church of St. Bartholomew, and procured at an expense of $103,000 the removal of the Egyptian Obelisk presented by the Khedive, thereby making possible its erection in Central Park, New York city. Two days before the failure of Grant & Ward, Grant borrowed from Mr. Vanderbilt, on an exchanged check, $150,000. The check went to protest, whereupon Gen. Grant offered to Mr. Vanderbilt, as security for the loan, all his swords, medals, works of art, and other gifts presented to him by foreign governments, in addition to deeds of certain real estate. After making many efforts to restore the property, all of which were declined by the Grant family, Mr. Vanderbilt's final proposition was accepted, that the presents should be transferred to Mrs. Grant during her life and at her death should be placed in the archives of the national government at Washington. By his will Mr. Vanderbilt left $10,000,000 to each of his eight children, one-half of each bequest to be held in trust. To his eldest son, Cornelius, he gave $2,000,000 in addition, and $1,000,000 to Cornelius's eldest son. The residuary estate was divided in equal parts between his two sons, Cornelius and William Kissam, subject to the payment of an annuity of $200,000 to the widow. His bequests for benevolent purposes amounted to $1,000,000, including gifts to the Vanderbilt University, the Metropolitan Museum of Art, the Young Men's Christian Association, missions of the Protestant Episcopal Church and St. Luke's Hospital. The death of William H. Vanderbilt occurred from apoplexy at his residence in Fifth avenue, its manner being at once tragic and affecting. In the midst of an interview with Robert Garrett, president of the Baltimore and Ohio Railroad, he suddenly fell forward on the floor unconscious. In five minutes he was dead. For two years he had not been in good health and had been under the care of his physician, but the death was totally unexpected and the news of it was a shock to the whole country. Mr. Vanderbilt was a lover of art, his collection of paintings being valued at over $1,000,000. The palace which he erected on the corner of Fifth avenue and Fifty-first street in New York city cost between $2,000,000 and $3,000,000, the double bronze doors which gave entrance to it alone being valued at $25,000. He was a vestryman of St. Bartholomew's Church for the last twenty years of his life, domestic in his tastes and habits and very fond of his home and family, with whom he spent much of his time. The date of his death was Dec. 8, 1885; his remains were buried in the massive family mausoleum at New Dorp, S. I.

VANDERBILT, Jacob Hand, steamboat manager, was born on the eastern shore of Staten Island, N. Y., Sept. 2, 1807, son of Cornelius and Phoebe (Hand) Vanderbilt. The common ancestor of the family, Jan Aertsen Van der Bylt, arrived in America about 1650, and took up his residence near Flatbush, L. I. His grandson, Jacob Van der Bilt, purchased from his father, of the same name, a farm on Staten Island and removed there with his wife, Eleanor, in 1718. He was the founder of the Staten Island branch of the Vanderbilt family. A few years before the birth of Jacob Hand, his father removed from the north to the east shore of the island and located in a settlement afterward known as Stapleton, where he owned a farm of forty acres of land. He operated one of the two ferry boats that were the means of communication with New York city, the boats being undecked periaugers with two long sails, which, if favored with a brisk breeze, made the direct route across the harbor to Whitehall slip, a distance of six miles, or if confronted by a calm or unfavorable winds would make their way by oars and poles over the Jersey shallows. The rival boat of the time was owned by his near neighbor Van Duzer. The mother of young Jacob was a woman of ability, force of character, and piety. She actively co-operated with her husband in all his enterprises, and to the qualities which she transmitted to her sons they were largely indebted for the prominence and influence which they subsequently attained. They received a fair common-school education, and at an early age began to "follow the water." At the age of eighteen, Jacob had the command of a steamboat, and from that time Capt. Vanderbilt was a prominent factor in the conduct of steamboat lines on the Hudson river and on Long Island Sound and the Connecticut river. In 1834 he was married to Euphremia Maria Banta, a descendent of Gen. Israel Putnam. She was a leader in society, beloved by the poor, and a woman of extraordinary personal and mental charms. She died in 1877. Capt. Vanderbilt lived in a beautiful home known as "Clove Hill," on the heights overlooking New York harbor and city. From 1864 to 1884 he was president of the Staten Island East Shore Railroad and Ferry. He was a man of action, of sturdy integrity, modest disposition, yet great force of character; kind of heart although brusque in speech, and always a comforter of the desponding. He was a great lover of fast horses, and was well known on the road both on Staten Island and in upper New York, where he was as prominent a figure as his brother, the commodore; Robert Bonner; or his nephew, William Henry Vanderbilt. Capt. Vanderbilt died at his home in Staten Island, March 19, 1893.

VANDERBILT, Cornelius, financier, was born at New Dorp, Staten Island, Richmond co., N. Y., Nov. 27, 1843, the eldest son of William Henry Vanderbilt. At the time of Cornelius's birth his father was engaged in farming at New Dorp, and it was there that the first years of the boy's life were passed. He received an excellent academic education and was, from his earliest years, a favorite with his grandfather, Commodore Vanderbilt, who watched his progress with great interest. The boy early gave indications of a talent for business, and, partly through the recommendation of his grandfather, was placed as a clerk in the Shoe and Leather Bank of New York, where he was made acquainted with the first principles of finance and the practical work of banking. The heads of the bank soon discovered that young Cornelius possessed faculties which, if properly encouraged and directed, could be made of great value to the institution. He was noticeably accurate and faithful in his work, industrious and indefatigable in the discharge of duty, close in attendance, and unflagging in zeal in the interest of the bank. Gradually, therefore, he was advanced and his salary increased, until his grandfather had him transferred to the private banking house of Kissam Brothers, in order that he might become acquainted with the brokerage business and the stock market, and learn features of the manipulation of money which he could not in an ordinary bank of deposit and discount. It was about this time that Cornelius first showed indications of those religious tendencies which have directed and governed his experience. Joining the Episcopal church, he at once showed himself to be earnest and constant in his desire to mould his life on true Christian principles. Meanwhile, he gained from his father the patience and self-discipline which had preserved the latter from irritation and recklessness under the disappointments which he must have felt at being comparatively late in life, misunderstood, or at least not fully appreciated, by the old Commodore. The will of the latter showed that the conduct and career of his young grandson, up to that period, had met with his approval. But long before this, Cornelius, having been appointed at the age of twenty-two years to a position in the office of the Harlem Railroad, began his practical study of railroad management and finance. In 1867 he became treasurer of the company, an office which he continued to fill for ten years. In 1877, after the death of Commodore Vanderbilt, who was succeeded by his son, William Henry, as president of the New York Central Railroad, Cornelius was made first vice-president, with entire control of the finances of the road, and his brother, William Kissam, second vice-president, in control of the traffic. Being thus brought into intimate relations with the heads of other departments of the Vanderbilt system, Cornelius became known for the special clearness of his financial knowledge, and for a quickness of perception which made any kind of financial statement, no matter how complicated, a simple affair for him to investigate or dissect. His remarkable memory enabled him to answer promptly and accurately any question which might be asked concerning the financial condition of the road or any other matter which came within his purview. Through his charge of the financial relations he also came in contact with the most prominent financiers, bankers, and railroad men of the country, who speedily recognized that he was a shrewd, able and far-seeing representative of his grandfather and father, and fully competent to follow them in the administration of their enormous financial interests. In May, 1883, William H. Vanderbilt retired from the presidency of the Vanderbilt roads, and Cornelius and his brother, William Kissam, resigned their vice-presidencies. Cornelius Vanderbilt became chairman of the board of directors of the New York Central and Hudson River Co. and of the Michigan Central, while William Kissam assumed the same position in the Lake Shore and Nickel Plate. James H. Rutter (q. v.) was the first president of the New York Central under the new arrangement, and

at his death was succeeded by Chauncey M. Depew
(*q. v.*) who, prior to this period, had held the position
of second vice-president and general counsel. The
experience of Cornelius Vanderbilt, up to this time,
had been very comprehensive; he had been first
vice-president and financial manager of the New
York Central, treasurer and vice-president of the
Michigan Central and Canada Southern, chairman
of the board of directors of the New York Central,
chairman of the board of directors of the Michigan
Central, president of the Canada Southern, and
treasurer and vice-president of the New York and
Harlem Railroads. In 1886 he was made president
of this last road, a position which he has continued
to hold ever since. In spite of the fact that his official connection with railroads is direct, and involves
constant daily labor of the most engrossing character, he is a director or trustee of as many public organizations, societies, and institutions perhaps as any
one man in New York. With religious organizations, his deep, serious, and conscientious nature has
brought him into special relations of prominence,
while as a benefactor in religious and charitable
works, his generosity has been equaled only by the
modesty of his method of giving. The most prominent
example of his munificence in this connection was his
gift of $100,000 toward the erection of a Protestant
Episcopal cathedral in New York city. He is a member of most of the clubs of New York, including the
Metropolitan, the New York Yacht Club, the Players' Club, the Union, the Knickerbocker, the Century, the Union League, the Country, and Tuxedo;
and at Newport, where he has a model farm, he interests himself greatly in local affairs, particularly

in the Casino, the Reading-room and the Improvement Society. He is a lover of art, and a good judge
of paintings. His elegant residence on Fifth avenue
possesses a well-chosen collection of the works of the
best modern painters, and he presented the Metropolitan Museum of Art with a valuable collection of
drawings by the old masters, as also with Rosa Bon-
heur's great painting of "The Horse Fair." But a
most important single benefaction—at once a remarkable and original instance of generosity and
consideration—was his gift to the employees of the
New York Central and Hudson River Railroad and
its leased and affiliated lines, of the club house at the
corner of Madison avenue and Forty-fifth street,
New York. This structure contains reading-rooms,
game rooms, a hall for general meetings, a gymna-

sium, bowling alleys, plunge bath, sleeping apartments, and the finest library owned by any club in
New York. The significance and value of this gift
have been thoroughly understood and appreciated
by the employees of the road for whose benefit it
was designed and has since been conducted. Mr.
Vanderbilt married in February, 1867, Alice
Gwynne, daughter of a distinguished Cincinnati
lawyer. They have had four sons and three daughters. The two eldest boys, William Henry and Cornelius, Jr., while in Cutler's Preparatory School,
New York city, edited and published a boy's newspaper, called "The Comet." For this enterprise a
large room at the top of their father's house was
supplied with cases and press and all the other material of a printing office, and placed at their disposal.
William died while a junior at Yale University.

VANDERBILT, William Kissam, second son
of William Henry and Maria Louisa Kissam Vanderbilt, was born Dec. 12, 1849, at Staten Island, N. Y.
As a boy he was thoroughly grounded in the usual
academic studies, and was then sent by his father to
Geneva, Switzerland, where he remained several years
completing his education,
and leading the ordinary life
of a student. On his return
to New York he was placed
in the office of Mr. C. C.
Clarke, Treasurer of the
Hudson River Railroad, at a
small salary; and his training for the vocation of a railroad manager was from that
time carried on thoroughly
and comprehensively. He
learned the routine work of a
bookkeeper; and for several
years progressed through
the various clerical grades
toward a mastery of the complicated and responsible duties of his prospective life.
He soon began to display
the qualities which had char-

acterized his father and grandfather; sharp per-
ceptive faculties, quickness of decision, excellent
judgment, and remarkable intuition and understanding of human nature. At the same time he
developed into a man of the world, interested in
social life, and with a definite leaning toward politics, becoming and remaining, from principle, an
adherent of the policy of the Democratic party. He
exhibited the possession of many of the characteristics which go to make one successful in a political
career, in which he would have doubtless risen to
eminence had he chosen to follow it. As he grew
to full manhood, he was placed according to the
policy of the Vanderbilts, in positions of trust and responsibility in connection with the great Vanderbilt
railroad system; thus, from 1877 to 1883 he was
second vice-president of the New York Central and
Hudson River Railroad; from 1882 to this writing,
president of the New York, Chicago, and St. Louis
Railroad; and from 1883 chairman of the board of
directors of the Lake Shore and Michigan Southern
Railway, of which he is the recognized head. Mr.
Vanderbilt has always been interested in the turf
and in yachting. Prominent in the Coney Island
Jockey Club when in this country, he has been
seen on the race-track on the occasion of all the
important events; while it is not improbable that he
will eventually possess a racing stable of his own.
Besides having built the Alva, which was sunk, and
the Valiant, steam yachts, he was a member of the
Colonia and Defender syndicates, and took a deep
interest in the matches for the America's Cup. His

handsome stone residence at Fifth avenue and Fifty-second street, New York, built by R. M. Hunt, and the "Marble House," at Newport, are evidences of his taste in architecture. Meanwhile, he has been generous in charity, and united with his brothers in founding the Vanderbilt Clinic, which cost more than half a million dollars. He was one of the or-

ganizers of the Metropolitan Club, and also a member of the Union and other leading clubs of New York. He has traveled extensively, making long voyages on his yachts, and is well known in the capitals of Europe. He married Alva Smith of Mobile, Ala., and has three children, the eldest a daughter, Consuelo; William Kissam, Jr.; and Harold.

VANDERBILT, Frederick William, the third son of the late William Henry Vanderbilt, was born about 1855. He early evinced a strong inclination for study and literature, and after going through the usual course of study, entered Yale, where he was graduated from the Sheffield Scientific School in 1878. With this solid foundation of learning he applied himself to the acquisition of a thorough business education. This he obtained in the offices of his father's railroad system, than which no better school for practical training could be found anywhere. Frederick Vanderbilt went through every department in the railroad service, mastering the general details of the whole business; and the heads of departments, in which he worked in a comparatively humble capacity, speak of his studious application and willingness to submit to the rules and regulations of the office in the very highest terms. He is extremely modest and unassuming in his demeanor and style of living. He is a type of the intelligent, well-informed, wealthy American gentleman. He is in no sense a club man, preferring domestic comforts above everything else, and spending most of his time at home, absorbed in his books and family. His house is at the corner of Fifth avenue and Fortieth street, the gift of his father, who in turn received it from the Commodore. For a long time it was regarded as the most magnificent residence in the city of New York. Mr. Vanderbilt does not devote himself much to business affairs. At the present time he owns one of the finest steam yachts in the world, the Conqueror, built in 1889 by Russell & Co., of Port Glasgow. The yacht is 203 feet in length, by 24 feet 7 inches beam, and draws 13 feet of water. Mr. Frederick Vanderbilt has a

home at Newport, known as "Rough Point," and an estate of 600 acres at Hyde Park, on the Hudson.

VANDERBILT, George Washington, philanthropist, was born in New Dorp, Staten Island, N. Y., Nov. 14, 1862, youngest son of William Henry and Maria Louise (Kissam) Vanderbilt. He was educated by a private tutor, and at the best schools. His tastes did not end him in the financial paths so successfully followed by his grandfather, father, and brothers, but rather led him to study and literature. Having inherited an ample fortune, he neither sought to squander his money nor to hoard it. He traveled extensively, and combined with the pleasures of travel the advantages it gave him for study, and thus accumulated both information and experience. He gave to New York city the Thirteenth St. Branch of the Free Circulating Library, which he founded, provided with a suitable building and appointments, on Jackson Square. When it was decided to remove the New York College for the Training of Teachers from its crowded quarters on University Place, Mr. Vanderbilt, one of its trustees, presented to the college an available and valuable site on Morningside Heights, adjoining the site selected for Columbia College. He presented to the American Fine Arts Society of New York the room in their building known as the Vanderbilt Gallery. He is a member of the Century Association, of the Metropolitan, City, Lawyers', Racquet, New York Yacht, New York Athletic, Players', and Grolier Clubs, and of the Society of the Sons of the American Revolution. In 1885 he became interested in the great beauty of the natural scenery of the mountain regions of western North Carolina, and especially that in the vicinity of Asheville, on the French Broad river, and he purchased 100,000 acres of mountain land and laid it out in a vast park, erecting a stately mansion, with stables, and laid out the grounds on a scale of magnificence not equaled in America. This estate he stocked with fine-blooded cattle, horses, and sheep, and now spends much of his time in personally superintending its

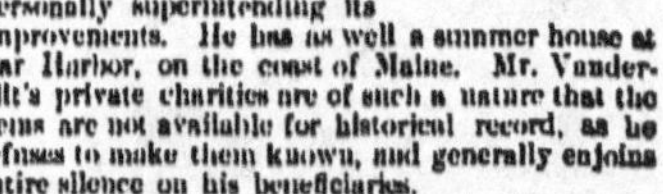

improvements. He has as well a summer house at Bar Harbor, on the coast of Maine. Mr. Vanderbilt's private charities are of such a nature that the items are not available for historical record, as he refuses to make them known, and generally enjoins entire silence on his beneficiaries.

VANDERBILT, Aaron, manufacturer, was born at Tomkinsville, Staten Island, N. Y., Jan. 29, 1844. He comes of another branch of Commodore Vanderbilt's family. His great-grandfather, John Vanderbilt, a resident of Staten Island, was a member of the legislature in De Witt Clinton's time. He had a son, Aaron, who married a Mary Simonson, whose ancestry were among the first settlers of Staten Island. From this union came Isaac Simonson Vanderbilt, who married a lady named Sarah Seguine, descended from a family of French Huguenots, who first settled and named that part of Staten Island known as Seguine's Point. Their son, Aaron, is the subject of the present notice. After leaving school he commenced his business career as a clerk in the office of a shipping and commission house in 1859, and subsequently served for some time in the merchant marine. He arrived from a voyage to the Mediterranean shortly after the breaking out of the civil war, and was appointed in the U. S. navy as a master's mate, and ordered to the U. S. sloop-of-war Savannah for instruction and drill; thence to the gunboat Vicksburg, doing duty as a guardship to the port of New York, and blockading the entrance of Cape Fear river, N. C. He took part in various engagements, and in the defence of Annapolis, Md.; and preparatory to the attack on the forts at the mouth of Cape Fear river, reconnoitered thirty miles of the coast and fortifications north and south of Cape Fear, and made drawings of the plan of the defences. He was then ordered to duty on the staff of Rear-Adm. David Dixon Porter, commanding the North Atlantic squadron, with the Malvern for his flagship, and participated in the battles of Fort Fisher in 1864 and 1865. Mr. Vanderbilt was present at the engagements with Forts Anderson, Strong, and Lee, and at the taking of Wilmington, N. C.; was then ordered to the Appomattox and James rivers, taking part in the siege of Petersburg and Richmond; was promoted to ensign after the second battle of Fort Fisher, and, after the capture of Wilmington, performed the duty of fleet signal officer during the command of Adm. Porter; and was one of the escort to President Lincoln on his entrance into Richmond at the fall of that city. After the close of the war he applied for and received an honorable discharge, and entered mercantile life again as a partner in the firm of James Moore & Co., built the Alligator Steam Saw Mills on the St. John's river, Fla., and established a line of sailing packets between New York and Jacksonville; besides being connected with a maritime firm running lines of sailing vessels to the Mediterranean. In 1877 he was appointed general superintendent of the Ward line of steamships, subsequently the New York and Cuba Mail Steamship Co., of which he was for many years a member of the board of directors. Mr. Vanderbilt has taken a very active part in the national work for the restoration of the merchant marine of the United States, and was one of the founders and organizers of the American Shipping and Industrial League in 1886, serving on the board of officers as its national treasurer, and representing it and the American shipping interests at Washington during the fiftieth and fifty-first congresses. His efforts in securing the passage of the U. S. Mail Subvention act and other legislation contributing to the American merchant marine in foreign trade, has been highly commended. To Mr. Vanderbilt is mainly due the credit of the establishment of the U. S. naval reserve as an auxiliary to the navy, as the national guard is to the army. As chairman of the committee on naval reserve of the board of trade of New York, he opened correspondence with the governors and adjutant-generals of the various states, and with the secretary of the navy, in respect to the proposed new branch of the service. A number of states passed acts creating state naval militia, and he secured the passage of a similar act by the state of New York in the spring of 1889, and induced the national government to grant an annual appropriation contributing to the support of the imitations, and providing ships of war for their instruction. He was also largely instrumental in securing the passage of the U. S. Mail Subvention act, providing for auxiliary cruisers in the event of war, as well as the introduction of a bill in the fifty-third congress to complete the work providing the enrollment of the sea-going officers and men of the merchant marine into the reserve, on ap-

plication and qualification. Mr. Vanderbilt has served as a member of the maritime exchange committee on international maritime conferences, which secured the act inviting and creating the International Maritime Congress at Washington for the better security of life and property at sea. Mr. Vanderbilt is now engaged in the manufacture of machinery, and is treasurer of the Wheeler Condenser and Engineering Co., of New York. He was a member of Gen. W. S. Hancock's memorable staff during the obsequies of Gen. U. S. Grant, and one of the guard of honor with the remains while lying in state. He is a companion of the military order of the Loyal Legion of the United States, a comrade of the Grand Army, member of the United States Naval Institute, at Annapolis, Md., and of the Army and Navy Club, of Washington; chairman of the committee on ocean transportation of the board of trade, and a member of the American Society of Mechanical Engineers. He was married in 1869 to Miss Lillie Wheeler, and has two daughters. His home is at New Brighton, Staten Island.

HOWE, Albion Paris, soldier, was born in Standish, Me., March 13, 1818. He entered the Military Academy at West Point in 1837; was graduated in 1841, and assigned to the 4th artillery. He served on garrison and frontier duty for a time, and then as professor of mathematics at West Point until the Mexican war. While in the Mexican campaign he occupied the staff position of adjutant of 4th artillery from Oct. 1, 1846, to March 2, 1855, and participated in many battles. For gallant and meritorious conduct at Contreras and Cherubusco, he received the brevet of captain, Aug. 20, 1847, a full captaincy being granted March 2, 1855. In the interim between the Mexican and civil wars he was on garrison duty, four years of the time being given as instructor at the Artillery School at Fortress Monroe. At the opening of the civil war he was appointed Gen. McClellan's chief of artillery in the army of the Potomac during the campaign on the peninsular in 1862, after having served in West Virginia in 1861. In 1862 he commanded a brigade of light artillery in the peninsular campaign; was brevetted major July 1st, for bravery at Malvern Hill, Va; lieutenant-colonel, May 3, 1863, for gallant action at Salem Heights, Va.; colonel, Nov. 7, 1863, for daring and meritorious work in the battle of Rappahannock Station, Va.; and brigadier-general and major-general, March 13, 1865, and further brevetted major-general of volunteers, July 13, 1865, for faithful and meritorious services during the war. Gen. Howe was on duty in Washington as chief of artillery in 1864-6, and was a member of the military commission that tried the conspirators against President Lincoln and his cabinet after the terrible assassination of Apr. 14, 1865. He was mustered out of the service Jan. 15, 1866, and retired June 30, 1882, with the rank of colonel of the 4th artillery, his commission dating from Apr. 19, 1882. During the latter part of his active military service he was stationed on the Pacific coast, where he held the rank of major.

BUSH, Joseph, artist, was born in Franklin, Ky., in 1793, son of Philip and Eliza (Palmer) Bush, of German ancestry. He early developed a taste for sketching, and at the age of seventeen was sent to Philadelphia, under the care of Henry Clay, and placed under the instruction of Thomas Sully. He remained there three years, and at the same time received an academic education. His most noted paintings are those of Gen. Zachary Taylor, Gov. John Adair, Dr. Benj. W. Dudley, and Judge Thomas B. Moore. He resided for many years in Lexington, Ky., where he died Nov. 11, 1865.

CONOVER, Charles Edwin, merchant, was born in Middletown, Monmouth county, N. J., in the old Conover homestead, Dec. 28, 1846, son of Azariah and Emily P. Conover, grandson of Hendrick Conover, great-grandson of Peter Albertse Kouwenhoven, great-great-grandson of Albert Willemce Conwenhoven, sixth in descent from William Gerotso Kouwenhoven, seventh in descent from Gerret Wolfesen Conwenhoven, and eighth in descent from Wolfest Garretson Van Couwenhoven, who emigrated from Amersfoort in the province of Utrecht in Holland, in 1630, with the colonists who settled Rensselaerwick, near Albany where he was employed by the patroon as superintendent of farms. He afterward resided on Manhattan Island, where he cultivated the company's "bowery" or farm No. 6, and in 1667 was enrolled among the burghers of New Amsterdam. Gerret Wolfesen Conwenhoven, his son, came with him to this country, and settled at Flatbush, L. I. Peter Albertse Conover or Kouwenhoven, the great-great-grandson of the emigrant, removed to Monmouth county, N. J., previous to 1699, where he acquired a large farm, which is still in the possession of his descendants. Charles E. Conover, the subject of this sketch, is descended on his mother's side from the Shermans of New England, a family from which many of the most distinguished men of the country have sprung. Mr. Conover was prepared for college at the Flushing (L. I.) institute, but the breaking out of the civil war interfered with his plans, and he was obliged to return home to assist his father on the farm. In 1864 he removed to New York city, and entered the employ of the Manhattan brass works as a salesman, where he remained three years, and later was employed by Wallace & Sons, manufacturers of brass and copper goods. In 1879 he engaged with the notion house of Banning, Chadwick & Co., and two years afterward became a partner. On the retirement of Mr. Chadwick in 1884, the firm was changed to Banning, Conover & Co. The death of Mr. Banning, the senior partner, in 1877, led to a dissolution of the firm, and in January, 1888, he started in the notion commission business in his own name, taking with him the important manufacturers' accounts of the old firm. Some months later he organized the C. E. Conover company, of which he became president and general manager, and conducted the business successfully up to the time of his death. He was a man absolutely tireless in energy, devoted to every interest committed to him; far-seeing and comprehensive in all his plans, he was not only able to guide business to success, but worked with the hardest to accomplish it. He was a member of the Holland society, and of the Lotos and Manhattan athletic clubs. In 1878 he married Carrie Chanfrau, daughter of Peter F. Chanfrau, and a niece of Frank S. Chanfrau, the celebrated actor. He died Jan. 9, 1891.

CONOVER, Jacob Dey, merchant, was born at the homestead farm, Middletown, Monmouth county, N. J., Jan. 26, 1860, son of Azariah and Emily P. (née Sherman) Conover, and youngest brother of Charles E. Conover. His father was a large and prosperous farmer, and resided on the homestead farm, which he inherited from his ancestors. Jacob D. Conover in his youth enjoyed excellent educational advantages. He was prepared for college at Flushing (L. I.) institute, intending to enter Columbia college, and passed a creditable examination. He decided, however, to adopt a business career, and in 1880 started in the real estate business in New York city. When his brother, Charles E., organized the C. E. Conover company in 1888, he became associated with him in the enterprise, and devoted himself assiduously to acquiring a knowledge of the business. He was the main stay of his brother during the early period of trying to establish a new house in the metropolis, where competition was sharp and strong, and when older houses in the notion business had been compelled to retire. During his brother's long illness he managed the business successfully, and soon after the death of the latter became his successor as president of the C. E. Conover company. He has fully maintained the high standing of the house, which is recognized as one of the stanchest firms in the business. Mr. Conover has

been twice married, his first wife being Susie H. Conover, by whom he had one child, Lester Dey. His present wife, to whom he was married in 1889, was Lillian Wild, daughter of Geo. H. Wild, and granddaughter of Horatio N. Wild, who was at one time a prominent New York politician, and a successful business man. Mr. Conover still resides at the old homestead of his ancestors, and is popular in society. He is a stanch republican, and has taken an active interest in local politics.

RIVES, William Cabell, U. S. senator and minister to France, was born in Nelson county, Va., May 4, 1793, grandson of Col. W. Cabell. He studied at the colleges of Hampden-Sidney and William and Mary, and received his legal and political training from President Jefferson. In the last year of the war with England he served for local defence with the militia. In 1816 he was a member of the Virginia constitutional convention, and in 1817-19 of the legislature, as again in 1822. He was in congress 1823-29, and minister to France 1829-32 and 1849-53; during his former term of service there he negotiated the treaty of indemnity, July, 1831. Most of the interval between these two periods, 1832-45, was spent in the senate, except some months in 1834-35; his resignation was caused by a difference with his constituents as to the removal of the deposits and the senate's vote of censure on the president, which was expunged in January, 1837. He had published: a "Life of John Hampden" (1845); "Ethics of Christianity" (1855), and some minor works; after his withdrawal from public life in 1853 he prepared the "Life and Times of James Madison," of which three volumes appeared in 1859-69, not completing the subject. He attended the peace conference at Washington in February, 1861, and was a member of the provisional Confederate congress at Montgomery, Ala. He was the father of Alfred Landon Rives, a distinguished civil engineer, and the grandfather of Mrs. Amélie Rives Chanler, the novelist. He died at his wife's estate of "Castle Hill," Albemarle county, Va., Apr. 26, 1868.

RIVES, Judith Page Walker, wife of William Cabell Rives, was born near Charlottesville, Va., March 24, 1802, and was married in 1819. She wrote: "The Canary Bird" (1835); "Souvenirs of a Residence in Europe" (1842); "Epitome of the Bible" (1847), and "Home and the World" (1857). She died at her birthplace Jan. 23, 1882.

WALCUTT, Charles Carroll, brevet major-general U. S. army, was born at Columbus, O., Feb. 12, 1838, son of John Macy and Mariel (Broderick) Walcutt (originally spelled Wolcott). His father, the son of William Wolcott, a revolutionary soldier, was a cabinet-maker, who removed to Columbus, O., in 1815, from Loudon county, Va.: he was a soldier in the war of 1812, and died in 1870. His maternal grandmother was a first cousin of the celebrated David Crockett. Gen. Walcutt was educated in the public schools of his native city, and at the Kentucky Military Institute, near Frankfort, Ky., where he was graduated in 1858. He then entered upon the avocation of civil engineering, and was elected county surveyor of Franklin county, O., in 1859. On the first call for troops in April, 1861, he raised a company of men, but Ohio's quota being full, they were not accepted. In June, 1861, he was commissioned major, and assigned to duty as inspector in West Virginia, on the staff of Gen. Hill. In 1862 he was made colonel, and July 30, 1864, was made brigadier-general, for bravery and especial gallantry at the battle of Atlanta, receiving the thanks of Gen. Frank Blair for saving the 17th army corps. Gen. Walcutt's service was most of the time with Gen. Sherman, and he participated in all of the engagements of that command. He was wounded at Shiloh in the left shoulder, and carried through life the bullet lodged there. He was at Vicksburg, Jackson, Miss., Missionary Ridge, Kenesaw, relief of Knoxville, Dallas, Burnt Hickory, and Noonday Creek. He was engaged in the battles of Ezra Chapel, Jonesboro', and Lovejoy stations, Ga., and was in command of the battle of Griswoldville, the only battle on Sherman's march to the sea. Here his command only numbered 1,300 effective men, and two pieces of artillery, while the enemy had 10,000 men, and eight pieces of artillery. After a severe engagement of five hours the Confederates retreated. Early in this action Gen. Walcutt was severely wounded by the explosion of a shell, and from that time was compelled to be carried in a captured carriage. For special gallantry in this action he was made a major-general by brevet. He was mustered out in February, 1866, and took charge of the Ohio penitentiary, and after remaining there a few months, he was appointed and accepted a commission as lieutenant-colonel of the 10th U. S. cavalry. He remained in this service about six months, when he resigned, and again resumed the position of warden of the Ohio penitentiary. In this capacity he served until July 1, 1869, his executive ability being of great service, as the institution, formerly an expense to the state, was made more than self-supporting. In May, 1869, he was appointed by Gen. Grant as U. S. collector of internal revenue, serving until July, 1883. In April, 1883, he was elected mayor of the city of Columbus, and was re-elected in 1885. In 1875 he was elected a member of the school board of Columbus, O., was its president for seven years, and remained a member until the term of 1894. During this time he devoted himself to the building up and making efficient the public schools of Columbus, which owe to him much of their present high standard. The Public-School Library, with its most beautiful and commodious building, with a well selected library of 23,000 volumes, was built during his term of service, there having been but

650 volumes in 1875. In this library Gen. Walcutt has taken a deep interest, and to his energy and zeal is largely due its prosperity. Gen. Walcutt since the civil war has been an active Republican, and influential in the councils of his party. He was chairman of the state Republican committee of 1872–73, and contributed to the election of Gen. Grant to the presidency. He was one of the Grant electors in 1868. He was for a number of years a member and president of the Franklin County Agricultural Society; a member of the Loyal Legion, was senior vice-commander, one of the charter members of the Ohio commandery; and a Knight-Templar Mason. As a soldier, Gen. Walcutt was a brave and efficient officer, commanding the respect of his superiors, and the warm, personal friendship of Gen. Sherman. As a citizen, he has been devoted to the advancement of the best interests of humanity, and active, zealous, and true, in the performance of those duties entrusted to his care. In May, 1860, he was married to Phœbe Neill, and three children have been born to them.

MILLER, Lewis, inventor and philanthropist, was born at Greentown, O., July 24, 1829. His father, John Miller, who was of German descent, removed from Maryland to Ohio in 1812, where he took up farm land, and engaged in the business of house-building. He was known for his strict integrity, and exerted great influence in the community. Young Lewis received his early education in the common schools, working at the same time on his father's farm, and later was sent to Illinois, to take an academic course. After completing his studies, he learned the plasterer's trade, which he followed for some time. He returned to Ohio in 1851, and became a partner in the firm of Ball, Aultman & Co., of Greentown, manufacturers of reaping and threshing machines. He learned the machinists' trade, and rapidly developed his inventive genius. In 1855 he invented the celebrated "Buckeye Mower," the distinctive feature of which was the "double-hinged floating bar," upon which all subsequent two-wheel machines are modeled. In the study and experiments necessary to perfect the labor-saving machines subsequently invented, which are covered by over 100 letters patent, he was largely assisted by his brother Jacob. From a small beginning, making only a few machines each year, Mr. Miller has lived to see the products of his genius, in the hands of industry all over the world; has manufacturing establishments at Canton and Akron, O., giving employment to 1,500 men, and an output yearly of $6,000,000. He was an earnest advocate of anti-slavery, and when the civil war was precipitated, aided the cause of the Union in every possible way. In 1878 he was a candidate of the Republican party for congress. In educational matters, he was throughout his life an active and

leading spirit. He was the first to conceive and project the "Chautauqua Movement," in which he was associated with Bishop Vincent. In 1873, in pursuance of the idea, they visited Chautauqua, and secured the use of the ground, where the first assembly was held in the August of that year. The proportions to which it has since grown are part of the history of religious, scientific, and literary culture. Mr. Miller was president of the assembly, the reading circle, the college of liberal arts, and the dozen other departments of this complex institution. He owned a cottage on the lake at Chautauqua, kept a steam yacht, and a park there bears his name. At his home in Akron, O., he was superintendent of the Methodist Episcopal Sunday-school for over forty years, where he carried out some original ideas, in the way of Sunday-school architecture, at his own expense. It is known as the "Akron style," and is the world's model to day. In 1866 he was made president of the board of trustees of Mount Union College, in Ohio, and his gifts to the college were numerous. He was also a member of the board of Wesleyan University, of Delaware, O., and Allegheny College of Meadville, Pa., and was active in the building of Buchtel College, at Akron, to all of which institutions he has been a substantial benefactor. In 1852 he married Mary V. Dau, and was the father of eleven children. His daughter Nina married Thomas A. Edison, the inventor.

LIPSCOMB, Andrew Adgate, author and educator, was born in Georgetown, D. C., Sept. 6, 1816. The father, Rev. William Corrie Lipscomb, was one of the first to secede from the Methodist Episcopal church on account of lay representation. He was a God-fearing man, who ruled his household with a rigid hand. Andrew was a thoughtful youth, and applied himself so closely to study that he undermined his health. His association with his aunt, Mona E. Cox, a woman of superior intellectual ability and high literary culture, guided the formation of his literary tastes and instilled him with his belief in women's intellect and capabilities. He received his education at the Georgetown Military Academy and at a classical school in the town, and when eighteen years of age, entered the Methodist ministry, and began preaching, being known as the "Boy Preacher." He became successively pastor of the churches of Alexandria, Baltimore, and Washington, and in 1842 accepted a call to Montgomery, Ala. After a few years of ministerial work, he was forced to resign his charge on account of failing health, and he established in that city the Metropolitan Institute for Young Ladies, which was, however, burned shortly afterwards, entailing great loss and disappointment. He then turned his attention to literature, and became a valued contributor to "Harper's Magazine." After a fifteen years' residence he accepted the presidency of the Female College at Tuskegee, Ala. Failing health compelled him to resign, and he was preparing to go abroad when he was offered and accepted the chancellorship of the University of Georgia. After filling this position for fourteen years, upon the death of his son, from whose loss he never recovered, he resigned, and became professor

of art and criticism in the Vanderbilt University, but his health again became precarious, and he was compelled to return to his home in Athens, having been made professor emeritus, which position he held until his death. His last years were spent in literary work. For forty years he was a regular contributor to the "Independent," "Methodist Recorder," and "Christian Advocate," and published "Studies in the Forty Days," and "Supplementary Studies." He also has written many beautiful hymns, and his sermons would fill volumes. He was a great student of Shakespeare, and was considered one of the best Shakespearean critics the country has produced. He was a valued friend of Longfellow, who once wrote to him in regard to slavery: "I can never make it

rhyme with 'Do unto others as you would have others do to you,' nor do I think you can when you meet it face to face." The New York "Independent" says that he is "one of the most brilliant writers of the South." He left many unpublished manuscripts, which his friends and admirers desired to have published. The degree of D.D. was conferred upon him by the University of Alabama, and that of LL.D. by Emory College. Dr. Lipscomb had the faculty of developing the best from every nature which touched his own, and it is said of him that "no man since Dr. Arnold has had such intellectual sway." Besides the works mentioned, he published "Our Country," ' The Social Spirit of Christianity," "Christian Heroism," "Lessons in the Life of St. Peter." He died Nov. 23, 1890.

ELZY, Arnold, soldier, was born at Elmwood, Somerset co., Md., Dec. 18, 1816, the son of Arnold Elzy Jones and Annie Wilson Jackson. At the age of sixteen Arnold entered the U. S. Military Academy at West Point, and was graduated there in 1837, at the same time being promoted second lieutenant in the 2nd artillery. After graduation he dropped his last name, and was thereafter known as Arnold Elzy. In 1845 he married Ellen, daughter of Henry Irwin, of Huntingdon county, Pa., and had one son. He served in the Florida war in 1837–38, in the Cherokee nation, while emigrating the Indians to the West, and on the northern frontier during the Canadian border disturbances. On Aug. 20, 1847, he was brevetted captain for gallant and meritorious conduct in the battles of Contreras and Churubusco, Mexico. He was present at the storming of Chapultepec, the assault and capture of the City of Mexico, 1847, and in the Florida hostilities against the Seminole Indians. He was made captain of the 2nd artillery in 1849. At the breaking-out of the war he resigned his position in the U. S. army, Apr. 25, 1861, and joined the Confederate army, with the rank of colonel. He was immediately assigned to a brigade under Gen. A. P. Stewart. At the first battle of Bull Run he distinguished himself, and after Gen. Kirby Smith was wounded he assumed the command, for which he was complimented by Gen. Beauregard, and promoted to a brigadier generalship by Jefferson Davis. He commanded the brigade through Stonewall Jackson's valley campaign, and at the battle of Cold Harbor was shot through the head, which ended his active service in the field. After his recovery he was promoted to major-general. At the end of the war he retired to a farm in Maryland, and died in Baltimore, Md., Feb. 22, 1871.

WINTHROP, Robert Charles, statesman, was born in Boston, Mass., May 12, 1807. He was the youngest son of Lieut.-Gov. Lindall Winthrop, a merchant of Boston, prominent in political and intellectual affairs, who was a great-grandson of John Winthrop, the younger, and who married the granddaughter of Gov. James Bowdoin. He was a descendant in the sixth generation from John Winthrop, the first governor of Massachusetts. Robert's early education was obtained under the most favored circumstances. His father personally directed it until he entered the Boston Latin School when he was nine years old. He was graduated at Harvard in 1828, on which occasion he delivered an oration on 'Public Station," which was almost a forecast of his future career. Upon his graduation he entered the office of Daniel Webster, and was admitted to the bar in 1831, and after a brief professional career became active in politics as a Henry Clay Whig. He was early interested in military matters, and served as captain in the Boston light infantry, as lieutenant of the ancient and honorable artillery, and as aide-de-camp to Govs. Davis, Armstrong, and Everett. In 1834 he was chosen representative to the Massachusetts legislature, and after four years' service on the floor was elected speaker, being the youngest speaker the house ever had. He was re-elected speaker the following year, and again in 1840, in which year he was elected a representative to congress by the Whig party, to which organization he belonged throughout his entire life. After he had served seven years, he was chosen speaker of the house for the session of 1848-49, but being a candidate again in 1850 for the speakership, was defeated by a plurality of two votes, after over sixty ballots had been taken. He represented Boston in congress for nearly ten years, during which time he greatly increased his reputation as a ready debater and accomplished parliamentarian. He delivered a series of impressive speeches upon leading questions of the day, which are still consulted as authorities. He offered the first resolution in favor of international arbitration by a commission of civilians. In 1850 he was appointed by Gov. Davis to succeed Daniel Webster in the U. S. senate when the latter resigned his seat to accept the appointment of secretary of state under Pres. Fillmore.

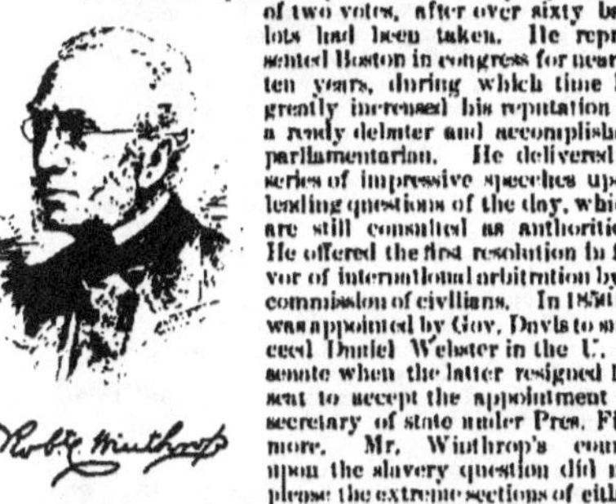

Mr. Winthrop's course upon the slavery question did not please the extreme sections of either party, and in 1851 he was defeated for re-election to the senate by a coalition of the minority parties. Upon his return to Boston he became the candidate of the Whig party for governor of Massachusetts, but was again defeated by the same coalition. Although he had a large plurality, a majority vote was required. When the state constitution was changed, requiring only a plurality, Mr. Winthrop declined to become a candidate, and devoted himself to literary and philanthropic occupations. The last political office he held was the place at the head of the Massachusetts electoral college, which, in 1851, gave the vote of the state to Gen. Winfield Scott. He was active, however, in presidential elections, and gave his voice in support of Millard Fillmore in 1856, of John Bell in 1860, and of Gen. McClellan in 1864, besides making memorable political addresses upon noted occasions. He was a favorite orator at great historical anniversaries, when his fervid eloquence and rare scholarship delighted all listeners. These productions were published in his four volumes of "Addresses and Speeches," issued, the first in 1852, and the last in 1886, which are considered as among the classics of the language. He also published "Washington, Bowdoin, and Franklin, as Portrayed in Occasional Addresses" in 1876, and memoirs of J. H. Clifford, Henry Clay, and other eminent men. Among the most admired are the orations at the laying of the corner-stone of the national Washington monument, July 4, 1848, and upon its completion in 1885, prepared upon the request of congress; his oration upon the life and services of James Bowdoin, delivered before the Maine Historical Society at Bowdoin College in 1849; a remarkably scholarly and high-minded address on "The Obligations and Responsibilities of Educated Men in the Use of the Tongue and Pen," before the alumni of Harvard University in 1852; a lecture on "Archimedes and Franklin," before the Massachusetts Charitable Mechanics' Association in 1853; an oration on the "Franklin Statue," in 1856; in memory of William

H. Prescott, in 1859; Josiah Quincy, in 1864; Edward Everett, in 1865; on the 250th anniversary of the landing of the Pilgrims, in 1870; at the centennial of the Boston Tea Party, in 1873; the Boston Centennial oration, in 1876; the oration at the unveiling of the statue of Col. Prescott, in Charlestown, in 1881, and the same year the oration on the centennial of the surrender of Yorktown. His speeches made on Boston common during the civil war were models of eloquence, and excited great patriotic enthusiasm throughout the country, and his eulogies upon the deaths of eminent men with whom he had been associated were marked with rare scholarship and discriminating appreciation. When the Whig party died, Mr. Winthrop became an independent voter, identifying himself with no party, but supporting such candidates as seemed to him at the time the best men and representative of the best principles. In his congressional career he admirably represented the Massachusetts sentiment of the day, favoring a sound financial policy, and protection to home industry, fighting the extension of slavery, and opposing the fugitive slave law. He deplored the widening breach between the North and South, and he did his best to close it; but when the war broke out he joined, heart and soul, with the Union cause. For twenty-five years Mr. Winthrop served the Boston Provident Association as its president; for thirty years he was president of the Massachusetts Historical Society; for eight years president of the alumni of Harvard, besides been chairman of the Poor of Boston, and holding many other offices of trust and honor. Besides his collected speeches and addresses, Mr. Winthrop's most important literary work embraces the biography of his great ancestor, "The Life and Letters of John Winthrop," in two volumes, published in 1864. He has been president of the board of trustees of the Peabody education fund since its first organization, and was the chosen counsellor of Mr. Peabody in several of his benefactions. On one of his visits abroad he received the degree of LL.D. from the University of Cambridge, which degree had been previously conferred upon him by both Harvard and Bowdoin. The

best picture of Mr. Winthrop's personality is given in his speeches and addresses, which are 180 in number, and stretch along from 1835 to 1879, like milestones along his path of life. What Dr. O. W. Holmes has been in poetry to great festal occasions, Mr. Winthrop has been in prose, and but few notable public gatherings have taken place at which his eloquence has not been one of its leading features. In the earliest years of his public life an anti-Catholic excitement ran high, and his sense of justice is shown in a speech in the Massachusetts house of representatives in favor of compensation for the destruction of the Ursuline convent at Mt. Benedict. In January, 1845, he made a great speech in the house of representatives against the annexation of Texas, upon the ground that it involved the extension of domestic slavery. In two subsequent speeches he also opposed the war with Mexico as an unjust war of conquest for the acquisition of territory. Mr. Winthrop's last speech in congress was in opposition to the fugitive-slave law, and was delivered in the senate Aug. 19, 1850. In the matter of the dispute with England over the Oregon boundary he strenuously urged an amicable settlement, and favored referring the question to arbitration. He advocated a comprehensive national system of river and harbor improvement, and a tariff that would protect labor, and enrich the treasury of the nation. While Mr. Winthrop was speaker of the house, ex-Pres. John Quincy Adams was stricken with illness in his seat, and died in the speaker's room. He made the official announcement of Mr. Adams' death to the house in a speech which was a model of terse eloquence and sincere feeling. A portrait of him, presented by the citizens of Massachusetts, is placed in the capitol at Washington, and commemorates at once his speakership and his Yorktown oration. Another portrait of him is placed in the hall of the Massachusetts Historical Society, and serves to signalize his worth and services to the history and honor of his native state. George T. Curtis says that Mr. Winthrop has been from his earliest youth an object of public regard as a person of high qualification for public service. The "North American Review" says: "Winthrop's addresses manifest large information and pure taste of the well-trained scholar, as well as the fluent manner and ready logic of the practical debater," and of his "Sir Algernon Sydney," we should be glad to see it put into the hands of every young man in the United States." Mr. Winthrop thrice married; his first wife was Eliza O. Blanchard; his second Laura, daughter of John Derby of Salem, and widow of Arnold F. Wells, and the third, the widow of John E. Thayer. In 1886 he suffered from a severe attack of pneumonia, from which he never fully recovered, and after a long and painful illness, he died at his home in Boston, Nov. 16, 1894.

KNOX, John, clergyman, was born near Gettysburg, Pa., June 17, 1790. His father was Dr. Samuel Knox, a physician of fine education and large practice. The boy was prepared for college by his father, aided by the minister of the church which the family attended. He entered the junior class of Dickinson College, Carlisle, Pa., and was graduated in 1811. At college he formed the purpose of undertaking a preparation for the ministry, and after graduation he entered the Theological Seminary of the Associate Reformed Church in New York. He received his license to preach in 1815. It was a rule in the Associate Reformed church, that after the licensure, a year should be spent in visiting the vacancies within the bounds of the church, as arranged by the synod, and after fulfilling his appointments, Mr. Knox received calls from three of the leading vacancies. He was, however, installed as one of the colleague pastors in the Collegiate Church in New York, before whose congregation he had preached to their entire satisfaction. In 1818 Mr. Knox married the eldest daughter of Rev. Dr. John M. Mason, who had been his instructor in the theological seminary. Dr. Knox became senior minister in the Collegiate Church in 1853, and continued to hold that position for nearly twenty-five years. He is described as having been a man of disciplined, earnest, and uniform piety, possessing remarkable simplicity and perfect integrity of character. He was also a man of sound judgment and practical wisdom. He was very industrious, and systematized the course of his duties in such a way that they never trenched upon each other. For a period of ministerial service approaching forty-two years, he was held in uninterrupted respect and friendship not only by the ministerial brethren and laymen of his own sect, but also by those of other denominations who knew him. He took a very active part in raising funds for the endowment of theological professorships in the seminary at New Brunswick. He generally had a place on the various boards which were organized by the general synod, and early after its board of corporation was organized he was chosen director. He was especially identified with the American Tract Society, and a member of its publishing committee, and was for many years chairman of the publishing, and also of the executive committee. He was president of the board of trustees of Leake and Watts Orphan House, and was a trustee of Columbia College, Rutgers College, and the College of Physicians and Surgeons. Dr. Knox met his death by an accident, through falling from the gable of his house onto the stone pavement in the yard below. He remained insensible for three days and died on Jan. 8, 1858.

SEDDON, James Alexander, lawyer, was born in Falmouth, Va., July 13, 1815. He was the son of Thomas Seddon, a merchant and subsequently a banker, who was descended from John Seddon of Lancashire, Eng., who was one of the early settlers of Stafford county, Va. His mother, Susan Alexander, was a lineal descendant from the earl of Stirling. Young Seddon's early education was much neglected on account of ill health, but he inherited a love of learning, and having access to a well stocked library, studied by himself, and acquired a knowledge of the classics and general literature, which became noted in after years. He entered the law department of the University of Virginia when twenty-one years of age, and after graduation began practice in Richmond, where his abilities attracted immediate atten-tion, and he became one of the foremost members of his profession in the state. His entrance to political life was in 1845, when he was elected by the Democratic party to congress, when he received a handsome majority, although the district was usually uncertain. He declined a renomination in 1847, because his views were not in accord with the platform of the nominating convention, when the candidate of the opposite party was elected. In 1849, however, he was re-elected, but his delicate health obliged him to decline another nomination, and he retired to Sabot Hill, his home on the James river, above Richmond. He took an active part in the debates during his service in congress, and was acknowledged to be the leader of his party. His debates upon the reform revenue bill, in which he advocated free trade, were models of strength and erudition, and commanded wide attention. The crisis of 1860 again brought him into active politics, and he was appointed, with John Tyler and others, a commissioner to the peace congress which, at the instance of the state of Virginia, was held in Washington. He was placed upon the committee of rules, and by the instruction of his state made the minority report, recommending the amending of the constitution according to the resolution which had been introduced into the senate by John J. Crittenden; to which was added a further article which expressly recognized the right of any state to withdraw from the Union. Upon the establishment of the Confederate government he became a member of congress, and was given the portfolio of secretary of war in the first cabinet of Jefferson Davis. His services were in the highest degree efficient. Under a mild exterior he possessed an unflinching will. In his contention with Gov. Brown, of Georgia, upon the subject of conscription, he showed the strength of his personality. The principle of state sovereignty, according to Gov. Brown, did not permit the general government to conscript the citizens of any state—carried out logically there could be no general government. Jealousies of this character had much to do with weakening the Confederacy even as early as 1862. Upon the fall of the Confederacy, Mr. Seddon retired from public life, and died in Goochland county, Va., Aug. 19, 1880.

THOMAS, Isaiah, printer, journalist and publisher, was born in Boston, Jan. 19, 1749. His father was Moses Thomas, who died in Isaiah's infancy. He was apprenticed at the age of six to Zachariah Fowles, a printer, serving eleven years. After a voyage to the West Indies and Nova Scotia, he returned to Boston and became a partner with his old master. They founded what is now the oldest paper in the state, "The Massachusetts Spy," but after three months the partnership was dissolved,

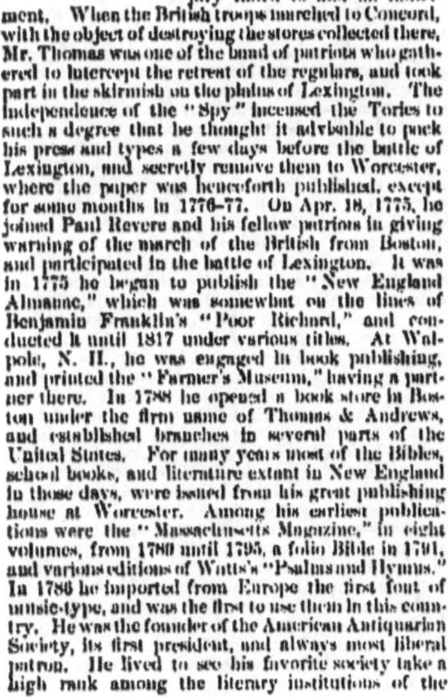

Thomas continuing the paper alone, and taking for his motto, "Open to all parties, but influenced by none." Being a Whig, the policy of the paper underwent a gradual change, and it became the organ of that party. So bold and spirited were his appeals on the subject of the oppressive acts of the British parliament towards the colonies, and in the advocacy of freedom, that in 1771 Gov. Hutchinson summoned Mr. Thomas to answer for an alleged seditious article published in the "Spy." He refused to appear, and the attorney-general was ordered to prosecute him, but the grand jury failed to find an indictment. When the British troops marched to Concord, with the object of destroying the stores collected there, Mr. Thomas was one of the band of patriots who gathered to intercept the retreat of the regulars, and took part in the skirmish on the plains of Lexington. The independence of the "Spy" incensed the Tories to such a degree that he thought it advisable to pack his press and types a few days before the battle of Lexington, and secretly remove them to Worcester, where the paper was henceforth published, except for some months in 1776–77. On Apr. 18, 1775, he joined Paul Revere and his fellow patriots in giving warning of the march of the British from Boston, and participated in the battle of Lexington. It was in 1775 he began to publish the "New England Almanac," which was somewhat on the lines of Benjamin Franklin's "Poor Richard," and conducted it until 1817 under various titles. At Walpole, N. H., he was engaged in book publishing, and printed the "Farmer's Museum," having a partner there. In 1788 he opened a book store in Boston under the firm name of Thomas & Andrews, and established branches in several parts of the United States. For many years most of the Bibles, school books, and literature extant in New England in those days, were issued from his great publishing house at Worcester. Among his earliest publications were the "Massachusetts Magazine," in eight volumes, from 1789 until 1795, a folio Bible in 1791, and various editions of Watts's "Psalms and Hymns." In 1786 he imported from Europe the first font of music-type, and was the first to use them in this country. He was the founder of the American Antiquarian Society, its first president, and always most liberal patron. He lived to see his favorite society take a high rank among the literary institutions of the

country, and made ample provisions in his will for its future support. It is indebted to him for its land and building, and a fund of $24,000 for its maintenance; 8,000 volumes to its library from his important collection; many tracts; and an unsurpassed and most valuable file of early newspapers. The library, which now contains upwards of 100,000 volumes, includes the Mather collection. He entered the ranks of authorship with a "History of Printing" (2 vols., Worcester, Mass.), which was well received, abounds in interesting anecdotes, and displays great and careful research. In recognition of his services to literature, Allegheny College in Pennsylvania conferred upon him the degree of LL.D. in 1818. Mr. Thomas died at Worcester, Apr. 4, 1831, aged eighty-two years; and has left a character distinguished for integrity, patriotism and philanthropy. In his "History of Worcester" (1837) William Lincoln says of him: "His reputation in future time will rest, as a patriot, on the manly independence which gave—through the fultitory stage and progress of the revolution—the strong influence of the press he directed toward the cause of freedom, when royal flattery would have reduced and the power of government subdued its action." A memoir by his grandson, B. F. Thomas, appeared in 1874. He was succeeded as manager of the "Spy," by his son Isaiah, Jr., who published it until 1819.

McKEON, John, lawyer, was born in Albany, N. Y., in 1804. He came of Irish stock, his father, Capt. James McKeon, being a member of the band of United Irishmen, who brought about the rebellion in 1798. After their abortive attempt, Capt. McKeon fled to America, with his family, and settled in Albany, N. Y. He fought during the war of 1812, and while John was still a child, went to the city of New York to reside, and remained there until his death. John received a good education, part of the time from a private tutor, who taught him the English branches and fitted him for college. He entered Columbia College and was graduated with high rank, especially in the classics, in 1824. He had already determined to make law his life profession, and began to study in the office of his brother James, who was then practicing in New York, before he entered college. Immediately after graduation, John entered the law office of the late Judge John L. Mason, where he qualified soon after reaching his majority and was admitted to the bar. From the beginning he was successful in practice, although in those days far less confidence was felt in young lawyers than there is at present. By the year 1830 John McKeon was established in a large and steadily increasing practice. He was a close student and worked hard at his profession, yet he had a taste for politics and soon became active and prominent in local campaigns. He attached himself to the Jefferson Democracy and being a fluent speaker and ready in debate, he soon made an impression upon the party in New York. When only twenty-eight years of age, he was elected to the state assembly, being the youngest member of that body. His conduct during his first term was so satisfactory to the party, that he was re-elected for the two following terms, and by that time had become well known throughout the state, while his law business grew in profit and importance with his political prestige. He served in congress from Dec. 7, 1835, to March 3, 1837. He was renominated, but in the next campaign native Americanism was a factor and any candidacy outside of that was bitterly fought. Mc-

Keon, however, fought back with great determination, being as bitter and fearless as were his enemies. He was defeated, but the failure only strengthened him in his determination to climb the heights which led to the summit of his political ambition. In 1840 he again ran for congress, and was elected. In 1843 he was again a candidate, but this time was defeated. In 1846 Mr. McKeon was appointed district attorney of New York county, and he was so popular in this office that he was elected for a second time. In 1853 he was appointed by Pres. Pierce, U. S. district attorney for the southern district of New York, succeeding Charles O'Conor in that position. In his new office Mr. McKeon displayed unusual energy and determination. He broke up the slave-trading and filibustering expeditions, which were at that time fitting out in New York, and was the cause of the dismissal by the president of the British minister, Crampton, from Washington, on account of recruiting in this country for the British army, in the Crimean war. At the close of his term as U. S. district attorney, he resumed his private practice, and made a name equal to any of his contemporaries at the bar. Two of his most noted clients were Richard B. Connolly, one of the principal actors in the ring frauds, and Edward S. Stokes, who was tried for the murder of Fisk. In 1881 he was elected district attorney of New York by a brilliant majority, and thoroughly reformed that office. Mr. McKeon married Mrs. Whitmore, a daughter of Commodore Sloat of the U. S. navy. His daughter married Mr. Hecker, the well-known New York merchant. He died in New York, Nov. 22, 1883.

BELL, Alexander Graham, inventor of the telephone, was born in Edinburgh, Scotland, March 3, 1847. He is the son of Alexander Melville Bell, a distinguished Scotch educator, the inventor of a system of "visible speech," which he has successfully taught to deaf-mutes, and the author of several text-books on shorthand and elocution, and the grandson of Alexander Bell, well-known as the inventor of a method for removing impediments of speech. The younger Bell received his education at the Edinburgh High School and Edinburgh University, and in 1867 entered the University of London. In 1870 his health having been impaired by over-study, he removed with his father to Canada and two years later settled in the United States, becoming first a teacher of deaf-mutes and subsequently professor of vocal physiology in the University of Boston. In 1867 he began to study the problem of conveying articulate sound by electric currents, and after nine years of research and experiments, completed the first telephone early in 1876. In that year it was exhibited at the Centennial Exhibition in Philadelphia, and pronounced "the wonder of wonders in electric telegraphy."

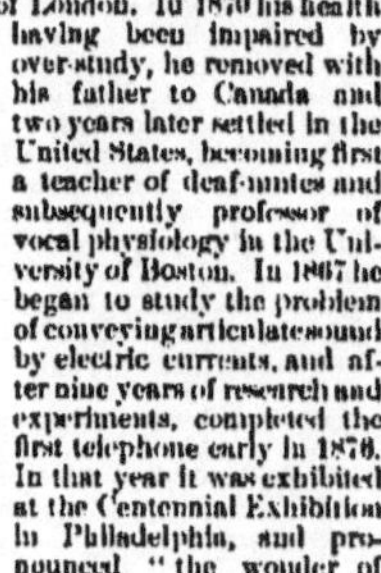

Mr. Bell filed his application for a patent at the patent office in Washington on Feb. 14, 1876, and it is a singular fact that an application for a patent for a speaking telephone, was received from Elisha Gray (q. v.) of Chicago, on the same day but a few hours later. The patent was granted to Mr. Bell on the ground of the difference in time and not because of any difference in the merits of the claims. The Bell Telephone Co. was organized in 1877, and in 1878 the first exchanges under the Bell patents, were established. In 1879 the new method of communication became firmly established as a commercial and social necessity, and since that time has come into use in all parts of the world. In the first eight years of the Bell Co.'s existence, $4,000,000 in dividends were paid the stockholders, and it is estimated that the dividends which have been paid since 1885 have greatly exceeded that amount. The validity of the Bell patents have been fiercely contested in the courts by rival inventors. The first important litigation by the Bell Co., upon its patents was in the suit of the American Bell Telephone Co., against Dowd. The latter was defended by the Western Union Co., owning the patents of Edison and others, and was defeated. The next case prosecuted was that of the American Bell Telephone Co. against Spencer, in the Massachusetts Circuit Court, which was decided adversely to the

defendant. The most bitterly fought contest over the telephone was that of Bell against Drawbaugh, the case lasting through several years, and being finally decided in Bell's favor. Drawbaugh, a Pennsylvania mechanic, some time about 1872 made a working telephone, using a cigar box, a glass tumbler, a tin can and other crude instruments. With this telephone, he claimed, he had carried on a conversation over a wire several hundred feet long, and when testimony was taken in Pennsylvania, more than a score of persons were found to testify that they had either heard of Drawbaugh's telephone or had actually used it. Some instruments said to be the original ones made by Drawbaugh were brought into court and exhibited, and it was shown that speech could readily be transmitted in an imperfect way with their aid. In Drawbaugh's statement it was said, that he was too poor at the time to take out the necessary patents, but the other side showed that he was not too poor to apply later on for patents upon other devices of comparatively no importance, and he was in communication during these years with men who would have advanced him money to complete anything so important as an apparatus for the transmission of speech. Suit was also brought against Mr. Bell by Elisha Gray, who claimed that Bell derived by accident or fraud, a knowledge of what was contained in a caveat filed by Gray describing a practical and useful form of telephone, a so-called liquid transmitter. This caveat was filed before Mr. Bell applied for his first patent, and it was charged that the patent examiner employed upon the case told Bell what Gray was doing, and how he did it. The lower court decided against Gray, dismissing the charge of official collusion, and the decision in this case, as well as in the others mentioned, was confirmed by the U. S. supreme court in March, 1888. The profits of his invention have made Mr. Bell a very wealthy man, and he now has a winter residence in Washington, D. C., and a summer home at Cambridge, Mass. Mr. Bell is the inventor of the photophone, which aims to transmit speech by means of a vibratory beam of light. It was first described by him before the American Association for Advancement of Science in Boston in 1880. He has also given much time and study to the problem of multiplex telegraphy, and to efforts to record speech by photographing the vibrations of a jet of water. He is an earnest advocate of teaching written language to deaf-mutes, and has embodied his views upon this question in frequent public addresses. He is a member of many scientific associations, and the author of a large number of papers upon scientific subjects. His wife, the daughter of Gardner G. Hubbard, is a deaf-mute, of whose education he had charge when she was a child.

SMITH, John, U. S. senator, was born in Hamilton county, O., in 1735. In his early days, the place where he lived was on the extreme western frontier of the country, and the opportunities for an education were of course very limited. Through the country schools of his neighborhood, however, he succeeded in becoming fairly well informed, and as he was gifted with much natural ability, he became a prominent man in the early history of Ohio. He joined the Baptist church, and grew to be known as a popular preacher, and in 1790 founded at Columbia the first church of that denomination in the state. He was elected a member of the first territorial legislature, which met in 1799, and the state being admitted into the Union in 1803, he was elected U. S. senator, and remained in that position until 1808. He was a Jeffersonian Democrat, and during the first part of his service in the senate was a close friend of Pres. Jefferson. In 1804 the president sent Senator Smith to Louisiana and Florida on a confidential mission, for the purpose of discovering the state of feeling with regard to the United States of the Spanish officers, who were there in official positions, in order that an idea might be formed as to the possible importance of their friendship in case of a war between the United States and France. Apparently Senator Smith conducted this mission satisfactorily, but he was unfortunately a warm personal friend of Aaron Burr, and when the latter fell under public odium, on account of his treasonable actions, Smith was involved in these, mainly because appearances were against him, and a motion was made for his expulsion from the U. S. senate. Smith absolutely denied having any connection with Burr's treasonable projects, and was generally believed by his constituents. The motion in the senate failed by one vote. Senator Smith died in Hamilton county, O., June 10, 1816.

CLAGGETT, John Thomas, first Protestant Episcopal bishop of the diocese of Maryland, was born Oct. 2, 1742, at White's Landing, on the river Pautuxent, in Prince George's county, Md. His father, the Rev. Samuel Claggett, was a clergyman of distinguished piety and talents, in Charles county, in the same state. At the period of his death, A. D. 1756, John Thomas, then thirteen years of age, was entrusted to the care of Mr. Philipson of Lower Marlborough in Calvert co., by whom he was prepared for his collegiate studies, which he pursued at Nassau Hall, Princeton. He was graduated there A. D. 1762, and immediately commenced the study of theology, which he prosecuted with very great success. He repaired to England, and was admitted by the bishop of London to deacon's order, on Sunday, Sep. 20, 1767, and to priest's order, on Sunday, Oct. 11, 1767. On his return to America he took

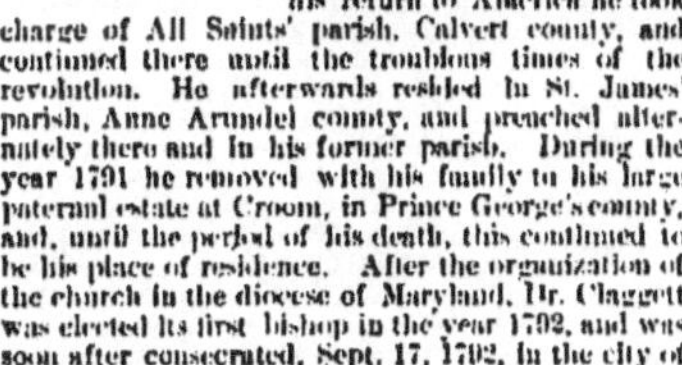

charge of All Saints' parish, Calvert county, and continued there until the troublous times of the revolution. He afterwards resided in St. James' parish, Anne Arundel county, and preached alternately there and in his former parish. During the year 1791 he removed with his family to his large paternal estate at Croom, in Prince George's county, and, until the period of his death, this continued to be his place of residence. After the organization of the church in the diocese of Maryland, Dr. Claggett was elected its first bishop in the year 1792, and was soon after consecrated, Sept. 17, 1792, in the city of New York, by the Rt. Rev. Dr. Provoost, assisted by Bishops Seabury, White, and Madison. His liberal education, extensive reading, retentive memory, commanding and impressive utterance, tender admonitions, affectionate appeals, and faithful exhibition of apostolic fervor, and of the truth as it is in Jesus, rendered him for many years eminent as a preacher, as a divine, and as a bishop. In the decline of life, however, he became very infirm, and was so incapacitated from performing the duties of his episcopate, as to require the aid of an assistant or suffragan bishop, the Rt. Rev. Dr. Kemp, who was consecrated Sept. 1, 1814. After having presided over the diocese of Maryland for twenty-four years, Bishop Claggett died, Aug. 2, 1816, having been an eminently successful teacher of the saving doctrines of the gospel, and in the language of his successor in the episcopate, "a true and genuine son of the church."

KEMP, James, second Protestant Episcopal bishop of Maryland, was born in Aberdeenshire, Scotland, in 1764. At an early age he was sent to the Grammar School of Aberdeen, and in 1782 was transferred to Marischal College. He continued to pursue his studies with the utmost diligence, and was distinguished through all the gradations of his collegiate course. At this time the faculty of Marischal College was adorned by some of the ablest men of the age; and the subject of this memoir had the advantage of the instruction of Profs. Skein, Copland, Hamilton, Beatle, and Campbell. He took his degree in 1786. Anxious, however, to avail himself of all the advantages of the institution, he continued his studies, attending the celebrated Dr. Campbell's lectures on divinity, and applying himself to the acquisition of the various branches of ornamental learning not usually embraced in a collegiate course. In April, 1787, he embarked for the United States, where he was soon employed as a private tutor in Dorchester county, eastern shore of Maryland, and, during the two years passed in this situation, he continued to prosecute his theological studies. Having abandoned the Presbyterian communion, in which he was educated, he was, in 1789, admitted to holy orders in the Protestant Episcopal church. In the following year he became rector of Great Choptank parish; and in 1813 succeeded the Rev. Dr. Bend as associate rector with the Rev. Dr. Beasley, of St. Paul's parish, Baltimore; having previously received the degree of D.D. from Columbia College, New York. Being elected by the convention of the church of Maryland, in 1814, to the office of suffragan bishop during the life of the Rt. Rev. Dr. Claggett, and as his successor in case he survived him, he was consecrated to the episcopal office Sept. 1st, of the same year. Bishop Kemp was a man of great modesty, scrupulously averse to everything like literary ostentation, and was esteemed one of the best scholars in the church. The jurisdiction of the church of the Eastern shore was committed to him, as his peculiar province, until 1816, when upon the death of Bishop Claggett he succeeded him as diocesan, and continued to discharge the duties of the office until his sudden and most lamented death, Oct. 28, 1827. This melancholy event was occasioned by the upsetting of a stage coach in which he was returning from Philadelphia, whither he had gone to participate in the consecration of the Rt. Rev. Dr. H. U. Onderonk. He died from the effects of his injuries on the morning of the third day following.

STONE, William Murray, third Protestant Episcopal bishop of Maryland, and twenty-third in succession in the American episcopate, was born in Somerset county, Md., June 1, 1779. He was a great grandson of William Stone, colonial governor of Maryland from 1648 until 1653 and a relative of Thomas Stone, signer of the declaration of independence and of John Hoskins Stone, governor of Maryland from 1794 until 1797. One of his collateral descendants, Frederick Stone, served in congress from 1867 until 1871, and has been since 1881 a judge of the Maryland court of appeals. Bishop Stone was graduated at Washington College, Maryland, in 1799. He was ordained deacon in 1802 and priest in 1803 by Bishop Claggett. With the exception of a short period spent in the rectorship of the church in Chestertown, Kent co., his ministry was confined to his native parish; and during several years in particular his faithful labors were crowned with much success. For fourteen years previous to 1828, he did not attend the conventions of his church; but, although he thus abstained from intermeddling in ecclesiastical politics, and confined himself to the duties and interests of his own parish, his modest worth was well known and duly appreciated by his brethren. In 1828, after the death of Bishop Kemp, there was no unanimity of opinion in regard to his successor. Repeated but unavailing attempts were made to fill the office, each party seeming resolved to adhere to its own candidate. In 1830 a committee of conference was chosen by the convention, and this committee nominated Dr. Stone, who was forthwith elected with great harmony, both of the other gentlemen withdrawing from the contest. His consecration was performed Oct. 21st, of the same year, in the city of Baltimore. During the seven years of his remaining life, he devoted himself with zeal and assiduity to the arduous and responsible duties of his station. He had, however, but a feeble and shattered constitution, and during his brief career in the episcopacy, was twice disabled by the fractures of his limbs. Yet, notwithstanding these infirmities and disabilities, all will bear testimony that he faithfully exerted his abilities in promoting the interests of the church of which he has been made one of the overseers. During the first year of his episcopate, as a token of personal respect, and in honor of the office he was elected to fill, the University of Pennsylvania conferred on him the degree of D.D. Bishop stone was distinguished by the passive meekness, the unaffected humility, and the lovely simplicity of his character. His course was not marked by brilliant actions; there was nothing in the attributes of his mind to occasion sudden bursts of admiration; but he possessed good common-sense talents, which were so sanctified by religion as to make him highly useful. His death occurred Feb. 26, 1838.

WHITTINGHAM, William Rollinson, fourth Protestant Episcopal bishop of Maryland, was born Dec. 2, 1805, in New York city. His grandfather was an English brass-founder, who emigrated to America in 1791, whose son, Richard, was associated with him in the foundry business. Richard was a scholarly man, while his wife, a daughter of William Rollinson, was a woman of marked character, whose love for their son William was so absorbing that she devoted herself entirely to his education. She studied Latin, Greek, and Hebrew in order to be able to instruct him, and she became so proficient that she gave instruction to a class of divinity students. He received no other instruction until he entered the General Theological Seminary in 1822, at the age of seventeen. He was so well prepared that he was asked who was his tutor, when he proudly answered, "My mother." All of William's friends were intelligent boys, one of whom became Cardinal McCloskey. During his college days, in addition to his studies, he wrote for the religious papers, and his reckless sacrifice of health in his zeal for study brought forth a touching protest from his fellow students. Upon his graduation, in 1825, he was appointed librarian and made a fellow of the college, and in 1827 he was made deacon, and then chaplain over a charity school connected with Trinity parish, and afterwards was transferred to Orange, N. J. On Dec. 17, 1829

he was ordained priest, and became rector of St. Mark's. He continued his ministrations and added to his work the editorship of a series of church works. He was, during this time, doing editorial work for the Sunday-school Union and the "Press." In 1831 he accepted a call to the rectorship of St. Luke's in New York city, when he resigned his salary from the Sunday-school Union and the "Press," although he retained his editorship. He also assumed the editorship of "The Churchman," which had been established in the early part of the year by Bishop Onderdonk, but the accumulation of his duties became such a drain upon his health that he was obliged to seek rest by a trip abroad. After fifteen months of travel he returned, apparently wholly recovered, and accepted the chair of ecclesiastical history in the General Theological Seminary, which he occupied until 1840, during a part of which time he also filled the chair of pastoral theology. Upon the death of Bishop Stone of the diocese of Maryland, after a warm contest, the opposing factions united upon Dr. Whittingham, and he was elected bishop of Maryland with only two dissenting votes, and was consecrated Sept. 17, 1840. He was zealous and self-sacrificing in the performance of his duties, and in his support of St. James' College at Hagerstown, which was founded in 1842 through

his efforts, he brought his family to dire necessity. He also was instrumental in founding the Church Home and Infirmary in Baltimore, an order of deaconesses, and the sisterhood of St. John in Washington. The Oxford movement, which was looked upon by many with distrust, was heartily indorsed by Dr. Whittingham, who was a prominent high churchman, and led to many controversies between himself and his clergy, which culminated in his presentment, in 1876, upon the ground that he ignored charges made against the rector of Mount Calvary Church who was an extreme ritualist, and whose practices, countenanced by the bishop, were distasteful to many of the parish. In 1852 he again made a European tour, during which he met the eminent dignitaries of the church, and among them the celebrated Dr. Keble. He made a second visit to Europe that year, and after his return devoted himself with his accustomed devotion to the duties of his charge. During the civil war although condemning the aggressive spirit of the anti-slavery party, Bishop Whittingham's sympathies were with the North, which cost him the support and confidence of many in whom he trusted. He openly rebuked a company of militiamen for an insult to the flag, and sent a circular letter of protest and remonstrance, when he learned that the prayers for the president of the United States were omitted from the services in some of the churches. In 1864 the General Theological Seminary invited him to a vacant chair in the institution, but he felt compelled to decline from a sense of duty to his bishopric. His long-continued disability necessitated a division of his labor, and upon his advice the new diocese of Easton was set off from Maryland; the Rev. William Pinkney D. D. was elected bishop, and consecrated in 1870, while Bishop Whittingham was ill in New Jersey. He was desirous of establishing a national church at Washington, where a cathedral was to be built at which he himself should officiate. His friends brought the project so near accomplishment that he went so far as to select a home for himself in Washington, but the arrangement was finally dropped to his great disappointment. In 1872 Bishop Whittingham was sent as representative of the American church to the congress of Cologne. which had for its object the advancement towards Christian unity on the part of the "Old Catholic" party. In 1873 he received an invitation to attend the third "Old Catholic" congress at Constance, and to the fourth congress at Freiburg, but was unable to accept either. His work may be summed up in the statement that everything done in the last half century was in a great measure helped by him. He held a high place in the regard of Western Catholics. Columbia conferred upon him the degree of S.T.D. in 1827. When the bishop attended the council in New York, in 1878, he taxed his strength severely, and his health, at best precarious, gave way, and he returned to Orange, N. J., where he died, Oct. 17, 1879.

PINKNEY, William, fifth Protestant Episcopal bishop of Maryland, was born at Annapolis, Md., Apr. 17, 1810, and was graduated from St. John's College in that city, in 1827. He began the study of law, but laid it aside that he might pursue that of divinity, which he did, partly at Princeton, N. J., and partly at the General Theological Seminary, New York city. He was ordained deacon in Christ Church, Cambridge, Md., Apr. 12, 1835, and priest at All Saints' Church, Frederick, Md., May 27, 1836. He received his first call from St. Andrews' Church, in Somerset county, Md.; afterwards, in 1838, he became the rector of St. Matthew's, near Bladensburg, Prince George's co., Md., and was pastor of that parish for seventeen years. In 1855 he was called to the rectorship of the Church of the Ascension, Washington, D. C., and continued to be its pastor even after he was elected assistant bishop of Maryland in 1868, and up to the time of his death. When Bishop Whittingham died in 1879, the assistant bishop became bishop by right of succession. He gave one-half his annual salary ($4,000) to poor and needy clergymen in his diocese. He was a firm believer in home missions, and the religion of the by-ways. as much if not more than in that of the "high places" in the synagogue. He died July 4, 1883.

PARET, William, sixth Protestant Episcopal bishop of Maryland, was born in New York city, Sept. 23, 1826. He was educated in the public schools and at Hobart College, where he was graduated in 1849. He was fitted for the ministry under the direction of Bishop Wm. H. Delancey, and was ordained as deacon in 1852 by Bishop Chase acting for the bishop of western New York and as a priest in 1853. In 1852 he was called to the rectorship of a church at Clyde, N. Y., where he remained until 1854. The following ten years he was rector of a church at Pierrepont Manor, N. Y.; and from 1864 until 1866 he was stationed at East Saginaw, Mich. Then, until 1884, he successively had charge of churches in Elmira, N. Y.; Williamsport, Pa.; and Washington, D. C. In 1884 he was chosen the successor of

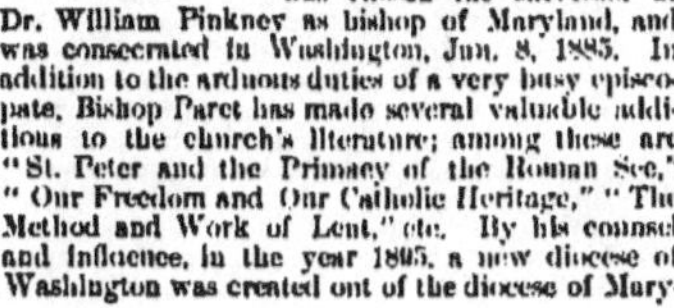

Dr. William Pinkney as bishop of Maryland, and was consecrated in Washington, Jan. 8, 1885. In addition to the arduous duties of a very busy episcopate. Bishop Paret has made several valuable additions to the church's literature; among these are "St. Peter and the Primacy of the Roman See," "Our Freedom and Our Catholic Heritage," "The Method and Work of Lent," etc. By his counsel and influence, in the year 1895, a new diocese of Washington was created out of the diocese of Maryland, and Bishop Paret, under the rights given him by the laws of the church, chose the remaining diocese of Maryland as his permanent work. He now (1896) resides in Baltimore, Md. Hobart College gave him the degree of D.D. in 1867, and that of L.L.D. in 1886. His brother, Thomas Dunkin Paret, born in New York city, Dec. 20, 1837, is the inventor of "tanite," a substance made from waste leather, which is extensively used in the manufacture of jewelry. He has been since 1867 president of the Tanite Co., at Stroudsburg, Pa.

DEXTER, Timothy, merchant, was born in Malden, Mass., Jan. 22, 1743. He early became an apprentice to the leather-dressing trade, in which he proved so proficient that in 1764 he began business on his own account in Charlestown, Mass. His subsequent great wealth was entirely the work of his own industry and shrewdness. The latter quality was especially displayed in the purchase of the depreciated Continental money, which, after Hamilton's funding system went into operation, became suddenly increased in value. With the accession of wealth Dexter's eccentricity of character asserted itself, and he made efforts both desperate and ridiculous to attain social prominence. He assumed the title of "Lord" and most earnestly endeavored to attract the notice of the good folk of first Boston and then Salem. Failing in this, he removed to Newburyport, where he purchased two large houses, one of which he afterwards sold at a profit, while the other he fitted up most extravagantly. The grotesque traditions concerning him, still current in the East, are almost incredible. His library was completely equipped with elegant books, his taste for literature, however, going no further than these same bindings. His art gallery was supplied in a like manner, he having commissioned a young connoisseur to purchase a number of paintings in Europe. Dexter unhesitatingly rejected all the masterpieces, and would only accept those that were worthless. He kept a poet laureate, whose rhymes, when unacceptable to his master, were rewarded with cuffs, blows, and sometimes pistol shots. Dexter's mansion was magnificent with minarets and other architectural devices alien to the quiet New England atmosphere. In his garden was a group of forty enormous columns, surrounded with mammoth statues of the world's great men, himself being included among the number, with the modest inscription, "I am the greatest man in the East." The cost of this freakish embellishment was about $15,000. His coach-and-four were of the most conspicuous style, and a crowd of wondering and jeering people generally followed him on his drives. Although so seemingly imbecile, he was nevertheless singularly successful in all business ventures, and attempts to trick him in such enterprises were sure, by either chance or cunning, to result in his eventual good fortune. A troublesome neighbor, his absurd conduct often brought horse-whipping and like attentions upon him. Happening to be in Boston when the news of the death of Louis XVI. was received, Dexter hastened to Newburyport and had the passing-bell tolled before the tidings of the monarch's death were circulated. He appeared as an author in the volume "A Pickle for the Knowing Ones." Upon one occasion he had a fine coffin made, a tomb prepared, and even went so far as to carry on a mock funeral. So strange a character was, moreover, not content with mere eccentricity for its expression. Dexter was dissipated to an extraordinary degree of abandonment, and although toward the end of his life he appeared to have shown some repentance for his many follies, yet nothing but absolute insanity can excuse him altogether. He died at Newburyport, Mass., Oct. 22, 1806. (See his life by S. L. Knapp.)

McVICKER, James Hubert, theatrical manager, was born in New York city, Feb. 14, 1822. As early as the age of ten he was obliged to work for a livelihood, and his school education as a boy was limited to a brief attendance at the public school. In 1837 he removed to St. Louis, Mo., where he learned the printer's trade, employing his leisure in study. He early exhibited a predilection for the stage. In 1843 he made his first appearance as an actor, in the St. Charles Theatre, New Orleans. He continued his professional career in that city, Cincinnati, Louisville, and St. Louis with steady advancement until 1848. In that year he was engaged by John B. Rice as principal comedian of the first theatre ever erected in Chicago expressly for the purpose of presenting theatrical performances. In 1849, the popular Yankee comedian, Dan Marble, having died, Mr. McVicker bought from his widow his plays and costumes and subsequently, commencing in 1852, made a tour of the United States in a series of Yankee impersonations. In 1855 Mr. McVicker married a daughter of the Rev. B. F. Meyers of Newark, O., and made his wedding tour to Europe. While there he filled a three months' engagement in London, appearing in a round of Yankee characters. In the course of this engagement he gave an order to the then popular dramatic writer, the late Mr. Charles Gayler, to write an American comedy, with the view of presenting a just conception of the New England Yankee. This comedy, called "Taking the Chances," was produced at Burton's Chambers Street Theatre, New York, in the spring of 1856. It proved to be a valuable addition to Mr. McVicker's repertoire, which embraced the leading comedy characters presented to the English-speaking public. The next effort to place the Yankee character before the public in a truly human conception was made by Mr. Joseph Jefferson when the "American Cousin" was produced by Laura Keene in 1858. It was then the "Peter Pomeroy" of Mr. McVicker and the "Asa Trenchard" of Mr. Joseph Jefferson that stamped the New England rustic a distinct human being. Constitutionally a lover of home life, Mr. McVicker in 1857 returned to Chicago to make it his permanent home and to devote his energies to theatrical management. On Nov. 5th of that year McVicker's Theatre was opened to the public, and has since continued under its founder's and proprietor's management. It was destroyed by the great fire of October, 1871, but was immediately rebuilt and reopened in August, 1872; the comedy, "Time Works Wonders," being the opening play. It is now one of the prettiest and most conveniently constructed theatres in the United States. Mr. McVicker has done more to impress his personality in the northwestern section of the United States than any other personage connected with the American stage. A leading trait in Mr. McVicker's moral and mental personality is the dignified pertinacity with which he magnifies his profession. He has at all times been its defender from the savage, uncalled-for, and fanatical attacks made upon it by many clerical gentlemen. He is the author of two pamphlets, "The Theatre, Its Early Days in Chicago," and "The Press, the Pulpit, and the Stage." The latter sets forth the view that, as a great moral instructor, the

stage is a worthy companion of the two other great social voices, the pulpit and the press, and quite as true to its mission. At the same time, Mr. McVicker is himself a fervid believer not only in the existence, but in the necessity, of great spiritual forces as the life-springs of earthly as well as heavenly things. He maintains that the highest art consists in a harmonious combination of realism with idealism, and that the greatest actor, like the greatest poet, is he who conveys the profoundest moral lessons in the most perfect artistic expression.

UPHAM, William, senator, was born at Leicester, Mass., Aug. 5, 1792. In 1803 his family removed to Montpelier, Vt. Young Upham studied at the University of Vermont, and then, in 1809, entered the law office of Cyrus Ward, of Montpelier. In 1810 he entered the office of Samuel Prentiss, and in 1813 was admitted to the bar. He began practice in Montpelier, and was highly successful. He was a member of the state legislature in 1827, 1828, and 1830, and in 1828 was elected state attorney for Washington county. In October, 1842, he was elected U. S. senator by the Whig party, and was re-elected in 1848. He died of smallpox, in Washington, D. C., Jan 14, 1853.

SMITH, John, founder of Virginia, was born in the town of Willoughby, Lincolnshire, England, in 1579. It is said of his early life that, while he could have acquired a good education at the free schools in England which existed at this period, he was of so daring and adventurous a nature that he cared but little for study, and having determined to become a sailor, had even sold his school-books and satchel to obtain the means to carry out this purpose. He already had the misfortune to lose his mother, and at this time his father died suddenly, which temporarily delayed his intention. He was in charge of guardians who proved, however, to be false to their trust; and who incited him to follow his own wishes with the hope of profiting by his running away, if he should do so, by obtaining the little property which his father had left him. He was, however, apprenticed to a merchant, but, as was anticipated, ran away when he was fifteen years of age, and visited France and the low countries, traveling for a part of the time as a servant to the young sons of the noblemen who were making a tour of the continent. He soon left this party, receiving on his departure a sum of money. At this time France was in the throes of war, which at length ended with the assassination of Henry IV. Young Smith enlisted as a soldier, and fought on the side of the Protestants, and when there was no more fighting in France he joined some English troops who were assisting the armies of Philip II. and the Duke of Alva, who were fighting in the Netherlands. He is said to have continued for four years in this service, when he became restless and took ship for Scotland. The series of extraordinary adventures which occurred at different periods during his life, began with this voyage. The vessel in which he sailed was wrecked, but he was in some extraordinary manner saved. After passing some time in Scotland, he returned to his native town, but only to remain there for a brief period. The association with old and new friends, which at first pleased and charmed him, at length began to pall upon his taste, and he determined to retire from the bustling world of

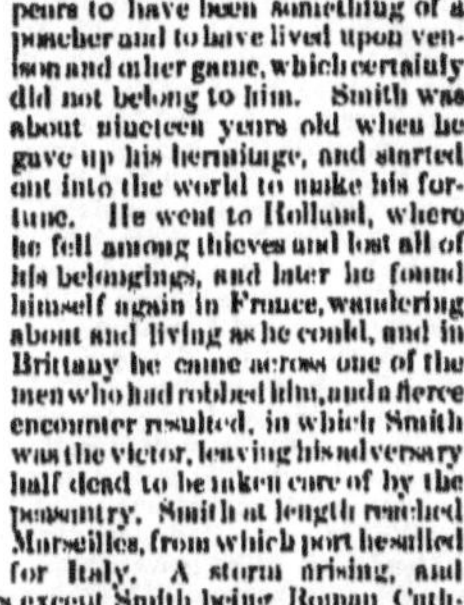

people altogether. He became a hermit, living in a hut in the seclusion of dense forests, where he read Marcus Aurelius and Machiavelli's "Art of War." It was a wild and erratic life which he lead, probably derived from his acquaintance with the old legends of "Robin Hood," and others similar to it. He is said to have had a horse and a servant, and occupied himself in imitation of what he had heard of the tourney, by riding about on his horse and tilting with his lance at whatever came in his way. He appears to have been something of a poacher and to have lived upon venison and other game, which certainly did not belong to him. Smith was about nineteen years old when he gave up his hermitage, and started out into the world to make his fortune. He went to Holland, where he fell among thieves and lost all of his belongings, and later he found himself again in France, wandering about and living as he could, and in Brittany he came across one of the men who had robbed him, and a fierce encounter resulted, in which Smith was the victor, leaving his adversary half dead to be taken care of by the peasantry. Smith at length reached Marseilles, from which port he sailed for Italy. A storm arising, and all the passengers except Smith being Roman Catholics, the elemental disturbance was laid to his charge as though he had been another Jonah, and he was at length cast into the sea. Fortunately he was a good swimmer, and succeeded in reaching the island of St. Mary's, from which he was taken off the next day by a French vessel, which had put in for a harbor during a storm. The captain of this vessel turned out to be a pirate who was on his way to Alexandria, at which port he discharged his cargo, and then cruised about the Mediterranean seeking his prey. After a bloody fight, which lasted two hours, they captured a Venetian merchantman, heavily laden with a cargo of silks, velvets, gold, spices and wines, and Smith received his share of the spoils, amounting to 1,000 sequins, which would be nearly $5,000 in modern money. Not wishing to continue in the piratical business, which did not approve itself either to his conscience or taste, Smith requested to be set ashore, and this request the captain willingly granted when they arrived at a port on Piedmont. Smith next visited Venice, and traveled through Italy, and in 1601, having a great desire to fight the Turks, he joined the Austrian army, and behaved himself with so much bravery and daring that he was soon put in command of a company of 250 cavalry. His services to the Austrians seemed to be without limit. He devised a telegraphic system of communication, and invented a bomb, which on being filled with some combination of chemicals, and thrown, by means of a sling, among the Turks, exploded, not only creating great consternation, but wounding and killing many of the enemy. But all his ingenuity did not prevent Smith from being taken prisoner by the Turks, and narrowly escaping with his life. He was held as a slave, but succeeded in killing his master and escaping into Russia. He now returned to England, after having a number of curious and exciting adventures, and found, on his arrival, that a deep interest had become prevalent in regard to the settlement of North America. The dazzling stories told of Cortez, in Mexico, and of Pizarro, in Peru, with the account given of such parts of Florida and the shores of the Mississippi as had been visited, had awakened an intense desire among Englishmen of an adventurous character to cross the ocean themselves, and seek their fortunes in these new and strange lands. Already Frobisher was exploring the coast of Labrador; Raleigh had successfully reached the Southern shore, which he named Virginia, after the virgin queen. So Smith, after a long delay, succeeded in forming a company, capitalizing it, and obtaining for it a patent or land grant, and with an expedition, comprising 105 men and three small vessels, he set sail Dec. 19, 1606. During the voyage, Smith, owing to his excitable disposition and determination to command, got into trouble with others of the party, and was put in irons, in which condition he remained thirteen weeks. They stopped at the West India islands for water, and then sailed north, but grew disheartened at not reaching land, and were about to return to England when a terrible storm drove the little fleet straight into Chesapeake bay. They landed at what is now known as Jamestown, Apr. 26, 1607, and proceeded to establish their colony. Smith immediately began explorations to discover the source of the James river, and by his kind treatment of the Indians insinuated himself into their good graces, making a league of friendship with Powhatan and others of the great chiefs. He soon acquired the real leadership of the colony, through his shrewdness and wise foresight. He was respected and feared by the Indians, and protected the colony from their depredations by his kind treatment and strong personality, even when they were provoked beyond endurance by the inhumanity of the settlers. He fortified Jamestown, and explored the Chickahominy river, and procured supplies of provisions by trading with Indians. At one time, owing to hostilities brought about by the settlers, they would have starved to death but for the exertions of Smith, who alone was able to

procure corn from the Indians. While on a mission of this kind he was captured by the natives, and carried before Powhatan, the chief, who, angered by the constant aggressions of the settlers, ordered him to be put to death. As he was about to be despatched with war clubs, his life, according to the well-known story, was saved by the intervention of Pocahontas, the king's favorite daughter. Smith made no allusion to this story of his rescue until Pocahontas's arrival in England as the wife of John Rolfe, when he wrote an account of it in a letter to Queen Anne. He was sent back to Jamestown, where he found the colony reduced to forty men, who were so disheartened that many of them were preparing to return to England, but, after a good deal of entreaty with the other leaders, he succeeded in preventing the abandonment of the plantation. During the next year Smith explored the whole country, from Cape Henry to the Susquehanna river, and drew a map of the bay and rivers, sailing about 3,000 miles. In 1608 he became president of the council, and, by enforcing strict discipline, greatly improved the condition of the colony. But the settlers were more bent upon gaining riches than in founding a colony, and they conspired to depose Smith, sending evil reports to England of his administration. Lord Delaware was made governor under a new charter, and three commissioners, Capt. Newport, Sir Thomas Gates, and Sir George Somers, were given power to rule the colony until his arrival. The vessel containing this authority was wrecked, however, and Smith remained in authority, and enforced it to preserve the colony from anarchy. In

1609 he was so injured by an explosion of gunpowder that he was obliged to return to England for proper medical treatment. Here, for a long time, his life was despaired of, and it was evident that it might take years for his health to be fully restored. As a matter of fact, he disappeared from the world, and was entirely lost sight of for five years. It is said that he devoted this period to study and reading, trying to make up the time which he had lost in his youth, when he had thrown away his opportunities for early

education. In 1614 Capt. Smith again sailed from London for North America, keeping well to the northward, and landing in a new country, which he called New England. They remained for six months on this coast, devoting their time to catching codfish, of which they obtained about 60,000, while from the Indians they bought about 10,000 beaver skins, besides a large number of other peltries. He subsequently made other voyages back and forth, had some adventures with pirates, awakened the first interest in the New England cod fisheries, and wrote and published a number of volumes describing the voyages which had been made to America, and relating the history of the Jamestown settlement, which was published under the title of "The True Travels, Adventures, and Observations of Capt. John Smith, in Europe, Asia, Africa, and America, from 1593 to 1629, together with a Continuation of his General History." His pen was very active in these later years, while his memory was clear and full with regard to his adventures. Nothing is known as to the circumstances surrounding the death of Capt. John Smith. It is said to have occurred among strangers, and in an obscure quarter in London, in 1631. Regarding Pocahontas, it is related that she was the victim of an infamous plot on the part of one Capt. Argall, commander of one of the English vessels, who succeeded in enticing her on board his ship, when he made her a prisoner, and held her for a heavy ransom. The Indian girl was only about eighteen years of age, and is said to have been very beautiful. During her captivity an English gentleman, John Rolfe, became enamored of her, and married her in the spring of 1613. Soon after her marriage Pocahontas received the rite of Christian baptism. In 1616 she sailed for England with her husband, and was there received with great hospitality and kindness, obtaining an audience at court, and awakening the interest of King James himself. Pocahontas, who had, no doubt, experienced great fondness for Capt. Smith, had several interviews with the latter after her arrival in England. In 1617 she was about to return to Virginia, when she grew suddenly ill, and soon

after died, leaving a son, Thomas Rolfe, from whom have descended many of the oldest and most respected families in Virginia, including that of John Randolph, of Roanoke. Pocahontas was buried at Gravesend, where she died, the certificate of her death reading : "1616, May 21, Rebecca Wrolfe, wyffe of Thomas Wrolfe, gent., a Virginia lady borne, was buried in the chancel."

VAN NESS, John Peter, member of congress, was born in Ghent, N. Y., in 1770. He went to New York city, and studied at Columbia College, where he was graduated, and afterward decided to adopt the profession of the law. He prepared for the bar, but the state of his health forbade his entering upon practice. In 1800 he was elected as a Democratic member of congress. He settled in Washington, D. C., and married Marcia, daughter of David Burns, a very wealthy man of that city, and on whose death Mr. Van Ness, through his wife, became very wealthy. He built a large and costly residence, where he entertained luxuriously. He was mayor of the city, trustee of a number of public institutions, and president of the Metropolitan Bank. His wife, who died in September, 1832, being one of the wealthiest heiresses in the District of Columbia, and a woman of fine education and accomplishments, was conspicuous in Washington society in her time. She was noted for her numerous charities, and besides founding the Protestant Orphan Asylum, gave the land upon which two churches were erected. She was the only woman in Washington who ever received a public funeral. He died in Washington, March 7, 1847. Mr. and Mrs. Van Ness were buried on the grounds of the Protestant Orphan Asylum, in a mausoleum built after the pattern of the temple of Vesta at Rome.

ALLIBONE, Samuel Austin, author, was born in Philadelphia, Pa., Apr. 17, 1816. He was for a considerable time engaged in business in his native city, but, being a man of liberal education and literary tastes, his leisure was devoted to literary pursuits, and it was as an amateur that he began the great work to which many of the best years of his life were devoted. He lived at this time on Arch street, above Ninth, in an old-fashioned continental house, in which the library was the conspicuous feature. His published writings consisted mainly of some contributions to theological controversy, he being an earnest member of the Protestant Episcopal church, and especially interested in Sunday-school work. His important works are: "Poetical Quotations from Chaucer to Tennyson," "Prose Quotations from Socrates to Macauley," "Great Authors of all Ages," "Union Bible Companion," "Explanatory Questions on the Gospels and the Acts." He also published a large number of religious tracts and articles in the current periodicals. The completion of the great "Critical Dictionary of English Literature and British and American Authors," the first volume of which was published in 1854, and which proved an undertaking of such magnitude that it gradually absorbed all his time, established his position as a leading authority in the line of research into which it led him. Its chief value consists in its accurate and exhaustive statements of the books written by each author, to which is added a comprehensive selection of critical judgments from the acknowledged censors of literature. The "Nation" says:—"He has accomplished a work for which every American scholar owes him hearty thanks." The second and third volumes of this work were not printed until after an interval of seventeen years, during which he had published an "Alphabetical Index to the New Testament," and several minor works, and had become the book editor and corresponding secretary of the American Sunday-school Union. In connection with his dictionary, which contains biographical and critical notices of no fewer than 46,000 authors, he compiled several volumes of poetical and prose quotations, and also indexes to several important publications, as well as a variety of religious tracts and hand-books. In 1879 he was appointed librarian of the then newly-endowed Lenox Library in New York, and removed to that city, where he lived until 1889, when failing health compelled him to go abroad. He died Oct. 2, 1889.

WOODBURY, Roger Williams, banker, was born at Francestown, N. H., March 3, 1841, the ninth generation from William Woodbury, who emigrated from Somersetshire, England, in 1628, and was one of the earliest settlers of Beverly, Mass. His education was obtained in the common schools, alternating with work in the cotton factories of Manchester. He then became a compositor. At the age of twenty, at the inception of the civil war, he enlisted as a private in the 3rd New Hampshire Infantry, and served until the end of the war. At twenty-three he was a captain and chief ordnance officer on the staff of Gen. A. H. Terry, in command of the expeditionary corps that captured Fort Fisher, N. C. He participated in some fifty battles, and was wounded at the battle of the Mine at Petersburgh, July 30, 1864. He removed to Denver, Col., in 1866, and there became the proprietor of the "Daily Tribune," and in 1872 of the "Daily Times," but disposed of the latter ten years later. He was the first president of the Denver chamber of commerce, and served three years, until, having entered the banking business, he voluntarily retired. While in that capacity he erected the chamber of commerce building, and established the first free public library and reading room in Colorado. This library has now (1895) 30,000 volumes, and Gen. Woodbury is chairman of the committee in charge. The Woodbury gold medal, awarded annually in the Denver high school for excellence in declamation, was established by him in 1875. He was six years regent of the State University of Colorado, and on his retirement the new dormitory was named Woodbury Hall in token of his services. In the Masonic fraternity he held many important offices. He organized the association which erected the elegant Masonic temple in Denver.

As a journalist and citizen he has been in the front rank in his adopted state, and has contributed much by public addresses, as well as by example, to establish it as a great commonwealth. He first applied the name of the "Centennial State" to Colorado on the passage of the enabling act in 1875. He has been the presiding officer of many associations, and possesses marked ability as an organizer. He is president of the Union National Bank of Denver.

COBB, George T., manufacturer and philanthropist, was born in Morris county, N. J., in October, 1813, the grandson of a revolutionary officer. His early education was limited to that obtained in the public district school, and as he had his own way to make in the world, when a lad of fifteen years he found employment in a country store, and afterwards in the iron works at Dover, N. J., where he soon mastered the business, and in time became established in the iron trade on his own account. In this business he was eminently successful, and he soon acquired a large fortune, which he generously distributed during his lifetime. Among his benefactions was the Evergreen cemetery in Morristown, a gift to his native town. To the same town he gave a school-house, costing $15,000, and a church, costing $75,000. In 1860 Mr. Cobb was elected as a Democratic representative in the thirty-seventh congress, serving from July 4, 1861, to March 3, 1863. In the three sessions that determined the policy and purpose of the civil war, Mr. Cobb gave the war measures of the administration his support so far as they were directed towards the suppression of the rebellion,

and in this offended a wing of his party. At the convention of 1862 he would have been renominated by his party, but when the convention had passed a resolution condemning the war, refused, Mr. Cobb then abandoned his party, and in 1865 was elected a state senator from Morris county on the Republican ticket. He was re-elected in 1867. In 1869 he was a candidate for U. S. senator, to fill the vacancy caused by the death of Senator William Wright. In the nominating convention he was opposed by Frederick T. Frelinghuysen, who was nominated by three votes over Mr. Cobb, and was elected. Mr. Cobb met his death in a railroad accident, on his return from Greenbrier, White Sulphur Springs, Va., on the Chesapeake and Ohio Railroad, Aug. 6, 1870.

WINCHELL, Alexander, scientist, was born at North East, Dutchess co., N. Y., Dec. 31, 1824, and was a nephew of Rev. James Manning Winchell, a well-known Baptist minister of Boston. His parents were in comfortable circumstances, and were of more than ordinary ability, having been teachers in the public schools of the town. They took unusual pains in the education of their son, which greatly helped his early development. By the time he was seven years old he had made considerable progress in arithmetic, being able to recite the entire multiplication table, and at sixteen, expressing a desire to teach, his father secured for him a position in a neighboring district school, where he taught in the winter of 1840. His active mind led him to continue his mathematical studies, which soon opened to him the study of astronomy. In 1843 he was assistant in Armenia Seminary, and the next year entered Wesleyan University as a sophomore. Here his ardor received such a check in the marking system, which favored a literal reproduction of the words of the text-book, that he refused to compete for honors. He was graduated in 1847, and declined a tutorship in mathematics in that institution, to become instructor in natural science in Pennington Seminary, N. J., where he remained a year, devoting his spare moments to the flora of the vicinity. From 1848 to 1850 he was teacher of natural science at Armenia (N. Y.) Seminary, where he gave his first lectures in geology; made a catalogue of the flora; observed solar spots, and began a series of meteorological observations. He then taught in several institutions in Alabama, and made a thorough study of the geology of that state, at the same time contributing scientific papers and collections to the Smithsonian Institution and other societies. He returned North in 1854, having been elected to the chair of physics and civil engineering in the University of Michigan. Not being satisfied with the text-books, he originated matter and methods, and as a branch of physics, he made meteorological observations, which he also reported to the Smithsonian Institution. The next year he was appointed to the newly-created chair of geology, zoölogy, and botany. In 1859–61, and again, after its reorganization after the war, in 1869–71, he was director of the geological survey of the state of Michigan, and among the results of his labors in the department of palæontology was the establishment of seven new genera and 364 new species, chiefly fossil. His active mind seemed to lead in every direction. He advocated the study of natural history in the lower schools of the state; determined the position of the salt waters of East Saginaw, and anticipated the vast development of the salt interest; pointed out the richness of the gypsum beds near Tawas, which were pronounced barren; published numerous geological papers, and a paper on the fruit-bearing belt of Michigan, calling attention to the climatic influence of Lake Michigan; studied the oil regions of the United States and Canada. In 1873 he was elected

chancellor of Syracuse University, but, finding the duties of the presidency interfering with his scientific work, resigned the position at the end of the year, and took the chair of geology, zoölogy, and botany in that institution. In 1875 he became professor of the same sciences at Vanderbilt University, Ky., but continued to lecture at Syracuse. His advocacy of the evolution theory, and of a belief in the existence of a preadamite race, while kindly received in the North, brought him into conflict with the board of trustees of Vanderbilt University, and in 1878 his resignation was requested. Professor Winchell replied: "If the board of trustees have the manliness to dismiss me for cause, and declare the cause, I prefer that they should do it." On his refusal to accede to the wishes of the trustees, on the grounds alleged, the lectureship was declared abolished. He was then unanimously recalled by the regents of the University of Michigan to the chair of geology and palæontology, which he retained until his death. Upon his return he began an extended syllabus of a course in geology, with copious references, which greatly contributed to the success of his department. At the same time his studies extended in every direction, and his contributions were of the greatest importance to the whole country. He was called to preside over the anthropological section of the American Association at Montreal, and spent the summer of 1880 in field work with the geological survey of Minnesota, studying the outcrops of over 890 localities. The observations of the survey were found to throw much light upon many of the problems of archæan geology. The next year's work included a survey of the original Huronian area, and the iron regions of Michigan, Wisconsin and northern Minnesota. He accumulated such a mass of data that for its examination he was obliged to decline all but the most important invitations to lecture. The results of this work were partially preserved in his report of the Minnesota survey, 1880. Although he was busily occupied with lectures, attendance on scientific meetings, and the preparation of plans for enlarging the laboratory, he was the leading spirit in the formation of the Geological Society of America, and in 1890 was elected its president. He also was active in establishing the "American Geologist."

His name is lastingly associated with American geology by his establishment of the Marshall group, and by fourteen new species discovered by him, if for no other reasons. In 1867 the degree of LL.D. was conferred upon him by Wesleyan University. Dr. Winchell lectured frequently outside of the class room, and did much to popularize science in this country. He was at one time editor of the "Michigan Journal of Education," and at the time of his death was senior editor of "The Geologist." He was a voluminous writer, and in addition to his reports on geology, he published, among other works, "Genealogy of the Family of Winchell in America" (1869); "A Geological Chart" (1870); "Michigan" (1873); "The Doctrine of Evolution" (1874); "The Geology of the Stars" (1874); "Reconciliation of Science and Religion" (1877); "Preadamites, or a Demonstration of Existence of Men before Adam" (1880); "Sparks from a Geologist's Hammer" (1881); "World Life, or Comparative Geology" (1883); "Geological Excursions, or the Rudiments of Geology for Young Learners" (1884); "Geological Studies, or Elements of Geology" (1886); "Walks and Talks in the Geological Field" (1886); "Shall We Teach Geology?" (1889). The predominant thought running through his works is the harmony between the indications and doctrines of science, and the central doctrines of the Christian religion. His "Geology of the Stars" was an attempt to extend the history of the earth, as recorded in the geological strata, so as to include the whole lifetime of a world. Dr. Winchell was, perhaps, the first man of science who could descend from that high and stately and unpopular style which was formerly thought necessary to dignify science, and in simple language tell the story of the landmarks of the world's growth. A large proportion of his books are scientific treatises for popular reading. Dr. Winchell died Feb. 19, 1891. During his last illness he promulgated a theory, which he believed would necessitate the essential modification of the La Placean nebular hypothesis, and which was his last legacy to science.

SPRAGUE, Charles, poet, was born in Boston, Mass., Oct. 22, 1791. His father, Samuel Sprague, a native of Hingham, where the family had lived for five generations, was one of the party that threw overboard the tea in Boston harbor. His mother, Joanna Brunton, was a woman of remarkably original powers of mind, and wielded great influence in the development of her son's talent. He was educated at the Franklin school, Boston, having for one of his teachers Lemuel Shaw, who became chief justice of Massachusetts. When ten years old he met with an accident, by which he lost the use of his right eye. He left school when only thirteen, and entered a mercantile house, and when twenty-five, was admitted to a partnership, which was continued until 1820, when he became teller in the State Bank. When the Globe Bank was established in 1825, he was chosen cashier, which position he re-

tained until his retirement from business life in 1864. Mr. Sprague's poetical writings consist largely of theatrical prize prologues. He was first brought into prominence by his poetical address at the opening of the Park Theatre, in New York, which was received with great enthusiasm. He increased his reputation by similar successes in Portsmouth, Salem, and Philadelphia. He composed a "Shakespearian Ode," which was read by him at the Boston Theatre in 1820, at a celebration in honor of the great dramatist. His chief poem "Curiosity," was delivered before the Phi Beta Kappa Society of Harvard in 1829, and the following year he recited a "Centennial Ode" on the celebration of the settlement of Boston. He also wrote a number of shorter poems, which have great poetical merit. His dramatic odes are elegant, polished compositions, possessing a refined eloquence which is characteristic of all his productions. Edwin P. Whipple says: "His prologues are the best which have been written since the time of Pope. His Shaksperian ode has hardly been exceeded by anything in the same manner since 'Gray's Progress of Poesy.' But the true power and originality of the man are manifested in his domestic pieces. 'The Brothers,' 'I See Thee Still,' and 'The Family Meeting,' are the finest consecrations of natural affection in our literature." The London "Athenæum" says: "Sprague has been called the 'American Pope,' for his terseness, his finished elegance, his regularity of metre, and his nervous points." Loring says: "Amidst a host of competitors, he received the prize six times for producing the best poem for the American stage, an instance unprecedented in our literary annals." His "Prose and Poetical writings" appeared in 1850. He died in Boston, Jan. 22, 1875.

THORPE, Thomas Bangs, author and journalist, was born at Westfield, Mass., March 1, 1815. He was the son of Thomas Thorpe, a clergyman, who died at the early age of twenty-six. After studying three years at Wesleyan University, he traveled in the southwest, and was in Louisiana, 1836–53, editing Whig papers in New Orleans and at Baton Rouge, and gaining some fame as a political speaker. In his youth he displayed a taste for painting, and executed "the Bold Dragoon" to illustrate Irving's story, when only seventeen years of age. It was exhibited in the American Academy of Fine Arts, and won universal admiration. Like Irving, he left the pencil for the pen, and turned his talent to descriptive writing. His first books, "Hive of the Bee Hunter" (1845; reprinted 1854), and "Mysteries of the Backwoods" (1846); written in the dialect and character of "Tom Owens," were praised by Griswold, and gave

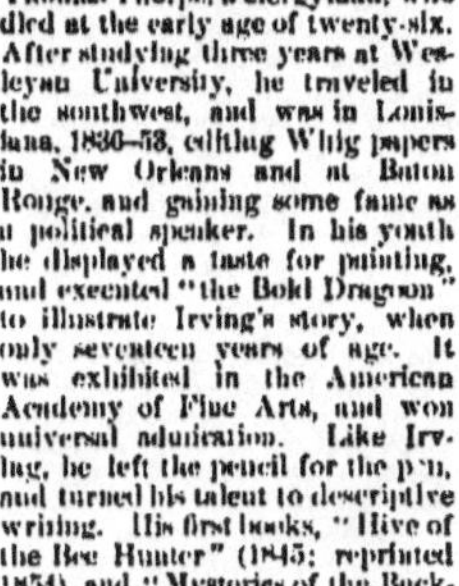
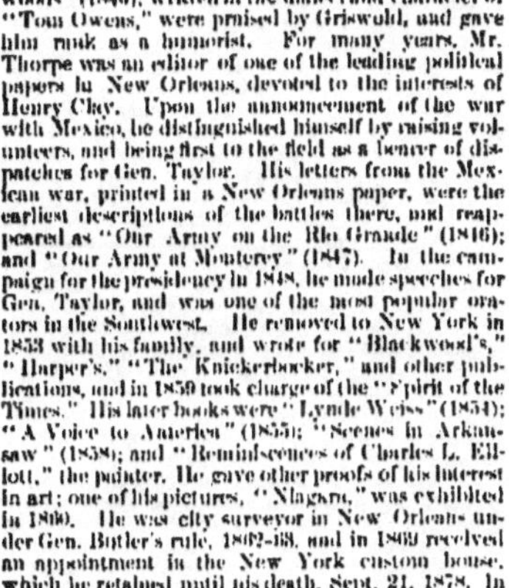

him rank as a humorist. For many years, Mr. Thorpe was an editor of one of the leading political papers in New Orleans, devoted to the interests of Henry Clay. Upon the announcement of the war with Mexico, he distinguished himself by raising volunteers, and being first to the field as a bearer of dispatches for Gen. Taylor. His letters from the Mexican war, printed in a New Orleans paper, were the earliest descriptions of the battles there, and reappeared as "Our Army on the Rio Grande" (1846); and "Our Army at Monterey" (1847). In the campaign for the presidency in 1848, he made speeches for Gen. Taylor, and was one of the most popular orators in the Southwest. He removed to New York in 1853 with his family, and wrote for "Blackwood's," "Harper's," "The Knickerbocker," and other publications, and in 1859 took charge of the "Spirit of the Times." His later books were "Lynde Weiss" (1854); "A Voice to America" (1855); "Scenes in Arkansaw" (1858; and "Reminiscences of Charles L. Elliott," the painter. He gave other proofs of his interest in art; one of his pictures, "Niagara," was exhibited in 1860. He was city surveyor in New Orleans under Gen. Butler's rule, 1862–63, and in 1869 received an appointment in the New York custom house, which he retained until his death, Sept. 21, 1878. In

proof of the fidelity of Mr. Thorpe's hunting scene, it is related that Sir W. D Stewart projected a hunting party in the West, and wished to secure his services to record their experiences. Mr. Thorpe could not accept, but he wrote a series of letters purporting to give an account of the doings of the party, which were accepted as genuine in this country and in Europe, Sir William himself pronouncing them correct descriptions, all the while supposing them to be written by one of the party.

SEWALL, Stephen, Hebrew scholar, was born in York, Me., Apr. 4, 1734, grand-nephew of Samuel Sewall. He was graduated at Harvard College in 1761. He taught school at Cambridge, and in 1762 became librarian and instructor in Hebrew at Harvard College. Two years later he was appointed first Hancock professor of Hebrew in Harvard. He was an active Whig during the revolution, and represented Cambridge in the general court in 1777. Prof. Sewall's lectures proved him to be one of the most learned men of his time. His published works are a Hebrew grammar; a Latin funeral oration on Edward Holyoke; "Young's Night Thoughts," translated in Latin, a volume of Greek and Latin poems; "The Scripture History Relating to the Overthrow of Sodom and Gomorrah, and to the origin of the Salt Sea." He left a Chaldee and English dictionary in manuscript, which is still in existence in the library of Harvard College. He spent the latter part of his life in retirement, and died in Boston, Mass., July 23, 1804.

CLAPP, Alexander Huntingdon, clergyman, was born at Worthington, Mass., Sept. 1, 1818, and was graduated at Yale College, 1842. He studied theology in the Theological Seminaries of Yale and Andover, and had charge of the Congregational Church at Brattleboro', Vt., 1846–53, and of the Beneficent Church, Providence, R. I., 1855–65. In 1865 he became secretary of the American Home Missionary Society, New York city, and in 1878 its treasurer. He has published some sermons, and is, since 1875, the New York editor of the "Congregationalist," Boston. He received the degree of D.D. from Iowa College in 1868.

TUCKERMAN, Joseph, clergyman and philanthropist, was born in Boston, Mass., Jan. 18, 1778, son of Edward Tuckerman, the founder of the earliest fire insurance company in New England. He was graduated at Harvard in the same class (1798) with Channing and Story, having shared his room with the latter; studied theology under Thomas Thacher, and was pastor at Chelsea, Mass., 1801–26. In 1812 he organized a Society for the Religious and Moral Improvement of Seamen, and later, the Benevolent Fraternity of Churches, under whose auspices he labored as minister at large in Boston from 1826. He visited England in 1816 and 1833, and made many warm friends there, among them Joanna Baillie and Lady Byron; his ideas took shape in the Tuckerman Institute at Liverpool, and were followed by Degerando in France. At home he was the author of the system of public charities which, according to E. E. Hale, "have proved sufficient for whatever exigency." Judge Story attested "the general excellence of his character, his zeal in all good works, and his diffusive benevolence." Though a Unitarian, he cared little for doctrinal or ecclesiastical distinctions. His fervor was carried to a point of picturesque intolerance; he blamed Channing for spending himself on the pulpit, and seemed "to disparage all forms of Christian ministry but the one in which he was so ardently engaged. His degree of D.D. was conferred by Harvard in 1824. He published: "Seven Discourses" (1811); eleven tracts for the Seamen's Friend Society; a prize essay on "Wages paid to Females" (1830); "Reports to the Fraternity of

Churches" (1831–32); "Gleams of Truth" (1835), and "Principles and Results of the Ministry at Large" (1839). Some of these were reprinted in 1874 with the title "Elevation of the Poor." He sought to regain health at Santa Cruz in 1836, and afterwards in Cuba, but died in Havana, Apr. 20, 1840. Memoirs of him were written in Boston by Dr. Channing, 1841, and in England by Mary Carpenter, 1849.

SILLIMAN, Augustus Ely, financier and author, was born at Newport, R. I., Apr. 11, 1807; son of Gold Selleck Silliman, the second, and brother of Benjamin Douglas Silliman. He went into business in New York at an early age, and having engaged in banking co-operated actively in establishing, in 1853, the powerful clearing-house association, and was one of the committee which for the first six years of its existence directed its proceedings. In 1857 he was elected president of the Merchants' Bank, and held that responsible position until May, 1868. His integrity and sound judgment were proverbial. He was independent and self-reliant in his opinions; absolutely sincere and truthful, not only in matters of importance, but also in the smallest affairs and conventionalities of life. He was noted for his conservatism in business, and for his energy, wisdom, caution, and firmness in financial crises, and possessed the unqualified respect, confidence and regard of all his contemporaries. In May, 1868 (as has been stated), Mr. Silliman was obliged, by impaired health, to retire from active business, and the step was regretted by the press and the public. The directors of the Merchants' Bank passed resolutions recording their sense "of the ability, devotion, and courteous bearing with which he had fulfilled every trust during a connection of over forty years with that institution;" adding that "no one in any financial community can point to a more pure and spotless record of unswerving fidelity to duty and honor. At the same time he received a testimonial in the form of a letter signed by the presidents and officers of the various banks of the city represented in the clearing-house association, testifying to the uniform courtesy and kindness which had characterized his intercourse with them; the zeal and constancy with which he had ever supported sound and conservative measures, and the influence he had exerted in establishing and giving character and dignity to the association. On retiring from business, Mr. Silliman devoted himself to astronomical and other studies, and to the enjoyment of literature and the fine arts, and to revising a volume published in his earlier days, entitled "A Gallop among American Scenery, or Sketches of American Scenes and Military Adventure," which received abundant praise for its brilliant descriptive passages and original style. A new and enlarged edition appeared in 1881. Besides this, Mr. Silliman published, in 1869, a translation, with notes, of Fénelon's "Conversations with M. de Ramsai on the Truth of Religion, with his Letters on the Immortality of the Soul and the Freedom of the Will." Among the public institutions of which Mr. Silliman was an active member, were the Century Club and the Long Island Historical Society, and the Mercantile Library Association of New York, of which he was for a time the president. His pronounced and firm opinions and convictions, polished manners, affectionate nature, playful humor, and great culture made him prominent in every circle into which he entered. He was particularly devoted to his mother who was a woman of rare qualities of mind and character, and in honor of her memory bequeathed to Yale College nearly $100,000 for the founding of an annual series, forever, of lectures in that university, "the general tendency of which may be such as will illustrate the presence and the wisdom of God as manifested in the natural and moral world." For several years Mr. Silliman was forced by ill health to withdraw from general society. He died in Brooklyn, May 30, 1884.

WHITE, Charles Abiathar, geologist, was born in North Dighton, Mass., Jan. 26, 1826. His father, who married Nancy, daughter of Daniel Corey of Dighton, was a son of Capt. Cornelius White of Taunton. This Cornelius White was the fourth in an unbroken genealogical line of six, bearing precisely the same name, five of whom lived in Taunton, but the line is believed to have originated in Boston. When Charles was in his thirteenth year the family removed to the then territory of Iowa, where he grew up to manhood, and where he began his scientific career. His early predilections were toward natural science, but, because of the lack of suitable schools in that region at the time, his education was largely self-acquired. He was graduated at Rush Medical College with the degree of M.D., and practiced medicine in Iowa City three or four years. In 1866 he became state geologist of Iowa by legislative appointment, which office he held until 1870. In 1867 he was chosen professor of natural history in the State University of Iowa, and held that chair until 1873, when he was called to a similar chair in Bowdoin College, Maine. While performing his duties at this college, he was appointed geologist and paleontologist to the U. S. geographical and geological surveys west of the 100th meridian, under Lieut. (now Maj.) Geo. M. Wheeler, and in 1875 he entered upon similar service in the U. S. geographical survey of the Rocky mountain region, under Maj. J. W. Powell. In 1876 he passed to a similar position in the U. S. geological survey of the territories, under Dr. F. V. Hayden. He remained with the latter survey until its suspension in 1879, at which time he became fully employed upon the paleontological collection of the U. S. National Museum. He had more or less complete charge of those collections from 1878 to 1894, inclusive, although engaged most of that time in other official work. He became attached to the present U. S. geological survey in 1881, and was detailed in that year to act as chief of an artesian wells commission upon the Great Plains, but he resumed his duties upon the survey, and continued them until 1894, when he resigned. He was commissioned by Emperor Dom Pedro II. to investigate the invertebrate cretaceous fossils collected upon the Brazilian geological survey, the results of which were published in Rio Janeiro in a large quarto volume, profusely illustrated. His travels connected with scientific work have been extensive, mainly in North America, but also in large part in the old world. He has spent fifteen seasons in explorations and field work, mainly in the Rocky mountain region. He has been a prolific writer, the titles of his published books and papers numbering above 200. These are mostly geological, but some relate to biology, medicine, and physics, respectively. Several of his publications have been translated into other languages. A contemporary writer says: "Among paleontologists, Prof. White ranks as the greatest living authority on mesozoic invertebrates, and as a geologist, his position is among the ablest investigators and expositors of his time." In 1880 he was elected a member of the U. S. National Academy of Sciences, and vice-president of the American Association for the Advancement of Science. He is corresponding member of the principal geological societies of Europe, and received the degree of LL.D. from the State University of Iowa in 1893.

WARRINGTON, Lewis, naval officer, was born at Williamsburg, Va., Nov. 3, 1782. He received a classical education, and was graduated at William and Mary College in 1798. He entered the navy as midshipman in 1800, and served under Preble in the war with Tripoli. He became a lieutenant in February, 1807, and was on the Chesapeake in her encounter with the Leopard, June 20th. In 1812 he sailed in the Congress with Com. Rodgers' squadron in vain pursuit of the British West India fleet. In 1813 he was made master, and placed in command of the Peacock, with which he took nineteen vessels, including the Epervier, captured off Cape Canaveral, Fla., Apr. 29, 1814, after a close contest of forty-two minutes; for this congress voted him a gold medal. Having made several prizes in the Bay of Biscay, he returned to New York in the fall, was commissioned captain, and sailed in Decatur's fleet. On June 30, 1815, he took the Nautilus and three more East India vessels in the straits of Sunda, a region until then avoided by American cruisers; these prizes had to be given up as peace had been declared before they were captured. After this he was in the Mediterranean, 1816-19; in command of the Norfolk navy yard, 1820-24 and 1832-39; of the West India squadron, 1821-26; and then of the new navy yard at Pensacola, where a town took his name. He was a navy commissioner 1827-30 and 1840-42, a president of the board in 1841, chief of the bureau of yards and docks 1842-46, and of that of ordnance from 1847 until his death, which occurred at Washington, D. C., Oct. 12, 1851.

GREENOUGH, Horatio, sculptor, was born in Boston, Mass., Sept. 6, 1805. His father, David Greenough, was a prominent merchant, and the boy had every advantage offered him for culture and education. His artistic tastes were early developed. When quite a child he became noted for his success in carving toys for his companions, and even at this early age made a very successful copy in plaster of a Roman head, taken from a coin. His evident talent attracted to him many friends, and he read books on art, and studied and worked, at the same time becoming thoroughly well informed on general subjects. It is stated that when a boy he could repeat 2,000 lines of English verse without hesitation or error. When fifteen years of age he was so fortunate as to encounter a French sculptor, who taught him how to model in clay. Then he went to Hartford, where he remained two years, when he became the friend of Washington Allston. It was during his collegiate course that Greenough designed the existing Bunker Hill monument. In 1825 he went to Florence, and then to Rome, and thereafter made his residence in Italy. In 1826 he returned to Boston, where he remained for a few months and executed the portrait busts of Pres. Adams, Chief-Justice Marshall, and others. He then returned to Rome, and was the first American student who settled there permanently. There he made the acquaintance and secured the friendship of the great Danish sculptor, Thorwaldsen. During a visit to Paris, Greenough executed a bust of Lafayette, which has been considered by good judges more truthful than that by the French sculptor, David. J. F.

Cooper was one of his first patrons, and gave him an order for an ideal group of the nude cherubs; this work was much admired in America. The influence of Allston, who had been his friend in youth, of Cooper, Everett, and R. H. Dana, secured for him, in 1835 a commission from congress for a statue of Washington. He spent nearly eight years upon this task, handling the theme poetically rather than historically, and never intending that it should be placed in the open air: it won high praise, but its location before the capitol did not satisfy the sculptor. Among his smaller and more literal portraits, produced at various periods, are busts of Henry Clay, Josiah Quincy, Josiah Mason, James Fenimore Cooper, Thomas Cole, Samuel Appleton, and John Jacob Astor. A man of genius, full of refined and poetic fancies, and no mere copyist, he excelled in heads of children, and in ideal subjects. Many of his best works are in private houses in Boston and elsewhere. Among those on sacred, legendary, or literary themes, are a bust of Christ, "The Guardian Angel," "The Angel Abdiel," "Lucifer," "Venus Victrix," the "Graces," and Byron's "Medora." About 1837 he received from the U. S. government a second commission, on which he labored at intervals until 1851; this work, "The Rescue," depicts a combat between a settler and an Indian. Partly to place it to his mind at Washington, but as much to escape from the political disturbances in Italy, he returned to his native land in the fall of 1851. Here, as abroad, he made many friends; R. W. Emerson esteemed his talk "both brilliant and deep," and greatly admired his scattered writings in prose and verse. Attacked by brain fever at Newport, he was taken for treatment to Somerville, Mass. A memorial volume (1853), was edited by H. T. Tuckerman, and contains his "Essays on Art." Some of his letters appeared in 1887. Two of his brothers attained eminence, one as an architect, the other as a sculptor. He died at Somerville, Mass., Dec. 15, 1852.

ADAMS, Milward, theatrical manager, was born at Lexington, Ky., Jan. 6, 1857, the son of Dr. Samuel L. Adams, who occupied the chair of anatomy and physiology in the Transylvania Medical College at Lexington, Ky., until the breaking out of the war, when he entered the U. S. army as surgeon. His grandfather built the first brick residence in Hamilton county, O., in a little town now a suburb of Cincinnati, O. In 1861, the family moved to Lebanon, O., where they resided until 1865, when they located at Danville, Ind., and there Dr. Adams died in 1869. Soon after his father's death Milward Adams went with his family to Chicago, and entered the employ of Wilson Bros. In January, 1872, he became associated with George B. Carpenter in the business of public amusements, both dramatic and musical, on the stage and the platform. This was entirely successful, and led gradually and naturally to an enterprise which turned out one of the most distinguished successes in Chicago real-estate operations. It was the building of the fine edifice known as the Central Music Hall, a new and profitable departure in its line. It has always been the meeting place of the Central Church, the largest Protestant congregation in Chicago. It has also been a prominent place of meeting of all public lectures and performances for charitable and other objects. Mr. Adams' association with Mr. Carpenter was dissolved in 1884 by Mr. Carpenter's death, at which time Mr. Adams assumed the sole management of Central Music Hall. In December, 1887, Mr. Adams quitted the Central Music Hall for a still more important enterprise, the management of the Chicago Auditorium, the grandest private building for public use in America.

Ale. Bernays

BERNAYS, Augustus Charles, surgeon, was born at Highland, Madison co., Ill., Oct. 13, 1854, the son of a prominent physician. His early education was superintended by his mother and an aunt, who carefully instructed him in German and French. His first schooling was received at a grammar school in St. Louis, Mo., and in 1872 he was graduated at McKendree College, Lebanon, Ill. In October of the same year he entered the University of Heidelberg, and was matriculated as a student in the medical department. He was kept closely at his studies for four years, and then passed the examination for the degree of M.D., in July, 1876, taking the highest honors. He was the first American-born student to take that degree, *summa cum laude*, at the University of Heidelberg, which fact was commented on in the English and American university magazines. After graduation, he served a term as assistant house-surgeon at the Academic Hospital at Heidelberg, under Prof. Gustav Simon and Hermann Lossen. In the autumn of the same year he published in the "Morphological Archives," edited by Gegenbaur, his first original memoir, "On the Development of the Auriculo-ventricular Valves of the Heart," which was soon followed by another equally original investigation on "The Development of the Knee-Joint, and of Joints in general." Both these memoirs are quoted in all exhaustive treatises on embryology and anatomy that have appeared since their publication. In 1877 Dr. Bernays went to England, and in the autumn of that year qualified for, and passed, the examination for the degree of Member of the Royal College of Surgeons of England, which is equal to the state's examination in Germany, and entitles the holder to practice anywhere in Great Britain and the colonies. In 1878 he began the practice of surgery in St. Louis, Mo., with his father, and in 1888 was elected professor of anatomy and clinical surgery in the College of Physicians and Surgeons of that city. Besides teaching anatomy, which is his special and most favorite work, he has been the leader in original surgery. A series of monographs, under the title of "Chips from the Surgeon's Workshop," have recorded the progress of his work. Some of his best known papers are, "Kolpohysterectomy," one of the first successful operations of the kind in the United States. In 1889 Dr. Bernays performed the first successful Cæsarean section in the State of Missouri, saving both mother and child. At the international congress of medicine, at Berlin, in 1890, where Prof. Bernays was secretary of the surgical section, he read a paper on the treatment of intestinal wounds, which caused much favorable comment, and was reprinted in every civilized country. Another contribution is, "A New Operation for the Treatment of Retroflexion of the Uterus." Prof. Bernays's practice is perhaps the largest of any surgeon in the West, and besides his private work, he devotes a great deal of his time to teaching surgery and operating in the charitable institutions of the city of St. Louis. The very latest contribution to surgery by Dr. Bernays is a paper published in the "Journal of the American Medical Association," May, 1894, entitled "The first Successful Case of Cæsarean Section for Placenta Prævia." He is professor of anatomy, surgical pathology, and clinical surgery in the Marion-Sims College of Medicine, and the Woman's Medical College of St. Louis. His reputation is wide-spread, and his cases come to him from every state in the Union. He is a member of numerous scientific bodies; a life member of the German Surgical Society of Berlin; a life member of the Anatomische Gesellschaft, and of the American Association for the Advancement of Sciences.

THOMPSON, Daniel Pierce, novelist, was born at Charlestown, Mass., Oct. 1, 1795. His grandfather, Daniel Thompson of Woburn, a cousin of Count Rumford, fell at Lexington. He was taken to Berlin, Washington co., Vt., in childhood, where he was brought up on a farm. He worked his way to, and through, college, being graduated at Middlebury in 1820. His early education was what a scanty attendance upon the public school afforded. Finding a water-soaked volume of the English poets, he dried the leaves and gained a glimpse of the world of literature. He was now intent upon getting an education. By the sale of some sheep, which he owned, he was enabled to begin his preparation for college, and by teaching school, and earning a few dollars here and there with incredible toil. While a private tutor in Virginia he studied law, and was admitted to the bar. After spending a few years in the practice of law, in 1824 he opened an office at Montpelier, Vt., and was made register of probate. In 1830-33 he was clerk of the legislature, and appointed compiler of the state laws enacted since 1824, in continuation of Slade's work. The volume appeared in 1835. While at college he contributed short tales and essays to the periodicals, and continued to write frequent articles for the magazines upon poetical and miscellaneous topics. Noticing the offer by the "New England Galaxy" of a prize for a tale, was his first incentive to the writing of fiction, and in competing for this prize, he wrote "May Martin; or, The Money Diggers," which gained the prize, and when printed in book form in 1835, had an enormous sale. He took an active interest in the anti-masonic controversy, and published a satirical novel aimed against the Free Masons, entitled, "The Adventures of Timothy Peacock; or, Free Masonry Practically Illustrated," which was issued under the pen-name of "A Member of the Vermont Bar." He was judge of probate for Washington county, 1837-40, clerk of the county court, 1843-45, and then of the supreme court, and secretary of state, 1853-55. With these peaceful avocations he combined a great deal of literary activity, which did much in the service of his adopted state, for most of his novels aimed to illustrate its traditions and popularize its early history. Of this character are: "The Green Mountain Boys" (1840), which embodied the more romantic incidents of the early history of Vermont; "The Rangers" (1850), was illustrative of the revolutionary history of Vermont, and was the result of a careful study of the time; and "Tales of the Green Mountains" (1852); "Locke Amsden; or, The Schoolmaster" (1845) was largely autobiographical, and was drawn from personal observations, intending to illustrate the art of self-culture; "Gaut Gurley; or, The Trapper of Lake Umbagog" (1857), crossed the border into New Hampshire, and "The Doomed Chief" (1860), into the region of King Philip. Mr. Thompson's other books were, "Lucy Hosmer" (1848); "Centeola, and Other Tales" (1864); and a "History of Montpelier" (1860). He contributed in youth to Zadoc Thompson's "Gazette of Vermont" (1824); and in his later years wrote sundry historical monographs and biographical articles. He was extremely popular as a lyceum lecturer, and was an accomplished orator on public occasions. He died at Montpelier, June 6, 1868.

REA, John Patterson, soldier and commander-in-chief of the G. A. R. (1887–88), was born at Lower Oxford, Pa., Oct. 18, 1840. He went to the village school, and then worked in a factory. In April, 1861, after removal to Ohio, he enlisted as a private in a three-months' regiment, the 11th Ohio infantry. When the three months were over, he joined the 1st Ohio cavalry as second lieutenant, and was promoted to be first lieutenant in 1862; captain in 1863; and in the same year was brevetted major for gallant services. During three years and four months' service in the 1st Ohio volunteer cavalry he was only eight days absent, and that was when he was taken prisoner. He was in all the battles and campaigns of his regiment, which was a part of Gen. Eli Long's cavalry brigade, army of the Cumberland; he served until ill health compelled him to resign, Nov. 23, 1864. In his twenty-fourth year he entered the Wesleyan University at Delaware, O., where he was graduated in 1867. Returning to Pennsylvania, he studied law, and was admitted to the bar in 1868.

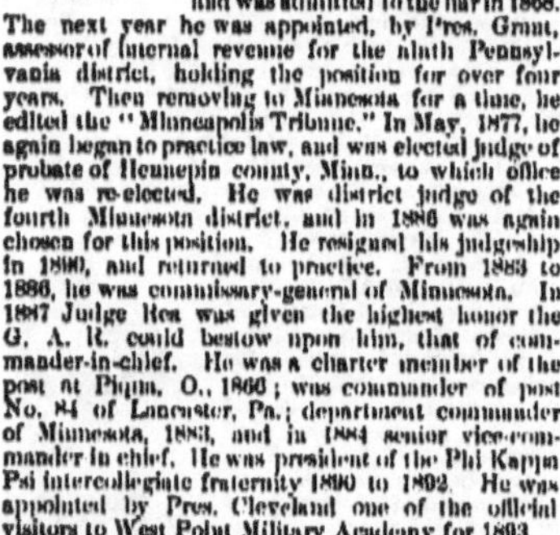

The next year he was appointed, by Pres. Grant, assessor of internal revenue for the ninth Pennsylvania district, holding the position for over four years. Then removing to Minnesota for a time, he edited the "Minneapolis Tribune." In May, 1877, he again began to practice law, and was elected judge of probate of Hennepin county, Minn., to which office he was re-elected. He was district judge of the fourth Minnesota district, and in 1886 was again chosen for this position. He resigned his judgeship in 1890, and returned to practice. From 1883 to 1886, he was commissary-general of Minnesota. In 1887 Judge Rea was given the highest honor the G. A. R. could bestow upon him, that of commander-in-chief. He was a charter member of the post at Piqua, O., 1866; was commander of post No. 84 of Lancaster, Pa.; department commander of Minnesota, 1883, and in 1884 senior vice-commander-in-chief. He was president of the Phi Kappa Psi intercollegiate fraternity 1890 to 1893. He was appointed by Pres. Cleveland one of the official visitors to West Point Military Academy for 1893.

CLARKE, Augustus Peck, physician, was born in Pawtucket, R. I., Sept. 24, 1833. His father, Seth Darling Clarke, was of the eighth generation in descent from Joseph Clarke, who, with his wife, Alice (Pepper) Clarke, came with the first settlers from Plymouth, England, to Dorchester, Mass., in 1630. Dr. Clarke's great grandfather, Ichabod Clarke, was a captain in the war of the revolution, and his grandfather, Edward Clarke, served in the war of 1812. Dr. Clarke's mother (née Fanny Peck) was sixth in descent from Joseph Peck, who came from Beccles, England, to Hingham, Mass., in the year 1638. Her father, Joel Peck, fought under Gen. Washington in the battle of Rhode Island, Aug. 27, 1778. Dr. Clarke completed his preparatory course in the University grammar school, Providence, R. I., and entered Brown University in September, 1856, receiving the degree of A.M. in the class of 1860. Before the close of his academic course he commenced the study of medicine under the direction of Lewis L. Miller, M.D., of Providence, entered Harvard University Medical School, and received the degree of M.D. in the class of 1862. In August, 1861, he was appointed assistant surgeon of the 6th New York cavalry, served under Gen. McClellan, in 1862, and was at the siege of Yorktown, and in the engagements at Mechanicsville, Gaines's Mill, and Peach Orchard. At the battle of Savage's Station, Va., June 29, 1862, he was made prisoner, but was allowed to continue his professional services, and remained with the wounded until all were exchanged. He was promoted to the rank of surgeon of his regiment, May 5, 1863, and served subsequently under Gens. Meade, Sheridan, and Grant, until the surrender at Appomattox. During four years' service he participated in upward of eighty-two battles and engagements, was frequently complimented in the reports of his superior officers, and "for faithful and meritorious service" was appointed brevet colonel. After the completion of his military service, in 1865, he traveled abroad, and attended the various medical schools and hospitals in London, Paris, Leipzig, and other great medical centres, for the purpose of fitting himself more particularly for obstetrical, gynecological, and surgical work. On his return, in 1868, he removed to Cambridge, Mass., where he soon established a high reputation as a practitioner. Dr. Clarke is a member of the Massachusetts Medical Society, and has been one of its councillors; a member of the American Academy of Medicine; American Medical Association, and vice-president of that body for 1895–96; American Association of Obstetricians and Gynecologists; president of the Gynecological Society of Boston, 1891–92; a vice-president of the Pan-American Medical congress, 1893; member of the Ninth International Medical congress, Washington, D. C., 1887; of the tenth, at Berlin, Germany, 1890; and of the eleventh, at Rome, Italy, 1894; before each of which he read papers; a delegate to the British Medical Association, in 1890, and to medical societies at Paris in the same year. He was one of the founders of the Cambridge Society for Medical Improvement, in 1868, and was its secretary from 1870–75; also a member of the American Public Health Association; of the military order of the Loyal Legion of the United States, and one of the board of officers of the latter in 1894–95.

After the close of the congress in Berlin he again visited the great cities of Europe, including London, Edinburgh, Paris, and Vienna, devoting himself to the study of their hospital service. While pursuing, in 1865–66, his medical studies under Messrs. Lemaire of Paris, and Creslé of Leipzig, he became impressed with the importance of adopting antiseptic measures for carrying on successful surgical work, and thus became one of the earliest advocates of this method of procedure, Dr. Clarke, in the midst of the multitudinous duties of his professional work, has been able to make important researches relating to gynecology, and to abdominal surgery, and has contributed articles frequently to different medical societies and journals, as well as to the public press. Among his contributions to medical literature may be mentioned: "Recto-Vaginal Fistula, its Etiology and Surgical Treatment" ("Journal of the American Medical Association," 1894). Dr. Clarke has been consulting physician to Middlesex Hospital and Dispensary since 1892, and professor of gynecology and abdominal surgery in the College of Physicians and Surgeons of Boston, Mass., since 1893, and dean of the faculty since 1884. He was president of the Cambridge Art Circle, 1890-91; member of Cambridge city council, 1871, '73, '74, and during the last year, was an alderman, and chairman of the committee on health. Dr. Clarke married, Oct. 23, 1861, Mary H. Gray, author and poet. They have two daughters.

CLARKE, Mary Hannah (Gray), author and poet, was born in Bristol, R. I., March 28, 1835, daughter of Gideon and Hannah Orne (Metcalf) Gray. She was a great-granddaughter of Col. Thomas Gray of Bristol, R. I., an illustrious officer in the revolutionary war, and a direct descendant of John Gray, an English gentleman, who traced his descent to the John de Gray, that came over with William the Conqueror. John Gray's son, Edward, born in 1623 in Stapleford, Tawney, Essex county, England, emigrated in 1643 to Plymouth, Mass., and became the richest merchant of the colony. Mrs. Clarke spent her early years at her father's homestead, a portion of the Mount Hope lands obtained from King Philip, the Indian chief. She was educated at the public schools of her native town, at Miss Easterbrook's Young Ladies' School in Bristol, and subsequently at East Greenwich Academy, R. I. She afterward went to Boston, where she devoted herself to the study of fine arts, including painting, poetry, and music. She was married, Oct. 23, 1861, to Dr. Augustus P. Clarke, surgeon of the U. S. army, and since widely known in this country as a writer on subjects pertaining to obstetrics and gynecology. At an early age Mrs. Clarke displayed marked literary talent. She wrote extensively for magazines and for the public press, and was the author of many dramas, lyric poems, and operettas. She assumed different pen names, but was chiefly known in print as " Nina Gray Clarke." The titles of some of her works are: " Effie, Fairy Queen of Dolls," for which she received the prize awarded by the Cambridge " Tribune " in 1880; " Prince Puss-in-Boots;" " Golden Hair and her Knight of the Beanstalk in the Enchanted Forest;" " Obed Owler and the Prize Writers;" " How I Came to Leave Town, and What Came of It;" " Edith Morton, the Sensible Young Lady;" " The Story that the Willow Basket Told to Faith Fairchild;" " English Lyrics," and " Home." Mrs. Clarke also composed a number of songs: " Were it not for Dreams," " Just Like Cinderella " (an operetta); " Jack Frost's Visit to the Fairies" (an operetta); " Twittering Swallow;" " Robin, Robin, Bold and Free;" " Down by the River;" " Not to Blame;" " Four-Leafed Clover." As an artist, the many pictures painted by her, in both water-color and oil, have commanded much attention from connoisseurs of art. Although endowed with many unusual gifts, she nevertheless sought to improve her talents by unremitting application of all her powers. She traveled extensively throughout Europe, visiting many of the chief cities for observation, and was thus enabled to gain from the masters an inspiration for greater work. She died in Cambridge, Mass., May 31, 1892. Her two daughters are graduates of Radcliffe College.

BOREN, Samuel Hampson, pioneer planter and financier, was born in Giles county, Tenn., Dec. 3, 1811, the son of Capt. James Boren (born Aug. 3, 1781, in Georgia). Mr. Boren's grandfather, Nicholas Boren, died in Gibson county, Ind., at the age of eighty. His wife was a Hampson, and from her Mr. Boren derived his second name. Mr. Boren's mother was originally Jane Blair, born in North Carolina, Aug. 27, 1791, the daughter of a very wealthy planter. Mr. Boren received only a limited academic education until the age of eighteen, when he thoroughly schooled himself in a college course while teaching as the principal of a small Tennessee school. In November, 1838, he removed from Tennessee to Nacogdoches, then the principal town in the Republic of Texas, where for sixteen years he led the life of a planter. In 1846 he volunteered from Nacogdoches and served in the Mexican war with distinction as a lieutenant of cavalry under Gen. Zachary Taylor, being in the battles of Monterey and Buena Vista. In 1854 he removed to Tyler, where he entered the cotton business. He was very successful, and in 1871, his son, Capt. B. N. Boren, took charge of a branch house in Galveston. Mr. Boren was one of the best financiers in Texas, and his opinion and advice were sought by capitalists and financiers. He made an extensive and valuable addition to the city of Tyler, and that city named one of its thoroughfares in his honor. He was a director in, and a chief promoter and original incorporator in both the Texas and St. Louis Railroad Co., and in the East Texas Fire Insurance Co. He was a director in a leading bank, and aided and encouraged, by generous donations, many enterprises that built up eastern Texas. Mr. Boren was a staunch Democrat, having been reared in the Polk and Jackson school of politics, and served as a delegate to three Democratic state conventions. He was a member of the Christian church and was a master Mason. On Feb. 21, 1839, in Nacogdoches,

Tex., he was married to Sarah A., daughter of Col. Benjamin Long, who fought under Gen. Jackson, being in the battles of the Horseshoe and New Orleans. In the winter of 1814 he was taken prisoner and kept on a man-of-war until the spring of the following year when he was exchanged. After the war he was colonel of militia in Bedford county, Tenn. He was handsome and popular, famous for his integrity and generosity. Mrs. Boren's mother, Mary Moore Dickson, was a granddaughter of Gen. Joseph Dickson, of North Carolina, a revolutionary officer. Mary Dickson Long, upon the death of her husband, Col. Benjamin Long, with her children removed in the winter of 1836 to the Republic of Texas, locating at Nacogdoches, the home of her cousin, J. Pinckney Henderson, the first governor of the state of Texas. Mrs. Boren was an accomplished and fascinating woman, and was pronounced by Gen. Thomas J. Rusk the handsomest young lady in the Republic of Texas. Mrs. Boren's brother, Col. Richard B. Long, was postmaster at Tyler during Pres. Cleveland's first administration; her nephew, R. B. Long, Jr., is mayor of Tyler, and another nephew, John B. Long, of Rusk, was a member of the fifty-second congress, from the second district of Texas. By his marriage with Miss Long, Mr. Boren had eight children, James N. (who was killed at the battle of Richmond, Ky., in 1863), Capt. Benjamin N., of Dallas (formerly of Galveston), and Richard L., of Colorado, Tex. Mrs. Franklin Newman Gary (see Vol. IV., p. 397), Mrs. Oliver Loftin, Mrs. James A. Pegnes, and Mrs. Charles Q. Goodman, all of Tyler, and Mrs. Sawnie Robertson of Dallas. Mr. Boren died Sept. 28, 1881, and Mrs. Boren died Aug. 10, 1888.

WILLIAMS, Ephraim, founder of Williams College, was born at Newton, Mass., Feb. 24, 1715. He was the son of a colonel of the same name (1691–1754), grandson of Isaac Williams, (1634–1708) by his second wife, and great-grandson of Robert Williams, who settled at Roxbury in 1638. After making several voyages he removed with his father to Stockbridge, Berkshire co. He was a captain in the French wars, serving in several Canadian campaigns, showing talent as a military officer. He had command of a line of forts on the west side of the Connecticut river, and lived at Fort Massachusetts on the Hoosick river, three or four miles east of the site of Williamstown. This was surrendered to the French and Indians in 1746, while he was absent on one of his northern errands, but was rebuilt and garrisoned in 1747. After the war he retired to Hatfield. In 1755 he was colonel of a regiment sent to join Sir W. Johnson in the expedition against Crown Point. With 200 Mohawks and 1,000 whites, among whom were several of his relatives, he advanced to attack Dieskau, fell into an ambuscade at Bloody Pond, near the head of Lake George, and was killed by the first fire, Sept. 8, 1755. His party retreated to the main body, and during the day repulsed the enemy in battle. Being unmarried and having, it is said, a presentiment of death, he had made his will at Albany, July 22d leaving his property to a school among the settlers near his home. This in time became valuable; trustees were appointed in 1785, a school was opened in 1791 and chartered in 1793 as a college, which, like the town, was named from its benefactor. He is commemorated by a rude monument set up in 1854 by the Alumni on the spot where he fell. His bequest for the purposes of education seems to have grown out of both his respect for learning and his affection for the settlers among whom his military life was passed. He was of a warm, generous disposition, with a winning ease and politeness, and though he was not much indebted to schools for his education, is said to have had a taste for books, and cultivated the society of men of letters.

FITCH, Ebenezer, first president of Williams College (1793–1815), was born at Norwich, Conn., Sept. 26, 1756, son of Dr. Jabez Fitch, a physician of considerable eminence, and Lydia (Huntingdon) Fitch. The son passed his childhood at Canterbury, Conn., which gave rise to the erroneous idea that he was also born there, a fact that was even engraved upon his tombstone. He was fitted for college by the Rev. Dr. James Cogswell, for some years a minister in Canterbury. From his earliest boyhood he contemplated entering the ministry, and his excellence in study and in conduct were marked, both at school and at home. He was graduated with honor at Yale College in the fall of 1777, a commencement which, owing to the distracted state of the country in consequence of the revolutionary war, was attended by but few. The next two years he spent in New Haven as a resident graduate, and a part of a year at Hanover, N. J., teaching an academy. In 1780 he received the degree of A.M., with the appointment of tutor in Yale College. This office he resigned in 1783 to form a mercantile connection with Henry Daggett, of New Haven, and in June of the same year he went to London to purchase goods, which, owing to his ignorance in business matters, were wholly unsuited to the simple wants of the Connecticut people, and, hence, involved him in serious pecuniary embarrassment, from which he was unable to extricate himself for a number of years. In 1786 he was a second time elected to the office of instructor in Yale College, and until 1791 officiated as senior tutor and librarian. During his tutorship he connected himself with the college church, and was licensed to preach in May, 1790. He was elected preceptor of the Academy of Williamstown, Mass., in 1790, and on Oct. 26, 1791, commenced teaching a school there, which subsequently attained great prosperity. In June, 1793, the institution at Williamstown, known as the Williamstown Free School, received from the general court of Massachusetts a charter for a college, and in August of the same year Mr. Fitch was elected president. The first commencement of Williams College was held on the first Wednesday in September, 1795, President Fitch having been ordained a minister of the gospel on June 17th previous. In 1800 he received the honorary degree of D.D. from Harvard University. He presided over Williams College with a marked degree of ability and success, for twenty-two years. Through his wise and prudent direction of its earlier affairs was the institution's later prosperity made possible. His most distinguishing characteristics were purity and benevolence, and through his personal aid many students without means of their own were enabled to obtain a college education. Upon his resignation from the presidency in 1815 he became pastor of the Congregational Church at West Bloomfield, N. Y., and remained there twelve years, and after resigning continued to preach occasionally until the time of his death, March 21, 1833.

MOORE, Zephaniah Swift, second president of Williams College (1815-21). (See Vol. V., p. 307.)

GRIFFIN, Edward Dorr, third president of Williams College (1821-36), was born at East Haddam, Conn., Jan. 6, 1770, the son of a prosperous farmer. He was prepared for college under the Rev. Joseph Vaill, of Hadlyme, entered Yale College in 1786, and was graduated with honor in 1790. On leaving college he became principal of an academy at Derby, Conn., and at the same time began the study of law. In the summer of 1791 a severe illness turned his thoughts in the direction of the ministry, and upon his recovery he relinquished the study of law, entered upon the study of theology under the direction of the Rev. Dr. Jonathan Edwards, of New Haven, and was licensed to preach Oct. 31, 1792. In January, 1793, he began to preach in New Salem, where a great revival of religion was brought about in consequence. His subsequent ministrations in other communities were equally successful. On June 4, 1795, he was ordained, and installed pastor of the Congregational Church of New Hartford. The winter of 1800 was spent in Orange, N. J., and in 1801 he entered upon a pastorate at the First Presbyterian Church of Newark, N. J., which continued for more than seven years. He received the degree of D.D. from Union College in 1808; in 1809 accepted the professorship of pulpit eloquence at Andover, and in 1811 took charge of the newly organized Evangelical Church on Park street, Boston. For a time he filled the chair of sacred rhetoric at Andover; in February, 1812, assisted at Salem in the ordination of the first five missionaries, who were sent into the foreign field by the American Board; and in the winter of 1812 delivered his celebrated Park street lectures. His return to Newark in 1815 was marked by a general and widespread revival of religion. In 1817 he published a notable

work on the atonement. In the spring of 1821 he was elected president of the college at Danville, Ky., and also to the same position in a college in Cincinnati, O., both of which offices he declined. In August of the same year he was chosen president of Williams College, "his reputation being precisely what was needed for the college at such a crisis," said Dr. Hopkins. This prediction was more than verified at the time when the legislature granted a charter for Amherst College in preference to Williams, an act which

threatened to seriously affect the latter's usefulness, but which was rendered harmless through the prompt and energetic conduct of President Griffin. He at once secured funds to the amount of $12,000—the first thousand of which was subscribed by himself—and so strengthened the institution in every possible way that its success was unassailable. At a later period of financial distress he voluntarily surrendered a considerable portion of his annual salary that the funds of the college might be unimpaired, an example that was immediately followed by the rest of the faculty. His administration was further marked by the organization of the Alumni Society of Williams College; by the erection of several new buildings—among them the college chapel; by the establishment of the professorship of rhetoric and moral philosophy; and by a distinct growth in the spiritual life of the entire community. Upon his retirement from official life Dr. Griffin returned for the third time to Newark. On May 17, 1796, he was married to Frances, daughter of the Rev. Joseph Huntingdon, of Coventry, Conn. Two daughters were born to them. He was a prolific writer, three volumes of his sermons having been published, while his contributions to religious periodicals were varied and numerous. He died Nov. 8, 1837, having preached the Gospel for forty-five years.

HOPKINS, Mark, fourth president of Williams College (1836-72), was born in Stockbridge, Mass., Feb. 4, 1802. He came of English ancestry, the

earliest American representative being John Hopkins, who settled in Cambridge in 1634. His son, Stephen, established himself at Waterbury in 1680, where he built a mill on what is now known as Mad river. Here his eldest son, John, became town clerk, and was the father of Timothy Hopkins, who became a person of great influence, officiating at various times as constable, selectman, grand juror, and moderator of the town meeting, and holding the office of justice of the peace for eight years, while he represented the town many times in the general court. He died in 1749. His son, Samuel, born in 1721, was the celebrated divine, whose theological doctrines created a new epoch in New England religious development. Another son, Mark, became a colonel of the Berkshire militia in 1776, and served in the war of the revolution, and was otherwise noteworthy as the first lawyer of Berkshire county. Mark's son, Archibald, was a farmer, who lived and died at Stockbridge—a man of lesser parts, perhaps, than his distinguished ancestors, but of rugged worth. He married a Mary Curtis, a true descendant of the early Puritans. To this couple was born Mark, and two younger brothers, Albert, who became a well-known astronomer, and Henry, whose early promise of distinction as an artist was nullified by premature death. Mark was fitted for college partly at Clinton, N. Y., partly by his uncle, Rev. Jared Curtis, then principal of Stockbridge Academy, and was for a short while an inmate of Lenox Academy. Before entering college he taught school at Richmond. In 1821 he entered Williams College, founded in 1755 by Col. Ephraim Williams, whose half-sister was the mother of Electa Sergeant, afterwards Col. Mark Hopkins's wife. The future president was thus connected by blood with the founder of the college. In 1824 he was graduated with the valedictory as B.A. The following year he became a tutor in the college, after having entered the medical school at Pittsfield, then in a flourishing condition. In the autumn of 1827 he resumed his medical studies, and was graduated from Berkshire Medical School in 1829, and in 1830 prepared to settle down in New York city as a physician. At that time, however, Dr. William A. Porter, professor of moral philosophy and rhetoric at Williams College, died, and the vacant chair was offered to Mark Hopkins, and was accepted by him after some hesitation. Thus began the connection which was to last for over half a century, and be productive of such great and enduring results. On Christmas Day, 1832, he married Mary Hubbell, of Williamstown, and in 1833 he was licensed to preach by the Berkshire Association. In 1836, despite the fact that he was but thirty-four years old, he had made so powerful an impression by his lofty character and scholarly attainments, that he was chosen to succeed to the presidency of the college in the place of Pres. Griffen, resigned. For thirty-six years he remained at the head of Williams College, and brought the institution to a high state of efficiency and merited prosperity, attracting pupils from far-off states by the mere virtue of his personal renown. Many high positions of influence and trust were offered him during these years, but he remained faithful to his

alma mater. Even when in 1872, he resigned the presidency, he continued to give his invaluable services as professor of intellectual and moral philosophy. He also retained the pastorate of the college church, the duties of which he had first assumed in 1836. As an educator, a governor, and a moral philosopher, Dr. Hopkins was one of the greatest men New England has produced. He was a believer in the study of physiology, as the true basis for the upbuilding of moral health, and as affording the groundwork for a complete understanding of the mind. This belief that the physical nature of man could not be ignored in the successful study of the intellectual led him to give his note for $600 to purchase an illustrating physical manikin, despite the fact that his salary did not amount to more than $1,100. He raised a portion of the necessary funds by lecturing during the winter, but further self-sacrifice on his part was made unnecessary when, in August, 1842, the college trustees voted to assume the cost of the manikin, and that Pres. Hopkins's note be cancelled. The president's heroic effort to pay for the manikin was typical of the man, who preferred to work noiselessly to accomplish his purposes, rather than ask assistance of anyone. This quality of quiet determination marked Pres. Hopkins's whole career. When, in 1868, a serious rebellion of the students against the faculty broke out during his temporary absence, it needed but a few masterly words from him and a little mingling with the malcontents to

restore harmony, which his consummate tact soon rendered permanent. Pres. Hopkins was a great believer in the Christian influences of a college education, and perhaps no college president ever sent out so great a number of young men imbued with the influences of their minister's moral and religious training. Many of them have written testimony of the fact in his declining years. As a philosopher, he was one of the acutest thinkers that the New World has produced, and it is perhaps a matter for regret that his absorbing duties as the head of a great college should have left him so little time to formulate to the full the philosophical system of which he was the father. His lectures on the "Evidences

of Christianity," published in Boston in 1846, and again in 1864, have attained to the rank of a text-book, as have also his "Outline Study of Man" (New York, 1873), and his work entitled "The Law of Love, and Love as a Law" (1869), which may be regarded as the fullest exposition of his system. The first effort of his to attract widespread attention was his master's oration on "Mystery," delivered in 1827, and published the following year in the "American Journal of Science and Arts." Other works from his pen are: "Miscellaneous Essays and Discourses" (1847); "Lectures on Moral Science" (1862), given first before the Lowell Institute; "Baccalaureate Sermons and Occasional Discourses" (1863); "Strength and Beauty" (1874), afterwards revised and republished under the title of "Teachings and Counsels" (1884); and his last production, a collection of lectures under the caption of "The Scriptural Idea of Man" (1883). His death occurred at Williamstown, Mass., June 17, 1887.

CHADBOURNE, Paul Ansel, fifth president of Williams College (1872–81), was born at North Berwick, Me., Oct. 21, 1823. He became an orphan at the age of thirteen, and thus early learned the lessons of industry and self-reliance, working in summer on the farm of an acquaintance of the family, and in winter acquiring the carpenter's trade under the same master, when not attending the district school. At seventeen he was apprenticed to a druggist at Great Falls, N. H., and there gained an elementary knowledge which was of service to him in his subsequent chemical studies. Determining to acquire a good education, he entered Phillips Exeter Academy, supporting himself by copying law papers. In 1845 he entered Williams College, where he was graduated class valedictorian in 1848. During these student days he acquired an ardent love of nature, and went rambling among the mountain scenery about Williamstown, studying the local flora, fauna,

and mineral treasures. After graduation, he taught for a while at Freehold, N. J.; then, in 1850, became principal of the High School at Great Falls, N. H.; was tutor at Williams College in 1851; and subsequently principal of East Windsor Academy, Conn., while pursuing theological studies at the Theological Seminary of Connecticut. In October, 1853, he was licensed to preach, and in the same year was appointed professor of chemistry and natural history at Williams College. In 1858 Dr. Chadbourne accepted the chair of chemistry and natural history at Bowdoin College, and continued to hold the two professorships concurrently for no less than nine years, besides performing similar duties in the Berkshire Medical College until its discontinuance, and in the Medical School of Maine. For twelve years he delivered courses of lectures at Mount Holyoke Seminary, and lectured also, from time to time, at the Smithsonian Institution, the Lowell Institute, and at Western Reserve College. His professorial labors were by no means confined to the class-room. His passion for scientific research was such that his pupils were invariably fired with his own enthusiasm, and accompanied him on long expeditions. Three of these, undertaken for the purposes of exploration and the collection of specimens, were particularly notable, and productive of rich results. The first was to Newfoundland in 1855, the second to Florida in 1857, and the last to Greenland in 1861. In 1859 Dr. Chadbourne traveled in Sweden, Norway, and Denmark and prolonged his journey to Iceland, and thence to Greenland for the purpose of studying geological formations, and more particularly in order to solve disputed problems in connection with geysers and volcanoes. In this year he was transferred to the chair of natural history, on account of the department of chemistry being placed under a separate head. In 1864 he was elected Massachusetts state senator, and made his mark in that legislative body. In 1866 he accepted an invitation to the presidency of the new Massachusetts Agricultural College at Amherst. He devised a new system of study, and decided the location of the college build-

ings, botanical museum, and plant houses; but at the end of seven months' tenure of office, disease of the lungs compelled him to seek a more genial climate. He became president of the State University of Wisconsin at Madison, and administered its affairs successfully for three years, when he removed to Utah, and visited the mining regions of the Rocky mountains. In 1872 he was elected president of Williams College, to succeed the revered Mark Hopkins, and returned to the scene of his former labors to render services of even greater and higher scope. His administration was productive of distinguished results, and marked an era of ever-increasing prosperity. The endowment was increased, the college grounds beautified, new buildings erected, and old ones repaired. Pres. Chadbourne impressed himself upon the students as a man of inexhaustible vitality, great resolution, high purpose, stern integrity, and unlimited devotion to work. He increased the interest of the public in the college, which his great predecessor had awakened, and thoroughly established their confidence in it as one of the foremost educational institutions of the country. The number of students, accordingly, rapidly increased, and the college was definitely placed upon a basis of assured prosperity. In 1881, however, Pres. Chadbourne resigned, in order to devote himself to important literary labors. During this year and 1882 he was mainly engaged in the editorial

supervision of two exhaustive works: "The Wealth of the United States," and "Public Service of New York." These labors he varied in the summer with researches as a mining geologist in North Carolina and Dakota, besides superintending some manufacturing enterprises of his at Williamstown. In January, 1882, he had received another invitation to the presidency of the Massachusetts Agricultural College, and finally, in the fall of the same year, he decided to accept it. Within a year the institution had taken a fresh start, gather-

ing around it new friends, and giving excellent promise of increased future usefulness, when Pres. Chadbourne was suddenly called away by death. He was a man of extraordinary force of character, of attainments as solid as they were varied, of a Christianity as genuine as it was vigorous. In public affairs he continued to take an active interest, even after his elevation to the head of Williams College, and was a delegate to the national Republican convention at Cincinnati in 1876, and a presidential elector in 1880. Various learned societies, both at home and abroad, enrolled him among their membership. He was given the degree of LL.D. from Williams in 1868, and that of D.D. from Amherst in 1872. His chief published works are: "The Relations of Natural History to Intellect, Taste, Wealth, and Religion" (New York, 1860); "Natural Theology," and "Instinct in Animals and Men" (Boston, 1867 and 1872); "Strength of Men, and Stability of Nations" (1873-77); and "Hope of the Righteous" (1877). Most of these are collections of lectures delivered before the Smithsonian Institution at Washington, and the Lowell Institute at Boston. Pres. Chadbourne died in New York city, Feb. 23, 1883.

CARTER, Franklin, sixth president of Williams College (1881——), was born in Waterbury, Conn., Sept. 30, 1837. He fitted for college at Phillips Academy, Andover, Mass., where he completed the course in 1855, being valedictorian of his class. The fall of that year he entered Yale, but on account of impaired health was compelled to leave at the end of his sophomore year. After two years of rest he resumed college work, entered the junior class at Williams, and was graduated in 1862. Early in 1863 he was appointed professor of Latin and French at Williams, and after eighteen months in Europe assumed the duties, continuing in charge until 1868 when he ceased to teach French. He retained the chair of Latin until 1872, when he accepted the pro-

fessorship of German at Yale University. He then spent a year in special study abroad and occupied the chair until 1881, when he was elected president of Williams College. Two years later he also became professor of Theology in that institution. He received the degree of M.A. from Williams and from Jefferson in 1864; from Yale in 1874; Ph.D from Williams in 1877; and LL.D. from Union in 1881. He has served as trustee in Andover Theological

Seminary and in Clarke Institute for deaf mutes. He was president of the American Modern Language Association and is a member of various literary and benevolent organizations. Some of his principal writings are: An edition of "Iphigenie auf Tauris" in Whitney's "German Texts," 1879; "A Biography of Mark Hopkins" in series of American Leaders, 1892; "The New Translations of Laäcoon;" "Mr. Lettson's Version of Middle German Epic;" "Science and Poetry;" "Bayard Taylor's Posthumous Books;" and various other works with articles contributed to the "New Englander." "On Begesmann's Views as to the Weak Preterit of the Germanic Verbs;" "Did Von Der Kurnberg compose the present form of Nibelungen Lied?" "On Wilmann's Theory of the Authorship of the Nibelungen Lied" were papers in the "Transactions" of the American Philological Association. He has published articles in "Modern Language Transactions" and the "American Journal of Philology." Dr. Carter has delivered many addresses before learned societies, and baccalaureate sermons before graduating classes. While scholarly in his tastes, he is eminently a man of affairs, and his work for the college has been one of notable progress. During his presidency he has added eighty acres to the college domain, secured over $1,000,000 for new buildings and enlarged endowments; nine new professorships and departments have been established, and the older professorships liberally furnished; and the number of students in attendance has been largely increased. As a teacher, Dr. Carter is a thorough master and a born leader. As the chief executive officer of the college he is quick in decision and promptly secures desired results.

HOPKINS, Albert, astronomer, was born in Stockbridge, Mass., July 14, 1807. He was a brother of the celebrated Mark Hopkins (q. v.). Like his brother he was precocious and entering Williams College in the junior class, was graduated when only nineteen. He then spent a year in the study of agriculture and civil engineering, and returned to his alma mater as professor of mathematics and natural philosophy in 1829. In 1834 he was sent abroad to make purchases of apparatus for the college. Having become interested in astronomy, he devoted much study to the science, and upon his return built an astronomical observatory entirely from his own means, which was eventually donated to the college. By this liberality Williams College was the first American college to enjoy the distinction of having an observatory in connection with its work. In 1869 a memorial professorship of astronomy with an endowment of $25,000 was established by David Dudley Field, with the stipulation that its income should be secured to Prof. Hopkins during his lifetime. Although the equipment of the observatory was not of the finest, Prof. Hopkins made many important discoveries, and contributed many important papers upon astronomical subjects to the transactions of the Royal Society of Great Britain. He had great versatility, giving instruction in French for a number of years, besides becoming a minister of the gospel. He was much devoted to his ministerial work, supplying the pulpits of the various churches in town and vicinity, besides acting as pastor of the college during much of the

time. He also built a missionary chapel almost entirely at his own expense, at White Oaks, where he devoted himself to philanthropic work, and in 1868 organized it into a church. He was moreover a great student of botany, and it was he who first organized scientific expeditions in connection with college work. He founded, while at Williams, a natural history society, and also an Alpine club. The degree of LL.D. was conferred upon him in 1859 by Jefferson College, and he was elected corresponding fel-

low of the Royal Astronomical Society of Great Britain. In 1841 he married Louisa, the daughter of Rev. Edward Payson. She was a highly gifted lady, who became celebrated as an author. She prepared the question books for the Massachusetts Sunday-school Union, and was the author of many books for the young. Prof. Hopkins died in Williamstown, May 24, 1872, surviving his wife ten years.

PINKNEY, Fredrick, author and statesman, was born at sea, Oct. 14, 1804, while his parents were returning from England to their native land. His education was obtained principally at the Baltimore College and at St. Mary's College, where he was graduated in 1825. He studied law under Judge Purviance, and was admitted to the bar in 1825. He was associated with his brother, Edward C. Pinkney, in the publication of the "Marylander," and was also editor of the "Chronicle," and assistant editor of the "Patriot," published in Baltimore, in which he published a number of poems and literary essays. Mr. Pinkney was for many years one of the commissioners of the High Courts of Chancery, and, after the abolition of that court, he was made one of the commissioners in the circuit court of Baltimore, which office he held at the time of his death. He was appointed assistant attorney-general under the administration of Atty.-Gen. Richardson, and held that office for thirty years. He died in Baltimore, Md., June 13, 1873.

VAN NESS, Cornelius, jurist, was born in Vermont, in 1803, the son of Gov. Cornelius P. Van Ness of that state. He went to Texas as a volunteer in 1836. While his father was American minister to Spain, Cornelius Van Ness was secretary of the Legation there, and acquired a knowledge of the Spanish language. As a lawyer in the western district of Texas, located at San Antonio, he stood well. His brother, a most gallant man, was a soldier on the frontier, a Santa Fé prisoner in 1841, and a Mier prisoner in 1842-43-44. From 1837 to 1842 he was a member of congress, and was rapidly rising in public esteem, when, in the summer of 1842, he was killed by a gunshot caused by the plunging of his horse.

BALLOU, Hosea, 2nd, the first president of Tufts College (1852-61), was born in Guilford, Vt., Oct. 18, 1796. He was the son of Asahel Ballou, and grand-nephew of Hosea Ballou, the famous Universalist preacher, who died in Boston in June, 1852. His childhood and youth were spent in Halifax, Vt., to which town his father removed soon after the birth of his son. He early manifested a desire for learning. He attended school in Halifax, acquired the rudiments of Latin under the tuition of Rev. Thomas H. Wood. The means of the father did not permit the sending of the boy to college.

The rising fame of his uncle was the occasion, no doubt of turning his attention early to the Universalist ministry. His first settlement was in the town of Stafford, Conn., where he remained four or five years. The Universalists of Roxbury erected a church which was dedicated in 1821, Hosea Ballou, Sr. preaching the sermon of dedication. It was at his suggestion, and largely through his influence, that a call was given to his young nephew to the pastorate in Roxbury. He was installed, July 28, 1821. Here he manifested not only great fidelity in the pastoral office but also those solid and scholarly qualities for which he was ever afterwards distinguished. In May, 1822, he became associated with the elder Ballou and Thomas Whittemore in the editorship of the "Universalist Magazine," a publication which for many years exerted a powerful influence. In 1824 Mr. Ballou proposed to Mr. Whittemore the collaboration of a history of Universalism, in which he was to write the ancient history of the doctrine, and Mr. Whittemore, the modern. The "Ancient History of Universalism from the Time of the Apostolic Fathers to the Reformation" was published in 1829, having been about five years in preparation. Mr. Ballou entered upon this task, for which he had extraordinary qualifications, with great avidity. It is the opinion of scholars that, so far as the first six centuries are concerned, he exhausted the subject. To Mr. Ballou also must be attributed the rise of the "Universalist Expositor," which afterwards became the "Universalist Quarterly." At first Hosea Ballou, Sr. was associated with him in the editorship of the magazine, but later on the Rev. T. Starr King was his associate. It was through this medium that Mr. Ballou communicated articles which for learning and vigor commanded the attention of scholars throughout New England. After a pastorate in Roxbury covering a period of seventeen years, he removed to Medford, where he was installed in June, 1838. His literary reputation continued to increase. Harvard University conferred upon him the degree of D.D. in 1845. In the autumn of 1847 Dr. Ballou gave the occasional sermon before the Universalist general convention which held its sessions for three years in the city of New York. In this sermon he took the ground that denominations live by their institutions and that no denomination can long command the confidence of the public that does not maintain at least one respectable college. The sermon produced so profound an impression that steps were immediately taken for the gathering of funds for a college. As the result of this movement, Tufts College was incorporated in 1852. The Rev. Thomas J. Sawyer, D.D. was first elected president, but he declined the office, and in May, 1853, Dr. Ballou was chosen to the place. After a prolonged tour abroad, visiting the different educational institutions of Europe, he gave some time to the inspection of the New England colleges, and entered upon his work at Tufts College in the latter part of 1854. The institution was first formally opened to students in the autumn of 1855. Dr. Ballou displayed great wisdom and prudence in the organization of the college. By his hands were laid the foundations out of which the present development of the institution has come. His determination was that the college should win its way to the confidence of the public only by adherence to the highest standard of scholarship. But the task was too great for his physical strength. In addition to the work of administration, he taught almost continuously from morning until night. His great attainments made him a rare teacher of history and the different departments of philosophy. Under this great burden of labor and responsibility his strength gave way, and in May, 1861, he died. During his pastorate in Stafford, Dr. Ballou married Clarissa Hatch of Halifax, Vt., who survived him about fifteen years. By her he had two sons and three daughters, all of whom are now dead.

MINER, Alonzo Ames, second president of Tufts College (1862-75). (See Vol. I., p. 315.)

CAPEN, Elmer Hewitt, third president of Tufts College (1875——), was born in Stoughton, Norfolk co., Mass., Apr. 5, 1838. He was named for the Rev. Elmer Hewitt, a Universalist preacher still living (1898) at an advanced age, in Weymouth, Mass. His father, Samuel Capen, was a substantial citizen of Stoughton, and for more than twenty years one of the selectmen. On his mother's side he is descended from the Shepards, probably Ralph Shepard, who came to this country in 1635, and from whom the Shepards of the Old Colony region are supposed to be descended; and he is of the American Capens who descended from a single family, Bernard, and his two sons Samuel and John, who settled in Dorchester in its early history. The ancestry has never been traced on the other side of the ocean. An old Bible has, however, been discovered in London containing the familiar names Bernard, John, and Samuel, ending probably with the Bernard who came to Dorchester. This carries the genealogy back to the beginning of the seventeenth century. Both paternal and maternal ancestors served as minute men and otherwise in the revolutionary struggle. He was educated in the old district school of Stoughton; the Pierce Academy, Middleborough; the Green Mountain Liberal Institute, South Woodstock, Vt.; and Tufts College, being graduated in the latter in 1860. While a student in college, in his senior year, he was elected to the Massachusetts legislature from Stoughton, and served one term, the youngest member of the body. Intending to adopt the law as his profession, he spent a year at the Harvard Law School, and read with Thomas S. Harlow of Boston, and in 1864 was admitted to the Suffolk bar. His inclination, however, was more towards theology than law, and after a short time in practice he determined to enter the ministry. Accordingly, he took a preparatory course with A. St. John Chambré, D.D., then a Universalist, subsequently becoming an Episcopalian, and in October, 1865, was ordained pastor of the Independent Christian Church of Gloucester, Mass.: the church founded by John Murray. He remained there four years, then went to St. Paul, Minn., for a year. He then became pastor of the First Universalist Church in Providence, R. I., installed in the autumn of 1870, and was there settled when he was called to the presidency of Tufts in March, 1875. His inauguration took place on the following June 2d. During his administration the college has had a remarkable development. The student body has increased nearly four-fold. Not only have new departments been added, but the older departments have been enlarged and strengthened. The teaching force of the institution has increased from sixteen in 1875 to seventy in the current catalogue (1895). The material resources have been considerably augmented, more than $600,000 having been added during the past decade. The special aim of Dr. Capen has been to put the college educationally in line with the movements and spirit of the age, and to bring it as closely as possible into relation with the public schools. The elective system has been introduced and carried to a high point of development, so that now the student, from the moment of his entrance to college, within certain broad groups of study, may choose his own course, and may advance as rapidly as his ability will permit towards a degree. Tufts was one of the first New England colleges, under Pres. Capen's lead, to abandon Greek as an indispensable requisite for a four-years' curriculum, and one of the first to offer the degree of A.B. without Greek. In 1875 a course leading to the degree of civil engineer had been organized, and a small number of students were in

attendance. This course has been strengthened, electrical and mechanical engineering have been added, and there are now (1896) over 100 students pursuing these branches. Some of the most distinguished engineers in the country have received their training here. For a number of years Dr. Capen advocated the equality of the sexes in education, and in the autumn of 1892 the college was opened to women on the same terms as to men. During 1893 a medical school was opened in Boston under the auspices of the college, and speedily achieved a marked success. Also the Bromfield-Pearson School for both technical and preparatory training has been established (1893–94), and a beautiful and commodious building erected for its use. Besides the enlargement and reconstruction of the older buildings, nine important structures have been added: the Goddard Chapel, built by Mrs. Mary T. Goddard as a memorial to her husband; the Barnum Museum of Natural History, built and equipped by P. T. Barnum at a cost of $100,000; the gymnasium, given by Mrs. Goddard; Dean Hall, a dormitory named in honor of Dr. Oliver Dean, one of the prominent benefactors of the college; Miner's Theological Hall, the gift of Dr. A. A. Miner; Paige Hall, a dormitory named in honor of Lucius R. Paige, D.D.; a hall for a commons building and dormitories combined; and Metcalf Hall, a dormitory for women.

Pres. Capen's specialty in teaching has been ethics and political economy. Through his handling of these subjects he has exerted a powerful influence on the thought and life of the students who have been under him. During his entire connection with the college he has also maintained an elective, three hours a week for the year, in ancient law and international law. This elective has been eagerly chosen by a large number of students. Dr. Capen is also the college preacher, conducting the daily morning prayers and preaching nearly every Sunday during term time. Before his election to the presidency he had won a reputation as an able and eloquent preacher. Among his official duties is the delivery every year of the baccalaureate sermon. These discourses have attracted considerable attention for their treatment of scholarly and timely themes, and many of them have been printed at the request of friends. He has given many addresses before educational bodies and has advocated many of the leading reforms in education. He has been a frequent contributor to magazines and newspapers. He wrote the articles in the work "Latest Word of Universalism" on the "Philosophy of Universalism." At the Universalist congress, held in Chicago in 1893, he contributed the paper on "Retribution." In a work issued in 1894 by the Universalist publishing house, entitled "Our Word and Work for Missions," the initial chapter is contributed by him on the "Principle of Missions." He contributed the section in the "People's Bible History" (H. O. Shepard Pub. Co., Chicago), on the title, "From the Call of Abraham to the Bondage of Israel." Dr. Capen is an attractive public speaker, and during the winter season he is in almost constant request at clubs, festivals, and other public gatherings. He is an earnest advocate of temperance, and has been often heard before legislative committees and on platforms throughout the New England states. In politics he is a Republican, and is frequently a participant in the political gatherings of that party. In 1888 he was a delegate from the fifth congressional district to the National Republican convention at Chicago. Dr. Capen is, and has been since its organization, president of the Commission on Admission Examinations established by the colleges of New England to maintain and promote uniformity in the requirements for admission; is a member of the Massachusetts State Board of Education; president of the Law and Order League of Massachusetts; and a trustee of the Universalist general convention. He received the honorary degree of D.D. from St. Lawrence University, New York, in 1877. He has been twice married, first to Letitia H. Mussey of New London, Conn., who died Sept. 5, 1872; and secondly to Mary L. Edwards of Brookline, Mass., by whom are three children living.

SHUFELDT, Robert Wilson, biologist, was born in New York city, Dec. 1, 1850, son of Rear-Adm. R. W. Shufeldt, and grandson of George A. Shufeldt, a distinguished jurist of New York. His mother was the youngest daughter of Rev. Dr. Abercrombie, the eminent rector of St. Peter's and of Christ's Church, Philadelphia, a friend of Gen. Washington, and author of works on moral philosophy and other subjects. As a child, young Shufeldt accompanied his father on a number of voyages, visiting England, Jamaica, Central America and Mexico. In 1861 his father, temporarily relieved from active service in the navy, was appointed American consul at Havana, Cuba. He took his family to that place, where the son attended a Spanish school. During the early part of 1864, Rear-Adm. Shufeldt was again on the active list of the navy and in command of the United States gun-boat Proteus, serving in the East Gulf squadron, and took his son with him as his secretary. The lad filled this position with credit for nearly a year, passing safely through many scenes of danger and excitement, and returning home just prior to the close of the civil war. During this cruise the first evidence of his interest in natural science was exhibited. After his return he was placed at school in Stamford, Conn. Close confinement, absence from field and forest, and severance from his favorite studies, brought at this early stage the prospect of an early close to his career. His room was a museum; the premises a zoölogical garden; he had made a private collection of some 500 birds and animals; and had a portfolio full of original colored drawings. The father, of strongly military tastes, found himself confronted with a puzzle similar in all respects to that presented to the father of the distinguished Audubon. Both dealt with the problem in pretty much the same way. Birds and animals were released, apartments cleared of rubbish, and things put away generally. The aspiring young naturalist was sent to an uncle, then living in Oconomowoc, Wis. There he rambled at pleasure; mounted a collection of birds; received every kindness from his uncle, who made him a present of Audubon's greatest work, and then returned him to his father as a "hopeless case." In the meantime the Stamford home was exchanged for a large farm. Outdoor life became the order of the day, and studies in botany and ornithology were resumed with vigor; but the duties which pertained to the farm were distasteful. Through his father's influence he was given a position in the American Museum of Natural History in New York, for the purpose of accompanying, as naturalist, one of the Polar expeditions then in preparation. The vessel set sail several days prior to the appointed time, and, by a telegram being placed in a country post-office, departed, and Shufeldt was left behind. In 1874 his father removed him from college, and before his graduation secured him a position in the U. S. naval hydrographic office in Washington; a position was subsequently obtained in the Army Medical Museum (the old Ford's Theatre). Thence he entered St. John's Hospital, Washington, and was given charge of the children's wards. While there he collected the largest unbroken series of thermometric and other observations upon children on record in medical literature. He was graduated M.D. at the Columbian University in 1876, and awarded the prize for the best thesis submitted: "A Series of Thermometrical Observations upon Children," and a few months later commissioned assistant-surgeon in the U. S. army. Soon after being commissioned he was detailed as a medical officer to Fort McHenry, Baltimore, Md. He soon after married Catherine Babcock of Washington, D. C., who died in 1892; and in 1895 he married Florence Audubon, granddaughter of the famous ornithologist. In 1877 he was ordered to duty at the Indianapolis arsenal and thence to service on the frontier against the Sioux in the department of the Platte. Five years of service on the frontier enabled Dr. Shufeldt to secure fine collections of the flora and fauna of the entire region. While at Fort Laramie he prepared the first series of scientific papers, a detailed monograph upon the "Osteology of the Burrowing Owl," afterward published in the govern

ment reports. This paper was followed by three or four more monographs, illustrated by plates and figures, drawn by the author, all upon similar subjects. In 1881 he returned to Washington and was placed in charge of the section of comparative anatomy at the Army Medical Museum. More scientific work rapidly appeared, and membership in a number of learned societies followed. He was also appointed honorable curator of comparative anatomy in the Smithsonian Institution. On Aug. 5, 1881, according to law, he became a captain and was ordered to New Orleans. While there he published some thirty scientific papers; personally made a collection of hundreds of specimens for the National Museum in Washington, and received his first corresponding membership in a learned foreign society—the Anthropological Society of Florence, Italy. He contributed to "The New York Medical Record" a searching article on the "Uselessness of Government Examinations" and other matters pertaining to the medical corps of the army. The article attracted widespread attention both at home and abroad. It was followed by an article from the pen of Elliott Coues—brilliant and bitter. This called out others and the system was thoroughly criticized. In 1883 he was again ordered to the charge of his department in the Army Medical Museum, and resumed the duties. In 1884 he went again to the frontier, and remained until January, 1886. During that time he wrote and published about 150 important books, memoirs and monographs. These included, "The Comparative Osteology of Arctic and Sub-Arctic Water Birds," "The Myology of the Raven," and many extensive contributions to the anatomy of birds, mammals, and fish. They were illustrated by upwards of 1,500 original drawings and photographs. Many of his papers on "Indians" were published by the government, while the majority of his anatomical ones appeared in the proceedings of the scientific societies of Europe.

Both the National Museum in Washington and institutions abroad rendered him valuable assistance. Army jealousies became rife, and the war department and the surgeon-general's office in particular, harbored a hostility toward him which became more and more bitter, and finally burst forth in fury. A tedious trial, lasting many weeks and costing the government thousands of dollars, ensued. The record of it, on file in the U. S. war department, was regarded as one of the most remarkable of the kind in the history of this or probably of any other county. The principle involved was "whether an officer of the medical corps of the army could devote himself to scientific studies during his time of leisure," and it was decided in the negative in the surgeon general's office. A few scientific men in the medical department sided with Dr. Shufeldt, but in the main the great bulk of the corps were against him. A nervous disease of the heart, from which Dr. Shufeldt had long suffered, became aggravated by the annoyances and disappointments he had undergone, and he made application for retirement. Another tedious trial was inaugurated. Dr. Shufeldt defended bravely, and succeeded at last in securing in 1889, the retirement to which he was justly entitled. During the time, the press, both at home and abroad, kept actively at work on Dr. Shufeldt's case, and the entire trial both interested and involved many holding the highest positions in civil and military life. His retire ment from the military service having been secured, Dr. Shufeldt purchased a suburban residence in Washington, where he entered upon the prosecution of his scientific work with vigor. He is a member of some twenty-five learned societies in the Old and New World. Dr. Shufeldt's life is a quiet one, engaged as he is upon a general work of several volumes on the "Osteology of Birds," now nearly completed. He enjoys the confidence of his many confrères in science, and is a correspondent of numerous of the most distinguished men of letters and learning.

FISK, Clinton Bowen, soldier, educator, and reformer, was born Dec. 8, 1828, at Clapp's Corners, now Greigsville, Livingston co., N. Y. His

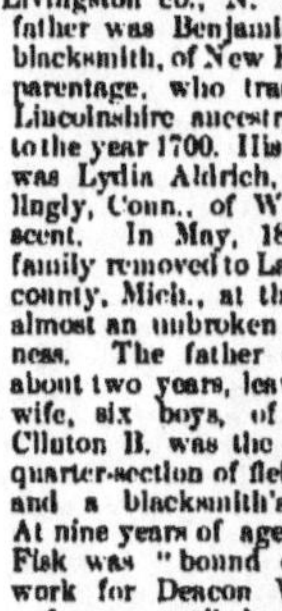

father was Benjamin Fisk, blacksmith, of New England parentage, who traced his Lincolnshire ancestry back to the year 1700. His mother was Lydia Aldrich, of Killingly, Conn., of Welsh descent. In May, 1830, the family removed to Lawrence county, Mich., at that time almost an unbroken wilderness. The father died in about two years, leaving his wife, six boys, of whom Clinton B. was the fifth, a quarter-section of field-land, and a blacksmith's shop. At nine years of age young Fisk was "bound out" to work for Deacon Wright, a farmer, until he should come to legal age. He was to have three months of "schooling" each year, for at least four years, and when of age was to be paid $200 in cash, with a horse, saddle, bridle, and two suits of clothes. Young Fisk was fond of knowledge, and spent many long winter evenings before the farmer's fire reading whatever he could lay hands upon. One of his first literary possessions was a second-hand copy of Shakespeare, which he bought of a farmer by two day's work, hoeing corn. Here, too, he imbibed hearty anti-slavery convictions. Leaving the farmer at the end of two years, he sought other ways to obtain an education to maintain himself and help his mother. At seventeen years of age he was a clerk in a store at Manchester, Mich.; at twenty he formed a business alliance with Crippen & Kellogg, a leading business firm at Coldwater, Mich. At twenty-two he married the daughter of the senior member of the firm, and Crippen & Fisk started an exchange bank the same year. In 1854 we find Mr. Fisk already a successful business man, and a father, actively engaged in church and in temperance work. He was a candidate for the office of justice in Coldwater on the "Maine law," or Prohibition ticket in 1855. During the financial crash of 1857 the banking firm of Crippen & Fisk paid dollar for dollar, every valid claim, but the doing this took a large share of Mr. Fisk's health, and a large share of his fortune. He then took the Western agency of the Ætna Insurance Co., of Hartford, Conn., with headquarters at St. Louis, Mo. Early in the civil war (1862), at St. Louis, he recruited the 33d regiment Missouri volunteers, at the request of Pres. Lincoln, and was commissioned its colonel. He was then appointed brigadier-general, with instructions to recruit a brigade. In 1863-64 Gen. Fisk was successively commander of the districts of Southeast and North Missouri, and in 1864 he drove the Confederate Gen. Price, with his army of 20,000, out of Missouri, and effectually saved that state to the Union. In 1865 he was made major-general of the Missouri militia

by Gov. Fletcher, and a few weeks later brevet major-general of U. S. volunteers by Pres Andrew Johnson, and in May, 1865, assistant commissioner of the bureau of refugees, freedmen, and abandoned lands for the states of Kentucky and Tennessee, with headquarters at Nashville. Here he addressed large assemblies of white and colored people in the open air, and was most instrumental in the establishment of relations of good fellowship between the whites and the newly made freedmen. Here he also organized freedmen's courts for the maintenance of the rights of the colored people, and issued a little volume, "Plain Counsels for Freedmen," which was published in large numbers, and given away by the Boston Tract Society. The Fisk School of Freedmen was opened Jan. 9, 1866, in some government buildings west of the Chattanooga depot, and from this humble beginning came the Fisk University of Nashville, Tenn. Gen. Fisk was president of its board of trustees. The famous Fisk Jubilee Singers, who, in the space of a few years raised $100,000 for the education of the negro, went out from it upon their noble mission. After the war was over (Gen. Fisk was mustered out of the U. S. military service Sept. 1, 1866) he returned to St. Louis, accepting an appointment tendered him by the governor of the state as state commissioner of the Southwest Pacific Railroad. Then he became vice-president of the old Missouri Pacific Railroad, and was such until 1877, having removed his residence to New York city in 1872. Here he won speedy recognition as a man of fine integrity, clear brain, strong character, quick, cool judgment, and unflagging zeal. His aid for commercial and philanthropic projects came to be sought on every side. In 1874 he was a fraternal delegate to the Methodist

Episcopal church South; in 1876 he was made a member of the book committee of the Methodist Episcopal church; and in 1881 was a delegate to the Ecumenical Council in London, Eng. In 1884 he delivered the address on missions before the Centennial Methodist assemblage at Baltimore, Md. His zeal for the Methodist church, and his activity in all his labors for her good was a marked feature of his busy life. In politics he was an uncompromising Abolitionist and Prohibitionist, running in 1886 as the Prohibition candidate for governor of New Jersey, and polling 20,000 votes; then as the Prohibition candidate for the U. S. presidency in 1888, and polling in the aggregate about 250,000 votes. He died at his residence in New York city, July 9, 1890.

STUART, Moses, "the father of Biblical learning in America," was born at Wilton, Conn., March 26, 1780, and educated in the Academy of Norwalk, Conn. In 1797 he entered Yale College, where he distinguished himself by his aptness for mathematics, and after graduation in 1799, he taught first in the Academy of North Fairfield, Conn., then in the High School of Danbury, Conn., studying law at the same time. He was admitted to the bar in 1802, and his rapidity and precision of thought as well as the ease and impressiveness of his speech, augured well for a successful legal career. But in the same year he accepted a tutorship in Yale College, and, after studying theology for three years under Pres. Dwight, he was, in 1806, ordained pastor of the First Congregational Church in New Haven, Conn. His pastorate, too, was a success. Nevertheless, in 1810, he was appointed professor of sacred literature in the Theological Seminary of Andover, Mass., and it is on his labors in this position, which he held for thirty-eight years, that his great fame rests. As professor of sacred literature he had to teach Hebrew, but in order to do that as he thought it ought to be done, he had to write a Hebrew grammar. For grammar, however, he had a great natural talent. On entering the Academy of Norwalk in his fifteenth year, he learned the whole Latin grammar in three days in order to be able to join a higher class. Within two years his Hebrew grammar was ready, and for more than two generations that book formed the foundation for all instruction in Hebrew in America. It was also introduced into England, having been republished by Dr. Pusey, regius professor of Hebrew at Oxford. But there was more in Moses Stuart than a mere grammarian. In order to make himself thoroughly conversant with that new departure in German theology which received the principal part of its motive power from the labors of the great German orientalists, Ewald, Rosenmüller, Gesenius, etc., he had also studied German, and he was one of the first among American theologians who understood German theology, and understood how to use it. Whatsoever might be the verdict of to-day with respect to the theological standpoint of Ewald, hardly should anybody like to deny that, viewed in its historical connection, it denotes a great progress. How much of superstitious illusion, theological prejudice, clumsy error, and pious fraud was not swept away, and how fresh and radiant looked the records of the Old Testament, when approached after the sweeping. This new power of progress, and this new source of health, Moses Stuart carried over into American theology, without carrying the standpoint into which they had crystallized along with them. He was eminently gifted as a teacher, and during the thirty-eight years of his professorship he had over 1,500 ministers among his pupils, besides 100 foreign missionaries, seventy college professors, and thirty Bible translators. His grammatical works are: "Grammar of the Hebrew Language, without Points" (1813); "Grammar of the Hebrew Language, with Points" (1821), often reprinted; "Grammar of the New Testament Dialect" (1834); besides some translations. His exegetical works are: "Commentary on the Epistle to the Hebrews" (2 vols., 1827–28); "The Epistle to the Romans" (2 vols., 1832); "The Apocalypse" (1845); "Ecclesiastes" (1851); "Proverbs" (1852). Of doctrinal or historical interest are: "Letters on the Divinity of Christ" (1819); "Letters on the Eternal Generation of the Son of God" (1822); "Critical History and Defense of the Old Testament Canon" (1845). In 1848 he retired on account of failing health, and died at Andover, Jan. 4, 1852.

ARMSTRONG, Samuel, governor of Massachusetts, was born in Boston, Mass., in 1784. He was educated in the common schools, and then became a bookseller's clerk. Later he engaged in business on his own account, also became publisher, and amassed a large fortune. He was noted for his enterprise and public spirit, was prominent in the municipal affairs of Boston, and at one time mayor of the city. In 1835 he was elected lieutenant-governor of Massachusetts, and when Geo. Davis resigned to enter the U. S. senate, succeeded the latter in the executive chair, serving until Jan. 1, 1837. He was a man of deep piety and a generous and earnest supporter of foreign missions. His sudden death prevented him from bequeathing his wealth to charitable and religious objects, as was his intention. He died in Boston, Mass., March 26, 1850.

LEE, Mary Elizabeth, author, was born in Charleston, S. C., March 22, 1813. Her uncle was Thomas Lee, a prominent judge of South Carolina. She attended a private school in Charleston in charge of A. Bolles, and developed great aptitude for the acquisition of languages. She became passionately fond of literary studies, but on account of ill health was compelled to give them up. At the age of twenty she became a contributor to the "Rosebud," edited by Mrs. Gilman, and shortly afterwards her first volume entitled "Social Evenings, or Historical Tales for Youth," was published by the Massachusetts School Library Association. She continued writing for Northern and Southern periodicals until her health utterly failed. She died in Charleston, S. C., Sept. 23, 1849. In 1851 a volume of her poems was published, with a memoir by Rev. Samuel Gilman.

HOTCHKISS, Benjamin Berkely, inventor, was born in Watertown, Conn., Oct. 1, 1826. His parents removed to Sharon when he was only three years old. He received a common-school education, and displaying an aptitude for mechanics, was apprenticed to and mastered the machinist trade. His career as an inventor began in 1856 with the invention of a rifle field-gun, which he sold to the Mexican government. Thereafter his studies and experiments were all in the field of ordnance, and before he died he attained a reputation second to that of no other designer of ordnance in the world. In 1860 a percussion fuse for projectiles and rifling belt designed by him were adopted by the U. S. government, and he removed to New York city and engaged extensively in their manufacture. During the civil war many thousands of Hotchkiss shells were used by the Union forces, being more generally used than any other except, perhaps, the Parrott shells. In 1867, while in Paris, he invented a metallic cartridge case, which was at once accepted and placed in use by the French government at St. Etienne. His sojourn abroad was an extended one, and before he returned to the United States he designed many improvements in rifles and cannon. His revolving cannon attracted much attention when completed, and is now used by the United States and principal governments of Europe and South America. In 1875, while traveling from Vienna to Bucharest, his attention was called by a Roumanian army officer, whom he met in a railway train, to the need of a magazine rifle. In half an hour he  sketched on the blank page of a newspaper a design for such a weapon. He sent the design to his workshop in Paris, and in three months the rifle was finished, and when put to the test won against all rivals. It is now (1891) the standard rifle of the U. S. navy and of England and France. In 1882 the firm of Hotchkiss & Co. was formed, with headquarters in the United States, and branch establishments in England, Germany, Austria, Russia, and Italy. During the nine years, ending in 1891, over 10,000 guns were manufactured and successfully tested at the different factories. In 1887 the Hotchkiss Ordnance Co. was formed with the three original partners as managing directors. By an arrangement with the U. S. government, factories were established in Hartford, Conn., where the company is extensively engaged in the manufacture of revolving cannon. The great inventor was engaged in improvements on this weapon when he died suddenly, in Paris. Mr. Hotchkiss had the reputation of being the most expert artillery engineer in the world, and out of the thousands of guns which were turned out by his factories up to 1890, only two had failed to reach the requisite results. He was a man of remarkable intellect, wide and exact information, indefatigable industry, and intense patriotism. He sought out obstacles only to conquer them. His tastes were Democratic, and his habits simple. He was married, and the father of several children. He died in Paris, France, Feb. 14, 1885.

McINTOSH, Maria J., author, was born in Sunbury, Ga., in 1803. She was of Scotch-highland descent. On the fall of the house of Stuart her great-grandfather, Capt. John More McIntosh, whose family fortunes had been greatly diminished by adherence to the cause of Prince Charles, sailed for the colony of Georgia in 1735. Her father, Lachlan McIntosh, was a major in the revolutionary war. Maria's education was largely obtained at home; what she received from schools was gotten at Sunbury Academy, which admitted pupils of both sexes. After the death of her parents, in 1835, Miss McIntosh made her home in New York, residing with her brother, Capt. James M. McIntosh, of the U. S. navy. The financial crisis of 1837 destroyed her large fortune, throwing her upon her friends, or her pen, for support. With characteristic independence she chose the latter. Her first idea was to translate from the French, but at the suggestion of a friend, that she should attempt a juvenile series of works, similar to the "Peter Parley" books, having a moral sentiment as a basis, the "Aunt Kitty Tales" were written. The story of "Blind Alice" was published in 1841, followed by "Jessie Graham,"

"Florence Arnott," "Grace and Clara," and "Ellen Leslie." These tales were collected into one volume, and published in 1847. Her first novel, "Conquest and Self-Conquest," appeared in 1843, followed by "Woman an Enigma" in 1844, "Praise and Principle" in 1845, "Two Lives; or, To Seem and to Be" in 1847, and in 1848 "Charms and Counter-Charms," considered her greatest work, and upon which her fame chiefly rests. Later, she wrote "The Lofty and the Lowly," depicting the life of the slave and master in the South, and "Woman in America, Her Work and Her Reward," the only didactic work published by the author, in which she deals with the duties and possibilities of women. Miss McIntosh was also a contributor to the magazines, and a collection of her articles, strung together by a slight thread, appeared under the title of "Evenings at Donaldson Manor." Miss McIntosh's books have enjoyed a high reputation both in America and England, where her "Aunt Kitty Tales" were first recommended by the tragedian, Macready, who took them home to his children, reading them himself with pleasure and enjoyment on the voyage. Her style is marked by ease and grace, with no attempt at description or local coloring; her object being to paint the mental life alone, and teach a pure morality. A well-known critic says of her work: "She desires to benefit her reader's heart, rather than to gratify his taste and charm his imagination; and that she aimed to express those lofty principles that showed the nobleness of simplicity and the holiness of truth." Her later works are: "Emily Herbert" (1855); "Rose and Lillie Stanhope," "Violet; or, The Cross and the Crown" (1856); "Meta Grey" (1858); and "Two Pictures" (1863). She died in Morristown, N. J., Feb. 25, 1878.

CUMMINGS, Thomas Seir, artist, was born in Bath, England, Aug. 26, 1804, but was brought to New York by his parents while still an infant. His father was a New York merchant, having established himself in that city soon after his arrival in this country. The boy received a good school education. When about fourteen years of age he came under the influence of Augustus Earle, "the wandering artist," and decided to follow that profession himself. His father, however, having different plans for his future, he was put into the counting-room, where he remained three years, studying art in his leisure hours. At the end of that period the father relented, and Thomas became a pupil of Henry In-

man, with whom he soon formed a partnership, which continued for five or six years. He then devoted himself almost entirely to the painting of miniatures in water-colors, and in early life he became one of the most eminent artists of his time in that art. These were, for the most part, portraits, many of the celebrities of the times being among his sitters. Of those that were not portraits may be mentioned: "The Bracelet," "The Bride," and the "Exchange of Queens," all of which have been frequently engraved. When a young man he was one of the students of the American Academy of Fine Arts, of which Col. Trumbull was president. Dissatisfaction with the treatment received at this institution, led Mr. Cummings and other artists, on invitation of S. F. B. Morse, to meet at his studio on Nov. 8, 1825, when the New York Drawing Association was formed, which, on Jan. 10th following, became the National Academy of the Arts of Design. Mr. Cummings was for forty years treasurer of the academy, which held its first exhibition on Broadway, near Reade street, in the year it was founded. He became vice-president in 1849. To his sound financial management much of the success of the academy is due, his ability saving it several times from dissolution. In recognition of this fact, he was presented with a service of plate by the directors at the close of his first twenty years of office. In addition to superintending the schools of the academy, he conducted for a number of years a private school of design. He was chairman of the building committee of two, of the present structure, which was completed in 1865 at a cost of $250,000. Shortly after the formation of the National Academy of Design, with Durand and Ingham, he organized the Sketch Club, a social body, whose first meeting was held at the house of Thomas Cole. In 1844 this club was reorganized as the Artists' Sketch Club, whose members in 1846 founded the Century. He succeeded Prof. Morse to the chair of the arts of design in the University of the City of New York. He was an active spirit in various literary, scientific, and charitable associations, and prominent in military circles. He was a member of the national guards of the state, and for many years commanded one of the New York city regiments. In 1838 Gov. Seward commissioned him a brigadier-general of the state militia. He was regarded as one of the soundest military jurists in the country. He was married in 1822. In 1866 he retired to a beautiful home at Mansfield Centre, Conn., passing a part of every winter in New York city with his wife and children. One of his daughters married the well-known fish painter, Wakeman Holberton. He contributed numerous essays and lectures to the literature of art. In 1865 he published "Historical Annals of the National Academy of Design," a trustworthy and valuable history of the foundation and progress of the Academy of Design during its first forty years. On the death of his wife, in 1889, he removed to Hackensack, N. J., where he died Sept. 24, 1894, in his ninety-first year.

SMITH, Joseph B., naval officer, was the son of Joseph Smith (1790–1877), an officer of the U. S. navy, who had served on Lake Champlain in 1814.

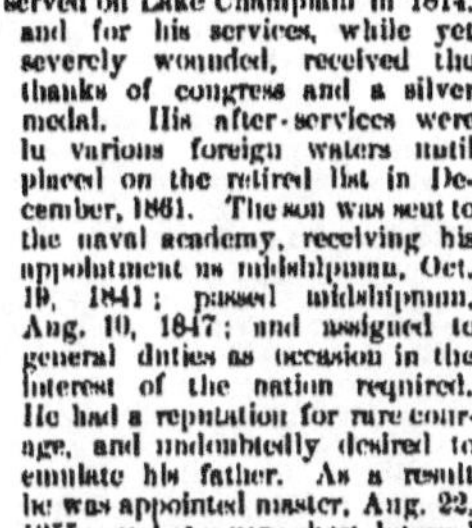

and for his services, while yet severely wounded, received the thanks of congress and a silver medal. His after-services were in various foreign waters until placed on the retired list in December, 1861. The son was sent to the naval academy, receiving his appointment as midshipman, Oct. 19, 1841; passed midshipman, Aug. 10, 1847; and assigned to general duties as occasion in the interest of the nation required. He had a reputation for rare courage, and undoubtedly desired to emulate his father. As a result he was appointed master, Aug. 22, 1855; and at a very short interval

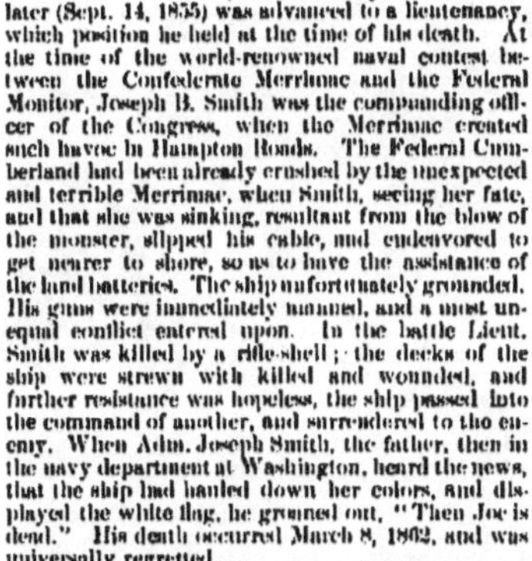

later (Sept. 14, 1855) was advanced to a lieutenancy, which position he held at the time of his death. At the time of the world-renowned naval contest between the Confederate Merrimac and the Federal Monitor, Joseph B. Smith was the commanding officer of the Congress, when the Merrimac created such havoc in Hampton Roads. The Federal Cumberland had been already crushed by the unexpected and terrible Merrimac, when Smith, seeing her fate, and that she was sinking, resultant from the blow of the monster, slipped his cable, and endeavored to get nearer to shore, so as to have the assistance of the land batteries. The ship unfortunately grounded. His guns were immediately manned, and a most unequal conflict entered upon. In the battle Lieut. Smith was killed by a rifle-shell; the decks of the ship were strewn with killed and wounded, and further resistance was hopeless, the ship passed into the command of another, and surrendered to the enemy. When Adm. Joseph Smith, the father, then in the navy department at Washington, heard the news, that the ship had hauled down her colors, and displayed the white flag, he groaned out, "Then Joe is dead." His death occurred March 8, 1862, and was universally regretted.

CLARE, Ada, actress and author, real name Jane McElhenry, was born in the South about 1835. She came of an excellent family, being a cousin of Paul Hayne, the poet. She made her début as an actress at the Academy of Music, New York, on Nov. 27, 1855, as Ophelia in "Hamlet," but she never achieved enduring success on the stage, and soon became better known as a writer than as an actress. A woman of great beauty and marked intelligence, but impulsive and indifferent to public criticism, she was for many years a distinctive and attractive feature of literary life in New York, and the boon companion of O'Brien, Arnold, Ward, Wilkins, Clapp, Thompson, and other journalistic free-lances of the day. She contributed frequently to the press, and published a volume entitled, "Only a Woman's Heart." She finally became the wife of Frank P. Noyes, and in her last years returned to the stage. She died on March 4, 1874, from hydrophobia, resulting from the bite of a favorite lap-dog. She is buried in Greenwood Cemetery, N. Y.

WALKE, Henry, rear-admiral U. S. navy, was born in Princess Anne county, Va., Dec. 24, 1808. He is of Dutch descent, and his ancestor, Anthony Walke, came to America prior to 1700 from England. His father, Anthony Walke, fifth of the name, removed from Virginia to Chillicothe, O., in 1811, and the son received an academic education in the latter place, among his classmates being William Allen and Allen G. Thurman. On Feb. 1, 1827, he entered the navy as midshipman, and his first service was in the Alert, under David G. Farragut, then a lieutenant. He was promoted to be passed midshipman in July, 1833, and lieutenant in February, 1839, and during the Mexican war participated in the capture of Vera Cruz, Tobasco, Tuspan, and Alvarado. He was commissioned as commander in 1855, and from 1858 until 1860 commanded the Supply, employed in African and West Indian waters. In 1861 he commanded her at Pensacola, and saved Fort Pickens from capture, thus enabling the Union forces to regain possession of Florida. When the Pensacola navy-yard was captured, though he had been previously ordered to Vera Cruz, he elected instead to convey the loyal paroled prisoners and their families to New York. For this he was court-martialed, and censured by the secretary of the navy, but the public and the press warmly commended him for his wise discretion. Walke commanded the gunboats Taylor and Lexington at the battle of Belmont, and effectively covered the retreat of the land forces under Gen. Grant. He commanded the Carondelet at the capture of Fort Henry, and for his services received the thanks of congress and the legislature of Ohio. He took part in the first bombardment of Island No. 10, on March 17, 1862, and then at night ran the gauntlet of the Confederate batteries, a feat that had been pronounced impossible by his superiors. This led to the capture of the batteries below the island,

and the immediate surrender of the latter, and rendered possible the opening of the blockade of the Mississippi. At the battle of Fort Pillow, May 11, 1862, the Carondelet led the Union fleet in attacking and defeating the Confederate gunboats. At Memphis, June 6, 1862, still under the command of Walke, she was in the front line of that successful battle, and July 15th bore the brunt of the battle with the Confederate ram Arkansas. Com. Walke was promoted to be captain on July 16, 1862, and assigned to the command of the Lafayette, with which he engaged in the passage of the batteries at Vicksburg. At the battle of Grand Gulf, on Apr. 29, 1863, he led the second division of Porter's fleet in the attack on the Point of Rocks, being ten hours under fire. Capt. Walke continued to render splendid service with the Mississippi squadron until Sept. 24, 1863, when he was assigned to the Sacramento, and sent in search of the Alabama. He followed her for many weeks, but found, when he arrived at Lisbon, that she had been sunk by the Kearsarge. He then blockaded the Rappahannock, a Confederate cruiser of the same class as the Alabama, for fifteen months at Calais, France, and intercepted her when she escaped into British waters, under British colors, following her nearly into Liverpool, whence his vigilance did not permit her to sail until after the close of the war. Capt. Walke was advanced to the rank of commodore July 25, 1866; created rear-admiral July 13, 1870, and on Apr. 26, 1871, was, at his own request, placed on the retired list. He was instrumental in defeating the notorious works of the first Navy Star Chamber Retiring Board of 1855, which, without just cause or a hearing, on *ex parte* evidence, had themselves and their abettors promoted by retiring and dismissing over 100 naval officers, some of whom were our most distin-

guished old heroes of the war of 1812 and their sons, without pay, or on half-pay or two-thirds full pay. He also refuted the complaint of the above board in a court of inquiry, was restored to his proper rank on the active list, and promoted to a commander from the above date. By the ambiguity of an act of congress the full pay of the restored officers was withheld, yet Walke faithfully and cheerfully performed all his duties as commander and paymaster of the store ship Supply, and rendered very important services at Pensacola and on the Mississippi flotilla; as did nearly all those officers who were retired, as Coms. William D. Porter and A. H. Kilty, who fought so faithfully and suffered so terribly for the Union, and many others too numerous to mention, but some of the relentless clique in that Navy Retiring Board were the bitterest secessionists, and fought against our government. After the war, Adm. Walke, for several years, at great expense and trouble, appealed to congress for the full pay due him, and he finally obtained a decisive act of congress, which not only restored the back pay to him, but to all the officers of the navy who had been retired, some of whose families were almost destitute of the means of living. Since his retirement he has resided in Brooklyn, N. Y. Rear-Adm. Walke published, in 1877, " Naval Scenes in the Civil War," accompanied by sketches drawn by himself.

DURFEE, William Franklin, engineer and gun inventor, was born in New Bedford, Mass., Nov. 15, 1833. He completed his education at the Lawrence scientific school of Harvard, and in 1853 engaged in business as an architect and engineer in his native town. He also for five years filled the office of city surveyor. In 1861 he was elected to the lower branch of the Massachusetts legislature, where he was secretary of the military committee, and a leader in securing the enactment of legislation necessary for a successful prosecution of the war. A resolution introduced by Mr. Durfee in the legislature, embodied the first formal proposal for the arming of colored troops. In 1862 he designed and perfected a gun for naval warfare, which was warmly praised by a government commission and anticipated by several years the " Destroyer." However, owing to the failure of the government to adopt it when it was brought to its notice, the inventor turned his attention to other matters, and the gun has never come into general use. In the summer of 1862 Mr. Durfee made a careful inspection of the iron ores of the Lake Superior region, to ascertain if they could be profitably employed in the manufacture of steel by the Kelly method, and as a result of his investigations temporary works were built at which steel ingots were produced, and from these ingots, in May, 1865, the first steel bars made in the United States were rolled. Following this, Mr. Durfee constructed an analytical laboratory at Wyandotte, Mich., and entered upon an exhaustive study of the chemical properties of ores. He introduced the Siemens regenerative furnace in the United States, and in recent years has successfully managed different steel plants. In 1876 he was one of the judges of machinery at the Philadelphia exhibition, and was rewarded with a medal for his services. In 1878 he constructed at Ansonia, Conn., furnaces for the refining of copper by the use of gaseous fuel, the first of their kind built in the United States to prove entirely successful. Since 1880 he has been general manager of the United States Mitis Co., engaged in the production, by new processes, of wrought iron and steel castings. Mr. Durfee is a member of different scientific societies, and a frequent contributor to scientific periodicals.

REQUA, Isaac Lawrence, mining engineer, was born in Tarrytown, N. Y., Nov. 22, 1828. His ancestors on his father's side were Huguenots, who, being driven from France, settled in the town of New Rochelle about 1680. From there the family removed to Tarrytown. During the American revolution the family took an active part on the side of the colonies, no less than twenty-two of the name being enlisted. Glode Requa, a great-grandfather, was captain of Tarrytown company 1st (South) regiment Westchester county militia. Mr. Requa was educated at Newman Academy in Tarrytown, and for some years worked on his father's farm. He removed to New York from Tarrytown, but on the news of the finding of gold went to California, arriving in 1850, by way of Cape Horn. Going to the interior, he engaged in mining, and continued in this business in California until 1860, when he went to Virginia city, Nev. Here he engaged in the milling and mining business. In 1867 he became connected with the Chollar-Potosi Mining Co., as superintendent. He continued in this capacity until he removed to Oakland, Alameda co., Cal. Mr. Requa has the distinction of having installed at the Chollar-Norcross-Savage shaft the heaviest mining machinery

used on the Comstock. This shaft is 3,250 feet in vertical depth. He was also superintendent of the Union Mill and Mining Co., controlling the majority of the stamp mills of the Comstock lode. In politics he was an old-line Whig until the formation of the Republican party. He was for twenty years chairman of the Republican state central committee, and was tendered the nomination for governor, which he declined, not feeling justified in relinquishing his mining and milling interests to enter upon a political career. Since removing to Oakland, Mr. Requa has become identified with banking and railroad interests, and is now president of the Central Pacific and the Eureka and Palisade Railroads, and of the Oakland Bank of Savings.

MAGELLAN, Ferdinand, explorer, was born at Villa de Sabroza, Portugal, in 1740. His real name was Magalhaes, but it was changed to Magallanes by the Spaniards. His boyhood was spent in the household of Queen Leonora, the consort of John II. of Portugal, and at an early age he devoted himself to the study of astronomy and navigation. For several years he was in active service in the East Indies. He is said to have given warning to Siqueira in 1510 of the plot of the people of Malacca, thus probably saving his countrymen from annihilation; and, along with Serrano, he commanded the ships sent out under Abreu for the discovery of the Spice Islands. On his return to the East, Magellan was sent to Aynmor, in Morocco, where, in an action, he received a wound which left him lame for the rest of his life, and which was the origin of the troubles that determined his future course. He applied to King Manuel for an increase of his pay, which was refused, and this so incensed him that, in company with Ruy Faliero, another malcontent of note, and a geographer and astronomer, he formally renounced his nationality, went to Valladolid in 1517, and offered his services to the court of Spain. He laid before Charles V. a scheme for reaching the Moluccas by way of the southern coast of America, instead of the usual route around the Cape of Good Hope, which plan was favorably received by both the emperor and the bishop of Burgos, and an agreement was entered into, stipulating that Magellan was to be admiral of the exploring fleet, and governor of whatever lands he should discover. No sooner had Manuel heard what Magellan had proposed to the Spaniards, than he felt the mistake he had committed, and made every possible effort to allure his alienated subject back to his allegiance, but without avail. Things had gone too far for Magellan to retrace his steps, and on Aug. 10, 1519, his fleet, consisting of five ships of from 60 to 130 tons, with 80 cannon and about 240 men, set sail from Seville. After a stormy passage of nearly two months the squadron reached what is now known as the bay of Rio de Janeiro, where its store of provisions was replenished. Sailing close to the coast, Magellan arrived at the mouth of the river La Plata, Jan. 12, 1520. When the fleet reached the port of St. Julian, on the Patagonia coast, three of Magellan's Spanish captains conspired against him, and it was only by a rapid execution of summary vengeance that he maintained his authority. Two leaders of the rebellion were killed and quartered, and a third was set ashore with a priest, who had also taken part in the revolt. These misfortunes were followed by the loss of one of the ships, although the crew escaped, and were distributed among the other vessels. On Oct. 21, 1520, he entered the strait between the American continent and Terra del Fuego. It being the festival day of St. Ursula and her eleven thousand virgins, he named it the Strait of the Eleven Thousand Virgins, which name was afterward changed to that of his own. At this time one of the ships abandoned him and returned home to Spain. The strait was passed on Nov. 28th, and Magellan pushed on for the Moluccas. Three months later (March 16, 1521) he discovered the group of islands known as the Philippines, which he took possession of in the name of the Spanish king. He was at first very successful in subduing the natives, but in an encounter with them on the island of Martan, he was killed. Only one of the vessels and fifteen men, in command of Sebastian del Cano, returned to Europe, reaching Spain Sept. 6, 1522; and thus the first circumnavigation of the earth was achieved. No record of his exploits has been left by Magellan himself. The best contemporary account is that of Antonio Pigafetta, a volunteer in the fleet. Magellan was killed Apr. 27, 1521.

DYER, Heman, educator and clergyman, was born at Shaftesbury, Vt., Sept. 24, 1810, and was graduated from Kenyon College, Gambler, O., in 1833. He was principal of Milnor Hall, 1835–40; teacher at Pittsburg, Pa., 1840–43; professor in the Western University of Pennsylvania, 1844–45; and its chancellor, 1845–49. In 1854 he was appointed editorial secretary of the Evangelical Knowledge Society, and in 1865 corresponding secretary of the American Church Missionary Society, New York city. He belongs to the Episcopal church, and received the degree of D.D. from Trinity College, Hartford, Conn., in 1843. In 1862 he declined the bishopric of Kansas, and in 1880 he was compelled to retire from active life by failing health. He published, "The Voice of the Lord upon the Waters" (New York, 1870); and, "Record of an Active Life" (1886).

LOCKWOOD, Frederick St. John, financier, was born in Norwalk, Conn., Aug. 23, 1825, the son of Col. Buckingham St. John and Polly (St. John) Lockwood, and seventh in descent from Robert Lockwood, who settled in Watertown, Mass., in 1630. A "History of the Lockwood Family in America," a copious volume of nearly nine hundred pages, was published in 1889. It is there shown that 147 Lockwoods, descendants of Robert, served as officers and privates in the revolutionary, and twenty-three in the colonial, wars. The St. John family, of ancient lineage, has intermarried with the Lockwood family in nearly every generation. Frederick was graduated from Yale in the class of 1849, and was a classmate of Timothy Dwight, now president of the university. He intended taking a legal course, and began the study of law in the office of Chief-Justice Butler, but the sudden death of his father, in February, 1850, which threw the whole care of his large estate in Ohio and Connecticut upon his shoulders, prevented his carrying out his original designs. From 1859 to 1862 he was bank commissioner. During the war he was on the staffs of Maj.-Gens. King and Russell. At the close of the war he represented Norwalk as a Republican in the legislatures of 1865 and 1866, and also in 1872. For many years he has been a director of the Danbury and Norwalk Railroad, and in 1892 was elected its president. Mr. Lockwood has been officially connected with many financial and industrial corpora-tions. From 1884–1890 he was president of the Fairfield County National Bank, and for more than thirty years a director of the Norwalk Savings Society, and was one of the incorporators of the Fairfield County Savings Bank. He is past-worshipful master of St. John's Lodge F. and A. M., of Norwalk, a Knight Templar, a member of the Norwalk Club, and of the Connecticut Society of the Sons of the American Revolution, being grandson of Capt. Eliphalet Lockwood, of the 1st company, 7th Connecticut regiment in that war. In religion he is a Congregationalist. He married, in 1866, Carrie, daughter of Frederick Ayres, and they have two daughters and one son, the latter, Frederick Ayres, being now (1894) a member of the senior class at Yale.

GRIMES, Byran, soldier, was born in Pitt county, N. C., Nov. 2, 1828, the son of Byran Grimes, a farmer, and grandson of William Grimes, a patriot of the revolution. Byran was brought up on the farm, and entered the University of North Carolina, from which he was graduated in 1848. He then engaged in farming, and was distinguished for his success and enterprise. He was a member of the convention of Raleigh which passed the ordinance of secession in 1861. He immediately entered the Confederate service, and was appointed by Gov. Ellis major of the the 4th regiment of the North Carolina state troops. He served gallantly throughout the whole war. He was with Lee at Sharpsburg and Gettysburg, and was severely wounded at South Mountain. He was promoted through the several grades of service, and attained the position of senior major-general of Stonewall Jackson's corps. His division made the last charge at Appomattox immediately before the final surrender to Gen. Grant. After the war he returned to his farm in Pitt county, and was the constant advocate of all improvements that were ushered in by the new order of things consequent upon the change in the labor system of the state. Gen. Grimes was twice married—first, to Bettie Davis, and, upon her decease, to Charlotte Bryan, daughter of the late John H. Bryan. On Aug. 14, 1880, while returning from Washington, N. C., to his home, in a buggy, he was fired upon by some miscreant in ambush, and killed. The alleged cause of the assassination was the impending testimony of Gen. Grimes in a forthcoming trial, which would incriminate certain persons who, it is supposed, took this means to close his lips forever.

WALKER, Thomas Barlow, philanthropist, was born in Xenia, Greene co., O., Feb. 1, 1840, the second son and third child of Platt Bayliss and Anstis Barlow Walker. The Walkers were of English stock, and settled during the early history of the country in New Jersey, his father leaving that state early in life for New York. The Barlows were also of sturdy parentage. His maternal grandfather was Thomas Barlow of New York, and two of his uncles were for many years judges, Thomas in New York and Moses in Ohio. His father died *en route* to California in 1849, and his mother was left to struggle with adversity with her four young children. From his ninth until his sixteenth year, Thomas led the usual careless life of the average frontier village boy. He was expert with the rifle and shot-gun and at the game of checkers. At sixteen the family removed to Berea, O., where better educational advantages were possible, and where Thomas's boyhood abruptly ended and earnest life began. From sixteen to nineteen his time was divided between work and study. After various business adventures, always attended with hard work and generally with success, he returned to his books and studies, and the next winter taught a district school in the adjoining township, where he had about sixty scholars, among whom were eight school teachers, some of them much older than he. About this time the war broke out, and with his associate students in the Baldwin University he volunteered as a soldier. Having failed to get sent to the front he, after waiting

several months, and while in search of employment, landed in St. Paul, and the next morning took the train to the city of Minneapolis. On Dec. 19, 1863, he was married to Harriet, youngest daughter of Fletcher Hulet. Dating from his marriage, the history of Mr. Walker is the history of Minneapolis. His first years were years of hardship, self-denial, and patient toil. The summer of 1863 was spent in railroading, after which, for some years, he gave his whole time to government surveys. In 1868 he began his venture in pine lands. As a consequence of his foresight, Mr. Walker to-day owns more valuable pine lands than any other man in the Northwest. In connection with these surveys and pine land enterprises, Mr. Walker has been, and is yet, extensively engaged throughout various sections of the Northwest in the manufacture of lumber. Mr. Walker is extremely liberal in the use of his wealth for the upbuilding of Minneapolis, or for purposes of charity or charitable work. Mr. Walker's whole life has been greatly moulded and influenced by reading the books of public libraries, beginning with the private library of Father Blake, a Catholic priest. Through Mr. Walker's influence and efforts the Athenæum Library was greatly improved. The reading-room was enlarged, an assistant employed, and hours lengthened. The library was also opened on Sunday, and the membership increased by allowing payment by installments. Mr. Walker purchased several hundred membership certificates, which he kept loaned out among his employees and others. In the rapid growth of the city he foresaw the demand for a library that should meet all the wants of our mixed population, and be free to all. At the same time it seemed unnecessary to maintain two separate libraries and duplicate the valuable stock of books now in the Athenæum. Mr. Walker proposed that the city by taxation establish a free library upon condition that the citizens contribute a certain large sum toward the erection of the building, and that the Athenæum, the Academy of Science, and the Fine Art Society, be given space in the building, in consideration of which the books of the Athenæum Library were to circulate upon the same terms as those of the public library, and to be drawn in the same manner. This was agreed to, necessary legislation secured, and Mr. Walker was the first to subscribe to the library fund. When the beautifully designed building was completed, Mr. Walker saw the realization of his desire of many years. The rapid growth of this institution during the six years which have now passed (1895) since it was first formally opened, makes its standing in circulation fourth among the public libraries of the country. The perfect harmony of action between the two boards of the library and the Athenæum, and the pride of the citizens in it, are the best possible witnesses to the wisdom of the board, and the liberal policy inaugurated by Mr. Walker. He has been annually elected president of the library board from its organization in 1885 to the present time, 1895. The liberal provision for art in this building is also due to Mr. Walker's devotion to its interests. From its inception he has been a staunch friend and supporter of the Art School, which has taken so high a rank among the educational interests of the city, and among the art schools of the country. On the walls of the spacious gallery he has placed examples of nearly all of his own private collection. The art gallery at his home has been pronounced the choicest collection of art treasures, for its size, in the United States, and is open to the public on all days but Sunday, a liberality highly esteemed and appreciated both by citizens and strangers. The fame of this gallery has gone throughout the nation, and even to Europe, and many are the expressions of surprise from Eastern connoisseurs over the un-

J. B. Walker

Mrs. T. B. Walker

looked-for treasures displayed upon its walls. Mr. Walker's home library consists of a large and carefully chosen collection of choice books. When Mr. Walker constructed his present residence in 1874 his large lawn was thrown open without a fence. This innovation has now become the custom adopted by a large portion of the citizens of Minneapolis. The benches placed around the lawn under the trees are occupied free by all classes of people during the entire summer. The Minnesota Academy of Natural Science is another institution much indebted to Mr. Walker's interest and patronage for its past support and present fortunate situation, for through his influence when the library building was designed, the needs and importance of this association were considered, and spacious and beautiful apartments were assigned to them. For several years Mr. Walker was a member of the board of managers of the State Reform School, where he made his strong practical business habits felt, and inaugurated many valuable changes, thus becoming a great favorite with its inmates. It was especially through the efforts of Mr. Walker that the Minneapolis Business Union was organized, which has been a leading factor in building up the business interests of the city, both in the line of manufacturing and wholesale trade. Mr. Walker was elected president of the union, which is composed of the wealthiest and most influential men of the city, and he has devoted a large part of his time, as well as a considerable amount of money, for the benefit of the city. He is the head of the Minneapolis Land and Investment Co. Mr. Walker was for many years president of the Flour City National Bank. Three years ago he organized a company, of which he is president, which constructed the Central City Market, which is, probably, the finest market building in the United States. In politics, Mr. Walker has always been a radical Republican, believing in a sufficient protective tariff to hold our money at home, so as to build up our manufactories for the employment of our workmen. He is a regular attendant of the Methodist church, of which his wife and several of his children are members. Through much doubt and questioning he has wrought his way up to a clear religious faith, a firm belief in the Bible as the rule of man's conduct, and the only safe foundation on which either men or nations can build. He has also taken pains to ground his growing children in the faith to which he has attained only by tiresome research. He has been the constant director of the education of his eight children, as well as their daily and close companion. From their earliest years they have been supplied with tools and machinery and shops, which have given the manual dexterity and practical knowledge of applied mathematics for lack of which a large percentage of men are at a disadvantage all their lives. As a result, the boys, while yet in their early years, became expert in the use of tools, and their beautifully outfitted shops form no inconsiderable part of their home. Remembering his own boyhood, Mr. Walker has encouraged the boys in all out-of-door amusements, especially hunting, which he has shared with them.

WALKER, Harriet Granger, reformer, was born in Brunswick, O., Sept. 10, 1841, youngest daughter of Fletcher and Fanny Hulet, natives of Berkshire county, Mass. Her grandfather, John Hulet, of Lee, Mass., was in the battle of Bunker Hill, and her great-grandfather (also John Hulet) built the first Methodist church in Berkshire county, if not in the state of Massachusetts. When Harriet was six years of age her parents removed to Berea, O., where she attended Baldwin University. At eleven years of age she joined the Methodist church, to which her family belonged, and with which she has

been prominently identified ever since. She early showed marked literary ability, and it was her girlhood ambition to write a book. During her school days she was a regular contributor to several periodicals. On Dec. 19, 1863, she was married to Thomas B. Walker, her schoolmate and companion since their sixteenth year. They took up a permanent residence in Minneapolis, Minn., where, during the first twelve years of their married life, Mrs. Walker devoted herself exclusively to her home and family cares, while her husband laid the foundation of his later business success. Mrs. Walker's work of public philanthropy began some twenty years ago, and to-day (1896) she is actively associated with most of the leading charities of Minneapolis, many of which she has been instrumental in organizing and maintaining with money and hard work. Out-side her immediate church work she, for the past nineteen years, has been the secretary of Bethany home for the reformation of fallen women. The city authorities made it appropriations from the public funds.

The Northwestern Hospital for Women and Children was organized by her about twelve years ago, and she is its president. It is under the sole management of women directors, and has a training-school for nurses, with women physicians. It owns one of the finest hospital buildings in the Northwest. Mrs. Walker brought together from the four leading Christian organizations of the city, the Woman's Christian Association, the Sisterhood of Bethany, and the two branches of the Woman's Christian Temperance Union, a joint committee which induced the police commissioners of Minneapolis to create the position of police matron, and to allow this committee the nomination of the incumbent by the payment of half her salary. She had visited and investigated the workings of matrons, or the want of matrons, in Boston, New York, Washington, Pittsburgh, Philadelphia, Cincinnati, Cleveland, Chicago, and Milwaukee, writing extensively upon the subject. She was one of the first to take up the work of the Woman's Christian Temperance Union. When that organization took up the political issue, however, she was for many years shut out from the work. Upon the division of the union, she joined the Non-partisan Woman's Christian Temperance Union, and took an active part in temperance again. She now holds the responsible positions of national vice-president and state president of the non-partisan organization, in each of which capacities her genius finds full play. In 1892 Mrs. Walker was elected president of a new organization called the Woman's Council, a delegate representative association of all branches of woman's work in Minneapolis. To her capable leadership is unquestionably due the astonishing growth and prosperity of this body. Seventy associations are represented, covering all departments of thought, study, and work in the fields of education, philanthropy, reform, medicine, art, music, the church, literature, history, and science. The Woman's Council now publishes a magazine. The Newsboys' Home is another charity to which Mrs. Walker's active influence has been lent; the Kindergarten Association has had her interest and support, and also the Children's Home, which is an outgrowth of Bethany Home. Mrs. Walker is equally active in her private charities. So much of her time is now required in the giving of advice and help to the unfortunate, that she has been obliged to institute regular office hours, and to employ a stenographer to carry on her correspondence. In all her work she enjoys the loving and admiring support of her devoted husband, whose example, as well as counsel, has been such an inspiration in all her work. She is also an earnest advocate of woman's suffrage. Her lectures, written for the Nurses' Training School, Christian Endeavor Society, and temperance work, have been published, and very widely copied and quoted. Several articles discussing and endorsing the Keeley cure for inebriety, one of which was read at the World's temperance congress in Chicago during the World's fair (1893), have been reprinted and largely circulated. She is a regular contributor to the "Trained Nurses' Magazine" of New York, and to the "Temperance Tribune," of which she is chairman of the publication committee. Through all her active life, however, Mrs. Walker's home duties have always been foremost. Her husband and eight children have been given precedence over every other demand, and, when her devotion to her large family, the care of her elegant home with its beautiful art gallery, and the large number of guests who enjoy the hospitality of that home are considered, it seems phenomenal that so large an amount of outside work could have been accomplished. Mrs. Walker has refused to give her time to society; her evenings are given to her family, yet among the women of the city of Minneapolis there is probably no other one so widely beloved and respected.

SPARKMAN, Stephen M., lawyer, was born in Hernando county, Fla., July 29, 1849. His father, Nathaniel Keightley Sparkman, was of Welsh and Scotch ancestry, his mother of a Georgia family, who were of French extraction. The Sparkman family settled in Florida in the early days of the Indian wars, in which Nathaniel K. Sparkman took an active part. At the time of the death of his father the son was only eight years old, but ere long became the mainstay and support of his widowed mother. Until his eighteenth year he lived on the farm, and his opportunity for acquiring an education was limited to the country school, aided by his own determined and persevering efforts in self-education. It is told of him that, after the day's work in the field, he was accustomed to study and read at night by the fitful blaze of a pine wood knot, and in the gray light of the early morning, before rising, he would snatch thoughts from his favorite authors to ponder over during the day while walking behind the plow. He taught school for two or three years. At the age of twenty-one he began the study of law, under H. L. Mitchell, afterward governor of the state of Florida. In 1872 he was admitted to the bar, where his great capabilities, together with his firmly acquired habits of intense application and untiring perseverance, soon made for him an enviable position, and the young lawyer pushed rapidly to the front ranks in his chosen profession. In 1875 he was married to Ellen Hooker of Polk county, and in August, 1879, located at Tampa, where he has continued the practice of law. In 1878 he was appointed state attorney for the sixth judicial circuit of Florida, which position he retained until 1887. As this service would indicate, he was an able and successful prosecutor, yet his preference was to defend. In 1890, upon the resignation of Gov. Mitchell from the supreme bench, Mr. Sparkman was tendered the appointment by Gov. Fleming, which he declined. In politics he is a Democrat, contributing liberally, in money and service, to the success of his party, but never seeking office. He was a member of a congressional committee for the first congressional district of Florida for six years, and chairman of that committee for two years, being at the same time a member of the state executive committee, of which he was elected chairman in 1892. In 1894 he was elected a representative in the fifty-fourth U. S. congress from the first congressional district of Florida.

FERRY, William Montague, soldier, was born at Michilimackinac, Mich., July 8, 1824, the elder son of Rev. William M. and Amanda White Ferry of Massachusetts, who were missionaries on the frontier. Mr. Ferry, Sr., was a Presbyterian clergyman, who established, and for a number of years maintained, the Mackinac Mission. In 1834 he removed with his wife and five children to the present site of the city of Grand Haven, Mich. They were the first white settlers in Ottawa county, Mich. Here the subject of this sketch grew to manhood, encountering all the excitements and vicissitudes incident to frontier life. He learned the trade of machinist and engineer. In 1855 he erected the Ottawa Iron Works, a large machine shop and foundry, and engaged largely in the manufacture of steam engines and sawing-machines. He soon became noted as a skilful draughtsman and practical engineer, and also is well known as an inventor, having taken out various patents on his inventions. In 1856 he was elected regent of the University of Michigan, retaining the position until the outbreak of the civil war. In 1861 he enlisted as a private in the 14th Michigan infantry, with which he served throughout the war, passing through successive grades of promotion to the rank of colonel. At the close of the war Col. Ferry returned to Grand Haven and resumed his business. He is a Democrat of the Jacksonian type, and in 1870 was a candidate for congress from the fifth congressional district of Michigan, and greatly reduced the majority in that Republican stronghold. He was secretary of the national Democratic convention held at Louisville, Ky., of which James Lyon of Virginia was chairman, which nominated Charles O'Connor for president and J. Q. Adams for vice president, and was the "straight" Democratic candidate for governor of Michigan for that year. In 1873 Gov. John J. Bagley appointed him a member of the constitutional commission for framing a new constitution for the state of Michigan. Col. Ferry was, in 1876, elected mayor of Grand Haven, Mich. In 1878 he removed to Park City, Utah, to devote himself to his mining interests. He there became an active member of the Liberal party. In 1888 he was chosen the member from Utah of the national Democratic committee for the succeeding four years, and served as such until 1892. He was nominated Democratic candidate for delegate to the fiftieth congress, the Liberal party not making a nomination that year, against John T. Caine, the Mormon candidate. Pres. Harrison appointed him one of the alternate commissioners from Utah of the Columbian World's Fair. Col. Ferry has taken an active part in educational affairs both in Michigan and Utah, and is ardently devoted to the interests of the public schools. He is noted for his literary ability, and as a writer has contributed largely to the political and historical history of Michigan, during the civil war and since, to the current literature of the day. His style is terse, almost to brevity, smooth, comprehensive, and vigorous. He was married, in 1851, to Jeanette Hollister of Grand Rapids, Mich. Religiously, Col. Ferry is a Presbyterian.

O'ROURKE, John Henry, builder and contractor, was born in Brooklyn, N. Y., Feb. 10, 1840. His father and grandfather were among the first Irish emigrants to that city, in 1828, settling on a small farm in Dean street, near Court, now the very heart of Brooklyn. The father, Patrick O'Rourke, a blacksmith, was one of the early contractors of the city. John H. O'Rourke attended the public schools, and obtained the rudiments of a practical education. At the age of nineteen he served with one James Ashfield, to learn the brick-mason's trade, and continued with him for about three years. In 1861 Mr. O'Rourke was attached to the engineering corps in the department of the Gulf, U.S.A., and served on government fortifications on the coast of Florida. He returned to Brooklyn about 1865, and began working as a builder and mason, and, in 1866, was appointed superintending mason for the park commissioners, a responsible position, which he filled most creditably until 1871. He then became contractor on his own account, and the following year built the 18th regiment armory. After that he erected numerous public buildings, stores, school-houses, business blocks, and private residences. He was considered one of the most enterprising men in his profession in Brooklyn. Although a Democrat, Mr. O'Rourke was never an active politician, yet he obtained much influence in his ward. He was a prominent member of the Catholic Knights of America. In 1872 he was married to Agnes L. Lennon of New York.

BISSELL, Joseph Bidleman, physician, was born at Lakeville, Conn., Sept. 3, 1859. He traces his ancestry back in a direct line to John Bissell, who settled at Windsor, Conn., in 1636. His father, Dr. William Bissell, was graduated at Yale in the famous class of 1853, and was subsequently graduated in medicine at the Yale medical school. He is a practicing physician at Lakeville, Conn., trustee of the Hotchkiss School, and a commissioner of the State Insane Asylum at Middletown, Conn. The son received his first education in the Rocky Dell Academy of Lime Rock, Conn., and afterward at Amenia Seminary, Amenia, N. Y., where he prepared for college. He entered Yale University in 1876 and was graduated in the scientific department in 1879. He then became a student in the medical department of Columbia College, where he was graduated in 1883, and was shortly afterwards appointed house surgeon in the City Charity Hospital of New York. Being desirous of attaining still higher proficiency in his profession, he crossed over to Europe in 1884, and pursued his studies and practiced surgery in the hospitals of the universities of Vienna and Munich. Shortly after his return he was appointed, in 1886, instructor of surgery at the New York Polyclinic, and in 1889 at the New York Postgraduate, Medical Schools, and Hospitals. In 1895 he received the appointment of chief surgeon to the outdoor department of St. Vincent's Hospital, with surgical work in the wards of the hospital. He is a member of the New York County Medical Society and a fellow of the New York Academy of Medicine, and from 1893 to 1895 held the position of president of the Society of Alumni of the City Charity Hospital. He has contributed various papers on surgical and medical topics to different journals and magazines, the most important of which are: "Pathological Anatomy of Club Foot," "Rickets," "Incontinence of Urine in Children," "Preventive Treatment in Seasickness," etc., etc. Dr. Bissell was a member at college of the Chi Phi Fraternity, and is now president of the Chi Phi Club of New York, as well as of the Omicron Trust Association of New Haven, which is now (1895) building a fine society clubhouse for the use of the local chapter of the fraternity. He is also a member of the Yale Alumni Association and of the University Club. Dr. Bissell married, Nov. 20, 1889, Josephine Hauck of Harrison, N. J.; they have three children.

COY, Edward Gustin, educator, was born in Ithaca, N. Y., Aug. 23, 1844. His father, Edward Gustin Coy, was connected with the Howe family, several of whom, in Vermont and  New Hampshire, bore honorable parts in the French and Indian wars. He was a plain man, yet possessed of a singularly pure and unselfish character, which was a constant inspiration and example to his children. His mother, Elizabeth Brown, was connected with the Corwins and Vances. Young Coy received a liberal education, and was graduated at Yale in 1869. He began at once to teach, and has engaged in no other calling. He was first a tutor at Yale, and, after a year's service, resigned to accept a professorship at Phillips Academy at Andover. He remained in this position until 1892, when he was elected head master of the Hotchkiss School in Lakeville, Conn. Prof. Coy was in Europe in 1883 and 1884, and gave some time to visiting and studying the historic parts of Greece. He spent a winter semester at the University of Berlin, hearing lectures on archaeology from Ernst Curtius, and on philology from Steinthal. Prof. Coy was married at New Haven, Conn., Nov. 25, 1875, to Helen E. Marsh, a great-great-granddaughter of Roger Sherman of Connecticut. In personal appearance Prof. Coy is tall, being over six feet high, finely proportioned, and erect and alert in bearing. He has made some valuable contributions to educational literature, among which may be mentioned "Greek for Beginners" (1880), and "First Greek Reader" (1881).

GAYARRÉ, Charles Étienne Arthur, the historian of Louisiana, was born in New Orleans, Jan. 9, 1805. He is of illustrious Spanish and French descent; one of his grandfathers came to Louisiana in 1766, as royal comptroller and commissary after the cession from France to Spain; the other was Étienne de Boré, one of Louis XV.'s mousquetaires, the first Louisiana planters to make sugar in 1795, and the first mayor of New Orleans in 1803. Educated at the College of Orleans (now extinct), he, in 1825, opposed some of the provisions of the criminal code prepared for Louisiana by Edward Livingston, and so successfully that the code was not adopted. In 1826–28 he studied law at Philadelphia under William Rawle, and in 1828–29 was admitted to the bar there and at home. In 1830 he was sent to the legislature, in 1831 appointed attorney-general, and in 1832 presiding judge of the city court. In January, 1835, when barely of senatorial age, he was elected to the U. S. senate, but, by reason of ill-health, could not take his seat, and spent eight years abroad. Returning, he re-entered the legislature in 1844, and there effected a reduction of the state debt. Again chosen in 1846, he was at the same time made secretary of state, a post which then included the superintendence of public education, and (with the state treasurer) the control of the city banks. During his seven years' tenure of this office, he built up the State Library, and enriched it with many documents procured from Spain.

Charles Gayarré

His "Histoire de la Louisiane" appeared in two volumes (1846–47); "Romance of the History of Louisiana" (1848); "Louisiana; Its History as a French Colony," two volumes (1851–52); and "History of Louisiana under Spanish Rule" (1854). The complete work, brought down to 1861, was published in four volumes in 1866, and reprinted in 1885. This work was a monument of painstaking industry and scholarship, and gave him place as one of the great historians of the country. In 1854 Mr. Gayarré put forth two lectures on "The Influence of the Mechanic Arts," and a play, "The School for Politics," for which the Louisiana "Courier" attacked him as unfaithful to the party. He refuted the charge in a letter to the Washington "Union," Oct. 23, 1854. In 1853 he had been an Independent Democratic candidate for congress, and was defeated by fraud. This practically closed his political career; henceforth he was little more than an adviser, for the opponent of corruption makes powerful enemies. In 1855 he exposed the American or Know-Nothing party, and destroyed its temporary dominion in New Orleans. In 1861 he defended the right of Louisiana to secede, and in 1863 read at Osyka, Miss., an address to the Confederate congress, urging the arming of the slaves, and a treaty with England and France, based on gradual emancipation. In 1866 he delivered in New Orleans a timely lecture on Oaths, Rebellion, and Armistices, and attended the convention held in Philadelphia to reconstruct the Democratic party. In 1867 he was nearly elected to the U. S. senate. His last official work was as reporter of the decisions of the state supreme court (1873), of which he prepared four volumes. In all the numerous public speeches which he was called upon to deliver on political and other subjects, and which were textually and at length recorded by the Louisiana press, Gayarré showed himself gifted with great oratorical powers. On presidential elections he more than once canvassed the state with such men as Pierre Soulé, Preston, and other eloquent speakers; and justice to him requires it to be stated that he accomplished with zeal and ability, and invariably at his own expense, all the missions with which he was intrusted by his party, inside and outside of Louisiana. It is a remarkable trait in Gayarré's political career that he never was the subject of any personal and vituperative attacks from the press, but on the contrary, was treated by these organs of public opinion not only with much consideration, but even with the utmost kindness, in spite of the prevailing bitterness of party feeling, except on one single occasion: that was on the publication of Gayarré's "School for Politics." Since the war he has published "Doctor Bluff," a two-act comedy; "Philip II. of Spain" (1866); "Fernando de Lemos; or, Truth and Fiction" (1872), and its sequel, "Aubert Dubayet; or, The Two Sister Republics" (1882), and numerous contributions to reviews, magazines, and newspapers. In his last years he wrote another historical novel, a "History of New Orleans," and a volume of reminiscences. Until within a year or two of his death he was a frequent and valued lecturer at home, and often declined invitations from the North, fearing the winter climate. Of his "Philip II.," the "Saturday Review" says: "Regarded, as it should be, simply as an inquiry into one of the most curious physiological problems which history suggests, it is a work of no ordinary interest." It was unfortunate for his own interests, and for those of literature, that his plan of going to Spain for some years was frustrated by the outbreak of hostilities in 1861. He might have preserved his handsome fortune, which was lost in the war, and he would have added much to the sum of available human knowledge. He survived to a great age, with faculties almost unimpaired, still earning his living by the pen, neglected by the state and general governments (his application for the naval office at New Orleans in 1865 was disregarded), but honored throughout the land by such as value chivalric independence, lofty purity in public and private life, great attainments, and eminent services to literature. He died Feb. 11, 1895, in New Orleans, La., where he lived his entire life.

ALSTON, William, revolutionary soldier, was born in Charleston, S. C., in 1757. He was a captain under Marion, a capable soldier, and a zealous patriot. After the war he served for many years in the state senate, and on one occasion was a presidential elector. He was the father of Gov. Joseph Alston. He died June 26, 1839.

OWEN, Robert, social theorist, was born in Newtown, Montgomeryshire, Wales, May 14, 1771, the son of a Welsh saddler. He does not appear to have had more than a merely commercial education to fit him for common business. At the age of ten he was sent to London, consigned to the care of an elder brother, to make his fortune. There he was employed as clerk in a dry-goods store, but finding the work uncongenial he entered the employ of David Dale, a prosperous cotton manufacturer. In 1797 he married Mr. Dale's daughter, Anne Caroline, and soon afterward became business manager of these mills, which he conducted for many years with great success. While in this business he set on foot a number of liberal and far-reaching plans for the benefit of the working people and their children. He built commodious and beautiful school-rooms, where, besides the regular branches, the children were regularly drilled in singing, dancing, military exercises, and deportment. He introduced sanitary reform, and was instrumental in reducing the hours of labor. A factory was, however, far too limited a sphere for his ambitions; he wanted to organize the world, and in 1816 Mr. Owen published "New Views of Society, or Essays on the Formation of Human Character," which was followed by other writings on the organization of society on the principles of socialism, in books, pamphlets, lectures, and other available forms until his death. His

Robert Owen

plans for the relief of pauperism found at first public favor; the leading journals and many eminent men gave him countenance, but his defiant attack on all forms of accepted religion at a great meeting in London brought an instant change. His socialism was identified with infidelity, and all his efforts thereafter were discredited in the popular mind. In 1824 he came to the United States, and purchased a large area of land on the Wabash river in Indiana, where he continued with the intention of establishing a colony, but after a trial of less than three years it proved a failure. He returned to Scotland, where a second attempt was made to carry out his cherished plan, with no better success. He then went to Mexico in 1828, but was unable to make the experiment there because of the Mexican government insisting, when making the grant of land, that the religion of the settlers should be the Roman Catholic. He visited the United States on several occasions, and took part in a debate with Rev. Alexander Campbell, of Ohio, on "The Evidences of Christianity," Mr. Owen taking agnostic ground. Besides a number of publications on his great life work, he published his autobiography in 1857. He appeared at the meeting of the Social Science Association at Liverpool in the autumn of 1858, with all his schemes as fresh as ever. He died a few weeks later at Newtown, Wales, Nov. 19, 1858.

DORSEY, Jesse Hook, lumber manufacturer, was born in Beallsville, Washington co., Pa., in 1849. His father, James Francis Dorsey, a clergyman of the Methodist Episcopal church, was an able preacher, and a distinguished revivalist, most of his labor being performed in western Pennsylvania. The son was educated in the public schools and Waynesburg College, where he was graduated in 1869. After leaving college he taught school for three years; then edited the Waynesburg "Independent" for two years, and left that to take charge of a large cotton plantation belonging to an uncle at Helena, Ark. He was successful in the management of the plantation, but his health breaking down through malarial fever, he went to Tampa, Fla. In 1882, he formed a partnership with James H. Wells, engaging extensively in the manufacture of lumber. The business was continued until 1893 with a partner, when Mr. Dorsey purchased and conducted the business alone. The Tampa Lumber Co. transacts the largest business of its kind in the state. Eighty men are employed in the mills, and 100 in the woods. The pay-roll for labor alone averages $2,000 a week. The company had their mills burned out twice in less than three years, resulting in a total loss, as no insurance was carried. Mr. Dorsey rebuilt after each fire, and purchased the mill of his only competitor, increasing the value of his plant to $50,000. Mr. Dorsey was married in 1878 to Emily Chalfant of Greenville, Pa., by whom he has three children. He is a member of the M. E. Church in Tampa, the superintendent of its Sunday-school, and was for some time president of the Young Men's Christian Association. He is also a member of the Florida annual conference of the M. E. church, and prominent in all work connected with his denomination. That Mr. Dorsey has been successful in all his enterprises, notwithstanding the misfortunes he has met with, is due to his integrity, quick perception, executive ability, and prompt business instincts. Being active in every good work to help his city, state, and fellow-men, he has won the confidence and respect of all his fellow-citizens.

BERKELEY, George, Protestant Episcopal bishop of Cloyne, Ireland, was born at Dysert Castle, near Thomastown, County Kilkenny, Ireland, March 12, 1684. His father was the son of an English royalist, who was rewarded for his loyalty to Charles I. by an official post at Belfast, Ireland, in the reign of Charles II. The peasantry of Kilkenny have their quaint stories of the Berkeley family. They tell that in his youth the philosopher kept a school in the neighborhood and taught his scholars that there was no spirit, and that when the body died the man was annihilated. He used, they added, to make the boys leap over the school benches until they were bruised and bleeding, and then explained that after the blood all ran out, there was an end of them. Another fancy, equally absurd, was that Berkeley's own corporeal remains were buried within the masonry of the battlements of Dysert. In 1696 he entered the Kilkenny School and was placed in its second class, the lowest class at that time being the first. This school, the "Eton of Ireland," was originally an appendage to the Cathedral of St. Canice. He matriculated at Trinity College, Dublin, March 21, 1700. In 1702 he was made a "scholar," the emoluments of one of their students not exceeding, at that time, the sum of £3. In the spring of 1704 he became a Bachelor of Arts, and took his master's degree in 1707. On June 9, 1707, he was admitted to a fellowship. His bent was already fixed. Berkeley and some of his college friends had formed a society to promote investigations in the new philosophy of Boyce, Newton and Locke. Early in 1707 he published two tracts, one an attempt to demonstrate arithmetic without the help of Euclid or algebra, the other consisting of "Thoughts on Some Questions in Mathematics," both written in Latin, and published in London, England. On the title page they were attributed to a "Bachelor of Arts in Trinity College, Dublin," but they are contained in all the editions of the Bishop's collected works, and are assigned to him as author, without dispute. Early in 1709 appeared the celebrated "Essay Toward a New Theory of Vision," with his name upon the title page. It attracted so much attention as to call for a new edition before the end of the year. The next (1710) began with his "Treatise Concerning the Principles of Human Knowledge," in which Berkeley boldly announced the great conception of which for years he had been full. The book was a systematic attack upon scholastic abstractions, especially upon abstract or unperceived matter, space, and time. Berkeley's leading

thought and method as a mental philosopher was thus published when he was young. None of his predecessors or successors resemble him in this to the same degree. His contention that the commonly received notion of the existence of matter is false; that sensible material objects, as they are called, are not external to the mixed, but exist in it, and are nothing more than impressions made upon it by the immediate act of God according to certain rules termed laws of nature, from which in the ordinary course of his government, God never deviates; and that the steady adherence of the Supreme Spirit to these rules is what constitutes the reality of things to his creatures, was not much regarded by the philosophers of the age. Lord Byron wrote thus of it:

"When Bishop Berkeley proved there was no matter,
He proved it was no matter what he said."

On Feb. 1, 1709, he had been ordained Protestant Episcopal deacon in the old chapel of Trinity College, his ecclesiastical service at this time being confined to an occasional sermon in the college chapel. In 1711 he published three sermons under the title, "A Discourse of Passive Obedience," a closely argued defense from the point of view of a philosophical advocate of high Tory principles, of the Christian duty of not resisting, as a nation, the supreme civil power, wherever placed. In 1710 he had been nominated a sub-lecturer at the college and in the same year junior deacon. In 1712 he visited England for the first time. At that date he had been a Junior Fellow and a tutor at the college for five years. His pay, however, did not probably exceed £40 per year, say £140 by the standard of the present day. On an April Sunday in 1713 he was presented at the court of Queen Anne in London by Dean Swift, and from March 14th to Aug. 5th of that year, was a contributor to Richard Steele's "Guardian," contributing to its pages fourteen essays. In them he appears as a free-thinking anti-free-thinker and tries to describe the believer in God and immortality by contrasts with the unbeliever in both. It was about this time that he was introduced by the Earl of Berkeley to Lord Atterbury, who, after listening to his conversation, was interrogated as to how he liked him. Atterbury, it is said, lifted up his hands in astonishment and replied: "So much understanding, so much knowledge, so much innocence and such humility, I did not think had been the portion of any but angels until I saw this gentleman." He now met Addison and Steele and Pope also. In November of the same year he became chaplain to Lord Peterborough, and accompanied him to the continent, returning in August, 1714. The next year he traveled as tutor

to the son of Lord Ashe, and was absent from England for five years. On his way home he wrote and sent to the French Academy the essay, "De Motu," in which he gives a full account of his new conception of causality, the fundamental and all comprehensive thought in his philosophy. In 1718 Mrs. Van Homrigh (Dean Swift's Vanessa) left him £4,000. She had only met him once at dinner. In 1721, when the great South Sea bubble burst, he published an "Essay Toward Preventing the Ruin of Great Britain," which shows the interest he took in practical affairs. In that year he returned to Ireland as chaplain to the Duke of Grafton and was made divinity lecturer and university preacher. In 1724 he was promoted to the rich deanery of Derry, with £1,100 per annum, and resigned his fellowship, but had hardly been appointed before he was using every effort to resign it, that he might devote himself to his project of founding a college on the islands of Bermuda. His scheme for this was published in 1725 and was entitled, "A Proposal for Converting the Savage Americans to Christianity." With great exertion he obtained a promise from the government of £20,000, and finally sailed in September, 1728, accompanied by friends and by his wife, daughter of Judge Forster, speaker of the Irish House of Commons, whom he had married in the preceding month. Their destination was Rhode Island, where they had resolved to await the promised government grant. Before sailing, Berkeley had poured out his feelings in the ode which ends with the familiar lines:

"Westward the course of Empire takes its way;
    The first four acts already past,
A fifth shall close the drama with the day:
    Time's noblest offspring is the last."

Three years of quiet retirement and study were spent in Rhode Island. Berkeley bought a farm there which he named "Whitehall," made many friends, and endeared himself to the inhabitants. He preached every Sunday at Newport while there, besides performing pastoral work. But as the British government did not fulfill its engagement in the matter of funds, the projector of the college was forced to give up his plan. This was doubtless after a call made in London upon Sir Robert Walpole, the English minister, by Bishop Gibson of London, in whose diocese Rhode Island was then included, and the bishop's begging to know whether the money would be forthcoming or not. "If you put this question to me as a minister," replied Sir Robert, "I must and can assure you that the money shall most undoubtedly be paid as soon as suits with public convenience; but if you ask me as a friend whether Dean Berkeley should continue in America, I advise him by all means to return to Europe and give up his present expectations." It was in September, 1731, that Berkeley complied with this advice, and sailed from Boston on his return to Great Britain. But he had become increasingly interested in the advancement of letters and learning in this country, not so much by travel and observation while he was in it, as by the visits of men who were able to give him facts concerning the condition of education in America, and after reaching his native land he put into execution the benevolent purposes which made him the revered patron of Yale and Harvard Colleges. To Yale College he presented 880 volumes, which are now kept by themselves in its library, as the "Berkeleian Collection;" to Harvard, valuable donations of Greek and Latin classics. The "Whitehall" farm, which has since become exceedingly valuable property, he conveyed to Yale College, for the provision and maintenance of three scholarships in Latin and Greek. These scholarships and prizes have been regularly awarded since 1733, and have been enjoyed by some of the most distinguished of the alumni of the college. In 1762 this farm was rented by the college authorities for 999 years. Soon after his return to England, Berkeley published: "Alciphron, or The Minute Philosopher," which he had written at Newport, R. I., examining the various forms of free-thinking in the age, and bringing forward, in contrast to them, his own theory, which shows all nature to be the language of God. This, having been written in America, became exceedingly popular in this country. In May, 1734, he was consecrated bishop of Cloyne in Ireland. Subsequently, the Earl of Chesterfield offered him the see of Clogher, double the value of that of Cloyne, where, also, fines to the amount of £10,000 were due, but the bishop declined the offer, saying to his wife, "I desire to add one more to the list of churchmen who are evidently dead to ambition and avarice." At Cloyne he published "The Analyst," attacking the higher mathematics as leading to free-thinking, and giving rise to sharp controversy. Then came "The Querist," a practical work on social or economic philosophy, in three parts. In 1752 he removed, with his family, to Oxford, England, where his son was studying, not being permitted by the King (George I.) to resign his bishopric. The King said that Dr. Berkeley should "die a bishop in spite of himself," but he allowed him to reside where he pleased, and at Oxford he died suddenly and painlessly, conversing with his family. His philosophical writings are still widely read, and his name is widely honored, especially in America. At New Haven, Conn., there is a memorial window in the Battell Chapel (Yale College). At Middletown,

Conn., the Protestant Episcopal denominational theological seminary is the Berkeley Divinity School, Berkeley, Cal., where the state university is situated, is named after him. At Newport, R. I., his influence is perpetuated in the Redwood Library and by his gift of an organ to Trinity Protestant Episcopal Church. In 1886 a beautiful memorial chapel was dedicated at Newport by Rt. Rev. Bishop T. M. Clark. It has been well said that Berkeley's was one of the purest and most beautiful human lives on record. The date of his death was Jan. 14, 1753.

GREGG, David, clergyman, was born in Pittsburg, Pa., March 25, 1846, son of David and Mary Gregg. His father, descended from the Scotch Covenanters of 1638, was for many years, and up to the date of his death in 1892, an elder in the Central Reformed Presbyterian Church, Allegheny city, Pa. The son was trained in the principles of that church, while his secular education was acquired, first at the public schools of his native city, and then at the Allegheny College, where he was prepared for entrance at the Washington and Jefferson College at the age of fifteen. He was graduated with honors in 1865. He then took a year's course at the Iron City Commercial College in Pittsburg, from which he was graduated in 1866. When, Gen. Lee invaded Pennsylvania in 1863 young Gregg enlisted as an emergency man. After his year's training in commercial business, he studied theology at the Theological Seminary at Allegheny, and was graduated in 1868. He then went abroad, and traveled in Great Britain and on the continent. While in Scotland he received two calls to take charge of churches there, but his affinities for America would not allow of his acceptance. Immediately after his return to America he refused the call of churches at Oil City, in Iowa, and in New York city, but by the repeated efforts of the congregation of the Third Reformed Presbyterian Church, New York city, he was finally encouraged to undertake the charge, in spite of his youth. In his work in this large congregation he was eminently successful. During the pastorate he expounded nearly every book of the Bible, and upon some of the books delivered as many as thirty lectures, each lecture costing him, on an average, three days' study. Many of these expository lectures were printed in full. He was, in addition to his pastoral duties, for thirteen years editor of "Our Banner," a monthly church magazine. During his pastorate in New York he was elected to the chair of the Moderator of the Covenanter Church, the youngest moderator that ever presided over that august body. He refused calls from Providence, Pittsburg, and Boston, but finally, in 1880, accepted the call from the Park Street Congregational Church, Boston, where A. L. Stone, W. H. H. Murray, and J. L. Witherow had been his eminent predecessors. There was said to have been not a single unpleasant thing in his pastorate in Boston. He left the church in a flourishing condition, both numerically and financially. His last foreign mission collection amounted to over $10,600. In 1890 he was asked to succeed Theodore L. Cuyler as pastor of the Lafayette Avenue Presbyterian Church, Brooklyn, and he accepted the call. In Brooklyn he has met with the same success that attended him in New York and Boston. His study is fitted up in the tower of the church, and has become historic. When his father died, in 1892, he disinherited this son, because he had left the

VI.—17

church of his youth. The son cheerfully acquiesced in his father's decision, because he recognized its judgment as based on principle, and in the closing hours of his life the father asked the son to pray with him as he lay on his dying couch, and the son poured out his earnest and tender prayers for his father. In 1893 Dr. Gregg's mother restored to him the share of the property withheld by his father's will. In 1889 the University of the City of New York conferred upon him the honorary degree of D.D. He was married in 1871 to Kate, daughter of Robert Etheridge, of Frankfort, N. Y., and they have two sons and two daughters. His published works include: "From Solomon to the Captivity," "Studies in John," and "Facts that Call for Faith." His sermons, "The Hollanders as Makers of America," "George Washington, the Father of Our Country," and his Fourth of July Oration at Woodstock, Conn., in 1891, have been widely published—the first having been translated and printed in Middleburg, Holland.

HOOPES, Benjamin, educator, was born in Chester county, Pa., March 26, 1820, of English ancestry. He was educated principally at the Friends' Boarding School, Westtown, Pa. When nineteen years old, he began to teach, having determined to make that profession his life calling. He conducted, as assistant and principal, various private, public, and boarding schools in Eastern Pennsylvania, and had for his pupils many of the children of Quakers, who largely made up the better class of the residents of that section of the state. He gave up his regular routine of instruction by ordinary methods to become superintendent and manager of a farm and training school for boys, in Bucks county, Pa., where he was a pioneer in the Swedish system of manual training and practical education of hand as well as head. His success at this manual labor school was the subject of investigation by educators from all parts of the country, and his methods have been adopted in the best equipped schools. After six years' labor in this field, he accepted the superintendency of the Pennsylvania Hospital at Philadelphia, where he has found a work that calls for an exercise of all the philanthropy and concern for his fellow man so largely developed by his experience in the school-room and on the farm.

CLEVELAND, Moses, colonizer, was born at Canterbury, Conn., Jan. 29, 1754. He was the founder of Cleveland, O. In selecting the site of which he showed much sagacity. He was graduated from Yale College in 1777, and in 1796 he headed an expedition despatched by the Connecticut Land Co. to block out into townships of five miles square, the whole of the Western Reserve—a tract of land extending along the shore of Lake Erie for over 100 miles west of Pennsylvania. At Conneaut, where he landed with a party of fifty, July 4, 1796, he presided at a patriotic banquet of bread, pork and beans and grog—the first Fourth of July celebration on the Western Reserve. A few days later  he smoked the pipe of peace with the Indians, and so far conciliated them with whisky and glass beads and impressed them by his stature and swarthy complexion that they gave him the name of Paqua, their favorite chief. On July 23d he ascended the Cuyahoga in command of a small reconnoitering party and fixed upon the site of the future Cleveland. After superintending the laying out of this town into building lots and providing for its settlement, he returned to Connecticut where, for the remainder of his life, he had a good law practice and a considerable local reputation as a member of the State Legislature and brigadier-general of the militia. He has been described as "cool, deliberate, and always self-possessed as well as brave and courageous amid threatening dangers, and especially popular with his associates." He died at Canterbury, Conn., Nov. 16, 1808.

JOHNSON, Edward Hibberd, electrical inventor, was born in Chester county, Pa., Jan. 4, 1846, son of Albert B. and Mary A. Johnson. His parents were both natives of the United States, descended from English ancestors. The son was educated in the schools of Philadelphia, and began business life as a telegraph operator, passing through 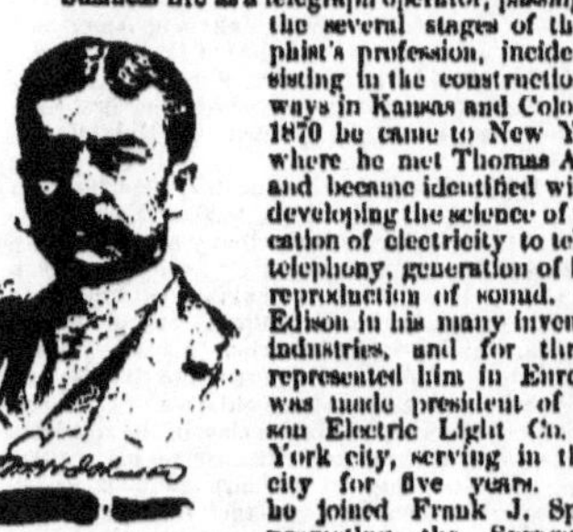 the several stages of the telegraphist's profession, incidentally assisting in the construction of railways in Kansas and Colorado. In 1870 he came to New York city, where he met Thomas A. Edison, and became identified with him in developing the science of the application of electricity to telegraphy, telephony, generation of light, and reproduction of sound. He aided Edison in his many inventions and industries, and for three years represented him in Europe. He was made president of the Edison Electric Light Co. of New York city, serving in that capacity for five years. In 1883 he joined Frank J. Sprague in promoting the Sprague Electric Railway and Motor Co., the pioneer of the popular trolley system. He is now president of the Interior Conduit and Insulation Co., founded largely on his own inventions. He was in 1894 engaged in promoting a new electric railway system, intended to revolutionize the methods of street transit in crowded cities. Mr. Johnson was married at Philadelphia, in 1873, to Margaret V. Kenney. They have three children. Their home is in Greenwich, Conn.

DULLES, John Welsh, clergyman, missionary, and editor, was born in Philadelphia, Pa., Nov. 4, 1823, and was graduated at Yale College in 1844. He studied theology in Union Theological Seminary, New York city, and went in 1848 as missionary to India, where he was stationed at Royapooram in the presidency of Madras. Though his powers proved well adapted to the work before him, the climate was so uncongenial to his health, that he was compelled to leave the field. After his return home he was secretary first of the American Sunday-School Union, 1854–57, and then of the Presbyterian (New School) Publication Committee. But after the reunion of the two branches of the Presbyterian church he became editorial secretary of its board of publication, editing all its periodicals, tracts, and books. He visited Europe in 1874, Egypt and Syria in 1878–79, and Algeria and Spain in 1884. He published "Life in India" (Philadelphia, 1855); "The Soldier's Friend" (1861); "The Ride Through Palestine" (1881); and received in 1872 the degree of D.D. from the College of New Jersey. He died in Philadelphia, Apr. 13, 1887.

COFFIN, Tristram, pioneer, was born in Brixton, England, in 1605, and thirty-seven years afterward emigrated to the colony of Massachusetts with his wife, five small children, a widowed mother and two unmarried sisters. He first settled at Salisbury, then at Haverhill, then at Newberry, and finally, about 1659, at Nantucket island, which he with nine associates, about that time, had purchased. In this small island he was the acknowledged chief. His energy, intelligence, philanthropy, and great public spirit lifted him prominently above the men of his time, and he became the founder of one of the most remarkable families in the United States. His extraordinary physical, mental, and moral qualities seem to have been continuously transmitted in a wonderful degree to his numerous descendants, who are found in all sections of the country, and number over 150,000 souls, many of them prominent in their respective social, business, and religious communities. One cannot examine the voluminous records of the family, covering a long period before its Puritan founder emigrated, and the 250 years since that time, without being confirmed in the belief that there are few, if any, families in the United States to-day that can boast of such a continuous line of distinguished men and women. Among them we find Benjamin Franklin, Lucretia Mott, Maria Mitchell, Charles J. Folger, Levi Coffin, Admiral Sir Isaac Coffin, Col. James Vanderberg, commanded by Washington; Capt. Israel Vail, killed at the battle of White Plains, and Capt. Reuben Coffin, who commanded the Seth Low while towing the Monitor from New York to the James River in 1862, bravely hurrying it over a dangerous sea against the protest of naval officers, and so providentially arriving in time to save a fleet of our best war ships from destruction. Tristram Coffin died Oct. 2, 1681.

TERRY, Eli, inventor and manufacturer, was born in East Windsor, Conn., Apr. 13, 1772, and was prominent above all other men of his time in the manufacture of wooden clocks. He was apprenticed to Thomas Harland, a brass clock maker in Norwich, Conn., where he acquired the rudiments of his trade. He had much ingenuity and innate talent, and before he was twenty-one years old, he constructed a few old-fashioned wooden clocks. In 1793 he removed to Plymouth, Litchfield county, and began the manufacture of this class of clock, working alone for a period of seven years. In 1800 he engaged a boy and a couple of young men to assist him. They began two dozen at a time, cutting the wheel with saw and jack-knife, by hand. Two or three times a year he took a trip, taking with him several clocks, which he sold for $25 each, for the movement only. In 1807 he purchased an old mill, which he fitted up for the purpose of making clocks by machinery. At this time a number of men in Waterbury formed a company, and made a contract with him—they furnishing the capital and he making the movements. He accumulated quite a fortune, for the times, by this arrangement.  The first 300 clocks that were ever started by machinery at one time in this country were made by Terry at his factory in the old mill in 1808. This was a larger number than had ever before been begun at one time in any place in the world. In 1810 he sold out his business to Seth Thomas and Silas Hoadley, his principal workmen, who entered into partnership, and two years later removed the factory to Thomaston. Terry, however, kept on making inventions in clock machinery, including a form of gravity escapement, which were sold to Thomas and other manufacturers. Later, with the aid of his sons, he established several large clock factories, and did an immense and successful business. He died in Terryville, Conn., Feb. 24, 1852.

GILMAN, Caroline Howard, author, was born in Boston, Mass., Oct. 8, 1794, daughter of Samuel Howard, a shipwright. Her father died when she was three years old, and her mother—a descendant of the Brecks, a well-known family of Boston and Philadelphia, retired with her children to the country. They lived in various towns in New England, and finally settled in Cambridge, Mass., where her mother died. At the age of sixteen Miss Howard commenced her literary career, producing "Jephtah's Rash Vow," and this was followed by "Jairus's Daughter," in the "North American Review." In 1819 she was married to Samuel Gilman, and they removed to Charleston, S. C., where he became pastor of the Unitarian Church. Dr. Gilman gained a wide literary reputation outside of his profession as the author of "The Memoirs of a New England Village Choir." In 1832 Mrs. Gilman commenced the publication of the "Southern Rosebud," a weekly juvenile newspaper, which she continued for several years. From this miscellany her writings have been collected and republished at various times. Among her better known writings, which have passed through many editions, are: "Recollections of a New England Bride;" "Recollections of a Southern Matron;" "Poetry of Traveling in the United States," made up of graceful humorous sketches of Northern and Southern life; "Verses of a Life-time," published in Boston, in 1849; "Tales and Ballads;" "Ruth Raymond;" "Oracles from the Poets," and "Oracles for Youth." She has also edited "The Letters of Eliza Wilkinson during the Invasion of Charleston," one of the most graceful personal memoirs of the revolutionary period. She published in 1860 a memorial of her husband. Mrs. Gilman's prose writings are natural and unaffected, with a cheerful vein of humor. Her poems are marked by their grace of expression, chiefly referring to nature, or the home-cherished affection. She died in Washington, D. C.

DE TROBRIAND, Philip Regis, soldier, was born at the Château des Rochettes, France, June 4, 1816. Upon becoming an American citizen he dropped his full name of Denis de Keredern, and title of Baron de Trobriand. His father was an eminent officer in the French service, and was military instructor in the College of Rouen. From his youth he was educated for a military career, being first sent to the College of St. Louis, in Paris, and subsequently he studied at the College of Rouen, under his father, and was finally sent to the College of Tours. The revolution of 1830 destroyed his military prospects, and he entered the University of Orleans, from which he was graduated in 1834, and two years later was graduated at Poitiers as Licencié en droit. He became a journalist and contributed articles upon miscellaneous subjects to the press. In 1841 he emigrated to the United States, and followed journalism until 1849, when he became editor and publisher of the "Revue du Nouveau Monde," in New York city, and in 1854 became associated in the editorship of the "Courrier des Etats-Unis." At the breaking out of the civil war he entered the Federal service as colonel of the 55th New York volunteers, was transferred to the 38th regiment in 1862, and was given command of a brigade of the 3rd army corps in 1862–63. He was engaged in the battles of Yorktown, Williamsburg, Fredericksburg, Chancellorville, and Gettysburg. In 1864 he was appointed brigadier-general, and given command of the New York city defences. He commanded a brigade of the 2nd army corps at the battles of Deep Bottom, Petersburg, Hatcher's Run, and Five Forks, and commanded a division in the campaign which terminated in Lee's surrender, in which latter service he was brevetted major-general of volunteers, in 1865. In 1866 he entered the regular army, and was made colonel of the 31st infantry. The next year he was brevetted brigadier-general, U. S. army, and given command of the district of Dakota. In 1869 he was transferred to the 13th infantry and given the command of the district of Montana. At his own request, on account of age, he was retired, March 20, 1879. Gen. De Trobriand is the author of "Les Gentils-hommes de L'ouest," and "Quatre Ans de Campagnes à l'armée du Potomac," two volumes.

ANDERSON, Alexander, the father of wood engraving in the United States, was born in New York city, Apr. 21, 1775. He had the educational advantages usual to the time, and at an early age conceived an ambition to become an artist; but, complying with the wishes of his father, he began the study of medicine, occupying his leisure in attempts at engraving. He entered the medical school of Columbia College, and was graduated M. D. when but twenty-one years of age. When only twelve years of age he began engraving on copper cents rolled out, and upon type-metal, with tools of his own invention, but this work he did so well that he was employed to execute some cuts for a book called the "Looking-Glass for the Mind." His earliest efforts were reproductions of the anatomical figures in his medical works, but he had a wonderful genius which enabled him, almost without any instruction, to achieve results which were masterpieces.

Soon afterward he learned that it was possible to engrave on wood, and he began working upon wood, and in 1798, he abandoned the practice of medicine, and devoted himself exclusively to the business of engraving. For about fifteen years he was the only wood-engraver in New York, and for the fifty years following 1812, was the leader in his art in this country, which he continued to practice as late as his eighty-seventh year. He engraved the illustrations for "Webster's Spelling Book," and made forty plates to illustrate an edition of Shakespeare. He engraved the cuts of Bewicks' "Birds" and Sir Charles Bell's "Anatomy." He was employed for many years by the American Tract Society. He died in Jersey City, N. J., Jan. 18, 1870, and soon afterwards a brief account of him and his work was published by Benson J. Lossing.

COATES, Kersey, pioneer, was born in Salisbury, Lancaster co., Pa., Sept. 15, 1823, son of Lindley and Deborah (Simmons) Coates, who were lifelong members of the Society of Friends. His father was a farmer, but deeming his son's talents adapted to a more intellectual life, gave him the advantage of a liberal education; and the young man attended school, first near home, and afterwards at Whitestown Seminary, in New York, completing his course at Phillips Academy, in Andover, Mass. After having finished his studies, he was appointed to the chair of English literature in the High School of Lancaster, Pa., where he taught for several years. When about twenty-five years of age, he entered the office of Thaddeus Stevens, an associate and personal friend of his father, with whom he remained until 1858, when he was admitted to the bar. In 1854 Mr. Coates went to Kansas, for the purpose of attending to real estate interests, and soon found himself among a desperate set of men from Missouri, Kentucky, Virginia, and Georgia, who determined to make Kansas a slave state. Mr. Coates was not long in taking position with the anti slavery faction, and for two years, while he remained on the border, the exercise of that inherent freedom of speech which had characterized his ancestors, made him constantly an object of hatred with the pro-slavery element, while to the free-state party his great personal fear-

lessness, his devotion to the cause of human rights, his legal skill and attainments, and his clear, cool head were a tower of strength. He was looked up to as an unusually strong and safe man, and was employed as one of the counsel for the defense of Gov. Charles Robinson, when that official was on trial for treason. The Kansas trouble over, he returned to Missouri, and located in Kansas City, where he lived during the remainder of his life. In 1855 he was married to Sarah Chandler, also of the Society of Friends, and a native of Pennsylvania. In 1856–57 Kansas City began to show signs of business life and activity, and Col. Coates, uniting his efforts with those of other enterprising citizens, newspapers were established, railroads projected, favorable legislation was secured, grand commercial enterprises were inaugurated, and important municipal improvements were started, the result of which was a stream of immigration that speedily filled up Kansas City, and overflowed into the adjacent counties of Missouri and Kansas. He engaged in banking, dealing in real estate, merchandising, and building. He was also prominent in securing legislative and municipal aid for the Missouri Pacific and Cameron Railroads. During the political contest of 1860 he was president of the only Republican club in western Missouri, if not the only one west of St. Louis, and on the day of the presidential election he was one of only seventy or eighty citizens who were willing to put themselves on record as "black Republicans." During the civil war he was a staunch supporter of the Union, and before the war closed, was made colonel of the 77th regiment of E. M. M., which, during 1863–65, rendered valuable and efficient service, and was especially useful during the "Price raid" of 1864. At the close of the war Col. Coates devoted his time and attention to rebuilding Kansas City, which had, during the war, lost nearly half its population. At that time not a railroad reached within thirty miles of the city. Leavenworth, its old rival, had prospered by the war, and claimed a population of 15,000. Nothing daunted, Col. Coates and his associates began where they had left off in 1861, interested Eastern capitalists in the various railroad lines projected before the war, and almost before the people of Leavenworth were aware of it, had renewed the Cameron branch of that road, had procured the charter for a bridge over the Missouri river at Kansas City, and induced a wealthy corporation to undertake the construction of it, had incorporated the Missouri River, Fort Scott, and Gulf Railroad, obtained for it a splendid endowment of land from the state of Kansas, and effected a treaty between the government and various tribes of the Indian nation, giving the company great advantages. Within five years after the war the population had increased over 600 per cent., and the im-

portance of its trade and commerce was recognized all over the country. In all these enterprises Col. Coates was prominent, and in many of them he was a leader. He was especially instrumental in securing the legislation in congress and the Kansas legislature, which resulted in the Missouri River and Fort Scott Railroad, of which he was president for several years. Besides his own handsome residence, he erected the elegant hotel known as the Coates House, and the Coates Opera House, one of the finest theatres in the West. He was one of the organizers of the Kansas City Industrial Exposition and Agricultural Fair Association in 1870, and when the Interstate Fair Association was organized in 1882, was elected its president. He died Apr. 24, 1887.

CLARKSON, Floyd, soldier, was born in New York city, Feb. 27, 1831, the son of Samuel Floyd and Amelia A. (Baker) Clarkson. His paternal ancestor, Matthew Clarkson, was secretary of the colony of New York under appointment of William and Mary, in 1688, and his paternal grandmother, Catharine Floyd, was a daughter of William Floyd, who was a delegate to the Continental congress from New York, and a signer of the Declaration of Independence. Floyd Clarkson was prepared for the University of New York at King & Feck's (afterwards Lyon's) school, in New York city. But after completing his academic course, he persuaded his father to allow him to enter business, and took a position with the firm of Tracy, Allen & Co., hardware merchants, and remained with this firm and its successor until he engaged in business on his own account. Mr. Clarkson was among the first of those who responded to Pres. Lincoln's call for troops in April, 1861, and went with his company (Co. 6, 7th regiment, N.G.S.N.Y.) to Annapolis, Md., thence to Washington, D. C. Mr. Clarkson had joined the 7th regiment on March 18, 1856. He was one of the number who built Fort Runyon at the westerly end of the Long Bridge, Va. He was mustered out on June 3, 1861, and at once began recruiting for the cavalry service. On Nov. 11, 1861, Mr. Clarkson was mustered into the service as major of the 6th New York cavalry, and the latter part of the month went with his regiment into active service, serving in the peninsular campaign, attached to the 2d corps, afterwards to the 4th corps. He resigned Oct. 13, 1862, and was again mustered into the service as major of the 12th New York cavalry Apr. 2, 1863, and was ordered with his regiment to New Berne, N. C., May, 1863. On June 4, 1864, Maj. Clarkson was appointed assistant inspector-general, on the staff of Brig.-Gen. Edward Harland, commanding the subdistrict of New Berne. He also occasionally served as inspector-general of the district of North Carolina, Brig. Gen. Innis N. Palmer commanding.

On Feb. 21, 1865, Maj. Clarkson resigned his commission as major of the 12th N.Y.V. cavalry, to take effect on March 13th, in order to avail himself of a business opportunity offered in New York city. The resignation was returned from the headquarters of the army of the Ohio, marked "disapproved." Brig.-Gen. Innis N. Palmer having placed on it the endorsement: "This cannot be approved at this time; Major Clarkson is too valuable an officer to be spared now." He continued to serve until the close of the war, and on Apr. 22, 1866, was brevetted lieutenant-colonel "for faithful and meritorious service." He was subsequently employed as cashier in the flour-commission house of George W. Van Boskerck, and as secretary of the Equitable Savings Bank. In 1873 he opened a real-estate office, and in 1884 associated with him his son, John V. B. Clarkson, under the firm name of Floyd Clarkson & Son. He was a trustee of the Union Dime Savings Bank of New York city, and president of the Riverside Bank. Col. Clarkson was an active member of the Republican party. He was married on Oct. 27, 1857, to Harriet, a daughter of John Van Boskerck, one of the old Hollandish business men of New York. Col. Clarkson died in New York city, Jan. 2, 1894.

HENTZ, Caroline Lee, author, was born in Lancaster, Mass., June 1, 1800. She was the daughter of Gen. John Whitney and sister of Gen. Henry Whitney, both officers in the U. S. army. Before she had reached the age of thirteen, she was the author of a poem, a novel, and a tragedy in five acts. In 1825 she married Nicholas M. Hentz, a French gentleman, who at that time was associated with Mr. Bancroft, the historian, in the Round Hill School, at Northampton, Mass., and who was soon afterwards appointed professor in the college at Chapel Hill, N. C. This position he occupied for several years, and then removed with his family to Covington, Ky. Here Mrs. Hentz wrote her popular drama "De Lara, or the Moorish Bride," for which she received a prize of $500, offered by the Arch Street Theatre, Philadelphia, where it was successfully produced for many nights. It was afterwards published in book form. From Covington Mr. and Mrs. Hentz went to Cincinnati, O., and in 1834 to Locust Hill, Florence, Ala., where for nine years, they had charge of a flourishing female academy. In 1843 they transferred this institution to Tuscaloosa, and in 1848 to Columbus, Ga., where Mrs. Hentz resided the remainder of her life. These frequent changes and the arduous duties connected with the school, afforded her little opportunity for literary labor, and she was not able to write with any degree of regularity, until her removal to Columbus. Here she wrote her second tragedy, "Lamorah, or the Western Wild," which was brought out in a newspaper, and afterwards produced on the stage at Cincinnati. In 1843 she wrote a poem, "Human and Divine Philosophy," for the Erosophic Society of the University of Alabama. In 1846 she brought out "Aunt Patty's Scrap-bag," a collection of short stories written for magazines, which was followed in 1848 by "Mob Cap," for which she received a prize of $200. Both of these books have been universally read and admired. Among her other works are: "Linda, or the Young Pilot of the Belle Creole," "Rena, or the Snow-bird," "Marcus Warland," "Eoline, or Magnolia Vale," "Wild Jack," "Ellen and Arthur," "The Planter's Northern Bride," and "Ernest Linwood." Her short poems are scattered throughout various periodicals, and are full of the tender warmth of the writer's nature. Her tragedy "De Lara" stands first among her poetical works, and holds high rank in the dramatic literature of America. Mrs. Hentz died in Marianna, Fla., Feb. 11, 1856.

GURNEY, Francis, lieutenant-colonel in the war of the revolution, was born in Bucks county, Pa., in 1738. He received the rudiments of an education in a country school near his home, but when only eighteen years of age he became excited by the news of the French and Indian war, and volunteered his services in the provincial army. He went to Canada, where he was thrown into association with Israel Putnam, and he is said to have been viewed by that officer in the light of an adopted son. Young, active, and emulous of distinction, Gurney is said to have been engaged by choice in every spirited and gallant enterprise undertaken against the enemy during this campaign. He was present at the capture of Louisburg on Cape Breton, June 25, 1758, and was one of those who went with the British fleet to attack the French West India islands, and assisted in the taking of Guadaloupe, Apr. 27, 1759. Returning from this expedition, young Gurney settled down in Philadelphia, where he obtained a business position, and was conducting a successful trade at the outbreak of the revolutionary war. In the years 1774 and 1775 he was one of the first to arouse to resistance his fellow-citizens. Having a good knowledge of tactics and the manual of arms, he became instrumental in the formation and disciplining of the military, although he at first refused to accept a commission. He at length, however, May 25, 1775, was made captain in a regiment of infantry, raised by authority of the province. In the following year he entered the regular service, and was appointed a lieutenant-colonel in the 11th regiment of the Pennsylvania line. While holding this command he was present, and behaved with great bravery, being slightly wounded, at the battles of Brandywine and Germantown. On account of unjust discrimination in regard to promotion, Col. Gurney resigned his commission, and was placed on the committee of safety for the city of Philadelphia and for the defense of Delaware river and bay; the vigilance and competency which he manifested in connection with these appointments, proved to be important in their effects, and placed him high in the confidence of his fellow-citizens. On the conclusion of the peace of 1783 he again entered into mercantile business in Philadelphia, in which he was successful, and in which he continued until a year or two before his death, when he retired, but in the meantime and for nearly thirty years he was constantly employed in the discharge of some public function, civil or

military. For a number of years he was warden of the port of Philadelphia, during which time he suggested and carried into effect many important improvements in the buoys and beacons of Delaware bay; and he is said to have been the inventor of certain improvements in the construction of these important articles, which are still in use. Col. Gurney was for a long time in the city councils, was one of the aldermen of the city, and president of the select council. He was for several successive years elected a member of one or the other body of the legislature of the state of Pennsylvania, in which he proved an able speaker and an industrious and useful member. He was a trustee of Dickinson College and of other institutions, county commissioner, church-warden, and one among the most active, skilful, and indefatigable of the militia officers of the state. He held a colonel's commission in this corps, from May 1, 1786 to March, 1799, when he was promoted to brigadier-general. In 1794, when it became necessary to call a considerable force into the field to suppress the whiskey insurrection in the western part of Pennsylvania, he commanded the 1st regiment of the Philadelphia brigade, amounting to about 600 men, whom he carried through a severe campaign of three months, with the loss of only two men. The last few years of his life were passed by Col. Gurney at his country-seat in the vicinity of Philadelphia, occupying himself with social intercourse and reading, until he died May, 25, 1815.

STONE, Wilbur Fisk, jurist, was born in Litchfield, Conn., December, 1833, of English ancestry, and is descended from some of the earliest settlers in Hartford Colony. In 1838 his father removed to western New York, and soon after to Michigan. As that region proved unhealthy, another change was made to Fayette county, Indiana. In 1844 he located in Iowa on the new government lands at Oskaloosa. After living on the farm for six years, Wilbur, at the age of eighteen, was sent to an academy in Rushville, Ind., where for two years he studied, supporting himself by serving as an assistant teacher. He then entered Asbury University, Greencastle, where he remained until the beginning of his senior year. While here, he earned his tuition by writing prize essays and teaching country schools during vacations. He then entered the senior class of the State University at Bloomington, Ind., and was graduated. He was subsequently graduated in the law department, having engaged for a year as college tutor in the classical department. After the completion of his law studies, he settled in Evansville, Ind., and for more than a year was the leading editor of the "Daily Enquirer." In the winter of 1859-60, he was assistant editor of the "Omaha Nebraskian." In the spring of 1860 he crossed the plains to Denver, and soon afterward passed up to the Tarryall diggings in the South Park, where the next

five years were passed in prospecting and mining at various points, and in practicing law. In 1861, when the territory of Colorado was organized, he was chosen to represent Park county in the legislature, which assembled in Colorado City in 1862, and he was re-elected in 1864. From 1862 to 1866 he held the position of assistant U. S. district attorney, under Gen. Sam E. Browne. In the winter of 1865-66 he was married to Sallie Sadler of Bloomington, Ind., and soon after settled in Pueblo, Col., where he engaged in the practice of law until 1877, when he was elected to the supreme bench of the state. Judge Stone was one of the early settlers in Cañon City, Fremont co., and in connection with Geo. A. Hinsdale, drafted the first code of laws for the people's court of that district. During the early days he wrote many letters for the territorial press over the pen-name "Dornick." In 1864 he wrote and published the finest description of Mount Lincoln that has ever appeared in print, and which was widely copied in the various literary newspapers of the land, reproduced in Hollisters' "Mines of Colorado;" in one or two of the books on Colorado published by Samuel Bowles of the Springfield "Republican," and by Col. Alexander McClure of the Philadelphia "Times." Mr. Stone and George A. Hinsdale were the first editors of the Pueblo "Chieftain," established in 1868. He was treasurer and corresponding secretary of the first board of trade, organized in 1869, wrote and delivered an historical review of Pueblo in 1876, for the National centennial records of the government at Washington. He was the first district attorney of the third judicial district, and held various positions connected with the educational and industrial institutions of Pueblo and the state. In connection with Gov. A. C. Hunt and Gen. William J. Palmer, he was one of the active promoters of the Denver and Rio Grande Railway; was its attorney until 1877, when he entered upon his duties upon the bench. In 1874, with H. C.

Thatcher, he effected the contract for the building and extension of the Atchison, Topeka and Santa Fé Railroad, from the eastern boundary of the state to Pueblo. He was a member of the constitutional convention in 1875, and named by the Democratic minority as their candidate for president of that body. He was chairman of the committee on judiciary department, and a member of several other important committees. Upon the ratification of the constitution framed, and the admission of the state in 1876, he was nominated by the Democratic party for associate justice of the supreme court, but was defeated with the rest of the ticket. In 1877, however, Judge E. T. Wells, who held the long term of nine years, resigned, and Mr. Stone was nominated for the position by a convention of the bar of the state, held at Colorado Springs, and was elected without opposition. He remained on the supreme bench until the expiration of his term in 1886, and in 1887 was appointed by the governor, judge of the criminal court at Denver, which office he held until that court was abolished by the legislative act of 1889. From that time until 1891 he was engaged in the practice of law. Under the act of congress of March 3, 1891, "The Court of Private Land Claims" was established for the settlement of the Spanish and Mexican land-grant titles, in accordance with the treaty of Guadalupe-Hidalgo, the court consisting of five judges appointed from different states of the Union, and its territorial jurisdiction, including Colorado, New Mexico, Arizona, Nevada, Utah, and Wyoming. Judge Stone was appointed one of the justices of said court, by Pres. Harrison. In pursuance of an order of the court, he went to Spain in the winter of 1894-95, in company with S. Mallet-Prevost, special assistant to the attorney-general of the United States, for the purpose of procuring evidence, on behalf of the government, from the royal archives at Madrid, to be used in the famous Peralta case in Arizona, a grant of over 12,000,000 acres of land, alleged to have been made in 1748, by the King of Spain to one of his barons. The fraudulency of the case was amply established by the evidence collected. Judge Stone has visited Europe five or six times with his wife and sons, and possesses a good knowledge of the French and German languages, as well as the Spanish. He is a classical scholar, a ready and felicitous writer, and much given to the humorous as well as the practical vein. He is a prominent member of the Society of Colorado Pioneers, and seldom fails to contribute a happy address at the annual banquets of the society.

ATWATER, Wilbur Olin, chemist, was born in Johnsburg, N. Y., May 3, 1844. He was graduated at Wesleyan University, Middletown, Conn., in 1865; later he studied chemistry at New Haven and received the degree of Ph.D. from Yale in 1869, after which he spent two years in study at the universities of Leipsic and Berlin and elsewhere in Europe, specializing in physiological and agricultural chemistry. During 1871-73 he held the chair of chemistry in East Tennessee University. In 1873 he was called to fill a similar appointment in the Maine State College. In the same year he returned to Wesleyan University as professor of chemistry, which position he still retains. On the establishment of the Connecticut Agricultural Experiment Station, the first one of these institutions in the United States, in 1875, he was made its first director, and the work was carried out in his laboratory in Wesleyan University. He had charge of this station until 1877, when it was removed to New Haven, and is still a member of its board of control. On the establishment of the Storrs (Conn.) Agricultural Experiment Station, in 1878, he was made its director, and still retains that office. The success of the experiment station movement was such that in 1887 an act was passed by congress providing for the establishment of these institutions in all the states and territories in the Union. Provision was likewise made by congress for a central bureau in connection with the department of agriculture in Washington for the scientific co-ordination of the work of these institutions. Prof. Atwater was called in 1889 to organize this establishment, to which, by his advice, the name of Office of Experiment Stations was given, and continued in charge of it until 1891. By this time the office was in good working order and its success assured, but the work had increased so that he could not continue its supervision and at the same time attend to his duties in Middletown. He therefore resigned the directorship but was made special agent of the department, in which relation he continues until the present time. In the year 1878 Prof. Atwater undertook some studies of the chemistry of fish in connection with the U. S. Fish Commission. Some time later he conducted, in behalf of the Smithsonian Institution, other studies of the chemistry of foods. These investigations were continued in various ways; public attention was attracted to the usefulness of results, and finally, in 1894, congress provided an especial appropriation to be used in the study of the economy of the food of the people of the United States. The responsibility for the investigation was given to the secretary of agriculture, who placed it in Prof. Atwater's charge. It is now being carried on successfully in different parts of the country. The legislature of Connecticut has also, by an act passed in 1895, provided an appropriation for the same purpose; it is given to the station of which Prof. Atwater has charge. He has also co-operated for several years with the U. S. department of labor in investigations of the economy of food. Prof. Atwater has made frequent visits to Europe in the interests of his specialty in science. His published papers are very numerous. The majority treat of the scientific investigations which have been carried out by himself and under his direction. They have appeared in scientific journals in the United States, France, and Germany, and in various government publications. More popular articles from his pen have been published in the "American Agriculturist," the "Century Magazine," the "Forum," and other periodicals. A book by him on "Methods and Results of Investigations on the Chemistry and Economy of Food" was published in 1895 by the government under authority of the secretary of agriculture.

FORD, Gordon Lester, journalist, was born at Lebanon, Conn., Dec. 16, 1823, the son of Lester and Eliza (Burnham) Ford, and a descendant of Capt. Thomas Burnham, one of the earliest settlers of Hartford, Conn. His early education was received in his native town, and at eleven years of age he went to the city of New York, and entered the store of his uncle, Gordon W. Burnham, as office boy. Later he gained employment with the firm that afterward became H. B. Claflin & Co. From the Claflin's he entered the U. S. marshal's office, under William Coventry H. Waddell. He studied law in the intervals of his daily work, and in 1850 was admitted to the bar in New York county. His great talent for business was early recognized, and led to his election to the presidency of the New London, Willimantic and Palmer Railroad, now a part of the Vermont Central system, and he managed the concerns of this road until it passed into a new control. He went to Brooklyn in 1856, and was soon identified with many of the institutions of that city. Until 1869 Mr. Ford practiced law in New York city, but in all other respects his interests were entirely centred in Brooklyn. In 1869 he was appointed U. S. collector of internal revenue for the third collection district, but was retired in 1873, for refusing to allow political

assessments. In 1878 he became business manager of the New York "Tribune," where he remained until 1881, and for a short time in 1883 he was president of the Brooklyn, Flatbush and Coney Island Railroad, but soon retired, and from that period was only concerned in the management of his private affairs. Mr. Ford was one of the founders of the Brooklyn Art Association, and was its treasurer through many years. He was a director in the Academy of Music almost from the beginning, and was long chairman of the executive committee, and was one of the founders of the Hamilton Club. Mr. Ford possessed one of the finest and most complete collections of autographs and autographic manuscripts relating to the history of this country in the world. Not less than 100,000 manuscripts and 50,000 volumes bear testimony to Mr. Ford's discrimination, and is, perhaps, his best monument. Such was the value of the collection, that from all parts of the country historical writers either asked admission to, or information from his library, and all its contents were as free to such as if it had been a great public institution. On Dec. 16, 1853, Mr. Ford married Emily Ellsworth Fowler by whom he had eight children. He died in Brooklyn, N. Y., Nov. 14, 1891.

LOVELL, Leander Newton, was born at Fall River, Mass., Nov. 15, 1835, the son of Leander Perkins Lovell and Ariadne Borden, both of whom were descended from early New England settlers, the Lovells having come from Great Britain in 1630, and the Bordens but little later. The father died in 1843, leaving the boy to the care of his mother, by whom he was sent to the common schools of Fall River, and later to the high school. In 1852 he came to New York to push his fortunes in the firm of Tisdale & Borden, at that time agents for the Borden Coal Mining Co., the Fall River Iron Works Co., and the Fall River line of steamers. In 1863 he was admitted to partnership with Col. William Borden, under the firm-name of Borden & Lovell. During the civil war the business frequently brought him into connection with the different branches of the service, though he held no commission. Col. Borden died in 1882, but Mr. Lovell continued the business under the old firm-name, and has brought it to a high degree of prosperity. He has risen to an important place in the mercantile community of New York, and is a member of the chamber of commerce, the Maritime Association, and the Society of Naval Architects and Engineers, besides being a trustee of the Atlantic Mutual Insurance Co., of the New York and Boston Lloyd's, director of the Ohio and Kentucky Railroad Co., and of the Old Colony Steamship Co. He is also president of the Borden Mining Co. and the Lovell Coal Mining Co. He became a member of the Union League Club early in its history, is a life member of the New England Society of New York; the New York Young Men's Christian Association, and of the Sons of the American Revolution. He was married Jan. 16, 1867, to Phœbe Durfee, by whom he has eight children. Mr. Lovell is a resident Plainfield, N. J., and an elder of the Crescent Avenue Presbyterian Church at that place; also member of the board of education. The versatility of his tastes is further shown by his active membership in the American Statistical Association and the American Academy of Political and Social Science.

DE LAND, Charles Victor, journalist, was born in North Brookfield, Mass., July 25, 1826. His ancestry dates from Sir Christopher De Land of Lambille, Côte du Nord, France, whence they emigrated in 1634, settling in Portsmouth, England, and later, in 1649–50, coming to New England. Paul De Land came from Salem to Brookfield in 1724, and the subject of this sketch is the fifth descendant born in that town. In the spring of 1830 his father went to Michigan, and settled in Jackson, then over forty miles from any other settlement. In 1830 a newspaper was established in Jackson, and young De Land began the trade of printer. After working for several years in the state printing-offices, in Detroit and Lansing, he returned to Jackson in 1849, and established the Jackson "Citizen," which he owned and edited until 1861. He was active in the organization of the Republican party in 1854, and his paper was one of its foremost agents in the campaigns of 1856 and 1860, in which years he was elected a member of the state senate, but left his seat in that body, and his newspaper work as well, to enter the army in April, 1861, serving until the close of the war, rising from the ranks to be brigadier-general by brevet. During this service he was three times severely wounded, and was twice a prisoner of war. After the war, Col. De Land removed to Saginaw, where he remained for eighteen years. He first established the "Daily Enterprise," but his health was too much shattered by his wounds to admit of newspaper work, and he soon retired to serve as a collector of internal revenue, and again in 1873 as state senator. Later, in 1876, he established the "Daily Herald," which was continued until consolidated in 1886 with the "Courier-Herald." In 1883 he retired to his old farm home near Jackson, Mich., to again recuperate his health. In 1888 he was a delegate from his state to the Farmers' National congress and in 1890 was grand vice-president of the order of the Patrons of Industry. In 1892 he was a Republican elector-at-large for president. In 1893 he was selected by the legislature to revise and compile the tax laws of Michigan, which work was completed and the revision enacted into law at the legislative sessions of 1893–95. In recognition of this work, the legislature of 1895 erected the bureau of "state tax statistician," at the head of which Mr. De Land was placed by the governor and legislature. Col. De Land has published many addresses and statistical articles that have attracted wide attention. A bold thinker and vigorous speaker, he has exercised a large influence in the political and industrial affairs of his party and state, and is held in high esteem by its citizens.

ORR, James Lawrence, governor of South Carolina (1866–68), was born in Craytonville, S. C., May 12, 1822. His paternal ancestors came to this country from Ireland in 1730, and both his father and grandfather served in the revolutionary war. He was educated in the schools of his native place until he attained his eighteenth year, when he entered the University of Virginia, where he was graduated, and afterwards began the study of law. He was admitted to practice in 1843, and opened an office in Anderson, and at the same time became editor of the "Anderson Gazette." In 1844 he was elected to the legislature by the Democratic party. He earnestly advocated giving to the people the election of presidential electors, who were at that time in South Carolina elected by the legislature. The measure was carried in the house, and defeated in the senate, but was subsequently made a provision of the constitution of the state. After serving two terms in the legislature, he was elected to congress in 1848, by an unprecedented majority, and re-elected each successive term until 1858, when he declined to serve longer. He entered the thirty-first congress to find a galaxy of political and intellectual greatness, such as never before or since was gathered into the national council. In the senate were Calhoun, Webster, Clay, Douglass, Benton, and others of world-wide reputation. While in the house were Winthrop, Toombs, Stevens, McDowell, Bayley, etc., who had been called together to discuss some of the greatest problems of the times. Mr. Orr was soon accorded a prominent position among these able statesmen, although he was then only twenty-six years old. His utterances on the slavery question at once gave him a foremost rank among the Southern representatives. He served as chairman of the committee on Indian affairs, and was active in securing legislation that sought the improvement of the condition of the semi-civilized Indians. When the anti-Catholic Know-Nothings swept the country in 1854, Stephen A. Douglass and James L. Orr were the first prominent men in the United States to make a bold and fearless assault on the party. Mr. Orr was elected speaker of the thirty-third congress, and presided with firmness. He was bitterly opposed to secession, but after fighting against it for sixteen years, and finding it at last triumphant, against his convictions, he followed the tide of his native state —of the two evils choosing what he considered the lesser —believing it better for all to engage in a common, though desperate, cause than that brothers should fight against brothers. The Southern Confederacy had no harder worker for its success than Mr. Orr. He raised and commanded one of the first Southern regiments, and was for several months in command of the harbor of Charleston.

He was elected a member of the Confederate senate in 1861, and early in the following year went to Richmond, where he remained in the discharge of his duties until the close of the war. During that time he devoted his earnest but ineffectual efforts to bring about a treaty of peace with the United States. He was the first governor elected under the constitution when South Carolina was rehabilitated, entering upon his duties in November, 1866. He exercised his rare powers and influence in bringing to some degree of order out of the chaos that followed upon the overthrow of the Confederate and state authority, and was so successful in promoting good feeling between the whites and blacks that during his entire administration no race riot occurred in South Carolina. His conciliatory course frequently enabled him to mitigate the vigor of military rule. Soon after retiring from the office of governor, he was elected, by the legislature, judge of the eighth circuit of South Carolina. In 1872 Pres. Grant appointed Mr. Orr minister to Russia. The climate proved too rigorous for his constitution, and he contracted a cold, from which he died at St. Petersburgh, May 5, 1873. His body was brought home, and buried in Anderson, S. C.

POLK, James Knox, eleventh president of the United States, was born in Mecklenburg, N. C., Nov. 2, 1795, of Scotch-Irish antecedents on both sides. His grandfather, Ezekiel Polk, was captain of a company of rangers during the war of the revolution, and did service in the woods and mountains, where he protected the border from invasions of the Indian allies of Great Britain. He was also an active member of the Mecklenburg convention, of which his brother, Col. Thomas Polk, as chairman, adopted what is termed the "Mecklenburg Declaration of Independence" long before the legislature of Virginia instructed her delegates to the Continental congress to vote for separation from Great Britain. He was subsequently a member of congress and colonel of the 4th Regiment of North Carolina

militia. Samuel Polk, the father of James K., was raised during the exciting times of the struggle for American independence. In 1794 he was married to Jane Knox, daughter of James Knox of Iredell county, N. C., a captain in the revolutionary war. In 1806 they removed with their family to the fertile valley of Duck river, in Tennessee. James, though not physically strong, was a lad of courageous disposition, and very early gave evidence of extraordinary intellectual powers. There were no schools near by, and but few books were available. His parents gave him all the assistance in their power, which was unfortunately little, but even with these limited resources he succeeded by his perseverance and industry in obtaining the foundation of a good education. He craved for further educational advantages, which for the time it seemed out of his father's power to give, and he therefore obtained a place for him in a country store. James K. Polk knew more of mathematics and books than most boys of his age, but had never evinced a taste for trade, and while recognizing the fact that if he became a merchant his fortune was assured, he felt that this was not the field in which he was called to labor. Recognizing the justness of his position, his father reconsidered his determination, and resolved to educate the promising boy at any price. His father died in 1827, having lived to reap the reward of the sacrifices he had made and money expended in the education of his son. Mr. Polk entered the law office of Felix Grundy at Nashville in 1819. That gentleman ranked among the leading lawyers of the day, and possessed an extensive political influence that reached beyond the limits of his state. Gen. Jackson was a frequent visitor at the law office, and completely captivated the heart of the young student, whose inherited prejudices, political training and social tendencies were in accord with those of his chosen leader. In 1820 James K. Polk was admitted to the bar and immediately returned to Maury county, where he opened a law office in the village of Columbia. He at once attained an almost phenomenal success, and part of the while practiced alone and at other times was associated with the first lawyers of the state. In 1822, when Maj. Lewis, quartermaster of the Tennessee militia, was pushing the claims and planning the nomination of Gen. Jackson for the presidency, he had agents and correspondents throughout the state. Among them was James K. Polk, whose political career actually began with this connection. In 1823 he was elected to the state legislature from the Duck River district, returned in 1824, and in 1825 was sent to the congress of the United States from the same district, and re-elected every succeeding term until 1839, when he resigned to become governor of Tennessee. He was married Jan. 1, 1824, to Sarah Childress, daughter of Joel Childress, a wealthy merchant of Rutherford, Tenn., who was in every way fitted to become the wife of this rising statesman, and to shine in the career which was opened to her. Mr. Polk was but thirty years old when he took his seat in congress, and had been elected as an active agent in the great Jacksonian democratic political campaign. Part of the policy adopted by Jackson and his adherents was that neither he nor they should take decided ground upon any exciting question during the campaign. Mr. Polk from the first was a free-trade advocate, a moderate strict constructionist, and opposed to internal improvements, and in these questions at least was ahead of his leader. The annexation of Texas was brought forth in the political canvass of 1824, and proved to be of greater importance than any other event in the political career of James K. Polk. The subject of annexation was made an issue of the campaign again in 1844, and Mr. Polk, who had always strongly favored it, replied to a letter written to him by the citizens of Cincinnati requesting his views on the subject, in these terms: "I have no hesitation in declaring that I am in favor of the immediate re-annexation of Texas to the government and territory of the United States. The proof is fair and satisfactory to my mind that Texas once constituted a part of the United States, the title to which I regard to have been as indisputable as that to any portion of our territory." In 1829, when Andrew Jackson presented his first message to congress, the long war in which he was engaged against the Bank of the United States commenced. From the beginning to the end of this struggle Mr. Polk was entirely in accord with the president. In 1833 he was appointed chairman of the Committee of Ways and Means, the leader of the house, where he acquitted himself ably, and strengthened his hold on the main body of his party, while he still retained good relations with the extreme southern wing. He was opposed to a protective tariff, and the state-rights men were all with him. In 1833, when President Jackson aimed his blow at the United States Bank, and decided that no more government funds should be deposited there, and that the money already on deposit must be withdrawn, a panic was threatened, and there was a majority in the senate ready to condemn the removal of the deposits. Mr. Clay introduced a series of resolutions censuring the president, and was supported by Calhoun, Tyler, and other strict constructionists. The president's conduct was as bitterly assailed in the house as it was in the senate, but Mr. Polk kept an administration majority in working order throughout the session, and, as chairman of the committee of Ways and Means, subsequently reported a series of resolutions fully sustaining the course of the president. He advocated them with rare skill and, Apr. 4, 1834, obtained a vote upon them, and through his efforts secured a complete victory for the president in the house of representatives. This was a great session in congress for James K. Polk. In 1835 he was elected speaker of the house, with a strong Jacksonian majority to sustain his rulings. He held this position until 1839. He took no part in the democratic national convention, called at Baltimore May 10, 1835, which nominated Martin Van Buren for president, and Richard M. Johnson for vice-president, but afterward gave his hearty assent to the action of his chief and party. He was opposed to the doctrines of the anti-slavery reformers, and, while speaker of the house, a memorable event occurred in the history of American politics, when the house adopted what was later known as "the gag rule," which was an effort to stop an aggravating flow of petitions, generally presented by John Quincy Adams, relative to the abolition of slavery. Jan. 18, 1837, a resolution was adopted by a vote of 129 to 69, "that all petitions relating to slavery, without being printed or referred, shall be laid on the table; and no action shall be had thereon." This immediately gave an impetus to the anti-slavery movement, and, before the close of the year, the abolition societies numbered 2,000, and their rejected petitions to congress bore 300,000 names. In 1839 Mr. Polk decided not to become a candidate for another congressional term, having accepted a nomination for governor of Tennessee, and returned home to enter upon a hard and uncertain canvass, and was triumphantly elected by a small majority of 2,500 votes. He made an excellent governor, and was again a candidate for that office in 1841, but before the election his defeat was certain. The change in the political feelings of the country that had elected William Henry Harrison president had also de-feated James K. Polk for governor of Tennessee, and placed James C. Jones, the whig candidate, in the executive chair of that state, but Mr. Polk had the satisfaction of reducing his majority to 3,000, against the 12,000 majority the whigs of Tennessee had given to Harrison. He was once more a private citizen, and resumed his law practice, which he found yielded him a larger income than he had ever derived from his official positions. He purchased a handsome residence in the aristocratic quarter of Nashville, and, with the assistance of Mrs. Polk, made his home a social centre, where he dispensed the most liberal hospitality. There was, however, a decided difference between the invitations extended to this mansion and the unqualified welcome given to all who chose to visit the Hermitage, and it was even asserted, detrimentally, that Mr. Polk had become a very aristocratic man to call himself a democrat. There were, no doubt, grounds for the charge, but it should also have been taken into consideration that the social position of the Jackson and Polk families had never been equal, either in Ireland or America. When the democratic convention assembled in Baltimore, May 27, 1844, James K. Polk had not been thought of as a nominee for president, though his name had been mentioned as a possibility for vice-president. The friends of Mr. Van Buren numbered more than one-third of the delegates present, and were in a position to name the successful candidate, though they found that Van Buren could not secure the necessary two-thirds vote. It was also ascertained that they were obstinately opposed to Cass, Johnson and Buchanan, and others who had been mentioned. The name of Mr. Polk was presented as a conciliatory candidate. It was at once accepted, and he was unanimously nominated. George Dallas was nominated for vice-president. After an exciting canvass Polk was elected over Henry Clay, his distinguished opponent, by a plurality of 40,000 on the popular vote, which did not include South Carolina, whose electors were selected by the state legislature. He received 175 votes in the electoral college, against 105 that were cast for Mr. Clay. As far as the presidential election could be regarded as an expression of popular feeling, the people of the United States were decidedly in favor of the annexation of Texas. Mr. Polk was an open advocate of the extension of the area of slavery, and had publicly expressed his views on the subject of annexation. He also believed that if the matter was not at once brought to issue there was imminent danger of the territory becoming a dependency or a colony of Great Britain. Mr. Calhoun, as secretary of state, signed a treaty of annexation Apr. 12, 1844, which met with numerous obstacles and delays, but March 1, 1845, the treaty was approved, and the following day signed by Mr. Tyler, who thus made things ready for his successor, and immediately despatched a messenger to Texas to announce the action of the U. S. government, and call for corresponding legislation on the part of Texas. March 4, 1845, Mr. Polk was inaugurated president of the United States, and his inaugural address left nothing unsaid that could have been desired by his party. He was particularly happy in the selection of his cabinet. James Buchanan, of Pennsylvania, was made secretary of state; Robert J. Walker, of Mississippi, secretary of the treasury; William L. Marcy, of New York, secretary of war; George Bancroft, of Massachusetts, secretary of the navy; Cave Johnson, of Tennessee, postmaster-general; and John Y. Mason, of Virginia, attorney-general. They were all able men, in perfect sympathy with Mr. Polk and the aggressive policy his administration must necessarily assume. March

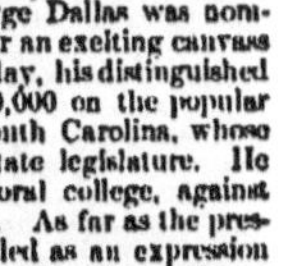

Statue of Freedom on Dome of Capitol

6th, the Mexican minister, Gen. Almonte, entered his formal protest against the annexation, asserting that it would sever from his country an integral part of her territory. On April 2d the American minister to Mexico was formally debarred all diplomatic intercourse, and June 4, 1845, the president of the Mexican republic, Gen. Herrera, issued a proclamation denouncing the act of annexation, and calling his fellow-citizens to rally in defence of their country. President Tyler had anticipated the Mexicans, and, early in 1844, began to collect a body of troops on the Texas border. There were some formalities to be undergone before the United States could legally land troops in Texas, or march them over the border. After rejecting the French-English-Mexican treaty, both houses of the Texan congress unanimously adopted joint resolutions of final consent and agreement to the act of annexation June 18, 1845. A convention of the people was summoned, and the act ratified on July 4th, and an act of congress was passed Dec. 29, 1845, by which Texas was admitted to the Union, and on the 31st another act was passed, extending the U. S. revenue system to the uncertain domain beyond the Nueces. Notwithstanding these decisive measures, the Mexican authorities did not declare war, and expressed a desire to negotiate concerning the disputed territory between the Nueces and the Rio Grande. The negotiations, however, amounted to little. President Polk and his party decided that the Texas which had been admitted to the Union was the identical ground which Napoleon had sold, and which was again lost by the ill-advised treaty of 1819, and the region to which the United States had just laid claim originally belonged to the United States, and, having been recently recovered, an American army could justly be sent to take possession. Gen. Taylor was therefore sent with five regiments of infantry, one of cavalry, and four companies of light artillery, to assert the old French claim, the rights given to Texas by Santa Anna, and the new title of the United States. The twenty-ninth congress of the United States had meanwhile assembled. President Polk's message was unusually long, and handled affairs of the greatest national importance. The failure of Mexico to pay claims provided for by existing treaties, and the outrages to which American citizens were subject, was forcibly put, while the subject of annexation received due consideration. The tariff question was presented in a manner that led to the adoption by congress of measures subsequently known as "the tariff of 1846." Next in importance to the great question of the Mexican war was the discussion between the United States and Great Britain regarding the Oregon boundary, which was settled to the satisfaction of all parties. May 7, 1846, the Mexican troops first opened fire on Gen. Taylor's command, at Palo Alto. There was no hesitation on either side, and a sharp engagement ensued, in which the American loss was nine killed and forty-five wounded, and the Mexicans, though greatly superior in numbers, were forced to retreat. Several other battles were fought, and the Mexican force retreated across the Rio Grande, and left the American army as occupants of what seemed to have been its exact destination, and sustained President Polk's assertion that the correct boundary of the old Mexican state of Texas was the Rio Grande river. He sent a special war message to congress, May 11, 1846, wherein he declared, without reference to the negotiations then pending, that Mexico had "at last invaded our territory, and shed the blood of our citizens on our own soil." War with Mexico was duly declared, and an act passed giving the president 50,000 men and $2,000,000 with which to carry it on. The whigs were all the while opposed to the war, and Abraham

Lincoln, who was at the time a member of the house, introduced what became known as the "spot resolutions," which called upon the president to designate the spot of American territory where the outrage had been committed, but, notwithstanding their opposition, the whigs generally supported the war until it was concluded. On Aug. 10, 1846, President Polk petitioned congress for the necessary authority and funds to purchase the territory from Mexico, in case opportunity should offer to do so by negotiation; his request was granted, and $30,000 were appropriated for his preliminary expenses, and $3,000,000 more allowed to be used at his discretion. The Wilmot proviso was added to this bill, which was to the effect that "neither slavery nor involuntary servitude shall ever exist in any part of said territory, except for crime, whereof the party shall first be duly convicted." The bill was passed, but reached the senate too late to be acted upon. The president vetoed a river and harbor appropriation bill, Aug. 3, 1846, because it savored too strongly of measures for internal improvements by the Federal government, against which he had declared himself in his first message. When the thirtieth congress was organized for business, December, 1847, the house was whig, with a whig speaker, while the senate was democratic. President Polk's message contained a review of the military situation, and suggested that the country should demand of Mexico indemnity for the past and security for the future. The Wilmot proviso again came up and was passed by the house, but the obnoxious amendment was struck out by the senate, and the entire matter returned to the house. There was a sharp contest, but California and New Mexico were already in American hands, and for fear of the risk of losing them the whigs yielded the point, and passed the bill without the proviso, and compromised by attaching the proviso to the act relating to Oregon. The political victory of President Polk's administration over the anti-slavery opposition was complete. He had always opposed the agitation of the slavery question in congress, and urged that temporary civil governments should be provided for California and New Mexico. Before the middle of September, 1847, the American army had captured the city of Mexico, and no organized Mexican army remained in any part of the apparently ruined republic. Another matter of almost equal importance to President Polk and the United States was that, for a while, there was no responsible government left in Mexico with which a binding treaty of peace could be made. The American troops continued in possession of the country, which they had partially conquered but did not care to retain, until an almost entirely new government was organized and prepared to discuss terms of peace. The aspirations of the annexation party were more than realized by the terms agreed upon. Texas, New Mexico, Arizona and California continued the property of the United States upon the payment of about $15,000,000 and a few minor considerations. The treaty of Guadalupe Hidalgo, signed in Mexico Feb. 2, 1848, was sanctioned by the United States March 10th of that year, and the Mexican war was at an end. The history of the administration of affairs under President Polk is hardly paralleled in the annals of the United States. The great political democratic party triumphantly brought about its declared policy under the leadership of its choice. A war for the acquisition of territory was led to a successful issue, while the whig party questioned and condemned all the victories won. Mr. Polk declined to accept a renomination and retired from political life when he resigned the office of president. Mr Polk was only fifty-four years old when he closed his remarkable political career, and no one realized how near was also the close of his life. His vitality had been reduced by the cares of his office, and he had suffered for a number of years with malaria. The cholera, which appeared in 1849, found in him a ready victim. He was a man of the most correct private character, of simple habits, brilliant intellect, and essentially fond of home life, the attractions in his home proving a greater charm than did the gayest society of the capital. He died in Nashville, Tenn., June 15, 1849. See "Eulogy on the Life and Character of the Late James K. Polk," by George M. Dallas; "James Knox Polk," by John S. Jenkins; "James Knox Polk," by William O. Stoddard.

POLK, Sarah Childress, wife of President Polk, was born near Murfreesboro, Rutherford Co., Tenn., Sept. 4, 1803, the daughter of Joel and Elizabeth Childress. Her father was a farmer in good circumstances. She was educated at the Moravian Institute, Salem, N. C., and shortly after leaving school, when but nineteen years of age, was married to James K. Polk, the rising young statesman, who had but begun his promising career. She accompanied her husband to Washington, and during the fourteen years of his service in congress she was a prominent figure in Washington society. Deeply interested in her husband's future, she acquainted herself with public affairs, and though never a politician as the term is applied at the present time she was better informed on the subject of national politics than most of the women who had preceded her as mistress of the White House. She was in the fittest sense of the term the helpmeet and companion of her husband, and was accustomed to look over the various journals of the day, and mark such passages as she deemed sufficiently important for his notice. She blended her life into his, and elevated him to her ideal. As a widow, by her devotion to her husband's memory, and calm, dignified demeanor she added to the influence of his life, and commanded the respect of all for herself. She was comparatively young when her husband died, and had both beauty and social ability, but determined to live out the life that was already full, instead of re-entering society which she was so eminently fitted to adorn. After her husband's death she remained in the house, "Polk Place," at

Nashville, Tenn., where the reverence in which she held her husband's memory was most apparent. She was universally beloved by all classes in Tennessee, and her small fortune in state bonds (all that she possessed), was exempted from repudiation, and in all the mutations of public credit that have occurred in Tennessee there was never any default of interest to the honored lady, who was one of the historic figures of America. President Polk left a large estate, but during the civil war it depreciated in value, and before her death she found herself well-nigh penniless. When a bill was introduced in congress to allow the widow of President Lincoln a pension of $5,000 a year, it lacked one vote in the senate to secure its passage; that was the vote of Senator Howell Jackson of Tennessee, who offered to vote for the bill, provided it was amended so as to give annual pensions of $5,000 to Mrs. Polk and the widow of President Tyler, as well as Mrs. Lincoln. The bill passed and became a law, and from that time to her death, Mrs. Polk lived on the pension. She died Aug. 14, 1891.

DALLAS, George Mifflin, vice-president and U. S. minister to Russia and England, was born in Philadelphia July 10, 1792, the second son of A. S. Dallas. He was graduated first from Princeton with the highest honors in 1810, read law with his father, and directly after his admission to the bar in 1813 went abroad as secretary to Gallatin, who was sent to St. Petersburg as a commissioner, the czar having offered to aid in negotiating a peace with Great Britain. This mediation being declined by England, Dallas went to London to arrange for a meeting elsewhere, and came home in 1814 with the British proposals, which were not admissible. After helping his father for a time at Washington, he began practice, became solicitor of the U. S. Bank, and in 1817 deputy attorney-general for his native city. He appeared as an orator July 4, 1815, in vindication of the recent course of the government toward England. He was mayor of Philadelphia in 1828, U. S. attorney for the eastern district of his state 1829–31, and in the U. S. senate to complete an unex-

pired term 1831–33. Here he was prominent as a defender of the bank which owed its existence to his father, and urged the renewal of its charter; but a little later he supported President Jackson in opposite measures. Declining a re-election he was attorney-general of his state 1833–35. In 1837 he was sent by President Van Buren as minister to Russia; some of his observations here were printed in the "Century Magazine" for May and June, 1891, with the title "At the Court of the Czar." After his return in 1839 he declined the post of U. S. attorney-general. The democratic national convention, which met at Baltimore in May, 1844, placed him on its ticket with J. K. Polk, and he presided in the senate 1845–49. The tariff bill of 1846 was in the direction of free trade; the vote upon it in the senate being a tie, Dallas gave his casting vote for the new measure, thus repealing the protective tariff of 1842, though he was previously understood to be a protectionist and was nominated on that basis. He explained his action by expressing a conviction that the change was desired by a majority of the states, and saying that he "did not feel at liberty to counteract by his single vote the general will." Besides his speech at the time he published a "Vindication" in a series of letters. After seven years of devotion to his practice he was sent in February, 1856, as minister to England, succeeding Mr. Buchanan, who was soon to be president. His first year in this post was harassed by the Central American question and the demand of his government for the recall of Sir J. Crampton, the British Minister at Washington; these points he settled with much ability and tact. He wrote a series of "Letters from London in the Years 1856–60," which were published by his daughter in 1869. The Life of his father followed in 1871. Returning in May, 1861, he denounced the "Pernicious Sorceries of Nullification and Secession." Allibone's "Dictionary of Authors" gives the titles of thirty speeches, letters, etc., which he put forth between 1811 and 1854; they include a "Vindication of President Monroe" in 1819, and a Eulogy on President Jackson in 1845. His last years were spent in retirement in Philadelphia, where he died Dec. 31, 1864.

BUCHANAN, James, secretary of state. (See Vol. V., p. 1.)

WALKER, Robert James, secretary of the treasury, was born at Northumberland, Pa., July 19, 1801, the son of Jonathan H. Walker, a revolutionary soldier and judge of the county, state and U. S. courts. He was graduated from the University of Pennsylvania, was admitted to the bar in 1821, and opened an office at Pittsburg, where he embarked in democratic politics, proposed Jackson in 1823 for the presidency, and married in 1825 a Miss Bache, a grandniece of Franklin and of A. J. Dallas. Settling in 1826 at Natchez, Miss., he published "Reports of Cases" in the state supreme court, and acquired much influence, which he used with tongue and pen, against the nullifiers, winning Madison's praise by his articles in the local paper, and inducing the legislature to denounce the South Carolina doctrines as treasonable. In 1836 he was sent to the U. S. senate, where he introduced the first Homestead bill, and that recognizing Texas as an independent state, opposed the U. S. Bank and a protective tariff, supported Jackson and Van Buren in the main, and urged the abolition of the slave trade. He freed his slaves in 1838 and steadily favored gradual emancipation. This point he kept in view when, during his second term in the senate, he proposed the annexation of Texas in a letter widely published in January, 1844. His services were gratefully remembered in Texas, where his bust was placed in the capitol. He had much influence with Tyler, and promoted the nomination of Polk, under whom he was secretary of the treasury, 1845-49. In this post he established the warehouse system, procured the creation of a department of the interior, effected a reciprocity treaty with Canada, and carried the moderate tariff in 1836. His late years were spent chiefly in Washington, in legal practice and minor public functions. In 1853 he declined the post of commissioner to open trade with China and Japan. In 1857 he went to Kansas as fourth territorial governor, but would not be used in forcing slavery on the new state "by fraud or forgery," resigned in 1858, and exposed the state of affairs before congress. In the troublous early months of 1861 he was a resolute and clear-sighted Unionist, urging prompt and decisive measures. Sent abroad as U. S. financial agent in 1863, he placed $250,000,000 of the 5-20 bonds, and prevented the sale of the second Confederate loan of $75,000,000. He was co-editor for a time of the "Continental Monthly," and wrote for it some papers on American resources, etc., which carried much weight. He urged the building of the Pacific railroad and the purchase of Alaska and the Danish West Indies, and opposed the impeachment of President Johnson and the application to his adopted state of the reconstruction measures. He died in Washington Nov. 11, 1869, leaving a very high reputation as a lawyer, financier, statesman and patriot.

MARCY, William Learned, governor of New York (1833-39), secretary of war (1845) and secretary of state (1853), was born in Southbridge, Mass., Dec. 12, 1786. Certain of his ancestors formed part of a company who, in 1729, being at that time residents of Medfield and adjoining towns in the colony of Massachusetts, obtained a grant of land in Worcester county, which they named New Medfield. In 1738 this section was incorporated as a town under the name of Sturbridge, and among its first settlers was Moses Marcy. He was of English descent, born in Woodstock, Conn., and married in 1723, to a Prudence Morris. In 1732 they removed to New Medfield, afterward Sturbridge, having a family of five children, which subsequently increased to eleven. In the act of incorporation of Sturbridge, Moses Marcy is styled "one of the principal inhabitants." He built the first grist-mill in the town, held a number of important local offices, was a colonel of militia, was appointed the first justice of the peace, and was the first representative sent by the town to the general court. He was a selectman thirty-one years, town clerk eighteen, and town treasurer eight years, not infrequently filling all these offices at once. During the old French war he fitted out soldiers for the army on his own responsibility and from his own private resources. He died Oct. 9, 1779, leaving an honorable name, a large estate and a numerous posterity. One of his grandsons, Jedediah Marcy, was the father of William Learned Marcy, and the husband of Ruth Learned. He was a farmer by occupation, held a command in the state militia and was a respectable citizen, highly esteemed in his neighborhood. He was in comfortable circumstances, and after his son William had gained all the advantages of instruction to be obtained in the common schools of his native town, he was sent to the Leicester Academy. Having completed his academic course, the young man entered Brown University, where he proved a careful and diligent scholar, correct in all his studies, while particularly excelling in the classics. While in college he enjoyed much miscellaneous reading and was able to cultivate his naturally refined literary taste. He was graduated in 1808, and removed to the city of Troy, N. Y., where he began the study of law. Being duly admitted to the bar, he commenced practice, but had hardly entered upon the active duties of his profession when war was declared against Great Britain and he offered his services to the governor of the state. He was lieutenant of an infantry company of Troy, which was first dispatched to the northern frontier, and there he had an immediate opportunity of seeing active service, as he was one of the detachment which captured the post of St. Regis and took the whole force of the enemy prisoners. After this engagement, Lieut. Marcy, with his company, joined the main army under Gen. Dearborn, and for a time was on the frontier, but in 1814 was ordered to the city of New York, where he remained until the close of the war, having attained the rank of captain and a highly creditable reputation. In 1816 Mr. Marcy was appointed recorder of the city of Troy, an office which he continued to hold until June, 1818, when he was removed on account of his frequently expressed dissatisfaction with the administration of Gov. Clinton. By this time Mr. Marcy had become thoroughly interested in politics and known as a member of the "Bucktails," as they were called, and in 1820 supported Gov. Tompkins in opposition to Mr. Clinton. He was for a time editor of the Troy "Budget," a daily newspaper which supported Martin Van Buren, and as the "Bucktails" or republicans, had a majority in the assembly, he was appointed in January, 1821, adjutant-general. Two years later he was made comptroller of the state and removed to Albany, in which city he continued to make his residence thereafter. Mr. Marcy was by this time a recognized member of the "Albany regency," which exercised for so long almost supreme political power in the state. The office of comptroller was particularly important at the time when Marcy filled it, owing to the heavy expenditures connected with the construction of the Erie and Champlain canals. In 1828 he powerfully contributed to the political revolution which resulted in the elevation of Gen. Jackson to the presidential chair and gave Martin Van Buren the governorship of the state of New York. On Jan. 15, 1829, Mr. Marcy was appointed one of the associate justices of the supreme court of the state, a position in which he conducted himself with credit to the court and to himself. He presided at the special circuit held at Lockport, in 1830, for the trial of the abductors of William Morgan, who exposed the secrets of the Masonic fraternity, and Marcy's course during these important and exciting trials, his urbanity, his firmness and his impartial decisions, were highly commended by men of all parties. Mr. Marcy was elected as a democrat to the United States senate, taking his seat in December, 1831. His reputation for ability had already been recognized in Washington, and he was complimented by being appointed to the important position of chairman of the committee on the judiciary, and to membership in the committee on finance. Early in his experience of the senate, Mr. Marcy found himself called from his seat to sustain the reputation of his friend, Martin Van Buren, against the aspersions of Henry Clay. In March, 1832, he spoke on the apportionment bill, in reply to Daniel Webster. In regard to the tariff, he was opposed to the surrender of the doctrine of protection, but in favor of removing the duties on non-protected articles, and he voted for the law of 1832, although he did not approve of all its provisions. In 1833 Senator Marcy resigned his seat to take the position of governor of the state of New York, to which he had been elected, and he continued to hold that office during three terms, or until 1839, when he was again nominated, but was defeated by William H. Seward. As governor of New York, Mr. Marcy showed himself neither a timid man nor afraid of incurring responsibility, but, being a shrewd observer and possessing an almost intuitive knowledge of men, he allowed the legislature of the state a wide latitude on all questions affecting the interests of their constituents, so long as the provisions of the constitution were not disregarded. In his annual message in 1834, Gov. Marcy advised extreme caution in the granting of bank charters, there being a sudden rush and demand for these on account of the United States bank veto of President Jackson. In the winter of 1834 a coalition of the national republicans and anti-Masons of the state of New York resulted in the adoption of the name of "Whigs," which was soon after taken by the entire opposition to the democratic party. At the election in 1834 Gov. Marcy received a majority of nearly 13,000 over the vote of Mr. Seward. In his annual message in 1835 he recommended a law which was afterward passed, providing for the suppression of bank notes under five dollars; and at the same time, by his advice, the legislature refused to grant any more bank charters. It was at this period that the rise of the abolition or anti-slavery party took place, a movement to which Gov. Marcy was always opposed, on the ground that it was calculated to foster sectional prejudices and ill feelings. Throughout his administration Gov. Marcy used all his influence in opposition to the speculative mania which was at that time in existence, and which resulted in the panic of 1837. On being defeated in the contest for the governorship in 1838, Gov. Marcy was appointed by President Van Buren one of the commissioners to decide upon the claims against the Mexican government under the convention of April, 1839, an office which he continued to hold until the powers of the commission expired, February, 1842,

when he practically retired for the time from public life. Gov. Marcy presided over the democratic convention at Syracuse, in September, 1843, and used his influence in the state in favor of James K. Polk's candidacy for the presidency. On the election of Mr. Polk, the friends of Gov. Marcy began to work in his behalf, and he was offered the place of secretary of war, which he accepted. As he held this position during the war with Mexico, its duties were unusually arduous, and it is claimed for him that to his ability as the head of the war department the country was greatly indebted for the brilliant results of the contest with Mexico. Indeed, he showed a peculiar fitness for the position he filled, both through the comprehensiveness of his mind and because of the force and energy of his character. During the administration of President Polk, Gov. Marcy held a very confidential relation with regard to the president, and was his most influential adviser. In 1848 he supported Gen. Cass for the presidency, and upon the expiration of Mr. Polk's term, he returned to Albany and resumed his position as a private citizen. In 1853 President Franklin Pierce appointed Gov. Marcy secretary of state, and he continued to hold the office through that administration. In this position he gained the reputation of being an acute and able diplomatist and a statesman fully competent to cope with those of the great powers of Europe. Important questions came before him, such as the Danish sound dues, the enlistment question, Central American affairs, and the exciting conditions which surrounded the release of Martin Koszta by Capt. Ingraham, commanding the sloop-of-war St. Louis, at Smyrna, in July, 1853. An elaborate discussion resulted in Washington between Secretary Marcy and M. Hülsemann, the *chargé d'affaires* at Washington, the conduct of Capt. Ingraham being fully approved by the United States government. At the end of President Pierce's administration in 1857, Mr. Marcy went to Ballston Spa, N. Y., where he was found dead on the evening of July 4, 1857, sitting in his library with an open volume before him.

BANCROFT, George, secretary of the navy. (See Vol. III., p. 160.)

MASON, John Young, attorney-general. (See page 7, this volume.)

JOHNSON, Cave, postmaster-general, was born in Robertson county, Tenn., Jan. 11, 1793. After having passed through the schools, he studied law, was admitted to the bar, and began to practice in Clarksville, Tenn. In 1820 he was made circuit judge, and continued in that position and in the practice of law until 1829, when he was sent to congress, where he remained until 1837. In 1839 he was re-elected to congress, and remained in the house of representatives until 1845, when President Polk appointed him postmaster-general, under date of March 5th. Mr. Johnson went out of politics with the close of the administration, and continued to devote himself to his private affairs during the remainder of his life. From 1850 to 1859 he was president of the Bank of Tennessee. He was a Union man in sentiment during the civil war, and was elected to the state senate of Tennessee on that basis in 1863, but was obliged to decline to serve on account of his advanced age and infirmity. He died in Clarksville, Tenn., Nov. 23, 1866.

CLIFFORD, Nathan, attorney-general. (See Vol. II., p. 473.)

TOUCEY, Isaac, attorney general (See Index.)

OLIPHANT, Laurence, author and barrister, was born at Ceylon in 1829, of an old Scotch family, the Oliphants of Condie. His father, Sir Anthony Oliphant, was appointed chief justice of Ceylon while Laurence was yet a child, and he was brought up in that Oriental possession of England. It was his father's intention to educate him in the mother-country, but when the time arrived for him to enter the universities, he persuaded Sir Anthony that a course of foreign travel would be much more to his advantage. He therefore missed the discipline and intellectual training that would probably have moulded him into a different man, and acquired a taste for travel and adventure that soon became the ruling passion of his life. His father's exalted office in Ceylon made his house the rendezvous of the most distinguished people who visited the colony, embracing all the bureaucracy of Hindostan, as well as the pleasure-seekers passing through India. Accustomed to society of this character from his infancy, he soon learned to play the host to brilliant companies in his father's absence. His manners were charming and he readily made friends. He soon developed special social qualities, and acquired the *savoir faire*, tact and address, necessary to a man of the world. His mind, though irregularly cultivated, was kind, penetrating, and of fine quality. The career of a barrister had been marked out for him. He studied, was admitted to the colonial bar, and frequently practised in the Cingalese courts before going to England to pass examination for the Scotch bar, where it was also necessary for him to qualify. His mother was a devout Christian woman, whose chief anxiety was for her son's soul, but he was an original and independent thinker, unwilling to take creeds on trust, and for the time being, put all thoughts of religion in the background. About this time he took a trip through Russia, which resulted in his acquiring fresh knowledge about the Russian shore and the Black Sea, and enabled him to write a particularly seasonable book upon his return, the Crimean war being then in sight. When the war was declared, his adventurous spirit of course led him to wish to join the army, but just at this time Lord Elgin offered him a position as private secretary with his mission to Washington, on the Oregon boundary question. He accepted this opening to a diplomatic career, and made himself extremely popular both in Washington and Quebec. Notwithstanding, his letters home gave strange accounts of the dissipation at this period in Washington, much of which is recorded in his "Episodes in a Life of Adventure." He was made Indian superintendent, which offered him further opportunities to pursue his desire for adventure. In 1855 he returned to England in sufficient time to go to the Crimea. At the end of this war his adventurous spirit again took him to America, where he joined Walker's filibustering expedition, but the timely intervention of an English man-of-war was the means of detaching him from that ill-starred undertaking. He next attached himself to Lord Elgin's mission to China, after which he went to Japan and was appointed chief secretary of the embassy under Sir Rutherford Alcock. For some time after this, he was employed ostensibly as traveling correspondent for the "Times," but was virtually engaged in secret political missions in different parts of Europe. This diplomatic service was soon abandoned, and he wandered among the revolutionary Poles, taking observations of the Schleswig-Holstein puzzle on the spot. He was supposed to understand that question better than any man in Europe. Upon his return to England he went much in society, and was welcomed with general cordiality. He was keenly observant all the while, and took notes for that virile satire, "Piccadilly," wherein he drew the portraits of the wholly worldly and the worldly holy. About this time he came under the influence of that extraordinary man, Thomas Lake Harris (*q. v.*), the founder of Brocton and Santa Rosa settlements, who held that there was but one course for true Christians, and that was to "live the life," at any cost or sacrifice. Oliphant at once joined the colony, abandoned his brilliant life and prospects, and for five years lived the life of a common laboring man, under a discipline well nigh as severe as that of La Trappe. At the end of this time he returned to society, embraced it with the same avidity as before, and was eagerly welcomed by the Prince of Wales, the queen, and the social world. The remainder of his life was spent vacillating between society and religious ecstasy. In 1870 he was sent on the continent by the "Times" as special correspondent during the Franco-Prussian war. He married, in Paris, Alice Le Strange, a beautiful girl of noble character, who became a sharer of his religious belief, and also placed herself under the spell of Harris, patiently enduring the many hardships and indignities he thrust upon her, sinking her fortune in the Brocton colony, only a pittance of which was saved from the wreck. Together they wrote the peculiar and almost incomprehensible book, "Sympneumata." He and his wife were both believed to have inclinations toward spiritualism, but he always denied the allegation. He died in London, Eng., Dec. 23, 1888.

AVERY, Rosa (Miller), author, was born in Madison, O., May 21, 1830, of Scotch and English ancestry. Her grandfather, Capt. Isaac Miller, was a soldier of the revolution and wounded at Bunker Hill; another kinsman, Gen. James Miller, was for a time aide-de-camp to Gen. Washington. Her father, Nahum Miller, was a pioneer anti-slavery agitator. The "Miller farm" was as noted for its hospitality to every one, white or black, who was in need of assistance or sympathy, as it was for its fine cattle and blooded stock, which claimed so much devotion and attention from Rosa as to cause her to be dubbed "Tomboy" by the minister and his wife, who told her she "should think more of beings who had souls to save, as there were no animals in heaven." "No animals in heaven!" repeated Rosa; "then the dear Lord knows if I go there, I will be dreadfully homesick for earth." While attending the Madison seminary, Rosa wrote stirring anti-slavery essays, which were met with derision and abuse. She never charged the sin of slavery to the door of the Southern people, but maintained that the spirit of slavery was everywhere present in any and every form of injustice. It was confined and sectional in the case of the poor blacks, because "Cotton was king," and so controlled New England manufactures, and the manhood of the entire nation paid tribute. Miss Miller was married Sept. 1, 1853, to Cyrus Avery of Oberlin, O. During their residence in Ashtabula, O., after marriage, Mrs. Avery organized the first anti-slavery society ever known in that village. Not a clergyman in the place would give notice of its meetings so late as two years before the war, and that, too, in the county home of Giddings and Wade, the well-known apostles of freedom. The leading men of wealth and influence were so indignant because the churches would not read a notice of her missionary effort for the "black heathen," that they counseled together and withdrew from their respective churches and built a handsome brick church edifice for the anti-slavery Congregational element. During the years of the civil war Mrs. Avery's pen was actively engaged in writing for various journals on the subject of Union and emancipation. She wrote under a male signature so as to command the greater attention. Her letters and other articles attracted the attention of Gov. Richard Yates of Illinois, James A. Garfield, James Redpath and Lydia Maria Child, all of whom sent her appreciative letters, with their portraits, which are still preserved as souvenirs of those stormy days. During ten years' residence in Erie, Pa., besides writing occasional articles for the newspaper world, she disseminated her views on social questions, love, matrimony, religion, in romance, to the high-school graduates, of which her son was a member, in their organ, the "High-School News," over the pen-name of Sue Smith, work which produced much and rich fruition in the years following. Mr. and Mrs. Avery removed to Chicago in 1877. While living in the city Mrs. Avery's special efforts were for social purity and equal suffrage. The many and ably written articles and responses to the opponents of suffrage for women which have appeared from time to time in the daily press under her signature have sown much seed broadcast in favor of equal suffrage, and have borne good fruit in favor of municipal school suffrage. At the time of the dedication of the Bartholdi statue, Mrs. Avery when called upon to respond to the sentiment of "Liberty," at a banquet of representative men and women, spoke as follows: "The idea of liberty for woman has become so prevailing, so penetrating, that even the stones cry out and take upon themselves the form of womanhood and proclaim 'Liberty Enlightening the World.'" Mrs. Avery is very domestic in her tastes, and few can equal her as a caterer or excel in domestic economy. Her "Rose Cottage," facing Lake Michigan, in Edgewater, a suburb of Chicago, is an ideal home.

EVRETT, Isaac, author and editor, was born in New York city, Jan. 2, 1820. He worked from his tenth year on the farm, in the mill or the lumberyard, as a bookseller and as a painter, but under the strong influence of Alexander Campbell he succeeded in also gaining an education, and in 1840 became pastor of the Church of the Disciples at Pittsburg, Pa. From 1840 until 1871 he there held various pastoral charges in the Church of the Disciples, being at the same time corresponding secretary of the Ohio Christian missionary society 1853–56, and its president 1868–71; corresponding secretary of the American Christian society, 1857–60, and its president 1874–76; and president of the Foreign Christian missionary society from 1875 until his death. In 1866 he started "The Christian Standard," Cincinnati, O., which in a few years he succeeded in establishing as the principal organ of his denomination. Among his other works are: "Spiritualism Compared with Christianity" (Warren, O., 1859); "Brief View of Christian Missions, Ancient and Modern" (Cincinnati, 1857); "First Principles, or the Elements of the Gospel" (1867); "Walks About Jerusalem, a Search after the Landmarks of Primitive Christianity" (1872); "Letters to a Young Christian" (1881); "Evenings with the Bible" (3 Vols., 1885–87); "Our Position: A Brief Statement of the Plea urged by the People Known as Disciples of Christ" (1885). He received the degree of M.A. from Bethany college, W. Va., 1867, and that of LL.D. from Butler University in 1886. He died at Cincinnati, Dec. 18, 1888.

MUNFORD, Morrison, journalist, was born at Covington, Tipton county, Tenn., June 25, 1842, son of Richard H. Munford, who in early youth settled in Tipton county, where he held the highest county offices, and was for some time a member of the state legislature. His wife was a daughter of Dr. Morrison, a prominent physician of Tennessee. He came of distinguished Virginia and Kentucky families, and was descended from Simon de Montfort, son of Crusader Simon de Montfort, and who was chief of the English barons in the time of Henry III. His paternal grandfather founded the town of Munfordville on Green river, Ky., where Morrison's father was born. He was educated in James Byer's Academy in his native town in an English and classical course and was admitted to the La Grange (Tenn.) Synodical College as a member of the

junior class in 1860. The civil war coming on, the college was closed, and the young man entered the Confederate army. He was wounded and taken prisoner at the battle of Stone river, Tenn. On being exchanged he was incapable of field service, and was detailed as medical purveyor at Atlanta, Ga., where he remained until the close of the war. In 1866 he attended lectures at the Missouri medical college under Dr. J. N. McDowell, who successfully removed the minié-ball from its lodgment against his spinal column. He had, before going to St. Louis, studied medicine for one year under Dr. L. P. Yandell of Louisville, Ky., carrying on a small farm and teaching school to enable him to attend medical lectures at St. Louis. In the spring of 1867 he assisted in establishing and editing the "Tipton Weekly Record." In the autumn he returned to St. Louis and entered his medical studies, and was graduated in 1868 with the degree of M.D. He did not take up the practice of medicine, as an offer from his uncle, an extensive land-owner in Kansas, to take charge of his property, free it from taxes, and establish the titles for a one-third interest was accepted by him, and after a long litigation, in which he was opposed by Senator Ingalls, although not a lawyer he prepared the brief for his side of the case, defended the claim and gained titles. Senator Ingalls afterwards published, in the "Kansas Magazine," a romantic sketch, founded upon this litigation, entitled "Regis Loisel." In August, 1871, Mr. Munford became secretary and general manager of the "Kansas City Times" company. He found the paper, then three years old, struggling for existence, and soon made it the leading journal of the West. With his paper he advanced the interests of Kansas City, and took the struggling city into account in every movement and advancement looking to the prosperity of his journal. They advanced hand in hand—the "Times" the mirror of the place—and through it Eugene Field, speaking of this community of interests, says: "Under every variety of embarrassment, financial, political, social and moral, Dr. Munford brought his newspaper up to prosperity and influence; presumably the world will never know of the actual tribulations which that accomplishment involved, the delays, the disappointments, the humiliations, the toils, the excitement, the wrong, amid it all one man, the genius of the enterprise, was confident and brave, and it was masterful, if erratic, valor that wrought out the victory. Dr. Munford was never a profuse writer, but a strong one, clear and concise in diction, elevating and beautiful in sentiment and never sacrificing truth for any purpose or person. He was a delegate to the national democratic convention of 1879-80 from his congressional district, and from the state at large in 1884, when Mr. Cleveland was nominated for the first time. Dr. Munford at this convention introduced a resolution looking to the early opening of the Oklahoma country to settlement. In 1870 he was married to Agnes E. Williams, a New England girl, early left an orphan and educated in the West at Monticello seminary. Their residence was one of the finest in the city, and as the habits of Dr. Munford were extremely domestic, it became largely his workshop, and his wife his associate, confidante and helper. They travelled extensively in Europe and over their own country, and their home became the repository of many rare and valuable works of art collected by them. Dr. Munford was a Presbyterian in religious creed, having united with that church when quite young. His mother and his wife were to him the two most sacred of all earthly objects, and his life was largely shaped by their lives. Dr. Munford died in Kansas City March 27, 1892.

BIGELOW, Lettie Salina, poet and author, was born in Pelham, Mass., July 30, 1849, a descendant in the eighth generation of John Biglo of Watertown, Mass. Her father, Rev. I. B. Bigelow, was an itinerant minister, and for half a century an honored member of the New England conference of the Methodist Episcopal church. He left active work in 1885, and made for himself and family a permanent home in Holyoke, Mass. Miss Bigelow's early education was in the cities and towns where her parents lived, and completed later at Wesleyan academy, Wilbraham, Mass., where she was a student for two years. Her prose sketches show remarkable power, her vocabulary is extensive, and her lecture on "Woman's Place and Power" has been widely quoted. She has written for the New York "Independent," Boston "Journal," "Wide-Awake," New York "Christian Advocate," "Zion's Herald," and many other papers. She published a serial story, but many of her early sketches were under a pseudonym. In 1872 she wrote a book of Sunday-school and anniversary exercises, which was published in New York, and had a large sale. In 1890 she became the editor of "True Light," a paper published in the interests of the Woman's Christian temperance union, of which her "Aunt Dorothy" letters formed a unique feature. But the routine of editorial work proved irksome, and failing health compelled her to resign the position. It is as a poet that Miss Bigelow prefers to be known. She early evinced a talent for versification, and in poetry her intense nature and eager soul finds the best outlet of expression. She has been for years closely identified with the cause of temperance, and whatever relates to the development of woman, or the enlargement of her opportunities, finds in her an earnest advocate. She is a woman of deep feeling, vivid imagination, and in conversation with congenial friends is delicately vivacious, sparkling, and entertaining.

DAVIS, Robert Stewart, journalist, was born at Philadelphia, Pa., in 1841. He was educated at Phillips academy, Andover, Mass., and at Yale college, where he was graduated in 1860. He immediately began the study of law under Judge Pierce of Philadelphia, relinquishing it in 1870 for one of the editorships of the Philadelphia "Inquirer," and subsequently serving in the same capacity upon the Philadelphia "Press." In 1863 he was war correspondent in South Carolina for the Philadelphia "Inquirer," and in 1864 was Washington correspondent for the "Inquirer," and, later, for the New York "Times." In 1865, with a capital of $5,000 he established the Philadelphia "Saturday Night," a weekly paper, which in five years, reached a circulation of over 200,000 copies. The most successful serial stories of this paper, which were the chief cause of its rapid increase in circulation, were written by him. These stories were some twelve in number, and were written between 1868 and 1879, during which latter year he sold out his interest in the "Saturday Night," and soon after joined in the formation of "Our Continent" company. Not satisfied with this venture, he withdrew from it, and Sept. 17, 1883, began the publication of the "Call." Because of its original features, namely, women's, children's and fashions' departments, the "Call" was immediately recognized as a first-class family newspaper, and met with great success. At first the price of the "Call" was two cents a copy, but as soon as white paper declined to such a cost as to enable Mr. Davis to reduce the price of the paper to one cent, he promptly did so, in 1888. This reduction added materially to an already extensive circulation. It was not necessary because of this reduction in price to curtail any of the literary and news features of the paper; and such was the increase in advertising that further editorial and news expenses were incurred to make the "Call" one of the best and most popular one-cent afternoon papers in America, a position which it has held for many years. Besides being the sole proprietor of the "Call" and giving his personal attention to its various departments, Mr. Davis has also won credit as a railroad man. In 1888 he became officially connected with the Philadelphia and Reading railroad, and President McLeod, recognizing his ability, soon made him manager of the Atlantic City railroad company, putting him in sole charge of the Reading's many interests in New Jersey. In this position Mr. Davis served with distinction for five years, dividing his time between the "Call" and the railroad. In 1893 he gave up the railroad, however, and devoted his subsequent time entirely to his newspaper property. During his residence in Philadelphia, Mr. Davis has joined in all the active measures for the advancement of that city. He is an active member of its leading clubs and literary associations. His wife, his home, his business, and microscopy are his most absorbing interests.

RUSH, James, author, was born in Philadelphia, Pa., March 1, 1786; son of Dr. Benjamin Rush. He was graduated from Princeton in 1805, took his degree of M.D. at the University of Pennsylvania in 1809, studied at Edinburgh for a time, and practiced for some years in Philadelphia. He married Phoebe Ann Ridgeway (1797-1857), a great heiress, who had one of the largest houses in the city and became its most notable leader of society. Dr. Rush in later years lived mainly in his study. His "Philosophy of the Human Voice" (1827) occupied a field then new, and gained much repute. He published also "Hamlet, a Dramatic Prelude" (1834), an "Analysis of the Human Intellect" (in two volumes, 1865), and "Rhymes of Contrast on Wisdom and Folly" (1869). He died in Philadelphia, May 26, 1869, leaving most of his estate to the city library on certain conditions, among which were the reissue of his books, to be sold at cost, five times within the next fifty years, the exclusion of all newspapers, and the occupation of a fine building on South Broad street, in the erection of which most of the money, about a million dollars, was expended. The location is such that the Ridgeway branch of the Philadelphia library has few visitors; but the library company places those of its books which are in demand in another building at Locust and Juniper streets, where they are in constant and extended use.

COCHRAN, Thomas Baumgardner, editor, was born in York, Pa., Aug. 21, 1845, removing with his parents to Lancaster in 1858. He is the eldest son of John J. Cochran. His grandfather, R. E. Cochran, was a member of the state constitutional convention of 1838, and died in Columbia, Pa., in 1854, being the first victim of the cholera epidemic, which visited that borough in the year named. His mother was Catharine Baumgardner, a daughter of Thomas Baumgardner, who came from Germany, and settled in York, Pa. Thomas Baumgardner Cochran, therefore, is of Scotch-Irish blood in the paternal, and Teutonic in the maternal line. Mr. Cochran was graduated from the Lancaster high school in 1861, and started in life as a printer's apprentice on the Lancaster "Union," published by his father. The paper was the organ of Thaddeus Stevens. After serving a full apprenticeship at home, he worked for some time in Philadelphia. During the legislative session of 1864 he was employed by George Bergner, of Harrisburg, as reporter for the "Legislative Record." In this capacity he served until 1872, when a vacancy occurred in the office of journal clerk of the senate, to which position he was unanimously elected. During the period between his first and last appointment just mentioned he corresponded for the Lancaster papers, and was thus almost continuously in practical journalistic work. During the presidential campaign of 1868 he formed a co-partnership with Capt. E. H. Rauch in the publication of "Father Abraham," a weekly republican paper, which obtained a large circulation. In 1870 he withdrew from this enterprise, read law, and was admitted to the Lancaster bar in 1873. While the legislature was in session, he served as journal clerk of the senate from 1872-76 inclusive. In 1877 he was elected to the chief clerkship of the senate, which position he held until 1889. During all these years he was actively engaged in politics, was a member of the republican state and county committees for several years, and, of the latter, chairman from 1886-88 inclusive. He was also a member of the Lancaster city council for one year, and of the Lancaster school board for twelve years ending November, 1889, when he declined a re-election. In March,

1889, he and his brother, Harry B. Cochran, purchased from John A. Hiestand the "Examiner" newspaper, the building in which it is published, and all the plant, which they afterward increased by the addition of new presses and other machinery, building up a business and paper second to no inland daily or weekly in the country. The "Examiner," one of the oldest journals of the state, had passed through many different ownerships, and absorbed a number of other newspapers, including "The Old Guard," published by Mr. Cochran's uncle, Theodore D. Cochran, in 1841; the Lancaster "Union," the property of Mr. Cochran's father, in 1863; and the Lancaster "Evening Express," in 1876. One of the owners of the latter was John H. Pearsol, Mr. Cochran's father-in-law. While a republican newspaper, the "Examiner" is conducted on liberal and independent lines, and has become one of the most influential journals in Pennsylvania. It is published daily and semi-weekly.

SWAIN, James Barrett, editor, was born in New York July 30, 1820. Being compelled to strike out for himself early in life, he did not have much opportunity for schooling, although he was a student from his earliest years. He engaged in the printing business when quite young, but when eighteen years of age he was made private secretary to Henry Clay, and assisted him in his correspondence during the campaign of 1839, which broadened his ideas, and the next year he formed a partnership with Horace Greeley (with whom he had had former associations in the printing business) to publish the "Log Cabin." This work gave him an opportunity to make himself known, and in 1843 he was asked to take editorial charge of the "Hudson River Chronicle," in Sing Sing. He was an indefatigable worker, and while thus engaged, he also obtained a position as a clerk in the state prison. In 1850 he was invited to become the city editor of the New York "Tribune," but the next year left it to become the editor of the "Times," and later, of the "American Agriculturist," but he continued to contribute political articles to the "Times," and in 1860-61 went to Washington to become its correspondent. He also edited a campaign paper, published in New York in 1856 by the National republican committee, and in 1877 he returned to his early paper, the "Hudson River Chronicle." In 1855 he was appointed railroad commissioner for New York state. During the war he served as first lieutenant in the 1st U. S. cavalry, and was promoted to the colonelcy of the 1st U. S. volunteer cavalry. Immediately after the war he was appointed engineer-in-chief of the national guard of New York; was given a position of weigher in the New York custom-house, and was made post-office inspector in 1881. Mr. Swain published in 1842 the "Life and Speeches of Henry Clay," prepared from notes gathered when he was private secretary, and in 1843, "Historical Notes to a Collection of the Speeches of Henry Clay." He is also the author of a military history of the state of New York.

HAGEN, Theodore, author, was born in Hamburg, Germany, Apr. 15, 1823. He studied the pianoforte and theory in his native place, and in 1841-42 completed his musical course in Paris. Thereafter he became a contributor to musical journals in France and Germany. Returning to his home, Hagen published a volume, entitled ' Civilization and Music," that abounds in thoughtful criticism. It was subsequently translated into the English language. Hagen came to the United States in 1854, and settled in New York city, where he published in succession several musical journals, of which he was chief editor and proprietor. In 1862 he established "The Weekly Review," devoted to music and literature, in which he permitted some of his associates to insert the most reckless criticism and personal abuse. Although an otherwise agreeable and able publication, it necessarily came to an early end. He published "Musical Novels" in 1848. Hagen died in New York city, Dec. 27, 1871.

FIELD, Kate, journalist, was born in St. Louis, Mo., in 1854. Her family was a distinguished one in England, dating back to the time of Elizabeth, when one of her ancestors, Nathaniel Field, was a fine actor and personal friend of Shakespeare. From England the family went to Ireland and in the rebellion of 1708 her grandfather, Mathew Field, who was a leading Roman Catholic of Dublin, lost all his property. He then emigrated to America and settled in Baltimore, becoming a publisher, and bringing out the first American Catholic almanac. He died early and the family moved to New York, where Kate Field's father, Joseph M. Field, obtained his early education. He afterward went upon the stage and became a great favorite in the West and in New Orleans, where he was one of the founders of the "Picayune."

He also wrote plays, some of which were produced with success. He founded and edited the "St. Louis Reveille," built Field's variety theatre in St. Louis, and married Eliza Lapsley Riddle, a charming actress. Mr. Field died suddenly and Mrs. Field died at sea while en route to England with her daughter. Kate Field early evinced artistic proclivities. She chose her own time for going to school, arranged to go there regularly, and then informed her parents that she had done so. She began to write at an early age, and her first article was printed when she was only eight years old. She was passionately fond of music and the stage, and aspired to become an opera singer. When very young she was taken to Italy, where she was left in charge of an English lady. Walter Savage Landor gave her lessons in Latin. Miss Field subsequently gained much reputation by her reminiscences of Landor in the "Atlantic Monthly." She was fond of riding but received a fall from her horse which seriously impaired her health. In 1874 she appeared on the stage in New York city, but, much to her regret, ill health compelled her to give up the profession of an actress. She was an excellent critic, however, and began to write articles on the drama for the New York "Tribune." When Dickens came to America, Kate Field heard him nightly and published a book, entitled "Pen Photographs of Dickens's Readings," which passed through several editions. About this time, she and her friends purchased John Brown's farm in the Adirondacks in order to rescue from ignominy John Brown's body, which was buried there. She returned to New York and lectured on the subject, following up her first venture on the platform with a eulogy of Dickens. She then sailed for England and remained several months abroad lecturing. She also went to Spain for the purpose of making Castelar's acquaintance, and wrote a series of letters for the "Tribune," called "Ten Days in Spain," which afterwards appeared in book form. Finding that her voice was returning, she studied singing in London with Garcia and William Shakespeare, the English tenor. While in London she produced a play called "Extremes Meet," which had considerable success. She also wrote many articles for leading journals and magazines, contributing to the London Times an article on the "Telephone" which led to her being placed in charge of the entire literary management of that invention. At Osborne house she sang to Queen Victoria through the telephone and had a telephone harp played in Shakespeare's house in Stratford which was heard in the London theatre. Returning home she wrote "Eyes and Ears in London," which met with a genuine success. Going west in 1883, she accidentally stopped at Salt Lake City, becoming so interested in Mormonism as to remain a year, when she returned east, and by her lectures on that subject brought about legislation that has led to changed conditions and the admission of Utah as a state. Several years later she visited Alaska and California, and by pen and speech has been of great service to the Pacific slope. In 1890 she established a literary and critical journal at Washington, with a branch office in New York, which she entitled "Kate Field's Washington," in which she continues her brilliant criticism of literature, the stage and politics. Through her efforts the tariff on art was reduced from thirty to fifteen per cent. in the McKinley bill, and has been put on the free list in the Wilson bill. She has been decorated by the French government with the palm of the academy, the highest honor given to a woman.

BALDWIN, John Davison, journalist and author, was born at N. Stonington, Conn., Sept. 28, 1809. He was educated by his own exertions and attended Yale college, graduating with the degree of A.M., after which he studied theology and was licensed to preach at the age of twenty-four. Having written for the magazines on archæology and kindred subjects, he later drifted into journalism, and in 1842 became editor of the "Charter Oak," a Hartford newspaper. He subsequently held the same position on the "Daily Commonwealth" in Boston, and also wrote for the "Advertiser," and in 1859 became the proprietor of the "Worcester Spy," which he conducted for more than twenty years. Between 1863 and 1869 he represented the Worcester district in congress by three successive elections. He was the author of a volume of poems, and of two volumes of antiquarian study, entitled "Prehistoric Nations" and "Ancient America." He died July 8, 1883.

LEGGETT, William, author and journalist, was born in New York city in 1802; son of a major in the war of independence. He was graduated from Georgetown college, D. C., in 1822, spent four years in the navy, and in 1825 published a book of verse, "Leisure Hours at Sea." In 1828 he started the "Critic," a weekly, which six months later was merged in the "Mirror." From 1829 to 1836 he was associated with William Cullen Bryant on the "Evening Post;" confining himself at first to literary topics, he soon won distinction as a political writer. Fearless, independent and combative, he defended freedom of speech for all; while other newspapers were calling down public wrath upon the abolitionists, he, though in no sympathy with their views, loudly condemned the outrages of 1835, and maintained the right to discuss slavery like any other subject. His "Tales by a Country Schoolmaster," reprinted from the "Mirror," appeared in 1835, as did his "Naval Stories." "The Plain Dealer," which he founded in 1836, was a literary but hardly a financial success, and died within a year. Failing health compelled his retirement to New Rochelle, N. Y., the residence of his wife's family, where he died May 29, 1839, soon after his

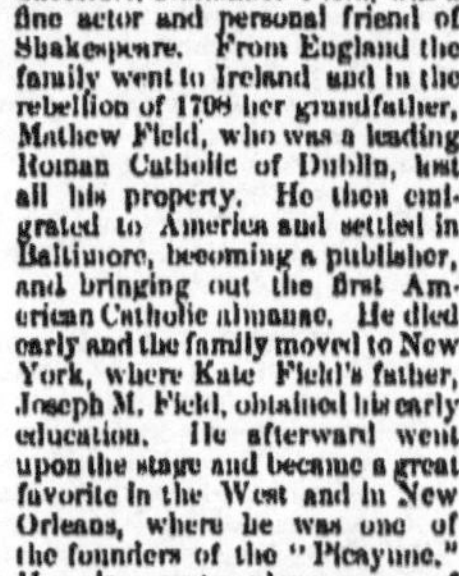

appointment as U. S. diplomatic agent to Guatemala. His "Political Writings" were collected in two volumes by T. Sedgwick, Jr., in 1840.

LEGGETT, William Henry, his nephew, was born in New York, Feb. 24, 1816, and was graduated from Columbia college in 1837, became a teacher and conducted the "Torrey Botanical Bulletin" 1870–80. He was a member of several scientific bodies, and died in New York in April, 1882.

LOGAN, Olive, author, was born at Elmira, N. Y., Apr. 16, 1841, the daughter of Cornelius A. Logan of Baltimore, and sister of Eliza Logan, the actress. Her father was an actor, and Miss Logan was brought up in the dramatic profession, often going on the stage when a little child in the arms of Booth and Forrest in "Figaro." She left the stage when sixteen, and studied abroad for several years. She married Edward A. Delile in 1857, and was divorced from him in 1865. In 1864 she returned to this country, and resumed her career as an actress, putting several comedies of her own writing on the stage. She gave up her profession finally in 1868, and, at the suggestion of

"Artemus Ward," began to lecture on popular topics, and is said to have had an income of $15,000 a year from this enterprise. In 1871 she married William Wirt Sikes, U. S. consul at Cardiff, who died in 1883, since which time she has resided much of the time abroad.

VERY, Jones, poet, was born at Salem, Mass., Aug. 28, 1813. In 1823–24 he made two voyages with his father, a sea-captain. At school he was described as "an eager student, a recluse, shy and introspective." Entering Harvard during the sophomore year, he was graduated in 1836, and was instructor in Greek there from 1836–38. At the close of this connection he had a peculiar mental experience, the effects of which are described in Emerson's diary of Oct. 26, 1838, two days after a visit from Very: "His position accuses society as much as society calls that false and morbid. The institutions, the cities which men have built, the world over, look to him like a huge ink-blot. His only guard in going to see men is that he goes to do them good, else they would injure him spiritually. He felt it, he said, an honor to wash his face, being, as it was, the temple of the spirit. He prized his verses, he said, not because they were his, but because they were not." Very's "Essays and Poems" appeared, at Emerson's urgency, in 1839. Their delicate and recondite character made little appeal to the popular taste, and the volume and its author were alike neglected. The Cambridge association (Unitarian) "approbated" him in 1843, but he rarely preached, and never took a charge nor even had a "call." Beyond occasional contributions to the Salem papers, the "Christian Register" and the "Monthly Magazine," he published nothing more. An acquaintance describes him (about 1850) "tall, thin, quiet, reserved, silent, serene, with somewhat the aspect of an extinct crater; he looked as if he belonged to another sphere." He was more than content to live in the strictest retirement, having "but one thought, the immanence of God; but one emotion, a desire that the spirit might be intrepid and confessed; but one interest, that men should turn their eyes toward the light." He was as much a transcendentalist as

Thoreau, less virile and more a mystic. His poems were highly valued by a select few. Bryant found in them "extraordinary grace and originality." R. H. Dana said they were "apart in American literature, deeply and poetically truthful." C. E. Norton called them "the work of an exquisite spirit: some are as if written by a George Herbert who had studied Shakespeare, read Wordsworth, and lived in America." Seven of them, in part cut down from sonnets, became more widely known in S. Longfellow and S. Johnson's "Book of Hymns" (1846); one of these, "Wilt thou not visit me?" has been greatly admired and extensively used. Very died at Salem, May 8, 1880. An enlarged edition of his poems, with a memoir by W. P. Andrews, appeared in 1883. See also a sketch of him headed "An Inspired Life," in the Century for October, 1882. His brother, Washington Very (1815–53), also wrote verses, and his sister, Lydia Louisa Anna Very (born Nov. 2, 1823), a teacher in the Salem schools, and an artist, published a volume of poems in 1856.

URE, William Andrew, editor, was born at West Farms, N. Y. (now part of New York city), Apr. 8, 1839, son of William Ure, a carpet manufacturer and a native of Scotland (1814–88). After acquiring a limited education at the common schools, the son worked in the carpet factory, and then in his uncle's shoe store, subsequently entering the employ of Mr. Bronson, a New York lawyer, who was largely interested in western lands. In the spring of 1857 he was sent to Nebraska to look after some property interests. There being no railroad through Iowa, he crossed that state alone, on horseback, and in the financial panic of that year the young man found himself suddenly thrown upon his own resources in a new and wild country. Turning to account whatever offered, he worked on a farm, and carried the United States mail to Fort Kearney. He at length fell a victim to a prevailing fever, but eventually recovered, and returned to New York in the latter part of 1858, where, Mr. Bronson having died, he again secured a situation in a shoe store. He next started on his own account in the real estate business, and soon became owner of a music store stocked with pianos, etc., the result of a real estate trade. He sold his stock, and then became a newspaper advertising agent, meeting with much success, part of the time in Washington, D. C. In 1867 he went to Newark, N. J., and taking a position on the "Journal," subsequently became city editor and associated press correspondent at Trenton. He was afterward business manager of the "Register," and in 1873 he, together with James W. Schoch, bought the "Sunday Call." By energy and sagacity he was mainly instrumental in making this paper the leading weekly of New Jersey, enabling him to acquire a comfortable fortune and retire from active business. He was elected alderman in 1875–76 as an independent democrat in a strongly republican ward. Always active in every movement toward the improvement of the city of Newark, he has been president of the West End improvement association and of the flourishing West End club since their organization. He was chairman of the board of directors of the Newark board of trade, and in January, 1894, was elected its president. Mr. Ure has been for many years a trustee of the Memorial Presbyterian church of Newark. His individual independence and sterling integrity stamped themselves upon his newspaper, and thus won the confidence of the public. Prominent in philanthropy, Mr. Ure is well known as the friend of the laboring man. In 1865 he was married to Martha L. Simonds. Of the five children born to them, two are living, a son and daughter.

STEINMAN, Andrew Jackson, editor, was born at Lancaster, Pa., Oct. 10, 1838, youngest son of John Frederick Steinman, of Lancaster, and his wife, Mary Smith Fahnestock, of "The Warren,"

Chester county, Pa. The son was educated at the Lancaster high school and at Yale college, where he was graduated in 1856. He studied law at the Albany law school and in the office of A. Herr Smith of Lancaster, and was admitted to the bar in 1859. As a democrat, he took great interest in politics, and devoted a large portion of his time for many years to that party, serving as secretary and chairman of the county committee, and member of the state committee. Other public positions than these he neither sought nor filled. The party, during the civil war, desired a daily organ in Lancaster, which was at length established by aid of the democratic county committee in 1864. The undertaking was unsuccessful financially until Mr. Steinman, through his interest in the party and his official connection with it, was induced to associate himself with Henry G. Smith, one of the editors, and to purchase an interest in the paper. For many years since that time he continued to edit and conduct the "Intelligencer," in connection with Mr. Smith and his subsequent associates, Mr. Hensel and Mr. Foltz. About 1880 Mr. Steinman became interested in resurrecting the principal iron industry of Lancaster, a rolling-mill plant, of which he shortly became chief owner and the chairman of the company. As the Penn iron company, limited, it was successfully established. On Jan. 25, 1882, Mr. Steinman was married to Caroline Morgan Hale, daughter of John M. Hale, of Reading, Pa. The three children born to them were christened Elizabeth Duncan, John Frederick, and James Hale.

GRAHAM, George Rex, publisher, was born in Philadelphia, Pa., Jan. 18, 1813. He was left an orphan when very young, and his education was limited to the opportunities afforded by the common schools. He learned the cabinet-maker's trade, but afterward studied law. He acquired a taste for literature, and contributed to the magazines, afterward becoming part owner of the "Casket," a magazine published at Philadelphia. Later he became sole proprietor of the publication. He also purchased the "Gentleman's Magazine," and consolidated the two journals under the name of "Graham's Magazine." He employed only the best writers, and the venture proved a great success. In 1840 he was induced to engage in copper-mine speculations, which caused his financial ruin. After a few years he again became proprietor of "Graham's Magazine," but was this time unable to make it successful. He wrote extensively for the newspapers until he lost his eyesight, when for three years he was a patient in an ophthalmic hospital. In 1888 his eyesight was partially restored. He died at Memorial hospital, Orange, N. J., July 13, 1894.

HOLT, John Saunders, author, was born in Mobile, Ala., Dec. 5, 1826. While yet an infant, he removed with his father to Woodville, Miss., and received his education first in New Orleans and then at Centre college, Danville, Ky. At the outbreak of the Mexican war in 1846, he enlisted as a private in Col. Jefferson Davis's regiment of Mississippi volunteers, and received honorable mention for bravery at Buena Vista. Subsequently he studied law, was admitted to the bar, and began the practice of his profession in Woodville in 1848, where he resided until his removal to New Orleans in 1851. Six years later he returned to Woodville, and when the civil war commenced joined the Confederate army, serving as a lieutenant until the cessation of hostilities. Afterward he resumed his law practice. In middle life he entered the field of literature, and wrote several novels illustrative of various phases of Southern character. Under the *nom-de-plume* of "Abraham Page," he published "The Life of Abraham Page, Esq." (Philadelphia, 1868); "What I Know About Ben Eccles, by Abraham Page" (1869), and "The Quines" (1870). Mr. Holt died in Natchez, Miss., Feb. 27, 1886.

DAWSON, Daniel L., poet, manufacturer and athlete, one of the most picturesque personalities in American literature, was born on a farm near Lewistown, Pa., in 1855. In the public schools, where he obtained his early education, he was noted for his love of literature, and at ten years of age won prizes for excellence in composition. Those who knew him then recognized that he possessed extraordinary mental powers, quickness of apprehension and capacity for rapid advancement in his studies. After his mother's death in 1868, his father removed to Philadelphia, and Daniel completed his education at La Salle college and the University of Pennsylvania, distinguishing himself as a student in both institutions. His father had established a foundry and boiler works at Gray's Ferry, in the southern part of Philadelphia, and in 1872, upon leaving college, Mr. Dawson became a partner in the business. His two elder brothers, who were members of the firm, died, and his father retired in 1879, when Mr. Dawson became sole proprietor. He continued the business with success during the remainder of his life, and the products of his manufacture were widely known for their excellence and durability. The income which he derived from his business made him comfortable, and gave him an opportunity to follow the bent of his mind by devoting much of his time to athletic sports and literary pursuits. Nature had endowed Dawson with a handsome form and a vigorous personality, for he was tall and superbly built and possessed great muscular strength. His grace and dignity of manner and sunny disposition, with the added charm of a brilliant intellect, endeared him to all his associates and made him one of the most popular men in Philadelphia. Honest, generous, sympathetic, with a soul as broad as his shoulders, a heart as stout as his arms—at times as tender as a child's—he won the affections of the people, and was a welcome guest in the most cultured and refined society. During his college days Dan Dawson gained prestige as an athlete and was a leader among his fellows. He continued to develop his muscular powers as a recreation and a delight, and after receiving careful training under skilled tutelage, he became one of the best all-around boxers in America. He had frequent bouts with amateur, and occasionally with professional, sparrers, and thus acquired a reputation for skill and prowess. But literature was his favorite diversion, and he drank deep at the fountain of knowledge. Books were his constant companions, carrying them with him wherever he went, spending his leisure time in absorbing their contents. He thus mastered the classic lore of the ancient Greeks and Romans, the beauties of the Norse mythology, and was an omnivorous reader of the best English literature. Already he had written some few fugitive verses which had been printed in the magazines, and one day his name was signed to a poem called "The Star of the Gnite" in "Lippincott's Magazine." It attracted attention outside of Philadelphia, and was favorably criticised in New York and Boston. "The Seeker in the Marshes, and Other Poems," is the title of a volume containing the best selections from Mr. Dawson's poetry. It was published in 1893, and was most favorably reviewed by the literary journals of the country. A second edition appeared in 1894. Few poets have surpassed Mr. Dawson in skillful and melodious versification. He died suddenly Oct. 31, 1893.

CAREY, Mathew, publisher, was born in Ireland, Jan. 28, 1760. His father was a baker, who, by careful management, accumulated quite a fortune, and was thereby enabled to give his son good educational advantages. When Mathew had attained the age of fifteen his father gave him the choice of twenty-five trades from which to make a selection; he chose that of a printer, and, though his father opposed this choice, he finally overcame all opposition, and went as an apprentice to Mr. McDonnell of Dublin, a printer and a bookseller. Mathew was a voracious reader, having from his earliest childhood devoured all books that came in his way. His first published production was written when he was but seventeen years old, and published in the "Hibernia Journal." The next, following in 1779, was a pamphlet, written in regard to the oppression of the Irish Catholics, which from its results proved one of the most important occurrences of his early life. It showed a comprehensive survey of the freedom which America was just then making such efforts to secure, not only for her own sons, but for the children of her adoption, and called other nations to emulate her glorious example. The pamphlet produced such an excitement that the duke of Leicester brought it up before the house of lords, and Sir Thomas Conelly before the house of commons, and it was denounced as treasonable and seditious. The father of the lad became alarmed, and Mathew was secretly sent to France. He there met Dr. Franklin, "who had a small printing-office at Passy, a village near Paris, for the purpose of reprinting his dispatches from America and other papers. Young Carey worked for a time for Dr. Franklin, and subsequently, with Didot Le Jeune, on the republication of some English books. While in France he made the acquaintance of the Marquis De Lafayette. At the expiration of a year he returned to his native land, the excitement having subsided, and in October, 1783, started a paper of his own, called the "Freeman's Journal," which was described by its editor as enthusiastic and violent. It soon obtained a large circulation, and had a great influence on the thought of the people, and the house of commons resolved to put it down. Mr. Carey was prosecuted for libel, and was committed to Newgate. When parliament adjourned he was given his liberty by the mayor of London. It was thought advisable

that he should leave Ireland, and, disguised as a woman, in order to escape the government officers, he embarked for America on Sept. 7, 1784, and arrived at Philadelphia on Nov. 15th of that year. The Marquis De Lafayette was then in America, and remembering the acquaintance he had with the young fugitive in France, and taking a lively interest in his welfare, called upon him at his lodgings, and wrote him a kindly letter, enclosing four one-hundred-dollar bills, making, however, no mention of the enclosure in his letter. Mr. Carey subsequently had the gratification of acknowledging this kindness by making Lafayette a handsome present, when he visited America in 1824 in broken fortunes. He moreover sent him a check for the full amount of the $400, which the marquis reluctantly accepted. The word "fail" was not in Mr. Carey's lexicon, and, undaunted by his previous experience, he at once started a paper in Philadelphia called the "Pennsylvania Herald," the first issue of which appeared on Jan. 25, 1785, which was the first newspaper in the United States to furnish correct reports of legislative debates, Mr. Carey acting as his own reporter. He became engaged in a bitter controversy with Col. Oswald, who edited a rival journal. The result was a duel, in which Mr. Carey, who had never drawn a trigger but once before in his life, was shot through the thigh-bone, and laid up for over a year. Mr. Carey's next venture was the "Columbian Magazine," from which he soon withdrew to start the "American Museum," which he conducted until 1787. He was married in 1791 to Miss B. Flahavan, a daughter of a worthy citizen, who had lost his fortune in the revolutionary war. He soon afterward began printing and bookselling on a small scale. In 1793 he was one of Stephen Girard's most efficient assistants during the yellow-fever epidemic that devastated Philadelphia. Mr. Carey wrote a thrilling account of the calamity, which was a history of "its rise, progress, effects, and termination." The same year he formed an Hibernian association for the relief of Irish emigrants. In connection with Bishop White and a few other American citizens, Mr. Carey formed the first American Sunday-school society. In 1802 he was elected by the senate a director of the Bank of Pennsylvania, which position he filled until 1805. He warmly advocated the renewal of the charter of the Bank of the United States, and wrote a number of vigorous articles for the press, and pamphlets which he published and distributed at his own expense. In 1814 he began the publication of the "Olive Branch," which he regarded as one of the most important steps of his life. The author's purpose was to endeavor by a candid publication of the follies and errors of both sides, to calm the embittered feelings of the political parties. In 1819 his "Vindiciæ Hiberniæ" appeared, which was a summary and denial of the charges against Ireland, for the part it was supposed to have taken in the massacre and conspiracy of 1641. The book has been pronounced by the highest authorities to be "the best vindication of Ireland that was ever written." He soon afterward began his essays in favor of the protective system of American industry, and was for a number of years an untiring champion of this policy. Mr. Carey took an active part in all the leading charities of his time. For many years he had a charity-list, on which were the names of hundreds to whom he gave regularly every two weeks. His last publication of any note was entitled the "Philosophy of Common Sense." He died at Philadelphia, Pa., on Sept. 17, 1840, at the age of eighty. His funeral showed the universal esteem in which he was held by all classes, and was, perhaps, with the exception of that of Stephen Girard, the largest ever held in Philadelphia.

MATHEWS, James Macfarlane, first chancellor of the University of the City of New York (1831-39), was born at Salem, N. Y., March 18, 1785. His father, David Mathews, came to this country some time before the Revolution, and enlisted at the commencement of the struggle for independence. The son displayed very early a taste for study, and was fond of books, which fact attracted the attention of his pastor, Dr. Proudfit, who encouraged him, and took special interest in his progress. In the academy he was popular with his teachers, and made such rapid progress that he entered Union College in 1801, two years in advance, graduating with a high reputation for scholarship. He returned to the former, and under the judicious instruction and advice of Dr. Proudfit, began studying for the ministry in the Seminary of Dr. John M. Mason, and was graduated in 1807, being one of the first who passed through that recently organized institution of the Associate Reformed Church. Dr. Mason discovered in his student special qualifications for the work of instruction, and at his solicitation young Mathews was, in 1808, called to the professorship of Biblical literature, a position which he filled with

marked ability, until he was called, in 1811, to take charge of the South Reformed Dutch Church, in Garden street, in New York, which was at the time but a struggling organization. In a very short time the church became one of great strength and influence, owing to his careful ministrations. Dr. Mathews continued in the active duties of this ministry until 1840, when he was released from pastoral work. He was one of nine gentlemen who met, Dec. 16, 1829, to consider "the establishment of a university in the city of New York on a liberal and extensive scale." He took a prominent part in the founding of the university, and, at the opening of the college in 1831, was chosen its first chancellor, which position he held for about nine years. His interest in its welfare, and the sacrifices he made to promote its prosperity, are important points in its history, and were warmly appreciated by his co-laborers in this great enterprise. Retiring in the year 1839 with a constitution very much broken by excessive labor, Dr. Mathews took a much needed rest, but soon turned his attention to preparing a course of lectures on "The Bible, and Men of Learning," and topics which attracted his attention while chancellor These were afterwards delivered in various cities of the country before intelligent audiences, and highly appreciated. They were subsequently published and widely circulated. In addition, he prepared, in 1864, a volume of great interest, embodying his recollections of eminent men and prominent events. He spent the later years of his life in works of general benevolence, interesting him chiefly in the cause of education, and promoting the welfare of young men, especially the medical students who came to the city to pursue their studies. He invited them in numbers to the hospitality of his home, and gained their confidence, which enabled him to befriend them with timely counsel. He was above the ordinary height, of erect form and fine physical development, and possessed a countenance of marked benevolence and intelligence. The bestowal of favors was a great gratification to him, and he would make great sacrifices in order to assist and oblige his friends. It was supposed by some that he was not easily accessible, or friendly, but with those who knew him he was a model of kindness and amiability. He was gifted with rare conversational powers, and in literary and social circles he was the centre of attraction, and often fascinated the company by his fund of information and timely anecdotes of men and events. As a preacher, he ranked among the most acceptable and impressive of his day. Among the pulpit celebrities of New York in the early part of the century, he held an honorable position, and maintained the reputation of being a solid, earnest, and powerful preacher. In 1819 Yale College conferred upon him the degree of D.D. After a lingering sickness, during which he preserved his wonted gentleness and serenity, he died Jan. 26, 1870, in New York city.

FREYLINGHUYSEN, Theodore, statesman and second chancellor of the University of the City of New York (1839-50). (See Vol. III., p. 401.)

FERRIS, Isaac, third chancellor of the University of the City of New York (1852-1870), was born in New York city Oct. 9, 1798, the son of Col. John and Sarah (Watkins) Ferris. His father was a lieutenant-colonel of artillery, and in command of the battery at Castle Garden during the latter part of the war of 1812, when Isaac served as bombardier. His early education was obtained under the tutelage of the celebrated blind classical teacher, Prof. Neilson. He was graduated from Columbia College in 1816, with high honors, and immediately became professor of Latin in the Albany Academy. Having taken up the study of theology under Rev. Dr. John M. Mason, he was graduated from the Reformed Dutch Church Seminary, at New Brunswick, N. J., in 1820, and one year later became the pastor of the church there. He was made trustee of Rutgers College in 1822. In 1824 he accepted a call to the Second Reformed Dutch Church, of Albany, N. Y. During his twelve years' ministry there he so endeared himself to the people that, when he died, nearly forty years afterwards, the church was draped in mourning for him. In 1833 he received the degree of D.D. from Union College, and in 1858 that of LL.D. from Columbia College. From 1836 to 1853 he was pastor of the Market Street Dutch Reformed Church, in New York city, then the fashionable church in the aristocratic old Seventh Ward. He was for many years president of the New York Sunday-school Union. He organized the board of foreign missions of the Dutch Church, and was its president. From 1840 until his death he was a trustee of the American Bible Society, and preached the sermon at the celebration of its fiftieth anniversary. He planned and organized the Rutgers Female College, and was for many years its president. In 1837 he became a member of the Council of the University of the City of New York, and in 1852 was made its third chancellor, succeeding Chancellor Frelinghuysen, who had resigned two years before. The university was by his efforts relieved of debt, which had seriously embarrassed it from its foundation. When Chancellor Ferris resigned his active duties in 1870, and became chancellor emeritus, he left the institution in a most flourishing condition. In the words of one of the university's most distinguished graduates, he was " wise in instruction, enthusiastic in encouragement, kindly in reproof, warm in praise, just in punishment; the white-haired chancellor was truly a model teacher, and, oh, rarer type, a wise man !" In appearance, Dr. Ferris was tall, broad-shouldered, and of commanding presence, combining great dignity with a most genial and kindly manner. He died at Roselle, N. J., June 13, 1873.

CROSBY, Howard, fourth chancellor of the University of the City of New York (1870–81). (See Vol. IV., p. 193.)

HALL, John, clergyman, and fifth chancellor of the University of the City of New York, was born of Scotch-Irish line in County Armagh, Ireland, July 31, 1829. At the age of thirteen he matriculated at Belfast College, where he distinguished himself by winning prize after prize in both the under graduate and the theological course, thrice and again being a prize man in Hebrew. Being licensed to preach when only twenty, he was enthusiastically elected to be " The Students' Missionary " in the western part of Ireland, and even in this humble position he showed the zeal and fidelity to duty which have gained for his later labors a national reputation. The character of his work was seen even outside the limits of his humble missionfield, and three years later he was installed pastor of the First Presbyterian Church at Armagh. Here he labored for five years, and in 1858 the Church of Mary's Abbey (now Rutland Square), in Dublin, prevailed upon him to accept a call, and here, as elsewhere, he

stood among the leaders. While in this charge he was editor-in-chief of " The Evangelical Witness," and advocated the cause of popular education; and in recognition of his services in this direction, the Queen bestowed upon him the honorary appointment of commissioner of education for Ireland, in which position he continued very acceptably during his residence at Dublin. The general assembly of the Presbyterian church in Ireland commissioned him their delegate to the Presbyterian churches of the United States in 1867, and, as a result of this visit, he was, after his return home, unanimously called to his present field of labor—the Fifth Avenue Presbyterian Church, in New York city. His labors in the new field began Nov. 3, 1867, where his success has been such as even his most ardent admirers could scarcely have predicted. The congregation rapidly increased in numbers and influence, and

a new church was erected in 1873–74 on the corner of Fifth avenue and Fifty-fifth street, fronting on Fifth avenue. This edifice, which is probably the largest Presbyterian church in the world, cost a round million of dollars. The congregation is one of the wealthiest owing allegiance to the Presbyterian system. About $125,000 a year is given for charitable purposes, and the mission work directly supported and carried on by this church ramifies in all directions. Strangers visiting New York, who happen into the regular services, are impressed with the chaste simplicity of the interior decorations of the church, the surroundings well comporting with the services themselves; and visitors carry away the feeling of having received a warm though unostentatious welcome. The preacher is very tall, and heavily built in proportion, and his smooth-shaven, kindly face, and striking figure clothed in the Geneva gown, hold all attention as he persuades and instructs the vast congregation. His sermons seem to be extemporaneous, but such is not the case; they are carefully written, either completely or in part, but he never takes the manuscript with him into the pulpit. According to the testimony of a member of his family, he preaches his sermons almost exactly as they are written. His pastoral work is done most systematically, and he gives notice from his pulpit of the parts of the city he expects to visit on given days. Until recently, the musical part of the services was led only by a precentor, but now (1891) the precentor is assisted by a male quartette. The singing is exclusively congregational. In 1881 Dr. Hall was made Chancellor of the University of the City of New York, succeeding the late Rev. Dr. Howard Crosby, and held the post for nearly ten years without drawing any salary. In the spring of 1891 he retired from the position, on account of increased demands upon his time in all directions. He was succeeded in the chancellorship by the vice-chancellor, the Rev. Henry Mitchell MacCracken, D.D., LL.D. Dr. Hall has received the degrees of D.D. and LL.D. In 1875 he was the Lyman Beecher lecturer in the Yale Theological School, where he has since that time been a special lecturer, delivering an annual course at that institution. He has been a large contributor to both religious and secular journals, and has also written several popular religious books.

MacCRACKEN, Henry Mitchell, clergyman, and sixth chancellor of the University of the City of New York (1891—), was born in Oxford, O., Sept. 28, 1840. His paternal great-grandfathers, both of Scotch blood, fought in the Revolution on the American side, Henry MacCracken falling in leading the defence of a post in the Susquehanna Valley. His mother was of English and Scotch-Irish blood; she founded a young women's school at Oxford, O., the seat of the Miami University. From this university

he was graduated in his seventeenth year, and became, first a teacher of classics, and afterwards a superintendent of public schools. He studied theology at the U. P. Seminary at Xenia, O., where he remained two years, and completed his course at Princeton, N. J., where he was graduated in 1863. He was immediately called to Westminster Church, at Columbus, O., of which he was pastor for four years, having a parish made up largely of professional men. He served upon a committee of three of the Ohio Synod, in founding the University of Wooster in 1866. In 1867 he went abroad upon leave of absence, acting as a deputy to the Free Church Assembly in Edinburgh, and the Assembly in Dublin. His address to the former was published. Deciding to resume study, he resigned his parish and spent a winter at Tübingen and Berlin Universities. Upon his return home he became pastor of the First Presbyterian Church in Toledo, O., and while filling this position, was active as an ecclesiast and writer. The General Assembly minutes of 1870 credit him with proposing the Presbyterian Tercentenary movement of 1872, which led to wide results. He published, among other writings, "Lives of the Leaders," a volume of 900 pages, chiefly from the German. In 1881 he was elected chancellor and professor of philosophy of the Western University of Pennsylvania. He was instrumental in removing this college in 1882 from Pittsburgh to Allegheny, and in placing it upon a more hopeful foundation. On July 4, 1884, he gave the historical address at the Scotch-Irish Reunion at Belfast, Ireland. In this year he was called to the University of the City of New York, first as professor of philosophy, then as executive officer, with the title of vice-chancellor, and, in 1891, upon the resignation of Chancellor Hall, he was made chancellor. Among the events of his administration have been the opening of the graduate Seminary; the founding of the School of Pedagogy; the alliance between the University and the Union Theological Seminary in 1890; the purchase of "University Heights," the new site of the University College and the School of Engineering, between Morris Heights and Fordham Heights, New York, in 1892; the removal of the college there in 1894; and the founding there of a system of college halls, including a library, which will have cost by 1896 over $600,000; also in 1894-95 the erection, at a cost of $700,000, of an eleven-story building on the east side of Washington Square, in which the topmost stories are adapted to the needs of the University School of Law and Pedagogy, the council room, and chancellor's office. He is vice-president of the Society for the Prevention of Crime, and as such nominated to its presidency Dr. Charles Henry Parkhurst in 1891. He was the formal mover in the general assembly of 1890 for a committee to revise the Westminster Confession. The degree of D.D. was conferred upon him by Wittenberg (Ohio) College in 1878, and LL.D. by his alma mater in 1887. Dr. MacCracken's untiring energy, wise discretion, and thorough knowledge of men, make him a safe counselor and a successful administrator. No one person in the sixty years' history of the University of the City of New York has done so much for its prosperity as a school of high learning, and this by a remarkable attention, both to the general management of the university, and also to the minutest details. Notwithstanding these increasing labors, his interest in all public questions has not failed, and his essays on educational and financial subjects have commanded general attention.

MOTT, Valentine, surgeon, was born at Glen Cove, L. I., Aug. 20, 1785. His first American ancestor, Adam Mott, who settled on Long Island about 1660, was one of the original disciples of George Fox, the founder of the Society of Friends. His father, Henry Mott, was a physician, practising in New York city and for a while at Newton, L. I., where the boy received a classical education at a private seminary. In 1804 young Mott became a pupil of his kinsman, Dr. Valentine Seaman, a skilled and enlightened physician, and a man of rare benevolence and humanity. Under his fostering care and guidance the young student became imbued with that intense love of his profession which animated him throughout his career. He remained with Dr. Seaman until 1807 when, after attending the full course of lectures at Columbia College, he was graduated from that institution. Ambitious to attain the highest rank in his profession, he went to London and placed himself under the tuition of Astley Cooper, who was then near the zenith of his fame. With him he spent his time principally in the study of practical anatomy by the dissective method, in and out of the hospitals, while diligently attending the lectures of some of the greatest surgeons of the day. He next spent a year at the celebrated school of medicine in Edinburgh, where he received instruction from some of the most skilful practitioners and teachers of the medical profession. In the autumn of 1809 he returned to New York, and in the following winter, after a private course of lectures on surgery, he was appointed by his alma mater to the chair of surgery. Three years later the medical faculty of Columbia College was merged in the College of Physicians and Surgeons, and Dr. Mott continued in the institution until 1826 when, in consequence of certain offensive actions on the part of the trustees, he and his colleagues, all men of distinguished ability, withdrew in a body and founded a new school under the auspices of Rutgers College. In 1830, however, the institution, in spite of a prosperous career, was compelled to close its doors on account of a defect in its charter respecting the granting of degrees. The four years which had elapsed since Dr. Mott left the College of Physicians and

Surgeons had sufficed to soften asperities, and he returned to that institution as professor of operative surgery and surgical and pathological anatomy, continuing there until failing health forced him to give up his labors and seek rest and relaxation. Accordingly, in 1835 he resigned, and in quest of renewed strength and vigor set sail for Europe, whither his reputation as one of the foremost surgeons of the age had preceded him. He hastened to London to greet his old master, Sir Astley, and afterwards visited several of the countries on the continent, returning to the United States after an absence of sixteen months. Finding that his health was not thoroughly re-established, he again embarked for Europe, and this time establishing his headquarters in Paris, made annual excursions into the countries bordering the eastern Mediterranean, and making a special visit to the ancient city of Epidaurus, the birthplace of Æsculapius, as the Mecca of his pilgrimage. In one of these journeys, when visiting Constantinople, he was called upon to remove a tumor from the head of Sultan Abdul Medjid, and was rewarded for his success in the operation by being invested with the Order of the Medjidieh. He finally bade adieu to Europe in 1841, completely restored to health, having been flattered everywhere with the homage of men in the most exalted walks in life; having been treated in Paris with especial courtesy and consideration by

the "Citizen King" and his family; and having enjoyed the distinguished companionship of the brilliant military surgeon, Baron Larrey, who had accompanied Napoleon through his marvelous career from battlefield to battlefield. During his absence from America, Dr. Mott had been unanimously elected in 1840 professor of surgery and president of the medical faculty of the University of the City of New York, and he continued in this office, besides being surgeon of the New York Hospital, until his resignation in 1850, when he once more crossed the Atlantic. Under his direction the school rose rapidly into prominence, the pupils in its classes ranging from 350 to 400 annually, and including many students from abroad. On his return in the autumn of 1851 Dr. Mott again entered the College of Physicians and Surgeons as professor of operative surgery and surgical anatomy, but abandoned this position in 1852 to become emeritus professor of surgery in the university, which office he held up to the time of his death. He was but thirty-three years old when he sprang at a bound into the foremost rank of the illustrious surgeons of his day by an operation which had never been performed before. This was the ligation of the innominate artery, a small vessel not much more than an inch in length, rising from the arch of the aorta, the great trunk of the arterial system, in fearful proximity to the heart. The operation was performed, May 11, 1818, upon a Massachusetts sailor named Michael Bateman, fifty-seven years of age, who was suffering from an aneurism of the right subclavian artery. Although after everything had seemed to go well and promise ultimate recovery, secondary hemorrhage set in on the twenty-third day and the patient expired of exhaustion on the twenty-sixth, the case fully proved the practicability and even the justice of the operation. The great German surgeon, Von Graefe, of Berlin, repeated it three years later, but again the patient perished, this time on the sixty-seventh day, and it was not until 1864 that the operation was successfully performed. In 1821 Dr. Mott excised the right side of the lower jaw of a young woman afflicted with osteo-sarcoma, after having secured the primitive carotid artery; and in three later instances successfully removed the bone at the temporo-maxillary articulation. In 1824 he performed, on a ten-year-old lad, an amputation of the hip joint, by which operation nearly a fourth of the entire human body is removed. This was long supposed to have been the first operation of the kind in America, but it subsequently came to light that Dr. Mott had been, unknown to himself, forestalled as far back as 1806 by Dr. Walter Brashear, of Bardstown, Ky. In 1827 he ligated the common iliac artery for an extensive aneurism of the external iliac artery, a most difficult operation attempted but once before, in 1812, by Dr. William Gibson, professor of surgery in the University of Maryland, and then without success. In the present instance, however, the patient recovered. The most arduous and dangerous operation ever performed by Dr. Mott, one he was wont to call his "Waterloo operation," was the excision, in 1828, of the collar bone for osteo-sarcoma. An immense tumor, the size of a man's doubled fist, had formed rapidly and contracted extensive and powerful adhesions, involving not only large arteries, veins, and nerves, but even the pleura and the lung itself. It was absolutely necessary to exclude air from the external jugular vein, the admittance of which would have placed the patient's life in instant jeopardy, so that vessel had to be secured by two ligatures. It was further found necessary to tie no less than forty arteries, "an occurrence," as Dr. Gross remarks, "probably without a parallel in the history of surgery," and made all the more remarkable by the fact of the patient's complete recovery. Yet more than thirty years elapsed before any other surgeon had sufficient faith in his knowledge, dexterity, and coolness, to perform a similar operation. In 1830 Dr. Mott had the rare satisfaction of curing a case of cleft-spine in a child n'ne years of age, when he removed a large tumor from the lower part of the back. This success he duplicated later in the case of an infant but nine days old, in which the cervico-dorsal region was involved. In 1841 his fame was still further augmented by the successful performance of an operation, which, though not the first of its kind, was by far the most considerable and difficult. This was the removal of an immense fibrous tumor, which filled up the entire nostril and dipped far down into the pharynx. In order to gain access to the growth, Dr. Mott had to divide the nasal and maxillary bones in front of the face. In the treatment of hare-lip and lockjaw he possessed peculiar skill, one aggravated case of the latter coming to his notice as early as 1812, when he was successful in effecting a restitution. After considerable reflection, he invented, in 1822, an instrument upon the screw and lever principle, with which to pry open the jaw after the modular tissues had been cut out. No surgeon, it may be confidently asserted, ever excelled him in the treatment of lithotomy. He concurred with his famous Scotch contemporary, Dr. Robert Liston, in his condemnation of the gorget, and invariably used the bistoury and the lateral method. Once he removed a stone weighing seventeen ounces, two drachms, the largest ever taken out of a living body; and altogether he operated no less than 165 times, losing only seven patients, a ratio of but one in twenty-three. The reputation of Dr. Mott as an operator had become worldwide long before his career closed. He possessed in the highest degree all the qualifications for a successful operator—keenness of vision, steadiness of nerve, and instant readiness of resource, combined with a physical hardihood that seemed capable of withstanding all sense of fatigue. His left hand was little less skilled than the right in the manipulation of the scalpel, in the dexterous use of which he was never excelled, and but seldom equaled. Yet with all these advantages he never would consent to perform an operation until he had become convinced of its absolute necessity. He loved not the knife for the knife's sake. His absolute conscientiousness, and, at the same time, his superiority to the great majority of the surgeons of his day, was further manifested in his thorough acquaintance with the science of therapeutics, which enabled him always to adopt such after-treatment of his patients as should most surely conduce to their rapid recovery from the effects of the operation. He invented not a few surgical and obstetrical implements, and was always an eager welcomer of the inventions and improvements of his contemporaries. One of his biographers, Dr. Samuel D. Gross, in his work published at Philadelphia in 1868, says of him: "Of the many thousand operations which he performed, only a very few need be specified to show that the great reputation founded upon them was justly deserved. The name of Churchill is not more indissolubly associated with the battle of Blenheim, or that of Wellington with Waterloo, than is the name of Valentine Mott with the history of surgery in the first half of the nineteenth century. What they, and others like them, accomplished with the sword, aided by hordes of soldiers, he accomplished silently and alone, with the knife. His victories and triumphs were no less real than theirs." As a lecturer his career was a somewhat checkered one, beginning with a private course on anatomy after his first return from Europe, and being continued at intervals in various schools and hospitals in New York. His lectures were never committed to memory nor even written out, but delivered from well-digested notes. Both subject-matter and illustrations were largely drawn from his own experience; theories, as such, receiving but scant courtesy. His prominence as a public teacher was early established, and thousands of diplomas bearing his signature attested his popularity and the affectionate zeal of his pupils, by whom he delighted in being surrounded, watching their progress with an unfeigned enthusiasm which could not fail to communicate itself to them. He collected a large museum of pathological specimens, the product principally of his own surgical operations, but the collection, with its illustrated catalogue, was consumed in the fire which destroyed the University Medical College in 1866. Dr. Mott was officially connected with many charitable institutions. Many of his most brilliant operations were performed in the New York Hospital, which he finally quit in 1850. For fifteen years subsequently he was senior consulting surgeon to Bellevue Hospital, and at various periods in his active career he was similarly connected with St. Vincent's, St. Luke's, the Women's, and the Hebrew Hospitals. Honors were showered upon him. The University of Edinburgh conferred upon him the honorary degree of M.D., and the University of the State of New York that of LL.D. in 1851. He was elected an Honorary Fellow by the Imperial Academy of Medicine of Paris, the Paris Clinical Society, the Medical and Chirurgical Society of London, the Medical Society of Brussels, and the King and Queen's College of Physicians of Ireland, which during two centuries of existence had elected but twenty-six foreigners to membership, and never previously an American. He was also made a Foreign Associate of the Institute of France, founded by Napoleon; a member of the medical societies of Berlin and Athens, and of numerous states of the Union. It is a matter for regret that Dr. Mott was strongly averse to literary composition. The only volume of any size which issued from his pen was published in 1842, on his return from his foreign tour, entitled, "Travels in Europe and the East." In the same year and the two following, he supervised the translation by Dr. Peter S. Townsend, of Prof. Velpeau's treatise on "Operative Surgery," a monument of learning and research, to which he wrote an elaborate preface, and contributed in addition several hundred pages of notes and illustrative matter drawn mainly from his own previously published cases and reports. Some of these had appeared as long ago as 1818 in the "New York Medical and Surgical Register," founded by him in conjunction with Dr. Alexander H. Stevens, on the model of the celebrated "Dublin Hospital Reports," but unfortunately the periodical failed to survive its first year. In his preface to Velpeau's work, Dr. Mott makes mention of his early and frequent use of the curvilinear incision, the superiority of which in operations on the jaws and in resections of the bones generally the eminent French surgeon clearly establishes, but fails to ascribe the main credit of the improvement to the genius of his American contemporary, to whom it rightly belongs. In 1862 Dr. Mott, at the request of the U. S. sanitary commission, prepared a paper on the use of anesthetics for the benefit of army surgeons, and shortly afterwards another, intended mainly for the use of wounded soldiers on the battlefield, on the means of suppressing hemorrhage in gunshot wounds. His other published writings consist almost exclusively of addresses and lectures, introductory or valedictory, with a few contributions to the "Transactions" of the New York Academy of Medicine, and one to the London Medical and Chirurgical Society, on a rare and peculiar skin tumor, which he was the first to describe, and to which he gave the name "pachydermatocele." From his pen we have also a "Sketch of the Life of Dr. Wright Post," and a "Eulogy" on his most intimate and life-long friend, Dr. John Wakefield Francis (1861). Beyond the notes with which he prepared his lectures, he left no MSS. "Mott's Cliniques," an abstract of his later clinical lectures, was published in 1860 by Dr. Samuel Ward Francis, a son of his friend. Dr. Mott married, in 1819, Louisa Dunmore Mums, who, after his death, purchased, at a cost of $30,000, as an enduring monument to the memory of her husband, a fine building at 64 Madison avenue, for the Mott Memorial Library, which, in 1866, was incorporated by an act of the legislature of New York. It contains, besides what remained of his valuable specimens of healthy and morbid anatomy, a library of 4,000 volumes on medical and surgical topics, to which all medical students and practitioners are admitted. Dr. Mott died in New York city, Apr. 26, 1865.

HAMMER, Frederick Oscar, secretary, was born in St. Paul, Minn., Aug. 11, 1866, son of Jacob Hammer, a prominent pioneer manufacturer of the city. He was educated in the public and private schools and at college, and was graduated in 1881. Shortly after leaving school he secured employment in the registry department of the post-office, and not finding it agreeable to his taste he resigned, and accepted the position of assistant secretary of the Hail and Storm Insurance Co. of St. Paul, which position he held until the dissolution of the company in 1888. His ability as secretary being recognized, he was made secretary of the Capitol Building Society, the Minnesota Savings and Loan Society, and the Germania Loan and Building Association, through which organizations, as the result of co-operative savings, at least 1,000 homes had in 1895 been secured and paid for beyond the limit of danger to investors, and besides he has charge of several private estates. He is a member of the Minnesota Building Association League, of the Commercial Club of St. Paul, and a number of other social organizations. Mr. Hammer was married on Apr. 10, 1890, to Lavanche Imogene, daughter of Edwin Barnum, of Loomis, Neb.

MARDEN, George Augustus, journalist, was born in Mont Vernon, N. H., Aug. 9, 1839, son of Benjamin and Betsey (Buss) Marden. His elementary education was obtained at the district school, and afterward, through his own persistent exertions, and by means of money earned at his trade as a shoemaker, and by teaching school, he fitted himself for college, matriculating at Dartmouth in 1857, and

was graduated in 1861. In November, 1861, he enlisted as a private in the 2d regiment, Berdan's U. S. sharpshooters, received a warrant as sergeant, and was afterward detailed as clerk at Col. Berdan's headquarters in Washington. He served, in 1862, in the army of the Potomac, with the 1st regiment of sharpshooters under Col. Berdan, and in July, 1862, was commissioned by Gov. Berry of New Hampshire first lieutenant and quartermaster of that regiment, which rank he held until September, 1864, when the regiment was mustered out of the service. Meantime, much of his service was as acting assistant adjutant-general of the brigade in which the regiment served, in which capacity he was in the battles of Chancellorsville and Gettysburg. Upon his return to his native state he studied law at Concord, and in 1865 became editor of the "Kanawha Republican," published at Charleston, W. Va. In 1866 he returned to New Hampshire, and edited, for Adjt.-Gen. Head, the history of the various state regiments. In 1867 he removed to Boston and took a position on the editorial staff of the "Daily Advertiser." In September of that year he joined in the purchase of the "Daily Courier" and the "Weekly Journal" of Lowell, and removed to that city and assumed the position of editor-in-chief of both papers. In 1872 Mr. Marden was elected a member of the Massachusetts house of representatives, serving one year (1873). In 1874 he was elected clerk of the house, and successively re-elected, serving nine consecutive years. In 1882 he was elected a member of the house, and served as its speaker for two terms (1883–84). In 1885 he was a member of the Massachusetts senate. In 1888 Gov. Ames appointed him a trustee of the Massachusetts Agricultural College, which position he resigned the same year, on being elected treasurer and receiver-general of Massachusetts for 1889. He was re-elected to the treasurership each successive year for four years—five years was the limit provided in the state constitution for the continuous service of an individual. Mr. Marden was a delegate from the seventh congressional district to the Republican national convention held in Chicago in 1880, and was one of the historic "Old Guard" of 306 who voted for the nomination of Gen. Grant for president. He was the first commander of Post 42 G. A. R., of Lowell, and is a member of the Massachusetts Commandery of the Loyal Legion of the United States. He was married, Dec. 10, 1867, to Mary, daughter of David Fiske, of Nashua, N. H., and they have two sons: Philip Sanford, who was graduated from Dartmouth College, class of 1894, and Robert Fiske, a member of the class of 1898, same college. On Jan. 1,

1895, the "Lowell Courier" and "Lowell Citizen" were purchased by a new corporation, and Mr. Marden was elected editor-in-chief of both papers. Mr. Marden was the poet for the Phi Beta Kappa Society at Dartmouth College at commencement in 1875, and of the Alumni Association of Dartmouth at commencement in 1886. He was a guest, and one of the speakers, at the annual dinner of the New England Society of New York Forefathers' Day in 1889, and again in 1891.

MENDENHALL, Richard Junius, banker and floriculturist, was born in Jamestown, N.C., Nov. 25, 1828, son of Richard Mendenhall, a tanner. His first American ancestor, John Mendenhall, was a companion of William Penn, and emigrated with him, settling in Pennsylvania. His early life was spent on his father's farm and at work in the tannery, and his literary education was acquired at the village school and at a Quaker boarding school at New Garden, N. C., and the celebrated Friends' School at Providence, R. I. When he was fourteen years old he served in the post-office at Greensboro', N. C. as a clerk, and afterwards in a store of his uncle's in his native village. He taught school for a time in North Falmouth, Mass., and afterwards was engaged in the building of a railroad tunnel in Ohio, engineering on a North Carolina railroad and with a surveying party in Iowa. He continued his studies in civil engineering during the winter of 1855–56 at Des Moines, Iowa, and the next year removed to Minneapolis, Minn., where he engaged in real estate speculation and banking. In 1858 he married Abby, daughter of Capt. Silas Swift, West Falmouth, Mass., and made his home in Minneapolis. At the town election in the spring of 1862 he was chosen town treasurer, and to float a currency script issued by the town, Mr. Mendenhall personally endorsed it and further met the financial needs of the times by putting in circulation the notes of Indiana banks which he personally agreed to redeem. In November, 1862, Mr. Mendenhall purchased one-half of the capital stock of the State Bank of Minnesota and removed it to Minneapolis. He was its president until it was merged into the State National Bank. He was also president of the State Savings Association. In the panic of 1873 the Savings Bank was compelled to suspend, but Mr. Mendenhall by personal sacrifice settled almost all just claims against it. He was for many years secretary and treasurer of the board of education of Minneapolis, and was largely instrumental in building up the public school system of the city. Mr. Mendenhall is a devoted student of entomology and botany. He is also an earnest promoter of agriculture and horticulture, and has held the office of president of the State Horticultural Society. His collection of choice exotics and many other rare and beautiful plants of the floral kingdom is the finest in Minneapolis if not in the entire Northwest; and when adversity overtook him he turned his knowledge and experience to account and largely increased the area of his houses for propagating and perfecting flowers, and became a floriculturist for profit and made the business largely remunerative. His attachment for the simple worship of the Society of Friends still continues, but does not debar him from the pleasure he derives from contributing liberally to the various denominations that appeal to him for help.

KEANE, John Joseph, bishop and educator, was born at Ballyshannon, county Donegal, Ireland, Sept. 12, 1839. He came with his parents to the United States in 1846. After finishing his common school studies, at the age of seventeen, he was engaged until his twentieth year in mercantile pursuits in the city of Baltimore, in the course of which he acquired business habits which were to be useful to him in his subsequent career. In 1851 he entered upon a classical course at St. Charles College, near Ellicott city, Md. His talents and previous studies enabled him to make the course there in three years instead of six, the usual period, and he was thus able to enter St. Mary's Theological Seminary, in Baltimore, in the autumn of 1862. In 1863 he took there the degree of bachelor of arts, in 1864 that of master of arts, and in 1865 that of bachelor of divinity. On July 2, 1866, he was ordained to the priesthood. He was then stationed as curate at St. Patrick's church in Washington, where he remained for twelve years. During this period he took a leading part in the organization of the Catholic Total Abstinence Union of America, and also of the Catholic Young Men's National Union. In February, 1878, he was chosen bishop of Richmond, Va., succeeding the Rt. Rev. James Gibbons, now archbishop of Baltimore and cardinal of the Holy Roman church, and received episcopal consecration on Aug. 25th of that year. While presiding over the diocese of Richmond, he occupied himself incessantly in preaching and lecturing, and especially in the organization of church work among the colored race in nearly every part of the diocese, and the establishment of schools and churches for them. In the second year of his episcopate, after correspondence with Cardinal Manning and Father Hawes of London on the subject, he established throughout the diocese the Confraternity of the Holy Ghost, writing pastoral letters and other papers calculated to arouse his people to an appreciation of that important devotion. In 1884 he took part in the Third Plenary Council of Baltimore, at which was decreed the establishment of a great national institution for post-collegiate and highly specialized education, to be called the Catholic University of America. He was chosen one of its directors, and subsequently was requested by the American hierarchy, and by His Holiness Leo XIII., to resign his diocese in order to devote himself entirely to its direction, and in 1886, accordingly, he was appointed rector of the university; on May 24, 1888, the corner-stone of its first building was laid, and on Aug. 20th of the same year he was transferred from the see of Richmond to the titular see of Ajasso. In 1889, in recognition of his distinguished talents and great learning, he received from Laval University the degree of doctor of divinity. In connection with the establishment of the university he paid several visits to Europe, for the purpose both of conferring with the pope regarding the great enterprise, and of studying the educational methods of the universities of the Old World. With this view he spent some time at Rome, Vienna, Munich, Bonn, Strasburg, Louvain, Lille, and Paris, and other great seats of learning, familiarizing himself with the system which it was proposed to transfer for the first time to American soil. Since the opening of the university on Nov. 13, 1889, he has devoted himself assiduously to its organization, the perfecting of its methods, and the enlarging of the sphere of its work.

His aim, and that of the founders, has been to make it a true university, devoting itself exclusively to post-graduate work. The one faculty thus far established, that of divinity, is open only to clergymen who have completed at least a three-years' seminary course of theology in addition to their collegiate studies. The faculty of philosophy, science, and letters, and the faculty of jurisprudence was opened in October, 1895, and is open to lay students who have taken their baccalaureate of arts in a first class college, or have made equivalent studies privately; other faculties will be added as soon as possible. Bishop Keane is one of the best known lecturers in the United States, especially on subjects connected with education, the institutions of the American republic, and temperance. In 1890 he delivered the Dudleian lecture at Harvard University. His breadth of view and of sympathy, his enthusiasm for lofty ideas, and his cheerful optimism have endeared him, no less than his finished oratory and his sturdy patriotism, to the whole American people, regardless of party or creed. He has frequently in the intervals of his long life contributed articles, mostly on educational questions, to the "North American Review," the "Forum," the "Catholic World," the "American Catholic Quarterly," and other periodicals.

BADEAU, Adam, soldier and author, was born in New York city, Dec. 29, 1831. He received his early instruction from private tutors, and then attended a boarding-school at Tarrytown, N. Y. As a young man he wrote dramatic criticisms for "Noah's Sunday Times," which were afterward collected under the title of "The Vagabonds." Young Badeau also served as a clerk in the New York street department through the influence of Gen. Bosteel. In 1862 he volunteered his services in the cause of the Union, and was appointed aide on the staff of Gen. Thomas W. Sherman. He was present at the siege of Corinth, May, 1862, and in the defenses of New Orleans from January to May, 1863. When Gen. Sherman was assigned to the command of the 2d division of the 19th army corps in the expedition to Port Hudson, La., Badeau accompanied him, and led an assault upon the Confederate works, May 27, 1863, in which he was severely wounded. In March, 1864, he was appointed military secretary to Gen. Grant, with the rank first of lieutenant-colonel, and afterward of colonel. The foundation was then laid of the intimate friendship between the two, which lasted twenty-one years, until Grant's death in 1885. Badeau was with the commander-in-chief in the Wilderness and Appomattox campaigns, and remained on his staff until March, 1869, when he was retired from the army with the full rank of captain, and the brevet rank of brigadier-general U. S. army. He had also received a similar brevet in the volunteer service. After Grant's first inauguration as president, Badeau was appointed secretary

of legation at London, and held the post from May to December, 1869. In the early part of 1870 he was sent to Madrid as the bearer of government despatches, and in May returned to London to fill the important position of U. S. consul-general in that city. Gen. Badeau continued to discharge the duties of this office until September, 1881, excepting the two years (1877-78) during which he was given leave of absence by the state department to accompany

Gen. Grant on his tour around the world. In 1875 he had been appointed U. S. minister to Brussels, and in 1881 to Copenhagen, but declined both appointments. From May, 1882, until May, 1884, he was consul-general at Havana. During his tenure of this office he accused the state department at home of corruption, and because he was refused an opportunity of substantiating the charge, promptly tendered his resignation. Shortly afterwards he was engaged to assist in the preparation of the personal memoirs of Gen. Grant, his work being very largely that of an amanuensis. When Gen. Grant suddenly relapsed into what ulti-

mately proved a fatal sickness, Gen. Badeau made a demand upon him to the effect that he should be paid a certain sum per month, and likewise be allowed a share in the profits of the book. Gen. Grant regarded that as a suggestion that Gen. Badeau should practically write his book, and that he (Gen. Grant) should assume the credit. This the general declined to do in a severe letter, as involving injustice to himself, and terminated the arrangement with Badeau. When Gen. Grant died Gen. Badeau made a demand upon the estate for the sum stipulated in 1884. In October, 1888, Col. Frederick D. Grant paid Gen. Badeau $10,000, and this was accepted as a settlement of the disputed claim. During the last years of his life he was a frequent contributor to the magazines and periodicals, and in these articles chronicled his experiences in Europe and the United States. The strain upon his eyes, occasioned by continuous application to literary work, had caused cataracts to form on both of them, and during the winter of 1894-95 he underwent several operations for their removal. He had not been in good health for some time, and each successive operation involved a loss of physical strength, but there was nothing in his condition to indicate that death was near at hand. For two weeks previous there had been some improvement in his general health, and for an hour or two prior to the fatal seizure he seemed to be in unusually good spirits. As an author, Gen. Badeau is best known by his admirable "Military History of Ulysses S. Grant" (Vol. I., 1868; Vols. II., III., 1881). The New York "Nation" has spoken of this work as follows: "It is not only a very full history of the military career of Gen. Grant, but also the completest and fullest history of our war. . . . . It is nowhere dull." The "Saturday Review" says: "The work is written with that soldierly respect for high qualities . . . which is the first characteristic of a good military history." Gen. Badeau has also published: "The Vagabond," a collection of essays (New York, 1859); "Conspiracy: A Cuban Romance" (New York, 1885); "Aristocracy in England" (New York, 1886); and "Grant in Peace, from Appomattox to Mt. McGregor: A Personal Memoir" (Hartford, 1887). He died of apoplexy in Ridgewood, N. J., March 19, 1895.

WALL, Stephen, Roman Catholic priest, was born in Kilmichael, county Cork, Ireland, in 1838. He was educated for the priesthood and after having been admitted to holy orders, came to America and was attached to the diocese of Pittsburgh, where he served in various churches with great acceptance. His last charge was as rector of St. Peter's church, Allegheny City. He was distinguished for his great learning, being a profound theologian and an erudite pulpit orator. He was vicar-general of the diocese, one of the diocesan consultors and chairman of the examinations. He received, during his synodal life, the degrees of D.D. and LL.D. from his alma mater. He died in Allegheny City, Pa., Aug. 21, 1894.

DOUGLAS, Orlando Benajah, physician, was born in Cornwall, Vt., Sept. 12, 1836, eldest son of Amos Douglas. He is the eighth in descent from Deacon William Douglas, of Scottish origin, who came from England to Boston in 1640, and in 1660 removed to New London, Conn. Dr. Douglas began his education at Brandon, Vt. At the age of eighteen, and subsequently, he taught school, and in 1858, in compliance with his mother's earnest wish, he commenced the study of medicine with his uncle at Brunswick, Mo. In 1861 Missouri was torn with dissension, and Dr. Douglas was on the point of starting for Illinois to complete his medical studies, but appreciating the need in Missouri of loyal men who would stand firmly by the government, he induced half a dozen young men to join him in Brunswick, where two hundred followed Price to the South, and they enlisted in the 18th regiment Missouri volunteers, organized by order of General Frémont, and, enduring the fortunes of war, went through Georgia to the sea with Sherman. He was appointed lieutenant (refusing a captaincy), and, later, adjutant of his regiment. By order of General Grant he was made acting assistant adjutant-general on General Bain's staff. He was wounded in the forearm while scouting in Missouri, Jan. 4, 1862, and at the battle of Shiloh, Apr. 6, 1862, was severely wounded in the left hip. He was for some months seriously ill; but, later, was assigned to duty in Cincinnati, O., and at Corinth, Miss. In February, 1863, he was honorably discharged, but afterwards served for eighteen months in the provost marshal's office at Concord, Mass. In 1870 he resumed his medical studies, and in 1877 was graduated from the University Medical College of New York. He served in De Milt Dispensary for two years. In 1877 he was appointed assistant sur-

geon in the throat department of Manhattan Eye and Ear Hospital, and since the spring of 1878, has had charge of the throat clinic of that institution three days of each week. In 1885 he was elected surgeon and director in this hospital. Here he has done important work, having devoted himself assiduously to the improvement of his department. More than 80,000 visits have been made by patients to his clinics in this hospital. Since his connection with it, the institution has grown to be one of the most prosperous of its kind in the country, and he has been identified with the marvelous progress made in this special department of medicine. Dr. Douglas has written several papers on his specialty, some of which have been published: one, "Is the Cure of Chronic Nasal Catarrh as Difficult as has been Supposed?"; another, "The Upper Air-Passages and Their Diseases." He was elected professor of diseases of the nose and throat in the Post-Graduate Medical School and Hospital in 1888; was treasurer of the Medical Society of the County of New York from 1879 to 1887, and was elected its president in 1890—at which time it was the largest medical organization of its kind in America. He was secretary of the Therapeutical Society of New York; chairman of the section on laryngology and rhinology in the Academy of Medicine, 1888; director in the Physician's Mutual Aid Association for ten years; treasurer of the New York Academy of Medicine from 1880 to 1893; member of the Medical Society of the State of New York; honorary member of the Vermont State Medical Society and other medical organizations. He is a member of the Masonic fraternity, surgeon of Reno Post, Grand Army of the Republic, companion of the first class of the Loyal Legion, and Fellow of the American Geographical Society. He is a Baptist, was for many years actively identified with the Young Men's Christian Association, was superintendent of Sunday-schools—and at one time superintendent of the largest Sunday-school in his native state—president of the State Sunday-School Association, and is interested in other religious and temperance work. Dr. Douglas resides in New York city, and has one son, Edwin Rust Douglas. In all his career he never sought position, asked for promotion, or solicited votes to elect him to any office whatever.

SWIFT, Lucian, Jr., journalist, was born at Akron, O., July 14, 1848. His father, a leading man in the Western Reserve, emigrated from Connecticut in early life, was a lawyer by profession and served in the courts of Summit county, and represented the people of that locality in the Ohio senate. His grandfather, Judge Zephaniah Swift, was chief justice of Connecticut for nearly twenty years, as well as author of a digest and several standard treatises upon branches of law. The first American ancestor of the family emigrated from England in 1635. At an early age young Swift removed with his family to Cleveland, where he enjoyed excellent educational advantages, and in 1867 was a graduate from the High School. He then entered the University of Michigan, and taking the special course in mining engineering, completed the three years' course of study in two years. His college fraternity was the D. K. E. Returning to Cleveland, Mr. Swift engaged in mercantile business for two years, but finding this uncongenial he, in the spring of 1871, turned his steps toward the West and obtained a position in the land department of the Northern Pacific Railroad, with headquarters at Minneapolis. He held this position until 1877, when he resigned, and soon after became cashier of the Minneapolis Tribune Co., which position he held until the fall of 1885, when he, with three other gentlemen, purchased the Min-

neapolis "Journal," and became manager, secretary, and treasurer, which positions he still holds. Mr. Swift has for many years been a board of trade director, also director and treasurer of the Minneapolis Exposition. In January, 1894, he was elected president of the Business Men's Union. Mr. Swift is also director of the Minneapolis and Commercial Clubs and holds the rank of colonel on the governor's staff. In 1877 Mr. Swift was married to Miss Minnie Fuller, daughter of Rev. George W. Fuller of Litchfield, Minn. Their only surviving child is a daughter, Grace.

RUTAN, Thomas Benton, builder, was born in Newark, N. J., Feb. 10, 1837, son of Henry A. Rutan, whose ancestors came to America from France before the revolutionary war, the name being originally Routin. He removed to Brooklyn in 1845, where he received a liberal education in the public schools. He afterwards became a mason and builder, and was doing a successful business when the war began. He then joined the Federal army; enlisting for three years in Company A, 139th regiment, New York volunteers, in September, 1862. He accompanied his regiment to Washington, thence to Fortress Monroe and Newport News. He participated in the second battle of Fair Oaks, Crump's Cross Roads, and a number of smaller engagements. In June, 1864, his regiment joined the Army of the Potomac, and was attached to the 1st brigade, 3d division, and 24th army corps, and took part in the battle of Cold Harbor and siege of Petersburg. He was subsequently detached as a sharpshooter, and served in that capacity until the close of the war. The brigade with which he was connected was the first to enter Richmond after its capture. He was mustered out as a sergeant, with his regiment, on June 19, 1865, and was finally discharged at Hart's Island on July 1st following. He returned to Brooklyn and resumed his former business, and soon became one of the leading builders and contractors, and some of the finest buildings in the city of Brooklyn were constructed under his supervision. He was appointed superintendent of construction of the Federal Building, now used for the post office and United States court-house, on Apr. 1, 1885, and served in that capacity until January, 1887, when he assumed the duties of city auditor, having been elected to that position at the January election, and was re-elected, and served until January, 1891. On June 18, 1892, he was appointed commissioner of buildings in place of Inspector Platt, deceased. Mr. Rutan is actively engaged in business as a contractor and builder. Among the many contracts placed with him may be mentioned the construction of the following buildings: Fourteenth regiment armory, Mount Prospect water-tower, the Brooklyn City Railroad building on Montague street, St. Augustine's Church, the new National City Bank building, and many other buildings of this character too numerous to mention. One of the most difficult contracts undertaken and successfully accomplished by Mr. Rutan, was the moving of the Thirty-ninth street ferry-house one hundred feet in one direction and thirty in another. Taking into consideration its size and weight and the distance the building had to be moved, and the many serious obstacles encountered, this was a most difficult piece of engineering, so much so, in fact, that many people predicted that it could not be done; however, Mr. Rutan confidently undertook the task, and moved the building, remodeled the same, and made it one of the finest structures of its kind in this country. Mr. Rutan is ex-president of the Master Masons' Association of Kings County. He is a past master of the Cornerstone Lodge, No. 367, F. and

A. M., of Brooklyn, and Constellation Chapter, R. A. M., and Clinton Commandery, No. 14, Knight Templar. He is also a member of Enterprise Lodge, Knights of Honor, and of the Democratic General Committee of Kings County. He is ex-president of the 139th Regiment Veteran Association of New York Volunteers. He was elected commander of Rankin Post, No. 10, G. A. R., in 1884, after having been but eight months a member, and was chairman of the Memorial and Executive Committee, G. A. R., of Kings County, in 1888, and also in 1890. He helped to organize Moses F. Odell Post in 1888, was elected its first commander, and was re-elected in 1889. He is also a member of the Constellation Club, and Cœur de Lion Encampment, Knights of St. John and Malta.

CHENEY, Moses, preacher and reformer, was born in Haverhill, Mass., Dec. 15, 1776, the second son of Nathaniel and Elizabeth Ela Cheney. His father, who fought at Bunker Hill, was a great-grandson of the heroine Hannah Dustin (q.v.), who, instructed by a fellow-captive, scalped nine Indians on Dustin Island, near Concord, N. H., and made her escape in March, 1697. Moses, a feeble child, unable to work out of doors until thirteen years of age, learned to read from his mother. The family library consisted of the Bible, Watts's psalms and hymns, and an English primer, and when he arrived at manhood he read and studied so thoroughly that he could repeat the Bible from beginning to end. At the age of eighteen the feeble boy was greatly

changed, being then a powerful man, six feet and an inch high, and having the strength of a giant. His home was at Sanbornton, N. H., whither his parents removed in 1780. Here, after a little primitive schooling, he learned the joiner's trade at twenty, and four years afterward married Abigail Leavitt, daughter of Moses and Ruth Leavitt, who was born at Exeter, N. H., March 1, 1781, and went to Sanbornton with her parents three years later. The young joiner worked at his trade in summer, and at sleigh-making in winter. Being ambitious to push forward, he overworked; and, in three or four years, his health was broken. Never afterward a laboring man, he turned to books. He paid his way at Gilmanton Academy by teaching singing, and studied medicine at home. He attained sufficient knowledge of medicine to practice it, and was at one time known as Dr. Cheney. But after the loss of his health and of two children, his mind ran continually in religious channels. For a year following his conversion, he was haunted day and night by the text: "Behold, I bring you good tidings of great joy, which shall be to all people." At thirty he began to preach, and never gave up preaching to the end of his life. No man in New England preached, prayed, and sang more hours for a round half-century than "Old Elder Cheney," as he was called after he was forty-five, on account of his hoary head, which, like Jefferson's, was originally red. He preached all over New Hampshire, and much of Massachusetts; a good deal in Chelmsford, Lowell, Beverly, and towns about; in Salem and in Groton, and a whole year in Littleton. He lived and preached a year in Brentwood, N. H.; preached in Portsmouth and Exeter, in Hampton and in Rye. Wherever he went, reformation followed him. In 1824 he removed from Brentwood to Derby, Vt., where he lived for many years. Elder Cheney was one of nature's preachers, magnetic

and irresistible. Tall, broad-chested, with a great head covered by snowy hair, and with blue eyes, and a clear, ringing tenor voice; once seen and heard, he was never forgotten. He was a devoted lover and supporter of music of all sorts, and knew all the psalms and hymns by heart; and in whatever company he sang, whether the music was sacred or secular, his high, pure tenor voice led all the rest. Five of his nine children—four brothers and a sister—constituted "The Cheney Family," so favorably known in concert circles in 1845, and for several years following. In politics he was a Jeffersonian Democrat. In religious faith he was originally a Baptist, but for the last twenty years of his life he was practically free from all sectarianism. A man of singular uprightness of character, of rare gifts, and of most varied and thrilling experiences for one whose lot was so humble, his life was one of exceptional and perpetual influence for good. He died at Sheffield, Vt., Aug. 9, 1850.

CHENEY, Simeon Pease, singer, was born in Meredith, N. H., Apr. 18, 1818, son of Elder Moses and Abigail (Leavitt) Cheney. His distinguishing gift of voice manifested itself in early boyhood. Between the ages of five and ten his singing astonished all that heard him. When a raw country boy he went to Boston, and sang in the old Odeon. Dr. Lowell Mason went to him immediately, and, putting his hand on his shoulder, said: "Sir, you have the best bass voice I have heard in America." Young and untrained as the members of the "Cheney Family" were when they gave their first concert, which took place in New York city in October, 1845, it is evident from the newspaper reports that they impressed experienced listeners with a new and refreshing order of musical talent. To Mr. Cheney's gift of voice was added a commanding, magnetic presence. He might have been distinguished as an orator, as many aver who heard him speak on music, on natural and religious topics, toward the close of his life. Owing to a peculiar distrust of his own abilities, an unfortunate diffidence which followed him through life, he rejected many flattering offers in New York and Boston, and returned to his country haunts and to the humble work of a teacher of singing-classes. To this hard life he held until within a few years of his death. Luckily he inherited the iron constitution of both the Cheneys and the Leavitts, and was so enabled to work on, even beyond the allotted three-score-and-ten. New England is greatly indebted to him, and to his brothers, Moses and Joseph, who, like him, passed from village to village, teaching the people to sing, to love and study and practice music. In June, 1847, Mr. Cheney married Christiana Vance, of Groveland, N. Y., a gentle, prepossessing woman, who had, too, her share of the gift of music. With her he lived in their beautiful home at Dorset, Vt., until her death, in 1860. Some sixteen years later, being a sufferer from nervous prostration, he went to California. It was there he compiled "The American Singing-Book." The author proved by his own compositions, scattered here and there, that his musical talents were not limited to the powers of a singer. But it was not until many years after the publication of "The American Singing-Book" that Mr. Cheney took up a line of musical investigation that causes one to regret perhaps more than before his disinclination to pursue any study with thorough method and patience. When in his sixty-sixth year he was persuaded to employ certain of his unused gifts in taking down the songs of the wild birds singing around him as he worked in the field, or sat in the shade of the lordly trees that gave the name to his home—"Maple Grove." The result was the unique volume, "Wood Notes Wild," the manuscript of which was just completed when sudden illness put an end to his life. The records of this little volume are highly original, a genuine contribution to the study of nature, and to the art and science of music. Of his two sons, John Vance Cheney, librarian of the Newberry Library, Chicago, is better known as a poet, and Albert Baker Cheney is teacher of vocal music at Emerson College of Oratory, Boston. In April, 1888, Mr. Cheney married Mrs. Julia (Clark) Hibbard, and made his home at Franklin, Mass., where he died May 10, 1890.

CHENEY, John Vance, poet, was born at Groveland, N. Y., Dec. 29, 1848, son of Simeon Pease and Christiana (Vance) Cheney. His father was the author of "Wood Notes Wild," and he, two of his brothers and a sister, formed the most gifted family of singers that have appeared before the American public. Elder Moses Cheney, grandfather of John, was an eloquent Baptist preacher, who, during a period of fifty years, preached more sermons, perhaps, than any man of his time in New England. Though John Vance Cheney was born in New York state, the family home was at Dorset, Vt.; and it was there that he obtained his primary education at the district school. Losing his mother when he was yet a child, he was brought up by two women remarkable for sagacity and strength of character — his grandmother, Eve Vance, and his aunt, Janet Vance. Later, he attended Burr and Burton Seminary, at Manchester, Vt., and Temple Hill Academy, at Geneseo, N. Y., graduating from the latter as valedictorian at the age of seventeen. He was soon afterward chosen assistant principal of this institution. He relinquished teaching to study law at Woodstock, Vt., where he remained three years. This was followed by a year's legal instruction in Haverhill, Mass.; after which he was admitted to the Massachusetts bar. He then went to New York city, and being admitted to the bar of that state, at once began practice there. During all these years he had from time to time written considerable verse, some of which, coming to the notice of Dr. J. G. Holland, the editor of the old "Scribner's Magazine," found favor, and appeared in that periodical. From that time Mr. Cheney has produced an extensive amount of poetry, conspicuous for its genuineness, for lightness of touch and grace of expression. Ill health forcing him to give up his legal profession, he made his home on the Pacific coast, where, in 1887, he assumed charge of the San Francisco Free Public Library. In this capacity his success was most gratifying; more progress in cataloguing, and in internal management generally, having been made during his first seven years of service than possibly in any other library in the country during the same period. In 1894 he accepted the position of librarian of the Newberry Library, Chicago, made vacant by the death of Wm. F. Poole. Besides his verse, he is the author of numerous essays on literary subjects, especially on poetry. The essays are characterized by extensive research, candor, and discriminative appreciation. All phases of his art are regarded with a seriousness approaching reverence. His published works, exclusive of magazine contributions, comprise, "Thistle-drift," poems (1887), "Wood-blooms," poems (1888), and "The Golden Guess," essays (1892). He has also edited his father's singularly original papers on bird music—"Wood Notes Wild," Simeon Pease Cheney (1892).

STRONG, Charles Dibble, publisher, was born in Somersetshire, Eng., June 10, 1808, the son of John and Elizabeth Strong. His parents emigrated to America in the spring of 1819, and located in the city of Montreal, Can., where the son was educated and grew to manhood. He served an apprenticeship with H. H. Cunningham, the largest bookbinder and stationer in Montreal, and being employed in its various departments, he had thoroughly mastered the business in 1828, when he removed to Boston. In 1829 Mr. Strong established himself as a bookbinder, and a few months later he opened a bookstore for the sale of religious books principally. This was the first store of that kind in New England. He soon increased his operations by publishing a large number of miscellaneous books. He led in the organization of the Wesleyan Association, which had for its object the establishment of a Methodist paper, to be published in the interests of New England Methodism, and he assisted in the re-establishment of "Zion's Herald," Boston. Mr. Strong became engaged in the specialty of issuing books to be sold by subscription, and was one of the publishers of S. G. Goodrich's "Peter Parley." Mr. Strong was a brilliant writer, and has done very efficient work for Methodism with his pen. In the summer of 1859 he removed to St. Paul, Minn., where he engaged in buying country produce and packing pork—being the first regular pork-packer

in that city. Shortly after, he opened a retail grocery store, which he conducted for two years. In 1860 he purchased a retail hardware store, which proved very lucrative. He afterward founded the extensive hardware store of Strong, Hackett & Co.

Mr. Strong has contributed extensively toward the growth of the city; he was one of the incorporators of the Chamber of Commerce, and was its vice-president for several years. Mr. Strong was married to Frances Wyman Gill in 1828. She died Sept. 19, 1843, leaving him nine children. His second marriage was to Mrs. Abigail Spurr FitzGibbon, and from this union there were five children. He united with the Methodist Episcopal church while a boy, and was always actively engaged in her cause. He was one of the strongest members of the Central Park Church, of St. Paul, and was for years president of its board of trustees, and was one of its most honored members until his death. His strong, generous heart was always ready to help the poor. His kindly nature, and his uniform, generous and sympathetic conduct, added to the purity of his private life, and his honorable record as a citizen and a Christian, have endeared him to all who knew him. He died Jan. 7, 1890.

STRONG, Abigail Spurr, reformer, was born at Annapolis, N. S., Aug. 23, 1811, daughter of Robert and Sarah (Harris) Jefferson, who were prominent Episcopalians, and later became Methodists. Their home was always open to the ministers of the gospel, and the poor and friendless. Her ancestry were quite distinguished, and bore honorable parts in the great events of their time. Henry Evans, who was her great-grandfather on her father's side, took the first squadron from Boston harbor to settle the province of Nova Scotia during the reign of Queen Anne. He named the harbor where he landed "Annapolis Royal," which afterward came to be known simply as "Annapolis." David Baldwin, who was brother of Mrs. Henry Evans (great-grandmother of Mrs. Strong), is said to have been among the first of the revolutionary soldiers who fired upon the British troops in the opening of the struggle for American independence. The only child of Henry and Elizabeth Evans married an English gentleman named Robert Jefferson, and the son of this couple, Robert Jefferson, married Sarah Harris, who was daughter of a celebrated surveyor and civil engineer, named John Harris, whose wife was Abigail Spurr, after whom the subject of this sketch was named. Miss Jefferson inherited the good qualities of her parents. She united with the Methodist church in 1831. She was married Aug. 24, 1835, to John G. FitzGibbon, who was educated for the Episcopal ministry of the Church of England, and was a graduate of Trinity College, Dublin. She and her husband moved to Boston, Mass., where he began to prepare for missionary work, while she identified herself prominently with the various organizations of her denomination. As early as 1820 Mrs. FitzGibbon united with, and became an active worker in, a temperance society, taking with her

into the organization twenty-four young ladies who were her intimate friends and associates. In 1836 they removed to Brooklyn, N. Y., where she continued her religious and reformatory work. She taught a private school near New York city from 1837 to 1843. Mr. FitzGibbon died in 1839, and his widow married, Oct. 29, 1843, Charles Dibble Strong, of Boston, Mass., a prominent and active Methodist, and a publisher of religious works. Mrs. Strong continued active in good works while she remained in Boston. Mr. Strong, on account of failing health, about 1859 determined upon a change of location, and after a visit West, decided upon St. Paul, Minn., as his future home. She joined her husband in August,

1860, in St. Paul, where she immediately identified herself with the old Jackson Street M. E. Church and Sunday-school, of which Rev. Dr. Chaffee was the pastor. Her constant efforts contributed more or less directly to the erection of the Mission Sunday-school, Grace M. E. Church, two German Methodist churches, and two Swedish Reformed Lutheran churches; in all of which work Mrs. Strong was one of the most active and inspiring leaders. She was the founder and first secretary of the "Home for the Friendless." When it was seen that there must be a reformatory department to this work, the "Magdalene Home" (since changed to the "Woman's Christian Home") was organized and placed in operation. This was the

germ of the "Bethany Home," which has become a successful institution. Mrs. Strong materially aided in this work. She was one of the organizers of the "Daughters of Rebecca" in 1865, and has been a member since, and was the first woman to occupy the chair of vice-grand in that organization. From the time of her joining the temperance society in 1829, she continued to be an active worker and identified prominently with the temperance cause and its various organizations—such as Good Templars, of which she was grand worthy vice-templar for Minnesota. Later, she was vice-president of the W. C. T. U. of St. Paul. During all these years she was an effective worker in the Jackson Street M. E. Church, afterward changed to, and now known as, the Central Park Methodist Church, to which she has contributed her time and money without stint. She is an important factor in the Woman's Foreign Missionary Society, and was its president for five years, and in the branch organization she has become a life member, patron, and a manager, always supporting this cause liberally in proportion to her means. Her husband died Jan. 7, 1890, whereupon she retired to her comfortable home, where she is still living.

KIRK, Nettie Madora, was born at Malden, Mass., May 1, 1854, daughter of Charles Dibble and Abigail Spurr Strong. Her father was a prominent Methodist and publisher of religious works, and her mother is a reformer, identified with the leading charitable organizations of St. Paul, Minn., and prominently connected with missionary and other leading societies. When a child, her parents removed to St. Paul, Minn., where she united with the Jackson Street M. E. Church (now Central Park M. E. Church), of which she was a life member. Early in life she evinced great musical talent. She attended public and private schools of St. Paul, and

after leaving school she was instructed by a private tutor. She studied vocal and instrumental music during leisure time, and became very proficient —especially as a singer. She assisted her mother materially in her religious work by rendering the necessary music and instructing the infant class in vocal music. In 1873 she was married to Alvah, son of Henry Kirk, of New York. They had three children, two sons and one daughter. Mrs. Kirk was of generous disposition, uniform and unassuming manners. She gave but little of her time to society, preferring to attend to her home duties with her husband and children. Her charities were widely distributed and greatly appreciated, by reason of the quiet methods employed. She died Feb. 25, 1880.

EATON, Margaret O'Neill, was born about 1796, and was the daughter of William O'Neill, who kept an old-fashioned tavern in Washington, in the early part of this century. It was kept in true southern style, and was a favorite stopping-place for public men of the day, notably Gen. Jackson, who always put up there. Peggy, as she was called, was a bright, lively girl, and the pet of the household from infancy. Under these circumstances she grew up a spoiled beauty, and with manners which did not escape public criticism. In early womanhood she married a man by the name of Timberlake, who was a purser in the navy. He committed suicide while on duty in the Mediterranean, and left his wife with two little children. Malicious tongues accused Senator Eaton of Tennessee, who had long been a boarder at O'Neill's tavern, of undue intimacy with the widow. On speaking to his intimate friend, Gen. Jackson, of his intention to marry her, he was counseled so to do, as a means of disproving the charges, and thus restoring Peg's good name. They were married in January, 1829. When Gen. Jackson was elected president of the United States, he made Senator Eaton secretary of war; and thus began the social war which completely changed the course of political events in the United States during the next half century. Mrs. Eaton now became one of the ladies of the cabinet, and held an important social position. The ladies of Washington, however, influenced by the tales which had been spread about her, refused to call upon her, or to recognize her official position. The first that Gen. Jackson knew of the outbreak of the scandal, was on his receiving a letter from Dr. Ely, a prominent clergyman of Baltimore, who asked the president to refuse her social recognition. This roused Gen. Jackson to the defense of his old friend's daughter, and he replied in letter after letter. He interviewed the purveyors of the scandal, and discussed it in his cabinet. Neither threats nor entreaties prevailed with the ladies; even his niece, Mrs. Donelson, then mistress of the White House, returned home rather than call on Mrs. Eaton. Martin Van Buren, then secretary of state, and an intimate friend of Senator Eaton's, called on Mrs. Eaton, and caused certain bachelor members of the diplomatic corps to do the same. Neither balls nor dinners given by them succeeded in breaking down the opposition of the ladies; and at last, in 1830, neither party yielding, President Jackson, worn out with the fight, sent Mr. Van Buren as minister to England, and later secured his succession to the presidency in 1836, in consequence of his behavior in this matter. He dissolved his cabinet, and thrust Mr. Calhoun into nullification.

Senator Eaton died not long after, leaving his wife very rich. She continued to live in Washington very handsomely and happily with children and grandchildren. Unfortunately she married, in her old age, a young Italian dancing-master, who spent her fortune, and bowed her gray head in poverty and sorrow. She died there Nov. 8, 1879, in her eighty-fourth year.

EDDY, Edward, tragedian, was born in Troy, N. Y., in 1822. He received his first training as an actor as a member of a company of amateurs in his native city. He made his début as a professional in Albany in 1841, and soon after became a member of a company playing in Baltimore. He first appeared in New York as "Othello" at the Richmond Hill Theatre in April, 1846. During the season of 1847–48 he was leading man at the National Theatre in Boston. On March 18, 1851, Mr. Eddy opened at the Bowery Theatre, New York, as "Richelieu." In 1854 he became manager of the Metropolitan Theatre, in 1856 he managed Burton's Theatre, and in the following year assumed the direction of the Old Bowery. Later he managed the Broadway Theatre. The last performance given in the latter play-house occurred on Apr. 12, 1859, and was for the benefit of Mr. Eddy. After abandoning management, he traveled as a star for a number of years. His last appearance was as the "Ragpicker of Paris." Eddy played as wide a range of parts as any actor of his time, but his acting was always wanting in quiet and repose. He was twice married. His first wife, Mary Matthews, an English actress, retired from the stage after their marriage, and died in New Orleans in 1865. His second wife, Henrietta Irving, is still upon the stage. He died on the island of Jamaica on Dec. 16, 1875, and his remains were taken to New York for burial.

GOODWIN, Nathaniel C., comedian, was born in Boston, July 25, 1857. He was educated in the public schools of Boston and intended for a commercial life, but early displayed a fondness for the stage, his clever imitations of leading actors being well remembered by his former schoolmates. He began his professional career by giving imitations of prominent people in drawing-rooms and at small entertainments, his powers as a mimic being droll, unctuous, and mirth-provoking, and it was while thus engaged that he attracted the attention of Stuart Robson, who had just resigned his position as leading comedian at the Globe Theatre, in Boston. Mr. Robson had secured a play entitled "Law in New York," which he induced John B. Stetson to produce at the Howard Athenæum, and young Mr. Goodwin was engaged at a salary of $5 a week, to enact the part of a bootblack and give imitations during the run of the piece. "Law in New York," which proved measurably successful, inaugurated Mr. Robson's brilliant career as a star, and also served to firmly establish Mr. Goodwin in popular favor. The latter, at the close of the engagement, was engaged by Josh Hart to appear at the Eagle Theatre, in New York city, at a weekly salary of $150. The following season he returned to Mr.

Stetson's management at the same salary. Later he appeared as Captain Dietrich, in "Evangeline." This was in 1876, and three years later Mr. Goodwin had entered upon his career as a star, which has continued successfully ever since. He was selected from all the comedians of the country to appear at the Cincinnati Dramatic Festival, 1883, where he essayed the characters of Modus in "The Hunchback," and the grave digger in "Hamlet." In 1890 Mr. Goodwin visited London, where he filled a long engagement and was received with every manifestation of approval, a piece of good fortune quite rare in the case of American actors who invite the endorsement of the English public. During the season of 1890 and '91, Mr. Goodwin was seen at the Bijou Theatre in "The Nominee," a pleasing comedy written for him by Leander Richardson, and in which he achieved one of the most prominent successes of his professional career. From the outset, Mr. Goodwin's advancement in the command of his art has been rapid and unretarded. Commencing as an imitator and mimic, he has gained all the time in finish and certainty of touch, in the refined unctuousness and the capacity for tone pathos, which are the most essential requisites of a great comedian, and in the development of those sympathetic qualities which come with years and contact with the world. His powers are still ripening and maturing, and he is one of the very few among the younger actors of America who can confidently be depended upon to keep fresh the splendid traditions of the elder Jefferson and of Hackett, Blake, and Burton. Among the plays in which he has been seen to advantage on the American stage are: "Hobbies," "Crusts," "Warranted," "Ourselves," "Major Wellington De Boots;" in comic opera: "Mascot," "Pinafore," "Patience," "Big Pony," "Cinderella at School," "Jack Sheppard," "Confusion," "Turned Up," "Bottom's Dream," "The Skating Rink," "Member for Slocum," "Gringoire," "Col. Tom," "Nominee," "A Gilded Fool," "The Bookmaker," "In Mizzourra," "Lend Me Five Shillings," "David Garrick," and "The Gold Mine," most of them written to fit his peculiar talents; and he has also successfully assumed many of the well-known characters of legitimate comedy. Mr. Goodwin has been twice married. His first wife, Eliza Weathersby, an accomplished actress, known and admired of all theatre-goers, died in 1887, and in 1890 he was married to Nella Baker of Buffalo. His professional earnings are large and he has a pleasant home in New York city and a delightful summer place at Ocean Spray, near Boston.

NEWMAN, John Philip, M. E. bishop, was born in New York city, Sept. 1, 1826. He completed his education at Cazenovia (N. Y.) Seminary, and after taking a course in theology entered the ministry of the Methodist Episcopal church in 1849. He filled various pastorates until 1860, when he went abroad, studied at the universities and visited different parts of Europe, Syria, and Egypt. Upon his return he filled pastorates in Hamilton, Albany, and New York city, and in 1864 was sent to the South, where, during five years of earnest and successful missionary labor, he established three conferences, two colleges, and a church journal. In 1869 he returned to the North, and until 1874 was chaplain of the U. S. senate. During this period he organized the Metropolitan Memorial Methodist Church in Washington and became its pastor. In 1874 he was appointed inspector of U. S. consuls in Asia, and while there employed, revisited Palestine. In 1876 he was again appointed pastor of the Metropolitan Church, Washington, and in 1879 was transferred to the Central Church, New York city. In 1882 he accepted a unanimous call to the pastorate of the Madison Avenue Congregational Church, New York city, but resigned in 1884 and was the spiritual adviser of Gen. U. S. Grant during the long illness that terminated in the latter's death. In 1885 Dr. Newman was a third time assigned to the pastorate of the Metropolitan Church, Washington, serving until 1887. In 1888 he was elected and consecrated a bishop of his church. In 1876 he was a member of the commission that re-established fraternal relations between the Methodist Episcopal church, North, and the Methodist Episcopal church, South. In 1881 he was a delegate to the Methodist Ecumenical Conference, held in London, and has sat on three of the general conferences of his church. He has frequently appeared on the lecture platform; delivered orations at the funerals of Gens. Grant and Logan; and ranks among the most eloquent pulpit orators of his time. Dr. Newman is the author of: "From Dan to Beersheba" (1864); "Babylon and Nineveh" (1875); "Christianity Triumphant" (1884); "Evenings with the Prophets on the Lost Empires," and "America for Americans" (1887). Rochester (N. Y.) University gave him the degree of D. D. in 1863; and Otterbein University, Westerville, O., and Grant Memorial University gave him that of LL. D. in 1881.

RUFFIN, Thomas, jurist, was born in King and Queen county, Va., Nov. 17, 1787, the eldest son of Sterling and Alice Ruffin. His early education was gained from a private tutor engaged in the family of his father, who fitted him for college. He entered Princeton at the age of fifteen, and was graduated in 1805. He entered the law office of David Robinson, an eminent lawyer of Petersburg, Va., at the same time with Winfield Scott. Two years later he removed with his father to North Carolina, and settled at Hillsboro', where he engaged in the practice of his profession. He served in the legislature in the years 1813, 1815, and 1816. He was chosen speaker in 1816, and in the same year was elected judge of the superior court, in which capacity he served two years, when he resigned. In 1825 he was again elected judge, serving for four years, when he was chosen one of the justices of the supreme court, serving until 1852, when he resigned. He was again elected in 1858, permanently retiring from the supreme bench in 1858, but served his fellow-citizens as presiding judge of the county court until the outbreak of the war in 1861. He had already opposed the nullification doctrine in 1832, and not only did not believe in the rights of secession, but combated the heresy declaring the sacred right of revolution the only remedy for the redress of the grievances of the South. He was elected to the state convention at Raleigh, which took action on the ordinance of secession, and, feeling it to be a duty to follow the fortunes of his state, voted for the ordinance, which was his last public service. In his office of justice of the supreme court for twenty years, and for many years its chief justice, Judge Ruffin's opinions established his reputation as one of the first jurists of the age. In person he was spare; uniform and neat in his dress; of striking presence, commanding and venerable. He resembled Thomas Jefferson, both in person and mental qualifications. The degree of LL. D. was conferred upon him in 1834 by the University of North Carolina. He died at Hillsboro', N. C., Jan. 15, 1870.

STEVENS, Robert Livingston, builder of the first ironclad, was born in Hoboken, N. J., Oct. 18, 1787. He was the son of John Stevens, the eminent engineer, and at the age of seventeen became his father's assistant. In 1815 he built the Philadelphia, a steamboat with a speed of eight miles, the fastest then known, and during the following seventeen years, by successive improvements, increased the speed of steamboats to fifteen miles an hour. He designed the ferry-boats and ferry-slips now in general use, made numerous improvements in the steam engine, as applied to navigation, and invented the gallows frame, the split waterwheel, and the balance valve. He was the first to use anthracite coal on steamboats, and in 1831 built the first marine  tubular boiler. In 1830 he visited England, and while there had made, from his own designs, the rails for the railway which, with his brother Edwin, he was building in New Jersey. He also brought with him, upon his return to the United States, the locomotive "John Bull," built by the Stevensons, which has been the type from which all subsequent improvements in the United States have been made. During the war of 1812 Mr. Stevens became interested in the subject of ordnance, and after repeated experiments perfected a percussion shell which proved successful when favorably tested and which was at once purchased by the government. Between 1814 and 1841 he made a thorough study of the use of iron-plating in the construction of war vessels and having successfully demonstrated that a four-inch-iron-plating would resist a sixty-four pound shot at thirty yards, he was, in 1842, given a contract by the government to build an iron clad steam-vessel. The rapid advances made in the construction of heavy ordnance necessitated frequent changes in the designs for the vessel, and as a consequence it was never completed, although work upon it was continued for a long period. It was, however, the first iron-clad vessel ever projected. Mr. Stevens died in Hoboken, N. J., Apr. 20, 1856.

ASBURY, Francis, Methodist Episcopal bishop, was born near Hemstead Bridge, in Staffordshire, a short distance from Birmingham, Eng., Aug. 20, 1745. His father, Joseph, and his mother, Elizabeth, are described as "amiable and respectable persons" of the middle class of population. Their religious affiliations are asserted by some to have been with the English Methodists at an early date, but this was not established. His father being in comfortable circumstances, Francis was placed at a tender age in the school of one Arthur Taylor, at Sneal's Green, in the vicinity of Barre, where the family had removed. At this school the teacher was savage in the extreme in dealing with his pupils, which resulted in young Asbury's removal from this institution to another part of the parish, and placed in one of the wealthy and fashionable families of the neighborhood. This has been spoken of by his biographer as a much sorer trial of his faith than any through which he had passed. Under this influence, to use his own language, ne "became somewhat vain," having naturally a light and joyous disposition, but "did not become openly wicked." Returning to the paternal roof in a few months, at the age of fourteen years he was indentured to a maker of "buckle chapes," or tongues, and labored with him diligently. A kind family, of which he became an inmate, now led him to recommence prayer, morning and evening. At Brownwich Church, too, he listened to the preaching of Ryland, Stillingfleit, Talboot, Hawes, and others, some of whom were among the most distinguished ministers and ornaments of the English pulpit. He read Whitfield's sermons, but up to this time his biographer (Strickland) asserts that he had not heard of the Methodists, although John and Charles Wesley had their movement well in hand. In reply to his inquiries concerning them, his pious mother directed him to a person who could give him the information he sought about them, and he accompanied that person to a neighboring town, to listen to their services. These he was surprised to find were not held in a church, but Asbury says, "it was better than a church; the people were so devout, men and women kneeling, and all saying Amen." He attended these meetings several times, making rapid progress in spiritual life. Forthwith he commenced leading religious services in the house of a friend, which were largely attended; but from fears of opposition and outbreak, were soon transferred to his father's dwelling. Here with fervency and power he exhorted those who were present to come and be saved from their sins. He identified himself with the Wesleyans, shortly taking license from them as a local preacher, and in the Methodist chapel he held forth the word of life to "wondering, weeping thousands." This was at the age of seventeen, and this local relation was sustained for several years, although in fact he was a traveling preacher. He also preached during the week three or four and often five times, far and near, until the age of twenty-one, when he was received into the Wesleyan conference, and appointed to labor on a circuit, according to the Wesleyan form. Having traveled circuits for five years, he was present at a conference at Bristol, Eng., Aug. 7, 1771, when Rev. John Wesley called for volunteers for religious labor in America, where at that time there were only three preachers. Asbury had been prayerfully considering this matter for a season, and "conferred not with flesh and blood," but immediately accepted the call. From that moment his heart was in the American colonies. Breaking the matter to his parents, and receiving their approbation, he embarked at Bristol, Sept. 4, 1771, for America, reaching Philadelphia, Pa., Oct. 27th, accompanied by Richard Knight, a young man in the Methodist connection, who had volunteered for the service in America. It was but five years since Methodism had been introduced into the North American colonies by the labors of Embury, Webb, and Strawbridge. The John Street Methodist Episcopal Church edifice in New York, the first of that order in America, had been dedicated by Embury, Oct. 30, 1768. At once Asbury began preaching in Philadelphia, passing from thence in a few days to Burlington, N. J., and thence to New York city. Here he met Boardman, the Methodist clergyman, in whose pulpit his first sermon in that city was preached on Tuesday, Nov. 13, 1771. Then he discoursed at Westchester, New Rochelle, Rye, East Chester, and Mamaroneck, N. Y., initiating the first regular circuit work in America. He says in his journal: "My brethren seem unwilling to leave the cities, but I will show them the way. I have nothing to seek but the glory of God, nothing to fear but his displeasure. I have come to this country with an upright intention, and through the grace of God I will make it appear. I am determined that no man shall bias me with soft words and fair speeches; nor will I ever fear the face of man, or know any man after the flesh, but whomsoever I please or displease, I will be faithful to God, to the people, and to my own soul." When the preachers met in Philadelphia to arrange work for the year 1772, of the few assignments (determined on by themselves), Asbury was sent there. Large congregations attended his ministry, but he did not limit himself to preaching in the city. Faithful to his purpose, in the development of the circuit system, he preached at Bohemia, Chester, and other places in Pennsylvania, also at Burlington, N. J., Wilmington, Del., Greenwich, Freeston, Gloucester, and other points. Within four months

he was summoned to New York, to aid in adjusting difficulties, and while there, in pursuance of his cherished intention, extended his labors to Staten Island, Kingsbridge, and elsewhere. Oct. 10, 1772, he received a letter from John Wesley, appointing him superintendent of the Methodist Societies in America. A call was now made upon him to spend the winter in Maryland, which he did, and to an officious rector of the Episcopal church, who came to one of his appointments demanding by what authority he preached, calmly responded by telling him who he was. In the dialogue which ensued the rector became enraged. Asbury steadily asserted his authority from God, and proceeded to preach, with the rector for a hearer. Quarterly conferences of preachers were now established by Supt. Asbury, who was stationed at Baltimore, Md. Neither did he here limit himself to ministrations in the city. Visiting New York in March, 1773, he attended the Episcopal church, for the purpose of taking the sacrament, in accordance with instructions from Wesley. In 1773 he met at Philadelphia, Thomas Rankin, an older Methodist preacher from England, who, by Wesley's appointment, superseded him as superintendent. He appears to have greeted Rankin in a sufficiently Christian spirit, but it was soon evident that the ideas of the latter did not comport with the practices of the American authorities. Singularly enough, Rankin objected to revivals of religion and creeds, while Asbury defended them. And these began to prevail in Virginia and in Maryland in connection with his own and with labors carried on by other Methodists. Five or six new circuits were now formed in Virginia. At the second annual preachers' conference, May 25, 1774, Asbury was located at New York; in 1775 at Norfolk, Va.; in May, 1776, he was too ill to attend, but was appointed to Baltimore as preacher for the year. At the conference in May, 1777, twenty out of the twenty-seven Methodist preachers in the colonies being in attendance, it was plain to these preachers that the lines had become clearly drawn between the colonists and the mother country, and some of the Englishmen being ill at ease, began to make arrangements for returning to their country. By this time, moreover, the Methodist laity were widely asking for the administration of the ordinances in their own religious assemblies. During the year 1777, Asbury was required to take an oath of allegiance to the state of Maryland, but could not conscientiously do so, because of its special form, although his sympathies were with the patriot cause. In March, 1778, because of this, he was obliged to leave the state, and he went to Delaware, where no such oath was exacted, finding refuge in the house of Judge Thomas White of Kent county. In April, 1779, he had a conference in his place of exile; Delaware was made a circuit, and he was appointed in charge of it. With his headquarters at

Judge White's, he faithfully performed the duties of his station. March 1, 1780, he attended a conference at Baltimore, as a citizen of Delaware, and under the protection of its governor. The southern Methodist preachers at this juncture organized a conference of their own, greatly to Asbury's annoyance, appointing a committee of their number to ordain the preachers and other members of conference, who should go forth and administer the ordinances among the people. In 1780, at the northern conference, he accordingly procured the appointment of a committee to visit the next southern conference and propose a suspension of all proceedings about ordinances for the current year. At the next year's conference (at Baltimore) the action of the southern brethren in 1780, as to ordinances, was rescinded, with but one southern vote in its favor. Asbury now laid before Wesley, in England, by letter, the exact condition of the Methodist people in America. When traveling through a wild region, that he might go over the bounds of his whole work, he found repose in the cabin of a friendly settler, his resting-place the top of a chest, his clothes his only covering. This was a mere sample of what now and afterwards made up his experience upon his constant journeys. Indeed, this fare was better than he frequently had. Often, to the end of his life, he slept upon the ground, or on rocks or on boards in deserted cabins, with nothing to eat. At the yearly conference of 1782 his appointment by Wesley as general superintendent of the Methodist church in America was unanimously confirmed. At the conference of 1784, held at Baltimore, eighty-two preachers were reported in the United States, and 13,740 members. Asbury was attacked by fever on his succeeding tour, and "suffered much, but still rode on, preaching the next day," one of the few men in ecclesiastical history who almost invariably allowed no personal, physical illness to interfere with the ordinary round of duty. By this time (November, 1784) Dr. Thomas Coke and Richard Whatcoat had been sent out to America by Wesley. Wesley had in Coke's case crossed the Rubicon in the matter of taking up authority, for he had consecrated him as a superintendent of the Methodist Episcopal church in America, and given to him letters of ordination under his hand and seal, accompanied by another, in which he appointed Thomas Coke and Francis Asbury joint superintendents of that body of believers. The revolutionary war having ended, the question of establishing a church independent of any foreign supervision whatever was naturally in order, and a general conference of the Methodists in America was called at Baltimore, Md., for Dec. 25, 1784. Their first act was to organize the Methodist societies of the country into the Methodist Episcopal church in the United States. The next to declare the office of bishop elective, after which a unanimous vote was cast in favor of Dr. Thomas Coke and Francis Asbury as the choice of the church. The latter was first ordained deacon, and then an elder, and then Dr. Coke, assisted by several elders, set him apart, by the imposition of hands, as bishop of the Methodist Episcopal church. But this ordination, although it gave Asbury, a new title, by no means increased his power or usefulness. In the entries in his journals he had previously given a simple statement of has preaching, associated with the exercise of his mind and the incidents of his travel. Now he records his acts in administering the sacraments. As a part of his experience he adds: "I am sometimes afraid of being led to think something more of myself in my new station than formerly," but it is doubtful if his fears were well grounded. In his journal he records many incidents of long, fatiguing rides over rough roads, crossing rivers and rugged mountains, sleeping in comfortless quarters (frequently three in a bed), and with half fare. In the first year of his bishopric he attended three conferences. New circuits were added—two in North Carolina, one in New Jersey, and another in Kentucky. Revivals prevailed in Maryland and in other parts of the country, the membership rose to 20,684, the traveling preachers to 117. In 1785 he brought forward at conference the desirability of founding a Methodist school, but Dr. Coke preferred the founding of a college, and secured the adoption of his views. Asbury did not withhold his co-operation, but, in company with his colleague, raised $5,000, and a corner-stone for Cokesbury College, named in honor of its founders, was laid at Abington, twenty-five miles from Baltimore, on June 5th, of that year, Asbury preaching the sermon, as he did in December, 1787, when the college was opened for students. This institution was in existence here for about ten years, and was then transferred to Baltimore, in consequence of the destruction of its building by fire. Asbury's devotion to its interests was intense. All its financial business fell upon his shoulders, while his annual salary as bishop was but $64 per year, and traveling expenses. Often his clothes were worn threadbare; he was shabby in appearance, and obliged to deprive himself of some of the comforts of life. But uncomplainingly, unless in behalf of his poor preachers, he went on his way, living not for himself, but consecrating all to God and the church. In 1787 the first Methodist ordination in the great valley of the Mississippi took place. About this time Asbury set himself to the management of the "Methodist Discipline," which had been first printed at Philadelphia in 1785. The second edition omitted stringent promises against the use of spirituous liquors by ministers and traveling preachers, and against the extirpation of slavery among the members of the Methodist Episcopal church. This revision was studious and elaborate, embracing Biblical research and logical acumen, and by it Asbury's mind was stamped upon the genius and institutions of American Methodists as effectually as was that of Wesley upon Methodism in England. The journey in 1788, on his tour to Georgia across the mountains to North Carolina, affords another glance at his perils by travel: "We were spoken to on the mountain on our way by most awful thunder and lightning, and accompanied by heavy rain. We crept for shelter into a little dirty house where the filth might have been taken from the floor with a spade. We felt the want of fire, but could get little wood to make it, and what we did get was wet. Coming to the river the next day, we hired a young man to swim over for the canoe, in which we crossed, while our horses swam to the other shore. We were compelled to travel an old road over the mountains. Night came on; I was ready to faint with a violent headache; the mountain was so steep on both sides, I prayed to the Lord for help. Presently a profuse sweat broke out upon me, and my fever entirely subsided. This," adds the bishop, "had been an awful journey to me, and this a tiresome day; and now, after riding seventy-five miles, I have thirty-five more to travel before I can rest a day." After this journey he grieved considerably, on reviewing it, that he was not able to pray more on the road. All the journeys were performed on horseback, or other primitive conveyances. At the next conference, at Petersburg, Va., to conciliate preachers who were disaffected with his exercise of Episcopal prerogatives, he addressed them a letter, saying: "I will take my seat in council as another member, and in that point, at least, waive the claims of Episcopacy; yea, I will lie down and be trodden upon rather than injure one soul." He was charged, more or less directly, with misappropriations of money. He replied by the most explicit exhibit of his doings, showing that he had never received a penny of the funds concerning which the

insinuations had been made, and the official who furnished the exhibit declared, "I think I never knew so disinterested a man as Mr. Asbury." Such was the pioneer bishop of American Methodism, such his labors up to 1790. Precisely such in kind, and almost in extent, did they continue to be, as he fulfilled his bishopric, unhasting, yet unresting, until he died. Besides the labors that have been enumerated, he laid the foundations of the Methodist Episcopal Book Concern; founded Methodist missions to the frontier settlements of the country; was the first man, it is claimed, on the American continent to introduce to it the Sunday-school system in the Methodist Episcopal discipline; revered, and was the personal friend of Washington; threw a steady and prevailing influence for the patriot cause in the struggle of the American revolution. Indeed, it has been said that the civil history of the United States might have been very different had Asbury failed to be on the ground to assume his office at the time he took it. When he passed away he left his denomination in the country 214,000 strong, controlled by bishops, with 2,000 preachers and itinerants. He died at the home of his friend, George Arnold, twenty miles south of Fredericksburg, Va., March 31, 1816, on his way to a general conference of the church at Baltimore, Md., literally worn out in the service of the great organization he had built up by consecrating to it all he had of life and energy. He was buried in Mr. Arnold's family burying-ground, but by request of the people of Baltimore, his remains were subsequently removed, and were deposited in a vault in the Eutaw Methodist Episcopal Church in that city, immediately beneath the pulpit. His journals (3 vols.) were published in New York in 1852.

SHAROOD, Charles K., manufacturer, was born in Livingston county, Mich., Oct. 10, 1849, son of William K. and Mary Sharood. His father was a blacksmith in moderate circumstances, and emigrated from England in 1848, locating in Livingston county. Mr. Sharood's maternal grandfather performed a distinguished part in the war of 1812, and his paternal grandfather was a prominent English divine. From his seventh to his fourteenth year he attended the district schools of his native county, and subsequently pursued his studies privately at such odd times as he could spare. In 1863 he entered the employ of his uncle, a shoe manufacturer, and two years later removed to Buffalo, N. Y., where he secured a situation in a wholesale shoe factory. From 1867–71 he was employed in various manufactories in New York state and thoroughly learned all branches of the shoe business. Owing to failing health he left his trade, and worked for an elevator dealer in Chicago for one year, and thence removed to Detroit, Mich., where he was employed first by

Robinson & Burkingshow, and then for nine years by Pingree & Smith, being promoted from time to time until he was made foreman of the concern. In the spring of 1882 Mr. Sharood entered into partnership with S. S. Crooks in Detroit, and they removed to St. Paul, Minn., bringing with them 110 operatives, and there organized the Minnesota Shoe Co. This was the first factory in the state that manufactured fine shoes. His thorough knowledge of the business and untiring energy so increased the demand for fine shoes that in 1883 he consolidated with C. Gotzion & Co., in order to carry on the business on a larger scale. The trade kept increasing until it reached the annual output of $800,000. In 1892 he sold out his interest, and formed the firm of Sharood & Crooks, and put at work over 400 men. Mr. Sharood is a member of the St. Paul Commercial Club, and a prominent Mason, being connected with nearly all the leading Masonic organizations of the city. He is a liberal contributor to charitable objects, and a public-spirited citizen ready to help the advancement of municipal reforms. He was married Sept. 23, 1875, to Alice, daughter of Norman Stafford, of Michigan.

HARRISON, Thomas Asbury, banker, was born near Belleville, Ill., Dec. 18, 1811, son of Thomas and Margaret Harrison. His father was a presiding elder in the Methodist Episcopal church, and for many years preached twice a week. Slavery was extremely repugnant to Mrs. Harrison, and though born and reared in a family of slave-holders, she persuaded her husband to leave their home and friends in the South and go North, so in 1809 the family removed to Illinois. The father first engaged in farming and later in milling, with successful results. Young Harrison's early education was meagre, being chiefly attained at a private school at Belleville. After leaving school he engaged for a time as a clerk in a store, but upon reaching his majority he went into the milling business with his father and brothers, and built the first Harrison mill in Illinois. This was mainly accomplished by means of borrowed money, and but a short time after the mill was finished, and while full of wheat and flour, it was consumed by fire, entailing an almost total loss, as there was not a dollar's worth of insurance on either the mill or its contents. The mill was at once rebuilt, Mr. Harrison working as a day laborer in order to save one man's wages. For some years the mills were run at but little above living expenses, and for a time at a positive loss, but the extra quality of the production, and the out-breaking of the Crimean war eventually changed the state of affairs, and the foundation of the Harrison fortune was laid. The firm pros-

pered for a number of years, and only sold out at a time when, in Mr. Harrison's judgment, the business was beginning to wane. That he was right in this opinion was confirmed by the ill fortune of his successor, whose failure may be partly accounted for, however, from the fact that he was compelled to hire four men to do the work that Mr. Harrison had accomplished alone. In 1860 Mr. Harrison took a

permanent residence in Minneapolis, Minn., where his brother had established himself some years previously. One of Mr. Harrison's first enterprises in Minneapolis was the buying of a piece of neighboring ground solely on account of a fence which obstructed his view, and which the owner persisted in maintaining. The deal proved to be most advantageous, however, for the subsequent rise in the value of that property alone gave him an independent fortune. His first investment of importance in Minnesota was in the First National Bank of St. Paul. Later he became a heavy stockholder in, and a director of, both the Chicago, Milwaukee, and St. Paul, and the St. Paul, Minneapolis, and Omaha railroads. In 1862 he and his brothers built Harrison Hall, the first substantial modern structure in Minneapolis, and the beginning of the era of substantial building in that city. In 1863 he and his brothers, H. G. and W. M. Harrison, entered into partnership with Joseph Dean, under the firm name of Joseph Dean & Co., which for many years was the largest and most important lumber firm in that city. Under their man-

agement the Atlantic and Pacific mills were built. When the civil war broke out, Mr. Harrison turned over thousands of dollars to the government, at first without so much as a scrap of paper to show for it. Mr. Harrison unfortunately became connected, through a money loan to a friend, with the State National Bank, of which he subsequently assumed the presidency, in the hope of putting its affairs in order, and when it failed he paid its liabilities out of his own pocket, though he was under no obligation to do so. He then organized the Security Bank, of which he was made president, and which under his careful management soon achieved prosperity, being to-day one of the strongest financial institutions in Minneapolis, a circumstance due in no small degree to Mr. Harrison's watchful care and the confidence in which he is held by the people. He continued as president of this bank until his death. In the year 1839, at Belleville, Ill., Mr. Harrison was united in marriage to Rebecca Greene, an educated and highly accomplished woman, who died Feb. 14, 1884, leaving five children, two sons and three daughters, of whom W. W. Harrison, Mrs. S. H. Knight, and Mrs. Dr. E. B. Zier are now living. Mr. Harrison was one to whom others would look for guidance and direction. Of a most generous disposition, he neglected no public enterprises, and was liberal to those who applied to him for aid. He was a life-long member of the Methodist church, and a generous friend of all churches and schools. For Hamline University his affection was deep and abiding, and many struggling students were through him enabled to obtain an education. He was a man of

Thomas A Harrison

unflinching integrity in all relations of life, sound judgment, and indomitable will, while in his judgment of men he was well nigh infallible. He died of malarial fever, Oct. 27, 1887.

POTTIER, Auguste, decorator and designer, was born at Coulommiers, in the department of the Seine-Marne, France, in 1823. He was apprenticed in Paris at the age of fourteen to a sculptor on wood, and after serving his time perfected himself further by every available means, when in 1847, he received a proposition to go to America. He came to New York and became connected with E. H. Hutchings & Son. In 1853 he formed an alliance with Gustave Herter under the firm name of Herter, Pottier & Co., and eventually established himself permanently in partnership with William P. Stymus, whose acquaintance he had made while they were both employees of Rochefort, the well-known cabinet-maker of that day. Pottier & Stymus opened their first workshop and salesroom upon the slender capital of $1,800, in 1859. They were the first to apply gilt as an ornament in place of charges and of bronze mouldings, and to introduce furniture inlaid with ivory and mother-of-pearl. In 1864 they removed to larger workshops, increasing the size of their salesroom on Broadway and in 1871 they became established in the large factory on Lexington avenue, between Forty-first and Forty-second streets, with which their best work was afterwards identified. Here were to be found departments of every kind organized on a scale commensurate with their importance. Mr. Pottier and his partner recognized the fact that the design of ornaments for use should be adapted, not imitated, from nature or from accepted types of good historic ornament. Hence the epoch of the Centennial, by the freedom it gave the decorator to present a new system to the public, was the special opportunity for that firm. The most notable feature of their furniture exhibit at the Centennial was a bedstead and bed of the period of Louis XVI. which cost $12,000 to manufacture. The bedstead was of amaranth wood, inlaid with American carved walnut. The entire piece of furniture was made up of innumerable carvings representing arabesques, flowers, and birds. An elaborately and beautifully carved walnut cabinet of the Renaissance period formed part of the same exhibit, which was afterwards presented by Mr. Pottier to the Metropolitan Museum of Art. In 1882 Pottier & Stymus opened warerooms at 485, 487 and 489 Fifth avenue, between Forty-first and Forty-second streets. After their factory on Lexington avenue was burned down in 1888, they built a new one immediately on the same site. Thus, from a very modest beginning, Mr. Pottier raised his business to the first rank by the same admirable courage and endurance with which he had met certain early discouragements, and to attain as a reward that position which he has shared with the houses of Marcotte, Herter Brothers, Cottier, and those other remaining few pioneers in the field of decoration whose labors are identified with the early history of the city.

Gustave Herter

HERTER, Gustave, decorator, designer, and founder of "Herter Brothers," was born in Stuttgart, Germany, in 1830, son of Christian Herter, a cabinet-maker and wood carver of note. After receiving a practical preparatory education, the son was employed for nearly two years by the eminent architect Leins, who built "The Villa," the palace at Berg for Queen Olga, young Herter designing the woodwork for it. Gustave Herter came to New York in 1848, and attracted the attention of Edward W. Hutchings, a leading cabinet-maker, through whom he formed business connections which led to his permanent establishment. Auguste Pottier became associated with him, under the firm name of Herter, Pottier & Co., the partnership continuing up to 1858. They were among the first to abandon cabinet-making proper, to give their exclusive attention to the larger province of decoration. In 1857 Mr. Herter organized the firm of "Gustave Herter," which he changed in 1865 to that of " Herter Brothers," upon the admission to partnership of his brother, Christian, who, as early as 1855, had been studying in Paris, where he had developed artistic abilities of great promise. In 1863 Mr. Herter married Anna F., daughter of William Frederick Schmidt, a shipping merchant, and a grand-niece of Robert Morris, of revolutionary fame. They have four sons. Mr. Herter executed contracts for architectural wood work, furniture, and decorations for many of the notable banks, office buildings, insurance companies, churches, and private residences erected in New York between 1855 and 1864. These early years were distinguished by marked changes in the world of decorative art, which paved the way for the improvements executed while the two brothers were partners. The purely architectural part of their interior work, including staircases, doors, and mantels, were made from rosewood many years before it became the fashion to have the entire interior of hardwood. The first interior made entirely of hardwood by " Herter Brothers " was that of the house of Henry Probasco, of Cincinnati, O., in 1865. The rosewood mania manifested itself in the rosewood staircase in the house of Robert L. Stuart, of New York. Color, however, became the feature of the Herter school of decoration, and in connection with hardwood floors, tufted ceilings, high wainscotings, came in favor as early as 1865; the change indicated was an innovation, the average taste being content with less impressive effects. Upon his retirement in 1870, Mr. Herter went abroad, where, with the exception of certain intervals, he resided until 1892, when he returned to New York, to make it his permanent residence. The standard he set up has been exceeded by none which has followed it, and equaled only by that introduced by his brother Christian, in whose achievements he witnessed the expression of those talents which, in extending the fame of both, were always a source of personal pride and pleasure to Gustave.

HERTER, Christian, artist, decorator, and designer. (See Vol. V., p. 320.)

OATES, Alice, actress and singer, was born in Nashville, Tenn., Sept. 22, 1849. She received her education at a Catholic school in Nazareth, Ky., and also had a careful musical training under competent instructors, in Louisville and New Orleans. In 1865 she became the wife of James A. Oates, an actor. Her début was made at the Theatre Comique in Cincinnati under her husband's management, and the following season she traveled through the West at the head of a concert company. Later she became the leader of a company that produced " Undine" and ' The White Fawn." At the Chicago Opera House on Feb. 9, 1869, she scored a success as Darnley in "The Field of the Cloth of Gold." After this she organized a company of her own, with which she traveled through the West, and then made her Metropolitan début at the Olympic Theatre, Chicago, on July 16, 1869, in "The Fair One With the Golden Wig." In August following she was seen at the same theatre in "The Daughter of the Regiment." Mr. Oates died in July, 1871, and in November, 1872, the widow married Tracy Titus, her business manager. She was divorced from Titus in 1875, and in May, 1879, she married Harry P. Watkins. From 1871 until 1886, she traveled almost continuously, appearing in comic opera and burlesque. Her talents as an actress were not of the first order, but she used them with grace and cleverness and was always received with favor. She died of softening of the brain, in Philadelphia, Jan. 10, 1887.

KIMBALL, Nathan, soldier, was born in Fredericksburg, Ind., Nov. 22, 1822, son of Nathaniel Kimball, and grandson of Nathan Kimball of Massachusetts. He served as captain in the war with Mexico. He was commissioned captain in the Indiana volunteers by Gov. Merton at the outbreak of the civil war, and later was made colonel of the 14th Indiana infantry. He fought at Cheat Mountain, and Greenbrier in 1861; was put in command of a brigade at Winchester, and commissioned brigadier-general Apr. 15, 1862, for the victory gained over "Stonewall" Jackson at Kearnstown, March 23d. At Antietam his brigade, the 1st of the 3rd division of the 2d corps, lost nearly 600 men, but stubbornly held its ground. At the battle of Fredericksburg he was severely wounded. On his recovery he was sent to Vicksburg, Miss., in command of the 3rd division 16th corps, up Yazoo river, where, on June 4, 1863, he had an engagement near Satartia, driving the enemy beyond Black river,

after which he remained in position at Haines Bluff until after the surrender of Vicksburg to Grant. In August, 1863, he was ordered with his division to Arkansas, where he remained until May 3, 1864, then ordered to join the army of the Cumberland, which he did on May 23, 1864, in command 1st brigade, 2nd division, 4th army corps. He engaged in the battles of the Dallas and New Hope Church, Georgia, and of Kenesaw Mountain, June 27, 1864; after Peach Tree Creek, July 20th, he was for gallantry in that engagement promoted by Gen. Thomas to the command of the 1st Division, 4th Army Corps, and took part in all engagements around Atlanta and battles of Jonesboro' and Lovejoy station, resulting in the surrender of the Confederate army, and in the capture of Atlanta. After the capture of Atlanta he was taken from field service to Indiana to aid in the suppression of the "Knights of the Golden Circle." His services in this duty resulted in the stamping-out of the organization in Indiana. He commanded the 1st division, 4th corps, army of the Cumberland at Franklin, Nov. 30th, and at Nashville Dec. 15, and 16, 1864. He was brevetted major-general Feb 1, 1865, and was mustered out of the service the following Aug. 24, 1865. In 1870–71 he was elected treasurer of Indiana, serving two terms, and was also a member of the legislature. In 1866 he took part in the organization of the G. A. R. of Indiana, and Nov. 22nd was its state commander. In 1873 he was appointed surveyor general of Utah Territory by Pres. Grant. He removed from Indianapolis to Salt Lake City, where he took an active part in the organization of the G. A. R. there, and became commander of the Utah department in 1888.

McALPIN, David Hunter, tobacconist, was born in Pleasant Valley, Dutchess co., N. Y., Nov. 8, 1816, and came to New York city, like many another, without means. His father was James McAlpin, who was one of the participants in the rebellion of 1798, and came to this country from Belfast, Ireland, in the early part of the century. The son speedily found employment with Mr. Hughes, a brother-in-law, and the proprietor of a cigar store on Catherine street, which was then the most fashionable business street in New York, where business property was actually more valuable than in any other part of the city. Buying out Mr. Hughes, Mr. McAlpin became associated with John Cornish, who was a manufacturer of tobacco in Avenue D. Through the energy, activity, and business sagacity of Mr. McAlpin, who had become the junior partner in the firm, Mr. Cornish soon acquired the small competency to which he aspired, and was willing to retire. Mr. McAlpin bought out his interest, and became the sole proprietor of the business. He was the first to introduce into the New York market the best Virginia tobacco. His originality is best shown by the name which he gave to this tobacco, a name which gave him an established position among the great tobacco manufacturers of the country: the "Virgin Leaf." His business prospered so greatly that in 1868 he purchased two entire blocks on Avenue D, near Tenth street, and built large buildings, which he filled with the most recent machinery. Mr. McAlpin has been married three times. His first wife, Frances Adeline Rose, bore him ten children; his second wife was Mrs. A. D. Chamberlain; and his third wife is a sister of the first Mrs. McAlpin. The manufacturing business of D. H. McAlpin & Co. has grown to such enormous proportions that it may be justly said that Mr. McAlpin has personally been one of the largest contributors to the prosperity of the city of New York.

He is a director in the Bank of the Republic, the Home Insurance Co., the Union Trust Co., the Rutgers Fire Insurance Co., of which he was one of the original incorporators, and is now vice-president; Standard Gaslight Co., and other large corporations. A great number of his investments have been made in real estate, and his ventures have almost uniformly brought tribute to his business sagacity. He is the owner of the entire plot running from Thirty-third to Thirty-fourth streets fronting on Broadway and adjoining the Astor properties, which extend through to Fifth avenue. The most noticeable building upon this is the well-known "Alpine" building. His house, at the corner of Fifty-third street and Fifth avenue, and the property at the corner of Fifty-fifth street and Broadway, which have greatly increased in value, form only a small part of the real estate which he owns in the central part of the city. Mr. McAlpin is a devoted member of his church, and very generous in its support.

QUINCY, Josiah, fourth mayor of Boston, was born there Jan. 17, 1802, eldest son of the president of Harvard. He was graduated at Harvard in 1821, studied and practiced law, was president of the city council 1834–37, and of the state senate in 1842. As mayor, 1845–49, he emulated the activity and enlarged the public spirit of his father, planning and promoting many improvements; his greatest service, and one of the most important ever rendered to the city, was the introduction of the Cochituate water. He was long treasurer of the Western Railroad and of the Boston Athenæum. His book, "Figures of the Past," appeared shortly before his death at Quincy, Nov. 2, 1882.

RIDPATH, John Clark, historian and author, was born in Putnam county, Ind., Apr. 26, 1840. Through his father he is descended from the Ridpaths of Berwick-on-Tweed, and through his mother from Gov. Samuel Matthews of Virginia. His parents came from Montgomery county, Va., and were poor; but the boy's diligence and quickness overcame all obstacles. He was the oldest in the family, and from childhood gave tokens of great talents and character. His early education was obtained under great difficulties, but his active mind took up the substance of books as if by intuition, and when he was eleven had gained all the old log school house could impart. His parents recognized his fondness for study and supplied him with a few books. From his twelfth to his sixteenth year he studied by himself, works on natural philosophy, including popular treatises on astronomy, the beginnings of chemistry, and the outlines of history. He was teaching at seventeen and also served as a clerk, hoping to obtain the means of completing his education. His father finally came to his rescue and furnished the means for his first year at Asbury (now De Pauw) University, where he was graduated in 1863, having gone through a six years' course in four years, meanwhile supporting himself by private tutoring, and beginning to make a reputation by contributions to the newspapers. His attainments in Latin and Greek were regarded as phenomenal, and it is related that at his examination he offered to read the whole of the "Agricola," when the professor stopped the examination and gave him 100 blind. He became principal of Thorntown Academy in 1864, and superintendent of schools at Lawrenceburgh in 1866. In 1869 he was called to the chair of English literature to his alma mater; this he exchanged in 1871 for that of *belles-lettres* and history. From his earliest boyhood Mr. Ridpath had had a profound interest in human story and the historical course was mastered with surprising facility, and he

went on, on his own account, with postgraduate study. In 1879 he was elected vice-president of the university; chiefly through his management it received its splendid endowment and its new name of De Pauw. All the official correspondence relating to these measures was conducted by him, and to him the final success of the project was ascribed by Mr. De Pauw and by the public. Mr. Ridpath became an author through the historical studies suggested by the work of his department. His "Academic History of the United States" appeared in 1874 and met with immediate success. This he abridged to his "Grammar School History," in 1876, which still holds its place as a text-book in the schools. His "Popular History," (1877), reached a sale of 350,000 copies, and was translated into German. Next came an "Inductive Grammar of the English Language" (1878); a monograph on "Alexander Hamilton" (1880); and the "Life and Work of Garfield" (1881); of which 75,000 copies were sold in

three months, and a German version made. It was followed by a monograph on the "Trial of Guiteau," (1882). His "Cyclopædia of Universal History," in three large volumes, (1880–85), has been eminently successful; a fourth volume has lately been added. His later works are "Beyond the Sierras" (1888); "Great Races of Mankind" (four volumes, 1891); and a "Life of Columbus." Dr. Ridpath has also contributed to magazines and reviews, and became, in 1880, one of the editors of the "People's Cyclopædia." He received the degree of LL.D. from the Syracuse University in 1880. In 1891 Dr. Ridpath was honored with a semi-centennial celebration of his birthday at which a large number of the notable men and women of the county participated. In 1863 Dr. Ridpath married Hannah R. Smythe and has three daughters and one son, who have in a measure inherited their father's talents.

ORNE, Caroline F., poet, was born at Cambridge, Mass., Sept. 3, 1818, the daughter of John Gerry Orne, who was a grandson of the patriotic William Azee Orne of Marblehead, and a great-nephew of Elbridge Gerry, vice-president of the United States. Her mother, Anna Stowe, was a descendant of Simon Stowe who settled at Watertown, Mass., in 1635, and in whose family the estate of Sweet Auburn, had descended from father to son until it became the celebrated cemetery known as Mount Auburn. The subject of this sketch received much of her intellectual training from her mother. Caroline was educated at some of the best schools of Cambridge and Boston, and early began to contribute articles both in prose and verse to magazines and periodicals. She has published two volumes of poetry, "Sweet Auburn and Mount Auburn" and "Morning Songs of American Freedom." From the last, several representative pieces have since 1874 found their way into various collections. Miss Orne was for seventeen years librarian of the Cambridge library, and during the greater part of that time selected the books annually added and always assisted in the selection.

MAC QUEARY, Howard, clergyman, was born near Charlottesville, Albemarle co., Va., May 27, 1861, son of Thomas Howard and Sarah Jane (Garland) Mac Queary. His father, a planter, lost all his property through mismanagement and died the year of the son's birth. Young Mac Queary, therefore, enjoyed but few advantages during his youth. He was enabled, however, to attend the parochial school of the neighborhood until he was thirteen, when on account of ill health, he began farming on a small scale. In five years his health being completely restored, he went to Washington and entered commercial life, supporting his mother as well as himself in this way. At the end of a year he entered Norwood High School and College, Nelson county, Va. (1880), having through the kindness of friends obtained a scholarship there. In 1883 he was matriculated at the Theological Seminary of the Protestant Episcopal Church, near Alexandria, Va., where he was graduated and ordained a clergyman in 1885, by the Rev. George W. Peterkin, bishop of West Virginia. By reason of his scanty means his educational career had been a long struggle. His first ministerial charge was at Fairmount and Morganstown, W. Va., where he built a church and was in other ways substantially successful. In Jan. 1882, he was called to Canton, O., and during this pastorate his theological views underwent a severe and radical change. From an advocate of the most orthodox doctrine he became a staunch supporter of the ideas of the more liberal Christians, such as Frederick W. Robertson, Frederick Denison Maurice, Charles Kingsley, Dean Stanley, and others. Mr. Mac Queary sought to reconcile the principles of evolution with the established creeds of theology in a volume entitled, "The Evolution of Man and Christianity" (1890). This publication, although containing nothing especially novel, aroused the fiercest opposition in the Episcopal church, and as a natural result the Rev. Mr. Mac Queary was summoned before the œcumenical council of that body, where, although he pled his cause with much eloquence, he was openly denounced as a heretic, and forbidden to preach. His congregation in Canton, however, who had become likewise affected by the change in the pastor's belief, refused to sustain this decision. He has since become a Universalist.

JUCH, Emma, soprano singer, was born in Vienna, Austria, in 1863. As an infant she was taken by her parents to New York city, where she received early singing lessons from her father, and later was educated by noted masters. Her operatic début was made in London, in Italian opera, in Thomas' "Mignon," which was followed by leading soprano rôles in the works of Verdi, Meyerbeer and others. There she continued three seasons, and after the close of her engagement returned to the United States. After singing at concerts and in operas during an extended term, in the principal cities of the Union, she proved herself equally well equipped for the interpretation of German, French, and Italian compositions. In 1889 Fräulein Juch formed an English opera company of her own, under the leadership of Mr. C. E. Locke, with which she toured through the greater part of the United States. She excels in the leading soprano parts of Wagner's musical dramas, and is an ideal representative of Margaret in Gounod's "Faust." In 1894 she was married to F. L. Wellman, assistant district-attorney of New York city.

BOYD, Trustin Brown, merchant, was born in Indianapolis, Ind., Dec. 25, 1853, son of David M. Boyd, one of the pioneer merchants of Indianapolis, having migrated to that city from Cincinnati, O., on horseback before the railroad was built. His paternal ancestors were of Scotch-Irish Presbyterian stock. His paternal grandfather was a chaplain of Gen. Harrison's army in 1811–14, and his mother was a second cousin of Pres. Polk. He was educated in the public and high schools of his native city, and at the age of sixteen left school to accept a position offered him in the freight department of the C. C. C. and I. Railway, where he served as clerk for two years, at the end of which time he was promoted to the office of cashier of the road at Indianapolis. He was married in 1876 to Emily, daughter of Oliver Tousey. He removed to St. Louis, Mo., in 1879, where he became a partner with the firm of Wilson Brothers, clothing merchants. In 1884 he purchased the entire interests of the business and conducted it under the firm name of T. B. Boyd & Co. He ranks as one of St. Louis' most progressive and public-spirited citizens. He was one of the organizers of the Mercantile Club, and is a director of the St. Louis Exposition, having been elected in 1885, and was made its president in 1893.

CORRIGAN, Thomas, capitalist, was born in Huntington county, Canada, Dec. 31, 1825, one of a family of twelve children. His parents were natives of Ireland, having emigrated to Canada in 1825,

where his father, a well-to-do farmer, was for twenty years commissioner of the district in which he lived. His mother was a sister of Mrs. Tarsney, mother of Congressman John C. Tarsney. After a few years spent on the farm and at the common schools, Thomas Corrigan went West, and purchasing land in Brown county, near the town of Hiawatha, Kan., commenced farming for himself. He gave this up at the end of a year, and engaged in transporting freight from St. Joseph, Mo., to Pike's Peak, it then being the time of the gold excitement. At the outbreak of the civil war he went to Leavenworth, Kan., and entered the employ of Rays & Steel, after which he was engaged in constructing the Kansas Pacific Railroad. From that time until 1874, he was identified as contractor with the construction of various western roads. He then built the Kansas city water works, and in the latter part of the same year started the building of a street railway, which was completed in 1875. Upon the purchase of one of the old street railways of Kansas City, which had been in operation for some years without profit to its owners, he put it upon a paying basis, and subsequently continued to purchase the stock of the other

street railways in that city until he became the owner of all of them but one. In 1883, after a long and successful ownership, his entire railway interest was sold out to a Boston syndicate known as the Metropolitan Street Railway Co., for $1,250,000. He next devoted his energies to the improvement of the Kansas City real estate, of which he held a large amount. Except for his service as police commissioner from 1874 to 1881, Mr. Corrigan never held public office. He belonged to the Catholic Knights of America, and was a prominent member of that religious body. In February, 1864, he was married to Katie McGinley of Shenington, Canada. Four daughters survived him. His estate was valued at $2,000,000, all earned by his own honest endeavor. He was never afraid of hard work, possessed a remarkable will and determination, and a strict integrity of purpose. In 1893, his health began to fail, and, after a brief vacation in Europe, he died at Kansas City, March 1, 1894.

BOARDMAN, George Nye, educator, was born in Pittsford, Vt., Dec. 23, 1825. He was fitted for college at Castleton Seminary, Castleton, Vt., entered Middlebury College in 1843, and was graduated in 1847. During the two years immediately succeeding his graduation he filled the office of tutor in the college. In 1849 he entered Andover Theological Seminary, where he was graduated in 1852, subsequently attending the lectures of Dr. N. W. Taylor of Yale Divinity School. In June, 1853, he was invited on the same day to the pastorate of the Congregational Church of South Danvers (now Peabody), Mass., and to the professorship of English literature in Middlebury College. He accepted the latter appointment, and occupied that chair for six years. In 1859 he accepted a call to the pastorate of the First Presbyterian Church in Binghamton, N. Y. In 1871 he resigned this pastorate to accept a professorship in Chicago Theological Seminary, and in September of that year he was inaugurated Illinois professor of systematic theology, which post he still holds. He has published occasional sermons and several review articles. The degree of D.D. was conferred upon him by Vermont University in 1867, and that of LL.D. by Lafayette College in 1889.

WOODFORD, William, soldier, was born in Caroline county, Va., in 1735. He distinguished himself in the French and Indian war. In 1775, when the Virginia militia assembled at Williamsburg, Va., he was commissioned colonel of the 2d regiment. At the Great Bridge, on the Elizabeth river, Dec. 9th of the same year, he fought the forces of Lord Dunmore, royal governor of the colony, and gained a victory. Dunmore had fortified a passage of the Elizabeth river, on the borders of the Dismal Swamp, where he suspected the militia would attempt to cross. At the Norfolk end of the bridge, Dunmore cast up his intrenchments, and supplied them amply with cannon. His forces consisted of British regulars, Virginia tories, negroes and vagrants, in number about 600. Woodford had thrown a small fortification at the opposite end of the bridge. Early in the morning, the royalists attacked the Virginians. After considerable manœuvering, a sharp battle ensued which lasted about twenty-five minutes, when the assailants were repulsed and fled, leaving two spiked field pieces behind them. The loss of the assailants was fifty-five killed and wounded; not a Virginian was killed, and only one of their men was slightly wounded. Woodford was afterward commander of the 1st Virginia brigade, having been appointed brigadier-general by the Continental congress. At the battle of the Brandywine, Sept. 11, 1777, he was severely wounded, but was in the action at Monmouth, N. J., June 28, 1778, and at the siege of Charleston, S. C., in 1780. Here he was taken prisoner by the British and sent to New York city, where he died on the 13th of November of that year.

BELCHER, Jonathan, colonial governor of Massachusetts, New Hampshire and New Jersey, was born at Cambridge, Mass., Jan. 8, 1682. He was a son of Andrew Belcher one of the provincial council, a man of wealth, who died in 1717, and a grandson of the Andrew Belcher who lived in Cambridge in 1648. He was graduated from Harvard university in 1699, his education being carefully supervised by his father. Shortly after he sailed for Europe, where he spent six years, and at the royal court of Hanover made the acquaintance of the Princess Sophia and of her son, subsequently George I. of England, so laying the foundation of his future honors. Returning to Boston, he became a merchant and a member of the provincial council. In 1729 he was sent as agent of the colony to England, this appointment, as Thomas Hutchinson declares in his history, having been secured in a manner that was not very creditable. The same year he was sent back to Boston as governor of Massachusetts and of New Hampshire, to succeed Gov. Burnet. Belcher was a man of society and of the world, loved intrigue and tortuous methods, and brought into politics some habits of trade, but he spent his money with an elegant liberality during the eleven years in which he occupied the governor's chair. He was for years, during Burnet's administration, the friend of high prerogative principles in the government, but finally embraced the popular side of the controversy between Burnet and the General court, about a fixed salary for the governor's office. It was in view of this that he was made colonial agent, but when he became a Massachusetts governor he reverted to his old position and insisted upon a fixed salary. Pursuing the controversy with the colonists, he excited such popular clamor against himself that in 1741 he was removed from office by the British authorities. He was able to vindicate himself, however, at the British court; no difficult task, when the main question was the support of one who had advocated kingly prerogative, and received the appointment of governor of the province of New Jersey. This he took in 1747, and here he maintained a successful administration until his death at Elizabethtown, N. J., Aug. 31, 1757. He extended the charter of the college of New Jersey, was its chief patron, and left to it a fine library.

COOPER, Susan Fenimore, author, was born at Scarsdale, N. Y., Apr. 17, 1813, daughter of James Fenimore Cooper. The greater part of her life was spent at Cooperstown, where she has won universal affection by founding an orphanage, which now gives shelter and a home to about a hundred friendless boys and girls, and has reared many useful men and women. She has written several books displaying talent of no common order. Her "Rural Hours" is descriptive of the scenery that surrounds her home, and which her father, in the "Pioneer," pictured as it was a hundred years ago. It, and her other works, "Rhyme and Reason of Country Life" and "Country Rambles," are admirable sketches of American out-door life, just as it is, with no coloring but that which all objects receive in passing through a cultivated and contemplative mind.

COOKE, Rose Terry, author, was born at West Hartford, Conn., Feb. 17, 1827. She is the daughter of Henry Wadsworth and Anne (Hurlbut) Terry. Her mother was the daughter of John Hurlbut, who was the first New England shipbuilder who sailed around the world. When Rose was six years of age her parents removed to Hartford, where she was educated at the female seminary and was graduated in 1843. Her father took special interest in her education, and she was made familiar with birds, bees, flowers and sunshine. Being so carefully trained at home, she became noted at school for her brilliancy, and the ease with which she learned. Soon after her graduation she began to write short poems and stories for various periodicals, and these, collected into volumes, have given her a wide reputation. She was a vigorous writer of stories respecting life in New England. She wrote vividly and possessed the power of strong characterization in a marked degree. She was not only thoroughly familiar with the history of New England, but with its social aspect as well; and this knowledge enabled her to reproduce what is quaint and amusing in early New England life with great spirit and grace. She has written several novels and is a constant contributor to periodical literature, both in prose and poetry. In the more than thirty years that she has been an author she has produced nothing which can not now be read with pleasure and profit. Many of her pieces of verse rank in poetic quality with anything written by an American poet, and there is scarcely a scrap-book in the country in which she is not represented. "The Two Villages," "New Moon," "An Answer," "The Fishing Song," and a score of others have made a place for themselves in the memory of every lover of true poetry. The volume, "Poems by Rose Terry Cooke" (New York, 1890), includes all that she has written in verse which she desired to preserve. In 1873 she was married to R. H. Cooke, a Connecticut manufacturer, of Winsted, Conn., where she resided until 1887, when they removed to Pittsfield, Mass., where she died July 18, 1892.

KING, Rufus, statesman, was born in Scarborough, Me., March 24, 1755. Richard King, his father, was the eldest son of John King, who came to America early in the eighteenth century, settled in Boston, and married Mary Stowell of Newton,

Mass. Richard King, who was born in Boston in 1718, engaged in the lumber business, and was one of the officers in Gen. Shirley's successful expedition against Louisburg, after which he settled in Scarborough, and became an extensive dealer in lumber, in which occupation, and as a merchant, he prospered, and became a man of influence in his town. He was twice married, and by his first wife, Isabella Bragdon of York, Me., had three children. Rufus, the eldest, received a careful education at the Byfield academy, and from there entered Harvard university, pursuing his studies elsewhere while the college buildings of the university were occupied for military purposes, and on the resumption of the exercises at Cambridge was graduated in 1777 with much distinction. He at once began the study of law under Theophilus Parsons at Newburyport, and by careful attention to business, and by the exercise of a gift of oratory, which he had assiduously cultivated, he, on entering upon the practice of his profession, in a short time gained the confidence of the people, and was sent, in 1788, to the general court of Massachusetts. Before this, in 1778, he became an aide to Gen. Glover in the short, but unsuccessful, expedition of Gen. Sullivan to Rhode Island. He was sent by the legislature of Massachusetts in 1784 to the old congress of the United States, then sitting at Trenton, N. J., and was re-elected to that body each year until it was dissolved, finally, under the new constitution. In April, 1784, Mr. Jefferson had proposed that in the northwest territory slavery should not exist after the year 1800. The suggestion not having been adopted, Mr. King moved, in 1785, that "there should be neither slavery nor involuntary servitude in the states described in the resolution of congress in April, 1784, otherwise than in the punishment of crime, whereof the party shall have been personally guilty; that this regulation shall be made an article of compact, and remain a fundamental principle of the constitution between the original states and each of the states named in the said resolve." This resolution was never acted upon, but became in 1787 part of the ordinance of that year, drawn and offered by Nathan Dane, Mr. King's colleague, while the latter was a member of the constitutional convention at Philadelphia. It kept out slavery, but it had attached to it, when adopted, the provision for the surrender of fugitive slaves, which was not in the resolution of 1785. Mr. King was appointed by the legislature of Massachusetts a commissioner to settle the boundaries between it and the state of New York, and to convey to the United States lands west of the Alleghanies, and by the congress in 1786, with James Monroe, to urge the state of Pennsylvania to pay her quota of the impost tax. In 1787 the legislature of Massachusetts sent him as one of their representatives to the convention, which met in Philadelphia, to revise the articles of the Confederacy. Here he bore a conspicuous part, and was one of the committee on style, by which the results of the deliberations received their final form before adoption as the constitution of the United States. He was afterward elected by Newburyport a deputy to the convention of Massachusetts to decide upon the adoption by that state, of the constitution, its final ratification in 1788 being largely brought about by his eloquence and familiarity with its provisions. While residing in New York, where the old congress sat during its last years, he gave up the practice of law, devoting himself to the public business, and in 1786 married Mary Alsop, the only daughter of John Alsop, who had been a member of the first congress, and a retired merchant of New York. As a consequence of this, in part, Mr. King became a citizen of the state of New York in 1788, and was chosen to its legislature, which met in 1789, where "he received the unexampled welcome of an immediate election, with Schuyler, to the senate" of the United States. He was fortunate in drawing the long term, and was rarely absent from his seat, efficiently promoting the establishment of the new government, and the measures and policy of what was known as the federal party. In 1794 a petition was presented to the senate against the right of Mr. Gallatin to a seat in that body, based on the ground that he had not been a citizen the required number of years. A warm debate ensued, in which Mr. King eloquently opposed Gallatin's admission, and which resulted in the latter's exclusion. Mr. King earnestly advocated sending Mr. Jay as a special envoy to England to settle the questions threatening the peace between the United States and Great Britain; and when a treaty was made with that country, he defended it in the senate and in writing, being the author of a number of letters concerning its commercial provisions, published by Alexander Hamilton, under the signature of "Camillus," and which had the effect of promoting its adoption. The careful study of maritime and international law required in the preparation of these, stood him in good stead in the various discussions in which he was soon to engage, and gave him confidence in his opinions upon the questions they involved. Having been re-elected to the senate in 1795, he continued to serve but a short time, and, having resigned his office, was appointed in 1796, by President Washington, minister plenipotentiary to Great Britain, in which capacity he continued during the administration of Mr. Adams and two years of that of Mr. Jefferson, being relieved only at his own request. In this long period of service he had the full approbation of his government, and secured many important modifications of the commercial relations between the two countries. He persistently sought to have a stop put to the unwarrantable impressment of our seamen by the British officers, but without success. While in England he won the confidence of the government there by his intelligent, courteous and firm presentation of the matters in discussion, and claimed and obtained for his country the respect due to one of the important powers of the world. Returning to America, he soon carried out a purpose he had planned for some years, and purchased a farm at Jamaica, on Long Island, to which he removed in 1805, and occupied himself in its improvement, in hunting and fishing, and, surrounded by a large and well-selected library, in the cultivation of an already well-stored mind, in study and observation of the political questions of the day, and in an extensive correspondence at home and with the valued friends he had made abroad. He was strongly opposed to the policy which brought on the war of 1812; but deeming it the duty of a good citizen to sustain his country, he was among the first to aid the government by his efforts and his means. In 1813 he was again elected to the United States senate from New York. When it was proposed to abandon Washington, after the ruthless destruction of the public buildings by the English, he denounced the suggestion in what is said to have been one of his most eloquent speeches. Earnestly seeking in congress to repair the finances of the government, consequent upon the war, he ever maintained the principles of the old federal party, and in 1816 was nominated, without his knowledge, for the office of governor of New York; he was, however, defeated, as he was also when a candidate for the presidency of the United States against Mr. Monroe. Although he had been a warm advocate for the establishment of the Bank of the United States, and was a director in it, he was opposed to a second bank, with the large capital of $50,000,000. He labored strenuously, and with success, to obtain a change in the commercial relations with Great Britain in the West Indies, being the author of the navigation law of 1818, which settled the future policy of the country. Always interested in the care of the public lands, he was instrumental in bringing about a change of their sale, by requiring the payments to be made in cash, though at a lower price, instead of credit. The application of the territory of Missouri to become a state brought out a very warm discussion, hinging upon the demand that slavery should be permitted there, and Mr. King took the lead in objecting to its extension into what was the common property of the United States. One of his speeches (imperfectly reported) during this debate, contained the following carefully prepared statement: "Mr. President, I approach a very delicate subject; I regret the occasion that renders it necessary for me to speak of it, because it may give offence, where none is intended. But my purpose is fixed. Mr. President, I have yet to learn that one man can make a slave of another. If one man cannot do so, no number of individuals can have any better right to do it. And I hold that all laws or compacts imposing any such condition upon any human being are absolutely void, because contrary to the law of nature, which is the law of God, by which he makes his ways known to man, and is paramount to all human control." As is well known, his efforts were unavailing; the state was admitted with slavery under the compromise offered by Mr. Clay, which he opposed, and which was afterward broken. Mr. King, upon the close of his fourth senatorial term, in 1825, left, as his last effort to put an end to slavery, a resolution, providing that where the proceeds from the sale of the public lands, which had been pledged for the extinguishment of the public debt, were freed from that obligation, they should be held as a fund to emancipate and remove slaves and free persons of color to a territory outside of the United States. It was never passed, and war alone settled the abolition of slavery forever. Mr. King was an influential member of the convention for the formation of a new constitution in New York in 1821. While desirous and determined at the end of his senatorial term to retire to private life, he was induced by President John Quincy Adams, in 1825, to accept the position of minister to Great Britain, with which country many interesting questions were pending. His former residence in England had made him many friends, by whom he was cordially received; but his health failing, he returned home the next year. Mr. King was much interested in agriculture, having imported a fine herd of Devon cattle. He was also active in promoting the cause of education, especially in Columbia college, New York city. He was also an able counselor in the promotion of the welfare of the Protestant Episcopal church, to which he had long been attached. He died in New York Apr. 29, 1827.

WORTHINGTON, Henry Rossiter, inventor, was born in New York city, Dec. 17, 1817. Nothing is related of his early life. His father was a merchant, doing business in the metropolis, and the boy at an early age assumed a position in his establishment. He developed at an early age a great interest in mechanics, as well as a talent for invention, and as early as 1840 was engaged in experiments looking toward the application of steam to canal navigation. His mind was already directed toward the kind of invention which was afterward to cause his name to be remembered, that of improvements in pumps. It was necessary, in regard to propelling canal boats, to overcome the difficulty of keeping the boiler full of water while the engine was not working, as in passing through locks. This was done at the time by a crude arrangement of a hand pump. But Worthington formed the idea of obtaining his power from the idle boiler and applying it to the furnishing of its own water. This he accomplished by means of a small steam cylinder with a pump attached, which, though a very simple mechanism, effected his purpose. In 1841 Mr. Worthington patented his independent feed pump, out of which grew the direct action steam pump, bearing his name, which he patented in 1849. In 1854, having invented a direct acting compound condensing engine, he set up the first one ever made in Savannah, Ga., and there also he built the first compound engine ever used in water works. The Savannah water works were built in 1853-54 by the city, the water being taken from the Savannah river by means of pumping to settling basins for low service, and to a tank for high service. Mr. Worthington put up here a Worthington pump, with a daily capacity of 5,000,000 gallons and was appointed engineer of the works. His success in the application of his new pumping device was so great that the Worthington pump was rapidly adopted throughout the country. He afterward invented the duplex pump, in which two pumps work side by side, and which has been brought into general use for supplying water not only to mills and factories but in cities and towns, while it is also extensively used on steamers for the purpose of feeding boilers, to extinguish fires, and for other uses. As the value and importance of his inventions grew, Mr. Worthington found it necessary to build manufactories and to establish a considerable plant for the construction of his pumping machinery. He took rank as a pioneer in his particular branch of hydraulic engineering. He was one of the founders of the American society of mechanical engineers, and a member of the American institute of mining engineers. He died in Tarrytown, N. Y., Dec. 17, 1880.

WENTWORTH, Benning, governor of New Hampshire, was born at Portsmouth, N. H., July 24, 1696, eldest son of Lieut.-Gov. John Wentworth. He was graduated from Harvard in 1715, became a leading merchant, made repeated voyages to England and Spain, sat for several terms in the assembly, and was made a councilor in 1734. He was the first governor of the province, and the longest in office of any in the colonies, receiving his commission in 1741, when New Hampshire was separated from Massachusetts, and holding it for twenty-five years. Under his rule may be traced the advance of aristocracy in contact and contrast with the free ideas and manners of the frontier. As early as 1757, he complained that "the prerogative of the crown is treated with contempt, the royal commission and instruction

rendered useless; the members of both houses are all become commonwealth's men, and not enough loyalists left to form a council." He lived in much state, and added to his wealth by the fees received, beginning in 1749, for large grants of land in what is now Vermont. In each of these he required a lot to be reserved for an Episcopal church. That region was claimed also by New York; the two governors came into collision in 1763-64, and the attempt to eject settlers under Wentworth's grants caused much trouble, which was not ended until the admission of Vermont as a state in 1790. Bennington was named in honor of the governor, and the 500 acres on which Dartmouth college stands were given by him in 1768. Longfellow's poem, "Lady Wentworth," refers to his second marriage in 1760, with Martha Hilton, who became his heir. He resigned at the age of seventy, in favor of his nephew, and died at Portsmouth, Oct. 14, 1770. (See Belknap's "History of New Hampshire.")

CONWELL, Henry, second R. C. bishop of the diocese of Philadelphia, was born in County Derry, Ireland, 1745. His family were the founders of a bourse in the Irish college at Paris, and it was at this institution he pursued his ecclesiastical studies. While a seminarian there, he attracted the attention of Benjamin Franklin. He was ordained a priest in 1776, was for a number of years engaged as a missionary in his native diocese, and was subsequently parish priest of Dungarvan. At the time he was appointed bishop of Philadelphia he was filling the important office of vicar-general of the diocese of Armagh. Dr. Conwell was consecrated bishop of Philadelphia by Bishop Poynter, vicar apostolic of the London district, on Aug. 24, 1820. He immediately sailed for America in company with Bernard Keenan, a young priest, who had applied for admission to his diocese. One of the first acts of

his administration was to suspend Rev. Wm. Hogan, a priest of doubtful character. Unfortunately, this priest had the trustees on his side, and troubles arose in the diocese, the effects of which were not eradicated for many years. Mr. Hogan appealed to Archbishop Maréchal, who declined to uphold him, investigations proving that Hogan had shown an inclination to renounce the doctrines of Catholicism and enter the Anglican church. His faculties were taken from him, and he was afterward excommunicated by Bishop Conwell. But this did not deter him from exercising ecclesiastical functions. A schism was inaugurated. The trustees retained possession of the cathedral church of St. Mary's, and reinstated Mr. Hogan, while the bishop and his household were obliged to take up their residence at St. Joseph's, a small church in the vicinity of St. Mary's. St. Joseph's thus became the pro-cathedral of Bishop Conwell. The trustees declined to pay the salaries of either the bishop or his priests, and he was thus without means of support, and unable to make the regular visitations of his diocese. In 1821 Bishop Conwell visited Canada, in hopes of obtaining some pecuniary assistance from the clergy of Quebec and Montreal, and also to arrange for the establishment of an Ursuline convent in Philadelphia. The Canadians liberally responded to his appeal, and a plot of ground was purchased for $40,000, on Ninth and Walnut streets, Philadelphia, upon which it was proposed to erect a suitable cathedral; ground for a new cemetery was obtained, and matters began to assume a more favorable aspect. The pews in St. Joseph's church were well rented, one to Joseph Bonaparte, and one to the king of Spain. In February, 1824, Bishop Conwell baptized the infant son of Prince Charles Julius Bonaparte and Princess Zenaida. Joseph Bonaparte was godfather, and the mother of the great Napoleon godmother, by proxy. In October, 1824, when Gen. Lafayette visited Philadelphia, the procession of the clergy which went in

a body to meet him, was headed by Bishop Conwell, and Bishop White of the P. E. church. Bishop Conwell in April, 1827, aroused new animosity by withdrawing the faculties of Rev. W. J. Harold. Bishop England, and other prelates who had before unsuccessfully attempted to act as mediators, were not brought into this controversy, which was referred to Rome, and Bishop Conwell was requested by the sovereign pontiff to repair to that city without delay. The Rev. William Matthews, rector of St. Patrick's church, Washington, D. C., was appointed administrator of the diocese. The administration of the diocese of Philadelphia by Bishop Conwell was practically closed when he sailed from New York for Havre, July 11, 1828. At the time of his departure there were thirty-two priests in the diocese. Bishop Conwell's explanations were not satisfactory to the Vatican, and he was admonished not to resume charge of his diocese. The Cardinal prefect solicited him not to return until all unpleasant feelings had been overcome, and the Papal nuncio repeated the advice. Notwithstanding these admonitions, he repaired to Philadelphia, but never regained jurisdiction of his see. He was present at the Council of Baltimore in 1829, but held no seat and took no part in the proceedings. He reached the age of nearly 100 years, and outlived all the bitter feelings that had clouded his episcopate, his declining years being solaced by the respect and veneration of the clergy and laity. He died at Philadelphia, Pa., Apr. 22, 1842.

COOK, George Hammell, scientist, was born in Hanover, Morris county, N. J., Jan. 5, 1818. After receiving a common-school education, he adopted, in 1836, the profession of civil engineer, but, not being satisfied with his attainments, he entered the Troy polytechnic institute, graduating in 1839. He afterward became professor of mathematics and natural philosophy in the Albany academy. In 1850 he was appointed principal of the academy, and held the office two years, resigning on his election to the chair of chemistry and natural philosophy in Rutgers college. The next year he was made assistant geologist of New Jersey. The office of state geologist had been allowed to lapse for several years, but a paper by Mr. Cook led to its reorganization, and in 1864 he was made its head. His work as state geologist was varied, and of great importance. The topographical maps of the state, which were published under his supervision have been adjudged the best of any published by the different states. The last of the series was recently issued, and he was at the time of his death engaged on his final report. Two volumes had been prepared, the latter now being in print. In 1864 the State scientific college was attached to Rutgers, and Dr. Cook, while retaining his professorship, became vice-president of the college. He was the organizer of the State board of agriculture, and, having been for a long time its secretary, became in 1886 chief director of the New Jersey state weather service. He was long president of New Brunswick's Board of water commissioners, was a member of the State board of health, and held many minor offices in the state. He had been active also in work elsewhere. In 1852 he was sent to Europe by the state of New York to make investigations that might aid in developing the Onondaga salt springs. He went again to Europe in 1870 to study certain geological subjects, and in 1878 was a delegate to the International geological congress, held at Paris in connection with the French exposition. He was the author of "Geology of New Jersey," and published annual reports as state geologist, besides contributing to the scientific journals of the country. He was a fellow of the American association for the advancement of science. He died at New Brunswick, N. J., Sept. 22, 1889.

KING, William, first governor of Maine (1820–
22) was born at Scarborough, Me., Feb. 9, 1768.
He was the seventh child and third son of Richard
King, by his second wife, Mary, daughter of Samuel Black of York. Richard King had been commissary in the army under Sir William Pepperell, at
Annapolis, Nova Scotia, in 1744. He afterward
engaged in business at Watertown, Mass., whence
he removed to Scarborough in 1746, and became a
wealthy lumber exporter. Probably no family in
the state has had more famous descendants than his.
Unlike his own brother, Cyrus, and his half-brother,
Rufus, the statesman, William King had few educational advantages. His early life was spent in working in a lumber mill in Saco. On reaching manhood
he obtained work in a saw mill at Topsham, Me. He
afterward became proprietor of a mill of his own,
and a few years later his increased means enabled
him, with his brother-in-law, to open a store in the
same town. In 1800 he removed to Bath, as the
Kennebec river offered superior advantages for lumbering and shipbuilding. There he resided for over
fifty years. Of good natural powers, strong-willed,
self-reliant, and ambitious, he became a wealthy
merchant and one of the largest ship-owners in the
United States. He organized the first bank opened
at Bath, and was its president. He owned much
real estate in Bath and other parts of Maine, including the whole town of Kingfield (in
Franklin county), which was named
for him. He was one of the incorporators and principal owners of
the first cotton mill in Maine, erected
at Brunswick in 1809. Politically,
William King was a Democrat, and
his abilities soon made him the
leader of the Maine Democracy;
his brothers were equally strong
Federalists. At this time political
feeling ran high; the embargo act
was paralyzing our commerce and
bringing poverty to owners of
shipping. Bath had its full share
of strife, and Mr. King took an important part in all political struggles, gaining from some the title of
the Sultan of Bath. He began his
political career by representing the
town of Topsham at the general
court in Boston in 1795 and 1796. In 1800 he was
elected representative to the Massachusetts legislature from Bath, for three years, and in 1807 and
1808 was elected senator to represent the Lincoln
district. His public record shows a desire to legis-
late for the people. The passage of two noteworthy
measures is due to him: the betterment act, which
compelled original proprietors of wild land and
speculators therein either to sell the same at its first
value to the pioneer settler who had cleared and cultivated it, or to pay them for the improvements they
had made; and the toleration act, of which he was
the father, which annulled the law that had compelled towns to support a minister. His most important public service, however, was the prominent
part he took for seven years in the struggle for the
separation of the district of Maine from Massachusetts. He presided over the convention that framed
the constitution for the new state. In 1820 he was
elected the first governor of Maine by an overwhelming majority; the duties of his position he discharged
with marked ability. In 1821, before completing
his term of office, he resigned to accept the appointment of the U. S. commissioner for the adjustment
of Spanish claims in Florida. In 1828 he was appointed commissioner of public buildings for Maine,
and was empowered to procure plans and estimates
for the construction of a state capitol at Augusta.

This work he brought to a successful conclusion, the
building erected being modeled after the Massachusetts state house. From 1831 to 1834 he was collector of customs at Bath. Gov. King was conspicuous as a military man. He was major-general of
militia, and held the commission of colonel of the
U. S. army, as recruiting officer of U. S. volunteers, in the District of Maine, upon the declaration
of war in 1812. In 1814
he recruited a regiment in
Bath, and was busy recruiting another when the war
closed. He was a promi-
nent Free Mason and was
first grand master of the
grand lodge of Maine. He
was a member of the board
of trustees, and personally
a strong friend of the
Maine Literary and The-
ological Institution, afterward chartered as Water-
ville College, now Colby
University. He is Maine's
representative among the national statuary at Washington. Gen. King was unfortunate in his last
years; loss of property, the death of friends and relatives, and a clouded intellect, combined to darken
the close of his life. In 1802 Gen. King married
Ann Frazier of Scarborough. One son, Cyrus W.
King, was born to them. He died in Bath, Me.,
June 17, 1852.

WILLIAMSON, William Durkee, second
governor of Maine, lawyer, politician, and historian,
was born in Canterbury, Conn., July 31, 1779. He
was the eldest son of George and Mary (Foster)
Williamson. George, a descendant of Timothy
Williamson, a freeman of the Plymouth Colony in
1647, was born in Middleborough, Mass., Jan. 15,
1754, and was a soldier in the revolution. His wife
was of the fifth generation in descent from Abraham
Foster, who came from Exeter, England, to Ipswich,
Mass., about 1635. While quite young, William D.
Williamson removed with his father to Amherst,
Mass. There he attended the common schools in
the winter, and for two summers worked on a farm
in Brooklyn, Conn. He taught school for two or
three years, and in 1800 entered Williams College,
but before completing his course changed to Brown
University, where he was grad-
uated in 1804. He at once began
the study of law in the office of S.
F. Dickerson at Amherst; he afterward studied at Warren and Bangor, Me. On being admitted to
the bar, he commenced practicing at Bangor in 1807. Being very
industrious and of much natural
ability, he met with marked success from the first. In 1811 he was
appointed by Gov. Gerry county-
attorney for Hancock, a position
that he occupied for seven years.
In 1816 he was elected to the senate of Massachusetts, and held
the office by successive elections
until the separation of Maine from
Massachusetts in 1820. He was
then chosen first and sole senator
to represent Penobscot county in the legislature of the
new state, and was soon elected president of the senate. On the resignation of Gov. King, who was
appointed commissioner under the Spanish treaty,
he became acting governor of Maine. This office
he did not hold for the full term, but having been
elected to congress, as a Democrat, from his district,
he resigned the governorship and took his seat in

the house in December, 1821. He held the position for one term, at the close of which, by a new division of the state into districts, the election fell to another portion of the territory. In 1824 he was appointed judge of probate for the county of Penobscot; this office he held until 1840, when the constitutional amendment took effect, limiting the tenure of all judicial offices to seven years. He then retired from public life. In religious faith Judge Williamson was a Congregationalist. He served as one of the overseers of Bowdoin College and of the Bangor Theological Seminary. From 1838 to 1841 he was a bank commissioner, and was for some years president of the Bangor Bank. He was first married, June 10, 1806, to Jemima Montague Rice of Amherst, Mass. She died at Bangor, June 22, 1822, leaving him four daughters and one son. On June 3, 1823, he married Susan Esther, daughter of Judge Phinehas White of Putney, Vt.; she died March 9, 1824, and the year following he married Mrs. Clarissa Emerson Wiggin of York, Me. No children were born of the last two marriages. The great labor of Judge Williamson's life was "The History of the State of Maine, from its First Discovery in 1602, to the Separation, A.D. 1820, Inclusive." All his leisure was given to the accumulation and selection of materials for this work. Though from a literary point of view the book does not rank very high, yet it is a treasure-house of facts relating to the early history of the state and is on that account invaluable to the student. It was published in two volumes of about 700 pages each in 1832, and a revised edition was issued in 1839. Mr. Williamson was an original member of the Maine Historical Society and many of his valuable MSS. are preserved in its archives. He was also a member of other societies, and contributed to the "American Quarterly Register," and to the "Collections of the Massachusetts Historical Society." He died in Bangor, May 27, 1846.

PARRIS, Albion Keith, third governor of Maine, the second by election (1822–27), was born in Hebron, Me., Jan. 19, 1788, being the only child of Samuel Parris and his wife, Sarah Pratt Parris of Middleborough, Mass. He was of English ancestry, being descended from Thomas Parris, of London.

Samuel Parris (born Aug. 31, 1755), was a revolutionary officer on land and sea; one of the first settlers of the town of Hebron; for several years judge of the court of common pleas for Oxford county; and in 1812 a presidential elector. Albion K. Parris spent the first fourteen years of his life on his father's farm. He entered the sophomore class at Dartmouth in 1803, and was graduated in 1806. After studying law in the office of Judge Whitman, at New Gloucester and at Portland, he was admitted to the Cumberland bar in 1809. He immediately began practising at Paris in Oxford county. In 1811 he was appointed attorney for Oxford county. In 1813 he represented Paris in the Massachusetts assembly. In 1814 he was state senator for Oxford and Somerset counties. From 1815 to 1819 he was a member of the national house of representatives. During his second term in congress, in 1818, he was appointed judge of the U. S. district court for Maine, to succeed Judge Sewall, who had held the office from the organization of the government. In 1819 he removed to Portland, was chosen a delegate to the state constitutional con-

vention, was treasurer of the convention, and served on the committee that drafted the constitution of the new commonwealth. In 1820 he was made judge of probate for Cumberland county. While holding this office, he was nominated for governor by the Democratic party, and elected in a triangular contest, at the age of thirty-three. He was four times re-elected, being governor of the state for five successive years, from 1821 to 1826. In his message at the beginning of his fifth term he positively declined a renomination. Under his able administration the state was quiet and prosperous. The most important matter arising to claim attention in this period were the treatment of the property shared by the new state with Massachusetts, and the northeastern boundary dispute with England. Gov. Parris was authorized by the legislature to procure all documents, maps, and surveys bearing upon the latter question. In 1825, when Lafayette visited the states, he cordially received and entertained him. In 1826, before the close of his last term, he was elected to the U. S. senate to succeed John Holmes whose term expired March 3, 1827. This position he resigned on being appointed, in June, 1828, associate justice of the supreme court of Maine. He devoted himself earnestly to the discharge of his new duties, and remained upon the bench until 1836, when he gave up his place to accept Pres. Jackson's appointment of second comptroller of the U. S. treasury. This last post he held faithfully for thirteen years, through the administrations of Van Buren, Harrison, Tyler, and Polk. On retiring from this position he returned to his home in Portland in 1850. In 1852 he was elected mayor of the city, but declined a renomination. In 1854 he was the Democratic candidate for governor, but was defeated by Anson P. Morrill, the first Republican governor of the state. Probably no other person in the history of the state has had so long and continuous a public career. For thirty-six years almost without interruption Gov. Parris was filling positions of the greatest importance and responsibility, and among his varied duties there were none that he did not discharge with credit to himself and his state. Though he was not a brilliant man, his ability, industry, and perseverance made his career a successful one. Throughout his life he was prominent in educational matters, and was in precept and example an earnest Christian. In religious faith he was Congregationalist. He was married, in 1810, to Sarah, eldest daughter of Rev. Levi Whitman of Wellfleet, Mass., who with three daughters and two sons, survived him. He died in Portland, Feb. 11, 1857.

LINCOLN, Enoch, fourth governor of Maine (1827–29), the third elected by the people, was born in Worcester, Mass., Dec. 28, 1788. His father, Levi Lincoln, was a member of congress, attorney-general of the United States, and for a time provisional secretary of state; he was lieutenant-governor of Massachusetts, 1807–8, and acting governor for some months after the death of Gov. James Sullivan. Two of his sons became governors of states, Levi, of Massachusetts, and Enoch of Maine. The latter, the subject of this sketch, entered the sophomore class of Harvard College in 1806, but voluntarily withdrew before graduation in 1808. On leaving the university, he began to study law with his brother Levi, who was an attorney in Worcester, and in 1811 was admitted to the Worcester county bar. He began to practice in Salem, Mass., but in 1812 removed to Fryeburg, Me. Here he pursued his profession, devoting his spare hours to literary work, and paying especial attention to the study of Indian languages; he always intended to publish a history of the Indian tribes of Maine, and collected a large amount of material for that purpose, which, however, he never carried out. In 1815 he was appointed assistant U. S. district attorney. An earnest Democrat, he was in 1818 chosen representative to congress to fill the seat resigned by A. K. Parris, and held the office from Nov. 16, 1818, to March 3, 1821. After Maine became a separate state, he was again elected to congress, serving from 1821 to 1826, when he resigned. In 1826 he was elected governor of Maine by the Democrats, and twice re-elected, serving until his death. He was very popular with the people. The most important matter of state calling for action during his terms as governor, was the question of the northeastern boundary between Maine and New Brunswick. He earnestly defended the state's right to the disputed territory, and maintained that the national government had no authority to cede any land without the state's consent. During his administration, and largely through his influence, Augusta was selected as the seat of the state government, the matter being decided by the governor and council in June, 1827. Gov. Lincoln was an earnest promoter of the cause of education, and gave his hearty support to the subject of internal improvements. In 1819 he removed to Paris, Me., where he succeeded Judge A. K. Parris, in his law practice, also succeeding him as member of congress, and later as governor of the state. It may be noticed that both were born in 1788. Early in 1829 Gov. Lincoln had declined a renomination, intending to settle down on a farm he had purchased in Scarborough, to enjoy a quiet life, and the pursuits of literature and science. But having been persuaded, though in feeble health, to deliver the oration at the laying of the corner stone of the capitol at Augusta, in July, 1829, he did not recover from the physical and mental strain. Gov. Lincoln was never married. In 1821 Bowdoin College gave him the degree of M.A. He delivered a poem at the Centennial celebration of the fight at Lovewell's Pond, and was the author of a poem, "The Village," describing the scenery of Fryeburg (1816). He contributed articles on the Indian languages, and the French missions in Maine to the first volume of the "Maine Historical Collections," and also left among his papers an unfinished manuscript on Maine's history and resources. He died at Augusta, Oct. 8, 1829. His remains are buried opposite the State House.

CUTLER, Nathan, fifth governor of Maine (1829-30), was born in Lexington, Mass., May 29, 1775. He was descended from James Cutler, one of the early settlers of Watertown, Mass., who removed to Lexington in 1648. Joseph Cutler, born in Lexington in 1733, in 1759 married for his second wife, Mary Read, who was the mother of the subject of this sketch. Joseph Cutler, being a farmer in very moderate circumstances, could do little for the education of his children, and offered Nathan a small farm; but the latter was bent on a profession, and managing to fit himself for college at Leicester Academy, entered Dartmouth, where he was graduated in 1798. After graduation, he took charge of the academy (now a college) at Middlebury, Vt., where he taught for two years, spending his spare time in the study of law with Judge Chipman of that place. He completed his studies in Worcester, Mass., and was admitted to the Worcester county bar in 1801. He first opened an office at Lexington, but soon removed to Maine, and at the advice of Judge Whitman of New Gloucester, established himself at Farmington in 1803. He entered heartily into the life of the town, holding various offices of trust. In 1807 he was instrumental in procuring a charter for an academy there, and was during life a member of its board of trustees. He represented the town in the general court of Massachusetts in 1809, 1810, 1811, and 1819; in the latter year, he was a delegate to the convention that formed the state constitution of Maine, and one of the committee on the "Style and Title" of the new state. In 1828 and 1829, he was a member of the Maine senate, from Kennebec county. In 1829 he was president of that body, by virtue of which office he became governor for the unexpired term of Gov. Lincoln, who was removed by death. In 1832 he was an elector-at-large for president, when Maine threw her ten electoral votes for Jackson and Van Buren. The last public office held by Mr. Cutler, was that of representative to the legislature in 1844. Mr. Cutler was married in September, 1804, to Hannah Moore of Weston, Mass., who bore him nine children, seven sons, and two daughters; she died in 1835. He died at Farmington, Me., June 8, 1861.

HUNTON, Jonathan Glidden, sixth governor of Maine, the fourth by election (1830-31), was born in Unity, N. H., March 14, 1781. He was the son of Josiah and Hannah (Glidden) Hunton, his father having been a major in the revolutionary army, and for many years town clerk of Unity. The family traces back its ancestry to Philip Hunton, who came from the Isle of Jersey, and is known to have married Elizabeth Hall of Exeter, N. H., in 1687. Jonathan G. Hunton was educated in the common schools. While a young man, he went to Readfield, Me., and studied law in the office of his uncle, Samuel P. Glidden, the first lawyer to establish himself in the town. He succeeded to his uncle's business, when the latter stopped practicing. In politics he was a National Republican, and when nominated in 1829 for governor of Maine, was a member of the executive council. He served as governor during 1830; he was renominated for another term, but failed of election. He was afterwards chosen state senator. A few years before his death he removed to Dixmont, Me., where he practiced law for several years, subsequently removing to Fairfield. Though previous to his election to the chief magistracy of the state, Gov. Hunton was not prominent, yet he made many strong friends by his conduct in public affairs, and received a largely increased vote on his second and unsuccessful candidacy. He was one of the first, if not the first, of Maine's chief magistrates to advocate the establishment of a state insane asylum, and the work of building that institution is believed to have been begun through his instrumentality. He was twice married; first to Betsy Craig, who died Nov. 7, 1819, and secondly to Mrs. Mary Glidden, his uncle's widow, who survived him ten years. Two children of his are mentioned, a son and a daughter, who both died young. He died suddenly at Fairfield, Me., Oct. 12, 1851.

SMITH, Samuel Emerson, seventh governor of Maine (1831-34), the fifth by election, was born in Hollis, N. H., March 12, 1788. He was the seventh child and third son of Manasseh Smith of Leominster, Mass., and Hannah, daughter of Daniel Emerson of Hollis, N. H. Samuel was fitted for college at Groton

Academy, and was graduated at Harvard in 1808. On leaving college he studied law with Samuel Dana, of Groton, and with his own brothers, Manasseh and Joseph, he was admitted to the Suffolk Bar at Boston, Feb. 25, 1812. He at once moved to Wiscasset, and began the practice of his profession, soon building up a fine business. Like the others of his family, he was a strong Democrat, and entered actively into politics. In 1819, the year before the separation of Maine from Massachusetts, he was chosen to represent Lincoln county in the Massachusetts legislature, and the year following he was elected to the legislature of Maine. In 1821 he was appointed chief justice of the circuit court of common pleas, and in 1822, when the circuit court system was abolished, he was made an associate justice of the new court. This position he held until 1830, when he was nominated and elected governor by the Democrats. He was twice re-elected, the period of his service covering the years 1831, 1832 and 1833. Perhaps the most important matter with which his administration had to deal, was the subject of the northeastern boundary, which had now for some years had been a bone of contention between Maine and New Brunswick. Worthy of note also in the state's political history at this time was the removal of the seat of government from Portland to Augusta, the legislature beginning its first session in the new state house at Augusta in January, 1832. In the last year of Gov. Smith's administration, the country was greatly disturbed by the nullification movements of South Carolina; and in his message of 1833 the governor took firm ground in support of the national government. In 1835, after his retirement to private life, he was again appointed to the bench of common pleas. In October of the same year he was appointed (with Chief Justice Mellen, and Ebenezer Everett, Esq.,) one of the commissioners to revise and codify the public laws; the first edition of the revised statutes was the result of their labors. He withdrew from the bench in 1837. In 1836 Gov. Smith removed from Augusta to his old home in Wiscasset, and there spent the remainder of his life upon his estate, in literary pursuits. Mr. Smith married at Augusta, Sept. 12, 1832, Louisa S., daughter of Henry Weld Fuller of that city. Five sons were born to them. He died at Wiscasset, March 3, 1860.

DUNLAP, Robert Pinckney, eighth governor of Maine, the sixth by popular election (1834–38), was born in Brunswick, Me., Aug. 17, 1794, the son of Capt. John and Mary (Tappan) Dunlap. His father was born in Dracut, Mass., 1738, a man of great strength and courage, a soldier in the French and Indian wars, a frequent representative in the general court of Massachusetts, and one of the first board of overseers of Bowdoin College. He was the eldest son of Rev. Robert Dunlap, born in Manilla, county Antrim, Ireland, who came to this country in 1736, and became pastor of the church in Brunswick in 1747. In 1788, Capt. John Dunlap married for his second wife, Mary, daughter of Richard Tappan of Newburyport, Mass., and their third son is the subject of this article. Robert P. Dunlap was graduated at Bowdoin College in 1815. He studied law in the office of Benjamin Orr of Topsham, and Ebenezer Morely of Newburyport, Mass., was admitted to the bar in 1818, and began to practice in his native town. Being possessed of ample means, he was not especially devoted to his profession, though

he continued practicing for several years. He was an old-school Democrat, and early turned his attention to politics. In 1821–22 he was representative in the legislature. He was state senator from 1824 to 1833, with the exception of the year 1829, when he was on the executive council. He was twice president of the senate, and as a presiding officer had few equals. In 1833 he was elected governor by the Democrats; at this election the Whigs made their first appearance under that distinctive title. Gov. Dunlap was three times re-elected, serving from 1834 through 1837. He was very popular. In 1843 he was elected representative to congress, and served two terms, being in the lower house until 1847. In 1848–49 he was collector of the Port of Portland; from 1853 to 1857 he was postmaster of Brunswick. For many years he was president of the board of overseers of Bowdoin College. Gov. Dunlap was a zealous Free Mason, and attained to the highest honors

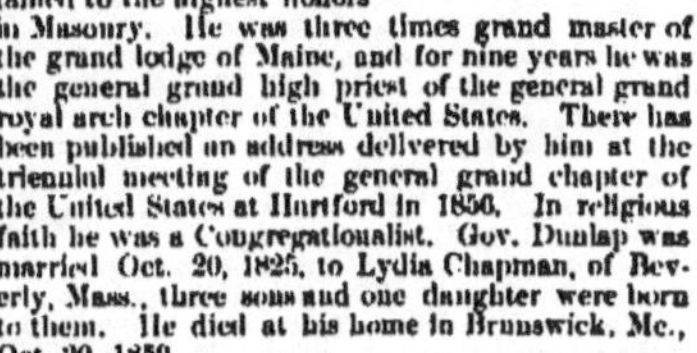

in Masonry. He was three times grand master of the grand lodge of Maine, and for nine years he was the general grand high priest of the general grand royal arch chapter of the United States. There has been published an address delivered by him at the triennial meeting of the general grand chapter of the United States at Hartford in 1856. In religious faith he was a Congregationalist. Gov. Dunlap was married Oct. 20, 1825, to Lydia Chapman, of Beverly, Mass., three sons and one daughter were born to them. He died at his home in Brunswick, Me., Oct. 20, 1859.

KENT, Edward, ninth and eleventh governor of the state of Maine (1838–39, 1840–41), was born in Concord, N. H., Jan. 8, 1802. He was the youngest son of William Austin Kent, a native of Charlestown, Mass.; his mother was a sister of Prentiss Mellen, the first chief justice of the state of Maine. Edward Kent was graduated at Harvard College in 1821, in the same class with Ralph Waldo Emerson, Josiah Quincy, and Robert Barnwell, of South Carolina. He at once began the study of law under Benjamin Orr, of Topsham, one of the most eminent lawyers in Maine; he also studied with Chancellor Kent, the most famous legal commentator in the United States. In September, 1825, he opened a law office in Bangor, Me., and soon built up a good practice. The routine drudgery of his profession was unpleasant to him, and he found relief from it in writing for the press and in political discussions. In 1827 he was admitted to practice in the supreme judicial court, and in the same year was appointed by the governor, chief justice of the court of sessions; this office he held until the close of 1828. He then formed a partnership with Jonathan P. Rogers, then acting as attorney-general of the state, and two years after formed another partnership with Jonas Cutting (afterwards associate justice of the supreme court), which lasted eighteen years. Judge Kent was very popular, and was elected to almost all the local offices of his adopted city. From 1829 to 1833 he was a member of the Maine legislature, where he at once made a state reputation. From 1830 to 1838 he was mayor of Bangor. In 1836 he was nominated by the Whigs for governor of the state, but was defeated by the Democratic nominee, Gov. Dunlap. In 1837 he was again nominated, and this time elected by a small majority. So close was the contest that the supreme court was compelled to decide the legality of some of the returns; the decision established his election and he was inaugurated Jan. 19, 1838. In his message he insisted that the northeastern boundary line should be run as authorized by congress, and that the national government should extricate the state from the difficulties arising from the dispute with New Brunswick. The Aroostook war occurring in the next two years, under the administration of Gov. Fairfield, brought this controversy to a crisis. In 1838 and 1839 Judge Kent was the Whig candidate for governor, but was each time defeated by John Fairfield, the Democratic nominee. In 1840 the two were again rival candidates. There was no election by the people, but the legislature, which was composed largely of Whigs, elected Judge Kent over his competitor. He served through the year 1841, and at its close was renominated, but was defeated by Gov. Fairfield. In 1843 he was appointed by the legislature one of the commissioners to decide the matter of the Maine boundary line under the Ashburton treaty. He unsuccessfully urged on Lord Ashburton and Sec'y Webster that the territorial integrity of the state should be preserved. He now returned to private life, resuming the practice of law at Bangor. In 1848 he was a delegate to the national Whig convention that nominated Gen. Zachary Taylor for the presidency; and in 1849 he was appointed U. S. consul at Rio Janeiro. This office he held until 1853. Returning again to the practice of his profession, he associated himself with his brother, George Kent, until 1859, when he was appointed by Gov. Lot M. Morrill to a seat upon the bench of the supreme court. In 1866 he was reappointed by Gov. Cony, and held the position up to 1873, when he retired to private life. On leaving the bench, he traveled with his family for twelve months in Great Britain and on the continent, being especially interested in Italy and Greece. In 1874 he returned to the practice of his profession in Bangor, engaging in several very important cases. The last public position held by him was that of president of the convention for amending the constitution of the state in 1875. In 1855 Waterville College, now Colby University, gave him the degree of LL.D. Gov. Kent was twice married. By his first wife, Sarah Johnston of Hillsburg, N. H., who died in 1853, he had several children, who all died comparatively young. In 1855 he was married to Abby Anne Rockwood, of Lynn, Mass.; now residing in New York city with her son, their only child. Gov. Kent died in Bangor, May 19, 1877.

FAIRFIELD, John, tenth and twelfth governor of Maine (1839–40, 1841–43), was born at Saco, Me., Jan. 30, 1797. He was the eldest child of Ichabod and Sarah (Nason) Fairfield, and grandson of Rev. John Fairfield, a graduate of Harvard and settled minister at Saco. He was educated in the common schools and at Limerick Academy. He first engaged in trade, making several trips to the South, but finally began the study of law in the office of Judge Shepley, and was admitted to the bar in 1826. In 1832 he was appointed reporter of decisions of the supreme court, and held the office three years. In 1835 he was elected to congress as a Democrat. In 1837 he was re-elected, and held the position until March 3, 1839, when he resigned. In the fall of 1838 he was elected governor of Maine, and re-elected in 1839, each time

defeating Edward Kent, who had been nominated by the Whigs. The election of 1840 was a very close one, and Gov. Fairfield was defeated by a very few votes. In 1841 and 1842, however, he was re-elected. On March 7, 1843, he resigned his position, to accept an election to the seat in the U. S. senate left vacant by the resignation of Reuel Williams. He held the position from Dec. 4, 1843, to his death, having been re-elected in 1845. During his congressional term occurred the Graves-Cilley duel, and with great courage he presented a resolution in the house, asking that a committee be appointed to investigate the circumstances of the affair. An exciting debate, which won him a national reputation, followed, and as the result Graves was expelled from the house. It was while Gov. Fairfield was chief magistrate of his native state that the Aroostook war occurred. Maine was thoroughly aroused, and her governor was foremost in vindicating the rights

of the people to the disputed territory. The legislature appropriated a large sum of money for carrying on the expected military operations. Though the result was tame, and the settlement unfair to the state, Gov. Fairfield's action greatly strengthened his hold on the affections of the people. His public record has been equaled by few; in twelve years he was twice representative to congress, four times chosen governor, and twice a U. S. senator. He was a plain, straightforward man, thoroughly upright in public and private life; his geniality, kindliness, and ready wit made him a favorite with all. Gov. Fairfield was married Sept. 25, 1825, to Anna Paine, daughter of Dr. Thomas G. Thornton, of Saco, Me. Nine children were born to them, and for these and his wife Gov. Fairfield cherished the deepest affection. Mrs. Fairfield died July 18, 1862. Gov. Fairfield was the author of "Supreme Court Reports" (Augusta, 1835–37). He died in Washington, D. C., Dec. 24, 1847. His death was quite sudden, being caused by blood-poisoning, the result, it was believed by many, of a mistake of his physician in treating a chronic trouble of the knee joints.

KAVANAGH, Edward, thirteenth governor of Maine (1843–44), was born at Damariscotta Mills, Me., Apr. 27, 1795. His father, James Kavanagh, a native of New Ross, Wexford county, Ireland, came to Boston in 1780. He married Sarah Jackson, of that city, and settled in Damariscotta Mills, where he engaged in the lumber business and ship-building. Edward Kavanagh was reared a Roman Catholic; he was educated at the Jesuit Colleges in Montreal and Georgetown, D. C., and was graduated from St. Mary's College, Baltimore, in 1813. He was for a time associated with his father in the lumber business, but his tastes did not incline him to a mercantile life. After the establishment of peace in Europe at the close of the Napoleonic wars, he went abroad for about two years, visiting the continent and the British Isles. On returning home, he began the study of law, and on his admission to the bar established himself in Damariscotta, where he became a sound and reliable counsellor. He was prominent in town affairs, being one of the selectmen of Newcastle from 1824 to 1827. In 1826 he was elected representative to the state legislature. He served as secretary of the senate of Maine in 1830. In 1831 he was one of a committee of two appointed by Gov. Smith to ascertain the number of persons settled on the public lands in the north of the state, a duty requiring a long and toilsome journey through the wilderness; this duty was ably and faithfully discharged. From 1831 to 1835, Mr. Kavanagh was a member of the national house of representatives, being elected as a Jackson Democrat. A candidate for re-election in 1834, he was defeated by his Whig opponent. In 1835 he was appointed by Pres. Jackson *chargé d'affaires* of the United States at the court of Portugal, a position for which his education, ability, religious faith, and previous continental travel thoroughly qualified him. The fruits of his labors there were the satisfactory settlement of many claims of American citizens, and the conclusion of a treaty of commerce and navigation between the United States and Portugal. His labors impaired his health, and in June, 1841, he resigned, returning to his home in Maine. He was elected to the state senate for the year 1842, and re-elected for the following year. In 1842 he was chairman of the joint legislative committee to whom the long-contested northeastern boundary question was finally referred; and he was chosen one of the commissioners to confer with the national authorities at Washington regarding the matter. The conference resulted in the adoption of the boundary line defined in the Webster-Ashburton treaty of 1842. On the resignation of Gov. Fairfield, March 7, 1843, to take the seat vacated by Renel Williams in the national senate, Mr. Kavanagh, who had been chosen president of the state senate, became chief magistrate, and discharged the duties of the position with faithfulness and ability for the remainder of the term. His health was now steadily declining, and he died in Newcastle, Me., Jan. 20, 1844. He was never married.

ANDERSON, Hugh Johnston, fourteenth governor of Maine (1844–47), was born in Wiscasset, Me., May 10, 1801. His father, John Anderson, was a native of county Down, Ireland, and had immigrated to America in 1789, immediately after his marriage. Upon the death of his father, in 1810, Hugh went to Belfast, Me., as a clerk in the store of his uncle, his father's brother, finally becoming a member of the firm. In 1827 he was elected clerk of court of Waldo county. In his early years he had taken part in the discussions of the political questions of the day, and had affiliated himself with the Democratic party, to whose principles he gave unfaltering allegiance throughout his life. His mother was a woman of noble piety and finely cultivated mind, under whose guidance he had received a good education; and as he was always of studious habits,

giving all his spare hours to study, he became a fine scholar in later years. Mr. Anderson was elected to congress in 1837, and re-elected in 1839. As a member of the committee on commerce, he distinguished himself by his devotion to duty and his exertions to promote the interests of his constituents, as well as those of his party. He won the friendship of Pres. Van Buren by his upright and able course in congress, a friendship that lasted during the life of the president. It was largely through Mr. Anderson's influence that Mr. Van Buren received the vote of the state of Maine in the convention which renominated him, and his defeat in that memorable contest was a keen blow to Mr. Anderson. But defeat did not dishearten the leaders of the party; they set to work to find the cause and repair the disaster to such good purpose that in the following year a Democratic governor was elected by a handsome majority. Mr. Anderson received the nomination, and was elected governor by his party in 1843, and re-elected in 1844 and 1845, retiring with the esteem of men of all parties. In 1847 he was a candidate for the U. S. senatorship, Hannibal Hamlin being his opponent, when it became evident that neither could be elected, Mr. Anderson withdrew, and James W. Bradbury of Augusta (Democrat), was elected. In 1852 he served with marked ability as commissioner of customs for the treasury department under the administration of Pres. Pierce; and was appointed by Mr. Buchanan, in 1857, to head a commission for the reorganization and adjustment of the affairs of the San Francisco mints, and make enquiry into other claims against the government. Edwin M. Stanton, afterward the famous war minister of Mr. Lincoln's cabinet, was associated with him in this work, and a warm friendship which only ended with the death of the great secretary, resulted; and, after two years' service in California, he returned to Washington, where he continued to reside until 1880, when he went to Portland, Me., where he died May 31, 1881. Gov. Anderson was most fortunate and happy in his domestic relations. In 1832 he married Martha J. Dummir, and to her wise counsel and ever ready sympathy he paid the tribute of being one great factor in whatever of success he had achieved. They had six children, two of whom died soon after he took up his residence in Portland, and he never recovered from the grief of the sad loss. Mrs. Anderson survived her husband by only a few months.

DANA, John Winchester, fifteenth governor of Maine (1847–50), was born in Fryeburg, Me., June 21, 1808. His father was Judah Dana, born in Pomfret, Vt., Apr. 25, 1772, a graduate of Dartmouth College in 1795. He was the grandson of Gen. Israel Putnam, and came to Fryeburg in 1798, being the first lawyer to settle in Oxford county. During his career, he was at different times executive counsellor, bank commissioner, member of the state convention that framed the constitution of Maine, judge of the court of common pleas, and for a short time U. S. senator. He was twice married, his first wife and the mother of all his children being Elizabeth, youngest daughter of Prof. Sylvanus Ripley, of Dartmouth College, and granddaughter of the first president, Wheelock, of the same college. Their son, John W. Dana, received his education at Fryeburg Academy, and early turned his attention to business, contrary to the desires of his father, who wished him to study law. Later on, however, he began to take a deep interest in politics and state affairs, being for many years an active Democratic politician. He was a member of both branches of the legislature, being in the senate during 1843 and 1844; the latter year he was president of that body. He was a thorough parliamentarian, and made a good presiding officer, but rarely took part in debate. He was elected governor by the Democratic party for the years 1847, 1848, and 1849. In 1853 he went to Bolivia, having been appointed by Pres. Pierce *chargé d'affaires* of the United

States ; on June 29, 1854, he was commissioned minister resident, and held the post until March 10, 1859. In 1861 he was again Democratic candidate for governor of Maine, but was defeated. After the breaking out of the civil war, he took a gloomy view of the situation and the country's future. His wife dying, he sold his property in Fryeburg, and went to South America to engage in sheep raising. A short time after, while acting as nurse in a plague-stricken district, he was attacked by cholera, and died at Rosario, Dec. 22, 1867. Gov. Dana married Eliza Ann, daughter of Maj. James Osgood of Fryeburg. Five children were born to them. One of his sisters, Abigail Ripley Dana, married Edward L. Osgood, and became the mother of James R. and Kate Putnam Osgood.

HUBBARD, John, sixteenth governor of Maine (1850–53), was born in Readfield, Me., March 22, 1794. His parents were natives of New Hampshire, and were among the pioneer settlers of Readfield,

having removed there in 1788. His mother was Olive Wilson, and his father, John Hubbard, was a physician who passed a laborious life as a country doctor in a new and thinly settled country. He was highly esteemed as a practitioner, and held a number of important positions in the community, and once represented his district in the general court of Massachusetts. He also had a farm which he placed in charge of his sons as soon as they were old enough to assume the responsibility. The subject of this sketch was, as a lad, remarkable for his physical strength, and took a prominent part in athletic sports. He had the management of his father's farm when

but a boy, and up to the age of sixteen his only schooling had been in the district schools during the winter months, and a two months' term at the academy. He worked until he was nineteen on the farm, devoting all his leisure to study. In 1813 he left home with the object of obtaining an education, and while preparing himself for college, made his expenses by filling the position of tutor in a private family. In 1814 he entered Dartmouth College, where he was graduated in 1816. In order to obtain money to pursue his medical studies, he devoted himself to teaching as soon as he had completed his collegiate course, and secured a position as principal at Hallowell College, Me., and subsequently taught in Virginia. In 1820 he entered the University of Pennsylvania for his medical course, and in April, 1822, received his diploma as a doctor of medicine and fellow of the Philadelphia Medical School. He began practice in Virginia, and in 1825 married Sarah H. Barrett of Dresden, Me., and in 1830 removed to Hallowell, Me., where he subsequently resided. Dr. Hubbard was always interested in politics, and identified himself with the Democratic party of his native state. In 1843 he was elected to the senate of Maine, and in 1849, was nominated and elected, by the Democratic party, governor of the state, and in 1850 was re-elected for a second term. Among the measures to which he directed the attention of the legislature were, the establishment of a reform school for young offenders, the foundation of an agricultural school, that suitable provisions be made for the establishment of a college for the education of females in the more advanced branches of study, etc., etc. He always made the subject of education paramount. He urged the encouragement of settlers, and the development of the southeastern portion of the state.

The result of his efforts was a marked increase in the settlement of the public lands. The temperance legislation was the most important subject that arose during his administration, and Gov. Hubbard signed the first act known as the Maine law. When Gov. Hubbard retired from his position as chief executive of Maine, he immediately resumed the practice of medicine. In 1852 he was appointed by the treasury department, a special agent to examine the custom houses in Maine, with a view to economical enforcement of the revenue laws, and in 1858 his services were extended through all the Eastern states. In 1859 Pres. Buchanan appointed him commissioner under the reciprocity treaty, concluded between America and England in 1854. One of the principal objects of this treaty was to settle disputes arising about the fishery boundaries, a question that is pertinent at the present time (1898). This was the last official position he filled. His latter years were saddened by the civil war, and although he lived to see the U. S. government retain its supremacy, he died before harmonious relations were established between the North and the South. He died at Hallowell, Me., Feb. 6, 1869.

CROSBY, William George, seventeenth governor of Maine (1853–55), was born in Belfast, Me., Sept. 10, 1805. He was seventh in descent from Simon Crosby, who came from Lancashire, England, in 1635, and settled at Cambridge, Mass. His father, Judge William Crosby, was an eminent jurist, and his mother was Sally, daughter of Benjamin Davis of Billerica, Mass. Young Crosby received his preparatory education at Belfast Academy, and entered Bowdoin College, where he was graduated in 1823, being the first person born in Belfast to receive a college education. Among his classmates were such eminent men as Franklin Pierce, William Pitt Fessenden, Henry W. Longfellow, Nathaniel Hawthorne, John S. C. Abbott, and others of genius and distinction. Mr. Crosby studied law with his father and began to practice in Boston, where he remained two years. He returned to Belfast in 1828, and continued to reside there permanently. From the first of his career, Mr. Crosby became prominently identified with the politics of his state. He was a Whig, believing that party to be the purest and most patriotic in the country. He was an active participant in the campaign for "Harrison and Reform," and in 1844 was a delegate to the national convention which nominated Henry Clay, and was one of his warmest supporters. When a department was established to remedy the existing defects in the common school system, Mr. Crosby was appointed secretary of the state board of education, and his active interest in the work resulted in the material advancement of the conduct of the public schools. In 1850 he was nominated by his party for governor of the state, but was defeated, and again in 1852, when, owing to the division in the Democratic party through the agitation of the Maine law and free soil issues, there was no choice of the people. The election was thrown into the legislature, and after a long struggle he was elected governor. He was re-elected in the same manner in the following year. Gov. Crosby administered the duties of his position acceptably, and his appointments to office were judicious. After the dissolution of the Whig party, Gov. Crosby took no active part in politics, though acting with the Democrats from that time. His sympathies were with the Union during the civil war, though he affiliated with

Andrew Johnson. He was defeated for congress as a Democratic candidate. In his profession Gov. Crosby was known as a man of integrity, rectitude, and impartial fairness. He chose rather to be the advocate of truth and justice, than the agent of power and oppression. He was an enthusiastic lover of nature, and the flowers and fruits of his garden were his untiring sources of recreation, while the woods and streams and lakes were his favorite haunts. He was prominent in all the educational, literary and charitable undertakings of his day. In religion he was a Unitarian. Gov. Crosby was an active Free Mason for forty years, and twice master of his lodge. In 1870 his alma mater, in which he was deeply interested, and of which he was a trustee for many years, conferred upon him the degree of LL.D. He was a member of the Maine Historical Society from 1846 to the end of his life. While at college he contributed fugitive poems to the newspapers, which were afterward published in book form. He was also the author of "Poetical Illustrations of the Athenaeum Gallery." He died in Belfast, March 21, 1881.

MORRILL, Anson Peaslee, eighteenth governor of Maine (1855-56), was born in Belgrade, Me., June 10, 1803, in a picturesque house, standing not far from the stream upon which was his father's mill. He received his education in his native town, putting to good account the short and infrequent terms of the district schools. He early began to assist his father in the mill, which was a combination of grist-mill, carding-mill and saw-mill, and even during his minority he won such a reputation for ability and integrity, that his endorsement upon his father's notes was honored in the money transactions necessary to the conduct of the business. Mr. Morrill was postmaster of his native town, and held other local offices while yet a young man. On reaching his majority he engaged in business for himself, keeping a general store in Belgrade. Here, too, he married Rowena M. Richardson, who lived to share his success and honors, and died at a ripe old age. Later Mr. Morrill removed to Belgrade Hill, and again to Madison, still continuing in the same line of business, that of a country storekeeper. In 1844 he took charge of a woolen mill at Readfield, then on the verge of ruin through mismanagement, invested all his savings in the stock of the company, to show his confidence in the enterprise, and eventually owned the factory. In 1853 he was elected to the state legislature by the Democratic party; in 1839 was made sheriff of Somerset county for one term, declining a reappointment, and held the office of land agent from 1850 to 1853. Mr. Morrill left the Democratic party on the prohibition issue in 1853. His early experiences in the business of keeping a country store, had so impressed him with the evils entailed upon the people, by the use of spirituous liquors, which at that time was one of the stock articles of trade that he became one of the first leaders in the organized temperance movement in the state. He was nominated for governor on the Prohibition and Free Soil ticket, and though defeated, he continued a life-long and ardent advocate of enforced prohibition in the state. He was again a candidate in 1854, and the result being undecisive, he was appointed by the state legislature to that office, being the first Republican governor of Maine. In 1860 he was elected to congress and took his seat in the ever-memorable extra session, convened July 4, 1861, at Mr. Lincoln's call for the means to suppress the civil war. Mr. Morrill did not feel that he could afford to neglect his business interests, and declined a renomination for a second term, and was succeeded by James G. Blaine, who then began his brilliant career. Mr. Morrill and Mr. Blaine were life-long friends; they were pioneers in the founding of the Republican party, and were members of the Republican national convention which nominated Fremont for the presidency in 1856. Mr. Morrill removed to Augusta in 1870, where he resided during the remainder of his life. In 1880, when in his seventy-eighth year, he was, through the insistence of his friends, again sent to the state legislature, serving with his wonted integrity. Gov. Morrill was president of the Maine Central Railroad from 1871 until he retired from business. Mr. Morrill was magnanimous, kind-hearted, charitable; subordinating all personal interests either in business, social or political relations to the most unswerving principle. Though known more widely as a leader in temperance and politics, he was liberal and progressive on all subjects, and an ardent student of modern research in the domains of thought and science. He was not a professor of religion in any outward sense, but was a devoted Universalist, and regular in his attendance on the church of that sect, and liberal in its support. He died, July 4, 1887, in Augusta, Me.

WELLS, Samuel, nineteenth governor of Maine (1856-57), was born in Durham, N. H., Aug. 15, 1801. He was a lawyer, and first settled in Waterville, Me., in 1826, remaining there until 1835; he had a large practice, and stood high at the bar and in the community. In 1835 he removed to Hallowell, where he resided until 1844, engaged in the labors of his profession. In 1836 and 1838 he represented Hallowell in the state legislature. In 1844 he removed to Portland and lived there three years. On Sept. 28, 1847, he was appointed by Gov. Dana an associate justice on the bench of the supreme judicial court of Maine. He continued in this office until March 31, 1854, when he resigned his commission. During his term of service he won an excellent reputation as a thorough jurist and impartial judge. Politically, he was a strong Democrat, and in 1855 was nominated by his party as its candidate for governor. He took up the duties of the office in January, 1856, and discharged them with marked ability. He was renominated at the close of the year, but, owing to the dissensions in his party on account of the slavery and temperance questions, he was defeated by Hannibal Hamlin, the candidate of the new Republican party. Mr. Hamlin received, in round numbers, 69,000 votes; Mr. Wells, 43,000, and Mr. Geo. F. Patten, the Whig candidate, only 6,500. This ended the career of the Whig party in Maine, and Gov. Wells was the last Democratic governor for more than twenty years. Being a strong party man, he took the defeat rather severely, and was not afterward prominent in Maine affairs. After a time he removed to Boston, where he spent the remainder of his days. He received the degree of A.M. from Colby University (then Waterville College) in 1833, and from Bowdoin College in 1838. He died July 15, 1868.

HAMLIN, Hannibal, twentieth governor of Maine (1857). (See Vol. II., p. 76.)

WILLIAMS, Joseph Hartwell, twenty-first governor of Maine (1857-58), was born at Augusta, Me., Feb. 15, 1814. His father was Reuel Williams, born in Augusta (then Hallowell), June 2, 1783, the son of Seth Williams, who emigrated to Augusta from Stoughton, Mass., in 1779. Reuel Williams was largely a self-made man; he became a member of the state legislature and senate, a U. S. senator, and was prominent in business and railroad matters. His wife was Sarah Lowell, daughter of Daniel Cony of Augusta. Joseph H. Williams was educated in the public schools and at a boarding-school at Wiscasset. He entered Harvard College in 1830, and was graduated in 1834; spent two years at the Dane Law School in Cambridge, and began to practice law at Augusta in 1837, succeeding to his father's extensive law business on the latter's election to the senate. He continued in practice twenty-five years, when the death of his father in 1862, leaving him a large estate to settle, made it necessary for him to give up the greater part of his law business. At about this time Gov. Washburn nominated him to a seat on the bench of the supreme court of Maine, but his avocations made it necessary for him to decline the honor. In his early years he was, like his father, an ardent Democrat, but in 1854, when chairman of the committee on resolutions of the Democratic state convention, he felt compelled to disapprove of the administration of Pres. Pierce, because of the latter's attitude towards the Missouri compromise. From that time he ceased to vote with the Democratic party as long as the interests of slavery continued to shape political issues. In 1856 he actively supported the Fremont ticket. On returning from a journey he found that, without his knowledge, he had been nominated for one of the state senators on the Republican ticket for Kennebec county. He accepted the nomination, was elected, and at the beginning of the session of 1857 was chosen to preside over the senate, thus becoming acting-governor, when, on Feb. 25, 1857, Gov. Hamlin resigned to accept the U. S. senatorship. Mr. Williams filled out the latter's term, but, though urged to become a candidate for the office on the following year, would not consent to accept the nomination, not favoring the prohibition plank in the platform of the new party. During the war he strongly supported all war measures, and was a valued adviser of the several governors who served through that period. He was in the state legislature for three years, 1864, 1865, and 1866; during the last two terms he was chairman of the committee on finance. In September, 1873, without his knowledge, and during his absence on a journey, he was elected to the legislature on an independent ticket. In 1877 he was the Democratic nominee for governor, but was not elected. He still resides in Augusta (1895), enjoying his home and large estate, and thoroughly respected by all. He was married, Sept. 26, 1842, to Apphia Putnam, daughter of the distinguished antiquarian and genealogist, Sylvester Judd of Northampton, Mass., and sister of Rev. Sylvester Judd, once a brilliant Unitarian pastor of Augusta. One son, who died at the age of two, was born of this union.

MORRILL, Lot Myrick, twenty-second governor of Maine (1858–60), was born in Belgrade, Me., May 3, 1813. He was one of a family of seven sons and seven daughters. He received his early education at the district schools, working in a saw-mill, and as clerk in a country store out of school hours. He early determined to be a lawyer, and to that end availed himself of every opportunity to study. At sixteen years of age he began to teach school, to increase his means of defraying the expenses of a college education. He entered Waterville College (now Colby) in 1833, but becoming impatient to prepare himself for his chosen profession, left college before the time he was to graduate, and entered the office of Judge Edward Fuller of Readfield. Mr. Morrill was admitted to the bar in 1837, and, entering into partnership with a fellow-student, Timothy Howe, began to practice in Readfield. Desiring a wider field for professional work, he removed to Augusta in 1841, and formed a partnership with James W. Bradbury; a connection which proved very congenial to both parties, and continued many years. Mr. Morrill was a Democrat in early life, but always opposed to the extension of slavery, and was a strong temperance man. He was elected to the state legislature in 1853, and again in 1854, and received a considerable vote against William Pitt Fessenden in the U. S. senatorial contest of that year. He was a member of the state senate in 1856, and president of that body the following year. During this session, Mr. Morrill opposed the attempted repeal of the prohibitory laws, and the removal of Judge Davis from the bench, in such vigorous speeches, as gained him a state reputation; and was a warm opponent of a resolution pledging the Democratic party of Maine to further concessions on the slave question in the territories. He was, notwithstanding, made a member of the Democratic state committee, but refused to act after the Cincinnati convention in 1856, which nominated Mr. Buchanan. He wrote in a letter to E. Wilder Farky, "The candidate is a good one, but the platform is a flagrant outrage upon the country, and an insult to the North." Mr. Morrill now allied himself to the Republican party, and was elected governor on that ticket in 1857 by a large majority. He was re-elected in 1858 and 1859. He was made U. S. senator in 1861, to fill out the unexpired term of Mr. Hamlin, on his resignation to accept the vice-presidency, and in 1863 was re-elected for the full term. In 1867 he was defeated by a single vote in the memorable Hamlin-Morrill senatorial contest of that year, but was soon called to fill the vacancy in the senate, caused by the death of Mr. Fessenden in September, 1869. He was again elected for the full term, but resigned in 1876 to accept the portfolio of the treasury under Gen. Grant's administration, an office he filled with distinction. So highly were his services appreciated, that Pres. Hayes gave him the choice of any position he might select, and on intimation that collector of customs for the port of Portland would be most congenial, he promptly received that appointment. Mr. Morrill was a noble man, and a faithful public servant. He was generous and warm-hearted, and in his public and private life the admiration of all who knew him. Mr. Morrill never fully recovered his health from a severe illness with nervous prostration in 1870, induced from overwork. He died in Augusta, Jan. 10, 1883.

WASHBURN, Israel J., twenty-third governor of Maine (1861–63). (See Vol. V., p. 400.)

COBURN, Abner, twenty-fourth governor of Maine (1863–64), was born in that part of the town of Canaan now called Skowhegan, March 22, 1803. His father, Eleazer Coburn, came to Maine in 1792, at the age of fifteen, from Dracut, Mass., and during his life was one of the most prominent citizens of the new region. In 1811 he represented his townsmen in the general court of Massachusetts, and afterward served several terms as senator or representative in the legislatures of Massachusetts and Maine. Gov. Coburn's mother (born Mary Weston), was descended from a Massachusetts family characterized by the best traits of Puritan character. Her grandfather, who came to Maine in 1772, lost his life as the guide of Benedict Arnold's expedition through the forests against Quebec. Abner Coburn's boyhood was spent on the farm and in assisting his father in land-surveying. His education was obtained at the district school and at Bloomfield Academy. He also taught for a short time. In 1825 he began to survey land on his own account, and in 1830, with his father and brother, Philander, formed the firm known as E. Coburn & Sons. Their business consisted in surveying and buying land, and cutting timber along the Kennebec. The greatest prosperity attended their efforts, and in 1845, when the father died, the two sons formed another firm, under the name of A. & P. Coburn, which was as prosperous as the old. They continued to purchase land up to 1870, when they were by far the largest landowners in the state, having 450,000 acres, or more than 700 square miles. Their operations were extended to the West, where at one time they held more than 60,000 acres of valuable timber land. Their sturdy integrity, combined with shrewdness and sagacity, made them leaders of industry along the Kennebec valley, and gave them a reputation throughout New England. Besides their lumber and land business, both brothers were prominently identified with the railroad interests of the state, and the now flourishing Maine Central Railroad owed much to their aid in its earlier days, when it consisted of two separate roads, the Kennebec and Portland and the Somerset and Kennebec. Abner Coburn was for several years president of the latter road, and after the consolidation he at one time owned 2,000 shares of stock. Mr. Coburn took an active part in politics. In early life he was a Federalist, later a Whig, and finally a Republican. As a Whig he was representative to the state legislature in 1838, 1840, and 1844. In 1852 he was on the electoral ticket when Gen. Scott was the Whig candidate for president. He was one of the founders in Maine of the Republican party. In 1855 he was on the council of Gov. A. P. Morrill, and in 1857 on that of Govs. Hamlin and Williams. In 1860 he was one of the presidential electors who voted for Abraham Lincoln. In 1862 he was nominated and elected governor of Maine by the Republican party, and served through the trying year of 1863 with distinguished patriotism and ability. His courage, wisdom, and unwavering loyalty to the Union gave Maine an administration that could not have been clearer or more efficient. He discharged his last public duty in 1884, when he was chairman of the Republican presidential electors. Gov. Coburn was prominent in philanthropic and educational movements. The Maine State College of Agriculture at Orono, Colby University (of whose trustees he was for years vice-president) at Waterville, and the Coburn Classical Institute in the same city, were greatly aided by him during his life, and the first two generously remembered in his will, the former receiving $100,000 and the latter $200,000. Though not a church member, he was strongly attached to the Baptist denomination, and aided it liberally. Among his bequests were $200,000 to the American Baptist Home Missionary Society, and $100,000 to the American Baptist Missionary Union. He died, Jan. 4, 1885, at Skowhegan, Me. He was never married.

CONY, Samuel, twenty-fifth governor of Maine (1864–67), was born in Augusta, Me., Feb. 27, 1811. He was descended from a Massachusetts family, being the fourth of the same name in the continuous line of descent. The first to bear the name was Deacon Samuel Cony, who was born in Boston in 1718, and removed to Maine from Shutesbury, Mass., in 1777. With him came his sons, Lieut. Samuel Cony, born in 1746, a revolutionary officer; and Daniel, also a revolutionary soldier, who after coming to Maine was a physician in Augusta, with an extensive practice; represented his town in the general court of Massachusetts; was a senator and member of the governor's council, and was one of the electors by whom Washington was chosen for his second presidental term. Gen. Samuel Cony, son of Lieut. Samuel, was born in Massachusetts in 1775; he was a merchant at Wiscasset and Augusta, and the first adjutant-general of Maine, holding the office for ten years. In 1803 he married Susan Bowdoin, daughter of his uncle, Daniel Cony, and from this union was born the subject of the present sketch. He enjoyed through his youth the advantages to be obtained in a family of culture and education. His early studies were carried on under private tutors and at China Academy. He first entered Wakefield College, but afterward removed to Brown University, where he was under the instruction of Pres. Wayland and where he was graduated in 1829. After leaving college he studied law with Hiram Belcher, at Farmington, Me., and Reuel Williams, at Augusta. He was admitted to the bar in 1832, and began to practice at Oldtown, Me. In 1835, at the age of twenty-four, he was a representative in the state legislature, and in 1839, at twenty-eight, was a member of the executive council of Gov. Fairfield. In 1840 he was appointed judge of probate for Penobscot county, an office that he held for seven years. In 1847 he was appointed land agent for the state; this position he held three years. In 1850

he was elected state treasurer, and re-elected for five successive years, which was the constitutional limit. The duties of this office made it necessary that he should return to Augusta which thereafter became his permanent residence. In 1854 he was elected mayor of the city. From his youth he had been a Democrat, but on the Lecompton question and other slavery issues he sided with Judge Douglas. On the breaking out of the war he became a war Democrat, and heartily supported every measure for suppressing the rebellion. In 1862 the Republicans of Augusta elected him to represent them in the legislature, where he was foremost in voting men and money to assist the cause of the Union. From that time he was ranked with the Republicans, and in 1863 he was nominated and elected by them governor of the state by a majority of 18,000 over Bion Bradbury, the Democratic candidate. He showed himself a worthy successor of Govs. Washburn and Coburn, the other war governors, and responded promptly to every call made by the national government for troops and supplies. He was twice re-elected, and in his last inaugural address at the opening of the legislature in January, 1866, announced that he would not accept another nomination. During the war Maine had sent to the front 71,558 men. Out of the 4,295 commissions issued by the executive of the state, Gov. Cony signed about 1,400. To his earnest patriotism and tireless labors much of the honor that Maine won during the civil war may justly be attributed. Gov. Cony was a man of fine personal appearance, and in private and public life a thorough gentleman. He was by nature strongly religious. Though he served his state so well in her time of need, his tastes were domestic, and his greatest happiness was found in his home, where his last few years were spent peacefully amongst his books and friends. He was twice married. His first wife, married Oct. 17, 1838, was Mercy H. Sewall of Farmington; she died Apr. 9, 1847, leaving him with two sons and a daughter. On Nov. 22, 1849, he married Lucy W. Brooks of Augusta, by whom he had two daughters and a son. He died in Augusta, Me., Oct. 5, 1870.

CHAMBERLAIN, Joshua Lawrence, twenty-sixth governor of Maine (1867-71). (See vol. I. p. 419.)

PERHAM, Sidney, twenty-seventh governor of Maine (1871-74), was born in Woodstock, Oxford co., Me., March 27, 1819. His father was Joel Perham, born in Paris, Me., in 1797, the son of Lemuel Perham, born in Upton, Mass., in 1760. His mother, Sophronia, was born in Paris, Me., in 1801, daughter of Rowse Bisbee, son of Galvin, who was a descendant of Thomas Bisbee, who came from England to Scituate harbor in 1634. Sidney Perham received his education in the district schools of his native town and at Gould Academy, Bethel. At the age of nineteen he began his labors as a teacher, and for fifteen years taught school during the winter months, and devoted himself to agriculture in the summer. During this time he took an active part in teachers' institutes and educational conventions. At the age of twenty-one he bought his father's homestead at Woodstock, and for twenty years following conducted farming operations on a comparatively large scale, making a specialty of sheep-raising. In 1853-54 he was a member of the Maine board of agriculture. He has always been a strong advocate of the cause of temperance, and in 1857 spoke in 200 towns urging the re-enactment of the repealed prohibitory law. He has also lectured on other subjects. At the age of twenty-two he was elected selectman of Woodstock, and afterward served the town in other offices. Politically he was a Democrat up to 1853, after which date he became one of the organizers of the Republican party, with which he has since been connected. In 1854 he was elected to the legislature, and at the opening of the session was chosen speaker, the first instance in Maine of a person with no previous legislative experience being elected to the office. In 1856 he was a presidential elector, voting with the others of his delegation for John C. Fremont. In 1858 he was elected clerk of the supreme court for Oxford county, and was re-elected in 1861; he resigned in January, 1863. In 1862 he was elected representative to congress, for the second Maine district, by about 2,500 majority, and in 1864 and 1866, re-elected by increased majorities. While in congress he was one of the pension committee, being chairman the last four years. The increase of claims created by the war made the duties of this position onerous, and necessitated the reorgan-

ization of the pension bureau on a broader basis. During Mr. Perham's term of service as representative he made several note-worthy speeches on the reconstruction of the states and on other subjects growing out of the war. In a speech delivered March 2, 1868, on the impeachment of the president, he arraigned Pres. Johnson for his violations of the constitution and laws; and on March 21, 1868, he spoke very ably on "Relief" from taxation and the national finances. He was faithful in the performance of all public duties and was regarded as a firm friend by the soldiers. In 1870 he was elected by the Republican party governor of Maine, by a majority

of over 9,000 votes; in 1871 he was re-elected by over 10,000 majority, and in 1872 by over 16,000. He advocated the reform of the jail system so that prisoners should be employed in some industrial pursuit; an industrial school for girls; the establishment of free high schools; and biennial elections and sessions of the legislature. All these measures were adopted, the first three during his administration and the last two. Since the founding of the industrial school he has been president of the board of trustees. From 1877 to 1885 he was appraiser for the port of Portland, resigning the position at the latter date. In 1891 he was appointed by Pres. Harrison a member of the commission for selecting a site for a dry-dock on the Gulf of Mexico. Since 1886 his winter home has been at Washington, D. C., his summers being spent at Paris Hill, Me. In religious faith Gov. Perham has always been a Universalist. He has often been president of the Universalist state convention and of the national convention. He has been for twenty-two years one of the trustees of the general convention, and a portion of the time president of the board. For several years he has been president of the board of trustees of Westbrook Seminary. Gov. Perham was married, Jan. 1, 1843, to Almena J. Hathaway of Paris, Me. They have three sons and two daughters, all living (1895) with the exception of one son, who died at the age of seven.

DINGLEY, Nelson, Jr., twenty-eighth governor of Maine (1874-76), was born at Durham, Androscoggin co., Me., Feb. 15, 1832. He was graduated at Dartmouth College in 1855. In 1856 he purchased the Lewiston "Weekly Journal," and adding a daily edition in 1863, became, and still is, its editor. In 1862-65, 1868, and 1873 he was a state legislator; and speaker of the house in 1863-64. In 1874 he was governor of Maine, and received the honorary degree of LL. D. from Bates College, and in 1894 received the same honor from Dartmouth College. He was re-elected governor in 1875. In

1876 he was a delegate to the National Republican convention. He was elected to the forty-seventh congress in 1881, at a special election to fill the vacancy made by the election of William P. Frye to the U. S. senate, and re-elected in 1882-94 to the forty-eighth, forty-ninth, fiftieth, fifty-first, fifty-second, fifty-third, and fifty-fourth congresses. Gov. Dingley's public life has been long, varied, and useful. Six times a member, and twice speaker of the Maine house of representatives, twice governor of his state, once delegate to a presidential convention, and eight times elected a national representative, covering twenty-four years of high office and illustrious service, his matured statesmanship and wide experience make him a valuable factor in the national councils. As an editor, he made his paper the leading Republican journal of his state. He has been one of the leaders of the powerful Republican party in New England. In congress he has taken an active part in the legislation upon shipping, the tariff, and currency. He has, during his entire life, been an ardent champion of the cause of temperance, and served as president of the Congressional Temperance Society. His long retention in exalted public trusts evinces his worth and ability, the esteem of his people, and the value of the New England practice of retaining disciplined men in place.

CONNOR, Selden, soldier and twenty-ninth governor of Maine (1876–79), was born at Fairfield, Me., Jan. 25, 1839. He was graduated at Tufts College in 1859, and was studying law at Woodstock, Vt., when the war began, but promptly threw down his books and enlisted, April, 1861, in the 1st Vermont. On the mustering-out of that regiment in August, 1861, he was commissioned lieutenant-colonel of the 7th Maine. In December, 1863, he became colonel of the 19th Maine, and by virtue of his rank commanded the first brigade, second division, second army corps, until the reorganization of the Army of the Potomac, March 23, 1864, when Gen. Gibbon was placed in command of the division, relieving Gen. A. S. Webb, who thereupon resumed command of the brigade. In the Battle of the Wilderness, May 6, 1864, he received a severe gunshot wound in the left thigh, necessitating the operation of exsection, which was performed at the field hospital. As soon as communication by water with Fredericksburg was reopened, he was conveyed to Washington where he remained in Douglass Hospital until August, 1865, when he was taken home on a stretcher. In April, 1866, the imperfectly knit bones were fractured anew by a fall. He was promoted brigadier-general of volunteers, June, 1864, and was mustered out of service Apr. 7, 1866, appointed assessor of internal revenues for the third district of Maine in 1868, and collector in 1874. In October, 1869, he married Henrietta, daughter of John Bailey of Washington. He was thrice elected governor of Maine, in 1875, 1876, and 1877, and nominated a fourth time in 1878, but owing to the rise of the Greenback party, failed to receive a majority of votes, as required by the state constitution. This threw the election upon the legislature, which, being controlled by a fusion of Democrats and Greenbackers, elected Garcelon, the Democratic candidate. The constitution has since been amended so that a plurality is sufficient to elect. In 1882 Pres. Arthur appointed Gen. Connor, U. S. agent for the payment of pensions in Maine, this office he held for four years. From the spring of 1887 until the fall of 1892 he was president of the Northern Banking Co., Portland. He has been commander of the department of Maine G. A. R., senior vice-commander of the G. A. R., and commander of the commandery of Maine, military

order of the Loyal Legion of the United States. He was elected president of the Society of the Army of the Potomac in 1890, and in October, 1895, junior vice-commander of the commandery-in-chief of the M. O. L. L. U. S. In October, 1889, he delivered the oration at the dedication of the monuments of Maine regiments on the field of Gettysburg. The degree of LL.D. was conferred upon him by Tufts College in 1876. In 1892 he was chosen president of the Maine State College by the trustees of that institution. Although the position was an important one and its duties would have been congenial to him and he was cordially urged by the officers and friends of the college to accept it, personal considerations compelled him to decline the office. In 1893 he was appointed adjutant-general of Maine by Gov. Cleaves.

GARCELON, Alonzo, thirtieth governor of Maine (1879–80), was born in Lewiston, Me., May 6, 1813, son of Col. William G. and Mary (Davis) Garcelon. His father was a prominent citizen of the town, and owner of a large farm on which the son worked during his youth, attending the town school in the winter. He afterward studied at the academies at Monmouth, Waterville, and Newcastle, and entered Bowdoin College in 1832, being graduated in 1836. During his course he earned money to pay his way by teaching school in winter. After graduation he taught three terms at the Alfred Academy, and then began the study of medicine at the Dartmouth Medical School, and under the private instruction of the famous Dr. Muzzey. When, in 1838, the latter was called to a professorship in the Medical College of Ohio, at Cincinnati, Mr. Garcelon accompanied him to take advantage of the greater facilities that a large hospital practice and numerous surgical operations would afford. Being graduated at this institution in 1839, Dr. Garcelon returned to Lewiston in October, and began the practice of his profession. He soon gained prominence as a physician, and built up a large practice. Politically he was reared a Whig, but his admiration of Pres. Jackson for the stand he took against nullification, led him to join the Democrats. Being strongly opposed to slavery, however, he afterward became a Free Soiler.

During the war he was a Republican, but not agreeing with the party in their reconstruction policy and their impeachment of Pres. Johnson, he withdrew and joined the Democratic party, of which he has since been a member. He represented Lewiston in the legislature in 1853 and 1857, and was in the state senate in 1855. In 1868 he was Democratic candidate for congressman. In 1871 he was elected mayor of Lewiston, being the first Democrat to hold that office. In 1878 he received the Democratic nomination for governor. There was no election by the people, neither of the three candidates in the field receiving a majority of votes, and the legislature, at the beginning of its session in 1879, chose Dr. Garcelon governor. He discharged the duties of the position with good judgment, firmness, and dignity. In the municipal and industrial progress of his native city Dr. Garcelon has been a prominent figure. He built the first mill in Lewiston, and was influential in obtaining railroad connections for the city. He was the first man to establish a newspaper there—starting the Lewiston "Journal" in 1847. It was largely through his efforts that Androscoggin county was formed, and the county-seat located at Auburn. He has always kept up his interest in agriculture, and has a fine farm in the northern part of Lewiston. Dr. Garcelon has been twice married: first, to Ann Augusta Philpot, of Somerset, N. H., by whom he had three sons and a daughter; his first wife died in December, 1857. On Jan. 13, 1859, he married Olivia N. Spear of Rockland, Me., who died some years ago, leaving one daughter.

DAVIS, Daniel Franklin, thirty-first governor of Maine (1880–81), was born in Freedom, Me., Sept. 12, 1843. His father, the Rev. Moses Franklin Davis, was a minister of the Christian Church, in charge of several small societies of that faith at and near Freedom. His mother Mary French, daughter of a minister of the Christian denomination, was related to the Brewsters and Frenches of the old colony of Massachusetts Bay. Young Davis received his education in the common schools of Stetson, to which town his father removed in 1854; but this was effectively supplemented by home study, in which his father and mother assisted him. His family being in limited circumstances, he had to engage at work on the farm, at home, and elsewhere; but anxious to fit himself for a profession, he kept up his studies, and effected an entrance at the East Corinth Academy in 1863. A company of troops being raised at his old home, he left school, and enlisted as a private soldier in October, 1863, and served until the close of the war. Having kept up his studies while in camp, he now entered the academy at Corinna, and later, the Kent's Hill Seminary. During this time he taught school in winter, and had private instruction from Prof. Sawyer of the Corinna Academy. In 1867 Mr. Davis began to read law with Lewis Barker, then a resident of Stetson, and was admitted to the bar of the state in 1868. He began to practice in East Corinth in 1869, and after holding some local offices and taking active part in the canvasses of the Republican party from time to time, was elected to the lower house of the state legislature in 1874. He represented Penobscot county in the state senate in 1878, and was elected governor of the state in 1879. He was renominated in 1880, but owing to the fusion of the Greenback and Democratic parties, was defeated in a very close contest by 130 votes. In 1881 he entered into partnership with Charles A. Baily of Oldtown, at Bangor, and has since devoted himself to the practice of his profession. He was subsequently collector of customs for the port of Bangor for four years. While still practicing law, much of his time is devoted to the management of timber lands in the state. Gov. Davis was married in East Corinth, Jan. 1, 1867, to Laura, only daughter of William Goodwin, of that place. Eight children were born to them, five sons and three daughters.

PLAISTED, Harris Merrill, thirty-second governor of Maine (1881–83), was born in Jefferson, N. H., Nov. 2, 1828. He was the son of Deacon William and Nancy (Merrill) Plaisted, and with his five brothers and three sisters, received the training to be derived from parents who, though not rich in worldly goods, were so in industry and piety. Deacon Plaisted was sixth in descent from Capt. Roger Plaisted, slain, with two sons, at Kittery by the Indians in King Phillip's War. Other noted names in the genealogical line are Col. John Plaisted, twenty years associate and chief justice of New Hampshire, and Judge Samuel Plaisted, Deacon William's father. Until the age of seventeen, Harris M. Plaisted remained at home, working on the farm and attending the district school; for the next three years he attended academies, spring and fall, and taught in the winter. He entered Waterville College in 1849, being graduated in 1853. While in college he taught the village school, was principal of the Waterville Liberal Institute, and superintendent of schools, elected by the town for three years. He was graduated at the Albany Law School in 1855, winning the first prize. He studied one year in Bangor, with A. W. Paine, and in 1856 began to practice law there. He was a member of Gov. Lot M. Morrill's staff for three years—1858, 1859, and 1860. After the breaking out of the civil war, he enlisted (August, 1861) in the 11th Maine. He was commissioned lieutenant-colonel Oct. 30, 1861, and colonel, May 12, 1862. During the peninsular campaign of 1862 he took part, as commander of his regiment, in the siege of Yorktown, the battles of Williamsburg, Fair Oaks, and the "Seven Days' Battles." He commanded his brigade in the siege of Charleston in 1863, and in the campaign of 1864–65 against Richmond and Petersburg. In this campaign his, "The Iron Brigade," lost, in killed and wounded, in fifty-nine days of fighting, 1,385 men out of 2,698. During his term of service his command never moved to the front without him. He was twice promoted by the president for "gallant and meritorious conduct in the field," and he received the highest commendation from Gen. Terry, his corps commander, and Maj.-Gen. Foster, his division commander. His popularity among his soldiers, and the esteem in which they held him, was shown by a resolution forwarded to him by one of his regiments after his return to Maine. In May, 1865, he returned to the practice of law at Bangor. In 1867–68 he represented that city in the legislature; in the latter year he was delegate-at-large to the national convention of his party. He was three times elected attorney-general of Maine—in 1873, 1874, and 1875,

and made a notable record. He was a member of the forty-fourth congress, but declined a renomination. In 1880 he was nominated for governor of Maine by the Democrats and Greenbackers, and was elected in a close contest for a two years' term. In 1883 and 1889 he was the Democratic candidate for the U. S. senate. In 1866 Gen. Plaisted delivered a very able oration at the laying of the corner-stone of Memorial Hall, Colby University. Since July, 1883, he has been editor of "The New Age," at

Augusta, Me. He has been twice married: first, Sept. 21, 1858, to Sarah, daughter of Chase P. Mason of Waterville. Three sons were born to them, Harold M., a graduate of Maine State College, 1881, and Stevens Institute of Technology, 1882, now a patent solicitor in St. Louis, Mo.; Frederick W., a graduate of St. Johnsbury Academy, and since 1885, one of the editors and proprietors of "The New Age"; and Ralph P., a graduate of Bowdoin College, 1894. Mrs. Plaisted died Oct 25, 1875, and Sept. 27, 1881, the general married Mable True, daughter of Francis W. Hill, of Exeter. One daughter has been born to them.

ROBIE, Frederick, thirty-third governor of Maine (1883-87), was born in Gorham, Me., Aug. 12, 1822. On both sides he is descended from the best English blood, his father's ancestors having come from England in 1660, and his mother's, the Lincolns, in 1637. His father, Toppan Robie, born in

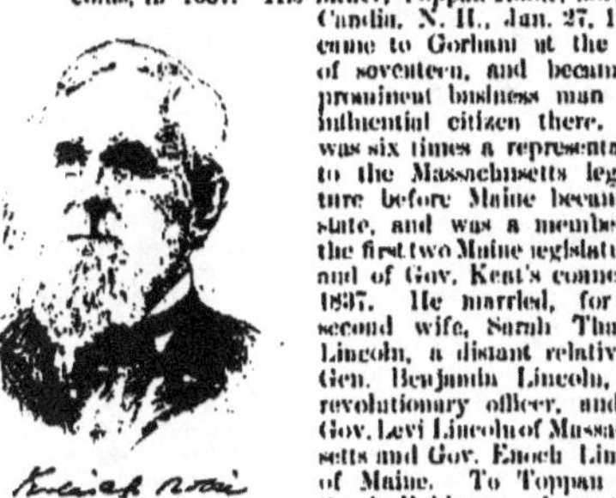

Candia, N. H., Jan. 27, 1782, came to Gorham at the age of seventeen, and became a prominent business man and influential citizen there. He was six times a representative to the Massachusetts legislature before Maine became a state, and was a member of the first two Maine legislatures, and of Gov. Kent's council in 1837. He married, for his second wife, Sarah Thaxter Lincoln, a distant relative of Gen. Benjamin Lincoln, the revolutionary officer, and of Gov. Levi Lincoln of Massachusetts and Gov. Enoch Lincoln of Maine. To Toppan and Sarah Robie were born three sons, with the youngest of whom we are at present concerned. Frederick Robie fitted for college at Gorham Academy and under private tutorship, and was graduated at Bowdoin College in 1841, at the age of nineteen. The same year he went South, and was principal of academies in Georgia and Florida. Having decided to be a physician, he studied medicine in the Jefferson Medical College in Philadelphia, receiving his degree of M.D. in 1844. He began practicing at Biddeford, Me., in April, 1844, and continued until May, 1855. He then removed to Waldoboro', Me., where he practiced very successfully for three years. In 1858 he returned to his native town of Gorham. At the breaking out of the civil war he was a member of the executive council of Gov. Israel Washburn; this position he resigned to accept from Pres. Lincoln the appointment of additional paymaster of U. S. volunteers. During the first two years of the war he was with the army of the Potomac, and in 1863 was stationed in Boston as chief paymaster of the department of New England. In 1864 he was transferred to the department of the Gulf, where he remained for more than a year. At the close of the war he was ordered to Maine to superintend the final payment of the soldiers of that state. For his services he received the brevet of lieutenant-colonel, Nov. 24, 1865. In 1866-67 he was a member of the Maine senate, and has ten times represented his native town in the legislature. In 1872 and 1876 he was speaker of the house. He was a member of the executive council of Gov. Davis in 1880, and of Gov. Plaisted in 1881-82. In 1882 he was nominated for governor by the Republicans, and elected by a plurality of nearly 9,000, which was largely increased in 1884, when he was re-elected. Politically, Gov. Robie has always been a Republican since the formation of the party. From 1868 to 1873

he was an active member of the Republican state committee. In 1872 he was a delegate to the National convention that nominated Gen. Grant for his second term. In 1878 he was appointed one of the commissioners to the Paris Exposition, and remained abroad a year. He has been identified with many business enterprises, is a director of the Portland and Rochester Railroad Co., of the Union Mutual Life Insurance Co., and of the First National Bank, Portland; of this last institution he is also president. He is a prominent member of the G. A. R. In agricultural pursuits he has always been greatly interested, and for eight years, from 1881, was worthy master of the Maine State Grange. Gov. Robie was married, Nov. 27, 1847, to Olivia M. Priest of Biddeford. Four children, three daughters and one son, have been born to them.

BODWELL, Joseph Robinson, thirty-fourth governor of Maine (1887), and business man, was born in Methuen, Mass., that portion now embraced in the city of Lawrence, June 18, 1818. His father, Joseph Bodwell, owned a small farm, and being in poor circumstances, young Joseph went to live with Patrick Fleming, in the town of Methuen proper, where he worked on the farm. He received little education in the district school, and at the age of sixteen hired out for $6 a month as a farm hand. A year later he began to attend school in the daytime and to work at the trade of shoemaking nights and mornings, often working far into the night. In 1838 he bought a farm at West Methuen, in company with his father, and they worked it together for ten years. When the improvements were begun on the Merrimac river at Lawrence, young Bodwell hauled the stone for the building of the dam from Pelham, N. H., where it was quarried. This was the beginning of those extensive operations in the stone business, with which he was afterward identified. In 1852, in company with Moses Webster, he went into the business on his own account, beginning operations on Fox Island, Vinalhaven, with one yoke of oxen, which he drove, tended, and shod himself. This was a most admirable location and the quality of granite very fine. The stone would be lifted into the hold of a vessel, and carried to New York, Boston, and other points at a cost which defied competition. Business increased

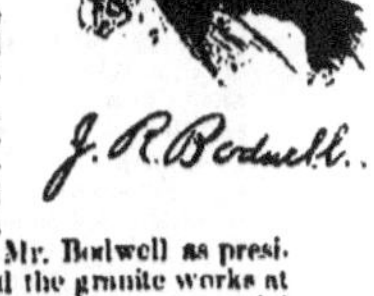

so rapidly, that in time a corporation was formed, with Mr. Bodwell as president and general manager, and the granite works at Vinalhaven became the largest and most successful in the country. Some of the finest government and public buildings in the country were built from stone cut at Fox Island quarries. In 1866 he removed to Hallowell, Me., and opened the Hallowell quarries. This granite is much lighter in color, more easily worked, and more suited to the lighter styles of architecture and monumental work. The great statue of Liberty, which surmounts the Pilgrim's Monument at Plymouth Rock, was cut at the Hallowell quarries. Mr. Bodwell was engaged in other large enterprises. He purchased a large farm, and engaged in stock-breeding and stock-raising; was in ice and lumbering operations on the Kennebec; projector and president of Bodwell Water Power Co. at Oldtown; and in several railroad operations, all of which were most successful. He took no part in politics, beyond what is incumbent upon a good citizen, but was for two years mayor of Hallowell and a representative in the city legislature. In 1880 he was a delegate to the Republican convention at Chicago. In 1880 he was nominated for governor of Maine, much against his will, and was elected. During the short term of his administration he conducted the business of the state in a manner highly satisfactory to his constituents. Mr. Bodwell never forgot the struggles of his own early life, and his sympathy and help were always extended to those similarly situated. Generous, warm-hearted, and broad-minded, he was no less lovable than he was energetic and enterprising, and his death was widely lamented. He died at his home in Hallowell, Dec. 15, 1887.

MARBLE, S. S., thirty-fifth governor of Maine (1887-89). (See index).

BURLEIGH, Edwin C., thirty-sixth governor of Maine (1889-93). (See Vol. I., p. 429.)

CLEAVES, Henry B., thirty-seventh governor of Maine (1893-), was born in Bridgton in 1840, and educated in the common schools and at the academy. He attended school in the fall and spring, working on the farm in summer, and in the woods, cutting and hauling wood and lumber, in winter. He enlisted in the summer of 1862 in company B, 23d Maine volunteers, a regiment of nine months' men. It was expected at that time, when the government called for nine-months' men, that the rebellion would be crushed before the expiration of the term of service. Young Cleaves served during the first enlistment with his regiment at Poolsville, on the Potomac, and at Harper's Ferry, and was advanced to orderly sergeant. The regiment was mustered out of service in the following July, by reason of the expiration of the term of service. Sergt. Cleaves at once re-enlisted for three years, and was appointed first lieutenant of company F, and a portion of the time was in command of company E, the officers of the latter company having been either killed or dis-

abled in action. The regiment was sent to New Orleans and attached to the army in the department of the Gulf. He participated in various engagements under Gen. Banks, and in the Red river expedition, and was with Col. Fessenden's regiment at Mansfield, Pleasant Hill, and Cane River Crossing, Col. Fessenden losing his leg in the latter action while the regiment was making a brilliant charge. The 30th suffered severely. At the close of the campaign in Louisiana, Lieut. Cleaves's regiment was transferred to Virginia, and he served during the remainder of the war in the army of the Potomac and in the Shenandoah Valley, under Gen. Sheridan. He was mustered out of service at the close of the war, and offered a commission in the regular army by Sec. Stanton, but declined. He made a notable reputation for personal valor, and, as it was feelingly remarked by one of his command, "a braver and better officer never drew a sword." Mr. Cleaves's first vote for president was cast for Abraham Lincoln while he was still in active service in Virginia, in 1864. At the close of the war he returned to his home in Bridgton, and worked for two years in a sash and blind factory and lumber yard. In January, 1868, he began the study of law, and in September was admitted to the bar. He formed a copartnership, and practiced in Bath for about a year, when he removed to Portland. Mr. Cleaves was a member of

the legislature in 1876-77, and chairman of the judiciary committee. In 1877 he was elected city solicitor, and during his two years of office tried many important cases. In 1880 he was made attorney-general of the state, and was twice re-elected, serving five years. During the first year he was instrumental in securing the passage by the legislature of a new tax act relative to the taxation of railroad and telegraph companies, designed to procure more revenue to the state from those sources. The taxes were duly assessed against these corporations; the railroads refused to pay, and suits were brought. The cases were carried to a successful termination by Mr. Cleaves, and all decided in favor of the state, nearly $100,000 being subsequently paid into the state treasury resulting from this litigation. During his term of office as attorney-general, he was engaged in the prosecution of some eighteen murder cases. Among the more notable was the case of Wallace and Benjamin Chadbourne at Dover, for the murder of Alvin Watson, the trial occupying some three weeks, and in which Byron Chadbourne, a celebrated deaf-mute, figured prominently. Mr. Cleaves is a prominent member of the G. A. R. and the Maine State Veteran Association. In the practice of his profession, and in matters of charity, he has always shown a great friendship for the "old soldier." His defense of William T. Best, in the extradition proceedings brought against him by the province of New Brunswick, excited great interest. Best served in the American navy, and it was claimed at the time that he was the first sailor who had lost a leg in the service. After his discharge from the navy he settled on Campobello Island. He was a member of the G. A. R. post at Eastport. In October, 1888, he had a controversy with Edward M. Batson, a resident of Campobello Island, and during the controversy Best drew his revolver and fired at Batson, wounding him in the face. Best took his boat and rowed to the American side, landing at Eastport, followed by Batson's father, armed with rifles, who kept up a constant fire upon Best. Best, standing in the stern of his boat, returned this fire with a small revolver which he had with him, but his shots fell short. The officers at New Brunswick commenced extradition proceedings against Best in the district court of the United States at Portland, charging that he attempted "feloniously and of malice aforethought" to kill Edward M. Batson. At the request of the Eastport G. A. R. post, Mr. Cleaves appeared for Best. The commissioner before whom the case was heard, after a protracted hearing, committed Best to jail, certified the proceedings to Washington, and a warrant was issued by the state department for the surrender of Best and his return to Campobello Island for trial there. The officer arrived from New Brunswick to take Best back to Campobello, but Mr. Cleaves applied for a writ of *habeas corpus*, claiming that the prisoner was illegally detained; that the proceedings before the commissioner were void; that the warrant issued by the secretary at Washington was illegal, and that no authority existed under the treaty for the surrender to the authorities at New Brunswick. Best, who had been confined in jail about sixty days, was brought into court and, after a protracted hearing, was discharged, to the great satisfaction of his old comrades, as well as his counsel, Mr. Cleaves. He returned to Eastport and has since lived there, in sight of Campobello. Gov. Cleaves attends High Street Congregational Church. He is generous and charitable, although a man of moderate means. He is tall, has a manly figure, a military bearing, and altogether a notable appearance. He is a good citizen, a genial gentleman, and Portland was proud to present to the state such an able chief magistrate.

HAYDEN, Hezekiah Sidney, capitalist, was born in Haydens, Windsor, Conn., Jan. 29, 1816, a descendant of the seventh generation from William Hayden, who came from Devonshire, England, to Windsor, about the year 1640, and from whom have descended many whose names are familiar in the early history of Connecticut. Obtaining his early education in the district school, he entered a country store at the age of sixteen, and two years later he joined his elder brother in Charleston, S. C., applying himself with such energy to his business, that on the retirement of his brother, in 1843, he took charge of the business himself, and conducted it successfuly for about fifteen years. During Mr. Hayden's residence in Charleston he came in daily contact with slavery, a subject which was then discussed with strong feeling both North and South, and while his feelings revolted against it, he believed the blacks were better provided for and happier than they would be if left to their own resources and therefore he deprecated the denunciation of the South by the abolitionists. He enlisted in many public enterprises for the religious instruction of the blacks, both slave and free, being for considerable time superintendent of a negro Sunday-school. In 1843 he, with his partner, Wm. Gregg, became owner of Jesse Young, a skilful jewelry-workman, of the value of $2,000, and became his full owner in 1846, on the retirement of his partner. Two years later he purchased Jesse's entire family, of the number of twelve persons, to prevent their separation. They were subsequently sent to New Orleans, and Mr. Hayden entered into $10,000 bonds to support them during life, and prevent their ever becoming a public charge, and he made good his promise supporting his charges until they were manumitted under the emancipation proclamation. Shortly after Mr. Hayden returned to Windsor, in 1858, he erected buildings for a Young Ladies' Institute, which has been conducted successfully. He has served in both branches of the state legislature: in the senate in 1866, where he served as chairman of the joint special committee, for the care and education of the orphans of soldiers, and in the house in 1868 and 1872, where he was on the joint standing committee on the school fund. He was judge of probate for twenty-seven years, until disqualified by the seventy years limit set by law for all judicial officers. He was appointed chairman of the trustees to select a site and erect buildings for a hospital for the insane; and has had supervision over the erection of nearly all the buildings now composing the Connecticut Hospital for the Insane at Middletown, which cost the state over $1,000,000. He served on the board gratuitously, voluntarily retiring in July, 1889. He is one of the trustees and the treasurer of the Loomis Institute, an educational institution to be established with its large fund at the old Loomis Homestead in Windsor, Conn. His enterprises and investments have added much to the growth and attractiveness of the historic old town of Windsor, in which he takes commendable pride as the home of his ancestors from their early settlement in this country. He has been an active member and large contributor to Grace Episcopal Church in Windsor, of which he is the senior warden. Mr. Hayden married, Oct. 9, 1848, Abbey S., daughter of Col. James Loomis of Windsor, a descendant of one of the first settlers of the town.

POOL, Maria Louise, author, was born at Rockland (then known as E. Abington), Mass., in 1845, daughter of Elias and Lydia (Lane) Pool. She received her education at the public schools of her native place. She began to write early, and before she was out of her teens became a contributor to the "Galaxy" and other magazines. In 1870 she removed to Brooklyn, and after fulfilling an engagement to write exclusively for a Philadelphia paper, she began a connection with the "Evening Post" and the "Tribune," of New York, which laid the foundation of her reputation. In the latter paper her sketches, dated from Ransom, were very favorably noticed for their almost photographic fidelity to New England country life, and their qualities of humor and pathos. Much of her journalistic work has had a new lease of life in book form, her published works consisting of "A Vacation in a Buggy" (New York, 1887); "Tenting at Stony Beach" (Boston, 1888); "Dally" (1891); "Roweny in Boston" (New York, 1892); "Mrs. Keats Bradford" (New York, 1892); "Katharine North" (New York, 1893); "The Two Salomes" (New York, 1893); "Out of Step" (New York, 1894); and "Against Human Nature" (New York, 1895). For a few years Miss Pool was a resident of Wrentham, Mass. She now lives in her native town, Rockland, Mass.

HAMMOND, Edward Payson, evangelist, was born in Ellington, Conn., Sept. 1, 1831. He is descended on his father's side from an old family who came to England with William the Conqueror, and whose name is registered on "The Battle Abbey Roll" at Hastings. His American ancestor was Thomas Hammond of Lavenham, England, who settled in Hingham, Mass., in 1635. His mother, Esther Griswold, was a descendant of Geo. Griswold of Kenilworth, Warwickshire, England. Mr. Hammond was graduated at Williams College in 1858, and afterwards studied theology in the New York Theological Seminary, and the Seminary of the Free Church, Edinburgh, Scotland. While a student at Edinburgh his evangelistic work began. He was invited by the ministry to hold meetings and special services in which they assisted him. Halls were hired that would hold immense audiences and tens of thousands who never entered the church were drawn to these meetings, and thousands converted. From 1861–66 Mr. Hammond held meetings in many of the states of the Union, and the cities of Canada. From Montreal, where audiences of thousands assembled nightly to hear him, he went to New York, and was ordained by the Presbytery of that city as an evangelist. In his teachings he was careful to state his belief in the doctrine of God's word, as far as possible, in Bible language, and it was therefore difficult for anyone to learn from his preaching to what denomination he belonged. In 1866 Mr. Hammond was married to Eliza Overton of Towanda, Pa., a great granddaughter of George Clymer, one of the signers of the Declaration of Independence; with her he visited the Holy Land, where he wrote "Sketches of Palestine." He traveled through the continent of Europe, holding meetings in Paris, Florence, and Naples. He spent some time in Scotland and Wales, and then went to London, where for sixteen weeks he held meetings in various parts of the city, including one week in Mr. Spurgeon's tabernacle. As a direct result of these services the Children's Special Mission was inaugurated. In 1875, Mr. Hammond accompanied by his wife, was sent by Gen. O. O. Howard to Alaska. He held meetings in Fort Wrangle and other places, and some

of the natives were converted. The results of his work were published, and Mr. Hammond did much to stimulate Christians of various denominations in this country and in Scotland to send missionaries there. The next year he held great meetings for twelve weeks in Washington, preaching each Sabbath from the steps of the capitol, where the presidents are inaugurated to audiences of 15,000 to 20,000. Wherever he went the people thronged to hear him, and multitudes were brought to Christ. Mr. Hammond has long been a writer for religious papers of various denominations, and he is associate editor of "The Worker." His numerous books and tracts have been published by such houses as the London Sunday-School Union, and The London Religious Tract Society, the Drummond Tract Society of Scotland, the Baptist Publication Society of Philadelphia, and the New York Tract Society. His book, "The Conversion of Children," has been translated into various languages. Within a few years it has appeared in the Tamil language, spoken by 15,000,000 people in Southern India. Rev. P. C. Headley in "The Reaper and the Harvest," a book of 550 pages, published by F. H. Revell, and in London by Morgan & Scott, gives an account of Mr. Hammond's labors.

CHILDS, Henry Warren, lawyer, was born in the village of Belgium, Onondaga co., N. Y., Nov. 24, 1848, son of Philander and Mary (Preston) Childs, whose ancestors came to America in early colonial days, settling in Massachusetts. His father became a resident of Onondaga county in 1850 and continued to reside therein, and mostly engaged in farming until his death, which occurred in 1876, and in his seventy-second year. His grandfather on his mother's side, Benjamin Preston, became a resident of the same county about the year 1810, and participated as a minute-man in the battle at Fort Oswego. The subject of this sketch resided with his parents until reaching his majority, attending in the meantime the district and village schools, Falley Seminary, Fulton, N. Y. and Central Conference Seminary, Cazenovia, N. Y., where he was graduated in 1871. He then engaged in teaching for several years in his native county. Later he took up the study of law, and was admitted to the bar in 1881, at, Syracuse N. Y., where he opened a law office in the same year. He removed, in 1883, to Fergus Falls, Minn., where he continued the practice of his profession. In 1887 he was appointed assistant attorney-general, and took up his residence at St. Paul. In 1892 he was elected attorney-general on the Republican ticket, and in 1894 he was re-elected to the same office. He delivered the Columbian address before the Minnesota Historical Society, at the state capitol in 1892. He was married in 1883 to Alberta A., daughter of Alanson Hakes, a citizen of his native county. He has one child, a son, James A., born in 1886.

CONLEY, John Wesley, clergyman, was born near Cedar Rapids, Ia., Nov. 20, 1852. When very young his parents removed to Floyd county, Ia., then the western frontier, and settled upon government land. He attended the district school in winter, working on the farm in summer. At the age of fifteen he entered the Cedar Valley Seminary at Osage, Ia., where he remained two years, teaching school afterward to procure the means to carry him through college. He was graduated at the State

University of Iowa in 1877, with the degree of A.B. Three years later the same institution gave him the degree of A.M. On entering college, it was his intention to prepare himself for the legal profession, but becoming converted and joining the Baptist church during his Sophomore year, he decided to enter the ministry. During his college life he was active in Christian work, and preached occasionally. He was licensed to preach, and was pastor of the Baptist Church in Downey, Ia., for one year, teaching school at the same time. In 1881 he entered the divinity school of the University of Chicago, where he was graduated in 1881, with the degree of B.D. During this time he preached for the Baptist Church of Hadley, Ill., having been ordained by a council of the church, thus defraying his expenses. Mr. Conley was married to Sarah Elizabeth daughter of Samuel Clyde of St. Ansgar, Ia., in 1878. She had been a fellow-student with him at college, and after marriage took the theological course with him. In 1887 Mr. Conley was called to the pastorate of the First Baptist Church at Joliet, Ill., where he labored with marked success for eight years. He was for three years pastor at Oak Park, Chicago, and at the same time instructor of the English New Testament in his alma mater. In 1892 he resigned his pastorate to accept the chair of missions in the divinity school of the University of Chicago, and the superintendency of city missions. In 1893 he accepted a call to the First Baptist Church of St. Paul, Minn., as opening to him a field of great promise, and entered at once upon the work, which has progressed wonderfully. As a preacher, Mr. Conley magnifies the doctrines of grace, and is aggressive and evangelistic. He keeps in close touch with current thought, and topics of interest, and is active in temperance reform. He is an extensive reader and progressive thinker, and has contributed largely to religious periodicals.

BRUCE, Sanders Dewees, soldier and editor, was born in Lexington, Ky., Aug. 16, 1825. His father, John Bruce, born 1770, in Northumberlandshire, England, of Scottish parents, was a direct descendant of Robert Bruce, the most famous of Scottish kings. His mother, Margaret Ross Hutton, born at Gibraltar in 1772. Col. S. D. Bruce was educated in the Transylvania University at Lexington, Ky., where he was graduated in 1846. In 1848 he engaged in mercantile business, which he continued until the opening of the civil war, when, being a staunch Union man, he offered his services to the government, and was appointed inspector-general of the Union Home Guard of Kentucky. He was subsequently instrumental in having the department of the Cumberland established, and it was due to his efforts that the army of the West secured the services of its two eminent commanders, Gens. William T. Sherman and George H. Thomas. He recruited the famous 20th regiment, Kentucky infantry volunteers, of which he was elected colonel. While in command of the post at Smithland, Ky., he built the fortifications at the mouth of the Cumberland river. He was afterward ordered to Louisville, Ky., and assigned to the command of the 22d brigade, Gen. Nelson's division, army of the Cumberland, marching at its head in the rapid advance to the battle-field of Shiloh. His brigade was the first in the army to take part in that critical battle, crossing the river under fire on the evening of Sunday, Apr. 6, 1862, to the relief of Gen. Grant's beaten and disheartened army. In this battle Col. Bruce was injured by the falling of his horse, and went on sick leave to Louisville, Ky. On his recovery he was assigned by Gen. Buell to the command of the post at Bowling Green, Ky., with orders to keep open the line of communication at that point, and there he directed the construction of the almost impregnable fortifications on College Hill. Later, as commander of the provisional brigade, he was ordered to Clarksville, Tenn., and cleared the obstructions from the Cumberland river below Fort Donelson, thus opening water communication with Nashville. He was subsequently placed in command of the post of Louisville, Ky., forwarding supplies and troops to Gen. George H. Thomas, and was of great assistance to him in winning the important battle of Nashville. Gen. Sherman recommended his promotion to brigadier-general, which was warmly endorsed by Gen. Grant; but, in view of Sec'y Stanton's prejudice to Southern men, the recommendation was never forwarded. In the summer of 1864 Col. Bruce was obliged to withdraw from the service, on account of heart-trouble, and having resigned his commission, went to New York city. There, after a period of recuperation, he founded, Aug. 5, 1865, the widely-known sporting journal, "Turf, Field and Farm," which is still under his editorial control. In this field Col. Bruce was thoroughly at home, being at that time, and ever since, the best living authority upon the pedigree and genealogy of thoroughbred horses, and in all matters relating to the turf and field sports. He is author and compiler of the "American Stud Book," of which six volumes have been issued; and has published "The Horse-Breeder's Guide and Hand-Book," and "The Thoroughbred Horse." Col. Bruce is a member of the Coney Island Jockey Club, in whose purposes and welfare he takes much interest. He also belongs to the American Geographical Society, and other sporting and social organizations in New York city, where he still resides.

KEPHART, Horace, librarian, was born at East Salem, Juniata co., Penn., Sept. 8, 1862. He was a descendant of Nicholas Kephart, a Swiss, who emigrated to Pennsylvania in 1747. He was graduated at Lebanon Valley College in 1879, and afterwards took a postgraduate course in Boston and Cornell Universities. In the winter of 1884 he went abroad, spending most of his time in Italy, preparing a bibliography of Petrarch from the materials collected by Willard Fiske. Upon his return to America, he was for a short time in the library of Rutgers College, and afterwards spent four years in that of Yale University. In 1890 he accepted the position of librarian in the Mercantile Library, St. Louis, Mo. He is a valued contributor to periodicals on historical and bibliographical subjects. The library, under his management, promises to become one of the best equipped in the West. He is yet but a young man, and is destined to become pre-eminent in the ranks of his profession. As a classifier of books, he is unequaled.

CROSS, Judson Newell, lawyer, was born in the town of Philadelphia, Jefferson co., N. Y., Jan. 16, 1838, son of Rev. Gorham Cross, Congregational minister of Richville, N. Y. His mother was Sophia Murdock of Townshend, Vt. When the son was seventeen years old he entered Oberlin College, Ohio. At the outbreak of the civil war he enlisted in company C, 7th Ohio Infantry, composed of Oberlin students, and was elected first lieutenant Apr. 29, 1861; was with his regiment through the several campaigns in West Virginia in 1861. At the battle of Cross Lanes in West Virginia, Aug. 26, 1861, he was severely wounded and taken prisoner, but was afterward recaptured by Maj. R. B. Hayes, at the battle of Carnifex Ferry, Va., Apr. 10, 1861. On Nov. 25, 1861, he was promoted to captain. He went to Cleveland, O., as a recruiting officer, and rejoined his regiment early in 1863, at Dumfries, Va. On Sept. 11, 1862, at Oberlin, O., he married Clara Steele Norton, a descendant of John Steele, the leader of the founders of Connecticut. In 1863 he was commissioned first lieutenant in the 5th veteran reserve corps, and afterward captain by Pres. Lincoln. He commanded the military post at Madison, Ind., with six companies of infantry, remaining until April, 1864, when he was made adjutant-general of the military district of Indiana at Indianapolis, and was ordered to Kentucky during Morgan's raid. In July, 1864, he was appointed assistant provost marshal on the staff of the military governor of Washington, and in November, 1864, provost marshal of Georgetown, D. C., and soon after special mustering officer, to muster for pay at Annapolis, Md., the 18,000 returned prisoners of war from Andersonville. He was honorably discharged March 16, 1865, and studied law at Columbia College Law School, and at the Albany Law School, graduating in the spring of 1866. He commenced the practice of law at Lyons, Ia., where for about ten years he was a partner of A. R. Cotton, M.C.; was the mayor of the city of Lyons in 1871; went to Minneapolis in October, 1875, and formed a law partnership with his old classmate, Judge H. G. Hicks. He was three times elected city attorney of Minneapolis, and held the office from 1883 to 1887. He was the author of the famous and novel patrol limits ordinance and charter provision of Minneapolis, which he maintained in  the courts, which limits the licensing of saloons to the immediate business centre of the city, about one-twelfth of the territory, where the saloons can be actively watched by the police. This was pronounced by Archbishop Ireland the best repressive license ordinance yet devised. He brought suits, also pioneers of their kind, and compelled the railroads passing through the city to depress their tracks about fourteen feet, and build iron bridges over four of the principal avenues of the city. He was appointed by the legislature a member of the first board of park commissioners of Minneapolis in 1883; and in 1885 Gov. Hubbard appointed him a commissioner to represent Minnesota at the funeral of Gen. Grant in New York. He was a member of the board of immigration commissioners who were sent to European countries in 1891 to observe matters in reference to immigration into the United States, and while in England he ferreted out, and reported to the government, the custom of sending prisoners out of English prisons to the United States, through the agency of the Prisoners' Aid Societies, at the expense of the British government. In 1895, in a letter to Pres. Dole of Hawaii, he urged voluntary annexation to the United States.

HUFF, George Franklin, banker and senator, was born in Norristown, Montgomery co., Pa., July 13, 1842, son of George and Caroline (Boyer) Huff. His paternal ancestry dates back to Baldwin Von Hoof (now written Huff), who resided on the family estates near the city of Passau, Bavaria. He was famous among the Bavarian knighthood and nobility, and lost his life in the first crusade in July, 1008, at the storming of Jerusalem. George F. Huff's paternal great-grandparents were natives of Berlin, Germany. Huff's Church, Berks county, Pa., is so called because of the donation of land at that place by them for a church site and burial grounds. George began to attend the public schools when he was four years old, and remained until he was seventeen, when he entered the shops of the Pennsylvania Railroad Co., at Altoona, to learn the trade of car-finishing. After three years he entered the banking house of Lloyd & Co., and in 1865, they sent him to Ebensburg, Cambria co., Pa. to establish a banking house. In that mission he was successful beyond the expectations of all concerned. In 1867 he removed to Greensburg, and established the Greensburg Deposit Bank of Lloyd, Huff & Co., with branches at Latrobe, Irwin, and Mt. Pleasant. These banks went out of business in 1873. In 1871 Mr. Huff organized the Farmer's National Bank of Greensburg, with a capital of $100,000, and was its first president, remaining at the head of the bank until 1874, when he took the active management of its business as cashier, and Gen. Richard Coulter was elected president. Subsequently the officers of the bank procured an act of congress changing its location and name. It then became the Fifth National Bank of Pittsburgh, and upon its removal to that city Mr. Huff was chosen vice-president, which position he held until 1876. In 1874 he helped organize the Greensburg Banking Co; was elected cashier and served until 1887. He is largely interested in the coke and coal industries of Westmoreland county, and was mainly instrumental in the establishment of the Greensburgh, Hempfield, Argyle, United Coal and Coke, Mutual Mining and Manufacturing, Manor Gas, Latrobe, and Carbon Coal companies, which furnish employment for many hundred men. Col. Huff also took an active part in organizing the Southwest Pennsylvania Railroad, whose main line passes through the heart of the Connellsville coal and coke region, and is a director of that company. He is identified with, and is director in, the Greensburg Electric Street Railroad Co., Greensburg Fuel Co., Greensburg Gas (illuminating) Co. He was first president of the Greensburg Steel Co.; of the Greensburg Electric Light, and Westmoreland Water companies; has been an important factor in the development of the Jeanette natural gas region, and the building of the town of Jeanette. At Burrell, the adjoining station, he donated several acres of land for a manufacturing site. To the material development of Greensburgh, no citizen of the place has contributed more than Senator Huff. He has built a fine residence, put up a block of buildings, and erected one of the finest and most imposing business buildings within the county. His "Rose Fountain Farm," which adjoins the borough, contains about 180 acres of land, and with its four miles of drive, handsome groves, large fish ponds, and springs of pure, cold water, has become the favorite drive and pedestrian resort for the citizens of Greensburg. Senator Huff was married, March 16, 1871 to Henrietta Burrell, of Greensburg, daughter of Jeremiah Murry Burrell, formerly judge of the tenth judicial district of Pennsylvania, and afterwards U. S. assistant judge of the territory of Kansas. To Senator and Mrs. Huff have been born eight children. Senator Huff is a progressive Republican, and "can justly claim a larger political following than any other man in his county." His political career commenced in 1880, when he came into national prominence in the Republican convention at Chicago as one of the "Old Guard," or "Immortal 306," which was led by the imperious and incorruptible silver-haired senator of New York, in support of the "Great Commander" for the presidential nomination. In 1884 Mr. Huff was the Republican candidate for state senator in the thirty-ninth senatorial district, comprising Westmoreland county. In 1887 he was nominated for congress in the twenty-first district, by the Republicans of Westmoreland county, but failed to secure the district nomination. Receiving the nomination in 1890, he was elected by a handsome majority. In 1894 he was nominated as one of the congressmen-at-large of Pennsylvania, and was elected by a majority approximating 244,000. Socially he is the same affable, approachable gentleman to high and low alike, and has won success and position in life by his intellectual ability, untiring energy, and indomitable perseverance.

POSEY, Thomas, soldier, was born on the Potomac in Virginia, July 9, 1750. Little is known of his origin. He seems not to have belonged to the distinguished colonial family of that name, whose first American founder was a member of the first Maryland house of burgesses, and another, Belain Posey, who saved all that was saved at the battle of Long Island. In 1869 his family removed to the western frontier of Virginia. He was assistant in the quartermaster's department in Lord Dunmore's Shawnee expedition in 1774, and participated in the battle with the Indians at Point Pleasant, the junction of the Kanawha and Ohio rivers, Oct. 10, 1774. He was commissioned by congress as captain in the Continental service, raised a company, and joined the 7th Virginia regiment, and took part in the battle at Gwynn's Island, July 8, 1776, in which Lord Dunmore was defeated. Later he was transferred to Col. Morgan's celebrated regiment of riflemen, raised in Virginia by Washington's especial command, and assisted at the surrender of Burgoyne. While Washington was at Valley Forge, this regiment was stationed at Radnor, near the line of the British, then in possession of Philadelphia, Capt. Posey being in command, and engaged in constant skirmishing. When Maj. Morris was killed, Capt. Posey was promoted to his place. This famous regiment joined the forces of Lafayette at the battle of Monmouth, and opposed the British right wing, doing glorious service. Afterwards, in command of the regiment during Col.

Morgan's absence, he was sent to subdue the Indians in Wyoming Valley, and gave them a severe chastisement at German Flats, Cherry Valley, and Schoharie, N. Y., driving them to the lakes, and wintering in the latter place 1778–79. He joined the main army at Middlebrook in 1779, by order of Gen. Washington, and commanded a battalion of Col. Fehriger's regiment, under Gen. Wayne. He was the first to enter the British works at the assault of Stony Point, and received the arms of the British officers. In 1779–80, being cut off from the whole Virginia line while home on a leave of absence, he was ordered to Charleston, S. C. Here he tried to get leave of Gov. Rutledge, to raise and command a regiment of militia, but not succeeding, he returned to Virginia, where he recruited and organized a regiment, of which he took command with the rank of lieutenant-colonel. While there he went to Yorktown, and was present at the surrender of Cornwallis. In 1781–82 he was ordered to join Gen. Greene in South Carolina, but the order was countermanded to join Gen. Wayne in Georgia, where he was engaged in many successful actions. In the night surprise of Wayne at Savannah by the British and Indians, under Gueristersigo, Posey, by his coolness and ability, brought order out of confusion, and saved the body, sabering several of the enemy with his own arm. When the British evacuated Charleston, he marched in with a battalion, to keep them from plundering as they left. After the peace, in 1783, he married the second time, and settled in Spottsylvania county, Va., and was county lieutenant and magistrate. In 1793 he was commissioned brigadier-general in the legion of the United States, and served under Gen. Wayne in the Indian campaigns in the Northwest. He resigned in 1793, and settled in Kentucky, and was a member of the senate in 1805–6. In the war of 1812 he was in Louisiana, and separated from the army to which he belonged, but he raised a company and acted as captain, though holding a major-general's commission. When Destréhan resigned his seat in the U. S. senate in 1812, Gen. Posey was appointed to fill the vacancy. When his term had expired, Pres. Madison appointed him governor of Indiana territory, a position he held until it became a state in 1816, when he was a candi-

date for the governorship, but was defeated. He was then appointed Indian agent, an office which he held at the time of his death. Gen. Posey was twice married. His first wife was a daughter of Samson Matthews, one of the prominent revolutionary leaders of Augusta county, Va., by whom he had one son, who was a captain in the war of 1812. His second wife was the widow of Maj. George Thornton, a grandson of Mildred Washington, and daughter of John Alexander, the founder of Alexandria, Va. By her he had several children. They have numerous descendants, many of whom are, by intermarriage with descendants of Mildred Washington, nearest by blood to Gen. Washington. In person Gen. Posey was six feet two or three inches high, and of magnificent physique; light brown hair, clear blue eyes, and of ruddy complexion. He died March 18, 1818, at the home of his son-in-law, Joseph Montfort Street, at Shawneetown, Ill. He left a letter to his children and grandchildren on the conduct of life, and a sealed letter, to be delivered to his wife after his death, the contents of which have never been revealed.

DEWEY, Chester, scientist and educator, was born at Sheffield, Mass., Oct. 25, 1784. His ancestors came from England in 1633, and settled at Dor-

chester, Mass.; then in Windsor, Conn. The family returned to Massachusetts, and settled at Westfield. Young Dewey received a common school and academic education, then entered Williams College, where he was graduated in 1806. He studied for the ministry, and was installed in his first charge at Tyringham, Mass., in 1808. He was appointed a tutor in Williams College the same year, and in 1810 was called to the chair of mathematics and natural philosophy, a position he filled for seventeen years. He was professor and lecturer on chemistry and botany in the medical colleges of Pittsfield, Mass., and Woodstock, Vt., for many years, and principal of the Collegiate Institute of Rochester N. Y., from 1836–50. When the Rochester University was established in that year, he was appointed professor of chemistry and natural philosophy. He resigned this position in 1860, as he felt unequal to the performance of continuous active work, but retained his connection with the institution, and served at his own convenience. Prof. Dewey devoted his entire life to scientific research, and was considered one of the first of American naturalists. His specialty was the study of grasses, and he discovered many new species which he described. He was a recognized authority on the class of "carices," and wrote an

elaborate monograph on the subject, which was the labor of over forty years. Many of his papers on scientific subjects were published in the "American Journal of Science;" those on the "Families and Natural Orders of Plants," attracting the attention of some of the leading European botanists, and leading to a correspondence with them. Meteorology also claimed his attention, and his weather observations were published in regular monthly reports. He wrote the "History of the Herbaceous Plants of Massachusetts," which was published by that state. His later writings were reviews on "The True Place of Man in Zoölogy," and "An Examination of Some Reasonings Against the Vanity of Mankind." Prof. Dewey lived in retirement after his eightieth year, and devoted himself to religious and benevolent works. The honorary degree of M. D. was conferred upon him by Yale in 1825; D.D. by Union College in 1838, and L.L.D. by Williams in 1850. He died in Rochester, N. Y., Dec. 5, 1867.

GRAHAM, David Brown, jurist, was born in Fairfield, Westmoreland co., Pa., Feb. 17, 1846, son of Andrew Graham, a merchant and farmer in moderate circumstances. His grandfather, Andrew Graham, emigrated from the north of Ireland about 1800, and settled in Westmoreland county, Pa., where he established himself as a merchant. The boy attended district school, worked on his father's farm and occasionally in the store until the age of sixteen, when he began teaching, and in the spring of 1862 he entered a business college, paying his tuition with the money he had earned and saved by teaching during the winter. He was graduated in 1863, and returned home to take care of his mother's farm and store. In 1864 he resumed his studies in an academy in his native village, and the same year enlisted in the 211th Pennsylvania volunteer infantry. He participated in the capture of Petersburgh, and served until the close of the war. In 1865 he resumed his studies at Westminster College, Pennsylvania, and was graduated in 1869 an A.B. He then taught in the academy, Fairfield, Pa., devoting his spare time to a general course of reading, and in 1870 he taught in the Ligonier Academy, Pennsylvania. He next entered the Albany Law School, where he was graduated in the summer of 1871, with the degree of LL.B. He located in Denver, Col., Sept. 1, 1871, where he opened an office and began the practice of law. In 1876 Mr. Graham was elected district attorney of the second judicial district at the first state election, and by re-election served, until 1883, when, owing to failing health, caused by over work, he declined a renomination, and spent one year in travel, and upon his return to Denver, resumed the practice of law. In 1889 he was elected judge of the second judicial district, from which position he retired in 1895, and again entered upon the practice of his profession. In 1894, when Gov. Waite attempted by the aid of the state militia to induct certain appointees into office, Judge Graham issued an injunction restraining the governor from so doing, maintaining that the governor's constitutional obligation to take care that the law be faithfully executed does not impose upon him the duty of forcibly inducting his

appointees into office, nor justify his calling upon the military forces of the state for such purpose, unless it be for the enforcement of judicial process. This decision was subsequently sustained by the supreme court of the state. He is prominently identified with the Masonic fraternity, and is a Knight-Templar and Shriner. He is a member of the Knights of Pythias, Odd Fellows, and G. A. R. Judge Graham has received the honorary degree of A.M. from Westminster College. He was married, Nov. 7, 1877, to Lucy A., daughter of Dr. Wm. Seeley, a pioneer of Colorado.

SARGENT, Franklin Haven, educator, was born in Boston, Mass., March 31, 1850, son of John Turner Sargent, a prominent Unitarian minister and active anti-slavery reformer of his day, who was graduated at Harvard College in 1827, and at the Harvard Divinity school in 1830. His alma mater conferred upon him the degree of A.M. in 1877. Mr. Sargent was the first to invite ministers of all other denominations to his pulpit. Mr. Sargent's original ancestor in America was William Sargent, who came to this country from Gloucester, England, before 1678. His descendant, Epes Sargent, was a colonel of militia before the revolution, and died in Gloucester, Mass., in 1762. Epes's son, Paul Dudley Sargent, soldier, born in Salem, Mass., in 1745, commanded a regiment at the siege of Boston, was wounded at Bunker Hill, commanded a brigade in 1776, fought throughout the war, and on the return of peace became an eminent jurist. His nephew, Winthrop Sargent, born May 1, 1753, died Jan. 3, 1820, attained the rank of major in the revolutionary war; was governor of the territory of Mississippi, 1798–1801, and an original member of the Society of the Cincinnati. Paul Dudley's nephew, Henry Sargent, an artist, was born Nov. 25, 1770, died Feb. 21, 1845, studied under Benjamin West in London, became adjutant-general of Massachusetts, and invented a plan for an elevated railroad. Henry's brother, Lucius Manlius Sargent, an author, born in Boston, Jan. 25, 1786, died June 2, 1867, was a man of considerable literary renown and a temperance lecturer for thirty years. His grandson, John Osborne Sargent, lawyer, was born Sept. 20, 1811; another grandson, Epes Sargent, born Sept. 27, 1813, died

Dec. 31, 1880, was a noted editor. Franklin Haven Sargent, was prepared for college in Chauncy Hall School, Boston, was matriculated at Harvard in 1873, and was graduated in 1877, just fifty years after his illustrious father. His chosen profession was elocution and pantomime, and upon leaving college he studied to perfect himself in the art and to fit himself as an instructor. To this end he entered upon an extended course of study under private tutors, and visited Europe to avail himself of the best teachers of the art in London, Paris, and Berlin. In 1880 he was appointed instructor in elocution at Harvard College, remaining in that capacity for two years. He left the college to take, in 1882, the position of dramatic director of the Madison Square Theatre, New York, then under the management of Rev. Dr. Mallory. He directed its high-class dramatic representations for two years, and in the production of plays, the care in the dialogue, and the perfection of the pantomimic effects, the Madison Square Theatre became the model for other managers. On leaving the theatre he founded the Lyceum School of Acting, (Oct. 1, 1884), the first institution founded in America devoted exclusively to training for the professional stage. This enterprise was afterwards renamed the American Academy of Dramatic Arts, and Mr. Sargent was elected its first president, which position he has since occupied. Mr. Sargent was also for three years manager of the Berkeley Lyceum, a theatre originally built for amateurs by the Berkeley Athletic Association, and opened Feb. 27, 1888, and here conducted the work of the academy. Mr. Sargent has been identified with all the productions of classical Greek plays in this country, whether presented by society leaders, college students, or professionally. He has been a specialist in the pantomimic methods developed by François Delsarte. In 1895 Mr. Sargent entered into an agreement with the Music Hall Co. of New York, Ltd., to manage a portion of the Carnegie Music Hall building and to make extensive alterations therein. All of Mr. Sargent's enterprises were on Oct. 1, 1895, removed to Carnegie Music Hall.

COBB, Amasa, statesman, was born in Crawford county, Ill., Sept. 27, 1823. He received his education in the common schools. He emigrated in 1842, to Wisconsin territory, and entered into the lead-mining business. When the Mexican war broke out in 1846, he enlisted as a private soldier and served until peace was declared in 1848. During this time he had studied law, and returning to Wisconsin commenced practice. He was elected district attorney of his county in 1850, and held the office for four years. In 1855 and 1856 was a member of the state senate; was appointed adjutant-general of the state in 1855, and re-appointed in 1857. Was returned to the state house of representatives in 1860, and again in 1861, when he was chosen speaker. In the war of the rebellion he took an active part; raising the 5th Wisconsin regiment of volunteers, of which he was commissioned colonel from 1861–62. Was elected a Republican representative to the thirty-eighth congress, and was chairman of the joint committee on enrolled bills, and member of the committee on the militia. During a recess of congress he raised the 43d regiment of Wisconsin volunteers, and was again commissioned as colonel. He commanded the regiment until mustered out in July, 1865. For gallant services at Antietam, Williamsburg, and Golden Farms he received the brevet rank of brigadier-general. Was again elected as a Republican to the thirty-ninth congress, in which he served on the committees of mines and mining, and District of Columbia; was re-elected to the fortieth and forty-first congresses, and served on such important committees as claims, public buildings and grounds, and military affairs; was a member of congress from Dec. 7, 1863, to March 3, 1871.

MATTHEWS, James Brander, lawyer and author, was born in New Orleans, La., Feb. 21, 1852. When he was only four years old his parents removed to New York city, where he has since resided. After receiving a thorough preparatory education, he entered Columbia College, and was graduated there, with the honor of class-poet, in 1871; he then entered the law school of this institution, at which he was graduated in 1873. A year later he was admitted to the New York bar. His taste for literature quite over-balanced his inclination toward the legal profession, and, in 1873, he began to write for the leading periodicals; his articles were eagerly accepted, and this encouragement led to more ambitious work on his part, and he soon launched into broader fields, meeting with the first success in his published books. Among which are: "The Theatres of Paris," "French Dramatists of the Nineteenth Century," "The Last Meeting," "A Secret of the Sea," "Pen and Ink," "A Family Tree." Mr. Matthews is a poet, essayist, and critic, and his writings preserve great literary and artistic merit. His early writings appeared under the pen-name of "Arthur Penn," which was, however, soon dropped. He has contributed largely to the periodicals upon his specialty of dramatic criticism. The "Nation" says: "Mr. Matthews's appreciation of French actors and of French plays shows judgment and taste;" and of his plays: "His characters stand out distinct and complete." His taste inclined more strongly to dramatic subjects and the drama; the result being: "Comedies for Amateur Acting;" "Actors and Actresses of Great Britain and the United States," which was written in connection with Lawrence Hutton; and plays whose worth has been attested on the stage in various cities, where they have uniformly been accepted with commendation by the people and press. Among the more noted are: "Margery's Lovers," a comedy in three acts, performed in London in 1884, and in New York in 1887; "A Gold Mine," a comedy in three acts, given in Memphis in 1887; New York, 1889; and in London, 1890. "On Probation," a comedy in four acts, produced first in Chicago in 1889. He was one of the founders of the Dunlap Society, the American Copyright League, the Authors' and Players' Clubs, and in 1890 was elected president of the Nineteenth Century Club, of which he had been acting vice-president for two years previous. Although a resident of New York, Mr. Matthews travels a great deal, and spends much of his time in England, where he is welcomed by the literary world of London. He became a lecturer on English literature at Columbia College, 1891-92; and professor of literature in the same institution in 1892. In addition to the works already mentioned Mr. Matthews has published: "With my Friends: Tales Told in Partnership" (1891); "Tom Paulding," "In the Vestibule Limited," "Americanisms and Briticisms" (1892); "The Story of a Story and Other Stories" (1893); "Studies of the Stage,"

"Vignettes of Manhattan," "The Royal Marine, an idyl of Narragansett" (1894); "Books and Play-books, Essays on Literature and the Drama," "His Father's Son, a Novel of New York," "Bookbinding, Old and New, Notes of a Booklover" (1895); "Introduction to the Study of American Literature" (1896).

SANDERS, Daniel Jackson, president of Biddle University, was born near Winnsboro', S. C., Feb. 15, 1847. His parents were slaves. At the age of nine he began to learn the shoemaker's trade, and within three years' time he was a skilled workman. At the outbreak of the civil war young Sanders and his parents were taken by their owners to a plantation some distance from Winnsboro', where shoemaking and farming were combined. At the close of the war the boy set forth to seek his fortune. He determined, first of all, to obtain a good education. To this end, he put himself under the instruction of two young men of the neighborhood, who were themselves preparing for college, there being neither public nor private schools for colored people at that time. In this way he gained a fair knowledge of arithmetic, geography, grammar, history, Greek, and Latin, working all the while at his trade of shoemaking. In 1869 he resolved to become a minister of the gospel, and, in the following year, he was ordained. His early ordination was the result of an ecclesiastical emergency, it being understood that he would continue his studies through the usual course. In September, 1871, therefore, he entered the junior class of the Western Theological Seminary, Allegheny City, Pa. His class numbered forty, all except himself and another, being white, and the graduates of well-known schools. His manly bearing, devotion to duty, and superior intellectual work, soon overcame all prejudices, however, and in 1874 he was graduated from the seminary with honor. For the next twelve years he was pastor of the Chestnut Street Presbyterian Church, Wilmington, N. C. He spent some time in Europe, where he did much preaching and lecturing on behalf of the Freedmen's mission board of the Presbyterian church. He was also instrumental in raising the $6,000 African scholarship fund of Biddle University, for the education of negroes located at Charlotte, N. C., and founded in 1869. On his return to America he resumed the pastorate of the church in Wilmington. In January, 1879, he established the

"Africo-American Presbyterian," of which he is still the editor. In 1891 he received the honorary degree of D.D. from both Lincoln and Biddle Universities, and in 1891 he was elected to the presidency of the latter institution. His accession to the presidency marked an era of prosperity, and in 1894 the institution had eleven instructors and 285 students. Dr. Sanders has been regarded as a leader in presbytery and synod. He was the first colored moderator of the Atlantic synod; served as moderator several times, of both Yadkin and Cape Fear presbyteries; served as stated clerk of Atlantic and Yadkin presbyteries, and is now the stated clerk of the Catawba synod. He has been three times a member of the Presbyterian general assembly, and was appointed by the Detroit assembly one of the fifty delegates to the Presbyterian Ecumenical council, which met in Toronto, Canada, in September, 1892. Through his editorial work upon the "Africo-American Presbyterian," Dr. Sanders is also well known as an able writer.

LOWREY, Clement J. G., Roman Catholic priest, was born in Pickaway county, O., Aug. 21, 1837, on the maternal grandparental homestead. His father, Daniel Lowrey, was of Swiss Republican ancestry, and lived to the advanced age of four score years, for more than fifty of which he was engaged in the active practice of medicine. His mother was a daughter of Jacob Teegardin, a thrifty pioneer farmer of German ancestry. The son was reared, instructed and trained in the Roman Catholic faith, his parents being both converts from Lutheranism. Their ancestors came to America prior to the revolutionary war. Our subject removed with the family to Iowa in the spring of 1845, settled at West Point, then the seat of justice of Lee county. His education was obtained at the common or free schools, select schools taught by teachers of more than ordinary merit, at Des Moines Valley College, St. Thomas Preparatory Seminary, Bardstown, Ky., where he made his humanity course, and at St. Vincent's College, Cape Girardeau, Mo., where he was graduated in June, 1862. Nov. 24, 1862, he was ordained to the priesthood in the cathedral of Dubuque, Ia., by the Rt. Rev. Clement Smythe, D. D., bishop of Dubuque. After being retained there in the capacity of parochial assistant, owing to the scarcity and pressing demand for priests in the northern part of this extensive diocese, he was commissioned to take charge of fourteen missions dispersed through the five counties, Allamakee, Winneshiek, Howard, Chickasaw, and Floyd, the first three bordering on Minnesota. Here he displayed a wonderful zeal and earnestness which won him the respect and affection of his own people; the good will and kindly regard of his many non-catholic friends and acquaintances. This enabled him to build, finish, refit, and improve several much needed churches in this vast territory. At the close of the year 1867 he was assigned by Bishop Hennesy to another extended field of labor, comprising Cedar Rapids, where he located, with twelve outlying missions, mostly along the railways centering there. Here, too, he exhibited the same zeal and disinterestedness which had attracted the attention of the bishop and induced him to make this selection for so responsible a position as this promising missionary field offered. In Cedar Rapids he built a substantial brick church in 1870, and in 1874 completed one of the most imposing and commodious Catholic institutions of learning at that time in the state. In the month of October, 1880, he was placed in charge of St. Paul's Church, Burlington, where he was instrumental in liquidating the residue of a debt, $2,800, incurred by his immediate predecessor. In 1887 Bishop Cosgrove selected him to fill a vacancy occasioned by the death of the late pastor of St. Francis de Sales Church, Keokuk. Here again he was confronted with an encumbrance, of years' standing, amounting to a little more than $1,000, which he readily removed and in addition expended a considerable sum, in the aggregate, for needed repairs and useful improvements, all accomplished in the short space of three years. Father Lowrey is strong and uncompromising in his religious convictions and has ever been ready, by trenchant contributions to the local press, to resent all wilful vilification of this church, as likewise to correct unwarranted misstatements and false representations of Catholic teaching whereby he felt insult was offered and injury inflicted upon his church and her membership. Tolerant of the well-grounded convictions of those who differ from him in faith, he on all occasions is considerate of their sensibilities, and ever studiously avoids giving offense to his non-Catholic friends who might chance to be among his audience. While he feels in duty bound to insist that Catholic parents, in the fulfilment of their conscientious obligation, shall give their children a right Christian education in the parochial school, yet he never disparages the public school system when urging compliance with this duty.

BRENNAN, Martin S., Roman Catholic priest, was born near Templemore, county Tipperary, Ireland, July 23, 1845. His parents emigrated to America when he was about three years old, settling in St. Louis, Mo. His ancestors, both paternal and maternal, were for several generations well-to-do farmers in the neighborhood of Templemore. His family in one line is descended from the chieftains of Castle Comer, in Kilkenny; and in another, the Waterford line from St. Brendan, or properly St. Brennan. His paternal grandfather was an officer on the side of the rebels in the battle of Vinegar Hill, during the rebellion of 1798. He was educated in the College of the Christian Brothers, St. Louis, and received, in 1865, a diploma of batchelor of arts from that institution. A few years later the same college conferred upon him the degree of M. A. and academic sciences. He made his theological studies in St. Vincent's College, Cape Girardeau, Mo., and was ordained a priest by the Most. Rev. Peter Richard Kenrick, in St. John's Church, St. Louis, Apr. 3, 1869. His first mission was Hannibal, Mo. He was subsequently placed in the parishes of Lebanon, Mo., the Cathedral, St. Patrick's, and St. Michael's, St. Louis. He was assistant pastor of St. Malachy's Church, St. Louis, for eleven years, where he was highly esteemed and beloved by the people, and when transferred to the rectorship of St. Thomas Aquinas, received from them a princely testimonial. He remained pastor of St. Thomas's for eight years, succeeding in removing its entire indebtedness, and was then promoted to the charge of St. Lawrence O'Toole's, a very popular parish, prominent for its fine parochial schools taught by the Christian Brothers and the Sisters of St. Joseph. The church is one of the largest and finest in the state, and the parish is probably the best organized in the West. Father Brennan has been delivering popular lectures on science for many years, and has written on scientific subjects for a number of magazines. His work, "Electricity and Its Discoverers," published in New York, was adopted as a reference book by the St. Louis public schools. His next work, "What Catholics Have Done for Science," became very popular, running through several editions. Another of his books, "Astronomy, New and Old," received the highest encomiums from scientists. Father Brennan is also professor of astronomy and geology in the Kenrick Theological Seminary. He excels as a master of ceremonies, and has officiated in that capacity at the consecration of a number of bishops, and on several other important occasions, notably, at the celebration of the golden jubilee of the episcopacy of the Most Rev. Peter Richard Kenrick, on Nov. 30, 1891, a most unusual ceremony, being only the third of the kind on record. The "St. Louis Republic," in 1891, in a newspaper contest to determine the popularity of various local clergymen to be determined by popular votes, delivered to Father Brennan tickets for a tour of Palestine and Europe. He headed the list during the entire contest, and was elected by nearly a quarter of a million votes. He wrote some very interesting letters from the different countries of Europe visited by him. On his return home he gave an illustrated lecture on his travels, in the grand music hall of the exposition building, to an audience of between 6,000 and 7,000. Father Brennan is a member of the St. Louis Academy of Science, of the Astronomical Society of the Pacific, and of the British Astronomical Association.

KEILTY, Francis M., Roman Catholic priest, was born in the town of Boyle, county Roscommon, Ireland, in 1830, a descendant from a good old Irish family. He lost his parents in early youth, and was

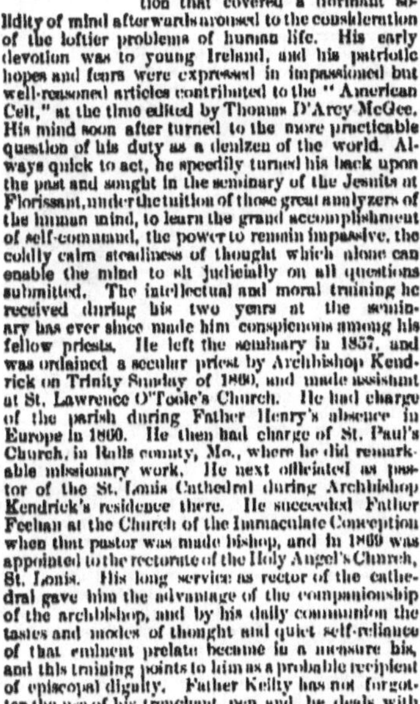

cared for by his sister, who resided in England. Under her care he received a good parochial-school education. He came to America when but a mere boy, and located at Cincinnati, O., where he attracted the attention of the Rev. Father Murphy, provincial of the Jesuit order, who had him educated at the St. Louis University, Missouri. After spending three years there he was sent to the Jesuit seminary at Florissant, Mo. As a student, he was physically stalwart, but possessed of a modesty of demeanor that was rare among the class. His nature was deeply religious and yet there was a poetry of thought and action that covered a dormant solidity of mind afterwards aroused to the consideration of the loftier problems of human life. His early devotion was to young Ireland, and his patriotic hopes and fears were expressed in impassioned but well-reasoned articles contributed to the "American Celt," at the time edited by Thomas D'Arcy McGee. His mind soon after turned to the more practicable question of his duty as a denizen of the world. Always quick to act, he speedily turned his back upon the past and sought in the seminary of the Jesuits at Florissant, under the tuition of those great analyzers of the human mind, to learn the grand accomplishment of self-command, the power to remain impassive, the coldly calm steadiness of thought which alone can enable the mind to sit judicially on all questions submitted. The intellectual and moral training he received during his two years at the seminary has ever since made him conspicuous among his fellow priests. He left the seminary in 1857, and was ordained a secular priest by Archbishop Kendrick on Trinity Sunday of 1860, and made assistant at St. Lawrence O'Toole's Church. He had charge of the parish during Father Henry's absence in Europe in 1860. He then had charge of St. Paul's Church, in Ralls county, Mo., where he did remarkable missionary work. He next officiated as pastor of the St. Louis Cathedral during Archbishop Kendrick's residence there. He succeeded Father Feehan at the Church of the Immaculate Conception when that pastor was made bishop, and in 1869 was appointed to the rectorate of the Holy Angel's Church, St. Louis. His long service as rector of the cathedral gave him the advantage of the companionship of the archbishop, and by his daily communion the tastes and modes of thought and quiet self-reliance of that eminent prelate became in a measure his, and this training points to him as a probable recipient of episcopal dignity. Father Keilty has not forgotten the use of his trenchant pen, and he deals with questions of the day through the secular press in a

positive manner. His views on the subject of "The Church and Politics," appearing in the "Republic" of St. Louis, Nov. 22, 1894, was a positive and able argument against the meddling of Catholic priests with politics. He also ably answered Ingersoll's question, "Is Suicide a Sin?" in an article over his name that appeared in the press, Sept. 4, 1894. Father Keilty has the finest private literary, philosophical, and theological library in St. Louis, excepting only that of the archbishop. His executive abilities are of the highest order. An eminent citizen, his classmate, says of him, "He is a father in the filial reverence of his children, and a brother in the eternal devotion of his friends."

O'BRIEN, James M., Roman Catholic priest, was born at Kennebunk, Me., Jan. 28, 1842. His father came from Tyrone, Ireland, and his mother, from Cork. His family removed to New Hampshire when he was an infant and settled at Keene. When old enough, he attended the public school there, passed through the respective grades and attended the high school for three years. Having finished school, a desire for travel caused him to visit several parts of Europe, South America, and the West Indies. Returning home during the war, and being under age, he went to Boston, and enlisted in Company H., 23rd Massachusetts volunteers. After active service he was discharged from the army because of wounds received at the battle of Whitehall, N. C. He entered St. Mary's College, Wilmington, Del., in 1865, and St. Mary's Seminary, Baltimore, Md., in 1869, where he spent four years in the study of philosophy and theology. He was ordained Jan. 6, 1874, for the diocese of Savannah, in the old Cathedral of St. John the Baptist, of that city, being the first priest ordained by Rt. Rev. W. H. Gross, D.D. He was sent immediately to Washington, Ga., to take charge of that parish and attend missions in fifteen counties. He labored most zealously and was indefatigable in his efforts to bring the consolations of religion to the few and widely-scattered Catholics. He purchased property and built a church at Athens and one at Sharon. In 1876 the Male Orphanage was removed from Savannah to Washington, Ga., and placed under his administration, which meant notonly the spiritual care of the orphans, but their support, which was secured by his personal efforts, collecting in the diocese. In 1877 he founded in Washington St. Joseph's Academy for young ladies. The domestic arrangements of the orphanage and

the academy were entrusted to the Sisters of St. Joseph. In 1879 he was sent to Atlanta, Ga., and given charge of the Church of the Immaculate Conception. During his administration the church was finished and frescoed, ground for a new church purchased, and St. Joseph's Infirmary established. In 1881 he was sent back to Washington, as the Orphanage had been brought into debt during his absence. This he soon cancelled and built a commodious house for the orphans and a new parish church. In 1889 he was sent to St. Patrick's Church, Augusta, where he was most successful in his labors for the congregation. The church was renovated, internally and externally, and a spire erected; but just when he was about to enjoy a rest from laborious building, much to the regret of his devoted parishioners, he was recalled to Washington to resume charge of the orphanage, once again involved in debt, which only superior business tact seemed able to remove. His record as a priest is one of zealous labors, not only as a financier, but as a warm-hearted, devoted father to the poor orphan boys. Kindly attentive to the congregations placed under his charge, he has formed temperance societies, and can well be proud of his efforts in the grand cause of temperance. A friend to rich and poor, he deserves all the honor and affection that the people of Georgia entertain for him.

JESSING, Joseph, clergyman, was born in Munster, Germany, Nov. 17. 1836, of Frisian parents, his ancestors having been for many centuries farmers in Northern Germany. When only a boy he entered the Prussian army, and was afterwards sent to a military academy in Westphalia. In the war

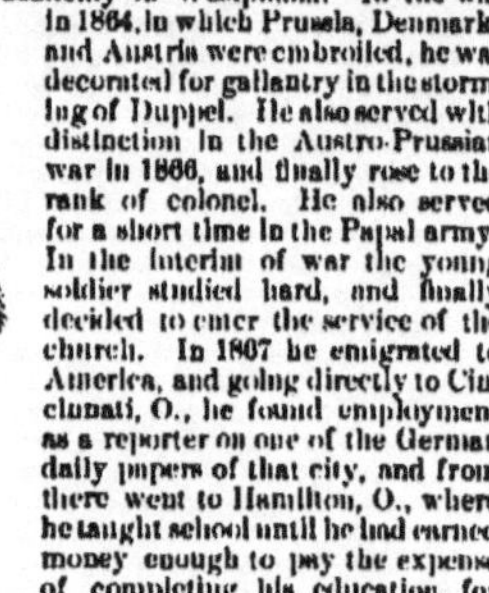

in 1864, in which Prussia, Denmark, and Austria were embroiled, he was decorated for gallantry in the storming of Duppel. He also served with distinction in the Austro-Prussian war in 1866, and finally rose to the rank of colonel. He also served for a short time in the Papal army. In the interim of war the young soldier studied hard, and finally decided to enter the service of the church. In 1867 he emigrated to America, and going directly to Cincinnati, O., he found employment as a reporter on one of the German daily papers of that city, and from there went to Hamilton, O., where he taught school until he had earned money enough to pay the expense of completing his education for the priesthood. Then he entered the Mt. St. Mary's Seminary on Price Hill, Cincinnati. He was ordained a priest by Bishop Rosecrans at Columbus in 1870, and was assigned to the pastorate of the little church at Pomeroy. Father Jessing's first step was to establish a little German paper which he named "Der Ohio Waisenfreund" "The Ohio Orphan's Friend." It was ably edited, and the circulation increased until it was a paying institution. He then started his orphanage with three German-American orphan boys in 1875. The four conducted the paper, doing all the work except that of foreman. Two years later he removed the paper to Columbus. The circulation steadily increased until it was the most extensive journal of any kind in central Ohio. By degrees land was bought in the heart of the city, and an orphanage was built called the Josephinum. The different trades were taught on a practical basis, and so well was it managed that the director and owner found it feasible to buy a hundred-acre farm within three miles of the city. There he placed an experienced farmer, and with a number of boys who seemed especially fitted for agriculture, he easily cultivated much of the vegetables and other farm products that were consumed at the asylum. The city property now occupies a four-acre tract in the heart of Columbus, there being nine fine brick buildings, including the manse and dormitories, the home for the Sisters, the school and chapel, the printing-office and press-rooms, a turning department, fitted with all the necessary machinery for the larger woodwork used in altar building, the wood-carving building, a boiler and engine house, the shoe shop and tailor shop, and a fine new five-story academy for the theological students, besides barns, stables, and chicken-houses. In 1887 Father Jessing founded a college in connection with the orphanage, which soon attracted students of the best class. George Kanne, of St. Louis, donated to the college $5,000, the interest of which

supports a scholarship. Five other scholarships were endowed by the contributions of many individuals, but aside from this the college has received no help except from Father Jessing. The course of study covers six years, and includes the usual classical and scientific studies leading to the degree of B.A., to which will be added hereafter two years of philosophy and four years of advanced theological and scientific study. Every student is required to become an accomplished German scholar. The final step of consecrating the institution to the work of the church was lately taken. Father Jessing, fearing that he might die and his property be scattered and diverted from the purpose for which it was collected, decided to turn it over to the Propaganda. Archbishop Satolli himself officiated for the pope, and accepted the trust. An incorporated company was formed, known as the Pontifical College Josephinum of the Sacred Congregation for the Propagation of Faith. Father Jessing, however, is one of the original incorporators and remains as rector of the college and president of the faculty.

McKEEVER, Edward M., Roman Catholic priest, was born in Pittsburgh, Pa., Feb. 10, 1849, son of William and Catherine Mullen McKeever. His parents on both sides belonged to families in Ireland that had followed farming for generations, his father coming from county Monaghan and his mother from county Tyrone. He went through the common school course at the school in charge of the Franciscan Brothers connected with St. Paul's Cathedral, and there began the study of the classics under Mr. J. McCann. He began to study for the priesthood at St. Michael's Seminary in March, 1868, and was ordained priest by Bishop Dominec, Dec. 20, 1871, being assigned the same day assistant pastor to St. Peter's Church, Allegheny. From there he was transferred to a newly-formed congregation at Derry, Westmoreland co., Sept. 20, 1873, but remained only until the following Monday, when he was appointed pastor of Sts. Simon and Jude's Church, Blairsville, Indiana co. There he remained until January, 1889, when he took charge of the Holy Family congregation, Latrobe, Westmoreland co., Pa. He left there in May, 1891, to be pastor of St. John the Baptist's Church, Pittsburgh, Pa. In these different places he discharged his duties in such a way as to win the esteem of the people and the approval of his superiors. Beside the work of the ministry, he has always taken an active interest in the temporal welfare of the communities where he has

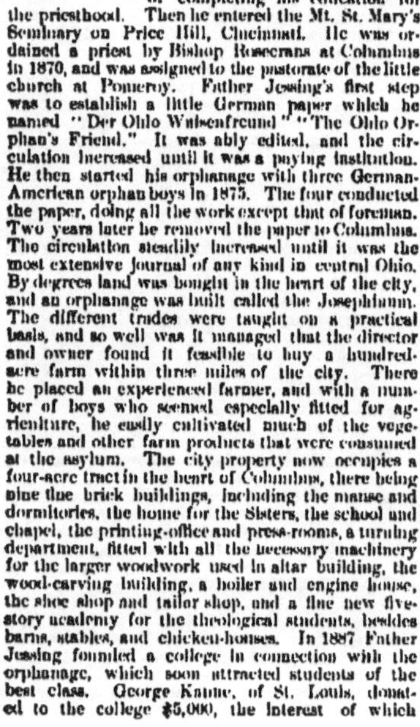

resided. Inspired by the great Christian precept of love of God and man, he has been able to walk hand in hand with all classes in endeavoring to secure what pertained to the public good. In the last week of August, 1889, he set sail for Europe, where he spent three months, visiting Ireland, England, France, Germany, Italy, and parts of the Austrian empire. While not known as a public writer, he is a man of decided views on all questions of general interest, as well as on matters affecting his church or the community where he happens to reside, and from time to time contributes articles on subjects of special interest to the periodicals.

O'REILLY, James Thomas, Roman Catholic priest, was born in Lansingburg, N. Y., May 1, 1851. His grandfather emigrated to this country in

1847 from Athboy, county Meath, Ireland, and died in 1886 at the age of ninety-six years. His father, Edward O'Reilly, served honorably in the civil war as a private in Company E., 68rd N. Y. volunteers up to the time of his death, which was from natural causes in the field. The son received his early education at a school conducted by the Christian Brothers in Troy, N. Y. In 1866 he entered the Augustinian College at Villanova, Penn., from which he was graduated in 1871, and having already entered the novitiate of the order of St. Augustine and made therein his solemn profession, he was ordained priest March 15, 1874. He was retained as instructor at his alma mater for the next two years. In 1876 he received the appointment of procurator. While serving in this capacity he also performed the duties of pastor of St. Denis Church, West Haverford, Penn. Here he displayed on a small scale that gift for administration and organization which is particularly demanded of the Catholic clergy and which was to distinguish him in his later career. He made many improvements in the church building, and erected a handsome parochial residence. In 1879 he was transferred to the pastorate of St. John's Church, Schaghticoke, N. Y. Here again he looked carefully after the upbuilding of the material as well as the spiritual interests of his flock and the church. He purchased a much-needed parochial residence and built a mission church at Johnsonville. Here he labored for seven years, when he was placed in charge of St. Mary's Church, Lawrence, Mass. At this point there existed a condition that, the Augustinian brotherhood felt, required the best head and heart they had at their command. For many years money had been received upon deposit from hundreds of the parishioners on the assumption that greater confidence could be placed in the priests than in the regular banks. The fathers, responsible for these accumulations, both as to principal and interest, employed the money in building an elegant stone church, and in otherwise improving the parish property. The same system had been pursued, also in the neighboring parish of the Immaculate Conception. As long as deposits were made in excess of withdrawals this course was smoothly pursued, but when in 1881 the conditions were reversed, failure and disgrace ensued. When Father O'Reilly took hold, the shortage to be made good was $425,000. It was his task to remove the suspicion and heal the distrust of the parishioners and church authorities alike; to unite and build up the scattered members of the church body, to re-organize the forces which were out of harmony. Upon his advent Father O'Reilly at once abolished the parochial residence of the Immaculate Conception and arranged to have his church and others attended from St. Mary's. These combined parishes number now some 16,000 souls and require the ministrations of eleven members of the Augustinian brotherhood. St. Mary's School was first opened in 1859. Chiefly under Father O'Reilly's fostering care it has grown to number 1,200 children. He has also built up schools in connection with St. Lawrence's Church and the Church of the Assumption. While Father O'Reilly attends most faithfully to the essential religious duties, his particular talent is shown in his management of affairs and of men. He has rendered conspicuous services to the general public by his advocacy of the cause of temperance and by his counsels during periods of labor troubles, when his influence among the mill operatives is always strongly exerted and felt. In 1886 he organized the Young Men's Catholic Association of Lawrence. In 1888 he introduced into Lawrence a teaching community of the Xaverian brothers in order to provide for the higher education of the boys in his charge, who, up to that time had been obliged to pass from Catholic instruction at the age of twelve. Early in 1892, the erection of a convent for the sisters of Notre Dame was begun as a result of his efforts. This has since been completed and stands as a fitting monument to the zeal of its founder. Father O'Reilly has been instrumental in organizing many societies designed to further in various ways the interests of his people in Lawrence. Among these are a court of the Massachusetts Catholic order of Foresters, a court of the Knights of Columbus, a conference of the society of St. Vincent de Paul, and the Merrimac Co-operative Bank. Among the special objects of his care and charity has been the Orphan Asylum of Lawrence. He is serving his third term as member of the Definitory of the Augustinian Order, and was duly elected as one of the three delegates to the general chapter of the order to be held in Rome in September, 1895. He is serving his second term as president of the Catholic Total Abstinence Union of the archdiocese of Boston. Father O'Reilly's present record is an augury of important future achievements in the cause of religion and humanity.

JUNCKER, Henry Damian, Roman Catholic bishop, was born at Fenetrauge, France, about 1810. He emigrated to America at an early age, and attached himself to the diocese of Cincinnati, where he made his theological studies. He was ordained a priest on March 10, 1834, and was appointed pastor of the Church of the Holy Trinity, the first German Catholic congregation established in Cincinnati. He was subsequently, for nearly two years, engaged in missionary work in Ohio, and in 1846 was made pastor of the Church of the Emanuel, at Dayton, and also had charge of several English churches, and a number of German congregations in the central part of Ohio. In 1857 Father Juncker was appointed first bishop of the newly created see of Alton, and on Apr. 26th, of that year was consecrated in Cincinnati, at St. Peter's Cathedral by Bishop Purcell. Finding the eighteen priests in his diocese entirely inadequate in number for the large territory it embraced, he went to Europe in 1858 to endeavor to secure more priests, and to provide for the many wants of his see. Within one year after his ordination Bishop Juncker had held four ordinations, increased the number of priests to forty-two, and built eight churches. During the second year he completed the handsome Cathedral of Sts. Peter and Paul, which was consecrated on Apr. 19, 1859, by Archbishop Kenrick, of St. Louis, assisted by a number of eminent prelates. Bishop Juncker had an arduous work before him, the visitations of his see in a new and growing country were long and laborious, often having to be made in the severest weather. He founded many new congregations, and was an earnest promoter of education. In 1868 the number of his clergy had increased to 100, with twenty-five theological students; the churches numbered 123, the parochial schools fifty-six, two colleges for boys, six academies for girls, two hospitals, and one orphan asylum. He also built a fine episcopal residence, which was designed to serve the additional purpose of an ecclesiastical seminary. Bishop Juncker was not only extremely popular with the members of his own church, but made many friends among those who were not of his faith, and frequently received from them generous contributions to assist him in his work. He was an able conversationalist, could speak fluently in several languages, and was a man of much energy and executive ability. He died at Alton, Ill., Oct. 2, 1868. (A sketch of his life may be found in Vol. II. Dr. Clarke's "Lives of the Deceased Bishops.")

KELLY, Patrick, first Roman Catholic archbishop of the diocese of Richmond, was born in Ireland. For a number of years before he was appointed bishop, he was professor, and also president, of Birchfield College, near Kilkenny, Ireland. On July 11, 1820, the Holy See erected Virginia into a diocese, locating the see at Richmond, and Dr. Kelly was appointed its first bishop. He was consecrated in the parish chapel of St. Mary, Kilkenny, by the Most Rev. Dr. Long, archbishop of Dublin, and was himself afterwards present as one of the assistant prelates at the consecration of Bishop England, of Charleston, S. C. Bishop Kelly arrived in Norfolk on Jan. 19, 1821, and for a time made his residence in Norfolk, on account of there being more Catholics in that city. There were seven churches in the diocese of Virginia, including the Cathedral Church at Norfolk, which was erected in 1800, and was the first cathedral of Virginia. The other churches were located at Richmond, Portsmouth, Martinsburgh, Winchester, Bath, and Shepardstown. The last four were missionary churches, attended by priests from Maryland. Bishop Kelly made efforts to obtain resident pastors for these parishes. There were no Catholic schools in the diocese, and the bishop was reduced to such pecuniary straits that he opened a school at Norfolk, and conducted it himself, in order to mitigate his impoverished condition. He was an untiring worker, and, in addition to his teaching, did the work of a missionary; but, in spite of his indefatigable efforts, found himself unable to minister to all the spiritual wants of his diocese, which covered such an extensive field. His health failed under the continued pressure, and Rome translated him to the episcopal see of Waterford and Lismore in Ireland. He died in Ireland, Oct. 8, 1829.

CHEVERUS, Jean Louis Anne Magdelene Lefebre de, first Roman Catholic bishop of Boston, was born in Mayenne, France, Jan. 28, 1768. He received his preparatory education at a college in Mayenne, and at the age of twelve decided to adopt a religious life, and received the tonsure from Mons. de Hercé, bishop of Dol. The bishop of Mans making his acquaintance, was attracted to him and offered to place him in the College of Louis le Grand in Paris, and at the age of thirteen he was preferred to the benefice of the priory of Torbechet by the count of the province, subsequently Louis XVIII. He entered the celebrated college of Louis le Grand, July 21, 1786, and defended a thesis in public so successfully that he received unqualified praise. After spending several years at this college he entered the Theological Seminary of St. Magloine, and October, 1790, was made a deacon, and on Dec. 18th of that year was elevated to the priesthood. For a while he was assistant priest to his uncle, who was parish priest of Mayenne, but upon the death of that relative, January, 1792, he was appointed to succeed him, and was also made vicar-general of the diocese of Mans. The terrible revolution which devastated France broke out about this time, and he was driven from Mayenne. With the Bishop of Dol and several other clergymen, he was placed under espionage at Lavalle, and subsequently imprisoned in the convent of the Cordeliers, from which he made his escape, and concealed himself in his brother's rooms at the college of Louis le Grand, where he remained during the terrible massacre of Sept. 2 and 3, 1792. He afterwards escaped in military dress with a passport bearing the name of his brother, whom he closely resembled, and went to England where he

was hospitably received. He remained there a few years, and soon acquired a fluent use of the English language. Afterwards at the invitation of his friend, Dr. Matignon, Father Cheverus joined him on the the mission in Boston, where at that time Catholicity gave little evidence of its subsequent prosperity in New England. He arrived there Oct. 3, 1796, and found in the whole of New England but three places of Catholic worship, a small chapel on School street, Boston, two old chapels on the Indian missions in Maine, and only three priests besides himself, who made missionary journeys to all the important towns in New England. He declined the pastorate of St. Mary's Church, in Philadelphia and went on a mission among the Indians in Maine, returning to Boston in 1798, when the yellow fever epidemic was at its height, to devote himself day and night to nursing the sufferers. In this way he endeared himself to both Catholics and Protestants alike, and so entirely did he win the heart of the people that when Pres. John Adams visited Boston, and was tendered a public banquet, the two highest places of honor at the table were given to the president and Father Cheverus. He was also given another testimonial of public esteem when the legislature had in preparation the formula of an oath to be taken by the citizens before voting; in order that it might contain nothing that would conflict with the consciences of Catholics it was submitted to him for revision and amendment, and when he had prepared his own formula and placed it before the legislature it was immediately accepted as a law. The little church in School street becoming too small for the rapidly increasing congregation, in connection with Father Matignon he opened a subscription for the building of a new church; this was headed by Pres. John Adams and had many other prominent Protestant citizens of Boston among its subscribers. On Sept. 29, 1803, the first Catholic church erected in Boston, the Church of the Holy Cross, was dedicated by Bishop Carroll. In 1808 the diocese of Boston was created, and Nov. 1, 1810, Dr. Cheverus was consecrated first bishop of Boston by Archbishop Carroll, in St. Peter's Cathedral, Baltimore; he had only the assistance of two priests for the entire territory of his large diocese. In spite of his personal popularity and wise management of the affairs of his diocese, it was not until 1818 that Catholicity began to show material signs of advancement in New England. May 21, 1817, he raised to the priesthood the Rev. Dennis Ryan, who was the first priest ordained in the city of Boston. About this time the Ursuline nuns established themselves in the diocese and opened the first Catholic school for young ladies, in Boston. In 1818 he purchased and dedicated St. Augustine's, the first Catholic cemetery in Boston, and built in the centre of the ground a small mortuary chapel as a mausoleum to his friend, Dr. Matignon, who had died Sept. 18th, of that year. In 1822 the number of churches in his diocese had increased to six; the Catholic population of Boston numbered nearly 2,500, and that of the diocese hardly more than 5,000. Bishop Cheverus' health now began to fail under the continual strain and hard labor attendant upon his episcopal duties, and he seriously considered the advisability of resigning his bishopric to a younger man of more robust health. In 1823 the see of Montauban, France, becoming vacant, King Louis XVIII. recalled him to that country and made him ordinary of that diocese. Father Cheverus left America much to the regret of himself and his friends, carrying with him the esteem and veneration of all classes. He at once assumed charge of the see of Montauban, and three years later, July 30, 1826, was appointed archbishop of Bordeaux, which diocese he successfully conducted for a period of ten years, and Feb. 1, 1830, was proclaimed a cardinal, on account of his merits and virtues and the zeal that he displayed in Boston, Montauban, and Bordeaux. He died July 19, 1830.

FENWICK, Benedict Joseph, second Roman Catholic bishop of Boston, was born near Leonardtown, Md., Sept. 3, 1782. The Fenwicks in America were the descendants of the Fenwicks of Northumberland county, Eng., and the founder of the family in the United States, Cuthbert Fenwick, was one of the Catholic pilgrims who emigrated to America with Lord Baltimore's colony. Joseph Fenwick was educated at Georgetown College, being one of the first students there. He was graduated with the highest honors, and afterwards filled a professorship in the college. Deciding to become a priest, he entered the Theological Seminary of St. Sulpice. In 1806, when the Society of Jesus was re-established

in the United States, and Georgetown College placed under its charge, Mr. Fenwick entered the novitiate of this order. On account of his brilliancy and erudition, and the great necessity for priests in this country, his term of studies was shortened, and on March 12, 1808, he was ordained a priest at Georgetown by Bishop Neale, coadjutor to Bishop Carroll. In 1809 he was sent to New York city, to minister to the wants of the Catholics in the city and its vicinity. In 1809, in connection with Father Kohlman, S. J., and four scholastics of the order, he established a Catholic school in the city of New York, which was called the New York Literary Institution. After the death of Bishop Concanen, Father Kohlmann was appointed administrator of the diocese, and Father Fenwick subsequently succeeded to the difficult position. He ably filled all the important duties of his office, and made an entire visitation of the diocese. In 1816 he was made vicargeneral by Bishop Connelly. The following year he was recalled from his missionary labors in New York, and made president of Georgetown College, and was at the same time rector of Trinity Church. He did not, however, remain there long, his services being needed elsewhere. For some time back troubles had existed in the church in South Carolina, and in 1818 Father Fenwick was appointed vicargeneral of that diocese, in the hope that he would be able to adjust the difficulties. By a happy exercise of good judgment and amiability he succeeded in effecting results that were satisfactory to all parties. In 1822 he returned to Georgetown College, and was appointed minister of the college and procurator-general of the Jesuits in this country, and in 1824 was again elected president of the college. In 1825 he was made spiritual director of the Carmelite Convent, and on May 10th of that year was appointed

to succeed Bishop Cheverus, of Boston. On Nov. 1, 1825, at the Cathedral of Baltimore, Father Fenwick was consecrated a bishop by Archbishop Maréchal. The diocese of Boston comprised the whole of New England, and besides the Cathedral Church of the Holy Cross, there were but three Catholic churches in the whole of New England suitable for use, and there were but two priests in his extensive field. One of his first acts was to establish schools for the religious education of the Catholic children of Boston. He founded a Sunday-school in connection with the Cathedral of the Holy Cross, which he himself taught; opened a day-school for boys; erected for the Ursuline Sisters the Convent of Mount St. Benedict at Charlestown, which has become one of the most celebrated institutions of learning in the country. Bishop Fenwick, as soon as practicable, undertook the visitation of his vast diocese, which, in those days of poor traveling accommodations, was an arduous task. He spent some time among the Passamaquoddy Indians of Maine. This tribe was the remains of the Abenakis, who were converted to Christianity in the early part of the seventeenth century, and visited the Indians of Old Town, and then went to Bangor, Damariscotta, New Castle, Whitefield, Portland, etc. In 1831 Bishop Fenwick again visited the Indians. He caused a number of new churches to be erected in his diocese, which rose in rapid succession, and were evidences of his zeal and the increase of the Catholic population in New England. On Aug. 11, 1834, the Convent of Mount St. Benedict was attacked by a mob, and burned during the night. The nuns had fortunately received warning, and escaped. In 1843 Bishop Fenwick founded the College of the Holy Cross at Worcester, and placed it under the control of the Jesuits. Bishop Fenwick now shared the labors of his episcopate with Bishop Fitzpatrick, who had been appointed his coadjutor. At the time of his death his diocese was in a most prosperous condition. There were fifty churches, supplied with priests, a college, orphan asylum, and a number of Catholic schools; and out of the original diocese a new bishopric had been created. "These are in truth imperishable monuments of the energy and greatness of his mind." He died at Boston, Mass., Aug 11, 1846, and was interred at Holy Cross College, in the establishment of which he had taken such a deep and heartfelt interest.

FITZPATRICK, John Baptist, third Roman Catholic bishop of Boston, was born in Boston, Mass., Nov. 1, 1812, of Irish parents, who settled in that city in 1805. They were represented to be persons of striking character and of personal appearance so venerable and prepossessing that they inspired respect from all with whom they came in contact. John Baptist's education was begun at home under the direction of his parents. He afterwards entered the primary and grammar schools of Boston, and subsequently attended the Adams and Boylston Schools. From both of these institutions he received the Franklin medals. In 1826 he entered the Boston Latin School, where he remained for three years, attaining the same distinction that had marked his career in the primary schools. His knowledge of Christian doctrine, of which he made a special study, was also superior. In September, 1829, he entered the Montreal College to prepare himself for the ministry of the Roman Catholic church. Mr. Fitzpatrick showed such efficiency in his studies that he was withdrawn from the rank of students and appointed professor of rhetoric and *belles-lettres*, subjects for which he had always evinced a special aptitude. In 1833, at the public exhibition of Montreal College, he maintained a discussion in Latin, Greek, French, and English, in the presence of four bishops and the governor of the province. He was graduated at the College of Montreal in 1837, and went to the Grand Seminary of St. Sulpice at Paris, to complete his ecclesiastical studies. He soon attracted attention at St. Sulpice, as he had done elsewhere, and his fine intellectual gifts received ready recognition. He was appointed to teach the catechism in French at the Church of St. Sulpice, to the sons of the aristocratic families in the Faubourg St. Germain, and was also chosen as one of the four or five masters to preside at theological conferences. Mr. Fitzpatrick was made a subdeacon in May, 1839, a deacon the following September, and on June 13, 1840, was ordained to the priesthood. The November following he returned to Boston and his first appointment was at the Cathedral. He was subsequently assistant pastor at St. Mary's and pastor of East Cambridge churches. In 1844 Dr. Fitzpatrick was appointed coadjutor to Bishop Fenwick, and was consecrated at Georgetown, on March 4th of the same year by Bishop Fenwick; Bishop Whelen of Richmond, Va., and Bishop Tyler of Hartford, Conn., assisting. From that time he relieved Bishop Fenwick from the more arduous of his duties. In 1846 Bishop Fitzpatrick attended the sixth provincial council of Baltimore. During his administration he was called to face a number of unfortunate and trying occurrences which took place in the diocese, principal among them were the blowing up of the Catholic Church which was being built at Dorchester, on July 4, 1854. On the 4th and 5th of the same month an anti-Catholic mob, led by a fanatic named Orr, broke into the churches, destroyed the pews, and otherwise demolished and fired the church in Bath, and about the same time a Know-nothing riot occurred at Manchester, N. H., which resulted in great destruction to church property, and much distress to the Catholic population. In October of the same year, the "Ellsworth Outrage" as it is known, took place, when a priest was cruelly assaulted, and injured by a mob of citizens. These were only a part of the numberless difficulties with which he had to contend. After returning from Rome, whither he went in 1854, Bishop Fitzpatrick engaged in his celebrated controversy with the Boston school board, which eventuated in a repeal of the laws obnoxious to Catholic pupils. So rapidly did the Catholic population grow under his administration, that in 1853 it became necessary to erect two new sees out of the Boston diocese. There were but forty churches and forty priests when he began his episcopate. At his death he left 300 churches and 300 priests, and had also built a large reformatory, a hospital, one of the finest orphan asylums in the United States, and Boston College which, under the care of the Jesuit fathers, has become famous as an institution of learning. Bishop Fitzpatrick also conceived and planned the new Boston Cathedral, and purchased a large and eligible lot for its location, but the fruition of his grand plans was left to his successors. He was a man of refined and cultivated tastes. "A beautiful trait of his character was a love of truth. This was recognized and felt by all who knew him and by none more than by those who knew him best," his biographer, Dr. Clarke, says of him. His long illness and protracted sufferings only served to bring out with greater lustre his many excellent traits. His death was worthy of his life, calm, resigned, devout, and noble to the last. His death produced a profound sensation in Boston and throughout New England, and was earnestly felt in every part of the country. Every honor was paid to his memory. As his remains were carried to the church, the bells of the city of Boston were tolled by the order of the mayor, and again during the funeral. People of all religions turned out by tens of thousands to show their sorrowful respect. His funeral was attended by ten bishops, and 140 priests; by the governor, mayor, and other officials, and by an immense concourse of people, including some of the most distinguished and literary men of the country. He died at Boston, Mass., Feb. 13, 1866. His biography may be found in Vol. II. "Lives of the Deceased Bishops," by Dr. R. H. Clarke.

WILLIAMS, John Joseph, fourth bishop of Boston, first archbishop. (See Vol. IV. p. 415).

FLAGET, Benedict Joseph, Roman Catholic bishop, Bardstown, Louisville, Ky., was born at Contournat, Auvergne, France, Nov. 7, 1763. His parents were farmers, of high respectability. He pursued his classical studies at the College of Billom, and as a child, had a foresight of his future life as a missionary, saying that "he would go far, very far, from home, and that they would see him no more." At the age of seventeen he entered the University of Clermont, and for two years attended the classes of philosophy and theology, acting during the time as the tutor of two wealthy young men with whom he resided, and defrayed his expenses at the university with the salary he acquired as tutor. On Nov. 1, 1783, he entered the seminary at Clermont for his theological studies, and at the same time joined the order of Sulpicians. While still under age, he completed his theological studies, and was sent to Issy, near Paris, where, at the termination of three years, he was ordained a priest. He was at once appointed professor of dogmatic theology in the Seminary of Nantes, and two years later was made professor of moral theology. He had filled this position but two months when the terrors of the French revolution compelled him to fly for protection to his family at Billom. He was for a time undecided what course to pursue. The situation of the church in America appealed strongly to his sympathies, and after much deliberation, he decided to go as a missionary to that country. In January, 1792, he left Bordeaux, in company with the Rev. Messrs. Badin, David, and Chicoisneau, and arrived at Baltimore on March 26th of that year, where they were warmly welcomed by Bishop Carroll, to whom they unreservedly offered their services. The Abbé Flaget was appointed to the mission of Vincennes, Ind., and immediately started on his laborious journey West. He remained at Pittsburgh for nearly six months, and was cordially received by Gen. Hayne, to whom he had carried letters of introduction. He did missionary work at Pittsburgh. As soon as circumstances permitted he left Pittsburgh, stopped for a time at Cincinnati, O., which was then only a fort, and went thence to Louisville, Ky., at that time a settlement containing but three or four rude cabins. He was cordially welcomed by Col. George Rogers Clark, who commanded the garrison of Corn Island, near the falls of the Ohio. He gave him an armed escort to accompany him to Vincennes, where he arrived Dec. 21, 1792. It would be hard to realize at the present time the deplorable condition in which he found the country that had been for so long a time without the ministration of a priest. The white settlers had begun to acquire the savage habits of the Indians, and the Abbé Flaget had not only to labor for their regeneration, but for that of the warlike Indian tribes as well. With a wonderful zeal and perseverance he overcame these obstacles, and when he was called to new fields of labor two years later, he left a record of deeds that was transmitted to future generations. In 1795 he was recalled to Baltimore, and was appointed chief disciplinarian and professor of French and geography in Georgetown College. He went with the Rev. Mr. Dubourg and the Rev. Mr. Brabant to Havana, Cuba, in 1798, to assist in the founding of a college on that island, to be placed under the care of the Sulpicians. Their efforts were, however, unsuccessful, and the Abbé Flaget contracted a severe illness, and was detained some time in Cuba. During his stay there he filled the office of tutor to the sons of Don Nicholas Calvo, a Spaniard of wealth and position. During his residence on the island he formed the acquaintance of Louis Phillppe and his two brothers. The citizens of Havana subscribed quite a sum of money for their relief, and selected the Abbé Flaget to present the purse to the exiled princes. In the autumn of 1801 he returned to the United States, and for the next eight years was stationed at St. Mary's College. In 1804 he applied to his superior to join the order of Trappist monks, the most rigid order in the Roman Catholic church, but he was destined for a higher purpose, and some difficulties falling in the way, he subsequently abandoned the idea. In 1807, when the four new sees of Boston, New York, Philadelphia, and Bardstown were created, Abbé Flaget was appointed bishop of Bardstown, and on Nov. 4, 1810, he was consecrated in the Baltimore Cathedral by Archbishop Carroll, and reached Louisville, Ky., on June 4, 1811, and arrived at Bardstown five days later. At the time he assumed charge of this see there was not more than 1,000 Catholic families in the whole state of Kentucky—but 6,000 Catholics in the entire population. There were two small churches, six in process of erection, and thirty congregations in his diocese. The episcopal palace of the new bishop was a log cabin, sixteen feet square. He resided with Father Badin at St. Stephen's (now Lorretto). His diocese covered a vast field, and extended to the borders of the great lakes and the banks of the Mississippi. His episcopal visitations were laborious missionary journeys. It has been said that "wherever Bishop Flaget pitched his tent, he there laid the foundations for a new church, and that each one of his principal halts was destined to become a bishopric"—Vincennes, in Indiana; Detroit, in Michigan; Cincinnati, in Ohio; Erie, in Pennsylvania; Buffalo, in New York. He would sometimes be absent from his episcopal residence as much as thirteen months, giving missions along his route at any point where he chanced to find settlements of whites, blacks, or Indians. His vast diocese and his extended absences made the appointment of a coadjutor indispensable, and accordingly the Pope appointed Father David titular bishop of Mauricastro, and coadjutor to the bishop of Bardstown. Bishop Flaget, soon after his elevation to the Episcopate, ordained the Rev. Mr. Chabrat, who was the first priest ordained in the West. He paid much attention to the establishment of a diocesan seminary, and in 1811 Mr. Thomas Howard donated a plantation for that purpose. Soon after Bishop David was appointed coadjutor the bishops removed their residence from St. Thomas Seminary to Bardstown, and on Aug. 8, 1819, consecrated the new cathedral in that town. Bishop Flaget was the first to propose the erection of an archiepiscopal see in the West. Notwithstanding the many labors required of him in his own diocese, he always found time to take an active part in the leading religious questions in the church. He was constantly in correspondence with Rome, and was consulted by the Propaganda upon important affairs. In 1829 he attended the first provincial council at Baltimore. In 1830, on account of failing health, he resigned his see, and Bishop David was appointed his successor. This transaction met with such opposition from both the clergy and laity in his jurisdiction that he was obliged to submit to a reversal. In 1833, during the cholera epidemic, he was untiring in his ministrations to those suffering from the disease. Without regard to sect or creed, and heedless of his own health, he attended the sick and dying. On June 29, 1834, he received the bulls announcing Dr. Chabart his second coadjutor. In 1835 he went abroad, and was received at Rome with every mark of respect by the pope, cardinals, and other persons of distinction. He returned to America during the summer of 1839. In 1841 his episcopal see was removed from Bardstown to Louisville, Ky. Bishop Chabart's health necessitated his resignation as coadjutor in 1847, and the following year Dr. Martin John Spalding was appointed coadjutor in his stead. The corner-stone of the new cathedral at Louisville was laid on Aug. 15, 1849. Bishop Flaget did not, however, live to see its completion, but, after great suffering, died in February of the following year. The diocese which he had found in such a desolate condition, was left to his successor in a prosperous state; there were some forty churches and chapels, twenty-six priests on the missions, with twenty otherwise occupied. A diocesan seminary under the charge of the Lazarists was established on a firm basis; the Jesuits and Dominicans were in the field; St. Joseph's College had been duly incorporated; St. Mary's was also incorporated, and in charge of the Jesuit fathers; St. Ignatius' Literary Institution in Louisville, was also under their care; Mount Merino Seminary, near Hardinsburg, was established, and female academies have been started at Bardstown, Morganfield, and Lexington, under the care of the sisters of charity; near Springfield, under the Dominican sisters, and the sisters of Lorretto had charge of the Lorretto Deaf and Dumb Asylum; an orphan asylum, and female academies at Lorretto, Bethlehem, Holy Mary, Calvary, and Gethsemane. He died at Nazareth, Ky., Feb. 11, 1850.

BIGOT, William Valentine, Roman Catholic priest, was born near Altkirch, Upper Elsass, Germany, Dec. 4, 1888, son of Anthony Bigot, a prominent architect, and Magdelena Besenfelder. When a youth of thirteen he entered the Gymnasium of Maria Stein (Switzerland), conducted by the fathers of St. Benedict, where he remained four years. At eighteen he entered the missionary institution of the Holy Ghost in western France (Bretagne), where he continued his studies, and prepared himself for missionary life. His philosophical and theological studies were completed in the Seminary of the Holy Ghost, rue Lhomond, Paris. After a five years' course at this institution he was ordained to the priesthood, May 22, 1864, by the Rt. Rev. Bishop Maupoint of St. Deny's (Reunion Island). After his ordination he was sent by his superior to Kaiserwerth, near Dusseldorf, Rhine Province, where, at the request of the Cardinal von Geisel, he was appointed to take charge of an institution for retired priests. He served in this capacity six years, from 1864 to 1870, when the war broke out between France and Germany. Anticipating nothing good for France, he removed from Kaiserwerth to Marienthal, near

Cologne, another similar institution of the order, to await the development of events. Upon the request of Bishop Hefele of Rottenburg, Wurtemburg, he was appointed military chaplain, to attend to the spiritual needs of the 18,000 French soldiers, who were held prisoners of Stuttgart, Ludwigsburg, and Asperg. He remained in this entirely Protestant country five months, enduring the severity of the winter, exposing himself to contagious diseases and to the hardships of the war. After the treaty of peace was concluded he was allowed to return to Marien-

thal, not to rest, but to take charge of the convent. At the same time he received orders from the German and French governments to collect the death certificates of French soldiers who had died in captivity, and within a short time he delivered to the French ministry at Paris a volume of 18,300 certificates. The French government forwarded to him 60,000 francs, with instructions to have monuments erected in all cemeteries where French soldiers lay buried. For his faithful services he was decorated with the cross of the legion of honor, and received a purse to be used for his recreation. Meanwhile, the May laws of 1873 had decreed that all Jesuit and similar institutions be abolished, and the members thereof be exiled. Consequently, he received, instead of an appreciation for his services, the decree of exilement. He received permission, however, to emigrate to the United States, there to serve as a missionary priest. In January, 1874, he reached Cincinnati, O., where he was cordially received by Most Rev. Archbishop Purcell, taken into the diocese, and placed in charge of the large congregation of St. Michael's, Loramie (Berlin), O. In the course of the twenty-one years' pastorate he built the substantial St. Michael's Church, admired for its beauty, solidity, and minor equipment, at a cost of $50,000.

CLANCY, William, Roman Catholic bishop, was born in Cork, Ireland. He took his theological studies at the College of Carlow, and was afterwards curate of that institution for six years. In 1829 he accepted the chair of theology at Carlow, which he occupied for the six years preceding his elevation to the episcopate. He also performed missionary labors in the city and county of Cork. In 1845 Dr. Clancy was appointed coadjutor to Bishop England, with the title of bishop of Oriense. He was consecrated by Bishop Nolan in the Carlow Cathedral on Feb. 1, 1835. Before completing his preparations to assume his duties in America, Bishop Clancy was taken seriously ill, and his departure was, on this account, for some time delayed. After regaining his heath, he devoted himself to obtaining missionaries for the diocese of Charleston. His efforts were successful, and a number of ecclesiastical students preceded him to America, and others followed. Bishop Clancy arrived at Charleston on Nov. 21, 1835, where he was warmly received by Bishop England. He performed the duties of coadjutor-bishop for two years; was present at the provincial council of Baltimore in 1837, and in the summer of the same year he was transferred to British Guiana. Shortly before he was translated to his new see he was engaged in an interesting correspondence with Washington Irving on the subject of a narrative, with a supposed historical foundation, which cast reproach upon the Catholics, and which Mr. Irving had incorporated in one of his works. Mr. Irving disclaimed all intention of wishing to throw discredit on the Catholic church, and avowed his freedom from prejudice, and agreed to correct the error in future editions of the work. Unfortunately, for some unknown reason, he never fulfilled the agreement. This interesting correspondence was published in the "London Catholic Magazine," and the "New York Freeman's Journal," in 1842. Bishop Clancy filled the position of vicar apostolic in British Guiana for two years, when, on account of feeble health, the climate having completely undermined his constitution, he returned to Ireland, where he died in the summer of 1847.

SHEEDY, Morgan Madden, Roman Catholic priest, was born in Liscarroll, Ireland, Oct. 8, 1853. His early studies were made in the Latin school of Charleville, where he was prepared for college. He entered St. Coleman's Fermoy, and, subsequently St. Patrick's College, Maynooth. He came on the invitation of the Bishop of Pittsburgh to America, in 1870, and was accepted in the diocese of Pittsburgh as a candidate for the priesthood. Immediately after his arrival on Sept. 23rd, he was ordained priest by Bishop Tuigg. He was for a time professor of theology and history in St. Michael's Seminary. In November, 1877, he was assigned to missionary work, at Parker's Landing, and in 1878 was transferred to Altoona as assistant at St. John's Church. Here he remained until March, 1881, when he was appointed pastor of St. Rose's, Carmelton, and St. Teresa's, Clinton, Pa. In 1885 he was made rector of St. Mary of Mercy's Church, Pittsburgh, Pa. He organized the parish school of St. Mary's, Duquesne Hall, and built a new church for the congregation. The welfare of young men was a special object of his concern, and he instituted a free library and reading-room, open to the public, irrespective of creed. He co-operated with Dr. Hodges, the rector of Calvary Episcopal Church, Pittsburgh, in Sunday afternoon concerts for the working people. He was the projector and founder of the Columbus Club, and for seven years a director. He originated the Pittsburgh Polytechnic Society, one of the flourishing literary societies of the city. He was for four years vice-president of the Catholic Total Abstinence Union of America, and the first president of the Catholic Summer School of America. He is, at present, chairman of the directory board of the Reading Circle Union, and treasurer of that association. In 1894, Father Sheedy, as the result of a public concursus, was named permanent rector of St. John's Church, Altoona, Pa., made vacant by the promotion of Very Rev. E. A. Bush to St. Peter's, Allegheny, to succeed Vicar-Gen. Wall. He is a regular contributor to various maga-

zines and periodicals; an active member of a number of scientific and historical societies, before which he has read, from time to time, valuable papers. He has lectured before the Academy of Science and Arts, Pittsburgh, taken a deep interest in the work of the Historical Society of Western Pennsylvania, of which he was vice-president. He is a close student of social science, and delivered before the Champlain Summer School a course of lectures on social problems in 1894. Father Sheedy is one of the great national priests of the Roman Catholic church, prominent in the large activities of the total abstinence movement, and of enlarged popular education. His career has been characterized throughout by a catholic spirit of the truest sort, which strives to encompass the good of all men.

O'CONNOR, Michael, first Roman Catholic bishop of Pittsburgh, Pa., was born in the city of Cork, Ireland, Sept. 27, 1810. His boyhood was spent in Queenstown, where he received his preparatory classical education in the Grammar school. He was an altar-boy in the cathedral of Bishop Coppenger, who was very partial to him, and had him to answer his private mass. Showing an early predilection for the ecclesiastical calling, he was sent to Rome, to study at the Propaganda, and was one of its most gifted and distinguished scholars. On July 27, 1833, young O'Connor won his doctor's cap and ring in a disputation of the most brilliant kind. The theses assigned him embraced all theology and scripture, the same test given to St. Thomas and St. Bounventure in the thirteenth century, when they became doctors of the University of Paris. It is said that when Dr. O'Connor came to receive the Pope's blessing, Gregory XVI. playfully twined his handkerchief round the young doctor's brow, saying, "If it were a crown of gold you would deserve it." Dr. O'Connor was ordained at Rome the same year, and appointed vice-rector of the Irish Ecclesiastical College in that city. During his ministry here he enjoyed the friendship and esteem of the Pope, and the high regard of Cardinal Wiseman, who predicted a great career for him. After an absence in Rome of ten years, he returned to Ireland in time to assist at his mother's death-bed. For three years he was pastor of Fermoy, and chaplain to the Presentation Convent in Doneraile. In 1838 he was a competitor for the chair of dogmatic theology in Maynooth College, but while deep in his preparation, Bishop Kendrick, of Philadelphia, sent his brother, on his way to Rome, to offer, and urge upon his acceptance, the presidency of the seminary of St. Charles Borromeo. He arrived in Philadelphia in 1839, and besides the duties of his office, had the care of the missions of Norristown and Westchester, visiting them twice a month. In 1841 he was sent as vicar-general to settle some church difficulties at Pittsburgh, and became pastor of St. Paul's Church. In 1843 the Provincial Council of Baltimore recommended the erection of a new see for western Pennsylvania at Pittsburgh, and Dr. O'Connor was nominated as bishop. He had for a long time desired to become a member of the Society of Jesus, and having an exalted conception of the duties of the episcopal office, shrank from accepting it. To escape the appointment, he hastened to Europe. But the letters of the American bishops had already reached Rome, and when he knelt at the feet of the Pope, and humbly preferred his petition to join the Society of Jesus, Gregory XVI. forbade him to rise until he consented to accept the new diocese of Pittsburgh. "You will be bishop first and Jesuit afterward." He was consecrated by Cardinal Franzoni, Aug. 15th, at St. Agatha's, the church of the Irish College at Rome. He passed through Ireland on his return to America, to obtain religious recruits. Five students, and three others far advanced, responded to his appeal, and seven sisters, of the recently founded order of our Lady of Mercy, accompanied him, to take charge of the parish schools and seminary for young ladies. Bishop O'Connor took an informal census of religion in his new diocese, and reported a Roman Catholic population of about 25,000, thirty-three churches (some still unfinished),

fourteen priests, and only two religious institutions. He was deeply impressed with the want of priests, and determined to appeal to the Catholic countries of Europe for more. To this end he set out for Rome in 1845, and returned with four presentation brothers, to found an Institute of their order, and take charge of the boys' school. Bishop O'Connor had great enterprise and business qualifications, and was very successful in financial investments. He purchased a large farm on the hill south of Birmingham for $18,000, which, sold in building lots, yielded a return of $100,000. St. Michael's Church, the Franciscan Convent, the Passionist Monastery, and St. Michael's Seminary now crown the hill. In 1850 the great work of the new cathedral was begun, and, despite the difficulties encountered, he was able to have it ready for consecration on June 24, 1855. In 1854, on summons of Pope Pius IX., Bishop O'Connor sailed for Rome, to take part in defining the dogma of the Immaculate Conception; and it is said that it was due to his learned suggestions that some changes were made in the wording of the decree. In 1860 Bishop O'Connor's resignation was accepted, and he entered the novitiate of the Society of Gorheim, in Germany. After two years he was permitted, by special dispensation, to take the four vows at once. Returning to the United States, he taught theology at Boston College. He was afterward Socius to the Provincial of the Jesuits, an office he held until his death. He was an accomplished linguist, and as a lecturer, and in his pulpit efforts he was most effectual. He was particularly interested in the colored people, and zealous in their behalf. He purchased the church and organized the colored congregation of St. Francis Xavier. In the spring of 1872 his health had so declined that he was sent to rest at Woodstock College, where he spent the remainder of his days. He said his last mass on the Feast of St. Michael, his patron. He died Oct. 18, 1872. His remains repose with the deceased members of the Society of Jesus, at Woodstock.

DOMENEC, Michael, second Roman Catholic bishop of Pittsburgh, was born in the city of Ruez, near Tarragona, Spain, in 1816. His father was of Moorish descent, wealthy, and of high social position. At the age of fifteen he accompanied his parents to France, and was entered at the seminary of the Lazarists in Paris. Here he met Father Timon, visitor-general of the Lazarists in the United States, at whose invitation, and the designation of his superiors, he joined the American mission, arriving at the Barrens in Missouri in 1838. Young Domenec continued his theological studies, becoming well versed in English, and acquiring some reputation as an orator. He was ordained to the priesthood in 1839. In 1845 he was sent to Philadelphia to take charge of the Seminary of St. Vincent, and was pastor of the Church of St. Stephen, at Nicetown, and later of St. Vincent de Paul, at Germantown. As professor, ecclesiastical teacher or missionary, he had been so successful, that he seemed called only to the higher spheres of usefulness and labor; therefore, when Bishop O'Connor resigned the episcopal office in 1860, Father Domenec was recommended as his successor, and he was consecrated in the Cathedral of St. Paul, in December of that year. The new incumbent found his diocese in good order, well supplied with priests and churches, and finely equipped institutions. While Bishop Domenec was opposed to debt, and his judgment was not so much at fault, he was not fitted to deal successfully with financial involvements, such as the panic of 1873 precipitated upon the diocese. In the plenteous period following the war, when debts should have been paid off, instead of more incurred, improvements upon the cathedral, and the building of churches, convents, and schools, had rolled up heavy obligations, which, in the crisis could not be met. The diocese had increased to such an extent that it was considered too large for a single bishop, and in 1875, it was divided by the erection of the new see of Allegheny, to which Bishop Domenec was transferred. Father Tuigg of Altoona, being appointed to the bishopric of Pittsburgh. This division was not well received in the diocese of Pittsburgh, as it left the churches and institutions most heavily in debt to the parent diocese, and making the financial situation more complicated. No satisfactory arrangement could be made on this side of the Atlantic, and an appeal was made to Rome, Bishop Domenec going to the Holy City to represent his own side of the question. Upon the judgment of the Holy See, that the diocese of Allegheny should be re-united to that of Pittsburgh, Bishop Domenec resigned. The decision was made in 1877, and Bishop Tuigg assumed the administration of the diocese of Allegheny. Thus Bishop Domenec was left a bishop without a charge. It was subsequently rumored that an exalted position in the American Church had been offered him. From Rome he went to Barcelona in the fall of 1877, preaching twice a week, in the churches of that city, attracting crowded audiences by his eloquence and great personal popularity. He left Barcelona to visit his native city prior to returning to the United States, and was taken suddenly very ill at Tarragona. His disease was putrid pneumonia. Before this, Bishop Domenec had enjoyed the most robust health. He never knew fatigue, and was never so well pleased, as when hard at work. He visited Rome several times, being present, at the invitation of Pius IX., at the canonization of the Japanese martyrs in 1862, and attended the Œcumenical Council of the Vatican in 1870. He died, Jan. 7, 1878.

TUIGG, John, third Roman Catholic bishop of Pittsburgh, Pa., was born in Donoughmore, Ireland, in 1820. He was educated in the missionary college at All Hallows, Drumcondra, and when Michael O'Connor went to Dublin in 1849, calling for volunteers for the missionary work in America, young Tuigg was the first to respond, reaching Pittsburgh in December, 1849. He finished his studies in St. Michael's Seminary, when he was appointed professor in the institution, where he remained until he was ordained, May 11, 1850, and appointed one of the assistants in St. Paul's Cathedral, at the same time appointed secretary to the bishop. He organized the St. Bridget's congregation, and with characteristic energy entered immediately upon the work of erecting a new church. But before it was completed he was transferred to mission work at Altoona, where he remained until 1876. He had been appointed vicar-general for the eastern part of the diocese. Upon a division of dioceses Father Tuigg was selected to preside over the see of Pittsburgh, and he was officially notified that the Pope would not accept any declination of the honor. In 1876 he was consecrated bishop of Pittsburgh. Upon his accession he found the property encumbered and the finances embarrassed by the panic of 1873, but with wise foresight and extraordinary ability he extricated the diocese from its difficulties, and gave new impetus to the zeal of his people. On the retirement of Bishop Domenec, the Allegheny diocese was added to his administration. The double burden was more than he could bear, and his

constitution gave way under a paralytic stroke. He went South, and partially recovering his health, resumed his labors, when he was again stricken, and forced to retire. The bishop combined in a rare degree the unusual qualities of firmness and gentleness, and possessed astonishing executive abilities, as the schools, convent, and splendid church of St. John bear witness. The united diocese contained 183 churches, and 191 chapels, convents and educational institutions. He was also ranked among the foremost preachers of the state. He died in Altoona, Dec. 7, 1889.

PHELAN, Richard, fourth Roman Catholic bishop of Pittsburgh, was born near the town of Bollyragget, county Kilkenny, Ireland, Jan. 1, 1828, son of a high-minded and well-to-do farmer, devoted to his country and to his family. Richard was the oldest of nine children, all of whom had the advantage of a good education. His earliest scholastic training was received from private tutors in his father's house and in the parish schools of the neighborhood. He pursued the higher branches of study at St. Kieran's College, Kilkenny, intending to enter the famous ecclesiastical school at Maynooth, but when he heard the call from the Rt. Rev. M. O'Connor, first bishop of Pittsburgh, for students to take up the work of the church in his diocese, he in December, 1849, left Ireland for America and proceeded immediately to Pitts-

burgh, where he resumed his studies in the old seminary of St. Michael's. The next three years he passed at St. Mary's Seminary, Baltimore, where he received minor orders and was ordained sub-deacon and deacon by Archbishop Kenrick. On May 4, 1855, he was ordained a priest by Bishop O'Connor in the cathedral at Pittsburgh. His first charge was a small mission at Cameron's Bottoms, Indiana county; it was while here that cholera visited Pittsburgh, and Father Phelan voluntarily relinquished his mission to care for the sick and dying in the plague-stricken city. Here he did heroic work until the danger was past, when he returned to his modest mission from which he was soon called as an assistant at St. Paul's Cathedral, where for four years he performed the arduous duties of curate in a great parish, as well as looking after the spiritual and temporal welfare of several small congregations in the outlying country districts. It was in these new parishes that his skill as a disciplinarian and peacemaker evidenced itself. Bishop O'Connor selected him to settle several serious disturbances notably at Freeport, where he was placed in charge of the church, and succeeded in quieting what promised to be a very serious revolt. He bought and paid for a parish house, improved the church, purchased ground and laid out a cemetery, and restored peace and harmony in the congregation. In 1868 he was appointed pastor of St. Peter's Church, Allegheny city, to succeed Very Rev. Tobias Mullen, who had been made bishop of Erie. Here he found a church inadequate to the wants of the congregation, and he at once set about to provide a new and handsome edifice, which he completed in three years at a cost of $150,000, and dedicated July 5, 1874. This was pronounced to be one of the finest churches in western Pennsylvania. During the life of Bishop O'Connor, Father Phelan was intrusted with the confidences of that prelate, and was selected for many important and delicate missions. Twice he administered the affairs of the diocese, once on the resignation of Rt. Rev. Bishop Domenec and again during the absence of Rt. Rev. Bishop Tuigg

In Europe. In 1883 he was made vicar-general of the diocese, and in 1885 coadjutor of the two sees of Allegheny City and Pittsburgh, with the right of succession to Bishop Tuigg. He was consecrated as titular bishop of Cibyra, Aug. 2, 1885. With all the responsibility and only part of the authority of a bishop, he did the real work of the diocese and he came through the ordeal with the respect and regard of the entire clergy. Just as he was preparing to leave Allegheny City to take up his residence at St. Paul's Cathedral, Pittsburgh, fire destroyed his beautiful St. Peter's Church and reduced his life work to ashes. This incident changed his plans, and he determined to remain and rebuild the church. This he successfully accomplished, and on Apr. 22, 1888, the cross on the steeple of the new St. Peter's Church gloriously reflected the rays of the morning sun over a twice-built monument of his priestly piety and energy. On the death of Bishop Tuigg in 1889, Father Phelan succeeded to the full bishopric of Pittsburgh. In June, 1891, he left the parish where he had spent twenty-five eventful years, and took possession of the episcopal residence at Pittsburgh. For sixteen years he attended the convicts of the Western Penitentiary, continuing his ministrations until the institution was removed. The Catholic inmates of all the public institutions in his diocese were provided by him with the comforts of religion. The diocese of Pittsburgh, through an existence of nearly half a century has greatly prospered, especially under Bishop Phelan's indirect and direct administration. In 1850, including the present diocese of Erie, it had twenty-five priests, thirty-five churches and a Catholic population of 40,000. In 1894 there were 205 churches, 170 secular and 120 regular priests, with a Catholic population of about 220,000. Although sixty-six years have passed, with forty years of pastoral solicitude and labor to his credit, Bishop Phelan is remarkably well preserved, and his kindly face, compact figure of medium height, strong features, and his dark hair slightly mixed with gray, are familiar to nearly every resident of Pittsburgh and to the entire Catholic population of his extended diocese.

LAMBING, Andrew Arnold, Roman Catholic priest and author, was born at Manorville, Armstrong co., Pa., Feb. 1, 1842, the son of Michael Anthony and Anne (Shields) Lambing. He is descended from Christopher Lambing, who emigrated to America about the year 1745, and settled in Nockamixon township, Bucks county, Pa. Young Andrew began work on a farm before he was eight, and in a few years found employment in public works, spending six years in fire-brick yards, with three or four months at school in winter; and two years in an oil refinery, a considerable part of which time he worked fifteen hours a day. At the age of twenty-one he entered St. Michael's Preparatory and Theological Seminary at Pittsburgh, where he finished his classical and theological course, and was ordained to the priesthood Aug. 4, 1869, by the late Bishop Domenec of Pittsburgh. He was first sent to teach in St. Francis' College, Loretto, Cambria co., and attend certain small missions, but in April, 1870, he was transferred to Kittanning, Armstrong co., where he remained nearly three years, and built a church in the country west of the river for the accommodation of those living in that part of the county. He was then transferred to Freeport, where he remained but six months, when he was called to the chaplaincy of St. Paul's Orphan Asylum, Pittsburgh, with a view of bettering the financial condition of that institution. But the financial crisis of 1873 destroyed all such hopes for the time, and he was placed in charge of the congregation of St. Mary of Mercy, Pittsburgh. While there he placed the schools under the care of

the Sisters of Mercy, purchased and remodeled a Protestant church for the congregation, and rendered other invaluable services. Having ministered to this congregation until October, 1885, he assumed pastoral charge of the congregation of St. James at Wilkinsburgh, where he still remains. In the fall of 1886 he opened a parochial school for the first time, and in the summer of 1888, he enlarged the church for the accommodation of the increasing congregation. In December of the same year the building was destroyed by fire and he at once fitted up the school house to serve the two-fold purpose of church and school, and occupied it on Christmas eve while the ruins of the burnt church were still smouldering. Father Lambing is the author of "The Orphan's Friend" (1875); "The Sunday-School Teacher's Manual" (1877); "A History of the Catholic church in the Dioceses of Pittsburgh and Allegheny" (1880); "The Register of Fort Duquesne, Translated from the French with an Introductory Essay and Notes" (1883); and "The Sacramentals of the Holy Catholic Church" (1890). He has also published a number of pamphlets. He wrote a considerable part of the "History of Allegheny County, Pa," in 1888; in the same year, he, assisted by J. W. F. White, of the Allegheny county bench, wrote the "Centennial History of Allegheny County," for the centennial celebration. In the summer of 1884 he started the "Catholic Historical Researches," a quarterly magazine devoted to the history of the Catholic church in the United States. It was afterwards transferred to a Philadelphia publisher, by whom it is still continued. In 1885 he procured from the Archives of the Marine at

Paris, a copy of the journal of Céloron's expedition down the Allegheny and Ohio rivers in the summer and fall of 1749. This he translated and annotated, publishing it in the "Researches." He is a regular contributor to several magazines, and has for a number of years been president of the Historical Society of Western Pennsylvania. He was president of the board to prepare the exhibit of the educational institutions of the diocese of Pittsburgh, for the Columbian Exposition, and is at present fiscal procurator of the diocese of Pittsburgh. He has inherited the health of his fathers; for, though more than twenty-six years on the mission, he has not been off duty a single day on account of ill health. In June, 1880, the University of Notre Dame, Indiana, conferred on him the degree of LL.D.

BUSH, Edward A., Roman Catholic priest, was born in Montreal, Canada, June 5, 1839, son of Edward Bush, a native of England and a convert to the Roman Catholic faith. His mother was Catherine Doran, a Catholic Irish woman. At the death of his parents, in 1851, he came to the United States under the care and protection of Rev. William Pollard, a near relative, and began his preparatory studies, at the desire of the first bishop of Pittsburgh, Rt. Rev. M. O'Connor, D.D., as a subject of that diocese. He entered St. Michael's Seminary and was, during his theological course, instructed by the distinguished scholars, Rev. James Keogh, D.D., and Very Rev. James O'Connor, D.D. He was ordained priest by Rt. Rev. M. Domenec, D.D., Feb. 7, 1863, and was assigned to duty as professor at the seminary. In 1864 he was appointed rector of St. Francis' College, Loretto, Pa., where he remained until 1868, when he was recalled to St. Michael's Seminary.

In March, 1870, he became rector of St. Michael's Church, Loretto, and soon after was made diocesan counselor by Bishop Domenec, and continued in that office by Bishops Tuigg and Phelan. In 1800 he was made rector of St. John's Church, Altoona, and appointed the same year, vicar forane of the eastern portion of the diocese. Here he remained until November, 1894, when he became rector of St. Peter's Church, Allegheny, Pa., and soon after was promoted to the vicar generalship of the diocese by Rt. Rev. R. Phelan, D.D., fourth of the eminent prelates who have governed the diocese of Pittsburgh.

REID, William J., clergyman, was born in South Argyle, Washington co., N. Y., Aug. 17, 1834, son of John and Elizabeth (McQuarie) Reid, descendants of Scotch families who emigrated to America in 1764–68, and settled on a tract of land located in what is now Washington county, N. Y., which was given by George IV. to the Duke of Argyle. He is the great-grandson of William Reid, 1738–1833, who was the first American ancestor of the family. After preparatory training in Argyle Academy, he entered Union College, Schenectady, N. Y., and was graduated in the class of 1855. During his college days he taught district schools in his native county, and after graduation he was for four years a professor in Whitestown Seminary, Oneida county, N. Y. He pursued his theological studies in the Allegheny Theological Seminary of the United Presbyterian Church, Allegheny, Pa., and was graduated in 1862, and soon after became pastor of the First United Presbyterian Church of Pittsburgh, Pa. He has been principal clerk of the general assembly of the United Presbyterian church since May, 1875; editor in chief of "The United Presbyterian," a religious weekly, published in

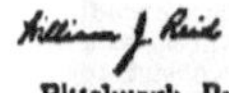

Pittsburgh, Pa., since November, 1887, and has taken part in the general work of his denomination, serving on many of its boards and committees, and representing it in the council of Presbyterian churches, which met in Belfast, Ireland, in 1884. Though his activities have been employed in these several departments of ecclesiastical work, his chief field of labor has been in the one congregation of which he has been pastor for thirty-three years. He has published, "Lectures on the Revelations" (1878); "United Presbyterianism" (1881), besides occasional sermons and articles in the religious press. He was married at Troy, Pa., Oct. 29, 1862, to Mary Bowen, whose family of Quaker descent emigrated from New England to Northern Pennsylvania.

LYNE, Wickliffe C., insurance manager and educator, was born near Richmond, Va., Sept. 22, 1850. His ancestors were of old English and Scotch stock, prominent in civil and ecclesiastical affairs of the old country as well as of Virginia in colonial times. His father, Robert Baylor Lyne, a graduate of Transylvania University, Kentucky, was a Virginia physician, a man of great public spirit and influence, and brother to the mother of William Lyne Wilson, author of the Wilson tariff bill, and postmaster-general in the cabinet of Pres. Cleveland. His great-grandfather, William Lyne, represented the county of King and Queen in the house of burgesses, composed of the most eminent men in Virginia, and was a member of the Virginia convention of 1775, made memorable by the first resolution planning the organization and defense of the colonies, in which Patrick Henry made his passionate speech for "liberty or death." He was also a member of the famous convention of 1788 with Madison, Jefferson, Henry, and Randolph, when Virginia ratified the Federal constitution, and the career of the American Republic virtually began. His father was John Lyne, colonel of "minute men," and prominent in state affairs after the war. The subject of this sketch received a thorough classical training under private tutors at Jefferson Academy. At sixteen he entered the sophomore class at Bethany College, West Virginia, and three years later was graduated with distinction, ranking first in the classics and science, though the youngest of his class. His alma mater subsequently conferred on him the honorary degree of A. M. in recognition of his successful work as principal of the Burgettstown Normal School and Academy, the Claysville Normal School and the Washington High School, and offered him the chair of Latin and Greek which had been filled for twenty years by Prof. Chas. L. Loos, president-elect of the Kentucky University. This he declined, and for five years labored as principal of one of the leading schools of Pittsburg. His services were engaged by Curry University to take charge for three years of the Saturday normal department in literature, history, and methods of instruction. Propositions to assume charge of one of the Pennsylvania normal colleges, and also of a normal college in Ohio, were offered him, but he declined both, as well as the superintendency of education of one of the large cities in the state, and accepted the management for western Pennsylvania of the National Life Insurance Co. of Vermont. In this field he built up so large and lucrative a business that his territory was enlarged to include Iowa and West Virginia, and his skill as an underwriter and manager was sought in various executive capacities by leading life insurance corporations. On the organization of the Pittsburgh Underwriter's Association, he was made

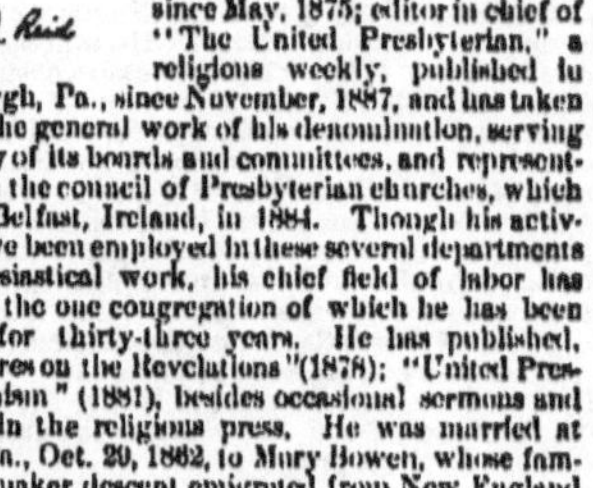

chairman of the executive committee, and next year was chosen president. Mr. Lyne is actively engaged in various business interests, operating extensively in real estate; is director of a national bank and of an insurance company; president of the Natural Gas Co.; director and vice-president of the board of trade of his resident town; and stockholder in a number of prominent corporations. As a member of the Academy of Science and Art, of the executive committee of the Mozart Musical Society, and trustee of the Pittsburgh Art Society, he is identified with the largest and most influential organizations promoting standards of public taste and enjoyment. He is a member of the Christian or Disciples' church, is superintendent of the Sunday-school, trustee and president of the official church board, a director of the Home and Foreign Missionary Societies and of the board of church extension, vice president of the Y. M. C. A. at Wilkinsburg, and has served as vice-president of the State Missionary Society of Pennsylvania. He is a trustee of Pittsburgh Academy and of Bethany College, has been secretary of the Alumni Association and twice honored with appointment as lecturer at commencement before its meetings. Mr. Lyne was married in 1878, to Mary Vowel, daughter of Addison Winters of Washington, Pa., and granddaughter of the only sister of the Brown brothers, founders of the noted American and European banking houses.

BROWN, Samuel Smith, financier, was born in Pittsburgh, Pa., Dec. 15, 1842, the son of William Henry Brown, who, in 1847, established the vast coal and coke interests which subsequently came under the ownership of his sons. Samuel Brown received his early education at common schools, and then entered Washington and Jefferson College, where he remained until the close of his junior year in 1861, and then joined company D, of the 10th regiment Pennsylvania reserves, with which he remained until its occupation of Fredericksburg, Va. There he contracted malarial or swamp fever, and was discharged at Washington, May, 1862. He soon recovered, and with Sherman's division was sent to Memphis, Tenn., directly after its capture, to take charge of the hay and coal transport for the first campaign against Vicksburg. After the close of the war he at once took an active interest in the business of his father, and made a thorough study of its vast details by actual service in its several departments, and in 1875, upon his father's death, took charge of it in connection with his brothers. He is a liberal patron of the turf, and has a string of celebrated racers. He owns an extensive farm and stables at Westport, Ky., and also owns the old Bascombe racing-track at Mobile, Ala., which he uses as the winter training quarters for his horses. He was the owner of Troubadour, winner of the Suburban handicap in 1886. He is also the owner of a controlling interest in a railroad in the South. In 1890 the Monongahela House, a celebrated hostelry of Pittsburgh, fell into difficulties, and Mr. Brown bought the property, and assumed the management. He was as successful in that as in his other business ventures, and made it one of the best paying hotel properties in the United States. Mr. Brown owns a delightful summer country-seat in the mountains above Uniontown, Pa. The coal and coke interests controlled by him include mining and shipping of the product of six mines, employing fifteen steam-boats, 1,000 barges, with retail yards at Cincinnati, Memphis, and New Orleans, and steamboat supply stations at Cairo, Ill., Natchez, Miss., Greenville, Miss., and Helena, Ark. Mr. Brown is a director of the National Bank of Commerce, Pittsburgh; and First National Bank, Dawson, Pa., a member of the Pittsburgh Coal Exchange, a member of the chamber of commerce, and president of the Ohio Valley Railway Co.

THOMAS, Joseph Dio, physician, was born in Pittsburgh, Pa., May 8, 1843, son of David and Rachel Thomas, both natives of Dolwen Fawr, near Carmarthen, South Wales, who emigrated to America about 1830 and settled in Pittsburgh. They had fourteen children. Joseph was educated in the public school of his native city, and on the outbreak of the civil war he enlisted in the army as a private in a battery of light artillery. At the end of the war he resumed his studies, taking a practical course in the Western University of Pennsylvania. He then became a student of medicine, studying first with Dr. George McCook, and afterwards at the Bellevue Hospital Medical College, New York city, where he was graduated in 1869. He then took a postgraduate course and commenced practice in South Side, Pittsburgh, in the same ward in which he was born. He is a member of the Allegheny County Medical Society, and has served one term as its president. He is a member of the Medical Society of the State of Pennsylvania; of the American Medical Association; and of the South Side Medical Society, of which he has been president. He was a member of the Pittsburgh board of health, and has served the board as its president; served one year as a member of the city council, and for a number of years as president of the school board. He occupies the chair of genito-urinary and venereal diseases, in the medical department of the Western University, and is a member of the board of trustees of the college. He was one of the founders and is a trustee and member of the surgical staff of the South Side Hospital. He made the tour of the Pacific coast in 1892, also in 1894 to the Medical Association at San Francisco, and in 1890 visited Europe. He contributed during this tour a series of letters to Pittsburgh papers, afterwards published as "A Souvenir of Europe." Dr. Thomas was married in April, 1870, to Sarah Lizzie, daughter of Abraham Keller; they have three children. Dr. Thomas has contributed to many valuable medical journals, his articles adding much to medical literature. In 1887 he delivered an address on "Hygiene" before the Medical Society of the State of Pennsylvania, at its meeting at Bedford, Pa. During his tour of Europe he visited England, Wales, Belgium, Germany, Switzerland, Italy, and France. He is a genial companion, entertaining, benevolent, generous to a fault, having a lovely home on the South Side. Surrounded by pleasing elements, he bids fair for years of usefulness.

NEEB, John Nicholas, journalist, was born in Allegheny City, Pa., March 19, 1851, son of William Neeb, a pioneer German of the state, proprietor of "Der Freiheits Freund." His education was acquired at Mt. Troy, near Allegheny City, afterward he attended the public schools, passing through the junior year at the Western University. In 1868, he became a journalist, soon attaining editorial management, and becoming a writer of distinction. At the age of twenty-one he became a member of the Allegheny county Republican executive committee, and henceforth took active part in politics. In 1875 he was elected a member of common council of Pittsburgh, and also served as a member of the Morganza reformatory board, being appointed in turn by Govs. Hartranft, Hoyt, Pattison, and Beaver. In 1890, he was nominated and elected as Republican state senator. He served through 1891 in both general and extra sessions. As a senator he served on many important committees, on all rendering valuable service. He was an active member of the Evangelical Reformed Church of Allegheny. He organized and was president of the Pittsburgh Press Club, and Y. M. Tariff Club. He was a congenial companion, firm in his convictions, of great determination and untiring activity, a quick thinker, and sound adviser. He died Feb. 19, 1898.

JOHNSON, Samuel, clergyman and first president of King's College (1754–63), was born at Guilford, Conn., Oct. 14, 1696, of English antecedents; his grandfather, Robert Johnson, having emigrated from Kingston-on-Hull, England, in 1637, and settled in New Haven, Conn. The subject of this sketch was one of the earliest students of Yale, having entered the college in 1710, nine years after it was established. He was graduated in 1714, and two years afterward, though still under twenty years of age, was appointed a tutor in the college. Yale having been removed during this time from its original seat at Saybrook, Conn., to New Haven, and for a time the young tutor had the charge of the institution. He only retained this position a short time, resigning to enter upon his ministerial work, and was ordained a clergyman in the Congregational church, and began his regular parish work at West Haven, Conn., in 1720. After two years he resigned, and in company with Timothy Cutler, rector of Yale, sailed for England, and in 1723 he was ordained a priest in the Protestant Episcopal church, soon afterward returning to America and becoming rector of the church at Stratford, Conn. He became acquainted with Dean Berkeley, during his sojourn in America, subsequently corresponding with him during his whole life, and it was through Mr. Johnson's influence that his donations were later on made to Yale. During Mr. Johnson's residence in Stratford he wrote several very learned treatises, published by Benjamin Franklin at Philadelphia in 1752, as text-books for the new University of Pennsylvania. He was also requested to accept the president's chair in the university, but declined. His active defence of Episcopacy brought him into controversy in 1725 with Rev. Jonathan Dickinson of Elizabethtown, N. J., afterward president of the College of New Jersey; with the Rev. Thomas Foxcroft, of Boston, and in 1732 with the Rev. John Graham of Woodbury, Conn., which continued for a period of four years. Pending the revival of Whitefield's work, he published a pamphlet for the period, an exposition of his views of divine sovereignty. This was answered by Mr. Dickinson, and afterward, to counteract what he considered the pernicious views that were spreading at the time he published a work on moral philosophy, entitled "A System of Morality." By 1744 his congregation had attained such proportions that it was deemed expedient to seek a new place in which to hold services.

At the earnest solicitation of the trustees of the new College of Kings, afterward Columbia, which was about to be established under Episcopal auspices in New York city, he removed thither in 1754. The charter had not then been granted, owing to opposition in the city to a sectarian institution, and he would not positively accept the presidential chair until that had been accomplished. But he at once began work, issued the first advertisement of the college in the "New York Gazette," June 3, 1754, and began teaching the first class of the college which contained eight students July 17th, the classroom being in the school house attached to Trinity Church. The charter finally passed the seals Oct. 31st, and the college being full-fledged in its corporate existence, he became its president. On June 1, 1758, his first wife died, but he resolutely turned from his family grief to attend to the preparations for the commencement, held on June 21st of that year, when the first eight students were graduated. In 1850 he moved into the college building, being the first to live in Kings, as forty-four years previously he had been the first to live in Yale, and soon the officers and students joined him and began to lodge and mess there. He filled the office of president until 1763, and during his entire term directed the institution safely through its initial troubles, regulated its course of study, solicited subscriptions for its endowment, and guided its policy. At the end of that time he resigned on account of advanced age and trouble in his family, and resumed his residence in Stratford, where he lived with his son, and in 1764 accepted the rectorship of his old parish, where he remained until his death, doing quiet parochial work and revising his earlier crudite writings. He compiled and published an English and Hebrew grammar, and a number of other learned works. His second wife died in 1763, a victim of small-pox, a disease of which he had an almost cowardly dread. Upon his resignation the governors of the college voted him an annual pension of £50, which, though not magnificent even for those days, represented a much greater value than the amount would do at the present time. In 1723 he was awarded the degree of M.A., from both Oxford and Cambridge, and in 1743 that of D.D. from Oxford. He died at Stratford, Conn., June 6, 1772.

COOPER, Myles, second president of King's College (1763–78), was born in England in 1735. In 1760 he was graduated at Oxford, and afterward became a fellow of Queen's College. He published a characteristic volume of verses, entitled, "Poems on Several Occasions," which, according to the custom of the day, treated variously of conviviality, sacred topics, and sundry sentiments. He explains in his preface that some of the poems were imitations and others were written by his friends. He came to

America in 1762, at the request of the archbishop of Canterbury, to old Samuel Johnson, president of King's College (now Columbia), and was made professor of mental and moral philosophy. The same year Dr. James Jay was made solicitor for the college in England. This arrangement brought nearly £6,000, including a special donation of £400 from his majesty George III. Joseph Murray about this time bequeathed £9,000 to the college, which helped to furnish the library, already started by the bequest of a collection of 1,500 volumes from Dr. Bristowe of England. Upon the resignation of Dr. Johnson, Myles Cooper was elected president of the college, Apr. 12, 1763, then being only twenty-eight years of age. Being a man of superior attainments and a fine educator, he raised the college to a standard above any in America. In 1763, about the time of

Pres. Johnson's resignation, a grammar school was established in connection with the college, and put in charge of Mr. Matthew Cushing, of Charlestown, Mass. In the same year new statutes were made, which provided "an habitation be assigned to each student in the college, and a penalty of 5 shillings for the first night of absence, 8 for the second, 12 for the third (or adequate exercises), and finally expulsion. Within fourteen days after his entrance a proper academical dress must be procured, in which he shall always appear (unless he have leave from the president or tutors), under the penalty of 2 shillings for the first offence, and so in proportion (or adequate exercises). Each student must attend morning and evening prayers in the college, and also public worship on the Lord's day, under penalty of 4 pence for each omission, or proportionate exercises. Three-quarters of an hour are allowed for breakfast, an hour and a half for dinner, and from evening prayers until bed-time for recreation. The money from fines is to be spent in books to reward the diligent. Tardiness at "studying" time shall bring a fine of 2 pence for the first half-hour, 4 for the second, etc. The outer gates are to be locked at 10 P. M. in summer, and 9 P. M. in winter. Coming in after this shall bring a fine of 6 pence for the first hour, 1 shilling for the second, etc. Getting through the college fence, or over it, shall bring the same penalties." These rules, however, did not apply to students of medicine. A lightning-rod, which was probably the first ever used in New York city, was placed on the college in 1764, and during that year trees were planted, and steps taken to beautify the college green. Music was first used at the commencement in 1765. The province in 1767 granted the college 24,000 acres of land on the east side of Lake Champlain, but unfortunately this princely grant being within the boundaries of what was subsequently Vermont, the property was lost. The medical school was at first founded in 1767, at the suggestion of Dr. Clossy, a distinguished tutor of the institution from Dublin. Pres. Cooper went abroad in 1771, and returned shortly before the revolutionary war. He gave his allegiance to the crown, and warmly advocated his Tory principles, both by speech and with his pen. He was credited with the authorship of an inflammable pamphlet, entitled: "A Friendly Address to all Reasonable Americans on our Political Confusions; in which the Necessary Consequences of Violently Opposing the King's Troops, and of a

General Non-Importation are Fairly Stated." Alexander Hamilton, then one of the younger students of Columbia, responded to this address anonymously, and fairly worsted Pres. Cooper, whose course greatly outraged the patriots. Public feeling finally became so strong that a mob was the result, which on May 10, 1775, entered to the college, intending to do violence to the president. He had, however, been forewarned, and half-dressed escaped over the college fence, and found refuge in the house of a friend in the suburbs of the city. The following day he boarded the Kingfisher, a British sloop-of-war, and sailed for England. In 1776 the committee of safety took possession of the college, and turned it into a hospital for the use of the American soldiers. All the pupils were dispersed. About 100 young men had already been graduated at the institution. The college was suspended until the war was over, when measures were at once adopted for its re-establishment. In 1784 the legislature of New York granted it a new charter under the name of Columbia College, and the regents of the University of the State of New York, appointed by the same act, took the institution under their control. The property of the old corporation was transferred to the new. No president was elected until 1787, on account of lack of funds. When Pres. Myles Cooper reached England in safety, after having escaped the fury of the mob in America, he was given two excellent livings—one in Edinburgh, where he lived principally, and the other in Berkshire. On Dec. 13, 1776, Dr. Cooper gave an address before the University of Oxford, "On the Causes of the Present Rebellion in America." This caused considerable political discussion. He also published a number of poems, one, which appeared in the "Gentleman's Magazine" for

July, 1770, was descriptive of his flight from America, and closed with the petition of a true, loyal Briton:

> "Nor yet for *friends* alone—for all,
> Too prone to heed sedition's call,
> Hear me, indulgent Heav'n!
> Oh, may they cast their arms away,
> To Thee and George submission pay,
> Repent, and be forgiven."

He wrote an "Address to the Episcopalians in Virginia," in which he advocates the appointment of bishops for the colonies, and published the "American Querist." Dr. Cooper died in Edinburgh, May 1, 1785, and was buried a few miles from that city, in a burying-ground where only the Episcopal ministers who die in that city are interred. He himself wrote a characteristic epitaph in verse for his tombstone.

JOHNSON, William Samuel, first president of Columbia (formerly King's) College (1792–1800), was born at Stratford, Conn., Oct. 7, 1727. His father was

Samuel Johnson, and his mother a daughter of Col. Richard Floyd of Brookhaven, L. I. William Samuel was prepared for college by his illustrious father, entered Yale and was graduated A.B. in the class of 1744. Though but seventeen years old at the time of his graduation, he was elected a "scholar of the house" under the bounty of Dean Berkeley. Mr. Johnson afterwards pursued his theological studies at home, and deciding to become a lawyer, on May 30, 1747, went to Cambridge for a course of lectures at Harvard College and also to be present at the commencement to receive the degree of M.A. He

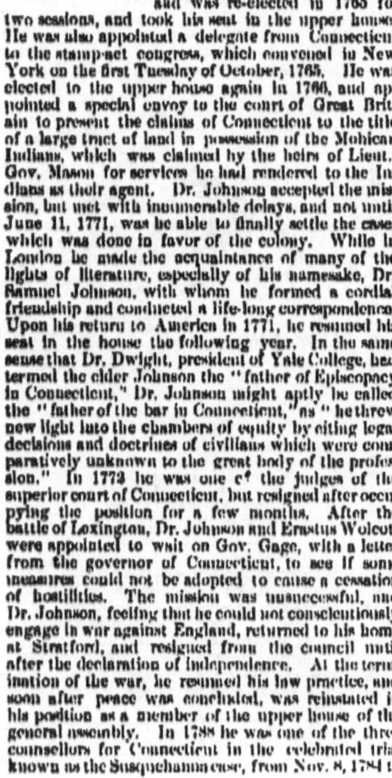

continued his studies on a large and liberal scale of his own devising, and soon attained a high standing in his profession, when the importance of the cases in which he became involved brought him prominently before the public. He was always, if possible, secured as counsel in the religious controversies which were at that time unfortunately forced upon churchmen in different parts of the colony, the utmost confidence being reposed in his good judgment and honesty. Mr. Johnson was elected in 1761 to represent the town of Stratford, in the lower house of the general assembly and was re-elected in 1765 for two sessions, and took his seat in the upper house. He was also appointed a delegate from Connecticut to the stamp-act congress, which convened in New York on the first Tuesday of October, 1765. He was elected to the upper house again in 1766, and appointed a special envoy to the court of Great Britain to present the claims of Connecticut to the title of a large tract of land in possession of the Mohican Indians, which was claimed by the heirs of Lieut.-Gov. Mason for services he had rendered to the Indians as their agent. Dr. Johnson accepted the mission, but met with innumerable delays, and not until June 11, 1771, was he able to finally settle the case, which was done in favor of the colony. While in London he made the acquaintance of many of the lights of literature, especially of his namesake, Dr. Samuel Johnson, with whom he formed a cordial friendship and conducted a life-long correspondence. Upon his return to America in 1771, he resumed his seat in the house the following year. In the same sense that Dr. Dwight, president of Yale College, had termed the elder Johnson the "father of Episcopacy in Connecticut," Dr. Johnson might aptly be called the "father of the bar in Connecticut," as "he threw new light into the chambers of equity by citing legal decisions and doctrines of civilians which were comparatively unknown to the great body of the profession." In 1772 he was one of the judges of the superior court of Connecticut, but resigned after occupying the position for a few months. After the battle of Lexington, Dr. Johnson and Erastus Wolcott were appointed to wait on Gov. Gage, with a letter from the governor of Connecticut, to see if some measures could not be adopted to cause a cessation of hostilities. The mission was unsuccessful, and Dr. Johnson, feeling that he could not conscientiously engage in war against England, returned to his home at Stratford, and resigned from the council until after the declaration of independence. At the termination of the war, he resumed his law practice, and soon after peace was concluded, was reinstated in his position as a member of the upper house of the general assembly. In 1788 he was one of the three counsellors for Connecticut in the celebrated trial known as the Susquehanna case, from Nov. 8, 1784 to

May 8, 1787. He was a delegate from Connecticut to the Continental congress, notwithstanding the neutrality of his position during the revolutionary war, and the aspersions cast upon his loyalty. At that time there was no man in the congress who possessed more statesmanlike views, or in whom there was more confidence reposed as a national legislator. Dr. Johnson was a member of the committee of five referred to by congress as a "grand committee," which was appointed to frame a federal constitution and "to devise such further provisions as were necessary to make the constitution of the Federal government adequate to the demands of the United States." He served as chairman of the committee, and among other measures he proposed, was that of forming the senate into a separate body. Dr. Johnson was appointed president of Columbia College, New York city on May 21, 1787, and thus became the first head of the institution under the new charter, as his father had been of King's under the royal charter. The college had fallen into decay during the war of the revolution, the regular course of instruction had been suspended, and its reorganization demanded the energies of a thoroughly efficient man. Mr. Johnson proved himself as able in the administration of the affairs of the college, as he had shown himself as a lawyer and a statesman. When he assumed the office there were thirty-nine students in the college, nearly half of whom were freshmen. The income of the college amounted to about £1,330. There were no faculties of law and divinity, and the faculties of arts and medicine consisted of three professors each. There was but one extra professor, a German, who served without a salary. In 1792, the medical school was established on a broader basis, seven medical professors being appointed, with Dr. Samuel Bard as dean. A grant of £7,000 was obtained from the legislature, and with an annuity of £750 for five years, foundations were laid for two new buildings, additional professors appointed, and the library was considerably augmented. The authorities had, however,

progressed more rapidly than was expedient, and when, at the end of the five years, the annuity was withdrawn, they were compelled to consolidate the professorships, and instead of completing the buildings, to dispose of the materials on hand. Mr. Johnson took cold in 1799, while returning through a snow storm from a meeting held in Trinity vestry to pass resolutions on the death of George Washington, and in consequence of this illness resigned his office on July 16, 1800. The senior professor of Columbia filled his place at the ensuing commencement. Though obliged by his position as president of Columbia to take up his residence in New York city, Dr. Johnson did not allow the duties of his office to separate him from his former constituents; his aid and counsels were still eagerly sought. He resumed his place in the Connecticut legislature in 1788, and the following year was elected U. S. senator from Connecticut. From his long residence in England and intimate acquaintance of the workings of both houses of parliament, he was one of the best qualified members of the senate. Finding that his duties in the senate interfered with his administration of the affairs of Columbia, he resigned his seat. Gov. Huntington, in accepting his letter of resignation, March 22, 1793, said: "I am sorry that Connecticut and the Union should be deprived of so able a councillor in that honorable body; but must believe on due deliberation you have discovered reasons sufficient to justify the measure you have adopted, and am satisfied that you will not fail, as opportunities shall offer to promote the happiness and prosperity of this state."

After resigning the presidency of Columbia, Dr. Johnson returned to his home at Stratford, where he passed the remainder of his life. He was not only consulted by eminent men upon legal and political affairs, but also upon literary, philological, and ecclesiastical matters. He was probably in his day unexcelled as an orator, was a man of commanding and attractive personal appearance, and superior mental attainments. He left some valuable contributions to literature. "He had a keen perception of what he dwelt upon in his public addresses to the graduating classes of Columbia College, that the first duty of man is owed to heaven, to his Creator, and Redeemer, and he practised that duty in all the posts of honor and responsibility which he was called to fill. He was on this account the more noble. For a Christian statesman is the glory of the age, and the memory of his deeds and virtues will reflect a light coming from a source which neither clouds can dim, nor shadows obscure." Dr. Johnson was awarded the degree of D.C.L. from Oxford in 1776, and that of LL.D. from Yale in 1778, being the first graduate of the last named college to receive the honorary degree in laws, as his father was first to receive the honorary degree in divinity. He was twice married. He died at Stratford, Conn., Nov. 14, 1819.

MOORE, Benjamin, third president of Columbia College (1801–1811) and bishop, was elected to the office upon the resignation of Rev. Charles Henry Wharton, of Philadelphia, whose official connection with the college lasted scarcely seven months, during which he was in attendance upon one commencement. (See Vol. I., 514.)

HARRIS, William, fourth president of Columbia College (1811–1829), was born in Springfield, Mass., Apr. 29, 1765. He entered Harvard College and was graduated in 1786, after having completed a course in theology. He was then licensed a Congregational preacher, but handicapped by failing health, decided to abandon pastoral work and took up the study of medicine. While thus engaged, the perusal of Hooker's "Ecclesiastical Polity" led him to give up Independency, and on October 16, 1791, Bishop Provoost ordained him deacon in Trinity Church, New York, and a priest the following Sunday. He became rector of St. Michael's Church at Marblehead, Mass., and also the conductor of the academy there, remaining until 1802, when he was made rector of St. Mark's Church, New York city, and established in close proximity to his rectory a school of classical studies. In 1811 he received from both Harvard and Columbia Colleges the degree of D.D. In the same year, upon Bishop Moore's resignation of the presidency of the last named institution, Dr. Harris was elected his successor. For a few years he divided his energies between this office and his church, but resigned the latter in 1816, owing to the discontinuance of the office of provost. This office had been created in 1811 on purpose, apparently for the Rev. John Mitchell Mason, whose Presbyterianism rendered him ineligible to the presidency in name, although in fact giving him the leadership of all the affairs of the college. Henceforth the duties and responsibilities of the presidential office devolved upon Dr. Harris, who, in spite of failing health, faithfully discharged them until the time of his death. His administration saw the complete organization and success of the Columbia Grammar School, one of his favorite plans. His published writings consist of three sermons only, among which is his farewell sermon to his parishioners of St. Mark's. He died Oct. 18, 1829.

DUER, William Alexander, fifth president of Columbia College (1829–42), was born in Rhinebeck, N. Y., Sept. 8, 1780, and was the son of William Duer, commissary-general, member of the revolutionary committee of safety, and noted as a statesman in the early days of the republic, and Catherine, daughter of Gen. William Alexander, claimant to the Scotch earldom of Stirling. He studied law in the office of Peter S. Duponceau in Philadelphia, and of Nathaniel Pendleton in New York, and was admitted to the bar in 1802. When war with France was imminent in 1798, he obtained appointment as midshipman in the navy under Stephen Decatur, but resigned upon the adjustment of the difficulty. He engaged in business with Edward Livingston, mayor and district attorney of New York, but upon the latter's removal to New

Orleans, formed a partnership with his brother-in-law, Beverley Robinson, the while taking active part in politics by his contributions to the "Corrector," a journal conducted by his friend, Peter Irving, in support of Aaron Burr. Later he removed to New Orleans, resumed his business relations with Mr. Livingston, and took up the study of Spanish civil law. His practice was successful, but finding the climate unhealthful, and having married a Miss Denning of New York, he resumed his residence in that city. In 1812 he opened an office in Rhinebeck, N. Y., and in 1814 was elected to the state assembly. He was appointed chairman of the committee on colleges and academies, and also of that which arraigned the constitutionality of the law, vesting the right of river navigation in Fulton and Livingston. On these committees he bore a prominent part in formulating bills from which are derived our present laws on common school income and the management of canals. He was also instrumental in efforts to check the abuses growing out of the old lottery system, and remained in the legislature until 1820. In 1822 he was elected judge of the supreme court for the third circuit, and held the office for seven years, resigning in 1829 to accept the presidency of Columbia College. He devoted himself to some needed reforms in the distribution of college studies, and devised a system by which one hour daily was added to the time of instruction. He himself took charge of the freshman class in English composition, and delivered lectures to the seniors on the constitutional jurisprudence of the United States. As executive head of the college, he was eminently successful, securing the respect of the students by his studied courtesy, which needed little discipline to enforce good behavior. Owing to ill health, he resigned in 1842, took up his residence in Morristown, N. J., and devoted himself to literature during the remaining years of his life. His lectures, "Constitutional Jurisprudence" and "The Inauguration of Pres. Washington" were published. He was also author of two pamphlets on the "Steamboat Controversy," and a life of his maternal grandfather, published by the New Jersey Historical Society, under title "Life of William Alexander, Earl of Stirling." He died in New York, May 30, 1853.

MOORE, Nathaniel F., sixth president of Columbia College (1842–49), was born at Newtown, Long Island, Dec. 25, 1782. He was the son of William Moore (1754–1824), a prominent physician and a nephew of Bishop Benjamin Moore, second president of Columbia. His early education was directed by Mr. Samuel Rudd, and entering Columbia, he was graduated in 1802. On this occasion he delivered the Latin salutatory with an oration, "De Astronomiae Laudibus." He immediately entered upon the study of law in the office of Beverley Robinson, a rising young lawyer of the period, and was admitted to the bar in 1805. He was, however, of far too retiring a disposition to distinguish himself in his profession, and limited his practice to the duties of notary and of master in chancery. In 1817 he was appointed adjunct professor of Greek and Latin to his alma mater, and three years later, on the death of Dr. Wilson, was made full professor in the same department. In 1835 he resigned his professorship, and with his sister made an extensive tour in Europe. On his return in 1837, the college purchased his library and appointed him librarian, but in 1839 he again went abroad, this time visiting Greece, Egypt, and Palestine. In 1842, upon the resignation of Pres. Duer, he succeeded to the vacant office, and discharged its duties with care and good success. He was the third layman who had held the presidency, but as there was no chaplain at the time was obliged to offer prayers at all public exercises. In 1849 he resigned, and made a third voyage to Europe in 1851, during which he visited the World's Fair in London, becoming much interested in the new art of photography, to which he subsequently devoted much study. Columbia graduated him LL.D. in 1825. He was author of several notable books, among them: "Ancient Mineralogy" (1834); "Remarks on the Pronunciation of the Greek Language" (1819), in which he defended the current Erasmian method as against the proposal to pronounce according to the rules of modern Greek; "Lectures on the Greek Language and Literature" (1835); "An Introduction to Universal Grammar" (1844); "Historical Sketch of Columbia College" (1849); and numerous pamphlets and articles. He died in the Highlands of the Hudson, Apr. 7, 1872.

KING, Charles, seventh president of Columbia College (1849–64), was born in New York city, March 16, 1789, second son of Rufus King. While the father was U. S. minister to England, he and his brother, James Gore, attended school at Harrow for five years, subsequently going to Paris to gain a perfect knowledge of the French language. He served as clerk in the banking house of Hope & Co., in Amsterdam, and returning to America in 1806 entered the employ of Archibald Gracie, merchant, becoming his son-in-law and partner four years later. In 1813 he was elected to the legislature of New York, and although earnestly opposed to the war with England, enlisted as a volunteer in 1814 and served until the cessation of hostilities. In 1815 he went abroad in the interests of his business, spending two years, but in 1823 his firm failed and Mr. King entered the field of journalism as part owner of the New York "American," of which in a few months, upon the retirement of Johnston Verplanck, he became sole proprietor and editor. He ably conducted this journal, having the support of many of the foremost writers and statesmen of the day, and making a marked departure from the current habit of publishing offensive personals and bitter, partisan editorials. He also established a literary and review department. This paper was in 1847 merged into the "Courier and Enquirer," which Mr. King edited for about a year, then retiring into private life. In 1849 he was chosen president of Columbia College, whose affairs he ably conducted for fifteen years. In 1851 the college was removed from its old location on College Place, and secured a plot west of Fifth avenue, between Forty-ninth and Fiftieth streets, pending the construction of buildings, taking up temporary quarters in the old Deaf and Dumb Asylum, east of Madison avenue, where, however, it continued permanently, owing to the stoppage of its plans by the civil war. Several movements toward scholastic extension were made, among them in 1857, a graduate school under Profs. Arnold Guyot and George P. Marsh, which continued only one year. The law school was founded in 1858, with Prof. Theodore W. Dwight as warden, and the school of mines began modestly in 1863 under Prof. Thomas Egleston. The medical department was also re-adopted in 1860. Pres. King received the degree of LL.D. from Princeton and Harvard. He resigned his office in 1863, owing to failing health, and going abroad almost immediately, died in Frascati, Italy, in October, 1867.

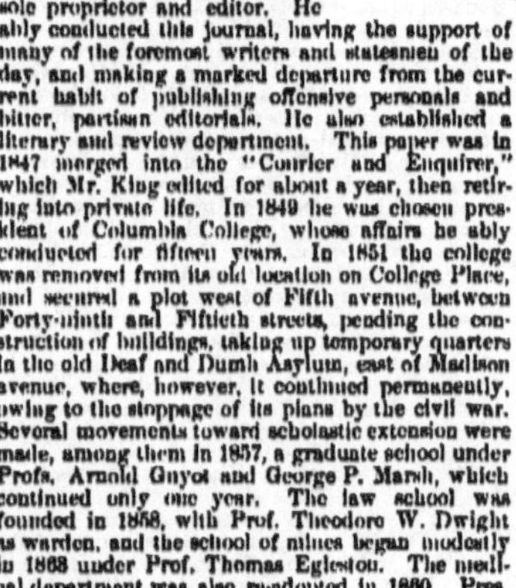

BARNARD, Frederick Augustus Porter, eighth president of Columbia College (1864–89), was born in Sheffield, Mass., May 5, 1809. He began the study of Latin at six years of age. Language, however, was not his favorite subject, and at Yale College, where he was graduated in 1828, he did his best work in mathematics and the sciences. After his graduation he taught in a Hartford grammar school, in Yale College (as a tutor), in the Deaf and Dumb Asylum at Hartford, and in the New

York Institution for the Instruction of the Deaf and Dumb, whose building was subsequently occupied by Columbia College. In 1837 he went South, and distinguished himself there both as an educator and as a courageous and outspoken defender of the Union.

In the University of Alabama he was professor of mathematics and natural philosophy for twelve years, and of chemistry and natural history for five, serving in the meantime on the commission which settled the long disputed boundary between Alabama and Florida, and delivering public addresses on a number of subjects. He built an astronomical observatory for this institution during his connection with it. In 1854 he became professor of mathematics, astronomy, and natural history in the University of Mississippi, and in 1856 he took orders in the Protestant Episcopal church. He was appointed president and chancellor of the university, holding office until 1861, when he resigned at the outbreak of the civil war. On arriving in Washington with his wife in 1863, after a long detention at Norfolk, owing to their inability to obtain passports, he was appointed director of printing and lithographing in the map and chart department of the Coast Survey, and continued in the position until 1864, when he was elected president of Columbia College, New York city. He served in that capacity until his resignation on account of ill health, May 7, 1888. His educational work in the South, while valuable, could not in the nature of the case be permanent. It is as president of Columbia College, therefore, that he will be longest remembered. During his connection of a quarter of a century with this institution, he transformed the old-fashioned college into one of the great universities of the country. One of his first acts upon assuming the office of president was to move for the erection of suitable buildings for the growing needs of the various departments. All the professors were consulted as to the special requirements of their classes, and as a result, the present imposing structures for the schools of arts, mines, law, and political science arranged in double quadrangle for the best utilizing of the limited space, by the architect C. C. Haight, were soon under way. The Law School, the School of Mines, the School of Political Science, the School of Library Economy, and the Barnard College for Women, are all largely indebted to his influence, and he was arranging for a University School of Letters and Philosophy at the time of his death. His scholarship covered a wide range, but his specialties were pure mathematics and the exact sciences, in which departments he published a number of important books and papers, written in a clear and graceful style. He was also editor-in-chief of "Johnson's New Universal Cyclopædia." His scholarship secured him many honors. He succeeded Agassiz as foreign secretary of the National Academy of Sciences, of which he was one of the fifty original incorporators. He was president of the American Metrological Society, of the American Association for the Advancement of Science, of the Board of Experts of the American Bureau of Mines, and of the American Institute, an honorary corresponding member of a number of foreign scientific asso-

ciations, U. S. commissioner to the Paris Exposition of 1867, and assistant commissioner general to the Paris Exposition of 1878. He published various valuable scientific text-books and standard works. He left the bulk of his property to Columbia College. Pres. Barnard held the honorary degrees of S.T.D., LL.D., L.H.D., D.C.L., Ph. D. He died in New York city, Apr. 27, 1889.

LOW, Seth, ninth president of Columbia College (1890–   ), was born in Brooklyn, N. Y., Jan. 18, 1850, son of Abiel Abbot Low, a noted merchant of that city. He received his early education at the Brooklyn Polytechnic Institute, and entered Columbia College, where his natural talent and aptitude were quickly developed, and was graduated in 1870 at the head of his class. During the last year in college he attended the lectures at the Columbia Law School, but did not continue the course, having accepted employment in his father's tea-importing establishment. After occupying in turn several important clerical positions, he became in 1875 a member of the firm, and soon thereafter a member of the New York Chamber of Commerce and other commercial bodies, frequently serving upon important committees. In 1881 he was nominated independent candidate for the mayoralty of his native city, and gained a splendid victory at the polls. Consequent on a highly successful administration he was re-elected in 1883, and his endeavors to purify the city government by introducing the method of civil service examinations for municipal offices and other needed reforms, gained for him an enviable national reputation. After the expiration of his second term he went abroad; then resumed active business until 1890, when he was elected to succeed Dr. F. A. P. Barnard as president of Columbia College. In the same year the University of the State of New York conferred upon him the degree of LL.D., and he was likewise honored

by Harvard College in 1890. Immediately after assuming the presidency of Columbia College, he began the work of raising the venerable institution to new life. Aided by his business experience, he began to manage its affairs with admirable prudence and judgment, and the result soon becoming obvious, he further added to the prosperity of the college by personal gifts and by donations obtained through his influence. In 1890 the several departments of instruction, hitherto separate and independent, were organically united and controlled by a university council created for the purpose, instead of by the several faculties as heretofore. By an act dated March 24, 1891, the College of Physicians and Surgeons was made an organic part of the corporation, having in the previous year, for the first time since the formation of the medical faculty in 1814, held its annual commencement with the other departments. The phenomenal growth of the institution was rapidly rendering the old quarters far too contracted, and the plan of removing to some site in the upper part of Manhattan Island began to be seriously agitated. A committee was appointed, which in 1892 reported favorably on the site of the Bloomingdale Asylum for the Insane, on the heights of Morningside Park, which was valued at $2,000,000. Pres. Low's active championing of the cause, rendered it possible to pay the required amount by 1894, and the work of preparing buildings suitable for occupancy at an early date was begun. He himself donated in 1895 the sum of $1,000,000 for the construction of a new library building. The work of rendering the university more efficient was further carried out in the establishment by the corporation, toward the close of 1893, of the Columbia Union Press, to publish valuable documents, etc., after the manner of the Oxford Clarendon Press. Mr. Low was instrumental in the foundation of the Brooklyn Bureau of Charities, and was its first president. He is president of the Archæolgical Institution of America, vice-president of the New York Academy of Sciences, and one of the organizers, and first president, of the Young Men's Reform Club of Brooklyn.

McVICKAR, John, educator, was born in New York city, Aug. 10, 1787. He was the son of a wealthy New York merchant, who gave personal attention to his son's education. The son was carefully reared, and after graduation at Columbia, in 1804, spent several years in England with his father, devoting most of his time to study at Cambridge. Upon his return he studied for the ministry, and in 1811 was ordained in the Protestant Episcopal ministry, and became rector of St. James' Church, Hyde Park, N. Y., where he remained until 1817 when he accepted the chair of moral philosophy, rhetoric, and *belles-lettres* in Columbia, which position he held for nearly fifty years. To his chair was subsequently added the evidences of Christianity. He was superintendent of the Society for Promoting Religion and Learning in New York, and labored earnestly to secure a training school for the diocese which resulted in the establishment of St. Stephen's College at Annandale. He was also chaplain to the U. S. troops at Governor's Island for nearly twenty years. In 1864 declining health made it desirable for him to retire from active college work, when he was honored with the title of professor emeritus. He had already received from his alma mater the degree of A.M. in 1818, and S.T.D. in 1825. Dr. McVickar's wife was a descendant of Samuel Bard, one of the old New York celebrities, the physician of Washington, whose father had been a captain of Franklin, and in 1822 he published "A Domestic Narrative of the Life of Samuel Bard," which was written with great skill, and is valuable for its reference to the early history of the country. Dr. Bard deserves mention in the history of education for his service to Columbia College after the revolutionary war. In his lectures on natural philosophy and for his earlier establishment of the Medical School in New York, then attached to the college of which he was professor of the theory and practice of medicine; also for his services to other medical institutions of the city. He retired to Hyde Park, where he gathered about him the celebrities of his time. In 1825 Dr. McVickar published "Outlines of Political Economy," and later a memoir of Bishop Hobart, entitled "Eighty Years," followed by "The Professional Years of Bishop Hobart." He was the author of numerous essays, addresses, reviews, and occasional publications. He held important positions in the church and in the diocese. As a college professor, Dr. McVickar pursued the higher interests of the subjects entrusted to him with original tact and ability. His course of instruction was eminently clear and practical, while he quietly led the pupil in the discipline of taste and philosophy. He died in New York, Oct. 29, 1868.

ANTHON, Charles, educator, was born in New York city, Nov. 19, 1797. His father, George Christian Anthon, a German physician was surgeon-general in the British army until the surrender of Detroit in 1788, and in 1796 a trustee of Columbia College: his mother was the daughter of a French officer. He entered Columbia College at the age of fourteen, and so far surpassed his classmates that he was twice awarded the gold medal, and was accordingly excluded from competition. He was graduated in 1815, studied law in the office of an elder brother, and was admitted to the bar of the supreme court of New York in 1819. His time, however, was given chiefly to classical literature, and the next year he was appointed adjunct-professor of Greek and Latin in Columbia College, which office he held for fifteen years. His series of classical publications did much to make available for popular purposes the researches of European scholars. His first work was a new edition of "Lempriere's Classical Dictionary," published in 1822, which was almost immediately reissued in England. In 1830 appeared his larger edition of Horace, accompanied by exhaustive English notes, which is believed to be the first attempt in this country at a critical edition of an ancient author In 1833 he issued a smaller edition for the use of schools and colleges. Virgil, Cæsar, and other ancient writers, have been illustrated by notes in the same attractive manner, which have been very popular. In 1835 he succeeded to the full professorship of the classics, following Prof. Moore, and at the same time was made head master of a grammar school attached to the college, which position he held until 1864, when he was retired. In 1831 Prof. Anthon received the degree of LL.D. from his alma mater. He died in New York city, July 29, 1867, after a devotion of forty-seven years of an obstinate and unflagging industry, an extraordinary knowledge, and a patient habit of accumulation, to the instruction of his students and the editing of books.

ANDERSON, Henry James, educator, was born in the city of New York, Feb. 6, 1799. His early education was received from a private tutor. Afterwards he entered Columbia College, and was graduated with honors in 1818. He then devoted his time to the study of medicine, and was graduated at the College of Physicians and Surgeons in 1823, and two years later received an appointment as professor of mathematics, analytical mechanics, and physical astronomy at Columbia College, succeeding Dr. Robert Adrain. He continued there for eighteen years, when, on account of the ill health of his wife, he went abroad, traveling extensively throughout Europe, Asia, and Africa. While visiting the Holy Land, he joined Lieutenant Lynch's exploring expedition to the Dead Sea and the river Jordan as geologist for the company. His "Geological Reconnoissance of Part of the Holy Land," was published by the government. Having, while in Europe, united with the Roman Catholic church, on his return to this country he actively engaged in  promoting the interests of Catholicism in New York city. In 1851 he was elected a trustee of Columbia College, and in 1866 emeritus professor of mathematics and astronomy. He was president of the Society of St. Vincent de Paul, and prominent in other church organizations. He went to Australia with the American scientific expedition sent there to observe the transit of Venus, and procured the necessary instruments at his own expense. On his return, he went to India to explore the region of the Himalaya mountains, and while there was stricken with a disease which caused his death, which occurred Oct. 19, 1875. Prof. Anderson is spoken of as a man whose character approached as near to perfection as is permitted to poor humanity. He was strong, able, modest, so versatile in his knowlege of languages that his students were afraid to wager what language he did not know. One day he was noticed listening to a strange conversation on the street; it proved to be Bohemian, which he had quietly added to his stock of tongues. His mathematical ability was still more noteworthy. Mr. A. S. Hewitt tells that he once went with the professor to make some observations at the observatory at West Point, when it was found that they had left behind some necessary and elaborate formulas. It was ten o'clock at night, and their only chance for the observations was early the next day. "Never mind," said the professor, "go to bed, and I'll see what I can do." By morning he had reconstructed all the formulas from the material furnished by his marvelous memory, and the observations were successfully made. His classical attainments commanded the exacting respect of Dr. Anthon, and he had found time also to train himself in out-of-door work, so that he had several times walked fifty miles in a day.

KUNZE, John Christopher, clergyman and educator, was born in Artern, Saxony, Aug. 4, 1744. He was educated at the Orphan House at Halle, and studied theology at the university of that city, when he became a teacher in Closter-Bergen near Magdeburg, and subsequently became inspector of the Orphans' Home at Gratz. In 1771 he was called to Philadelphia by the Lutheran congregations, and ministered to St. Michael's and Zion churches for fourteen years. He was one of the first to advocate educating German youth in English. While in Philadelphia he established a theological seminary which was, however, shortly closed by the revolutionary war. During the occupation of the British his churches were also employed as a hospital and garrison church. He was appointed in 1780 professor of oriental languages and literature in the University of Pennsylvania, which also conferred upon him the degree of M.A. in 1780 and that of D.D. in 1783. The next year he accepted the call of the German Lutheran Church in New York, where he remained until his death. In 1784 he accepted the chair of oriental languages and literature in Columbia College which he retained for three years, but was again appointed to the same position in 1792,

when he remained for seven years. He was a remarkable Hebrew and Arabic scholar, and his learning was recognized by the Jewish rabbis who often consulted him. He composed a hymn-book of German hymns translated into English verse, which mostly preserved the original metres. He also composed a liturgy and catechism in English, and was held in high esteem as one of the most learned divines of the country. On the formation of the second synod of the American Lutheran church, he was elected its first president, a position he accepted, to assist him in carrying out his liberal ideas as to the adopting the use of the English language in churches and education. He lived to see his views generally adopted. In addition to historical essays, sermons, and addresses, he published "Concise History of the Lutheran Church," "A Table of New Construction for Calculating the Great Eclipse Expected to Happen June 16, 1806." He died in New York city, July 24, 1807.

KEMP, John, educator, was born in Achlossan, Scotland, Apr. 10, 1763. He was a wonderfully precocious child, and imbibed knowledge so easily that he was graduated at the Aberdeen University when only eighteen years of age. His attainments were so great that he was admitted to the Royal Society of Edinburgh before he was twenty-one. In 1788 he emigrated to Virginia where he remained two years, when he removed to New York and was appointed teacher in Columbia College. He gave such satisfaction that the following year he was made professor of mathematics, and in 1795 was transferred to the professorship of geography, history, and chronology. He identified himself with the growth and progress of the country, and his earnestness wielded an important influence in moulding the views of De Witt Clinton on topics of internal improvement and national policy. His interest in the subject of water ways led him, in 1810, to make a journey to Lake Erie to satisfy himself upon the feasibility of the canal, which he pronounced practicable in advance of the surveys. Prof. Kemp served the college for a long period with signal ability, and died in New York city, Nov. 15, 1812.

DWIGHT, Theodore William, lawyer and educator, was born at Catskill, N. Y., July 18, 1822. His father was Benjamin Woolsey Dwight, physician and merchant, second son of Timothy Dwight, president of Yale College (1795–1817). He was, therefore, a first cousin of the present Timothy Dwight, who became president of Yale in 1886. He attended Hamilton College, Clinton, N. Y., and was graduated, with honors, in 1840. He entered the Yale Law School, but in 1842 was elected to a tutorship in Hamilton College, which he held until 1846. Two years later he was made professor of law, history, civil polity, and political economy in the same institution. This chair he filled most acceptably for ten years, during which time, in addition to per-

forming the regular duties of his professorship, he founded and most successfully conducted a department of law at Hamilton. In 1858 he went to Columbia College, New York, to become professor of municipal law, and at once attracted wide attention. The scheme of organizing a regular law school at Columbia was much talked of by the college authorities, and when the plan materialized, Prof. Dwight was unanimously chosen its warden. He literally made the Columbia Law School; to it flocked a multitude of students, on account of his reputation as the most successful of American teachers of law. He delivered special courses of lectures on his chosen subjects at Cornell University from 1869 until 1871, and at Amherst College from 1870 until 1872. He was a conspicuous member of the constitutional convention held by the state of New York in 1867, chairman of its committee on charities, and one of its judiciary committee. In 1874 he was president of the State Prison Association, and also one of the New York committee of seventy. On Dec. 30, 1878, he was chosen by Gov. Dix as a member of the commission of appeals, which the two following years (1874–75) assisted the court of appeals in clearing its docket. When, in 1880, five of the professors of the Andover Theological Seminary were accused of heteroxy before the board of visitors, Prof. Dwight acted as their counsel. His services in this case alone turned the eyes of the whole country upon him, and his argument was published. He has published a number of important treatises on various legal questions, and was for some time associate editor of the "American Law Register," published in Philadelphia. He has also written "Influence of the Writings of James Harrington on American Political Institutions" (Boston, 1887); edited Henry Sumner Maine's "Ancient Law" (New York, 1864); and was the legal editor of "Johnson's Cyclopædia," for which he wrote a considerable amount of original matter. After a long and distinguished career at the Columbia Law School, during which time he was the mainstay of that institution, Prof. Dwight retired in June, 1891, and was made professor emeritus. The method of instruction which he had originated, and successfully followed for thirty-three years, during which over 10,000 students were under his instruction, was soon after superseded by a different one. Immediately the alumni of Columbia Law School met together, and formed a committee, which issued appeals to all who had been students under Dr. Dwight, with the result that the New York Law School, designed to perpetuate his method of instruction, was incorporated, and the Dwight Alumni Association organized. A staunch Republican from the birth of the party, Dr. Dwight's interest in the uplifting of the unfortunate and the reformation of the vicious was recognized by governors of both political parties. Gov. Hoffman appointed him a member of a commission of five to establish a reformatory, which, by his deciding vote, was placed at Elmira. Gov. Fenton placed him on the board of state charities, of which he became the vice-president. In 1878, by appointment of Gov. Robinson, he represented the state of New York at the international prison congress in Sweden. He also took an active part in organizing the State Charities Aid Association. In spite of his labors as educator, lawyer, and citizen, Dr. Dwight's devotion to scholarly studies was never interrupted. He delivered many literary addresses, and was master of the Greek, Latin, German, and Italian languages. The Dante Society, lately organized in this city, chose him as its first president. He declined the presidency of a number of colleges, and many offers of high political place. He was the first president of the University Club of New York, and long a member of the Century Club. He was an active trustee of Hamilton College, the American Geographical Society, the New York Juvenile Asylum, etc., a member of various societies for political reform, and the first vice-president of the Bar Association. In religious belief he was a Presbyterian, attending Dr. Parkhurst's church. He received from Rutgers College in 1859 the degree of LL.D., and the same honor was conferred upon him by Columbia in 1860, and by Yale only a few days before his sudden death. He married, in 1847, Mary Bond, daughter of Asa Olmstead of Clinton. Three children were born, of whom only one survives, a daughter, who is the wife of Dr. Edward L. Partridge. He died, of sciatica, at Clinton, Oneida co., N. Y., June 28, 1892.

BAKER, George Hall, librarian of Columbia College, was born at Ashfield, Mass., Apr. 23, 1850. He fitted for college at Williston Seminary, Easthampton, Mass., and was graduated there in 1870. He was graduated at Amherst College in 1874, and spent the following year in postgraduate study in that institution. The following two years and a half were spent in travel and study in Europe, mainly

Columbia College Library.

at the University of Berlin, carrying out the line of studies, entered upon at Amherst, in history and public law. During these years special attention was paid to the study of modern European languages, with most of which Mr. Baker was conversant. After his return to this country he settled for some time near Boston and engaged in private teaching, writing, and study. Early in 1883 Mr. Baker joined the editorial staff occupied on the Century Dictionary in New York, and continued there until, in August, 1883, he joined the staff of Columbia College Library as assistant librarian. In this position, with special charge of the reference work and the department of buying, he remained until 1888, when he became acting librarian and then, in 1899, librarian in chief. Under Mr. Baker's administration the library was much more than doubled in size, until it now numbers 210,000 volumes and has been almost entirely recatalogued and largely rearranged, while its use and value have increased in even larger ratio than its numbers. During the years 1885 to 1889 Mr. Baker was lecturer in the School of Political Science in Columbia College on the bibliography of history and political science.

BOWDEN, John, clergyman and educator, was born in Ireland, Jan. 7, 1751. His father was in the British army, and he accompanied him to America at an early age and was placed at Princeton for two years, when he returned to Ireland with his father. But he came back to America in 1770 and was graduated at Kings College in 1772, where he studied for the ministry. He went to England in 1774, where he was ordained, but returned to become assistant minister of Trinity Church. He was not in sympathy with the patriot cause, and being warned to leave Norwalk, where he had retired at the beginning of the revolution, he fled to Long Island and returned to New York, then in the hands of the British.

Throat troubles obliged him to seek health in the West Indies, but not obtaining the desired relief he settled in Stratford, Conn., and soon after took charge of the Episcopal Academy at Cheshire, Conn., where he remained for six years. He was elected bishop of Connecticut in 1796, but on account of his precarious health he declined to undertake the responsibilities and duties of the office. He was elected professor of moral philosophy, *belles-lettres*, and logic in Columbia College in 1802, which position he held during the remainder of his life, receiving from the college the degree of S.T.D. in 1797. He is remembered as "a scholar, a reasoner, and a gentleman . . . having pure taste, deep and accurate erudition, and logical acuteness." Dr. Bowden published many works of importance to his denomination; notably "The Apostolic Origin of Episcopacy." He died in Ballston Spa, N. Y., July 31, 1817.

WILSON, Peter, educator, was born in Ordiquhill, Scotland, Nov. 23, 1746. His youth was spent with a cultivated clergyman, who imbued him with a love for the classics, and he devoted himself specially to this department of literature during his course at the Aberdeen University, and won a wide reputation for classical scholarship while even a mere youth. In 1763 he emigrated to America, and after spending some time as a teacher in New York, was appointed principal of the Hackensack Academy. His own and his wife's name are still to be seen, cut in stone, over the front windows of his residence. He became intensely interested in the political movements that preceded the revolution, and was elected a member of the New Jersey legislature in 1777, and in 1788 was appointed to revise and codify the laws of that state. He was elected to the chair of Greek and Latin in Columbia in 1789, which position he held until 1820, with the exception of three years, during which time he was principal of Erasmus Hall, Long Island. Upon his resignation he was given a pension for his long and meritorious services. Union College conferred upon him the degree of LL.D. in 1798. He published several important text-books which have had a wide use in the educational institutions of the country, notably "Rules of Latin Prosody," "Introduction to Greek Prosody," and "Compendium of Greek Prosody," together with editions of the classics. His health failed, and he died in Barbadoes, N. J., Aug. 1, 1825.

FITZSIMMONS, Thomas, soldier and statesman, was born in Ireland in 1741. The victim of oppression, he emigrated to America, probably in 1765, settled in Philadelphia, Pa., and there engaged in mercantile pursuits. He married the daughter of Robert Meul of Philadelphia, who was the great-grandfather of U. S. Gen. George G. Meade, commander of the Federal forces at Gettysburg, Pa., in July, 1863. Fitzsimmons formed a partnership with his brother-in-law, an eminent Philadelphia merchant and shipowner. In the American revolution Mr. Fitzsimmons was an ardent patriot, raising and commanding a military company. In the movements connected with the battles of Trenton and Princeton, N. J., he was on the field, and was also a member of the state council of safety, and of the navy board. In 1780 his house subscribed £5,000 to supply the necessities of the army. In 1782 he was a member of the Continental congress and a leader in its financial debates. For years after the conclusion of peace he was a member of the Pennsylvania assembly. In 1787 he was chosen as delegate to the convention to frame the U. S. constitution. He opposed universal suffrage, and insisted that the privilege of voting ought to be restricted to freeholders. He favored giving congress power to tax exports as well as imports, and also making the U. S. house of representatives co-ordinate in authority with the senate and the president, in the making of treaties. He was elected to the U. S. house of representatives from Philadelphia when the national government was formed, and held his seat until 1795. Mr. Fitzsimmons was a strong advocate of a protective tariff. He was trustee of the University of Pennsylvania, and a founder and director of the Bank of North America in Philadelphia, where he died, Aug. 26, 1811.

BUSH, George, theologian, was born in Norwich, Vt., June 12, 1796. He was graduated at Dartmouth in 1818, then studied theology at Princeton, officiating meanwhile, during one year as tutor in Nassau Hall. Then being ordained a minister of the Presbyterian church, he went as a missionary to Indiana. Having returned in 1829, he was, in 1831, elected professor of Hebrew and Oriental literature in the University of New York. At this time he began a career of authorship by writing a "Life of Mohammed," which was soon followed by a series of commentaries on the books of the Old Testament, that attained a wide circulation. His other works have been numerous. He occupied for years a position of unusual prominence as a preacher, teacher, and biblical scholar, and was one of the most progressive men in the Presbyterian church ; but at last he overstepped the lines of strict orthodoxy and became a convert to the theological system of Swedenborg, assigning as a reason that it enabled him to solve many of the difficulties of the orthodox faith. To the doctrine of the Trinity he adhered, because he believed it was taught by the Bible. Upon the division of attributes among the three personages of the Godhead, he did not agree with the Presbyterian church. Here Swedenborg's theories, framed with Bush's own conscientious care, lest the letter of Scripture should be exceeded, came to his assistance and gave him great comfort. Doubting the authority for a belief in the resurrection of the body, he again

found sympathy in Swedenborg. Experimenting largely in mesmerism, but learning only of its manifestations, without such of its underlying principles as have since been demonstrated, he realized that mental communication could be established between two different natures without the use of speech as a medium ; this discovery prepared him to accept Swedenborg's theory of spiritual communication and influence. Deeply interested in all scientific research as to the nature of life, yet failing in the then imperfect state of scientific knowledge to obtain any prospect of a solution, he found refuge in Swedenborg's belief that all life is a continual influx from the Deity. The Swedish seer's theory that love is the motive of all divine action was then an almost unheard of idea in the orthodox church, and the great-hearted author eagerly embraced it. The nature of Christ, which was then, as now, a great subject of wonder among thinking men, is explained by Swedenborg as the result of the Divine Spirit making its abode in a material form. This latter, the issue of Christ's mother, being the only attribute of humanity which Jesus possessed ; here again Bush found a belief more acceptable to him than the orthodox view. He died Sept. 19, 1859.

FARWELL, Charles Benjamin, senator, was born near Painted Post, Steuben co., N. Y., July 1, 1823. His earliest American ancestor, on the paternal side, came from England to Massachusetts in 1640, and his first American ancestor on his mother's side, a London merchant, settled in New England about the same time. He was born on a farm, received his early education in the common schools, and when out of school performed the usual labor of a farm boy, and completed his course of study at Elmira Academy, which he left, when he was fifteen years of age, to accompany his family to Ogle county, Ill. There he joined a public land-surveying party, with which he was connected about three months out of each year for four years, the remainder of his time during that period being devoted to farming. In January, 1844, he went to Chicago, then little more than a village, where he obtained a clerkship in the office of the county clerk of Cook county, and at a later date became teller in one of the pioneer banking institutions of the city. In 1853 he was elected county clerk of Cook county, and filled the office for eight years. At the end of that time he was engaged in mercantile pursuits, becoming a partner in the firm of John V. Farwell & Co., and in 1891, when the business was incorporated, he was made president of the corporation. He was appointed a member of the first state board of equalization of Illinois in 1867, chairman of the Cook county board of supervisors in 1868, and national bank examiner in 1869. In 1870 he was elected a representative in congress as a Republican over John Wentworth, Democrat, by 5,000 majority, and served as a member of the committee on banking and currency, and as chairman of the committee on manufactures. Early in his congressional career, he became conspicuous among the financiers of the house of representatives, one of the first measures which he introduced, and pushed to its passage, being an amendment to the national banking law, removing the restrictions which had prior to that time limited the number of national banks. Under the law, as amended on Mr. Farwell's motion, any regularly organized association of individuals having the requisite capacity, was enabled to establish a national bank. In 1875, as a member of the committee on banking and currency, he aided in perfecting the act providing for the resumption of specie payments, Jan. 1, 1879, being fixed upon as the date of resumption, at his suggestion. He served in the forty-second, forty-third and forty-fourth congresses, and declined a further renomination. In 1880, however, he was again elected, and served as a representative in the forty-seventh congress, declining a re-election. On the death of Gen. John A. Logan, he was elected in 1887 to the U. S. senate, and served as a member of that body until March 4, 1891, when the Democrats, having secured control of the Illinois legislature, elected his successor. As a senator, he sought to secure legislation which would insure the perpetuation of the national banking system, and the abolition of the government sub-treasury system. He frequently predicted that these two provisions must ultimately be incorporated into the financial legislation of the country, and declared it to be the only legislation necessary to perfect our financial system. He held that the government funds, locked up in the sub-treasuries, and thus kept out of circulation, should be deposited, upon good and sufficient security, with the banks of the country, and thus made available at all times for the demands of trade. His belief was, that with provision made for keeping these funds in circulation, and for a flexible volume of national bank currency, the finances of the country would be placed in the best possible condition. With his brother, John V. Farwell, he built up a colossal business in Chicago. He was one of a syndicate that built the state house at Austin, Tex., and has been connected with various other successful financial ventures. He is a careful student of literature and art, and has a large collection of rare volumes, especially on ethnology and oriental literature, as well as well-selected classical works of the sixteenth century.

WELCH, Charles Clark, pioneer and business man was born in Pamelia, Jefferson co., N. Y., June 14, 1830, of Scotch, English, and French extraction. His father, Charles Welch, Jr., was the first white male child born north of the Black river in the state of New York. Mr. Welch spent his early boyhood on his father's farm, and attended the public schools. At the age of fifteen he entered an academy to prepare himself for the vocation of teacher, which pursuit he subsequently entered and followed advantageously until 1850, when he started for California via the isthmus. He engaged in placer mining in Placer county, and in other parts of California, with fair success for the succeeding two years. He was a stockholder and part owner of one of the first quartz mills near Nevada, Cal. In June, 1852, he sailed

for Sydney, Australia, and after engaging for one year in successful mining operations, and gaining some valuable experience, he left Melbourne, Australia, via Cape Horn, and arrived in New York after a voyage of ninety days. In December, 1855, he located in Chicago, and embarked in a general real estate and brokerage business. In the spring of 1860 he left Chicago for Colorado, traveling across the plains, via Fort Kearney, on the first tri-weekly coach established on that line. Locating in Gilpin county, Col., he began mining in Nevada and Russel gulches, and subsequently extended his operations in Gilpin, Boulder, and Clear Creek counties, and was superintendent of various mining companies. He helped to originate measures for the extension of Colorado's railway system from Golden to Denver, and held the position of auditor of the road until its completion to Golden in 1870, when he became a director, and was for a time, vice-president of the road. In May, 1872, a construction company was formed, of which Mr. Welch was one of the trustees, to complete the Colorado Central Railroad from Golden to Julesburg. After building the road from Golden to Longmont, and grading nearly the entire length, 230 miles, work was suspended, but the line was subsequently completed. In the fall of 1874 he contracted with the Pueblo and Salt Lake Railroad Co., now Santa Fé system, to grade, tie, and bridge their road from Pueblo to West Las Animas, a distance of eighty-five miles, taking his pay in Pueblo county bonds. He cut 250,000 ties on and near the present site of Leadville, and floating them down the Arkansas river, through the celebrated Grand Canon to West Las Animas, a distance of about 250 miles, completed his contract in February, 1876. In July, 1877, he was placed in charge of the construction of the Colorado Central Railroad from Longmont *via* Fort Collins to Cheyenne, a distance of seventy-six miles, completing the same on Nov. 1, 1877. He was president of the Denver and Santa Fé Railroad during its construction, and for some years after, and is still a director of the company. In 1877 he became extensively engaged in coal-mining on Coal Creek, Boulder co., opening the Welch coal mine, and having some three miles of railroad track laid in it. In the fall of 1879 he sold his stock in the company to Jay Gould, reserving a royalty on all coal mined. The mine is now owned by the Louisville Coal Mining Co., of which Mr. Welch is one of the principal stockholders. In 1878 he was one of the organizers of the Handy Ditch Co., and was made its president. He irrigates from this ditch, about 2,000 acres of his own land. In January, 1880, he was elected president of the Cambria Fire Brick Co. of Golden, Col. In 1872 Mr. Welch was elected to the Colorado territorial legislature from Jefferson county. In 1885, in connection with others, he organized the Golden Ditch and Flume Co., and was made its president. This is one of the most expensive ditches for its capacity in the state, and irrigates a large tract of land lying between Golden and Denver. He was president and one of the principal promoters of the Denver, Lakewood, and Golden Railroad. He owned a large tract of improved land, on which he raised, in one season over 30,000 bushels of wheat. Mr. Welch worked persistently to secure the passage of the bill authorizing the construction and maintenance of the State School of Mines, located at Golden, and gave the ground on which the first building was erected, and for years after he watched and cared for its interest. The phenomenal success of this institution is a source of great satisfaction to him. He was married, May 22, 1876, to Jeanette, daughter of H. S. Darrow of Michigan, and has two children, a son and a daughter.

HOVEY, Harriette Spofford, educator, was born on the island of Nantucket, her ancestors on the mother's side being the Folgers and Coggeshalls of that island and Rhode Island; and on the father's side, the Spoffords and Farnhams of Essex county, Mass. Eleazer Folger, one of her ancestors, was a brother of Abiah Folger, the mother of Benjamin Franklin. Her parents removed, while she was yet a child, to North Andover, Mass., and settled beside the "Great Pond," where she grew up, and from which she trudged on foot to Abbott Academy, five miles away, for schooling. At the academy she was recognized as a superior scholar, and early attracted the attention of Dr. Barnas Sears, then secretary of the Massachusetts board of education, who, before the completion of her studies, recommended her for preceptress of Framingham Academy, one of the oldest and best institutions of its class in the state. Here she entered upon her life-work in educational pursuits, which were continued in Illinois. After her marriage to the president of the State Normal University of Illinois, Gen. Charles Hovey, and his enlistment, together with some 200 of his students, in the Federal forces in 1861, she spent nearly six months in camp, and then going back to her home, turned her house into a hospital and became a nurse to invalid soldiers, especially those who had been students in the university. She was Dr. John Phil

brick's assistant in preparing the United States educational exhibit for the Paris Exposition of 1878. She is now, and has been for thirteen years, in charge of the division of correspondence and records in the national bureau of education at Washington, where her devotion to education, her system and order, and her care-taking talent, find ample scope. In this division, in addition to the preparation of correspondence, is kept a record, carefully indexed, of all letters and documents exchanged with the tens of thousands of correspondents scattered the world over, and here, as nowhere else, may be learned the addresses of the great teachers and educators. As indicative of the amount of work done in this one division of the bureau, it may be stated that over 28,000 letters were sent out in connection with the Columbian educational congresses alone. Of her three sons, one died in infancy, Alfred is in business, and Richard is devoting himself to literature.

HOVEY, Richard, author, was born in Normal, Ill., May 4, 1864, son of Charles Edward and Harriette (Spofford) Hovey. He traces his ancestry on the father's side, back to Daniel Hovey who settled in Ipswich, Mass., in 1637, and to the Cushmans and Allestons, who came over in the Mayflower, and to the Arnolds, who claim descent from Cadwalader and the Welsh kings; and on the mother's side, to Gamelbar de Spofford, whose family antedates the conquest, and to John Coggeshall, first governor of Providence Plantations, and to the Folgers of Nantucket. His father, Charles Edward Hovey, founded the State Normal University of Illinois and was its president from 1857–61, when he entered the army as colonel of the 33rd Illinois Infantry. He was promoted to brigadier-general in 1862, and to major-general by brevet in 1865, for gallantry at Arkansas Post. Although born in Illinois, Richard spent his early life in Washington, D. C. He was educated at Dartmouth College, where he was graduated, with a Phi Beta Kappa key, in the class of 1885. He wrote "Hanover by Gaslight," a class history for Sophomore year, and was an editor of "The Dartmouth," and of "The Aegis," undergraduate publications. After leaving college, he studied theology at the Episcopal General Seminary in New York city, and while there, acted as assistant to Father Brown of the Church of St. Mary the Virgin. His first literary venture of note was the publication, in 1890, of "The Laurel," now out of print. This was followed in 1891, by "Launcelot and Guenevere," which has met with a favorable reception,—indeed, it was characterized by a leading New York paper, as "the ablest and most poetic drama of the Arthurian period since Tennyson's." Encouraged by the reception extended to this poem, he published another in 1893, entitled "Seaward," an elegy on the death of Thomas William Parsons, which was even more cordially noticed by the press. His essay on the Mephistophiles of Marlowe as compared with the Mephistopheles of Goethe, read at Dr. Davidson's School of Philosophy, attracted much attention among scholars and critics, while his articles in the "Independent," on the "Technique of Poetry," present a new view of that matter. Among his other writings are "Gandolfo," a twelfth century tragedy, "Songs from Vagabondia," prepared in collaboration with Bliss Carman, a translation from the French, of Maeterlinck's plays, and a translation

from the German, in collaboration with François S. Jones, of Karl Gutskow's "Uriel Acosta." He is a member of the Society of the Sons of the Revolution, and of the Cosmos Club of the district of Columbia.

EVANS, George, senator, was born in Hallowell, Me., Jan. 12, 1797. He received his early education at Hallowell and Monmouth academies, and in his sixteenth year entered Bowdoin College as a sophomore; was graduated in 1815, and entered the office of Frederick Allen for the study of the law; was admitted to the bar in 1818, and began the active practice of his profession at Gardiner. He afterwards returned to Hallowell, where as a criminal lawyer and advocate he won distinction and honor, being considered one of the most eminent members of the bar of his county. For eloquence and ability he was second to none of his compeers, and certain of his cases have become historical. But it was as a statesman he gained his national reputation. He entered political life early in his career, and was elected to the legislature in 1825, being returned for four consecutive years; was chosen speaker of the house in his last year, and performed the duties of the office with great tact and skill. In 1829 he was elected representative to congress over Reuel Williams of Augusta, after a warmly and closely contested canvass—winning by barely 200 majority. After serving in the house for seven terms, he was elected to the senate, where he took his seat in 1841. Though his party (Whig) was in the minority, and he was only second on the committee of ways and means, he exerted a commanding influence, and often by his address and ability carried measures in a body of which a large majority were his political opponents. This was in the days when such men as Webster, Clay, Crittenden, Calhoun, Dayton, Silas Wright, Rives, Benton, and Preston made the history of the senate illustrious. Mr. Evans was very effective on questions of political economy; was chairman of the committee of finance, a position Mr. Clay had declined, assigning as a reason that "Mr. Evans knew more about the tariff than any other public man in the country;" and in 1846 Mr. Webster, referring to a recent address of Mr. Evans which he called "the incomparable speech," made the assertion that he understood the subject of finance as well as any gentleman connected with the government since the days of Crawford and Gallatin. The power and effectiveness of Mr. Evans's speeches in congress on the complicated questions of that memorable period was universally conceded. The most notable were on the Protective System, in 1832; on the removal and establishment of a national bank, in 1834; on the failure of the fortification bill, in 1836; the question of the Northeastern boundary, in 1838; and on the bill to issue treasury notes, in 1841. When Gen. Taylor received the nomination for the presidency, Mr. Evans was one of the prominent candidates for vice-president, and but for a secret influence exerted by a few from his own state to whom he had made himself obnoxious by his agency in securing the ratification of the Ashburton treaty and from other causes, he would have received the treasury portfolio. He was, however, appointed chairman of the important commission on Mexican claims. After serving in congress for eighteen years,

VI.—23

Mr. Evans returned to his own state and the practice of his profession. He was made attorney-general of the state in 1853–54–58 and took a leading position at the bar. He was entirely free from the devices which too often obtain with members of the profession, and disgrace alike both court and bar, and he won the general respect and confidence of the people. He was the first president of the Kennebec and Portland Railroad, and brought to that enterprise the benefit of his powerful organizing and administrative abilities. It is said he never prepared an address for the press or wrote a word of his political speeches. He was a member of the board of overseers of Bowdoin College and of the board of trustees for twenty-two years. He was uniformly active in the duties of these offices, and always prominent at commencement or other public exercises. In 1847 the college conferred upon him the highest honor in its gift, the degree of LL.D. On retiring from public and professional life he took up his residence at Portland, where he died, Apr. 5, 1867, leaving a wife and three children.

FOSTER, Robert Sandford, soldier, was born in Vernon, Jennings co., Ind., Jan. 27, 1834, son of Riley Foster and Sarah J. Foster. He received a fair business education, and at the age of sixteen engaged with an uncle at Indianapolis, Ind., in the mercantile business, which pursuit he followed until the breaking out of the civil war, when he joined the Federal forces, and was mustered into the U. S. service, as captain of company A, 11th Indiana regiment volunteer infantry. He served in this capacity until July 3, 1861, when he was commissioned major of the 13th regiment Indiana volunteers, and with this regiment took part in the eventful campaigns in western Virginia and the Shenandoah Valley. His regiment was daily engaged with the Confederate forces, and during the campaign the first battle of Winchester or Kernstown was fought between Stonewall Jackson's forces and Shields' division, Shields defeating Jackson, and driving his army down the Shenandoah Valley to Staunton. He was engaged with his regiment in the various campaigns in the Shenandoah and Luray valleys. In 1862 his regiment was ordered to the army of the Potomac, and joined McClellan's forces, July 4, at Harrison Landing. He was promoted successively as lieutenant-colonel and colonel of the 13th Indiana. He was in command of a brigade during all the operations and battles occurring around Suffolk, among them the siege of Suffolk by Gen. Longstreet in 1863. On June 13, 1863, he was commissioned brigadier-general of U. S. volunteers, and was ordered, with his brigade, to the department of the South. He arrived at Folly Island, S. C., in the summer of 1863, and was engaged on Morris and Folly Islands during the siege of Fort Wagner and Fort Sumter. He was assigned, with his brigade to duty in Florida, during the fall of 1863, and in the spring of 1864 was ordered North with his brigade and was made chief of staff of the 10th army corps. He was engaged in the operations against Richmond from the south side of the James river, landing at Bermuda Hundred. He was engaged in the operations in front of Richmond and Petersburg, and commanded one of the assaulting columns against the Confederate works at Petersburg, and finally in the pursuit and capture of Lee's army at Appomattox. For service in this latter campaign, he was brevetted major-general of the U. S.

volunteers. He was detailed as a member of the commission that tried the conspirators and assassins of Pres. Lincoln. He resigned from the army September, 1865, and returned to Indianapolis. He has held important offices since he left the service, among them U. S. marshal for the district of Indiana, appointed by Pres. Garfield. He was married in May, 1861, to Margaret R. Foust, and had two children, a son and a daughter. His wife died June 7, 1891.

TORREY, John, botanist, was born in John street, New York city, Aug. 15, 1796. He received his early education in the public schools. In his youth he had a strong liking for mechanics, and at one time thought seriously of becoming a machinist, but he was more attracted to chemistry, and finally determined on the study of medicine. In 1815 he began to study in the office of Dr. Wright Post, and was graduated at the College of Physicians and Surgeons in 1820. It was the practice of physicians of that day to prepare their own prescriptions, and it was the duty of the office students to compound the prescriptions. Prof. Torrey found this early training in the manipulation of chemicals of immense value to him in after life, as was also his mechanical talent of great service in enabling him to devise apparatus for the illustration of his lectures. He opened an office in New York city, and for a time devoted himself to the practice of medicine, giving his leisure to the study of botany and kindred scientific pursuits. Finding the profession of medicine uncongenial, he he did not try very earnestly to become established in it, and in 1824 he entered the U. S. army as assistant-surgeon, at the same time filling the office of professor of chemistry in the U. S. Military Academy at West Point. Henceforth Dr. Torrey's scientific life was two-fold. As a botanist he is best known to the world, but it was as a chemist that he found his remunerative occupation. Up to the day of his death, he was either engaged in teaching chemistry, or employed in some position for which his profound chemical knowledge peculiarly fitted him. In 1827 he was appointed to the chair of chemistry in the College of Physicians and Surgeons, which he held until 1854, being also professor of chemistry at Princeton during a portion of this time. On the establishment of the U. S. assay office in New York in 1854, he was appointed assayer, and held that position of great responsibility until his death. He was often consulted by the treasury department on matters relating to the coinage and currency, and at various times was sent on special missions to visit the different mints. He was also consulting chemist to the Manhattan Gas Co., and was frequently engaged as adviser in establishments where profound chemical knowledge was requisite. Prof. Torrey was an enthusiastic mineralogist in early life, and he made many important contributions upon that science to "Silliman's Journal." He was one of the founders of the New York Lyceum of Natural History, and was one of the eleven charter members of that institution. He was elected president early in the history of the lyceum, and filled the office for several years. There is a botanical paper from him in the first number of the "Annals," and some of his most important contributions to science enrich the earlier volumes of this publication. Prof. Torrey's botanical career commenced while he was still a student of medicine. His first botanical publication, "A Catalogue of Plants Growing Spontaneously Within Thirty Miles of New York," was presented to the lyceum in 1817, and published in 1819. This work is now exceedingly rare, and fugitive copies offered at sales of libraries bring fabulous prices. This catalogue is regarded as a remarkable performance, considering the youth of the author, barely twenty-one years of age. Botanists of the present day (1895), who go over the same ground, marvel at its completeness. An idea of the city's remarkable growth may be gathered by reading some of the author's favorite resorts, such as "Love Lane," "Bog near Greenwich," and "Swamp behind the Botanic Garden," places long since covered by solid blocks of brick and brown stone; and also a glimpse of what New York must have been in the author's youth, to learn that a certain rare plant was found "in sandy fields above Canal street." Dr. Torrey was chosen a trustee of Columbia College in 1856, and was made emeritus professor of chemistry and botany. For several years prior to 1861 he was engaged in herbarium work, and upon his removal to Columbia College, he presented his large and valuable collection to that institution. This herbarium, embracing 50,000 specimens and including many typical varieties, was put into complete order by his own hands; and he brought to the drudgery of determining, arranging, and labeling the large mass of unassorted material that was the accumulation of years, the same industry and zeal that marked more congenial work. As it is, in some respects, the most important herbarium in the country, botanists have reason to be grateful that he was spared long enough to put it in proper condition for study and reference. The botanical collections of the Wilkes exploring expedition were divided between Drs. Torrey and Gray, Dr. Gray taking the extra-American share, while Dr. Torrey elaborated those collected upon the Pacific coast. But the civil war delayed the publication of his memoir, and stopped all appropriations for such work. The proposition to publish was revived the winter before his death; but though he attempted to prepare it for the press during a period of amendment of his fatal illness, his strength was unequal to the task. It was published posthumously, under the supervision of Dr. Gray, his friend and associate for many years. Any enumeration of Dr. Torrey's scientific labors would be incomplete without reference to his great educational work for others in science. Whatever the professorships he filled, he was always a loved instructor to his students. His influence was not confined to the class-room, but out of it as well; and to the circle of young men under his charge, who never came to him in vain for sympathy and encouragement, he gave what was better than pecuniary aid—comfort, hope, and help in its best and most enduring sense. Many who have become most eminent in science began their careers under his teachings. He was largely influential, as trustee of Columbia and Princeton, in giving prominence to scientific studies in these institutions; and it was through his influence more than that of any other one person, that the "School of Mines" was established. An association, formed of the botanists of New York and vicinity, to which they gave the name of the Torrey Botanical Club, met at his house; and when it became so large as to be incorporated, Dr. Torrey was the first president elected under the charter. One who had long known him said after his death: "He is the only man I ever knew of whom it could be said he was truly lovable." It was not given to many to possess the peculiar personal attractiveness that was his. There was that about him which invited confidence, and in advance promised sympathy. He was a devoted Christian, but let his Christianity appear in his every relation in life, rather than obtrude it upon others by his profession. So deeply grounded was his faith in Christianity, that he was never troubled by any fear that science might weaken his belief. Knowing that all truths are accordant; that the research in any domain of science can never reveal anything that will disprove God as the author and controller of all, he remained throughout his entire life a devout Christian. The degree of A.M. was conferred upon him by Yale in 1823, and that of LL.D. by Amherst in 1845. He contributed many papers to scientific periodicals, and to the societies of which he was a member. Many plants bear his name: *Torreya Taxifola*, an ornamental shade tree in the Southern states; *Torreya Californica*, of California; *Torreya Nucifera*, of Japan, and the *Torreya Grandis*, of northern China. A sketch of his life by his pupil, life-long friend and associate, Asa Gray, was contributed to the "Biographical Memoirs" of the National Academy of Sciences (Washington, 1877). His most valuable botanical publications, besides those mentioned, are "A Flora of the Northern and Middle United States" (1824), "The Flora of North America" (John Torrey and Asa Gray, 1838), of which only one part, the "Compositæ," was finished; and a "Catalogue of Plants Collected by Lieut. Fremont in an Expedition to the Rocky Mountains" (1845). He died in New York city, March 10, 1873.

VAUGHAN, Alfred J., soldier, was born in Dinwiddie county, Va., May 10, 1830. He was graduated at the Virginia Military Institute in 1851, and adopted civil engineering as his profession. Going west, he located at St. Joseph, Mo., where he made the survey of the Hannibal and St. Joseph Railroad. Afterward he received the appointment of deputy U. S. surveyor for the district of California, and on his return, settled in Mississippi, until the breaking out of the civil war. Gen. Vaughan was opposed to the dissolution of the Union, yet, when his adopted state, Mississippi, and his native state, Virginia, seceded, his course was determined. Joining a company at Moscow, Tenn., he was elected captain, and from this time on was engaged in every fight, under Gens. Polk, Bragg, and Joseph E. Johnston, including the battles of Belmont, Shiloh, Richmond, Perryville, Murfreesboro', Chickamauga, Missionary Ridge, and the 100 days' fighting from Dalton to Atlanta, Ga. During these years he had steadily risen in rank, and finally, at the battle of Chickamauga, was made brigadier-general on the field, by Pres. Davis. He served with courage and distinction until the fight near Marietta, Ga., on July 4, 1864, where he lost a leg. After the war, returning to his home in Mississippi, he engaged in farming until 1872, and afterward as general agent of the National Grange, organized the state granges of Mississippi, Arkansas, and Tennessee, serving as master of the first named for several years. In 1873 he opened a mercantile house in the city of Memphis, but owing to a disastrous combination of financial panic and yellow fever epidemic, he was forced to abandon the business five years later. In 1878, the people of Shelby county becoming tired of machine rule in politics, nominated an independent ticket, and for the office of clerk of the criminal court of Shelby county, placed Gen. Vaughan on it, with the result that he received 10,889 votes to his opponent's 4,688. He was re-elected, without opposition, in 1882, being the regular Democratic nominee. This was the only civil position Gen. Vaughan ever held. A man of extremely polite and affable manners, with all his gentleness and charity, he was

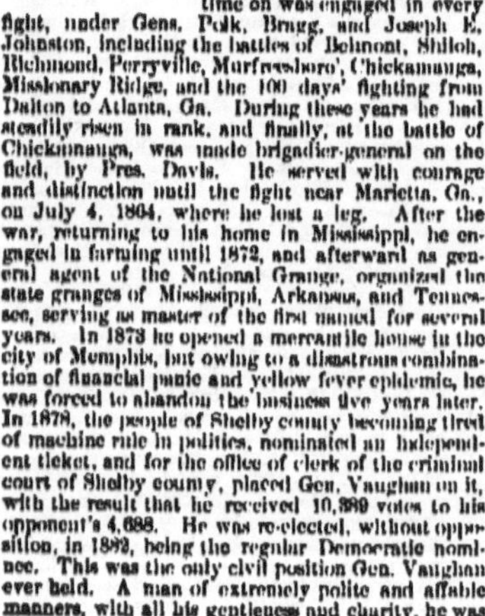

yet one of the strictest disciplinarians in the army, and was possessed of courage so lofty that his men instinctively looked for him in the front when danger was to be met.

SPAULDING, Elbridge Gerry, financier and "father of the greenbacks," was born at Sumner Hill, Cayuga co., N. Y., Feb. 24, 1809, and is of the seventh generation of descendants from Edward Spaulding of Lincolnshire, England, who came to this country in 1630, and settled in Massachusetts. Of this family one branch emigrated to Maryland in the seventeenth century, and one of its members became noted as Roman Catholic bishop of Baltimore. His grandfather fought in the memorable battle of Bunker Hill, and his father fought four years in the revolutionary war, and was one of the pioneer settlers of central New York from New England. This son received an academic training at Auburn, and on attaining his twentieth year entered the office of Timothy Fitch of Batavia, as a student. He remained with him three years, when he removed to Attica, and entered the office of Harvey Putnam. In 1834, having been admitted to practice in the court of common pleas of Genesee county, he went to Buffalo and became a clerk in the law office of Potter & Babcock, leading attorneys of that city; here he was admitted two years later to the bar of the supreme court, and in 1839 became a counsellor of that court and a solicitor in chancery. He subsequently became a partner in the law firm of Potter & Babcock, the partnership being dissolved in 1844, when the business was assumed by Mr. Spaulding. The practice was a very lucrative one, but too heavy for one to manage, and Mr. Spaulding formed a co-partnership with John Ganson, whom he induced to leave Canandaigua and settle in Buffalo. They formed the law firm of Spaulding & Ganson, which continued for four years, when Mr. Spaulding retired from practice. Meanwhile, in 1837, he had married a daughter of G. B. Rich, proprietor of the Bank of Attica, and became its legal adviser and attorney. He recommended the removal of the bank from Attica to Buffalo, where it carries on business under the name of the Buffalo Commercial Bank; Mr. Spaulding being a large stockholder. Mrs. Spaulding lived but a few years after her marriage, and died leaving no issue. He married again a Miss Strong, by whom he had three children, Edward R. and Samuel S. Spaulding, who now occupy positions in the bank over which their father presides, and a daughter married to Frank Sidway, cashier of the same institution. On his second wife's death, Mr. Spaulding married her sister, a widow of the late Clark Robinson. At the time of his retirement from professional life Mr. Spaulding was instrumental in securing the removal to that city of the Farmers' and Mechanics' Bank of Batavia, which has been organized under the state law, and was continued on that footing after its establishment in Buffalo, and of which Mr. Spaulding became a stockholder, and afterwards president and chief proprietor. In 1836 he was city clerk of Buffalo; in 1841 he was alderman, and in 1847 he was chosen mayor by the Whig party. Through his influence the Buffalo Gas Light Co. was organized, a general sewerage system for the city was introduced, and plans for the enlargement of lake and canal facilities by the formation of the Erie and Ohio Basins were adopted. In 1848 he was elected to the state assembly, and in 1849 a representative in the thirty-first congress, serving on the committee on foreign relations. He opposed the Missouri compromise measures of 1850. In 1853 Mr. Spaulding was elected state treasurer of New York, and being *ex officio* a member of the canal board, he succeeded in securing the adoption of measures for the enlargement and improvement of the canals, involving the expenditure of $9,000,000. In 1860 he was a member of the congressional executive committee for the conduct of the political campaign, which resulted in the election of Abraham Lincoln. Having been chosen in 1858 to represent Erie county in the thirty-sixth congress, and

re-elected in 1860 to the thirty-seventh. He served four years on the committee of ways and means, and occupied a conspicuous position in national legislation during the civil war. Mr. Spaulding was entrusted with the duty of preparing the bills necessary to meet the financial emergency, and he drafted the greenback or legal tender act and the national-currency bank bill. His official duties as chairman of the sub-financial committee of ways and means frequently brought him into contact with the president, and their acquaintance grew into a close and abiding intimacy. On the promotion of Sec'y Chase to the position of chief justice of the U. S. supreme court, the president announced that, "If the state of New York had not been represented in the cabinet, I should have tendered Mr. Spaulding the position of secretary of the treasury." In 1869 he published the "History of the Legal Tender Paper Money Issued During the Great Rebellion," which is, and will always probably remain the standard authority on that subject. In 1876 he delivered before the Banking Association an able review of "One Hundred Years of Progress in the Business of Banking." He is a life member of the Historical Society and the Young Men's Association, and a member of the Society of Natural Sciences, the Buffalo Club and other institutions. His official connection with local enterprises has been large and important. He has been associated with the International Bridge company as president, the gas-light company, and the street railroads. Mr. Spaulding retired from active business some years ago, and has since resided in summer at his beautiful country seat, "River Lawn," on Grand Island, where he maintains a well-appointed estate, containing 360 acres.

HOFFMAN, Eugene Augustus, Protestant Episcopal clergyman, was born in New York city, March 21, 1829. He is sixth in descent from Martinus Hoffman, who was an emigrant from Holland to the American colonies in 1640, since which date the annals of both church and state in New York show that members of the Hoffman family have rendered constant and conspicuous services, both military and civil, first to the colonial government, and afterward to the republic. His father, Samuel Verplanck Hoffman, born in New York in 1802, practiced law until 1828, when he founded the great dry-goods commission house of Hoffman & Waldo. Eugene Hoffman received his first education at Columbia Grammar School, whence he entered Rutger's College, and was graduated there in 1847. He then went to Harvard University, and received the degrees of B.A. and M.A. in succession. In 1848 he entered the General Theological Seminary in New York city, and was graduated three years later, being ordained deacon shortly afterward by Bishop Doane of New Jersey. After two years spent in energetic mission work in Elizabethport, N. J., he accepted a call to the rectorship of Christ Church, Elizabeth, N. J., in the spring of 1853, where he established one of the earliest and most successful free churches in America. He remained at Elizabeth ten years, and during this time he erected churches at Millburn and Woodbridge, N. J., and exerted a powerful influence over neighboring parishes. In 1863 he became rector of St. Mary's, Burlington, N. J., then heavily encumbered with debt, on which it was unable even to pay the interest. In a single year Dr. Hoffman wiped out its entire indebtedness, amounting to something like $23,000. After this signal proof of his ability, he was invited to the important rectorate of Grace Church, on Brooklyn Heights, but the keen air of the place seriously affected his health, and in 1869 he accepted the rectorship of St. Marks in Philadelphia. Here he remained for ten years; his incumbency being marked by almost unexampled prosperity. The communicants increased from 400 to 1,000, while the annual amount of the offerings averaged $40,000. A commodious rectory was built, and Dr. Hoffman established the first working-men's club in the country. In 1879 he was elected to the office of dean of the General Theological Seminary, after having twice declined the nomination. The institution was languishing for lack of funds; the professors' remuneration was inadequate; the buildings were unsanitary and unadapted to the needs of the hour. Dr. Hoffman in the sixteen years which have since elapsed has wrought a marvelous change by his administrative ability, added to his personal devotion and energy, and with the munificent assistance of others, whose active interests he has succeeded in enlisting in behalf of the seminary, he has built up

the institution to a condition of assured prosperity. New and spacious buildings have arisen in Chelsea Square; numerous endowments for professorships, fellowships, and instructors have been established; and a splendid edifice, the Chapel of the Good Shepherd, has been erected by the dean's mother, Glorvina Rossell Hoffman, as a memorial to her husband. Dean Hoffman is a member of numerous religious and charitable organizations; is chairman of the building committee of the Cathedral of St. John the Divine, president of the board of Trinity School, and has represented the diocese of New York in the last six general conventions. He is, further, a member of the Archæological Institute of America, of the American Institute of Christian Philosophy, the Metropolitan Museum of Art, the American Museum of Natural History, the American Geographical Society, the New York Historical Society, and the New York Genealogical and Biographical Society. The degree of D.D. was conferred upon him by Rutgers College in 1863, Racine College in 1882, the General Theological Seminary in 1885, Columbia College in 1886, and Trinity College in 1895. In 1890 he received the degree of D.C.L. from King's College, Nova Scotia, in 1891 that of LL.D. from the University of the South, Sewanee, Tenn., and in 1894 from Trinity University, Toronto, Canada. His multifarious duties have left him little leisure for literary composition, but he is the author of a "Manual of Devotion for Communicants," and numerous sermons, and has contributed various articles to reviews.

BUCKLEY, Edward, lumberman, was born in Devonshire, England, Aug. 8, 1842. He is of English ancestry, of the yeoman class, his father owning and tilling his own land. He was brought to America by his parents when a mere lad, they locating in Milwaukee, Wis., where he was educated in the public schools. When fourteen years old he was apprenticed to learn the trade of tinsmith, and followed that trade until 1862, when he enlisted as a private in the 24th Wisconsin regiment, and served during the entire civil war; his most notable battles being, Chaplin Hills, Murfreesborough, Franklin, Nashville, Chickamauga, and the Atlanta campaign. He followed his trade after his return from the war, and in 1867 located in Manistee, Mich., where he established a general hardware business, conducting it until 1880, when he joined in a partnership with William Douglas, as Buckley & Douglas, to carry on a general lumbering business, which was succeeded, Dec. 31, 1892, by the corporation, the Buckley & Douglas Lumber Co., of which he became president and treasurer. He also became interested in, and is president of, the Manistee and Northeastern Railroad Co. He owns and controls large tracts of pine and other timber lands in Michigan and Minnesota. Mr. Buckley is president of the Unitarian Society, Olympian Club, Manistee Driving Park Association, and is a Mason of the highest order. In 1869 he was married to Mary D. Ruggles of Manistee. She died in New York city in 1885, leaving no children. In 1894 he was married to Jennie Sloan of Thomasville, Ga. Mr. Buckley is a Republican in politics, and prominently identified with the work of the party in city and state, but not as an office-seeker or holder.

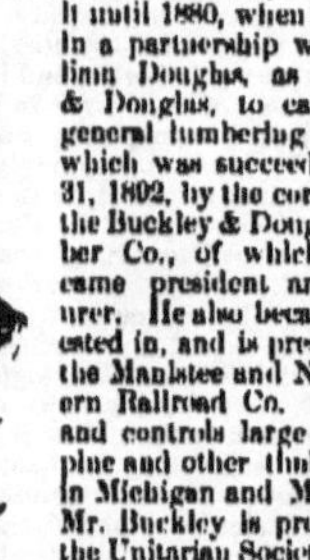

LIVINGSTON, Charles Ondis, manufacturer, was born in Contookville, N. H., Dec. 10, 1841, eldest child of Ondis Livingston, a native of Scotland, and Christina Linstrom, a native of Sweden. At an early age the son was obliged to go to work to help support the family. Desiring to procure a more profitable home, the father went West, and was never heard from, and the eldest son was hired out to farmers for his board and clothes and the privilege of attending school in winter. As this privilege came but rarely, his school education was confined to two winter terms at a country school of the most primitive kind. He supplemented this by having an open spelling-book beside him on the bench, while he pegged shoes during the seasons of ice and snow, in order to add to the scanty earnings of his employer. He would glance at the book occasionally, pick out a word, and after committing that to memory, would select another, and so on, until he mastered the book. He was therefore his own teacher, and studied under difficulties so great, that most lads of his age would have given up all attempts at an education. He worked on farms and pegged shoes in winter for several years, and then learned the wheelwright's trade in Manchester, N. H. In three years' time he became a thorough mechanic, and, on leaving his employer, traveled as a journeyman. On the breaking out of the civil war he enlisted with the three months' volunteers, and went to Washington. On the expiration of his term of service he returned home, joined the quarter-master's department as a mechanic and wagon master, and accompanied Sherman's expedition against Port Royal, S. C. He was at the assault on Port Royal Ferry, Jan. 1, 1862, and was injured by the fire from a masked battery. He subsequently became attached to the Army of the James, helped to dig the Dutch Gap canal before Richmond, and saw general service in South Carolina, Georgia, and Florida. On the surrender of the Confederate armies, he came to Jacksonville, to grow up with the town, and it is now said of him that he has built more houses than any other man in it outside of the contractor; and if stores and houses make towns, he has done as much as any one to make Jacksonville. Besides he has done a great deal for Tampa and West Palm Beach, Florida.

Mr. Livingston never took an active part in politics, but was always a hard worker in business and religious matters. He is now the oldest furniture man in the state, having started in 1869. In April, 1865, he opened a grocery store, but as he gave credit to almost everybody, he was compelled to close his doors at the end of two years and seek other employment. Mr. Livingston got a second start in business by buying a little stock of furniture, and in this line he made a fortune inside of twenty years, becoming one of the wealthiest men in the state. He retired from the furniture business in 1885, and devoted himself for six years to looking after his real estate and buildings. From 1872 to 1879 he ran a line of schooners plying between Boston and Jacksonville; he ran three steamers on the St. John's river, from 1872–76; and was the first man to bring an ice machine to Florida and produce ice by steam power. He made ice a necessity instead of a luxury of life, by selling the article at a price within the reach of all, and in that way became a public benefactor. Mr. Livingston had great mechanical and executive ability, could draw the plans of a structure, erect a house, make a buggy, or make a shoe for man or beast, plow a field, plumb a house, manufacture a harness, buy and sell goods, all with equal facility. For some years he was president of the Livingston Furniture Manufacturing Co., one of the largest of its kind in the state at that time. He was a Mason, a trustee of the Methodist Episcopal church, and a warm supporter of all charities irrespective of creed or race. Mr. Livingston was twice married; first in 1885, to Roxina Arey of Woodsville, N. H., and a second time to Martha, daughter of C. E. Johnson of Doylestown, Pa. The latter marriage took place at the World's Fair in Chicago, Sept. 19, 1893.

FLEMING, James Ezekiel, manager, was born at Columbus, O., July 24, 1836, son of Algernon Sidney Fleming of Clinton county, Pa., whose father was a member of the committee of safety of 1777, on the west branch of the Susquehanna river. The family settled in America in 1616; our subject's great-grandfather being John Fleming, Earl of Wigton, Scotland, who purchased for his son 1,000 acres of land in Pennsylvania in 1760. On the maternal side, he is descended from the Carskaddens, old shippers of Londonderry, Ireland, who also emigrated to America previous to the revolution, the

house being still in existence. James was educated at the private schools of Rumsey, Muhlenberg co., Ky., and at Flemington, Clinton co., Pa. On leaving school, he took a mercantile position in Philadelphia, and just before the outbreak of the civil war began reading law in the office of Samuel N. DuBoice of that city. With the opening of the war he recruited a cavalry troop that was attached to the 11th Pennsylvania cavalry, and in December of the same year he was made first lieutenant of company H, and engaged in picket, out-post, and outlug. On May 30, 1862, he was wounded on the Black Water, Va., captured, and held as prisoner of war for five months at Petersburg, Va., Salisbury, N. C., and in Libby Prison. Capt. Davidson and Lieut. Fleming were ordered to be held as hostages, it being alleged that the regiment to which they belonged, while on a raid, had committed acts in violation of the rules of civilized warfare. On the day of the first exchange of prisoners at Libby Prison, under the first cartel, information was conveyed to Lieut. Fleming that early that morning two officers had been sent to the hospital. Lieut. Fleming suggested to Capt. Davidson that they answer to the names of these absent officers, which was done, and they succeeded in getting away. He was afterwards exchanged, and, on account of his wounds, was ordered on staff duty, being first assigned to Gen. Alfred Gibbs's staff of Peck's division, and subsequently to the staff of Gen. Isaac J. Wister, whom he accompanied on the expedition to capture Jeff. Davis. On Jan. 14, 1864, he was promoted captain, and ordered to report to Gen. William Farrar Smith, commanding the 18th army corps, and who was relieved by Gen. E. O. C. Ord. Capt. Fleming remained on Gen. Ord's staff until February, 1865, when he resigned on account of his wounds. On his return home, Gov. Curtin of Pennsylvania appointed him lieutenant-colonel and assistant inspector-general, but the war coming to an end, he did not muster in. He soon removed to North Carolina, where he engaged in the planting and shipping of cotton, and took a prominent part in the reconstruction of the state. He was appointed military sheriff by Gen. Sickles, and in that capacity organized a body of ex-Confederate soldiers, and broke up the gangs of highwaymen that infested that section of the country. From 1868 to 1872 he remained on his plantation, after which he again came North, and was sent by the Wilkes Barre Coal and Iron Co. to Newark, N. J., to establish and superintend a branch of their business. As a citizen of Newark, he was a member of the board of freeholders and councilmen; a member of the board of trade, and its treasurer; a member of the Essex Club, and a member and one of the governors of the Country Club; also member of the board of managers of the Soldiers' Home for Disabled Soldiers of New Jersey. In June, 1890, he organized the Essex troop of light cavalry, becoming its commander. During the Columbian parade in New York city, Oct. 12, 1892, this troop was recognized as the finest cavalry organization in the line. On Apr. 25, 1859, Mr. Fleming married the daughter of Richard Penn Smith of Philadelphia, a granddaughter of William Moore Smith, one of the commissioners of claims of the war of 1812, as appointed under the sixth article of Jay's treaty. She was also a great-granddaughter of the Rev. William Smith, D.D., founder of the University of Pennsylvania. Mr. Fleming has continued in the service of the Coal and Iron Co. for twenty-two years.

KNIGHTON, Frederick, clergyman and educator, was born in Derby, England, Nov. 2, 1812, son of Thomas Knighton, who, with his family, came to America and settled near Mendham, N. Y. Here he prepared for college at the school of the Rev. A. E. Fairchild, being graduated with honor at Princeton College in 1837. He subsequently studied law under James A. Green at Princeton, and also taught for some years in a classical school at the same place. In 1844 he entered Princeton Theological Seminary, and being graduated in 1847, was licensed to preach the gospel by the Presbytery of East Hanover, Va., in April of the same year. Ordained by the Presbytery of West Jersey on Nov. 1, 1851, he was installed pastor of the Gloucester City Church on Nov. 11th, which charge he resigned a year later. Upon removing to Belvidere, N. J., he became, from 1854–73, the stated supply of the First Presbyterian Church at Oxford, N. J. Under his charge both the material and spiritual welfare of this church were greatly strengthened, a new edifice was erected, and large accessions were made to the membership. During the civil war Dr. Knighton served a nine months' term as chaplain of the 11th regiment of New Jersey. His scholarly tastes and attainments peculiarly fitting him for an instructor, he taught in Fredericksburg and Alexandria, Va., in Camden, Belvidere, Oxford, and Cranbury, N. J., also in Milford and Stroudsburg, Pa., in which latter place he spent the last twelve years of his life. He was the author of several text-books of education: "Primary Grammar," "Outlines of History," etc. He received the degree of Ph.D. from Princeton College, being the first of that institution's graduates to be so honored, and that of D.D. from Wells College, N. J. In 1879 he entered into a copartnership with William R. Bennett of Stroudsburg in the business of tanning and currying, which he continued until his death. He never entirely relinquished his ministerial labors until forced to do so from failure of physical

strength. Dr. Knighton was a man pre-eminent both in the professor's chair and in the pulpit. His capacity for hard work, his firm convictions, and his integrity of purpose also insured him success in business, just as they insured life and prosperity to many a feeble church and parish. In recognition of what such abilities were worth to the cause of education, it was the desire of his many friends that he should some day assume the headship of one of the first institutions in the country, a responsibility which, owing largely to his neglect to avail himself of the legitimate and ordinary means to secure it, was never given him. He died on Sept. 9, 1888.

FLINT, Timothy, author, was born in Reading, Mass., July 11, 1780. His early education was received in his native town, and he entered Harvard, where he was graduated in 1800. He devoted two years to theological study, and was then ordained pastor of the Congregational Church of Lunenburg, Mass. He was fond of scientific study and experiments, and, on account of his chemical work, was charged by ignorant persons with counterfeiting coin. Feeling ran high and culminated in his bringing suits for slander to establish his innocence. This, with political differences, engendered ill feeling among his parishioners, and he relinquished his charge in 1814, and after preaching in various localities in New England, went as a missionary to the Mississippi Valley, where he spent some seven or eight years. He was the first Protestant minister to administer the communion in the city of St. Louis. In 1822 he visited New Orleans, and after traveling from place to place, in pursuit of his missionary duty, was forced by ill health to return to the North, where he devoted himself to literature. In 1826 he published an account of these wanderings, under the name of "Recollections of the Last Ten Years Passed in the Valley of the Mississippi," which met with immediate success, and he followed it the same year with "Francis Berrian, or the Mexican Patriot." His third work was "The Geography and History of the Mississippi Valley," which appeared in two volumes in Cincinnati in 1827. The next year he published "Arthur Clenning," and several other stories of Indian life. His next work was "Lectures upon Natural History, Geology, Chemistry, the Application of Steam, and Interesting Discoveries in the Arts" (Boston, 1832). Mr. Flint then went to New York, and upon the retirement of C. F. Hoffman from the editorship of the "Knickerbocker Magazine," succeeded him for a few months. About this time he translated Droz's "The Art of Being Happy," with additions of his own, and also a novel, entitled "Celibacy Vanquished, or the Old Bachelor Reclaimed." He removed to Cincinnati in 1834, where he became the editor of the "Western Monthly Magazine" for three years, besides contributing to it a number of essays and stories. The next year he contributed to the "London Athenaeum" a series of "Sketches of the Liberation of the United States." He afterwards removed to Red River in Louisiana, but ill health obliged him to return to New England in 1840. While passing through Natchez he was buried for some hours in the ruins of a house blown down by a violent tornado, which increased his illness, and on his arrival at Reading became rapidly worse, and died there Aug. 18, 1840.

PEALE, Charles Wilson, artist and author, was born in Chestertown, Md., Apr. 16, 1741. His father, Charles Peale, was master of the county school and occasionally occupied the neighboring pulpits. Upon the death of his father when he was nine years old his mother removed to Annapolis, and placed him at school; but before he was thirteen he was apprenticed to a saddler, in which calling he afterwards established himself in business. While visiting Norfolk, Va., he saw a portrait which made such an impression upon him that upon returning home he attempted a likeness of himself. He took lessons in painting from Hesselius, a German painter, to whom he gave a saddle for the privilege of seeing him paint. His success won the admiration of influential friends, who placed funds at his disposal that he might go to England. He studied under John Singleton Copley at Boston, and in 1770 went to London and became a pupil of Benjamin West. While there he also studied modeling in wax, casting, and modeling in plaster, engraving and miniature painting. Upon his return he paid off all his debts "but those of gratitude," by painting the portraits of his benefactors as he had promised. He established himself in Philadelphia in 1776, and displayed his patriotism by contributing emblematical insignias for public displays at Newburyport and New England. Upon the mustering of militia in Philadelphia, he was made a lieutenant of one of the companies, which he soon filled by his energy, and was later made captain, and led his company at the battles of Trenton and Princeton. His fearlessness was noted, and he was selected one of fifty to remove the public stores, when Philadelphia was threatened with capture. He was one of six deputed to arrest those suspected of disloyalty, or, to obtain their parole, and he was one of three appointed to take possession of and sell confiscated estates. During this time he pursued his vocation of an artist, and snatched subjects for landscapes, and from surrounding faces secured portraits which are now numbered among the country's most valued possessions. He never lost an opportunity to secure a portrait or sketch of the eminent individuals he came in contact with, and had collected a large number of portraits. He  became interested in politics, and having been elected a member of the legislature in 1779, was one of the main advocates of the act for the gradual abolition of slavery. In 1801 his attention was turned to natural history from the finding of a mammoth in Ulster county, N. Y., and he began the collection of natural curiosities, which, with a number of portraits, he opened, in 1802, "Peale's Museum," himself giving lectures on natural history. He had previously, in 1791, endeavored unsuccessfully to lay the foundation of an art-academy in Philadelphia, but his efforts did ultimately assist in the foundation of the Pennsylvania Academy of Fine Arts, to seventeen of the exhibitions of which he contributed. His versatility was remarkable, and to his other accomplishments he added that of authorship. Among his publications are: "Building Wooden Bridges," "Discourse Introductory to a Course of Lectures on Natural History," "Epistles on the Means of Preserving Health," and "Domestic Happiness." Peale's fame, however, rests mainly upon his achievements as a portrait painter, and the circumstances of his association with Washington, who gave him fourteen sittings. He was the only portrait-painter at the time, and his genius was in great demand. The first of the fourteen portraits of Washington by Peale, was in the uniform of a Virginia colonel, and is the only one now extant of those painted before the revolution. One was painted in 1780 for Princeton College. His last portrait of Washington, executed in 1783, he retained until his death. Of the only two cabinet portraits known to exist, one, a three-quarter face, was painted for the father of Adm. Kilty. The other is in the possession of the family of Henry Randall. Among his other portraits are those of Hancock, Morris, Steuben, Franklin, Green, Gates, Jefferson, Hamilton, Monroe, Jackson, Calhoun, Clay, besides many other eminent men. He greatly admired a portrait of Lord Baltimore at Annapolis, thought by him to be by Van Dyke, and he secured it from the alderman of the city in exchange for six portraits of the governors of Maryland to be painted by him. He painted "Christ Healing the Sick," when eighty-one years of age, and finished a portrait of himself when eighty-three. Upon his death, which occurred in Philadelphia, Feb. 22, 1827, he left a collection of 269 original portraits and historical scenes.

FARRINGTON, Samuel Putnam, merchant, was born at Hopkinton, N. H., Jan. 29, 1819, son of Benjamin E. Farrington, a well-to-do farmer. His grandfather, Samuel Farrington, was a soldier in the revolutionary war, and built the first frame house erected in Concord, N. H., which is still (1896) standing. The boy was educated at the public school of his native town, and at the age of fourteen entered the Gilmanton Academy and was graduated at the age of seventeen. His school life was alternated with work on his father's farm mornings and evenings, and during vacations. Country life having no attraction for this ambitious lad, he went to Boston, and obtained employment as a clerk in the dry-goods business. He remained in this one establishment for three years, when he went to Florida, to try his luck in business, for two years. Upon his return to Boston, he engaged with Clark, Sweet & Co., wholesale dry-goods commission merchants, and was made a partner in the concern. In 1850 he sold his interest, on account of ill health, and went to Chicago. He entered the wholesale grocery business there, first as assistant, and afterwards as full partner. In 1857 he retired from business, but in 1859 was persuaded to join the firm of Day, Allen & Co., continuing as an active partner until 1867, when he formed the copartnership of Farrington & Schmahl. Upon the death of Mr. Schmahl, in 1879, the firm name was changed to S. P. Farrington & Co., and so continued until 1884. He then removed to Minneapolis, Minn., and there established the grocery house of Harrison, Farrington & Co., afterwards Winston, Farrington & Co., of which firm his son, L. H. Farrington, is a member. Mr. Farrington was married in 1841 to Frances H. Perkins of Wakefield, N. H. She died in 1848, and in 1853 he married Harriet L., daughter of Benjamin Mackay. He is a prominent member of the Presbyterian church, and takes an active interest in a number of charitable and benevolent institutions.

RUTHERFURD, Lewis Morris, astronomer, was born Nov. 25, 1816, in Morrisania, N. Y. His grandfather, John Rutherfurd, was a nephew of Lord Stirling, through whom he traced his ancestry for 700 years. On his mother's side he was a direct descendant of Lewis Morris. As a boy he showed his mathematical bent of mind and was precocious beyond his years. He entered the sophomore class of Williams College when only fifteen years old, and was graduated in 1834, when he began the study of law with William H. Seward in Auburn, and was admitted to the bar in 1837, and became associated with John Jay, and after his death with Hamilton Fish. But his tastes inclined him to physics, and he abandoned the law and devoted himself to scientific research and experiment principally in the direction of astronomical photography. He had, while at college, developed great proficiency, being made assistant to the professor in chemistry, in which capacity he had prepared with his own hands special apparatus for class lectures, and had reconstructed a telescope from scattered parts found in a lumber room. He had abundant

means, which were added to by his marriage, so that he was able to devote his life to professional work, travel, and study. He spent several years in Europe during which he studied optics under Prof. Amici, the most distinguished adept in that science. Upon his return he built an observatory in New York, which was the finest and best equipped private astronomical observatory in the country. He made with his own hands an equatorial telescope, and devised original means of adapting it for photographic use by means of a third lens, which, being placed outside of the ordinary object glass, converted the telescope into a photographic instrument. He devised and constructed a measuring machine for star plates, arranged to determine the position, angle, and distance from a central star, with which he determined the positions of thirty-one stars in the pleiades. This was improved in 1868 by using a glass scale, one division of which was equal to ten revolutions of the micrometer screw. Mr. Rutherfurd pursued his photographic work for twenty years, and was the originator and introducer of the photographic method of observation. To him also is due the idea of an object-glass for employing the chemical rays rather than visual ones. He invented a photographic corrector for adapting an ordinary object-glass to securing sharp definitions upon the sensitive plate. He personally planned the construction of these instruments, and superintended the construction of the lenses, which were made at his own house, by methods devised by himself. He also was the first to introduce the precautions by which the sensitive film is guarded against distortion, and was the first to devise and construct micrometer apparatus for measuring impressions on the plate. It is stated that he took such pains in the construction of the threads of the screws of his micrometer that he was engaged three years upon a single screw. Mr. Rutherfurd labored at the photographic method of observation for many years without the sympathy or encouragement of astronomers generally, but in 1865 he placed the results of his measurements in the hands of Prof. Gould, who computed and verified them, and presented a memoir embodying the results of his observations to the National Academy of Sciences, when the value and importance of his labors were recognized and acknowledged. In January, 1863, he published a paper in the "American Journal of Science," which was an attempt at classifying the stars according to their spectra, and which was the first work in this direction since Bunsen and Kirchhoff. In 1864 he presented to the National Academy of Sciences a photograph of the solar spectrum over eleven feet long, which contained three times the number of lines heretofore noted on the charts of Bunsen and Kirchhoff. In the course of his spectrum work Mr. Rutherfurd found,

as in his photographic experiments, that his instruments were not sufficiently delicate, and, therefore, with his accustomed ingenuity, devised a ruling machine which was able to work finer gratings than those of Nobert, whose gratings were at that time considered the best in existence. He succeeded in making about 17,000 lines to the inch which has only been surpassed by Prof. Rowland. It is with these improved facilities, which were developed by his own ingenuity, that he was enabled to produce such remarkable results, which are the more remarkable because his work was all done before the discovery of the dry-plate process, which has so greatly helped astronomical research in recent years. His photographs of the moon in clearness of detail surpassed all other prints. During the later years of his life Mr. Rutherfurd's health was delicate, and he was not able to endure the confinement of sedentary labor, and was obliged to give up active research, which was a sore trial to his energetic spirit. When he realized his inability for further work, he gave his instruments and photographs to Columbia College. His telescope is now mounted in the observatory of the college. The collection of astronomical photographs contains 175 photographs of the sun, 174 of the solar spectrum, 435 of the moon, and 604 of star-clusters, which was considered to have such value that it is preserved in fireproof vaults. The computation of the measures undertaken by the college authorities was published only a few days before his death, but too late to be verified by him. Prof. Gould says of Mr. Rutherfurd that "we owe to him not merely the first permanent records of the relative positions, at a given moment, of all the celestial objects impressed upon the sensitive plates, but the means and the accomplishment of the actual conversion of these records into actual numerical data." In 1858 Mr. Rutherfurd was made a trustee of Columbia College, and became one of its most active and hardworking members. He was one of the original members of the National Academy of Sciences upon its incorporation by act of congress in 1863, and was an associate member of the Royal Astronomical Society. In 1867 he was president of the American Photographical Society, which during his administration became the photographic section of the American Institute, and subsequently served as its first vice-president for many years. He was appointed American delegate to the International meridian conference held in Washington, D. C., 1885, and was one of its most active members, preparing and presenting the resolutions which embodied the results of their labors. In 1887 the French Academy of Sciences elected him a member of the International conference on astronomical photography to be held in Paris, and he was appointed by the president of our National Academy of Sciences its representative to the same conference, but his delicate health compelled him to decline serving. He also received numerous decorations and honors from the learned societies of the world. His death was the result of a cold taken when on his way to his country home in Florida, and was hastened by the shock caused by the death of his daughter. He died at his country home, Tranquility, May 30, 1892. Mr. O. G. Mason says of him: "His dislike of ostentation and show was a conspicuous trait of his character. He was never known to wear any one of the many decorations, emblems of rank, or acquirements which had been conferred upon him."

JOSEPH, Antonio, member of congress, was born at Taos, N. M., Aug. 25, 1846. His father, by birth a Portuguese, came to America in 1837, his mother of Spanish and French descent, was born in the United States. Both parents emigrated to New Mexico in 1840, and lived there until they died. They are both buried in the Masonic graveyard, near Taos. The son received his early education at Lux's Academy, in Taos. He afterward attended for two years, Bishop Lamuy's School in Santa Fé, N. M., with a subsequent four years' course at Webster College, in St. Louis county, Mo. On the completion of a commercial course at Bryant & Stratton's Commercial College, St. Louis, Mo., he entered upon a mercantile career. He was county judge of Taos county, N. M., for six years, a member of the territorial legislature for six years, and was a senator in the territorial legislature. He was

elected to the forty-ninth congress, and re-elected to the fiftieth, fifty-first, fifty-second, and fifty-third congresses.

COLT, Caldwell Hart, yachtsman, was born in Hartford, Conn., Nov. 24, 1858, son of Samuel Colt, the celebrated inventor and manufacturer. He was educated in part under private tutors, at St. Paul's School, Concord, N. H., and at the Sheffield Scientific School of Yale University. With a tutor, Mr. Bradley, he took extended trips in California and Colorado, and made the tour of Europe before he had attained his twentieth year. In these boyhood days he excelled as a hunter, and brought home with him various trophies of his skill as a marksman. But his greatest pleasure in early manhood was found on the sea, and as a yachtsman, as the master of the Dauntless, and the commodore of his yacht club, he was best known. Mr. Colt purchased the Dauntless in 1882, and in August of that year started on an extended cruise across the Atlantic for European waters. In 1885 with the Dauntless he defended the Cape May and Brenton's Reef cups against the Genesta to prevent the American trophies going unchallenged to the Briton. His old schooner he knew to be no match for the sleek cutter, but he at least made a plucky effort to retain them. In 1887 he sailed the Dauntless against the Coronet, owned by Mr. Bush, in an ocean race from Bay Ridge, New York harbor to Queenstown, Ireland. The Dauntless was twenty years older and one-third smaller than the Coronet, and was defeated by one day and two hours. On the thirteenth day out the Dauntless made the unprecedented record of 328 miles. In 1888 Mr. Colt was elected vice-commodore of the New York Yacht Club, and in 1892 commodore of the Larchmont Club, and was re-elected in 1893. He was also a member of the Eastern, St. Augustine and Biscayne Bay Yacht Clubs, and an honorary member of several European yacht clubs. He took a lively interest in the public affairs of his native city. In 1888 he was

elected vice-president of the Colt's Patent Fire Arms Co., holding the position for two years. He died at Punta Gorda, Fla., Jan 21, 1894, after a brief illness. His devoted mother caused to be prepared and printed, a beautifully designed volume as a memorial, which she thoughtfully placed in the hands of each of his more intimate companions and friends, and in which are preserved the various and tender tokens received by her on the occasion of his death.

TOURO, Judah, merchant and philanthropist, was born in Newport, R. I., June 16, 1775. His parents and relatives belonged to the Jewish faith, to which religion he adhered throughout his life, though he contributed liberally to many Christain enterprises. His father, Isaac Touro, was a native of Holland, and minister of the synagogue at Newport since 1762. In 1798 he made a Mediterranean voyage as supercargo, and narrowly escaped a French privateer. After a few years in Boston, he went to New Orleans, in 1802, where he prospered greatly through thrift and industry. In 1815 he served as a soldier under Gen. Jackson at the battle of New Orleans, receiving a wound from which he never entirely recovered. Mr. Touro was very eccentric in his habits. During his entire residence in New Orleans it is stated that he never left its limits, excepting as a soldier in 1815. A brother of his having been thrown from a carriage in Boston and killed,

Mr. Touro was never known to enter a carriage thereafter. He endowed several synagogues and churches throughout the country, and bequeathed over half his fortune amounting to $1,000,000, to charitable objects, both Hebrew and Christian. Mr. Touro died in New Orleans, La., Jan. 18, 1854.

PUMPELLY, Raphael, geologist and author, was born at Owego, N. Y., Sept. 8, 1837. He is the son of William Pumpelly, who was descended from a French Huguenot family of previous Italian origin. On the maternal side he is descended from Sir Richard Empson, the minister of Henry VII., Gov. Thomas Welles of Connecticut, and the colonial New England families of Pynchon, Pitkin, Talcot, Treat, Jonathan Edwards, etc. Returning to America after studying from 1854 to 1860 in France and at Freiberg in Germany, he passed a year in charge of mines in Arizona during the Apache war, being one of the very few who escaped the general massacre. On reaching California he was engaged by the government of Japan to explore a part of that empire, and to advise with reference to the introduction of foreign methods. Visiting China in 1864, he accomplished several geological expeditions at his own cost into western China, on the upper Yangtze Kiang, and to the Mongollan Plateau. Passing the winter at Peking, as the guest of Mr. Burlingame, he undertook for the Chinese government an examination of the coal fields of part of northern China. Traveling at the head of an imperial commission, with an escort of military and civil mandarins, and coming daily into official and social intercourse with local officials of all grades, he obtained an insight into the methods of the government, and the difficulties of its relations to the people. This and similar experiences in Japan, and an acquaintance with the diplomatic problems obtained during his residence in Peking, made the British and American ministers request him to write an essay on "Western Policy in Eastern Asia," which appeared in the "North American Review" in 1867. Through his extended scientific journeys, and the sifting of several thousand volumes of Chinese geographical works, in which he was aided by native scholars, he was enabled to construct the first geographical map of China and of part of Mongolia, and to show for the first time the immense extent of the Chinese coal fields, and the superior quality of its coals, and to predict the prospective dominating position of China in the manufacturing and commercial world. Leaving China, he made a geological section across the Plateau of Mongolia and the Gobi desert. After passing several winter months in Irkutsk, he traversed Siberia to Europe and America, thus finishing in 1865 a five years' journey around the northern hemisphere at a time of great interest in each country: the Apache war in Arizona; the disturbances that broke up the feudal system in Japan; the Taiping rebellion in China; the Polish rebellion in Russia. The varied observations and adventures of this journey gave rise to his narrative "Across America and Asia." On his return to America he became professor of mining engineering in Harvard University. In 1869 to 1871 he was state geologist of Michigan, and during 1872–73 director of the geological survey of Missouri. In 1873 he was elected member of the National Academy of Sciences, and in 1879 took charge of the special department of the tenth census for the mining industries. At the same time he conducted for the national board of health an extended investigation into the capacity of soils to remove bacteria from filtering currents of water and air. In 1881 he organized and directed the northern transcontinental survey—a topographical and economic survey of the northwestern territories, of which the greater part of the results are yet unpublished. From 1884 to 1890 he had charge of the "Archæan" division of the U. S. geological survey, and directed the mapping of the geology of western New England. He was American vice-president of the international geological congress at Washington in 1891. Among his more important contributions to purely theoretical geology, are his study of the "Metasomatic Development of the Copper Rocks of Lake Superior," and the theory that over-long unsubmerged regions the rocks become deeply disintegrated, thus preparing the way for a very rapid removal by ice during glacial periods from the glacial drift, and by wind, to be deposited as loess at a distance when the region becomes arid through climatic changes. This theory he extended later, showing the derivation, through ozogenic movements, of many obscure schists from such disintegrated masses. Besides numerous contributions to scientific and literary periodicals, he published: "Geological Researches in China, Mongolia and Japan," "Across America and Asia," "Geological Survey of Michigan Copper Rocks," "Geological Survey of Missouri Iron Ores and Coal Fields," "Mining Industries, Vol. XV. of Tenth Census," "Geology of the Green Mountains in Massachusetts, U. S. Geological Survey."

GUNTHER, Ernest Rudolph, capitalist, was born in one of the seven houses known as "Gunther Row," on Fourteenth street and Second avenue, New York city, in June, 1862, son of William Henry Gunther. Christian Gottlieb von Gunther, his grandfather, son of the celebrated surgeon of the king of Saxony and first cousin to the Prince von Gunther of his day, who was prominent in the royal courts of Prussia and Saxony, became a resident of America. He was twice married, his first wife being a widow with four children, two sons and two daughters, whose name was changed to Gunther; one of them, Charles Godfrey Gunther, being mayor of New York in 1863. By this marriage he had two sons, William Henry, father of Ernest Rudolph Gunther, and F. Frederick Gunther. By his second marriage he had two sons, Elsner and Bernard. Ernest Rudolph Gunther is a fine musician, a clever conversationalist, and of marked intellectual tastes. He is a member of the Union League and other clubs, and socially is extremely popular. As a patron of the arts, he is well known in New York society, the frequent musicales at his residence, being events of each season. He is an enthusiastic collector, and among many other rare and beautiful objects in his possession, may be seen the two coats-of-arms of the family, and the four ancestral miniatures which his noble grandfather brought with him to his adopted country.

SAY, Thomas, naturalist, was born in Philadelphia, Pa., July 27, 1787, the son of Benjamin Say, a physician and a member of the Society of Friends.

and grandson of Thomas Say, a Philadelphia merchant and philanthropist. The subject of this sketch was placed under the control of the Society of Friends at an early age, but conceived a strong dislike for his teachers, which was doubtless the cause of the great distaste he evinced for study at this time, although he afterwards showed such a predilection for it. After leaving school he was first employed in his father's drug store, and subsequently established in business with John Speakman, who was a member of the Academy of Natural Sciences of Philadelphia. Through the influence of his business associate, Mr. Say was persuaded to become a member of the society, and his life as a scientist began from that date. He connected himself with the academy Apr. 16, 1812, the association having been organized in January of that year, and up to the time of his admission was more of a social than a scientific organization; but from that date the plan of its management was changed, and it soon took its rank among the first scientific associations of the world. Soon after he became a member of the academy he began the investigations which he continued during his entire lifetime, upon the American fauna, and not long afterwards abandoned his business and gave himself up entirely to scientific pursuits. In 1818 he visited Georgia and Florida on a collecting expedition, and the following year was appointed naturalist on Long's expedition to the Rocky Mountains, he subsequently returned to Philadelphia, and was afterwards a member of Long's second expedition, which explored the sources of the Mississippi. In 1825 he returned to New Harmony, Ind., where he remained during the rest of his life, doing considerable scientific work, both in writing and collecting. His two chief works are his "American Entomology," and his "American Conchology." His numerous papers were published in the journal of the Academy of Natural Sciences, Philadelphia, Pa., "Transactions of the American Philosophical Society," Maclurean Lyceum, "Nicholson's Encyclopædia," the "American Quarterly Review," etc. His collection and library became the property of the Philadelphia Academy at his death, where many of the specimens are still preserved with his original labels. It is probable that he described more new species during his career than any other scientist with the exception of John Edward Gray, and Francis Walker, of the British Museum. He possessed a clear insight, a keen discrimination in selecting the salient features of the form before him, and his work never caused confusion in synonymy, and is easily recognized, and almost every form that he described, is at present [illegible] worked without books and with[illegible] and has been styled the [illegible] died at New Har[illegible]

born [illegible]
[illegible]
[illegible]

Augustus Soemüller, merchant of New York, where they afterwards resided. Her third work, "Reginald Archer," was produced in 1871, but met with considerable adverse criticism. Besides the novels mentioned, she wrote for the periodicals, and also published a collection of miscellaneous essays in 1878. Her life was a quiet, domestic one, and there was very little change of incident in it, but her vivid imagination, extended reading, intense love of music, and above all the deep religious feeling which pervaded her whole life, are shown in the books upon which she lavished so much of her short earthly existence. Her health having become enfeebled, she soon afterwards made a trip to Germany, France, and Italy, and while in Stuttgart, she died, Dec. 10, 1878.

CLARKE, Charles John, business man, was born in Pittsburgh, Pa., March 15, 1833, son of Thomas S. and Eliza (Thaw) Clarke. His father was a man of fine mind, great executive ability, and splendid business qualifications. Original and far-sighted in business matters, he did much to advance and develop many important financial and commercial enterprises of his day. While leading a life of wonderful business activity he devoted much of his time and gave liberally of his means to religious, charitable, and kindred objects, until called from his labors Oct. 19, 1867. Charles J. Clarke, after finishing his collegiate education at Jefferson College, in 1852, became a clerk in the office of Clarke & Thaw, who were engaged in the transportation business. Here, under the guidance of his father, he received a thorough business education, to which he attributed his business success in life. Ten years prior to the death of his father, in 1867, he became a member of the firm of Clarke & Co. After that period he become successor to his father's interest, and the firm was continued in business with his uncle, William Thaw, as his associate, until November, 1874, when it was dissolved, and he retired from active business. While Mr. Clarke inherited considerable property from his father, he acquired from his example and training thorough business habits that proved to be of much value. From the moderate inheritance received from his father and from the profits derived from his interest in the business, he has, by wise and judicious investments in real estate, in railroad and other securities, amassed a large fortune. He has been prominent alike in business and public enterprises, and, in an unostentious way, has given liberally of his time and means to educational, charitable, and religious institutions. His counsel and advice are much sought after, yet among the many positions of honor and trust occupied by him, he has never accepted one for a money consideration. Among other positions he has filled those of president of the Allegheny Cemetery; also of the School of Design for Women; and for sixteen years of the Mercantile Library Hall Co.; and is vice-president of the Pennsylvania College for Women. He has been a trustee of the Western University of Pennsylvania, the Home for the Deaf and Dumb, the Young Men's Christian Association, the Pittsburgh Bethel Home, and the Homœopathic Hospital; is a director of the Pittsburgh Safe Deposit and Trust Co., the Western Insurance Co., and a member of the chamber of commerce of Pittsburgh. Mr. Clarke was married Feb. 12, 1857, to Louisa, the daughter of John B. and Mary Semple.

PARRISH, Edward, first president of Swarthmore College (1868–70). (See Vol. V., p. 348.)

MAGILL, Edward Hicks, second president of Swarthmore College (1871–89), was born in Solebury, Bucks co., Pa., Sept. 24, 1825. His family had for several generations been members of the religious Society of Friends, and his parents, Mary Watson and Jonathan Paxson Magill, each frequently appeared in the ministry. The son was educated at the schools near his home, at a private boarding-school, and for two years at Westtown. At the age of sixteen he began to teach in the public school at Solebury. After teaching eight years, during one year of which (1848–49) he was instructor in Benjamin Hallowell's well-known school at Alexandria, Va., he determined to secure a collegiate education, and after a year of preparation (1849–50) at Williston Seminary, Easthampton, Mass., he entered the freshman class at Yale on the day he was twenty-five years of age. The next year he left Yale for Brown University, where he was graduated with the degree of A.B. in 1852. He also holds the degree of A.M. from Brown University, conferred after three years subsequent study, and a later honorary degree of LL.D. from Haverford College. Immediately after Prof. Magill's graduation at Brown University he became a teacher of classics in the High School of Providence, R. I. (1852). From 1854–59 he was principal of the classical department of this institution; in 1859 was sub-master of the Boston Public Latin Grammar School; and in 1867 he became principal of the preparatory department of Swarthmore College. As this college, then new, was not ready to receive students until 1869, Prof. Magill spent the following two years in study and travel in Europe. In 1871 he succeeded Edward Parrish as president of the college, which position he held over eighteen years, resigning at the commencement of 1889. His resignation was only accepted with the proviso that he should spend the next year abroad in study, and with full pay. This he did, chiefly in Paris in the study of the French language and literature, and upon his return to America, in 1890, he accepted the professorship of the French language and literature at Swarthmore. The name of Pres. Magill is most closely connected with the steady growth and prosperity of the institution with which he has been so long identified. A marked feature of his administration was his advocacy of Dr. Wayland's ideas with respect to the "New (Elective) College System." With a view to stimulating Friends to a fresh interest in education, Pres. Magill, in the summer and autumn of 1886, made an extended tour among members of that religious society, delivering lectures upon "The Advantages of a Modern College Course of Study." This trip carried him as far west as Iowa, and included Friends in Canada. A year later a similar journey was made among Friends in Maryland, Virginia, and Pennsylvania. This had a great effect upon the college attendance, which from 123 rose in two years to 170. During the year 1887–88 Pres. Magill originated a movement to obtain funds for the endowment of one or more professorships. He started a conditional subscription for that purpose, no money being payable unless $40,000 was secured that year. By June over $160,000 had been secured, and four professorships were endowed. At a meeting in Harrisburg, in 1887, Pres. Magill proposed a permanent association of Pennsylvania colleges, which

was subsequently organized during the same summer at Franklin and Marshall College, and is now a flourishing organization, under the title of "The Association of Colleges and Preparatory Schools of the Middle States and Maryland." In 1886 Pres. Magill received the honorary degree of LL.D. from Haverford College. His published works include: "A French Grammar" (1865, twelve editions); "An Introductory French Reader" (1867, five editions); "French Prose and Poetry" (1869); "A Short Method of Learning to Read the French Language" (1892). To illustrate the principles of wide, rapid, and yet accurate reading, which are laid down in the volume last named, Dr. Magill is now engaged upon a "Modern French Series" of annotated texts, of which volume I. ("Stories by Francisque Sarcey"); volume II. ("Sur la Pente," by Mme. de Witt); and volume III. ("La Fille de Clémentine, ou Le Crime de Sylvestre Bonnard," by Anatole France), have already appeared; and volume IV. ("Jean Mornas," a romance based upon the modern science of hypnotism, by Jules Claretie, of the French Academy), appeared in the autumn of 1894. This series, by some of the most distinguished of the writers of France of the present day, is being very favorably received.

DE GARMO, Charles, third president of Swarthmore College (1891–), was born at Mukwango, Wis., Jan. 7, 1849, of Quaker ancestry. He was brought up on a farm, receiving his education and afterward teaching in the neighboring schools. He was graduated at the Illinois State Normal School in 1873, whither, after a brief period as principal of one of the state public schools, he returned to assume a seven-year's charge of one of the model departments. During this time, in conjunction with Edmund J. James, later of the University of Pennsylvania, he established and conducted the "Illinois School Journal," subsequently known as the "Public School Journal." From 1883–86 Prof. De Garmo studied at the universities of Jena and Halle, in Germany, receiving the degree of Ph.D. from the latter institution. For the succeeding four years he occupied the chair of modern languages at the Illinois State Normal School. He was then called to the chair of philosophy and pedagogy in the State University of Illinois, and in 1891 he became the president of Swarthmore College, which under his administration is worthily extending its fame. Pres. De Garmo is prominently known as one of the leading exponents in the United States of the Herbartian thought in education; being president of the Herbartian Society for the scientific study of

education. This society is officially connected with the National Educational Association, of which Pres. De Garmo is an active member, one of its council, and director for the state of Pennsylvania; he has been president of the normal-school section. He has delivered numerous addresses on educational themes before this association, besides taking a prominent part in the discussions of the department of superintendence during the mid-winter meetings. In addition to frequent magazine contributions, he has published: "Essentials of Methods;" "Lindner's Empirical Psychology" (translation); "Lange's Apperception" (edited); "Herbart and the Herbartians;" Ufer's "Introduction to Herbart's Pedagogy" (edited); translation of Herbart's "Umriss der Pædagogischen Vorlesungen" (annotated).

BOND, Elizabeth Powell, dean of Swarthmore College, was born in Clinton, N. Y., Jan. 25, 1841, daughter of Townsend and Catharine (Macy) Powell, members of the Society of Friends; her mother being a descendant of the Macys who settled on Nantucket in 1660. She is the sister of Aaron M. and George T. Powell; the former for several years editor of the "Anti-Slavery Standard," and a prominent social reformer; the latter a well-known agriculturist, and at one time a director of the Agricultural Institute of the state of New York. Her childhood was spent in Ghent, N. Y., whither her parents had removed in 1845. At fifteen she was an assistant in the Friends' School in Dutchess county; at seventeen, was graduated at the State Normal School at Albany, N. Y., and after a year's study at the Claverack Institute, taught two years in public schools in Mamaroneck and Ghent, N. Y. Afterward, for three years, she conducted a home school in the house of her parents, having among her boarding pupils colored and Catholic children. She early developed the spirit of a reformer, and began active work in behalf of temperance; was identified with the abolitionists, and occasionally spoke at anti-slavery and woman's suffrage meetings. In the summer of 1863 she attended Dr. Dio Lewis's normal class in gymnastics in Boston, and next year she conducted classes in Cambridge, Boston, and Concord. Soon after the opening of Vassar College in 1865 she was appointed teacher of gymnastics, continuing in the position for five years; when she was employed as superintendent of the Free Congregational Sunday-school in Florence, Mass. In 1872 she was married to Henry Herick Bond (see volume II., p. 508), forthwith resigning most of her public work, though for a time editing with her husband the Northampton "Journal." She was selected a trustee of the Florence Kindergarten at its organization, and continued until 1891. The years 1879-81 were spent in the South in search of health for her husband, who died in 1881. In 1885 she became resident speaker of the Free Congregational Society, preparing written discourses for its Sunday meetings, and performing the social duties of a pastor. In 1886 she accepted the position of matron at Swarthmore College (a title changed in 1891 to dean), where she is still (1895) employed. Her son, Edwin Powell Bond, was graduated at Swarthmore in 1894, and is now in business in Frankford, Pa.

LINDSAY, John Summerfield, clergyman, was born in Williamsburgh, Va., March 19, 1842, son of Thomas Lindsay, an official in the Lunatic Asylum of that place. He comes of an ancient Scotch family, probably of the same branch as Sir David Lindsay, and his American ancestors served as soldiers in both the revolutionary war and the war of 1812. His early education was obtained at a private school, where he was prepared for college. He was graduated at William and Mary College in 1860, and the University of Virginia in 1866. He served as a minister of the Methodist Episcopal church for a short time in his youth, and acted as chaplain to the University of Virginia from 1865 until 1867. He then studied for the ministry of the Protestant Episcopal church, at the Theological Seminary of Virginia, and was graduated there in 1869 when he took his orders and was made rector of St. James Church, Warrenton, Va., and later of St. John's Church, Georgetown, D. C. From 1887 to 1889 he was rector of St. John's Church, Bridgeport, Conn. In 1889 he removed to Boston and became rector of St. Paul's Church. He is a member of the standing committee of the diocese of Massachusetts, a deputy to the general convention, and has twice been elected a bishop, each time declining the promotion. From 1883 until 1885 he was chaplain of the U. S. house of representatives. He has published several occasional review articles, sermons and addresses. William and Mary College conferred on him the degree of D.D. in 1881, and the University of the South in 1895. He was married in 1877, to Caroline W. Smith, who was born in Virginia, and brought up in Baltimore.

BRISTED, Charles Astor, author, was born in New York city, Oct. 6, 1820. He was the son of Rev. John Bristed and Magdalene B., the oldest daughter of John Jacob Astor. He was carefully trained until he entered Yale, where he took several prizes, and was graduated with honor in 1839. He afterwards spent five years at Trinity College, Cambridge, England, gaining the classical prize the first year and several other prizes, being graduated in 1845 with high honors, and elected foundation scholar of the college. He returned to the United States in 1847, and married the daughter of Henry Brevoort. He amused himself contributing articles, poetical translations, critical papers on the classics and sketches of society to various journals, and in 1849 edited "Selections from Catullus," for school use. In 1850 he published "Letters to the Hon. Horace Mann," being a reply to some strictures upon the characters of Girard and Astor. In 1852 a collection of his sketches of New York society appeared in the "Fraser Magazine." At the same time he published "Four Years in an English University," in which he described in a knowing collegiate style the manners, customs, and mode of

life but little understood in this country. Mr. Bristed exhibits in his writings a keen appreciation of the world of men and books. His wide scholarship makes his essays valuable, and his criticisms display the best qualities of a trained university man. He also published many clever poetical translations from the classics. He returned to America and resided at Washington, D. C., where he married as a second wife a member of the Sedgwick family. He was a frequent contributor to the "Galaxy," under the pen-name of "Carl Benson," and published "The Interference Theory of Governments," a book denunciatory of tariff and prohibitory liquor laws, and "Pieces of a Broken-down Critic." Mr. Bristed died in Washington, Jan. 15, 1874.

SCRIBNER, Charles, publisher, was born in New York city, Feb. 21, 1821. His grandfather, Matthew Scribner, a graduate of Yale College, was a Congregational minister, settled near Boston, Mass., and his father was Uriah R. Scribner, a successful New York merchant. Charles Scribner entered the University of the City of New York in 1837, continued there a year, and then entering Princeton College, was graduated there in 1840. He studied law with Charles King, of New York city, but his health broke down before his completion of study, and he made a trip to Europe. Returning to New York, he formed a partnership with Mr. Isaac D. Baker in the publishing of books, the firm beginning its business in Park Row, New York city.

From the first there was the distinction between this house and the others into which it grew, and other famous American publishers—it has never owned or been connected with a printing establishment. The first work which gave a success to the old house of Baker & Scribner was "Napoleon and his Marshals," by Rev. J. T. Headley, published in 1846. It was followed the same year by two others from Mr. Headley's pen, "Washington and his Generals" and "The Sacred Mountains." Over half a million of these works have been sold. This firm also became the publishers for Mr. N. P. Willis, Donald G. Mitchell, and J. G. Holland. Mr. Scribner being a Presbyterian, and a man of deep religious convictions, naturally undertook the publication of religious works, among others, the theological books of the Alexanders, Rev. Dr. Charles Hodge, and Rev. Dr. W. G. T. Shedd, Pres. Noah Porter, Rev. Dr. Horace Bushnell, Rev. Dr. Henry B. Smith, and Dr. James McCosh. In 1857 Mr. Scribner associated with himself Mr. Charles Welford, and organized the importing house of Scribner & Welford. About this time, moreover, the educational department of the house was thoroughly organized, and such books as Guyot's geographies, Sheldon's readers, Cooley's physical science, etc., were issued. This branch of business becoming very extensive, was sold in 1883 to Messrs. Ivison, Blakeman, Taylor & Co. The firm of "Charles Scribner" succeeded that of Baker & Scribner, Mr. Baker having died in 1848. Some years later Mr. Andrew C. Armstrong became a partner, and the style of the firm was changed to Charles Scribner & Co. In 1864 the first volume of the almost colossal "Commentary on the Holy Scriptures," by Rev. Dr. J. P. Lange, and extended to twenty-six volumes, was issued. In 1865 the issue of "House and Home," a monthly magazine, edited for years by Rev. Dr. J. C. Sherwood, and then by Mr. R. W. Gilder, began. This magazine was superseded (November, 1870) by "Scribner's Monthly," which was issued under the company name of Scribner & Co. Dr. Josiah G. Holland was its editor, and Mr. R. C. Smith its business conductor. The two gentlemen last named were also part owners. Mr. Charles Scribner having died, the firm was again reorganized, now as Scribner, Armstrong & Co., the partners being J. Blair Scribner (son of Charles), A. C. Armstrong, and Edward Seymour. Mr. Seymour dying in 1871, on July 12, 1878, the firm name was changed to Charles Scribner's Sons, Mr. Armstrong having retired. J. Blair Scribner died in 1879, and then the present house of Charles Scribner's Sons was formed, which has since continued, with Charles Scribner and Arthur H. Scribner as partners. In 1881 they sold their interest in the magazine so closely connected with their house to a new corporation, and it became the "Century Magazine." By the terms of sale, Messrs. Scribner were not to publish any magazine as competitor or rival for the term of five years from the date of this sale. But in January, 1887, they issued the first number of the now widely-known "Scribner's Magazine," with E. L. Burlingame as editor, and J. B. Millet as curator of the art department. This periodical is a magazine of general literature in the widest sense of the term, has no special lines, and is not the organ of a clique or coterie. The place it holds in American literature is already well assured. In the subscription department of the house among its most important publications have been: "Scribner's Statistical Atlas," "The Game Fishes," and the "Upland Game Birds and Waterfowl of the United States," "American Yachts," the "Trouvelot Astronomical Drawings," "Bryant's Popular History of the United States," Lieut. Greely's "Three Years of Arctic Service," and last, but by no means least, H. M. Stanley's "In Darkest Africa," published in 1890. The Messrs. Scribners also sell exclusively in the United States the authorized subscription edition of the "Encyclopædia Britannica," of which over 2,000,000 volumes have been sold in this country. Mr. Scribner died at Luzerne, Switzerland, Aug. 26, 1871.

PACKARD, John Hooker, physician, was born in Philadelphia, Pa., Aug. 15, 1832. His father was Frederick A. Packard, a philanthropist. His earliest American ancestor was Samuel Packard who came over in 1634. He was educated at the University of Pennsylvania, studied medicine under Prof. Joseph Leidy, took the degree of M.D. in 1853, and taught anatomy, surgery, and obstetrics for fifteen years. On June 8, 1858, he was married to Elizabeth, daughter of Charles S. and Indiana F. Wood. During the war he was an acting assistant surgeon, U. S. A., attending surgeon at the Christian street and Satterlee U. S. A. Hospitals, and consulting surgeon to those at Beverly, N. J., and Haddington, Pa., surgeon to the Episcopal Hospital from 1863 to 1884, to the Pennsylvania Hospital since 1884, and to St. Joseph's Hospital, Philadelphia, since 1880.

He was secretary of the College of Physicians of Philadelphia for fifteen years (1862-77); vice-president of same (1885-88); Mütter lecturer in the college from 1864 to 1866. He is a member of the American Medical Association, and State Medical Society of Pennsylvania, and County Medical Society of Philadelphia; and one of the founders of the Pathological and Obstetrical Societies of Philadelphia, and twice president of each; he is an original member of the American Surgical Association, and two years its treasurer. He has written, besides contributions to medical journals, a translation of Malgaigne's "Treatise on Fractures" (1859); "Hand-book of Minor Surgery" (1863); "Lectures on Inflammation" (1865); "Hand-book of Operative Surgery" (1870); articles on "Poisoned Wounds," and "Injuries of Bones," in Ashhurst's "Cyclopædia of Surgery" (1881); and on "Colotomy" and "Fractures and Dislocations," in Keating's "Cyclopædia of the Diseases of Children"

(1889). For many years he was engaged in general practice, but afterwards gave his attention almost altogether to surgery.

ATKINSON, George H., missionary, was born at Newburyport, Mass., May, 10, 1819, the eighth child of William and Anna Atkinson. His early years were spent in farm work and in obtaining such schooling as he could get, and in 1839, he entered Dartmouth College, where he was graduated in 1843. From there he went to the theological seminary at Andover, was graduated in 1846, and appointed by the American board of commissioners of foreign missions to do missionary work among the Zulus, but upon the earnest solicitation of the American Home Missionary Society, this appointment was rescinded and he was sent to Oregon, at that time the only territory on the Pacific coast. On Oct. 8, 1846, he married Nancy Bates, of Springfield, Vt., by whom he had six children. On Jan. 24, 1847, Mr. Atkinson was ordained at Newbury, Vt., the home of his parents and in the following October, sailed from Boston, via Cape Horn and the Sandwich Islands for his mission. At Honolulu he was obliged to wait three months for a vessel bound for Oregon, and it was not until June 12, 1848, that he crossed the Columbia river bar in a Hudson's Bay Co.'s vessel. He settled in Oregon City, where he remained for fifteen years as pastor in a Congregational church. He then became pastor of the First Congregational Church of Portland, Ore., and remained with that church for ten years. Mr. Atkinson devoted himself in all his leisure time to pushing forward the cause of education in the territory, and it was through his efforts that the public school system was established by the legislature in 1849. He was himself school superintendent at Portland, and rendered efficient and active service in building up the excellent system of public schools which was eventually established in that city. He founded in Oregon, the academy which afterwards became the Pacific University, of which he was one of the original incorporators, and for more than forty years secretary of its board of trustees. In 1872, Dr. Atkinson became general missionary for Oregon, and in 1880 superintendent of home missions for Oregon and Washington. He died in Portland, Ore., Feb. 25, 1889.

MELINE, James Florant, author, was born in the U. S. garrison at Sackett's Harbor, N. Y., in 1811, his father, a Frenchman of Swedish extraction, was at the time a lieutenant in the U. S. army. He was educated at Mount St. Mary's College, but was unable to complete the course, being forced by the death of both his parents to earn his own living. He went to Cincinnati, where he became a teacher of music, one of the professors in the Athenæum, and an assistant-editor of the "Catholic Telegraph." He also studied law at odd moments, and was admitted to the bar. Soon after he made an extended trip to Europe. On his return he engaged in the practice of law for a term of years, but finally exchanged this for banking, in which he continued until 1860, having in the meantime made a second visit to Europe for purposes of study and holding there several foreign consulates. In July, 1862, he entered the Federal army as major and judge advocate on the staff of Maj.-Gen. Pope, serving throughout the war, and acquiring the rank of colonel. In 1865 and 1866 he accompanied Gen. Pope on an official tour through the West and Southwest, and from 1866 to 1868, he was chief of the bureau of civil affairs in the third military district (Georgia, Alabama, and Florida), at the same time acting as regular correspondent of the "Cincinnati Commercial" and the New York "Tribune." He spent the remainder of his life in New York city, in literary pursuits, being a frequent contributor to the New York newspapers and to the "Galaxy," "Nation," and "Catholic World." In the winter of 1872–73 he delivered a course of lectures on English literature at Seton Hall College, the College of the Christian Brothers, and the Academy of the Sacred Heart. He is the author of "Two Thousand Miles on Horseback," and of "Mary, Queen of Scots and her Latest Historian," a scathing criticism of one of the best-known works of the historian, Froude. He died in New York city, Aug. 14, 1878.

COFFIN, William Anderson, artist and author, was born in Allegheny City, Pa., Jan. 31, 1855. He is a direct descendant in the eighth generation from Tristram Coffin, who came to Massachusetts from Devon, England, in 1642, and afterward became possessor of the greater part of Nantucket Island. His son, Tristram, Jr., settled in Newbury, Mass., where his house, built in 1652, is still standing and occupied by his descendants. Our subject's grandparents removed thence to Ohio in 1815, where his father, James Gardner Coffin, a prominent business man of Pittsburgh, Pa., was born the following year. William A. Coffin entered Yale College, and was graduated with the degree of A.B. in 1874. While a senior he began the study of drawing in the art school of the university, and resumed it during the term of 1875–76. In 1877 he went to Paris, where he became a pupil of Léon Bonnat and studied nearly five years, finally returning to America in 1882. He exhibited in the Paris Salon in 1879, 1880 and 1882, and his pictures are now "exempt" from examination by the jury of admission. He began exhibiting at the Society of American Artists in New York in 1881, and has since been a regular contributor, as also to the National Academy of Design, the American Water-Color Society, the New York Water-Color Club, and other exhibitions, in New York, Boston, Philadelphia, Chicago, etc. In 1886 he was elected a member of the Society of American Artists, and was its secretary for five years from 1887. He is a member of the Architectural League of New York, and was its vice-president for two years. He was one of the founders of Municipal Art Society, holding the office of first vice-president; also one of the founders of the American Fine Arts Society. He was awarded the second Hallgarten prize at the Academy of Design in 1886 for his picture "Moonlight in Harvest;" and in 1891 received the Webb prize for landscape at the Society of American Artists for his picture "The Rain," which was purchased by a committee of gentlemen and placed in the Metropolitan Museum of Art, New York. At the Paris Exposition in 1889, where he exhibited four pictures, he was awarded a bronze medal by the international jury. He was a member of the fine arts jury at New York for the Paris Exposition of 1889, and exhibited six landscapes. Some of his best known paintings are: "A Modern Painting Academy;" "An Inn in Brittany" (Paris Salon, 1879); "The Mandolin Player;" "Le Père

Jean" (Paris Salon, 1880); "After Breakfast" (owned by Thomas B. Clarke, N. Y.); "Early Moonrise," and "The September Breeze" (W. Seward Webb); "A July Evening" (Andrew Carnegie); "Evening" (Wm. E. Dodge); "Starlight" (Richard W. Gilder); "Sunset" (Mrs. John L. Gardner, Boston), and many others. He is also well known as a writer on subjects connected with art, having been art critic of the "Evening Post" and "Nation" for five years, 1880–91. He wrote for the "Nation" a series of critical articles on the fine arts at the Paris Exposition of 1889, and another series on the Columbian Exposition of 1893. He has contributed critical and biographical articles to the "Century," "Scribner's Magazine" and "Harper's Weekly," and has delivered lectures on art in various parts of the country. He was one of the judges of award at the Cotton States and International Exposition (fine arts department), at Atlanta, Ga., in 1895. He has a studio in New York city, and another on the slope of the Alleghanies in Somerset county, Pa. He is a member of the Players and City Clubs of New York.

FENN, Harry, artist, was born in Richmond, Surrey, England, Sept. 14, 1837, where his father, James Fenn, was engaged in business. He was connected with a titled family on the parental side. He was educated at Richmond. At a very early age he displayed an unusual aptitude with brush and pencil, struggling alone to train his eye for form and color through boyhood. He then took lessons in drawing, and soon became a skilful artist. His first work was as a wood engraver, but he soon abandoned that for the pencil. When about nineteen he came on a visit to America, ostensibly to see Niagara. The visit lasted for six years, when he went to Italy for a short term of study. He devoted himself to illustrating from nature, and soon made a wide reputation for his work. Returning to the United States, Mr. Fenn made an extended tour in 1870, gathering material for "Picturesque America." So great had been the success of "Snow-Bound," and "Ballads of New England," the first illustrated gift-books produced in this country, that Messrs. Appleton & Co. ventured the large undertaking involved in the production of the picturesque series. The "Picturesque America" had its origin in Mr. Fenn's overhearing an Englishman sneeringly say that the scenery of America had nothing picturesque about it. Mr. Fenn remarked in the hearing of the heads of the house, "If they will make it worth my while, we will show the young man if there is anything picturesque in America." Nothing more was said about the subject until several months had elapsed, and Mr. Fenn had forgotten the incident, when he received a letter from the Appletons, asking him to come over and talk to them about that suggestion he had made. The interview resulted in the inception of that magnificent publication. About this time Harry Fenn helped to organize the Water-Color Society of New York. In 1873 he went to Europe, to make sketches for "Picturesque Europe," and subsequently spent two winters in the Orient for the last of the trio, "Picturesque Palestine, Sinai, and Egypt." He returned to America in 1881, and has since that time spent his energies in water-color painting and illustrating, reaping the harvest of experience of travels in Europe, Asia, Africa, and America. Mr. Fenn has an extraordinary capacity for work. Of a nervous temperament, he has a

power of sticking to things, which has enabled him to produce an enormous amount of work, and placed him in the foremost rank in the artistic world. He resides in Montclair, N. J., where he has built a handsome residence. Most of his summers are spent in some picturesque neighborhood, of mountain or lake scenery, so attractive to the artist mind; or in travel abroad or at home. In religious faith Mr. Fenn is a Congregationalist, and is an active member of the First Congregational Church of Montclair. He was married to Miss Marian Tompson, in Brooklyn, N. Y., Sept. 5, 1852.

NEEDHAM, Charles Austin, artist, was born in Buffalo, N. Y., Oct. 30, 1844, son of Elias Parkman Needham, inventor. He was brought to New York when four years old, educated mainly in the public schools of the city, and passed the examination for admission to the Free Academy (afterward known as the College of the City of New York). In this institution he distinguished himself in art studies and in natural science, winning in 1862 the Ward medal for natural history, at the expense, however, of all his other classes. He was not graduated, as an inborn distaste for systematic methods, added to his ambition to engage in active business, would not wait for the laggard step of a college course. He engaged in the manufacture of condensed milk, an industry then in its infancy. He afterward joined his father in the manufacture of reed organs, as a partner, and here developed not only administrative but constructive genius. He introduced, and had patented, a number of important inventions. The cares of business, as the duties of school life and the play of childhood, never won his mind from his love of art, and his pencil was always busy, and his studio was his retreat when he sought recreation. For years he devoted his evenings to study under a master. Though always chafing under conventional methods, he became proficient in drawing, in painting in oil and water-colors, and in etching. He made a careful study of portraiture, and called to his aid the camera, with which he soon became an expert, and has since contributed instructive articles to the literature of photography. Mr. Needham's works in all the departments of his art have been exhibited at the annual displays in the National Academy of Design. They have been exhibited as well by the American Water-Color Society, the New York Etching Club, the Water-Color Club, and other special art institutions in New York and Brooklyn, the Boston Art Club, the Art Institute of Chicago, the St. Louis Museum of Fine Arts, and the art exhibitions in Philadelphia, Detroit, and Indianapolis. At the Columbian World's Fair in Chicago, in 1893, he exhibited three pieces—the oil paintings: "Mott Haven Canal, New York," "Near Factory Hollow, Turner's Falls, Mass."; and the water-color: "Dream of Autumn." The latter picture was placed by request of the World's Fair art committee in charge of the selection from the works exhibited at the Academy of Design by the American Water-Color Society. His "Mott Haven Canal" is probably one of the most effective of his productions. In 1895, when it was exhibited at the Mechanics' Building in Boston, it was aptly characterized as a "grand picture," setting forth the "magnificence of the commonplace as means to an end."

Alexr. Young

YOUNG, Alexander, manufacturer, was born in county Donegal, Ireland, Aug. 26, 1798. At an early age he emigrated to America, landing in Philadelphia July 15, 1821. He already had some knowledge of the malt distilling business, and being desirous of learning the art of extracting whiskey from raw grain, he obtained employment in J. W. Dower's distillery on the Schuylkill river, giving for his instruction $50 in cash, and many months' services. He soon acquired a thorough knowledge of the business, and determined to try his own fortune as a distiller. Although he had held a subordinate position, and for only one year, he had nevertheless saved money enough to purchase a small still, and he commenced business for himself. After one year he went into partnership with John Maitland, and for two years they carried on the business together, producing a very pure and excellent kind of malt whiskey, which still retains its then worthy celebrity. They also, at one time, distilled New England rum from molasses, and were the first firm to discover the process by which a large increase of spirit was obtained from the grain, having produced fourteen quarts of pure whiskey from fifty-six pounds of grain. In 1825 John Maitland secured a large building at the corner of Charles and South streets, Philadelphia, formerly used as a theatre—the Apollo. At a cost of $20,000 he fitted up this building as a distillery, thus inaugurating, with Mr. Young as foreman, a much larger enterprise than their former one. For twelve years they continued in this way, making important discoveries and improvements in the business, and founding, as it afterward proved, one of the largest and richest establishments in Philadelphia. In 1837 John Maitland's son, William J. Maitland, went into partnership with Mr. Young, these two continuing the business until the death of Maitland in 1847, when Mr. Young bought out the establishment for $20,000. Ten years later Mr. Maitland, Sr., died, but at that time he had no connection with Mr. Young. As soon as the business came entirely under the control of the latter, he at once commenced to enlarge and improve it, spending in a few years over $60,000 on the building and machinery, and adding every improvement and extension that could increase the value of the whole. Mr. Young was perhaps one of the few distillers who could truly claim that he made his whiskey from pure, sound grain. He purchased only the best rye, barley, corn, and wheat; buying and selling only for cash, and distilling from hops and pure water. So careful was he about the latter article that he had an artesian well dug on his own premises, which threw up seventy gallons a minute of the purest water for distilling purposes. The business founded by Mr. Young has grown to great proportions, and is now successfully handled by members of his family. Thousands and thousands of gallons of the purest whiskey, known as "Young's Pure Malt Whiskey," are annually distilled and sold, and the greatest care is maintained to keep up the pristine purity of the product. The extensive plant occupies the old site at Charles and South streets, between Fourth and Fifth streets, Philadelphia. Mr. Young was a man of plain parts and dress, modest demeanor, and thoroughly scrupulous and honest. His wealth and position were won by his own energy and industry, and his name has become the synonym for probity and uprightness. He died Nov. 24, 1884, leaving three sons and one daughter, and a large number of grandchildren.

COX, Samuel Sullivan, statesman, was born in Zanesville, O., Sept. 30, 1824. His grandfather was Gen. James Cox, of Monmouth, N. J., a soldier in the Revolution, who fought in the battles of the Brandywine, Germantown, and Monmouth. Mr. Cox's father was Ezekiel Taylor Cox, a prominent Democrat, and in 1832–33 a member of the Ohio senate, who, in 1818, married the daughter of Samuel Sullivan, state treasurer of Ohio, after whom he named his son. The latter, after studying in the public schools of Zanesville, entered the Ohio University, at Athens, and afterwards Brown University, Providence, R. I., where he was graduated in 1846. Having determined to adopt the law as his profession, Mr. Cox went to Cincinnati and entered the office of a Mr. Worthington, and from that time until 1851 devoted himself to the study of law. In the latter year he crossed the ocean, and traveled through Europe; and, on his return, published a description of his tour, which he called "The Buckeye Abroad." Mr. Cox had natural gifts in the direction of literature, and, even while in college, he was able to assist in maintaining himself by his literary work, besides obtaining prizes in classics, history, literature, and political economy. In 1853 he went to Columbus, O., where he assumed the position of editor of the "Ohio Statesman," and from this time forward interested himself in political affairs. It was shortly after this period that the *sobriquet* of "Sunset" Cox began to be applied to him. The occasion for this was an article he wrote entitled, "The Great Sunset," and in which occurred the following passage: "What a stormful sunset was that of last night! How glorious the storm, and how splendid the setting of the sun! We do not remember ever having seen the like on our round globe. The scene opened in the West, with the whole horizon full of golden inter-penetrating lustre, which covered the foliage and brightened every bough in its own rich dyes. The colors grew deeper and richer until the golden lustre was transformed into a storm-cloud full of finest lightnings, which leaped in dazzling zigzags all over and around the city. The wind arose in fury. The tender shrubs and giant trees made obeisance to its majesty—some even snapped before its force. The strawberry beds and grass plats 'turned up their whites' to see Zephyrus march by. Then the rains came, and the pools and gutters filled rapidly and hurried away; the thunders roared grandly, and the fire-bells caught the excitement and rang with hearty chorus. The South and the East received the copious showers, and the West at one time brightened up into a border-line of azure worthy of a Sicilian sky." This

style of writing was a new feature in Ohio journalism, and as the title "Sunset" chanced to agree with Mr. Cox's two initials, and as the article in question achieved a wide newspaper popularity, he was ever after alluded to in the press as "Sunset" Cox. From his entrance into journalism and political life Mr. Cox was a Democrat. In 1855 President Pierce offered him the position of secretary of legation at the American Embassy in London. He declined this position, but afterwards accepted that of secretary of legation at Lima, Peru; but on his arrival at the Isthmus of Panama, while *en route* there, was seized by an attack of the local fever, and was obliged to return home; whereupon he resigned the office. In 1857 Mr. Cox began his long period of legislative service, having been elected to congress on Dec. 7th from the old Licking-Franklin district of Ohio. It happened that his speech on the Lecompton constitution, was the first delivered in the new hall of representatives in the capitol at Washington, on the day when it was first occupied for legislative business, Dec. 16, 1857. In the debate on the important questions under consideration Mr. Cox soon made an impression upon the house. His active mind and keen foresight anticipated the possible consequences of raising a sectional issue, and from this time forward he used his best efforts to accommodate the questions at issue, and provide, if possible, for a peaceful solution of them. During the administrations of Buchanan and Lincoln, including the stirring years of the civil war, Mr. Cox was three times re-elected to congress from Ohio. During the war he sustained the government by voting for money and men to put an end to it, although he not infrequently differed from the policy of the administration. In 1863 Mr. Cox was the Democratic candidate for speaker of the house of representatives in opposition to Schuyler Colfax; but, as the Republican party was in the majority in the house, he was defeated. In 1865 Mr. Cox published a volume entitled, "Eight Years in Congress," in which he presented his observations and experience while a member of the house of representatives up

to that time. He was defeated in his district in Ohio for a re-election in 1865. He was married in early life to Julia Buckingham, a young lady of Muskingum county, O. He had by this time obtained a national reputation, not only as an able representative in congress, but as a brilliant, humorous, and popular campaign speaker. He foresaw that Ohio was going to be a Republican state, and wishing to live where his party held the supremacy, in 1866 he changed his residence from Ohio to New York city. The wisdom of this change was made apparent by his election, in 1868, to the forty-first congress as representative of New York city. In 1869 Mr. Cox paid another visit to Europe, during which excursion he traveled through Italy and northern Africa. He busied himself in writing during his tour, and on his arrival in London on his way home, published an account of his journey, entitled, "A Search for Winter Sunbeams." This work was afterward reprinted in the United States. In 1870 he ran against Horace Greeley for congress, beating him by about 1,000 votes. Two years later he was defeated by Lyman Tremain for congressman-at-large; he was, however, elected to the same congress, to fill the vacancy caused by the death of James Brooks. From this time forward, up to the day of his death, Mr. Cox was re-elected continuously as a member of congress from the city of New York. At the opening of the forty-fifth congress, in 1877, Mr. Cox was once more a candidate for the speakership, and, although he was never elected to that position, his knowledge of parliamentary law, and his appreciation of the amenities of legislative intercourse, made his services extremely valuable, and he frequently served as speaker *pro tem*. During the forty-fifth congress Mr. Cox took upon himself, by special resolution, the work of the new census law, which he successfully advocated, being also the author of the plan of apportionment adopted by the house. The ability with which he handled this important matter drew

from Gen. Francis A. Walker, the distinguished statistician and economist, who superintended the tenth census, a graceful and most flattering public testimonial. In his treatment of legislative questions, Mr. Cox was a close student of every subject which would throw any light upon them. He always aimed at obtaining for the people of the United States the widest liberty of industry, trade, and self-government. He was the introducer and champion for many years of an important bill concerning the life-saving service, and finally witnessed its passage; and also introduced and carried through a bill for the protection of immigrants, and for the inspection of steamships, which put an end to many scandalous abuses. His work in congress also brought about the raising of the salaries of letter-carriers, and the granting them a vacation without loss of pay; an action which made the letter-carriers of the country his firm friends for all time. During all the long period in which Mr. Cox was a metropolitan congressman, he took a prominent part in almost every important debate which occupied the attention of the house, sustaining the interests of the city of New York by every means in his power. He opposed high tariff and monopolies. Mr. Cox was for many years a regent of the Smithsonian Institution. He was on important special committees of the house, such as the one appointed to investigate the doings of "Black Friday," and the one on the Ku-Klux-Klan troubles. In the summer of 1881 he made his third trip to Europe, during which he visited Holland, Norway, Sweden, Russia, Turkey, Egypt, and Greece. One of the first acts of President Cleveland, on taking his seat in the presidential chair, in 1885, was to appoint Mr. Cox minister to Turkey, which resulted in the most happy manner. He made a very favorable impression upon the Sultan, and, during his stay in Turkey, was successful in clearing up several diplomatic complications. He resigned, however, at the end of one year, and at the close of his embassy, both Mr. and Mrs. Cox were decorated by the Sultan. On his return to the United States he was re-elected to congress. Besides the works mentioned, he has published, "Puritanism in Politics" (1863); "Why We Laugh" (1876); "Arctic Sunbeams" (1882); "Orient Sunbeams," and "The Three Decades of Federal Legislation" (1885). His death was felt as a national loss. It occurred just after his return from a visit to the four new states of the Northwest, which, in congress, he had been largely instrumental in creating. The strain of this long journey, with its sightseeing and public speaking, proved to be more than his constitution could bear, and he died at his residence in New York, No. 13 East Twelfth street, Sept. 12, 1889.

WHEELER, John Hill, historian, was born in Murfreesboro', N. C., Aug. 6, 1806. His first ancestor in America was Joseph Wheeler, a son of Adm. Sir Francis Wheeler, who, armed with a grant of land from Charles II. given to his father as a reward for faithful services, emigrated from England with his wife and young son, Ephraim, and settled in New Jersey where the city of Newark now stands. Ephraim Wheeler's son, John Wheeler, born in 1744, was the first American of the family. His parents gave him an excellent education and he became a prominent physician. He accompanied Gen. Montgomery on his expedition to Quebec and took part in the battle in which his general was killed. Dr. Wheeler also accompanied Gen. Greene in his southern campaign, remaining with his command until the end of the war. The genial climate of the South lured him to make his home there, and with his family he settled in Murfreesboro', N. C., where he died Oct. 14, 1814. His son, John Wheeler, was born in 1771, and in his youth was engaged with David Longworth as a publisher and book seller in New

York city. He afterward removed to Berten county, N. C., and from there to Murfreesboro', his birth place, where he engaged in business as a merchant and shipper until his death, Aug. 7, 1882. He was the father of John Hill Wheeler, the historian. The latter was educated at the Columbian University, Washington, D. C., being graduated in the class of 1826. He received from the University of North Carolina the degree of A. M. in 1828, having pursued his law studies under Chief-Justice Taylor of North Carolina. He was elected a member of the state legislature in 1827, a year before he was admitted to the bar. In 1830 he was nominated for congress, but defeated by an older and more experienced candidate. In 1831 he was secretary of the board of commissioners under the treaty with France to adjudicate the French spoliative claims under the Berlin and Milan decrees. In 1836 President Jackson appointed him superintendent of the U. S. mint at Charlotte, N. C., holding the office until 1841. In 1842 the state legislature elected him state treasurer. For the next ten years he devoted himself to collecting material for and preparing his "History of North Carolina," published in 1851. In 1852 he was elected to the state legislature, and in 1853 President Pierce appointed him U. S. minister to Nicaragua. The revolution in that country and the advent of Willie Walker and his followers and their establishing of a liberal government with their leader as president, were incidents of Mr. Wheeler's ministration. He thought he saw in Walker's movement and in the government he proposed to establish, the only hope for the peace of the country and promptly recognized his authority. Secretary Marcy disapproved of his actions and he asked to be recalled. The president refused to recall him. He, however, resigned his mission in 1857 and made his home in the national capital, retaining, however, his loyalty to his native state, and acknowledging his legal residence to be North Carolina, the name of which was always coupled with his own upon his door-plate. He engaged in statistical labors and made a journey to Europe to gather material for an enlarged "History of North Carolina." He was author of "A Legislative Manual of North Carolina" (1874); "Reminiscences and Memoirs of North Carolina" (published after his death at Columbus, O., 1884). He also edited Col. David Fanning's "Autobiography" (1861). He died in Washington, D. C., Dec. 7, 1882.

ANTHONY, Daniel Read, pioneer and editor, was born at South Adams, Mass., Aug. 22, 1824. His parents were Daniel and Lucy Anthony, of whom the father belonged to the Society of Friends. He was a man of resolute will and remarkable force of character, who died at the age of sixty-nine at Rochester, N. Y., leaving one son, besides Daniel Read Anthony, and five daughters, among them Susan Anthony, a leader of the woman suffrage movement in the United States. His maternal grandfather, Daniel Read, of South Adams, Mass., served in the war of the American revolution, and died at the age of eighty-three years. The subject of this sketch was educated at a common school at Battenville, N. Y., until he was thirteen years old, when he went to an academy (at Union Village, N. Y.) for six months, and then labored for his father in his cotton mill as a clerk, and in his flour mill. When he was twenty-three years of age he removed to Rochester, N. Y., taught school for two winters, and was then engaged in the insurance business until the outbreak of the civil war. In July, 1854, he visited the state of Kansas with the first colony sent out by the New England Emigrant Aid Society, under command of Eli Thayer, of Massachusetts, and while there helped to found the city of Lawrence. He located permanently in Kansas, at Leavenworth, in June, 1857, and has resided there until the present time. In 1861 he became lieutenant-colonel of the 1st Kansas cavalry, afterward known as the 7th Kansas Volunteers. In June, 1862, being in command of Brig.-Gen. R. B. Mitchell's brigade, with headquarters at Camp Etheridge, Tenn., he issued his "General Order, No. 26," declaring: (1) that "The impudence and impertinence of the open and armed rebels, traitors, secessionists, and southern-rights men, in arrogantly demanding the right to search our camp for fugitive slaves, has become a nuisance, and will no longer be tolerated. Officers will see that this class of men who visit our camp for this purpose, are excluded from our lines. (2) Should any such persons be found within our lines, they will be arrested and sent to headquarters. (3) Any officer or soldier of this command who shall arrest and deliver to his master a fugitive slave, shall be summarily and severely punished, according to the laws relative to such crimes." He carried out the letter and spirit of this order, with his own command, and refused to countermand it when ordered to do so by Gen. Mitchell, who thereupon had him arrested for insubordination. The senate of the United States taking cognizance of the matter, directed President Lincoln to communicate, at his discretion, to their body any information in his possession as to the reasons of this arrest; and within sixty days from its having been made, U. S. Gen. Halleck restored Col. Anthony to active duty, being fully satis-fied that public sentiment sustained his course. He resigned from the U. S. service after having been in it a little more than a year. In March, 1863, he was elected mayor of Leavenworth by a large majority, and signalized his administration by clearing the city and its outskirts of gangs of lawless characters who up to that time had kept the people of Leavenworth, who were loyal to the U. S. government, in constant terror. This was done in the abatement of the nuisance by heroic treatment: the houses which sheltered the miscreants being burned, one after the other, while several of the most prominent and respectable citizens stood guard over the premises until all were destroyed. Subsequently, valuable and permanent public improvements were made, and the city, freed from an incubus which had hampered its advancement, made decided growth in population. A conflict between the energetic mayor and U. S. Gen. Ewing, commanding the district of the Border (1863) over the seizure of some horses in Leavenworth by Gen. Ewing's detectives, this federal officer having previously put the district under martial law, brought on Mayor Anthony's arrest by Ewing for "interfering with the military authorities of the United States in the discharge of their duties," but after being taken to Kansas City, thirty miles away, and held as a prisoner for a few hours, Mayor Anthony was unconditionally released and brought back to Leavenworth the next evening. Here he was greeted by almost all the population of the city, and the speech he made to them exhibited the independence of the man, and reflected the spirit of the "times that tried men's souls" in that region and period. He said, in part: "Men of Leavenworth: Yesterday I was brutally arrested and marched out of town with two thieves at my side, followed by a company of soldiers with cocked revolvers pointed at my back. To-night I return to Leavenworth, my home, escorted by a committee of ten of your truest and best men, sent by you to Kansas City, to demand my release and the revocation of the order declaring martial law. . . . . Yesterday I marched between two thieves. To-day their heads lie in the dust. Yesterday martial law reigned in Leavenworth. To-day it is scattered to the four winds of heaven. Yesterday we were despondent. To-day we are triumphant." The worthy mayor, in point of fact, had relied for support in the position he had taken upon the orders of the general commanding the department to protect him in refusing to be interfered with in the discharge of his own duties by the agents of a subordinate officer; and the order of Ewing, declaring martial law in Leavenworth, than which no community had been, as a whole, more loyal to the union, was countermanded simultaneously with Anthony's release. The rest of his municipal administration was marked by the prevalence of law and order. In 1868 he was chairman of the Kansas Republican state convention, and since then has had various honors bestowed upon him by his fellow-citizens. His record as a journalist may be succinctly set down: In January, 1861, he established the "Leavenworth Conservative;" in March, 1864, his purchase of the "Bulletin" was consummated, and in 1871 he bought the Leavenworth "Times." In 1876 he became the owner of the Leavenworth "Commercial," and then, having control of the newspaper "situation," united all the morning papers of the city under one proprietorship and management, in "The Leavenworth Times," now one of the most extensive and profitable newspaper establishments in the West. The intensity of the personal contests in which Col. Anthony has been engaged in the border life of which he has long been a part, is illustrated by the fact that on May 10, 1875, he was assaulted and shot by an opponent, the bullet passing through his shoulder and lodging in his body. His recovery from the effects of the injury has been regarded as making his case one of the most notable in the record of gunshot wounds. Col. Anthony married Annie E. Osborn, of Edgartown, Mass., Jan. 21, 1864.

O'NEIL, Daniel Edwin, physician, was born at Shark River, N. J., Nov. 26, 1847. He was descended from revolutionary ancestors, who fought

the Hessians, and who have been subsequently identified with the growth of this country. He was educated at Manhattan College, from which he was graduated in 1868, when a predilection for a medical career led him to enter the medical department of the University of the City of New York, from which he was graduated in 1869. Later, he became a special student of Dr. A. L. Loomis. He commenced practice in 1869 as house surgeon at St. Vincent's Hospital, and shortly afterward settled in Hudson street, New York city, in which same block he has remained for twenty-four years. Dr. O'Neil has devoted himself particularly to obstetrics, in which specialty he has achieved a wide reputation, and obtained an extensive practice, which has sometimes included 300 obstetrical cases in a single year. He has been called in consultation in many of the critical operations in his specialty. He was appointed, in 1875, visiting and consulting physician to St. Joseph's Home for the Aged. Dr. O'Neil is a member of the Medico-Legal Association, and several other medical societies. In 1884 he married Anna Eliza Redmond, daughter of a New York merchant. He

is devoted to his profession, and attributes his success to his assiduity in the performance of its duties.

COBB, Thomas Reed Rootes, lawyer, and younger brother of Howell Cobb, the statesman, was born at Cherry Hill, Jefferson co., Ga., Apr. 10, 1823. His grandfather, Howell Cobb of Virginia, was a distinguished Georgia congressman from 1807 to 1812. His father, John A. Cobb, and his mother, Sarah Rootes of Virginia, were married in a house in sight of which their son was killed. Thomas was graduated with first honors at the Georgia State University in 1841, with the highest mark ever taken there, and was admitted to the bar and began a large law practice at Athens, Ga., in 1842. He became one of the university trustees and took an active interest in the cause of education. He was reporter of the Georgia supreme court from 1849 to 1857, when he resigned; one of the original codifiers of the Georgia code of 1863, doing an important part of that work, which has

been the law of Georgia for thirty years; delegate to the Georgia secession convention, January, 1861, and member of the secession ordinance committee, and chairman of the committee on the constitution; author of the state Confederate constitution under which Georgia was governed seven years; member of the Confederate provisional congress, and on the committee that drafted the permanent Confederate constitution, of which historic paper his widow has the original copy; and though not a candidate, he received a strong vote for C. S. senator. He was commissioned colonel of Cobb's Legion, August, 1861, and brigadier-general C. S. army, November, 1862. Gen. Cobb was one of the greatest lawyers, not only of Georgia, but of the South, with marvelous industry, acumen, and learning, herculean power of work, and a creative mind for originating codes and constitutions. He was profoundly versed in legal principles, and a prodigious master of legal lore, and, taking the foremost rank as an advocate, became a legal authority in his state. He took no part in politics until Lincoln's election impressed him with the danger to slavery and southern equality in the Union, when he threw himself into the effort for a separation as the best hope of southern institutions. His enthusiasm and influence were irresistible, and carried the state. Alex. H. Stephens, who was on the other side, compared the eloquent Cobb to Peter the Hermit, and ascribed to his potential power the success of secession. He displayed capacity and heroism as an officer and made a brilliant reputation. His death before he was forty years old, on a great battlefield in the zenith of his usefulness, was a loss to his cause and a shock to his state. He was a zealous member of the Presbyterian church and an active religious worker. He took a deep interest in education and founded the Lucy Cobb Institute at Athens, Ga., named after his daughter, which has become one of the leading female colleges of the country, and curiously he began the project on an anonymous suggestion in the press by his own sister. He published a "Digest of the Laws of Georgia" (1851); "Inquiry into the Law of Negro Slavery in the United States" (1858); "Historical Sketch of Slavery from the Earliest Periods" (Philadelphia, 1859), and some able papers for a state scheme of public schools. His library was one of the finest in the North, and contained valuable books in all languages, bought to verify the statements in his writings. He married Marion McHenry, daughter of Chief-Justice Lumpkin, in Lexington, Ga. Among his children are the wives of Henry Jackson, Hoke

Smith, and A. L. Hull. His moral, domestic, and social excellencies were as beautiful as his intellectual powers were extraordinary. He was killed at the battle of Fredericksburg, Dec. 13, 1862.

MILLER, William, founder of the sect of Adventists or "Millerites," was born Feb. 5, 1782, at Pittsfield, Mass. He was the son of Capt. William Miller, who fought in the revolution and in the war of 1812. On his mother's side, he was descended from Elnathan Phelps, a popular Baptist clergyman of Pittsfield, from whom he inherited his strong religious temperament and morbid tendencies. Although he was obliged to remain on the farm, he early had a craving for books and learning, and saved money from chopping wood to buy "Robinson Crusoe" and the "Adventures of Robert Boyle." His energy of character made him prosperous, and he acquired a farm of 200 acres. At the beginning of the war of 1812 he became recruiting officer, and after serving in the field, was made captain at Plattsburg. After the war he held various offices of honor in his town, being at different times justice of the peace, constable, and sheriff. He was a great admirer of Hume, Voltaire, and Tom Paine, and supported their doctrines, but in after years he became converted to Christianity and joined the Baptist Church at Low Hampton; when he became intensely interested in the study of the Bible, to such an extent that, as he wrote of himself, "I lost all taste for other reading." Without any guide or assistance other than the Concordance and a Polyglot Bible, he studied word by word, from Genesis to Revelation, and became convinced that he had been given the key to unlock the mystery of the prophecies which foretold the end of the world and of all things temporal, and the beginning of the millennium. This date he fixed between the equinoxes of 1843-44, when Jesus Christ would appear in person to judge the world. While he was never ordained, the Baptist Church at Low Hampton licensed him to preach, and he went through the country preaching in groves and public places to multitudes, who flocked to hear him demonstrate the mystical problem of the 2,300 days of Daniel's vision, proving the exact time when the "third woe" must be sounded. In 1839 he made his first appearance in Boston as a prophet—"a reed shaken with the palsy." He helped to organize the "Signs of the Times," afterward the "Advent Herald," the first Millerite organ. John Greenleaf Whittier, in describing his meetings, says, "Suspended in front of the rude pulpit were two broad sheets of canvas, upon one of which was the figure of a man, the head of gold, the arms of silver, the belly of brass, the legs of iron, and the feet of clay; on the other was depicted the wonders of the Apocalypse, the beasts, dragons, the scarlet woman seen by the seer of Patmos—Oriental types, figures, and mystic symbols translated into staring Yankee realities, and exhibited like beasts in a traveling menagerie." The connection between the seventy weeks of Daniel and the 2,300 days was the point of his argument, which was the interpretation of the "time, times and a half" of Daniel, upon which his calculations of destruction rested. The clew which Miller thought he had found was in the fact that the tenth day of the seventh month was that of the great day of atonement. On March 14, 1844, Father Miller closed the diary of his labors, and reckoned up his 3,200 lectures given since 1832. When, March, April, and May had come, he acknowledged his disappointment, but not his unbelief.

Then October was the month set. "The Lord will certainly leave his mercy-seat on the 13th, and appear visibly in the clouds of heaven on the 22nd. During this interval secular business was suspended among the Adventists. Muslin for ascension robes was freely given away, tradesmen closed their shops, and all repaired to the fields, while the ungodly disturbed the meetings with rotten eggs, crackers, and toy torpedoes. When the sun rose on the 23d the sad prophet could only say, "Here I mean to stand until God gives me more light, and that is to-day, to-day, and to-day, until He comes." There were many offshoots of the fanaticism. In their disappointment, some asserted that the Lord *had* come, and closed the door of mercy to the sinner. Then arose a contention between the orthodox and the "shut door" party as to which should win over Father Miller. Those who were opposed to the churches, and called upon believers in the blessed hope to come out of her, and who were chiefly from Cape Cod, made a joint convention at Groton with the Adventists, which was the name adopted by the new sect. Many returned to the churches, but the majority, some 50,000, still clung to their leader, and held to the doctrine of a speedy appearing. Many of Father Miller's sermons and lectures were published, and his "Dream of the Last Day" had a wide circulation. This sect, under various names, has been increasing in the country, and has made an impress upon the thought and sentiment of New England. Father Miller returned to Low Hampton, where he died Dec. 20, 1849.

POUJADE, Joseph, legislator, was born in Marion county, Ore., Oct. 6, 1852, son of T. C. Poujade, a native of Ohio, who was a pioneer trader on the Pacific slope. His mother was a native of Illinois, and a woman of culture and force. On the paternal side he comes of French and English ancestry, and on the maternal, of Irish and Scotch blood. His boyhood life was nomadic; and the territory embraced in the states of Oregon, Washington, and Idaho became familiar as he, with his parents, traversed the mountains and plains on horseback. Among his earliest playmates were the children of the Indian tribes. Living in 1862 on a ranch on the Nez Percé Indian reservation, this solitary white child became an object of curiosity; and in summer, during the Indian encampment, he became the involuntary chief of forty or more Indian children of his own age. If by chance an arrow from his bow lodged in a tree, the anxiety to return it to their leader invariably led to a wild scramble and savage fight, did not the young chief name the favored one who should climb the tree to recover it. Years afterward these same children, under the leadership of another Joseph of their own color, did savage work that horrified the civilized world. Afterwards the evolution of trade and civilization led the youth with his parents to California, Southern Idaho, and Nevada, in which latter state he made his home after he reached manhood. His parents had given him a good education, and he was well equipped to take his first earnest position in business life as a reporter on the Pioche "Record." Afterwards he engaged in merchandising and in mining and reducing ores. In 1879 he was married to Laura Gill, a native of Indiana. In 1884 he was elected a member of the state senate, serving two sessions. During his second session, 1887-89, he was elected president *pro tem.*, and distinguished himself as an efficient and impartial presiding officer. In 1888 he was admitted to the bar,

and began the practice of law at Pioche. In the same year he was elected, and served in 1889, as a member of the state assembly. In 1890 he was elected lieutenant-governor of the state, and became *ex-officio* president of the senate, adjutant-general, and state librarian. He made a brilliant record in each of these widely different official positions. Notwithstanding his efficiency and success, party faction, through a misuse of the word "silver" by his opponents, overwhelmed him in 1894, when he was the Republican candidate for judge of his district. The state of Nevada owes much to him for its admirable statutory laws, and the militia of the state, through his care and forethought as adjutant-general, has been brought to as near an actual service discipline as is practicable with an American citizen soldiery. By a system of target practice, which was materially improved under his administration, they were made efficient sharpshooters in each arm of the service, and claim in this respect to lead the world. In the state library Lieut.-Gov. Poujade accumulated 4,000 bound volumes, principally on subjects of law, making the state library a doubly valuable collection of over 84,000 bound volumes.

BOWDITCH, Nathaniel, mathematician, was born in Salem, Mass., March 26, 1773. His parents were in straightened circumstances, and unable to give the boy advantages of education other than were afforded by the common schools of the town, and from these he was withdrawn when only ten years old, to assist his father, who was a cooper. He had shown great aptitude for mathematics at school, and continued his studies during his spare hours, preferring his study room to play. At the age of thirteen he was apprenticed to a ship chandler, where he remained until he was twenty-one. During this time he mastered arithmetic and elementary algebra by

himself, and meeting a retired sea-captain, he took from him lessons in navigation. In 1790 he began the study of Latin without a teacher, in order to make a study of Newton's "Principia," and afterwards learned to read French in the same way. He did not confine his studies to mathematics, although it was his favorite pursuit. Having no one to direct his reading, he read "Chambers's Cyclopædia" from beginning to end. He was a great admirer of Shakespeare, and was thoroughly acquainted with the Bible. He seemed to have a wonderful facility for acquiring languages, which he mastered for the pleasure of reading their literature. When twenty-two he shipped as clerk in the ship Henry, and spent about nine years in a sea-faring life, during which he made five voyages to the East Indies, Portugal, and Mediterranean ports, serving as supercargo, and afterwards as master. During all this time he devoted every moment to his studies, and it is related of him that, in an engagement with a privateer, when he was called upon for powder, he was found sitting on the powder-keg working out a problem upon a slate. He had a remarkable knowledge of navigation, and made quite a reputation for himself by bringing his ship into Salem harbor in a snow-storm which obscured all landmarks, being guided by his reckoning, which he took from an instant's glimpse of Baker's Island light. He was engaged to correct Morris's work on navigation, but found that it contained so many mistakes that he concluded to make an entirely new one, which resulted in his new "American Practi-

cal Navigator," which was published in 1802, and immediately adopted as the standard in this country, and to a large extent in England and France. His fame as a mathematician spread abroad, and Harvard University conferred upon him the degree of M.A., which gave him more pleasure than all his subsequent honors, for the honor came upon him as a surprise, while listening to the college exercises. In 1804 he gave up the sea, and was made president of Essex Fire and Marine Insurance Co. of Salem, Mass., which position he held until 1823, when he was induced to take the position of actuary in the Massachusetts Hospital Life Insurance Co., of Boston, at a liberal salary, that enabled him to bring out his publications, which lack of means had heretofore made impossible. He was offered a professorship in Harvard in 1807, one in the University of Virginia in 1818, and one in West Point in 1820, but he declined them all, to pursue his favorite work, which he hoped eventually to publish. During his stay in Salem he made charts of the neighboring harbors, and contributed papers on astronomy and kindred subjects to the American Academy. He also contributed many articles to "Rhee's Cyclopædia," and began his greatest work, a translation of Laplace's "Mécanique céleste," which he accompanied with a copious and profound commentary, occupying more than half the work, explaining obscure portions, giving valuable historical information, and bringing the work down to date. To publish such a work was enormously expensive, but Bowditch refused to publish it by subscription, and devoted his savings to this purpose, he and his family practising for years the most rigid economy. In 1829 the first volume appeared, dedicated to his wife, stating in the preface that, "without her approbation the work would not have been undertaken." The second volume appeared in 1832, the third in 1834, but the fourth was not issued until after his death. The fifth, which was a supplemental volume added by Laplace many years after to the original work, was brought out under the supervision of Prof. Benjamin Pierce. This gigantic work, upon which Dr. Bowditch's fame rests, was the first entire translation of the great original, and was elucidated in a manner which commands the admiration of men of science. It was said that there were but two or three men in the country at that time able to read and appreciate the original work. Harvard University conferred upon him the degree of LL.D. in 1816, and at his death he was a member of the Royal Societies of London and Edinburgh, the Royal Academies of Palermo and Berlin, the Royal Irish Society, the Royal Astronomical Society of London, and the British Association. During his later years he was a trustee of the Boston Athenæum, president of the American Academy of Arts and Sciences, and a member of the corporation of Harvard University. He was also twice elected to the state executive council of Massachusetts, and held many offices of honor and trust. He was a great lover of poetry, particularly admiring Bryant, considering the "Old Man's Funeral" one of the most beautiful compositions in the English language. Dr. Bowditch's career is one of the most remarkable in American history. Notwithstanding the very limited advantages of education, and his engagement through life in laborious employments for the support of his family, yet by his extraordinary genius, and almost equally extraordinary economy of time, he made great acquisition in learning and science, gained a knowledge of the Latin, Greek, Italian, Spanish, French, Portuguese, and German languages, and made himself the most eminent mathematician and astronomer America has yet produced, and did more for the reputation of his country among men of science abroad than has been done by any other man, except, perhaps,

Franklin. A eulogy of him was delivered by Prof. Pickering before the American Academy, May 29, 1858, which included an analysis of his scientific publications and of his mathematical contributions to the knowledge of the world. Another was delivered by Judge Daniel A. White, in Salem, Mass., at the request of the corporation of that city. A full list of his mathematical papers will be found in the "Mathematical Monthly," Vol. II., published in Cambridge, Mass. He was stricken down in the midst of his work, and died March 16, 1838. His resting-place in Mount Auburn cemetery is marked by a beautiful tomb, upon which is his statue. His library is still preserved intact in Boston.

ALGER, Cyrus, gun manufacturer, was born in West Bridgewater, Mass., Nov. 11, 1781. He received a common school education, and developing a fondness for mechanics, learned the machinist's trade and later became an iron founder. He was engaged in business for some years at Easton, Mass., and in 1809 removed to South Boston and established the plant which became, in 1817, the South Boston Iron-works, now one of the oldest iron and ship-building concerns in the United States. Between 1812 and 1814 Alger supplied the greater portion of the cannon balls used in the second war with Great Britain and also engaged extensively in the manufacture of ordnance, the excellence and durability of which gave him a high reputation. He was an accomplished metallurgist and patented numerous improvements in the manufacture of iron, bronze, and other metals. In 1834 he completed the first gun ever rifled in America, and a few years later he succeeded in casting the first perfect bronze cannon ever made by an American artisan. He also cast and finished the mortar "Columbiad," at the time the largest cast-iron gun that had ever been manufactured in the United States. Alger secured patents, among other things, for the cylinder stove, for a method for making cast-iron chilled rolls for an improved timefuse for bombs and grenades. He took an active part in public affairs, was a member of the First Council elected in the city of Boston, and in 1824 and 1827 was chosen alderman. He died in Boston, Feb. 4, 1856.

ARCHER, Branch T., Texas patriot, was born of an ancient family in Farquhar county, Va., Dec. 13, 1790. He was educated for the medical profession in Philadelphia, and practised in Virginia until 1831, when he removed to Texas and became prominent in the political movements that led to Texan independence. In 1835 he presided over the convention of settlers called to consider the subject of independence, and was one of the then three commissioners sent to Washington to solicit aid from the United States. In the following year he was speaker of the Texan house of representatives, a member of the congress of 1836, and subsequently, until 1842, secretary of war for the new republic. He was a man of commanding presence, distinguished as an orator, and beloved for the nobility of his character. Archer county, Tex., was named in his honor. He died in Brazoria, Tex., Sept. 22, 1856.

ALLEN, Moses, clergyman, was born in Northampton, Mass., Sept. 14, 1748. He studied at Princeton College, where he was graduated in 1772, and was licensed by the presbytery of New Brunswick, N. J., Feb. 1, 1774. He was a personal friend of James Madison, and during 1774 passed some time at his residence, and was solicited to spend the winter there, but declined. He was ordained in 1775, in March, at Christ's Church parish, about twenty miles from Charleston, S. C. He remained there until June 8, 1777, when he removed to Midway, Ga., where he settled, and took charge of a church. In 1778 Gen. Augustine Prevost, with a detachment of the British army, passed through that section, and burned the meeting-house and almost every dwelling-house in the neighborhood, dispersed his society, and destroyed the crop of rice then in stacks. In December Mr. Allen was taken prisoner at the time of the reduction of Savannah by the British. He was chaplain of the Georgia brigade, and was denied the privilege of his parole—his earnest exhortations from the pulpit and his courageous conduct in the field having aroused the special animosity of the British. He was incarcerated on board a prison-ship for a number of weeks, his condition being loathsome and harsh to that degree that he determined to risk his life in an effort to obtain his liberty. He threw himself into the river on the evening of Feb. 8, 1779, and endeavored to swim to an adjacent point, but was drowned in the attempt. His body was washed onto a neighboring island, where it was found by some of his friends. Both as a soldier and minister of the gospel he attained to the highest reputation during his life, and his death at the early age of thirty was generally lamented.

RICHARDS, Samuel, artist, was born at Spencer, Ind., Apr. 22, 1853. He was educated in the academy of that town, and from his earliest boyhood determined to become an artist. His first pencil sketches were from nature, although he was also successful in portrait and caricature. At an early age he left school, and entered the employ of Allison Bros., who kept a large general store. Meanwhile, he continued to draw, although his studies were practically unaided. He first awakened to a full realization of the possibilities within him by reading "Chapman's Book of Drawing," which he procured at a price that must have cost him much self denial. He now began to paint as well as to sketch, and later he resigned his clerkship and devoted himself to his art exclusively. 

For a time he studied at Indianapolis, under Prof. Theodore Lietz, and upon returning home, did much creditable work in portrait-painting. Later, he removed to Franklin, Ind., where he met and married Louise Parks, daughter of a Baptist minister, and where he formed a lasting friendship with James Whitcomb Riley, the "Hoosier" poet, then a sign painter. Up to this time Mr. Richards had supported himself by his art, but realizing that he could fulfil his ambitions only by thorough and long-continued study abroad, he, in 1880, sailed for Antwerp. For seven years he toiled in the art schools at Munich, devoting four years to work in the still-life drawing class, although he might have passed to the painting class at the end of the second year. He won many medals for excellence in work, the merit of his genius even reaching the ears of John Ruskin, who asked for an examination of his pictures, returning them with a highly complimentary letter. His "Peasant Stories," painted during this period, subsequently became the property of Senator McPherson, of New Jersey, while the "Italian Boy," and numerous copies of Murillo, won him much praise from his instructors and friends. In 1875, while reading Longfellow's "Evangeline," he had become inspired to paint a picture illustrative of that poem. Lack of technical knowledge had alone prevented him from at once carrying out the project, although many sketches were made with a view to ultimate achievement. At length, in 1887, having mastered the technicalities necessary to its construction, his ideal began to assume form and color. For two years he worked unremittingly upon the painting, until his health at length gave way under the strain. He recovered sufficiently to complete the work, however, which was exhibited with notable success in Munich, Paris, and subsequently at Boston, Philadelphia, and Indianapolis. It was purchased in 1891 for $6,000, by Bela Hubbard, who presented it to the Art Museum at Detroit, Mich. The picture illustrates Evangeline finding Gabriel in the hospital, and in both conception and expression it is acknowledged to be a masterpiece of pictorial art. It is directly "against the light," one of the severest tasks of the painter's skill, by which Mr. Richards has conclusively proved himself to be the master-workman as well as the poetic genius. After the completion of "Evangeline" the artist, although daily expected to die, recovered sufficiently to be removed to Davos Platz, among the Alps, Switzerland. Here his health was in part restored, and he painted "The Day Before the Wedding," which, technically considered, is his greatest work, and which became the property of Mrs. Platt, of Chicago. At Davos, also, he became close friends with John Addington Symonds, and the famous physician, Dr. Ruedi. Mr. Richards returned to America in 1891, proceeding at once to Denver, Colo., where he hoped to regain his strength. He accepted the directorship of the Denver Art League, but, warned by returning disease, was compelled to resign at the end of a year. He had been also forced to decline an appointment at the head of the Boston Art School, and another as head of the art department of the Leland Stanford, Jr., University, of California. His illness continued to prey upon his system, and erelong he fell a victim to it, dying in the flower of his manhood and genius, at Denver, Nov. 30, 1893.

COOK, James, navigator, was born at Manton, Yorkshire, Eng., Oct. 28, 1728. His father was first an agricultural laborer, and then a farm bailiff. At

thirteen years of age he was apprenticed to a haberdasher at Straiths, near Whitby, but quarreled with his master, went as apprentice on board a collier belonging to the port, and was soon appointed mate. In the year 1755 he entered the English navy, and, having distinguished himself, he was appointed successively master of the sloops Grampus, Garland, and Mercury. In the Mercury he sailed on the river St. Lawrence, in Canada, and was present at the capture of Quebec. He was also engaged in sounding and surveying the river, and published a chart of the channel from Quebec to the Atlantic ocean. In 1762 he was present at the recapture of Newfoundland. Early in 1763 he was engaged in surveying its coasts; in 1764 he was made marine surveyor of Newfoundland and Labrador. His observations on a solar eclipse made at one of the Burger islands, near cape Ray, about this time, added to his growing reputation, and he was shortly appointed to conduct an expedition for making observations on an impending transit of Venus, and prosecuting geographical researches in the South Pacific ocean. He sailed as lieutenant in the Endeavor, a vessel of 370 tons, with several scientific men on board, among them Sir Joseph Banks. On Apr. 13, 1769, he reached the island of Tahiti, erected an observatory, and made the necessary astronomical observations. Then sailing southward, he reached the New Zealand Islands, but his attempts to get to the inland were foiled by the hostility of the natives. Cruising about New Zealand for six months, he traced the channel which divides it into two islands, and sailed thence to the present Australia—then called New Holland. He was in sight of Botany Bay Apr. 28, 1770. The natives here were also hostile, so much so that he could only take possession of the island on the coast, in the name of Great Britain. He next sailed for New Guinea, where he put in for repairs to his vessel. On June 11, 1771, having returned to England, he was made a captain by King George III., and appointed to the command of the ship Resolution, 462 tons burthen, and of a smaller ship, called the Adventure, with 193 men, all told. With these he set sail from Plymouth, Eng., July 13, 1772, on a voyage in which it was hoped to discover a great southern continent. He reached the Madeira islands on the 29th of the same month, and then proceeded to the Cape of Good Hope. Thence Cook explored the waters of the Pacific or Southern ocean within the parallels of latitudes which had been marked out for him, but found no land, and abandoned the search, sailing for New Zealand on Jan. 17, 1773. Wintering among the Society islands, he made further explorations to the eastward and northward, navigating the southern tropics from Easter island to the New Hebrides, and discovering the island which he called New Caledonia. He made one more fruitless attempt to find the continent, and then reached England, July 30, 1774. Here he was at once made post-captain, and appointed to the charge of Greenwich Hospital. He was unanimously chosen to the Royal Society, and made the recipient of the Copley gold medal for the best experimental paper that had appeared during the year. Capt. Cook forthwith offered to conduct a government expedition for the discovery of a northwest passage to Asia in the northern arctic regions. The Resolution and the Discovery were quickly equipped and placed under his care, and he was instructed to sail first into the Pacific ocean through the chain of islands which he had lately visited, and on reaching New Albion, to proceed north as far as latitude 65°, and try to find a passage to the Atlantic. Sailing in June, 1776, he first cruised in the South Pacific, discovering several small islands. In the spring of 1777 he bore away to the Friendly islands, where he continued for several months, sailing northward in January, 1778. After leaving these islands, he discovered the Sandwich islands (now Hawaiian), to which he gave their name—the Earl of Sandwich having taken great interest in the expedition. Sailing around and charting them, he reached the coast of America in March, 1778, and followed its line to the northward, penetrating into what is now known as Cook's Inlet. Then he sailed for Behring strait, but found there only an impenetrable wall of ice. He returned to the Sandwich islands to winter. On the night of Feb. 13, 1779, one of the Discovery's boats was stolen by a native. In order to recover it, Capt. Cook attempted his usual expedient of seizing the person of the king until reparation should be made. On the 14th he landed, and a struggle ensued between him and his marines and the natives. The English were forced to retire to their boats. Cook was the last to retire. As they reached the shore he was struck from behind and fell. Rising immediately, he resisted those who pressed upon him, but, single-handed and alone, was soon overpowered and slain. Capt. Cook was, as it has been truly said, a navigator of the very highest order. His personal qualities rendered him a favorite with his crew. His valuable researches into the nature and use of antiscorbutic medicines, proved of the greatest utility. Distinguished honors were paid to his memory in England, and in other European countries and courts, and a suitable pension was assigned to his widow. The date of his death was Feb. 14, 1779.

WILSON, Henry Parke Curtis, physician, was born at Workington, Somerset co., Md., March 5, 1827, son of Henry Parke Curtis and Susan (Savage) Wilson, and grandson of John Curtis Wilson, of Westover, Somerset co., Md. His father was for many years state senator of Maryland, and was descended from Ephraim Wilson, who came to this country in the early part of the eighteenth century, and settled on the eastern shore of Maryland. He was a Scotch-Irishman, who, leaving his own country because of religious persecution, became one of the founders of the first Presbyterian church in America. By will, he prohibited his descendants from worshiping God by any other than the Presbyterian faith, a command which has been generally obeyed. Young Wilson's education was chiefly obtained at Princeton College, from which he received the degree of A.B. in 1848, and that of A.M. in 1851. He commenced the study of medicine in Northampton county, Va., in 1848, under Dr. William G. Smith, and attended one course of medical lectures at the University of Virginia, completing his medical education at the University of Maryland, where he was graduated in March, 1851. He next spent a year and a half as resident physician in the hospital of the University of Maryland, after which, upon entering practice, he was appointed physician in charge of the Baltimore City and County Almshouse, from 1,000 to 1,500 patients being under his charge. Here, in the opportunities offered for every variety of practice, were laid the foundations of subsequent success in his profession. Dr. Wilson was one of the founders of the American Gynecological Society, and in 1889 was its president. He was also one of the founders of the Baltimore Obstetrical and Gynecological Society, and its president in 1887 and 1888; president of the Medical and Chirugical Faculty of Maryland in 1881, president of the Baltimore Academy of Medicine in 1880, member of the British Medical Association, vice-president of the British Gynecological Society, and honorary fellow of the Edinburgh Obstetrical Society. He has been surgeon-in-charge of the Hospital for the Women of Maryland since 1882, consulting gynecologist to St. Agnes Hospital since 1879, and consulting surgeon to Johns Hopkins Hospital since it was opened in 1889. In 1857 and 1858 he was surgeon in charge of the Baltimore City Almshouse. Dr. Wilson was the first to introduce the science of gynecology in his section of the country, and for some years was the only gynecologist in Baltimore, there now being over thirty. He was the second Maryland surgeon to perform a successful ovariotomy; was the first physician in that state to remove the uterine appendages by abdominal section, as well as to perform the operation for division of the cervix uteri (Sims' operation). He was the second physician in the world to remove, by cutting into pieces, a large intrauterine fibroid tumor filling the whole pelvis, the patient recovering after all other methods had failed. Moreover, when performing this operation he had no knowledge of the previous operation, it not having been published. In 1880 Dr. Wilson performed abdominal section with remarkable success in removing a living child from the abdominal cavity. He has invented a number of surgical instruments for the surgery peculiar to women. His chief medical papers are: "Ovariotomy during Pregnancy," "The Hand as a Curette in Post-Partum Hemorrhage," "Sub-Sulphate of Iron as an Antiseptic in the Surgery of the Pelvis,," "Division of the Cervix backwards in some forms of Antiflexion of the Uterus with Dysmenorrhœa and Sterility," "The President's Annual Address before the American Gynecological Society in 1889," "Foreign Bodies left in the Abdomen after Laparotomy," "Hysterectomy with a new Clamp for Removal of Large Uterine Tumors," "Twin Pregnancy; One Child in the Uterus and the Other in the Abdomen," "Paquelin's Thermo-Cautery with Wilson's Antithermic Shield," "Uterine Dilatation with a New Instrument." Dr. Wilson is a fellow of the Maryland Historical Society, and has been an elder in the Presbyterian church nearly thirty years. In 1858 he was married to Alicia Brewer Griffith, of Baltimore. They have six living children: Dr. Robert Taylor, Henry Parke Curtis, William Griffith, Henrietta Chauncey, Alicia Brewer and Emily Griffith Wilson.

SHAW, William Conner, physician, was born near Turtle Creek, Allegheny co., Pa., Feb. 7, 1846, son of William and Theresa (Conner) Shaw, of Scotch-Irish descent. His paternal ancestors were originally from Scotland and located in county Down, Ireland, about 1648. The first American ancestor, Samuel Shaw, married Sarah Lowry and brought his family to the New World about 1765 and settled in central Pennsylvania. Their youngest son David bought a farm in Allegheny county and married Jane Ekin, a native of York, Pa., who lived to be 102 years old. Their youngest child, William Shaw, married Theresa, daughter of Rev. William Conner and granddaughter of Cornelius Conner, a recruiting sergeant, afterwards major in the revolutionary war. His father, Cornelius, Sr., who came from Virginia and married Eliza Carroll, and two brothers, John and Thomas, were also in the revolutionary army. William Conner Shaw received his early education in the district school near his father's farm, and employed all his time out of school working in the fields or about the barn. In 1864 he was sent to Newell Institute, Pittsburgh, where he prepared for the sophomore class of Washington and Jefferson College. He was graduated in the class of 1869 as A.B., receiving the A.M. in course in 1872. He then took up the study of medicine and was graduated from Bellevue Hospital Medical College as M.D. in 1872. He then studied with Dr. Howe of New York city, entered the competitive examination for Bellevue Hospital, and entered the hospital as provisional junior assistant in October, 1872. He also served as ambulance surgeon and fever examiner. At the end of six months he was assigned permanently to the second surgical division. While house surgeon he was appointed clinical assistant to Dr. Stephen Smith, which position he resigned at the expiration of his term of service at the hospital, Oct. 1, 1874. He then opened an office in Pittsburg, Pa., and met with more than ordinary success. Dr. Shaw has been called as an expert in numerous medico-legal cases of more or less celebrity. From 1876 to 1882 he was physician to the Pittsburg Free Dispensary and was made a life member of the institution. From 1876 to 1887 he was physician and surgeon to the Mercy Hospital. He has been surgeon to the Pennsylvania and the Pennsylvania, Cincinnati, and St. Louis Railroads. He is a trustee, physician and obstetrician to Bethesda Home, chief medical examiner for the Equitable Life Insurance Society, as well as of other life and accident companies.

He is president of the Pittsburg Medical Library Association and a member of the local, state, and national medical associations, and of the Scotch-Irish Association of America, and also of the state of Pennsylvania. On Nov. 1, 1877, Dr. Shaw was married to Martha, daughter of J. C. Lewis, a son of George Lewis, a Welshman, who built the first rolling-mill in western Pennsylvania. Dr. Shaw is ruling elder of the First United Presbyterian Church of Pittsburg, and is a member of the committee of ways and means of the general assembly of that church.

PAQUIN, Paul, physician, was born at St. Andrews, Argenteuil, Canada, in 1860, son of Jullen Paquin, a farmer of French origin but a native of Canada. The son's mother-tongue was French. He was raised on the farm and attended French and English schools. He was entered at Bourget College, Rigaud, but on the death of his father, in 1875, he was obliged to leave college and earn a livelihood for his mother and six brothers and sisters, working on the farm left by his father. This he succeeded in doing, and in the meantime, keeping up his studies as best he could, he was finally able to leave the care of the farm to younger brothers and take a course in comparative medicine at the McGill University, Montreal, from which he was graduated in 1881. He had also the advantages of *l'École de Médecine et de Chirurgie,* Montreal, the Medical department of the University of the State of Missouri, affiliated with the Missouri Medical College, St. Louis, Mo., between 1878 and 1887, and had studied human and comparative medicine, taken special laboratory courses, and pursued investigations in histology, physiology, hygiene, and bacteriology. The University of the State of Missouri and the Missouri Medical College jointly conferred upon him the degree of M.D. He then pursued special courses at Cornil and Ranvier's laboratory of pathology, Paris Medical School, and at the conferences of Pasteur's Institute, Paris, on pathology and bacteriology, where he was sent by the University of the state of Missouri in 1886, shortly after Pasteur's announcement of his inoculation against hydrophobia. Dr. Paquin founded and was the first director of the laboratories of pathology and hygiene in the Missouri State University before the buildings were destroyed by fire in 1892. In connection with this institution he established "The Bacteriological World," the first journal in the English language devoted exclusively to bacteriology, also the vaccine laboratory of the university, which has since become private property under the name of the Paquin Vaccine Laboratory. He is the author of "The Supreme Passions of Man," a physiological and psychological study of certain attributes of human nature; "The Microscopical Diagnosis of Tuberculosis," a manual for the analytical diagnosis of consumption; "The Basis of Character and the Diseases of Personality," a monograph which has caused profound discussion in its views of the causes of crime and the treatment of criminals. Dr. Paul Paquin was the first to apply the serum therapy in the treatment of tuberculosis (pulmonary and general consumption). His experiments and researches on consumption began at the State University of Missouri in 1889, and the results thereof attracted universal attention in January, 1895, when he brought before the St. Louis Medical Society several cases of consumption

which had been in the third (last) stage, some of them bed-ridden, and had then seemed cured. Dr. Paquin is considered the discoverer of the technique to immunize and apply the blood serum of the horse in consumption.

JAY, John Clarkson, physician, was born in New York city, Sept. 11, 1808, son of Peter Augustus Jay, lawyer (see Vol. III., 462), and grandson of John Jay, U. S. chief-justice (see Vol. I., 20). He was educated in the best preparatory schools of his native city, and was graduated from Columbia College with the class of 1827, and from the College of Physicians and Surgeons in 1831, and served the usual time in the New York Hospital. Besides his medical practice, Dr. Jay was well known in the scientific world as a specialist in conchology, and his collection of shells was at the time the most noted in the United States; and with his costly library on the subject, was subsequently purchased by Catharine Wolf, and presented to the American Museum of Natural History, where it is known as the Jay collection. He was one of the founders of the Lyceum of Natural History, afterward the New York Academy of Science, being elected a fellow in 1832, and he was its librarian in 1833, and its treasurer from 1886 to 1843. He also, as a member of the purchasing committee, purchased at auction in 1835 the lot (25 x 100 ft.), on the west side of Broadway, near Prince street, for $11,000, and an adjoining lot at private sale, for a like sum. He also obtained a loan of $25,000, which enabled the society to erect their lyceum building. He was the leading spirit in the enterprise, and the building erected was the largest for its purpose in the United States—far more commodious than that occupied by its older sister society in Philadelphia. The property was subsequently sold by the society in a commercial crisis for $37,000, and was sold by the owners in 1867 for $200,000, justifying Dr. Jay's forecast as to the ultimate value of the property as an investment. He was one of the founders of the New York Yacht Club; from 1859 to 1880 a trustee of Columbia College; one of the early presidents of the old New York Club; and one of the early members of the Union League Club. He was married in 1831 to Laura, daughter of Nathaniel Prime, a well known banker, and shortly after his marriage he gave up his medical practice and engaged in the banking business for a short time. Upon the death of his father, in 1842, the country seat at Rye, N. Y., embracing over 400 acres of land, became the property of Dr. Jay, and he retired from business life in the city and took up his residence on the estate early in 1843. During his more vigorous years Dr. Jay was much interested in aquatic sports, and was the owner of the famous yacht Coquille. Dr. Jay is the author of "Catalogue of Recent Shells" (1835); "Descriptions of New and Rare Shells," and of later revisions of his catalogue, in which he enumerated about 11,000 well-marked varieties, and about 7,000 well-established species. He wrote an article which was made the government report on the shells collected by the expedition of Com. Perry to Japan in 1853–54, and placed in the Jay collection among the treasures of the Natural History Museum. His son, John Clarkson Jay, Jr., is a well-known physician of New York city. He died at his home, "Rye," at Rye, Westchester co., N. Y., Nov. 15, 1891.

JAY, John Clarkson, physician, was born at Rye, N. Y., Oct. 20, 1844, the son of John Clarkson Jay and Laura Prime, and great-grandson of the celebrated Chief-Justice John Jay. He was educated at Dudley's School, Northampton, Mass., at Charlier's French Institute, and at Columbia College Grammar School. He entered the collegiate department of Columbia in the class of 1865, but left at the end of the freshman year (standing sixth in his class) to enter the medical department of the College of Physicians and Surgeons, from which he was graduated in 1865. He served in the army during the civil war; was acting assistant surgeon, U. S. army, 1864–65; serving at the Armory Square U. S. General Hospital, Washington, D. C., and also at the Sedgwick U. S. Army General Hospital, New Orleans. For several years he served as attending physician at the New York Dispensary, and contributed greatly to the founding of the New York Free Dispensary for sick children, and is now (1891) and has been for a number of years attending physician to the out-patient department of the New York Hospital, and for nine years past has been a vestryman in the Church of the Heavenly Rest. He was a member of the aisle committee, and took an active part in the centennial celebration of the inauguration of George Washington, held in New York city, May, 1889. He has been successfully engaged in the practice of medicine in New York since 1868, and has contributed valuable articles at various times to medical literature. He is proficient in the French and German languages, and has several times been abroad. Since 1871 he has been a member of the Medical Society of the City and County of New York, a member of the Society of the Sons of the Revolution, a member of the Colonial Society, etc. On Dec. 12, 1872, he married Harriette Arnold Vinton, daughter of Maj.-Gen. David Vinton, U. S. army.

SENN, Nicholas, physician, was born at Buchs, canton of St. Gall, Switzerland, Oct. 31, 1844. He emigrated with his parents to America when nine years old, settling at Ashford, Fond du Lac co., Wis. He was educated at the Fond du Lac grammar school, from which he was graduated in 1864, with high honor. He then taught school for three years, at the same time attending lectures at the Chicago Medical College. He was graduated from there in 1868, winning first prize in the graduating thesis, the subject being: "Modus Operandi of Digitalis Purpurea." For one and a half years he served as house physician in Cook County Hospital, subsequently practicing medicine for five years in Fond du Lac county, Wis. In 1874 he took up a permanent residence in Milwaukee. In 1878 he visited Europe, to attend a course of lectures at the University of Munich, receiving at graduation the degree of *Magna cum Laude*, after which he visited several noted universities in Europe, returning to Milwaukee in the fall of 1878. In 1874 he had been appointed attending surgeon of the Milwaukee Hospital, which position he held for many years. He was appointed professor of surgery in the College of Physicians and Surgeons of Chicago in 1884, serving three years in that capacity. He was elected professor of principles of surgery and surgical pathology in the Rush Medical College of Chicago in 1887, and of practical and clinical surgery in 1890; also professor of surgery in the Chicago Policlinic. He is attending surgeon of the Presbyterian Hospital, and surgeon-in-charge at St. Joseph's Hospital. He is an honorary fellow of the College of Physicians of Philadelphia; permanent member of the German Congress of Surgeons; honorary member of La Academie de Medicina de Mexico; of the D. Hayes Agnew Surgical Society, in Philadelphia; of the Ohio State Medical Society; of the Minnesota State Medical Society; corresponding member of the Harveian Society, London; member of the American Surgical Association; of the American Medical Association; of the British Medical Association; of the Illinois State Medical Society; Chicago Medical Society (of which he is president at the present time); of the Brainard Medical Society; the Verein Deutscher Ærzte, in Milwaukee; and of

the Association of Military Surgeons of the United States. He was appointed surgeon-general of Wisconsin by Gov. Peck in 1890, and now holds the same position in Illinois under Gov. Altgeld. Dr. Senn has written largely on surgery and medicine, his subjects being the result of his own original investigation and practice. Among his best known publications are: "The Surgical Bacteriology," which has been translated into the French, Italian, and Polish languages; "Intestinal Surgery," translated into German; "Experimental Surgery," treating of his own original experience; "Principles of Surgery," a text-book for students and practitioners; "Tuberculosis of Bones and Joints;" and a "Syllabus of Surgery." He has, perhaps, the largest private medical library in America. In 1869 Dr. Senn was married to Aurella Millhouser of La Crosse, Wis.

SUTPHEN, John Thomas, physician, was born in Middletown, O., Sept. 29, 1840, son of Carlton Waldo Sutphen, a prosperous merchant. He traces his lineage on his father's side to Derrich J. Von Zutphen, his first American ancestor, who landed on Manhattan Island with Henry Hudson; on his mother's side to Commandant Carrick, who was one of the special officers of William of Orange. He was educated at the public school of Middletown, O., and entered the Ohio Wesleyan University, Delaware, in 1865. He left college when in his junior year and engaged as a clerk in a grocery store, and afterwards as a mining engineer in the Southern Ohio Coal Co. He began the study of medicine first with W. D. Linn, and continued his studies at Hahnemann Medical College, Philadelphia, where he was graduated as M.D., March 10, 1871, and at once took up the active reputation of his profession, in which he has gained the reputation of a leading physician and surgeon in the Miami Valley. In political faith Dr. Sutphen is a Republican, and for several years was vice-president of the Republican League of the United States. In July, 1872, he

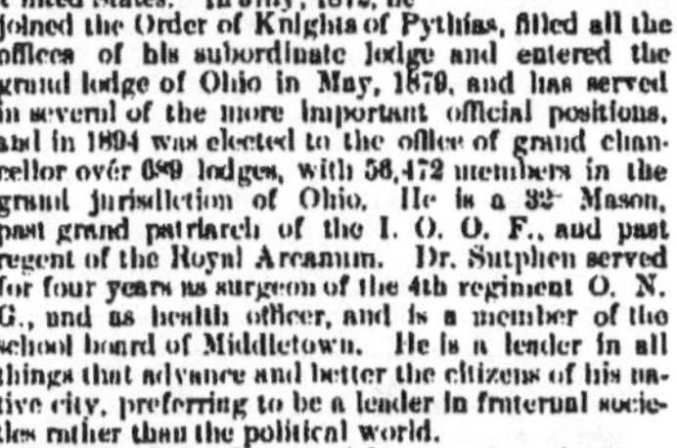

joined the Order of Knights of Pythias, filled all the offices of his subordinate lodge and entered the grand lodge of Ohio in May, 1879, and has served in several of the more important official positions, and in 1894 was elected to the office of grand chancellor over 689 lodges, with 56,472 members in the grand jurisdiction of Ohio. He is a 32° Mason, past grand patriarch of the I. O. O. F., and past regent of the Royal Arcanum. Dr. Sutphen served for four years as surgeon of the 4th regiment O. N. G., and as health officer, and is a member of the school board of Middletown. He is a leader in all things that advance and better the citizens of his native city, preferring to be a leader in fraternal societies rather than the political world.

GRAY, John F., physician, was born in Sherburne, Chenango co., N. Y., in 1804. When twenty years of age, he removed to New York city, and became the pupil of Dr. John Ward Francis. The following year he was appointed assistant surgeon in the navy; and as it was necessary that he should be a graduate or licentiate in order to hold this position, he was accorded a license by the County Medical Society. Shortly afterward he was appointed assistant physician in the New York Hospital. In 1827, after several years of successful practice, he became acquainted with Dr. Gram, the pioneer of homœopathy in this country, and through his arguments, illustrated by cases from practice, he became a convert to the doctrines of Hahnemann. He was subsequently a practitioner of that system, and enjoyed an extensive and lucrative practice. He died June 4, 1882.

WHEATON, Charles Augustus, physician, was born at Syracuse, N. Y., March 17, 1858, son of Charles and Ellen Birdseye Wheaton. His father was a prominent iron manufacturer and an original abolitionist, being a co-laborer of Gerrit Smith. In 1858 he removed to Northfield, Minn., where he died in 1882. In 1861 the son was brought to Northfield, Minn., where he obtained his preparatory education at Carlton College, attending until 1870. Shortly after he received an accidental gunshot wound,

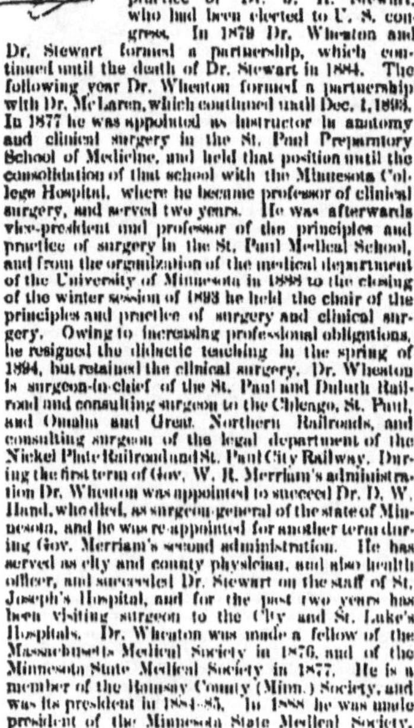

which confined him to bed for five months, and practically changed his whole career. After recovering he went to St. Paul, and obtained employment in an express office, which position he held for three years. During this period he spent his leisure time in studying medicine. In the fall of 1873 he entered the medical department of Harvard University, graduating in 1876. As the result of a competitive examination, he was selected as one of the internes in the Boston City Hospital, which position he held eighteen months. In the spring of 1877 Dr. Wheaton returned to St. Paul, and took charge of the extensive practice of Dr. J. H. Stewart, who had been elected to U. S. congress. In 1879 Dr. Wheaton and Dr. Stewart formed a partnership, which continued until the death of Dr. Stewart in 1884. The following year Dr. Wheaton formed a partnership with Dr. McLaren, which continued until Dec. 1, 1893. In 1877 he was appointed as instructor in anatomy and clinical surgery in the St. Paul Preparatory School of Medicine, and held that position until the consolidation of that school with the Minnesota College Hospital, where he became professor of clinical surgery, and served two years. He was afterwards vice-president and professor of the principles and practice of surgery in the St. Paul Medical School, and from the organization of the medical department of the University of Minnesota in 1888 to the closing of the winter session of 1893 he held the chair of the principles and practice of surgery and clinical surgery. Owing to increasing professional obligations, he resigned the didactic teaching in the spring of 1894, but retained the clinical surgery. Dr. Wheaton is surgeon-in-chief of the St. Paul and Duluth Railroad and consulting surgeon to the Chicago, St. Paul, and Omaha and Great Northern Railroads, and consulting surgeon of the legal department of the Nickel Plate Railroad and St. Paul City Railway. During the first term of Gov. W. R. Merriam's administration Dr. Wheaton was appointed to succeed Dr. D. W. Hand, who died, as surgeon-general of the state of Minnesota, and he was re-appointed for another term during Gov. Merriam's second administration. He has served as city and county physician, and also health officer, and succeeded Dr. Stewart on the staff of St. Joseph's Hospital, and for the past two years has been visiting surgeon to the City and St. Luke's Hospitals. Dr. Wheaton was made a fellow of the Massachusetts Medical Society in 1876, and of the Minnesota State Medical Society in 1877. He is a member of the Ramsey County (Minn.) Society, and was its president in 1884–85. In 1888 he was made president of the Minnesota State Medical Society, and president of the Minnesota Academy of Medicine in 1892. He has been a member of the American Medical Association since 1884. Dr. Wheaton is a 32nd degree Mason, being a member of the Paladin commandery of the Sir Knights and of the Ancient; and he accepted the Scottish Rite for the southern jurisdiction of the United States, and is also a member of Osman Temple of the Mystic Shrine. He is a member of the St. Paul Commercial Club, and a number of other social clubs of similar character. Dr. Wheaton is a liberal but judicious supporter of charitable organizations of the city. He has valuable real estate holdings, and has contributed largely towards the growth of the city. Dr. Wheaton is one of the leading surgeons of the Northwest, and his whole professional career has been most successful. In 1879 he was married to Ursula, daughter of Dr. J. H. Stewart.

CHAPMAN, William Carroll, physician and editor, was born in Hartford, Ky., June 17, 1863. His grandfather, David Chapman, was the first male child born in the state of Kentucky south of Green river, and near the present site of Bowling Green, the house in which he was born having been built to answer the purposes of a fort, provided with port-holes to aid the inmates in defending themselves from the Indians. He died in 1884, at the age of ninety-five years. The grandson was educated in the private schools of Hartford until he was thirteen years old, when he entered Cecilian College, where he attended until within a few months of his time for graduation, when ill health compelled him to forsake his studies and seek rest and recuperation. In 1879 he took up the study of medicine under Dr. S. L. Berry, a learned physician of his native town, and at the same time pursued a special course in chemistry, anatomy, and physiology at the Hartford College. He then attended three courses of lectures at the College of Physicians and Surgeons, Baltimore, Md., and was graduated an M.D. in 1884. Upon graduating, he received the appointment of assistant demonstrator of chemistry in the laboratory of the college, and was also made resident physician of the Maternity. During the summer of 1883, while yet a student, he was assistant in the Charity Eye and Ear Hospital in Baltimore. Upon returning to Kentucky, he practiced medicine at Cecilia, and was attending physician and surgeon to the Hardin County Almshouse. In 1885 he removed to Louisville, and continued his practice in that city. Dr. Chapman is assistant to the chair of clinical medicine and to the chair of chemical physiology in the Kentucky School of Medicine, secretary of the publication committee of the Kentucky State Medical Society, editor of the "Medical Progress," secretary of the Jefferson County Medical

Society, and a member of the Mississippi Valley Medical Association. He is the author of "Consumption and the Prophylactic Treatment," "Resorcin as an Antipyretic," "The Toxic Effect of Tobacco Vapor," and other scientific papers. He is devoting special study to the diseases of the upper gastro-intestinal tract. Outside of his professional studies, Dr. Chapman has written in both prose and verse for the current literary magazines. "The Severed Chord," "O Time," "In the Autumn," "Hyacinthus," and "Under the Linden" have given him more than a local reputation.

HANRAHAN, John David, physician, was born in Rathkeale, county Limerick, Ireland, Jan. 18, 1844, son of James and Ellen (O'Connor) Hanraban. His father removed with his family to New York city in 1850, where the son became a pupil of the public school and the Free Academy. He then entered the New York Medical University, where his studies were interrupted in 1861 by his entering the U. S. navy as assistant surgeon. He served in the Potomac flotilla until Aug. 23, 1863, when the vessel on which he was serving was captured, and all on board made prisoners. After six weeks' imprisonment in Richmond he was paroled. While a paroled prisoner in Washington he attended a course of lectures at the medical department of the Georgetown University. In 1864 he was exchanged, and ordered to duty in the North Atlantic squadron, where he served until discharged in July, 1865. He received his diploma from the medical department of the New York University in 1867, and practiced in New York city until the spring of 1869, when he removed to Rutland, Vt., and built up an extensive practice. Outside of his professional duties Dr. Hanrahan has been county commissioner, trustee of the village of Rutland, as well as the president of the board, and village president. He was appointed president of the Rutland county pension board in 1885 by President Cleveland. President Harrison continued him in office. He resigned in 1893 to accept the postmastership of Rutland by appointment from President Cleveland.

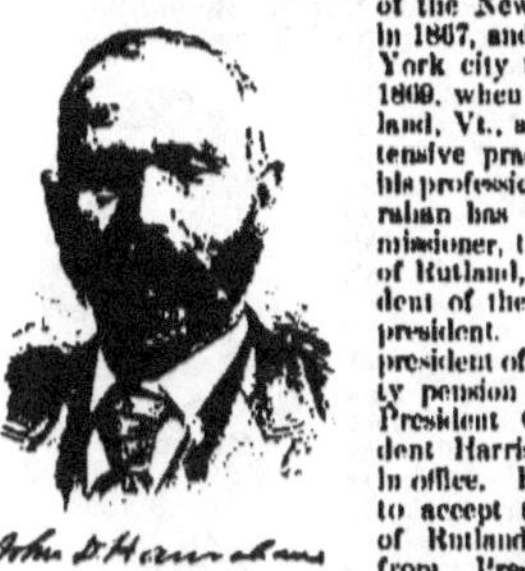

Dr. Hanrahan is a strong Irish nationalist, a potential factor in the Rutland Land League, and a delegate to all the national conventions. He has served as chairman of the Rutland county Democratic committee, and as a member of the state committee. He was a delegate to the Democratic national conventions of 1884 and 1888, and chairman of the delegation in 1892. Dr. Hanrahan is a member of the local G. A. R. post, and has served on the staffs of Commanders-in-chief Veazey, Palmer, and Weissert, and has been medical director of the department of Vermont. He is director of the Rutland Hospital, and consulting surgeon of the Fanny Allen Hospital (Hotel Dieu), Winooski, Vt. In his religious creed he is a Roman Catholic, worshiping with the congregation of St. Peter's in Rutland. Dr. Hanrahan was married Feb. 12, 1870, to Mary, daughter of Bernard and Elizabeth (Dolpin) Riley, of Willingford. She died in April, 1882. On Oct. 31, 1883, he was married to Frances, daughter of Dr. John and Mary (Hughes) Keenan, of Rutland. There have been six children born as a result of the second marriage.

HORNER, William Edmonds, physician, was born in Warrenton, Va., June 3, 1793. He was a grandson of Robert Horner, who emigrated from England to America and settled in Maryland before the revolution. He received his education at a private school and subsequently studied medicine, and was graduated from the University of Pennsylvania in 1814. He served as assistant surgeon in the war of 1812, and was stationed most of the time at Buffalo, where he witnessed considerable military service, of which he published an account soon after he resigned in 1815. He was appointed prosector of anatomy under Wistar in 1815. In 1819 he was made adjunct professor under Dr. Philip Physick, and at the resignation of Dr. Physick he was elected to the chair of anatomy, which position he held until his death. His first work, the "American Dissector," was published soon after he was made adjunct professor to Dr. Physick. This was followed in 1826 by his "Special Anatomy and Histology," the result of his personal researches in microscopical anatomy. A full description is given in this work of the tensor tarsi muscle, which he claimed to have first noticed, but which had really been described as early as 1822 by Rosenmüller of Germany. In 1839 he joined the Roman Catholic church, and two years later founded St. Joseph's Hospital, to which he bequeathed his valuable library. During the cholera epidemic of 1832 he was a prominent member of the Philadelphia city sanitary board, and on account of the important services he rendered, the citizens presented him with a silver pitcher. His work, "Pathological Anatomy," is valuable on account of the elaborate descriptions it contains of the changes which take place in the mucous crypts of the bowels in Asiatic cholera. Shortly before he died he published, in conjunction with his son-in-law, Dr. Henry H. Smith, an "Anatomical Atlas." Besides his numerous contributions to medical literature, he left at his death a number of manuscripts on these logical and literary subjects. He was the most accomplished anatomist America ever produced. He willed his fine anatomical collections, worth $2,000, to the University of Pennsylvania, where it is contained in the Horner and Wistar Museum. He died at Philadelphia, Pa., March 13, 1853.

JAMISON, Alcinous Berton, physician, was born at Wooster, O., Sept. 1, 1851, son of O. E. Jamison, a prominent farmer of Allen county, Ind. His first American ancestor, David Jamison, emigrated from Scotland, and located in Delaware before the revolutionary war. He served seven years under Washington, and his stone residence in Delaware was used by Washington as a storehouse for army supplies. His son, Richard Jamison, served under Anthony Wayne in the war with the Indians in Ohio and Indiana. His mother was Ann, daughter of James Springer. Her first American ancestor, Christopher Springer, came from Sweden in the colonial days, and purchased a large tract of land in Delaware, which he leased to tenants on leases of ninety-nine years. He was a nobleman of great wealth, and returned to Sweden, the land descending to his eldest son Carl, the father of James. On part of this tract the city of Wilmington was built. Alcinous was educated primarily at the district school, supplemented with a course at Fort Wayne College and the Indiana State Normal School. He was graduated in medicine from Fort Wayne College of Medicine in 1878. His first years were devoted to general

practice, first at Portland, Ind., 1877, from which place he removed in 1878 to Decatur, Ind., in 1882 to Grand Rapids, Mich., in 1883 to Detroit, Mich., and in 1885 to New York city, where he practices as specialist in the treatment of diseases of the anus and rectum. He published in 1892 a treatise, "The Anus and Rectum, their Physiology, Anatomy, and Pathology," which in three years passed through three editions. In his specialty he has invented many instruments and appliances for his own use, some of which he has patented. Dr. Jamison was married June 17, 1891, to Mary Ernestine, daughter of Xavier and Althea (Keyser) Schmid. Her father emigrated from Switzerland, and was a prosperous New York merchant. Her maternal grandfather, Ernest Keyser, served in the war of 1812, and was one of the few millionaires of his day. In his prosperity he has not forgotten others, and a prominent state senator acknowledges that he owes his present high standing to help furnished by Dr. Jamison, while two successful physicians at least have been helped through college through his beneficence.

BUTTLER, Charles Voorhees, physician, was born at New Brunswick, N. J., Jan. 18, 1860, son of George Buttler, a prominent manufacturer of that

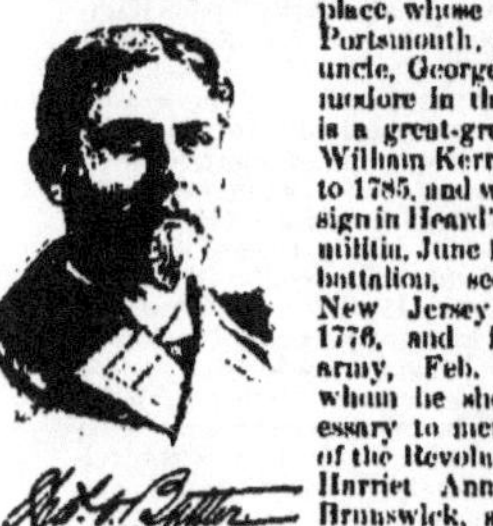

place, whose ancestors came from Portsmouth, England, and whose uncle, George Buttler, was a commodore in the English navy. He is a great-great-great-grandson of William Kerr, who lived from 1720 to 1785, and who was appointed ensign in Heard's brigade, New Jersey militia, June 14, 1776; in the fourth battalion, second establishment, New Jersey militia, Nov. 28, 1776, and in the Continental army, Feb. 17, 1777, through whom he shows the lineage necessary to membership in the Sons of the Revolution. His mother was Harriet Ann Voorhees of New Brunswick, a descendant of the Haviland family of England. Her ancestors came to this country from Holland, in 1620, and her relatives belong to the Holland Society, of New York. Dr. Buttler received his earlier education at the high school and Rutgers College of New Brunswick, and the U. S. naval school at Annapolis, Md. He studied medicine at the medical department of the University of the City of New York, and was graduated Apr. 4, 1893. The following month he settled at Elizabeth, N. J., shortly afterward removing to Norwich, Conn., where he afterward successfully practiced his profession.

LOMAX, William, physician, was born in Guildford county, N. C., March 15, 1813. His ancestors were among the first who colonized America, and both his great-grandfathers

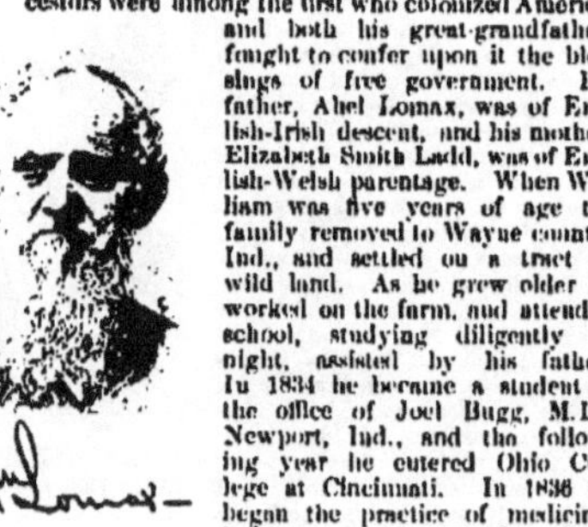

fought to confer upon it the blessings of free government. His father, Abel Lomax, was of English-Irish descent, and his mother, Elizabeth Smith Ladd, was of English-Welsh parentage. When William was five years of age the family removed to Wayne county, Ind., and settled on a tract of wild land. As he grew older he worked on the farm, and attended school, studying diligently at night, assisted by his father. In 1834 he became a student in the office of Joel Bugg, M.D., Newport, Ind., and the following year he entered Ohio College at Cincinnati. In 1836 he began the practice of medicine, in partnership with Dr. John Foster, remaining with him ten years. During the years 1847–48 he attended lectures at the Indiana Medical College, and subsequently entered the University of the City of New York, graduating in 1850. He then resumed practice in Marion. At the beginning of the civil war he began enlisting volunteers, and obtained the first appointment ever issued by Gov. Morton. He accompanied the 12th Indiana Infantry, and, as far as other duties would permit, remained with it throughout the war. He was found to possess superior skill, and was called to act in the capacities of surgeon-in-chief of the division

and medical director of the 15th army corps. At the close of the war he returned to Marion. Dr. Lomax was a member of the Indiana State Medical Society, and has been identified with all its history, having been admitted at its first annual meeting, and in 1856 he became its president. He has devoted himself to surgery with great enthusiasm, acquiring a national reputation. Among his most difficult operations is included the flap amputation below the knee, which he effected fifteen years before the earliest recorded operation of the kind. He was a member of the Methodist Episcopal church, a Republican, and Free Mason, in which society he had taken all the degrees conferred in this country. Dr. Lomax died at his home in Marion, Ind., Apr. 27, 1893.

McGUIRE, Frank Augustine, physician, was born in New York city, July 1, 1851. He was the son of James McGuire, a native of the north of Ireland and a merchant of New York, his mother being the daughter of Daniel Joshua Thom-

as, a native of Wales, a veteran of the war of 1812, (American side) and a long resident of New York city. He received his early education in De La Salle Institute and Manhattan College, and began the study of medicine in the University Medical College of the City of New York, from which he was graduated after a four years' course in February, 1877. He began practice in the city achieving a high reputation and establishing a lucrative practice. He is the author of several important papers, viz.: "Acute Croupous Pneumonia not an Infectious Disease," "Koumiss in the Treatment of the Summer Diarrhœas of Infancy," "Report of the Third American Case of Hæmodriosis, or Bloody Sweating" before the New York Neurological Society, and "Case of Tumor of the Corpus Callosum." He is a member of the County Medical Society, Physicians' Mutual Aid Association, Medical Jurisprudence and State Medicine, Manhattan Medical and Surgical, Liederkranz and Linnæan Societies, president of the Celtic Medical, ex-president of the Metropolitan Medical, and vice-president of the Westcolong Park and Delaware River Association for the preservation of game. He married Emma, daughter of Alexander Denmark of New York, Aug. 16, 1873.

POST, Alfred Charles, physician, was born in New York city, Jan. 13, 1806. He was the son of Joel Post, an eminent merchant, of the old firm of J. & J. Post, New York, and had his country-seat at Fairmount, now forming part of the Riverside Park, and embracing the site of Gen. Grant's tomb. Alfred was prepared for college by the time he was twelve years of age, and did enter Columbia College two years later, graduating in 1822. His uncle, Dr. Wright Post, an eminent surgeon, took him into his office as a medical student, and he also took a course of instruction in the College of Physicians and Surgeons, at which he received the degree of M.D. in 1827. He then went to Europe to complete his medical education, and studied at Paris, Berlin, and Edinburgh. On returning in 1839, he began the active practice of his profession in New York, and continued in it up to within a week of his death. He devoted himself chiefly to surgery, and as early as 1836 was made one of the attending surgeons of the New York Hospital, and later became connected with the medical staffs of St. Luke's and the Presbyterian Hospitals. He was one of the founders of the medical department of the University of the City of New York, where he held the chair of surgery and pathological anatomy, and at the time of his death was president of the medical faculty and emeritus professor of clinical surgery in that institution. For fifty-one years he was connected with the New York Hospital, where he was consulting surgeon at the time of his death. He was also consulting surgeon of the Woman's Hospital. Had he lived, he would have been made one of the board of managers of the New York Hospital in the spring of 1886. Dr. Post was a member of the New York Academy of Medicine, and its vice-president. He was president of the Pathological Society, and a member of the county and state medical societies of New York, and of many foreign societies. In 1872 he received the degree of LL.D. from the University of the City of New York. He held positions in a number of religious and charitable organizations, was a life-long member of the Presbyterian church, and an elder in the Church of the Covenant. He was also president of the New York Medical Missionary Association, and one of the directors of the Union Theological Seminary. He was a physician and surgeon of a deservedly high character and wide reputation. Dr. Post was an able writer on professional subjects, and contributed to the transactions of the medical societies many valuable papers. An important work of his, published in New York in 1840, was on "Strabismus and Stammering." He was the first man in the United States to operate for stammering, and he devised a new method of performing bi-lateral lithotomy. He possessed great mechanical ingenuity and inventive talent, and devised a number of valuable instruments and appliances for surgical use. During the latter part of his life he was greatly interested in plastic surgery, and made reports of many important operations of his own in that line. Dr. Post married, in 1832, Harriet, daughter of Cyrenius Beers, whom he survived nearly nine years. One of his sons, George E. Post, of the Presbyterian mission at Beyrut, Syria, became a distinguished surgeon. Dr. Post died in New York, Feb. 7, 1886.

SCHOONOVER, Warren, physician, was born in Honesdale, Pa., Feb. 17, 1838. He is the son of Daniel Schoonover, Honesdale, and is descended from the first settlers of Wayne county, Pa. After receiving his early education in the schools of his native town, he entered Union College, from which he was graduated in 1864. During the interims of study he engaged in teaching and farming, but having a great inclination for the medical profession he went to New York and entered the College of Physicians and Surgeons, from which institution he was graduated in 1867, and the following year he began practice in New York city. After graduating in medicine he was appointed house-physician to the Charity Hospital, New York, in which institution he served a term of eighteen months. He was appointed house physician and secretary of the board of managers of the North-Eastern Dispensary in 1873, which position he still holds. Dr. Schoonover has contributed a number of reports of special cases and several important papers to the medical press, which have given him a high reputation in the profession, and secured for him a large practice. He is a member of the American Academy of Medicine and of the American Medical Association; he is also a member of the New York County Medical Association, and the New York Physicians' Mutual Aid Association. In 1870 he married Amanda M. Mathewson of New York city.

BENTLEY, Edwin, physician, was born in New London county, Conn., July 3, 1824, son of George W. Bentley. He was educated at public school and by private tutors, and was graduated an M.D. in 1848. He practised his profession in Norwich, Conn., with marked success. At the outbreak of the civil war in 1861 he was mustered into service as assistant surgeon, 4th Connecticut infantry, June 6, 1861. He was appointed surgeon U. S. volunteers, Sep. 4, 1861, and honorably mustered out Jan. 4, 1866. He received the brevet of lieutenant-colonel March 13, 1865, for faithfulness and meritorious service during the war. He served in the army of the Potomac in Fitz-John Porter's division, until the autumn of 1862; was in charge of the general hospital at Alexandria,

Va., being subsequently made superintendent of hospitals at that place, to April, 1866; was post-surgeon at Russell barracks, D. C., until mustered out of the volunteer service; was appointed assistant surgeon, U. S. A., Feb. 8, 1866, service being continuous from the volunteer to the regular; made captain and assistant surgeon, July 28, 1866; and major and surgeon, July 12, 1879. He was on duty at Russell barracks, D.C., to December, 1868; at Lincoln barracks, D. C., to April, 1869; then as post-surgeon at Point San José, Cal. to January, 1871; from Apr. 17, 1873, with batteries B., C., and G., 4th artillery, on the Modoc expedition and at the headquarters of Gen. Gillem, on the south side of Tule lake, transporting wounded at the conclusion of the war from the field hospital, of which he was in charge and Fort Klamath, Ore. He rejoined his proper station at Point San José, where he remained post-surgeon until 1874; and was on duty at Alcatraz island at the presidio of San Francisco, Cal., and at Camp Bidwell, Cal. In February, 1875, he was appointed recorder of the medical examining board and attending surgeon at San Francisco, Cal. In 1876 he was on leave of absence to enable him to study mental diseases and morbid anatomy of the nervous system, being superintendent of the Napa Insane Asylum, California. In February, 1877, he was on duty with the 16th Infantry, at New Orleans, La., where, finding an epidemic of small-pox producing much alarm among the troops of the command, he established a post hospital, by order of the commanding general. For his success in its management he received a special letter of commendation from the medical director of the department. In 1877 he was on duty as post-surgeon at Little Rock barracks; on duty in Pennsylvania during the labor strikes; and was medical director of the department of Arkansas. In 1884 he was post-surgeon at Fort Clark, Tex., and post-surgeon at Fort Brown, Tex., in 1886; being retired July 3, 1888. He was professor of anatomy in Pacific Medical College, California, and has been professor of surgery in the Industrial University of Arkansas since its organization.

ROBERTSON, Samuel Empey, physician, was born in Hollen, Ontario, Can., June 16, 1860, the oldest son of Samuel Robertson, a merchant and afterwards a private banker, who was a native of Glasgow, Scotland, and emigrated to upper Canada in 1841. He was one of the pioneer settlers of the rich section called the Queen's Bush, in what is now Western

Ontario, and became one of the leading men of that part of the Dominion. He was at different times mayor of Harriston, reeve of the township of Maryborough, and for twenty-five years a magistrate. The son was educated at the public school of his native town, Brantford Collegiate Institute, and at Toronto University, from the latter of which he was graduated in arts in 1882. He then entered his father's banking house, but remained in that business only one year, having determined to follow the medical profession, for which his collegiate course in arts at the Toronto University had been most advantageous as a preliminary. He accordingly removed to New York and studied medicine at Bellevue Medical College, graduating in 1886. He settled in Newark, N. J.; at once began the practice of his profession; and was for several years attached to the staff of St. Michael's Hospital in that city. Being remarkably successful in his work, he soon built up a large and lucrative practice both in medicine and surgery, and took a high standing in the profession. He belongs to the Essex County District Medical Society, the Practitioners' Club, and the Wednesday Club. He has also belonged to the Masonic fraternity since reaching the age of twenty-one years, of which order his father was a prominent member, being a Royal Arch Mason, and holding prominent offices in the order. In 1883 Dr. Robertson was married to Hannah Chambers, of Harriston, Ont., and has had three children.

BARCLAY, Robert, physician, was born at St. Louis, Mo., May 8, 1857. His father, David Robert Barclay, born in Pennsylvania, author of the well-known "Barclay's Digest" of the decisions of the supreme court of Missouri (St. Louis, 1868), was the eldest surviving male in the direct American line of this ancient and celebrated Scotch-English family, retracing his lineage directly through many generations to Roger de Berkeley of Berkeley Castle, county of Gloucester, father of Theobald de Berkeley (born 1010), who lived in the time of the Conqueror. Of this line, John Barclay, first, emigrated to America in 1682, with his brother David, who died upon the voyage. Both were brothers of Robert, first governor of East Jersey (1683), and sons of Katharine Gordon, of royal Scotch lineage, and David Barclay (born 1610), who was a colonel under Gustavus Adolphus, and was afterward celebrated among the Friends, or Quakers, as the "Barclay of Ury," immortalized in verse by the poet Whittier. Dr. Barclay's mother, Mary Melinda Barclay, vice-president-general of the Daughters of the American Revolution (1893), business manager of their official organ, the "American Monthly Magazine," was born at St. Louis, Mo., and was the daughter of Mary Thomas, a Virginian, and Elihu Hotchkiss Shepard, of Halifax, Vt., formerly professor of languages in the St. Louis College, who, when sixteen years old, served his country at Sackett's Harbor and Queenstown, at Lundy's Lane, and afterwards went through the war of 1812, and served in three campaigns in the Mexican war of 1846, where he was a captain. In 1864 he enlisted in the "Old Guard." He was the original promoter, a founder, and first secretary of the Missouri Historical Society; and was the author of "Shepard's History of St. Louis and Missouri" (1673-1843). Among his ancestors are Ralph Shepard, Malden, Mass., passenger on the Abigail in 1635; Kenelm, brother of Gov. Edward Winslow of Plymouth and descendant of John Winslow, 1400, emigrant, it is stated, in 1629, in the Mayflower on her second voyage; Ellen Newton, passenger on the Ann in 1623, who married, first, John Adams, of the Fortune, and second, Kenelm Winslow; Peter Warden of Yarmouth, Mass. (born 1568), who came over before 1638; Elder Thomas King, who emigrated to America in 1634-35; Andrew Dalrymple, of the British army, emigrant about 1724; and others who served in the colonial and revolutionary wars. The grandfather of Capt. Elihu Shepard was closely related to Gen. Shepard, who, in 1787, in Shay's Rebellion, so gallantly defended the arsenal at Springfield, Mass. Robert Barclay attended school in St. Louis until 1870; afterward at the Episcopal High School, Alexandria, Va., until 1876. One of the very few of his class admitted unconditionally, he entered Trinity College, Hartford, Conn., in 1876. Here, after winning the first chemical prize, and securing an appointment for commencement, he was graduated as B.A. in 1880. Among his fellow-collegians he was prominent in many popular undergraduate institutions—musical, literary, athletic, etc.; his record as a pedestrian, for example, having since remained unequaled there. After a three years' course of study at the College of Physicians and Surgeons, New York, he was graduated M.D. in 1883. The degree of M.A. was then conferred upon him by Trinity College, Hartford, Conn. He was elected a member of the American Association for the Advancement of Science, August, 1881, and of the Medical Society of the County of New York, October, 1883. In December, 1883, he was elected assistant aural surgeon of the New York Eye and Ear Infirmary, serving (with re-election) until October, 1885, when he resigned the position, upon removing from New York to St. Louis. He was licensed to practise medicine in St. Louis, Nov. 16, 1885; was elected a member of the St. Louis Medical Society, Dec. 12, 1885; of the Mississippi Valley Medical Society in 1886; of the American Medical Association in 1886; of the Medico-Chirurgical Society of St. Louis, January, 1888; of the Medical Association of the State of Missouri, April, 1888; of the American Otological Society, July 16, 1889; of the National Association of Railway Surgeons, Oct. 26, 1893; and of the Southwestern Association of Railway Surgeons, on the same date. By the St. Louis Medical Society he was appointed delegate to the American Medical Association in 1888 and 1889. His attention was given exclusively to otology, aural surgery, and diseases of the ear, in which he has obtained an international reputation. He was appointed aural surgeon to the principal sanitary institutions of St. Louis. Although declining an appointment as lecturer in medical colleges, he contributed freely to medical society proceedings and current otological literature. Of his writings, the best known are: "Difficulty of Operation in the Depth of the Ear Canal; New Instruments for Surmounting It," "Acute and Chronic Otitis Externa," "Acute Diseases of the Middle Ear," "Closure of the Ear by Growths of Bone, Operation, Cure; Three Cases;" "The use of the Paper Disc, Case Histories;" "Relation Between Diseases of the Teeth and Ears," "Abscess of the Brain in its Relation to Inflammation of the Middle Ear," "The Whistle Signal: A Plea for the More Safe Management of Railroads;" "Practical Suggestions on the Removal of Foreign Bodies from the Ear," "Precepts of Aural Practice, with Illustrative Cases;" "Diphtheria of the Ear," "Ear Affections of Typhoid Fever," "Wax in the Ear," "Use of Pyoktanin in Ear Disease," "Hearing Without the Cochlea," "Facial Paralysis with Ear Troubles," "The Standard of General and Special Practice of Medicine," "Abscess of the Middle Ear," "Foreign Bodies in the Ext. Aud. Canal," "Noises in the Head and Ears," "Aural Polypi," "Disques on Papier," "Behavior of the Ear in Fracture of the

Base of the Skull," " How to Cure the Profound Deafness of Chronic Aural Catarrh," " Rupture of the Drum-Head by Blows upon the Ear,"etc. Of his instrumental devices, the most noted are the aural speculum, and the shaft-and-handle for aural instruments, which facilitate difficult and delicate operation in the depth of the ear canal. In 1886 Dr. Barclay married Miss Minnie G. Hamilton, of Hartford, Conn. They have three sons—Robert Hamilton, Shepard Gibson, and McClelland.

LOVE, Isaac Newton, physician, was born Sept. 18, 1853, at Barry, Pike co., Ill., the youngest son of Isaac N and Nancy (January) Love, the former having come from old Virginia, of English descent, and the latter from Kentucky, of French origin. The son attended the schools of his native town ; his father having died when the lad was two years old, and his mother about ten years later, he was sent to St. Louis to become a member of the family of his relative, Dr. John T. Hodgen, the leading surgeon of St. Louis for many years. He had exceptional facilities for the study of medicine and surgery, and, with special preparation, commenced when quite young. He was graduated in medicine in 1872. After a competitive examination, he was appointed assistant resident physician in the St. Louis City Hospital, where he remained two years. Following this he served as assistant to Dr. Hodgen, and was associated in practice with him for one year. He was appointed city physician of St. Louis under the administration of Mayor James H. Britton, and served in that capacity one year. He then engaged in private practice. In 1878 he married Florence N., a daughter of Judge John F. Williams, of Marshall, Tex. He served as adjunct-teacher in the department of physiology in the St. Louis Medical College for several years, during which time his private practice grew steadily. The department of diseases of children in St. Louis seemed to have been unrepresented, and he determined to devote himself to a special study of the department. His practice has been for years largely among children, and he has made a reputation at home and abroad ; in the former field by his work and in the latter through his contributions to the literature of the profession. He has been since its incorporation professor of clinical medicine and diseases of children in the Marion Sims College of Medicine. For a number of years he was also a contributor to the medical journals of the country, and an associate editor upon several. In 1890, having been elected president of the American Medical Editors' Association, he determined to establish a journal of his own, and the first number of the " Medical Mirror," of St. Louis, was issued in January, 1890. Dr. Love is consulting physician to the City and Female Hospitals of St. Louis, and is one of the attending physicians of the Rebekah Hospital. He is the author of several brochures, notably one entitled, " Practical Points in the Management of Some of the Diseases of Children." He is a member of the American Medical Association, and in 1893 was elected vice-president. In 1887 he was secretary of the section on diseases of children in the Ninth International Medical Congress, and the same year president of the Mississippi Valley Medical Association. He is a member of the Medico-Chirurgical Society of St. Louis, and the State Medical Society of Missouri, and one of the incorporators of the first

VI.—25

Pan-American Medical Congress, held in September, 1893, in the city of Washington, D. C. He is also a member of the board of trustees, and assistant secretary-general of that body, and honorary president of the section on diseases of children in the congress.

GREEN, William Cowan, physician, was born at Wilmington, N. C., June 12, 1851, son of James G. and Caroline E. (Cowan) Green, both natives of North Carolina. His father was a graduate of the University of North Carolina and a railroad manager. Both parents were of Quaker stock, and gave the son a careful training and liberal education, acquired largely in the best schools of St. Louis, to which city he removed during his early manhood. He served in the junior reserves of the Confederate army during the civil war, and was married in 1878 at St. Louis to Mellona, daughter of Jonathan B. and Jane (Smith) Moulton. He was graduated at the St. Louis Medical College in 1883, and commenced practice immediately afterward in that city. He is vice-president of the Ex-Confederate Home of Missouri for the eleventh congressional district and has been for six years a member of the board of education, and vice-president of the St. Louis public library. Dr. Green is a member of the Protestant Episcopal church; of the American Medical Association; of the St. Louis Medical Society; and other medical associations. He is an occasional contributor to medical journals, and ranks as one of the leading physicians of St. Louis.

BELL, Theodore S., physician, was born in Kentucky, in 1807. His early boyhood was a mere struggle for the means of existence, and was beset by hardships that would have daunted a less indomitable spirit. He did not attend school a year altogether, and he had the most meagre advantages for the acquisition of book knowledge; but he read all the books he could procure, and had an admirable mother, who, when his day's work was over, taught him the rudiments of an English education, and later, when he was accustomed to toil fourteen hours in the day as a tailor's apprentice, instructed him at night in history and the higher branches. When he was about fifteen years of age he listened to the preaching of Alexander Campbell, and that aroused him to a sense of the true meaning of life, and inspired him with an ambition to be a true man, and of some use in the world. The medical profession would, he thought, afford a wider field for the exercise of his abilities than a tailor's bench, and, therefore, he devoted all his leisure hours to the study of medical science, and in due time received his diploma, and was admitted to practice in Louisville. His unassuming worth made him many friends, and his professional skill brought him a crowd of patients, and in the course of time he was appointed professor of medicine and hygiene in the University of Louisville, and editor of the Louisville " Medical Journal," positions which placed him in the front rank of his profession. During the yellow fever epidemic of 1878, he did yeoman's service, saving many lives. But his professional duties did not engross his attention. He was active in other fields, engaged in every work that would promote the good of the community. He was one of the founders of the first public library in Louisville, the first musical society, the first mechanics' association, the first institute for the blind, and a recognized leader in every enterprise that was calculated to further the growth of intelligence and good morals. When the trying time of the civil war came, and one-half of his friends cast in their lot with the Confederacy, he stood so steadfastly by the Union that, hearing of it, Pres. Lincoln sent him a musket with this inscription upon it: "From A. Lincoln to Dr. T. S. Bell, for his unswerving loyalty;" and yet he never lost a friend because of any difference of political opinion. He neither sought nor acquired wealth. He was too busy in the pursuit of a higher good, both for himself and for others, to dwarf his mind by the accumulation of riches. He lived an ideal life, void of events, and yet filled with good deeds; and he was one of those men who in this time of luxury, avarice, and corruption, are to be the salvation of this country. He died at Louisville, Ky., Dec. 28, 1884.

BUTLER, William Morris, physician, was born at Malue, N. Y., March 26, 1850, and was educated at Cortland Academy and Hamilton Col-

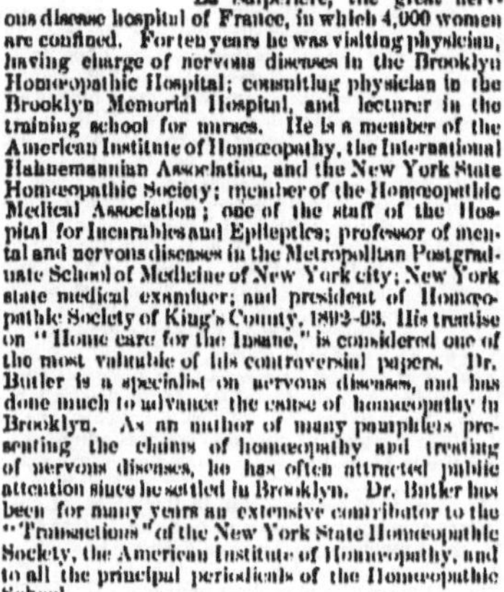

lege, receiving his degree from the New York College of Physicians and Surgeons, and from the American Institute of Homœopathy. He settled in Brooklyn, N. Y., in 1883. Prior to that time he had been connected with the State Homœopathic Hospital for the Insane at Middletown for nine years; he received its first patient. During his term of service he was given one year's leave of absence to study abroad. He passed the winter of 1877-78 attending lectures in the School of Medicine of Paris, and taking a special course of lectures under Dr. Charcot and private clinical instruction in La Salpérière, the great nervous disease hospital of France, in which 4,000 women are confined. For ten years he was visiting physician, having charge of nervous diseases in the Brooklyn Homœopathic Hospital; consulting physician in the Brooklyn Memorial Hospital, and lecturer in the training school for nurses. He is a member of the American Institute of Homœopathy, the International Hahnemannian Association, and the New York State Homœopathic Society; member of the Homœopathic Medical Association; one of the staff of the Hospital for Incurables and Epileptics; professor of mental and nervous diseases in the Metropolitan Postgraduate School of Medicine of New York city; New York state medical examiner; and president of Homœopathic Society of King's County, 1892-93. His treatise on "Home care for the Insane," is considered one of the most valuable of his controversial papers. Dr. Butler is a specialist on nervous diseases, and has done much to advance the cause of homœopathy in Brooklyn. As an author of many pamphlets presenting the claims of homœopathy and treating of nervous diseases, he has often attracted public attention since he settled in Brooklyn. Dr. Butler has been for many years an extensive contributor to the "Transactions" of the New York State Homœopathic Society, the American Institute of Homœopathy, and to all the principal periodicals of the Homœopathic School.

PECK, George Bacheler, physician, was born in Providence, R. I., Aug. 12, 1843, the eldest son of George Bacheler and Ann Power (Smith) Peck. His father was a descendant in the sixth generation through the eldest son, Joseph Peck of Hingham. Norfolk co., England, who came to America in 1638 with his wife, three sons, a daughter, and five servants, and settled in Hingham, Mass. His father's brother, Solomon Peck, was professor of Latin in Amherst College, and for twenty years (1840-1860) foreign secretary of the American Baptist Missionary Union, and another brother, William Peck, was a pioneer homœopathic physician of Cincinnati, O. His mother was a daughter of John Knowles and Marcy Wilbur Smith of Providence, R. I. The son was educated in the public schools of his native place and in Brown University, from which he was graduated in 1864 with a civil engineer's diploma dated six months earlier. The university honored him with the degree of A.M. in 1867. In the civil war, which was in progress during his college course, he participated after graduation. He raised a company of volunteers to help refill the 2nd Rhode Island Infantry, then serving in the 6th corps, army of the Potomac. He was made second lieutenant and was wounded at Sailor's Creek, Va. He was honorably discharged, July 5, 1865. He served from 1863 to 1871 in the Providence Marine Corps of Artillery, as corporal and in successive grades and commissions to and including that of major. From 1876 to its disbandment in 1879, he was surgeon of the battalion of light artillery division Rhode Island militia. After the war young Peck engaged as a clerk in his father's coal and wool yard, but, disliking business, he entered Hahnemann Medical College, Philadelphia, and attended a winter and summer course of lectures. The next year he attended the Yale medical department, receiving a diploma in 1871. He then spent one year in the study of practical chemistry, determinative mineralogy, and assaying at the Sheffield Scientific School. From August, 1872, to June, 1874, he was assistant chemist at the U. S. naval torpedo station, Newport, R. I., and during the fall of 1874 was temporarily in charge of the chemical department of the University of Vermont. He commenced the practice of medicine June 1, 1875, in his native city. He was secretary of the Rhode Island Homœopathic Society for seven years, and has served two years as vice-president and two years as president of that organization. He was for many years an active member of the Western Massachusetts Homœopathic Society, and twice its vice-president. In 1879 he became a member of the American Institute of Homœopathy and has been five times chairman of the bureau of obstetrics, and three times its secretary. His reports to this bureau, as well as to the bureau of pedology, were published in the leading homœopathic

Geo. B. Peck.

journals. He is an honorary member of the New York and Missouri Homœopathic Medical Societies. He obtained the charter for the Rhode Island Homœopathic Hospital, and has been its admitting physician and a director since the opening. He is medical director of the Rhode Island Department, G. A. R., a companion of the military order of the Loyal Legion, a prominent Mason in its highest degrees, and for fifteen consecutive years one of the Providence school committee. He has also been president of the Rhode Island Soldiers' and Sailors' Historical Society since January, 1892. Dr. Peck is a prominent layman in the Baptist denomination and has held the office of moderator of the Narragansett Baptist Association, the only layman enjoying such a distinction in that state. He has contributed to the military history of the Rhode Island volunteers, to the history of the Baptist church in Rhode Island, and to the daily and religious press on various subjects of current interest.

SCHABERG, Herman Henry, physician, was born at Rotterdam, Holland, May 16, 1848. His father, Herman H. Schaberg, though born in Holland, was the son of German parents. His mother, Mary Van Oversteeg, was of Holland parentage. The son's education was begun in his native city at four years old, and, when at the age of nine he came with his parents to America and settled in Kalamazoo, Mich., in August, 1857, he was, except in English, so far advanced in his studies as to rank with the grammar school pupils of that city. After three years of study at Kalamazoo, he entered the preparatory department at Hope College, Holland, Mich., completing the first term of his sophomore year. He then returned to Kalamazoo, and was matriculated at Kalamazoo College, where he remained until 1896, when he was obliged to discontinue his college work and assist in his father's business.

After three years as his father's assistant, he clerked in the drug store of Charles D'Arcambal, of Kalamazoo, in which business he continued for eight years, having charge of a drug store at Mendon, Mich., for one year. During a large share of the time he was in the drug business, he spent his spare moments in the study of medicine under the preceptorship of Dr. Logie of Kalamazoo, and when in 1876, he entered the Detroit Medical College, Detroit, Mich., he was sufficiently advanced to secure one year's credit. Having no money to pay for his college course while in Detroit, he served as night clerk in E. Stevens' drug store, and in this way met his expenses. During the years 1877-78, he was assistant to Dr. J. H. Carstens, chief of free dispensary at Harper's Hospital, and St. Mary's Free Hospital, Detroit, who was his preceptor while at college. On March 5, 1878, he received the degree of M.D., and contrary to the advice of his friends, he returned to Kalamazoo, and opened an office, where after a hard struggle at first, his native perseverance soon won for him a practice second to none in the city. Politically, Dr. Schaberg is a Democrat, and although from time to time urged to take office, he was obliged to refuse because of his practice. He served as township health officer for five years, and city health officer one year. He is president of the Holland News Publishing Co., director in the Home Savings Bank, and director in the local branch of the Capitol Building and Loan Association of Lansing, Mich. Fraternally, he is an Odd Fellow, a member of and medical examiner for the Knights of Honor, Royal Arcanum, and Ancient Order of United Workmen. He is also a member of the Kalamazoo Academy of Medicine, Michigan State Medical Association, and the American Medical Association. May 31, 1881, he was married to Nellie, daughter of Jacob Van Heusen, of Portage, Mich.

REESE, John James, physician and toxicologist, was born at Philadelphia, Pa., June 16, 1818, the son of Jacob Reese, a prosperous merchant, and Leah James Reese, a descendant of Major John James of the revolutionary army. In 1836 young Reese was graduated as a bachelor of arts in the University of Pennsylvania, receiving his A.M. and M.D. degrees in 1839. He at once began a career of success, rising rapidly in his profession, and acquiring a national reputation by his discoveries in toxicology. In 1841 he was elected to the Philadelphia County Society, and, in 1850, he became its treasurer. The American Medical Association elected him a member in 1852; in 1855 he became a member of the Medical Jurisprudence Society of Philadelphia, and at the same time he was made a member of the New York Medical Society. He filled many important positions in Philadelphia, among others, visiting physician to St. Joseph's Hospital, Girard College, medical supervisor of the Philadelphia Orphan Asylum, and, from 1854 to 1859 he was professor of medical chemistry in the old Pennsylvania College. He was assistant surgeon to the U. S. army from 1861 to 1865, being surgeon-in-chief of the Christian Street Hospital, Philadelphia. He was subsequently, for many years, associated with the firm of Booth, Reese & Camac, analytic chemists, of Philadelphia. Prof. Reese made important contributions to medical literature, his published works including an "Analysis of Physiology," an "American Medical Formulary," a "Manual of Toxicology," and "A Text-book of Medical Jurisprudence and Toxicology." He also edited the seventh American edition of "Taylor's Medical Jurisprudence." In 1877, he won a triumph in toxicology in the trial of Mrs. Wharton, of Philadelphia, who was accused of poisoning Gen. Ketchum of Baltimore. He was also called upon to give expert testimony in other famous cases. In 1865, when the "Auxiliary Faculty of Medicine" was established in the University of Pennsylvania, Dr. Reese was elected professor of medical jurisprudence and toxicology, which position he held until failing health obliged him to resign in 1891. He was married to the daughter of Prof. Gibson of the University of Pennsylvania. He died at Atlantic City, N. J., Sept. 4, 1892.

DOUGLAS, George, physician, was born in Franklin, Delaware co., N. Y., May, 7, 1823. His paternal ancestors were direct descendants of the celebrated William Douglas of Scotland, the progenitor of the "Good Sir James of Douglas" who perished in Spain in 1330, while on a journey to the Holy Land with the heart of Robert Bruce. The family coat of arms is that of the Earls of Angus. His academic education was acquired at the Delaware Literary Institute, his medical studies in the Geneva Medical College, and at the University of New York, where he was graduated an M.D., in 1845. He commenced the practice of his profession at Oxford, N. Y., in 1846, doing, in the commencement, what were then considered remarkable feats in surgery, and entered at once upon a large and lucrative practice. During the civil war he was appointed surgeon of the examining board of the nineteenth district, state of New York. In 1854 he was united in marriage to Ada E. Frink of Onondaga county, N. Y. After her death, which occurred in 1862, he married, in 1866, Jane A., daughter of William Mygatt, a distinguished financier of Oxford, N. Y. She died in 1894. In 1877 he retired from active

practice, and spent much time in travel, having twice made the tour of Europe, visiting most of its hospitals. He also visited all the states and territories of this country and Canada. Dr. Douglas has served as president of the Chenango County Medical Society, is a member of the New York State Medical Association, and for twenty-five years of the American Medical Association, is an honorary member of the California State Medical Society. He also served as a member of the Ninth International Medical Congress, Washington, D. C., and of the Centennial International Medical Congress, Philadelphia, 1876. He was a delegate from the

National Medical Association to the World's Medical Congress at Berlin, Germany, 1890. He read a paper descriptive of this congress before the members of the New York State Medical Association, 1891, which was favorably commented upon, and published in the transactions of that year. He is a member of the Rocky Mountain Medical Association, and in 1892 was elected president of this organization. He was also a member of the Pan-American Medical Congress which convened for the first time in 1893, at Washington, D. C.

MOORE, James E., surgeon, was born in Clarksville, Mercer co., Pa., March 2, 1852, the son of Rev. George W. Moore, a Methodist minister of sterling qualities and a member of the Erie conference for thirty years.

His mother is a descendant of the old German family of Zeiglers. He had good opportunities for early education, attending the public school nine months each year until he was fifteen years old. He then attended the Academy at Poland, O., where he remained three years. The following year was spent in teaching and studying medicine. The next year, 1871–73, he studied in the medical department of the University of Michigan at Ann Arbor. During vacations he always engaged in some sort of industry, in the rolling mill, on the farm, at the furnace, or in selling goods, as it was his ambition to be independent of his father's help. His second course in medicine was taken at Bellevue Hospital Medical College, New York city, where he was graduated in 1873. He then went to Fort Wayne, Ind., where he remained two and a half years, establishing a fair practice. In 1875 he returned to New York city to spend seven months in studying in the college and hospitals. While on his journey from New York city he met Dr. B. F. Hamilton, of Emlenton, Pa., nephew of Dr. Frank Hastings Hamilton. They formed a partnership and soon built up a flourishing general practice, which continued during their partnership of three years. The next three years and a half Dr. Moore practiced alone. He removed to Minneapolis in August, 1882, and formed a partnership with Dr. Ames, who had an enormous practice in surgery and had entered in politics, which prevented him from attending to it. This afforded Dr. Moore a good chance to exercise his skill in surgery, and he met with remarkable success during their four years' partnership. In 1886 Dr. Moore went to Europe, studying in some of the largest hospitals on the continent and in London. In Berlin he was a close attendant upon Dr. Von Bergman's clinic. While in London, he studied at the Royal Orthopædic Hospital, and was shown special favors by Sir Richard Barwell, at Charing Cross Hospital. Besides this study abroad he has made yearly visits to the hospitals in New York and Philadelphia, taking special instruction in surgery and particularly in Orthopædic surgery at the New York Orthopædic Hospital. Soon after his return from Europe he discontinued his general practice, and since 1888 he has confined himself exclusively to surgery, being the first practitioner in the Northwest to confine himself to that specialty. In 1885 Dr. Moore was elected professor of orthopedic surgery in the Old College hospital. He held the same position in the St. Paul Medical College during its school career, and now holds a like position in the medical department in the University of Minnesota. He is attending surgeon for St. Barnabas Hospital. He is also consulting surgeon for the Northwestern and City Hospitals, and orthopædic surgeon for the St. Mary's and the Asbury Methodist Hospitals. He takes great interest in his work at the Northwestern Hospital, and has helped that institution in many ways. He is an active member in the Hennepin County Medical Society, in the Minnesota State Medical Society, in the Minnesota Academy of Medicine, and has twice been vice-president of the Minnesota State Medical Society. He is a member of the American Orthopædic Association, and of the congress of American Physicians and Surgeons, and through his articles on Orthopædics is well-known abroad. He is a constant correspondent of medical journals, both East and West.

CARSTENS, John Henry, physician, was born in the city of Kiel, in the German province of Schleswig-Holstein, June 9, 1848. His father, John Carstens, a merchant tailor, was an ardent revolutionist, and participated in the various revolts in the memorable years of 1848–49. He had been captured, and was imprisoned when his son was born; some months after he was released, and fearing that he might again be imprisoned, he, with his family, left in the dead of night for America, and settled in Detroit, Mich. His earlier education was received in the public schools of Detroit, supplemented by six years' attendance at the German-American Seminary. He excelled as a student, and took high rank in his studies, especially those pertaining to natural sciences and mathematics. Before he had attained his fifteenth year he was compelled to engage in business, and after some time devoted to lithography, he entered a drug store, becoming proficient in the various details of the business, and then began the study of medicine, his name being first on the matriculation book of Detroit Medical College. After his graduation, in 1870, he was immediately put in charge of the college dispensary, and a few years later he held the same position in St. Mary's Hospital Infirmary. He was appointed lecturer on minor surgery in the Detroit Medical College in 1871, and afterwards lecturer on diseases of the skin, and clinical medicine.

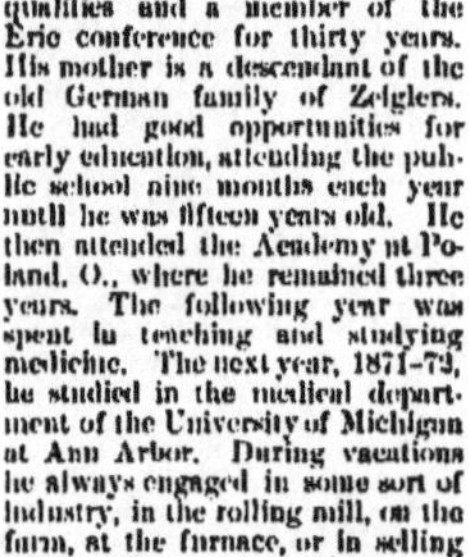

He has lectured on diseases of women and children, differential diagnosis, nervous diseases, physical diagnosis, pathology, chemistry, materia medica, and therapeutics. His taste and practice gradually tended to the diseases of women, and after holding a professorship of materia medica and therapeutics in the Detroit Medical College for some years, in 1881 he accepted the professorship of obstetrics and clinical gynecology, and on the consolidation with the Michigan College of Medicine, he was appointed to the same position in the Detroit College of Medicine. Both as an organizer and as an earnest, effective worker, he has rendered valuable aid in gaining victories for the Republican party. He was elected in 1875 a member of the board of education, and re-elected in 1876. In 1877 he was elected president of the board of health. On the organization of the Michigan Republican Club, he was elected a director. In 1892 he was selected by the state convention as presidential elector for the first district of Michigan, and ran about 300 ahead of the ticket. His contributions to medical literature have been various and extended. Nearly all of his articles have been extensively copied by medical journals in this country and Europe. He holds the position of chief of staff and gynecologist to Harper Hospital, attending physician at the Woman's Hospital, and obstetrician to the House of Providence. He is a member of the American Medical Association, and of the Michigan State Medical Society, of which he was vice-president in 1885; ex-president of the Detroit Medical and Library Society, a member of the Detroit Academy of Medicine, and of the British Gynecological Society, honorary member of the Owosso and Kalamazoo Academy of Medicine, and the Northwestern District Medical Society, and president of the American Association of Obstetricians and Gynecologists. In 1891-92 he was president of the Detroit Gynecological Society. His practice is now limited to abdominal surgery and diseases peculiar to women. He was married Oct. 18, 1870, to Miss Hattie Rohnert.

MARCY, Henry Orlando, surgeon, was born in Otis, Mass., June 23, 1837. His ancestors were of colonial stock, and were prominent participants in the development of the new country. His great-grandfather and grandfather fought side by side in the revolutionary war, and his father, at the age of eighteen, was a soldier in the war of 1812. The son received his preparatory and classical education at Wesleyan Academy, in Wilbraham, and at Amherst College. He was graduated in the medical department of Harvard University in 1863, and at once entered the U. S. medical service, being commissioned assistant surgeon in the 43d Massachusetts volunteers, and served with distinction until the close of the civil war, having been rapidly promoted from surgeon of brigade and division to that of medical director in the department of the South. Dr. Marcy married Sarah E. Wendell, of Somersworth, N. H., and settled in Cambridge, Mass., where he devoted a considerable portion of his time to chemistry, as an assistant in this department of Harvard Medical College. In 1869, accompanied by his wife, he went to Europe, and entered the University of Berlin, devoting himself largely to the study of surgery, and in 1870 became Mr. Lister's first American pupil. Convinced of the correctness and value of the principles of the antiseptic methods of wound treatment, Dr. Marcy at once became the ardent advocate of the then revolutionary methods of surgical procedure. He established a private laboratory for the investigation of bacterial infection in wounds, also a hospital for the demonstration of the new teaching. It is generally accepted that to him, more than any other, is due the merit of having established the scientific rationale of modern wound treatment, and caused the rapid adoption of the new practice to be disseminated in America. Since 1876 he has been an annual contributor to the American Medical Association. At the International Medical Congress, in London, in 1881, he was invited to open the discussion before the most distinguished body of surgeons ever assembled in defense of the principles of antiseptic surgery. In 1882 he published a translation of the works of the late Prof. Ercolani, of Bologna. Dr. Marcy was one of the presidents of the International Medical Congress, held in Washington in 1887. He is a member, active or honorary, of many of the special medical societies in Europe and America, and in 1884 he was president of the American Academy of Medicine. In 1887 Wesleyan University conferred upon him the degree of LL.D. In 1892 he was elected president of the American Medical Association, the representative body of the medical profession of America. His

publications have chiefly related to surgical subjects, the most important of which are: "Plastic Splints in Surgery" (1877); "Cure of Hernia by the Antiseptic Use of the Animal Suture" (1878); "Histological Studies of the Development of the Osseous Callus in Man and Animals" (1881); "Aspiration of the Knee Joint" (1879); "Best Methods of Operative Wound Treatment" (1882); "Comparative Value of Germicides" (1882); "The History and the Surgical Treatment of Uterine Myoma" (1882); "The Peritoneum, its Anatomy, Physiology and Methods of Restoration after Injury" (1889). His most important publication, issued in 1892, is a quarto volume on the "Anatomy and Surgical Treatment of Hernia," illustrated.

LAWRENCE, Joseph Joshua, physician, was born in Edgecombe county, N. C., Jan. 28, 1836. He is of revolutionary ancestry on both the paternal and maternal sides; his fourth-removed paternal grandfather was of Anglo-Norman descent, and a native of Norwich, England. The son of this old ancestor was Frank Lawrence, a noted Indian fighter, and his son, Joseph Nathaniel Lawrence, was a lieutenant of the Continental army under Washington. His son was Joshua Lawrence, an eminent Baptist minister and author, who was the father of Bennett Barrow Lawrence, a prominent cotton planter in ante-bellum days, and father of Joseph Joshua. His mother was Martha Frances, daughter of Judge Jesse Cooper Knight, her mother's revolutionary ancestor was Augustin Clement de Villeneuve, Chevalier de Bar thelot. He was a captain of French troops under Lafayette, and was killed at Yorktown, in 1781, fighting

for the American cause. After receiving a university and medical education, Dr. Lawrence was married on May 3, 1860, to Josephine, daughter of B. F. Edwards, of North Carolina. He was captain in the Confederate army during the civil war. He practiced medicine in his native state a short time after the close of the war, and then removed to St. Louis. In 1873, he commenced the publication of the "Medical Brief," which has now the largest circulation, and is financially the most prosperous of any medical publication in the world. Dr. Lawrence is devoted to the material prosperity of St. Louis, and is a great believer in its future, as is witnessed by his owning several valuable pieces of St. Louis real estate. He is noted for his universal good humor, his optimistic views, and his practical business ability. He is one of the vice-presidents of the Business Men's League of St. Louis.

KIRKBRIDE, Thomas Story, physician, was born in Morrisville, Bucks co., Pa., July 31, 1809. His ancestor, Joseph, came to America as one of the colonists with William Penn. Thomas was educated in the school of the Society of Friends, then in the University of Pennsylvania, where he was graduated in the medical department in 1832. He became resident physician of the Friends' Asylum for the Insane at Frankfort, Pa., and then for two years had charge of the insane in the Pennsylvania hospital in Philadelphia. In 1835 he determined on general practice and continued it for five years. In 1840 he became superintendent of the newly established hospital in Philadelphia, where he remained until his death. He was the first man to insist upon and carry out the plan of separate buildings for the sexes among the insane, and raised $355,000 in Philadelphia and vicinity for the carrying out of his plans. He was a close student, devoting himself particularly to the study of insanity. He aided in founding and was for several years president of the Association of Medical Superintendents of the Insane, as well as being a member of many medical societies in America and Europe, not devoted to questions regarding insanity. In his various reports, pamphlets, books, and publications, he has treated in a very learned, as well as practical, way regarding the construction, heating, and ventilation of hospitals for the insane. He was a contributor to the "American Journal of Medical Sciences" and the "American Journal of Insanity." He also published "The Construction, Organization, and General Management of Hospitals for the Insane" (1884), and "Appeal for the Insane." His death occurred in Philadelphia, Pa., Dec. 16, 1883.

McLOUGHLIN, John, physician, was born in Canada in 1784, of Scotch-Irish parentage. He was employed as a physician by the Northwest Fur Co., in the first quarter of this century, and was stationed for a time at their posts in Canada. When, after a stubborn competition, the Hudson Bay Co. coalesced with its formidable rival, the Northwest Fur Co., in 1821, Dr. McLoughlin was made governor of all this territory in the great Northwest, with headquarters at Vancouver. All power was vested in him; more than 1,000 attachés of the company, and more than 100,000 Indians were subject to his authority. Dr.

McLoughlin was a rigid disciplinarian. He won the confidence of the Indians by his just and honest dealings with them. They were not allowed to be subjected to other treatment than that accorded a white man or woman. He served his employers with faithfulness and fidelity, and his conduct to the early American settlers was on broad Christian lines. If the records of both men were fully written, Dr. McLoughlin is entitled to as much praise in history for his treatment of the Indians as William Penn. But it is for his kindness to the early settlers of Oregon that Americans should honor his memory. Privations, weariness, and sickness were incidents of the journey across the plains prior to 1850, and to the immigrants arriving at the Columbia river, he was the Good Samaritan. He is said to have lost standing with his company and government because of his kindness to American immigrants. Great Britain claimed and was anxious to hold the territory occupied by the Hudson Bay Co., and when rebuked for his sympathy with the Americans, by the director of the company, he resigned his position and removed to Oregon City. He lived to verify the maxim that republics are ungrateful, for the government of Oregon took from him the valuable claim he occupied in Oregon City. He died at that place in 1857, and is buried in the Catholic cemetery. No marble shaft marks the spot, but what is better, his memory is lovingly and gratefully held in the hearts of the people.

MEIGS, Charles Delucena, physician, the son of Josiah Meigs, was born on the island of St. George, one of the Bermudas, February, 1792. His ancestors were of New England stock, people of moderate possessions, and "were well inured to daily labor, and to habits of simplicity and economy." He was graduated at the University of Georgia, 1809, and there for a time studied medicine under Dr. Thomas Hanson Marshall Fendall, and served as apothecary boy and apprentice, assisting his master in various kinds of labor, such as bleeding, cupping, blistering, etc. He subsequently attended lectures in the University of Pennsylvania, from which he received his degree of M.D. in 1817. He began practicing in Augusta, Ga., where he soon acquired a good practice, but owing to his wife's aversion to slavery, after two years residence in Georgia, he removed to Philadelphia, where he settled permanently. He received at first little practice there, and devoted his ample leisure to hard professional study, the acquisition of general literature, and to reviewing his classical knowledge. He evinced much force as a debater in the Philadelphia Medical Society, and in the College of Physicians of Philadelphia, and became one of the first editors of the "North American Medical and Surgical Journal." For several years he lectured on midwifery in the Philadelphia School of Medicine, and published in 1831, a translation of Velpeau's celebrated treatise on midwifery. In 1838 he published his first original work "Practice of Midwifery," which was followed, in 1847 by "Woman, her Diseases, and Remedies," and in 1849 by "Obstetrics, the Science and the Art." In 1850 appeared his "Certain Diseases of Children," and in 1854 a "Treatise on Acute and Chronic Diseases of the Neck of the Uterus," and his elaborate work on "Childbed Fever" also appeared in this year. He also contributed a paper on "Fibroid Tumors of the Uterus," to the transactions of the American Medical Association, and translated a treatise on "Diseases and Special Hygiene of Females" by Colombat de l'Isère. Many of his writings reached a third and a fourth edition. Besides his vast literary work, he had for many years a large practice in obstetrics, and was for a long while the acknowledged leader in the branch, not only in Philadelphia, but in the United States. In 1841, he was appointed professor of obstetrics, and diseases of women and children, in the Jefferson Medical College of Philadelphia, which position he retained until 1861, when he virtually retired from practice, and purchased a small farm twelve miles from Philadelphia, which he named Hamanassett after a small stream in Connecticut, near which his forefathers had settled. Here he gave himself up almost entirely to agricultural pursuits, literature, and the contemplation of philosophy. He was a member of numerous medical and social organizations in Philadelphia, but rarely attended social gatherings. In 1827 he was elected a fellow of the Philadelphia College of Physicians, and filled the office of censor, 1841-48, and was vice president in 1848. In 1818 he was awarded the honorary degree of M.D. from Princeton. He died at his country place, Hamanassett, Delaware co., Penn., June 22, 1869.

SMITH, Joseph Mather, physician, was born at New Rochelle, N. Y. March 14, 1789. His father was a distinguished physician of New Rochelle, and his mother a daughter of Samuel Mather, belonged to a prominent New England family, some of whom were among the founders of Harvard University, and many of whom were eminent in medicine and divinity. After having received his general education, Joseph began to study medicine in the office of his father in 1808. Here he remained three years, when he was licensed to practice by the Medical Society of Westchester county, of which his father was president. He settled in New York, and was for several years associated with Dr. William Baldwin. In 1815 he was graduated at the College of Physicians and Surgeons. Having a taste for literature, Dr. Smith, in company with Mott, Duprey, Bliss, and others, organized the New York Medical and Physical Society, and under Dr. Smith's supervision was published a volume of "Transactions," in 1817. He continued in successful practice, contributing frequently to the medical publications, and in 1824 published his "Elements of the Etiology and Philosophy of Epidemics," a work of so learned and logical a character that it attracted the most profound attention everywhere, and was pronounced at the time to be fifty years in advance of the medical literature on its subject. Dr. Smith did not believe in contagion in regard to the propagation of yellow fever, the plague, dysentery, typhus, and other fevers. He considered that these diseases were never communicated by a specific contagion, but were uniformly produced by a miasmal poisoning generated by materials entirely distinct from the human body. He also believed that when many persons ill with yellow fever or plague were crowded into small and ill-ventilated apartments, and cleanliness was neglected, the disease which would result would be typhus. In 1826 Dr. Smith was appointed to the chair of the theory and practice of physic in the College of Physicians and Surgeons in the city of New York, succeeding in that chair the illustrious David Hosack, who, with his colleagues, Mott and Francis, had gone out of the college and organized a new medical school. Dr. Smith continued in this professorship until the year 1855, during which time he delivered four important introductory discourses which were published. In May, 1847, Dr. Smith, as chairman, prepared the report of the committee of practical medicine for the American Medical Association at Philadelphia. In 1850 he published the "Transactions of the American Medical Association," his "Sources of Typhus Fever, and the Means Suited to their Extinction." In 1857 he read a paper before the New York Academy of Medicine upon "Puerperal Fever; its Causes and Modes of Propagation." He also published in 1860 as a report to the American Medical Association, "The Medical Topography and Epidemics of the State of New York." In 1855 Dr. Smith was established in the chair of materia medica in the college, which he continued to hold until his decease, his connection with the institution lasting for almost forty years. In the meantime he had received other honors, in 1829 being appointed by the common council of New York consulting surgeon to the Bellevue Hospital, which he, however, declined. In the same year he was appointed attending physician to the New York hospital, a post which he held up to the time of his death. In 1854 he was president of the New York Academy of Medicine, of which he was one of the early promoters. In 1864 he was appointed president of the Common Council of Hygiene of the Citizen's Association of New York. He married in May, 1831, Henrietta M. Beare, daughter of Capt. Henry A. Beare, British navy, who, with three sons and two daughters, survives him. Dr. Smith died on Apr. 22, 1866.

PHYSICK, Philip Syng, "The father of American surgery," was born in Philadelphia, Pa., July 7, 1768. His father was a man of vigorous intellect, strict integrity, and enlarged views, who held the office of keeper of the great seal of Pennsylvania, by appointment of the king, and who after the revolution acted as the agent of the Penn family, taking charge of their estates. He himself possessed a considerable fortune, and was therefore enabled to afford his son the best advantages of education. At the age of eleven years the boy was placed in the Friends' Academy, in Philadelphia, under the care of Robert Proud. He made great progress, and in due time entered the collegiate department of the University of Pennsylvania. In 1785 he was graduated, and at once began to study medicine with Dr. Adam Kuhn, who had been a pupil of the renowned Linnæus, and who was at that time professor of the theory and practice of medicine, in the University of Pennsyl-

vania. While studying with Dr. Kuhn the young man attended the lectures of the university, but was not graduated in medicine at that institution. After studying three and a half years, he went with his father to London, in 1788, and became a private pupil of the great John Hunter. Here he had access to the lectures of Clarke, Osborne, Baillie, Home, and Cruikshank. He was so successful in winning the confidence and regard of Dr. Hunter, that the latter procured for him the post of house-surgeon in St. George's Hospital. The young man continued to hold this post during the year for which he was elected, and conducted himself with such gratifying results that, on leaving, he received the diploma of the Royal College of Surgeons, and also the handsomest personal testimonials as to his conduct and abilities. For several months young Physick remained with Hunter, residing in his house, and assisting him in his professional business. In May, 1791, he went to Edinburgh and attended the lectures of the university in that city for a year, taking his degree of M.D. in May, 1792. He now returned to Philadelphia and began the practice of medicine. The following year an epidemic of yellow fever gave Dr. Physick ample opportunity to display his medical knowledge, his ability, and his courage. Having volunteered, he was elected physician to the Yellow Fever Hospital, which was established at Bush Hill. Here the zeal, energy and high medical qualifications which he displayed brought him public recognition, and in 1794 he was appointed one of the surgeons of the Pennsylvania Hospital. In the same year he was made physician to the Alms House Infirmary. All of these honors naturally increased his professional business, which now became very lucrative. In 1798, Philadelphia being again scourged with yellow fever, Dr. Physick again assumed his post of resident physician at the Bush Hill Hospital. He was twice afflicted with this terrible disease and came near losing his life. On his leaving the institution, the management presented him with a service of silver plate in ac-

knowledgement of "their respectful approbation of his voluntary and inestimable services." In 1800 Dr. Physick was urged to lecture on surgery before the university, as there was no separate chair of surgery in its faculty. He consented, and in this way began his important career as a public teacher. In 1805, a professorship of surgery having become imperative, the trustees of the institution created the chair and elected Dr. Physick to fill it. At this time Philadelphia was the American centre of medical education and ability, and Dr. Physick became formally associated with Barton, Wistar, Chapman, Dewees, Coxe, and other leading medical men of that city. As a lecturer, Dr. Physick was grave, dignified and impressive; as a teacher he was, both in matter and method, severely practical, teaching only that which he had himself thoroughly learned, mainly by the aid of his dissecting knife. While Dr. Physick had now reached his highest fame as a teacher, it was also the period of his largest practice as a physician, and the amount of work which he accomplished was extraordinary. In 1819 Dr. Physick was transferred from the chair of surgery to that of anatomy, and in this post he remained until 1831, when his failing health obliged him to retire, the institution conferring upon him the honorary title of emeritus professor of surgery and anatomy. During most of the years of Dr. Physick's great professional labor, he was himself a very sick man. The two attacks of yellow fever; in one of which he was bled to the amount of 176 ounces, tried his constitution terribly. He suffered also from dyspepsia, from frequent and severe attacks of catarrh, and from nephritic calculi. Yet, during all this disorder of his health, he did his work, as it appeared, to the full extent of his mental powers, and with comprehensive demand on all of his experience. Dr. Physick was married in the year 1800, to Elizabeth Emlen, a daughter of one of the most distinguished ministers of the Society of Friends. By this marriage he had four children; two sons and two daughters. Dr. Physick was extraordinary among practitioners in the ability and success with which he performed great operations in surgery. One of these, and one of the most important in his experience, was performed in 1831, after he had retired from general practice, and had refused to act in such cases. This operation was upon the late Chief-Justice Marshall. The operation was lithotomy, the result being a prompt and perfect cure through the removal of one thousand calculi. Justice Marshall was at this time seventy-six years of age, and the operator, sixty-three. Of course the hazard attending such an operation, great in itself, was considerably increased by the advanced age of Justice Marshall, besides which the responsibility, in the case of a man of such eminence and so valuable to the country was greatly enhanced. Dr. Physick was president of the Phrenological Society of Philadelphia in 1822, and of the Philadelphia Medical Society in 1824. He introduced many valuable instruments and methods. In 1825 he was made a member of the Academy of Medicine of France. In 1836 he was elected an honorary fellow of the Royal Medical and Chirurgical Society of London. Dr. Physick's last operation was made on Aug. 13, 1837, and was upon the eye in a most delicate case. From this time forward the symptoms and sufferings of his own disease increased rapidly. Dropsy of the chest set in, and after protracted suffering he died in Philadelphia, Dec. 15, 1837.

ROOT, Arthur Lewis, physician, was born in Gilbertsville, Otsego co., N. Y., May 24, 1859. He was prepared for college at the academy of his native town, and was graduated at the medical college of the University of the City of New York in 1883. Dr. Root was attached to the staff of the Ward's Island Hospital for eighteen months, being interne for six months, house-physician for six, and house-surgeon for six, acquiring in this period an immense amount of clinical experience. He subsequently commenced practice in New York city, and immediately began a career of uninterrupted success. He has a natural aptitude for the practice of medicine, being unusually able in grouping facts and diagnosing disease. He possesses in addition an untiring industry and devotion to his calling, and also a winning and sympathetic manner which endears him to his patients and inspires their confidence. He was for some years a pupil of Dr. Egbert Guernsey in the principles and practice of homœopathic theory, and seems to have been also an apt pupil of that distinguished practitioner in all the qualities of heart and manner which make the true physician. Dr. Root is a member of the Clinical Club, and the West End Medical Society, and one of the staff physicians of the Hahnemann and Metropolitan Hospitals. He is a Republican in politics, and a well-known member of the Colonial Club. Dr. Root married Oct. 23, 1888, Frances Robinson of New York, a most agreeable and accomplished woman.

CHAMBERLIN, Jehiel Weston, physician and surgeon, was born at Rock Falls, Wis., Oct. 29, 1857, son of George Harris and Antoinette (Weston) Chamberlin, and grandson of Preston Chamberlin, M.D., who pursued the practice of medicine and surgery in northern New York, where he enjoyed a long and active life. His father having become early imbued with an idea of the opportunities offered by the great West, migrated about the year 1850, and was one of the pioneers of Wisconsin, and settled at Rock Falls, where he has since been very successful in mercantile life. He is a direct lineal descendant of Richard Chamberlin, who was the first of the name in this country, being one of the earliest settlers of Sudbury, Mass., where he died in 1673. Among his ancestors was Joseph Chamberlin, who was a soldier in King Philip's war, and in the great swamp fight, December, 1675. Also Nathaniel Chamberlin, who was in the French and Indian wars of 1752–1755 and 1759, during which time he was captured, and held a prisoner for two years. Also Joseph Chamberlin, who was a lieutenant in the revolutionary wars, serving from 1775 to the end of the war. The doctor received his early education in the district schools at Rock Falls, and subsequently entered Galesville University, where he pursued a three years' course. During his earlier years he was actively engaged in his father's business, thereby receiving a business education. In 1878 he began the study of medicine, under the preceptorship of Dr. Dwight W. Day, and in 1879 was matriculated at Rush Medical College, at which institution he was graduated in 1882. He took several private courses of instruction, under able tutors, in diseases of the eye and ear, and also has a diploma from the Illinois Charitable Eye and Ear Infirmary. He afterwards went to Europe, and began a course of study in the Royal London Ophthalmic Hospital under Mr. John Couper, Mr. R. Marcus Gunn, Mr. John Tweedy, and Mr. Edward Nettleship, afterwards acting as assistant to these surgeons. He also visited, for purposes of instruction, Berlin, Paris, and Vienna, at which last place he pursued the study of his specialty, under the most prominent instructors there. Returning to this country in 1884, he located in St. Paul, Minn., where he engaged in the practice of his profession. Besides attending to a large private practice, he is oculist and aurist on the staff of the City and County Hospital, of which staff he is secretary. He is also oculist and aurist on the staff of St. Luke's Hospital, and the Babies' Home, and lecturer in the Training School for Nurses in St. Paul. He is a member of the County Medical and Pathological Societies, the Minnesota Academy of Medicine, and the Minnesota State Medical Society. He is a member of the Sons of the American Revolution, and is prominently identified with the various Masonic bodies of Minnesota. Dr. Chamberlin was married in October, 1887, to Clara A., daughter of Martin and Elmina Smithe, and has two sons, Ralph Weston and Harold Smithe Chamberlin

PRIME, Benjamin Young, physician, was born at Huntington, L. I., Dec. 30, 1733. He was graduated at the college of New Jersey in 1751, studied medicine with Dr. Jacob Ogden, Jamaica, L. I., and began his practice at Easthampton, L. I.

In 1756–57 he was tutor at his alma mater, receiving the thanks of the trustees, and a special testimonial, when he resigned his position. Yale College gave him the honorary degree of A. M. in 1760. On June 16, 1762, he sailed for England from New York, to visit European medical schools. On its voyage the vessel was attacked by a French privateer, and in the engagement Dr. Prime was wounded. At London and Edinburgh, and at Leyden in Holland, he attended medical lectures, receiving his diploma from the university of the last named city, July 7, 1764. Returning to America during the following November, he took up the practice of surgery in New York city. Here he espoused the cause of the American colonies in the differences with Great Britain, with great ardor, using his literary talents, which were neither few or uncultivated, in fanning the flames of patriotism. On the passage of the stamp act by the British parliament, he wrote "A Song for the Sons of Liberty in New York," which was extensively used for this purpose. Removing to Huntington, L. I., to watch over his father's declining years, he was obliged, at the opening of the revolutionary war, to fly to Connecticut with his wife and one child, where he remained, at New Haven, and at Wethersfield, until 1783, three children being born to him during this exile. Their departure was so sudden that Mrs. Prime had no place in which to conceal the family silver, save their well. Hastily gathering it into a canvas sack, she sank it in the well, and it was safely recovered after a seven years' deposit, upon her return to Huntington. Dr. Prime died suddenly at that place, Oct. 31, 1791.

WESTBROOK, Albert Ernest, physician, was born at South Woodbury, O., Dec. 17, 1840. He is of German ancestry, two brothers, John and Leonard Westbrook, having emigrated from their native country in early times; one of them settled in the North and the other in the South. His father, Solomon Westbrook, was a native of New York, but removed with his wife, Mathena, to Ohio in 1816. Here he found employment, first as a carpenter and afterward as a hotel-keeper, until 1836. He then rode on horseback to New Orleans, where he engaged in the practice of medicine for about one year, when he returned to Ohio, traveling in the same manner. Shortly thereafter he made the round trip to Canada, on horseback. In 1849 he went from Missouri to San Francisco on foot, being three months on the road. After two years of labor in the mines, with indifferent success, he returned to Ohio, thus accomplishing the remarkable feat of having traversed the country from lakes to gulf on horseback, and nearly from ocean to ocean on foot. The son was educated first at Mt. Hesper Seminary, where he was in almost constant attendance from eight to eighteen, then at the Ohio Wesleyan University. After completing his collegiate education he read medicine under Dr. I. H. Pennock of Morrow county, O., preparatory to entering the Cincinnati College of Medicine and Surgery, where he was graduated Feb. 23, 1862. In August of the same year he entered the 106th Ohio volunteer infantry as surgeon, and served in the field and hospitals until the close of the war. He was on detached duty at Gallatin, Tenn., where he had charge of the Post Hospital, and was medical director on the staff of Brig-Gen. E. A. Payne. He had charge of Forts Negley, Huston, and Morton, at Nashville, and was on duty in the hospital in Stevenson, Ala., for a time, serving as surgeon in the 68th

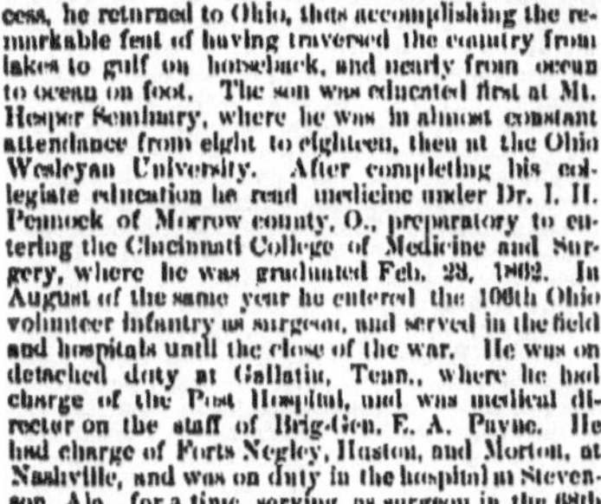

New York volunteer infantry. Dr. Westbrook is a member of the American Medical Association, the Ohio State Medical Society, and the Delaware County Medical Association, having served as president of that organization. In 1865 he opened an office in Ashley, O., where he has since resided. He has always found place at the front of every movement looking toward the moral and educational elevation of his community. For nine years he was a prominent member of the village board of education. Dr. Westbrook has been twice married; first, in 1866, to Amanda E., daughter of Judge S. T. Cunard, a prominent jurist, of Mt. Gilead, O.; and in 1888 to Rose M., daughter of Capt. L. M. Cunard of Mt. Gilead.

FOSTER, Eugene, physician, was born in Augusta, Ga., Apr. 7, 1850, the twelfth child of John Foster, who served twenty years as councilman, and one term as mayor of the city of Augusta. His mother was Miss J. E. M. Zinn, whose father was an honored revolutionary soldier. Eugene Foster was prepared by a thorough academic training, to make the most of his fine opportunities when he came to study medicine. He was graduated at the Medical College of Georgia in 1872. By continued application to the study of his profession, by careful attention to unusual clinical and hospital opportunities, and by a rapidly growing, and representative class of general practice, he has come to be one of the most highly qualified and prominent physicians, not only in the city of Augusta, where he has always resided, but in his state. The positions with which he has been

honored by his native state, mark him a man of exceptional ability. In 1884 he was elected president of the Medical Association of Georgia, and is now chairman of the board of censors of the association. He was president of the Richmond County Medical Society, and is now professor of principles and practice of medicine and state medicine in the medical department University of Georgia; visiting physician to City Hospital; president of the Alumni Society, medical department of the University of Georgia, and a member of the World's Congress of Medico-Climatology. He is, and has been for five years, a member of the board of trustees of the Lunatic Asylum of Georgia, and has done much to place this noble charity on its high plane of efficiency. He is a member of the Augusta Academy of Medicine; of the Medical Association of Georgia; of the American Medical Association; of the American Public Health Association; of the New York Medico Legal Society, and the American Academy of Political and Social Science. In 1880 he was unanimously elected president of the board of health of Augusta, and has been unanimously re-elected to this position in 1884, 1888, 1892. Upon his re-election to the presidency of the board, in 1884, the members of that body, as a testimonial of their personal regard and high appreciation of his services to his native city, presented him an elegant gold watch, chain, and seal, on which were engraved the sentiments of the donors. He is still president of the board of health in Augusta, and by his experience and special studies is one of the highest authorities in the South, on sanitation and its collateral bearings. His library is said to be one of the finest private libraries south of Baltimore. He has written much and ably upon the leading lines of his profession, and his opinions have obtained a flattering reception. He is the writer of several of the leading chapters in "Buck's Reference Hand book of Medical Sciences," and is the author of the article on vaccination, in vol. IX. "Transactions of the American Public Health Association." Numerous articles from his pen are to be found in the volumes of "Transactions of the Medical Association of Georgia." He writes after most careful preparation, and his wide, general reading adds life and clearness to what would otherwise necessarily be very technical and abstract discussions. He is an exceedingly able expounder of the germ theory of disease, having by diligent, laborious, and extensive research fitted himself to dispassionately, and discriminately speak upon what is probably, the most radical new standpoint of his profession.

EDWARDS, Charles Jerome, insurance manager and political economist, was born in Wayne county, N. Y., May 8, 1866. He is a descendant of Benjamin Edwards, a Welshman, who settled in the Massachusetts colony in 1760, and was a soldier in the war of the revolution. On the maternal side he is descended from Robert Chapman who came from Hull, England, in 1642, and settled in Saybrook, Conn., and was for forty-three terms a member of the Connecticut legislature, and for nine years an assistant deputy in the legislature, serving altogether more times than any other man in the history of the state. Mr. Edwards was educated in the common schools, and at the age of twenty became connected with the Equitable Life Assurance Society, as an agent, and two years later he became metropolitan manager for that company, and is at present (1896) so connected. Since 1892 Mr. Edwards has been active in the Democratic politics of Brooklyn and New York state, identified as a strong supporter of Mr. Cleveland, as opposed to Mr. Hill. The efforts of Cleveland's friends in New York state to secure his nomination for the presidency in 1892 brought Mr. Edwards prominently before the public, and, together with Edward M. Shepard, Charles S. Fairchild, and William R. Grace, he became a controlling power in the movement which ended in Mr. Cleveland's nomination in the national convention in Chicago. During that period he was foremost in organizing Kings county in the interest of the "anti-snapper" movement, which was opposed to Mr. Hill's nomination, and was a delegate to the Syracuse convention which sent a protesting delegation to the Chicago convention, he being one of such delegation. He has since that time been a confidential adviser, and one of the leaders, of the Cleveland Democracy. He was active in the presidential campaign as president of one of the largest Democratic clubs in Brooklyn, and was selected as the chairman of the committee appointed to devise a plan for continuing the organization of the Kings county Cleveland Democracy. Acting upon Mr. Edwards's recommendation, the Brooklyn Democratic Club was organized, and he became the chairman of its executive committee. It was under his management that the Independents fought the machine Democracy in the campaign of 1893, in support of Charles A. Schieren's candidacy and election to the mayoralty. He was also prominent in the Kings county Democratic re-organization, carried out under the auspices of the committee of 100 in 1893 and 1894, acting as its secretary. At the formal organization of the new Democratic party in Kings county, he was elected secretary of the gen-

eral committee, and for the first year he assumed practically its entire management and operations, and is at present vice-chairman of that organization. He was a delegate to the state conventions held at Saratoga, 1894, and in Syracuse, 1895, and had charge of the campaign of the reform Democracy in Brooklyn in the campaigns that followed. Mr. Edwards was married on Aug. 26, 1890, to Edith, daughter of Frederick S. Wendell of Portsmouth, N. H. In 1895 he was appointed commissioner of elections in the city of Brooklyn, the youngest man ever appointed there to a position, and the wisdom of his selection was made manifest of such importance through the reforms which he introduced in the board of elections.

COLE, Cordelia Throop, reformer, was born in Hamilton, N. Y., Nov. 17, 1833, the daughter of George A. and Deborah (Goldsmith) Throop. Her mother dying when Cordelia was two years old, she was taken in charge by her grandparents, Richard and Ruth Goldsmith. She received her education in what was then Hamilton Academy, now Colgate Seminary, and, being of a religious turn of mind, had decided to go as a missionary to India when her school days were over; but this mission was subsequently abandoned, by reason of marked change in religious belief. She was for four years principal in a private seminary for young people in Keokuk, Ia., and accepted later a similar position in the North Illinois Institute at Henry, Ill. Here, in 1856, she 
was married to William Rainey Cole. In 1863 Mr. and Mrs. Cole, with their three young boys, went to Cambridge, Mass., where Mr. Cole took a course in Harvard Divinity School, was ordained as a Unitarian minister, and went to Mt. Pleasant, Ia., which has since been their home. From 1876 to 1884 she was secretary of the Iowa Unitarian Association, as work she could do from the home centre, being otherwise wholly devoted to the duties of home and the education of her seven children. An important part of her work at this time was the development of the post office mission, a now firmly established branch of Unitarian work in all new fields. She was often called to fill vacancies in the pulpit of the denomination, and on two occasions gave the charge at ordination services. In 1885 she was made state superintendent of the Iowa W. C. T. U., of the department of the "White Shield and the White Cross." She handled the subject with great delicacy and power, and has delivered hundreds of addresses in Iowa and other states. She was at one time assistant to Miss Willard, but on the division among the workers, growing out of the political affiliations of the large body, she resigned. After the non-partisan organization of the National W. C. T. U. she accepted the position of national superintendent, still maintaining her allegiance to the Iowa work. She is at present (1896) general secretary of the Iowa Prohibitory Amendment League, a state body which has its headquarters at Mt. Pleasant; vice-president for Iowa of the American Purity Alliance, and with her husband edits the "Champion of Progress," a state paper, published at Mount Pleasant. Mrs. Cole has made many valuable contributions with her ready pen to the work of temperance and social purity; and has frequently addressed large audiences on these subjects. Her home at Mt. Pleasant is the centre of hospitality and active effort to "make life less difficult for others."

MERCER, Jesse, Baptist minister, founder of Mercer University, was born in Halifax county, N. C., Dec. 16, 1769. His great-grandfather came from Scotland to Virginia about 1700. His grandfather removed to Wilkes county, Ga., 1767. His father, Silas, was an able Baptist preacher. Jesse was immersed in a barrel of water. At nineteen, in 1788, he married Sabrina Chives, who died in 1826, and before he was twenty was ordained as minister. His main education was gained after his marriage, and he became a fair linguist. He began as pastor of Sardis Church, Wilkes county; then, in 1796, took Phillips Mills Church, now in Taliaferro county, which he served thirty-nine years, baptizing 230 persons; and the same year, Bethesda Church, Greene county, serving thirty-one years; and Powell's Creek Church, Hancock county, in 1797, serving twenty-eight years. He removed to Powellton in 1818, and to Wilkes county in 1826. In 1818 he organized a church at Eatonton, and was its pastor six years. He married Mrs. Nancy Simons in 1827, who died in 1841, and the same year organized a church in Washington, Ga., of which he was pastor until his death. In 1833 he bought the "Christian Index," published in Philadelphia by Dr. Brantley, and removed it to Washington, Ga., and in 1840 the paper was tendered to the Baptist state convention, and removed to Penfield. He was clerk of the Georgia Baptist Association from 1795 to 1816, and moderator from 1816 to 1839, and moderator of the Georgia Baptist state convention regularly until 1841, when prevented by feeble health, and was a member of the convention executive committee. He was unceasingly active in missionary labor. He was profoundly interested in education, being active in establishing Mount Zion College, in Richmond county, Ga.; he contributed liberally to a Baptist college in the District of Columbia, and was so ardent a friend and administrator of, and liberal contributor to, Mercer University, that this great and successful institution bears his honored name. Mr. Mercer was the greatest of Georgia Baptist ministers. He was of impressive appearance. He was intellectual, benevolent, firm, and gentle. His mind was clear, strong, and original, and his oratory had these qualities. He had fine capacity of analysis and illustration, immovable convictions, and the highest moral courage. His heart was instinct with noble aims, and his whole life a beautiful exemplification of the purest and most practical Christianity, and his death called forth a universal grief. He died Sept. 6, 1841.

SANDERS, Billington McCarter, first president of Mercer University (1833–39), was born in Columbia county, Ga., Dec. 2, 1789. His parents were Ephraim and Mary Sanders. He was graduated at the South Carolina College, Columbia, S. C., in 1809. He taught school two years, farmed twenty years, was licensed in 1823, and ordained in 1825. He preached until 1833, when he occupied a log cabin in the now lovely village of Penfield, and began Mercer Institute (now Mercer University), remaining president until 1839, and organizing this valuable college. He was the vital instrumentality in building the institution in its initial years. He preached fifteen years as pastor, was clerk several years, and moderator nine years of the Georgia Association; chairman of the executive committee of the Georgia Baptist convention, and president six years; editor of the "Christian Index," and delegate to the old Triennial convention, and the Southern Baptist convention. Mr. Sanders was a shining Baptist light for twenty-five years. Not logical or eloquent, he was earnest and persuasive. He had piety, common sense, energy, business judgment, and principle. He was twice married; to Martha Lamar in 1812, and to Cynthia Holliday in 1824, having twenty-two children. He died at Penfield, May 12, 1852.

SMITH, Otis, second president of Mercer University (1839–43). (See Index.)

DAGG, John Leadley, third president of Mercer University (1844–54), was born at Middleburg, Va., Feb. 13, 1794. At fifteen he became religious, and was baptized in 1812. He bore arms as a private in the U. S. army when the British attacked Washington, D. C. He preached first in 1816, was ordained in 1817. He was lamed in 1819, by leaping from a window, the floor giving way. In 1824 he was called to the church in Richmond, and in 1825 to Philadelphia, where his voice failed him in 1834. He then took charge of the Haddington College; in 1836 of the Alabama Female Athenæum at Tuscaloosa, and in 1844 became president of Mercer University, continuing until 1854. Dr. Dagg was a persuasive preacher, a surpassing college executive, a learned and strong writer, and the highest type of a Christian. Physically feeble, his sermons were most impressive, quiet, dignified, natural; his deliverances carried remarkable effect. He had marked intellectual powers, a varied and solid scholarship, and a gentle affability, combined with resolute firmness that made him loved and revered. He gave dignity to the new college. He published: "Manual of Theology," "Elements of Moral Science," "Church Order," and "Evidences of Christianity." He died at Hayneville, Ala., in 1881.

CRAWFORD, Nathaniel Macon, fourth president of Mercer University (1854–65), was born in Oglethorpe county, Ga., March 22, 1811. He was the son of the great statesman, William H. Crawford, who was of Scotch-Irish descent, and his mother, Susannah Gerdine, was of a French family. He lived in Washington, D. C., until fourteen years of age, while his father was U. S. senator, and was graduated at the Georgia State University in 1829, with the highest honors, among such men as Bishops Pierce and Scott and Chancellor Waddell. Dr. Church, the college president for thirty years, said he never saw a student with such powers of getting knowledge. He studied law under his father, and was admitted to the bar, but never practiced. He became professor of mathematics in Oglethorpe University, Ga., in 1837, and remained until 1841, and was ordained in 1844. He was pastor of the Baptist Church in Washington, Ga., in 1845; in Charleston, S. C., in 1846; professor of biblical literature in Mercer University in 1847–54, and president to 1856; professor of moral and mental philosophy, University of Mississippi, to September, 1857; professor of theology in the Baptist Seminary, Georgetown, Ky., to July, 1858; president of

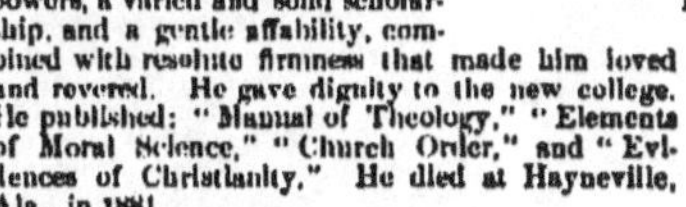

Mercer University to 1865; and president of Georgetown College, Ky., to 1872. Mr. Crawford had vast attainments and marvellous learning. His scholarship was as accurate as it was extensive. He mastered  everything—half a dozen languages, mathematics, sciences, history, poetry, metaphysics, law, politics, and theology. He was educated in, and joined, the Presbyterian church, and when he was about thirty he renounced the church of his fathers and became a Baptist, under the conviction that nothing was baptism but immersion. He wrote a work called "Christian Paradoxes." He died at Tunnel Hill, Ga., Oct. 27, 1871.

TUCKER, Henry Holcombe, fifth president of Mercer University (1866-71), was born in Warren county, Ga., May 10, 1819. His grandfather, Isaiah Tucker, removed from Virginia to Georgia in 1761. His mother's father, Rev. Henry Holcombe of Virginia, was a great pulpit orator, and the father of the Georgia penitentiary system, and founder of the Savannah Female Orphan Asylum, and Mount Enon Academy, an originator of the Georgia Baptist convention, and publisher of "The Analytical Repository," the first Baptist periodical in the United States. Henry was graduated at the Columbian College, Washington, D. C., in 1838. He was in mercantile business in Charleston, S. C., from 1839 to 1842, was admitted to the bar in Forsyth, Ga., in 1846, and practiced law until 1848. He married, in 1848, Mary C. West, whose death occurred within a year, driving him to the Bible for comfort, and impelling him to the ministry. He taught for three years at the Southern Female College, Lagrange, Ga., and was ordained in 1851; declined, in 1853, the presidency of the North Carolina Wake Forest College; became pastor of the Alexandria (Va.) Baptist Church in 1854; married Sarah O. Stevens; was professor of *belles-lettres* and metaphysics in Mercer University from 1856 to 1862; editor of the "Christian Index" in 1866; and the same year president of Mercer University until 1871; chancellor of the Georgia State University from 1874 to 1878, when he was again made editor of the "Christian Index."  He received the degree of D.D. from the Columbian College in 1860, and of LL.D. from Mercer University in 1876. Dr. Tucker was one of the most original thinkers of the South. He preached during his entire career after his ordination, and his sermons were always striking and powerful deliverances. Positive, sincere, independent, he was a leader in thought. Dr. Tucker was one of the remarkable men of his day. He wrote many pamphlets and sermons, and a book in 1868, "The Gospel in Enoch." He died in Atlanta, Ga., in 1889.

BATTLE, Archibald J., sixth president of Mercer University (1871-89), was born at Powelton, Ga., Sept. 10, 1826. His father was a wealthy North Carolina planter, who removed to Eufaula, Ala. Archibald was graduated at the University of Alabama in 1846. He professed religion at thirteen; was married to Mary E. Guild of Tuscaloosa, Ala., in 1847. He took charge of the Eufaula Academy; was tutor of ancient languages at the Alabama University in 1850; professor at the East Alabama Female College in 1852; licensed to preach the same year; ordained in 1853; became pastor of the Tuscaloosa Baptist Church in 1855; Greek professor of Alabama University in 1856; president of the Alabama Central Female College in 1860, founded by himself; president of the Judson Female Institute, Marion, Ala., in 1865; president of Mercer University, 1871-89. In 1879 he was pastor for an interim of the First Baptist Church of Macon. He received the degree of D.D. from Howard College, Alabama, and Columbian College, Washington, D. C., in 1872, and the University of Georgia in 1873. Dr. Battle has been one of the eminent instructors of the South. Every institution he has presided over has flourished. An able  preacher, an accomplished *belles-lettres* scholar, a profound metaphysician, a wise administrator, and rare Christian gentleman; he has taken the foremost rank among the best college presidents of the country. He published "Human Will."

NUNNALLY, Gustavus Alonzo, seventh president of Mercer University (1890-93), was born in Walton county, Ga., March 24, 1841. His parents, William Branch Nunnally and Mary Hale Talbot, of Virginia, settled among the first in Walton county. He was graduated at the State University of Georgia, Athens, in 1859, at eighteen, with second honor, the youngest graduate of the institution, missing the first honor only because of two months' absence from sickness. In 1860 he became professor of mathematics in Hamilton Female College; and in 1861 principal of the Johnston Institute, Walton county, to 1868, except that he served a while during the war as quartermaster, 9th Georgia state troops, under Col. P. H. Mell. He entered the ministry in 1865, and preached in the county churches of his vicinity, blending with it mechanics, trading, farming, editing, and the duties of county school superintendent. In 1876 he accepted the call of the Baptist Church at Rome, Ga.; in 1884 took charge of the church building department, inaugurated by the Southern Baptist convention in connection with the home mission board; in 1885 he was called to the Baptist Church, Eufaula, Ala.; in 1887 took charge of the Baptist interests in Anniston, Ala.; and was elected, in 1890, president of Mercer University, Macon, Ga., to succeed Dr. Battle, who resigned. Dr. Nunnally is one of the foremost among preachers and educators of Georgia. He is essentially a creative spirit, and full of zeal, energy, and executive ability. During his pastorate in Rome, the old house was torn down, and one of the handsomest churches in the state erected; and in Anniston he organized a large congregation, and led it to build a beautiful, $75,000, sandstone house of worship, increasing both congregations over 200 members each. During his brief administration of Mercer University, he has raised funds to erect new buildings, doubling the capacity of the college; the new, completed structure containing six large recitation-rooms, and as many offices, a chapel with 800 sittings, and library for 20,000 books. He increased the endowment, and $50,000 is expected to be soon raised, while the patronage has more than doubled. He has a power for stimulating enthusiasm, and inducing liberality. He pushed the Baptist church building department so vigorously that it was suspended, for fear its success would imperil the missionary boards, diminishing their needed funds. He is an original and argumentative preacher, earnest, fluent, and analytical. To literary finish, he adds practical judgment and financial ability. His social qualities are delightful. He married in 1859, Mary Briscoe, of Walton county, Ga.

GAMBRELL, James Brueton, eighth president of Mercer University (1898–), was born in Anderson county, S. C., Aug. 21, 1841. In 1843 his parents removed to Tippah county, Miss., then a very new country, where he grew up much in the style in which youth of the old-time South was reared, upon a plantation. He received his education in the county schools, pursuing at the same time a course of reading, the books being bought with the price of coon-skins, the prizes of nightly excursions through the great forests. By this means he acquired what was then the best library in the community in which he lived. His habit was to convey a book to the field, and placing it on the fence, read a few lines as the horse turned at the end of a furrow, and think over them while plowing the next round. He united with a Baptist church in his fifteenth year. He was prepared for college by Rev. Mr. Laird, a Cumberland Presbyterian minister, and afterward pursued his studies at Lowell's Academy at Cherry Creek, Miss. While at this school his state seceded from the Union, and he joined the Confederate army as a private soldier in the 2d regiment Mississippi volunteers. After serving some months in the line, he was promoted to the rank of sergeant, and placed in command of a company of scouts attached to Hill's corps. For conspicuous gallantry on the field he was promoted to the rank of captain, and sent west to raise a company of scouts for special service in Tennessee. Later he was transferred with his command to the army of northern Virginia, and participated in most of the great battles of that army. Here he met Mary T. Corbelle, a daughter of one of the oldest and most aristocratic families in Nansemonde county, Va., and on Jan. 13, 1864, at midnight, just within the Federal lines, they were married. During the year immediately succeeding the war, Capt. Gambrell began anew the pursuit of his education, with the help of his wife, a most accomplished woman. He says of her, "She has been my greatest earthly blessing and helper." This experience greatly stimulated his zeal in education; teaching set his mind on fire. A few years later he entered the University of Mississippi at Oxford, to pursue classical studies, and was graduated in 1876. During this time he was pastor of the Baptist congregation of Oxford, having been ordained to the work of the ministry in 1867. He was elected in 1877 editor of the newly established "Baptist Record," which position he filled for fifteen years, doing much work along many other lines in connection with his editorial labors; was secretary of the mission board for the Baptist state convention for two years, and connected vitally for

many years with the temperance movement throughout the nation. Through his instrumentality a gift of $10,000 was made by the American Educational Society to the University of Mississippi, and was the nucleus upon which an endowment of $75,000 was raised for that institution. He has been, since the close of the war, of the conciliatory group of public men in the South, and has addressed large assemblies in the North on many public questions with favor. Few lectures perhaps have had a wider reading than his famous address on "The White Side of a Black Question," delivered at Martha's Vineyard in 1891. He was elected president of Mercer University without solicitation in 1898, and has administered the position with marked distinction. The degree of D.D. was conferred on him by Furman University and that of LL.D. by Wake Forest College in 1893. Personally Dr. Gambrell is a man of remarkable magnetism. Plain, earnest, candid, and sincere, his words carry with them a weight too sadly rare in public men.

CROLY, Jane Cunningham ("Jenny June"), was born at Market Harborough, England, Dec. 19, 1831. She is of Scotch-English parentage. Her father was a Unitarian preacher. She was educated mostly at home, wrote stories and little plays as a girl, and acted them with her girl friends; began her journalistic life about 1850, the year before her marriage to D. G. Croly, a journalist on the New York "Press." Mrs. Croly began her work with no intention of doing more than "help to make a footing," but at once attracted attention, and won a place. At that time there were no departments for women on the press, and no women employed in regular salaried positions. Mrs. Croly made a field for herself, and one into which other women soon entered. She was at one and the same time the associate-editor of the New York weekly "Times" and "Messenger;" on the staff of the daily "Times," and "World;" a contributor to the "Democratic Review;" New York correspondent of New Orleans "Delta," and Richmond

"Whig;" and wrote the fashion departments of "Graham's Magazine," Frank Leslie's "Weekly," and "Monthly," and included the dramatic, the literary editorship, a special woman's department, and one-third the editorial page in her work on the weekly "Times." Mrs. Croly did the first work on the Demorest publications. She edited "Demorest's

Magazine " for twenty-seven years; was the regular New York correspondent of the Baltimore " American " for fifteen years; and for a syndicate of from twenty to twenty-five journals for over thirty years. She originated the system of duplicate correspondence. Her latest venture was the founding of a paper of original design called the " Woman's Cycle," which after a year of life was purchased and merged in the " Home-maker " of which she has become sole editor, devoting all her time to this work. Mrs. Croly has published several books: " Talks on Woman's Topics;" " For Better or Worse;" a practical cook book ; manuals of knitting, needle-work, etc. She is also known in Europe and America as the original founder of the first and most famous woman's club in this country, " Sorosis" of New York, and she was its first elected president, and afterwards its president for ten successive years. She is perhaps the best-known club and committee woman in the United States, and the most fertile in ideas. Above all she represents the all-round club idea, and the fellowship of woman, and probably no woman in the United States has done so much to bring this about.

TESLA, Nikola, electrician, was born in 1857, at Smiljan, Lika, in Servia. He is descended from an old and representative family of Servia. His father was a minister in the Greek church, who held the highest ecclesiastical rank open to a married clergyman, while his mother was  a woman of remarkable skill and ingenuity in the construction of looms, churns, and the machinery required in a rural home. Her brother is metropolitan of the Greek Church in Bosnia. Nikola received his early education in the public schools of Gospich, when he was sent to the higher Real Schule at Karlstadt, where, after a three years' course, he was graduated in 1873. He devoted himself to experiments in electricity and magnetism, much against the wish of his father, who had destined him for the ministry, but his native genius was too strong in the direction of mechanics, and he was allowed to continue his studies in the Polytechnic School at Gratz, with the intention of becoming a professor of mathematics and physics. He inherited a wonderful intuition, which enabled him to see through the intricacies of machinery, and despite his instructor's demonstration that a dynamo could not be operated without commutators or brushes, he was not convinced, and began experiments which ultimately resulted in his rotating field motors. In the second year Mr. Tesla relinquished the idea of becoming a teacher, and took up the engineering course. Upon the completion of the course, after a short sojourn at home, he began the study of languages at Prague, and later at Buda-Pesth, to qualify himself thoroughly for the engineering profession. He served for a short time as an assistant in the government telegraph engineering department, and then became associated with M. Puskas, who had introduced the telephone into Hungary. He invented several improvements, but not being able to reap the benefit of his ideas he sought a wider field, and went to Paris, where he secured employment as an electric engineer with one of the large companies engaged in electric lighting. During this period he endeavored to apply the rotary field principle to practical use, but having learned of the encouragement given to an inventor in the United States, he abandoned Europe, and set his face westward. Upon his arrival in the United States, he immediately found congenial employment in the Edison works, deriving great benefit and stimulus from Mr. Edison, for whom he has always had the profoundest admiration. Finding it impossible, however, to carry out his own ideas, he left the Edison works to join a company formed to place his inventions upon the market. He now perfected his old discovery of the rotary field principle, and succeeded in adapting it to the circuits then in operation, and in an exhibition of motors, illustrating a paper first read before the American Institute of Electrical Engineers in New York in 1888, triumphantly proved the correctness and value of his invention. In a subsequent lecture before the same society, in 1891, he demonstrated beyond question a distinct departure in electrical theory and practice, the practical results of which will revolutionize electrical science. Mr. Tesla was the first to conceive an effective method of utilizing the undulating current. It occurred to him, that if instead of a bar of iron, made magnetic by an electric current passing round it, he should use an iron ring, and use two alternating currents, so regulated that one would be positive when the other was negative, he could by means of wires, wrapped alternating about the ring, produce a magnetic current, which would travel around the ring in accordance with the frequency of the alternations in the electric currents, and a piece of iron placed within the magnetic field of the ring could be revolved by the changing poles of the magnetized ring. This converts electrical into mechanical energy more simply, effectively, and economically than by the direct current. The power now wasted in the steam engine is conserved by his " mechanical and electrical oscillator," an invention which vibrates the armature on the principle of the steam pump. Mr. Tesla's discoveries formed the basis of the attempt to utilize the enormous water power at Niagara Falls, and also underlay the combination of the Westinghouse and Baldwin companies to run a through railway express by electricity. Formerly electric energy could only be transmitted a few hundred feet, but by his invention, Mr. Tesla believes that it is possible to place 100,000 horse-power on a line at Niagara and deliver it at New York or Chicago with a loss in energy of less than twenty-five per cent. Mr. Tesla's work ranges far beyond the vast departments of polyphase currents and high potential lighting, and includes a great many other inventions in arc-lighting, transformers, pyro-magnetic generators, thermo-magnetic motors, improvements in dynamos, new forms of incandescent lamps, electrical motors, condensers, unipolar dynamos, the conversion of alternating into direct currents, etc. An account of his inventions has been given by T. C. Martin, editor of the " Electrical Engineer." Not all of Mr. Tesla's researches have been among machines, for he is a metaphysician, and has also something of his father's gift of oratory. He has also published a collection of his lectures delivered in New York, London, and Paris. The destruction of his workshop by fire in 1895, gave the world an anxious moment until it was learned that it was a loss of only a few dollars, and of " some sentiment." As for his machines, Mr. Tesla said, he could make them over in his shop, without availing himself of Mr. Edison's courteous and generous offer of the resources of his establishment at Orange, N. J. Illustrative of the world's estimation of his abilities, the New York " Sun" declared that " the men living at this time who are more important to the human race can be counted on the fingers of one hand ; perhaps on the thumb of one hand."

PARSONS, Richard Chappell, lawyer, was born at New London, Conn., Oct. 10, 1826. His family was among the earliest and most distinguished in New England. Four of his direct ancestors were graduated at Harvard College, and preached the gospel in New England. His grandfather, Rev. David Parsons, D.D., of Amherst, N. H., married a niece of William Williams, signer of the Declaration of Independence, and a cousin of Jonathan Edwards. He received a liberal education, and removed to Ohio in 1845, where he began the study of the law at Norwalk in the office of C. L. Latimer. He was admitted to practice in 1851, and the same year entered into partnership with Hon. R. P. Spalding, under the style of Spalding & Parsons, which soon took rank among the foremost law firms in Cleveland. Mr. Parsons was elected a member of the city council in 1852, and in 1853 was chosen president of that body. In 1857 he was elected a member of the legislature of Ohio, and re-elected in 1859. This legislature of 1860 was the first Republican general assembly chosen in Ohio. Mr. Parsons was elected speaker, and served two years. In 1861 he was offered, by Pres. Lincoln, the mission to Chili, which he declined, accepting the position of consul of the United States to Rio Janeiro. He resigned this place in 1863, and was appointed by Mr. Lincoln collector of internal revenue at Cleveland. In 1866 he was made marshal of the supreme court of the United States, and served six years. He was elected to congress in 1873. In 1872 he was offered by Pres. Johnson the governorship of Montana or the place of assistant secretary of the treasury, both of which he declined. Among his services in congress was securing the construction of a harbor of refuge at Cleveland, at a cost of $1,800,000. While editor of the Cleveland "Daily Herald" Col. Parsons began a series of articles in favor of removing Hudson College from Hudson, O., to Cleveland. He also urgently solicited some prominent citizens to subscribe a half million of dollars necessary for the removal. Mr. Parsons also took active efforts to enlist the trustees of the college in the project, and Rev. Dr. H. C. Haydn led the way favoring the removal. The trustees voted in favor of removing the college, provided the necessary means could be provided. Soon afterward Amasa Stone of Cleveland, offered to give the entire sum of $500,000, provided the college should be named after his son, Adelbert Stone, who died before completing his college term. The trustees accepted this arrangement, and the Hudson College was transferred to Cleveland. Adelbert College is now a part of the Western Reserve University which includes a college for women of over 100 students. The establishment of this university at Cleveland has already produced most remarkable benefits to the city. For many years Mr. Parsons has been specially prominent in matters of lake improvements, and has the reputation of securing the building of more light-houses, life-saving stations, break-waters, fog signals, and clearing obstructions in rivers and harbors than any other man living. Mr. Parsons joined the Free Soil party in 1848, and was one of its earliest leaders. In 1847 he became the principal owner and editor of the Cleveland "Daily Herald," and for three years the paper, under his care, was among the most influential in the West. Some of his addresses and speeches have been published in book form. He married the only daughter of Judge Samuel Starkweather.

FLIESS, William Maynard, mining engineer, was born in Prussia, Sept. 7, 1833, the son of Dr. Jules Robert Fliess, a celebrated physician who, on coming to America, settled in Baltimore, Md. In 1855, during the yellow fever epidemic in Norfolk, Va., Dr. Fliess was conspicuous in ministering to the yellow fever victims, and became a martyr to the scourge. He was buried by the citizens, and his name placed on the monument in the Norfolk cemetery. His wife, Joan Maynard Fliess, was a leading church-woman, and devoted much time to charity. The son was educated largely by his mother, and was sent to England to complete his education. He then studied law, but not having an inclination to practice that profession, became a distiller, and afterwards a mining engineer, and investor in mining properties. Mr. Fliess was chairman of the law committee, of the committee of seventy, who broke up the old Tweed ring in the city of New York. He de-

clined the nomination for alderman-at-large in 1872, and the appointment as governor of Utah, proffered by Pres. Grant during his administration. He was one of the first New York capitalists to open mines in Utah, and is largely interested in California, Montana, and Utah mines. He is president of the California Mining and Water Co., of the Hollywood Distillery Co., of the St. Joseph and Kansas Railroad, and an officer, and member of various clubs and social associations. Mr. Fliess was married, in 1863, and is a member of the Church of the Heavenly Rest (Protestant Episcopal), New York city. He is a thorough business man, a good public speaker, an enthusiastic fisherman, and an excellent rifle shot.

GRIFFITH, Harrison P., educator, was born in Laurens county, S. C., Feb. 25, 1837. His ancestors came to America from Wales. He was brought up on a farm, educated in the common schools, attended Furman University two years, and was married to Amanda P. Lanford of Spartanburg, S. C., June 18, 1861. In August, 1861, he entered the Confederate army as captain in the 14th South Carolina Volunteers. In the Battle of the Wilderness, in 1864, he was so disabled by two wounds as to be of no further service in the field, and so was assigned to post duty. He returned to his farm, where he remained until 1872, when he established a high school at Woodruff, S. C., which he successfully conducted until 1881, when he was elected principal of Cooper-Limestone Female Institute, by the Spartanburg Baptist Association. This school was, at the time, the property of Peter Cooper of New York, who had acquired the property and donated it to the association on condition that a school should be maintained there. Prof. Griffith faithfully administered the trust, and built up a flourishing school. He is an eloquent and magnetic public speaker, and popular with all classes, creeds, and political parties. He is an able educator, and has done much towards building up the fortunes of the new South. He is the author of a number of papers.

TOWNSEND, William Penn, manufacturer, was born in Pittsburgh, Pa., Apr. 13, 1817, son of Robert and Deborah (Colman) Townsend of New Brighton, Pa. The family is among the oldest in the state, being descended from Richard Townsend of Gloucestershire, England, and his nephew, Joseph, who came to America with William Penn in the ship Welcome. They landed near the site of Chester, Oct. 24, 1682, and Richard soon after built a mill at Chester Creek. Joseph Townsend, born in Berkshire, England, settled on a grant of 882 acres of land near Westchester, Pa., in 1725, and died in 1766. He married Martha Woolerson of England. Their son Joseph married Lydia Reynolds of Chichester in 1739, and was the father of Benjamin Townsend, who in 1784 married Jemimah Booth of Uniontown, Pa., and was the grandfather of our subject. His son Robert was born in Westland, Pa., Apr. 9, 1790, and in 1816 married Deborah, daughter of Thomas and Elizabeth (Mayes) Colman of Norwich, England. He owned and operated the first wire-mill west of the Alleghany mountains, which he built at Fallston, Pa., in 1828. He died in New Brighton, Oct. 1, 1897. Their son, William Penn Townsend, received a common school and academic education, and in 1834 entered his father's warehouse in Pittsburgh. In 1840 he became a member of the firm. His father retired from the firm in 1861. In 1866 he associated with him in the business his two sons, Charles C. and Edward P. Townsend, under the firm-name of W. P. Townsend Co. He retired from active business in January, 1894. During its entire history the house founded by his father and firmly established by himself and his sons, has enjoyed an unbroken record of honor and success. In his personal relations Mr. Townsend exhibited the highest character and the strictest integrity. He enjoyed the highest respect of all who knew him. He was earnest and active as a member of the Presbyterian church, and contributed largely to benevolent enterprises. He was married, March 2, 1841, to Sarah A. Champlin of Elbridge, N. Y., and had two sons and three daughters. He died at his home at New Brighton, Pa., Sept. 27, 1894.

SHEEDY, Dennis, financier, was born in Ireland, Sept. 26, 1846. His father, John Sheedy, was a farmer in comfortable circumstances, who emigrated to this country, with his family, while Dennis was an infant, and settled in Massachusetts. Young Sheedy was early thrown upon his own resources by the death of his father, and even then displayed remarkable foresight and business sagacity in the management of his affairs. He attended school in the winter, and was a clerk in a store in summer. In 1863 he removed to Denver, then a town of village proportions, and secured employment in a mercantile house. The following year he went to Montana, and embarked in mining and merchandise business, in which he was phenomenally successful. With a roving disposition, and the desire to make a mark in the world, he engaged in business successively in Salt Lake City, Utah, Lemhi City, Idaho, and other western states and territories, and proved the fallacy

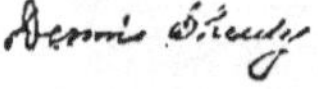

of the proverb of the "rolling stone" by the success of all his ventures and investments. In 1869 he made a tour through the Eastern and Southern states, including a horseback ride of over 600 miles in southwestern Texas, where he invested and dealt extensively in cattle. During the seventies he made Kansas his headquarters, his herds of cattle at one time reaching 32,000 heads. In 1881 he located in Denver, Col., and became a large stockholder and a director of the Colorado National Bank of which he has been vice-president since 1882. He soon became president and general manager of the Globe Smelting and Refining Co., and was instrumental in arranging with the railroads for reduced rates on lead, ore, and other mine products, thus admitting them to the smelters of Colorado. In 1892 Mr. Sheedy was chosen manager of the Denver Union Real Estate, Live Stock and Investment Co.; was treasurer of the Colorado Mining Exchange, Western Patent Co., and has displayed inventive genius by a number of valuable inventions of his own. He was elected in 1894 president of the Denver Dry Goods Co., and still holds the office. In 1882 he married Katherine Ryan of Leavenworth, Kan., a woman of rare culture, who largely interested herself in the various charitable and social functions of the capital city. She died in 1895, leaving two children. Mr. Sheedy has traveled widely throughout the United States and the West Indies. He has one of the finest libraries in the city, filled with the latest works in literature, history, and science. He is liberal and unostentatious in his charity, and prominent in all public enterprises. His speeches before the state legislature and public assemblies stamp him as a fine scholar, a deep thinker, and a man of astute understanding in the conduct of public affairs. Mr. Sheedy is tall and erect in person, well-formed, and has the air of the scholar. He is liberal in his views, and his quickness in grasping opportunities makes him a leader of men.

WESTON, John Burns, clergyman and president of the Christian Biblical Institute, Stanfordville, N. Y., was born in Madison, Me., July 6, 1821, a descendant of the first settler of Somerset county. His minority was spent on a farm. His school privileges were small, even for a country district, but by

studiously improving his leisure moments under the instruction of his father, he was fitted, at seventeen, for teaching school. Besides the ancient classics, he read largely in French, and was prepared for advanced standing in college classes. His circumstances did not allow him to enter college, and under a conviction of duty, at the age of twenty-two, he entered the ministry of the Christian denomination, of which he has been a member since his fourteenth year. The following ten years were devoted to ministerial work, varied with service as office editor of the "Herald of Gospel Liberty," published at Newburyport, Mass., and in an agency for the establishment of Antioch College. In the meantime he studied German and Hebrew. Upon the opening of Antioch College, under the presidency of Horace Mann, in 1853, he resigned his pastorship at Portland, Me., and went to Ohio and entered the college. Here he took the studies of both the classical and elective courses, at the same time teaching a class in the institution. In 1857 he was appointed a member of the faculty, and was associated with Pres. Horace

Mann until his death in 1859. Mr. Weston continued on the faculty of Antioch until 1881, at first as principal of the preparatory department, and afterwards as professor of Greek. Sometimes he was acting president, and frequently filled vacancies in other professorships, especially in philosophical, historical, and classical departments. In some of the critical periods of its life the college owed its continuance to his self-sacrificing labors and assumption of responsibilities. During this period he also gave courses of lectures to the theological classes of Wilberforce University of Xenia, O. He is one of the original members of the American Philological Association and of the Ohio Association of College officers. In 1881 he was appointed president of the Christian Biblical Institute. Besides his work as an educator, all measures of public beneficence, religious advancement and moral reform have found in him an active advocate and supporter. The degree of D.D. was conferred on him in 1884 by two colleges, Antioch, where he delivered the oration on the unveiling of the statue of Horace Mann, and Union Christian College.

HARTRIDGE, Augustus Griffin, lawyer, was born in Jacksonville, Fla., May 27, 1869, son of Dr. Theodore Hartridge, a native of Savannah, Ga., but who removed to Florida in early life, married Susan, daughter of Madison L. Livingstone of Abbeville, S. C., and became one of the most prominent physicians and leading citizens of Jacksonville. The Hartridge family is of English descent, one of their ancestors having been a lord of the admiralty in the last century. Augustus was educated at the public schools of Jacksonville, and was graduated at its high school in 1886, when seventeen years old. He

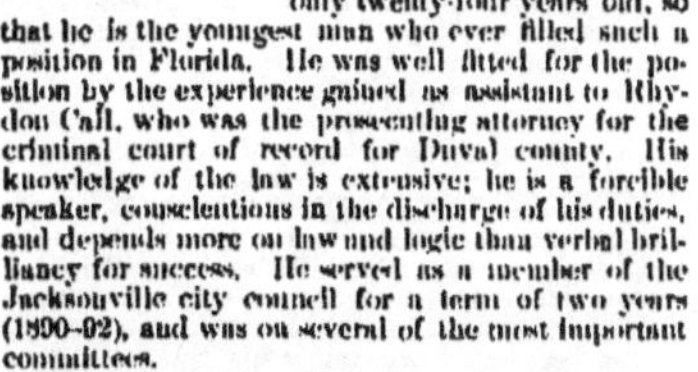

then entered the military academy in Charleston, S. C., for a year, and, on returning home, began the study of law in the office of his brother, John E. Hartridge, in Jacksonville. He was admitted to the bar in the U. S. court, June, 1890, and afterward practiced in his native city. He has been prominently identified with the state national guard, having been first lieutenant of the Jacksonville light infantry, and the adjutant of the 1st battalion for two years. He was appointed state's attorney for the fourth judicial district by Gov. Mitchell, May 27, 1893, when he was only twenty-four years old, so that he is the youngest man who ever filled such a position in Florida. He was well fitted for the position by the experience gained as assistant to Rhydon Call, who was the prosecuting attorney for the criminal court of record for Duval county. His knowledge of the law is extensive; he is a forcible speaker, conscientious in the discharge of his duties, and depends more on law and logic than verbal brilliancy for success. He served as a member of the Jacksonville city council for a term of two years (1890-92), and was on several of the most important committees.

STUBBS, John Christian Spayd, railway manager, was born at Ashland, O., May 31, 1847. He is the fifth generation born in America descended from Thomas Stubbs, an Englishman of Quaker ancestry, who came to this country in 1716, and married Mary Minor, in Chester county, Pa., in September, 1720. His father is J. D. Stubbs of Ashland, O., who married Mary Jane, daughter of Rev. David Gray, one of the pioneer Methodist preachers of Ohio. His father served in the civil war as reg-

VI.—26

imental quartermaster of the 42d Ohio (Gen. Garfield's regiment); was afterward captain and assistant quartermaster of volunteers on the staff of Gen. James A. Garfield; and later served as depot quartermaster at Nashville and Johnsonville, Tenn., Raleigh and Newbern, N. C., and Charleston, S. C. In 1866 he was chief quartermaster of the department of North Carolina. The son's preliminary education was received at the common schools of Ashland, and was interrupted by the breaking out of the civil war, when he accompanied his father into the field; though, because of his youth, he was not allowed to take part in the fighting, but was given a clerkship in the quartermaster's department in 1863, and continued in that work, performing various duties, from check clerk to chief clerk, until August, 1868, when he returned to Ohio. In the spring of 1869 he took service as clerk in the general freight office of the Pittsburgh, Cincinnati and St. Louis Railway Co., of which his uncle, D. S. Gray, was general manager. In October of the following year he entered the service of the Central Pacific Railroad Co., as chief clerk in the general freight office at Sacramento, Cal., and advanced rapidly to the position of freight traffic manager; and, in 1884, on declining a similar position on the Atchison, Topeka and Santa Fé Railroad, was promoted to the office of general traffic manager, which put in his charge the general direction, throughout the whole system, with its leased lines, of both passenger and freight traffic. In 1889 he accepted the second vice-presidency of the Chicago, Milwaukee and St. Paul Railroad Co., but, a month later, was recalled to the Southern Pacific Co., successor to the

Central Pacific Railroad Co., as fourth vice-president. Not long after, he was made third vice-president. Mr. Stubbs's activities were not confined to railway management, however. In 1881 he was elected president of the board of education of the city and county of San Francisco, and served in that capacity during the whole term of the board. Despite the meddling of the politicians, he inaugurated valuable reforms in school administration, and pushed them through to the great and lasting benefit of the educational system and institutions of the city and county. Mr. Stubbs owes his success to unremitting diligence in mastering the details of his particular branch of business, to his loyalty to the interest of his employers, and to his excellent administrative ability and good judgment in the selection of able assistants. He married, Aug. 14, 1871, Mary, daughter of Jacob Patterson of La Crosse, Wis., and Sacramento, Cal., by whom he has six children.

HEALD, Charles Mercer, railroad manager, was born in Baltimore, Md., July 5, 1849. His father, William Heald, who was born in Wilmington, Delaware, in 1788, and died in Baltimore in 1868, was a prominent and successful merchant. His mother was Belinda Eleanor, daughter of Col. John H. Simmons of Frederick, Md. She was born in 1810, and died in 1881. The death of his father caused the son to leave Yale College, where he had been pursuing his studies for over two years, and to return to Baltimore, where he shortly afterwards embarked in mercantile life. In 1872 he entered the service of the Baltimore and Ohio Railroad Co., in which he was rapidly promoted until he became general agent at Locust Point, Baltimore, the great terminal of the Baltimore and Ohio system, where are located several grain elevators, also coal piers and bonded warehouses, and where large numbers of ocean steamers receive, and discharge, cargoes of merchandise, grain, cattle, and thousands of immigrants are landed annually, making the position of general agent at this place one of the most important in the service. He left the company in 1876, and was for a time business manager of the Baltimore "Gazette," and later engaged again in mercantile pursuits; but his inclinations were still in the direction of the great field of transportation, and especially in the line of railroad management, and about Jan. 1, 1878, he was appointed cashier to the receiver of the Long Island Railroad Co., and two years later the title and duties of general ticket agent were added. In 1881, when the road was sold and an entire change made in the management, he returned to the service of the Baltimore and Ohio, but only remained a few months, when the new management of the Long Island Railroad Co., tendered him the place of general traffic manager of all its lines, which he accepted, and continued to fill until November, 1886, when he was appointed assistant to the general manager of the Philadelphia and Reading Railroad Co., and afterwards freight traffic manager of that company. On Feb. 1, 1889, he was elected president of the New York, Susquehanna and Western Railroad Co., and retired from the presidency Feb. 1, 1890. On March 1, 1890, he was appointed general manager of the Detroit, Lansing and Northern, and the Chicago and West Michigan railways, which comprise about 1,000 miles of railroad. His headquarters and residence are at Grand Rapids, Mich.

NEWHOUSE, Samuel, railroad president, was born in New York city, Oct. 14, 1853, son of Isaac Newhouse, who was a pioneer merchant of the anthracite coal region of Pennsylvania. He obtained his education in the Central High School of Philadelphia, and then began reading law in the office of A. W. Winton, of Scranton, Pa., and later with Edward N. Willard of the same place. He remained with Mr. Willard until 1873 when he was made clerk of the courts of Lucerne county, Pa., which position he held until 1879, when he removed to Leadville, Col., and engaged in the freight transportation business before railroads were built in the region. He took machinery into the mountains and handled the merchandise throughout that vicinity. In 1886 he began mining in the San Juan region of southwestern Colorado, where he operated successfully several large properties. In 1888 he removed to Denver, Col. In 1889 he went to England and began to float the stock of several large enterprises, the most important of which was the Newhouse Tunnel between Idaho Springs and Central City. This tunnel when completed will be four and a half miles long, and will cut through about 300 gold veins. The expense of its construction will reach over $2,000,000 when completed. Mr. Newhouse owns a half interest in the tunnel, and the other half belongs to the English capitalists who are furnishing the money. He is the originator of the Denver, Lakewood, and Golden railroad, started in 1891, and in 1894 was made president of the company. He was married, Jan. 1, 1883, to Ida H. Stingley, daughter of Hiram Stingley of Virginia.

JOHNSON, Lorenzo M., railroad manager, was born in the city of New York, Jan. 22, 1843. His father, Rev. Lorenzo Dow Johnson, was descended in a direct line from John Alden and Priscilla Mullins, who were among the first to land at Plymouth in 1620, while his mother was a descendant of Thomas Burges, who landed at Salem, Mass., in 1627. The home of his parents was in Plymouth county, Mass., where he lived and went to school, and worked on the family farm until 1860, when he was appointed an aid in the U. S. coast survey. He was engaged in this service during a survey of Mobile Harbor; the projected canal across the base of Cape Cod; office work in Washington and volunteer guard duties; until assigned Sept. 27, 1861, to duty in the pay-department of the army. In this capacity he was with the Army of the Potomac at the capture of Yorktown, and during the Seven Days' Battles on the Peninsular, and at the capture of Vicksburg, Dec. 13, 1863. At the end of that year, he was ordered to the Pacific coast *via* the Isthmus, and while there traveled over Oregon, Washington, and Idaho. After an examination at the state department, he was appointed one of the thirteen consular pupils, Sept. 12, 1867, under a law intended to create a permanent consular and diplomatic service, and was assigned to duty in Syria, where he served as vice-consul at Beirut, Jaffa, Jerusalem, and Damascus, and was promoted from consul, July 13, 1870, to consul-general at Beirut. After extensive travels in Asia and Europe, he returned to America in 1871, and entered Yale University, being graduated

in 1874 with the degree of B.A., and in 1875 as civil engineer. Going immediately to Iowa, he entered, Sept. 1, 1874, the service of the Keokuk and Des Moines Railway Co., where he passed through the various grades of engineer, chief engineer, paymaster, acting general superintendent, and assistant-general superintendent. Accepting the appointment of general manager of the Cairo and St. Louis railroad, Dec. 7, 1877, he remained there until Jan. 1, 1881, when he was appointed assistant to the president of the Pullman Palace Car Co., having charge of disbursements and construction, meanwhile becoming vice-president of the Cairo and St. Louis Railroad Co. On Dec. 1, 1883, he accepted the appointment of general manager of the Mexican International Railroad Co. To this has been added the management of the Construction Co. in Mexico, and the three coal companies which have been developed under his charge, now producing annually about 300,000 tons of coal, and 40,000 of coke, the only product of this class in the republic of Mexico; and of the Hacienda de Soledad of 225,000 acres, stocked with 10,000 cattle. He was married, Apr. 22, 1878, to Helen Wolcott, daughter of Gen. Hart L. Stewart of Chicago. He is a member of the American Society of Civil Engineers, the Chicago Club, Sons of the American Revolution, New England Society, and other scientific and literary societies.

THURSTON, Charles Baldwin, railway president, was born in New York city, Apr. 2, 1832. He was a son of Peter Kipps Thurston, a well-known pianoforte manufacturer of that city, and a grandson of Rev. Peter Thurston, who came from London to New York in 1767. The father dying when he was a young lad, be afterwards made his home with his uncle, Justice David W. Baldwin of Newark, N. J., attending the school of William Walton, where he received his primary education. After attending the academy at Chatham, N. J., under the instruction of Prof. Forgus, for two years, he returned to Newark and finished his school education under Nathan Hedges, a celebrated teacher. He then entered himself as a medical student with his cousin, Dr. Dennis E. Smith of Brooklyn. Becoming acquainted, while there, with Dr. Geo. Wood, a well-known and skilful dentist, whom he often assisted in his laboratory, be finally decided to apply himself exclusively to dentistry. For this purpose he again returned to Newark and engaged with Dr. John Hassell, a dentist having a large practice and an excellent reputation. After completing his studies there, he commenced the practice of dentistry himself in Newark and was remarkably successful, achieving some very fine results in dental surgery and establishing for himself an enviable name. In consequence of applying himself too closely to his profession, his health failed, and he gave it up in order to associate himself with his uncle in the paint and varnish business. Their factory was in Newark, with branch offices in Chicago and New Orleans. The business not being congenial to his taste, he severed his connection with it early in 1865 and went, *via* Panama, to California and Nevada, to look after some mining interests. He returned east by the Nicaragua route in 1867, making his residence in Jersey City, N. J., and accepted the agency of several leading insurance companies. In the course of this business he secured control of the insurance of a number of large railroad companies, and among them that of the United New Jersey and Camden and Amboy Companies. When these lines were leased by the Pennsylvania Railroad Company, he became associated with A. L. Dennis in looking after the general interests of that company, and is its special agent for the care of their real estate in New Jersey, New York and Brooklyn. He was also made director in a number of companies controlled by it. In 1872 he was elected trustee and secretary of the associates of the New Jersey Company, which position he still holds (1894). In 1882 he was elected president of the Jersey City and Bergen Railroad Company (whose lines were leased in 1893 to the Consolidated Traction Company). Judge Knapp of the supreme court of New Jersey, in 1888, appointed him as one of the park commissioners of Hudson county, and he was elected president of the board, which position he held as long as it continued in existence. Judge Werts (afterwards governor of New Jersey) appointed him to succeed William Muirheid as one of the commissioners of adjustment of Jersey city. He was president of the Fayetteville Water, Light and Power Company of Fayetteville, N. C., of the Jersey City Chain Works of Jersey City, N. J., of the Port Richmond, S. I., and Bergen Point, N. J., Ferry Company, the Millstone and New Brunswick Railroad Company, and of the American Employers' Liability Company of New Jersey, which insures the legal liability of employers or companies, for death or injury, as the result of accidents to employees —the first company in America to cover that business exclusively. He is also a member of the managing committee of the Boston Lloyd's and of the Assurance Lloyd's, and is a director and trustee in a large number of corporations, and receiver of others. He is a member of the Jersey City Club and the Carteret Club of Jersey City and of the Sullivan County Club, the Lawyer's Club, and the Metropolitan Museum of Art of New York. On Apr. 14, 1859, he married Lida, daughter of James J. Armour of New York. They have no children. Mr. Thurston has long been a prominent member of the Masonic fraternity.

BURT, Grinnell, railroad manager, was born at Bellvale, N. Y., Nov. 7, 1822. He is the seventh descendant from Henry Burt, who came from England and settled in Roxbury, Mass., in 1638, and who afterward was one of the original founders of the city of Springfield, Mass. His father, Benjamin Burt, was the son of James Burt, who was one of the prominent men of Orange county. Our subject received his early education in the village public schools, and after spending several years in Ohio returned to New York and began the study of law, developing such qualifications that his legal friends urged him to make the practice of law his profession and apply for admittance to the bar. But his inclination was for the organization and development of railroads, and as early as 1852 he became identified with the building of a road from Newburg to the Delaware. In 1859 Mr. Burt organized the Warwick Valley Road from Greycourt, on the Erie Railroad, to Warwick, N. Y. In 1878 he organized the Wawayanda road, extending the Warwick Valley Road to McAfee, which in 1881 was extended to Belvidere on the Delaware. In 1882 these various roads were consolidated, under the corporate name of Lehigh and Hudson Railroad, over which, in their separate or consolidated capacity, Mr. Burt has been both president and manager from 1859, being the oldest railroad president in continuous service in the state. While thus employed, he was also active in developing the Middletown, Unionville and Water Gap Road, which, as president, he rescued from financial embarrassment. In 1878 he built forty miles of the Pittsburgh and Western Road, of which he was for a time superintendent of construction. In 1883 he was president of the Cincinnati, Van Wert and Michigan Road, which was extended 100 miles under his administration, and was for several years president of the Kanawha and Michigan Railroad. He was one of the committee which so successfully reorganized the Toledo and Ohio Central Road, and was also largely instrumental in the successful reorganization of the New Jersey Midland Road. In 1875 Gov. Tilden appointed him one of three commissioners to remove

obstructions on the Delaware river, which was accomplished with less expenditure than the amount of the appropriation, a result so unusual as to call for general commendation. Mr. Burt has been identified with various projects for bridging the Hudson river, and has held many responsible public positions. He has served for many years as president of the Middletown State Homœopathic Hospital, and since his residence in the town of Warwick has held many offices of trust and responsibility. Mr. Burt has independent notions and an aggressive spirit, and has achieved success where more pliant men would have failed. His rugged honesty of purpose has never been questioned, even when he has been most bitterly assailed. He is a keen observer of men and affairs, and is original in thought and action. As a public speaker, he has a remarkable faculty for direct and pointed argument. He has always been a favorite with the employees of the roads he has managed, and his firmness and impartiality has averted all disagreements, so that no strike has ever occurred on any of his lines. He is emphatically a self-made man, and by his strong principles and executive ability he has risen to be considered one of the most successful railroad managers in the country.

RICKER, Robert Edwin, railroad superintendent, was born in Portland, Me., March 27, 1828. When six years old his mother was left a widow with three children. He received his early education in the public schools of his native town, and when sixteen entered the employ of James Hall, civil engineer, whom his mother had married. He entered the railway service in 1845, as assistant engineer on surveys and location of the Atlantic and St. Lawrence road. The next year he was engaged in locating and constructing the Essex road from Salem to Lawrence, in which position he showed such capacity that two years later he was given charge of the surveys and location of the Portsmouth and Concord road. In 1849 he located and constructed the Great Falls and Conway Railway. In 1840 he accepted service on the Kennebec and Portland road, having at the same time charge of the location and construction of the extension from Yarmouth to Portland. In 1850 he was the principal assistant engineer of the Rochester and Syracuse Air Line Railway. His next great work was locating and constructing the famous White Mountain carriage road. In 1854 he was engaged in the survey and location of the Utica and Binghampton road. In 1856 he became chief engineer of the Detroit,

Monroe and Toledo road, and was made division superintendent until 1858, when he accepted the position of superintendent and engineer of the Louisville, New Albany and Chicago Railway, where he remained until 1861, when he was made superintendent and engineer of the Terre Haute and Indianapolis road. At the breaking out of the war he received a commission as colonel and was made military superintendent of all the railroads running into Indianapolis, Ind., which position he held until the close of the war. In 1866 he became superintendent of motive power and machinery of the Pennsylvania road, but the next year transferred his services to the New Jersey Central road as superintendent and engineer, which position he filled until November, 1876. He was appointed and acted as one of the judges of machinery at Philadelphia Centennial. For the next two years he engaged in the railway and supply business, but could not long keep from his profession, and in 1880 he entered the service of the New York Elevated as general manager, and remained there for four years, when he was made general manager of the Gilbert & Brush Co.'s works at Troy. In 1884 he was made general superintendent and chief engineer of the Denver and Rio Grande road, and in 1888 accepted the general superintendency of the St. Louis, Iron Mountain and Southern Railway, holding that position until June, 1893, at which time he gave up on account of failing

health. Col. Ricker had experience in every kind of railroading, and achieved a wide reputation for executive ability, being regarded one of the best railroad men in the country. In 1854 Mr. Ricker married Ellen S., daughter of Josiah B. Sawyer, of Portland, Me. She was a woman of exceptional force of character, which had a marked influence upon her husband's career. He died May 17, 1894, leaving two daughters.

ROUSE, Henry Clark, railway president, was born in Cleveland, O., March 15, 1853, only son of Edwin Coolidge and Mary Miller Rouse, grandson of Benjamin and Rebecca Elliott Cromwell Rouse, seventh in descent from Sir Anthony, father of Francis Rouse, speaker of the Long Parliament under Cromwell in 1658, and fourteenth in descent from Sir Robert LeRouse, knight baronet under Edward, the Black Prince. His grandfather, Benjamin Rouse, born in Boston, Mass., March 23, 1795, was a celebrated philanthropist and pioneer evangelist and an early settler in northern Ohio. Joseph Rouse, the father of Benjamin Rouse, was born June 22, 1773, the second son of Benjamin Rouse, Sr., who was born in England, June 25, 1736. Our subject's paternal grandmother, a native of Salem, Mass., was president of the Soldiers' Aid Society of Cleveland, the first organized, went to the front during the civil war, and visited various military hospitals. In recognition of these patriotic services, her figure in bronze with her name inscribed, was placed on the soldiers' monument in Cleveland. Her son, Edwin Coolidge Rouse, born in New York city on Aug. 12, 1827, was prominent in the material development of the city of Cleveland for more than thirty years. In 1865, as captain of the 150th regiment, O. N. G., he commanded Fort Totten, one of the defenses of Washington. Upon the organization of the Sun Fire Insurance Co. of Cleveland he became its secretary and treasurer, and in 1875 was elected president. For five years he was president of the Cleveland board of underwriters; was first president of the American District Telegraph Co. of Cleveland; a member of the national board of fire underwriters, and on its executive committee until his death, Feb. 1, 1877. His only son, our subject, received an academic education, and two years' instruction under private tutors. In 1874 he entered his father's office, and upon the death of the latter, assumed entire charge of the business, being perhaps the youngest fire insurance manager in America. In 1882 he gave up fire-underwriting and erected the first large apartment house in Cleveland, organizing the venture under the title of Lincoln Apartment House Co., becoming himself managing director. The commercial depression of 1883 called out his superior business talents in rescuing the Joel Hayden Brass Co. of Ohio from what seemed hopeless bankruptcy. This led to his election as president of the Hayden Co., operating large brass works at Haydenville, Mass., and in 1884, of the United Brass Co. of New York, then the leading brass manufacturers in the country. He also held official positions in the Britton Iron and Steel Co. of Cleveland, and the Lorian Manufacturing Co. In 1885 he joined a syndicate for the construction of the Chicago, Wisconsin, and Minnesota Railroad, and shortly after withdrew from his other interests and devoted himself entirely to railroading. In 1891, upon the reorganization of the Missouri, Kansas, and Texas Railway Co., Mr. Rouse was made chairman of its board of directors, and the property was turned over to him by the receivers. In 1892 he was elected president, and another recognition of his abilities came in 1893, when he was appointed receiver of the Northern Pacific, a position he still holds. These systems are two of the largest in the United States, aggregating 7,000 miles of road. In addition to these vast official duties he is chairman or president of sixteen railroad companies and director in twenty-six other lines and kindred organizations operated in the interests of the Missouri, Kansas and Texas and Northern Pacific railroads; director in the American Steel Barge Co. and several southwestern coal companies. Mr. House enters into no new enterprises without intimate knowledge of its resources and possibilities. His capacity for acquiring minute information of details has caused his services to be eagerly sought for in large and difficult enterprises. He is a member of the Union, Roadside, and Athletic Clubs of Cleveland, of the Country Club of Glenville, and of the Metropolitan, Riding, Racquet and Tennis, and Lawyers' clubs, and the Down-Town Association of New York city. He is the owner of the schooner yacht Iroquois, a member of the Shelter Island and New York Yacht clubs, and vice-commodore of the Seawanhaka and Corinthian Yacht Clubs of New York.

DODDRIDGE, William Brown, railroad manager, was born in Circleville, O., Oct. 19, 1848. His father was Nathaniel Willis Doddridge, who emigrated from Virginia and settled in Ohio in the thirties. Originally the family came from England, to Virginia, prior to the days of the American revolution. His mother was Annie E. Brown, whose ancestors were also Virginians and Marylanders, descended from the Scotts of revolutionary fame; in the right of whom he is a member of the Society Sons of the Revolution. He received his education in the common schools of Columbus, O. When eight years of age he lost his father, and from that time until he was fourteen was cared for in a more or less unsatisfactory manner by relatives, living first with one family, then with another. Upon arrival at that age, he determined to throw off all restraint, and be no longer dependent upon the doubtful charity of relatives. He secured a position as messenger in the Western Union Telegraph office at Columbus, O., at a salary of $15 per month, and from that date was independent. He applied his energies during spare moments to the study of telegraphy. It was a year of stirring times during the great rebellion. Columbus, O., was a rendezvous for troops and scene of organization of armies. In the discharge of his duties he came into daily contact with such persons as Gov. David Todd, John Brough, Sec. Salmon P. Chase, and others of national reputation. At the end of about a year's service as messenger, he was promoted and sent to Zanesville, O., as an assistant to the office manager. While in Zanesville, he became attracted toward railroad service and obtained a position upon what was then known as the Pittsburg, Columbus and Cincinnati Railroad, in the year 1866. At this time he had become an expert operator. The year following, having no strong home ties to bind him to his native state, he decided to go to what was then the far West. He resigned his position with the Pittsburg, Columbus and Cincinnati Railroad, and proceeded to Omaha, Neb. The Union Pacific Railroad was then in process of construction. He obtained with that company a position as local agent at Columbus, Neb. It was here that his ability began to be exhibited. He was rapidly promoted, serving through various minor positions at different points upon the rapidly-developing railroad system. He was married in Nebraska in 1870 to Frances L. Barnum. In 1878 he was advanced to the important position of division super-

intendent at the western section of the Union Pacific Railroad. In 1881 he was made general superintendent of the Idaho, division of the same property, with headquarters at Ogden, and had a large part in the construction of the Oregon Short Line and Utah and Northern Railroads. On account of changes in Union Pacific management in 1884, he resigned his position with that company and engaged with the Anaconda Copper Smelting Co. of Montana, as business manager, to which territory he removed. In 1886 he again returned to railroading, becoming superintendent of the Central Branch Union Pacific Railroad at Atchison, Kan., a property controlled by the Missouri Pacific Railway Co. Almost immediately his jurisdiction was increased by the addition of the western division of the Missouri Pacific Railroad. In 1889 he was made general manager of the St. Louis, Arkansas and Texas Railroad, at that time an insolvent and broken-down property. For years Mr. Doddridge has been well known in railroad circles in the West, and had the credit of very great efficiency in whatever position he engaged to fill. When George J. Gould became president of the Missouri Pacific Railway Co. in 1893, Mr. Doddridge was appointed general manager of the entire system, which position he still occupies. Mr. Doddridge's career has been remarkable, showing what can be accomplished by indefatigable will and perseverance; from the lowest positions he has worked himself up to almost the highest place in the railroad world. He has great force of character which is shown by all the lines of his face, while his presence is agreeable and his manner quiet. While yet a young man he is considered one of the most successful managers of the country.

KNIGHT, Edward Collings, merchant and railroad president, was born near Camden, N. J., Dec. 8, 1813. His first ancestor in this country was Giles Knight, who came in the Welcome with William Penn, in 1683, and settled at Byberry, near Philadelphia. His father died when he was ten years old, and the son after leaving school became a clerk in a store in South Camden. In 1836 he established a grocery store on Second street, Philadelphia, giving his mother an interest in the business. A few years later he obtained an interest in the schooner Baltimore, and was engaged in the importation of coffee and other products of the West Indies to Philadelphia. In September, 1846, he removed to the southwest corner of Chestnut and Water streets, and there carried on the wholesale grocery, commission, importing and refining business, first alone, and subsequently as E. C. Knight & Co. In 1846 this firm became interested in the California trade, and owned and sent out the first steamer that ever plied the waters above Sacramento City. This firm also originated the business of importing molasses and sugar from Cuba to the United States, and for many years was extensively engaged in refining sugar, owning two large molasses houses and two large sugar refineries in Philadelphia. Mr. Knight was long identified with large commercial enterprises, and served as a director in numerous financial institutions and railroad companies. He possessed clear perception, excellent judgment, and marked ability in the conduct of large affairs. These qualities enabled him to grasp the general features of an enterprise, and at the same time retain a full knowledge of its details. His name was a synonym for integrity and honor in the city, where for more than half a century he was a successful merchant and public-spirited citizen. It was largely through Mr. Knight's instrumentality as chairman of a committee of the board of directors of the Pennsylvania Railroad Co. that the American steamship line between Philadelphia and Europe was established, and he became its president. He was president of the Bound Brook Railroad from 1874 to 1892; was president of the Central Railroad of New Jersey from 1876 to 1880; and was twenty years president of the North Pennsylvania Railroad. He was a member of the Electoral College which chose Abraham Lincoln president of the United States in 1860, and in 1873 was a member of the Pennsylvania Constitutional Convention. In 1883 he was appointed a member of the Fairmount Park Commission, and in 1882 was president of the Bi-Centennial Association, and one of the most active promoters of the celebration that was held that year in commemoration of the founding of Pennsylvania by William Penn. He died in Philadelphia in 1892.

HUNTINGTON, Collis Potter, railroad builder, was born in Harrington, Conn., Oct. 22, 1821. He is descended from the Huntingtons of Connecticut, who were the progenitors of Benjamin, the jurist; Samuel, the signer of the declaration of independence; Daniel, tutor at Yale and Congregational minister; Frederick Daniel, Protestant Episcopal bishop, and Daniel, the painter. His father was a farmer, with a family of nine children, of whom Collis was the fifth. He was brought up as the average farmer's son of his time, with many more hours of manual training than of mental. Four months each year at the village school, until he was fourteen, was the extent of his mental education. He then hired out at farm work for one year, receiving $7 per month. His instinct for business, and that in a larger field than was afforded him by farm work, led him to New York city, where he obtained credit for a small invoice of goods, with which he began his career as a merchant. He spent six years traveling through the South and West, selling his goods, and at the same time collecting notes for Connecticut clock-manufacturers. This experience gave him a thorough knowledge of the topography of the country, and proved of great value in his future railroad enterprises. When he reached his majority he had saved a considerable sum of money, and with it he went into partnership with his brother, as general merchant, at Oneonta, N. Y. His store was one of the largest in that part of the country, and his business prospered, where his rivals prophesied failure on account of his apparent recklessness in giving credit, but his knowledge of human nature stood him in hand, as it did in later life in larger transactions, and he made very few bad debts. A motto which, even so early, ruled his business transactions, and to which he often referred, was, "Trust all in all, or not at all;" adding that "A man will fill the niche you put him in," and "If you show a man that you believe in him, he will in turn try to show that you are not mistaken." In 1849 he drew out of the business $1,200, and with it set out for the gold fields of California, which had been discovered the year before, and to which thousands had preceded him. He went by way of the Isthmus. Possibly no man of the great number of adventurous spirits

who had gone to the new El Dorado, was better equipped by nature and training to undertake its hardships. He was of Herculean strength and stature, and in perfect health. It had been his habit every year to saw, split, and pile up, for his own consumption, twenty cords of wood, doing the work before breakfast. His muscles were like iron, and it was an every-day practice in the store for him to pick up a barrel of flour by the chime and place it on his shoulders. Not a drop of liquor or a cigar had touched his lips. He was energetic, determined, enterprising, and thoroughly self-reliant. Delayed on the Isthmus many days, young Huntington gave himself to neither dissipation nor idleness. He walked across the Isthmus during his stay twenty times, making the twenty-four miles' journey in a morning and evening walk, resting during the heat of the day. He traded in such commodities as had a market among the emigrants and natives, and when he finally took passage for San Francisco, his $1,200 had grown, during the three months' detention, to $5,200. In the fall of 1849 Mr. Huntington commenced business in Sacramento, in a tent, with such articles as were in demand by the miners. The large use of shovels, picks, and other hardware, led to determining his line of business. With the increase in trade, and the need for carrying a larger stock of goods, to take advantage of cheaper freight by sailing vessels around the Horn, Mr. Huntington became associated with Mark Hopkins, which association continued for twenty-four years, until the death of Mr. Hopkins. This partnership was a model in that it was not marred by a single misunderstanding or unkind word between the partners, and with a credit extended to an apparently unlimited extent, the losses were a minimum, which fact should be recorded as an evidence of the commercial integrity of the early Californians, not generally found in a new and shifting population made up so largely of the adventurous. Mr. Huntington, as early as 1849 was an advocate of a speedy projection and completion of a railway across the Sierra Nevada mountains. This project was so gigantic that he was, with other early advocates, called "Pacific-railroad-crazy." As a business proposition, it staggered the wisest financiers of the community, but Huntington went steadily onward, and in 1861 the Central Pacific Railroad Co. of California, became a *bona fide* corporation, with Huntington, Stanford, Crocker, and Hopkins as moving spirits. Mr. Huntington, empowered with full authority, went East, and in New York and Washington set the financiers and lawmakers in active co-operation, and a contract with the government, by which he agreed to construct a railroad and telegraph line from the Pacific coast to a point where it would meet the Union Pacific Railroad, was made and executed. His laconic telegram, "We have drawn the elephant, now let us see if we can harness him," announced his success to his associates in Sacramento. Mr. Huntington and his associates pledged their personal fortunes and their credit to the success of the road, and while the country was in the throes of civil war and financial depression, the bonds of the road were sold, the funds raised, the last spike which connected the Central Pacific with the Union Pacific, was driven, and the dream of Huntington became a reality. Not content with this gigantic achievement, Mr. Huntington planned and perfected the whole Southern Pacific Railroad system, with over 8,900 miles of steel track, and built and acquired a system east of the Mississippi river by which the Southern Pacific Railroad and the Chesapeake and Ohio, and other railways, form a continuous line, nearly 5,000 miles long, from Portland, Ore., to Newport News, Va., which developed a multiplicity of steam water-lines connecting the Pacific coast through vessels that find abundant and safe harbor at Newport News, with every commercial port in the Old World, including a steamship line on the Pacific to China and Japan. At Newport News he erected the largest dry-dock and ship-yard in America, where the largest cruisers for the U. S. navy, and war ships for the republic of South America, are built and fitted out. For a few years the great railroad builder enjoyed the unique experience of riding in his private car over his own lines from ocean to ocean, or from Newport News, on the Atlantic coast, *via* New Orleans, to San Francisco, and a third of the way across the continent again, *via* the Central Pacific, to Ogden, Utah. By the year 1890, however, Mr. Huntington had disposed of all his railroad interest east of the Mississippi river, in order that he might devote his energy to the interest of the Southern Pacific Co., in whose future he has unbounded confidence. Mr. Huntington's whole life has been one of self-imposed and cheerful labor. The secret of his unimpaired faculties and healthy organism is well told by himself when he says, "I do not work hard, I work easy."

MELLERSH, Thomas, railroad secretary and comptroller, was born Aug. 2, 1856, at Hawkley, Eng. His father was William Mellersh, a barrister and gentleman farmer, who was born at Sand Hill, 1809, and died at Tigwell, 1868. Thomas's early training was received in Petersfield British School, after which he was educated by private tutors. He early displayed proficiency in mathematics, and entered the railway service as clerk in the London accountant's office of the London, Brighton and South Coast Railway in 1871. His accuracy and devotion to duties soon won promotion, and after being a clerk in the ledger-department, he was given a position in the secretary's office, and in 1875 was made assistant cashier in the season-ticket office, and later, was returned to the secretary's office as corresponding clerk. In 1880 he was appointed assistant auditor and traveling auditor of the Alabama Great Southern Railroad, with headquarters at Chattanooga, Tenn., and the following year became acting auditor and assistant auditor of the Alabama, Great Southern, Vicksburg and Meridien, New Orleans and Northeastern, and Vicksburg, Shreveport and Pacific Railroads. In 1882 he was removed to Cincinnati, to become general bookkeeper of the Cincinnati, New Orleans and Texas Pacific Railroad, where he remained three years, when he became chief clerk in the comptroller's office of the Queen and Crescent Railroad system, and was made assistant comptroller in 1887. He removed to New York in 1888, to take charge of the accounting department of the American Cotton Oil Trust, but in a few months returned to his former occupation, and undertook the position of secretary and auditor of the San Francisco and Northern Pacific Railroad, at San Francisco, Cal.; and in 1891 became the comptroller, as well as secretary, of the same road. In 1882 Mr. Mellersh married Harriet Blakemore, the daughter of Milton McClure, of Illinois. His quick perception of the intricacies of accounts, has given him a reputation as one of the expert accountants in railroad financial management.

REINHART, Joseph W., railroad president, was born at Pittsburgh, Pa., Sept. 17, 1851. His father was Aaron Grantley Reinhart, who was descended from a long line of old Pennsylvania Dutch and English families. His mother is Katherine McHenry, whose paternal and maternal grandfathers and great grandfathers were pioneers of Pennsylvania, Maryland, and Kentucky. He received his education in the Western University of Pennsylvania. He entered the railway service when eighteen years of age, as a clerk in the office of the division superintendent of the Allegheny Valley Railroad, at Pitts-

burgh, where his aptitude for affairs was so marked that he was rapidly promoted. In 1875 he was made superintendent of transportation and rolling-stock. In 1880 he was offered the auditorship of the Richmond and Allegheny Railroad, and removed to Richmond, Va., and achieved such success that he was offered the general auditorship of the New York, West Shore and Buffalo Railway of New York, when his ability in financial affairs began to show itself, and when the road went into the hands of receivers, he was retained by them in the same position. After closing up the receivers' accounts, in 1886, he was made general passenger and ticket agent of the Lake Shore and Michigan Southern Railway at Chicago, in which place he reorganized the passenger department. He resigned this position in one year, to locate in New York, to act as expert for several railroad corporations. On Nov. 1, 1888, he went to Boston to make an inspection and report upon the Atchison Railroad. He made a thorough investigation of the accounts, which were presented in the famous 140-page report. Mr. Reinhart later made an inspection of every part of the Atchison system, presenting to the board, early in 1889, his recommendations to amalgamate the scattered properties and work them as one railroad system. This being adopted, resulted in a large increase of earnings and reduction of working expenses. He then gave his attention to the financial con-

dition of the property. It had $173,-000,000 bonds outstanding of forty-three separate and distinct issues, with various rates of interest, while its annual fixed charges were $12,000,000, with net earnings of about $6,500,-000. In two weeks' time he conceived and wrote out the financial reorganization known as "Circular 63," which was presented to the board, promptly accepted, and on Oct. 15, 1889, was offered to the company's investors for acceptance. Mr. Reinhart then, as fourth vice-president and head executive financial officer, pushed the plan through, and inside of two months he reported to the board its complete success. This not only placed the company on a sound financial basis, and reduced its bond issues from forty-three to two, but it also saved the vast property from almost innumerable receiverships and disintegration. A remarkable feature of this reorganization was the increase in market-value of all securities involved without foreclosure of any of the many corporate interests in the system. In 1890 he was made first vice-president, and in 1893 he became a director and president. In addition to this office, he became a director and president of the Gulf, Colorado and Santa Fé Railway; the St. Louis and San Francisco Railroad; St. Louis, Kansas City and Colorado Railroad; Atlantic and Pacific, Colorado Midland Railway; Wichita and Western Railway; Southern California Railway; New Mexico and Arizona Railroad, and Sonora Railway, limited. Mr. Reinhart has had a remarkable career, and achieved the reputation of being one of the most successful executive officers in handling railroad property in the United States. In May, 1893, Mr. Reinhart was selected by a joint commission of the U. S. congress as chief expert for the commission in the revision of the work of the executive departments of the government. Under his direction such changes were made and systems adopted that the government is now carrying on its work, for that part alone to which attention was given, at a saving of over $830,000 per annum. Mr. Reinhart was married to Lizzie Taylor Allison, at Sewickley, Pa. Oct. 21, 1875,

HARVARD, John, clergyman and founder of Harvard College, was born in High street, Southwark, London, England, in November, 1607, son of Robert Harvard, a butcher, and his second wife, Katherine (Rogers) Harvard. Of his early life we know nothing whatsoever, and it was only after the most diligent research that he was finally identified with the John Harvard whose baptism on Nov. 29, 1607, is entered in the records of St. Saviour's parish, Southwark. The name seems to have been by no means unusual, and to have been borne by various persons in Somerset, Dorset, Wilts, Middlesex, Warwick, and Devon. It was, however, variously alternated with Harvey, Harvye, Harverd, Harverie, Harver, and Harwood, in accordance with the somewhat uncertain spelling then in vogue. His mother, we are informed, was "possessed of some property," and, being ambitious for her son, sent him to the Puritan College of Emmanuel in the University of Cambridge in or about 1627. The records of neither college nor university contain further mention of him than his signatures attached to the three "articles," acknowledging the royal supremacy, and accepting the English liturgy and the articles of religion, upon qualifying for the degree of A.B. in 1631, and subsequently for that of A.M. in 1635; and the entry in the index of the matriculates of Emmanuel College: "Harvard, Jno. P., MID., A.B. 1631, A.M. 1635." That he was, however, as he has been described, a "well-trained and accomplished scholar of the type then esteemed" would seem to be evidence dby his master's degree. Shortly after his final graduation he was ordained a dissenting minister, and in 1637 married Ann, daughter of Rev. John Sadler of Sussex, and sailed for New England. He was admitted an inhabitant of the Massachusetts Bay colony, Aug. 1, 1637, and on Nov. 2d was made a freeman, and awarded a grant of land in the city of Charlestown, where he occasionally exercised his ministerial functions. Although a new-comer and of feeble health, his personality and abilities seem to have made him prominent. We learn from official records that in April, 1638, he was appointed one of a committee "to consider of some things tending towards a body of laws," and find him variously mentioned by his contemporaries as "reverend," "godly," and a "lover of learning." But his career was cut short, and he succumbed to consumption, Sept. 26, 1638, leaving a widow, who subsequently became the wife of Rev. Thos. Allen, pastor of the Second Church in Charlestown. By a nuncupative will he bequeathed one-half of his small estate of £1,700 and his library of 260 volumes to the recently founded school in Newtown (Cambridge), thus becoming the actual founder of the college subsequently called by his name. His library, from the catalogue still preserved, seems to have been an excellently chosen collection of classical and theological authors. Of this act one early writer among the colonists relates that "After God had carried us safe to *New England*, and wee had builded our houses, provided necessaries for our liveli-hood, rear'd convenient places for God's worship and setled the Civill Government: One of the next things wee longed for and looked after was to advance *Learning*, and perpetuate it to Posterity; dreading to leave an illiterate Ministry to the Churches, when our present Ministers shall lie in the Dust. And as wee were thinking and consulting how to effect this great Work; it pleased God to stir up the heart of Mr. *Harvard* (a godly Gentleman and a lover of Learning, there living amongst us) to give the one halfe of his Estate (it being in all about 1,700l.)

towards the erecting of a Colledge, and all his Library; after him another gave 800l. Others after them cast in more, and the publique land of the State added the rest; the Colledge was, by common consent, appointed to be at *Cambridge* (a place very pleasant and accommodate and is called (according to the name of the first founder) *Harvard Colledge*"—("New England's First Fruits, etc.:" London, 1643). The bequest, small though it seems, enabled the college to go into immediate operation on the basis of the ancient institutions of England, and has made our country proud to write herself the debtor of this Puritan divine. To use the words of Pres. Quincy, "The noblest and purest tribute to religion and science this western world has yet witnessed was made by John Harvard in 1638." The general court of the colony, held in Boston, Sept. 8, 1636, Gov. Henry Vane presiding, voted to give £400 toward the new college, indicating "200l. to bee paid the next yeare & 200l. when the worke is finished, & the next Court to appoint wheare and wt building." Another court, held in Newtown on "the 2th Day of the 9th mo." (November), 1637, Gov. Winthrop presiding, decreed that the site should be in that place, and subsequently appointed a committee of twelve, including the governor, "to take order for a colledge at Newetowne." At another session, held an the "2d Day of the 3d Mo." (May), 1638, the name of the town was changed to Cambridge; and finally, "on the 18th of the First Mo." (March), 1638–39, it was ordered "that the colledge agreed vpon formerly to be built at Cambridg shallbee called Harvard Colledge." In the meantime the beginnings of the college had been made and a master chosen.

EATON, Nathaniel, first master of the school afterwards called Harvard College, was born in England about 1609, son of a clergyman and younger brother of Theophilus Eaton (1591–1658), first governor of New Haven colony, and Rev. Samuel Eaton (1597–1665). He was educated at Francker, in the province of Friesland, where he is said to have joined the Society of Jesus. He emigrated to America with his brothers in 1637, and was almost immediately, on account of his reputation for learning and piety, appointed first master of the recently founded school at Newtown. He was intrusted with the donations to, and the management of, buildings for the college. One usher assisted him, Nathaniel Briscoe, whom Gov. Winthrop describes as "a gentleman born to be his usher," and the students were boarded and lodged in his own home near the site of the old president's house. During his management of affairs the first building of the college was begun, and his scholarship and executive ability was so satisfactory to the authorities that the general court of the colony in 1639, deeded him 500 acres of land upon the stipulation that he should retain the office for life. With the students, however, the matter was different; complaints about bad food and ill treatment grew greater and more numerous, also the suspicions of his avarice and dishonesty, until finally in September, 1639, Eaton was "convened before the

magistrates" for many offenses, but particularly on the charge of beating his usher, Briscoe, "with a cudgel" 200 stripes about the head. He made so full and eloquent a confession of all his misdeeds that the elders were impressed, and prayed for his release, but "on account of the scandal of his conduct to religion," he was fined 100 marks, ordered to pay £60 to the injured Briscoe, and at once dismissed from office. When questioned upon the charge of providing poor food for, and ill-treating the students, he protested that this was the fault of his wife. She was visited by the elders, and also made a confession replete in references to her "negligence," which seems to have evoked a similar good feeling, although she was probably not brought to public trial. Mather pays him the tribute of saying: "He was a Rare Scholar and made many more such; but their Education truly was in the School of Tyrannus." He was immediately excommunicated by the church in Cambridge, but soon afterward leaving

about £1,000 in debts, escaped to Virginia, where he is said to have essayed the rôle of parish minister. He subsequently returned to England, and, upon the restoration of Charles II., conformed to the established church, obtained a living at Biddeford, Devonshire, and became a violent persecutor of nonconformists. He was finally convicted for debt without benefit of clergy and, as Cotton Mather feelingly remarks, "did at length pay One Debt, namely, that unto nature by death." He died in a London prison late in 1660.

DUNSTER, Henry, first president of Harvard College (1640–54), was born in Lancashire, England, probably in 1612. He was educated at Magdalen College, Cambridge, at the time a resort of Puritan scholars, and was there graduated in 1634. The persecution he might expect at home as a nonconformist, no doubt determined his emigration, and he left England for the New World about 1635. Upon his arrival in Plymouth he was recog-

nized as a man of remarkably pure character and profound scholarship, and the magistrates found in him an able successor to Nathaniel Eaton, under whose oversight the college building had been erected. The new master was already established as pastor of the Cambridge Church, and had some valuable holdings in real estate. He was young, unmarried, and determined, and was inducted into office in August, 1640, as the first president of Harvard College. He found the college property to consist of a single building, and less than three acres of land. The organization had no "laws, liberties and orders" as afterward devised by him, and no governing board. He framed a course of instruction "adequate to every department of the civil or sacred service of the country, and not inferior to that of the distinguished schools of Europe." His fame as an instructor brought to the college many students sent from England to receive their education. The course of studies included all the contemporaneous learning as presented in the English universities. The general scheme of government and degrees were also adopted, although omitting the pompous ceremonials. Science, as we understand it, was quite unknown, but the degree of acquaintance with Greek, Latin, and Hebrew required of a candidate for the bachelor's degree was profound. Examinations in all branches were frequent and severe, especially before commencement, when the graduating class was required to prepare disputations and orations in all the learned languages. Under Pres. Dunster's administration, Syriac and Chaldee were added to the curriculum, and thorough instruction was given in logic, metaphysics, and especially divinity. During the first century of its life the college remained true to its original conception as a school for the preparation of a learned and able ministry; as embodied in its ancient motto "In Christi Gloriam." This aim is also set forth in one of the early college laws prepared during the administration of Pres. Dunster, "Let every student be plainly instructed, and earnestly pressed to consider well, the maine end of his life and studies is, *to know God and Jesus Christ which is eternall life*, Joh. 17. 3, and therefore to lay *Christ* in the bottome, as the only foundation of all sound knowledge and Learning." The first commencement was held on the second Tuesday in August, 1642, and was an event of historic importance to the colony. In the same year the general court had passed an act establishing the board of overseers of the college to consist of the governor, deputy-governor, the magistrates, and ministers of Cambridge, Watertown, Charlestown, Boston, Roxbury, and Dorchester. After some years of trial this body was found to be too large for immediate supervision, and in 1650 the college was made a corporation to be governed by the president, five fellows, a treasurer and bursar, with right to elect successors, and known as the president and fellows of Harvard College who were responsible only to the board of overseers. Pres. Dunster afforded financial help to the college by donating 100 acres of land towards its support, besides giving his official services for

a succession of years. The charter for the college was probably obtained by Pres. Dunster in 1642, and the later one of 1650, was entirely through his personal petition. He also built the president's house, and obtained relief for the institution from the general court. He labored for fourteen years bravely, faithfully, and loyally. Upon him was placed the responsibility of laying the foundation of the first and greatest of America's universities. He framed the charter, organized the code of laws for the government, nursed it in its cradle, sustained it in financial straits, and aided needy students who sought its doors. His labors and sacrifices were never appreciated by his age and time, and an intolerance that afterwards seemed unaccountable, made him one of the earliest martyrs in our land to the principle of free thought and speech. In 1654 the college authorities took exception to his public proclamation made in his church at Cambridge, of grave doubts in his mind as to the validity of infant baptism. For this offense he was not only forced to resign the presidency of the college, but the grand jury indicted him as a heretic, and he was sentenced to public admonition and placed under bonds for future good behavior. The grand jury afterwards prosecuted him for neglecting to baptize one of his own children. Upon being required to resign the office in October, 1654, Pres. Dunster presented to the general court in November, a series of "Considerations," setting forth reasons why he should not be compelled to vacate the president's house—he had built it himself at considerable sacrifice—pathetically pleading the illness of his wife and children, and the impossibility of removing many of his goods in safety. The appeal could not but awaken the humanity of the magistrates in spite of the fact that his coöperation with the Evil One in his heretical views on infant baptism had been detected; and he was allowed to remain until the following March. He then removed to Scituate, where he continued in the ministry up to the time of his death. By his will he directed that his body be interred at Cambridge, and he magnanimously left legacies to the very persons who had been most active in securing his resignation of the presidency of the college. Through his excellent Oriental scholarship he was intrusted with the revision of the literal version of the Psalms known as the "Bay Psalm Book." The first printing office in the colony was set up in his house from which the first publication was the "Freeman's Oath." He died in Scituate, Feb. 27, 1659. His life has been written by Rev. Dr. Jeremiah Chaplin (Boston, 1872).

CHAUNCY, Charles, second president of Harvard College (1654–72), was born at Yardleybury, England, about 1592. He was educated at the noted Westminster School, London, and was in attendance at the time of the gunpowder plot. He entered Trinity College, Cambridge, and was graduated in 1613. Upon becoming a fellow, he accepted a professorship of Hebrew and afterwards of Greek there. He then took a pastorate at Marston-Laurence, Northamptonshire. He became vicar of Ware in 1627. His nonconformity to the rules of the church, and open expression of dissent, brought him before Bishop Laud, who required him to make submission in Latin. He was afterwards brought before the high commission court in 1635, charged with characterizing the altarrail as "a snare to men's consciences." For this offense he made recantation in open court, but is said to have over after regretted the act. He was finally silenced in 1637, and took refuge in New England, landing at Plymouth in May, 1639. His purpose to preach was opposed by the colonists, on account of his peculiar views on baptism and communion, but about 1641 he settled as a minister in Scituate, Mass., where he struggled under insufficient support for twelve years, when he received an invitation from his congregation in Ware to return. On reaching Boston, intending to sail for England, he was offered the presidency of Harvard College, made vacant by the resignation of Henry Dunster, and accepted, Nov. 27, 1654. He was far past the prime of life, with a wide experience as pastor and teacher, added to great natural abilities. His views on baptism were

"of the contrary extreme" from those of his predecessor. He was an advocate of immersion for infants and adults, alike, and also held the heretical belief that the Lord's supper should be administered in the evening, but as he was conservative and yielding in his disposition as touching his doctrinal views, he better met the requirements of the college directors. Under his direction the college greatly prospered for seventeen years. But, although upon assuming the office the general court had bound itself to provide "a liberal maintainance," he made two ineffectual petitions on the subject to that body. In the second instance, after the court had refused his requests, the deputies favored the appropriation of £5 a quarter out of the public treasury for his compensation, but the vote being referred to the magistrates, it was returned marked: "the magistrates consent not thereto." Finally, after his death, his son, Elnathan Chauncy, presented a petition to the court, memorializing his father's services and privations, and asking that one of his sons, who, "through the Lord's afflicting hand," was "distempered," be provided for. Then, rather tardily, did the magistrates decree that the arrearges of the late president's salary be paid in money and, the deputies agreeing, further voted £10 per year for the care of the afflicted son. His learning was profound, his industry untiring, and he was also a physician of considerable skill. He had six sons, all Harvard graduates. He was an early riser, up at four o'clock in the morning, winter and summer; preached plain sermons to the students and townspeople; was laborious in duty, manfully holding that the student, like the commander, should fall at his post. He has a reputation as a divine and a scholar. He published several sermons, notably "Advantages of Schools," "A Faithful Ministry," a volume of twenty-six sermons on "Justification" and "Anti-Synodation." His writings passed into the hands of his step-daughter, whose husband, being a pieman, used them to line his pastry. His sermons were largely published. In one of them he characterizes the wearing of long hair as heathenish and one of the sins of the land. He died at Cambridge, Feb. 19, 1672. Pres. Chauncy is accredited with being the ancestor of all in this country that bear that name, whether spelled Chancey or Chauncey.

HOAR, Leonard, third president of Harvard College (1672–74), was born in England in 1630. It has been said that his father was a wealthy London banker, who died soon after his arrival in New England, whither he had immigrated with his wife and five children. His mother died in Braintree, Mass., Dec. 21, 1664. He was educated at Harvard College, being graduated in the class of 1650. Like many of the graduates of Harvard at this time, he, upon the execution of Charles I., went to England. He took a course at Cambridge, and was given by that celebrated university the degree of M.D. in 1671. He took orders in the established church, and had a parish at Wanstead, Essex, until he was ejected for nonconformity in 1662. He married Bridget, a daughter of John Lisle, the regicide. He returned to Massachusetts in 1672, bearing letters from several dissenting ministers in England recommending him to the vacant presidency, and preached in the South Church as assistant to Thomas Thatcher. On Sept. 10, 1672, he was installed president of Harvard College, and at once introduced in the institution a system of technical education before unknown in America. He organized an experimental garden and orchard, established a workshop, and built a chemical laboratory. His innovations in these directions did not take deep root, but the seeds were planted that resulted in the present system of technical training, so popular and effective. Although ushered into office under most auspicious circumstances, his administration began at once to be marked with all sorts of insubordination on the part of the students, which excited great dissatisfaction among the friends of the college. Finally, in 1674, the general court summoned the corporation, overseers, president and students, and, after a full hearing of the case, passed the extraordinary resolution, "that if the affairs of the College be found in the same languishing condition at the next session, the president is concluded to be dismissed without further hearing." The insubordination of the students is attributed by Cotton Mather and others to the influence of certain persons who "made a figure in that neighborhood," who had encouraged the discontented youths in their efforts "to strive to make him odious;" and the "emulation of some expecting the preferment" is given as the cause. Certain it is that Urian Oakes and three of his colleagues on the corporation withdrew from that body and, in spite of all pressure brought to bear on them, returned to their office only on March 15, 1674, the very day Pres. Hoar presented his resignation. Hoar did not long survive the chagrin of this unhappy ending of his official life and, having long been a victim of consumption, died at Barnstable, Mass., Nov. 28, 1675.

OAKES, Urian, fourth president of Harvard College (1675–81), was born in England in 1631, son of Edward and Jane Oakes of Cambridge, Mass., and was brought to America in 1634. He received a liberal education, and was particularly proficient in astronomy. While yet a mere lad, he made, and published in Cambridge, a series of astronomical calculations that would have been creditable to a professional astronomer. Being destined for the min-

istry, he entered at Harvard, and was graduated in the class of 1649. He then took a course in theology, and was ordained to preach the Gospel. He had a charge at Roxbury, Mass., for a time, and then went to England, which offered to nonconformist clergymen, at this time, a promising field, by reason of the execution of Charles I. He was settled in a parish at Tichfield, Hampshire, where, in 1662, he, as a nonconformist, was forbidden to preach. He afterwards found a new congregation. In 1671 he returned to America to accept a call from the church at Cambridge, Mass., whose pulpit had been made vacant by the death of Jonathan Mitchell in 1668. Upon the resignation of Pres. Hoar he,

as a fellow of Harvard College, assumed the duties of president, but was not formally inaugurated until Feb. 2, 1680. He was a noted Latin scholar. He published several sermons, a Latin eulogy, and an elegy in English verse on his friend, Thomas Shepard. During his administration, the first collection of books was greatly enlarged by the library of Theophilus Gale, an eminent philologist, philosopher, and theologian. Cotton Mather, making a pun on the president's name, pronounced the college, under his administration, a "rendezvous of happy druids." Oldmixon says of him: "This man, excepting that he was very religious, does not seem to have had any extraordinary qualities worthy the station to which he was advanced." He died in Cambridge, Mass., July 25, 1681.

ROGERS, John, fifth president of Harvard College (1682–84), was born in Coggeshall, England, in January, 1631, son of Nathaniel Rogers, afterwards a celebrated clergyman of Ipswich, Mass., and a descendant of John Rogers, the martyr, burned at Smithfield during the reign of "Bloody Mary." He came to America with his father in November, 1636, and located at Ipswich, where he received his primary education. He was admitted to Harvard in the class of 1649, and upon his graduation, like Prests. Hoar and Chauncy, he studied both medicine and theology. He first preached in his father's church at Ipswich as his immediate successor, and was associated with John Norton in the ministry to that church up to the time of the death of that noted preacher. Upon the resignation of Pres. Hoar, he was unanimously elected to succeed him, but, on his refusal, Urian Oakes was chosen. When Pres. Oakes died he was again elected president, May 27, 1682; was "solemnly inaugurated" Aug. 12, 1683; and served until the time of his death. There is no record of his work in the college that marks his personality, and as his administration extended over only two years, his influence or methods probably made but small change in the settled policy of the institution. He was a man of much sweetness of temper, and his "real piety set off with the accomplishments of a gentleman, as a gem set in gold." He married Elizabeth, only daughter of Maj.-Gen. Daniel Denison of Ipswich, whose wife, Patience, was a daughter of Gov. Thos. Dudley. They had five children, one daughter, Margaret, becoming the wife of John Leverett, eighth president of Harvard College. It is recorded that in December, 1705, the provincial legislature ordered two pamphlets that had been sent them by John Rogers and his son, John, to be burned by the hangman of Boston. This would point to opposition on the part of the Rogers to the legislative action regarding the governor's salary. Pres. Rogers died in Cambridge, Mass., July 2, 1684, the day after commencement, when, on account of his "sudden visitation by sickness." Rev. William Hubbard of Ipswich, was appointed by the overseers to manage the exercises and confer the degrees.

MATHER, Increase, sixth president of Harvard College (1685-1701) was born in Dorchester, Mass., June 21, 1639, the youngest of six sons of Richard Mather, a celebrated New England clergyman and the progenitor of the Mather family in America, and his first wife, Katherine Holt. He was educated at home until he was admitted to Harvard, and was graduated in the class of 1656. Like so many graduates of Harvard of the time, who chose the ministry for a profession, he sought a field for labor in England, following the example of his brothers, Samuel and Nathaniel. He took his second degree (A.M.) at Trinity College, Dublin, in 1768. His first charge was at Great Torrington, Devonshire, and he was selected at the instance of John Howe, one of Cromwell's chaplains. In 1659 he became chaplain of the English garrison stationed on the Island of Guernsey.

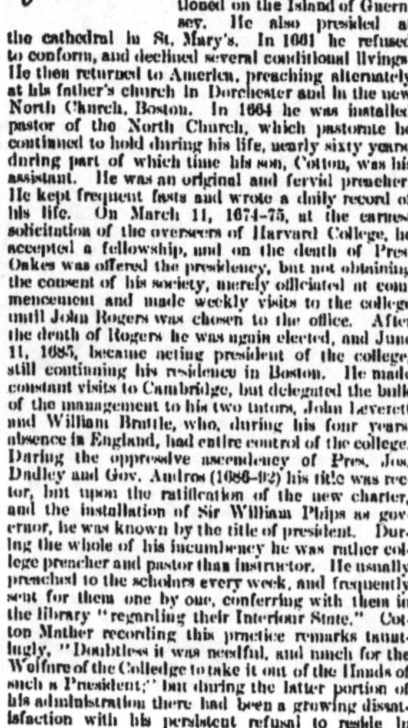

He also presided at the cathedral in St. Mary's. In 1661 he refused to conform, and declined several conditional livings. He then returned to America, preaching alternately at his father's church in Dorchester and in the new North Church, Boston. In 1664 he was installed pastor of the North Church, which pastorate he continued to hold during his life, nearly sixty years, during part of which time his son, Cotton, was his assistant. He was an original and fervid preacher. He kept frequent fasts and wrote a daily record of his life. On March 11, 1674-75, at the earnest solicitation of the overseers of Harvard College, he accepted a fellowship, and on the death of Pres. Oakes was offered the presidency, but not obtaining the consent of his society, merely officiated at commencement and made weekly visits to the college until John Rogers was chosen to the office. After the death of Rogers he was again elected, and June 11, 1685, became acting president of the college, still continuing his residence in Boston. He made constant visits to Cambridge, but delegated the bulk of the management to his two tutors, John Leverett and William Brattle, who, during his four years' absence in England, had entire control of the college. During the oppressive ascendency of Pres. Jos. Dudley and Gov. Andros (1686-92) his title was rector, but upon the ratification of the new charter, and the installation of Sir William Phips as governor, he was known by the title of president. During the whole of his incumbency he was rather college preacher and pastor than instructor. He usually preached to the scholars every week, and frequently sent for them one by one, conferring with them in the library "regarding their Interiour State." Cotton Mather recording this practice remarks tauntingly, "Doubtless it was needful, and much for the Welfare of the Colledge to take it out of the Hands of such a President;" but during the latter portion of his administration there had been a growing dissatisfaction with his persistent refusal to reside in

Cambridge and devote his whole time to the college. This was probably the occasion of the passage of the law by the general court in 1701, that no man should act as president who did not reside in Cambridge. Almost immediately upon the passage of this law Pres. Mather resigned. Previous to this, in 1692, the management of the inward affairs of the college with the title of vice-president had been given to Rev. Charles Morton, a graduate of Oxford University, an accomplished teacher and member of the board of overseers. This gentleman, however, died the next year, and in July, 1700, Rev. Samuel Willard succeeded to the office and title of vice-president. Mather's administration served to increase the endowments to the college from generous friends in England, rather than to improve the literary advancements of the students, as he spent but a few months at Cambridge near the close of his official life. His political services to the Massachusetts colony and his long and successful pastorate of the old North Church are more powerful credentials to his fame than his college presidency. During his administration, however, the attendance was largely increased, and the first endowed fellowship was founded through the donations of Thomas Hollis of London. In 1692 he proposed a charter for the college, which met the approval of the general court, but was vetoed in England. He several times attempted to procure a charter from the king but was prevented. In 1699 Lieut.-Gov. William Stoughton erected, at a cost of £1,000, the first hall bearing his name, which lasted until 1780, and was succeeded, in 1805, by a new building bearing the same name. The influence of Mather led rather to the establishment of a sectarian character to the college. It was at the outset deemed unnecessary to specify any religious principles for the college; it being merely an outgrowth of the religious life of the colony which was also the dominant element in its gov-

ernment. Consequently the original charter was silent upon points of religious faith. The original seal "Veritas," was changed to "Christo et Ecclesiæ;" the orthodox party sought control of the college, and a struggle between rival theological interests began. Pres. Mather was pre-eminently a disciplinarian, and is said to have "required a Conforming to the Statutes of the College, with a Stedy Government and Faithful Discipline." He was at first of the same opinion as his son Cotton Mather, in regard to the witchcraft trials, but later he published a book called "Cases of Conscience Concerning Witchcraft and Evil Spirits Personating Men," in which he acknowledged the inadequacy of "spectre evidence." He had, however, great faith in signs, omens, and prodigies, and frequently essayed the rôle of prophet. On one occasion a fire broke out and destroyed his church and many houses on the very evening after he had vehemently predicted such a scourge, from the pulpit. He also wrote several sermons and treatises on the malefic influences of comets, calling them "preachers of divine wrath." In 1682 Charles II. attempted to recall the charter which had been granted to the colony of Massachusetts Bay, threatening *quo warranto* proceedings in case of refusal. Mather opposed the surrender on the ground that if overpowered the responsibility would rest upon their oppressors. In 1684, Gov. Andros having ordered the surrender of the colonists' charter in the preceding year, he went to England, spoke in behalf of the colony, and returned to America in 1692, bringing with him a new charter from William and Mary. He made a favorable impression upon the king, and was allowed to name the governor and lieutenant-governor and first board of council to be appointed by the king. For this service he received the thanks of the colony, and Harvard conferred upon him the degree of D.D. (under the new charter giving it university powers), the first that was ever conferred in this country. This was the only doctor's degree given by Harvard College for seventy-nine years, until 1771, when Rev. Nathaniel Appleton of Cambridge was graduated S.T.D. The charter thus obtained united the colonies of Massachusetts and Plymouth and continued until the revolution. In 1662 Dr. Mather married Maria, daughter of Rev. John Cotton, by whom he had ten children. He was a voluminous writer, and published in all 136 volumes, many of which are preserved in the Antiquarian Society of Worcester. His life was written in 1724 by his son Cotton. He died in Boston, Aug. 23, 1723.

WILLARD, Samuel, seventh president of Harvard College, known by the title of vice president (1701–07), was born at Concord, Mass., Jan. 31, 1640, son of Maj. Simon Willard, founder of Concord. He was graduated at Harvard College in the class of 1659. He then studied theology, and was, in 1663, ordained as minister at Groton, Mass., where he succeeded Rev. John Miller. Here he was deeded a house and land, with the understanding that he should remain pastor for life, and faithfully served the society until the village was burned by the Indians during King Philip's war, early in 1676. He then removed to Boston, where, in 1678, he became colleague of the famous Thomas Thatcher, rector of Old South Church, and upon the latter's death the following October, succeeded to the pastorate, holding it until his death. His ministrations were so acceptable that it was remarked that "his removal to Boston was any compensation for the disasters of King Philip's war." Edward Randolph wrote of him in 1682: "We have in Boston, one Mr. Willard, a minister, brother to Maj. Dudley; he is a moderate man, and baptizeth those who are refused by the other

churches, for which he is hated." His "moderation" was further shown by his conduct during the persecution of the alleged witches. In company with the Rev. Joshua Moodey, he visited Philip English and his wife, who were in prison awaiting trial at Salem, consoled them, and doubtless sympathized with Moodey's successful zeal in assisting them to "escape from the forms of justice, when justice was violated in them." A story, illustrating his humor, relates that his son-in-law, Rev. Samuel Treat, of

Eastham, having preached in his pulpit a sermon distasteful to the congregation, from its faulty delivery, he was requested not to permit any more from that source. Willard, however, borrowed the sermon, and some weeks later preached it himself, and by his capital delivery, so delighted his people that they requested its publication, remarking how superior was his treatment of the text to that of his son-in-law. When Gov. Andros assumed control of the colony in 1686, he demanded that the Church of England services be held in South Church, and being refused, commanded the sexton to ring the bell, which he was frightened into doing. Thereafter, for three years, Episcopal services were held in the building every Sunday morning, Mr. Willard's congregation being obliged to wait until their completion. On the first Sunday Andros promised to allow them possession of the building at 1:30 P.M., but kept them waiting until long after two o'clock, while he and his staff prolonged their devotions. Afterward he was accustomed to suit his own convenience about the hour of services, greatly to the annoyance of the good people of Mr. Willard's society. It is surprising that in this age of inflammable religious prejudice, no violence resulted from this high-handed measure, but Willard's wise counsels doubtless guided his people, and both parties came to evince a desire to accommodate one another. He was early made a fellow of Harvard College, and in 1700 became its vice-president. On the resignation of Pres. Mather in 1701, he succeeded to the control of the institution, but continuing his residence in Boston, and the active pastorate of South Church, he was, according to the resolution of the general court, debarred from the title of president, and was never inaugurated. After resuming the responsibilities in the college, he associated with himself, as the assistant rector of South Church, the Rev. Ebenezer Pemberton. Early in his presidency the printing establishment in Cambridge was discontinued, by the death of Samuel Green, who had conducted it for fifty years. In most respects Mr. Willard's administration was able, and characterized by his usual scholarship and moderation. He had the confidence of the authorities of the colony, and the support of its best representatives. He wrote and preached ably against the witchcraft delusion, and, besides numerous sermons, published an "Answer to the Anabaptists" (1681); "Mourner's Cordial" (1691); "Peril of the Times," "Love's Pedigree," and the "Fountain Opened" (1700). His masterpiece was the "Compleat Body of Divinity, in 250 Lectures on the Shorter Catechism," edited by his successors, J. Sewell and T. Prince, which appeared in a folio of 914 pages in 1726. Prof. C. F. Richardson of Dartmouth, prefers his English to that of the Mathers, and credits him with "an evenly-balanced mind, a logical plan, a clear style, and some imagination." Pemberton speaks of him as "a sage patriot in Israel." He was twice married: first, on Aug. 8, 1664, to Abigail, daughter of John Sherman of Watertown, and second, to Eunice, daughter of Edward Tyng, about 1679. He had twenty children, eight by the first wife and twelve by the second. Of his descendants, none bear the name of Willard, save only the descendants of his grandson Samuel (H. U., 1723), who was father of Joseph Willard (H. U., 1765), later president of the college. He died in Boston, Mass., Sept. 12, 1707.

LEVERETT, JOHN, eighth president of Harvard College (1707–24), was born in Boston, Mass., Aug. 25, 1662, grandson of Sir John Leverett, colonial governor of Massachusetts. He was educated in the preparatory schools of Boston, and was graduated at Harvard College in the class of 1680. This class numbered five graduates, Richard Martyn, James Oliver, William Brattle, and Percival Green being the others. Leverett took up the study of law, and was admitted to the bar, and practiced in the courts of Massachusetts with marked success. Harvard, in 1692, conferred upon him the degree of S. T. B. His learning was extensive and varied, and the Royal Society of London elected him a fellow, an honor at that time seldom accorded to colonial scholars. Besides his position as instructor in Harvard College, which he held for many years before he came to its presidency, he held offices in the colonial government as justice of the supreme court, speaker of the legislature, member of the council, and commissioner to the Indians. In 1707 he was sent by the colonial government as a commissioner to Port Royal, N. S., and was the same year elected president of Harvard College, to succeed Vice-pres. Willard. In his administration of the office of president, Leverett was not in sympathy with the rigid sectarianism and severe clerical discipline of the Puritan generation which had preceded him, and to which the great body of orthodox believers still adhered. On the death of Pres. Willard, Cotton Mather fully expected that he should be chosen to succeed to the vacant office, seeming to consider himself possessed of a sort of pre-empted claim, and was so annoyed at the choice of John Leverett that he and his father addressed letters on the subject to Gov. Dudley, " breathing a spirit of abuse and virulence," and concluding with expressions of " sad fears" regarding the safety of his soul and kindly admonition that " in the methods of piety he would reconcile himself to heaven." Gov. Dudley replied that he considered himself sufficiently intelligent to discriminate between personal animosities and pastoral advice. Increase Mather immediately withdrew from the board of overseers, and Cotton attended but once, and then to thwart Gov. Dudley, whom he hated. This opposition finally resulted in the formation of a party that strove unceasingly to bring discredit upon all measures instituted by Leverett, and to weaken his influence—a plan was even formed to dissolve the corporation, so as to bring about the removal of the new president. He was publicly accused of omitting to give expositions of the Scripture in the college hall, a charge which he indignantly denied. However, a petition addressed by him in 1720 to the house of representatives, stating his difficulties and need of necessary support, was utterly ignored by that body, which led him to suppose it their intention to " starve him out of the service." But for the firmness of Shute, the royal governor, this movement, backed, as it was, by a majority of the general court, of the overseers of the college, and of the high Calvinists generally, would undoubtedly have been successful. The opposition continued through sixteen years, but in August, 1723, it wholly disappeared; the result being not only the triumph of the president and corporation, but the strengthening of the new theological party formed by the Brattles, Benjamin Coleman, and Leverett, and which became dominant in the colony. Leverett is spoken of as a man of exceptional ability and scholarship, and indeed showed much of excellent quality in his conduct throughout the trying period of his administration. He had to battle against the odds of insufficient means, his repeated petitions for adequate support obtaining no very

generous response, and died with a debt of nearly £1,500. He had already sunk much of his personal property in colonization schemes in Maine. Under his administration the number of students was doubled, the endowments increased, and the college was more prosperous than at any previous time in its history. A long array of acts of liberality to the college by the Hollis family date from this time— Thomas Hollis, his two brothers and nephew, successively gave money, philosophical apparatus, and rare volumes, which are to-day among its most valuable literary treasures. The Hollis professorship of

divinity was founded in 1721, and Edward Wigglesworth chosen first incumbent. During his administration also, the building now known as Massachusetts Hall was erected by the college to accommodate the increasing number of students. Pres. Leverett was twice married: first, to Mrs. Margaret Berry, daughter of Pres. John Rogers, by whom he had nine children; and second, to Mrs. Sarah (Crisp) Harris. The hostility which had pursued him throughout his administration, however, wore upon a not over rugged constitution, and hastened his death. Although his official life had been filled with trouble by the acts of his associates in office, his funeral was attended by many of his most active opponents, Increase Mather being one of the pallbearers. Immediately after the funeral, however, the vexations of the Mathers began afresh. They had confidently expected that one of them would be chosen to succeed Leverett, but, according to their diaries, the overseers saw fit to insult them by successively electing to the office Joseph Sewell and Benjamin Coleman, both of whom declined, and finally Benjamin Wadsworth, who accepted. Upon the election of Coleman, Cotton Mather wrote in his diary: " The Corporation of our Miserable Colledge do again (upon a Fresh Opportunity) treat me with their accustomed Indignity and Malignity." Pres. Leverett died May 3, 1724.

WADSWORTH, Benjamin, ninth president of Harvard College (1725–37). was born in Milton, Mass., in 1669, seventh son of Capt. Samuel Wadsworth, an early martyr to the cause of civilization, he having been killed by the Indians in a battle fought at Sudbury, Mass., Apr. 18, 1676, and his memory perpetuated by a monument erected on the spot by his son. After a thorough preparatory training young Wadsworth was admitted to Harvard in the class of 1690, and was graduated with that class, the largest that had ever left the college. He then took a course in theology, was licensed to preach, and made assistant teacher in the First Church, Boston, November, 1693. He became colleague pastor on Sept. 8, 1696. He was made a fellow of Harvard College, serving until July 7, 1725, when he was inaugurated president to succeed John Leverett. He held the post up to the time of his death. During his administration donations from home and abroad in money, books, silver-plate, apparatus, and the like were being constantly received. To these gifts the general court added £1,700, and in 1725 voted the sum of £1,000 to build a new house for the president, and also increased his salary; but through depreciation in the value of currency, the salary paid rarely exceeded in value £150 English money. The benefactions of Thomas Hollis also continued unabated: in 1726 he founded the professorship of mathematics and natural and experimental philosophy, which bears his name, and with his approval Isaac Greenwood was chosen its first incumbent. In his death, which occurred in 1731, Harvard lost one of its most generous and devoted benefactors. As a theologian, Pres. Wadsworth held some theological opinions not current in his day. He was also a great student of the Bible and a celebrated textuary, able to adorn any point with numerous quotations from Holy Writ. He always preached plain, practical sermons, avoiding points in debate, and was seldom drawn into controversy. Pres. Elliot, in an address delivered on the 250th anniversary of the First Church, Boston, quotes Pres. Wadsworth as saying in a sermon preached in 1711: "'Tis of the mere undeserving mercy of God that we have not all of us been roaring in the unquenchable flames of hell long ago, for 'tis no more than our sins have justly deserved." Again he says that "nothing is more grating, cutting, and enraging to the devil than to have the gospel faithfully preached to men." "But," says Eliot, "when Dr. Wadsworth in a sermon entitled 'The Saint's Prayer to Escape Temptation,' told parents how to bring up their children, he gave advice good for all times, which the latest as well as the earliest president of Harvard College might gladly adopt as his own." There is no doubt that Pres. Wadsworth was more of a preacher than an educator, and made a better pastor of a church than a master of a school. In his administration of the affairs of the college, however, was witnessed the gathering of the rich fruitage of the toils, sacrifices, and faithful devotion of the early presidents of Harvard College, and his term closed with the first century of the history of the college. The growing "worldliness" among the students prompted the authorities to take immediate measures for its suppression, and a new body of laws was finally formulated for the college, forbidding, among other things on pain of penalties, the dispensing of roast meats, prepared dishes, plumcake or distilled liquors, or "unseemly dancing" by the students on commencement day; especially mentioning that any attempt to "evade" the statute by "plain cake," would cause the offender to "forfeit the honors of the college." During Pres. Wadsworth's administration the board of overseers was faced by a perplexing dilemma: Rev. Timothy Cutler, formerly of Yale College, having become an Episcopalian, was appointed rector of Christ Church, Boston, and forthwith made strenuous efforts to obtain a place on the board. His success would certainly have ended the sectarian control in the college, and great excitement prevailed among the authorities. He was finally thwarted in his efforts, and a law was passed that none but Congregational ministers were entitled to become overseers. Cutler had previously been ejected from his tutorship in Yale for preaching a sermon denying the validity of presbyterian ordination. He was a person of overbearing pride and haughtiness. Although in failing health

at the time of his appointment, Pres. Wadsworth faithfully stood by his post, preferring, as Tutor Henry Flynt expressed it in his eloquent mortuary oration, to "wear out rather than rust out." He died at the presidents' house in Cambridge, March 16, 1737.

HOLYOKE, Edward, tenth president of Harvard College (1737–69), was born in Boston, Mass., June 25, 1689. He was a grandson of Rev. Elizur Holyoke, a representative to the general court of the colony of Massachusetts. He was trained in the best schools of the city, prepared for college, and was admitted to Harvard in the class of 1705. He was graduated with high honors, such as entitled him to take a place as tutor in the college when he was twenty-one years old. He held this position, in connection with that of librarian, for four years, when he was made a fellow of the corporation, and served in that honorable capacity for three years. Meantime he had taken up the study of theology, and was ordained pastor of the Marblehead Congregational Church in 1716. He served that church for twenty-one years. In 1737, upon the death of Pres. Wadsworth, the corporation of Harvard looked for a successor who

would combine all the excellencies of the late president, yet one whose religious principles coincided more naturally with the catholic spirit which characterized the government of the seminary. The choice fell upon Holyoke, and as he had acceptably filled the positions of tutor and fellow, proving himself a very superior officer, neither obstinate nor flexible in temperament, the election gave universal satisfaction, and he commenced his administration under the most favorable auspices. His learning was extensive, his judgment sound, his manner dignified, his temper firm and gentle. He was not, says a contemporary, "deficient in any of the good qualities which are requisite to make a good president." He won great popularity by his liberal conduct in rendering aid to deserving students, and in his generous contributions to the pecuniary resources of the institution. During his administration George Whitefield made his first visit to Harvard College, and Pres. Holyoke commended him in his convention sermon of 1741. When Whitefield, in 1742, in his journal reflected on

the morals of the college, and the want of religious feeling among the faculty, Pres. Holyoke resented the imputation in a pamphlet, entitled "The Testimony of the President, Professors, and Students of Harvard College Against the Rev. George Whitefield and His Conduct." In it he characterized Whitefield as "an enthusiast, an uncharitable person, and deluder of the people," and "an itinerant and extempore preacher." The college prospered under his administration. Though the destruction of the old

Harvard Hall by fire was a serious disaster, as it involved the loss of the library, yet sympathy for the loss called forth renewed benefactions, which were of great assistance to the college. The first endowment for special annual lectures was made at this time by Paul Dudley, of great reputation on the bench, who in 1751 founded the course bearing his name, providing in his will the sum of £100 as a foundation. Four are delivered, in succession, one each year, on "Natural and Revealed Religion," "The Church of Rome," and "The Validity of Presbyterian Ordination." The first of these was delivered by Pres. Holyoke, by the special provision of the founder's will, but having a disinclination to appear in print, rare among New England clergymen, his discourse was never published. The college gained distinguished honor by the publication in 1761 of "Pietas et Gratulatio," a complimentary volume, published with much elegance in quarto, celebrating the death of George II., and the accession of George III. The writers were nearly all alumni of the college, and their scholarship was a credit to the institution. Pres. Holyoke wrote the first poem in "Pietas et Gratulatio," and published three volumes of "Sermons." His term as president of Harvard College terminated with his death, which occurred in Cambridge, Jan. 1, 1769.

LOCKE, Samuel, eleventh president of Harvard College (1770–73), was born in Woburn, Mass., Nov. 23, 1732. He was educated for the ministry, and, after a preparatory training, was matriculated at Harvard in the class of 1755, and was graduated. He then took up the study of theology, and was ordained a minister at Sherborn, Nov. 7, 1759, where he served as pastor of the Congregational Church for ten years. In 1769 he was twice elected to the presidency of Harvard College, but declined the office each time. He was again elected in March, 1770, and accepted. He was the youngest candidate ever succeeding to the office. His early life having been spent in a parish remote from the literary centre of Boston, he was lacking in that culture that comes from frequent contact with equally talented men. He was a man of generous catholic disposition, fine talents, and a clever thinker. Little has been preserved concerning his life or of his administration of the affairs of the college. He resigned his chair in December, 1773, suddenly and voluntarily. The reason for his withdrawal seems to have been some moral delinquency, but as to its nature the historian of the college fails to make record. He spent the remainder of his life in retirement. Harvard conferred upon him the degree of S.T.D. in 1773. The only publication accredited to his authorship is his convention sermon of 1772. He died in Sherborn, Mass., Jan. 15, 1778.

LANGDON, Samuel, twelfth president of Harvard College (1774–80), was born in Boston, Mass., Jan. 12, 1723. He was graduated at Harvard in the class of 1740 an A.M. He, upon graduation, engaged in teaching at Portsmouth, N. H., where he studied theology, and was licensed to preach. He received from the crown the appointment of chaplain of a regiment, and took part in the capture of Louisburg. On his return to New Hampshire, he was made assistant to James Fitch, pastor of the North Church of Portsmouth. He was ordained pastor in 1747, and ministered to the church until 1774, when he was called to the presidency of Harvard, to succeed Samuel Locke, who had resigned. He came to the office just as the war of the revolution was brewing, and being an ardent patriot, his administration of the affairs of the college led to opposition from the Tory students. This grew with the growth of the spirit of revolution, until in August, 1780, he tendered his resignation. Although the reports of the visiting committee always spoke of the satisfactory state of the college, and while his conduct amid great difficulties and dangers was characterized by zeal, activity, and fidelity, he gave as his reason for resigning the charge, that the cares of the office were becoming burlensome to him, and that "he had reason to hope that during his administration he had accomplished somewhat for the advancement of religion and literature." That the rebellious conduct of the students who were politically opposed to him had received encouragement from some who were connected with the government of the institution was never doubted. His biographers charge him with a lack of dignity, and a want of judgment and spirit, essential to the successful administration of the affairs of a college. No valid charge, however, was ever brought either against his character or his administration, and the students united in offering very complimentary resolutions upon the announcement of his resignation. Dr. Langdon the next year became pastor of the Congregational Church at Hampton Falls, N. H. In 1788 he was a delegate to the New Hampshire colonial convention that adopted the constitution of the United States. He is reported as having led its debates, and as doing much to remove prejudice against its adoption. He was the first president of the college selected from outside the province or commonwealth of Massachusetts. The University of Aberdeen conferred on him the degree of S.T.D. in 1762, and he was a fellow of the American Academy of Arts and Sciences of Boston from its foundation. He published several theological works and sermons, and in 1761 assisted in preparing and publishing a map of New Hampshire. He died at Hampton Falls, N. H., Nov. 20, 1797.

WILLARD, Joseph, thirteenth president of Harvard College (1781–84), was born in Biddeford, Me., Jan. 9, 1738, the second son of Samuel Willard (1705–41), a clergyman in Biddeford, from 1730 until his death, and great-grandson of Samuel Willard (1640–1707), vice-president of Harvard College (1701–07). He was left fatherless when three years old, and became a sailor, making several coasting voyages. Through the generosity of friends, he was prepared for college, and was graduated in the class of 1765 with high honors. The next year he was made a tutor in the college, and afterwards a fellow remaining on the college faculty until 1772, when he was ordained minister in the First Congregational Church in Beverley, Mass., as colleague with Joseph Champney. He remained in Beverley until 1781, when he was elected president of Harvard College, to succeed Samuel Langdon, who had resigned. He was installed into office Dec. 19, 1781, at a time when the spirit of discipline was weak and the college seriously embarrassed. Under his administration the discipline improved, finances greatly increased, and the institution was rendered prosperous and free. He enjoyed the full confidence of the faculty, the respect of the students, and the approbation and support of the public. In 1785 the college conferred on him the degree of S.T.D., and in 1790 Yale gave him LL.D. He was vice-president of the American Academy of Arts and Sciences of Boston, a member of the American Philosophical Society, and a member of the Kön. Gesellsch. Wissensch. Göttingen. He was a superior Greek scholar, and left a Greek grammar in manuscript. He died in New Bedford, Mass., Sept. 25, 1804.

WEBBER, Samuel, fourteenth president of Harvard College (1806–10), was born in Byfield, Mass., in 1759. His early life was spent upon a farm, and by hard labor, many privations, and much earnest effort, he prepared himself for college, and

Samuel Webber.

was graduated at Harvard with the class of 1784, with special honors in mathematics. He then took a course in theology, and was ordained a minister in the Congregational church. In 1787 he was made tutor at Harvard College, and two years after was promoted to the Hollis chair of mathematics and natural philosophy, which he held for fifteen years. Upon the death of Pres. Willard, Sept. 25, 1804, Fisher Ames was elected to the presidency of Harvard, but declined in 1805, when the choice fell to Prof. Webber, who was inaugurated in 1806. He was not gifted with the brilliant powers which fascinated the contemporaries of Fisher Ames, but he was learned, faithful, industrious, and devout. His early life on a farm had deprived him of a training calculated to give him the ease of manner and courtly dignity that characterized his predecessor, but he was urbane and gentle, and his administration was popular and successful. Through grants from the legislature, and numerous private contributors, the treasury of the college, during his tenure, was an index of the high degree of public favor the institution enjoyed. Dr. Webber served as one of the commissioners, appointed to settle the boundary-line between the United States and the British provinces. He was vice-president of the American Academy of Arts and Sciences of Boston, and a member of the American Philosophical Society. In 1806 Harvard conferred on him the degree of S.T.D. He was author of a "System of Mathematics," intended for use in Harvard, which was for a long time the only text-book on mathematics used in New England colleges. He also published a "Eulogy on President Willard" (1804). He died at Cambridge, Mass., July 17, 1810.

KIRKLAND, John Thornton, fifteenth president of Harvard College (1810–28), was born in Herkimer, N. Y., Aug. 17, 1770, son of Samuel Kirkland, a celebrated Congregational minister and Indian missionary, who, at the time of the revolution, was instrumental in attaching the Oneida tribe of the Six Nations to the patriots' cause, and for his influence and labor received from Gen. Washington especial mention in a letter addressed to congress in 1775. He afterward founded the present town of Kirkland, N. Y., and established the Hamilton Oneida College for the education of American and Indian youths. The son was graduated at Harvard in the class of 1789, and studied theology under Stephen West at Stockbridge, Mass. He changed his religious views before he completed his course, and returned to Cambridge to prepare for the ministry of the Unitarian church. He in the meantime was tutor in metaphysics at Harvard. In 1794 he was ordained and installed pastor of the New South

Church, Boston, and was continued in that charge until elected to succeed Samuel Webber as president of Harvard College in August, 1810. He found the institution in a flourishing condition, and at once sought to further increase the number of students and instructors, and to demand higher qualifications from both. New departments of instruction were opened, two new professional schools added, and the others greatly enlarged, and three new buildings were erected. During his administration the college received in donations and bequests nearly $400,000, which sum surpassed in amount the increase of the college property for any similar period until the opening of Pres. Eliot's administration. His success was largely due to his personal magnetism and elevated character. In 1814 a professorship of Greek literature was founded by Samuel Eliot, who appropriated $20,000 for the purpose. The gift was anonymous, and the professorship did not bear his name until his death in 1820. The presidents of Harvard from the beginning to Kirkland were clergymen, and while it has always been broad in its teachings, it preserved a religious atmosphere. In the religious opinions of its conductors and its plan of education, Harvard has faithfully represented the times through which it has passed. A glance at its catalogue will show its early proficiency in the studies connected with sacred literature and natural philosophy. Established in Puritan times, it has necessarily suffered a disintegration of the staunch orthodoxy of the Mathers and Chaunceys, and at the beginning of the cen-

tury virtually passed over to its present Unitarianism, though its officers are of nearly all shades of religious belief. Kirkland resigned the presidency on account of ill health in April, 1828. He published: "Eulogy on Washington" (1789); "Biography of Fisher Ames" (1809); "Discourse on the Death of Hon. George Cabot" (1823). He received the honorary degree of A.M. from Dartmouth in 1792, and from Brown in 1794. The College of New Jersey gave him S.T.D. in 1802; Brown made him LL.D. in 1810. He was vice-president of the American Academy of Arts and Sciences of Boston, and a member of the Massachusetts Historical Society. He lived for more than twelve years after his retirement from the president's chair of Harvard; his death occurring in Boston, Apr. 24, 1840. George Bancroft paid this merited tribute to his memory: "He was suited to any high public office, was ever the honored companion of statesmen, and fit to be the peer of the best of them; but he was satisfied with bringing the university, over which he presided, into a condition more worthy of the arts and sciences which he undertook to teach."

QUINCY, Josiah, sixteenth president of Harvard College, was born in Boston, Mass., Feb. 4, 1772, only son of Josiah and Abigail (Phillips) Quincy. He was educated at the celebrated Phillips Academy, Andover, making a thorough preparation for Harvard, where he was graduated in the class of 1790 with the highest honors. He determined to take up the profession of law, and studied with William Tudor, then the leader of the Boston bar. He was admitted to practice in 1793. His tastes led him to devote considerable of his time to the study of politics and state-craft. Inheriting from his father unusual power as an orator, young Quincy was selected, on July 4, 1798, to deliver the annual oration in the Old South Meeting-House. His effort gained for him such a reputation that the Federalists selected him as their candidate as representative in the U. S. congress in 1800. The opposition ridiculed their choice on account of his extreme youth, and made as their campaign cry, the suggestion for a cradle in which to rock the baby Quincy—he was consequently defeated. In 1804 he was elected to the state senate, and in the autumn election, the same year, was chosen to represent his district in the U. S. congress. As a state senator he was conspicuous in his activity in urging Massachusetts to suggest to congress an amendment to the Federal constitution, striking out the clause that permitted the slave states to count three-fifths of their slaves in arriving at a basis of representation. This was the most radical proposition ever suggested by a statesman, preliminary to secession, and could it have been effected at that time it would have resulted in the disruption of the Union. Mr. Quincy contended that the existence of slavery in the United States was sure to bring on civil war, and he dreaded its consequences. He did not see that civil war was far preferable to peaceable secession, and he honestly advocated the measure so as to purge the Federal constitution of any recognition of the existence of slavery as a right. In congress he opposed Jefferson and Madison and all measures advocated by them. The embargo fell under his bitterest opposition, and also the war of 1812, which measure, however, he finally accepted in a notable speech on the U. S. navy, made in the house of representatives, Jan. 25, 1812. He opposed the annexation of the territory of Louisiana, and predicted if the Federal government acquiesced it, it would only provide for slave states in the Southwest, and asserted the right of Massachusetts and the other Northeastern states to withdraw from the Union in such an emergency. This remarkable speech was delivered Jan. 4, 1811. In 1813 he declined a re-election to congress, and was elected the same year to the state legislature as a senator, and in 1820–21, as a member of the lower house, was elected its speaker. In 1820 he was a member of the state constitutional convention. In 1822–23, while he was judge of the municipal court of Boston, he refused to find libel in a publication of the truth in a good cause, and without malice. He was elected mayor of Boston in 1823, serving until the end of 1828. His administration of the affairs was phenomenal in the matter of reform measures instituted, and the vigor with which he carried them out. He also secured many municipal improvements, notably, the great Quincy market house. On June 2, 1829, he was inducted into the office of president of Harvard College, to succeed Pres. Kirkland, and brought to that office the indomitable energy which characterized him throughout life. During his administration the second centennial of the founding of the college was celebrated in September, 1836. The paper which he prepared for the occasion upon the history of the college and university was afterwards elaborated into a work of two volumes, and has ever since remained the standard history of Harvard University. It has been said of his administration that " he was as prompt, as unwearied, and as punctilious in the discharge of his duties as president of the university, as he had been in every previous trust," and that during his term of office he instituted a system so perfect that the college might well live by it for a century to come. He improved the discipline of the college, gave new impetus to the law school, secured the building of Gore Hall, and founded the astronomical observatory. He formed elective studies, and established the rule that offenses against public peace and order, committed by students, are to be dealt with by the police and the courts. He retired from the presidency of Harvard to his farm at Quincy in his seventy-fourth year, August, 1845. Gore Hall was named in honor of Christopher Gore, who had been governor of the state, and U. S. commissioner to England, under the Jay treaty, and who left to the college a bequest of $100,000. The narrative might be carried out at great length enumerating the bequests and legacies, the dates of college buildings, the foundations of scholarships and professorships through long series of incumbents more or less eminent. Pres. Quincy has written an extended history of the college in two volumes, which gives the minutiæ of administration, and an admirable history of the growth of education and opinion in the United States. The last of his political acts was in connection with the presidential campaign of 1856, when he used his utmost endeavors to secure the election of John C. Fremont. He published, in 1825, a memoir of his father. In 1851 he published "History of the Boston Athenæum"; in 1852 a "Municipal History of Boston," and in 1858, a life of John Quincy Adams. He was given the honorary degree of A.B. by Yale in 1782, and the honorary degree of A.M. by

Gore Hall

the College of New Jersey in 1796. Harvard made him an LL.D. in 1824. He was an overseer of Harvard, a member of the Massachusetts Historical Society, and of the American Philosophical Society. He was president of the Boston Athenæum, 1820–30, and a vice-president of the American Academy of Arts and Sciences, Boston. He lived to see the civil war, which he had predicted for sixty years, and in his last days saw slavery abolished; and the right of secession which he had so early advocated, put to the test and defeated, and the stability of the Federal Union maintained beyond the power of any section to disturb. Ever engaged throughout his long career in some public service to his state or country, his life, coeval with the nation, has a peculiar historical value. He was honored by every learned society in the land, and upon his death, the noblest and highest united in doing honor at his bier. Richard H. Dana, Jr., said, " When a boy I met a man in the street, who, from his style, I felt sure was Mr. Quincy. I raised my hat to him and received a generous bow in return. It was he, and he could be recognized anywhere by anyone on the lookout for a high character among the highest." He died at his home in Quincy, Mass., July 1, 1864.

EVERETT, Edward, seventeenth president of Harvard College (1846–49). (See Vol. I., p. 113.)

SPARKS, Jared, eighteenth president of Harvard College (1849–53). (See Vol. V., p. 433.)

WALKER, James, nineteenth president of Harvard College (1853–60), was born in Burlington, Mass. (then a part of Woburn), Aug. 16, 1794. He was graduated at Harvard with the class of 1814, studied theology, and was, from 1818 to 1839, pastor of the Unitarian Church in Charlestown. He was successful as a pastor and lecturer, and did much good in advocating and encouraging school and college education. He was a close student of literature and philosophy, and was, from 1831 to 1839, editor of the "Christian Examiner," the official organ of the Unitarian church. In 1839 he was chosen Alford professor of moral and intellectual philosophy in Harvard College, and was raised from that position to the president's chair in 1853, to succeed Pres. Sparks, who had resigned. Harvard had gained rapidly in public favor, as well as in efficiency, during the administrations of Presidents Everett and Sparks, and it was during the term of the latter that the office of regent was created, and Pres. Sparks, in the division of duties, had made the office of president less trivial as to functions, and to operate more as a balance-wheel in the complicated machinery of the college, and to bear upon the education and moral well-being of the students at large, rather than to fill the chair of higher professorship. He alone, of all the presidents of Harvard in its earliest days, directed his attention to each class in the several departments, attending at least one exercise in each term, and informing himself of the condition of every department in the university, and bringing himself into intimate personal relation with

every officer and teacher. The custom thus established afterward became the rule of the university, and as Pres. Walker had, as a member of the faculty, been a witness of its effective working, he was ready to carry forward the reform. The personal attachment he had formed as Alford professor, he retained and enlarged as president, and at the same time won the undivided support of his associates. Among the improvements introduced during his administration were the erection of the Appleton chapel, Boylston Hall, and the Gymnasium. The Museum of Comparative Zoölogy was also founded. He resigned the office in 1860, and engaged in literary pursuits. He left his valuable library and $15,000 in money to the college. Harvard conferred on him the degree of S.T.D. in 1835; LL.D. was given him by Yale in 1853, and by Harvard in 1860. He was a member of the Massachusetts Historical Society, and a fellow of the American Academy of Arts and Sciences of Boston. He published, among numerous sermons, lectures, and addresses, three series of lectures on "Natural Religion," and a course of Lowell Institute lectures on "The Philosophy of Religion;" "Sermons Preached in the Chapel of Harvard College;" a "Memorial of David Appleton White," and a "Memoir of Josiah Quincy." After his death a volume of his "Discourses" was published. He was the editor of several college text-books. He died in Cambridge, Mass., Dec. 23, 1874. A mural

monument was erected to his memory in Harvard Church, in Charlestown, May 14, 1883.

FELTON, Cornelius Conway, twentieth president of Harvard College (1860–62), was born in West Newbury, Mass., Nov. 6, 1807. He was descended in direct line from ancestors who originally settled in Danvers in 1636. He was prepared for college at the Franklin Academy, Andover, and entered Harvard when only sixteen years of age. To meet his college expenses, he was obliged to teach winter schools in his sophomore and junior years, at one time teaching at Round Hill School, Northampton, Mass., under George Bancroft. He was early devoted to literary composition, and was one of the conductors of the "Harvard Register" during his senior year. He was graduated in 1827, and during the next two years taught the High School at Genesee, N. Y., when he was appointed Latin tutor in Harvard, and the next year Greek tutor. Two years later he was given the Greek professorship, and in 1834 received the appointment of Eliot professor of Greek literature, succeeding Mr. Everett and Mr. Popkin. In April, 1853, he made a year's tour in Europe, visiting the art centres and making a study of their antiquities. His objective point was Greece, where he spent five months, visiting the most celebrated places for the purpose of illustrating ancient Greek history and poetry, and in studying at Athens the remains of ancient art, the present language and literature of Greece, the constitution and laws of the Hellenic kingdom, and in attending courses of lectures at the university. He was an ardent admirer of the modern Greeks, by whom he was known as the "American professor." Dr. Felton's scholarship was broad, embracing the principal languages and literature of of modern Europe as well as ancient, besides quite a knowledge of Oriental literature. Few men have been allowed so high a position in one department, with so generous a culture in all. Besides numerous contributions to periodical literature, Dr. Felton published a large number of works upon general literary topics. He edited the Iliad with Flaxman's illustrations, and translated Menzel's "German Lit-

erature." In 1840 he published a Greek reader, and during the next few years a number of classical text-books, besides a number of poetical translations for Longfellow's "Poets and Poetry of Europe." In 1849 he translated Prof. Arnold Guyot's "Earth and Man," which went through numerous editions in this country, and was reprinted in four distinct editions in England. Besides he published a revised edition of Smith's "History of Greece," with a continuation from the Roman Conquest to the present time.

One of his later labors has been the preparation of an edition of Carlisle's "Diary in Turkish and Greek Waters." He also published selections from modern Greek authors in prose and poetry. Besides teaching classes, he has delivered many courses of lectures on comparative biology and history of the 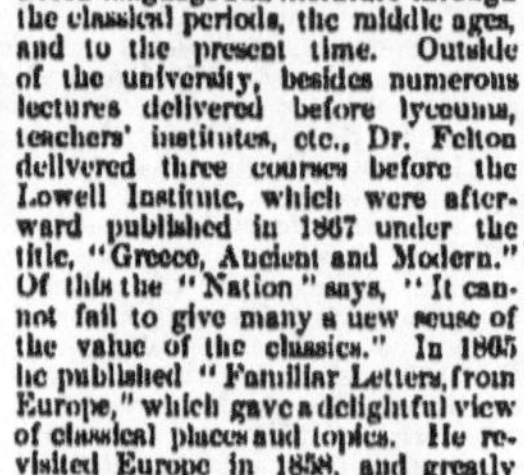 Greek language and literature through the classical periods, the middle ages, and to the present time. Outside of the university, besides numerous lectures delivered before lyceums, teachers' institutes, etc., Dr. Felton delivered three courses before the Lowell Institute, which were afterward published in 1867 under the title, "Greece, Ancient and Modern." Of this the "Nation" says, "It cannot fail to give many a new sense of the value of the classics." In 1865 he published "Familiar Letters, from Europe," which gave a delightful view of classical places and topics. He revisited Europe in 1858, and greatly extended his researches into Greek antiquities. In 1860, by the concurrent voices of all friends of the university, he was chosen president, to succeed Pres. Walker. He not only maintained the institution in the high standard it had attained, but in everything that was good and noble he added to the reputation it had already won. Pres. Felton's supervision of the university was of but short duration, but he brought to his work a scholar's enthusiasm. He did not confine his attention to the technicalities of his profession, but illustrated its learned topics in a liberal as well as an acute literal manner. At the same time he found time to write critical expositions upon the current scientific and popular literature of the day. As an orator he was skilful and eloquent. In 1856 he was elected regent of the Smithsonian Institution, and was also a member of the Massachusetts board of education. He was a fellow of the American Academy of Arts and Sciences of Boston, a member of the Massachusetts Historical Society, corresponding member of the Archæological Society of Athens. The degree of LL.D. was conferred upon him by Amherst in 1848, and Yale in 1860. On his way to Washington, to attend a meeting of the regents of the Smithsonian Institution, in the early part of 1862, he was stricken with heart disease, and died at the house of his brother, Samuel Morse Felton, Chester, Pa., Feb. 26, 1862.

HILL, Thomas, twenty-first president of Harvard College (1862–68), was born in New Brunswick, N. J., Jan. 7, 1818,  the son of Thomas Hill, an Englishman, a Unitarian, who came to America to enjoy larger freedom of thought, speech, and action, engaged in the business of tanning leather, and was also judge of the court of common pleas. He married, in 1797, Henrietta Barker, a grandniece of Joshua Toulmin, an eminent Unitarian minister. The son was left an orphan at an early age, was educated by his sisters, and when old enough to work was apprenticed to a printer for three years. On completing his term of apprenticeship in 1833, he attended school at the Lower Dublin Academy, near Philadelphia, of which his oldest brother was principal, and at the end of one year was apprenticed to an apothecary in New Brunswick. He commenced his preparation for college in 1838, and in August, 1839, was matriculated at Harvard College for the class of 1843, having studied under Rev. Rufus P. Stebbins, and at the Leicester Academy. His high standing in mathematics and physical science secured for him the offer of a high position in the National Observatory in Washington, and Prof. Peirce persistently attempted to dissuade him from the ministry. He, however, attended the divinity school, entering the middle class, and was graduated in 1845. He was then settled for fourteen years as minister of the Unitarian Church at Waltham, Mass. In 1859 he succeeded Horace Mann as president of Antioch College, Yellow Springs, O., and during his incumbency was also pastor of the Church of the Redeemer at Cincinnati, which was seventy miles from the college, and which service he performed in order to make up the deficit in his salary consequent to the financial straits of the college. He resigned the presidency in 1862. He was elected president of Harvard College the same year to succeed Pres. Felton. He had the respect and confidence of the entire faculty, and the scientific teachers recognized in him their rightful head. The academic council was started at his suggestion, and the university lectures were first opened to the public. He held the office until 1868, when he was compelled by ill health and domestic afflictions to resign. He retired to Waltham, Mass., and in 1871 was elected to the state legislature. He then accompanied Louis Agas-

siz to South America on his well-known expedition, and bore no small part in the explorations which have given it a permanent place in the history of science. Upon his return he accepted the pastorate of the First Parish Church of Portland, Me., over which society he was enstalled in May, 1873. Dr. Hill devoted much study to mathematical problems, and displayed great originality and fertility in the investigations of curves, and added greatly to the known number of curves, simplified their expression, and by introducing new combinations, vastly extended the field of research. He was one of the foremost investigators in natural science and an accomplished classical scholar, especially conversant with Hebrew and cognate Oriental languages. Dr. Hill was married, in 1845, to Anne Foster, daughter of Josiah and Mary Sparhawk Bellows of Walpole, N. H. She died in 1864. In 1866 he married Lucy Elizabeth, daughter of Otis and Ann Pope Shepard, of Dorchester. She died in 1869. His oldest son, Henry Barker, was graduated at Harvard in 1869, and is professor of chemistry and director of the chemical laboratory of that university. Dr. Hill published "A Treatise on Arithmetic;" "Geometry and Faith;" "First Lessons in Geometry," and numerous lectures, sermons, and text-books. Harvard conferred on him the degree S.T.D. in 1860, and Yale made him D.C.L. in 1862. He was a fellow of the American Academy of Arts and Sciences;

a member of the American Philosophical Society; of the Massachusetts Historical Society, and of the Portland Natural History Society. His address, entitled "Liberal Education," delivered before the Phi Beta Kappa Society of Harvard, is original in thought, compact in reasoning, and a masterpiece of analysis. He included all possible sciences under the following heads, and claimed that the natural development of the human mind was in the order named: mathematics, natural history, history, psychology, and theology. In May, 1891, he made his annual visit to the Divinity School, Meadville, Pa., to deliver a course of lectures before the students, and upon his return homeward, while at his daughter's home in Waltham, Mass., he died Nov. 21, 1891.

ELIOT, Charles William, twenty-second president of Harvard College(1809–   ), was born in Boston, Mass., March 20, 1834, the only son of Samuel Atkins Eliot, mayor of Boston, Mass., representative in the U. S. congress from Aug. 22, 1850, to March 3, 1851, and treasurer of Harvard College from 1842 to 1853. Through his mother's family he is allied to the Lyman family, which has held a distinguished position in New England history. The son was prepared for college at the Boston Public Latin School, entered Harvard in the class of 1853, and was graduated with high honors. In 1854 he was appointed tutor in mathematics, and, while filling the position, he continued the study of chemistry in the laboratory of Prof. Cooke. In 1857 he delivered a course of lectures in chemistry at the Medical School in Boston. In 1858 he was made assistant professor of mathematics and chemistry, the grade of assistant-professor being then first created. In 1861 he was relieved from his duties as mathematical tutor, and placed in charge of the chemical department of the Lawrence Scientific School. He went abroad in 1863, and spent two years in visiting the public institutions of France, Germany, and England, making himself acquainted with their organization, plans of study, and government. He at the same time devoted much of his leisure to the study of chemistry. While in Vienna, in 1865, he received from the Massachusetts Institute of Technology, then in course of organization under direction of Prof. W. B. Rogers, the offer of the chair of analytical chemistry, which he accepted. After holding the chair until 1868, he again visited Europe, studying in France during most of his vacation of fourteen months. Upon his return to America he was elected president of Harvard University, to succeed Pres. Hill, who had resigned in 1868, and was duly inducted in the office in the spring of 1869. His administration during the twenty-six years that have passed has been one of extraordinary brilliancy, and the university has enjoyed a prosperity heretofore unknown. The fame of the institution has become thoroughly national, and the name of its illustrious president is known and honored throughout the civilized world. "The light first kindled by the munificence of Harvard has spread onward to our own time, illuminating the course of our fathers, and concentrating a brighter radiance on the paths of the children." Mr. Eliot's accession marks an epoch in the history of the university. The chief aim of the faculty, and the governing boards had been to perfect it as a college of the normal New England type, the elective system had been introduced reluctantly for the latter half of the academic course; and the established curriculum had admitted only side-paths closely parallel with the main track. Mr. Eliot's determina-

tion from the first was to build upon the ancient foundation, a veritable university, open to real learners of every sort, and of every grade above that of school boys. The system which may be called his is at once strict and broad, imperative in its requirements, yet beyond all precedent liberal in the extension of its privileges. No student can receive a degree in the academical department, without having passed a thorough examination in a prescribed number of carefully planned courses; but the candidate for an academic degree has an unrestricted range of choice among courses, comprising every department that can be regarded as belonging to a liberal education. At the same time, special courses may be pursued, apart from the regular classes, by all persons who are able to avail themselves of

them. A more healthful system of discipline has been introduced, petty details of conduct are no longer subjected to rigid rule, and while there is less tolerance than ever before for disorder and immorality, large classes of college offenses have ceased to exist because no longer prohibited. These changes have so far met the demands of the outside public, that from the time that Mr. Eliot commenced his work of reformation while the number of undergraduates has been much more than doubled, there has been a perpetual inflow of funds from private benefactions into the college treasury, so that more new buildings have been erected than were built in the whole of the previous century; many old foundations have been increased, and several new endowments created. As a writer, Mr. Eliot has been known chiefly by educational reports, essays, addresses, which have the merit of concise and vigorous statement, of reasoning based whenever possible on admitted facts, of directness of aim, and of close adaptation to the specific end in view. On other occasions and subjects he shows himself master of a style pure, clear, and strong, of easy and graceful flow, and indicative of conversance with the best models of classical English, a style distinctively his own, but enriched and colored

by large and generous culture. As a speaker he has none of the arts, but a rare wealth of the best gifts of the practiced orator, always commanding close attention, and impressing not himself, but his thoughts, arguments, and feelings, forcibly upon his hearers. In private and social life he has the entire respect and confidence of all who know him, and the affectionate regard of all who enjoy his friendship and intimacy. The college graduated a class of 129 in 1870. The class of 1879 had 193 members, and that of 1888, 240. Williams College, and the College of New Jersey each conferred on him the degree of LL.D. in 1869. Yale conferred on him the same degree in 1870. He is a fellow of the American Academy of Arts and Sciences of Boston, a member of the American Philosophical Society, and of the Massachusetts Historical Society. He is a frequent lecturer on occasions of public interest, and an authority on higher education. His remodeling of Harvard after the liberal plan of an elective curriculum as enjoyed in the universities of the Old World, and his introduction and maintenance of a liberal university system which opened the doors of Harvard to over 4,000 students in 1894, are a few of the achievements of Pres. Eliot.

GOODWIN, William Watson, Eliot professor of Greek literature in Harvard College, was born in Concord, Mass., May 9, 1831, son of Hersey Bradford and Lucretia (Watson) Goodwin. His father was

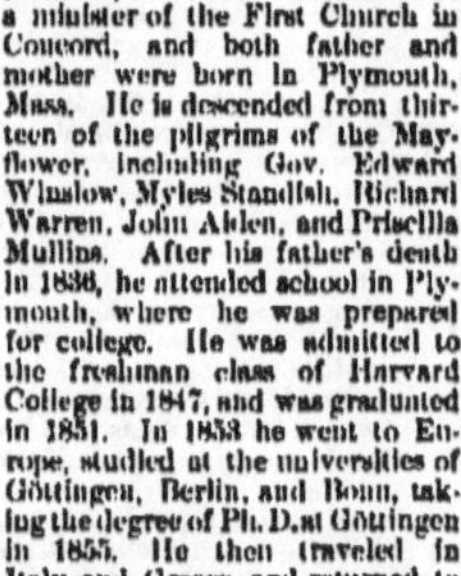

a minister of the First Church in Concord, and both father and mother were born in Plymouth, Mass. He is descended from thirteen of the pilgrims of the Mayflower, including Gov. Edward Winslow, Myles Standish, Richard Warren, John Alden, and Priscilla Mullins. After his father's death in 1836, he attended school in Plymouth, where he was prepared for college. He was admitted to the freshman class of Harvard College in 1847, and was graduated in 1851. In 1853 he went to Europe, studied at the universities of Göttingen, Berlin, and Bonn, taking the degree of Ph.D. at Göttingen in 1855. He then traveled in Italy and Greece, and returned to

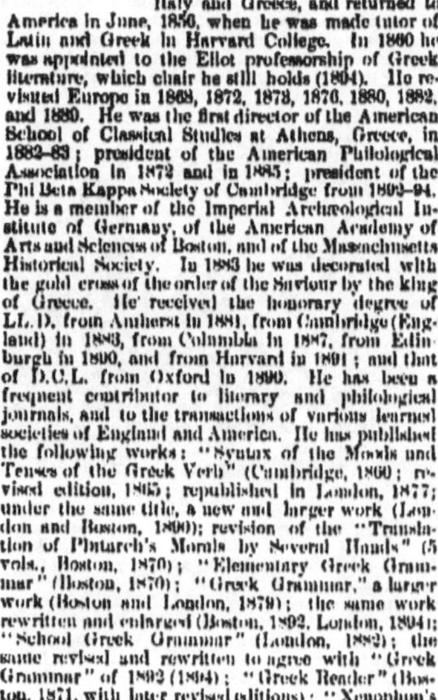

America in June, 1856, when he was made tutor of Latin and Greek in Harvard College. In 1860 he was appointed to the Eliot professorship of Greek literature, which chair he still holds (1894). He revisited Europe in 1868, 1872, 1873, 1876, 1880, 1882, and 1889. He was the first director of the American School of Classical Studies at Athens, Greece, in 1882–83; president of the American Philological Association in 1872 and in 1885; president of the Phi Beta Kappa Society of Cambridge from 1893–94. He is a member of the Imperial Archæological Institute of Germany, of the American Academy of Arts and Sciences of Boston, and of the Massachusetts Historical Society. In 1883 he was decorated with the gold cross of the order of the Saviour by the king of Greece. He received the honorary degree of LL.D. from Amherst in 1881, from Cambridge (England) in 1883, from Columbia in 1887, from Edinburgh in 1890, and from Harvard in 1891; and that of D.C.L. from Oxford in 1890. He has been a frequent contributor to literary and philological journals, and to the transactions of various learned societies of England and America. He has published the following works: "Syntax of the Moods and Tenses of the Greek Verb" (Cambridge, 1860; revised edition, 1865; republished in London, 1877; under the same title, a new and larger work (London and Boston, 1890); revision of the "Translation of Plutarch's Morals by Several Hands" (5 vols., Boston, 1870); "Elementary Greek Grammar" (Boston, 1870); "Greek Grammar," a larger work (Boston and London, 1879); the same work rewritten and enlarged (Boston, 1892, London, 1894); "School Greek Grammar" (London, 1882); the same revised and rewritten to agree with "Greek Grammar" of 1892 (1894); "Greek Reader" (Boston, 1871, with later revised editions); "Xenophon's

Anabasis," Books I.-IV., edited with Prof. J. W. White (Boston, 1877; London, 1880); same with text reprinted, and notes rewritten, and with an introduction (1894).

WARREN, John Collins, surgeon and educator, was born in Boston, Aug. 1, 1778, eldest son of Dr. John Warren. He attended the Latin School, 1786–93; was graduated at Harvard in 1797, studied medicine and French under his father, and then spent three years in the hospitals of London, Edinburgh, and Paris. Returning at the end of 1802, he assisted in his father's practice, and the next year sometimes made fifty visits in a day. From 1806 to his death he occupied a single house, No. 2 Park street. In that year he was made adjunct professor of anatomy and surgery at Harvard, and in 1815 succeeded to the chair and to the chief part of his father's extensive practice. In 1811 he joined others in founding the "New England Journal of Medicine and Surgery," which, in 1828, was merged in the "Boston Medical and Surgical Journal." With Dr. James Jackson he raised most of the funds for building the Massachusetts Medical College, which was opened in 1816. He was a founder of the Massachusetts General Hospital, and as its principal surgeon was in daily attendance from its opening in 1820 until his death. He was one of the founders of the McLean Asylum for the Insane, president of the Massachusetts Medical Society, 1832–36; and later of the Boston Society of Natural History. Inheriting or emulating his father's talents, energy, and public spirit, he gained a similar position in the community, and equal repute as an operator, but considered it his province rather to follow European precedents, with which few in the country were so well acquainted as he, than to attempt originality. He would not use the knife until other remedies had been tried, and when he did use it, he very rarely failed. He was the first American surgeon to operate

for strangulated hernia, and to use ether (1846); his example and influence in both these cases led to great results. Apart from his professional labors, he was active and zealous in the service of St. Paul's Church, which he joined in 1820, of the Bunker Hill Monument Association, and of the Massachusetts Temperance Society, of which he was president in 1827; he was even accused of "intemperance in the temperance cause." He went again to Europe in 1837 and 1852. He formed a valuable collection of specimens in comparative anatomy, osteology, and paleontology, to which he added, in 1845, the finest mastodon yet known, of this he published an account in 1852. His works include many medical and scientific treatises, and a "Genealogy of Warren" (1854). He died in Boston, May 4, 1856, providing by his will that his body be given to the Medical College, and his skeleton placed in its museum. His life, by his brother Edward, appeared in two volumes in 1859–60.

WATSON, Sereno, botanist, was born at East Windsor Hill, Conn., Dec. 1, 1826. He was graduated at Yale in 1847, and subsequently taught at various places in New England, Pennsylvania, and New York, studying medicine at intervals at East Windsor, and at the medical department of the University of the City of New York, completing his studies at Quincy, Ill., under the direction of his brother, Louis Watson. In 1856 he accepted the position of secretary of the Planters' Insurance Co., in Greensboro', Ala. At the outbreak of the civil war he tendered his resignation to the company, and returned North. He afterwards engaged in literary work, and was associate editor, with Dr. Henry Barnard, on the "Journal of Education," published at

Hartford, Conn. During his residence in the South he became interested in botany, and in 1868 was appointed botanist to the U. S. geological exploration on the 40th parallel, which was organized by Clarence King. In 1869 Dr. Watson returned to New Haven, Conn., and began the examination of the material collected in the herbarium of Prof. Daniel C. Eaton, in Yale College. He removed to Cambridge in 1870, and completed his study in the herbarium of Prof. Asa Gray. His results were published in Vol. V. on "Botany," in the series of reports of the geological exploration of the 40th parallel. This ended his connection with the exploration, and established his reputation as a botanist. Prof. Ferdinand V. Hayden subsequently assigned him the greater part of the botanical work of the geographical and geological explorations and surveys west of the 100th meridian. In 1874 he was given special charge of the herbarium at Cambridge, of which he was curator at the time of his death. From 1881–84 he was instructor of photography at Harvard, and after the death of Prof. Gray, in 1888, he conducted the active prosecution of the systematic work of the herbarium. In conjunction with Prof. John M. Coulton of Wabash College, he prepared a revised edition of Dr. Gray's "Manual of the Botany of the Northern United States," and also undertook the editing and finishing of the "Synoptical Flora of North America." In 1878 he was awarded the honorary degree of Ph.D. by Iowa College, and in 1889 was elected a fellow of the National Academy of Sciences. He was one of the resident fellows of the American Academy of Arts and Sciences, and a fellow of the Association for the Advancement of Sciences. He was a man of retiring disposition, and at the time of his death, was the fifth oldest active officer of Harvard University. Absorbed in his special duties at the herbarium, he seldom made the acquaintance of those who were

not interested in his work, and was personally known to but few. He died in Cambridge, Mass., March 9, 1892.

TOY, Crawford Howell, educator, was born at Norfolk, Va., March 23, 1836. The family came from England early in the eighteenth century, settled in New Jersey, and thence passed to Maryland and Virginia. He was graduated at the University of Virginia in 1856, and then taught three years; studied for a year, 1859–60, at the Southern Baptist Theological Seminary, Greenville, S. C.; was professor of Greek in Richmond College, Va., in 1861; served two and a half years in the Confederate army; was a professor in the University of Alabama, 1864–65; studied at the University of Berlin, 1866–68; was professor of Greek in Furman University, Greenville, S. C., 1868–69; and was transferred in 1869 to the chair of Old Testament interpretation in the Southern Baptist Theological Seminary. This post he held for ten years, removing with the seminary from Greenville to Louisville, Ky., in 1877, and resigning in 1879 on account of change of theological opinions. Since 1880 he has been Hancock professor of Hebrew and other oriental languages, and Dexter lecturer on biblical literature at Harvard. He translated the commentary on Samuel in the Lange series, 1877, and has published a "History of the Religion of Israel" (1882, fifth edition, 1887); "Quotations in the New Testament" (1884); "Judaism and Christianity" (1890); and many magazine articles on linguistic, ethical, and biblical-critical subjects.

PALMER, George Herbert, educator, was born in Boston, Mass., March 19, 1842. At the age of twelve years he entered Phillips Academy, Andover, but three years later, on account of failure of his eyes, was obliged to discontinue his studies. He made a voyage to Egypt, and upon his return was engaged in business in Boston. In 1860 he was matriculated at Harvard College, and being graduated in course, was appointed sub-master of the Salem High School, where he continued one year. From 1865 to 1867 he was a student in the Theological Seminary in Andover, going thence for two years of study to Tübingen, Germany. Returning again to Andover Seminary, he was graduated in 1870. For the next two years he was tutor in Greek at Harvard College, being made assistant professor of philosophy in 1873, and full professor ten years later. In 1889 he succeeded Prof. Francis Bowen as Alford professor of natural religion, moral philosophy, and civil polity. As an instructor Prof. Palmer is a great favorite, his wide scholarship, pleasing style, and poetic touch rendering his lectures both interesting and profitable to his pupils.

He is active in all causes for the welfare of the students; sits in many of the important committees of the faculty, and has been curator of the Grey collection of engravings. He has published a translation in metrical prose of the twelve books of Homer's "Odyssey" (1884), and a volume entitled "The New Education" (1887). The degree of A.M. was conferred on him by Harvard in 1867, and that of LL.D. by Michigan University in 1894, and by Union in 1895. In 1871 he was married to Ellen M. Wellman of Brookline, Mass. She died in 1879. In 1887 he was married to Alice Elvira Freeman, president of Wellesley College.

THAYER, Joseph Henry, biblical scholar and educator, was born in Boston, Nov. 7, 1828, and was graduated at Harvard College, Cambridge, Mass., in 1850. He studied theology in Andover Theological Seminary, Massachusetts, and was successively pastor of the Congregational Church at Salem, Mass., 1859-62; chaplain of the 40th regiment, Massachusetts volunteers, 1862-64; professor of sacred literature in Andover Theological Seminary, 1864-82; lecturer, 1883-84; and since 1884 Bussey professor of New Testament criticism and exegesis in the Divinity School of Harvard University. He was a fellow of the university, 1877-84. Besides contributions to theological reviews and the American edition of Smith's "Bible Dictionary," he has published "A Grammar of the Idiom of the New Testament," after Winer and Luenemann (Andover, 1867); a translation of Buttmann's "Grammar of the New Testament Greek" (1873); "A Greek-English Dictionary of the New Testament," after Wilke's "Clavis Novi Testamenti" (New York, 1886). He has devoted much time and loving labor to editing the works of the late Prof. Ezra Abbot, whom he succeeded in the Bussey professorship, publishing his "Notes on Scrivener's Plain Introduction to the Criticism of the New Testament" (Boston, 1885), and a volume of selections from his published writings, under the title of "Critical Essays" (Boston, 1888). He has also superintended the production of the new edition of Prof. E. A. Sophocles' "Greek Lexicon of the Roman and Byzantine Periods" (New York, 1887). He was a member of the American committee of the New Testament company on Bible revision in 1881. He received the degree of S.T.D. from Yale in 1873, and from Harvard in 1884.

LOVERING, Joseph, scientist, was born in Boston, Mass., Dec. 25, 1813, the son of Robert Lovering, a surveyor by profession, and his wife Elizabeth Simonds (Young) Lovering. He was educated at the public schools of his native town, and afterwards prepared for college by Rev. James Walker, who was subsequently president of Harvard College. In 1830 he entered the sophomore class of Harvard College, in which he was graduated in 1833, delivering the Latin salutatory oration at the commencement. In 1835 he was awarded the degree of A.M., and delivered a valedictory address in Latin upon this occasion. After teaching a year in Charlestown, he entered the Harvard Divinity School, and meanwhile continued the study of mathematics. In 1836 Mr. Lovering was appointed tutor in mathematics and physics, and in 1838 succeeded Prof. Farrar in the Hollis chair of mathematics and natural philosophy, which he held until 1888, when, having completed his term of fifty years as professor, he resigned and was made emeritus. During the absence of Prof. Cornelius C. Felton he was acting regent in 1853-54, and succeeded him as regent when the former became president of Harvard, resigning this position in 1878. In 1884 he was appointed director of the Jefferson Physical Laboratory, which position he held for four years. Prof. Lovering was identified with the growth and progress of Harvard Astronomical Observatory, having been connected with it since 1840, when it was but in its incipiency, the astronomical work then being done in the Dana House at Cambridge. When the United States coöperated with the Royal Society of London in making simultaneous observations on terrestrial magnetism in Great Britain and the colonies, one of the three stations in the United States was located at Cambridge, and the observations there were made under the direction of Profs. Bond and Lovering. From 1807-76 Prof. Lovering had charge of the computations for determining transatlantic longitudes from telegraphic observations on cable lines to Prof. Peirce, superintendent of U. S. coast and geodetic survey. He gave nine courses of twelve lectures each on astronomy and physics before the Lowell Institute, Boston, and shorter courses at the Charitable Mechanics Institute, Boston; the Peabody Institute, Baltimore, M.D.; the Smithsonian Institute, Washington, D. C.; and in various New England towns. He was a prolific contributor to scientific journals, his papers numbering over a hundred. Prof. Lovering was also associated with Benjamin Peirce in the publication of the "Cambridge Miscellany of

Mathematics and Physics." He was a member of the National Academy of Sciences, the American Academy of Arts and Sciences; of which he was at various times corresponding secretary, vice-president and president; was a member of the American Association for the Advancement of Science, and was from 1864-73 its permanent secretary, and during that time edited fifteen volumes of its proceedings. He was later made president of the association, and delivered his retiring address at Hartford in 1874 in which he reviewed the development of the physical sciences. He was also a member of the Buffalo historical Society, of the American Philosophical Society; of the Cambridge Thursday Club, and a trustee of the Peabody Museum of Archæology and Ethnology. Harvard conferred on him the degree of LL.D. in 1879. For some years prior to his death Prof. Lovering lived in retirement. It has been fitly said of him "That in his death Harvard has met a serious loss as has the scientific world which benefited so much by his investigations. Behind him, however, he has left results so well organized that the students of the present day can press forward to a consummation of the results which their teacher and exemplar did an incalculable amount to bring about and for the perfection of which he has given the vitality of his mind and body." Prof. Lovering's death was caused by influenza, and occurred at his home in Cambridge, Mass., Jan. 18, 1892.

JAMES, William, educator, was born in New York city, Jan. 11, 1842. He is the son of Henry James, the Swedenborgian author and theologian, and brother of the novelist. His early education was obtained in his native city and in Europe. In 1861 he entered the Lawrence Scientific School, Harvard University, and in 1863, the Harvard Medical School. He accompanied the Thayer expedition to Brazil in 1864-65, and on his return resumed the study of medicine, partly in Germany, being graduated M.D. in 1869. In 1872 he was appointed instructor in anatomy and physiology in the Harvard Medical School, becoming assistant professor of physiology in 1876. In this connection his attention was much occupied with psychological study, especially in its physiological aspects. He was one of the founders of the American Society for Psychical Research in 1884. In 1885 he was appointed assistant professor of philosophy in Harvard College, devoting most of his courses to psychology. Upon the enlargement of that department of study, he was made professor of psychology in 1889. Prof. James has published a number of papers in various periodicals, and is author of "Principles of Psychology," (2 vols. New York, 1890). In 1876 he married Alice Gibbens of Boston.

PICKERING, Edward Charles, director of the Harvard College Observatory, was born in Boston, July 19, 1846, the son of Edward and Charlotte (Hammond) Pickering, and great-grandson of Col. Timothy Pickering, secretary of state under Washington. Edward was graduated at the Lawrence Scientific School, Harvard, in 1865, and was Thayer professor of physics in the Massachusetts Institute of Technology, Boston, 1868-77. While there he devised plans for the physical laboratory of that institution, and introduced a system of teaching physics called the "laboratory method." His text-book, illustrative of the method, is still in use. During that period his scientific work consisted largely of researches in physics, chiefly the polarization of light and the laws of its reflection and dispersion. In 1870 he invented a telephone receiver which he publicly exhibited. He also devoted his attention to astronomy, and his studies in this branch of science formed an excellent preparation for the position which he now holds. He was a member of the nautical almanac party, observing the total solar eclipse of Aug. 7, 1869, at Mount Pleasant, Ia., and in the following year was a member of the United States coast survey expedition to Xeres, Spain, to observe the total solar eclipse of Dec. 20, 1870. In this expedition he had charge of the polariscopic and photometric observations. He was appointed director of the Harvard College Observatory in 1876. Under his directorship the institution rose to the high rank it holds as one of the foremost observatories in the world. The corps of assistants has increased from six to forty. Over thirty quarto volumes of annals have been published, and an auxiliary observing station established near Arequipa, Peru, South America. His principal work for several years, after accepting the directorship of this institution, was the determination of the brightness of the stars. He prepared, and published, a catalogue called the "Harvard Photometry," which gives the magnitudes of over 4,000 stars, and a latter work which gives the magnitudes of about 21,000 stars. He measured Jupiter's satellites photometrically, while they were undergoing eclipse, from 1878-91, also the satellites of Mars, and other faint objects. He has devoted some time to surveying mountains. The results were published in the journal of the Appalachian Mountain Club, of which he was one of the founders, and also president in 1877 and 1882. In 1882 his attention was directed to astrophotography, and since then he has followed up this branch of astronomy, and from it has obtained valuable results. Vol. XXVI., part 1, and Vol. XXVII. of the "Harvard College Observatory Annals," are the first detailed publications of the results of these investigations, being preceded by a memoir on stellar photography and a series of annual reports. These volumes form part of the "Henry Draper Memorial" and Vol. XXVII. is called the "Draper Catalogue." It describes the photographic spectra of over 10,000 stars. Photographic charts of the entire sky, and photographs of the spectra of all the brighter stars have also been obtained either at Cambridge or at the observing stations in South America. The Royal Astronomical Society of London, of which he is an associate, in 1886 awarded him the gold medal for his photometric researches. He is a member of the National Academy of Sciences, and received the Henry Draper medal for his work on astronomical physics; is also a member of other scientific societies in the United States, Great Britain, and Europe. He received the degree of S.B. from Harvard in 1865, and A.M. in 1880; LL.D. University of California, 1886; and University of Michigan, 1887. He married Elizabeth Wadsworth, daughter of Jared and Mary C. (Silsbee) Sparks, at Cambridge, Mass., March 9, 1874.

PICKERING, William Henry, astronomer, was born in Boston, Mass., Feb. 15, 1858. He is a great-grandson of Timothy Pickering, adjutant-general on the staff of Gen. Washington, and a member of his cabinet, who was himself a great-grandson of John Pickering, the first American ancestor, who settled in Salem, Mass., 1630. William Henry was educated in Boston, and was graduated at the Massachusetts Institute of Technology in 1879, and for one year experimented upon marine electrical devices at home. From 1880 to 1886, he was instructor of physics in that institution. In 1878 he observed his first total eclipse of the sun in Denver, Col., and ascended the Half Dome in Yosemite Valley. In 1882 he ascended several of the Alps in Switzerland. In 1886 he went to the West Indies with his family, in order to observe the total eclipse of the sun. In 1887 he was appointed assistant at Harvard College Observatory, and placed in charge of the newly established Boyden department. Later in the same year he visited Colorado in search of a suitable site for an observatory, to be used in connection with that at Cambridge. In the winter of 1888-89 he went to California and observed the total eclipse of the sun in the northern part of that state. Later he visited the southern portion of the state, and selected as a site for an observatory, Mount Wilson, near Los Angeles.

This station was occupied for over a year and several thousand photographs of the heavens were secured from it. In December, 1890, he was made assistant professor of astronomy, and that year established in Peru, South America, Harvard's Southern Observatory near the city of Arequipa. From this station many thousand photographs have been obtained, and numerous visual observations have been made upon the moon and the planets, especially Mars. He established a meteorological station upon Mt. Chachocomani, at an altitude of 16,650 feet, and an ascent of Mt. El Misté, 19,400 feet, was successfully accomplished. He also made a survey of the Andes in Bolivia, and obtained the altitudes of some twenty of the highest points upon the American continent. In 1893 he returned to the United States, by way of the Straits of Magellan and Europe, incidentally observing a total eclipse of the sun in Chili, and making a redetermination of the altitude of Mount Aconcagua. In the spring of 1894 he established the Lowell Observatory at Flagstaff, Arizona, the work at this point having been chiefly upon Mars and the satellites of Jupiter. Among his more important published works are, "Walking Guide to the Mount Washington Range" (1882).

MINOT, Charles Sedgwick, biologist and educator, was born in West Roxbury, Mass., Dec. 23, 1852. He was graduated at the Massachusetts Institute of Technology, in the department of chemistry, in 1872, then pursued the study of biology in Leipsig, Paris, and Würzburg, and at Harvard, where he received the degree of S.D. in 1878. He was appointed instructor in oral pathology and surgery in 1880; assistant-professor of histology and embryology in 1883, and in 1892 professor of histology and human embryology at the Harvard Medi-

cal School. He was actively instrumental in founding the American Society for Physical Research, and for several years was prominent in its work; but becoming convinced of the fallacy of many theories advanced by the parent society in London, he withdrew from active participation. He published several papers on the subject, notably one entitled "The Psychical Comedy," in the "North American Review," which expresses his negative position on the subject. Dr. Minot has made considerable research; principally on the physiology of the muscles and respiration, and on the phenomena of growth, death, and age, in their biological aspects. In 1887 he invented a form of microtome, which makes sections automatically for microscopic study, and is now generally used in biological and medical laboratories in all parts of the world. He has contributed a large number of papers to scientific journals on his subjects of special research, and in 1892 published his principal work, "Human Embryology," which has been translated into German by Dr. S. Kaestner, and published in Leipsig. He is a corresponding member of the New York Academy of Science, of the Philadelphia Academy of Arts and Sciences, and of the British Association for the Advancement of Science; was general secretary of the American Association for the Advancement of Science in 1885; vice-president for its section of biology in 1890, and president of the American Society of Naturalists in 1894. He has been a trustee of the Marine Biological Laboratory at Wood's Holl since its foundation in 1888, and has taken an active part in the development of that institution.

NORTON, Charles Eliot, critic and educator, was born in Cambridge, Mass., Nov. 16, 1827, son of Rev. Andrews Norton, D.D., a well-known author and divine of Unitarian connection. He was graduated at Harvard College in 1846, and began practical life in a Boston house engaged in the East India trade. In 1849 he went to India, and spent some time traveling in that country and in Europe. In 1855 he assisted Prof. Ezra Abbot in editing his father's writings, spending thereafter a year or two in European travel. During the civil war he was ed-

itor of the Loyal Publication Society's papers, and in 1864–65, of the "North American Review." After five years' sojourn in Europe he returned to America, and in 1875 was appointed professor of the history of art in Harvard University, a position he has continued to hold with credit and distinction. Harvard awarded him the degree of A.M. in course, and the honorary degree of LL.D. in 1887. He also received the degree of Litt.D. from Cambridge (England) University in 1884, and of L.H.D. from Columbia in 1888. Among his published writings are: "Considerations on Some Recent Social Theories," "The 'New Life' of Dante," "Notes of Travel and Study in Italy," "Historical Studies of Church-Building in the Middle Ages," "The Carlyle-Emerson Correspondence," and a "Life of James Russell Lowell." As an art-critic Prof. Norton is both forceful and scholarly; as an instructor he instils a genuine enthusiasm for his subject, lecturing to large classes. He is a member of the Massachusetts Historical Society, fellow of the American Academy of Arts and Sciences, of the Imperial German Archæological Society, and other learned bodies.

SHELDON, Edward Stevens, philologist and educator, was born at Waterville, Me., Nov. 21, 1851. His father, Rev. David Newton Sheldon, was at that time a Baptist clergyman, and president of Waterville College, now Colby University. In 1856 he joined the Unitarians. Our subject received his early education in Bath and Waterville, Me., in the latter place being under the tuition of J. H. Hanson, well known as a teacher and author of text-books in Latin. In 1867 he entered Colby University, but leaving at the end of the first year, he entered Harvard College, and was graduated in 1872 with highest honors in modern languages. Until the end of 1873 he was a proctor in the college, and then receiving a Parker fellowship, he went abroad to continue his

studies in the Romance and Germanic languages. He remained abroad until the summer of 1877, studying mostly in Germany, but traveling also in Switzerland, Italy, and France. Upon his return to America he was appointed instructor in modern languages in Harvard College; in 1878, tutor in German; in 1884, assistant professor, and in 1894, professor of Romance philology. He has published a "Short German Grammar for High Schools and Colleges" (1879); a paper on "Some Specimens of a Canadian French Dialect Spoken in Maine" ("Transactions of the Modern Language Association of America," Vol. III., 1887); "The Origin of the English Names of the Letters of the Alphabet," and "Further Notes" on the same subject, ("Harvard Studies and Notes in Philology and Literature," Vols. I., II., 1892–93); and since 1889 has been a contributor to "Dialect Notes," the publication of the American Dialect Society, and to other philological periodicals. The etymologies of Webster's "International Dictionary" were prepared by him in revision of the etymologies of Webster's "Unabridged

Dictionary." He also contributed a small amount of other material to the same work. He is a member of the Modern Language Association of America, the American Philological Association, and some other philological societies; was secretary of the American Dialect Society (organized through his initiative) 1889-93, and president of the same in 1894-95. He was married, in 1884, to Katherine H. Hinckley of Poughkeepsie, N. Y.

GOODALE, George Lincoln, botanist, was born at Saco, York co., Me., Aug. 3, 1839. His father, S. L. Goodale, for about twenty years the secretary of the Maine Board of Agriculture, is widely known as the author of a standard work on the "Breeding of Domestic Animals," and as an agricultural chemist. His mother was a lineal descendant of Rebecca Towne (Nourse), of witchcraft times in Salem. During his preparation for college he served as apprentice in an apothecary store, and acquired a good knowledge of the pharmacy of that day. He entered Amherst College in 1856, and was graduated in 1860 in the class with Prof. Estey and Pres. Francis A. Walker. After graduation he remained for a year connected with the college, as assistant in chemistry and botany. In his senior year he began the study of medicine with Dr. A. Smith of Amherst, but toward the end of 1861 joined the Portland School for Medical Instruction as a pupil, attending courses at the Medical School of Maine and at Harvard. He received his medical degree at Harvard University in 1863, reading at graduation a thesis on "Anthrax Malignus." Later in the year he was given the same degree by Bowdoin College. From this date until 1865, he practiced medicine in Portland; served as city physician, and gave lectures in the Medical School on anatomy, and afterward on surgery and materia medica. During the winter of that year he attended, as private pupil, in New York, the special classes of Dr. Frank Hamilton, Austin Flint, the elder, and Dr. Shrady; but in February of 1864 his health was so much impaired that he relinquished practice and study, and went by the way of Panama to California. After having executed certain commissions in the inspection of mining property, he visited the principal points of botanical interest in the state, ascending Mount Shasta with a party in August. He accepted, in 1868, an instructorship in Bowdoin College and the Medical School of Maine. His connection with these two institutions lasted until 1871, during which period he held the chair of materia medica in the Medical School, and of applied chemistry and natural science in the college. At the invitation of Prof. Asa Gray, he became assistant in botany in the summer school of 1871, and later in that year was appointed university lecturer in Harvard. In 1872 he was promoted to the assistant professorship of vegetable physiology, and in 1877 to the professorship of botany. On the death of his teacher, the late Asa Gray, he was appointed to the vacant Fisher professorship of natural history. Many of his vacations have been passed in Europe in the study of economic and physiological botany. Prof. Goodale is a member of the council of the university library, member of the faculty of the university museum, and director of the botanic garden of the university. Among the societies to which he belongs may be mentioned: Phi Beta Kappa, of Amherst; American Society of Naturalists (of which he has been president); American Physiological Society, Society of American Anatomists, the German Botanical Society, the Academies of Philadelphia and of New York, the American Academy of Arts and Sciences, the American Philosophical Society, and the National Academy, Washington. He has been president of the American Association for the Advancement of Science, and of the Boston Society of Natural History. Prof. Goodale's contributions to science have been chiefly physiological and botanical. In addition to these publications, reference may be made to his work as associate editor of the "American Journal of Science," and to his four series of lectures before the Lowell Institute in Boston. By his activity as a teacher and lecturer he has been successful in exciting a good degree of interest in his department in the city of Boston, and he has been enabled in this way to secure large sums of money for the botanical garden, herbarium, and museum. With a portion of this money there has been built an extensive addition to the Agassiz Museum, which accommodates amply the magnificent cryptogamic collections and commodious laboratories of Prof. W. G. Farlow, the laboratories of morphological, physiological, and economic botany, and the museums of botany. For the purpose of augmenting the material for the latter, Prof. Goodale made an extensive tour through the Orient, making large collections of objects illustrating the commercial botany of the present day, obtained from the principal countries of Europe and the East, and from the southern hemisphere. In addition to the degrees already mentioned, Prof. Goodale has received that of M.A. and LL.D. from Bowdoin and from Amherst.

LANGDELL, Christopher Columbus, dean of the Harvard Law School, was born in New Boston, N. H., May 22, 1826. His paternal great-grandfather came from England, and located in Beverly, Mass., whence he afterward removed to New Boston, being one of its earliest settlers. His maternal grandfather was born in Londonderry, Ireland, of a Scotch-Irish family, and, as a child, came with his parents to New Boston. In April, 1845, our subject entered Phillips Academy, Exeter, N. H., completing the course in September, 1848, when he entered the sophomore class at Harvard College. Leaving during the junior year, he commenced the study of law in Exeter, N. H., and in November, 1851, entered the Harvard Law School. He received the degree of LL.B. in 1853, and in December of the following year began the practice of his profession in New York city. In February, 1870, he received the appointment of Dane professor of law in the Harvard Law School, which office he still holds (1805), and immediately returned to Cambridge. At the annual commencement of that year the university conferred upon him the honorary degree of A.B., as of the class of 1851, and in the following September he was made dean of the law faculty, and so continued until 1895. In 1854 he received the honorary degree of A.M. from Harvard, and in 1875 that of LL.D. from Harvard and Beloit (Wis.) colleges. He has published: "Selection of Cases on the Law of Contracts" (1870); "Cases on Sales" (1872); "Summary of Equity Pleading" (1877); "Cases in Equity Pleading" (1878). He is a fellow of the American Academy of Arts and Sciences and of other learned bodies.

NISBET, Charles, first president of Dickinson College (1785–1804), was born in Heddington, Scotland, Jan. 21, 1736. He took the theological course at the University of Edinburgh, was graduated in 1760, and began immediately to preach. His first charge was a Presbyterian church at Montrose, and his eloquence soon gained him a more than local reputation. During the war of the revolution his sympathies were with the colonists, which caused dissatisfaction among his people, and gained him some obloquy. When Dickinson College, Carlisle, Pa., was established in 1783, Dr. Nisbet was called to the presidency. He landed in this country in June, and was inaugurated July 4, 1785. Some difficulty arising with the faculty in the conduct of affairs, particularly in the arrangement of the studies, he resigned in 1786, but a reconciliation being effected, he was re-elected the same year, and held the position up to the time of his death. Dr. Nisbet was a profound scholar, and besides administering the affairs of the college, delivered lectures on systematic theology, philosophy, logic, and *belles-lettres*. His works were published after his death, and a memoir, by Dr. Samuel Miller, in 1840. His library of rare and valuable books was presented to Princeton Theological Seminary. He died at Carlisle, Pa., Jan. 18, 1804.

DAVIDSON, Robert, second president of Dickinson College (1804–09), was born at Elkton, Md., in 1750. He received his education at Newark Academy, Delaware, and was for a time a tutor in that institution. In 1774 he was appointed professor of history and *belles-lettres* in the University of Pennsylvania, and in the same year was ordained to the ministry, and became assistant to Dr. Ewing in the First Church. A poetic dialogue composed by the young divine was recited at commencement, before the Continental congress, and in July, after the battle of Bunker Hill, he delivered before several companies of the Continental army, a ringing sermon, from the text, " And many fell down, for the war was of God" (Chron. V., 22). On the occupation of Philadelphia by the British in 1777, he retired to Delaware. In 1784 Dr. Davidson removed to Carlisle, Pa., as pastor of the Presbyterian church, a connection he retained during the rest of his life. By his benignity and tact he healed divisions in the church, and brought harmony out of the differences between the "old and new lights." When Dickinson College was reorganized in 1785, Dr. Davidson was elected vice-president, and appointed to the chair of history and *belles-lettres*. In 1796 he was chosen moderator of the general assembly. Upon Dr. Nisbet's death, in 1804, he became president of the college, and discharged the duties of the office until 1809, when he resigned to devote himself to his parochial charge exclusively. Dr. Davidson was a distinguished scholar, and a fine linguist, being more or less familiar with eight languages. He had considerable talent in music and drawing, and was especially interested in astronomy. He was the inventor of an ingenious apparatus for solving astronomical problems, a cosmosphere or compound globe. As a preacher he was unaffected, but clear and forceful, with more of the didactic than the oratorical or eloquent in his style. His rank as a counsellor is to be judged by the importance of the committees in which his name appears, among the records of the old synod. He was one of a committee with Drs. Allison and Ewing. Messrs. Blair and Jones, appointed in 1785, to prepare a new version of the Psalms. Dr. Davidson's writings include "An Epitome of Geography in Verse," which the students committed to memory and recited; "The Christian's A. B. C.," a metrical version of the 119th psalm; and "The Psalms in Metre," published in 1812. He also published a volume of sermons and orations. He died in Carlisle, Pa., Dec. 13, 1812.

ATWATER, Jeremiah, third president of Dickinson College (1809–15). See index.

MASON, John Mitchell, fourth president of Dickinson College (1821–24), was born in New York city, March 19, 1770. His father was a minister of the Scottish church, who personally instructed his son and prepared him for college. The son was graduated at Columbia in 1789, and continued his theological studies at the University of Edinburgh. He was recalled, the following year, by his father's death, and was chosen to succeed his father as pastor in his church in New York, and soon became the recognized leader of the American Reformed denomination. He went to England in 1801, by order of the synod, to induce other clergymen of his faith to come to the United States. During his ministerial career, he was associated from 1811 to 1816, with the government of Columbia College as provost. His high qualifications for the administration of the college are shown in the college statutes, adopted under his sway, and the report upon the state of the college attributed to his pen, which was a vigorous presentment of his ideas of college duties and discipline. He had pronounced views, and believing that the ministers of his denomination should be educated at home, he inaugurated a movement which resulted in the establishment of the Union Theological Seminary, and was appointed the first professor, when it was opened in 1804. He established the "Christian Magazine" in 1806, in the pages of which he conducted the celebrated controversy with Bishop Hobart, upon the claims of the episcopacy. He resigned his pastorate in 1810, and formed a new congregation, as his affiliation with the Presbyterians, had given offense to some of his denomination. Charges were preferred against him in 1811, but the synod refused to condemn him. Failing health obliged him to sever his connection with Columbia in 1816, and seek a change of air in a visit to Europe, where he spent a year, and upon his return resumed his ministerial duties until 1821, when he was elected president of Dickinson College, Carlisle, Pa. Here he remained for three years, when his health again became impaired, and he was compelled to resign. When Dr. Atwater resigned the presidency in 1815, various efforts and expedients in management were resorted to, to repair the exhausted finances of the college, but none succeeded, and the college was closed for six years. It was thought that the great reputation of Dr. Mason would revive an interest in its affairs, and the college was reopened. Dr. Mason was unremitting in his efforts to increase the financial strength, but the state of his health was such that he was compelled to relax his labors. During his administration he inaugurated new methods, and prepared the way for its future success. He had great reputation for robust eloquence, and was a powerful preacher and controversialist. Dr. Robert Hall of

England, upon hearing him preach, was so impressed by the flow of eloquence that he remarked, "I can never preach again." He was called the prince of pulpit orators. His advocacy of open communion gained for him great distinction in the religious world. His writings, consisting mostly of sermons, were published in four volumes by his son. He was a great admirer of Hamilton, and contemplated writing a life of him. He delivered an oration upon the occasion of Hamilton's death, which commanded wide attention. The University of Pennsylvania conferred upon him the degree of D.D. Dr. Mason was one of the founders of the American Bible Society, and for several years held the office of its foreign secretary. He died in New York city, Dec. 29, 1829.

NEILL, William, fifth president of Dickinson College (1824–29), was born near McKeesport, Pa., in 1778, amid the hardships of pioneer life. His parents were massacred by the Indians while he was a child, and he went to live with relatives. He received all the

advantages of education the times and conditions afforded, and was graduated at Princeton College in 1803. He was afterward a tutor in the college for a time. In 1805 he was ordained over the Presbyterian Church in Cooperstown, N. Y.; was pastor of the First Church of Albany in 1809, and of the Sixth Church of Philadelphia from 1816–24. He was chosen moderator of the general assembly in 1815. In 1824 he was called to the presidency of Dickinson College, which he held until 1829, when he became secretary of the Presbyterian board of education, and was pastor of the Germantown church for eleven years, raising it to a most prosperous condition. He retired from all active labor in 1842, and removed to Philadelphia, where he resided until his death. The degree of D.D. was conferred upon him by Union College in 1812. Dr. Neill was editor of "The Presbyterian" for several years, and contributed extensively to religious periodicals. His published works are: "Lectures on Biblical History" (1846); "Exposition of the Epistle to the Ephesians" (1850); "Divine Origin of the Christian Religion" (1854); and "Ministry of Fifty Years with Anecdotes and Reminiscences" (1857). He died in Philadelphia, Aug. 8, 1860.

HOW, Samuel Blanchard, sixth president of Dickinson College (1830–32), was born in Burlington, N. J., Oct. 14, 1790. He was graduated at the University of Pennsylvania in 1810, and at the Princeton Theological Seminary in 1813; was ordained in 1815, and installed pastor of the Presbyterian Church of Salisbury, Pa. Subsequently he had charges at Trenton and New Brunswick, N. J. In 1823 he was called to the Independent Church of Savannah, Ga., where he remained until appointed president of Dickinson College in 1830. Dr. How administered the affairs of this institution for two years, when he took charge of the First Reformed Dutch Church of New Brunswick, N. J. Failing health compelled his resignation of this pastorate in 1861. Dr. How was a Presbyterian of the old school, and not afraid to espouse an unpopular cause. He defended slavery, and when the classis of the German Reformed Church of North Carolina desired to join with the Dutch Reformed, published a volume advocating its admission by that body, entitled "Slaveholding not Sinful." The degree of D.D. was conferred upon him in 1830 by Union College. Dr. How was a voluminous writer, and published many sermons and addresses. He is the author of "The Gospel Ministry" (1838); "Tribute on the Death of Mrs. Jane Kirkpatrick" (1851); "Sermon on the Death of Rev. Dr. Jacob J. Janeway" (1858); and "Funeral Sermon on the Death of Littlejohn Kirkpatrick." He died in New Brunswick, N. J., Feb. 20, 1868.

DURBIN, John Price, seventh president of Dickinson College (1833–45), was born near Paris, in Bourbon county, Ky., Oct. 10, 1800. The respective families of his paternal grandfather, born at Havre de Grace, Md., and of his maternal grandfather, who was a native of Georgia, settled in the Blue Grass state among the first who emigrated thither. His father, Hozier Durbin, was a farmer by occupation, who, in 1799, married Elizabeth Nunn. The first born was reared on the farm, and, up to his fourteenth year, enjoyed but meagre educational advantages. At that age he was apprenticed to a cabinet-maker of Paris, Ky., and with a portion of his scanty earnings he bought books with which to supplement his limited knowledge. It was not long before the desire to be a preacher mastered him, and at the age of eighteen he joined the Methodist church, and shortly entered upon the Limestone circuit, remaining there with Walter Griffith about eight months. In 1819, he was appointed to the Greenville circuit in the northwestern part of Ohio. He now pursued his studies with increased ardor, at first entirely unaided, subsequently at Miami University while preaching at Hamilton, O., and in 1824 was enabled to enter Cincinnati College, at which he was graduated with honors in 1825, and the same year was offered, and accepted, the chair of languages in Augusta College, Kentucky, which he filled for two years, when he was elected professor of natural science at Wesleyan University, Middletown, Conn. In January, 1832, he was made chaplain to the U. S. senate,

and in May, of the same year, was elected editor of the "Christian Advocate Journal" of New York. In the following year he was elected president of Dickinson College, and held this position with distinction until 1845. He employed his vacations, largely in extensive travels abroad, particularly in the Orient, where he visited Egypt, Palestine, Syria, and Asia Minor. In 1844 he was the leader of the Philadelphia delegation to the Methodist convention of that year, and took a prominent part in the anti-slavery discussions. In 1845 he accepted the pastorate of Union Church in Philadelphia, and was elected presiding elder of the Philadelphia district. He was elected secretary to the Missionary Society of the Methodist Episcopal church in 1850, which post he held until 1872, when he declined re-election. Several European missions, notably those in Bulgaria, as well as Hindoo missions, owe their existence in large measure to his unceasing labors which also infused fresh life into the workers in the Chinese missionary field. Through the adoption of his plans the annual contributions to the missionary funds of the church were increased six-fold. Dr. Durbin was noted as an eloquent and powerful preacher, as well as a wonderful organizer and administrator, and from 1844 few men wielded as great influence as he in the counsels of his church. Nor was his pen idle, numerous contributions appearing in the various religious and secular periodicals. He was the author of a few books of travel. "Observations in Europe" (New York, 1844); "Observations in Egypt, Palestine, Syria, and Asia Minor" (1845), and he edited with notes "Wood's Mosaic History of the Creation" (1881). Dr. Durbin was twice married: first on Sept. 6, 1827, to Frances B., daughter of Alexander Cook of Philadelphia; the second time to his deceased wife's younger sister, 1839. He died in New York city, Oct. 18, 1876.

EMORY, Robert, eighth president of Dickinson College (1845-48). See index.

PECK, Jesse Truesdell, ninth president of Dickinson College (1848-52) and Methodist Episcopal bishop, was born in Middlefield, N. Y., Apr. 4, 1811, and was of a famous ministerial family. His paternal and maternal grandfathers were soldiers in the war of the revolution, serving with distinction. He received his education at Cazenovia Seminary, N. Y., where his brother, the Rev. George Peck, was principal. He joined the Oneida conference in 1832, and served as pastor until 1837, when he was principal of Gouverneur Wesleyan Seminary until 1841, and of the Troy Conference Seminary, at Poultney, Vt., from 1841 to 1848. He was a delegate to the general conference in 1844, when the slavery controversy was brought to a crisis, culminating in a division of the Methodist Episcopal church into a Northern and Southern body. Dr. Peck so distinguished himself in the debates on this burning question, as to bring him to the front ranks of Methodist ministers. In 1848 he was elected president of Dickinson College, and served until 1852. He was secretary and editor of the Tract Society in 1854, to fill the unexpired term of Rev. Abel Stevens. Dr. Peck returned to the pastorate in 1856, and was stationed for a time in New York, when he was transferred to San Francisco, in 1858. He was pastor and presiding elder

in San Francisco, Sacramento, and Santa Clara for eight years; also president of the board of trustees of the University of the Pacific, and of the State Bible Society. He was elected bishop in 1872, and was a delegate to the Methodist Ecumenical conference in London in 1881. Bishop Peck returned to the East in 1874, and had charges at Peekskill, Albany, and Syracuse. At the latter place he was one of the founders of the Syracuse University, was president of the board of trustees, and chairman of the building committee. He made the tour of the continent in 1881, and studied educational systems. He is the

author of "The Central Idea of Christianity" (1855); "The True Woman" (1857); "What Must I Do to be Saved?" (1858); and "The Great Republic" (1868). He died in Scranton, Pa., May 20, 1876.

COLLINS, Charles, tenth president of Dickinson College (1852-60), was born in North Yarmouth, Me., Apr. 17, 1818. He was graduated at Wesleyan University, Middletown, Conn., in 1837, and is chiefly distinguished by his labors as an educator. After his graduation he taught for a year in the High School at Augusta, Me. On the establishment of Emory and Henry College, at Emory,

Va., in 1838, Dr. Collins was made president, and held the office until 1852, when he was called to the presidency of Dickinson College. He retired in 1860. From this time until his death he was president of the State Female College, near Memphis, Tenn. He preached in the Methodist church, and contributed largely to Methodist journals. A discourse on "Methodism and Calvinism Compared" was published in 1849. He died in Memphis, Tenn., July 10, 1875.

JOHNSON, Herman Merrill, eleventh president of Dickinson College (1860-68), was born in Butternuts, N. Y., Nov. 15, 1815. He was graduated at the Wesleyan University of Connecticut, in 1839, and in the same year was appointed professor of ancient languages in St. Charles College, Missouri, which he held until 1842. He then accepted a like position in Augusta College, Kentucky, where he remained until 1844, when he was called to the chair of ancient languages and literature in the Ohio Wesleyan University. During Dr. Johnson's first year in this then recently opened institution, he was its acting president, organizing its curriculum, and adding a course of Biblical study as a means of education to its ministerial work. In 1845 he was ordained to the ministry of the Methodist Episcopal church. He severed his connections with the Wesleyan University in 1850 to become professor of philosophy and English literature in Dickinson College, and in 1860 was called to the chair of moral science. In the same year he accepted the presidency of the college, a position he filled with great honor and executive ability until his death. In 1852 the Ohio Wesleyan University conferred upon him the degree of D.D. Dr. Johnson edited "Orientalia Antiquaria Herodoti," and contributed many articles to the "Methodist Quarterly Review," and other religious journals. He published an edition of the "Clio" of Herodotus, in 1850, and was engaged on a German work on synonyms at the time of his death. He died in Carlisle, Pa., Apr. 5, 1868.

DASHIELL, Robert L., twelfth president of Dickinson College (1868-72). See index.

McCAULEY, James Andrew, thirteenth president of Dickinson College (1872-88), was born in Cecil county, Md., Oct. 7, 1822. His early education was defective and irregular, but he acquired the English rudiments, and had a great fondness for books. His family removed to Baltimore, and at the age of seventeen, young McCauley entered a mercantile house. At the end of two years his desire for a liberal education was gratified, and he took a preparatory course in the classical academy of Dr. J. H. Dashiell. In 1847 he was graduated with honor at Dickinson College, and for the ensuing two years was private tutor in one of the oldest families in Maryland. During his college life the conviction had come to him that the Christian ministry was his destined vocation, and in 1850 he was admitted to the ministry of the Methodist Episcopal church, at the session of the Baltimore conference. At this session that body decided to establish, under its auspices, a secondary school of high grade for women, and to him was assigned the responsibility of inaugurating and conducting the enterprise. From the first it was a notable success, and the history of the school is attestation to the thoroughness and wisdom of his work. The cares of administration involved labors so excessive, that at the end of four years he was compelled to relinquish the trust on account of impaired health. After a brief rest he entered the pastorate, and for eighteen years had some of the most important charges in the cities of Baltimore and Washington. He was residing in Washington as presiding elder of the district,

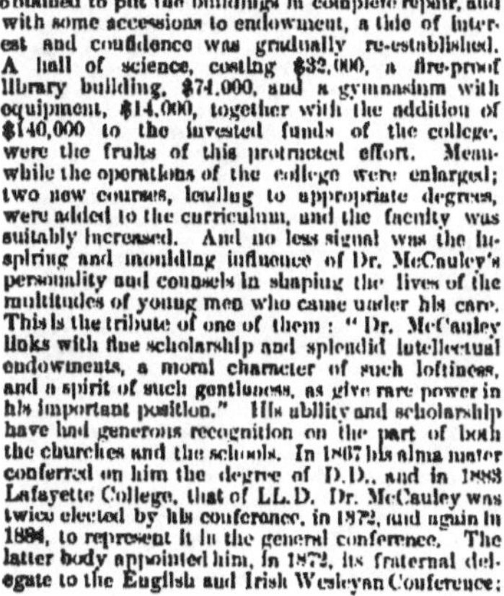

when called to the presidency of Dickinson College in 1872. There was little in the condition of the college to inspirit him at the time of his accession. Owing largely to the war, the patronage and income had undergone decline; the buildings were not only unsightly from want of repair, but were without many of the requisites of comfort—more depressing still, a feeling of distrust was causing many to despond with regard to the future. But Pres. McCauley faced the difficulties with giant courage, and through a decade worked strenuously for their removal. Through personal solicitations a fund was obtained to put the buildings in complete repair, and with some accessions to endowment, a tide of interest and confidence was gradually re-established. A hall of science, costing $32,000, a fire-proof library building, $74,000, and a gymnasium with equipment, $14,000, together with the addition of $140,000 to the invested funds of the college, were the fruits of this protracted effort. Meanwhile the operations of the college were enlarged; two new courses, leading to appropriate degrees, were added to the curriculum, and the faculty was suitably increased. And no less signal was the inspiring and moulding influence of Dr. McCauley's personality and counsels in shaping the lives of the multitudes of young men who came under his care. This is the tribute of one of them : " Dr. McCauley links with fine scholarship and splendid intellectual endowments, a moral character of such loftiness, and a spirit of such gentleness, as give rare power in his important position." His ability and scholarship have had generous recognition on the part of both the churches and the schools. In 1867 his alma mater conferred on him the degree of D.D., and in 1883 Lafayette College, that of LL.D. Dr. McCauley was twice elected by his conference, in 1872, and again in 1884, to represent it in the general conference. The latter body appointed him, in 1872, its fraternal delegate to the English and Irish Wesleyan Conference;

and in 1874, in association with Bishop Harris, he made this fraternal visitation to the satisfaction of the churches on both sides of the water.

REED, George Edward, fifteenth president of Dickinson College (1888–), was born in Brownville, Mo., March 28, 1846. His father, a Wesleyan Methodist minister in Devonshire, England, came to the United States with his family in 1840, joining the East Maine conference of the Methodist church, in whose service he continued up to the date of his death in 1852. On his mother's side, Dr. Reed is descended from Mrs. Rose, a celebrated local preacher, under the supervision of John Wesley, the founder of Methodism. Soon after the death of the father, the family, consisting of the mother and nine children, removed to Lowell, Mass. Here the son attended the public schools, working during the intervals of the terms in stores, or upon farms. Compelled to leave school for lack of means, he became a " runner-boy" in the office of the Lawrence Mills, afterwards entering the works in the capacity of "bobbin-boy." In January, 1865, he entered

Wilbraham Academy, Massachusetts, where in the incredibly short space of six months, toiling early and late, sleeping but four hours in each twenty-four, he prepared himself for college, entering the Wesleyan University, Middletown, Conn., in September, 1865, and being graduated with honor in 1869. He then studied theology in Boston University, was ordained minister of the Methodist Episcopal church in 1870, and for eighteen years served with distinction in various pastorates, as follows: Willimantic, Conn. (1870–72); Fall River, Mass. (1872–75); Hanson Place Church, Brooklyn, N. Y. (1875–78); Stamford, Conn. (1878–81); Nostrand Avenue Church, Brooklyn, N.Y. (1881–84); Hanson Place Church, Brooklyn, N. Y. —second time—(1884–87); New Haven, Conn. (1887–89), when he was elected to the presidency of Dickinson College. On leaving the Hanson Place Church in 1887, Dr. Reed was honored with a public reception, tendered by friends outside the religious body with which he had been associated, in recognition of his distinguished services in various fields of religion,

philanthropy, and reform. At the great gathering held in the Brooklyn Tabernacle, the Rev. Dr. Talmage, pastor, eulogistic addresses were made by the Rev. Drs. Talmage, Cuyler, Thomas, and Col. A. S. Bacon, with commendatory letters from the Rev. Drs. Storrs, Cuthbert Hall, and others, after which Dr. Reed was presented with an elegant testimonial, commemorative of the occasion. Dr. Reed's administration of Dickinson College has been a commanding success, the number of students having doubled within three years, and the prestige of the college largely augmented. In 1870 he married Ella F. Leffingwill of Norwich, Conn., a lineal descendant of Myles Standish, the historic "captain of Plymouth." In 1886 he received the degree of D.D. from his alma mater, and in 1889 Lafayette College conferred the degree of LL.D. A man of splendid physique, fine presence, and affable manners; of remarkable power, both in the pulpit and on the platform, Dr. Reed has also demonstrated an extraordinary capacity to attract and influence young men. These qualities, coupled with indomitable energy, and large power of organization, have been the salient features of a successful career, constituting him a live man at the head of a live institution.

McCLINTOCK, John, theologian and author, was born in Philadelphia, Pa., Oct. 27, 1814. He was graduated at the University of Pennsylvania in 1835, and in 1836 was appointed to the chair of mathematics in Dickinson College, Carlisle, Pa. He became professor of Greek and Latin in 1840, a position he held for eight years. Previous to his graduation he had preached in the New Jersey conference of the Methodist Episcopal church, and in 1848 he was elected by the general conference to edit the "Methodist Quarterly Review," which he did for eight years with scholarly ability, giving to that journal a high literary tone and character. His essays on the philosophy of Comte attracted the French philosopher's notice, and led to a correspondence between them. Dr. McClintock was a delegate, in company with Bishop Simpson, to the Wesleyan Methodist conference of England, in 1856, and also to the assembly of the Evangelical Alliance at Berlin, the same year. In 1857 he became pastor of St. Paul's Church, New York city, and was soon known as one of the most popular and elegant preachers of the metropolis. On the expiration of his term, in 1860, he sailed for Europe, and had charge of the American chapel in Paris during the civil war. At the Wesleyan missionary anniversary held in London during this time, he availed himself of his position as speaker to affirm his reliance in the harmonious relations between England and the United States. He also contributed letters to the "Methodist" which kept his countrymen apprised of the state of European opinion on that great conflict. On his return Dr. McClintock was again appointed pastor of St. Paul's Church, but was soon compelled to resign, owing to delicate health. He was chairman of the central centenary committee in charge of the centennial anniversary of American Methodism in 1866; and when Daniel Drew founded the Drew Theological Seminary at Madison, N. J., in connection with that event, Dr. McClintock was its first president, and retained his connection with the institution until his death. The degree of D.D. was conferred on him by the University of Pennsylvania in 1848, and that of L.L.D. by Rutgers in 1866. Besides his contributions to periodical literature, and an important series of Greek and Latin text-books in connection with Rev. George R. Crooks (1836-40), Dr. McClintock was engaged for the last years of his life on a "Cyclopædia of Biblical, Theological, and Ecclesiastical Literature" (12 vols.), which is a monument of scholarship and theological learning. This was begun in 1853, in conjunction with Dr. Strong, who has gone on with the work, which was not completed

at Dr. McClintock's death. Among other publications are; Neander's "Life of Christ" (1847), translated in connection with Carolus E. Blumenthal; "Sketches of Eminent Methodist Ministers" (1852); "The Temporal Power of the Pope" (1853); and a translation of Bungener's "History of the Council of Trent" (1858). "Living Words," a collection of sermons by Dr. McClintock (1870), and "Lectures on Theological Encyclopædia and Methodology" (1873), were issued after his death. He died in Madison, N. J., Mar. 4, 1870.

MAVERICK, Samuel Augustus, patriot and statesman, was born in Pendleton, S. C., July 25, 1803. John and Samuel Maverick, brothers, were original settlers of Charlestown, S. C., 1670-80, and John was a member of the first colonial parliament of that state. From John, Samuel A. Maverick was descended, and his mother was Elizabeth, daughter of Gen. Robert Anderson, a captain in the revolutionary army. Samuel Augustus was graduated at Yale, studied law in Winchester, Va., removed to Alabama, and thence in 1835 to Texas, at that time a province of Mexico. In the fall of that year he was wrongfully imprisoned at San Antonio, and sentenced to be shot by the Mexican general, but he managed to escape, and joined the insurgent Texan forces

under Gen. Burleson. He took an active part in the siege and successful storming of San Antonio, and it was into his arms that the insurgent leader, Col. Milam fell, mortally wounded. In 1836 Mr. Maverick was elected to the convention, which on March 2, 1836, established the republic of Texas. In the troublous years which followed, Mr. Maverick played a conspicuous part in settling the affairs of the country and allaying the passions of conflicting ambitions. In 1839 Mr. Maverick was elected mayor of San Antonio. In 1842 he was captured by Santa Ana's forces, and confined with others in the castle of Perote, near the city of Mexico, where he and his companions suffered severe privations. He was a member of the Texan congress when the republic was merged into the United States in 1845, and entered the first legislature of the Lone Star State. Yet he was never anxious for office, assuming it solely from a sense of duty, and although more than once spoken of for governor, he always peremptorily declined the honor in advance, and would not permit the use of his name. He became a member of the secession convention in 1861, and he, Judge Devine, and Col. Luckett were appointed a committee to seize and transfer the forts, arms, and other belongings of the U. S. government, which service was accomplished fearlessly and without bloodshed. When at the close of the war, Devine and Luckett were imprisoned, Mr. Maverick was merely placed under arrest, respect being paid to his advanced age and prompt surrender. During his lifetime Mr. Maverick accumulated an immense estate of grazing land amounting to 385,000 acres, which, however, averaged in value at the time of his death, not more than 30 cents per acre. His life was spent in good and honorable deeds, his great influence being ever on the side of right and justice. He was courteous and gentle in manner, and loved by all who knew him. On Aug. 4, 1836, Mr. Maverick married, at Tuskaloosa, Ala., Mary Ann Adams, a great-granddaughter of Gen. Andrew Lewis of Virginia. He died at San Antonio, Sept. 2, 1870.

Residence of Martin Van Buren.

VAN BUREN, Martin, eighth president of the United States, and governor of New York (1829–30), was born at Kinderhook, N. Y., Dec. 5, 1782. His father was a farmer in moderate circumstances; his education was acquired at local schools, and at fourteen he entered a lawyer's office. Admitted to the bar in 1803, he removed to Hudson in 1807, and was surrogate of Columbia county 1808–1813. In 1807 he married Hannah Hoes, who died in 1819. A Jeffersonian from boyhood, he had taken part in a convention at eighteen, and by 1811 was a declared enemy of the U. S. Bank and the "money power." In the state senate 1812–20, he supported Gov. Tompkins, and for a time DeWitt Clinton, but was mostly in opposition to the latter. He was attorney-general 1815–1819. In 1816 he removed to Albany, entered into partnership with B. F. Butler, and became a regent of the state university. In 1818, with Marcy and others, he established the so-called "Albany regency," which for twenty years exercised a controlling influence in the politics of the state. In 1819 he brought order out of local chaos, and showed magnanimity in promoting the election to the U. S. senate of Rufus King, whose opposition to the extension of slave territory was more pronounced than Van Buren's. Two years later he became King's colleague. Before taking his seat he bore a prominent part in the N. Y. constitutional convention of 1821, where he opposed the election of judges, defended the supreme court, then composed of his political foes, and advocated a property qualification for the right of suffrage, to be extended equally to negroes. In the U. S. senate he was long chairman of the judiciary committee, and a member of that on finance. He voted to restrict the admission of slaves into Florida, urged the abolition of imprisonment for debt, supported W. H. Crawford for president, voted for the tariffs of 1824 and 1828, without discussing them, tried in vain to alter the constitutional arrangement of the electoral college, favored a general bankrupt law, but opposed the bill of 1826, and aimed at the equal distribution of internal improvements. Throughout he was a strict constructionist and a defender of state rights. Re-elected in 1827, he resigned the next year to become governor of New York. In this office he suggested and urged the safety-fund banking system which was adopted in 1829, and vainly advised what has since been found necessary in other states, the holding of elections for state officers at a different time from that for president and representatives. In 1829 President Jackson, who thought, with Marcus Aurelius, that life can be made desirable only by spending it with persons who share one's principles, rewarded Van Buren's zealous support by making him secretary of state. As such his chief service was the settlement of difficulties with England concerning the West India trade. In June, 1831, he was sent as minister to England, but the senate, in the following winter, refused, by the casting vote of Calhoun, its president, to confirm the appointment, alleging as a reason for this unusual action a reflection on a previous administration in one of the late secretary's papers. The other party much resented this indignity put by the whigs upon their second favorite, and Verplanck said it would make Van Buren president. He soon had his revenge in being nominated and elected vice-president. Though fully in sympathy with the measures of Jackson's stormy second term, he wisely kept aloof from the noise and dust of party strife, and presided in the senate with exemplary courtesy, dignity and fairness, qualifying himself for the solitary step higher which remained to his ambition. He was elected president in 1836 by a small popular majority over three competitors, but with 170 out of 283 electoral votes. His fortunes in the White House were sadly unlike the placid course of his vice-presidential life. The financial disasters which enemies of the late administration had been predicting as inevitable results of its policy, and which Jackson's supporters ascribed, possibly with as much reason, to the late bank and its mismanagement, now overwhelmed the country, and the man in power of course received the blame. To meet these difficulties he convened congress in September, 1837, and urged a bankrupt law for corporations, the non-payment to the states of the last instalment of the surplus, and especially his favorite and lasting idea, the independent treasury system; this was twice defeated in the house after passing the senate, but became a law June 30, 1840, to be repealed in 1842, and permanently reinstated in 1846. Aside from this main victory, he carried the pre-emption bill, settled some troubles on the Canadian border, and endured with outward calmness the dwindling of his popularity and the virulent attacks of his enemies. Calhoun said in the senate that "justice, right, patriotism, were mere vague phrases" to this "practical politician." And yet he had adhered firmly to his own ideas of what was just and patriotic, and in some cases deliberately injured his own interests in so doing. Von Holst credits him with "courage, firmness, and statesmanlike insight" in the matter of his financial policy. The democrats had no more available candidate in 1840, but he was defeated by 140,000 popular majority, receiving, of 294 electoral votes, but 60, representing seven states. Disdaining to resume the legal practice which he had abandoned long before, he retired to Lindenwald, an estate near his native town, and became "the sage of Kinderhook." His unconcealed opposition to the annexation of Texas diverted the nomination to Polk in 1844, and fitted him to head the free-soil ticket, if not to lead the movement in 1848. He was put in the field over his refusal in advance, by a convention at Utica in June, and another at Buffalo in August. Though he carried no state, he contributed to the defeat of Cass and polled over 290,000 votes, where the Liberty party had had but 7,000 in 1840, and 60,000 in 1844; thus marking the entrance into politics, as a not inconsiderable factor, of principles which twelve years later were to sweep the country and overthrow the slave-power. The ex-president's later life was wholly uneventful. He was loyal to his party and to the Union; he gave no sign of restiveness, under his long exclusion from the scenes and activities in which he had played a leading part; he did not become embittered or soured, nor did he "despair of the country." Except for two years of foreign travel, 1853–55, he lived in dignified and apparently contented, happy retirement at Lindenwald, and died there greatly honored and respected by his neighbors. Though a zealous partisan, he had no bitterness of temper; he was on terms of personal amity with Clay, one of his chief political foes, and visited Ashland in the year after his withdrawal from office. His lack of enthusiasm and magnetism, the calm and uniform suavity of his manners, and his astuteness as a political manager, especially in his earlier years, led to his nickname of "the fox." But it is apparent from his career that he had convictions and the courage of them, and was able on occasion to sacrifice preferment and popularity to the duties of statesmanship. He won high rank as a lawyer, was an able and persuasive, though not a commanding speaker, and inclined to verbosity as a writer. Beyond state papers and speeches, he left nothing but an incomplete "Inquiry into the Origin and Course of Political Parties," published in 1867. His life, meagre as it was in elements of striking interest or moral impressiveness, has been repeatedly handled by W. H. Holland, W. Emmons, F. J. Grund (German), and D. Crockett, in the campaign of 1836; M. Dawson, 1840; W. L. Mackenzie and others, 1846. Of more value are the sketch by W. A. Butler, 1862, and the volumes by W. O. Stoddard, in "Lives of the Presidents," and E. M. Shepard, in the "American Statesmen" series, both 1888. That by George Bancroft, published in 1889, was written long before. None of his predecessors and successors in office, except Washington and Lincoln, have been more abundantly written about. He died July 24, 1862.

VAN BUREN, Angelica, wife of Abraham Van Buren, was born in Sumter District, S. C., about 1820, a daughter of Richard Singleton, a prominent planter. She was presented to President Van Buren by her cousin, Mrs. Madison, wife of President Madison, while she was attending school at Philadelphia in 1837. This introduction led to her marriage to the president's son Abraham in 1838, and the following New Year's Day she made her appearance as mistress of the White House. Her youth and beauty made her at once popular, and a trip to England the following summer and the advantage of the presence of her uncle, Andrew Stevenson, at the court of St. James as U. S. minister gave her exceptional advantages. She extended her

visits to the continent and returned to Washington in the fall, fully equipped to resume her place as the first lady in an exceptionally brilliant society assembled at the capital of the republic. Mrs. Van Buren retained her position in society up to the time of her death, which occurred in New York city Dec. 29, 1878.

JOHNSON, Richard Mentor, vice-president of the United States, was born at Bryant's Station, Ky., Oct. 17, 1781. His early education was limited. He had four years at grammar school and finished his education at Transylvania University. He began to practise law when he was only nineteen years of age. At twenty-two he entered into public life. At this time he was practising at a place called Great Crossings, Ky. He was elected to the state legislature in 1804, and after serving two years in that position was elected to a seat in the house of representatives as a republican. He was re-elected to congress, and, with the exception of a few months, served from 1807 until 1819. Immediately after the adjournment of congress in 1812 he returned home where he organized three companies of volunteers, which being combined with another, he was placed in command of the whole, and took part in the battle of the Maumee where he killed an Indian chief, supposed to be Tecumseh. Afterward the

question, "Who killed Tecumseh?" passed into a saying, and the fact has never been positively settled. After the fall of Tecumseh the Indians continued a brisk fire while retiring, but a regiment brought up by Gov. Shelby soon silenced them, while a part of Col. Johnson's men having flanked them, the rout became general. At the moment when Johnson's regiment made their charge, Gen. Proctor with about fifty dragoons fled from the field. His carriage and papers were taken. It is said that his flight was so rapid that in twenty-four hours he found himself sixty-five miles distant from the battle-field. Col. Johnson was carried from the field almost lifeless. He passed through incredible fatigues, severities and privations during his passage from Detroit to Sandusky and from thence to Kentucky, being carried over a distance of 300 miles, through the wilderness, in the winter, suspended between two horses. He remained about two months in Kentucky, when he had so far recovered from his wounds that he was able to repair to Washington and resume his seat in congress. The fame of his exploits had preceded him, and at the capital he was received with distinguished testimonials of respect and admiration. On his way to the house he was cheered by the populace, and congress passed a joint resolution ordering that he should be presented with a suitable testimonial for his eminent services. In 1819, at the close of his congressional term, Col. Johnson was elected to the U. S. senate in place of John J. Crittenden, who had resigned. At the end of his first senatorial term he was re-elected and served until March 3, 1829. From this time until 1837 he was continuously elected a member of the house of representatives. At the election of Martin Van Buren to the presidency Col. Johnson was the candidate for vice-president, and was chosen by the senate to that position, no choice having been made by the electoral college. At the end of his term of service he returned home, but was afterward again sent to congress, and was a member of that body at the time of his death. In 1844 Col. Johnson was appointed Indian commissioner. He died in Frankfort, Ky., Nov. 19, 1850.

FORSYTH, John, secretary of state, and fifteenth governor of Georgia (1827–29), was born in Frederick county, Va., Oct. 22, 1780. His father, born in England, was a revolutionary soldier, who removed to Georgia in 1784. John was graduated from Princeton in 1799, studied law under Mr. Noel, and was admitted to the bar in Augusta, Ga., in 1802. He was appointed attorney general of the state in 1808, elected representative to congress in 1813, 1815, and 1817, U. S. senator in 1818, resigning in 1819 to accept an appointment as U. S. minister to Spain. In 1823, while in Spain, he was elected representative to congress, and again in 1825; governor of Georgia in 1827, and U. S. senator in 1829, in place of J. M. Berrien. He was a delegate to the anti-tariff convention at Milledgeville, Ga., in 1832, and resigned as U. S. senator in 1834 to be appointed secretary of state by President Andrew Jackson. He was reappointed by President Van Buren, and served until March 3, 1841. Gov. Forsyth was a great lawyer, orator, diplomatist and statesman; in fact, Georgia has had no more brilliant public man. During his ten years as congressman, two years as governor, seven years as senator, four years as foreign minister, and seven years as secretary of state—thirty years, in all, of consecutive public life in the most varied service—he handled the most vital and difficult subjects of national and international interest with a broad and profound statesmanship. As attorney-general of Georgia he exhibited marked legal ability, and achieved high distinction. He was, in every arena, an orator of commanding eloquence. He was handsome, courtly, and fluent, and had a musical, magnetic voice, ex-

tensive knowledge thoroughly at his command, a lofty spirit full of sympathy with humanity, and a remarkable faculty of offhand discussion. Besides, he was a deep thinker. In congress he powerfully antagonized the policy of nullification, and supported with vigor and eloquence Henry Clay's compromise measures. He stood stanchly by the rights of Georgia, and his report on the original compact with the United States to extinguish the Indian title to territory in Georgia was a masterful paper. He championed President Jackson in the debate on the removal of deposits from the United States Bank. As U. S. minister to Spain he brought to a successful termination the negotiations for the cession of the valuable state of Florida to the United States by the Spanish government. As the premier of two able presidents, whose administrations have become noted, he carried on some of the most important transactions with foreign powers that the government has engaged in since the war of 1812, maintaining the national honor and interest with consummate tact and statesmanship. The legislature of 1841 passed appropriate resolutions upon his death, and one of the finest counties of Georgia and one of the most attractive and flourishing towns of that state bear his distinguished name. He died in Washington, D. C., Oct. 21, 1841.

WOODBURY, Levi, secretary of the treasury. (See Vol. II., p. 471.)

POINSETT, Joel Roberts, secretary of war, was born in Charleston, S. C., March 2, 1779. He came of Huguenot ancestry. Immediately after the close of the revolutionary war his parents took him to England, and there he remained until 1788, when the family returned to Charleston, and the boy was sent to school in that city. In 1793 he was placed under the tuition of Dr. Timothy Dwight, at Greenfield Hill, Conn., where he remained for nearly two years. He was then sent to England, and was at school near London for some time, when he went to Edinburgh, where he studied medicine. His health failing, he was sent to Lisbon, where he remained for a winter, and then passed some time in the military academy at Woolwich, studying mathematics, fortification and gunnery. In 1800 he returned to Charleston and began the study of law, but soon after returned to Europe, and, with the exception of a brief visit to the United States, on the occasion of the death of his father, Mr. Poinsett continued to travel on the Continent and in Asia until 1809. On his return, President Madison sent him to South America for the purpose of investigating the condition of the people of that country, and to establish with them friendly relations. He accomplished this object, and was in that country during the war of 1812. On his return he was elected to the South Carolina legislature, and was afterward a member of congress, serving in 1821. In 1822 he was sent to Mexico on a special mission, and in 1825 went to that country as United States minister. He remained in Mexico until 1829, during which time he negotiated a treaty of commerce, and displayed a great deal of personal courage while resisting what amounted to actual persecution on account of the interest which he took in establishing Masonic lodges in the city of Mexico. On his return to the United States, Mr. Poinsett sided with President Jackson in his opposition to the nullification measures of South

Carolina, in speeches, and published articles setting forth his adherence to the national government. He also organized a military company of the supporters of the administration in Charleston, which, by the authorization of the president, was supplied with arms and ammunition from the government stores in the harbor. His talent as a military leader had been demonstrated in South America, when at the head of a force furnished him by the republican authorities of Chili, he attacked the Spaniards and retook the American merchant vessels which had been seized on the rumor of war between the United States and Spain. He was in Valparaiso during the engagement between the Essex, Phœbe, and Cherub, and being prevented from embarking by the British naval authorities, crossed the Andes and arrived home after the declaration of peace. He held the portfolio of secretary of war during the administration of Pres. Van Buren, and did efficient work in reorganizing the ordnance department of the service, and strove earnestly to secure aid from congress, for the state militia organizations. Upon the expiration of his term in this office, he retired into private life, although occasionally expressing his views upon current issues in the public press. He strongly opposed the Mexican war. Mr. Poinsett was well known as a clear, concise, and energetic public speaker, and one possessed of considerable magnetism. He was throughout his life devoted to science and literary pursuits, making many valuable observations especially in botany, in the various foreign lands in which he traveled. He made valuable collections of natural history specimens, which he presented to scientific societies in the cities of New York, Philadelphia, and Charleston. The *Poinsettia pulcherina*, an indiginous Mexican flower, was named for him on his introducing it into the United States. He founded the Academy of Fine Arts in Charleston, S. C., and built the museum of the National Institution. He was a prominent Mason and a member of several scientific and literary societies. He published numerous articles and brochures. His best-known literary production is the book "Notes on Mexico, made in 1822, With an Historical Sketch of the Revolution" (Phila., 1824). The degree of LL. D. was conferred on him by Columbia College in 1825. He died in Statesburg, S. C., Dec. 12, 1851.

DICKERSON, Mahlon, secretary of the navy. (See Vol. V., p. 295.)

PAULDING, James Kirk, secretary of the navy. (See Vol. VII.)

KENDALL, Amos, postmaster-general. (See Vol. V., p. 296.)

NILES, John Milton, postmaster-general, was born in Windsor, Conn., Aug. 20, 1787. He received only a fair education at the common schools of his neighborhood, but being ambitious, and determined to rise, he applied himself to the study of law, and with such success that he was admitted to the bar, although not until he was thirty years of age. He then began to practice law, having settled in Hartford, but finally finding that to make his fortune in that profession would probably be a slow and very laborious piece of work, he cast about him for something else to do, and established the Hartford "Times." He surrounded himself with capable editors and business men, and soon made the "Times" a power in the New England states. It was a democratic paper, and its influential support of Gen. Jackson gave him many votes in the eastern states. Soon after his inauguration, Gen. Jackson appointed Maj. B. H. Norton, who was the editor of the Hartford "Times," postmaster of Hartford, as a reward for the service of the paper during the preceding campaign. Against this, however, Mr. Niles, who was the publisher of the paper, protested, and

even went to Washington, armed with powerful credentials, and worked upon Gen Jackson with such effect that the latter dismissed Norton from his position, replacing him by Mr. Niles, an act which originated a term very much used in politics for twenty years thereafter of "Nortonizing." To Norton, however, he gave a good position in the Boston custom-house, a measure which was entirely satisfactory. Mr. Niles was appointed to the U. S. senate in 1835, and served four years, and again in 1843, serving six years. In 1840 he was appointed by President Van Buren postmaster-general, but only held the position about a year. In 1851 Mr. Niles went to Europe, and on his return went out of politics and retired to private life, devoting himself mainly to agriculture and horticulture. He amassed a considerable fortune, and in his will bequeathed $70,000 in trust to the city of Hartford, directing that the income therefrom should be devoted to the worthy poor. He had a fine

library, which he bequeathed to the Connecticut Historical Society. Mr. Niles published a number of works, including "The Independent Whig" (1816); "Gazetteer of Connecticut and Rhode Island " (Hartford, 1819); "History of the Revolution in Mexico and South America, with a View of Texas" (1829); "The Civil Officer" (New York, 1840). He died in Hartford May 31, 1856.

BUTLER, B. F., attorney-general. (See Index.)

GRUNDY, Felix, attorney-general, was born in Berkeley county, Va., Sept. 11, 1777. His father was an Englishman, who emigrated to this country and for a time roved about, seeking a satisfactory locality whereon to settle. When Felix was two years old, the family lived in Pennsylvania, in Berks county, near what is now Brownsville, but which was at that time a wild country, overrun with Indians. They lived there only a year, when they removed to Kentucky, and there suffered greatly from Indian attacks. Three of Mr. Grundy's sons, of whom there were seven, Felix being the youngest, were killed by the savages. Of course, under the conditions of frontier life, it was impossible to receive even the most meagre education, excepting at the family fireside. It is said that the young Grundys obtained their instruction from the mother, who appears to have been a woman of ability, and very earnest in the discharge of her duties. After a time Felix was sent to an academy, and having been well grounded in the English branches, and a little in the classics, he determined to study law. He was admitted to the bar, and in 1799, when he was twenty-two years of age, was elected a

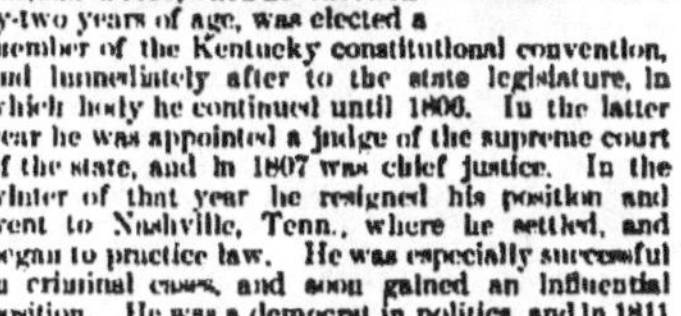

member of the Kentucky constitutional convention, and immediately after to the state legislature, in which body he continued until 1806. In the latter year he was appointed a judge of the supreme court of the state, and in 1807 was chief justice. In the winter of that year he resigned his position and went to Nashville, Tenn., where he settled, and began to practice law. He was especially successful in criminal cases, and soon gained an influential position. He was a democrat in politics, and in 1811 was elected by that party a member of congress, and re-elected two years later. He resigned in 1814, and continued to practice law during the war period and until 1819, when he became a member of the legislature of Tennessee, and the following year one of the commissioners appointed to settle the Kentucky boundary line dispute. In 1829 he filled out the unexpired term of John H. Eaton, in the U. S. senate, the latter having been appointed secretary of war. He was personally favored by Mr. Jackson in 1832, when he was up for the election for the senate, and was successful. In 1838 Mr. Grundy was appointed by President Van Buren attorney-general, and served in that office about a year, when he resigned, and again entered the senate. Mr. Grundy was a "tariff-for-revenue" man, and opposed to so-called protection. Personally, Felix Grundy was greatly admired, being a man of fine personal appearance, of a social and agreeable disposition, and an able and eloquent orator. His most finished oration was that delivered on the deaths of Jefferson and Adams. He was extremely popular, and the legal literature of the southwest is filled with anecdotes about him. His last political act was to speak in Tennessee in favor of Van Buren against Harrison. He died in Nashville, Tenn., Dec. 19, 1840.

GILPIN, Henry Dilwood, attorney-general, was born in Lancaster, Eng., Apr. 14, 1801. He descended from an English family, settled in Kentmore, Westmoreland Co., his ancestors having emigrated to this country in 1696, and settled on the borders of Chester and Delaware counties, on the banks of the Brandywine. The Gilpins were all Quakers. Joshua Gilpin visited Europe, where he spent seven years traveling on the continent, and devoting himself particularly to botany. In 1800 he married Mary Dilwood, the daughter of a banker at Lancaster, and remained there until shortly after the birth of his son, Henry D., when he returned to the United States. The family remained in this country until 1811, when they returned to England, and young Henry was for four years in a private school in that country. In 1816 the family finally settled permanently in Philadelphia, and Henry was sent to the University of Pennsylvania. He took the academic course, studied law, and after a period in the office of Joseph R. Ingersoll, was admitted to practice at the bar in 1822. In the meantime he had occupied the position of secretary of the Chesapeake and Delaware Canal Co., which owed its existence to the suggestion of his grandfather. Henry's great ability as a lawyer grew to be recognized, and in 1830 his successful management of an important international case gave him a wide reputation. This

case involved the official standing of two Portuguese ministers, each of whom had been duly accredited to this country by one of the two conflicting governments of Portugal. Mr. Gilpin's sagacity and judgment in this matter secured for him the high regard of President Andrew Jackson, and the confidence of the supreme court. In 1832 he was appointed to succeed Mr. Dallas as U. S. district attorney at Phil-

adelphia, a position which he held to the satisfaction of all concerned during the next five years. At the same time he was one of the government directors of the U. S. Bank, and gave great assistance to President Jackson in his efforts to suppress that monopoly. His attitude toward the bank, however, and his strong democratic principles interfered with Mr. Gilpin's advancement, as, when the president appointed him governor of the territory of Michigan, the senate refused to confirm the appointment. In 1837 President Van Buren appointed Mr. Gilpin solicitor of the treasury, and on Jan. 10, 1840, he was appointed attorney-general of the United States, having reached that elevated position while still under forty years of age. As the chief prosecuting officer of the United States government Mr. Gilpin was noted for the distinguished power and ability which he showed in handling the gravest and most important cases. Mr. Gilpin retired from political life at the close of President Van Buren's term of office. He had acquired a competency through the successful practice of his profession, and he now determined to devote the remainder of his life to the interests of literature and art, and to such social demands as might be made upon him. He had already given evidence of special literary taste and capacity, having from 1826 to 1832 edited the "Atlantic Souvenir," which was the first of a long series of literary and art volumes published yearly, and commonly called "Annuals." He also pub-lished in 1826 his "Biography of the Signers of the Declaration of Independence," of which a new edition was speedily called for. He contributed freely to the "American Quarterly Review," the "Democratic Review;" and the "North American Review." He edited and superintended the publication of the "Madison Papers," which were published in three volumes, octavo, in 1840, under the auspices of congress. Mr. Gilpin also edited or prepared "Opinions of the Attorneys-General of the United States" (1841); "A Northern Tour, being a Guide to Saratoga, Lake George, etc." (1825); "Autobiography of Walter Scott, compiled from Passages in His Writings" (1831); a translation of Chaptal's "Essays on Import Duties and Prohibitions" (1841); "Life of Martin Van Buren" (1844); besides a large number of published addresses, speeches, and reviews. He also published "Reports of Cases in the U. S. District Court for the Eastern District of Pennsylvania, 1828-36" (Philadelphia, 1837). During the latter part of his life Mr. Gilpin made an extensive tour through Great Britain and the continent of Europe, Egypt, and the East, and while abroad received distinguished attentions from the most eminent scholars and public men. Mr. Gilpin was for a considerable time director and afterward president of the Pennsylvania Academy of Fine Arts, director and vice-president of the Historical Society of Pennsylvania, trustee of the University of Pennsylvania from 1852 to 1858, and a director of Girard College from 1850 to 1858. At his death he bequeathed to the Chicago Historical Society the sum of $57,000, and gave his large and valuable library to the Historical Society of Pennsylvania, accompanied by a gift of money sufficient for the erection of a building in which to preserve the collection. Mr. Gilpin married, in 1835, Eliza Johnston, widow of J. S. Johnston, U. S. senator from Louisiana. Mr. Gilpin died in Philadelphia Jan. 9, 1860.

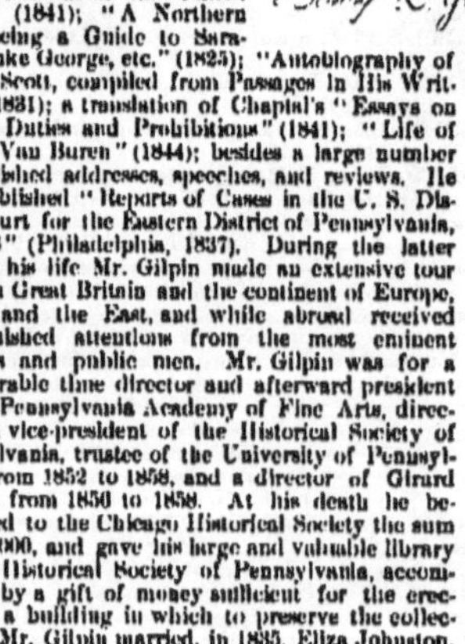

LUNT, George, author, was born in Newburyport, Mass., Dec. 31, 1803. His father was a well-to-do merchant, who gave him every advantage, and he was graduated at Harvard in 1824 with high honors. He studied law in his native town, being admitted to the bar in 1831, and in 1848 pursued his profession in Boston. He was prominent in local politics, and was elected representative and subsequently senator to the Massachusetts legislature. He was prominent in the convention that nominated Taylor to the presidency, and under his administration was appointed U. S. district attorney, which position he held through the administration of Fillmore. He devoted much of his time to literature, and, after resuming the practice of his profession, for a while became editor in association with George S. Hillard of the Boston "Courier." In 1839 he published a volume of "Poems," followed in 1840 by "The Age of Gold, and Other Poems," and in 1854 by "Lyric Poems, Sonnets, and Miscellanies." He was also author of a novel, entitled, "Eastford; or, Household Sketches." His practice was in the state courts, and he was counsel before congressional committees in the adjustment of French claims. In his later years he rendered efficient service in securing appropriations for the construction of harbors of refuge, notably at Scituate. He was eminent as a public speaker, and delivered many orations in the interest of the Whig party, to which he belonged in early life. Upon the dissolution of the Whig party he became a Democrat. Besides orations and addresses, he published: "Three Eras of New England;" "Radicalism in Religion;" "The Union, a Poem;" "The Origin of the Late War;" and "Old England Traits." He died in Boston, May 17, 1885.

CLARK, Nathaniel George, clergyman, was born at Calais, Vt., Jan. 18, 1825. His academic education was received in Montpelier, Vt., and he was graduated at the University of Vermont, in the class of 1845. After graduation he taught in academies at Keene, N. H., and at Montpelier until 1848, when he entered upon a course of theological study at Andover. Being graduated in 1852 he went abroad and spent nearly a year at Halle, and a short time at Berlin, returned in the Spring of 1853 to accept the professorship of Latin and English literature in the University of Vermont, which position he held for ten years. In 1863 he accepted the chair of English literature, rhetoric, and logic in Union College, and in 1865 was elected a secretary of the American board of commissioners for foreign missions, with a view to his succeeding the Rev. Rufus Anderson as secretary in the foreign department, which position he has held to the present date. He was given the degree of D. D. by Union College in 1867, and of LL. D. by the University of Vermont in 1875. In connection with his duties as secretary of the board of foreign missions, he has served as trustee of general institutions in this country as well as abroad; of Mt. Holyoke Seminary, Wellesley College, and the Mission Colleges at Harpoot and Aintab in Turkey, and Jaffna in Ceylon. His attention, however, has been almost exclusively devoted to the care of the mission fields of the American board, but in addition to the general supervision of evangelistic work, his efforts have been directed to the development of woman's work, to self-supporting institutions in native communities, and to the establishment of higher institutions in missionary fields, with a view to an able and efficient native university. He has published several essays on the subject of missions, and also a work entitled "The Elements of the English Language."

ASHE, John, soldier, was born in Grovely, N. C., in 1720. He was for several years a member of the colonial assembly, and its speaker from 1762–65. He was the first to propose a general provincial assembly; a suggestion which subsequently took form in the colonial congress. When the stamp act was passed in 1765, he was strongly opposed to it, and was one of an armed force that compelled the resignation of the stamp master. He was zealous in the cause of the colonies from the first of their struggle for independence, and, in 1775, recruited at his own expense 500 men, with whom he attacked and destroyed Fort Johnson. For this act he was publicly denounced as a rebel. In 1778 he was appointed brigadier-general, and served under Gen. Lincoln. In the following year he was given a separate command, and ordered to drive the British from Augusta, but was surprised and defeated by the enemy under Gen. Provost, at Brier Creek, March 4th, when he retreated to Wilmington. When Wilmington was captured by the British in 1781, Gen. Ashe was taken prisoner, and his death is said to have been hastened by the cruel treatment he received. He died Oct. 24, 1781, from small-pox contracted while in prison. Asheville, and Ashe county, in North Carolina, were named in his honor.

WELLS, Horace, one of the discoverers of anesthesia, was born in Hartford, Windsor co., Vt., Jan. 21, 1815. He began the study of dentistry at Boston in 1834, and its practice at Hartford, Conn., in 1836. Desirous to render the extraction of teeth painless, he expressed, in 1840, the idea that this might be done by the aid of nitrous oxide gas. On Dec. 10, 1844, he attended a lecture by Dr. G. Q. Colton, on "laughing gas," and observed that a man who had inhaled the gas was unconscious of pain. On the next day he tested its efficacy in his own person, and exclaimed, "A new era in tooth-pulling!" From that day he used the gas in his practice. It had been discovered by Priestly in 1790, and Sir H. Davy's belief that it could be used in surgical operations was published in his "Researches" in 1800; but no one was enterprising enough to put it to the test until Wells, early in 1845, went to Boston and attempted a demonstration before Dr. J. C. Warren's class. Unnerved by the responsibility he had assumed, he removed the gas too soon, and was hooted from the room as an imposter. Grief and shame brought on a long illness, and this failure not only postponed for months the greatest alleviation of human sufferings ever brought about by science, but transferred the chief honor as an anæsthetic to sulphuric ether. Its properties had long been turned to the amusement of students in New England and the South. Dr. Crawford W. Long of Georgia applied it in surgical cases in 1842, but made no claim to the discovery until others were in the field. Dr. Macy, of Hartford, a friend of Wells, used it in a successful operation in January, 1845; but its importance was first realized, and the credit of its introduction gained, by Dr. W. T. G. Morton, who had been a pupil and partner of Wells in 1841–43. He gained from Wells in 1845 the belief in nitrous oxide gas, but was persuaded by Dr. C. T. Jackson to use ether instead, and applied it Oct. 10th and 17th, 1846, in both dental and surgical operations. "Letheon" was patented ten days later, and a quarrel with Jackson ensued, each claiming from the French Institute the honors of the discovery. Poor Wells, anxious for his share, went to Paris in December, 1846, and obtained some recognition from the Medical Society there. Returning in March, 1847, he published a "History" of the discovery, made some experiments with chloroform (the similar uses of which had been announced by Florenes in January, 1847, and were applied by Sir J. Y. Simpson ten months later), and went to New York to push his claim; but his mind was unhinged by his troubles and by arrest on a disgraceful charge, and he died by his own hand. Truman Smith defended his cause in the U. S. senate in 1853, and in "An Examination," 1859, and "An Inquiry," 1867. He died Jan. 24, 1848. His statue stands in Bushnell Park, Hartford.

KINNE, Aaron, clergyman, was born in Norwich, Conn., Sept. 24, 1744. He was graduated at Yale College in 1765, and ordained in October, 1770. Soon after his ordination he accompanied the Rev. Samuel Kirkland as a missionary to the Oneida Indians. After this he took charge of a congregation on Long Island. He was made bishop of his people at Groton, Conn., Oct. 19, 1769, where he remained until 1798. He was chaplain at Fort Griswold during the massacre of Sept. 6, 1781, when Col. Ledyard was killed, and the fort taken by the British led by Benedict Arnold. From Groton, Mr. Kinne went to Winsted, Conn., and in 1804 he removed to Egremont, Mass., in both places being pastor of the Congregational churches. He afterwards went to Alford where, while having charge of the church, he was elected to the legislature and served two terms. In 1775 he was principal of the Morris School at Lebanon, an institution which led to the later organization of the college now at Hanover, N. H., and under the trusteeship of Dartmouth College. Mr. Kinne published the following theological works: "The Sonship of Christ," "A Display of Scripture Prophecies" (1813); "Explanation of the Types, Prophecies, Revelation, etc." (1814); and an "Essay on the New Heaven and Earth" (1821). He died in Tallmadge, O., July 9, 1824.

GORRINGE, Henry Honeychurch, naval officer, was born in Barbadoes, W. I., Aug. 11, 1841, son of an English clergyman of the established church. He came to the United States at an early age, and entered the merchant-marine service. At the outbreak of the civil war he enlisted in the national service as a common sailor, July 13, 1862, and by 1865 had risen, through successive promotions, to the rank of acting-volunteer lieutenant. On Dec. 18, 1868, he became lieutenant-commander, and from 1869 to 1871 was in charge of the sloop Portsmouth, of the South Atlantic squadron. He was employed in the hydrographic office in Washington, D. C., from 1872 until 1876, when he was sent with the Gettysburg on special service in the Mediterranean. While here, he contributed a number of letters to the New York

"Nation." Com. Gorringe's chief claim to public notice was his connection with the transportation and erection of the Egyptian obelisk, presented to the United States by the Khedive Ismail in 1879. He began these operations on Oct. 16th at Alexandria, where, with the assistance of 100 Arabs, he had by Nov. 6th removed 1,780 cubic yards of earth from around the obelisk's pedestal. He next invented a simple machinery by which the monolith was removed from its pedestal, and placed in a horizontal position, Dec. 6, 1879. The mechanism by which the obelisk was confined in the Dessony, the iron steamer purchased from the Egyptian government, into which the obelisk had been introduced by means of a hole in one side of the hold, was also the original device of Com. Gorringe. The obelisk arrived in New York, July 25, 1880. By means of iron tracks and cannon balls, it was conveyed from the North river to Central Park, where, on Jan. 22, 1881, it was erected on the same pedestal on which it had rested in Egypt. The height of the shaft is sixty-nine feet. It was erected by Thotmes III. at Heliopolis about 1600 B.C., and removed to Alexandria in 22 B.C. The total expense of its removal to New York and erection in Central Park was $103,732, paid by William H. Vanderbilt. Subsequently Com. Gorringe published a "History of Egyptian Obelisks." He also criticised the existing state of naval affairs with such freedom that he was called to account by the department, upon which he tendered his resignation, which was accepted. For some time after he was engaged in the formation and support of the American Ship-Building Co., an enterprise which, through want of capital, eventually failed. Some months before his death he received a severe injury by jumping from a railroad train. He died in New York, July 7, 1885. He is buried at Sparkill, on the Hudson, N. Y., his monument being an exact copy, on a smaller scale, of the obelisk that he so successfully transported from Egypt.

MILES, George Henry, poet and author, was born in Baltimore, Md., July 31, 1824. At the age of nine he was sent to Mount St. Mary's College, Emmittsburg, and was graduated there in 1842. He studied law in the office of J. H. B Latrobe, and subsequently practiced that profession in Baltimore, but without developing any great liking for it. He was passionately fond of literature and poetry, and as a boy he wrote verses of considerable merit. At the age of twenty he competed for a prize of $1,000, offered by Edwin Forrest for a tragedy, producing his play of "Mohammed," which was accepted. From this early success he decided to give up his law practice, and commenced to write plays for the leading actors of the day. His tragedy "De Soto," written for the actor, J. E. Murdock, and also a comedy entitled "Mary's Birthday," were successfully produced in New York city. Besides these he wrote "The Seven Sisters," "Senor Valiente," and the dramatization of Holmes's "Elsie Venner," which, however, were not so successful. He wrote, meanwhile, many stories, which were generally Catholic in tone and principle; the first one, "The Truce of God: A Tale of the Eleventh Century," was published serially in the "United States Catholic Magazine." "The Governess" appeared shortly afterwards, and another story, "Loretto," won a $50 prize offered by the "Catholic Mirror." In 1851 Mr. Miles was sent to Spain by Pres. Fillmore on official business. In 1864 he again visited Europe, and upon his return wrote a series of sketches, "Glimpses of Tuscany," and "Christine: a Troubador's Song," which was afterwards published in a book of poems in 1866. In 1859 he was appointed professor of English literature in Mount St. Mary's College, and removed from Baltimore to Thornbrook, a cottage near Emmittsburg, where he passed the remainder of his life. Among his other publications may be mentioned: "Discourse in Commemoration of the Landing of the Pilgrims of Maryland" (1847); "Christmas Poems" (1866); and "Abou Hassan, the

Wag, or the Sleeper Awakened " (1868). In 1870 he published a paper on " Hamlet," in the " Southern Review," and afterwards in pamphlet form, which won for its author an extended notice among the English critics. In February, 1859, he married Adaline Tiers of New York. After a short illness, he died at his home at Emmittsburg, July, 23, 1873, and was buried in the churchyard of St. Mary's College.

CLARK, Alvan, optician, was born in Ashfield, Mass., March 8, 1804. His father, Abram Clark, was a well-to-do farmer, who gave his son more than ordinary educational advantages. After completing his education, he went to Lowell, where he studied engraving, and became an engraver of blocks used

in printing calico. He followed this occupation for nine years, when he removed to Boston, and opened a studio for portrait-painting. He painted a portrait of Webster, and achieved a wide reputation and a large success. As a youth he had always been interested in mathematics, amusing himself in working out intricate problems, and when, in 1844, a neighboring optician came to him for advice, as to the best method of obtaining a proper curve in making a lens, he worked out the problem, and became so much interested in this line of work, that he gave it his attention, and eventually became a manufacturer of telescopes. He turned the energies of his mind to the perfecting of the lenses, and was the first person in the United States to overcome the difficulties of the achromatic lens, and achieved such skill that the most important telescopes of modern times have been made at his factory at Cambridgeport, Mass. Many of the glasses for European telescopes were also sent to him to be ground. The firm would not seek orders, nor issue a price-list, nor exhibit their instruments, yet they received and executed orders for four telescopes, each of which at the time was the largest instrument then known. The first, an 18-inch object glass, was ordered for the University of Mississippi in 1860, but eventually went to Chicago; the second was for the naval observatory at Washington, in 1870; the third was a 30-inch glass for the Pulkova observatory in Russia, in 1879; the fourth was a 36-inch glass for the Lick observatory in California, in 1886, which cost $50,000, unmounted. Dom Pedro, the emperor of Brazil, when visiting the United States in 1876, said there were three persons in Cambridge he wished to see, Longfellow, Agassiz, and Alvan Clark. Mr. Clark made numerous inventions for the improvement of telescopes, notably the double eye-piece for measuring small celestial arcs. He also became an expert astronomer, and made many discoveries which have been enumerated in the " Proceedings of the Royal Astronomical Society." In 1863 he received the La Lande prize of the French Academy for his valuable discoveries. The degree of A.M. was conferred upon him by Amherst, Chicago, Princeton, and Harvard. He associated with him his sons, who have continued the business even with greater success and reputation. Mr. Clark died in Cambridge, Aug. 19, 1887.

LE VERT, Octavia Walton, author, was born in Bellevue, near Augusta, Ga., in 1810. Her grandfather, George Walton, was one of the signers of the Declaration of Independence. Her father was his second son, who married Sally Minge Walker of Georgia, and removed to Pensacola in 1821, where he became territorial secretary under Gen. Jackson, and upon his retirement was for a time acting-governor. Octavia was much in the society of the officers of the war-ships which rendezvoused at this point, thus acquiring an ease of manner remarkable in one so young. Her mother and grandmother, both women of intellect and culture, vied with each other in developing her early life, and at twelve she could converse in three languages, and was often taken to her father's office to interpret his foreign despatches. She never was a pupil in any school, but was taught by an old Scotch teacher, who was a fine classical scholar and linguist, under whose tutelage she acquired Greek and Latin, and became proficient in French, Italian, and Spanish. When the new capital was established, the selection of a name was given to her, and she named it Tallahassee, a Seminole word meaning " beautiful land," which made her a favorite with the old Indian chief, who called her " the white dove of peace." Lafayette, when visiting the South, wished to meet her grandmother, but she was obliged by old age and infirmities to decline the interview, and sent Octavia to represent her. When Lafayette saw the child, he burst into tears and caught her to his breast, exclaiming : " The living image of my brave and noble friend." He held her on his knee, listening, delighted and spellbound, to her fluent use of his native tongue, and when she retired blessed her and said : " A truly wonderful child ! She has been conversing, with intelligence and tact, in the purest French. I predict for her a brilliant career." In 1833-34 she made a tour of the United States, having the *entrée* to the most select circles of the large cities, and everywhere was the reigning belle. Journeying by stage coach, she met a strange gentleman, who became greatly interested in her conversation. Good breeding forbade that they should ask each other's name, but he joined in telling anecdotes, and described a bull-fight in Spain, when Octavia exclaimed " where have I heard that before ?" The stranger said, " You cannot have heard it before, for it has never been recorded, and you have never been in Spain." Octavia thought for a moment, and then said : " You are Washington Irving." " Why do you think I am Washington Irving ?" he replied. " Because whoever told me of this incident said Washington Irving was by his side when it occurred." A friendship immediately sprung up between the two, and she was a frequent guest at " Sunnyside." At one time, when she was leaving, her host said : " I feel as if the sunshine were all going away with you, my child." She had great conversational powers, and made personal friends with many of the eminent men of the day, such as Clay, Calhoun, and Webster. She frequently reported their speeches, and is said to have done it so accurately  that she was often asked to read them from her portfolio. She was at that time called the " belle of the Union," and while she knew how to preside in fashionable drawing-rooms, she also knew how to minister to the sick and suffering, which was her frequent employment. While visiting among the poor in Mobile, she met a kind-hearted and handsome physician, named Henry Le Vert, a son of Dr. Claude Le Vert, the fleet surgeon under Rochambeau. Dr. Le Vert's mother was related to Adm. Vernon, for whom Lawrence Washington named Mount Vernon, and it was largely through the personal exertions of Madame Le Vert, the granddaughter of George Walton, that Mount Vernon was built. In 1836 she married Dr. Le Vert, and resided with him at Moble. She visited Europe in 1853, on the invitation of the Duke of Rutland, and again in 1855, when she wrote the letters to her mother which were, upon the advice of Lamartine, afterwards published, under the title of "Souvenirs of Travel." She next translated Dumas' "Musketeers," and the "Pope and the Congress." She also produced "Souvenirs of Distinguished People," and "Souvenirs of the War," but a painful accident prevented their being completed. She was devoted to her mother, who survived until 1864, and to her colored servants, who when freed by the war refused to leave, and begged to be allowed to remain and work as before. She opposed secession, but remained in Mobile after the death of her husband in 1860, and devoted herself to the soldiers during the entire war. Upon the conclusion of the war she went to Washington to urge the pardon of her friend, Gen. Beauregard. Crushed by the sorrows of her bereavement, she led a quiet and secluded life, but visited New York for a while with her two daughters, where she was the centre of a literary and fashionable circle. She died in Augusta, Ga., March 13, 1877.

MOFFAT, David Halliday, capitalist, was born in Washingtonville, Orange co., New York, July 22, 1839. He received a common-school education, leaving home at the age of fifteen to take the position of messenger in the New York National Exchange Bank. A year later he made his first western move, going to Des Moines, Ia., where he was engaged as clerk in the banking firm of A. J. Stevens & Co. Another remove toward the mountains found him in Omaha, Neb., acting as cashier in a bank at that place. Four years later the Pike's Peak gold fever broke out, and Mr. Moffat joined the ever-swelling procession that wended its way over the plains in 1860, toward the mecca of fortune-seekers. Arriving in Denver, he found it a mere prospectors' camp, giving slender promise of its magnificent future. Together with C. C. Woolworth of New York, he engaged in the stationery business, which, during the six years they were together, proved remarkably prosperous and remunerative. In 1866 he accepted the position of cashier

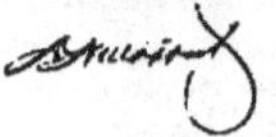

of the First National Bank of Denver, of which institution he afterward became, and still remains, the president. It has grown during his connection with it from a comparatively small business into one of the most respected and conservative banking institutions in the country, and is looked upon as the strongest and most extensive bank between Chicago and San Francisco. During his long residence in Denver, Mr. Moffat has become identified with every progressive enterprise in the state. His name appears in the incorporation of most of the public institutions, and the construction of the Denver Pacific Railroad, tapping the main line of the Union Pacific at Cheyenne, which gave the city of Denver its first railroad, was largely due to his efforts. He was also largely responsible for the building of the South Park Railroad, a narrow-gauge line which still carries much freight between Leadville and Denver. He was identified with the construction of the New Orleans Railroad, connecting Colorado with the gulf, and opening a new field for its products. In 1884 he accepted the presidency of the Denver and Rio Grande Railroad, and much of the progress and excellent condition of that road is due to his energy and splendid executive ability. Besides his many other interests, Mr. Moffat has given much attention to mining as a legitimate business. He de-

velops his properties in the best manner, and has been wonderfully successful, many times refuting the idea that the success of mining-operations was a matter of luck, instead of being due to a safe and systematic investment. He is looked upon as a leading mining man of his state, and has interests in many of the most valuable of the Colorado mines. Among them, possibly, the best known are: the Maid of Erin, Henriett, and Resurrection, at Leadville, the Victor at Cripple Creek, and the Amethyst at Creede. He is a man of wealth, and with widespread interests, yet he is one of the most popular and approachable of men. He is public-spirited to a great degree, and only recently subscribed $50,000 toward the building of a mining and industrial exposition in the city of Denver.

SHEA, John Dawson Gilmary, historian, was born in New York city, July 22, 1824, the son of James Shea, who was a native of Ireland, and at one time tutor to the sons of Gen. Schuyler of revolutionary fame, and later was principal of Columbia College Grammar School. His mother was a descendant of Nicholas Upsall, who emigrated to America with Gov. Winthrop in 1630, and settled in Boston. Young Shea was educated by the Sisters of Charity and at Columbia College Grammar School, subsequently studying law, and in 1846 was admitted to the bar. During his youth his attention was called to the early Catholic missions among the Indians, and he began to collect material for a general history of the Catholic church in the United States. In order to facilitate his historical researches he studied the Indian languages and pub-

lished grammars and dictionaries in this tongue entitled, Library of American Linguistics. When he was but fourteen years old an article from his pen, on Cardinal Albornoz, appeared in the "Young Peoples Catholic Magazine." He was a man of great versatility, and was well informed upon almost every subject. He was a fine classical scholar, familiar with most of the modern languages, and knew history, ancient, medieval, modern, ecclesiastical, and secular, with a thoroughness that was a surprise even to those who were acquainted with his fund of historical knowledge. But it was with the history of North America, to which he had devoted so many years of deep study, that he was most thoroughly acquainted. He went to the bottom and found out the real facts, and as far as these could be ascertained, his writings were valuable for their entire reliability as to dates, facts, and statements. At the time of his death he was engaged upon his greatest work, the "History of the Catholic Church in the United States." This history which represents many years of honest, laborious, intricate, and difficult research in various out-of-the-way resources, and in many languages, is a veritable treasure-house, and without its aid future generations would have been left in the dark as to what Catholic Christianity had accomplished in the United States. His writings were confined chiefly to historical subjects. Dr. Shea was completing the last volume of his "History of the Catholic Church in the United States," and was also editor of the "Catholic News," when he died. He received the degree of LL.D. from St. John's College, Fordham, St. Francis Xavier's College, New York city, and Georgetown College, D. C. He died at his home in Elizabethtown, N. J., Feb. 21, 1892.

ANDREWS, Stephen Pearl, philosopher, was born in Templeton, Mass., March 22, 1812. While yet an infant his father, Rev. Elisha Andrews, a Baptist clergyman, removed to Hinsdale, where Mr. Andrews's boyhood was passed. He was educated at Amherst College, and at nineteen years of age emigrated (as was then said) to Louisiana, where he studied law with an elder brother who had preceded him there. While preparing for admission to the bar he supported himself by teaching Greek and Latin. He married Mary Ann Gordon, a native of Norwich, Conn., who was an inmate of the young ladies' seminary where he taught. He practiced law in New Orleans for four years and was the first counsel retained by Mrs. Gaines in her famous suits, and commenced the actions which occupied the attention of the courts for the following years. While in New Orleans, and surrounded by slaveholding influences, both he and his brother became ardently devoted to the cause of abolition. His brother had married a Southern lady who owned a large plantation and more than 100 slaves. She also became convinced of the wrong of slavery, and they removed to southern Illinois, taking their slaves with them. They settled upon the public land, where they built houses for their negroes, whom they freed. In 1839 Stephen Pearl Andrews removed to Houston, Tex., where he entered upon the practice of law, becoming widely known, popular, and suddenly rich in lands. His purpose in going to Texas was to agitate in favor of making it a free state. He persistently refused to engage in suits which involved slave property, or even to become a citizen of Texas, because of the objectionable pro-slavery clause in the constitution. His impetuous and logical eloquence gained for him a wide reputation and the credit of a standing at the head of the bar, and the public were proud of his ability, while on the other hand, his seemingly reckless and fanatical opposition to their favorite institution, aroused a feeling so intense that it came very near costing him his life. His career in Texas furnishes the only instance during those ominous anti-abolition times when an avowed and active abolitionist of Northern birth maintained his footing in the midst of a Southern population. Near the close of 1843 Mr. Andrews resolved to make a more public and decided effort to overthrow the institution of slavery in Texas. For a time it seemed as if he was about to succeed, but, when the hostile party became thoroughly aroused, he was mobbed and finally driven from his home in the middle of the night on the alternative of being hanged if he was found in the city within an hour. With his wife and infant child he rode in the night for twenty miles across a prairie so flooded that the water came to the hubs of his buggy wheels, and narrowly escaped drowning in a stream they were compelled to cross. This experience did not deter him from his purpose. He determined to go to England, where the World's Anti-Slavery convention was just about to hold its sessions, in the hope that with the aid of the British Anti-Slavery Society he might raise sufficient money to pay for the slaves and make Texas a free state. He was cordially received in London by Lord Aberdeen, Lord Brougham, Lord Campbell, Lord Palmerston, and other influential men, and his scheme was taken up and favorably considered by the British government, but after months of consultation the project was abandoned through fear that it would lead to war with the United States, as the knowledge of it was already being used to strengthen the movement that ultimately led to the annexation of Texas and to the Mexican war. On returning to America, Mr. Andrews went to Boston and became a leader in the anti-slavery movement there. He was a remarkable speaker, having an almost unequalled command of language and facility of expression. As an orator of that time, he ranked with Wendell Phillips, who then labored with him in the same cause. While in England he learned of phonography, and during seven years after his return he devoted his attention to its introduction, and was the founder of the present system of phonographic reporting. He removed to New York in 1847, published a series of phonographic instruction books in co-operation with Augustus F. Boyle, and edited two journals in the interest of phonography and spelling reform, which were printed in phonetic type, the "Anglo Saxon" and the "Propagandist." Stephen Pearl Andrews was a man of vast learning. He had an intimate knowledge of thirty-two languages, several of which he spoke fluently. He was a master of Greek and Latin, a thorough Sanskrit and Hebrew scholar, and was credited with being the best Chinese scholar in this country when, in 1850, he published a work entitled "Discoveries in Chinese." He was the author of a system of teaching languages, and published, in collaboration with George Batchelor, a "French Instructor," which has been widely used. As a young man in Louisiana, he believed that he had hit upon the germ of a great discovery—that of the unity of all science and philosophy, the discovery, in a word, of the unity of law in the universe. He planned also at that day the reform of English orthography, and other minor enterprises, which he afterward endeavored to realize. He came later to the study of the great thinkers of all schools, and he proposed no less than to found the ultimate reconciliation of them all, not by a superficial eclecticism, but by a radical adjustment of all the possible forms of thought, belief, and idea. The same principles to which he looked for this immense result, furnish also, he informed us, the basis and guidance for the construction of the scientific universal language, the one destined to take the place of the many languages which now cover and cumber the earth. This universal science he denominated Universology, the elements of which are contained in a large work called "The Basic Outline of Universology." The new language he called Alwato (Ahl-wah-to), and his philosophy at large, as a doctrine of many-sidedness and reconciliation, is known as Integralism. The practical institution of life, which he advocated and labored to inaugurate—neither mere individualism nor mere communism—he called the Pantarchy. As a result of the publication of his "Sovereignty of the Individual," "Science of Society," "Love, Marriage and Divorce," the latter being a discussion between Henry James, Horace Greeley, and Stephen Pearl Andrews, Mr. Andrews had, as early as 1853, assumed the position of the leader of radical thought upon social questions. At that time society was still held in the bonds of bigotry and superstition which, though strained, were not yet broken, and questions of social and religious liberty that are now openly and freely discussed were then, for the most part, forbidden subjects, or were only to be secretly discussed. Mr. Andrews's bold utterances alarmed many of his friends, and for many years he pursued his studies sustained only by a small circle of faithful followers. He lived, however, to see the first promises of the harvest of which his radical thought may be called the seed. In 1882 he instituted a series of conferences known as the "Colloquium," for the interchange of ideas between men of the utmost diversity of religious, philosophical, and political views. Among those associated with him in this were Prof. Louis Elsberg, Rev. Dr. Rylance, Rev. Dr. Newman, Rabbi Gottheil, Rev. Dr. Sampson, Rev. Dr. Collyer, Prof. J. S. Sedgwick, T. B. Wakeman, and Rabbi Huebsch. Mr. Andrews was a prominent member of the Liberal Club of New York, and for some time was its vice-president. His contributions to periodicals are numerous. He was a member of the American Academy of Arts and Sciences, and of the American Ethnological Society. His works include "Comparison of the Common Law with the Roman, French or Spanish Civil Law on Entails and other Limited Property in Real Estate" (New Orleans, 1839); "Cost, the Limit of Price" (New York, 1851); "The Constitution of Government in the Sovereignty of the Individual" (1851); "Love, Marriage and Divorce, and the Sovereignty of the Individual; a Discussion, by Henry James, Horace Greely, and Stephen Pearl Andrews" (edited by Stephen Pearl Andrews, 1853); "Discoveries in Chinese; or, the Symbolism of the Primitive Characters of the Chinese System of Writing as a Contribution to Philology and Ethnology and a Practical Aid in the Acquisition of the Chinese Language" (1854); "Constitution or Organic Basis of the New Catholic Church" (1860); "The Great American Crisis," (a series of papers published in the "Continental Monthly," 1863–64); "A Universal Language" ("Continental Monthly," 1864); "The Primary Synopsis of Universology and Alwato" (1871); "Primary Grammar of Alwato" (Boston, 1877); "The Labor Dollar" (1881); "Elements of Universology" (New York); "Ideological Etymology" (1881); "Transactions of the Colloquium with Documents and Exhibits" (vols. I. and II., New York (1882–83); "The Church and Religion of the Future" (a series of tracts, 1885). His unpublished works will fill several volumes. His manuscripts have been collected and arranged, and it is intended that they shall be published. Mr. Andrews was twice married, but was, for many years before his death, a widower. He had four sons by his first wife, two of whom survived him. The date of his death, which occurred in New York city, was May 21, 1886.

PINKNEY, Edward Coate, author, was born in London, Oct. 1, 1802. He was the son of William Pinkney (q. v.), who was minister to England at the time of his birth. He spent the first nine years of his life in London, where he was carefully educated, and upon his return to his father's home in Baltimore entered college, but before completing his course entered the U. S. navy, when only fourteen years old. After serving six years he had a serious quarrel with his commanding officer, and challenged him to fight a duel. The commodore considered it the result of the exuberance of youth, and ignored it utterly, which so roused young Pinkney that he openly posted Com. Ridgely in the streets of Baltimore. He resigned, and began the study of law, and was admitted to the bar in 1824, but, from his poetical inclinations, did not make headway in his profession. He published a volume of verses in 1825, which were full of exquisite taste and susceptibility. A few of these are still remembered, notably "Health," and "The Picture Song." Pinkney's most ambitious effort was "Rodolph," a poem, a powerful sketch full of beauty, although the moral was decidedly questionable. Throughout his poems runs a vein of sullen melancholy, hinting of his disappointment with himself and the work. As an evidence of the estimation in which his genius was held, he was requested to sit for a miniature portrait which was to be used in a collection of the five greatest poets of the day, and Edgar A. Poe adjudged him the finest of America's lyric poets. In 1825 he went to Mexico, intending to join their navy in their struggle for independence, but became involved in a quarrel with a native, whom he killed in a duel, and was obliged to flee the country. Upon his return from Mexico, in recognition of his scholarship, he was appointed professor of rhetoric and *belles lettres* in the University of Maryland. In 1827 he became editor of "The Marylander," a political paper established in the interest of John Quincy Adams, and displayed an ability in dealing with public questions that was quite surprising for one of his years, but a few months after his health failed. A volume of his poems appeared in 1825. Among them were "The Indian Bride," and "On Italy," which was especially admired. He had fretted away his life from disappointments and had no desire to live, and after several months' illness he died, Apr. 11, 1828.

DILL, James Horton, clergyman, a son of James and Ruth (Cushing) Dill, was born in Plymouth, Mass., Jan. 1, 1821. He was educated at Yale College and Seminary, and entered the ministry in Winchester, Conn., where he served six years, and afterwards settled in Spencerport, N. Y. He began there a systematic work of visiting the entire region round about, with a view to awakening a popular interest in the faith and order of the Pilgrims, and chiefly through his indirect agency the large and influential Plymouth Church of Rochester was organized and a house of worship built. He delighted to make journeys, at his own suggestion and expense, as a general missionary of the good cause, which led one of his contemporaries to declare that "Mr. Dill had done more to establish Congregational churches in western New York than any other man in twenty years." He remained in Spencerport nearly eight years, and dually removed to Chicago, where he became pastor of the South Congregational Church. After a three years' occupancy of the pulpit, he offered his services, from motives of patriotism, to the army of the Republic soon after the breaking out of the war, and, joining the "railroad regiment" from Illinois, died in the service of his country. Mr. Dill was one of the most earnest and useful men in the Congregational denomination either East or  West. His efforts for the building of new churches, together with his industry in gathering the statistics of the denomination, made him one of the staunchest pillars of Western Congregationalism. Mr. Dill married Catherine, daughter of Capt. Jeremiah Brooks of Cheshire, Conn., a descendant of Henry Brooks, who, with his brother John, came from England and settled in New Haven colony about 1670. He died from sickness contracted in camp, Jan. 14, 1863.

DILL, James Brooks, lawyer, was born in Spencerport, N. Y., July 25, 1854, eldest child of Rev. James Horton and Catherine (Brooks) Dill. When four years of age his parents removed to Chicago. Upon the death of his father, in 1863, he removed with his mother to New Haven, Conn., and continued his studies in the elementary branches. From 1868 to 1872, he studied at Oberlin, O., then entered the freshman class at Yale, being graduated in 1876. Being wholly dependent on his own exertions, for support, after graduation he taught in Samuel Clements' School near Philadelphia, at the same time studying law with E. Copee Mitchell. Mr. Dill came to New York in 1877, and became an instructor in Steven's Institute in Hoboken; being graduated in the University Law School in 1878 as salutatorian of his class, with the degree LL. B.; and was at once admitted to the bar of New York. He made a special study of corporation law, and in 1879 won an important corporation case, establishing a doctrine new to New York as to the stockholders' liability. His business immediately experienced a marked increase, and within the next ten years he became known at the bar of New York as a corporation lawyer, and subsequently became an authority on corporation law. His business ability was marked, and that, combined with a clear legal mind, rendered his services valuable to many large and influential corporate interests. On his marriage, in 1880, to Miss Mary W. Hansell, daughter of a Philadelphia merchant, Mr. Dill made his home in Orange, N. J. He interested himself actively in the municipal and social development of the Oranges, organizing the People's Bank, of which he has been a director and the counsel from the beginning. He also assisted in the organization of the Savings Investment and Trust Co., of which he became vice-president and director. He is a director in the Seventh National Bank of New York city, the Corporation Trust Co. of New Jersey, the New England Street Railway Co. of Boston, the American School of Architecture at Rome, the Central Teresa Sugar Co., and other corporations. The pertinacity and determination which have enabled Mr. Dill to meet and successfully overcome obstacles are characteristics traceable to his Scotch ancestors, while his taste and aptitude for the law are derived from Caleb Cushing, the celebrated Boston lawyer, of whom he is a direct descendant.

COOKE, Augustus Paul, naval officer, was born in Cooperstown, N. Y., Feb. 10, 1836, son of Abner Cooke, Jr., and Catherine (Nichols) Cooke. He was appointed to the Naval Academy in 1852, and was graduated in 1856. During his first sea-service, in the home squadron, he participated in the capture of Walker, the filibuster, at Greytown, Nicaragua. In 1859 he received his warrant as passed midshipman, and made a cruise on the coast of Africa, in the San Jacinto, assisting in the capture of several slavers. He was commissioned lieutenant in 1860. When the rebellion occurred, the ship, then under the command of Capt. Wilkes, returned to the United States, capturing on the way the rebel commissioners, Mason and Slidell. In January, 1862, he, as executive officer of the Pinola, captured the blockade-runner Corn, and then the Pinola proceeded to join Farragut's squadron. Lieut. Cooke was several times under fire on the Pinola, while that vessel was assisting in breaking the chain-barriers which obstructed the Mississippi, and was present at the bombardment and passage of Forts Jackson and St. Philip, the destruction of the rebel flotilla, and the capture of New Orleans. He was also present at the first bombardment of Vicksburg, the passage of the batteries there, and the engagement with the rebel ram, Arkansas. In August, 1862, he was made lieutenant-commander, and ordered to command a vessel in Buchanan's flotilla, to operate, in conjunction with the army, in the Bayou Teche. In January, 1863, he went up the Teche, supporting Gen. Weitzel's brigade, and assisted in the destruction of the enemy's gun-boat Cotton. Here Lieut-Com. Buchanan was killed, and the command of the flotilla devolved upon Lieut.-Com. Cooke. During the Red river expedition, in 1863 he crossed troops over Berwick Bay, and transported Gen. Grover's division through Grand Lake, and landed it at Indian Bend, under fire, without accident. Next morning, at daylight, the flotilla under Cooke was attacked by the Queen of the West, and another gun-boat armed with rifled cannon, and with sharp-shooters behind cotton-bales. Cooke very promptly went to meet them, and his shells soon set fire to the cotton-bales of the Queen of the West, which was soon in flames, with her people leaping overboard to escape death from fire. Her consort, seeing this, turned, and having superior speed and lighter draft than Cooke's vessels, escaped. The officers and ninety men of the Queen of the West were picked up. About twenty were lost. There were no casualties in the flotilla. His next operation was the capture of Butte a la Rose, on the Atchafalaya, driving off the supporting gun-boat, and taking the garrison, with a large quantity of stores and ammunition, clearing the Atchafalaya from the gulf to the Red river; and by this route he proceeded to join Adm. Farragut, then at the mouth of the Red river. Gen. Banks made special acknowledgement to Lieut.-Com. Cooke for his success in these operations. His next service was in the Red river with Porter's fleet; followed, in the winters of 1863–64, by block-

ading Matagorda Bay and the coast of Texas. In July, 1864, he was detached from duty in the Gulf, and ordered to the Naval Academy, serving in the practice-ships Marion and Savannah. In May, 1867, he was made navigator of the steam-frigate Franklin, Capt. Pennock, which went to Europe as Admiral Farragut's flag-ship. This was a remarkable and interesting cruise, from the attention shown the admiral in every country he visited, especially in Russia and Sweden. In October, 1868, he was detached from the Franklin, and made executive officer of the Ticonderoga, on the same station. Upon his return home he was, in 1869, appointed head of the department of ordnance at the Naval Academy, and published a text-book on gunnery, long used by the cadets. Lieut.-Com. Cooke was commissioned commander in 1870; served at the Torpedo station, and in command of the torpedo-boat Intrepid, and afterwards the Alarm. Later he commanded the steamer Swatara. He was made captain in 1881, while stationed at Mare Island, Cal., and commanded the Lackawanna, on the Pacific station, in 1884–85. He next served at the navy-yard, Brooklyn, in command of the Vermont, and afterwards as captain of the yard. In 1888 he took command of the Franklin, at Norfolk. In 1890 he was relieved, and ordered to New York as president of the board of inspection of merchant vessels. Capt. Cooke was retired from active service in 1892, at his own request.

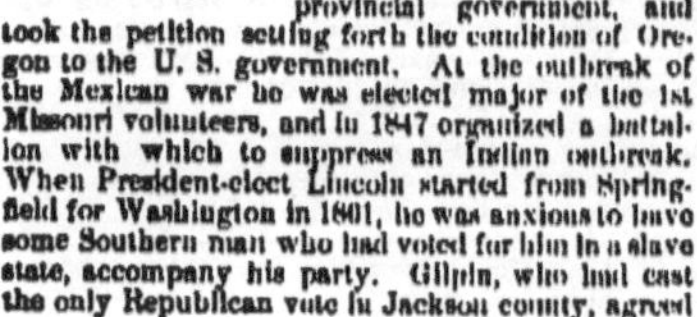

GILPIN, William, first territorial governor of Colorado (1861–62), was born Oct. 4, 1822, the son of Joshua Gilpin and Mary Dilworth. His great-great-grand-father came to America in 1695, and settled in what is now Delaware county. William Gilpin received his early education in England, and after a stay there of two years he came to Philadelphia, Pa., entered the University of Pennsylvania and was graduated two years later. Through the influence of Pres. Jackson he then obtained admission into West Point Academy, and shortly after his graduation, in July, 1836, was commissioned second lieutenant in the 2d Dragoons, U. S. A. In 1838 he was promoted first lieutenant, and went to the Florida war. After its close he resigned his commission, and for a year had charge of the "Missouri Argus" at St. Louis. He was elected secretary of the general assembly of Missouri, and having been admitted to the bar, began the practice of law at Independence, Mo. In 1843 he proceeded to Oregon City, where he was instrumental in organizing a provincial government, and took the petition setting forth the condition of Oregon to the U. S. government. At the outbreak of the Mexican war he was elected major of the 1st Missouri volunteers, and in 1847 organized a battalion with which to suppress an Indian outbreak. When President-elect Lincoln started from Springfield for Washington in 1861, he was anxious to have some Southern man who had voted for him in a slave state, accompany his party. Gilpin, who had cast the only Republican vote in Jackson county, agreed to make one of the party, and was one of an 100 men who slept in the White House as personal guard to the president. He was, subsequently, appointed governor of Colorado by Pres. Lincoln, as the one indispensable man for the place, and although unaided by the new administration, he succeeded in saving the territory to the Union. He was succeeded, in 1862, by John Evans of Illinois. At the time the Pacific Railway was thought by many to be a chimerical project, Gov. Gilpin did much to advance the idea both with tongue and pen. He was married in 1874, to Mrs. Julia Pratt Dickinson, by whom he had three children. Gov. Gilpin was a profound scholar, a deep thinker, and brilliant speaker. In person he was full six feet high, and of striking presence; his graceful mein and courteous manner reminding one of the thorough-bred soldiers and statesmen of Continental times. Gov. Gilpin is the author of " The Central Gold Region " (1860); "Notes on Colorado" (1870); "The Mission of the North American People" (1874), and " The Cosmopolitan Railway, Compacting and Fusing Together all the World's Continents " (1891). He died Jan. 19, 1894.

EVANS, John, second territorial governor of Colorado (1862–65), was born near Waynesville, O., March 9, 1814, son of David and Rachel Evans. His great-grandfather was among the early Quaker settlers in Philadelphia, and was a manufacturer of tools, whose sons, Benjamin and Owen Evans, carried on the same trade, Owen Evans being the inventor of the screw auger. Benjamin, the father of David Evans, removed to South Carolina, and married Hannah Smith, but left there soon after on account of his anti-slavery principles, and settled with his family in the "wilderness" of Ohio, where they continued to manufacture screw augers, and became extensive farmers. David carried on that business until 1835, when he became a merchant, finally retiring from business, and investing his earnings in various enterprises by which he became wealthy. John, the eldest son, was brought up on the farm, and grew accustomed to work with the rest of the farm laborers, and attended the district school when work on the farm was not pressing. Upon reaching his majority he went to Philadelphia, where he took a course at the Clermont Academy, and in 1836 began the study of medicine, being graduated M.D. in 1838. His first practice was among the pioneer settlers along the Illinois river. Early in 1839 he returned to Ohio, and was married to Hannah, daughter of Joseph Canby, an eminent physician and uncle of Gen. E. R. S. Canby, U. S. A. (see Vol. V., p. 838). They settled in Attica, Ind., where he acquired a reputation as a skilful physician and as a financier. His attention, as a physician, was early directed to the deplorable condition of the insane of the state, and their need of proper medical treatment. In 1841 he proposed to the people of Indiana, through the public press and their legislature, to levy a tax of one cent on the $100 on the cash valuation of the taxable property of the state, payable in state scrip, then current but depreciated, and with the proceeds build an insane asylum. The proposed measure passed the legislature, and Dr. Evans was appointed by the commissioners the first superintendent of the institution, and was instructed to visit and examine the plans of the various insane asylums of the country. In carrying out the scheme, he received the advice and aid of the great philanthropist, Dorothea L. Dix. He removed to Indianapolis, the state capital, and, in addition to his official duties, conducted a large private practice. In recognition of his ability, Dr. Evans was, in 1845, elected to a chair in the Rush Medical College, Chicago. He removed to that city, and held the professorship for eleven years, and prominently identified himself with the state and national medical associations. In 1848–49 Dr. Evans, during the cholera epidemic, prepared and published a monograph, maintaining, in opposition to the theories of the medical profession, that the disease is communicable, and showing that its lines of march pursue the lines of travel, and advocating a strict quarantine. In 1865 he urged upon congress the establishment of a national quarantine, quoting largely from his monograph. For a number of years he edited the "Northwestern Medical and Surgical Journal" of Chicago, and was founder of the Illinois General Hospital of the Lakes,

subsequently transferred to the Sisters of Mercy, and named Mercy Hospital. Dr. Evans was largely instrumental in establishing the Methodist Book Concern, and "Northwestern Christian Advocate" in

Chicago, and was one of the original promoters of the Methodist church block. He was one of the projectors of the Chicago and Ft. Wayne Railroad. By shrewd management, he secured its right of way into the city, and very valuable lands for its depots and extensive yards, and for many years acted as its managing director in Chicago. By judicious investments in Chicago realty, he laid the foundation of his subsequent fortune. In 1852–53 he served as a member of the city council of Chicago, and introduced the ordinance appointing a superintendent of public schools. He was chairman of the committee on public schools, and was one of the promoters of the establishment of the first high school. Dr. Evans, during his residence in Attica, formed the acquaintance of the renowned Bishop Simpson, and through his eloquent preaching, was converted, and united with the Methodist Episcopal church. He earnestly supported the admission of laymen as delegates to the general conference, and since 1864, when, for the first time, laymen were admitted as delegates, he has been elected delegate to all the general conferences. In 1853 he advocated the founding of the Northwestern University, and, in connection with others, selected a suburb of Chicago for its site, which was afterwards named Evanston in his honor. He succeeded so far in executing his plans that the

Northwestern University was established. He formulated a bill, and, through the assistance of Bishop Simpson, secured its passage by the legislature, of Illinois perpetually exempting its property from taxation. Dr. Evans' foresight in buying property located in the heart of the city, and his wisdom in reserving from sale one-quarter of every block in Evanston for endowment, makes it one of the wealthy institutions of the country. For this institution he endowed the chairs of Latin and mental and moral philosophy with $50,000, and subsequently increased the endowment to $100,000. He was the first president of the board of trustees, and occupied the position for forty-two years. In 1861 Dr. Evans, in a public controversy with Judge Scates of the supreme court of Illinois, advocated the emancipation of the slaves, and their enlistment in the army, as a war measure. His theory and arguments were largely copied and commented on. In 1855 he was a candidate for congress from Chicago, and one of the speakers at the first Republican convention at Aurora, Ill., but was defeated by the Know-nothing party because he refused to subscribe to their platform. He was a delegate to the Republican national convention, assembled in Chicago, Ill., June 17, 1860, which nominated his personal friend, Abraham Lincoln, for the presidency. Pres. Lincoln, in 1861, tendered him the governorship of Washington territory, which he declined. In 1862 he was appointed and succeeded Gov. Gilpin as governor of the territory of Colorado. He raised two regiments, which, together with Gov. Gilpin's regiments, he enlisted in the Union army. These prompt measures saved the whole territory for the Union. In 1863 Gov. Evans was commissioned to visit the Indians on the plains. He gathered the Ute tribes at Conejos, and, through the influence of Elbridge Gerry, grandson of the historical Elbridge Gerry, formed a treaty which settled the difficulty with most of the tribes. In 1865, realizing that any immediate attempt to civilize the Indians must prove futile, he advocated the plan for their gradual civilization, by distributing cattle, sheep, and horses among them, and inducing them to adopt the habits of pastoral life. In spite of his patriotic course, Gov. Evans did not escape the slanders of enemies, and Andrew Johnson requested his resignation in 1865. A thorough inspection of the records by his successor and enemies left his character unblemished, and a congressional committee completely exonerated him from all blame. In 1863 he inaugurated the plan for building the Colorado Seminary, which became the University of Denver, and was chartered in 1864. Through his efforts, the legislature forever exempted its property from taxation. Afterwards Dr. Evans rescued it from a sale for debt, and presented it to the university. His donations in land and money to this institution amounted to over $150,000. In 1865, when the first state organization of Colorado was perfected, the legislature sent him to the U. S. senate, where he requested admission to the sisterhood of states. Not being in political accord with Pres. Johnson on his reconstruction policy, the action of congress was twice thwarted by the president's veto, and, discouraged, Dr. Evans withdrew from political life. The Union Pacific Railroad having failed to build into Denver from the East, it created great consternation all over the state, and many of the citizens were discouraged, and threatened to leave. Thereupon Dr. Evans, in 1869, procured from congress the passage of the Denver Pacific land grant, by which he built a road from Cheyenne to Denver, 106 miles, connecting the territory with the Union Pacific Railroad. He was made president of the road, and directed its affairs for several years. Upon the completion of the road in 1870, the people of the state, at a celebration held

in Greeley, named one of the highest peaks of the Rocky mountains, within the boundaries of the state, Mt. Evans, and in 1895 the state legislature, upon Dr. Evans' eighty-first birthday, renamed the mountain in his honor, in recognition of his long and eminent services to the state. Soon after he built the South Park Railroad, extending it eventually 150 miles to Leadville, which, for the first time, opened up regular and direct communication between Denver and that great mining region. He also conceived the Denver, Texas and Gulf Railroad, and inaugurated its great mission of making Denver the importing and commercial centre of the Rocky mountains. It was for this end that he afterwards secured for Denver the location of the U. S. custom house.

Dr. Evans was the principal organizer and largest stockholder of the Denver City Electric Railway Co., started in 1885, and subsequently consolidated as the Tramway Co., which is one of the best equipped street railway systems of the United States, and was among the first to use electricity as a motive power. He has been very active in improving and building up the city, having erected both the first three and eight-story buildings. In 1877 he built the Evans' Chapel, a beautiful stone structure, in memory of

his oldest daughter, Josephine, wife of Judge S. H. Elbert, afterwards governor of Colorado. Dr. Evans' benefactions have extended to all the early churches of Denver, irrespective of creed. He was one of the organizers of the chamber of commerce and board of trade. He donated land in Evans sufficient to secure the removal of the state capitol from Golden City to Denver. His first wife died in 1850. In August, 1853, he married Margaret P., daughter of Samuel Gray of Maine. They had two sons and two daughters, one of whom died when five years of age. He has an extensive ranch near the base of Mt. Evans, where he indulges his taste for rural life, so firmly implanted in the boy on the farm near Waynesville, O. Dr. Evans' services to Colorado and the country at large are incalculable. Although past his eightieth year, he is still actively engaged in business, and shows no trace of mental weariness. His simple habits, easy accessibility, and cheerful disposition, added to the purity of his private life, and his honorable record as a Christian and a citizen, have endeared him to all who know him, and he is properly called the "grand old man" by the citizens of his adopted state.

CUMMINGS, Alexander, third territorial governor of Colorado (1865–67). (See index.)

HUNT, Alexander Cameron, fourth governor of Colorado territory (1867–69), was born in New York city, Dec. 25, 1825. In 1836 his father removed to Freeport, Ill., where Alexander received such education as the district schools afforded. At the age of sixteen, the boy determined upon leaving home to seek his fortune in the West. He became one of the pioneer settlers in California, prospered in business, and returned to Freeport, about 1850, a rich man. He invested his money in grain and commission business; married Ellen E. Kellogg, of White Pigeon, Mich.; was mayor of Freeport in 1856, and in the following year lost his all in the commercial crash. In 1858, attracted by the Pike's Peak gold craze, he crossed the plains by ox team in 1859, with his wife and child. They took up their abode in a log cabin without door or window, in a rude settlement called Auraria, in Colorado, now the city of Denver, and opened a restaurant. Hunt's generosity, however, was such that his supply of provisions ran out prematurely. He then engaged in the lumber business, in which he met with better success. It is noteworthy that he never interested himself in mining, although it was the excitement aroused by the discovery of gold which had drawn his steps Westward. He was elected presiding judge at the vigilance committee trials in 1860, and two years later was appointed U. S. marshal, which office he held until 1866. During this time he was active in opposition to the military political ring, which sought to secure the admission of Colorado as a state with a population of less than 25,000. Pres. Johnson, in 1867, appointed him governor of the territory of Colorado, as well as *ex officio* superintendent of Indian affairs, in which latter capacity he was successful in maintaining friendly relations with the tribes, and in 1868 brought about the treaty by which the Utes ceded to the United States all lands east of the 107th meridian. His policy as governor was marked by vigor and promptitude. In 1869 he was removed from office by Pres. Grant to make room for Gen. Edward M. McCook. He then turned his energies to railroad enterprise, then the absorbing topic of the day, and

in company with Gen. W. J. Palmer, who was in charge of the construction of the Kansas Pacific Railroad, originated the Denver and Rio Grande system, of which he subsequently became a director, and did much for the development of the country through which the road was to pass, by founding new towns and investigating new routes. Dr. William A. Bell joined the enterprise in 1871, and the three men together brought it through threatening bankruptcy to triumphant success. In 1880 Ex-Gov. Hunt lost his wife, a daughter, and two of his sons, and, utterly prostrated with grief, left his home and drifted with Gen. Palmer to Mexico. Here the two companions entered upon an investigation of the railroad possibilities of the country, which resulted in the construction of the International Railroad. Gov. Hunt had soon accumulated another fortune estimated at $500,000, and in 1883 he dissolved partnership with Palmer, and engaged in coal-mining and railroading enterprises in Texas, which, however, failed. His health began to break down with his failing fortunes, and he went North. He was stricken with paralysis in Chicago in 1891, while on his way to Colorado, and lay for two years and nine months helpless and even speechless, so that his death came as a welcome release. He died May 14, 1894, at Washington, D. C., and was buried in the Congressional Cemetery. A son and a daughter survive him.

McCOOK, Edward Moody, fifth and seventh governor of Colorado (1869–73, 1874–75), was born in Steubenville, O., June 15, 1835. His grandfather, George McCook, was an Irishman of Scotch descent, who, being involved with the United Irishmen in 1790, fled to the United States. His father was John McCook (*q. v.*), a physician of eminence, who married Catherine J. Sheldon of Hartford, Conn. John and his brother, Daniel (*q. v.*), were familiarly known as the "fighting McCooks," distinguished as the "tribe of John and the tribe of Dan." Edward was educated in the public schools, and when sixteen settled in Minnesota, but upon the breaking out of the Pike's Peak gold excitement, went to the Rocky mountains, when the entire surrounding country was Arapahoe county, Kan. (The illustration shows the first house with glass windows ever built in the Rocky mountains.) In 1859 he represented that district in the territorial legislature of Kansas, during which time the state of Kansas was formed, leaving the Pike's Peak country without government, when he went to Washington and secured the organization of the territory of Colorado, which has since become a state. When the first shot was fired at Fort Sumter he hastened to Washington and joined the Kansas Legion, which, with the Kentucky Legion were the only loyal commands in that city. As communication with the North had been cut off by the state troops of Maryland, McCook volunteered to carry Gen. Scott's dispatches; and, though Baltimore was in a state of insurrection, succeeded in getting through, and bringing back return dispatches, walking all the way back on the railroad ties. For this service, he was, May 8, 1861, commissioned second lieutenant in the 1st cavalry, and in 1862 was promoted to the first lieutenancy. He served as senior major in the 2d Indiana cavalry until the battle of Shiloh, when he was made colonel of the regiment. He received the brevet of first lieutenant in the regular army in 1862 for Shiloh, Tenn.; captain for Perryville, Ky.; major, in 1863, for Chickamauga, Ga.; lieutenant-colonel, in 1864, for cavalry operations in east Tennessee; colonel, in 1865, for capture of Montgomery, Ala., which was the capital of the Southern Confederacy. He was also brevetted brigadier-general in 1865, for services in the field, and major-general the same year for conspicuous gallantry. At Mossy Creek, with one division, he attacked two of Jackson's divisions, and captured eight battle-flags, 2,500 prisoners, and all of their artillery. He commanded the cavalry of the army of the Cumberland through the entire Atlanta campaign. Gen. McCook's most conspicuous service was in penetrating the enemy's line to prevent Gen. Taylor from reinforcing Gen. Hood, then shut up in Atlanta. He, with only 2,100 men, destroyed Hood's entire transportation train of 800 wagons and 8,000 horses and mules, which had been sent to the rear of Atlanta for safety, and captured three generals and over 200 field and line officers, besides a large body of men. On his return he encountered 4,000 of Wheeler's cavalry and two brigades of infantry, through which he was forced to cut his way, swimming the Chatta-

hoochee river, rejoining the main army at Marietta, with a loss of 900 men and one-half his escort. He then proceeded South to the gulf, and received the surrender of all the troops in Georgia and Florida, amounting to over 10,000 men, and remained there as military governor of Florida until June, 1865. Being unaware of the surrender of Lee, the 2d brigade of his command, under Col. La Grange, assaulted and captured West Point, Apr. 17, 1865, which was the last battle of the war. Upon his return to the North Gen. McCook married a granddaughter of Charles Thompson, the first secretary of the Continental congress. In 1866 he resigned his command to accept the appointment of minister to the Hawaiian islands, and during his term, nego-

tiated a treaty of commercial reciprocity. In 1869 he was appointed by Pres. Grant governor of the territory of Colorado, which he found in great disorder. He organized a school system, and established a board of immigration, which greatly benefitted that section. Gen. McCook was instrumental in bringing the first railroad into Denver. He organized the water works, and was identified with all the large enterprises of the city, and was at one time the largest real estate owner in this section, and the largest taxpayer in Colorado. He was the first to advocate woman's suffrage, which is now an accepted fact. His greatest service to the territory was in securing the transfer of the Ute Indians to Utah, which permitted the development of the rich mineral and agricultural lands which were opened for development and settlement, but which had been previously locked up in reservations. Gov. McCook lived to see fulfilled his prediction, which he made when assuming the gubernatorial chair, that within twenty-five years Colorado would no longer be on the frontier. At the earnest request of Pres. Grant he accepted the appointment of governor a second term, declining the postmaster-generalship. He was largely interested in the European telephone syndi-

cate, and at one time was one of the purchasers of the celebrated Batopilas mines, the richest silver mines in Mexico. Gen. McCook's literary attainments and oratorical powers were of such a high order that, on the death of Gen. Thomas, he was selected to deliver the funeral oration.

ELBERT, Samuel Hitt, sixth governor of Colorado (1873–74), and second chief justice, was born in Logan county, O., Apr. 3, 1833. His first American ancestor emigrated from Devonshire, England, and was located prior to 1683 on the "Eastern Shore," Maryland, where he owned a large plantation, which is still in the hands of one of his descendants. His paternal great-grandfather, Dr. John Lodman Elbert, was a surgeon in the American revolution; was voted a large tract of land for his services by the legislature of Maryland, and was a member of the order of Cincinnati. His mother was of Huguenot origin and her ancestors settled in Virginia. His father, John Downs Elbert, was an eminent physician and surgeon, with honorary degrees from the medical colleges of Cincinnati and Philadelphia. At the age of seven his parents removed to Iowa, where young Elbert passed his boyhood, working upon the farm, and attending the public schools. In 1848 he entered the Ohio Wesleyan University, being graduated with high honors in 1854. He began the study of law at Dayton, O., being admitted to the bar in 1856. In the spring of 1857 he began the practice of his profession at Plattsmouth, Neb. He soon acquired a

reputation as an able attorney, and in May, 1860, was elected a delegate to the Republican national convention assembled in Chicago, Ill., June 17, 1860, which nominated Abraham Lincoln for president. He took an active part in the presidential campaign of that year, and was elected a member of the council of the Nebraska legislature. In 1862 he was appointed by Mr. Lincoln secretary of the territory of Colorado, and during his incumbency per-

formed on several occasions the functions of governor, and promoted the mobilization of the 2d and 3d regiments for the suppression of the rebellion, and the protection of the territory against invasion by the Indians. In June, 1865, he married Josephine, daughter of Gov. John Evans of Denver, Col. She died in 1868. In 1866 he re-entered upon the practice of law, and in 1869 was elected to the territorial legislature. In 1870 he was elected secretary, and in 1872 chairman of the Republican territorial central committee. He is accredited with having first thoroughly organized the Republican party of Colorado, and was appointed governor of that territory in 1873 by Pres. Grant. As governor he was earnest in promoting plans for the development of the material resources of the country and thoroughly identified himself with the people in all their interests. He gave a great deal of his time to the study of irrigation, believing that it was a problem upon the successful solution of which the prosperity not only of Colorado, but of all the western states largely depended. Through his efforts a convention assembled in the summer of 1873, at Denver, composed of delegates from all the states and territories west of the Missouri river, to consider the subject of irrigation. In 1874 he went abroad, visiting all the principal capitals of Europe, and upon his return in 1876 he was elected a justice of the supreme bench of Colorado, serving as chief justice from 1880 to 1883. At this time his alma mater conferred on him the degree of LL.D. In 1885 he was re-elected, but resigned in 1889 owing to failing health, and again went abroad. His career as a judge was characterized by thorough research, and his decisions are highly regarded by the profession.

ROUTT, John Long, eighth and fourteenth governor of Colorado (1875–79, 1891–93), was born in Eddyville, Caldwell co., Ky., Apr. 25, 1826, son of John Routt, a farmer in moderate circumstances. His grandfather, Daniel Routt, fought as a soldier in the war of 1812, and his maternal grandfather was a distinguished patriot in the war of the American revolution. His father died while the boy was a mere infant, and the care of the family devolved on the mother, who removed with the family to Bloom-

ington, Ill., in 1836, where he was educated in the public schools, and when of suitable age was apprenticed to a builder and machinist to learn the trade. He continued in that business until 1851, when he began dealing in public lands and town property, in which he met with varied success. In

1860 he was elected sheriff of McLean county, and in 1862 resigned the office to accept a captaincy in the 94th Illinois infantry, which regiment he was largely instrumental in raising. His first service was in Arkansas and his first battle that of Prairie Grove. His regiment then joined Grant at Vicksburg, and Capt. Routt distinguished himself in a special service personally requested by Gen. Grant, by which he procured ammunition at great peril from a magazine sixteen miles distant and supplied the troops, thus rendering a whole brigade effective. Grant characterized the exploit as "one of the best responses to an order during the war," and after the war at a reunion, meeting the then Gov. Routt, Gen. Grant remarked, "I know Capt. Routt; he is the man who got the ammunition for me at Vicksburg." After the war he returned to Bloomington and found he had been elected treasurer of McLean county. He served for two terms and declined a third nomination. In 1869 Pres. Grant appointed him U. S. marshal for the southern district of Illinois, and in 1871 made him second assistant postmaster, which position he held until February, 1875, when the president made him governor of the territory of Colorado. He had the honor of reorganizing the discordant elements of his party and making it the party in power, preparing the territory for admission into the Union in 1876 as the "Centennial" state, and without solicitation he was nominated by acclamation by the first Republican state convention as its candidate for governor, and was duly elected and inaugurated Nov. 3, 1876. During his administration he established the credit of the state, and state warrants that when issued sold at 75 per cent., continued to appreciate and sold before his term expired at 12 above par. As president of the state land board he secured to the state some of the best land under the grants of congress, and organized the work of the board. He declined a renomination,

and engaged largely in mining. In 1883 he was elected mayor of Denver, and in 1890 was nominated and elected governor by a large majority, in spite of his earnest wishes not to be a candidate. He was a member of the capitol board of managers appointed to build the state capitol, and, largely through his influence and skill as an architect, it resulted in the erecting of one of the finest capitol buildings in the United States. Mr. Routt was married in the fall of 1845 to Hester, daughter of J. Woodson. She died in 1872. In 1875 he was married to Eliza Franklin, daughter of Franklin Pickerel, who is an acknowledged leader of society and largely interested in the various charities of the capital city. As wife of the governor during two administrations, she made a large circle of acquaintances and became greatly beloved and justly popular. They have one child, a daughter.

PITKIN, Frederick Walker, ninth governor of Colorado (1879–83), was born in Manchester, Conn., Aug. 31, 1837 son of Eli and Hannah Pitkin.

His father was a prominent citizen of that town, who came from a line of old and honored ancestry. His first American ancestor, William Pitkin, born near London, in 1635, settled in Hartford in 1659, was a member of the general court, and member of the colonial council. His grandson, William, was governor of Connecticut (1766–69). The son was prepared for college under careful instruction, and was matriculated at Wesleyan University, Middletown, Conn., in 1854. He was graduated with the class of 1858 with honors, and then entered the Albany Law School, where he completed his course of study and was admitted to the bar in 1859, and the same year located in Milwaukee, Wis. He was a member of the law firm of Palmer, Hooker & Pitkin. Too close application to office work and study, necessitated by the prosecution of a large practice, undermined his health, and he was obliged to withdraw from business altogether in 1872. He made a trip to Europe in quest of health. Finding no benefit, he spent a winter in Florida with no better results. He was then advised

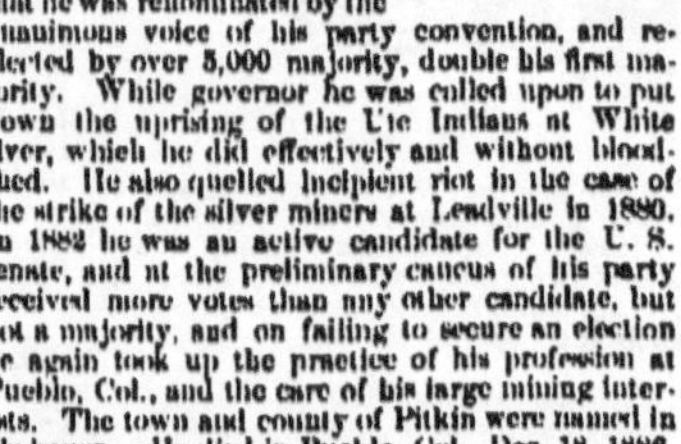

to test the climate of Colorado, and in three years' camp life, roughing it in the high mountains of Southern Colorado, he recuperated so far as to be able to engage in business in the development of the rich mines in that section. In 1878 he became the unanimous choice of the Republican party of the state for their candidate for governor, to succeed John L. Routt, and he was elected by the largest majority ever given a Republican candidate in the state. His administration of the affairs of the state in troublesome times was so satisfactory that he was renominated by the unanimous voice of his party convention, and reelected by over 5,000 majority, double his first majority. While governor he was called upon to put down the uprising of the Ute Indians at White river, which he did effectively and without bloodshed. He also quelled incipient riot in the case of the strike of the silver miners at Leadville in 1880. In 1882 he was an active candidate for the U. S. senate, and at the preliminary caucus of his party received more votes than any other candidate, but not a majority, and on failing to secure an election he again took up the practice of his profession at Pueblo, Col., and the care of his large mining interests. The town and county of Pitkin were named in his honor. He died in Pueblo, Col., Dec. 18, 1886.

GRANT, James Benton, tenth governor of Colorado (1883–85), was born in Russell co., Ala., Jan. 2, 1848, son of Thomas McDonough Grant, a prominent physician, born in North Carolina, and a large planter and slave owner in Alabama. His grandfather, James Grant, a native of North Carolina, was an extensive planter, and his great-grandfather, James Grant, emigrated from Scotland in 1746, and located first in Norfolk, Va., removing to Halifax county, N. C. The son was educated at the neighborhood school in his native state. The civil war forced him to help in the support of the family by working on the plantation of his father, and served in the Confederate army during the last year of the war. After the war he helped to build up the stricken fortunes of the family by hard manual labor, and in 1871 he removed to Iowa, and attended the agricultural college, and took a supplementary course in civil engineering at Cornell University, New York. From Cornell he went to Freiburg, Germany, where he took a course in mineralogy and kindred branches at the celebrated School of Mines of that place, which consumed two years. He returned to the United States by way of Australia and New Zealand, where he for five months studied the practical operations of mining as pursued in those countries. Upon arriving at San Francisco in 1870 he went to Gilpin county, Col., where he purchased and operated the Clarissa mine. In 1867 he engaged in assaying at Clear Creek, Col., for one year, and in 1878 removed to Leadville, where, with the assistance of his uncle, James Grant, who had already been at the expense of educating his nephew, he established smelting works under the firm-name of J. B. Grant & Co. James Grant sold his interest in January, 1880, to Eddy & James, and the business was then carried on under the name of the Grant Smelting Co. In 1882 this company was consolidated with the Omaha Co. under the name of the Omaha & Grant Smelting Co., of which he was made vice-president. He is also vice-president of the Denver National Bank. In 1882 he was nominated by the Democratic party of Colorado as their candidate for governor and was elected, the only Democratic candidate ever elected to the gubernatorial chair of the centennial state, and gave an independent and satisfactory administration to the state affairs. Gov. Grant was married, Jan. 19, 1881, to Mary, daughter of K. E. Goodell, and granddaughter of Gov. Matteson, of Illinois.

EATON, Benjamin Harrison, eleventh governor of Colorado (1885–87), was born Dec. 15, 1833, in Coshocton county, O. His ancestors were Quakers of English descent. His father, Levi Eaton, was a farmer in moderate circumstances. The son attended the common schools of his native county until the age of sixteen, when he entered West Bethford Academy, and three years later he was graduated and began teaching, which he pursued for several years. In 1854 he removed to Louisa county, In, where he engaged in farming and teaching, and during the gold excitement in 1859 he removed to Colorado, and continued prospecting and mining for three years; from thence to New Mexico, where he engaged again in farming; from thence in 1864 he located near Greeley, where he commenced farming, and also began the construction of irrigating canals, having formerly studied the subject of irrigation in New Mexico. He was eminently successful in his undertakings, and ranks as one of the largest farmers in the state, and has one of the finest flour mills and warehouses. His farm of 14,000 acres has yielded for the last eight years not less than 100,000 bushels of cereals, and 150,000 bushels of potatoes per annum. He has recently begun the construction of a reservoir at Cacha la Pointre river, which will have a capacity of 1,000,000,000,000 cubic feet, and will irrigate 30,000 acres when completed. He was school director and justice of the peace for a number of years, and was penitentiary commissioner for four years. In 1872 he was elected to the territorial legislature, and served as councilman one term, when he was elected to the senate. He was county commissioner for six years, and

the founder of the town of Eaton. In 1884 he was elected governor of Colorado, and served two years. He married Delila, daughter of James Wolfe, of Ohio, in 1856. She died in 1857, leaving one son. In 1864 he married Rebecca Jane, daughter of Abraham Hill, of Louisa county, Ia. They have two children.

ADAMS, Alva, twelfth governor of Colorado (1887–89), was born in Iowa county, Wis., May 14, 1850, son of a Kentuckian farmer, from New York state. His early education was obtained in the most ordinary of country district schools. On account of an invalid brother, the family decided to seek a milder climate, and with a horse team and a "grasshopper wagon" they crossed the plains in the spring of 1871, stopping in the then recently founded town of Greeley, Col. They soon after moved on to Denver, when young Alva, needing employment for the earning it would bring, took the first that offered, that of hauling ties which were the first that were used in the construction of the Denver and Rio Grande Railroad, from the mountains south of the city. In July of the same year he went to Colorado Springs in the employ of Mr. C. W. Sanborn, proprietor of a small retail supply of lumber and hardware. Colorado Springs was then but the germ of a small colony, with considerable distances between its fixed inhabitants. In October, Mr. Adams purchased the entire business

for $4,000. This business increased rapidly under Mr. Adams's marked ability, and in 1872 Joseph C. Wilson was admitted as a partner. Soon after Mr. Adams went to Pueblo and there established a branch house. Later the partnership was dissolved, Wilson taking the business at Colorado Springs. In 1873 Mr. Adams became one of the trustees of South Pueblo. In the meantime he had established branch hardware stores in the San Juan country. In 1876 he was elected to the first state legislature, where he made an excellent record, and he was nominated for governor first in 1884, again in 1886, when he was elected by about 2,400 majority. He was inaugurated January, 1887. During his wise administration the whole state enjoyed the utmost prosperity. In 1891 he was elected president of the Pueblo Savings Bank, which position he still holds (1899).

COOPER, Job Adams, thirteenth governor of Colorado (1889–91), was born Nov. 6, 1843, of English and Dutch descent. His grandfather, Thomas Cooper, was a paper manufacturer, and his father, Charles Cooper, was a mechanic in comfortable circumstances, and in later years a farmer. He came to America in 1820, and located first in New Jersey, then in Ohio and afterward went to Bond county, Ill., where Job A. Cooper was born. At ten years of age he went to school at Knoxville, Ill., and later entered Knox College, where he was graduated with high honors in 1865. His studies in college were temporarily broken off by a call for volunteer soldiers to suppress the rebellion, and he entered the service as second sergeant of company C, 137th Illinois infantry; was in Memphis when Gen. Forest made his raid upon that city in August, 1864, and continued in the service until his regiment was mustered out. After his graduation he studied law; was admitted to the bar of Illinois, establishing himself at Greenville, and in 1868 was elected clerk of the circuit court and recorder of Bond county, in which capacity he served four years. In May, 1872, he removed to Denver, then a place of village proportions, and began in the practice of law, but in April, 1876, accepted the vice-presidency of the German National Bank. In the same year he became cashier, and the history of the growth and prosperity of this institution is identical with and constitutes a part of his own history. In the capacity of banker through a period of twelve years his business abilities and sterling integrity became widely and favorably known, and out of his business office, Nov. 6, 1888, he was elected governor of his state by an overwhelming majority, against T. M. Patterson, by happy coincidence, on the forty-fifth anniversary of his birth. In 1893 he built the Cooper Building, costing $300,000, an office building which is second to none in the city in beauty. He has built extensively, and has contributed considerably toward the growth and prosperity of the city of Denver. His honesty and incorruptibility as a public officer, his broad and liberal views on all questions of public polity, distinguished him as an executive, as his public-spiritedness, enterprise, and far-sightedness had as a citizen. Retiring from office, he accepted the presidency of the National Bank of Commerce in Denver. He was married Sept. 17, 1867, to Jennie O., daughter of Rev. Romulus E. Barnes of Galesburg, Ill. He is identified with the leading charitable organizations of the city and is a member of the Masonic fraternity. He was one of the promoters and a director of the U. P. D. and G. R. R., and is a stockholder of a large number of enterprises of the city, as well as a mine owner in the Cripple Creek district and a stockholder in other mines of the state. He has four children, one son, Charles J. Cooper, and three daughters. His son is at present (1896) attending Knox College, Illinois.

WAITE, Davis Hanson, fifteenth governor of Colorado (1893-94), was born in Jamestown, N. Y., Apr. 9, 1825, son of Joseph and Olive Davis Waite. His father, a native of Vermont, was a lawyer and district attorney of Chatauqua county, and with his wife removed to New York state in 1845. The son was educated at the village school and the Jamestown Academy, after which he took up the study of law in his father's office. He removed in 1850 to the West, locating in Fond du Lac, Wis., and in 1851 removed to Princeton, and was engaged in merchandising. In 1856 he was elected as a Republican to the Wisconsin state legislature. In 1857 he removed to St. Louis, Mo., and soon after to Houston, Texas co., Mo., where he engaged as teacher in a high school. At the outbreak of the civil war the sentiment of the people of Missouri made it necessary for him, as a Union man, to leave the state, and he removed to Warren, Pa., and afterwards to Jamestown, N. Y., where he was admitted to the bar, and became editor and part proprietor of the "Chautauqua Democrat," a Republican organ of the county, and he afterwards became proprietor of the "Jamestown Journal." In 1876 he sold out his newspaper and removed to Larned, Kan., where he engaged in ranching and in the practice of law. In 1879 he was elected to the state legislature on the Republican ticket, and, as a member of the house, cast the deciding ballot that re-elected Senator Ingalls in 1879. He removed to Leadville, Col., in 1879, where he practised law, and in 1881 located at Aspen, Col., where in addition to his law practice he published the "Union Era," a reform paper. He was the first superintendent of schools in Pitkin county. In February, 1892, he was a delegate to the St. Louis conference which organized the Peoples' Party, and was a delegate from Colorado to the national convention at Omaha, July 4, 1892, which nominated Weaver and Field. He represented his state on the platform committee in the convention. On July 27, 1892, he was nominated for governor of Colorado, on the Peoples' ticket, and as the result of the canvass the state was carried by the fusion electoral ticket by 15,000 majority against a Republican majority of 15,000 two years before, and his plurality for governor was 5,816 as against the Republican and the White-Wing Democratic candidates. He was endorsed by the Free Coinage Democrats and by many Republicans, and taking advantage of the universal sentiments of the people of Colorado in favor of the free coinage of silver, his election was their triumph. Gov. Waite was inaugurated Jan. 11, 1893. His party measures were opposed by the state legislature, which was hostile to his reform recommendations, and many of the oppressive laws, notably those in favor of the creditor class, were continued. In December, 1893, he called a special session of the state legislature and made various reform recommendations. Although opposed and thwarted by political opposition on the part of the legislators themselves, they did consent to adopt amendments to the attachment and trustee laws, and to reduce the cost of collection of taxes —reforms more important to the general welfare than were passed at any two previous sessions of the legislature. The execution of the reform measures affecting the city government of Denver was opposed by the incumbent city office-holders who were removed, and the militia of the state had to be called out by the governor in order to enforce the laws and maintain order. The prompt action of the governor was sustained by the decision of the supreme court, and the new officers were placed in possession of their offices and introduced the many contemplated reforms in the government of the city. He promptly and effectively settled numerous disputes between miners and mine-owners that at times threatened civil war and bloodshed, and, either by arbitration or by the presence of the state militia, restored order. Gov. Waite, however, found that he had the money power of the state opposed to him, and although renominated in 1894 and receiving a total of 75,000 votes, while in 1892 he was elected although receiving but 44,000 votes, he was defeated by 19,000 majority. The Populists had given the women of Colorado the right of suffrage, and in this election they first largely exercised it to the defeat of the party that enfranchised them. These, aided by many Democrats, who deserted their own party ticket and voted for the Republican candidate, elected McIntire by a plurality of 19,708. After the inauguration of Gov. McIntire, Ex-Gov. Waite continued to reside in Denver, and is now engaged in lecturing. He was married in 1851, to Frances E., daughter of Robert Russell, Russelburg, Pa. They had three children. After the death of his wife, which occurred Nov. 7, 1880, he was married, Jan. 8, 1885, to her cousin, Mrs. Celia Maltby, and they have one son, Frank H. Waite.

McINTIRE, Albert Washington, sixteenth governor of Colorado (1895——), was born in Pittsburgh, Pa., Jan. 15, 1853, son of Joseph Philips and Isabella A. (Wills) McIntire. His grandfather, Thomas McIntire, was born in Wilmington, Del., and with his brothers was engaged in the transportation business in Maryland.

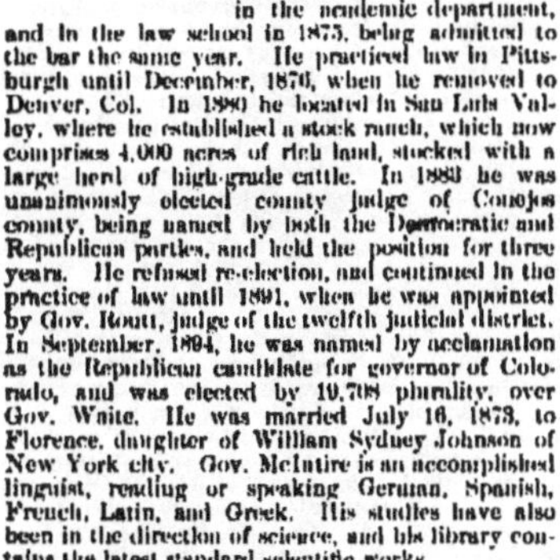

Their property was destroyed at the time the British burned Washington, while he was serving as an officer of volunteers during the war of 1812. His maternal grandfather was state attorney in Pennsylvania. Both his paternal great-grandfathers fought as patriots in the war of the American revolution. His first American paternal ancestor came from Ayrshire, Scotland, about 1745. His maternal ancestors came from Belfast, Ireland, in 1790, and from England earlier. He prepared for college at Newell's Institute in Pittsburgh, entered Yale in 1869, was graduated in 1873 in the academic department, and in the law school in 1875, being admitted to the bar the same year. He practiced law in Pittsburgh until December, 1876, when he removed to Denver, Col. In 1880 he located in San Luis Valley, where he established a stock ranch, which now comprises 4,000 acres of rich land, stocked with a large herd of high-grade cattle. In 1883 he was unanimously elected county judge of Conejos county, being named by both the Democratic and Republican parties, and held the position for three years. He refused re-election, and continued in the practice of law until 1891, when he was appointed by Gov. Routt, judge of the twelfth judicial district. In September, 1894, he was named by acclamation as the Republican candidate for governor of Colorado, and was elected by 19,708 plurality, over Gov. Waite. He was married July 16, 1873, to Florence, daughter of William Sydney Johnson of New York city. Gov. McIntire is an accomplished linguist, reading or speaking German, Spanish, French, Latin, and Greek. His studies have also been in the direction of science, and his library contains the latest standard scientific works.

FORMAN, Joshua, founder of the city of Syracuse, was born at Pleasant Valley, Dutchess co., N. Y., Sept. 6, 1777, son of Joseph and Hannah Forman. Young Joshua having displayed a strong tendency to study, received a good preliminary education, and in 1793, entered Union College, in Schenectady, where he was graduated with honor. On leaving college he began to study law in an office in Poughkeepsie for two years, when he established himself in the city of New York, and completed his law studies in the office of Samuel Miles Hopkins. Soon after his admission to the bar, he was married to Margaret, daughter of Boyd Alexander, M. P. for Glasgow, Scotland. In the year 1800 Mr. Forman settled in Onondaga Hollow, where he began the practice of law, in which he was uniformly successful, becoming popular throughout the county.

In 1807 Mr. Forman was elected to the legislature, where he became prominent as the projector of the Erie Canal. In 1813 he was appointed judge of the Onondaga county common pleas court, a position which he held, with dignity and credit to himself, for the next ten years. In the meantime he had, in 1807, erected the first grist-mill on the Oswego river, this resulting in facilitating the settlement of that section of the state. In 1809 he founded the celebrated Plaster Co. at Camillus. In 1821 Judge Forman succeeded in obtaining the passage of a law, in pursuance of which Onondaga Lake was lowered about two feet, by which means the marshes in the neighborhood were drained, and the surrounding lands improved. In 1822 he began salt manufacture, in which he introduced the making of solar salt. Judge Forman was practically the founder of Syracuse. In 1818 he laid out the city of Syracuse, and removed there in the following year, remaining until he had laid the foundation for a flourishing town. In 1826 he removed to a point near New Brunswick, N. J., where he opened and worked a copper mine. Soon after he was summoned by Gov. Martin Van Buren to Albany, to draw up the safety fund act, which had become necessary, for the purpose of regulating the banking system of the state, at this time exceedingly defective. In 1829, in company with others, Judge Forman bought from the state of North Carolina land in Rutherfordton, N. C., and in adjoining counties, and took up his residence at the village of Rutherfordton, where he made great improvements. He died at this village, Aug. 4, 1848, his remains being removed to Oakwood cemetery, Syracuse.

GOODRICH, Alfred Bailey, Protestant Episcopal clergyman, was born at Rocky Hill, Hartford co., Conn., March 22, 1828. He was educated at Trinity College, Hartford, and Berkeley Divinity School, and was ordained deacon in 1853 by Bishop Brownell, of Connecticut, and priest in 1854 by Bishop Williams. He officiated for a few months at St. Peter's Church, Plymouth, Conn., and for five years at Millville, Mass. While there he founded the Society for the Increase of the Ministry, a general society of the Episcopal church for the education of young men for the ministry. In August, 1859, he became rector of Calvary Church, Utica, N. Y., and has held that position ever since. During his rectorship the parish has grown steadily in membership and prosperity, and is at present one of the strongest churches in the city. In 1867 Hamilton College made him D. D.

He was secretary of the undivided diocese of western New York two years, and has held the same office in the diocese of central New York since its organization in 1868. He is a member of its standing committee. For ten years he was president of the second missionary district of the same diocese, and was one of its representatives in the centennial convention of the Episcopal church in Philadelphia, 1883. He is a member of the federate council of the five dioceses of New York state, and of the general missionary council of the Episcopal church. He is author of a service and tune book for Sunday-schools, and, in connection with Dr. Gilbert, organist of Trinity Chapel, New York, of a hymnal for choirs and congregations, both extensively used. He has been a contributor to many periodicals and religious publications. On Dec. 27, 1847, he married Elizabeth A. Meigs of Hartford, Conn.

DU PONT, Gideon, planter, was born in South Carolina in 1712, the younger son of Abraham Du-Pont, a great uncle of Du Pont de Nemours, who left France on account of the Huguenot persecution and came to America in 1695. South Carolina owes her successful rice culture to Gideon Du Pont, who was an experienced and intelligent planter on the banks of the Santee. He first conceived and successfully carried out the idea of causing water to overflow and cover to a certain depth the fields devoted to the culture of this cereal, thereby killing the weeds which before his time had always stifled the rice plants. Refusing to take out any patent, he and his family were never pecuniarily benefited by his agricultural successes.

DU PONT DE NEMOURS, Pierre Samuel, statesman and author, was born in Paris, France, Dec. 14, 1739, of Huguenot parentage. His public services began in 1762, when he was employed by the Duke of Choiseul, by Bertin, comptroller-general of the finances, and by Trudaine the Elder, in connection with various questions relating to agriculture and commerce. Two pamphlets of his, published in 1763, criticising a new scheme of taxation, attracted the attention of the celebrated Quesnay, who instructed him in the principles of the science of political economy. The Economists, as the followers of Quesnay were called, waged unrelenting

warfare against the errors and abuses that stifled commercial enterprise and ruined the tillers of the soil. With a rare capacity for work, which had gained him great distinction in his youthful studies, Du Pont quickly became a favorite pupil of Quesnay, and did more than any one else to give currency to the doctrines of the school. His first important book, "De l'Exportation et de l'Importation des Grains," appeared in 1764, and had a great success. Turgot, then Intendant of Limoges, sought the acquaintance of the young author, who became his most intimate friend. Laverdy, Bertin's successor, continued to employ Du Pont, and in 1765 named him editor of the "Journal de l'Agriculture, du Commerce et des Finances," a semi-official publication, which under Du Pont's direction became so imbued with the doctrines of the economists as to give offense and force his retirement from the editorship during the following year. In 1767 Du Pont published the "Physiocratie," a compendium of Quesnay's system, and in May, 1768, he succeeded Baudeau as editor of the "Ephémerides du Citoyen," the organ of the school. Here his personality soon made itself felt in interesting articles advocating the liberty of the press, the removal of all restrictions from commerce and labor, the abolition of slavery and of the exclusive privileges of the French East India Company, and the suppression of the oppressive tax called "Corvée." Although employed by Laverdy and Invau, a man of his character could not fail to be obnoxious to a minister like the Abbé Terray, who dismissed him from the public service and forbade the publication of the "Ephémerides." Abroad, however, Du Pont found appreciation and respect. The kings of Poland and Sweden and the Margrave of Baden conferred various titles and decorations upon him, and in 1774 he went to the first-named country at the instance of King Stanislaus Augustus to organize a general system of National education. Later in the year, when Turgot succeeded Terray

as comptroller-general, Du Pont was named inspector-general of commerce, and formally ordered by Louis XVI. to return to France. At the head of that bureau in the ministry of finance, to which all measures of importance were referred, "the right arm of Turgot," as Du Pont was styled, took a most prominent part in the various measures of reform which that minister instituted. The famous "Report on Municipalities," which was essentially a programme of a liberal constitution, was the work of Du Pont, although Turgot did not remain long enough in office to submit it to the king. Upon Turgot's disgrace, in 1776, Maurepas, his successor, placed Du Pont upon the retired list and banished him to the country, where he busied himself with agricultural and literary pursuits until recalled to active duty by Necker in 1778. Like Turgot, Du Pont had always been an ardent advocate of the cause of American liberty, and he was now employed by Vergennes in the task of conducting secret negotiations with the English representative, Dr. Hutton, which led to the treaty of 1783, by which Great Britain formally recognized the independence of the United States, and later, in the still more delicate undertaking of arranging the terms of the very liberal commercial treaty which France and England signed in 1786. In recognition of these services he was made councillor of state. In his capacity of inspector-general of commerce he satisfactorily adjusted with Jefferson, then U. S. minister to France, the pending commercial differences between the two powers, notably the vexatious and injustice which American commerce had experienced from the French custom houses and at the hands of those in charge of the royal tobacco monopoly. Du Pont was a member of the Commission of Agriculture instituted by Vergennes, and was appointed secretary-general of both the Assemblies of Notables, 1787–88, in which capacity he drew up the various measures of reform that Calonne and his successor, Fourqueux, presented. Having thus incurred the animosity of the clergy, on the accession of Archbishop Brienne to the ministry, the personal influence of Louis XVI. alone saved him from a second banishment. A member of the states-general from Nemours at the beginning of the revolution, and later, of the constituent assembly, of which he was twice elected president, he belonged to the party which advocated a constitutional monarchy. The radical fiscal reforms made by the assembly were the work of Du Pont, whose fearless opposition to the creation of an irredeemable paper currency nearly cost him his life at the hands of the mob, Sept. 2, 1790. After the dissolution of the assembly he edited the "Correspondence Patriotique" and published various pamphlets in the interest of law and order, among others his memorable letters denouncing Pétion, mayor of Paris. On Aug. 10, 1792, Du Pont de Nemours and his son were at the palace among the armed defenders of the unfortunate Louis XVI., and though lucky enough to make their escape unhurt from the garden of the Tuilleries, were marked by the Jacobins for subsequent destruction. Thanks to the astronomer Lalande and his assistant, Harmand, the father was hidden in the dome of the observatory of Paris until Sept. 2nd, when he was able to reach Cormeilles, near Paris, where he remained in disguise for a month, only arriving at his home, Bois des Fossés, on Nov. 9th, after a most painful and dangerous journey. Finding himself in comparative safety there, he wrote his "Philosophie de l'Univers," but was finally arrested and imprisoned July 20, 1794, the death of Robespierre, which occurred soon after, alone saving him from the guillotine. As soon as he was released, Aug. 24, 1794, he renewed his opposition to the Jacobins, appearing in print with his "Plaidoyer de

Lycias," which compared the enormities of the terror with an episode in Grecian history, and with his "Constitution pour la Republique Française" (1795) and other productions. He also founded and edited the "Historian," a political journal. He was elected to the Council of the Ancients, 1795, and became its president in 1797; but when the Jacobins broke up the councils with Augereau's troops, Du Pont de Nemours was again imprisoned and his property pillaged and destroyed. In 1799 he emigrated with his family to America, where he was received with much consideration and, at Jefferson's request, prepared a work on national education in the United States. The author's plan, though not carried out in the country for which it was intended, has been partially adopted in his native land. Returning to France in 1802, Du Pont de Nemours was instrumental in promoting the treaty of 1803, by which Louisiana was sold to the United States. On Nov. 1, 1803, Jefferson wrote to him: "The treaty which has so happily sealed the friendship of our two countries has been received here with general acclamation. For myself and my country, I thank you for the aid you have given it, and I congratulate you upon having lived to give this aid, to complete a transaction replete with blessings to millions of unborn men." Strongly opposed to Napoleon, Du Pont refused to hold office under his government, but became president of the Paris chamber of commerce and devoted the rest of his time to various charitable institutions and to literary and scientific research, chiefly for the Institute of France, of which he was a member. Among the numerous publications of his latter years may be mentioned "Sur le droit de marque de cuirs" (1804), and "Sur le banque de France avec une theorie des banques" (1806), which, after being seized by the French police, was republished in London, 1811, with preliminary notes. His last work was the "Examen de Malthus et lettre à Say" (Philadelphia, 1817). In 1814 he was secretary of the provisional government that prepared the return of Louis XVIII., but when Napoleon escaped from Elba in 1815, Du Pont de Nemours rejoined his sons in America, where he died at the Eleutherian Mills, near Wilmington, Del., on Aug. 7, 1817, beloved and respected by all who knew him. As Schelle has well said, there have been profounder thinkers and more able writers than Du Pont de Nemours, but none have surpassed him in love of truth for truth's sake, and in disinterested and continuous effort to promote the welfare of his fellow men. Du Pont de Nemours married, Jan. 26, 1764, Nicole-Charlotte Marie-Louise Le Dée de Rencourt, who died in 1784. His second wife, who survived him, was Françoise Robin, widow of the celebrated Poivre.

DU PONT DE NEMOURS, Victor Marie, diplomat and manufacturer, was born in Paris, France, Oct. 1, 1767, eldest son of Pierre Samuel Du Pont de Nemours. At the age of sixteen he entered the bureau of his father, who was then inspector-general of commerce, and from June, 1785, to January, 1787, traveled over a large portion of the kingdom collecting statistics in regard to French agriculture, commerce, and manufactures for the information of the minister of finance. He was appointed attaché of the French legation to the United States in 1787, returning after two years to France at the outbreak of the revolution and becoming aide-de-camp to Lafayette when the latter was in command of the national guard. In 1791 he was sent back to America as second secretary of legation, and acted as first secretary from October, 1792, until the following April, when Minister Ternant ordered him to France to demand fuller instructions from the committee of public safety. Mr. Genet, however, had sailed for America as French minister in Ternant's place when

Victor Du Pont reached Paris in June, and the latter remained without employment until the close of 1794, when he was assigned to duty in the ministry of foreign affairs. In 1795 he was promoted as first secretary of legation and came to the United States for the third time. In the following July he was sent to the South by Minister Adet as acting French consul for North Carolina, South Carolina and Georgia, in consequence of the deplorable condition of French interests in those states. His appointment was confirmed by the directory, and the following year he was named French consul at Charleston, where he gave so much satisfaction to his superiors that in the beginning of 1798 he was appointed consul-general of France at Philadelphia. Pres. Washington having refused him an exequatur on account of the grave difficulties then existing between the French Republic and the United States, Victor Du Pont returned to Europe with his family, and finding that his father and brother had decided to emigrate to America, he left the diplomatic service and sailed with them for the New World in September, 1799, arriving at Newport, R. I., Jan. 1, 1800. In connection with other members of his family, he established and directed the business house of Du Pont de Nemours, Fils et Cie at New York, recrossing the ocean in 1801 and visiting France and Spain in the interests of the firm. The business was very successful until 1805, when the house failed on account of heavy advances made to refit a French squadron, which had put into New York Harbor in a disabled condition, and to purchase subsistence stores for the French troops at San Domingo, payment of the drafts on the French Treasury to make good the loans being refused by the personal order of Napoleon, who could

not let this opportunity pass of displaying his animosity against Du Pont de Nemours. The zeal of the members of the firm for the interests of their native land having thus brought about their financial ruin, Victor Du Pont retired with his family in 1806 to Angelica, Genesee co., N. Y., then a new settlement in the forests, and three years later he joined his younger brother, Irénée Du Pont, on the Brandywine river, near Wilmington, Del., where he established a cloth manufactory, and passed the remainder of his life. During the war of 1812 he served as captain of a company of Delaware volunteers. Victor Du Pont married, Apr. 9, 1794, Gabrielle Josephine de la Fite de Pelleport, and left two sons, Charles Irénée, who succeeded him in the direction of the cloth manufactory, and Samuel Francis, rear-admiral of the U. S. navy. His appointment by the government as a director of the Bank of the United States, and his election to the Delaware legislature, attest the respect and esteem which he enjoyed until his sudden death in Philadelphia, Jan. 30, 1827.

DU PONT, Charles Irénée, manufacturer, was born at Charleston, S. C., March 29, 1797, eldest son of Victor Marie Du Pont de Nemours, who was French consul. there. When about a year old he accompanied his parents to France and returned with them to the United States upon their emigration to America in 1799. When he was nine years old his father removed from Bergen Point, N. J., where he lived while in business in New York city, to Angelica, N. Y., leaving there in 1809, and establishing himself at Louviers on the Brandywine river, near Wilmington, Del. After being educated at Mt. Airy Seminary, Germantown, Pa., he was associated with his father in the manufacture of cloth, and on the latter's death, succeeded to the charge of the business, which he continued until his retirement in 1856. He was also actively engaged in agricultural and banking enterprises, was one of the originators of the Delaware Railroad, and a member of the Delaware legislature. He married, on Oct. 6, 1824, Dorcas Montgomery Van Dyke of New Castle, Del., who died in 1839; and secondly, in 1841, Ann Ridgely, of Dover, Del., who survived him. He died Jan. 31, 1869.

DU PONT, Samuel Francis, naval officer. (See Vol. V., p. 50.)

DU PONT DE NEMOURS, Eleuthere Irénée, manufacturer, was born in Paris, France, June 24, 1771, younger son of Pierre Samuel Du Pont de Nemours, his unusual baptismal names being those selected by his godfather, the celebrated Turgot. He was brought up in the country at Bois des Fossés, in what is now the department of Seine et Marne. His tastes turned early towards agricultural and scientific pursuits, which prompted his father's friend, Lavoisier, whom Turgot had appointed superintendent of the government powder works (Régie Royale des Poudres et Salpetres) to take him in charge and secure his reversion, or right of succession, to that important post. This led to his going to the royal mills at Essonne to acquire a practical knowledge of the manufacture of gunpowder, where he remained until his whole career was seemingly changed by the events of the French revolution. On June 8, 1791, his father, who had been a leading advocate of constitutional monarchy in the constituent assembly, founded a large printing and publishing-house in the interest of the conservative party, and summoned his son Irénée, as he was commonly called, to take charge of the new enterprise. Thus at the age of twenty the latter became the superintendent of a great business necessarily connected with the political troubles of those stormy times. He was thrice imprisoned and frequently exposed to great personal danger—particularly on the fatal day of Aug. 10, 1792, when he accompanied his father to the palace of the Tuilleries to defend the king's person. Both were fortunate enough to get away unharmed, and Irénée Du Pont succeeded in escaping to the country, where he remained for some time in concealment at Essonne. After the reign of terror, he supported his father in his courageous opposition to the Jacobins, who, when beaten at the polls, Sept. 5, 1797, called in Augereau's troops to overthrow the government, his father being again imprisoned and the printing-house sacked and destroyed by the mob. Despairing of the political future, and ruined in fortune, Irénée Du Pont, with his father and brother and their families, sailed for America, arriving at Newport, R. I., on the first day of the present century. Some months later an accidental circumstance called his attention to the bad quality of the gunpowder made in the United States, and gave him the first idea of undertaking its manufacture. He went back to France in January, 1801, revisited Essonne to procure plans and models, and returned to the United States in August with some of the machinery. It is noteworthy that he was urged by Thomas Jefferson, his father's friend, to locate in Virginia, and that he declined on account of the effects which the institution of slavery had produced upon the character of the white race. Similar reasons deterred him from establishing himself in Maryland, and after inspecting sites at Paterson, N. J., and several other places, he bought in June, 1802, a tract of land with water power upon the banks of the Brandywine river, four miles from Wilmington, Del., and arrived there with his family July 19th. As early as 1810, his gunpowder works, known as the Eleutherian mills, and still in operation, had a capacity of 600,000 pounds per year, and during the war of 1812, in which he served as a captain of Delaware volunteers, they were able to furnish the entire powder supply for the American armies. The business, conducted from the start under the firm name of E. I. Du Pont de Nemours & Co., steadily grew, and at the time of Irénée Du Pont's sudden death, from cholera, in Philadelphia, Oct. 31, 1834, his mills were the most important of their kind in the United States. Inheriting that spirit of broad philanthropy, which was so marked a characteristic of his distinguished father, amid the incessant toil of an active and engrossing business career, Irénée Du Pont never forgot for a moment the duties he owed to his fellow men. He was not only foremost in the development of agriculture and industrial enterprise about him and in every measure of local improvement, but found time to serve as a director in the Bank of the United States; to take part in the philanthropic labors of the American Colonization Society; and to associate his life with innumerable acts of private benevolence. Irénée Du Pont married in Paris, on Nov. 26, 1791, Sophie Madeleine Dalmas, who died in 1828. His three sons, Alfred Victor, Henry, and Alexis Irénée, successfully continued his manufacturing enterprises.

DU PONT, Alfred Victor, manufacturer, was born in Paris, France, Apr. 11, 1798, the eldest son of Eleuthere Irénée Du Pont de Nemours. He came to America with his parents in 1799, and after passing two years at Bergen Point, N. J., went to Delaware on July 19, 1802, his father having bought a property near Wilmington, for the purpose of establishing a gunpowder manufactory. When very young he was sent to school at Mt. Airy, Germantown, Pa., and in 1814, entered Dickinson College, remaining until the discontinuance of that institution, in the fall of 1816. He then went to Philadelphia, remaining there two years under the instruction of private tutors. His father had meant him to complete his education in France, but the losses incident to the disastrous explosion of 1818 prevented this, and made it necessary for him to return home and go to work. Alfred Du Pont and his brother-in-law, Antoine Bidermann, assisted Irénée Du Pont in the manufacture of gunpowder until the latter's death in October, 1834, after which Mr. Bidermann had the general direction of the business until his withdrawal in 1837, when Alfred Du Pont became the head of the firm. Ten years later, he and his brothers, who were associated with him, had to face the enormous loss of life and property incident to the great explosion of 1847. Alfred Du Pont retired from business in 1850, his health having been very much impaired during the last years of his life. The only public office he ever held was that of presidential elector in 1845. While the force of circumstances rendered Alfred Du Pont's life comparatively uneventful, the man himself was most remarkable. To the scientific ability so strongly developed in his father he joined the literary and scholarly tastes of his grandfather, Du Pont de Nemours, from whom came also, in perhaps somewhat of an accentuated form, his characteristic individualism and originality. His heart, like his father's and his grandfather's, was full of liberality and generosity, and he was ever prominent in deeds of kindness and benevolence to the poor and afflicted. Alfred Du Pont was married, in 1824, to Margaretta

Elizabeth Lammot, by whom he left a large family. His two elder sons, Eleuthere Irénée (born Aug. 3, 1829, and died Sept. 17, 1877), and Lammot, both became prominent members of the firm of E. I. Du Pont de Nemours & Co. He died Oct. 4, 1856.

DU PONT, Henry, manufacturer, was born at the Eleutherian Mills, near Wilmington, Del., Aug. 8, 1812, second son of Eleuthere Irénée Du Pont de Nemours. In 1822 he was sent to school at Constant's Mount Airy Seminary, Germantown, Pa., which, in 1826, became a military school under the direction of Col. Roumfort. He left there in 1829, upon his appointment as cadet at the U. S. Military Academy, West Point, where he was graduated in 1833, becoming brevet second lieutenant of the 4th U. S. artillery. Joining his company at Fort Monroe, Va., he was soon after ordered on frontier duty with a battalion of his regiment at Fort Mitchell, in the Creek Indian country, Alabama. On July 15, 1834, he resigned his commission in the army at the instance of his father, Irénée Du Pont, and returned to Delaware to assist him in the manufacture of gunpowder. After Irénée Du Pont's sudden death in Philadelphia in the following October, Henry Du Pont aided his brother-in-law, Mr. Bidermann, and afterwards his elder brother Alfred, in the management of the business, which successfully weathered the great financial depression of 1837. When, in 1850, Henry Du Pont became the head of the firm of E. I. Du Pont de Nemours & Co., his executive ability soon made itself felt, and from that time until his death he was the controlling spirit of the enterprise, which, under his direction, assumed proportions of very great magnitude. In addition to the vast consumption of gunpowder in the avocations of peace, the mills sent large quantities abroad in 1855, for the use of the English troops in the Crimea and supplied the U. S. government during the war of the rebellion. During his long and successful business career, Henry Du Pont was found equal to every emergency; industry, enterprise, fair-dealing and liberality being the characteristics of his management of affairs. A Whig in politics, he cast his first vote for Henry Clay in 1836, and although, in 1860, after the dissolution of the Whig party, he supported Bell and Everett, when the rebellion broke out his patriotic and law-abiding character made him a staunch advocate of Pres. Lincoln, and he became one of the leaders of the Delaware Republicans, and was their candidate for presidential elector, in 1868, 1870, 1880, 1884, and 1888. In his eyes political work was a patriotic duty, and he performed it faithfully and conscientiously, serving for more than forty years as inspector of elections and challenger at the polls. His military service in the state began as aide-de-camp to Gov. Cooper in 1841. On May 16, 1846, Gov. Temple appointed him adjutant-general of the state, which office he held until May 11, 1861, when he was appointed by Gov. Burton major-general of forces raised and to be raised in the state of Delaware. In accepting the office, Gen. Du Pont stipulated that he should have absolute control of the armed forces of the state, and his first order, which compelled every man in the state military service to take an oath of allegiance to the United States or to surrender his arms, at once drew a line between the supporters of the government and the disloyal spirits who were counting upon the chances of Southern success and secretly discussing the question of taking Delaware out of the Union. Although the latter had influence enough to induce Gov. Burton to interfere and suspend the above order, upon Gen. Du Pont's application, Gen. Dix, commanding the U. S. troops at Baltimore, sent an armed force to Delaware to maintain the supremacy of the general government. With many other family characteristics, Henry Du Pont inherited the strong agricultural tastes of his father and grandfather. He was probably the largest as well as the most popular land-owner in the state of Delaware, always displaying an almost fatherly solicitude for the interests of his tenants and employees. Decided in opinion, liberal in thought, wise, prudent, and sagacious in business, and generous in private life, he took an active interest in the local affairs of his community, and was always the firm friend and advocate of public improvement. He married on July 15, 1837, Louisa Gerhard, who survived him. He died Aug. 8, 1889.

DU PONT, Alexis Irénée, manufacturer, was born at the Eleutherian Mills, near Wilmington, Del., Feb. 14, 1816, youngest son of Eleuthere Irénée Du Pont de Nemours. He was sent to Mr. Dwight's school in New Haven, Conn., and after completing his education at the University of Pennsylvania in Philadelphia, returned home to help his brothers in the gunpowder business, in which he continued until his death. Ardent and impulsive by nature, he put his whole soul into whatever he undertook, and though cut off at a comparatively early age, his characteristic enthusiasm and generosity had been long displayed in connection with religious matters, in which he took a very deep interest. Alexis Du Pont married, in December, 1830, Joanna, daughter of Francis Gurney Smith, of Philadelphia, who survived him. His three sons, Eugene (born Nov. 16, 1840), Alexis Irénée (born June 5, 1843), and Francis Gurney (born May 27, 1850), are active members of the firm of E. I. Du Pont de Nemours & Co. He died Aug. 21, 1856, the result of injuries received in an explosion of the mills.

DU PONT, Henry Algernon, soldier, was born at the Eleutherian Mills, near Wilmington, Del., July 30, 1838, son of Henry Du Pont. In 1853 he went to Dr. Lyons's boarding school near Philadelphia, and in 1855 entered the University of Pennsylvania, leaving college a year later to go to West Point, as cadet at the U. S. Military Academy. He was graduated there at the head of his class, May 6, 1861, and appointed second lieutenant of the corps of engineers, and May 14, 1861, first lieutenant 5th U. S. artillery. On July 6, 1861, he was made regimental adjutant, and was acting assistant adjutant-general of the troops in New York Harbor, April, 1862, to July 4, 1863, from which date he was in command of light battery B, 5th U. S. artillery in the field, being promoted captain 5th U. S. artillery, Mar. 24, 1864, and taking part in the battle of Newmarket, Va., May 15, 1864. Chief of artillery, department of West Virginia, May 24, 1864, he commanded the artillery during Hunter's Virginia campaign at the battle of Piedmont, June 5, 1864; engagement at Lexington, June 11; affair near Lynchburg, June 17; battle of Lynchburg, June 18; and affairs at Liberty, June 19, and Mason's Creek, June 21, 1864. Made chief of artillery, army of West Virginia, July 28, 1864, he served in Sheridan's campaign in the valley of Virginia, commanding artillery brigade of Crook's corps in affairs with the enemy at Cedar Creek, Aug. 12th, and Halltown, Aug. 23d, 25th and 27th; action at Berryville, Sept. 3d; battle of Opequan (Winchester), Sept. 19th; battle of Fisher's Hill, Sept. 22d; affair at Cedar Creek, Oct. 13th; and battle of Cedar Creek, Oct. 19, 1864. He was brevetted major to date from Sept. 19, 1864, for gallant and meritorious conduct at the battles of Opequan and Fisher's Hill, and lientenant-colonel Oct. 19, 1864, for distinguished services at the battle of Cedar Creek. After the war he commanded light battery F, 5th U. S. artillery, and, at various times, the posts of Fort Monroe, Va., Camp Williams, Va., Sedgwick Barracks, D. C., and Fort Adams, R. I.; and was a member of the board of officers which assimilated the tactics for the three arms of the service. Col. Du Pont resigned from the army, Mar. 1, 1875, and since May 5, 1879, has been president of the Wilmington and Northern Railroad Co.

CLARKE, McDonald, poet, was born in Bath, Me., June 18, 1798. He is an obscure poet, and little is known of his early life beyond the date of his birth, and that he was a playmate of the poet Barnard. In the preface to one of his volumes of poems he records his first appearance, Aug. 13, 1819, on Broadway, New York, which was henceforward the principal haunt and inspiration of his whimsical muse. He earned the sobriquet of "The Mad Poet," being one of that order of wits, as Dryden has it, whose "genius is divided from madness by a thin partition." He was constantly seen on Broadway, his blue coat and military bearing, enhanced by his

marked profile, making him a conspicuous and striking figure. He had no vices, and was amiable in his very weaknesses. He was always most gentle in his manners and deportment, and was a regular attendant at Grace Church, on Broadway, then, as now, the fashionable Episcopal church of the city. It was his hobby to fall in line with all the belles of the city, and to commemorate their beauties and worth in his verses. However well-meant these effusions on the part of the poet, they were annoying. His poems helped to support him, but the number of editions and present scarcity show that he must have eked out the revenue necessary to supply his humble wants, by subscriptions or the charity of publishers and friends. While his poems are erratic and whimsical, they are marked by much of tenderness, purity, and delicacy, and the simple, honest nature of the man, his brilliant flights, and frequent sharp witticisms, won a certain tenderness and respect from those who had any feeling in the matter. On one occasion some one remarked in his hearing that his brains were a little zig-zag, which called out the following impromptu:

"I'll tell —— in the way of a laugh,
 Since he has dragged my name in his petulant brawl,
That most people think it is better by half
 To have brains that are zig-zag than no brains at all."

A bit of autobiography, written two months before his death, will illustrate his erratic style, "Begotten among the orange groves, on the wild mountains of Jamaica, West Indies. Born in Bath on the Kennebec River, State of Maine, 18th June, 1798. 1st Love, Mary H. of New London; last Love, Mary G. of New York; intermediate sweethearts without number. No great compliment to the greatest Poet in America—should like the change tho'; had to pawn my Diamond Ring (the gift of a lady), and go tick at Delmonico's for Dinner. So much for the greatest Poet of America. The greatest Poet ought to have the freedom of the City, the girls of the gentry gratis, grab all along shore, the magnificent Mary, and snucks with all the sweet sisters of song." Clarke is the author of the celebrated couplet, quoted in various forms:

"Now Twilight lets her curtain down,
 And pins it with a star."

Some of the titles to the volumes of his published poems are: "A Review of the Eve of Eternity, and other poems" (New York, 1820); "The Elixir of Moonshine, by the Mad Poet" (1822); "The Gossip" (1825); "Poetic Sketches" (1826); "The Belles of Broadway" (1833); "Death in Disguise" (a temperance poem, 1833); "Poems" (1836); and "A Cross and a Coronet" (1841). He met a tragic death in the cell of the city prison, March 5, 1842. A policeman had found him on the street in a destitute, and apparently demented, condition, and taken him to jail for safety. He was found drowned by water from an open faucet. His simple monument is in Greenwood Cemetery at "The Poets Mound, Sylvan Water."

STEES, Washington Moore, merchant, was born in Columbia, Lancaster co., Pa., March 28, 1826, son of Benjamin and Lydia (Greenawalt) Stees, and grandson of Philip Lorenz Greenawalt, who emigrated to America in 1749, locating in Lancaster county, Pa., where he took up 100 acres of land. He participated in the revolutionary war, and upon the organization of the associated battalions was commissioned colonel of the 1st battalion of Lancaster county. He fought in the battles of Germantown, Brandywine, and Monmouth, and was complimented by Washington for his remarkable bravery and gallantry in the battle of Germantown. On Dec. 16, 1777, he was appointed by the state to take subscriptions for the continental loan, and May 6, 1778, the assembly of the state appointed him one of the agents for the forfeited estates. He spent £60,000 sterling of his own money in supplying the army with food, blankets, etc., at Valley Forge. He died Feb. 28, 1802, at Lebanon, Pa. Mr. Stees obtained his education in Lebanon and Little Academy. After serving an apprenticeship in Philadelphia in the furniture business, he removed to St. Paul, Minn., in the spring of 1850, and commenced the furniture business in a modest way, but his business increased so rapidly that two years later he erected a large brick block, and in 1870 he erected a still larger building. This was the oldest and largest furniture store in the state. In 1884 he sold out his furniture business and retired. Mr. Stees

had great confidence in the future of St. Paul, and invested all his ready cash in real estate with flattering results. He was the first chief of the fire department, and served one term as county commissioner. Mr. Stees contributed extensively toward the growth of the city. No one knew the extent of his private charities. He bequeathed $2,000 to each of the five principal charitable organizations of the city. Mr. Stees was married to Ann Kirk of Pennsylvania, who removed with him to St. Paul. He died in St. Paul, Jan. 30, 1890.

SHORTALL, John G., lawyer, was born in Dublin, Ireland, Sept. 20, 1838, son of John and Charlotte (Towson) Shortall. When he was between two and three years old, his parents emigrated with their family, joining an elder branch long settled in New York. After the death of his parents he was employed by Horace Greeley, and the two or three years passed in the editorial rooms of the New York "Tribune" proved a period of rare education. In the summer of 1854, following the advice of Mr. Greeley, he went West, locating first in Galena, Ill., where he was engaged for a short time by the Illinois Central Railroad Co., in the completion of the survey and construction work between Scales's Mound and Galena. Going thence to Chicago in the late autumn of 1854, he was engaged for a few months upon the Chicago "Tribune," and then withdrew to enter the office of J. Mason Parker, where he began the study of real-estate law and titles, which profession he afterwards followed. At that time Mr. Parker was engaged in preparing the real-estate abstract books, afterwards known as the "Shortall & Hoard Abstracts," and which are now the property of the Title Guarantee and Trust Co., of which Mr. Shortall is a director. Upon the completion of the abstract books, in 1856, Mr. Shortall leased them, and began the business of making abstracts of title to real estate. In October, 1871, the county records were entirely destroyed by the great fire. At that time there were three abstract firms in Chicago, each of which saved a large part of its valuable records, but no complete set, and it was decided to consolidate all the evidences of title extant. Moneyed men relied upon the accuracy of the books and the skill and integrity of the owners, and, thus confident, loaned the hundreds of millions of dollars necessary to the rebuilding of the city. Mr. Shortall continued with his associates in the conduct of the business until 1873, when the property was leased to Messrs. Handy & Co., and Mr. Shortall retired from active participation in it, though still retaining his holdings and interest. On Sept. 5, 1861, Mr. Shortall was married to Mary Dunham, daughter of John N. Staples of Chicago. Mrs. Shortall died in August, 1880, leaving one child, John Louis, born May 1, 1865, surviving. Since his retirement from active business, Mr. Shortall has devoted the major part of his time to public affairs, doing all in his power to aid the promotion of the city's welfare. He is a constant patron of fine arts, and was one of the directors of the old Philharmonic Society, and afterward president of the Beethoven Society during almost its entire existence. He is a member of the Chicago and Chicago Literary clubs, and also one of the honorary members of the Amateur Musical Club of Chicago. He is a writer of intelligence and force, and has made valuable contributions to papers and periodicals. In 1880 he was appointed by the school board one of the appraisers of school property, and in 1886 was appointed appraiser of the school lands by Mayor Harrison. In 1883 Mr. Shortall was appointed a director of the Chicago Public Library, served three terms as president, and conducted negotiations on behalf of the board, which resulted in securing Dearborn Park as the site of the Public Library building, and in the successful adjustment of all opposing claims. Under his administration, the plans of the superb new library building were selected, after large competition, and the necessary appropriations of money made by the city. He was originally appointed a director by Mayor Harrison, and reappointed by Mayors Harrison, Cregier, and Washburn, successively. He has been president of the Illinois Humane Society since 1877, and was one of its original organizers. He is also an honorary member of the Pennsylvania Society for the Prevention of Cruelty to Animals. During the World's Columbian Exposition, Mr. Shortall, as the chairman of the men's committee on moral and social reform of the auxiliary congresses, assisted in the important work of that committee, and organized and conducted the humane congress in October, 1893, which was so successful. He also arranged the humane exhibit of the American Humane Association, of which he was president, in the Liberal Arts Building, for which it obtained a medal and diploma. Possessed of a warm and sympathetic heart, reaching out in charity and love to the worthy helpless, the suffering, and the needy, his name has become synonymous with good works.

MENETRY, Joseph, missionary, was born in the canton of Freiburg, Switzerland, Nov. 28, 1812. Sept. 29, 1836, he entered the Society of Jesus, and two years after his entrance, offered himself for the Indian missions of the Rocky mountains. He arrived in Oregon, Aug. 13, 1847, and passed to other missions established in Idaho, Washington, and Montana. He labored zealously and successfully among the Colville, Spokane, Cœur d'Alene, Pen d'Grelles, Kootenay, Kalispel, Blackfeet and Flathead Indians. In every Indian mission where he worked, may be seen (1896) numerous and lasting monuments of his zeal, industry, toils, and endurance. He was founder of St. Ignatius' mission, the first pastor of Frenchtown, and for many years ministered to the spiritual wants of the Catholic people scattered over what was known as Hellgate Valley. In 1874, he was stationed at Helena, and was for three years one of the fathers attending the missions and visited, as his special missionary task, the Boulder, Missouri, Crow Creek, Gallatin Valley, and other outlying stations. Few missionaries have done more to propagate religion and civilization among the Indians. He died at St. Ignatius' Mission, Montana, in 1891.

CLARKE, John Hopkins, senator, was born in Elizabeth, N. J., Apr. 1, 1789. His father was Dr. John Clarke, and his mother was a daughter of Com. Esek Hopkins, first commander-in-chief of the U. S. navy. When quite young John removed to Providence, R. I., upon the decease of his father, where he was fitted for college under the tuition of Tristram Burgess. He entered Brown University, and was graduated in 1809, when he began the study of law in the office of his tutor, and was admitted to the Rhode Island bar in 1812, soon afterward receiving the appointment of clerk of the supreme court of Providence county. He practiced law but a comparatively short time, preferring the business of manufacturing to that of the legal profession. For some years he resided in Cranston, where he engaged in business in his newly chosen vocation. He returned to Providence in 1824, and with the exception of a few years, during which he lived in Pontiac and Warwick, he continued his residence in Providence during the remainder of his life. He was sent in 1836 as a representative to the general assembly, and for many years was an active politician in the state. Mr. Clarke was always interested in public affairs and in 1847 was elected to  the U. S. senate, where his sound sense, his positive views, and force of character commanded the respect of his associates. Subsequent to his retirement from the national senate, he represented Providence for one year in the state senate, and in 1864 was in the lower house of the assembly. He was able, by his strong personality and varied abilities, to wield a wide influence upon this time, both of the commonwealth and of the congress of the U. S. He was twice married, his first wife being Elizabeth Bowen of Pawtucket, to whom he was married in 1811; and his second, Susan Carrington Miles, of Middletown, Conn., to whom he was married in 1829. He had a large family of children, one of whom is James H. Clarke of Providence. He died in Providence, Nov. 23, 1870.

RENWICK, James, architect, was born at Bloomingdale, N. Y., November, 1818. On the paternal side he is of Scotch lineage, while his maternal ancestors are of old Knickerbocker families, his mother being a daughter of Henry Brevoort, of the Bowery and his father Prof. James Renwick of Columbia College, who in addition to his other varied accomplishments had mastered the study of architecture. His son inherited this taste and was given every opportunity to develop and cultivate his genius. At the age of thirteen he entered Columbia College, where he was graduated when eighteen years old. He accepted a position as assistant engineer on the Croton Aqueduct, and superintended the building of the distributing reservoir between Fortieth

St. Patrick's Cathedral

and Forty-second streets, New York city. He volunteered to furnish a plan for the fountain in Union Square and superintended its construction, which the property owners around the Square agreed to erect. He was the successful one of the competing architects for the plan and erection of Grace Church, which when completed was so satisfactory to all concerned, that his reputation was at once established, and he immediately fell into a large and lucrative business. He was architect of Calvary Church, Fourth avenue, the Church of the Puritans, Union Square, and many business and private residences. He was chosen by the board of regents architect of the building of the Smithsonian Institute, Washington, D. C., and was also appointed architect to the board of charities and correction of the city of New York, which position he retained until 1874. In 1873 he competed for the plan of the new Roman Catholic Cathedral and was victorious. It is the most beautiful, chaste and imposing church edifice in this country, and stands pre-eminent among his works, the grandest monument to his genius. Among his other works are the Corcoran Art Gallery, Washington, D. C.; the City Hospital; Small-pox Hospital; Workhouse; Lunatic and Inebriate Asylums on Ward's Island, Vassar College of Poughkeepsie; the Cardinal's residence, Madison avenue, N. Y.; the Young Men's Christian Association; Booth's Theatre, and a number of other fine buildings and churches of superior design and workmanship. Mr. Renwick was a great lover of art, and has collected a large number of paintings from all quarters of Europe, which embraces examples of the best known artists. Mr. Renwick was known as one of the best art connoisseurs in New York, and many of his paintings are masterpieces. In his will he directed that the larger part of his collection of paintings, and also a bust of himself, should be given to the Metropolitan Museum of Art upon condition that it should be known as the "James Renwick Collection," and that within one year a separate room or alcove should be set aside for the collection, and be open to the public during the hours set apart for the admission of visitors to the museum.

HUNT, Richard Morris, architect, was born in Brattleboro', Vt., Oct. 31, 1828. He was the son of Jonathan Hunt, who was at one time a member of congress, and was a brother of the celebrated artist Wm. M. Hunt (q. v.). He was graduated at the High School, Boston, Mass., in 1843, leaving immediately afterward for Europe, where he entered the atelier of Samuel Darier, Geneva, Switzerland, in 1844. In 1845 he studied with Hector Lefuel, and the following year entered the École des Beaux Arts, where he remained some time, and then spent several years in traveling in Europe, Asia Minor, and Egypt. He returned to Paris in 1854, and was appointed Inspecteur des Travaux by the government, the appointment directing his energies upon the construction of the buildings connecting the Tuileries with the Louvre. Lefuel was in charge of this work, and he gave Mr. Hunt the Pavillon de la Bibliothèque for his province. This was practical training in the French school of academic architecture, which takes splendor, dignity, and a certain monumental feeling as the most necessary merits of its construction. In 1855 he returned to America with a foreign experience that is unique in the annals of American architecture, and soon opened an atelier on the plan of the French architectural ones, where a number of the now leading professional men studied. His powers were soon recognized, and he had scarcely settled in New York before he was invited to share in the completion of the Capitol at Washington. He served for six months as assistant to Thomas U. Walter, the architect in charge, when he returned to New York, and founded the practice which he carried on to the day of his death. He did not strike out in new lines, but he was overflowing with vitality. How far he could go in the direction of mere elegance and sensuous beauty he showed in Mr. W. K. Vanderbilt's house on Fifth avenue and Fifty-second street. It is an enchanting revival of old French motives, and stands alone for exquisite finish and daintiness. As being aware that it was a masterpiece, the contractor

caused a statue of Mr. Hunt, dressed as an artisan, to be represented in stone upon the apex of the house. The Astor house on Fifth avenue and Sixty-fifth street, and the Gerry house near by, are admirable illustrations of what can be done for American architecture with French ideas. These ideas made him more successful with city houses than with country dwellings, and the best things he did in country architecture, like the "Breakers" of Newport, were modifications of his accustomed style. But better than either city or country houses were Hunt's public buildings. In the Administration building of the World's Fair at Chicago he struck the grandiose note of a formal magnificence of academic and official dignity. It was this building that brought Mr. Hunt the gold medal of the Royal Institute of British Architecture, which is regarded as one of the chief prizes of architectural merit in the world. Mr. Hunt added much to the artistic side of the fair, and his energy and taste was of incalculable service to the army of workers concentrated in Jackson Park. For a long time Mr. Hunt divided with H. H. Richardson the position of personal supremacy in architectural inspiration; but since Richardson's death the style, which promised to form itself into a school, has gradually given place to the abstract principles which Mr. Hunt taught his countrymen. He did not mould their styles to his, but he drilled them in the logic of architecture, in those elements which are independent of temperament, and in this inspiration he was one of the most remarkable artists of his time. His genius has been recognized both abroad and at home, and many honors have been conferred upon him, among the most conspicuous of which are: associate of the Academie des Beaux Arts, of which he had been for years an honorary and corresponding member; chevalier de la Legion d'Honneur; honorary and corresponding member of the Royal Institute of British Architects; and also of the Ingenieur und Architecten Verein; associate member of the Institute of France; and president of the American Institute of Architects; member of the Société Centrales des Architecten Français; and academician of St. Luke, Rome. The degree

of LL.D. was conferred upon him by Harvard in 1892. Among his more important works may be mentioned: the Lenox Library; the Tribune building; the Coal and Iron Exchange of New York city; the pedestal for the Statue of Liberty; and the residences of Gov. Levi P. Morton, at Rhinecliff on the Hudson; Henry G. Marquand, New York city, also country house at Newport; Ogden Goelet at Newport; Archibald Rogers, Hyde Park; George W. Vanderbilt at Biltmore, N. C.; Maturin Livingston, New York city; C. O. D. Iselin, New York city; and Marble House for W. K. Vanderbilt, Newport, R. I.; the Presbyterian Hospital, New York city; Yorktown Monument; U. S. Naval Observatory at Washington, D. C.; Fogg Art Museum, Cambridge, Mass.; and Vanderbilt Mausoleum, Staten Island. Mr. Hunt served on the juries of the Exposition Universelle in Paris, 1867, and at the Centennial Exposition at Philadelphia in 1876. After an illness of two weeks be died at Newport, July 31, 1895.

WAGNER, Albert, architect, was born in Possneck, Germany, March 14, 1848. He received his early education in the select schools of his native town, and he concluded his studies at the Polytechnic of Stuttgart and Munich Academy, under the supervision of Profs. Lubke and Fischer. When only twelve years of age, young Wagner, taking private lessons from Architect Schenke, determined to make architecture his profession. His first practical experience was under Prof. Von Holzt, in Riga, when he assisted in designing and building the stations along the line of the railroads of the East Sea provinces. After working successfully, and gaining much valuable experience in Europe, the young architect and engineer determined to try his fortune in the New World. He arrived in New York in 1871, and found occupation in designing interior decoration. A few years after, Mr. Mullet, the government architect, invited him to prepare model designs for all the office furniture to be used throughout the government buildings, which problem he accomplished with excellent results. Mr. Wagner again sought the more extended field of New York for his labors, and took engagement with the celebrated architect, Leopold Eidlitz, with whom he continued to work for over four years. After this period he concluded to establish his own office. He speedily made an impression, and many sections of the city are now adorned by handsome specimens of his genius. Among the many buildings which he has designed are the Central Turnvereinhalle, and the Puck building, including the entire block, gaining a first prize premium for both; the Walton building, the Henry Iden block on University Place, the Strobel, Bloomingdale, McCreery, Meyers, and Heywood buildings; also numerous handsome business buildings in the dry-goods district, and in the manu-

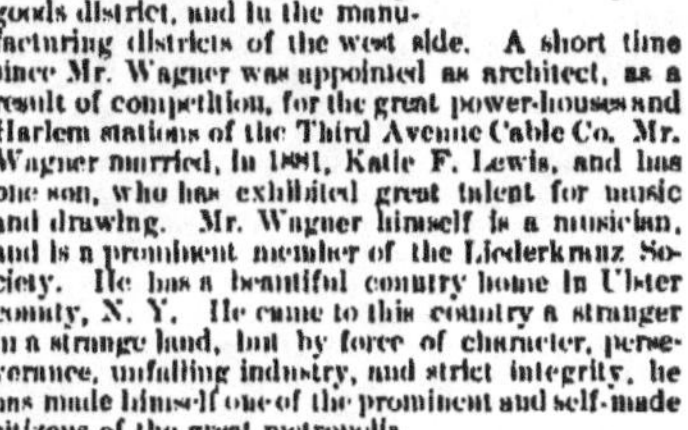

facturing districts of the west side. A short time since Mr. Wagner was appointed as architect, as a result of competition, for the great power-houses and Harlem stations of the Third Avenue Cable Co. Mr. Wagner married, in 1881, Katie F. Lewis, and has one son, who has exhibited great talent for music and drawing. Mr. Wagner himself is a musician, and is a prominent member of the Liederkranz Society. He has a beautiful country home in Ulster county, N. Y. He came to this country a stranger in a strange land, but by force of character, perseverance, unfailing industry, and strict integrity, he has made himself one of the prominent and self-made citizens of the great metropolis.

SANDERSON, John Philip, journalist and soldier, was born in Lebanon county, Pa., Feb. 13, 1818. He began practice as a lawyer in 1839; was elected to the Pennsylvania legislature in 1845 and to the state senate in 1847; was editor of the Philadelphia "Daily News," 1848–50; and published "Views of American Statesmen on Foreign Immigration," 1843; and "Republican Landmarks," 1856. He was appointed chief clerk of the war department, March 4, 1861, passed within a year or two to a lieutenant-colonelcy and was made colonel of the 13th U. S. infantry, July 4, 1863. On February, 1864, he was assigned to duty as provost-marshal-general of the department of the Missouri. His exposure of the Knights of the Golden Circle led to the breaking up of that order. Col. Sanderson died at St. Louis, Mo., Oct. 14, 1864.

DANA, James Dwight, geologist, was born in Utica, N. Y., Feb. 12, 1813. He early showed a taste for scientific research, and desiring to be under the instruction of Prof. Benjamin Silliman, who had gained the reputation of the foremost scientist of the time, he entered Yale College. During the regular course of study at Yale, he evinced a special love for the natural sciences, without neglecting his classical and mathematical pursuits, in the latter of which he distinguished himself. He was graduated with honor in 1833, and was appointed instructor of mathematics to midshipmen in the U. S. navy. While engaged in this service upon the warships Delaware and United States, he visited Turkey, Greece, Italy, and France. During 1836-37 he was assistant to Prof. Silliman in Yale College, where he devoted himself to his favorite study. He received the position of geologist and mineralogist on the Wilkes exploring expedition, which was sent by the U. S. government to the Pacific ocean. He sailed in the Peacock in 1838, and remained with the vessel until it was shipwrecked at the mouth of the Columbia river, when he was transferred to the Vincennes of the same expedition. He was gone three years and ten months, having in charge the zoölogical department, including crustacea and corals, besides the departments of mineralogy and geology, to which he was nominally appointed. During the next thirteen years, from 1842-54, he was occupied with the study of the material he had collected, making his own sketches, and preparing for the publication of his reports of the expedition for the government. In 1844 he married Henrietta Frances, the third daughter of Prof. Silliman. The result of his work has been embodied in his "Report on Zoöphytes," a quarto volume of 740 pages, in which 230 new species are described; the "Report on the Geology of the Pacific," and the "Report on Crustacea," each illustrated by a folio volume of plates, which were published by the government, the edition being limited unfortunately to only one hundred copies. The drawings in these reports were made almost entirely by Mr. Dana himself. In 1850 he received from Yale College the appointment to the Silliman professorship of natural history and geology, but did not enter upon the active duties of his professorship until 1854. In 1864 the title of the professorship was changed to that of geology and mineralogy, on account of lectures upon natural history being given by another professor. While engaged in preparing the last two of his reports in 1846, he became one of the editors of the "American Journal of Science and Art," and since the death of the second Prof. Silliman in 1885, he, as the senior editor, has continued its publication with his son, Edward S. Dana. The Wollaston medal was conferred upon him in 1872 by the Geological Society of London, and later the Copley medal by the Royal Society of London. He is a member of the Royal Society of London, the Institute of France, the Royal Academy of the Lincei of Rome, and the Royal Academies of Berlin, Vienna, and St. Petersburg, and was one of the original members of the Academy of Science of the United States. In 1854 he was president of the American Association for the Advancement of Science. The University of Munich, at its fourth centennial in 1872, gave him the degree of Ph.D.; Harvard, in 1886, gave him the degree of LL.D., and the University of Edinburgh the same degree in 1890. In 1893, on account of ill health, he resigned his professorship, and was made professor emeritus. He also gave private lectures and instruction at home, and invaluable advice on geological and zoölogical subjects in the Peabody Museum. While strength remained he was unable to resist the temptation to perform his accustomed duties. The London "Athenæum," speaking of his work on mineralogy, says: "This work does great honor to America, and should make us blush for the neglect in England of an important and interesting science." His papers contributed to the "American Journal of Science," and to the "Transactions" of scientific societies amount to hundreds of titles. He has also published a number of important works, among the most noted being: "System of Mineralogy," "Manual of Mineralogy," "Coral Reefs and Islands," "Manual of Geology," "Text-Book of Geology," "Corals and Coral Islands," "Geological Story Briefly Told," "Characteristics of Volcanoes, with Contributions to Facts and Principles from the Hawaiian Islands." Prof. Dana held one of the most eminent positions in American science, and was the acknowledged master in three extensive departments of mineralogy, geology, and zoölogy, having made original researches of the highest value in all these fields of study. He died of heart-failure in New Haven Apr. 14, 1895, maintaining his intellectual vigor to the last. He was the last member of the "old guard" professors, of which the late President Porter and the late President Woolsey were two of the most prominent.

WALKER, Edward Dwight, author, was born in New Haven, Conn., in 1858. He was graduated from Williams College in 1876, after which he entered the employ of Harper & Brothers in an editorial capacity. In 1878 he became editor of the "Cosmopolitan Magazine," with which he remained connected until his death. He was a frequent contributor to the magazines, and the author of "Reincarnation," which secured him an election to the Authors' Club. He was drowned while fishing on the Roanoke river, North Carolina, in June, 1890.

CROUSE, George Washington, manufacturer, was born at Tallmadge, O., Nov. 23, 1832, the son of George and Margaret H. (Robinson) Crouse. His grandfather, who was of German descent, was killed in battle, fighting for American independence. The maternal line is of Irish extraction, the ancestry emigrating from the north of Ireland. George was one of a family of ten children, his father being a hard-working farmer. His early years were spent on the farm, attending the common district school in the winter months, until he was seventeen years of age, when he was enabled to secure a position as teacher in a school, and taught five successive winter terms. He had become very proficient in mathematics, and in November, 1855, Mr. Sister, a friendly neighbor, having been elected county treasurer, offered him a position as deputy treasurer in his office at Akron. His peculiar fitness and diligent, conscientious performance of his duties made him many friends, and in addition to his duties as deputy treasurer, he was made deputy county auditor; in 1858 he was elected county auditor, and re-elected in 1860. A short time prior to the expiration of his second term, a vacancy occurred in the treasurer's office, whereupon the county commissioner appointed him treasurer. The A. and G. W. Railway (now the Erie) having been completed to Akron, Mr.

Crouse accepted a position as its agent at Akron, doing this work in addition to his work as treasurer. In 1863 C. Aultman & Co., of Canton, determined to build a branch factory at Akron, and Mr. Crouse was tendered the financial management of the enterprise, which he accepted, and with J. R. Buchtel erected the large building, he wholly attending to the financial management. This was the initial manufacturing establishment of Akron, and to Mr. Crouse's ability as a manager of men, his sagacity and promptness in the discharge of his many duties, is largely due the success of the "Buckeye" Mower and Reaper Works, one of the largest in the land. In 1865 a stock company was formed, he being made secretary and treasurer, continuing as such until 1885, when he became its president, continuing as such up to the present time (1892). The Buckeye Mower and Reaper Works have made over 200,000 machines and was one of the factors that contributed largely to the success of the Union arms in the civil war, supplying the place of the young men that went out in the defense of the flag by its labor-saving machinery. In 1872 he was elected county commissioner, serving one term. He was a member of the city council of Akron and served as its president; a member and president of the board of education, he has always taken a deep interest in educational matters, and has been one of the trustees of Buchtel College, and the donor to the college of the gymnasium that bears his name, Crouse Gymnasium. In politics he has always been an active republican, and as chairman of the county central committee, and other positions influential in and one of the leaders in the party. In 1885 he was elected to the state senate and served with honor one term. In 1886 he was elected to represent the Akron district in the Fiftieth congress. In that congress he served on the committee on commerce and the committee on war claims, that grew out of the war of the rebellion. His marked business capacity and experience specially fitted him to this laborious and delicate duty, and he brought to its performance the painstaking fidelity that has marked his business career, making him a most useful member of that body. In 1863, and for a number of years following, he was secretary of what was known as the Akron Board of Trade, an informal organization of the best citizens to encourage the location of manufacturing enterprises in that thriving, busy city. He has assisted directly as stockholder or indirectly with his influence, the Whitman and Barnes Manufacturing Co., the Akron Rubber Works, the Thomas Phillips & Co. Paper Mill, the Akron Iron Co., Woolen and Felt Co., the Diamond Match Works, the Stove Works, the Sellagear Works, and various other successful enterprises, which have received an impetus from the organizing and clear-sighted business ability of Mr. Crouse. In 1879 he assisted in organizing the Bank of Akron, and from that time until 1889 was its president. Oct. 18, 1859, he married Martha K., daughter of Edward and Clementine (Kingsley) Parsons of Brimfield, O. This union has brought them five children. Mrs. Crouse is a lady that exerts a strong home influence quietly and without ostentation, commanding the highest regard of those with whom she may be thrown in contact, and devoted to the happiness and best interests of her family, and dispensing the liberal hospitalities of their home. It has been by no fortuitous circumstances that he has reached his honorable position, but the result of assiduous attention to duties, strict integrity in all business relations, an ability to control and command the respect of his fellow-citizens, kindness to, and consideration for, the large number of men in his employ, a public speaker able to command by his presence and familiarity with questions of public interest the respectful attention of any audience, generous and affable, ever having in view the best interests and advancement of mankind, he has always been ready to respond to all demands that charity makes upon him, having been a liberal contributor to the erection of every church and charitable enterprise in his city, and he is held in the highest regard by his fellow-countrymen, and the declining years of his life will bear rich fruit for the benefit of mankind.

SKILTON, George Curtis, business man, was born at Charlestown, Mass., Apr. 28, 1833, the son of George and Caroline Skilton, a daughter of Rev. Jared Curtis. He was educated at the public schools of Charlestown, and in 1855 was graduated from the high school of that place. He was subsequently for one year employed with the firm of Daniel Deshon & Son, at Boston, Mass., who were large ship-owners. He was afterward engaged as bookkeeper for the grain firm of G. W. & J. B. Hagar at Boston, and later accepted a position on the Cincinnati and Chicago railroad. On Oct. 22, 1857, he removed to Richmond, Ind., to enter upon his new duties. The road had been in operation but a short time, and the country was comparatively new. Mr. Skilton was obliged to fill various offices and initiate new employees in their duties. During the two years that he was connected with the road he occupied the positions of general passenger agent, conductor and treasurer. In 1859 on account of ill health he was obliged to sever his connection, and returned East

where in 1860, in partnership with his father, he engaged in the vinegar business, the style of the firm being George Skilton & Son: the firm subsequently became Skilton, Foote & Co. The civil war was then going on, and they made a specialty of furnishing the navy with pickles, and secured the largest contracts that were awarded for this class of business. They made it a rule to furnish a better quality of pickles than the specifications demanded, and not one of the many thousands of packages furnished was rejected. Soon after the war closed they began to make a specialty of the manufacture of pickles, and adopted a trade-mark for their products. The "Bunker Hill Brand" was soon launched upon the market, and in a short time became known from Maine to California. The secret of the firm's success came from always observing the golden rule, and a firm determination to be in the foremost rank of the trade. In 1863 Mr. Skilton purchased a farm of 100 acres in Bedford, Mass., which was a part of Gov. Winthrop's estate of 1,700 acres. He has since resided on the farm, and has devoted his time and capital to making it one of the model farms of Massachusetts. The place is stocked with the celebrated Holstein-Freisian cattle. He has also devoted considerable attention to breeding colts from the most approved strain of American trotting horses. Mr. Skilton has served as a member of the common council of the city of Sommerville, as member of the Board of Health and board of aldermen. He is a prominent member of the Masonic order, and has a high standing in the community in which he resides as an honest, able business man, and a popular, spirited citizen.

GAYNOR, William Jay, jurist, was born in 1851, at Whitestown, Oneida co., N. Y., which was the birthplace of his father, Kendrick K. Gaynor, a farmer, and also of his mother. His father was a member of the small society of Abolitionists in that locality, led by Beriah Green and other co-workers of Garret Smith, and voted in 1844 for James G. Birney, the first Abolitionist candidate for president of the United States. The son worked on the farm and had no schooling except an occasional month or two at the district school, except that he also managed to take a term or two at the Whitestown Seminary, then an educational institution of considerable repute. When still a mere boy, he left home; afterward taught school, and then was a tutor in Boston, all the while attending lectures and continuing his studies in classics and mathematics. He went to Brooklyn, N. Y., in 1873, and began the practice of the law in 1875, having been employed for about two years on Brooklyn and New York newspapers. He almost immediately took a prominent place at the bar, and his practice grew to very large proportions. He was the counsel in the case of the Royal Baking Powder Co. in 1887, involving the right of minority stockholders, which attracted attention throughout the country and is now cited as a leading authority; and for the property-owners in the cases involving the validity of the charters of the elevated railroad companies in Brooklyn. In the case of Supervisor O'Brien against Thomas McCann for an alleged libel growing out of charges of corruption against the board of supervisors, in connection with the making of the improvements on the county buildings, the brilliancy of his defense attracted wide attention. He was afterward instrumental in having five of the supervisors indicted, but the district attorney never prosecuted them. When in December, 1889, Mayor Chapin and the comptroller and auditor of Brooklyn had entered into an agreement to purchase the plant and assets of the Long Island Water Supply Co. for $1,250,000, Mr. Gaynor remonstrated, nominally on behalf of Mr. Ziegler, a tax-payer, on the ground that the price was excessive. Mayor Chapin took no notice of the objection, whereupon Mr. Gaynor brought an action for an injunction. His initial argument of the statutory and constitutional questions involved in the case before the supreme court, was conceded to be one of the ablest ever heard in the courts. He afterwards argued it on appeal with equal ability. The result was the prevention of the attempted purchase. As a criminal lawyer he made a successful defence of Armstrong, Laughlin, McGinness, Tarkinter, and Darwin J. Meserole, all of whom were indicted for murder. He has been a frequent writer on legal and other subjects, and contributed to the "Albany Law Journal;" "The Arrest and Trial of Jesus from a Legal Standpoint;" "The Constitutional Limitations of the Taxing Power," and "The Construction of Wills as to the Charging of Debts and Legacies on Realty." In national politics he is a Democrat. In December, 1890, he was appointed judge advocate on the staff of Gen. McLeer of the 2d brigade of the National Guard of the state of New York, with the rank of major. He was prominently named by both Democrats and Republicans as a nominee for mayor in the election of 1891. In 1893 he declined the nomination for mayor of Brooklyn, but was nominated by the Republicans and Independent Democrats for justice of the supreme court, for the second district of the state of New York, which nomination he accepted after first declining, and was elected by a majority of 32,000. Among the various frauds he was instrumental in exposing, were the so-called Columbian frauds, and the street railroad franchise frauds, with the result that the public not only elected him, but also Mr. Schieren, whom he supported for mayor. He thus completely overthrew the Democratic ring in Brooklyn, thus earning the name of "Ring Breaker." He originated the movement and carried it on single-handed for four years. Previous to that he had been studious and retiring, taking no part in government matters, but he was all the while a close observer, for nothing seems to have escaped his notice. He opened his speech at a great reform meeting by saying that long silence often gave one the right to speak. His action in securing the conviction of John Y. McKane for fraudulent registration and election corruption at Gravesend and Coney Island, is a matter of history. His decisions against the abuses of the police power, and in favor of individual liberty when he became judge, attracted wide attention. He said from the bench: "Every citizen has the right to arrest any one committing a criminal offense in his presence, but as we do not all want to be acting as policemen we club together and hire and pay men for that purpose, but we do not thereby make them our masters but our servants." In the fall of 1894 he was offered the Democratic nomination for governor, but declined when the party leaders refused to accept his proposed platform. He said things had to be "lifted up" to carry the state, but the machine leaders could not see it. The convention then, without his permission, nominated him for judge of the court of appeals of the state of New York, but he declined it; this made the fourth time he had declined to run for high office. He is now serving his fourteen years' term on the bench of the supreme court. In January, 1895, the great strike of the employees of the electric railroads occurred in Brooklyn. The men claimed that they were compelled to work more than ten hours a day contrary to law, and were insufficiently paid. After the cars had stood idle for several days, an application was made to the supreme court by a citizen for a mandamus to compel the companies to run their cars. The decision of Judge Gaynor was deemed the clearest exposition of the law on the duties of railroad companies to the public which had been rendered, and was published in full throughout the country. He treated the case wholly from the standpoint of the public, and held that the duty of a railroad company was to the public first, and to its stockholders second; and that if it wanted to supersede its employees by others who would work cheaper, it could not stand idle meanwhile, but must run its cars at the best price obtainable. Being afterwards called upon by the state board of mediation and arbitration to state his opinion of what caused the difference between the companies and their men, he pointed out that the companies were not only bonded and capitalized far beyond the actual investment, but that they were also leased to a traction company formed in West Virginia, and with a paper capital of $30,000,000, which represented nothing, or, as he said, which "had neither a dollar nor a day's work back of it," the same being an inducement to the persons in control to cut down expenses, without regard to the rights of the public or of employees, in order to pay dividends on the sham stock to make it worth par, and thus enrich themselves at the expense of others. He said the fault was with the laws which permitted such things; that while the cause existed the results would follow, and that, therefore, there was no use of examining into the immediate dispute about which no two seemed to agree. This letter also received national attention.

NORTON, William Edward, artist, was born at Boston, Mass., in 1853, of English ancestry. At an early age he removed with his parents to Charlestown, Mass., where he attended the public schools. Before he was able to talk, he showed a taste for drawing, and at fourteen began the study of art at the Lowell Institute, in Boston, under Mr. Carleton and Mr. Hollingsworth. This was much against the wishes of his people, who wished him to follow some more lucrative occupation, and on leaving school, he entered the employ of a shipping firm as clerk. His distaste for figures, however, soon led him to leave this situation, and apprentice himself to a Mr. Needham, house, sign, and fresco painter, although still devoting his evenings to the study of art and science at Lowell Institute. Here he also began the study of anatomy under Dr. Rimmer, continuing it at the Harvard Medical College, and later, at the Royal Academy, London, and the École des Beaux Arts, Paris. After serving two years at his trade, his love for the sea induced him to become a sailor, which calling, after many and varied experiences, both afloat and ashore, he relinquished; and at the age of twenty-two, to a studio in Boston, and began his career as a marine painter. It was some years before he secured recognition, during which time he endured many hardships and discouragements, although cheered and aided by the substantial appreciation and instruction of such artists as William M. Hunt and George Inness. At the end of ten years, his success being then established, he sold at auction 108 pictures and sketches, and with the proceeds went to Europe, where he first traveled extensively upon the continent, and later took a studio in London. In the following spring he sent three pictures to the Royal Academy, all of which were accepted and well placed. Shortly afterwards he went to Paris, and entered the studio of M. Jacquesson, also availing himself of the criticism of M. Vollon. Four years afterwards he returned to London, having also spent much time in Italy, studying the old masters. The subjects of Mr. Norton's paintings are chiefly of the sea and sailors. He has been a constant exhibitor at the Royal Academy and other exhibitions in Great Britain. His work has been most favorably received and commented upon, and he has been awarded two gold medals from expositions.

WEIR, John Ferguson, artist, was born at West Point, N. Y., Aug. 28, 1841, son of Robert W. Weir, at that time professor in the U. S. Military Academy. After some years spent at boarding school, he studied under several instructors of the Military Academy, and took up art under his father. In 1861 he went to New York, and began his professional career as an artist. His first picture exhibited at the National Academy of Design, "The Interior of His Father's Studio," gained for him some reputation, and secured his election as associate of the academy. In 1865 he completed a large picture, "The Gun Foundry," which was the chief attraction of the academy exhibition of that year, gaining him a unanimous election as academician, a rare occurrence in the annals of the institution. This picture was sold to Robert P. Parrott, for the sum of $5,200, and was exhibited at the Paris Exposition in 1867. The following year he married Mary, daughter of J. W. French, D.D., professor of ethics and law in the

VI.—30

U. S. Military Academy. In 1868 he completed another large picture, "Forging the Shaft," which increased his reputation. The picture was exhibited at the academy, and also at the Paris Exposition in 1878, and was sold to Mr. Derby, the publisher, for $4,000. In 1868 Mr. Weir went abroad, and remained until the fall of 1869. While absent, he was elected to the office of dean of the School of Fine Arts at Yale University, and on returning home, entered upon the duties of his office, proceeding to build up that institution, which now holds the first rank among similar institutions in this country. Since 1869 Mr. Weir has continued to preside over the School of Fine Arts, while continuing the exercise of his profession. Among his principal works are: "By the Sea," "Venice," "Returning from Work," "The Confessional," "Storm and Sunshine," "Tapping the Furnace," "Christ on the Sea of Gennesaret," etc. Mr. Weir is not restricted to one class of subjects, but practices equally genre, landscape, and portrait painting. Among the portraits painted by him are those of Dr. Wells Williams, Adm. Farragut, Pres. Eliphalet Nott, Col. Alden, Pres. Dwight, and a large group of the theological faculty at Yale. He has given attention to sculpture also, producing a statue of the elder Benjamin Silliman, which, in 1884, was placed in front of Farnam College at Yale, and a seated figure of Pres. Woolsey. Mr. Weir has been an occasional contributor to the magazines, and has published, "The Way: The Nature and Means of Revelation."

HALLWIG, Gustav, artist, was born in Dresden, Saxony, in 1819. When quite young he began the study of art, and upon his graduation from college in 1828, determined to devote himself to the profession of painting. His parents were much averse to this, however, but every spare moment obtainable he spent in sketching. In 1829 he went to Berlin, arriving one bitter winter night, after many days of hard travel on foot. Upon making application at the Berlin Academy, he was several times refused. Undaunted by disappointments and discouragements, however, he again presented himself at the academy, and requesting the professor to be seated, drew forth his sketch book and in an astonishingly short time had finished a striking portrait of the astonished gentleman. This proof of his talent at once secured him admission, and he was placed under the especial charge of Prof. Hartman. In 1837, Mr. Hallwig was elected instructor in the Berlin Academy. He also devoted much time to the writing of magazine articles and art critiques. In 1845 he returned to Dresden, where his brush soon won for him yet more fame and fortune. Since 1872 Mr. Hallwig has made his home in Baltimore, Md., where he has established an enviable reputation as one of the foremost artists of America, his work being confined chiefly to landscape and cattle painting. He is a frequent contributor to the periodicals.

HALLWIG, Oscar, artist, was born in Dresden, Saxony, March 20, 1838. After completing a course of study in the schools of his native city he entered the Royal Academy of Fine Arts, where he remained for five years as special pupil of Director Schnorr von Karolsfeld, receiving during that time several first medals for his work. When he came to America, art being then in its infancy, there was little encouragement for one who had just taken up his palette and brush. Mr. Hallwig, however, painted a portrait of Miss Moale, one of the belles of Baltimore, which when placed in one of the prominent windows of the city created such a furor, the street was actually blockaded by crowds anxious to get a glimpse of it. His talent as a portrait painter was at once recognized, and the success which has since crowned his efforts began. He went to Chicago in 1870 and fitted up a magnificent studio at a cost of $30,000, lining the walls with his most valuable paintings. He was, however, so unfortunate as to be a victim of the great fire a year later, when his studio, with all its contents, was completely destroyed. He returned to Baltimore in 1878 and has since made it his home. He has painted portraits of the leading people of the country, and his work has been admired whenever exhibited. In 1873 he was awarded the first premium at the St. Louis art exhibit. His portraits are strikingly natural and show keen observation. He succeeds in bringing out in his work the chief characteristics of his subject in fine drawing and refined coloring.

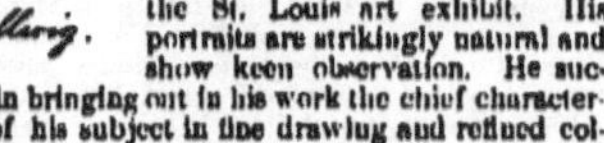

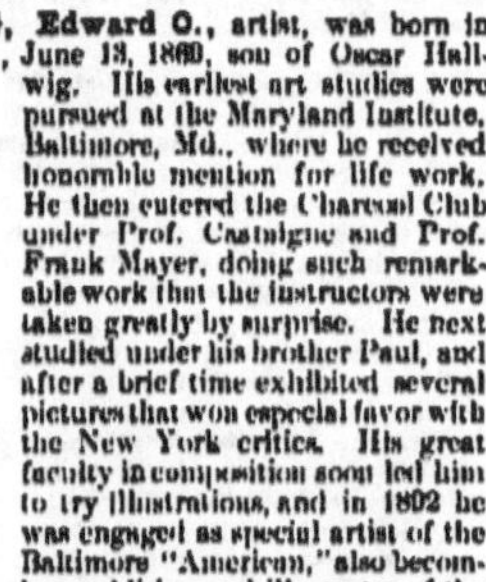

HALLWIG, Edward O., artist, was born in Baltimore, Md., June 13, 1860, son of Oscar Hallwig. His earliest art studies were pursued at the Maryland Institute, Baltimore, Md., where he received honorable mention for life work. He then entered the Charcoal Club under Prof. Castnigne and Prof. Frank Mayer, doing such remarkable work that the instructors were taken greatly by surprise. He next studied under his brother Paul, and after a brief time exhibited several pictures that won especial favor with the New York critics. His great faculty in composition soon led him to try illustrations, and in 1802 he was engaged as special artist of the Baltimore "American," also becoming publisher and illustrator of the Sidney magazines.

HALLWIG, Paul, artist, was born in Baltimore, Md., Dec. 18, 1865, son of Oscar Hallwig, a well-known portrait painter of that city. He received his general education at the public and private schools of his birthplace, and in 1883 began the study of art under his father. At the same time he became a pupil of the Maryland Institute Art School, where by diligence and artistic ability he won honorable mention, a prize of $100, and his diploma. Going abroad, he made his home at Munich, studied under Prof. Loetz, and for four years was a pupil of the Munich Royal Academy of Fine Arts, winning during that period several bronze and finally a gold medal. He then studied in private under Prof. Fritz A. Kaulbach, one of the most famous portrait painters, and also under the distinguished Prof. Nauen. Returning to his native city in 1889, he brought with him a fine collection of studies of the German peasantry, which are remarkable for their strength and boldness, and which have been greatly admired. He immediately received commissions to paint the portraits of many of the leading people of Baltimore, among them W. W. Taylor, president of the Union Bank; James J. Whedbee, of Whedbee & Dickinson; Rev. J. J. B. Hodges,

rector of St. Paul's Protestant Episcopal Church; and Mr. and Mrs. Augustus Alberts, Jr. After a short stay in Baltimore, he returned to Munich to paint the portraits of a number of prominent people in that city. Out of several hundred artists Mr. Hallwig was selected by Luitpold, the prince regent of Bavaria, to paint a life-sized portrait of him to decorate the art gallery of his palace, which picture received such special attention, and occasioned so much favorable comment that he was then commissioned to paint a life-sized portrait of the heir apparent to the crown, Prince Ludwig, of Bavaria, and also portraits of the Princess Gisela, Rupprecht, Graf Holsten, Baron Seymnsky, and many more of the court notables. After a visit to the Saxon court, where he met with extraordinary success, painting among others the royal family of King Albert, Mr. Hallwig went to Paris, where he put the finishing touches to his artistic education, studying under the most distinguished portrait painters. The different papers devoted paragraphs to the latest work of this most prominent artist, and the "Chronicle des Arts Critiques" counts him among the very best of portrait painters. In 1801 he was recalled to Baltimore by the retiring mayor of the city, Robert C. Davidson, to paint his portrait, to be placed in the collection in the city council chamber of the City Hall.

Mr. Hallwig has painted the portraits of many other prominent people, among which may be included a wonderful likeness of Mr. Mayo H. Thom, Mrs. Ernault Williams, and her daughter Eleanor; Mr. and Mrs. Hazelyte; President Cushing, of the Maryland Institute; Mr. McD. Richardson, president of the Baltimore Savings Bank; Gen. Felix Agnus; Prof. Smith, of the State Normal School; a life-size portrait of Louise Morris (daughter of John B. Morris), now Mrs. Frederick Gebhard, of New York city; Councilman John B. Bland; Cardinal Gibbons; John T. T. Ford, the veteran theatrical manager; Mr. Enoch Pratt, Mr. C. W. Conkling; President Grover Cleveland; and a life-size portrait of Edwin Booth in Hamlet costume, hanging in the reception-room at the City Hall; also portraits of Congressman Isador Raynor; Gov. Frank Brown, of Maryland; and Mayor Ferdinand C. Latrobe. In 1893 Mr. Hallwig was engaged as special artist to decorate the City Hall with portraits. He has been likewise commissioned for the State Hall at Annapolis.

HALLWIG, William, C., artist, was born in New York, March 25, 1870. From his earliest childhood he evinced marked artistic ability, and in 1885 he began study at the Maryland Art Institution under Prof. Adams and Prof. Hugh Newell, graduating therefrom in 1888. He also studied at the Peabody Institute, and in 1890 came to New York city, and took

several courses at the Art Students' League. His advance has been constant, and, considering his youth, unprecedented. He has painted some fruit pieces, which received special mention at the World's Fair, in Chicago, 1893, and excited much favorable comment.

JOUETT, Matthew Harris, artist, was born in Mercer county, Ky., Apr. 22, 1788, son of Capt. John, a revolutionary soldier, and Sally (Robards) Jouett. His uncle, Matthew Jouett, for whom he was named, was clerk of the first legislative body that assembled west of the Allegheny mountains, and was killed during the war of the revolution. Matthew Harris Jouett at first studied law, the practice of which proved distasteful to him, and he gave it up to devote his time to art, for which he had considerable talent. His studies were interrupted by the war of 1812, and he entered the army to serve in the northwest campaign. After the war he began to paint with renewed zest. He was wonderfully successful as a self-taught man, but feeling the need of a master, he, in 1816, went to Boston to be under the instruction of Gilbert Stuart, which was the beginning of a life-long intimacy between them. He returned to Lexington where, in a short time, he won considerable distinction as a portrait painter. Among his best pictures are those of La Fayette, which belongs to the state of Kentucky, Henry Clay, John C. Crittenden, Gov. Isaac Shelby, and James Morrison. Mr. Jouett was a thoroughly ideal artist, with a high-strung poetic temperament, vivid imagination, and a most sympathetic nature. He died in Lexington, Ky., Aug. 10, 1827.

STANLEY, James M., artist, was born at Canandaigua, N. Y., Jan. 17, 1814. He was thrown upon his own resources at an early age, spending the greater part of his boyhood in Buffalo, N. Y. In 1834 he removed to Michigan, and in 1835 commenced the profession of portrait painting in Detroit.

He went to Chicago in 1837, residing there and at Galena, Ill., for the following two years, during which time he painted portraits of the Indians, and took sketches of the Indian country in the region of Fort Snelling, Minn. Subsequently, he followed his profession in New York city; Philadelphia, Pa.; Baltimore, Md.; and Troy, N. Y. In 1842, having in the meantime become imbued with a love for Indian scenes and adventures, he traveled extensively over the western prairies, painting the portraits, in full costume, of the leading warriors around Fort Gibson, Arkansas, and in Texas and New Mexico. He accompanied the Kearney and Emory expeditions across the Rocky Mountains, and after performing much important labor for the U. S. government in California, visited Oregon, and traversed the greater portion of the Columbia river, taking a large number of sketches of the scenery along the route, and transferring them to canvas. He next spent over a year in the Sandwich Islands, and from 1851 to 1863 lived in Washington, D. C., after which he took up a permanent residence in Detroit, Mich. During his stay in Washington Mr. Stanley placed in the Smithsonian Institute a large and valuable collection of portraits of the leading Indian chiefs of America, which, when a portion of the building was destroyed by fire in 1865, was burned with it. As the collection was the result of eleven years' travel and labor, the loss was inestimable. The gallery comprised 152 paintings, chiefly life-size, of the prominent chiefs and leading men of forty-two distinct tribes. Mr. Stanley's personal knowledge of nearly all the existing tribes ranked him as one of the highest authorities in matters concerning Indian life and character. He was instrumental in securing to the government many relics and curiosities of aboriginal civilization, the greater part of which, however, were lost at sea

during transportation. One of his most important paintings, "The Trial of Red Jacket," was exhibited in all the principal cities of America, and many of Europe, being finally placed in Detroit. Valuable, both historically and artistically, it was appraised at $30,000, and was popularized by faithful chromo reproductions. Several of his pictures, representing events in the history of Michigan, were likewise reproduced in chromo-lithographs. His portraits of distinguished men from all parts of the United States won him deserved renown. Wherever he resided, Mr. Stanley was most zealous in his efforts to cultivate a love for art, being the organizer of the Western Art Association, and one of the founders of a gallery of paintings that in later years became a permanent and valuable acquisition to Detroit. He died from heart disease, Apr. 10, 1872.

COPLEY, John Singleton, painter, was born in Boston, Mass., July 3, 1737. His parents, both of English extraction, had emigrated from Ireland in the previous year. He commenced to draw in the nursery, making coarse drawings on the walls and rough sketches in his school books. According to his own account, which his mother confirms, he received no instruction whatever, and never saw a good picture until he left America, but Mr. W. H. Whitmore of Boston has endeavored to show that he was instructed by his stepfather, Peter Pelham, the portrait painter and engraver, who died in 1751, and probably also by John Smibert. He early "saw visions" of beautiful forms and faces, which he strove to reproduce as best he could, from colors and brushes of his own making. At the age of sixteen he was executing portraits of considerable merit, and in 1755 Washington sat to him for a miniature. In 1760 Copley sent to Benjamin West in London, without name or address, a portrait of his half-brother, Henry Pelham, with the request that it be placed in the exhibition rooms. Upon its reception, West, who was then high in the royal favor, exclaimed, "It is worthy of Titian himself!" The painter being unknown, he could only say that the picture, now known as "The Boy and the Flying Squirrel," must be the production of an American, because the frame over which the canvas was stretched was made from American pine. Though contrary to the rules of the academy to place any picture by an unknown artist upon its walls, it was admitted from West's influence and its own artistic merit. The reception of this picture influenced the whole course of Copley's life. His friends urged him to go to England in the pursuit of his avocation, and West invited him to his own house. But the separation from his aged mother was not to be thought of, and the project was postponed, though not abandoned. In 1776-77 he sent over other works for exhibition which attracted great admiration and established his European reputation. In 1769 he married Susannah Farnum, daughter of Richard Clarke, a wealthy merchant of Boston, and agent of the East India Co. It was to this Mr. Clarke that the tea was consigned, upon which was levied the obnoxious tax which so enraged the colonists, and it was because he, as a royalist, refused to send it back, that it was thrown overboard by the angry mob in the disguise of Mohawks. Copley's wife was a lineal descendant from Mary Chilton, the first woman to set foot on American soil from the Mayflower. She was a woman of great personal beauty, both in face and figure; her character was in keeping with her person, and she exercised the happiest influence over the home circle. Her lineaments are met with continually through the whole course of Copley's work. He bought a farm of seven acres on Beacon Hill, which he chose for its beautiful view, and upon which there was but one house. Here their four children were born, including the son who became lord chancellor of England. Copley wished to educate this son to be a painter, but he had no taste nor talent for the profession, and is said to have retorted to his father's importunities, that he preferred that future generations should speak of "Copley, the father of the lord chancellor, not of Copley, the son of the painter." At length the painter could no longer resist the importunities of his friends, and in 1774 he left his aged mother, wife, and family and embarked for England, not because of royalist tendencies, but to perfect himself in his art. He was warmly welcomed by West, and after a few weeks' stay in London, visited Italy, where, for a year, he reveled in the splendors of the world's masterpieces. On returning to London, he was joined by his family and settled in a handsome house in which himself, father-in-law, and son lived and died. Copley's reputation had preceded him, and he was immediately overwhelmed with work, and reached the highest rank in his profession, being given a royal commission to paint "The Three Princesses." His first important subject-picture was "The Youth Rescued From a Shark," which he presented to Christ's Hospital School. In 1790 he was elected a member of the Royal Academy, after having been an associate two years, and presented on his admission, as is customary, a picture entitled "The Tribute Money." He now turned his energies to the painting of historical pictures, particularly relating to some incident of the day. A happy selection of subject was "The Death of Lord Chatham," an impressive subject in which the portraits of the peers were carefully studied from life. From this an engraving was made by Bartolozzi, which had an extraordinary success in America as well as England. A still finer group is "The Death of Major Pierson." These two pictures are in the National Academy. In 1790 he executed the immense "Siege of Gibraltar," now in the Guildhall. His portrait of "Lady Frances Wentworth" is a picture of rare excellence, now in the Lenox Library in New York. A romance is attached to her memory which is the basis of a poem by Nora Perry. She was engaged to her cousin, John Wentworth, who, in a lover's quarrel, went away and returned to find her married, but she married him within a week after her husband's death. Among Copley's numerous other works may be mentioned: "Charles I. Demanding the Surrender of the Five Members" (now in Boston); "Charles I. Signing Strafford's Death Warrant," and "The Assassination of Buckingham." To the end of his life he pursued his art with unwearied energy. Copley's historical subjects are more original, spirited, and realistic than those of his friend and countryman, Benjamin West, with whom he is commonly classed, and they are distinguished by far richer and finer coloring. His composition is simple and effective, and drawing careful and accurate. In religious and poetical subjects he was less successful. His portraits, full of individuality, excellent in modeling and coloring, are in themselves enough to justify a great reputation; and in artistic qualities the finest of them may be said to approach the works of Reynolds and Gainsborough. In August, 1815, he was attacked with paralysis, and died on Sept. 9th of that year.

WILES, Irving Ramsay, artist, was born in Utica, N. Y., Apr. 8, 1861. He began the study of art with his father, Lemuel Wiles, and later entered the Art Students' League of New York, working under James Carroll Beckwith and William Merritt Chase. In 1882 he went abroad and studied in the Julian Academy in Paris, with Boulanger and Lefebvre and later with Carolus Duran, working in Paris two years in all. He received a medal for painting in the school in Paris, and exhibited in the Salon of 1884. He also went to Italy to study the old masters, where he painted many Venetian scenes in water-color and in oil. Since then he has lived in New York during the winter, in the summer assisting his father at his School of Art at Silver Lake, N. Y. He has chiefly busied his brush with portrait and figure painting, while his illustrations are well known to all readers of the leading magazines, appearing from time to time in the "Century," "Harper's," "Scribner's," "The Cosmopolitan," etc. As a member of the Society of American Artists, he has been for five years its treasurer. He is an associate of the Academy of Design, a member of the American Water-color Society, the Water-color Club, and the Pastel Club. He received the Hallgarten prize at the Academy of Design for "The Corner Table;" the T. B. Clarke prize for "The Sonata," now in the collection of Mr. W. T. Evans; *mention honorable* at the Paris Exposition, and medal at the Columbian Exposition.

Among his best known paintings, besides those above mentioned, are: "Portrait of My Father and Mother," "Sunshine and Flowers" (portrait of woman and child); "Memories" (in the collection of Mr. Andrew Carnegie); "Noon" (in the collection of Mr. T. B. Clarke); "Among Canada Thistles" (in the collection of Mr. G. W. English); "Sunshine in the Studio" (owned by Mr. C. D. Miller); "Discouraged" (owned by Mr. Havemeyer); "Girl in Black" (owned by Mr. William M. Chase); "The Green Gown" (owned by Dr. Dudley Tenney). All of Mr. Wiles's work is characterized by a charming simplicity of idea and treatment. "Memories," exhibited at the academy in 1891, and now in the possession of Mr. Andrew Carnegie, is an admirable example of these qualities of his art.

OCHTMAN, Leonard, artist, was born at Zonnemaire, in the province of Zeeland, Holland, Oct. 21, 1854. His father was a decorative painter, and the boy, assisting his father and in companionship with him, soon displayed a love of art. In 1866 the family came to America and settled in Albany, N. Y., where, in his sixteenth year, Leonard entered an engraving office as a draughtsman. At twenty-three he opened a studio in Albany, continuing it for about two years; then entered the Art Students' League, New York city, for the winter course of study. In his chosen line of work, landscape painting, he is entirely self-taught. The summer of 1885 found him traveling in England, France, and Holland, and on his return he took a studio in New York, where he spent his winter seasons. Upon his marriage in 1891 to Mina Fonda, his pupil, he purchased a few acres of picturesque land in Connectient and erected a studio and home, where he spends his summers, drawing about him a class of earnest students. Mr. Ochtman's first attempt at exhibition in the spring of 1892, at the National Academy of Design, was his picture "Early Autumn," now owned in Albany. Since that time he has been a constant exhibitor. He is a member of the Society of American Artists, the American Water-Color Society, the New York Water-Color Club, the Salmagundi Club, and the Brooklyn Art Club; and has received many honors. In person Mr. Ochtman is of medium height and slender, with brown beard and eyes, and hair now tinged with gray. He is quiet, unassuming in manner, with simple tastes, and love of fun; never happier than when entertaining friends, especially those of kindred tastes.

VEDDER, Elihu, artist, was born in Varick street, New York city, Feb. 26, 1836. His parents were first cousins, and came from the Schenectady family of Vedder. His mother died when he was sixteen years old, and his father (who had already been there for several years) continued to live, until 1870, in Cuba, when he took up a permanent residence in St. Augustine, Fla. The son's first art instruction was received during a year spent at Sherbourne, N. Y., with the painter, Mathison. In 1856 he went abroad, spending a winter in Paris, in the atelier of Picot. In April, 1857, he went to Italy, where he remained for four years, principally in Florence. At the outbreak of the civil war in 1861, Mr. Vedder at once returned to New York city, where he was desirous of enlisting in the Federal army, but was prevented by the condition of his left arm, which had been permanently injured by the accidental discharge of a companion's gun while out duck-shooting in 1856. During the civil war the young artist gained a precarious living in New York and Boston, although he was so far successful as to be elected, in 1863, an associate of the Academy of Design. In December, 1865, he returned to Paris, spending the following summer in Brittany, and a year later removing to Rome, where he has since resided altogether, although making frequent brief visits to America. The most striking quality of Mr. Vedder's work as an artist is its pre-eminent ideality, which displays to a very marked degree his superlative powers of imagination. He has been the subject of endless and varied criticism, the first such to recognize his peculiar individuality having appeared in Jarvis' "Art Idea," in 1856. A list of his best-known works includes: "The Monk on the Gloomy Path," "The Crucifixion," "The Lost Mind," "Death of Abel," "A Scene on the Mediterranean," "Greek Actor's Daughter," "Old Madonna," "Cumean Sibyl," "Young Marsyas," "A Questioner of the Sphinx," "Sleeping Girl," "A Venetian Model," "A Pastoral," "Nausicaa and her Companions," "Waves off Pier Head," "Le Mistral," "The Lair of the Sea-serpent," "The Roc's Egg," "Fisherman

and Djinn," "Dominican Friars," and "The Italian Woman." The last six paintings all hang in the Boston Museum of Fine Arts. Mr. Vedder's illustrations of Edward Fitzgerald's translation of the "Rubaiyat of Omar Khayyam" (1884) won him worldwide renown, while not less notable were his designs for a ceiling and wall-panels for the dining-room of C. P. Huntington's residence at Fifty-seventh street and Fifth avenue, New York city (1892). His latest work (August, 1893) is a decorative panel for the memorial art building at Bowdoin College, erected by the Misses Walker of Boston. On July 13, 1869, Mr. Vedder was married to Caroline, daughter of E. H. Rosekrans of Glen's Falls, N. Y.

SARTAIN, John, artist and engraver on steel, was born in London, England, Oct. 24, 1808. When but ten years old he left school, in which he had

learned but little, and at twelve began a career of active industry, first as a pyrotechnist with Sig. Mortram, who was also assistant scene painter at the principal theatre in London. Such was the reliability of the child's character and timely attention to his duties, that he was relied upon the same as a man, except when a man's strength was needed. At the age of fourteen, he was apprenticed to John Swaine to learn the art of line engraving, and at the end of a year he displayed such skill, that the eminent art critic, William Y. Otley, entrusted him with the execution of the plates for his work entitled, "The Early Florentine School," published in 1826. In 1828 he commenced the practice of mezzo-tinto, and thereafter mingled both styles with the addition of stippling in all his plates. His eagerness in the pursuit of knowledge made ample amends for the deficiencies of his early education. He married Susannah Longmate Swaine, daughter of his first master in steel engraving, and in 1830 the young artist and his bride set sail for America, and settled in Philadelphia. He is the founder in America of that branch of engraving on steel known as mezzo-tinto. Besides engraving, he engaged professionally in painting in oils, in water colors and in miniature on ivory. For quite a while he made vignette designs for the embellishments on bank notes, and also made designs on wood for that branch of engraving. In 1848 he became sole proprietor and editor of Campbell's "Foreign Semi-Monthly Magazine." In 1843, when the name of the scientist was but little known on this side of the Atlantic, he printed Agassiz's article, "A Period in the History of our own Planet." He engraved plates for the "Eclectic Magazine," and in 1848 he purchased a half interest in the "Union Magazine," a New York publication which became known throughout the country as "Sartain's Magazine," and during the latter part of its career he was its editor. His industry was indefatigable, and the variety of his capacity approximates the incredible. There was hardly an annual published this side of the Atlantic that had not its plates created from his prolific brain. His large framing prints are also numerous; among the more important are: "Christ Rejected," "The Iron Worker," and "King Solomon," "Civil War in Missouri," "Homestead of Henry Clay," "The Battle of Gettysburg," and many others, all of worth. He has held membership in numerous associations; was for twenty-three years director of the Academy of Fine Arts; controller of the Artist's Fund; manager and director in various prominent institutions in Philadelphia, and vice-president of the School of Design for Women, having declined the presidency. He was chief of the bureau of art at the International Exhibition in Philadelphia, in 1876, and has received numerous medals, decorations, titles and honorary memberships in foreign countries. His architectural knowledge and taste is frequently called on, in aid of important projects.

He is prominent in the order of Free Masons, having received forty-six degrees of its mysteries, is past master of his lodge, and past high priest of his chapter. He was chief of the art department at the American exhibition in London. His children have inherited his wonderful talent, and have attained a distinguished reputation in the world of art. Samuel Sartain, the eldest son, is known throughout the United States for his inimitably engraved portraits, as well as other able works on steel. William Sartain, the next son, is a prominent painter in New York city, an associate of the National Academy of Design, president of the Art club of New York, and was for some years professor in the life class of the Art Students' League and Cooper Institute, and was one of the founders of the New York Society of American Artists, and a prominent exhibitor at the periodical exhibitions of America. Emily Sartain, the daughter, is principal of the School of Design for Women in Philadelphia, is a practical engraver, etcher, and portrait painter, and has studied all the branches of the profession; has spent four years in the studios of Paris, and two winters in Italy, besides studying under her father and other eminent artists; was art editor of the "Continent," and the possessor of numerous medals, certificates and diplomas, including one from an East Indian maharajah, and one from the London Society of Literature, Science, and Art, and is her father's daughter in every sense of the word, possessing to a rare degree the art of making art practical. She was a member of the international jury of awards in the art department of the Columbian Exposition at Chicago in 1893. Henry Sartain, another son, also received an art education, but adopted plate printing as an occupation in which he gained an extended reputation.

MULLER-URY, Adolph Felix, portrait painter, was born in Airolo, Switzerland, Feb. 28, 1862, the son of a prominent lawyer. Developing artistic qualities at an early age, he was in 1871 sent to Stans, Switzerland, where the Swiss painter, Deschwanden, took charge of him in 1877. After three years' hard work he went to Munich to the Royal Academy of Fine Arts, where he studied with Strehuber, Gahl, and Benzur. In Munich he changed his idealistic tendency for the realistic interpretation of art. Encouraged by the success of his early work he visited Rome in 1881, making copies and studies of old masters. He painted many religious pictures, and received portrait orders from a number of prominent people, including Cardinals Hergenroether and Hohenlohe, sculptors Ackermann, Spillhofer, and others. His first exhibit at the International Exhibition, called "The Surprise," was sold on the opening day. He then went to Paris, where he remained for two years a pupil of Cabanel, and, after visiting Holland, came to America in November, 1887, and after travelling throughout the country opened a studio in New York city. He went to Europe in 1888 and 1891, and again in 1894, to study the master portrait painters, visiting London, Paris, Madrid, Florence, Venice, Holland, and Switzerland. He has traveled considerably throughout the United States, but his permanent studio is in New York city. Among his important portraits are Cardinal Gibbons, archbishop of Baltimore, Mons. Satolli, Archbishop Ireland, Chauncey M. Depew, exhibited at the Paris Salon, 1889, Prests.

Ruchonnet and Hammer of the Swiss Republic, the children of J. J. Hill of St. Paul, and Mlle. Calve, and a full size portrait of Gen. Grant, representing him on the field of battle, which is considered by many the best portrait of him in existence. A "Mater Dolorosa," an interpretation of suffering and sorrow, was painted in 1895. Mr. Muller-Ury's pictures are after the style of Velasquez, Rembrandt, and Titian. His portraits are remarkable for their boldness and likeness to life.

HOVENDEN, Thomas, artist, was born at Dunmanway, county Cork, Ireland, Dec. 28, 1840. From a very early age he evinced a strong attraction for art, and attended the Kensington department of the Cork School of Design for a few years. In 1863 he came to the United States, but the civil war had turned men's minds away from all less stern subjects, and finding there was no demand for pictures, the young artist went into business as a frame dealer, and in the following year became a student in the New York Academy of Design. He set up a studio in 1868 in the house of a friend, H. Bolton Jones, at Baltimore, but it was not until 1872 that he began to follow art as a profession. In 1874 he went to Paris, and entered the studio of Cabanel, upon whom his talent made so strong an impression that the great 
French artist assured him that if he would remain with him he would achieve the highest rank among the painters of the day. Mr. Hovenden did remain until 1880, when he returned to America. While pursuing his art studies in France, he met Helen Corson, a descendant of one of the oldest families of Friends in eastern Pennsylvania, who was also studying art there, and they were married after their return to America. His first notable painting was a "Breton Interior of 1793," which depicted a family sharpening swords and casting bullets to prepare for resistance against the Republicans in that year of the reign of terror. This picture was exhibited in Europe, and established Hovenden's transatlantic reputation. In 1881 he was elected an associate of the National Academy, a member of the American Water-Color Society, of the Society of American Artists, and in 1882 was made an academician. In 1883 he was elected to membership in the Philadelphia Society of Artists, and in 1885 became a member of the New York Etching Club. He resided at different times in New York, Baltimore, Philadelphia, Washington, and at his home at Plymouth Meeting, Montgomery co., Pa. It was while returning from there on the evening of Aug. 14, 1895, that the artist met a hero's death, being instantly killed by a railroad train at what is known as the "Trenton cut-off" of the Pennsylvania Railroad, while attempting to save a little ten-year-old girl from being run over. His end was all the sadder from the fact that the sacrifice of his life proved useless, as the child met her death beneath the wheels of the engine which crushed out the artist's life. Hovenden ranked among the very highest of American artists. He was a member of the national jury for the admission of pictures at the Chicago Columbian Exposition of 1893, and was a member of the international jury of awards in art on the same occasion. One of his best-known paintings, "Breaking Home Ties," has been engraved probably oftener than any other American work, and is to be found literally in thousands of homes. This painting was one of the most notable at the World's Fair. Among his other works are: "The Two Lilies"

(1874) ; "A Brittany Woman Spinning," and "Pleasant News" (1876); "The Image Seller" (exhibited in the Paris Salon of 1876) ; "Thinking of Somebody," and "News from the Conscript" (1877); "Pride of the Old Folks," and "Peasant Soldiers of La Vendée, 1793" (1878); "In Hoc Signo Vinces" (published by Goupil in Paris, 1880) ; "Elaine" (commenced in Paris and finished in New York, 1882); "Last Moments of John Brown" (1884); "Taking His Ease" (1885) ; and in later years "Their Pride" (a negro picture); "In the Hands of the Enemy," "Bringing Home the Bride," "When Hope was Darkest," and "Jerusalem the Golden." Of these most critics concurred in esteeming "Elaine" as Hovenden's masterpiece. As a powerful allegorical picture, it stands unrivaled among the productions of American genius. In all of his important works, however, there is his own individuality in the perfect mastery of detail, which makes him the commanding figure he is, and will remain.

THAYER, Abbott Henderson, artist, was born in Boston, Mass., in 1849, a descendant, through both his parents, of more than 200 years of New England ancestors. The fourth in the line from the earliest ancestor was Jedediah Thayer, a lieutenant in the 25th Continental regiment in 1776, and afterwards a captain under Kosciusko, at West Point. The sixth, the grandfather, was Gideon French Thayer, the eminent teacher, and founder of Chauncy Hall School in Boston. Abbott's maternal grandfather was Phinehas Henderson, an able and distinguished lawyer, of Keene, N. H. His father was William Henry Thayer, M.D. Until the age of eighteen, young Thayer lived in the country, with full opportunity for the study of nature. The privilege was improved. Out-door life, in woods and fields, gave him a good physical and mental development, and a preparation for artist life. He began early to draw, and work in water-colors. Animals were his subjects, and at eight years of age his water-colorings of birds were good. From fifteen to eighteen years of age, he was a pupil of Chauncy Hall School. During this period he began to use oils, and much of his time out of school was given to painting. He began to paint dog portraits, upon orders, and sold them at first for $10; but before he left school was receiving $50, and had more orders for dogs and horses than he could attend to. All this was the outcome of native taste. His summers were spent in the country, painting landscapes and animals. His subjects included lions, tigers, and wolves, painted at Central Park, and other animals as occasion afforded. In 1875 he married, and went to Paris, where he remained four years, painting in L'École des Beaux Arts, under Lehmann at first, and afterward for three years under Gérôme. His work in Paris turned his attention in a new direction. His pictures have been exhibited in New York, Boston, Philadelphia, and Chicago, and in Paris, Munich, and London. They are distinguished by their strength of character and imagination. He is a sincere student of nature, and endeavors to reproduce with truthfulness whatever he attempts. His reproductions are spiritualized. His paintings have been exhibited at the Society of American Artists, of which he has been a member from its organization in 1879. Among them are "The Lady and Horse," "The Woman and Swan," "The Angel," "The Virgin Enthroned," and "A Virgin." Besides these have been landscapes, two of which were engraved, one for "Scribner's Monthly," and the other for Hamerton's "Graphic Arts of the Nineteenth Century." In 1878, while in Paris, he sent to the annual exhibition of the National Academy of Design in New York, a painting, of which one of the art-critics wrote the following: "One of the most interesting pictures in the exhibition is Mr. Thayer's 'Sleep.' It is a small canvas, and its elements are few and simple. An infant is lying in its crib, with its arms encircling a small pug, which like itself, is fast asleep." Of the Exhibition of 1882, it is said, "The most striking and successful picture of the exhibition is Mr. Thayer's "Lady and Horse," a masterly composition, admirable as a piece of portraiture, and showing dignity, breadth, and largeness of style in its treatment. It is a portrait of a lady in a plain, unornamented dress of quiet olive green, standing with one arm thrown around her horse's head. The light of the picture brings the face, with its refined and agreeable expression, into sufficient relief, but from that point is subdued away, and maintains and denotes the general harmony of the composition." In 1891 and 1892, "The Virgin Enthroned" was exhibited, first in the Museum of Fine Arts in Boston, and later in New York. The "Virgin Enthroned" is regarded as Mr. Thayer's best work. In 1893 he exhibited another picture, with the same figures in action. The artist has named it "A Virgin." The young girl is advancing, leading a child in each hand. During several years, Mr. Thayer received a limited number of pupils, who have exhibited a development highly creditable to his method of teaching, suggestive, with an attention to radical principles.

FOOTE, Mary Anna Hallock, novelist and artist, born at Milton-on-the-Hudson, N. Y., Nov. 19, 1847, where her father's family had lived on the same land since the grant from Queen Anne to Capt. Bond, from whom the Hallocks bought their tract when it was a forest wilderness. Her parents and grandparents on both sides were of English Quaker descent. She was educated at Poughkeepsie Female Collegiate Seminary. She early showed indications of a talent for drawing, and in her seventeenth year was sent to New York to the School of Design in Cooper Institute. She spent three winters in New York at Cooper Institute, and one winter in the studio of Samuel Frost Johnson, studying color. She also received special instruction in de-

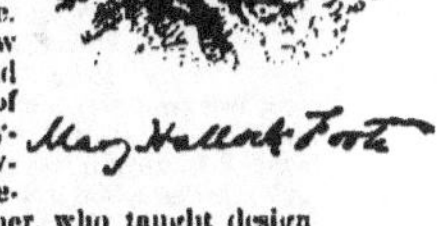

sign from Dr. William Rimmer, who taught design and anatomy at the Cooper Institute; and in drawing on wood from W. J. Linton, the English artist. Her life was exceedingly simple, sheltered, and quiet until her marriage on Feb. 9, 1876, with Arthur De Wint Foote, a civil engineer, who at the time of her marriage was in charge of mining work in California. When her husband's business made it necessary for her to travel extensively, living or stopping at New Almaden and Santa Cruz, Cal., Leadville, Colo., and other places, and scenes very unlike those of her early home. The experience thus gained she has utilized with great judgment and rare literary ability; after Bret Harte, no one else has given more vivid and effective delineations of the wilder and rougher phases of Western life. Besides "The Led Horse Claim," "John Bodewin's Testimony," "The Last Assembly Ball," "In Exile and Other Stories," "The Chosen Valley," "Coeur d'Alene," "The Cup of Trembling and Other Stories," she has published sundry short stories. Her too infrequent productions in the "Century" and other magazines are eagerly noted by discerning readers, who expect from her a higher combination of matter and treatment than they usually find elsewhere. She has illustrated her own tales, and various books and articles, always with point and force. She has also illustrated Longfellow's "Hanging of the Crane," "Skeleton in Armor," Whittier's "Mabel Martin," Hawthorne's "Scarlet Letter." She has three children.

DUNLAP, William, artist, was born in Perth Amboy, N. J., Feb. 19, 1766. The storm of the revolution naturally produced great confusion in New Jersey, and young Dunlap's education was almost utterly neglected until his father removed to the city of New York in 1777, at that time in the hands of the British. While in New York, the boy had the misfortune to lose one of his eyes by an accident. In the meantime he had shown great expertness in copying prints in India ink, and this accident appeared under the circumstances to be a misfortune which might imperil all his future career, as it was his intention to become a painter. By determination and industry, however, he succeeded in overcoming the difficulty, though habituating himself to drawing, using his pencil almost incessantly, under instruction from an artist. He was seventeen years of age when he began portrait painting, and in 1783 went to Rocky Hill, N. J., a short time before the disbanding of the Continental army, this being Washington's headquarters at the time when he issued his "Farewell Address to the Army." Here young Dunlap was privileged to paint the portrait of the commander-in-chief. In 1784 he went to England, where he became the pupil of Benjamin West. He remained abroad three years, and on returning to New York began portrait painting, but made little success. He accordingly abandoned art and took to literature, more especially dramatic writing. In 1789 he produced on the stage his play entitled "The Father." He continued to do literary work of a desultory character until 1796, when he became connected with the management of the Old John Street Theatre, and two years later was manager of the Park Theatre, and there produced his tragedy, "André," which proved a success. Here he remained for several seasons, but was eventually financially ruined. In the meantime, when not engaged in theatricals, he interested himself in certain business connections, and had married a sister of the wife of Dr. Dwight, of Yale College. For a time also he painted portraits in Albany and in Boston. He also wrote the memoirs of George Frederick Cooke, the celebrated English actor, and was for a time editor of a magazine called the "Recorder." In 1814 he was appointed paymaster-general of the militia of the State of New York, a post which he continued to hold for two years. He then began to paint regularly for a living, sometimes traveling from place to place in the United States and Canada, painting portraits with success, and at others devoting himself to the higher walks of art. He produced a series of large paintings, including "Christ Rejected," "Bearing the Cross," "Calvary," and "Death on the Pale Horse," which were publicly exhibited throughout the country and attained considerable reputation. Another work from his brush, entitled "The Historic Muse," was greatly admired. Mr. Dunlap became best known as the founder and early vice-president of the National Academy of Design in New York. In 1830 he began to lecture on fine-art topics, and attracted much attention. He also published, in 1832, a "History of the American Theatre," which was followed by his history of the "Arts of Design in the United States." In 1833 Mr. Dunlap received a complimentary benefit at the Park Theatre, from which he obtained about $2,500, a very large sum in those days. In 1839 he published the first volume of a "History of the State of New York." The second volume was unfinished at the time of his death. The latter part of his life was made comfortable and happy through the attention of his friends, who placed him beyond the reach of want by means of an exhibition of paintings for his benefit. Mr. Dunlap died in New York city, Sept. 28, 1839.

MILLET, Francis Davis, artist, was born at Mattapoisett, Mass., Nov. 3, 1846, son of Asa Millet, a well-known physician of East Bridgewater, Mass. He was fitted for college in the schools of Bridgewater, and as the civil war was then in progress, and the lad was too young to enlist as a volunteer soldier, he learned to drum, and enlisted as a drummer boy in the 60th Massachusetts regiment, with which he served between five and six months, when he returned to school and was matriculated at Harvard in the class of 1869, with which he was graduated. Having decided to devote himself to the profession of art, he, in 1871, went abroad to attend the Royal Art Academy, Antwerp. He studied under Van Lerius and De Keyser, and at the end of his first year won the silver medal of honor, and at the end of his second year, the gold medal. This rapid progress had never before been accomplished at the academy. While in Antwerp he was appointed secretary of the Massachusetts commission to the World's Fair at Vienna, and served as one of the jurors at the exhibition. He was at the same time correspondent of a New York newspaper. He afterwards visited Hungary, Roumania, and Constantinople, and studied art in Rome, Capri, and Venice for two years. At the breaking out of the Russo-Turkish war, in 1877, he was in Paris and accepted an offer from the New York "Herald" to go to Roumania as war correspondent, serving first this paper and then the London "Daily News" throughout the campaign, crossing the mountains in the winter with Gourko. He also sent illustrations to the London "Graphic." He received from Roumania the iron cross, from Russia the military crosses of St. Anne and Stanislas, and the war medals of Russia and Roumania. In 1878 he was a juror of fine arts at the World's Fair, Paris. In 1885 he received a medal at the Exposition at New Orleans, and in 1887, one from the American Art Association. He designed the costumes for the representation of the "Œdipus Tyrannus" of Sophocles, given by Harvard students at Cambridge, in 1880. His portraits of Charles Francis Adams, Jr., and of Samuel L. Clemens were exhibited at the National Academy in New York in 1877, also "Bashi Bazouk" (1878); "The Window Seat" (1884); and "A Difficult Duet" (1886). In the spring of 1892 he accepted the position of director of decoration of the World's Columbian Exposition at Chicago, and served in that capacity during the periods of construction and of operation. Shortly after the opening of the exposition he took charge of all the ceremonies, festivities, and entertainments of all kinds as director of functions, and performed the duties of this office in addition to those above spoken of. He spends his summers in Broadway, Worcestershire, England, and his winters in New York city. He is a member of the National Academy of Design and the American Water-Color Society of New York, and the Royal Institute of Painters of London, also an honorary member of the American Institute of Architects.

TURNER, Charles Yardley, artist, was born in Baltimore, Md., 1850. He is descended from a family the older members of which belonged to the Society of Friends. His grandfather, John Turner, owner of Andover Mills, at the head of the Chester river, Kent co., Md., and his grandfather on his mother's side, Joseph Turner, were cousins, the latter was owner of the old mill property at Woodbury, Baltimore co., Md. He established a lumber business in Baltimore, John C. Turner, son of John Turner and the father of Charles Y. Turner, being a member of the firm. Charles Y. Turner was educated at the public schools in Baltimore, Md., and began his art studies at the Maryland Institute, where he was graduated in the night school. He failed to obtain the Peabody prize, although he was graduated in the artistic department, because he had been studying architecture. In 1872 he went to New York city, where he commenced at the beginning in the Academy schools, but his advance was so rapid, he obtained honorable mention in the life class to which he had been promoted before the close of the session. Entirely dependent upon his own resources for an education, he worked during the day in a photograph gallery and pursued his artistic studies in the evening. He spent three winters in the National Academy schools, taking a bronze medal and a prize in money. During the fourth winter he was elected a member of the board of control of the Art Students' League, of which he was one of the founders and incorporators, and the next year he was made vice-president. In 1876 he went abroad, returning to New York in 1881. He studied in Paris under J. Paul Laurens, M. Munkacsy and Léon Bonnat. His summers were mainly spent in Dordrecht, Holland, where he found the subject of his famous picture, "The Grand Canal at Dordrecht." His first exhibition was at the Water Color Society, 1882, where his "Dordrecht Milkmaid" was one of the events of the exhibit, which was readily sold, and led to the appreciation and disposition of his other works at fair prices. His reputation was assured, and honors were soon showered upon him. He was elected a member of the Water-Color Society, a member of the Society of American Artists, and afterwards chosen, first an associate of the Academy, and then full academician. He is also president of the Salmagundi Club, secretary of the Society of American Etchers. His Puritan subjects are particularly fine, and great favorites. Among the more noted, are "The Courtship of Myles Standish," "John Alden's Letter," "The Bridal Procession," "Martha Hilton," etc., etc. Some of these have been etched, and are among the most popular etchings in the market, and from this source he obtains a handsome royalty. At the age of forty-six he has now (1896) a reputation that many an older artist might envy.

LOW, Will Hicok, artist, was born in Albany, N.Y., May 31, 1853. His father, Addison Low, was a contracting engineer, with scholarly tastes, while his mother, Elirva Steele, was the daughter of Samuel Steele, the veteran educator and a lineal descendant of Richard Steele of "Spectator" fame. On account of ill health, his schooling was intermittent, and most of his time was spent in drawing, when he should have been studying. When seventeen years old, he visited New York, and submitted a drawing to Mr. Bowen of the "Independent," who agreed to accept it if drawn on wood. This was his first attempt on wood, but when completed he received a check for $50, which was his start in life. His father met with serious financial reverses at this time, which threw the young man upon his own resources, and for two years he drew for the illustrated papers in New York. Although without other schooling than the study of nature, without direction he did such acceptable work that he attracted the attention of the Harper's and Appleton's, which gave him his first step to better things. He added to his income by a weekly letter to the "Albany Times" and found time to paint a picture in oils, which was exhibited in 1872. Recognizing the need of study, he went to Paris in

1870 through the kind efforts of his friend, E. S. Palmer, the sculptor, and after a few months' study under Gérôme, he became a pupil of Carolus-Duran, in whose studios he began work in color. For two years he struggled on with many discouragements, earning an irregular livelihood from work sent to America, but he persevered. From a sudden inspiration he began painting "Reverie," a life-size figure of a woman with a greyhound, for the Salon. Although discouraged by his master, he completed it in six weeks, and it was accepted, which greatly encouraged him. It is now in the possession of John Boyd Thatcher. The next year he exhibited in the Salon, a full length portrait of Albani in the character of "Lucia di Lammermoor," and a landscape entitled "Le jour de Mort," now belonging to Smith College. In 1874 he met Robert Louis Stevenson, who exercised over him an influence akin to worship, and they soon became inseparable friends. After five years' study in Paris, Mr. Low returned to New York to find art circles agitated over the attitude of the National Academy of Design, towards the new generation of artists, who, like Mr. Low, had sought knowledge abroad. The outcome was the establishment of the Society of American Artists, of which Mr. Low became a member. Time and mutual forbearance healed the misunderstanding, and the National Academy of Design in its present friendly rivalry lends the benefits of competition. To this institution, also, Mr. Low was elected a member in 1891, and has contributed to the exhibition of both. To the former he exhibited the picture from the Salon, "A Gray Day on the Seine" (owned by Isaac T. Williams); "Calling Home the Cows," "Skipper Ireson" (owned by John Boyd Thatcher), "Arcades," "Chloe," "Narcissa," "'Neath Apple Boughs," "In an Old Garden," "The Portrait" (a rendering of the old Greek story of the invention of painting); "Aurora" (which is now in the Metropolitan Museum, New York). To the exhibition of the National Academy of Design he has contributed "Portrait of

Mrs. L." "Men are April when they Woo," "Telling the Bees," "By the Fountain," "May," "Purple and Gold," "Love Disarmed." "Skipper Ireson" was a large composition of some forty figures, undertaken when he held the notion that he should confine himself to American subjects, and before his maturer judgment showed him that sentiments of humanity and not the local customs give the painter his best opportunity. Upon Mr. Low's return to America, he practically had to begin his art life over again, with much the same struggle for existence that he had known before he went to Paris, and was forced to return to illustrating work for magazines, when by right of talent he should be painting. In 1879 he was associated with John LaFarge, with whom he did decorative painting, and acquired his first knowledge of stained glass. He was the principal assistant in the painted decoration of the home of Cornelius Vanderbilt. In 1881 he accepted the position of teacher in the antique and life classes of the Women's Art School of Cooper Union, where he continued three years, and formed the first class in painting from life which the school ever had. In 1885 came the turning point in his career. J. B. Lippincott & Co., attracted by his talent, gave him a commission to illustrate Keats' "Lamia" which he did with all his heart. This work made so great a success in both America and England that the artist was commissioned to illustrate the "Odes and Sonnets" in the same way. The terms were so liberal that Mr. Low decided to execute the work in Europe, and after an absence of ten years, returned to Paris, where he renewed his intimacy with Stevenson. It was during this visit that Stevenson was brought into fame by Gladstone's statement that he was so delighted with "Treasure Island," that although worn out from work in the house of commons, he sat up all night devouring it. After spending five months in Paris he went to Florence and then returned to New York, where he finished the "Odes," which repeated the success of "Lamia," so far as the critical estimate of his work is concerned, and gave him a wide reputation. For these illustrations of Keats he received a medal from the Paris Universal Exposition of 1889. He engaged in making cartoons for stained glass windows for several churches, and painting the canvasses which were exhibited as before stated. Work now poured in upon him. In 1892 he was commissioned to paint the ceiling for the Hotel Waldorf, and again went to Paris. Upon his return he was commissioned to design the Diploma of Awards for the World's Fair. The direction of Mr. Low's work has remained essentially the same and has an excellence peculiarly its own. He has made the new design of the one dollar bill for the U. S. government. Mr. Low in late years, has met with considerable success in the field of literature, his articles on art subjects finding a welcome acceptance by the leading magazines.

LIPPINCOTT, William Henry, artist, was born at Philadelphia, Pa., Dec. 6, 1840. He is the son of Isaac Lippincott and Emily Hoover, his ancestry being English on his father's side and Dutch on his mother's. He commenced the study of art at the Pennsylvania Academy of Fine Arts, and became a designer of illustrations for publications, and later a scenic artist, in which latter vocation he won an extended reputation. He practiced scenic art for some six years, still continuing his studies at the easel, and in 1874 went to Europe, completing his higher artistic studies in Paris as a pupil of Léon Bonnat. He remained in Paris until 1882, when he returned to America and established his studio in New York city, though he has since made various professional excursions abroad and in the United States. He is a member of the American Water-Color Society, and of the New York Etching Club, and an associate member of the National Academy of Design, from 1884. For three years he held the professorship of the painting class at the National Academy, and is well known as one of the most competent instructors in his art in the United States. He is a painter of portraits, figures, compositions, and landscapes, an exhibitor at the Paris Salon, and a regular contributor to the American art exhibitions, and he continues to devote a portion of his time to scenic painting, to illustrating for the publications, and to etching. His most important pictures are: "Un jour de Congé" (Paris Salon, 1879); "The Duck's Breakfast" (Centennial Exhibition, Philadelphia, 1876); "The Pink of Old Fashion" (American Water-Color Society, 1882); "Helena" (National Academy of Design, 1883); "Afternoon Tea" (N. A.D., 1885); "Infantry in Arms" (N.A.D., 1887); "Love's Ambush" (N.A D., 1890). See "Artists of the Nineteenth Century and their Works" (Clement & Hutton), "Cyclopædia of Painters and Painting" (Champlain & Perkins), etc.

READ, Thomas Buchanan, artist and poet, was born in Chester county, Pa., March 12, 1822. His father was a farmer in reduced circumstances, and the boy's youth was spent in poverty and hardship. He had but little schooling, but devoted all his spare moments to reading, of which he was passionately fond. Upon his father's death, in 1839, his mother apprenticed him to a tailor, but he ran away and took service with a cigar-maker in Philadelphia. He soon tired of that humdrum life, and after following many employments, drifted to Cincinnati, O., where he was befriended by the sculptor S. V. Clevenger. Having gained some rudiments of artistic and general education, he roamed about the country, painting signs, and occasionally portraits, and at one time held an engagement with a theatrical troupe at Dayton. He afterward learned to paint in oils, and made rapid progress in portrait-painting. He returned to Cincinnati the next year, and attracted the attention of Nicholas Longworth, who recognized his talents, and assisted him to open a studio as a portrait painter. He gained some reputation from having painted the portraits of distinguished men, such as Benjamin Harrison. When business was dull he wandered from town to town, painting signs, giving public entertainments, and even returning to cigar-making when all else failed. Thinking he could find a wider field for his talents, he removed to New York in 1841, but failing of meeting immediate success, he went the next year to Boston. Here he made his first attempts at literary work, publishing in the "Courier," several lyric poems, and contributing some desultory pieces to the periodicals. He moved about in a restless way, painting and writing, but finally, in 1846, settled in Philadelphia, where he published his first volume of poems. The next year he published "Lays and Poems," which was followed by "Female Poets of America." He wrote a prose romance, entitled "The Pilgrim of the Great St. Bernard," which was published serially in a magazine, but was afterwards issued in book form. His restless spirit led him to visit Europe in 1850, and again in 1853 with his wife and daughter, where he devoted himself to the study and practice of art in Florence and Rome, where he had his first real opportunities for artistic study. Read had great original talent, and his work is notable in view of his sad lack of early advantages. His paintings deal mostly with allegorical subjects, and teem with poetic fancies, with which his mind was full. He had, however, a much greater facility of expression in poetry than in painting. The best known of his pictures are: "The Spirit of the Waterfall," "The Lost Pleiad," "The Star of Bethlehem," and "Cleopatra and her Barge." He painted portraits of Mrs. Browning, the ex-Queen of Naples, George M. Dallas, Henry W. Longfellow, and others. The group of Longfellow's children, so popular in photograph form, was the production of his brush, also "Undine," and "Sheridan's Ride." This illustrated his most famous poem, which was written for the elocutionist, J. E. Murdock, and was read throughout the country for the benefit of the sanitary commission. His genius of expression seemed to flow in every direction, and he did some good work also in sculpture, producing a bust of Sheridan which commanded universal admiration. While abroad he produced "The New Pastoral," which is the most elaborate of his compositions. It presents a constant succession of truthful and pleasing images in the healthy vein of Goldsmith and Bloomfield. It is a series of thirty-seven sketches, describing the beautiful regions of Pennsylvania along the Susquehanna. It portrays the pioneer life of a family of emigrants, and is so truthfully drawn that it is no less valuable to history as it is attractive as poetry. It was handled with an artist's eye for natural and moral beauty. Though he lived much abroad, his spirit responded quickly to home throes and patriotic occasions. During the civil war he returned to America and wrote many patriotic songs, which he himself recited to the soldiers in the camp, and for their benefit in the North. In 1856 he published "The House by the Sea," which was more dramatic, and attracted wide attention. Then appeared "Sylvia," "A Voyage to Ireland," and "A Summer Story," which consisted chiefly of war poems. In 1857 a collection of his "Rural Poems" appeared in London. A choice edition of Read's poems, delicately illustrated by Henry Meadows, was published by Trübner in 1852, and his "Complete Poetical Works" were published in Boston in 1860. His last long poem was "The Good Samaritan." Mr. Read divided the later years of his life between Cincinnati, Philadelphia, and Rome, but spent the greater portion of his time in the latter city. His earlier poems are the inspiration of foreign song and story, two of the most exquisite of which are "Drifting" and "The Closing Scene." It was upon one of his visits to this country that the artist-poet died. He was stricken down with pneumonia, and after a short illness, died in New York, May 11, 1872.

SANDHAM, Henry, artist, was born in Montreal, Canada, in 1842, of English parentage. At an early age he determined to become an artist, which wish was so strongly opposed by his father that the boy, in order to achieve his ideal, left home, and began, unaided, to work out the problem of his life. He therefore secured a situation in a large business house devoted to the sale of art products, spending every leisure moment, and most of his nights, engaged in study. Aided and encouraged by artist friends, his talent was speedily developed. His works soon found a place in the collections of connoisseurs and art patrons; one of his pictures was selected by the Princess Louise, as a representative painting for the national gallery at Ottawa, and in 1880 he was elected a member of the Royal Canadian Academy. In the year following, and in order that he might devote himself wholly to his art, Mr. Sandham retired from active business, withdrawing as full partner from the house where, a few years previously he had occupied but a subordinate position. After visiting England and France, for the purpose of art study, he settled in Boston, where he devoted himself principally to book illustration, making such rapid progress that he soon occupied a leading position among American illustrators. He did not, however, neglect his painting, and being a steady and rapid worker, has produced as many pictures each year as those artists who are known only by their pictures. Indeed, few American painters have contributed so largely to collections in the United States and Canada as Mr. Sandham;

portrait-painting having been one of his most fruitful fields of endeavor. "The Dawn of Liberty," a large historical painting, finished in 1886, was purchased by the Lexington Historical Society, and now hangs in the Lexington town hall. Among others of Mr. Sandham's pictures are: "Gathering Sea Rack," "Return from the Hunt," "Salmon Fishing on the Godbout Beacon Light, St. John Harbor" (now in the Canadian national gallery), "On Montreal Mountain" (owned by the Ontario Society of Artists), "The Battle of Lexington," Portrait of Robert Swan (in the Winthrop School, of Boston), Portrait of Joseph T. Duryea, D. D., "Zuni Chiefs," "Santa Barbara," "Marine Subject," "Shelter Island Landscape," "The Camp Steps at San Gabrielle," "Fishing Camp," "Restegouch," "Founding of Maryland," etc. By virtue of strength of color, vigor of line, and virility of form, Mr. Sandham ranks among the best American artists, while in the clear, unclouded art sense, he is unequaled.

OPPER, Frederick Burr, artist, was born in Madison, Lake co., O., Jan. 2, 1857. His father emigrated from Austro-Hungary when a young man, and engaged in mercantile pursuits in this country. His mother was a Miss Burr, of Madison, O., and belonged to the Stratford branch of the Burr family, the founder of which, Benjamin Burr, was one of the original settlers of Hartford in 1635. He received his education in the public schools of Madison, and when fourteen entered the printing office of the Madison "Gazette." After working there for nearly a year he removed to New York city, and while employed in a mercantile establishment, made during his leisure, sketches, which he sold to humorous publications. He practiced drawing, and attended one term of the evening class, Cooper Union. He gave up his position in the store, to work for publications, among them "Wild Oats," "Budget of Fun," and "The Comic Monthly." About this time he formed the acquaintance of Frank Beard, a talented designer, and entered his studio as a pupil and assistant, and several of his drawings appeared in the old "Scribner's" (now "Century"), and "St. Nicholas Magazine." In 1877 he was regularly engaged on the artistic staff of Frank Leslie's publishing house as a humorous draughtsman, and at times also one of the special artists. He remained there until he joined the staff of "Puck" in 1881, where he has since remained (1894). In this periodical the greater part of his work has appeared, probably more than 3,000 drawings. Two collections of these drawings have been published in book form, entitled "Puck's Opper Book" and "This Funny World." They have met with an extensive sale. His taste in drawing is in the direction of realism and the humorous actualities of real life, and his subjects are as far as possible based on truth and nature, which enhances greatly their artistic and commercial value.

FULLER, George, artist, was born at Deerfield, Mass., Jan. 16, 1822. He had no early artistic advantages, but at twenty he became a pupil of Henry Kirke Brown, at Albany, N. Y., whose portrait he subsequently painted, and the exhibition of which picture in New York, in 1857, was the means of making him an associate national academician. In 1859 he left New York for a short trip to Europe for study and travel, in the course of which he was strongly impressed by the study of the old masters, especially the works of Correggio, whose delicacy of sentiment and refinement of color appealed to his feelings more than the stronger and more masculine productions of other Italian painters; but, unlike most Americans who pursue their studies abroad, he did not identify himself with any of the schools then in vogue. Mr. Fuller did not have the pushing qualities which are so often necessary to secure recognition, and during his residence in New York he received but little encouragement. Therefore, on the death of his father, soon after his return to this country, he felt it his duty to withdraw from his artistic career to his native village, and devoted the larger part of his time and attention to farming and looking out for the family. Although his sojourn of the best years of his life on a country farm would appear to have been fatal to his progress in art, yet, on the contrary, it doubtless had a beneficial effect on him. He did not by any means wholly throw up his chosen work, although the duties of a farmer's life prevented any continuous application to painting. It was during this sojourn in the country that he was able to accomplish what perhaps would have been impossible if he had depended on his painting for his support—the development of a method by which he could express his appreciation of the charm in mysterious effect of light, and his acute sense of beauty of form. After fifteen years of farm-life he went to Boston, and became a professional artist, meeting with large success. He was a member of the Boston Art Club, the St. Botolph Club, and the Paint and Clay Club. He was preëminently an idealist, possessed of a genius for dreamy, light-effects, somewhat akin to Corot's. He believed that the province of art was to depict the beauties of nature, not its defects. He had an exceptional gift for subordinating unimportant details in figure, portrait, and landscape. Among his best-known works are, "Winifred Dysart," the masterpiece of his types of the loveliness of maidenhood; and "Arethusa," than which no more chaste and poetical rendering of the female figure has been seen in modern times. He died at Brookline, Mass., March 21, 1884. The same year the Boston Art Museum gave a memorial exhibition of his paintings.

REID, Robert, artist, was born at Stockbridge, Mass., July 29, 1863, of old New England stock. His father, Jared Reid, Jr., was well known for thirty years as a teacher and head of the famous Edward Place School for boys. The historic Jonathan Edwards' House was his birth place. His mother was of the old Massachusetts Dwight family, a descendant of Brig.-Gen. Joseph Dwight. Young Reid began the study of art in the school of drawing and painting, Museum of Fine Arts, Boston, in the winter of 1880, where for three years he was assistant instructor; went to New York and studied at the Art Students' League for the winter; became a member of the board of control of that institution; went abroad in October, 1885, and studied for four years in the Académie Julien, under Boulanger and Léfebvre, and had a studio for the summer in Etaples pas-de-Calais; exhibited every year in the Salon, and last in the Exposition of 1889; was a member of the Paris Association of American Artists, and returned to New York, in July 1889. He has become well known as a portrait painter, and more recently made great success with mural decorations, being one of the eight New York artists who painted the frescoes of the domes of the Liberal Arts Building in the World's Fair Exposition, for which he received one of the medals struck in honor of the master artists of the world's Columbian Exposition. His latest decorations are for the interior of one of the great ocean Greyhounds, building by the Cramps for the new American line, the International Navigation Co. This is a very important work, marking as it does a new departure in marine architecture and decoration. Mr. Reid's pictures and portraits are well-known and owned in all parts of the country. He has recently turned his attention to the painting of the nude, and his latest picture painted for Stanford White, Esq., was one of the successes of the spring exhibition of the Society of American Artists, of which Mr. Reid is a member. Mr. Reid is one of the instructors of painting at the Art Students' League and the Cooper Institute. He is a member of several clubs in New York, among them the Players and Fencers.

MERRILL, Frank Thayer, artist, was born at Boston, Mass., in 1848. Much of his talent is to be attributed to his mother, who not only herself possessed the genuine art-instinct, but strove to foster it in her son. Young Merrill was educated in the public schools of Boston, and subsequently studied art in his native city at the Lowell Institution and at the Museum of Fine Arts. With the exception of a few months abroad, during which time he studied in Paris, his entire life has been spent in Boston. He has been chiefly occupied with illustrations for books and magazines, finding opportunity for but little performance in other branches of his art. He brought back from Europe, however, a number of water-color studies from the costumed model and scenes in the George Eliot country. Among Mr. Merrill's earliest work as an illustrator, were drawings made for "Pioneers in the settlement of America," a large historical work to which many of his fellow craftsmen contributed. For Longfellow's "John Endicott," one of the "New England Tragedies," published in an edition of the poet issued some years since, Mr. Merrill furnished a number of illustrations of the persecutions of the Quakers in the Boston of 1665, and a little later he drew nearly 200 pictures for Miss Alcott's "Little Women." In company with E. H. Garrett, Mr. Merrill illustrated "Curfew Must not Ring To-night," and with J. J. Harley, Mark Twain's tale of "The Prince and the Pauper." He subsequently made many illustrations for a series of George Eliot's works, and Moore's "Lalla Rookh." His work

has, however, largely concerned itself with standard editions of the English classics, including, besides that of George Eliot, already mentioned, Bulwer, Thackeray, Blackmore, Longfellow, Holmes, Whittier, etc. He has also produced a large number of drawings for illustrated editions of Dumas. Other publications that have been enriched by designs from Mr. Merrill's pencil are: Thackeray's "Mahogany Tree;" Longfellow's "Courtship of Miles Standish;" "My Days and Nights on the Battlefield;" Scott's "Lay of the Imprisoned Huntsman;" Edward Everett Hale's "The Man without a Country;" Irving's "Rip Van Winkle" (which drew forth a letter of warm appreciation from Joseph Jefferson), with hundreds of pictures for juvenile magazines, etc.

TICKNOR, George, author and educator, was born in Boston, Mass., Aug. 1, 1791. He early showed great taste for reading, and upon being fitted for college by his father, Elisha Ticknor, a successful merchant of Boston, entered Dartmouth as a junior, at the age of fourteen, and was graduated in 1807, having, as he thought, learned very little. His general studies were continued nearly three years longer, under Dr. Gardiner of Trinity Church, and in 1810 he began to read law in the office of an eminent lawyer of Boston, and was admitted to the bar in 1813. He practised for one year, and then being able to consult his tastes, determined that his avocation lay in the direction of a literary life, as his father's means were sufficient to enable him to follow his bent. After a winter jaunt through Virginia, and a visit to Jefferson at Monticello, he sailed for Europe in April, 1815, and spent nearly two years at Göttingen, giving his main attention to languages. His appointment to a chair at Harvard in 1817 did not necessitate his immediate return, but gave a special direction to his studies, which were carried on in Paris, Rome, Madrid and other European capitals, where he studied the literatures of each country. While abroad he met Goethe, Humboldt, Mme. de Staël, Chateaubriand, Bunsen, Niebuhr, Scott and other persons of distinction, and collected a valuable library, which by additions grew to be one of the finest collections in the country, especially so in Spanish literature, on which it was not excelled even in Europe. Mr. Ticknor returned in June, 1819, his character matured by unusual experience of men, with rare learning and accomplishments, and with a taste cultivated and disciplined by acquaintance with the best society of Europe. He was inducted at Harvard, Aug. 10th, as Smith professor of the French and Spanish languages and literatures, and college professor of *belles-lettres.* In this double post, which he held for sixteen years, at a small salary, he did good and abundant work, organized his new and important department, and bore a leading part in those reforms which changed Harvard from an old-fashioned college to a modern university. Its literature had previously hardly extended beyond the classics; but Ticknor's lectures on Dante, Shakespeare, Milton, Goethe, etc., stimulated his students and drew auditors from without. More than half his instructions, he said, were "given voluntarily, neither required nor contemplated by the statutes." In 1825, returning from a southern trip, during which he had visited Madison and Jefferson, he found in Philadelphia Drs. Follen and Beck, needy exiles from Germany, and procured tutorships for them at Harvard. Resigning his chair in 1835, he spent three years in Germany, Italy, France, etc., meeting Metternich and Wordsworth, and carrying on the preparation of his great work. "The History of Spanish Literature" appeared in three volumes at the close of 1849 in New York and London, and within three years appeared in German and Spanish translations. Its recognition was rapid and extensive, both by scholars and the reading public. A London critic said there were "not six men in Europe able to review it." Motley called it "an honor to yourself and to American literature." Hallam wrote, "It supersedes all others, and will never be superseded." Rogers exclaimed, "How these Bostonians do work!" Three subsequent editions have appeared at home, two of them revised and enlarged. Feeling his debt to libraries abroad, Dr. Ticknor took a leading part in establishing the Boston Public Library. He induced Mr.

Everett to join him in this enterprise, and they formed the sub-committee which drew up a report initiating the project in 1852. The library was opened in 1854, in two small rooms, with 12,000 volumes, from which humble beginning it has grown to its present magnificent proportions. Dr. Ticknor gave it fourteen years of zealous labor, and in 1856-57 spent more than a year abroad, chiefly in its interest, often staying so late at the Berlin booksellers' shops with Karl Brandes, that they needed special police permission to go home unmolested. He presented the library with many volumes during his lifetime, and willed to it his fine collection of Spanish books. While the civil war was in progress, he was a liberal contributor to the Federal cause,

both in money and in other ways possible to a man seventy years of age. During his earlier period, he found solace in writing the life of his friend Prescott, the historian. The book appeared in 1864, and was described by Lord Carlisle as "simple, complete, unaffected, and thus entirely suited to the character and qualities of its subject." Bancroft, with his usual enthusiasm, called it "a sermon to the young, and a refreshment to the old, the best monument that one man of letters ever raised to his friendship for another." Mr. Ticknor received the degree of LL.D. from both Harvard and Brown in 1850, and from Dartmouth in 1858. Though not a profound or originative mind, he had fine powers of acquisition and retention, great industry, a resolute will, a calm, steady judgment, and a dominating regard for truth. The purity and dignity of his character commanded general respect. He embodied the quieter and more conservative ideals of Boston, and illustrated in his entire life the virtues of the gentleman and scholar. His "Life, Letters and Journals," appeared in two volumes in 1876. The "Nation" said of Mr. Ticknor, "Probably no American led a life richer in that class of associations and interests which belong properly to literary biography." The "Saturday Review" said of him, "In every capital of Europe he had not only acquaintances but friends, and at home he seemed to have known every eminent contemporary." He died in Boston, Jan. 26, 1871.

SPOFFORD, Ainsworth Rand, librarian of congress, was born at Gilmanton, N. H., Sept. 12, 1825. He is a lineal descendant of John Spofford of Yorkshire, England, who settled at Georgetown, Mass., in 1638, and is a son of Rev. L. A. Spofford, a clergyman of New Hampshire, and later a missionary in several western states, and founder of a number of churches. He obtained a good English and classical education under a private tutor, and in his early youth developed that innate love for literature and absorbing passion for books which gave bent to his later career. In 1844 he went to Cincinnati, O., where he became a bookseller and publisher. He spent his leisure time in studying the modern languages and in literary pursuits, and in 1850 was one of the founders of the Literary Club, a vigorous intellectual organization of that city. In

1859 he became an assistant editor of the Cincinnati "Daily Commercial." Mr. Spofford removed to Washington in 1861, where he was appointed first assistant in the library of congress. His eminent fitness marked him for promotion, and in 1864 he was made librarian-in-chief, which office he has since held. The law of 1870, which makes the national library the office for all records of copyright, and the permanent depository for all copyright publications, was enacted through his influence. When Mr. Spofford entered the library in 1861, it had but 70,000 volumes. This number has been increased (1894) to nearly 700,000 volumes and 220,000 pamphlets. About 25,000 volumes are added annually. The library at present is in the capitol. In his annual report for 1872 Mr. Spofford first called attention to the fact that a new library building was an absolute necessity. He repeated this suggestion until favorable action was taken by congress in the passage of a bill appropriating $585,000 for the purchase of a site. Four acres of land were obtained about 500 yards east of the capitol, and upon this site a magnificent library building, the finest in the world, has been erected at a cost of $6,000,000. It is built of New Hampshire granite, while marble from every quarter of the globe is represented inside. The counsels of the librarian were largely followed in the planning of the building, which is designed to meet the demands of the library of congress for a century, having a capacity of 4,500,000 volumes. Mr. Spofford has acquired a wide reputation not only for his executive and administrative ability in the judicious management of the library, but also for his vast and comprehensive knowledge of books and their contents, and his wonderful capacity to give direction to legislators and others who desire to obtain information from the books of the library. His long experience, extensive reading, excellent scholarship, retentive memory, and fine literary judgment have aided him in successfully performing the onerous duties of his responsible office. He has achieved honorable distinction in his chosen field of work, both as a scholar and a librarian. Mr. Spofford has written extensively for the periodical press on historical, economic, and literary topics. He has published catalogues of the library of congress; "The American Almanac and Treasury of Facts," an annual compiled from official

sources from 1878 to 1889; "The Library of Choice Literature" (ten volumes, 1881-88); "Library of Wit and Humor" (1884); "Manual of Parliamentary Rules" (1884); and other works. He has also contributed articles to a number of the standard cyclopædias. He is a member of numerous learned societies. Amherst College gave him the degree of LL.D. in 1884.

POOLE, William Frederick, librarian, was born at Salem, Mass., Dec. 24, 1821, a descendant of John Poole, who was in 1635 the leading proprietor of Reading, Mass., named for the English town from which he came. William was the second son of Eliza Wilder, of Keene, N. H., and Ward Poole, who carried on a tanning business in Salem. The third son, Henry Ward Poole (A. M., Yale College), was a man of considerable note as a professor in the National College of Mines in the city of Mexico, and as a writer on the abstruse mathematical laws of musical sounds, contributing extensively to the knowledge of the subject as presented in A. J. Ellis's translation of Helmholtz's "Sensations of Tone." William received his early education at the common schools of Danvers. When he was about twelve years of age, he left school, and took up, successively, the jeweler's business and his father's trade of tanning. The practical knowledge of leather that he thus obtained, served him in good stead in later years, with respect to bookbinding, upon which he was an acknowledged authority. At seventeen he resumed his studies, and in 1842 entered Yale College. At the close of the first year, lack of means obliged him to teach for three years, after which he returned to college, and was graduated in 1849. His love of books and the fact that he was older than most of his fellow-students, had gained for him the position of assistant librarian, and afterward librarian of his college society, the "Brothers in Unity," which owned an exceptionally fine collection of books, numbering nearly 10,000 volumes. It was while thus engaged, that Mr. Poole, observing that the exceedingly valuable literary material embodied in many magazines and reviews was almost unused, undertook the compilation of a simple index to such contents. The result of his labors proved so useful that he was eventually induced to publish it, and in 1848 there appeared a small octavo of 154 pages, indexing 560 volumes, and with the compiler's name modestly omitted from the title page. No sooner was the publication of the work announced, than orders from abroad exceeded the entire edition. For some time after his graduation,

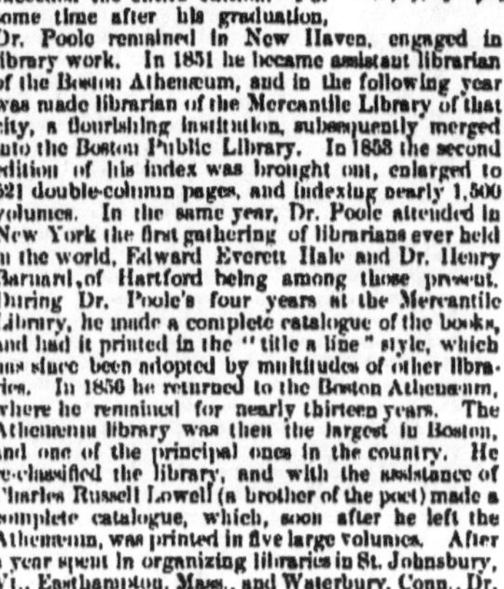

Dr. Poole remained in New Haven, engaged in library work. In 1851 he became assistant librarian of the Boston Athenæum, and in the following year was made librarian of the Mercantile Library of that city, a flourishing institution, subsequently merged into the Boston Public Library. In 1853 the second edition of his index was brought out, enlarged to 521 double-column pages, and indexing nearly 1,500 volumes. In the same year, Dr. Poole attended in New York the first gathering of librarians ever held in the world, Edward Everett Hale and Dr. Henry Barnard, of Hartford being among those present. During Dr. Poole's four years at the Mercantile Library, he made a complete catalogue of the books, and had it printed in the "title a line" style, which has since been adopted by multitudes of other libraries. In 1856 he returned to the Boston Athenæum, where he remained for nearly thirteen years. The Athenæum library was then the largest in Boston, and one of the principal ones in the country. He re-classified the library, and with the assistance of Charles Russell Lowell (a brother of the poet) made a complete catalogue, which, soon after he left the Athenæum, was printed in five large volumes. After a year spent in organizing libraries in St. Johnsbury, Vt., Easthampton, Mass., and Waterbury, Conn., Dr.

Poole in 1869, took charge of the public library at Cincinnati, remaining there until 1873, when he was called to the prospective Public Library of Chicago. Here, his abilities found full scope in the organizing and building up of this great institution, which soon ranked second only to the Boston Library. At the end of the fourteen years consumed by this work, Dr. Poole took charge of the Chicago Newberry Library of Reference, an institution, which, founded by a bequest of nearly $3,000,000 from Walter L. Newberry, presented the best opportunity yet offered in this country, for the organization of a fine reference library. Dr. Poole contributed many papers to the reports issued by the U. S. bureau of education, one of which, "The Organization and Management of Libraries" (1876), had been extensively used, as the only available practical manual of library work. The methods he advocated, while of the simplest, were at the same time most effective. He was an earnest exponent of the soundest and sanest views, as to the function of the public library, and its relation to the community. His arguments against the exclusion of good fiction from public libraries were no less clear and conclusive. With respect to the library structure, his ideas were most progressive. In 1881 a circular by him was issued by the U. S. bureau of education, in which he outlined a building so different from all previous library architecture, that but few were courageous enough to accept it. That it has slowly but surely gained adherents, however, is proven by the fact that the Newberry Library building was planned in accordance with his long-cherished views. Besides these many technical publications, Dr. Poole's work as a critic of American history-writing occupies no small place, and has been most valuable in the establishment of important historical data. In 1887 he was elected president of the American Historical Association, and in 1882 received the honorary degree of LL. D. from the Northwestern University. His chief claim to recognition rests, however, upon the "Index" to periodical literature already referred to. As a result of urgent demands for a later edition of the "Index," which was then twenty-three years behind the times (and was still said to be the most useful single volume in many libraries). Dr. Poole, in 1876, formed a plan for a co-operative method of continuing it. Over fifty librarians shared the undertaking, which was, however, so large an enterprise, that it was not until 1882 that the third edition appeared, a royal octavo volume of 1,442 pages, indexing 6,205 volumes, which was twelve times as many as the first edition, and four times as many as the second. Two five-year supplements, issued in 1887 and 1892, have given this "Index" the proportions of a monumental work. To Dr. Poole, more than to any other one man does American librarianship owe its character as a distinct calling. On Nov. 22, 1854, Dr. Poole was married to Fanny M. Gleason. He died at Evanston, Ill., March 1, 1894.

RICE, William, clergyman and librarian, was born in Springfield, Mass., March 10, 1821. He is a lineal descendant in the seventh generation of Edmund Rice, who, born about 1594, emigrated from England to Sudbury, Mass., in 1639, removing later to Marlboro, where he died May 3, 1663. His grandfather, Nathan Rice, was a revolutionary soldier whose wife, Hephzibah Allen, a relative of the famous Ethan Allen, was a native of Concord, Mass., and lived there at the time of the Concord fight. Dr. Rice's father, William Rice, was born in Belchertown, Mass., in 1788. He went to Wilbraham when a boy and lived there till 1817, when he removed to Springfield, and engaging in business as a merchant, became a most honored citizen. He was elected register of deeds in 1830, and county treasurer in 1838, which office he held for many years, regardless of the changes of party. The mother of Dr. Rice,

Jerusha Warriner, was a lineal descendant of William Warriner who settled in Springfield in 1640. Dr. Rice received his education in the Springfield public schools and at Wesleyan academy, Wilbraham. He was graduated with honor from the latter when he was nineteen. One year later he joined the New England conference of the Methodist Episcopal church, and at once assumed charge of the church in North Malden. For sixteen years he continued this charge, meanwhile receiving many of the best appointments in the conference. Ill health at length compelled him to give up his work as a pastor, and he returned to Springfield in 1857. He was popular as a preacher, and his tact and ready sympathy made him eminently successful as a pastor. Alive to all present issues, he was especially interested in the anti-slavery agitation. In 1856 he was elected to the general conference of the Methodist Episcopal church, and was at that time one of the anti-slavery leaders in the controversy relating to slavery in the church. In 1876 he was again a delegate to the general conference, and was made a member of the committee for the revision of the Methodist hymnal. Of this committee he was an active and efficient member, and when the revision was completed, the work was published under his editorial supervision. He is the author of a "Pastor's Manual," and an octavo volume, "Moral and Religious Quotations from the Poets." Dr. Rice is a leader also in the educational work of the Methodist church. He was elected a trustee of Wesleyan Academy in 1859, was secretary of the board of trustees for eighteen years, and has been the president for twelve years. Wesleyan University, Middletown, Conn., conferred upon him the degree of A.M. in 1853, and in 1876 the degree of D.D. Since 1875 he has been one of the trustees of that university. These offices are not held by Dr. Rice as merely nominal trusts. He is active in the councils and committee work of both the academy and university, and has contributed efficiently to the growth and prosperity of both institutions. For eighteen years, too, he was a member of the Massa-

chusetts board of education, and for the same period was the most active member of the Springfield school committee. Dr. Rice's principal work, however, has been in connection with the Springfield City Library. Three years after his return to Springfield he became secretary and librarian of the City Library Association, having now (1895) occupied these positions for more than thirty-four years. He has had entire charge of the selection and classification of the books and the general supervision

of the library. His wide range of reading, liberal
views, cultivated taste, and sound judgment have
eminently fitted him for such work, and it is almost
wholly his efforts that have given the City Library of
Springfield so high a rank. The library first started
in rooms in the city hall. Dr. Rice at once began to
solicit subscriptions to its funds and donations of
books. A suitable building was at length erected
in 1871, at a cost of $100,000. A few years
later, before the library was made free, Dr. Rice
made an effort to ensure the adequate growth
of its reference department by securing endowments. As a result of this movement $30,000
had already, by 1894, been paid in and invested and
more than $100,000 in addition has been given in
legacies, which will come into the possession of the
association in the near future. The latest undertaking of Dr. Rice has been in connection with the
erection of a new art building. This building, now
nearly completed, and which cost $125,000, provides
not only for an art collection, but also for a museum
of natural history, with rooms for lectures and
study. At the annual meeting of the City Library
Association in 1892, Dr. Rice was honored by a
unanimous resolution to christen the new art building in his name. At his urgent request, however,
this resolution was recalled, although another was
immediately substituted, that "the present library
building of the City Library Association shall be
known henceforth as the William Rice Building, in
honor of the man whose devotion to the city and the
institution inspired its erection, and whose service
has filled it with treasures of knowledge and wisdom
for the free use of all the people." In 1843 Dr.
Rice was married to Caroline L. North, daughter of
William North, of Lowell. Their children are Rev.
William North Rice, Ph.D., LL.D., professor in
Wesleyan University; Edward H. Rice, A.M., for
several years a teacher in the public schools; Rev.
Charles F. Rice, D.D., a minister in the New England
conference of the Methodist church; and Caroline
L. Rice, A.M., wife of Prof. Morris B. Crawford,
of Wesleyan University.

BRETT, William Howard, librarian of the
Cleveland Public Library, was born in Trumbull
county, O., July 1, 1846. He is of New England
descent on his father's side,
being the seventh generation
from William Brett, who came
to Plymouth from England in
1630. Among his ancestry are
the New England families of
Alden, Howard, and Foote. On
the other side he is of Dutch
descent, his mother being a
Brokaw. He attended the public schools in Warren, O. During the civil war he shared, with
most boys of that time, the prevalent war fever, and made several unsuccessful attempts to
enter the army, each time being
either refused as too young,
or else reclaimed by his father. He finally succeeded in
April, 1864, in getting into the
171st Ohio regiment, and after the expiration of its
term of service, re-enlisted in the 196th Ohio, and was
mustered out with this regiment after the close of
the war. He then attended school at the University
of Michigan, and at the Wesleyan Reserve College.
In 1871 he went to Cleveland and engaged in the
book business, having spent the intervals of his
school life in the same occupation. In 1884 Mr.
Brett assumed charge of the Cleveland Library, in
which capacity his work has been notable. Finding the library small and ineffective, he added

greatly to its size, his influence making it a powerful factor in the development of the city. He has
widely extended its influence in educational lines,
and has been of invaluable assistance to the public
schools in providing for and influencing the reading
of the pupils. One phase of this school work is
the sending of books freely to teachers, who in turn
give them to the pupils who most need them. Mr.
Brett's mind is essentially a progressive one, but he
is always ready to welcome suggestions from others.
His work has been patiently thorough. He was
not discouraged because the first few years did not
show all that he might have hoped for; he was content to wait, and while he waited he continued his
progressive work. Recently, the evidences of his
influence have been very marked. While, for example, the annual number of books drawn was, four
years ago, but 200,000, it is now (1894), 450,000.
There are some 80,000 volumes in the library, and
the number is constantly increasing. It is the only
large public library in the country in which the plan
is followed of allowing free general access to the
cases. Branch libraries have been established,
under his direction, which are connected by messenger and telephone service with the main building.
Mr. Brett has made the library among the best in
America, also establishing his own reputation as a
competent and thoroughly qualified librarian. He
has been a frequent contributor to the "Library Journal" and to the Cleveland papers, and occasionally to
some of the literary journals.

GREEN, Samuel Swett, librarian, was born
in Worcester, Mass., Feb. 20, 1837. His parents
were James Green, son of the second Dr. John Green
of Worcester, and brother of the third Dr. John
Green of the same place, and Elizabeth (Swett)
Green. Through his father he is descended from
Thomas Green of Malden, who came to this country
about the year 1635 or 1636, and from Thomas Dudley, the second governor of the colony of Massachusetts Bay. Through his mother he is descended from
Ralph Sprague, who came to Charlestown in 1629
from Upway, Devonshire, England. The son was
graduated from the Worcester High School in 1854,
and from Harvard College in 1858. In 1859 he visited
Smyrna and Constantinople. Remaining two years
in Worcester on account of ill health, in the autumn
of 1861 he entered the divinity school of Harvard
University, and was graduated from that institution
in 1864. He took the degree of Master of Arts in
1870 at Harvard, and in 1877 was chosen an honorary member of the Phi Beta Kappa Society connected
with that university. In 1864 Mr. Green became
bookkeeper in the Mechanics' National Bank, Worcester, and a few months later, teller in the Worcester
National Bank, in which position he remained several
years. He declined the cashiership of the Citizens'

National Bank, Worcester, and a position in the Worcester County Institute for Savings. Mr. Green became a director of the Free Public Library, Worcester, Jan 1, 1867, and four years later, Jun. 15, 1871, was chosen librarian of the same institution. He has held various offices in the American Library Association, of which he was one of the founders. Having been elected president of the association in 1891, he presided at the meetings held in San Francisco, Oct. 12th–16th of that year. In May, 1892, he was chosen one of the original ten members of the new council of the Association. He was a delegate of the American Library Association to the International Congress of Librarians held in London in October, 1877, was a member of the council of that body, and took an active part in the discussions carried on in its meetings. Before the close of the congress, the Library Association of the United Kingdom was formed, of which association Mr. Green was chosen an honorary member in July, 1878. He was for many years a member of the committee appointed by the overseers of Harvard University to make an annual examination of the library; he also gave annual courses of lectures on public libraries as popular educational institutions, to the students of the School of Library Economy, when that school was connected with Columbia College, New York city. In October, 1890, he was appointed by the governor of Massachusetts an original member of the state board of free public library commissioners. In November, 1890, he assisted in the formation of the Massachusetts Library Club, and was elected first vice-president. He was a member of the advisory council of the world's congress auxiliary of the World's Columbian Exposition on a congress of librarians; and at Chicago presided over that congress at the meeting on the second day of its sessions. Mr. Green is a fellow of the Royal Historical Society of great Britain; a member of the American Antiquarian Society; a member of the council of the latter body; and a member of the American Historical Association; of the New England Historic Genealogical Society; and of the Colonial Society of Massachusetts. He is a trustee of Leicester Academy, and a trustee of the Worcester County Institute for Savings; one of the founders and first president of the Worcester High School Association, and has been president of the Worcester Indian Association and of the Worcester Art Society, and treasurer of the Worcester Natural History Society. Mr. Green is a member of the art commission of the St. Wulstan Society, Worcester, and of the Sons of the Revolution, and lieutenant-governor of the Society of Colonial Wars. He has written constantly for the "Library Journal" since its establishment, and has made many contributions to the proceedings of the American Antiquarian Society, besides contributing to other magazines and periodicals.

BASSETT, Homer Franklin, librarian, was born in the town of Florida, Berkshire co., Mass., Sept. 2 1826, son of Ezra and Keziah (Witt) Bassett. When he was ten years old his father removed to Ohio and settled on a farm in Rockport. The son worked on the farm most of the time until he was twenty years old. His school advantages were limited, though by working to pay his expenses while at school he spent a few terms at the Berea Sem-

inary. Later he was in the College Preparatory School at Oberlin for nearly a year. Overwork, however, obliged him not only to leave the school a few weeks before the end of the year, but forced him to give up his long-cherished plan of taking a college course. In 1849, when leaving Oberlin, he managed to exchange some recently purchased college text-books for a copy of "Wood's Botany." This simple act proved to be a turning point in his life. The book opened to him a new world, and the study of botany and kindred branches of natural history from that time occupied the leisure hours of a busy life. His health remaining poor, he spent the next summer in western Massachusetts, and in the fall visited relatives in Connecticut. Here he was urged to teach the winter school in a small district in the town of Wolcott. This was the beginning of his work as a teacher. He spent sixteen years in the school room, the last eight in a large private school in Waterbury, Conn. About 1862 he began the study of insect life, confining himself almost entirely to the gall-producing insects of the Hymenoptera, the Cynipidæ. He has discovered and described a large

number of species, and has learned several interesting and important facts regarding their habits. When the Silas Bronson Library was founded in 1870 he applied for the position of librarian. Mr. W. I. Fletcher was appointed, however, as having a prior claim, but when in August, 1872, he resigned, Mr. Bassett was asked to take his place. He found in the Bronson library in 1872, about 13,000 volumes. These he rearranged, catalogued, and classified to the gratification of the board of agents and the public, and instituted many reforms in the conduct of the routine management. The original building in which the books were kept being much too small, a new library building was erected and occupied in 1894.

In 1895 the books on the shelves numbered over 52,000 volumes, besides a vast accumulation of unbound pamphlets and journals. Yale College graduated him M.A. in 1894.

BROWNING, Eliza Gordon, librarian, was born at Fortville, Ind., Sept. 23, 1856, of Welsh-Scotch ancestry. She was educated in the public schools of Indianapolis, giving much time also to the study of music, which, upon leaving school, she taught for two years. In 1880 she entered the Public Library of Indianapolis, and three years later became the librarian's first assistant. In 1882 she was elected librarian to fill a vacancy, in which capacity she proved so successful as to ensure her being twice re-elected. On Dec. 28, 1893, she was elected president of the Indiana Association of Librarians, and since 1892 has been a member of the American Library Association. Miss Browning is one of the charter members and Chapter registrar of the Daughters of the American revolution of the Caroline Scott Harrison chapter of Indianapolis.

VAN DYKE, John Charles, librarian, was born at New Brunswick, N. J., Apr. 21, 1856, son of Judge John Van Dyke of the New Jersey supreme court, and grandson of Prof. Theodore Strong, the well-known mathematician. He was fitted for West Point academy at sixteen, but declined to accept the appointment. He studied at Columbia College, and was admitted to the New York bar in 1877, but immediately abandoned the study of law for literature. In 1878 he became librarian of the Sage Library at New Brunswick, a position which he ably fills. He has been for years a writer and lecturer on art matters, and has spent many summers in European galleries and universities. He holds the professorship of the history of art in Rutgers college, and has given courses of university lectures at Princeton, Columbia, Harvard and many other institutions of learning. As an editor he has been connected with several art reviews, several of the New York dailies, and is the editor of the series of college text-books entitled, "College Histories of Art." Besides many magazine articles Prof. Van Dyke has published the following books: "Books and How to Use Them" (N. Y., 1883); "Principles of Art" (N. Y., 1887); "How to Judge a Picture" (N. Y., 1888); "Serious Art in America" (N. Y., 1889); "Art for Art's Sake" (N. Y., 1893); "History of Painting" (N. Y., 1894). Mr. Van Dyke is a member of the Authors' Club and many other societies. In 1888 in recognition of his contributions to art and literature, Rutgers college awarded him the degree of L.H.D.

HOSMER, James Kendall, author and librarian, was born at Northfield, Mass., Jan. 29, 1834. He studied at Harvard College, being graduated in 1855, when he was chosen class poet. A few years of quiet study followed, during which Mr. Hosmer prepared himself for the ministry. In 1860 his ordination took place, and he received a call to be pastor of the First Church at Deerfield, Mass. When the civil war broke out, the voice of duty seemed to the young minister to call to the battlefield rather than to the pulpit, so he joined the Federal ranks as a corporal in the 52nd regiment Massachusetts volunteer militia, seeing service in Louisiana, and taking part in the siege of Port Hudson. At the close of the civil strife Mr. Hosmer adopted the profession of teaching, and for twenty-six years devoted himself to his new duties, becoming successively professor of rhetoric and English literature in Antioch College, Ohio, in 1866; professor of English and history in the State University of Missouri, in 1872; and professor of English and German literature in Washington University, St. Louis, in 1874, which latter position he held for eighteen years. During all this time Mr. Hosmer was not idle with his pen, for he wrote a number of works, mainly of an historical nature, the most important being a "Short History of German Literature" (1878, Charles Scribner's Sons); "Samuel Adams" (American Statesmen Series, 1885, Houghton, Mifflin & Co.); "Stories of the Jews" (Story of Nations Series, 1886, G. P. Putnam's Sons); "Young Sir Henry Vane" (Houghton, Mifflin & Co., 1888); a "Short History of Anglo-

Saxon Freedom" (Charles Scribner's Sons, 1890); and "Thomas Hutchinson, Royal Governor of Massachusetts" (Houghton, Mifflin & Co., 1896); besides two or three novels. His works, which show considerable research and conscientious study of a high order, brought Prof. Hosmer into notice, and prompted the trustees of the public library at Minneapolis, in 1892, to offer the author the position of chief librarian, which, after some natural hesitation occasioned by his reluctance to leave the scene of so much of his useful labors, with its pleasant associations, he finally accepted.

KING, James L., librarian, was born in La Harpe, Hancock county, Ill., Aug. 2, 1850. His boyhood was passed in his native town, excepting two years during the civil war, which were spent in the South with his father, Col. S. W. King, an officer of the 50th Illinois Infantry. At the close of the war he resumed his studies at the La Harpe Academy, where a limited education was obtained. In 1867 he was an apprentice in the office of the Carthage (Ill.) "Gazette," where he learned the trade of a printer. When he had attained the age of nineteen he was the owner and editor of the "Home News," a weekly paper published in La Harpe. Later he engaged in the book and stationery business, and in 1870 com-

menced the publication of the "Headlight," the first paper to be established at the new town of Creston, Ia. He removed to Topeka, Kan., in the year 1871, engaging in newspaper work until 1876, when he entered the Topeka post-office. Here he remained for seventeen years, filling through promotion every position in the office, and receiving the appointment of postmaster in 1889 from President Harrison. Upon the completion of his four years' term as postmaster, he took up miscellaneous newspaper work until 1894, when he was appointed to be state librarian. Mr. King was married Oct. 10, 1877, to Elizabeth, daughter of Edwin B. and Celestia J. Coolbaugh, of Towanda, Pa.

VINTON, Frederic, bibliographer, was born in Boston, Mass., Oct. 9, 1817. His ancestry may be traced to John Vinton, who settled in Lynn, Mass., toward the close of the first half of the seventeenth century, lineal descendants of the Huguenots, who fled after St. Bartholomew's to England, and later to America. The third and fourth generations in this country were owners and operators of the iron works and blacksmith shop at Braintree, Mass., probably the first iron works established in this country. His paternal grandmother was closely related to Pres. John Adams. He spent the greater part of his boyhood in Braintree, and was graduated at Amherst College in 1839, and at Andover Seminary in 1843. Delicate health prevented him from continuing in the ministry, and for nearly a decade he devoted himself to teaching. In 1852 he compiled a catalogue of a library of 6,000 volumes, belonging to his brother Alfred, president of the chamber of commerce, St. Louis, Mo.; this was at the time the finest and largest collection of books west of the Alleghanies. He henceforth devoted his life to the profession of bibliography, of which he may be called one of the creators. In 1856 he was appointed first assistant-librarian of the Public Library of Boston, and 1865, first assistant in the Congressional Library at Washington, D. C., and in 1873 librarian at Princeton College. In these various positions he published volumes of catalogues and supplements, which are classical, particularly the subject-catalogue of the library of Princeton, the most complete work of its kind extant. It is regarded by critics as marking an epoch in bibliography. At the time of his death he had in preparation an analytical index of scientific periodical literature of all languages, designed to be to science what Poole's Index is to *belles-lettres*. He was a man of singular purity and nobility of character, and scrupulously faithful in the performance of his duty. He died at Princeton, N. J., Jan. 1, 1890.

DANA, John Cotton, librarian of the Denver Public Library, was born at Woodstock, Windsor co., Vt., Aug. 19, 1856, son of Charles Dana, a merchant. On his paternal side he is descended from Richard Dana, who emigrated to the United States about 1640, and who was the ancestor of all of that name in this country. He received his early education in the public schools of the neighborhood, and afterwards entered Dartmouth College, New Hampshire, and was graduated there in the class of 1878. He soon afterwards began the study of law, which he was soon forced to give up on account of ill health, and went to Colorado to live. Here he was employed as a surveyor and civil engineer for three years, when he returned to the East to continue his

legal studies, and in 1883 was admitted to the New York bar. He had practiced his profession for only one year when poor health again drove him West, where he resumed his out-of-door occupations as surveyor and civil engineer. He was married in Denver, Col., in 1888, to Miss Waggener of Kentucky. When the new public library of Denver was opened in 1889, in connection with the Denver High School, Mr. Dana was placed in charge of it, which position he has continued to fill until the present time (1896).

CRUNDEN, Frederick Morgan, librarian, was born at Gravesend, England, Sept. 1, 1847. On the paternal side his ancestry is English. In his infancy his parents removed to St. Louis, Mo., where soon after his father died. He was then reared under the sole direction of his mother, a woman of great energy and ability, and possessing rare self-denial and practical sagacity. Young Crunden received his education at the public schools of St. Louis, and was graduated at the High School in 1865 as valedictorian of his class. He also received the scholarship awarded by the Washington University for the best scholar in the graduating class of the school. During his college course Mr. Crunden was obliged to teach in order to defray his expenses. Immediately upon graduation, he was appointed instructor in the academic department of the university. Later, he held the principalship of one of the city grammar schools, afterward returning to the university, where he was first instructor in mathematics and elocution, and subsequently professor of elocution. In 1868 he received the degree of A.B., and in 1872 that of A.M. In 1877 he was appointed librarian of the Public Library of St. Louis, which position he still holds. As a librarian, he has had the good fortune to be in a section where there are no inherited prejudices, so that there is both need and opportunity for the progressive library management, which he has given to the public. From the first his aim has been to multiply the inducements to systematic reading, and to afford all possible assistance to seekers for information. In addition to these duties, Mr. Crunden is an active promoter of literature in St. Louis, and well known in literary circles. He has also served the interests of the

library by frequent articles in the daily press, and has contributed extensively to the "Library Journal," and other periodicals. He is a member of the St. Louis Academy of Science, Missouri Historical Society, and the St. Louis Artists' Guild. In 1890, at the annual meeting of the National Association of Librarians, he was elected its president. His latest and largest achievement has been that of making the St. Louis Library free, which was only accomplished after years of patient and persevering endeavor. The library now ranks, however, among the best of such institutions. In 1894 he was offered the charge of the Newberry Library, Chicago, but declined the invitation.

CAPEN, Edward, librarian, was born at Dorchester, Mass., Oct. 20, 1821. He is the third son of Rev. Lemuel and Mary Ann (Hunting) Capen, with ancestry on his father's side reaching back in Dorchester to the year 1630. While he was quite young his father removed to South Boston, where, at the Hawes School, he was fitted for the Boston Latin School in 1832. There he was graduated with a Franklin medal to enter Harvard College in 1838. A member of the Phi Beta Kappa Society, he was graduated in the class of 1842, attending the Cambridge Divinity School in the class of 1845. He engaged for one year as minister over the Unitarian Society in Westford, and at the end of that period was invited to settle as pastor of the parish, but felt obliged to decline the position owing to the inadequacy of the salary. One year more he spent in the ministry with little success, owing to his sympathy with the views of Theodore Parker, at that time a drawback to a settlement in the ministry of his denomination, but now rather a recommendation. In October, 1847, he felt constrained to seek a living in some other occupation, and was fortunate enough to secure a position with Dr. John Collins Warren as private secretary. His occupation here was congenial, consisting, as it did, in reading aloud from the popular science of the day, both medical and general, and in being present to assist at many surgical operations. In 1849 his name was registered as a student of the Harvard Medical School, and he attended the lectures of Dr. Oliver Wendell Holmes in anatomy, and Prof. John W. Webster in chemistry. It was his fortune to be present at the last lecture delivered by Dr. Webster, before the murder of Dr. George Parkman. In 1850 he accompanied Dr. Warren, who was then president of the American Medical Association, to attend its annual meeting in Cincinnati, and in 1851, the year of the first great exhibition, he went to London and Paris with him. In January, 1852, he secured the position of secretary of the school committee of the city of Boston, with the assurance that, during the year, the office of librarian of the Boston Public Library would be conferred upon him. He was chosen to fill the position in May, 1852. In 1853 the duties

of librarian demanded the surrender of the office of secretary. The library was opened to the public in Mason street, and Mr. Capen prepared, under the direction of the trustees, its first catalogue and its first six reports to the city council. The building in Boylston street was soon after commenced under the direction of a commission of which Robert C. Winthrop was chairman and Mr. Capen secretary. This building was dedicated in 1858 and the library removed to it. Prof. Charles C. Jewett was placed at the head as its superintendent, but Mr. Capen was annually chosen for several years unanimously by the city council, and afterwards by the trustees, to fill the office of librarian. In this position he remained until the expiration of twenty-two and one-half years from the date of his first election, and performed acceptably to the public the contining duties connected with the circulating department. It was said of him, intended as a compliment, that he represented the "Democratic element" in the library management. He certainly made it his earnest endeavor to furnish all needed facilities to those who frequented the library. In November, 1874 Mr. Capen was elected to the office of librarian of the Public Library of Haverhill, Mass., and he still (1896) occupies that position. Mr. Capen was married in July, 1850, to Ann Augusta, daughter of John and Mary (Webb) Saville of Quincy, by whom he has one daughter, a graduate of Smith College.

POOLE, Fitch, librarian, was born in Danvers, Mass., June 13, 1803. He was educated in the local schools, but early had a desire to become a journalist. While at school he began contributing to the press, and this he continued until the founding of the Danvers "Wizard," in 1859, when he became its editor, and continued in that position until 1868. In 1841 Mr. Poole was elected to the legislature, and besides held several responsible local offices. He was much interested in the advancement of his native town, and founded the Mechanics' Institute Library, which in after years became known as the Peabody Institute. He was made custodian of this library in 1856, which position he retained until his death. He wrote a number of ballads, satirizing the times, which won great popularity. He was highly educated, and did much to encourage the establishment of public libraries in Massachusetts. He died in Peabody, Mass., Aug. 19, 1873.

JONES, Gardner Maynard, librarian, was born at Charlestown, Mass., June 27, 1850, but a year later his parents removed to Dorchester, Mass. He was graduated at the Dorchester High School in July, 1866, and in May, 1867, entered the employ of the "Old Corner Bookstore," Boston. He served various

firms for twenty years, and his dealings with libraries showed him the importance and attractions of librarianship. To fit himself for a new career, after a short European tour, he entered, in January, 1888, the library school attached to Columbia College. In November, 1888, he left it to become the cataloguer and classifier of the Boston Book Co. In February, 1889, he was engaged to complete the catalogue of the Salem Public Library; in April he was made librarian, and in July the library was opened to the public. In addition to the usual reports, finding lists, and supplements, he has edited a monthly bulletin contain-

ing lists of new books, special reading lists, and editorials on literary and library topics. Mr. Jones has been an active member of the Massachusetts Library Club since its foundation, was elected its first secretary in 1890, and its president in 1893. He has contributed valuable reports and papers to the meetings of the American Library Association and prepared the "List of Subject Headings for use in Dictionary Catalogues," lately issued by one of its committees. He also published "A Rough Subject Index to the Publications of the Essex Institute" (Salem, 1890).

WOODCOCK, William Lee, lawyer, was born in Wells Valley, Fulton co., Pa., Oct. 20, 1843, and is the son of John and Sarah (Alexander) Woodcock. His is an old Lancashire family, whose descent may be traced back over four centuries. The name of "John Woodcocke of Kureden, gentleman," appears among the jurors in many inquisitions in the first half of the seventeenth century. His contemporary Dr. Kureden, a well-known antiquary, says, "There is another fayr-built hous upon the lower Kureden green, commonly called the 'Crow Trees,' being the antient inheritance of Mr. John Woodcoc, and his family, for 400 or 500 years." His father, Thomas Woodcock, was owner of "Crow Trees," in 1609, and was probably son of Richard Woodcock of Leyland, who died in 1592, and to whose children were paid part of the tithes of Coerden. To this family belonged Rev. John Woodcock, a Franciscan priest, whom Baines mentions among the "Worthies," of Lancashire, and who was executed, in 1646, for adhering to the Roman Catholic church. John Woodcock, of Kureden, married Margaret Fox, and had two sons, William and Thomas. Thomas, in 1788, married Ellen Spencer, heiress to the Newburg property, in the parish of Ormskirk, and the house now known as "Woodcock Hall." A branch of this family still resides in England, Thomas, gentleman, residing at Belmore place, near London. They had a large family of children, among them Isaac, who, in 1774, came to America, and settled in Wilmington, Del. He died in 1849. His son, John Woodcock (1800–74), our subject's father, was a farmer and tanner in Wells Valley, Pa., and served as steward, and class-leader in the Methodist church, for over half a century. A Republican in politics, he held office as school director and justice of the peace. William L. Woodcock attended the public schools, Martinsburg Academy, and Allegheny College, Meadville, Pa. He read law in the office of his brother, Samuel M. Woodcock at Altoona, being for one term principal of the Phillipsburg High School, and was admitted to the bar of Blair county, in 1865. He immediately began practice in Altoona, and has been most successful. He is attorney for several building and loan associations, and is one of the leading lawyers of the Blair county bar. He is also engaged in the banking business, and has invested largely in real estate in Altoona; owns the Arcade building, one of the largest business blocks in the city, besides a number of desirable houses and building lots. He is also interested in large timber tracts in Fulton county, and the coal regions of the Alleghany mountains and Indiana county. At the outbreak of the war he enlisted as a private in the 77th Pennsylvania regiment, was transferred to the signal corps, and promoted to lieutenant, but mustered out at the end of thirteen months, on account of ill health. Mr. Woodcock has always been especially active in the First Methodist Church of Altoona, of which he has been a steward and trustee for twenty years. He is president of the home chapter of the Epworth League, and for three years was honored with the presidency of the Fourth General Conference District League, which embraces several states. He has devoted much energy to Sunday-school work, and six years ago, erected Belmore Hall in the seventh ward, for mission school purposes. He takes particular pride in this institution, of which he is super-intendent, and through his earnest efforts the membership has increased to over 400 scholars, and a church has grown out of the school. An edifice has been erected, known as the Walnut Avenue Methodist Episcopal Church.

MORTON, Julius Sterling, secretary of agriculture of the United States, was born in Adams, Jefferson co., N. Y., Apr. 22, 1832, and is the son of Julius Dewey and Emeline (Sterling) Morton. His paternal ancestors were among the earliest settlers in New England, being passengers on the Little Ann, the first ship after the Mayflower. Our subject's parents removing to Michigan in 1834, he attended a private school at Monroe, until fourteen years of age, and was then sent to a Methodist seminary at Albion, in that state, and there prepared for college. In 1850 he entered Michigan University, where he remained through most of his course, but was graduated at Union College in 1854. He was married, in October of the same year, to Caroline Joy French of Detroit, Michigan, and immediately thereafter settled in Bellevue, Neb. Ter. He, however, remained at that point only a few months. He then removed to what is now Nebraska City, and became a member of the Town Co., which surveyed and established that town. Adjacent to the town site he took up a claim of half a mile square of the public land, as a pre-emptor. Upon that place, which is known as "Arbor Lodge," he has resided ever since, and there, in 1881, his wife died. Mr. Morton has been a practical farmer and lived upon the same place more than forty years. He originated "Arbor Day," and the thousands of trees thriving in the once woodless prairies of the West, are many of them living witnesses to the beneficence of this new anniversary. Mr. Morton was an original member of the Nebraska Territorial Board of Agriculture, and of the Territorial Horticultural Society, and has acted as president of both associations. He was likewise a charter member of the Nebraska State Historical Society, and is now its president, and was appointed a commissioner to the Paris Exposition of 1889. He is a forcible speaker and writer. During his college days he was a frequent contributor to the Detroit "Free Press," and in later years, to the Chicago "Times." He was the first editor, and the founder, of the Nebraska City "News." An uncompromising Democrat, he has pushed his views to their logical consequence. Four times, without solicitation on his part, he was made unanimously the candidate of his party for the governorship of Nebraska, and twice in a similar manner nominated for congress. At every senatorial election since the state was admitted, he has received more or less votes for U. S. senator. When a member of the legislature he opposed wild-cat banks, and during the next year was defeated for re-election because of his opposition to those financial fallacies. In 1858 Pres. Buchanan appointed him secretary of the territory of Nebraska, and he became, under a provision of law, the acting governor, upon the resignation of Gov. William A. Richardson. At the senatorial election in Nebraska, during the winter of 1892–93, forty-five Republican members of the legislature in caucus, declared that they would support Mr. Morton for U. S. senator, in preference to any populistic candidate. In 1893 Pres. Cleveland appointed Mr. Morton secretary of agriculture. He was inducted into that office March 7th, of that year, and has since discharged the duties appertaining thereto with his characteristic vigor and intelligence.

DARLING, Charles W., soldier, was born in New Haven, Conn., Oct. 11, 1830. His family is of New England origin, having intermarried with the families of Pierpont, Noyes, Chauncey, Ely, Davis, and Dana. His great-grandfather, Judge Thomas Darling, a graduate of Yale, and an eminent jurist, married Abigail Noyes, granddaughter of Rev. James Pierpont of New Haven, one of the founders of Yale College. His grandfather, Dr. Samuel Darling, of the same city, also a graduate of Yale, married Clarinda, daughter of Rev. Richard Ely of Saybrook, Conn. His father, Rev. Chauncey Dar-

ling, who was graduated at Yale College and at Princeton Theological Seminary, entered the ministry and settled in New York. He married Adeline E., daughter of William Dana of Boston, and granddaughter of Maj. Robert Davis, an officer of artillery in the war of the revolution. The boyhood years of Gen. Darling were devoted largely to study under the guidance of a private tutor. After matriculation in the classical and mathematical department of the University of the City of New York, he passed through its regular curriculum, and subsequently received the honorary degree of A.M. from Hamilton College. In 1857 he married Angeline E., daughter of Jacob A. Robertson of New York. The grandfather of his wife was Archibald Robertson, the Scotch artist, who, while a guest of the first president, painted from life the celebrated miniatures on ivory of Gen. and Martha Washington. Soon after his marriage Mr. Darling and his wife visited Europe on a tour of instruction and pleasure. On his return to the United States he connected himself with the National Guard of New York, and when Edwin D. Morgan was elected governor, he was appointed a member of his staff. He also identified himself with political matters, was president of one of the Republican organizations of New York city, and by his decision of character, he united many discordant elements in the party. During the New York riots, in 1863, his discharge of difficult and dangerous duties won the warm approbation of the civil and military authorities. In 1864 Col. Darling was appointed aide-de-camp on the staff of Maj.-Gen. Benjamin F. Butler, then in command of the army of the James, and was assigned to special duty. In 1865, when Reuben E. Fenton was elected governor, Col. Darling received an appointment on his staff as assistant paymaster-general, a position of much responsibility during the war. In 1867, on the re-election of the governor, he was appointed military engineer-in-chief of the state of New York, with rank of brigadier-general. In 1869 Gen. Darling again visited England, and was there the recipient of many courtesies, among which was an invitation to visit Aldershot with the Prince of Wales, the Duke of Cambridge, and Lord Elcho. He subsequently traveled extensively through Europe, Asia, and Africa, and his journeyings abroad covered a period of about ten years. On his return to this country he and his wife removed from New York to Utica, and his connection with the Oneida Historical Society, as its corresponding secretary, has been a great source of interest to him, and profit to others. Possessing independent means, he has been

able to gratify his tastes and his scholarly attainments, while his varied information on a wide range of themes is evident in all his writings. His elegant monographs, brochures, essays, etc., handsomely printed, are usually designed for private distribution. He was president of the Young Men's Christian Association of Utica for several years, and is now a ruling elder in the First Presbyterian Church of Utica. He was a member of the advisory council of the World's congress auxiliary of the Columbian Exposition, on historical literature. He is a Son of the Revolution, and is connected, either as honorary or corresponding member, with many historical and scientific societies. He is also a member of the American Authors' Guild, and an associate member of the Victoria Institute of London, England. He has, furthermore, been the recipient of a decoration of the first class, granted by the Society of Science, Letters, and Art of London, for gratuitous service rendered in connection with historical literature. The medal is of gold, in the form of a Maltese cross, handsomely engraved, with an appropriate inscription, and suspended by a blue silk corded ribbon, attached at the top by a bar of gold. He is also honorary secretary, at Utica, for the Egypt Exploration fund of Great Britain and the United States.

CAMDEN, Johnson N., senator, was born in Lewis county, W. Va., March 6, 1828, son of John S. Camden, a successful business man, and twice a member of the Virginia legislature. His father, Henry Camden, had removed from Maryland to that portion of Virginia west of the Alleghany mountains (now Lewis county, W. Va.), about the close of the eighteenth century. He left five sons, to whom he gave only such education as pioneer life afforded, and who all grew to be vigorous, successful men. John S. Camden removed with his family to Sutton, the county-seat of Braxton county when that new county was first formed in 1837, and here the son was educated in the way of the rural backwoods life of the period, passing much of his time in fishing, hunting, and acquiring a thorough knowledge of woodcraft, and a considerable insight into the mineral resources of this section. When he was seventeen years old he was appointed a cadet to the

U. S. Military Academy, West Point, where he remained two years, and then resigned, to take up the study of law. He was admitted to the bar in 1851, and appointed commonwealth's attorney for Braxton county in the same year. The next year he was elected to the same office for Nicholas county. Soon finding a better field for success, and one more to his liking, in the development of the natural resources of this section, he gave up the practice of the law, and surveyed and secured by purchase, or lease, numerous large tracts of undeveloped lands. In 1854 he was made assistant in a branch of the Exchange Bank of Virginia, established at Weston, and remained with the bank for three years. In 1858 he resigned, and again took up the development of the lands and the practice of law. He had just undertaken the production of oil from cannel coal, when the discovery of petroleum at Burning Springs, W. Va., directed him to that new enterprise as a more promising field. He purchased one-half interest in the tract of land on which the oil had been discovered, and the venture was a great success, and led to the general development of the mineral and natural resources of the state. He was made president of the First National Bank of Parkersburg, when it was established in 1862. He at the same time became interested in slack-watering the Little Kanawha river from Parkersburg to the oil district at Burning Springs, and soon thereafter established a large refining plant at Parkersburg, under the name of the Camden Consolidated Oil Co. This was soon after consolidated with the Standard Oil Co., and Mr. Camden was made an active director and member of the executive committee of that corporation, resigning upon his election as a U. S. senator in 1881. In 1882 he was instrumental in organizing the Ohio River Railroad Co., building a railroad from Wheeling, on the east bank of the Ohio river, by way of Parkersburg and Point Pleasant, to Huntington, a distance of 250 miles. Later, he organized and built the railroad from Fairmount to Clarksburg, along the west branch of the Monongahela river, opening up an extensive coal field which marketed over 1,000,000 tons of coal and coke annually. He also developed large lumber interests, by extending the road from Clarksburg south to the Elk and Gauley rivers, with a branch up the Buckhannon river, making an aggregate of 225 miles of road, and owning 150,000 acres of timber land. Mr. Camden is president of the Monongahela River and the West Virginia and Pittsburgh Railroads, and of the Gauley and Pickens Companies. His party gave him the Democratic nomination for governor in 1868, and again in 1872. In 1868, '72, and '76 he was a delegate to the Democratic national conventions. In 1880 he was elected U. S. senator, taking his seat March 4, 1881, and serving until March 3, 1887. In 1893 he was elected to fill the vacancy caused by the death of Senator John E. Kenna, taking his seat Jan. 28, 1893. His term of service expired March 3, 1895. He was married, in 1858, to Anna, daughter of Judge George W. Thompson of Wheeling, W. Va. Their son, Johnson N. Camden, Jr., married Susan Preston Hart of Kentucky, and resides at Spring Hill, near Versailles, Ky., and their daughter, Anna, married Gen. B. D. Spilman of Parkersburg, W. Va.

HAWTHORNE, Frank Warren, journalist, was born in Bath, Me., July 1, 1852, educated in the public schools of that city, and at Bowdoin College, being graduated in 1874. Only a few weeks after his graduation, a serious accident to his father necessitated his taking charge of the latter's business, temporarily, and for the succeeding eleven years he was associated in his business. In the meantime his natural taste for literature, and trend toward a newspaper career, led him to make occasional contributions to magazines and the press. In March, 1881, upon the occasion of the celebration of the 100th anniversary of the settlement of the town of Bath, Me., Mr. Hawthorne read an original poem, which was favorably commented upon. He is an earnest Democrat, a political faith inherited from his father and his grandfathers on both sides. He took an active part in the political campaigns of 1876 and 1880 in Maine. Gov. Plaisted, soon after his inauguration in 1881, gave Mr. Hawthorne an appointment on his military staff, with the rank of lieutenant-colonel, a position which he held until the inauguration of Gov. Roble, in 1883. Early in October, 1885, Col. Hawthorne was induced to go to Florida, and three months later, associated with John P. Varnum, he established the

"Morning News," at Jacksonville. Later, he became secretary and treasurer of the News Publishing Co., and in May, 1887, when the Florida Printing and Publishing Co. was organized, with a capital of $100,000, and purchased both the "Morning News" and the "Evening Herald," Col. Hawthorne became the associate editor of the consolidated newspaper, "The News-Herald." On May 1, 1888, the Florida Publishing Co., a reorganization of the Florida Printing and Publishing Co., purchased the "Florida Times-Union," and stopped the publication of the "News-Herald." Mr. Hawthorne continued as associate editor of the "Times-Union," and was in this position at the outbreak of the famous yellow fever epidemic of 1888. He remained at his post throughout the memorable siege of five months, almost miraculously escaping the fever, although every other member of the editorial and business staff was stricken with the disease, the editor and the city editor falling victims to it. Out of the sixty-five employees of the establishment, over thirty of those who remained in the city had the fever, and five died. Upon the death of Editor Martin, early in October, 1888, Mr. Hawthorne came into editorial charge of the paper, with a staff broken in numbers and in health, and in addition to conducting the policy of the paper, he performed the Florida news service of the Associated Press. In March, 1890, he became managing editor of the "Times-Union," and continued in editorial charge of it until Dec. 1, 1893, when he resigned, to engage in general newspaper and magazine work, still retaining his residence in Jacksonville.

MOON, George Temple, merchant, was born in Brooklyn, N. Y., July 6, 1857, son of John R. and Kate E. Moon. He was educated in the public schools of his native city, and at the Brooklyn Polytechnic Institute. He engaged with A. T. Stewart & Co., in 1877, as a clerk. In 1880 he left the dry-goods business to accept a position with his grandfather, then engaged as a wholesale commission merchant and shipper of fresh fish, in Fulton market. In 1885 he succeeded to his grandfather's interest in the business, and in 1888, upon the death of Mr. Lamphear, he became, by purchase, the successor to the firm of Moon & Lamphear. He was married, in 1878, to Sara L. Conely. He was for a time trustee and Sunday-school superintendent of the South Baptist Church. By reason of removal of residence, he afterwards joined the Central Congregational Church. Mr. Moon is a director in the Fulton Market Fish-Monger's Association, and in the Centennial Transportation Co. He is a member of the Hanover Club, of which he was an incorporator, and for three years a director. He is a member of the Royal Arcanum, and was for five years an official in the grand council. He is also a member of the American Legion of Honor, an associate member of Grant Post, G.A.R., and a member of the Stuyvesant Heights Republican Club, Brooklyn, N. Y.

SEWALL, Joseph Addison, first president of the University of Colorado (1877–88), was born in Scarborough, Me., in 1830. His early education was received at home, and he was graduated at Harvard in 1852, receiving the degree of M. D. The first year after graduation was spent in the practice of his profession in Bangor, Me. On account of ill health he went to Illinois, where he was for a time, the principal of the high school in Princeton, and afterwards he practiced medicine in La Salle county. He then went back to Harvard, and completed the scientific course, and received the degree of Ph. D. In the fall of 1860 he was appointed professor of natural science in the State Normal University of Illinois. In 1877 he received the honorary degree of LL. D. from Knox College, Galesburg, Ill., and in the same year went to Colorado as president of the Colorado State University at Boulder. Dr. Sewall served in this capacity for ten years. In 1888 he resigned, and accepted the chair of natural science in Denver University. This position he resigned in 1892, retaining his professorship in the medical school. Dr. Sewall has since had the charge of the U. S. Experimental Grass and Forage Station in Garden City, Kan.

HALE, Horace Morrison, second president of the University of Colorado (1887–92), was born at Hollis, Hillsboro' co., N. H., March 6, 1833, the fourth son of John and Jane (Morrison) Hale. His paternal and maternal ancestors were early settlers of New England. His grandfather, David Hale, was at the early age of sixteen, a soldier in the revolutionary war, and his great-grandfather, Col. John Hale, was on Col. Prescott's staff at the battle of Bunker Hill. His mother was a lineal descendant of John Morrison, one of the pioneers of New Hampshire. In 1837, his father, who was a mechanic and inventor of note, removed from Hollis to Rome, N. Y., and in 1840, to North Bloomfield, N. Y., where the family remained until the father's death in 1852. In the spring of 1839 Horace entered Genesee Wesleyan Seminary at Lima, N. Y., and the following year was admitted to Genesee College, where he remained through the junior year, teaching in the winters and working in the fields and shops in the summer vacations. At the close of the junior year he took a letter of honorable dismissal, and entered the senior class of Union College, Schenectady, N. Y., where he was graduated in 1850. Literally penniless, in 1852, young Hale worked his way through college without receiving the slightest pecuniary assistance. Good health, business tact, and pluck carried him through, and he at once accepted a position to teach in the Union School at West Bloomfield, N. Y. In the fall of 1857 he went to Nashville, Tenn., to teach in the public schools, and after one term he was assigned to a principalship, and ultimately was placed in charge of the Howard School of 750 pupils. On Aug. 4, 1859, he married Martha Eliza, daughter of Leonard and Hannah (Reed) Huntington, and they have one son, Irving, who was graduated at West Point in 1884, with the highest record ever made in that institution. In the fall of 1861 the family removed to Detroit, Mich., and Mr. Hale entered the law office of C. I. Walker as a student, where he remained until his admission to the bar in 1863. His health failing from over work, he went to Colorado, crossing the plains with a horse and buggy in company with his brother, and devoted four years to outdoor labor. In 1865 he returned to New York for his family, crossing the plains both

ways with a mule team. The western trip consumed forty days from St. Joseph, Mo., owing to the hostility of Indians. In 1868 he accepted the principalship of the Central City, Col., public schools, which he retained until 1873, having in the meantime been elected superintendent of schools of Gilpin county. In 1873 Gov. Elbert appointed him superintendent of public instruction of Colorado, to fill a vacancy, and reappointed him for two years in 1874. He was continued in this office by Gov. Routt, until the admission of Colorado as a state in 1876. While superintendent for the territory, he framed and got through the legislature a revised school law, which has proved to be well adapted to the peculiar wants of the state. In 1877 he was recalled to the manage-

University of Colorado

ment of the Central City schools, which position he held until July, 1887. After an aggregate service of fifteen years, he resigned, to accept the presidency of the University of Colorado, tendered him by its board of regents. This honorable position was not only wholly unsought, but was at first declined, and finally accepted, after earnest solicitations by his friends and the friends of the university. The affairs of the university were most carefully and ably managed during his administration, which lasted for nearly five years, when he resigned to retire from active business. The Hale Scientific Building was named in his honor. In 1889 Iowa Wesleyan University conferred upon him the degree of LL. D. At the state election of 1878 he was elected by the Republican party, a regent of the state university for six years. In 1882, while superintendent of the Central City schools, he was chosen mayor of the city, and was re-elected in 1883. Not one of the public offices ever held by Mr. Hale was sought by him, yet, at one and the same time, he was state regent, county superintendent of schools, city mayor and principal of the city schools. Few schoolmasters can show a record superior to his, nearly forty years of continuous school work, a quarter of a century of which has been in but three different schools. He was never asked to resign, nor was it ever intimated to him that his resignation would be acceptable. Dr. Hale is president of the Charity Organization Society of Denver, Col.

BAKER, James Hutchins, third president of the University of Colorado (1892–), was born at Harmony, Me., Oct. 13, 1848. His early education was obtained in the district school and the academy of his neighborhood, and he prepared for college in Nichols' Latin School, Lewiston. In 1870 he moved to Lewiston, having entered Bates College in that city the year before. He was graduated in 1873. After graduation he engaged in teaching, and was for a time the principal of the Yarmouth High School. He left this position in 1875, and went to

Colorado to take charge of the Denver High School. His influence there was felt from the first. He kept abreast of the most advanced methods of the times, and was quick to adopt their most desirable features, and apply them, with whatever modifications seemed necessary in his own field of work.

During his administration of seventeen years the attendance increased from fifty to 700, and a high school building was constructed second to none in the United States. In 1882 Mr. Baker was offered the presidency of the Colorado State Agricultural College, but decided to remain in the high school. In 1888 he was alumni orator at his alma mater. He has been an active member of the State Teachers' Association, and was president of the association in 1890. In 1888 he was elected a member of the national council of education. In 1890 he was made chairman of the national committee on the relation of high schools to colleges. In 1891 his leadership was acknowledged by his election to the presidency of the national council of education, the highest educational council known to this country. In January, 1892, Mr. Baker was called to the presidency of the University of Colorado, where he also occupies the chair of Ethics. He received, the same year, the degree of LL.D. from his alma mater. The university, under his direction, has undergone a wonderful change for the better, the attendance having trebled during the first three years of his administration. Pres. Baker was a member of the committee of ten which made the famous report on secondary education in the United States, and was the one who originated the scheme of such an investigation. He is author of an elementary psychology, published in 1890, besides various valuable papers and addresses. His "Elementary Psychology" is extensively used as a text-book in high schools, academies and normal schools. In addition to his regular work, which has always been of such a nature as to consume much time, he has been a constant student in his own special lines of psychology and ethics, besides branching upon many kindred subjects.

HUBBARD, John Barrett, soldier, was born at Hallowell, Me., Feb. 4, 1837, the eldest son of John Hubbard. He was prepared for college at the academy of his native town, and in 1853 entered Bowdoin College, at which, in 1857, he was graduated with high honors. He subsequently studied law with Edward Fox, who was afterwards judge of the U. S. district court at Portland, Me. In October, 1861, Mr. Hubbard was appointed first lieutenant of the 1st Maine battery of mounted artillery, and Dec. 18th, of the same year, was mustered into the U. S. service, and ordered to the department of the Gulf with the first expedition sent for the capture and occupation of New Orleans. In September, 1862, Lieut. Hubbard was selected as adjutant-general of Gen. Godfrey Weitzel's command, and was commissioned by the war department captain and assistant adjutant-general, with rank from Oct. 27, 1862. He served with ability and credit in the department of the Gulf, and participated in the Lafourche campaign, the first Teche campaign, and the siege of Port Hudson, where he was killed in battle in the first assault of that place, May 27, 1863.

CORNWELL, William Caryl, banker, was born in Lyons, N. Y., Aug. 19, 1851, son of Francis E. Cornwell, a prominent lawyer of Buffalo. On his mother's side he is descended from the Livingstons, of Livingston, N. Y. His education was obtained at the public schools of Buffalo, and at the age of seventeen he entered the banking house of H. N. Smith as a clerk. Upon the organization of the Bank of Buffalo, in 1873, Mr. Cornwell was made bookkeeper and correspondent, and was cashier from 1877 until 1892, when he withdrew from active connection with the bank, but retained his directorship. He then organized the City Bank, and was made president of the institution. The City Bank opened for business in 1893, and in that perilous year steadily grew through the panic period, accumulating over $1,000,000 in deposits by fall. The petition blank for the repeal of the purchase clause of the Sherman act, known as the "Buffalo petition," was originated by Mr. Cornwell, and had great weight in deciding final action. It was sent to thousands of banks in the United States, the signatures of their customers obtained, and forwarded to Washington. Mr. Cornwell has con-

tributed several important papers to the literature of banking. His pamphlet on "Free Coinage" had a wide circulation, and his papers on "Currency Reform and Bank Circulation," and the "Gold Standard," rank with the best economic productions in America. His "Currency and Banking Law of Canada" is of especial interest, in view of the necessity of changes in our own banking law. Mr. Cornwell's address before the American Bankers' Association in New Orleans in 1891, on "Canadian Bank Currency," became the student's reference on the subject, both in the United States and Canada. In 1894 he was invited, with other prominent bankers and financiers, to appear before the committee of the house on banking and currency, pending action upon the Carlisle bill, and his testimony received wide publicity through the press, and he was complimented for its high character by members of the committee. He was one of the founders of the New York State Bankers' Association in 1894, and was elected its first president. The constitution of this association limits the term of office to one year, but during his incumbency the membership increased from 112 to 400, making this the largest of all state associations, and on retiring was made honorary member of the council of administration. Mr. Cornwell was for several years vice-president of the Bank of Niagara, Niagara Falls, N. Y., and chairman of the Buffalo clearing-house committee for the first three years of the existence of that organization. In 1891 he was elected vice-president for the state of New York of the American Bankers' Association, and in 1894 member of the executive committee of that association for three years. Mr. Cornwell is a student of art and art literature, and uses both brush and pen with facility. He studied art at the Julien School, Paris, and was a pupil of Lefebvre and Boulanger. Mr. Cornwell was married, in 1873, to Marian W., daughter of Dr. H. N. Loomis, a noted physician of Buffalo.

ROOT, John Gilbert, financier, was born in Westfield, Mass., Apr. 20, 1835. He was the son of Silas Root, a solid and influential farmer, and one active in promoting the interests of the community. His early education was obtained in his native town, and at the age of twenty he removed to Hartford, Conn., and became connected with the Bank of Hartford County (now the American National Bank), and served them faithfully for fourteen years, when he became treasurer of the Hartford Trust Co. In January, 1871, he was elected cashier of the American National Bank. He held that position acceptably until 1883, when he was chosen president of the Farmers' and Mechanics' National Bank, and still serves in that position. This is one of the old banks of Hartford (organized in 1834), and, aided by careful management and conservative methods, is one of the leading, sound financial institutions in the city. Mr.

Root has held, and still holds, many positions of trust. He is a trustee of the Mechanics' Savings Bank, director of the Orient Insurance Co., and director, secretary, and treasurer of the Spring Grove Cemetery Association, and is officially connected with other enterprises. He was captain of the 22d regiment Connecticut volunteers, and saw active service. He is past commander of Robert O. Tyler post, G. A. R., Governor's Foot Guards, and president of the Veteran Association. He is a leading Mason, has taken the thirty-second degree, is past grand commander of Washington commandery, Knights-Templars, past master of Hartford lodge, and for many years has been grand treasurer of the Connecticut grand lodge and of the grand chapter. In 1888 he was elected mayor of Hartford, and proved an able and conscientious chief magistrate, and his administration was one that reflected credit on the city, being conducted on strictly business methods.

LAMBERT, Asher, mechanical engineer, was born near Lambertville, N. J., July 4, 1864, son of John Lambert, a prosperous farmer, living on a part of the old Lambert estate, whose wife was a daughter of Eden B. Hunt, of Stockton, N. J. His ancestor, a descendant of John Lambert, of English parliamentary fame in the time of Cromwell, settled in Connecticut in 1715, and with his four sons removed to New Jersey in 1746, settling two miles north of Coryell's Ferry, now the city of Lambertville. His great-grandfather, John Lambert, was acting governor of New Jersey. Asher Lambert received a public school education, and at the age of eighteen left his home with little capital besides his mechanical ability, and a confidence and full reliance in

his own powers. He apprenticed himself to Joseph S. Mundy of Newark for three years, after which he did contract work for three years more, when he was made superintendent of Mr. Mundy's shops. Desiring a greater opportunity for advancement, Mr. Lambert joined the stock company of Crook Bros. of Newark, hoisting engine manufacturers, as superintendent. On the death of the president and treasurer, William A. Crook, Mr. Lambert bought his stock and became vice-president and treasurer, a position he now (1896) holds, together with that of managing engineer. Though only thirty years of age, Mr. Lambert, already occupies a prominent place among mechanical engineers and manufacturers. He has made numerous inventions, and instituted many labor-saving devices of great practical value, especially in bridge building. A marked talent for mechanics and a scientific knowledge of everything to do with machinery, great executive ability, and business capabilities, bid fair to place him in the front ranks of those who have distinguished themselves in his line of work. Mr. Lambert was married in 1889 to Mary Van Doiah, the daughter of George Prall Wilson of Lambertville.

WOLCOTT, Henry Roger, financier, was born at Long Meadow, Mass., March 15, 1846, son of Rev. Samuel Wolcott, a Congregational minister, and brother of Edward Oliver Wolcott, U. S. senator from Colorado. His school education was acquired at the schools of Providence, R. I., Chicago, Ill., and Cleveland, O., in which cities his father was located as pastor. He served in different positions in banks in Cleveland for four years, except a short time in 1864. When eighteen years old he enlisted in a Cleveland regiment for 100 days' service, and was sent to the defense of Washington, D. C. He was transferred, by his own request, to the 140th Ohio regiment, and served until the regiment was mustered out, in the fall of 1864. He then engaged in business in Springfield, Mass., and in Chicago, and in 1869 removed to Colorado, locating at Black Hawk, where he engaged in mining, and in 1870 became associated with the Boston and Colorado smelting works. He continued his connection with the company for seventeen years, and during the last several years was general manager. In 1878 he was elected

state senator from Gilpin county, and was an active member of the state legislative sessions of 1879 and 1881. In the last session he was president *pro tem*. of the senate, and, by reason of the death of Lieut.-Gov. Robinson during the absence of Gov. Pitkin from the state, was acting governor. In 1888 he was chairman of the state delegation of the National Republican convention at Chicago. Mr. Wolcott has been a director of the Equitable Life Assurance Co., of New York since 1880. He was one of the charter members of the Denver Club, and has served as its president most of the time since its organization. He is president of the Denver, Utah and Pacific Railroad, and was for ten years vice-president of the First National Bank of Denver. He donated to Colorado College, Colorado Springs, a large sum of money, and built the Wolcott observatory for the use of the college. He has large private interests in lands, mines, and smelting works in Colorado and Montana. Mr. Wolcott has, for many years, persistently refused to accept any public office.

MEAD, Warren Hewitt, lawyer, was born in Genoa, Cayuga co., N. Y., Nov. 25, 1836, son of Lockwood and Susan (Miller) Mead, and grandson of Hewitt Mead, who settled in Cayuga county, shortly after the American revolution, having removed from Fairfield county, Conn.; was a soldier in the war of 1812, and died in the service at Sackett's Harbor, N. Y. The progenitor of this branch of the Mead family in America, was William Mead, who came from England about 1685, and settled in Connecticut, where the village of Greenwich was afterwards built. Solomon Mead, a graduate of Yale College in the class of 1788, and a celebrated Presbyterian theologian, and John Mead, a brigadier-general of the Continental army, conspicuous in the battles around New York, were of this branch. His mother was a daughter of Peter Miller, a sturdy Pennsylvanian of German stock. The son received a liberal education in the public school, and at Cazenovia Academy, where he was graduated in 1857. He then engaged in teaching a school in Bradfordsville, Ky., under charge of the Christian or Campbellite denomination. The school was broken up by the advent of the civil war in 1862, and he assisted in recruiting the 6th Kentucky cavalry for the Federal army. He served in the organization as first lieutenant, and participated in the various campaigns against the Confederates in 1862-63. He was with Rosecrans at the battle of Franklin, Tenn., where he captured two Confederate spies, who were subsequently shot. At the battle of Chickamauga, he was captured near Crawfish Spring, and was held a prisoner of war for eighteen months, being incarcerated at Macon, Ga., Columbia, S. C., and in Libby prison, Richmond. He was placed under fire of the guns of Gen. Gilmore during the bombardment of Charleston, S. C., and suffered a severe attack of yellow fever, and afterwards was taken to Columbia, S. C. On the approach of Sherman's army to that city, in February, 1865, he, with other prisoners, while being transported northward, cut their way out of a freight car with pen knives, and made their escape near Winnsboro'. He was recaptured, befriended by a Confederate officer from Kentucky, and again effected his escape into the lines of Sherman's army in North Carolina. On May 15, 1865, he rejoined his regiment at Nashville, Tenn., and was mustered out of the service, July 14th, following. He then completed a course of legal study, carried on during his imprisonment, and in December, 1865, was admitted to the bar at Louisville, Ky. On March 7, 1866, he was married to Frances A., daughter of Henry C. Hughes of Geddes, N. Y., and removed to Northfield, Minn., where he practiced his profession for three years, and then opened a law office in St. Paul, where he has since followed his profession. Mr. Mead is counsel for some of the largest corporations of the city. In 1877 he was elected a member of the state legislature, and re-elected in 1878 for two years. He is Republican in politics, a Presbyterian in religious creed, and a total abstainer, and an earnest advocate of temperance reform. He has traveled extensively in the Old World, and in all parts of his own country.

GRIGGS, George King, railroad manager, was born in Henry county, Va., Sept. 12, 1839, of English ancestry. At the age of fourteen years he began as clerk and salesman in a country store, and became a cadet in the Virginia Military Institute in 1857-58. He removed to Cascade, Pittsylvania county, Va., in 1860, and entered mercantile business, and was married to Sallie B. Boyd, Apr. 21, 1861. In June, 1861, he went to Richmond, Va., enlisted as captain of a volunteer company in the service of the Confederate states, and participated in most of the battles of the civil war fought by the army of northern Virginia. He was wounded many times, severely in the charge with Pickett's division at Gettysburg, Pa., and Drewry Bluff, Va. He was commissioned as captain, major, lieutenant-colonel and colonel in the 38th regiment of Infantry, Virginia volunteers, and surrendered at Appomattox Court House, in charge of the brigade. On returning home at the close of the war, he found employment, first as a school teacher, then as a merchant, and in 1877 went to Danville, Va., as secretary and treasurer of the Grange warehouse for the sale of leaf tobacco. In 1881 he was appointed secretary and treasurer of the Danville and New River Railroad, then being constructed. The duties of assistant superintendent were soon added. In 1886 he was made superintendent, secretary, and treasurer. In 1891 the road was sold, and the name changed to the Danville and Western, and Col. Griggs appointed general superintendent, treasurer, paymaster, purchasing agent, and to other official duties, which he has continued to fill until the present date. By his first marriage he had seven children, five boys and two girls, all living and profitably employed. He was married a second time on Sept. 11, 1894, to Mrs. Alice W. Burch, who was Miss Boatwright. He has been an official member of the Baptist church since 1860, a member of the Masonic order, being a past master; a past high priest of Euclid Chapter, and past eminent commander of Dove commandery, Knights-Templars. Col. Griggs is a man of great executive force and rare judgment, and to his abilities is largely due the success of the railroad under his management.

SWAIN, Joseph, educator, was born at Pendleton, Ind., June 16, 1857. His training for college was obtained in the academy of his native town. He was graduated at Indiana University, in 1883, and immediately elected assistant in mathematics in his alma mater. During his college life he won the personal friendship of David Starr Jordan. The names of Jordan and Swain are associated in the publication of numerous scientific papers printed by the National Museum. In 1885 he was elected associate professor of mathematics, with a year's leave of absence. The year was spent in study in Edinburgh University, Scotland, where he obtained entrance to the Royal Observatory. His association with Piazzi Smyth is described in a paper entitled: "An experience with the Astronomer Royal of Scotland." From 1888 to 1891 he was professor of mathematics in Indiana University, and in 1891 Dr. Jordan called him to the head of the department of mathematics in Leland Stanford University. Two years later Dr. Swain was persuaded to accept the presidency

of Indiana University. Since then, his efficiency, adaptability, liberal ideas, broad sympathies, and general knowledge, have brought to the institution the greatest success of its history. The enrollment of 772 students, and the marked advance in the educational standards during this time, indicate the character and methods of Pres. Swain.

HOMANS, Sheppard, actuary, was born in Baltimore, Md., Apr. 12, 1831, the son of I. Smith Homans, founder and editor of the "Bankers' Magazine." He was educated at St. Mary's College, and at Harvard University. At the university he gave special attention to the study of astronomy and mathematics, and while still a student, was given charge, by the U. S. government, of an astronomical expedition to England, with the object of determining the exact difference of the longitude between Liverpool, Eng., and Boston, Mass. He made two visits to Europe for that purpose, and the efficiency and thoroughness with which he did the work, led to his appointment as an officer of the coast survey. After this he served as an astronomer on several government exploring expeditions across the continent, and in 1855 he was tendered the responsible position of actuary of the Mutual Life Insurance Co., of New York, which he accepted. At that time American life companies depended wholly upon foreign life tables, but Mr. Homans at once devoted himself to an investigation of the laws of American life by making a careful analysis of the mortuary experience of the great company with which he was connected. The result was the construction and publication, in 1850, of the "American Experience Table," which has been adopted as the standard for valuation by many of the states, and by every American life company. About this time Mr. Homans and his assistant, Mr. D. P. Fackler, devised and applied to the distribution of the surplus of the Mutual Life Insurance Co. the famous "contribution plan," by which each insured person shares in the surplus in proportion to his contributions thereto. This plan was received with universal favor, and gave him a high reputation in both this country and Europe. In 1861 Mr. Homans was sent to Europe by the Mutual Life Insurance Co. to study the workings of the British life offices, and again in 1869 as the representative of that company and of American life insurance at large, for the especial purpose of being present at the statistical congress assembled at the Hague. The reception then extended to him gave full assurance of the appreciation in which his labors in the cause of life insurance were held in Europe. The interchange of his ideas with those of leading European actuaries was another step toward breaking down that barrier of self-sufficiency which leads every nation to regard its own policy as the best, and also another step in opening up the way for life insurance on either side of the ocean to measure its defects, and profit by the experience gained on the other side. Unquestionably, the eminence that was early gained by the Mutual Life Insurance Co. of New York was largely due to the industry, ability, and foresight of Mr. Homans. In 1871 he severed his connection with that company, continuing, however, its consulting actuary, and acting also in a like capacity for a number of other companies. In 1875 he organized the Provident Savings Life Assurance Society of New York, became its president, and introduced the system of renewable term assurance, which gives the maximum amount of protection for the premium paid, thus affording, as the company puts it, "The maximum of security and the minimum of cost." During its twenty years of business the Provident Life Assurance Society has achieved a phenomenal success, and it ranks among the best established life institutions in this country. Mr. Homans is best known as an actuary, and in that capacity he has laid all life insurance managers, and all policy-holders, past, present and prospective, under personal obligations, which are acknowledged by all who have knowledge of the subject. At a meeting of American actuaries, held in March, 1889, Mr. Homans was unanimously elected president of the Actuarial Society of America. There is no one for whom life underwriters have a kinder feeling, or a deeper respect than for Mr. Homans, and among the people generally there is probably no man in the country who is more widely known or more highly esteemed. Of him personally it has been said, "He is genial and cultivated in his address, and by the absence of all ostentation, exhibits the truest marks of his scholarly attainments."

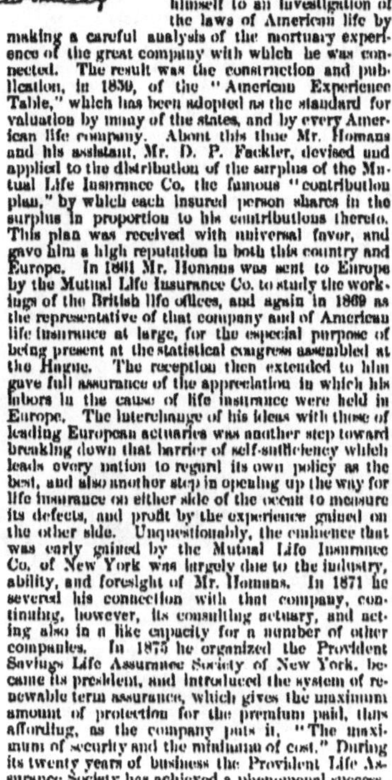

CROWE, John Finley, clergyman, was born in Green county, Tenn. (then a part of North Carolina), June 16, 1787. He was graduated from Transylvania University, and subsequently went to Princeton for his theological studies. In 1817 he was ordained to the ministry by the Presbytery of Louisville, Ky., and from 1815–23 was a teacher and stated supply at Shelbyville, Ky. From 1823–32 he was pastor of a church at Hanover, Ind., being principal of Hanover Academy from 1827–33. He founded Hanover College and the Indiana Theological Seminary, and was vice-president of the college, besides filling the professorships of rhetoric, logic, political economy, and history from 1832–60. Dr. Crowe devoted his last life's interest to the college. He planned it and worked for it with a zeal and devotion that never wavered, and even through its greatest struggles, and the trials of its darkest days, he was ever confident and hopeful of the ultimate success of the institution. He was a faithful, humble, and successful preacher, and a courteous Christian and gentleman of the kindliest spirit, revered and beloved by his pupils and friends. He died at Hanover, Ind., Jan. 17, 1860.

BOUTON, Emily St. John, journalist, was born in New Canaan, Fairfield co., Conn. On her father's side her ancestry is traced directly back to the distinguished French Huguenot, Nicholas Bouton, Baron Montague de Naton, one of whose sons, Noel, became marshal of France, while another, John, came to the United States and was the progenitor of all of the name on this side of the Atlantic. The family bore a prominent part in the Revolution among the Connecticut patriots. On her mother's side Miss Bouton was of English extraction. While she was yet a child her father removed to Sandusky, O., from whose public schools she was graduated at a very early age. After graduation Miss Bouton filled the position of assistant high-school teacher in Milan, O., then in Tiffin, O., and later in Toledo, O. Then followed two years of successful work in Chicago, during which time she occupied the chair of English literature in the Central High School of that city. She relinquished that position, however, on account of failing health, and went to California for change of scene and rest. Returning to Toledo in 1877, Miss Bouton became a member of the editorial staff of the Toledo "Blade," a position she continues to fill at the present time. Although she has become endeared to many thousands of American homes as household editor of the paper, Miss Bouton has, as the literary editor, won a reputation as a critic of high order. Her criticisms, always broad and just, possess a remarkable finish and delicacy of perception. Recognition from her pen is of value to both authors and publishers. Throughout all her work, which embraces the broad field of political, literary, and editorial writing, Miss Bouton evinces a mind trained to the clearest and most logical reasoning, united to the largest sympathy. The author of several successful books on home topics—one of which, entitled "Health and Beauty," has passed through many editions—of many pretty stories and poems, and clever letters and essays, her style is marked by a clearness and grace indicative of the author's personality. Miss Bouton takes a firm and prominent stand among the progressive women of the age who are working for equal rights for their sex. Her labors are to a large extent directed toward the enlargement of woman's sphere through the harmonious development of individual character. Her home is a most pleasant one, situated in a beautiful residential portion of Toledo, where she takes pleasure in dispensing hospitality to her friends. Surrounded by the evidence of a refined and cultured taste, with a family circle consisting of a widowed sister and two nephews, Miss Bouton leads a busy life, devoted to the practical advancement of the theories she advocates in her writings as helpful to the interests of humanity.

FARMAN, Elbert Eli, jurist and diplomat, was born at New Haven, Oswego co., N. Y., Apr. 23, 1831. On the paternal side he is descended from an old Maryland family of planters, that settled near Annapolis, in 1674; and on his maternal side from Leonard Dix, one of the original settlers of Wethersfield, Conn., and from Thomas Wells, also one of the settlers of that town, (1635), and the first colonial treasurer of Connecticut, who was afterwards secretary, deputy governor, and governor of that colony, and twenty-four years one of the judges of the general court; and the writer, and one of the enactors, in 1642, of the severe criminal statutes that have given rise to the tradition of the existence of a criminal code commonly called the "Blue Laws."

He prepared for college at the Genesco Wesleyan Seminary, and was graduated at Amherst in 1855, and three years later received his degree of A. M. Immediately on leaving college he took an active part in public political discussions, in support of John C. Frémont in the presidential campaign of 1856. He studied law at Warsaw, N. Y., and was admitted to practice in 1858. From 1865 to 1867 he traveled and studied in Europe. On his return, in January, 1868, he was appointed by Gov. Fenton district attorney for Wyoming county, and elected for the two following terms to the same position, serving until 1875. In March, 1876, he was appointed by President Grant diplomatic agent and consul general at Cairo, Egypt. He held this position until July 1, 1881, when President Garfield on the last day of his public service, on the personal recommendation of Secretary Blaine, designated him as one of the judges of the mixed tribunals of Egypt. This was a life position, with a liberal salary, but he resigned in the fall of 1884, and returned to the United States, taking an active part in the republican campaign of that year. In 1880, while holding the position of agent and consul-general, Mr. Farman and Geo. S. Batcheller

were appointed by President Hayes delegates on the part of the United States, to act on an international commission instituted to revise the judicial codes of Egypt for the use of the mixed tribunals. He was engaged in this work one year. In January, 1883, he was designated by President Arthur as a member of the International Commission, organized to determine the amounts to be paid to the people of Alexandria for damages arising from the riots, bombardment, burning, and pillage of that city in June and July, 1882. This commission examined, in eleven months, over 10,000 claims, and awarded upon them over $20,000,000. During this work he continued to hold his position in the courts, generally sitting one day in a week. Mr. Farman was the U. S. representative in Egypt during the most interesting period of its modern history. He was in Cairo during those eventful times that led to the dethronement of the Khedive Ismail Pasha, and the installation, in his place, of his son Tewfik, and afterward he witnessed the riots at Alexandria, and the bombardment and burning of that city. When Gen. Grant visited Egypt Mr. Farman presented him to the Khedive, and acted as interpreter at all their interviews. He also accompanied him on his famous voyage of the Nile. While consul-general he sent to the department at Washington voluminous reports upon the agriculture, people, commerce, politics, and finance of Egypt, many of which have been published. By direction of the department of state at Washington, made at his suggestion, he negotiated with Egypt a treaty relating to the extinction of the slave traffic in that country and its provinces. Although this treaty was completed, and verbally assented to by the Egyptian government, it failed of execution on account of a sudden change of the ministry. He took, in other ways, a deep interest in the condition of the slaves in that country, and on his application and through his personal efforts in their behalf at different times, fifteen slaves were liberated by the government on the ground of their ill treatment by their owners. He successfully conducted the negotiations for the increase of the number of American judges in the mixed tribunals, and Philip H. Morgan, afterward U. S. minister plenipotentiary and envoy extraordinary to Mexico, was appointed to the position thus created. He also conducted the negotiations for the obelisk, and to his friendly personal relations with the Khedive, Ismail Pasha, and the members of his ministry, and his diplomatic skill, New York city is indebted for the gift of that ancient monument. Mr. Farman also made while in Egypt extensive collections of ancient coins, scarabs, bronzes, objects in porcelain, and other antiquities, which he has since classified. Some of these collections are loaned to, and are now on exhibition in, the Metropolitan Museum of Art in New York city. In 1892 Amherst College conferred upon him the degree of LL. D. On his leaving Egypt, he received from the Khedive the decoration of "Grand officer of the imperial order of the Medjidieh," a distinction rarely conferred. Mr. Farman is a member of the Union League Club, of the Society of Sons of the Revolution, and of the New York Bar Association. He has been twice married. His first wife was Lois Parker, a niece of Rev. Joel Parker, D.D., of New York city. He married for his second wife, in 1888, Adelaide, daughter of David H. Frisbie, of Galesburg, Ill., and has three children. After his return from Egypt, he delivered an occasional lecture and made political speeches, but has been principally engaged in the management of his private affairs.

WILLIAMS, George Walton, banker and merchant, was born in Burke county, N. C., Dec. 19, 1820, son of Edward and Mary (Brown) Williams. When fourteen years old, George lost his mother, and having a desire to enlarge his sphere of action, he left home for Augusta, 150 miles distant, and engaged as a clerk in the grocery business. Young Williams's genius for business rapidly developed, and at the age of twenty-one he purchased the interest of a partner about to withdraw, and the new business firm, Hand & Williams, was established. In 1852 their business had accumulated a large surplus capital, and Mr. Williams established in Charleston, S.C., the wholesale grocery house of Geo. W. Williams & Co., both houses were conducted on strictly temperance principles. When twenty-three years old he was elected a director of the State Bank of Georgia at Augusta, and in that well-managed institution he gained his first knowledge in banking. At the time of the outbreak of the civil war Mr. Williams was the head of two of the largest commercial houses of the South, an alderman of the city of Charleston, and chairman of the committee on ways and means, which position he held during the entire war. He was director of the Bank of South Carolina, also of two railroad companies, besides being the financial counselor of a host of friends. During the war his charity supplied thousands with daily food, and on the landing of the Federal troops he saved from the fire with their help enough food to feed 20,000 people for four months. At the close of the struggle Mr. Williams erected warehouses in the burnt district for the storage of cotton, opened a banking house, and was soon in the full swing of business. He was also instrumental in saving the property of his first partner from confiscation, when during the war Mr. Hand was residing in the North, holding it in trust, and handing over to him more than $1,000,000, after fifteen years. Mr. Williams has traveled extensively in the United States and Europe, and has presented in literary form some of his vast experience. His "Letters to Young Men" are profitable reading to any who may wish to emulate his example. Mr. Williams was married in 1843 to Miss Wightman, a sister of Bishop William May Wightman of the Methodist Episcopal church. She died in 1854. He married his second wife, Miss Porter of Madison, Ga., in 1856, by whom he had two sons associated with him in business and in the Carolina Savings Bank, of which they are respectively vice-president and cashier. His two daughters are Mrs. P. Calhoun and Mrs. W. P. Carrington. Mr. Williams is a Methodist, and in politics an independent. He has a summer home in the Nacoochee valley, Ga., where he first earned the capital with which he started his business life, and where wealth and toil combine in making an ideal summer resting place from the cares of business. He has published, for gratuitous distribution, "Making and Saving," a book for the young business man, and a more pretentious work, "Sketches of Travels in the Old and New World."

HULL, James Clark, clergyman, was born in Fayette county, W. Va., Feb. 24, 1856, the son of Joseph and Rebecca Hull. His ancestors were from New England, having come there from Leeds, England, before the period of the revolutionary war. His immediate ancestors were natives of the rugged mountains of Pendleton county, Va., and were noted for their longevity, and an education quite in advance of their unfavorable environments. He was ten years old at the introduction of the free-school system in West Virginia. Without a dollar of help he made his own way in getting an education, working as a day laborer to purchase a library, until he was able to teach school. He attended Marshall College, Huntington, W. Va., a part of two years, and after teaching in Fayette and Roane counties, went to Kansas in the fall of 1879. After teaching with success in Woodson county, he entered the South Kansas conference of the Methodist Episcopal church in March, 1881, and was appointed to Madison, where he remained for two years, raising the money and building a new church, and, in general, promoting the interests of the work. In 1881 he was married to Alice Anderson, one of his former pupils. He was next stationed at Yates Centre, and after remaining there, with excellent results to the church, for two years, was transferred to the West Virginia conference, and stationed at Chapline Street Church, Wheeling; and after two years, to St. Paul's Church, Fall River, Mass. During this time he had carried through courses of Hebrew, under Dr. Harper; and of Greek, under Dean Wright; and in his second year at Fall River, was graduated at the Chautauqua School of Theology, with the degree of B.D. The hard study, together with very taxing pulpit and pastoral duties, had at this time impaired the health of Mr. Hull, and, on the advice of his physician, he took comparative rest. During this time he traveled among the mountain regions of the United States, and did extensive newspaper writing. He rendered, at various times, valuable service as a supply, going from Minneapolis, Minn., one winter, to Des Moines, Ia., where he supplied the pulpit of the First Methodist Episcopal Church for sixteen Sundays in succession. In the fall of 1898 he accepted the pastorate of the Clinton Avenue Methodist Episcopal Church of St. Paul. Mr. Hull is a ready extemporaneous speaker, and a leader in temperance reform since his participation in the campaign for prohibition in Kansas, in 1880.

ELY, Smith, lawyer, was born at Hanover, Morris co., N. J., Apr. 17, 1825. He is descended from ancestry notable in the defense of the country. His maternal grandfather, Judge Aaron Kitchell, and his grandfather, Moses Ely, were soldiers in the revolutionary war, while two more remote ancestors,

Richard and William Ely, were in the colonial army during the French and Indian wars. His father, Epaphras C. Ely, a leather merchant, served in the war of 1812. After receiving his preliminary education, he began the study of law in the office of Frederic De Peyster, and was graduated at the law school of the University of New York. After following mercantile pursuits, he entered political life, and was elected to the New York state senate in 1857, being the first Democrat elected from his district. At the outbreak of the civil war he was elected to the board of county supervisors, to which, at that time, belonged the important function of raising money, and enlisting men to carry on the war. He held the office for eight years, distinguishing himself for his vigorous opposition to the prevailing extravagance, and was, in 1867, re-elected as an independent candidate in opposition to the regular party nominees, being supported by every newspaper in the city. The same year he was made commissioner of public instruction. In 1870 he was elected to congress, and was placed by Speaker Blaine, on the committee on railroads. He was re-elected in 1874, when he served on the committees on foreign relations, public buildings, and expenditures of the treasury, of which latter committee he was chairman. While serving in congress, the different Democratic factions united in nominating him as candidate for mayor of New York, against Gen. John A. Dix, when Mr. Ely was elected by over 55,000 majority. His administration was characterized by wise and judicious execution of his trusts,

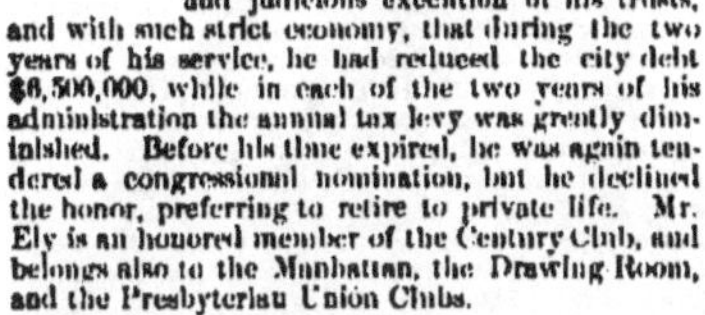

and with such strict economy, that during the two years of his service, he had reduced the city debt $6,500,000, while in each of the two years of his administration the annual tax levy was greatly diminished. Before his time expired, he was again tendered a congressional nomination, but he declined the honor, preferring to retire to private life. Mr. Ely is an honored member of the Century Club, and belongs also to the Manhattan, the Drawing-Room, and the Presbyterian Union Clubs.

FERRIS, Morris Patterson, lawyer, was born in New York city, Oct. 8, 1855, son of Rev. Isaac Ferris, D.D., LL.D., chancellor of the University of the City of New York, and Letitia Storm. His American ancestor John Ferris, came from Leicestershire, England, in 1640, and settled first in Fairfield, then a part of the New Haven colony, and removed to Westchester, N. Y., about 1654, being one of the first patentees and trustees of that town, granted under Gov. Nichols, Feb. 15, 1867, from James, Duke of York, and confirmed under Gov. Fletcher, from William III., King of England, Apr. 16, 1680. The Ferris family came originally from Normandy. Henri de Feriers, the son of Gunlehelme de Ferris, a Norman, obtained from William the Conqueror large grants of land in the counties of Leicestershire, Staffordshire, and Derbyshire. On his mother's side, Morris P. Ferris is descended from the Van Wycks, one of the old Holland Dutch families of Manhattan Island. His maternal great-grandfather served in the war of the revolution, and the Continental troops were encamped on his farm during most of the war. Mr. Ferris was prepared for college at the University Grammar School, was a member of the class of 1874, at the University of the City of New York, and was graduated at the University Law School in 1876; was admitted to the bar and commenced practice the same year. He soon after became

associated with John A. Taylor, who was corporation counsel of the city of Brooklyn under Mayor Seth Low. He separated from the firm, and opened an office by himself in 1891. He has for many years enjoyed a successful practice. He is a member of the Lawyers' and Delta Phi clubs; of the New York Historical Society; Long Island Historical Society; New York Genealogical and Biographical Society; Society of Colonial Wars, and Society of the War of 1812, of which last he is the registrar; also the Society of the Sons of the Revolution. He was the founder and first president of the Garden City Club. He was one of the earliest members, and for several years one of the executive committee, of the Brooklyn Young Republican Club. He married, in 1870, Mary Lanman, daughter of Col. John De Peyster Douw of Poughkeepsie, N. Y. Mrs. Ferris is a very clever and entertaining writer, contributing extensively to "Harper's Monthly," the "New England," and other leading magazines.

HAYES, Joseph Magnor, merchant, was born in Cincinnati, O., Feb. 17, 1846. Five years afterward, however, his parents removed to Illinois, finally locating in Peoria, where young Hayes received his education attending public schools and afterward Fay's Academy, which latter he left to enter a commercial college in Chicago, where, among his other studies, he took a course in commercial law. Being graduated at this college fully equipped theoretically, he entered into practical business in Chicago at the age of nineteen. Fortunately for himself, he practiced economy from the start, and his savings, coupled with the result of speculation in real estate, enabled him to begin business on his own account at the age of twenty-four. It was in December, 1870, that he commenced a small business venture, but had scarcely gotten fairly under way when the great Chicago fire of October, 1871, swept his business out of existence. A man of less energy and grit might have been overwhelmed by such early misfortune, but Mr. Hayes had the courage necessary to bank on the future, and the very next day after the fire he purchased the lease, stock, and fixtures of a small business house on the edge of the burnt district, and immediately started to New York to complete arrangements for a new beginning. Notwithstanding the large loss by the fire, the indebtedness of the firm was paid in full, leaving but little to recommence business. Confidence in his integrity and ability was however established, and he was enabled to

complete the year 1871 in Chicago. The year following the conflagration was a very trying one for the fire sufferers, owing to the scarcity of business buildings, and as Mr. Hayes had no money to invest in the construction of a new one, he determined upon removing to St. Louis. The struggle here to establish himself and recoup the loss by fire was a long one, but after three years the business was gotten fairly under way, and since 1875 its growth has been constant and its prosperity unbroken. In 1886, with a view of interesting some of the faithful employees, the firm was incorporated under the title of the Joseph M. Hayes Woolen Co. Mr. Hayes has infused his personality into every department, with the result that the house is now one of the greatest in its line in the United States, its trade reaching from Duluth on the North to the gulf on the South, and from the Ohio on the East to the Pacific Coast on the West. The house is known for its solidity and unvarying integrity, and its responsibility is unimpeachable The business has become an expression of Mr. Hayes' character. He is a man of the most rugged integrity, honorable and just in all relations of life, quiet and unassuming, possessed of great reserve force, with an executive talent highly developed. Between him and his employees the kindliest feelings exist, as evidenced by the fact that many of them have been with him for years. Mr. Hayes is a director in the Continental National Bank and the Missouri Savings and Loan Co. He was married, October 29, 1873, to Sarah E. Hoyle, and they have eight children living.

CROOKS, Samuel Stearns, manufacturer, was born in Hopkinton, Mass., Apr. 30, 1851, son of John Stearns and Emily Mellen (Parker) Crooks. His ancestors were Scotch Presbyterians, dwellers in Argyleshire, Scotland. They settled in Antrim, and Londonderry, Ireland, about 1618. In 1718 a colony of 100 families, including the Crooks, emigrated to America, settling in Portland and Boston, while some of the colony became the original settlers of Londonderry, Derry, Derryfield, and other pioneer towns in New Hampshire, and eighteen families settled upon the highlands of Hopkinton, Mass., in 1719 and among them Samuel Crooks, the American progenitor. His great-grandson, Samuel, born in Hopkinton, Aug. 22, 1792, married Emeline, daughter of Jonathan and Hannah (Thayer) Stearns. He was a farmer, and the father of John Stearns Crooks, born May 29, 1819, who was apprenticed to the bootmakers' trade in 1839, and subsequently taught the trade to his two younger brothers, Samuel and Abram, and they afterward became successful manufacturers. At a very early age Samuel Stearns Crooks began helping his father in various branches of boot-making, and acquired a very thorough knowledge of the business during his school days, by working in the factory before and after school hours, and during the vacations. He was graduated at the Hopkinton High School in 1869, and then taught a district school one term, after which he had charge of a graded school two terms. In 1870 he conducted a saw and grist-mill, and machine shop for a short time, when he took a position in a machine shop at Natick, Mass., for the purpose of learning the machinists' trade. Returning to Hopkinton, Mass., he was engaged in a shoe factory until October, 1872, when he removed to Detroit, Mich., and soon after accepted the position of foreman in the upper leather department at Pingree & Smith's shoe manufactory, which position he left June 18, 1883, to establish in St. Paul, Minn., in partnership with Charles K. Sharood, the Minnesota Shoe Co., manufacturers of fine shoes, taking with them over 100 people from Detroit, Mich. They established the first manufactory for fine shoes in the state of Minnesota. Early in 1885 the company consolidated with the jobbing firm of C. Gotzian & Co.; the partners continued with the firm. The business soon had an annual output of $750,000. In June, 1892, they withdrew and started the business known as Sharood & Crooks, manufacturers of all varieties of fine shoes and slippers. Previous to the advent of Mr. Crooks in St. Paul, less than 100 persons were employed in manufacturing shoes, while in 1894, there were more than 2,000. Mr. Crooks was married to Caroline A. Coryell, Sept. 8, 1875, and has one son.

ROGERS, John, pioneer settler of Minnesota, was born March 10, 1827, in county Tyrone, Ireland. His father was Owen Rogers, a cattle-merchant, and his mother Ellen Grimes, the daughter of a well-to-do farmer of that county. Mr. Rogers acquired his early education in his native country, afterward assisted in his father's business, later engaging in the same occupation on his own account. In 1845, having determined to seek the opportunities presented in America he came to the United States. Arriving at New Orleans, he remained there a short time, went later to St. Louis, and finally to Galena, where he became assistant steward in a hotel, and after four years, in the spring of 1849, removed to St. Paul, then but a village of 200 inhabitants, the capital of the newly-created territory of Minnesota. Here he engaged in the hotel business, and became actively identified with the future progress of St. Paul, taking part in public affairs as member of the city council and board of education. Mr Rogers was twice married, his first wife being Ann Hartnet of Galena, and the second Adelia Carney of St. Paul. He has six sons and two daughters living.

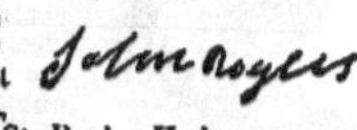

JACKSON, Samuel McCartney, business man, was born in Kiskiminitas township, Armstrong co., Pa., Sept. 24, 1833. He is of Irish-Scotch descent, his ancestors emigrating to this country in colonial times. His grandfather, James Jackson, was a soldier in 1812. Samuel received his education in the common schools of his county, and at the Jacksonville Academy. He engaged in farming and other pursuits until the breaking-out of the civil war, when he entered the Federal army as captain of company G, of the 11th regiment of Pennsylvania reserves. He was successively promoted to major, lieutenant-colonel, and in 1862 was colonel of the regiment, and participated in all the battles of the army of the Potomac, up to the crossing of the James river in 1864. For bravery and general meritorious service he was brevetted brigadier-general from May 6, 1864. In 1871 he engaged in the banking business, which he followed with remarkable success until 1885. He next launched out in iron manufacturing, and by close attention and honorable dealing prospered, and commanded the respect and confidence of the community. He was a member of the lower house of the legislature from Armstrong county in 1868, and was elected to the state senate in 1875. He was afterward collector of internal revenue for the twenty-third district, and elected state treasurer in 1893. In the various public offices in which he has served, he discharged the duties with

great credit to himself and fidelity to the people, but of all the achievements of a successful life, Col. Jackson looks back with the greatest pride and satisfaction to his record as a soldier in the service of his country. He was married, in 1860, to Martha Byerly of Apollo, Pa., who died in 1864. He married again in 1868, Mary E. Wilson of Clarion, Pa. Col Jackson is, in religious faith, a Presbyterian, and member of session of the Apollo Presbyterian Church.

HOOKER, Thomas, clergyman, was born at Marfield, Leicestershire, England, July 7, 1586. His father, Thomas, appears to have come to Marfield from Blaston in the same county, in some capacity as overseer of the large landed properties of the Digby family, and his family is thought from this and from other known facts, to have been of honorable standing. Young Hooker received his preparatory training for the university in the school at Market-Bosworth, about twenty-five miles west from Marfield, close to the celebrated Bosworth field where Richard III. was slain. It was about a year before Hooker's going to the university, that James I. succeeded to the English throne. Two months after the King's accession, young Hooker was at Cambridge University, and in Emmanuel College, which was practically a Puritan institution. He was a student here for certainly seven years, occupying a fellowship, and for a part of the time engaging in some form of clerical work. After the reception of his master's degree, he was at Emmanuel as a Dixie "fellow." Hooker spent some time at the university acting as catechist and lecturer, and there his lectures gave him immediate and wide distinction as a powerful exponent of gospel truths. The period covered by his active Christian ministry in England is thought to have been from 1618 to 1630. He was appointed at first to the rectorship of the little parish of Esher in Surrey, the living being a donative one, worth about £40 a year. Its patron was Francis Drake, kinsman of the great admiral, who received the new rector into his family. Here he married Mrs. Drake's waiting-woman, Susanna. About 1626 he became lecturer in connection with the Church of St. Mary at Chelmsford, Essex, the office being one of the most characteristic outgrowths of the Puritan movement in England, its purpose being to secure a more efficient preaching service than could often be had from the legal incumbent of a benefice. They were, of course, obnoxious to the English church party, and May, 1629, the dominant (church) party, headed by Bishop Laud, began ecclesiastical proceedings against him. The Vicar of Braintree, about this time, writing to Bishop Laud's chancellor declared of Hooker: "This man surpasses them all (other ministers and lecturers) for learning and some other considerable partes . . . gains more and far greater followers than e'l before him." Hooker went to London in answer to summons, and was put under bonds to appear again when called for. The issue was that he was compelled to lay down his Chelmsford lectureship and retire to Little Baddin, about four miles away, where "at the request of several eminent persons he kept a school in his own hired house." His employment there cannot have been of long duration, and is chiefly memorable for having brought to him the assistance in his school, of John Eliot, afterwards "Apostle to the North American Indians." He finally was cited to appear before the high commission court at London, on July 10, 1630, but did not go, and his bond was forfeited by his Chelmsford friends. He secretly boarded a vessel and fled to Holland, residing first at Amsterdam, then Delft, where he was connected for two years in the ministry of the Scotch Presbyterian church with John Forbes. Thence he went to Rotterdam and had some sort of ministerial association with Rev. Hugh Peter and Rev. William Ames. After the death of the latter he completed the book which Mr. Ames had begun, "A Fresh Suit Against Human Ceremonies in God's Worship" (2 vols). With Rev. Samuel Stone, Puritan lecturer at Towcester, England, Hooker took out to the Massachusetts Bay Colony, a company of English men and their families, arriving in Boston, Mass., Sept. 4, 1633. On Oct.

11th, Hooker and Stone were ordained, respectively, pastor and teacher of the church at Newtown, Mass., (now Cambridge). Thursday (church) lectures were speedily established in Boston, Dorchester, Roxbury, and Newtown. The influence of Hooker in colonial affairs grew apace, and among other offices of a semi-public character which he discharged, he was asked by the colonial authorities to argue the points in debate between them and the celebrated Roger Williams, in their proceedings against him; this he did, and Williams was banished from the colony. There was, however, from the first, a certain uneasiness which manifested itself at Boston, regarding the situation of the people at Newtown, all the causes of which it is now difficult to trace. Local jealousy may have given rise to friction, for Newtown's tax was as large as Boston's. Certain it is that the disagreements culminated in the removal of Mr. Hooker and almost the entire population of Newtown to Hartford on the banks of the Connecticut river. May 31, 1636, saw the new emigrants upon their journey from eastern Massachusetts to the banks of the Connecticut. They struck out into the almost pathless woods, and were soon in a wilderness marked only by signs of Indian trails. On the spot where the beautiful city of Hartford stands to-day, Mr. Hooker's company rested, and a church building was forthwith erected which was used for ninety-nine years. The town, with Windsor and Wethersfield its neighbors, was at first governed by a commission appointed by Massachusetts, but on May 1, 1637, a "Genrall Corte" was held "att Harteford," and formal, local, and popular government of the Connecticut plantations was established. Mr. Hooker who had all the influence, not to say authority, derivable from his office, as well as his weight of character, was henceforward until his death, a powerful force in the settlement. He had to do with the first New England Synod (August, 1637), which dealt with the case of Mrs. Anne Hutchinson, being one of its two moderators. He was concerned in the tentative movement towards

a confederation of all the New England colonies which marked the year 1637, and in the same year was at the front in the establishment of the written constitution of popular government, which the first few weeks of the year 1639 were to see formally adopted by Connecticut. His part in this, is indeed, in some sense, his most distinguishing and abiding monument, for the instrument is in reality, very largely the offspring of his jealousy for popular liberty. It stands in sharp contrast, in important respects, with the spirit of the government of Massachusetts Bay, that was not, and was not intended to be, Democratic. Gov. Winthrop having affirmed: "Democracy, I do not conceive that ever God did ordain as a fit government either for church or commonwealth." The contention that the first pastor of the Hartford Church was Connecticut's first great legislator is sustained by a volume of evidence. And John Fiske said of this Connecticut constitution of 1639: "It was the first written constitution known to history that created a government, and it marked the beginnings of American Democracy, of which Thomas Hooker deserves, more than any other man, to be called the father. The government of the United States to-day, is, in lineal descent more nearly related to that of Connecticut than to that of any other of the thirteen colonies." Shortly after the adoption of the constitution, Mr. Hooker visited Boston in company with Gov. Haynes of Connecticut, to confer with the Massachusetts authorities in respect to the formation of a colonial confederation. In 1643 he was invited with Cotton of Boston, and Davenport of New Haven, to sit in Westminster (England), Assembly of Divines, and "advise about the settling of church government," but declined, and counselled the others that he "liked not the business nor thought it any sufficient call for them to go 3,000 miles to agree with three men." He was, however, a moderator of the council at Cambridge, Mass. (Sept., 1643), which left the "Cambridge Platform" as one of the landmarks of Congregational polity in New England. A closing labor of his life was the preparation of a "Survey of the Summe of Church Discipline" (published in 1648); this duty having been assigned to him by the Cambridge synod or council. It was in the midst of these ever busy labors that he died at Hartford, Conn., from an "epidemical sickness," July 19, 1647. No portrait of Hooker remains. The state of Connecticut, years since, in commemoration of one to whom she owes so much, placed in her capitol at Hartford his striking statue by Niehaus, in the making of which the artist compared the likenesses of the various members of Hooker's lineal posterity, thus affording a not improbably fair representation of the great founder of the colony. Mr. Hooker was not in primary purpose an author of books, but of his published writings some thirty are extant. In the sermons which they have preserved to the world the most robust Calvinism is everywhere implied and incidentally expressed.

ADAMS, Franklin George, secretary of the Kansas State Historical Society, Topeka, was born in Rodman, Jefferson co., N. Y., May 13, 1824. He was brought up on a farm, and received a common school education. At the age of nineteen he went to Cincinnati, and taught five years in the public schools. He attended lectures at the Ohio Medical College, and in the law department of Cincinnati College, where he was graduated in 1852, being admitted to practice at the Ohio bar the same year. He removed to Kansas in March, 1855, with a colony which settled at Ashland, Riley co.; lived at Leavenworth in 1856, and at Atchison from 1857–61 in law practice. He was a member of the Leavenworth constitutional convention in 1858; probate judge of Atchison county in 1858–59; register of the U. S. land office, Lecompton and Topeka, 1861–64; clerk of the U. S. district court, Topeka, 1863; secretary of the State Agricultural Society, 1863–64; U. S. Indian agent for the Kickapoos, 1865–69. He was editor of the "Squatter Sovereign" newspaper, Atchison, 1857; of the "State Record," and also of the "Kansas Farmer," Topeka, 1863; "Atchison Free Press," 1864–68; "Waterville Telegraph," 1871–72. At Cincinnati he was author of several minor publications relating to the spelling reform, including "The Lives of the Presidents," in phonotypic print. He was author of the "Homestead Guide" (Waterville, Kan., 1873). From 1875–94 he was chairman of the educational committee of the Kansas State Grange, and made numerous reports, which were published by that body. In February, 1876, at the beginning of the work of the Kansas State Historical Society, he was appointed secretary, a position which he still holds. All the work of this notable society has been done under his management. The library contains (1896) 80,000 volumes, besides 10,000 manuscripts, 1,200 pictures, and a large collection of maps and historical relics and mementoes in every form. Mr. Adams has made all of the reports, and compiled all of the volumes of "Collections of the Society;" eight biennial reports (1875–92), and four volumes of "Collections," 1875–90. This institution is maintained by the state, its library and collections are the property of the state, and are kept in rooms in the state capitol at Topeka.

SMITH, Nelson, lawyer, was born in Middletown, Delaware co., N. Y., Sept. 29, 1832. His father, Samuel Smith, was a practical millwright and civil engineer. Mr. Smith's early paternal ancestors in America came from England, and his maternal ancestors from Holland. His paternal great-grandfather, Abel Smith, was born on Cow-Neck, North Hempstead, L. I., Oct. 31, 1702, married Ruth Jackson, June 19, 1730, and died Apr. 25, 1757. Ruth Jackson was the daughter of Samuel Jackson, and granddaughter of Col. John Jackson, who was a member of the  Colonial general assembly of New York, 1693–1700, lieutenant-colonel of militia, 1700, and judge of the court of common pleas, Queens county, 1724. Her great-grandfather was Robert Jackson, one of the original settlers of Hempstead, L. I., a member of Gov. Nicoll's convention, 1665, and well known in colonial history. Through his maternal great-grandfather, Harmonus Dumond, Mr. Smith is descended from Katrina Schuyler Dumond, daughter of David Schuyler, mayor of Albany, 1705–07. He was educated at the Delaware Academy, afterward taking special courses in New York city. He studied law with Samuel Gordon, a distinguished lawyer, and a representative in the twenty-seventh and twenty-ninth congresses, and with William Murray, afterward judge of the supreme court. He was admitted to the bar, and commenced practice in New York city in 1855, and was, soon after, admitted to practice in the supreme court of the United States. Mr. Smith took an active part in support of the Democratic cause in the national campaigns of 1884, 1888, and 1892, and of the campaign of education to promote the reform of the tariff. He contributed many articles and made numerous speeches, which were printed and circulated as educational documents. In the campaign of 1892 he was chosen an elector of president and vice-president on the Democratic ticket, and in 1893 was elected a delegate from the city of New York to the constitutional convention of the state of New York, which assembled at Albany, May 8, 1894, and continued its sessions until Sept. 29th. He is credited with many of the reforms effected by the judiciary article of the revised constitution, notably the creation of the new court called the "Appellate Division of the Supreme Court." He was for four years (1890–94) chairman of the general committee of Tammany Hall, which position he resigned in January of the last named year. He has also held the position of chairman of the central branch of the Irish Land League of America. As a lawyer, Mr. Smith has had a wide practice, and the reported cases in which his name appears as counsel, embrace nearly the entire range of the law. He is a member of the American Bar Association, the State Bar Association, the Association of the Bar of the City of New York, the Law Institute, and of the Press, Manhattan, Reform, and Democratic Clubs.

INDEX.

A

American Independence first conceived, I. 17, Otis, J.

American Scott, I. 399, Cooper, J. F.

Ames, Adelbert, soldier, IV. 354.

Ames, Fisher, statesman, II. 382.

Ames, Oakes, congressman, II. 199.

Ames, Oakes A., manufacturer, II. 200.

Ames, Oliver, governor, I. 122.

Amherst College. Presidents:
Gates, M. E., sixth, V. 309.
Hitchcock, E., third, V. 308.
Humphrey, H., second, V. 308.
Moore, Z. S., first, V. 307.
Seelye, J. H., fifth, VI. 157.
Stearns, W. A., fourth, V. 309.

Amherst, Jeffary, rev. soldier, I. 101.

Ammen, Daniel, naval officer, IV. 393.

Ammen, Jacob, soldier, IV. 391.

Ammidown, E. H., merchant, III. 246.

Amory, Thomas J. C., soldier, IV. 283.

Amundson, John A., lawyer, V. 495.

Anderson, C., attorney-general, III. 191.

Anderson, Alex., wood engraver, VI. 259.

Anderson, Galusha, educator, I. 303.

Anderson, George B., soldier, IV. 418.

Anderson, Henry J., educator, VI. 347.

Anderson, Hugh J., governor, VI. 310.

Anderson, James B., clergyman, IV. 62.

Anderson, James P., soldier, IV. 129.

Anderson, Joseph, senator, II. 11.

Anderson, Mary, actress, I. 243.

Anderson, Richard C., soldier, VI. 42.

Anderson, Richard C., statesman, VI. 115.

Anderson, Richard H., soldier, IV. 295.

Anderson, Robert, soldier, IV. 179.

Anderson, Robert H., soldier, IV. 130.

Anderson, Thomas McA., soldier, IV. 410.

Anderson, William, soldier, IV. 352.

Andover first named, I. 18, Osgood, S.

Andre, John, British soldier, I. 48.

Andrew, James Osgood, bishop, I. 521.

Andrew, John Albion, governor, I. 116.

Andrew, Samuel, educator, I. 164.

Andrews, Alexander B., R. R. pres., II. 482.

Andrews, Elisha B., educator, I. 303; I. 308.

Andrews, Garnett, lawyer, IV. 184.

Andrews, Geo. Leonard, soldier, V. 46.

Andrews, John, college provost, I. 342.

Andrews, Newton L., educator, V. 429.

Andrews, Sherlock J., jurist, VI. 11.

Andrews, Stephen P., philosopher, VI. 442.

Andrews, Timothy P., soldier, IV. 321.

Andros, Sir Edmund, colonial gov., VI. 90.

Angell, James Burrill, educator, I. 251.

Angell, William G., inventor, II. 392.

Angier, Nedom L., physician, II. 349.

Ansbacher, A. B., manufacturer, II. 515.

Ansorge, Chas., musical conductor, V. 280.

Anthon, Charles, educator, VI. 347.

Anthony, Daniel R., pioneer, VI. 371.

Anthony, Susan B., reformer, IV. 403.

Apostle of the Indians, II. 422, Eliot, J.

Appleton, Daniel, publisher, II. 509.

Appleton, Daniel & Co., II. 509.

Appleton, Daniel S., publisher, II. 510.

Appleton, George S., publisher, II. 510.

Appleton, James, father of prohibition, V. 433.

Appleton, Jesse, educator, I. 417.

Appleton, John A., publisher, II. 510.

Appleton, Samuel, merchant, V. 127.

Appleton, William H., publisher, II. 510.

Archer, Branch T., pioneer, VI. 375.

Archer, Henry M., R. R. manager, VI. 136.

Archibald, George D., educator, II. 125.

Arctic Explorers:
Brainard, D. L., III. 286.
Danenhower, J. W., III. 284.
DeLong, G. W., III. 282.
Gilder, W. H., III. 287.
Greely, A. W., III. 285.
Grinnell, H., III. 281.
Hall, C. F., III. 281.
Hayes, I. I., III. 280.
Kane, E. K., III. 288.
Lockwood, J. B., III. 286.
Melville, G. W., III. 283.
Nindemann, W. F. C., III. 284.
Peary, R. E., II. 63.
Rodgers, F., V. 14.
Schley, W. S., IV. 394.
Schwatka, F., III. 285.

Arkell, James, manufacturer, I. 367.

Arkins, John, journalist, I. 268.

Armistead, Lewis Addison, soldier, V. 15.

Armstrong, George W., merchant, II. 152.

Armstrong, Jas. F., naval officer, IV. 315.

Armstrong, John, statesman, I. 48.

Armstrong, P. B., insurance pres., I. 256.

Armstrong, Samuel, governor, VI. 245.

Armstrong, Samuel C., educator, I. 436.

Arnett, Benjamin W., bishop, III. 499.

Arnold, Benedict, rev. soldier, I. 53.

Arnold, Benedict, suspected of treachery, I. 45, Brown, J.; treachery, I. 49, Andre, J.

Arnold, Lewis G., soldier, IV. 297.

Arnold, Richard, IV. 399.

Artemus Ward, pen-name, I. 425, Browne, C. F.

Arthur, Chester A., U. S. pres., IV. 247.

Asbury, Francis, M. E. bishop, VI. 293.

Ashboth, Alexander S., soldier, IV. 413.

Ashburn, George W., soldier, IV. 399.

Ashby, Turner, soldier, IV. 296.

Ashe, John, soldier, VI. 438.

Ashe, Samuel, governor, IV. 421.

Ashmead, Henry G., author, IV. 93.

Ashmun, George, lawyer, VI. 162.

Ashmun, Jehudi, missionary, VI. 195.

Ashu, capture of the sloop, I. 51, Hale, N.

Associated Press, origin of, I. 127, Beach, M. Y.

Astronomers:
Barnard, E. E.
Brooks, W. R., V. 197.
Burnham, S. W.
Campbell, W. W.
Davidson, G.
Gould, B. A., V. 108.
Holden, E. S.
Kirkwood, D., IV. 349.
Langley, S. P., III. 338.
Loomis, E.
Lovering, J., VI. 424.
Mitchell, M., V. 236.
Mitchel, O. M., III. 440.
Newcomb, S.
Peirce, B.
Pickering, E. C., VI. 425.
Pickering, W. H., VI. 425.
Rutherfurd, L. M., VI. 360.
Swift, L., IV. 302.
Williams, S., I. 257.
Walker, S. C., V. 72.
Young, C. A., VI. 189.

Atkinson, Byron A., merchant, III. 68.

Atkinson, George H., missionary, VI. 367.

Atkinson, Henry Morell, banker, V. 223.

Atkinson, John M. P., educator, II. 26.

Atkinson, Thomas, P. E. bishop, VI. 52.

Atkinson, William Elrie, lawyer, V. 183.

Atlantic Monthly, The, illus. Publisher, I. 281, Houghton, H. O.; Editors, I. 282, Howells, W. D., Fields, J. T.; I. 283, Aldrich, T. B., Scudder, H. E.

Attwood, Julius, banker, II. 343.

Atwater, Amzi, pioneer, VI. 21.

Atwater, Wilbur Olin, chemist, VI. 262.

Aubry, Leander J., manufacturer, II. 223.

Audenried, Joseph C., soldier, IV. 227.

Audubon, John J., naturalist, VI. 75.

Angur, Christopher C., soldier, IV. 337.

Augustus, John, philanthropist, VI. 52.

Austell, Alfred, financier, I. 536.

Austin, Jane G., author, VI. 62.

Austin, Moses, pioneer, V. 157.

Austin, Samuel, educator, II. 39.

Austin, Stephen F., statesman, VI. 71.

Authors' club, I. 367, Boyesen, H. H.

Averell, William W., soldier, IV. 231.

Avery, Alphonso C., jurist, III. 424.

Avery, Benjamin Park, journalist, I. 319.

Avery, Elroy, McKendree, educator, V. 18.

Avery, Henry Ogden, architect, I. 157.

Avery, Isaac Wheeler, lawyer, III. 234.

Avery, Rosa Miller, author, VI. 271.

Avery, Samuel P., art connoisseur, I. 157.

Avery, Waitstill, rev. patriot, VI. 72.

Ayres, Romeyn B., soldier, IV. 255.

B

Babbitt, Edwin B., soldier, V. 31.

Babcock, George H., engineer, V. 304.

Babcock, Orville E., soldier, IV. 411.

Bache, Alex. Dallas, educator, III. 348.

Bache, Franklin, chemist, V. 346.

Bache, Theophylact, merchant, I. 496.

Bachman, Solomon, merchant, III. 421.

Backus, Henry C., lawyer, VI. 164.

Backus, Truman Jay, educator, V. 375.

Bacon, Delia Salter, author, I. 477.

Bacon, Edward P., merchant, II. 234.

Bacon, F., piano manufacturer, II. 447.

Bacon, Frederick H., lawyer, VI. 125.

Bacon, George A., agriculturist, V. 383.

Bacon, James Terrill, merchant, III. 210.

Bacon, Joel Smith, educator, III. 152.

Bacon, John W., civil engineer, VI. 174.

Bacon, Leonard, clergyman, I. 176.

Bacon, Nathaniel, colonial leader, V. 337.

Bacon, Sherman J., merchant, III. 256.

Bacon, Thomas Scott, clergyman, V. 305.

Bacone, Almon C., educator, III. 310.

Badeau, Adam, soldier and author, VI. 283.

Badger, Geo. E., secretary, III. 40, 305.

Badger, Joseph, missionary, VI. 70.

Badger, Milton, clergyman, VI. 80.

Badger, Oscar C., naval officer, V. 333.

Baer, William Jacob, artist, V. 469.

Bagley, John Judson, governor, V. 274.

Bailey, Ezra B., financier, VI. 124.

Bailey, Gamaliel, journalist, II. 417.

Bailey, George M., journalist, V. 354.

Bailey, Guilford D., soldier, IV. 364.

Bailey, Jacob, rev. soldier, I. 46.

Bailey, James M., humorist, VI. 24.

Bailey, James S., manufacturer, III. 138.

Bailey, Joseph, soldier, V. 394.

Bailey, Silas, educator, I. 302.

Bailey, Theodorus, rear-admiral, II. 106.

Baird, Andrew D., soldier, IV. 154.

Baird, George W., inventor, I. 415.

Baird, Henry Carey, publisher, V. 314.

Baird, John Faris, clergyman, II. 478.

Butler, Benjamin W., governor, I. 119.
Butler, Benjamin F., soldier and statesman, V. 297.
Butler, Charles, philanthropist, V. 84.
Butler, Edward, rev. soldier, I. 44.
Butler, John George, clergyman, I. 384.
Butler, Matthew C., senator, I. 298.
Butler, Percival, rev. soldier, I. 44.
Butler, Pierce, senator, II. 162.
Butler, Richard, merchant, I. 352.
Butler, Richard, rev. soldier, I. 44.
Butler, Thomas, rev. soldier, I. 44.
Butler, William M., physician, VI. 386.
Butler, William O., soldier, VI. 183.
Butler, Zebulon, rev. soldier, I. 52.
Butterfield, Daniel, soldier, IV. 128.
Butterworth, H., journalist, II. 111.
Buttler, Charles V., physician, VI. 382.
Button, Henry H., physician, III. 339.
Byford, Henry T., physician, II. 155.
Byford, William H., physician, II. 13.
Byrne, William, merchant, V. 303.

C

Cabaniss, Elbridge G., jurist, II. 137.
Cabaniss, T. B., congressman, V. 283.
Cabell, Samuel J., congressman, II. 264.
Cabell, William H., governor, V. 444.
Cable, George W., author, I. 533.
Cable, the laying of the ocean, IV. 452, Field, C. W.
Cabot, George, statesman, II. 5.
Cadillac, Antoine de la M., explorer, V. 172.
Cadwalader, John, rev. soldier, I. 39.
Cady, Ernest, manufacturer, V. 227.
Cahill, LeRoy, inventor, V. 117.
Cake, Henry L., soldier, V. 352.
Caldwell, George C., chemist, IV. 482.
Caldwell, James, soldier, V. 91.
Caldwell, John Curtis, soldier, V. 243.
Caldwell, Samuel Lunt, educator, V. 235.
Caldwell, Tod R., governor, IV. 428.
Calhoun, Edmund R., naval officer, IV. 295.
Calhoun, John C., statesman, VI. 83.
Calhoun, Patrick, R. R. president, I. 528.
California, governors of:
　Bartlett, W., sixteenth, IV. 113.
　Bigler, J., third, IV. 106.
　Booth, N., eleventh, IV. 110.
　Budd, J. H., nineteenth.
　Burnett, P. H., first, IV. 105.
　Downey, J. G., seventh, IV. 108.
　Haight, H. H., tenth, IV. 109.
　Irwin, W., thirteenth, IV. 110.
　Johnson, J. N., fourth, IV. 107.
　Latham, M. S., sixth, IV. 108.
　Low, F. F., ninth, IV. 109.
　Markham, H. H., eighteenth, II. 415.
　McDougall, J., second, IV. 106.
　Pacheco, R., twelfth, IV. 110.
　Perkins, G. C., fourteenth, IV. 111.
　Stanford, L., eighth, II. 129.
　Stoneman, G., fifteenth, IV. 112.
　Waterman, R. W., seventeenth, IV. 113.
　Weller, John B., fifth, IV. 107.
Caloric engine invented, IV. 47, Ericsson, J.
Calvert, George H., author, V. 357.
Calvin, Delano C., lawyer, V. 151.
Call, Wilkeson, senator, II. 431.
Callender, Walter, merchant, III. 269.
Cameron, Alexander, lawyer, IV. 63.
Cameron, James, soldier, IV. 136.
Cameron, James Donald, statesman, IV. 25.

Cameron, James Donald, senator, I. 218.
Cameron, Robert A., soldier, IV. 296.
Cameron, Simon, statesman, II. 78.
Cameron, Wm. Ewan, governor, V. 455.
Camden, Johnson M., legislator, VI. 488.
Camm, John, educator, III. 233.
Cammerhof, John C. F., bishop, V. 485.
Camp, David N., educator, II. 380.
Camp, E. C., lawyer, I. 478.
Campbell, Alexander, theologian, IV. 161.
Campbell, David, governor, V. 449.
Campbell, George T., physician, IV. 236.
Campbell, Geo. W., statesman, V. 372.
Campbell, James, postmaster-gen., IV. 251.
Campbell, J. A., associate justice, II. 472.
Campbell, James E., governor, I. 470.
Campbell, Jere. Rockwell, V. 66.
Campbell, Samuel L., educator, III. 164.
Campbell, Thomas J., educator, II. 268.
Campbell, W. H., clergyman, III. 402.
Campbell, William, rev. soldier, I. 62.
Canby, Edward R. S., soldier, V. 393.
Candler, Allen D., manufacturer, II. 121.
Candler, Warren A., educator, I. 521.
Cannon, Henry W., banker, I. 158.
Capen, Edward, librarian, VI. 483.
Capen, Elmer Hewitt, educator, VI. 241.
Capen, Francis L., meteorologist, V. 303.
Cardenas, Louis F., R. C. bishop, V. 423.
Cardinal, first Amer., I. 195, McCloskey, J.
Carey, Henry C., political economist, V. 24.
Carey, Joseph M., senator, I. 462.
Carey, Mathew, publisher, VI. 278.
Carhart, Henry Smith, electrician, IV. 435.
Carleton, Frank H., lawyer, VI. 101.
Carleton, Will, poet, II. 505.
Carlisle, John G., congressman, I. 461.
Carlton, Henry H., congressman, II. 145.
Carnahan, J., educator, clergyman, V. 467.
Caroline Thomas, pen-name, Dorr, J. C. R., VI. 56.
Carow, Isaac, merchant, I. 498.
Carpenter, Elisha, jurist, V. 243.
Carpenter, Esther Bernon, author, II. 449.
Carpenter, F. W., merchant, III. 257.
Carpenter, Matthew H., senator, IV. 22.
Carpenter, R. C., educator, IV. 430.
Carr, Elias, governor, IV. 430.
Carr, Joseph B., soldier, IV. 389.
Carr, Julien S., manufacturer, I. 186.
Carrington, Edward, soldier, V. 54.
Carrington, Paul, jurist, V. 161.
Carroll, Alfred L., physician, III. 122.
Carroll, Anna Ella, patriot, V. 193.
Carroll, Daniel, statesman, II. 389.
Carroll, David L., educator, II. 24.
Carroll, David W., jurist, V. 115.
Carroll, Howard, journalist, III. 309.
Carroll, John, archbishop, I. 480.
Carroll, Samul Sprigg, soldier, V. 51.
Carrow, Howard, lawyer, IV. 497.
Carson, Alexander N., clergyman, IV. 114.
Carson, Christopher, explorer, III. 278.
Carson, Hampton Lawrence, III. 264.
Carson, Joseph, pharmacist, V. 346.
Carstens, John H., physician, VI. 388.
Carter, Franklin, educator, VI. 239.
Carter, Lorenzo, pioneer, III. 296.
Carter, Samuel P., rear-admiral, II. 104.
Carter, William T., financier, VI. 160.
Cartwright, Peter, clergyman, VI. 61.
Carver, Jonathan, traveler, I. 476.
Cary, Alice, author, I. 535.
Cary, Annie Louise, singer, I. 426.
Cary, Archibald, patriot, V. 106.
Cary, Phœbe, author, I. 535.

Casey, Lyman R., senator, I. 291.
Casey, Silas, naval officer, IV. 321.
Casey Silas, soldier, IV. 279.
Casey, Thomas L., soldier, IV. 279.
Cashen, Thomas V., manufacturer, V. 422.
Cass, Lewis, statesman, V. 3.
Cassel, Abraham H., antiquarian, III. 276.
Castro, Henry, pioneer, III. 268.
Caswell, Alexis, educator, I. 307.
Caswell, Lucien B., lawyer, III. 356.
Caswell, Richard, governor, IV. 419.
Cathcart, Charles W., senator, IV. 364.
Catlin, George, painter, III. 270.
Catlin, Isaac Swartwood, lawyer, III. 346.
Catron, John, statesman, II. 470.
Cattell, Alexander G., senator, II. 35.
Cauldwell, Leslie Giffen, artist, III. 432.
Cauldwell, William, journalist, I. 237.
Cayvan, Georgia Eva, actress, II. 453.
Cecil, Elizabeth Frances, III. 266.
Century Magazine, The, publisher, I. 311, Smith, R.; editors, I. 311, Holland, J. G.; I. 312, Gilder, R. W.; I. 313, Johnson, R. U.
Cerberus of the Treas., I. 22, Ellsworth, O.
Cesnola, Luigi Palma di, soldier, I. 422.
Chadbourne, Paul A., educator, VI. 234.
Chaffee, James F., clergyman, VI. 115.
Chaffee, Jerome Bunty, senator, VI. 199.
Chalmers, James R., soldier, IV. 353.
Chamberlain, J. L., educator, I. 419.
Chamberlain Observatory, illus., I. 461.
Chamberlin, Ed. P., merchant, II. 400.
Chamberlin, Franklin, lawyer, II. 417.
Chamberlin, H. B., R. R. president, I. 460.
Chamberlin, J. W., physician, VI. 392.
Champney, Benjamin, painter, IV. 269.
Chancellor, Eustathius, physician, V. 152.
Chandler, A. B., pres. postal tel., III. 171.
Chandler, Wm. E., secretary, IV. 250.
Chandler, Zachariah, secretary, IV. 18.
Chanler, Amelie Rives, author, I. 366.
Channing, Wm. E., clergyman, V. 458.
Chapin, Aaron Lucius, educator, III. 164.
Chapin, Alfred Clark, mayor, I. 525.
Chapin, Chester Wm., V. 497.
Chapin, Edwin H., clergyman, VI. 89.
Chapin, Samuel, I. 525, Chapin, A. C.
Chapin, Stephen, educator, III. 132.
Chapman, Henry T., Jr., financier, IV. 344.
Chapman, John A. M., clergyman, IV. 461.
Chapman, Maria W., reformer, II. 315.
Chapman, Nathaniel, III. 294.
Chapman, William C., physician, VI. 280.
Chappell, Absalom H., author, VI. 187.
Charlton, Robert M., senator, IV. 191.
Chase, Denison, inventor, IV. 494.
Chase, Geo. Lewis, underwriter, V. 213.
Chase, Pliny E., astronomer, VI. 53.
Chase, Salmon P., jurist, I. 28.
Chase, Samuel, jurist, I. 24.
Chase, Waldo E., manufacturer, III. 435.
Chase, William T., clergyman, VI. 19.
Chauncy, Charles, clergyman, V. 168.
Chauncy, Charles, educator, VI. 410.
Cheadle, Joseph B., congressman, II. 162.
Cheever, Henry Martyn, lawyer, V. 91.
Cheever, Samuel, jurist, II. 498.
Chemical Bank, I. 262, Williams, G. G.
Cheney, Chas. Edward, I. 31, Fuller, E. W.
Cheney, John Vance, poet, VI. 289.
Cheney, Moses, preacher, VI. 288.
Cheney, Simeon Pease, singer, VI. 261.
Cheesebrough, Robert A., mfr., III. 164.
Cheshire, Joseph B., clergyman, VI. 53.

O

Pease, Calvin, educator, II. 42.
Peavey, Frank H., capitalist, VI. 43.
Peck, F. W., philanthropist, III. 355.
Peck, George B., physician, VI. 386.
Peck, George W., governor, II. 442.
Peck, Jesse T., educator, VI. 430.
Peck, John Hudson, III. 251.
Peck, John James, soldier, IV. 356.
Peck, Theodore Safford, soldier, V. 492.
Peckham, William G., lawyer, I. 477.
Peffer, William Alfred, senator, I. 299.
Pegram, John, soldier, V. 52.
Pegram, William H., educator, III. 447.
Peirce, Thomas May, educator, V. 28.
Pelham, Thomas W., financier, II. 229.
Pendleton, Edward W., lawyer, V. 280.
Pendleton, George, merchant, VI. 112.
Pendleton, George H., lawyer, III. 278.
Pendleton, Nathaniel, III. 273.
Penn, John, governor, II. 277.
Penn, William, III. 377, Smith, M.
Penn, H. C., second wife of founder, II. 277.
Penn, John, oldest son of founder by second wife, II. 277.
Penn, Richard, third son of founder by second wife, II. 277.
Penn, Richard, second son of third son of founder, II. 277.
Penn, Thomas, second son of founder by second wife, II. 277.
Penn, William, founder, II. 275.
Penn, Wm., oldest son of founder, II. 277.
Penn, Wm., second son of founder, II. 277.
Pennach, Alex. M., naval officer, IV. 280.
Pennington, William, governor, V. 206.
Pennington, William S., gov., V. 204.
Pennsylvania, University of. Provosts:
Andrews, J., fourth, I. 342.
Beasley, F., fifth, I. 342.
DeLancey, W. H., sixth, I. 342.
Ewing, J., second, I. 341.
Goodwin, D. R., ninth, I. 344.
Harrison, C. C., eleventh.
Ludlow, J., seventh, I. 343.
McDowell, J., third, I. 342.
Pepper, W., I. 345.
Smith, W., first, I. 340.
Stille, C. J., tenth, I. 344.
Vethake, H., eighth, I. 344.
Vice-provosts:
Adrain, R., I. 347.
Alison, F., I. 346.
Frazer, J. F., I. 348.
Krauth, C. P., I. 349.
Magaw, S., I. 347.
Patterson, R., I. 347.
Patterson, R. M., I. 347.
Rittenhouse, D., I. 346.
Wylie, S. B., I. 348.
Pennsylvania, governors of:
Beaver, J. A., twenty-seventh, II. 293.
Bigler, W., nineteenth, II. 288.
Bryan, G., second, II. 280.
Curtin, A. G., twenty-second, II. 290.
Dickinson, J., fifth, II. 281.
Findlay, W., tenth, II. 285.
Franklin, B., sixth, I. 328.
Geary, J. W., twenty-third, II. 291.
Hartranft, J. F., twenty-fourth, II. 291.
Hastings, D. H., twenty-ninth, V. 27.
Hiester, J., eleventh, II. 285.
Hoyt, H. M., twenty-fifth, II. 292.
Johnston, W. F., eighteenth, II. 288.
Logan, J., II. 276.
McKean, T., eighth, II. 284.
Mifflin, T., seventh, II. 283.

Pennsylvania, governors of—Con.
Moore, W., fourth, II. 281.
Packer, W. F., twenty-first, II. 289.
Pattison, R. E., twenty-sixth and twenty-eighth, I. 278.
Penn, J., first, II. 277.
Penn, W., founder, II. 275.
Pollock, J., twentieth, II. 289.
Porter, D. R., sixteenth, II. 287.
Reed, J., third, II. 280.
Ritner, J., fourteenth, II. 286.
Schulze, J. A., twelfth, II. 286.
Shunk, F. R., seventeenth, II. 288.
Snyder, S., ninth, II. 284.
Wharton, T., Jr., first president, II. 280.
Wolf, G., thirteenth, II. 286.
Penrose, Boies, lawyer, II. 444.
Penrose, Richard A. F., physician, II. 443.
Pepper, William, educator, I. 345.
Pepperrell, Sir William, soldier, III. 330.
Percheron Horse, introduction into U. S., I. 156, Walters, W. T.
Percival, Chester S., educator, II. 232.
Perham, Sidney, governor, VI. 315.
Perit, Pelatiah, merchant, I. 499.
Perkins, Bishop W., senator, III. 302.
Perkins, Charles G., inventor, IV. 290.
Perkins, Charles H., inventor, II. 271.
Perkins, George C., governor, IV. 111.
Perkins, T. H., philanthropist, V. 245.
Perry, Alexander J., soldier, IV. 99.
Perry, Amos, II. 297.
Perry, Matthew C., naval officer, IV. 42.
Perry, Oliver H., naval officer, IV. 288.
Perry, William S., P E. bishop, III. 469.
Peter Parley, pen name, V. 355, Goodrich, S. G.
Peters, Bernard, editor, I. 157.
Peters, Madison C., clergyman, II. 501.
Peters, R., railroad manager, III. 192.
Petersburg, battle of, IV. 7, Grant, U. S.
Petroleum V. Nasby, pen-name, Locke, D. R., VI. 26.
Pettigrew, Richard F., senator, II. 202.
Peyton, John Howe, jurist, IV. 88.
Peyton, John Lewis, author, IV. 89.
Peyton, John Rowze, IV. 88.
Peyton, Robert L. Y., jurist, V. 158.
Peyton, Wm. Madison, lawyer, IV. 89.
Phelan, Richard, R. C. bishop, VI. 337.
Phelps, Amos A., clergyman, II. 327.
Phelps, Edward John, diplomat, V. 411.
Phelps, Elizabeth Stuart, author, II. 433.
Phelps, John Smith, governor, V. 10.
Phelps, Thomas S., naval officer, IV. 341.
Philadelphia College of Pharmacy. Presidents:
Bullock, C., sixth, V. 344.
Ellis, C., fourth, V. 344.
Lehman, W., second, V. 343.
Marshall, C., first, V. 343.
Parrish, D., fifth.
Smith, D. B., third, V. 343.
Phillips, Adelaide, singer, VI. 149.
Phillips, Lewis S., manufacturer, II. 495.
Phillips, Wendell, orator, II. 314.
Phinizy, Charles H., educator, V. 485.
Phips, Sir William, colonial gov., VI. 96.
Physick, Philip S., physician, VI. 391.
Pickering, Edward C., astronomer, VI. 425.
Pickering, Timothy, statesman, I. 12.
Pickering, William H., astronomer, VI. 425.
Pickens, Andrew, rev. soldier, I. 70.
Pickett, George Edward, soldier, V. 49.
Pidge, John B. G., clergyman, III. 355.

Pierce, Benjamin, soldier, III. 410.
Pierce, Franklin, president of U. S., IV. 145.
Pierce, George Foster, educator, I. 311 and V. 396.
Pierce, Gilbert Ashville, senator, I. 294.
Pierce, Henry L., manufacturer, IV. 305.
Pierce, Jane Means, IV. 146.
Pierce, S. P., manufacturer, III. 204.
Pierpont, Francis H., governor, V. 453.
Pierpont, John, clergyman, VI. 155.
Pierpont, James, clergyman, I. 162.
Pierrepont, Edwards, attorney-gen., IV. 21.
Pierrepont, Henry Evelyn, V. 142.
Pierson, Abraham, educator, I. 164.
Pierson, William, physician, V. 111.
Pike, Albert, lawyer, I. 527.
Pike, Zebulon M., soldier, II. 517.
Pillsbury, Fred C., mill-owner, VI. 137.
Pillsbury, Parker, reformer, II. 325.
Pinckney, Charles, statesman, II. 11.
Pinckney, Charles C., soldier, II. 303.
Pine, J. X. P., manufacturer, III. 290.
Pinkerton, A., detective agency, III. 204.
Pinkerton, Alfred S., lawyer, VI. 193.
Pinkney, Edward C., author, VI. 443.
Pinkney, Frederick, author and statesman, VI. 240.
Pinkney, William, att'y-gen., V. 373.
Pinkney, William, bishop, VI. 224.
Pinney, Norman, educator, V. 159.
Pintard, John, philanthropist, III. 461.
Pitcher, James R., underwriter, II. 199.
Pitcher, Nathaniel, governor, III. 45.
Pitkin, Frederick W., governor, VI. 450.
Pitman, Benn, phonographer, IV. 87.
Pittsburgh, R. C. bishops of:
Domenec, M., second, VI. 336.
O'Connor, M., first, VI. 336.
Phelan, R., fourth, VI. 337.
Tuigg, J., third, VI. 337.
Pittsburg Landing, battle of, I. 369, Johnson, A. S.
Plaisted, Harris M., governor, VI. 317.
Plankinton, John, capitalist, I. 241.
Platt, Charles, jurist, II. 449.
Platt, Franklin, geologist, V. 181.
Platt, Henry Clay, lawyer, V. 501.
Platt, Orville H., senator, II. 339.
Pleasanton, Alfred, soldier, IV. 164.
Pleasants, James, governor, V. 447.
Plumb, David Smith, manfr., V. 241.
Plumb, Preston B., senator, II. 420.
Poe, Edgar Allan, poet, I. 463.
Poe, Ebenezer W., merchant, IV. 91.
Poe, Orlando Metcalfe, soldier, V. 53.
Poe's house at Fordham, illus., I. 464.
Poinsett, Joel R., statesman, VI. 435.
Poland, Luke Potter, senator, V. 253.
Poliuto, pen-name, I. 156, Wilkie, F. B.
Polk, James Knox, U. S. president, VI. 265.
Polk, Sarah Childress, VI. 265.
Polk, William M., physician, II. 102.
Pollock, James, governor, II. 289.
Pomeroy, Mark M., journalist, II. 507.
Pomeroy, Seth, rev. soldier, I. 54.
Pond, James B., lecture manager, I. 240.
Pool, Maria Louise, author, VI. 330.
Poole, Fitch, librarian, VI. 484.
Poole, William F., librarian, VI. 474.
Pooley, Thomas R., physician, I. 395.
Poor, Daniel W., clergyman, IV. 374.
Poor, Enoch, rev. soldier, I. 76.
Poore, Henry R., artist, V. 316.
Poorman, Christian L., lawyer, IV. 76.
Pope, Albert Augustus, mfr., I. 446.
Pope, O. C., editor, III. 73.

Stone, David Marvin, journalist, I. 265.
Stone, Ebenezer W., soldier, IV. 390.
Stone, Horatio O., merchant, III. 356.
Stone, James H., journalist, I. 159.
Stone, James Samuel, clergyman, V. 147.
Stone, John Marshall, governor, II. 301.
Stone, Lucy, reformer, II. 318.
Stone, Melville Elijah, journalist, I. 215.
Stone, Ormond, astronomer, VI. 194.
Stone, Thomas T., clergyman, II. 364.
Stone, Wilbur Fisk, jurist, VI. 262.
Stone, William M., P. E. bishop, VI. 222.
Stoneman, George, governor, IV. 112.
Stonewall Jackson, IV. 125, Jackson, T. J.
Storrs, Charles Backus, educator, II. 326.
Story, Emma Eames, singer, V. 404.
Story, Joseph, jurist, II. 468.
Story, William W., author and sculptor, V. 417.
Stow, Frederick H., banker, V. 432.
Stowe, Harriet E. (Beecher), author, I. 423.
Stratton, John, manufacturer, III. 120.
Stranahan, James S. T., III. 433.
Stratton, Charles C., governor, V. 207.
Strauch, Peter D., manufacturer, II. 36.
Strawbridge, Wm. C., lawyer, III. 277.
Streett, David, physician, II. 187.
Stribling, Corn. K., naval officer, IV. 335.
Strickler, Givens B., clergyman, II. 350.
Stringham, Silas H., rear-adm'l., II. 100.
Stripling, Joseph Newton, lawyer, V. 182.
Strong, Abigail S., reformer, VI. 290.
Strong, Caleb, governor, 1745, I. 110.
Strong, Charles D., publisher, VI. 289.
Strong, George C., soldier, V. 352.
Strong, William, jurist, I. 33.
Strout, Sewall Cushing, lawyer, V. 91.
Stryker, William S., soldier, III. 424.
Stuart, Alexander H. H., statesman, VI. 182.
Stuart, Gilbert Charles, artist, V. 324.
Stuart, Jas. Ewell Brown, soldier, IV. 51.
Stuart, Moses, Hebrew scholar, VI. 244.
Stubbs, J. C. S., railroad man'r, VI. 401.
Stuhr, Wm. Sebastian, lawyer, VI. 195.
Sturges, Jonathan, merchant, III. 350.
Sturdis, Frederic R., physician, IV. 198.
Sturgis, Samuel Davis, soldier, IV. 464.
Stuyvesant, Peter, governor, V. 138.
Stuyvesant, Peter G., III. 462.
Suffolk resolves, I. 58, Warren, J.
Sullivan, James, governor, 1744, I. 110.
Sullivan, John, rev. soldier, I. 56.
Sully, Alfred, financier, III. 365.
Sully, Thomas, artist, V. 215.
Sulzer, William, legislator, III. 369.
Sumner, Charles, statesman, III. 300.
Sumner, Increase, governor, 1740, I. 109.
Sumner, Chas., elected senator, IV. 14, Wilson, H.
Sumner, Edwin V., soldier, IV. 183.
Sumner, Jethro, rev. soldier, I. 57.
Sumter, Confederate cruiser, IV. 340, Semmes, R.
Sumter, Thomas, rev. soldier, I. 79.
"Sun," The, I. 127, Beach, M. Y.; I. 128, Dana, C. A.
"Sunday Mercury," I. 237, Cauldwell, W.
Sunderland, Le Roy, author, V. 354.
Super, Charles W., educator, IV. 444.
Sutcliffe, John, architect, II. 499.
Sutphen, John T., physician, VI. 379.
Sutro, Florence E., V. 461.
Sutro, Otto, musician, II. 159.
Sutro, Theodore, lawyer, III. 14.
Sutter, John A., pioneer, IV. 191.

Swain, David L., governor, IV. 424.
Swain, James Barrett, editor, VI. 274.
Swain, Joseph, educator, VI. 481.
Swan, Joseph Rockwell, jurist, V. 183.
Swarthmore College. Presidents:
  De Garmo, C., third, VI. 364.
  Magill, E. H., second, VI. 364.
  Parrish, E., first, V. 348.
  Bond, E. P., dean, VI. 365.
Swayne, Noah H., jurist, IV. 156.
Swayne, Wager, soldier, IV. 156.
Sweeney, P. B., III. 389, Hall, A. O.
Sweet, Alexander E., humorist, VI. 31.
Sweney, John Robson, musical composer, IV. 350.
Swift, Ebenezer, surgeon, V. 177.
Swift, Lewis, astronomer, IV. 302.
Swift, Lucian, Jr., journalist, VI. 287.
Swinburne, Ralph E., physician, II. 506.
Swing, David, clergyman, III. 16.
Swisshelm, Jane Grey, reformer, II. 318.
Sykes, George, soldier, IV. 280.
Sykes, Martin L., R. R. president, III. 329.
Sylvester, Richard H., journalist, III. 325.

T

Taft, Alphonso, statesman, IV. 24.
Taft, Charles P., journalist, I. 239.
Taggart, John Henry, journalist, V. 402.
Taggart, Wm. Marcus, journalist, V. 402.
Taintor, Henry Fox, manufacturer, I. 452.
Talbot, John, missionary, III. 460.
Talbot, Joseph C., P. E. bishop, III. 466.
Talbot, Matthew, governor, I. 223.
Talbot, Samson, educator, I. 302.
Talbot, Silas, naval officer, III. 501.
Talbot, Thomas, governor, I. 119.
Talleyrand's attempt to bribe U. S. envoys, I. 26, Marshall, J.
Taliaferro, Wm. Booth, soldier, V. 216.
Tallmadge, Benjamin, rev. soldier, I. 90.
Tallmadge, James, statesman, III. 493.
Tallmadge, N. P., senator, III. 444.
Talmage, T. DeWitt, clergyman, IV. 26.
Tammany, Sons of Saint, III. 377, Smith, M.; first wigwam, III. 378, Willett, M.
Tammany, Tamanend, Tamemund, III. 377, Smith, M.
Taney, Roger B., jurist, I. 27.
Tanner, Benjamin T., bishop, III. 89.
Tanner, Henry O., III. 89.
Tanner, James, com'r of pensions, I. 287.
Tansley, John O., surgeon, III. 296.
Tappan, Arthur, reformer, II. 320.
Tappan, Benjamin, senator, V. 403.
Tappan, Henry Philip, educator, I. 249.
Tappan, John, merchant, II. 321.
Tappan, Lewis, philanthropist, II. 321.
Tappan, Wm. Bingham, poet, V. 241.
Tariff for revenue only, Phrase, I. 468, Watterson, H.
Tarkington, Joseph A., physician, V. 159.
Tattnall, Josiah, governor, I. 221.
Tattnall, Josiah, naval officer, V. 488.
Taulbee, William Preston, III. 460.
Taylor, Alfred, naval officer, IV. 230.
Taylor, Barton S., librarian, V. 475.
Taylor, Bayard, author, III. 454.
Taylor, Charles H., journalist, II. 192.
Taylor, Charlotte de B., author, II. 164.
Taylor, George, patriot, V. 431.
Taylor, George H., author, VI. 45.
Taylor, George H., physician, V. 494.

Taylor, George S., manufacturer, III. 212.
Taylor, Henry Genet, physician, V. 497.
Taylor, James Monroe, educator, V. 235.
Taylor, John, soldier, II. 236.
Taylor, Margaret S., IV. 370.
Taylor, Moses, IV. 451, Field, C. W.
Taylor, Richard, soldier, IV. 331.
Taylor, Stephen Wm., educator, V. 427.
Taylor, Wm. R., naval officer, IV. 219.
Taylor, William M., clergyman, II. 189.
Taylor, William V., naval officer, IV. 154.
Taylor, Zachary, U. S. president, IV. 369.
Tazewell, Henry, senator, II. 6.
Tazewell, Littleton W., governor, V. 443.
Teague, Samuel W., capitalist, II. 187.
Teall, William W., financier, VI. 94.
Telautograph, IV. 454, Gray, E.
Telegraph inventor, IV. 449, Morse, S. F. B. IV. 450, Vail, A.; alphabet, IV. 450, Vail, A.
Telfair, Edward, governor, I. 219.
Teller, Henry M., secretary, IV. 250.
Tellier, Remidius, educator, II. 266.
Temple, William G., naval officer, IV. 367.
Ten Eyck, John C., senator, II. 95.
Tennent, Wm., Sr., educator, V. 469.
Tenney, Asa W., lawyer, II. 334.
Tenney, Samuel, physician, V. 175.
Terhune, Mary V., author, II. 122.
Terrell, E. H., minister to Belgium, I. 367.
Terry, Alfred H., soldier, IV. 69.
Terry, David S., I. 32, Field, S. J.
Terry, Eli, inventor, VI. 238.
Terry, John Taylor, merchant, III. 230.
Tesla, Nikola, electrician, VI. 398.
Texas, republic of, IV. 61, Houston, S.
Texas Siftings, Sweet, A. E., VI. 31.
Thacher, George, congressman, II. 197.
Thacher, John B., manufacturer, II. 396.
Thacher, Oxenbridge, lawyer, V. 229.
Thacher, Peter, clergyman, VI. 197.
Thacher, Thomas, clergyman, V. 229.
Thatcher, Henry K., naval officer, V. 44.
Thatcher, Oxenbridge, I. 19, Quincy, J.
Thatcher, Samuel C., clergyman, V. 64.
Thaxter, Laighton, Celia, author, I. 445.
Thayer, Abbott H., artist, VI. 471.
Thayer, John Milton, governor, I. 471.
Thayer, Joseph Henry, bib. scholar, VI. 424.
Thayer, Simeon, soldier, V. 226.
Thebaud, A., educator, II. 265.
Thomas, Amos R., educator, II. 196; III. 461.
Thomas, Arthur L., governor, I. 413.
Thomas, Benj. Franklin, jurist, V. 230.
Thomas, Charles M., physician, III. 483.
Thomas, David, manufacturer, III. 360.
Thomas, David W., merchant, II. 399.
Thomas, Douglas H., banker, I. 160.
Thomas, Ebenezer S., journalist, V. 391.
Thomas, G., deputy governor, II. 279.
Thomas, George Henry, soldier, IV. 48.
Thomas, Isaiah, journalist and author, VI. 220.
Thomas, James R., educator, I. 519.
Thomas, John, rev. soldier, I. 81.
Thomas, John, manufacturer, III. 124.
Thomas, John R., song writer, V. 230.
Thomas, Joseph D., physician, VI. 340.
Thomas, Lemon, merchant, IV. 353.
Thomas, Philip F., statesman, V. 6.
Thomas, Philip, I. 160, Thomas, D. H.
Thomas, Robert P., pharmacist, V. 347.
Thomas, Samuel, manufacturer, III. 360.

U

PRESS NOTICES.